Agatha Christie

Miss
Marple
and Mystery

The Complete
Short Stories

HARPER

HARPER

An imprint of HarperCollins*Publishers*
77–85 Fulham Palace Road
Hammersmith. London W6 8JB
www.harpercollins.co.uk

This collection first published 2008
9

Copyright © 2008 Agatha Christie Limited
(a Chorion company). All rights reserved.
www.agathachristie.com

*The publishers would like to acknowledge the help of Karl Pike
in the preparation of this volume.*

ISBN 978 0 00 728418 4

Typeset by Palimpsest Book Production Limited,
Grangemouth, Stirlingshire

Printed and bound in Great Britain by
Clays Ltd, St Ives plc

Mixed Sources
Product group from well-managed
forests and other controlled sources
www.fsc.org Cert no. SW-COC-1806
© 1996 Forest Stewardship Council

FSC is a non-profit international organisation established to promote the
responsible management of the world's forests. Products carrying the FSC
label are independently certified to assure consumers that they come
from forests that are managed to meet the social, economic and
ecological needs of present and future generations.

Find out more about HarperCollins and the environment at
www.harpercollins.co.uk/green

Contents

Stories featuring Miss Marple appear in **bold**

Author's Foreword to Miss Marple and the Thirteen Problems

These problems were Miss Marple's first introduction to the world of detective story readers. Miss Marple has some faint affinity with my own grandmother, also a pink and white pretty old lady who, although having led the most sheltered and Victorian of lives, nevertheless always appeared to be intimately acquainted with all the depths of human depravity. One could be made to feel incredibly naïve and credulous by her reproachful remark: 'But did you *believe* what they said to you? You shouldn't do that. *I* never do!'

I enjoyed writing the Miss Marple stories very much, conceived a great affection for my fluffy old lady, and hoped that she might be a success. She was. After the first six stories had appeared, six more were requested, Miss Marple had definitely come to stay.

She has appeared now in several books and also in a play – and actually rivals Hercule Poirot in popularity. I get about an equal number of letters, one lot saying: 'I wish you would always have Miss Marple and not Poirot,' and the other 'I wish you would have Poirot and not Miss Marple.' I myself incline to her side. I think, that she is at her best in the solving of *short* problems; they suit her more intimate style. Poirot, on the other hand, insists on a full length book to display his talents.

These *Thirteen Problems* contain, I consider, the real essence of Miss Marple for those who like her.

AGATHA CHRISTIE
Penguin edition, 1953

The Actress

'The Actress' was first published as 'A Trap for the Unwary'
in *The Novel Magazine*, May 1923.

The shabby man in the fourth row of the pit leant forward and stared incredulously at the stage. His shifty eyes narrowed furtively.

'Nancy Taylor!' he muttered. 'By the Lord, little Nancy Taylor!'

His glance dropped to the programme in his hand. One name was printed in slightly larger type than the rest.

'Olga Stormer! So that's what she calls herself. Fancy yourself a star, don't you, my lady? And you must be making a pretty little pot of money, too. Quite forgotten your name was ever Nancy Taylor, I daresay. I wonder now – I wonder now what you'd say if Jake Levitt should remind you of the fact?'

The curtain fell on the close of the first act. Hearty applause filled the auditorium. Olga Stormer, the great emotional actress, whose name in a few short years had become a household word, was adding yet another triumph to her list of successes as 'Cora', in *The Avenging Angel*.

Jake Levitt did not join in the clapping, but a slow, appreciative grin gradually distended his mouth. God! What luck! Just when he was on his beam-ends, too. She'd try to bluff it out, he supposed, but she couldn't put it over on *him*. Properly worked, the thing was a gold-mine!

On the following morning the first workings of Jake Levitt's gold-mine became apparent. In her drawing-room, with its red lacquer and black hangings, Olga Stormer read and re-read a letter thoughtfully. Her pale face, with its exquisitely mobile features, was a little more set than usual, and every now and then the grey-green eyes under the level brows steadily envisaged the middle distance, as though she contemplated the threat behind rather than the actual words of the letter.

In that wonderful voice of hers which could throb with emotion or be as clear-cut as the click of a typewriter, Olga called: 'Miss Jones!'

A neat young woman with spectacles, a shorthand pad and a pencil clasped in her hand, hastened from an adjoining room.

'Ring up Mr Danahan, please, and ask him to come round, immediately.'

Syd Danahan, Olga Stormer's manager, entered the room with the usual apprehension of the man whose life it is to deal with and overcome the vagaries of the artistic feminine. To coax, to soothe, to bully, one at a time or all together, such was his daily routine. To his relief, Olga appeared calm and composed, and merely flicked a note across the table to him.

'Read that.'

The letter was scrawled in an illiterate hand, on cheap paper.

Dear Madam,
I much appreciated your performance in The Avenging Angel last night. I fancy we have a mutual friend in Miss Nancy Taylor, late of Chicago. An article regarding her is to be published shortly. If you would care to discuss same, I could call upon you at any time convenient to yourself. Yours respectfully,
Jake Levitt

Danahan looked slightly bewildered.

'I don't quite get it. Who is this Nancy Taylor?'

'A girl who would be better dead, Danny.' There was bitterness in her voice and a weariness that revealed her 34 years. 'A girl who was dead until this carrion crow brought her to life again.'

'Oh! Then . . .'

'Me, Danny. Just me.'

'This means blackmail, of course?'

She nodded. 'Of course, and by a man who knows the art thoroughly.'

Danahan frowned, considering the matter. Olga, her cheek pillowed on a long, slender hand, watched him with unfathomable eyes.

'What about bluff? Deny everything. He can't be sure that he hasn't been misled by a chance resemblance.'

Olga shook her head.

'Levitt makes his living by blackmailing women. He's sure enough.'

'The police?' hinted Danahan doubtfully.

Her faint, derisive smile was answer enough. Beneath her self-control, though he did not guess it, was the impatience of the keen brain watching a slower brain laboriously cover the ground it had already traversed in a flash.

'You don't – er – think it might be wise for you to – er – say something yourself to Sir Richard? That would partly spike his guns.'

The actress's engagement to Sir Richard Everard, MP, had been announced a few weeks previously.

'I told Richard everything when he asked me to marry him.'

'My word, that was clever of you!' said Danahan admiringly.

Olga smiled a little.

'It wasn't cleverness, Danny dear. You wouldn't understand. All the same, if this man Levitt does what he threatens, my number is up, and incidentally Richard's Parliamentary career goes smash, too. No, as far as I can see, there are only two things to do.'

'Well?'

'To pay – and that of course is endless! Or to disappear, start again.'

The weariness was again very apparent in her voice.

'It isn't even as though I'd done anything I regretted. I was a half-starved little gutter waif, Danny, striving to keep straight. I shot a man, a beast of a man who deserved to be shot. The circumstances under which I killed him were such that no jury on earth would have convicted me. I know that now, but at the time I was only a frightened kid – and – I ran.'

Danahan nodded.

'I suppose,' he said doubtfully, 'there's nothing against this man Levitt we could get hold of?'

Olga shook her head.

'Very unlikely. He's too much of a coward to go in for evil-doing.' The sound of her own words seemed to strike her. 'A coward! I wonder if we couldn't work on that in some way.'

'If Sir Richard were to see him and frighten him,' suggested Danahan.

'Richard is too fine an instrument. You can't handle that sort of man with gloves on.'

'Well, let me see him.'

'Forgive me, Danny, but I don't think you're subtle enough. Something between gloves and bare fists is needed. Let us say mittens! That means a woman! Yes, I rather fancy a woman might do the trick. A woman with a certain amount of *finesse*, but who knows the baser side of life from bitter experience. Olga Stormer, for instance! Don't talk to me, I've got a plan coming.'

She leant forward, burying her face in her hands. She lifted it suddenly.

'What's the name of that girl who wants to understudy me? Margaret Ryan, isn't it? The girl with the hair like mine?'

'Her hair's all right,' admitted Danahan grudgingly, his eyes resting on the bronze-gold coil surrounding Olga's head. 'It's just like yours, as you say. But she's no good any other way. I was going to sack her next week.'

'If all goes well, you'll probably have to let her understudy "Cora".' She smothered his protests with a wave of her hand. 'Danny, answer me one question honestly. Do you think I can act? Really *act*, I mean. Or am I just an attractive woman who trails round in pretty dresses?'

'Act? My God! Olga, there's been nobody like you since Duse!'

'Then if Levitt is really a coward, as I suspect, the thing will come off. No, I'm not going to tell you about it. I want you to get hold of the Ryan girl. Tell her I'm interested in her and want her to dine here tomorrow night. She'll come fast enough.'

'I should say she would!'

'The other thing I want is some good strong knockout drops, something that will put anyone out of action for an hour or two, but leave them none the worse the next day.'

Danahan grinned.

'I can't guarantee our friend won't have a headache, but there will be no permanent damage done.'

'Good! Run away now, Danny, and leave the rest to me.' She raised her voice: 'Miss Jones!'

The spectacled young woman appeared with her usual alacrity.

'Take down this, please.'

Walking slowly up and down, Olga dictated the day's correspondence. But one answer she wrote with her own hand.

Jake Levitt, in his dingy room, grinned as he tore open the expected envelope.

Dear Sir,
I cannot recall the lady of whom you speak, but I meet so many people that my memory is necessarily uncertain. I am always pleased to help any fellow actress, and shall be at home if you will call this evening at nine o'clock.
Yours faithfully,
Olga Stormer

Levitt nodded appreciatively. Clever note! She admitted nothing. Nevertheless she was willing to treat. The gold-mine was developing.

At nine o'clock precisely Levitt stood outside the door of the actress's flat and pressed the bell. No one answered the summons, and he was about to press it again when he realized that the door was not latched. He pushed the door open and entered the hall. To his right was an open door leading into a brilliantly lighted room, a room decorated in scarlet and black. Levitt walked in. On the table under the lamp lay a sheet of paper on which were written the words:

Please wait until I return. – O. Stormer.

Levitt sat down and waited. In spite of himself a feeling of uneasiness was stealing over him. The flat was so very quiet. There was something eerie about the silence.

Nothing wrong, of course, how could there be? But the room was so deadly quiet; and yet, quiet as it was, he had the preposterous, uncomfortable notion that he wasn't alone in it. Absurd! He wiped the perspiration from his brow. And still the impression grew stronger. He wasn't alone! With a muttered oath he sprang up and began to pace up and down. In a minute the woman would return and then –

He stopped dead with a muffled cry. From beneath the black velvet hangings that draped the window a hand protruded! He stooped and touched it. Cold – horribly cold – a dead hand.

With a cry he flung back the curtains. A woman was lying there, one arm flung wide, the other doubled under her as she lay face downwards, her golden-bronze hair lying in dishevelled masses on her neck.

Olga Stormer! Tremblingly his fingers sought the icy coldness of that wrist and felt for the pulse. As he thought, there was none. She was dead. She had escaped him, then, by taking the simplest way out.

Suddenly his eyes were arrested by two ends of red cord finishing in fantastic tassels, and half hidden by the masses of her hair. He touched them gingerly; the head sagged as he did so, and he caught a glimpse of a horrible purple face. He sprang back with a cry, his head whirling. There was something here he did not understand. His brief glimpse of the face, disfigured as it was, had shown him one thing. This was murder, not suicide. The woman had been strangled and – she was not Olga Stormer!

Ah! What was that? A sound behind him. He wheeled round and looked straight into the terrified eyes of a maid-servant crouching against the wall. Her face was as white as the cap and apron she wore, but she did not understand the fascinated horror in her eyes until her half-breathed words enlightened him to the peril in which he stood.

'Oh, my Gord! You've killed 'er!'

Even then he did not quite realize. He replied:

'No, no, she was dead when I found her.'

'I saw yer do it! You pulled the cord and strangled her. I 'eard the gurgling cry she give.'

The sweat broke out upon his brow in earnest. His mind went rapidly over his actions of the previous few minutes. She must have come in just as he had the two ends of cord in his hands; she had seen the sagging head and had taken his own cry as coming from the victim. He stared at her helplessly. There was no doubting what he saw in her face – terror and stupidity. She would tell the police she had seen the crime committed, and no cross-examination would shake her, he was sure of that. She would swear away his life with the unshakable conviction that she was speaking the truth.

What a horrible, unforeseen chain of circumstances! Stop, was it unforeseen? Was there some devilry here? On an impulse he said, eyeing her narrowly:

'That's not your mistress, you know.'

Her answer, given mechanically, threw a light upon the situation.

'No, it's 'er actress friend – if you can call 'em friends, seeing that they fought like cat and dog. They were at it tonight, 'ammer and tongs.'

A trap! He saw it now.

'Where's your mistress?'

'Went out ten minutes ago.'

A trap! And he had walked into it like a lamb. A clever devil, this Olga Stormer; she had rid herself of a rival, and he was to suffer for the deed. Murder! My God, they hanged a man for murder! And he was innocent – innocent!

A stealthy rustle recalled him. The little maid was sidling towards the door. Her wits were beginning to work again. Her eyes wavered to the telephone, then back to the door. At all costs he must silence her. It was the only way. As well hang for a real crime as a fictitious one. She had no weapon, neither had he. But he had his hands! Then his heart gave a leap. On the table beside her, almost under her hand, lay a small, jewelled revolver. If he could reach it first –

Instinct or his eyes warned her. She caught it up as he sprang and held it pointed at his breast. Awkwardly as she held it, her finger was on the trigger, and she could hardly miss him at that distance. He stopped dead. A revolver belonging to a woman like Olga Stormer would be pretty sure to be loaded.

But there was one thing, she was no longer directly between him and the door. So long as he did not attack her, she might not have the nerve to shoot. Anyway, he must risk it. Zig-zagging, he ran for the door, through the hall and out through the outer door, banging it behind him. He heard her voice, faint and shaky, calling, 'Police, Murder!' She'd have to call louder than that before anyone was likely to hear her. He'd got a start, anyway. Down the stairs he went, running down the open street, then slacking to a walk as a stray pedestrian turned the corner. He had his plan cut and dried. To Gravesend as quickly as possible. A boat was sailing from there that night for the remoter parts of the world. He knew the captain, a man who, for a consideration, would ask no questions. Once on board and out to sea he would be safe.

At eleven o'clock Danahan's telephone rang. Olga's voice spoke.

'Prepare a contract for Miss Ryan, will you? She's to understudy "Cora". It's absolutely no use arguing. I owe her something after all the things I did to her tonight! What? Yes, I think I'm out of my troubles. By the way, if she tells you tomorrow that I'm an ardent spiritualist and put her into a trance tonight, don't show open incredulity. How? Knock-out drops in the coffee, followed by scientific passes! After that I painted her face with purple grease paint and put a tourniquet on her left arm! Mystified? Well, you must stay mystified until tomorrow. I haven't time to explain now. I must get out of the cap and apron before my faithful Maud returns from the pictures. There was a "beautiful drama" on tonight, she told me. But she missed the best drama of all. I played my best part tonight, Danny. The mittens won! Jake Levitt is a coward all right, and oh, Danny, Danny – I'm an actress!'

The Girl in the Train

'The Girl in the Train' was first published
in *Grand Magazine*, February 1924.

'And that's that!' observed George Rowland ruefully, as he gazed up at
the imposing smoke-grimed façade of the building he had just quitted.

It might be said to represent very aptly the power of Money – and
Money, in the person of William Rowland, uncle to the aforementioned
George, had just spoken its mind very freely. In the course of a brief ten
minutes, from being the apple of his uncle's eye, the heir to his wealth,
and a young man with a promising business career in front of him, George
had suddenly become one of the vast army of the unemployed.

'And in these clothes they won't even give me the dole,' reflected Mr
Rowland gloomily, 'and as for writing poems and selling them at the door
at twopence (or "what you care to give, lydy") I simply haven't got the
brains.'

It was true that George embodied a veritable triumph of the tailor's
art. He was exquisitely and beautifully arrayed. Solomon and the lilies of
the field were simply not in it with George. But man cannot live by clothes
alone – unless he has had some considerable training in the art – and
Mr Rowland was painfully aware of the fact.

'And all because of that rotten show last night,' he reflected sadly.

The rotten show last night had been a Covent Garden Ball. Mr Rowland
had returned from it at a somewhat late – or rather early – hour – as a
matter of fact, he could not strictly say that he remembered returning at
all. Rogers, his uncle's butler, was a helpful fellow, and could doubtless
give more details on the matter. A splitting head, a cup of strong tea, and
an arrival at the office at five minutes to twelve instead of half-past nine
had precipitated the catastrophe. Mr Rowland, senior, who for twenty-four
years had condoned and paid up as a tactful relative should, had suddenly
abandoned these tactics and revealed himself in a totally new light. The

inconsequence of George's replies (the young man's head was still opening and shutting like some mediaeval instrument of the Inquisition) had displeased him still further. William Rowland was nothing if not thorough. He cast his nephew adrift upon the world in a few short succinct words, and then settled down to his interrupted survey of some oilfields in Peru.

George Rowland shook the dust of his uncle's office from off his feet, and stepped out into the City of London. George was a practical fellow. A good lunch, he considered, was essential to a review of the situation. He had it. Then he retraced his steps to the family mansion. Rogers opened the door. His well-trained face expressed no surprise at seeing George at this unusual hour.

'Good afternoon, Rogers. Just pack up my things for me, will you? I'm leaving here.'

'Yes, sir. Just for a short visit, sir?'

'For good, Rogers. I am going to the colonies this afternoon.'

'Indeed, sir?'

'Yes. That is, if there is a suitable boat. Do you know anything about the boats, Rogers?'

'Which colony were you thinking of visiting, sir?'

'I'm not particular. Any of 'em will do. Let's say Australia. What do you think of the idea, Rogers?'

Rogers coughed discreetly.

'Well, sir, I've certainly heard it said that there's room out there for anyone who really wants to work.'

Mr Rowland gazed at him with interest and admiration.

'Very neatly put, Rogers. Just what I was thinking myself. I shan't go to Australia – not today, at any rate. Fetch me an *A.B.C.*, will you? We will select something nearer at hand.'

Rogers brought the required volume. George opened it at random and turned the pages with a rapid hand.

'Perth – too far away – Putney Bridge – too near at hand. Ramsgate? I think not. Reigate also leaves me cold. Why – what an extraordinary thing! There's actually a place called Rowland's Castle. Ever heard of it, Rogers?'

'I fancy, sir, that you go there from Waterloo.'

'What an extraordinary fellow you are, Rogers. You know everything. Well, well, Rowland's Castle! I wonder what sort of a place it is.'

'Not much of a place, I should say, sir.'

'All the better; there'll be less competition. These quiet little country hamlets have a lot of the old feudal spirit knocking about. The last of the original Rowlands ought to meet with instant appreciation. I shouldn't wonder if they elected me mayor in a week.'

He shut up the *A.B.C.* with a bang.

'The die is cast. Pack me a small suit-case, will you, Rogers? Also my compliments to the cook, and will she oblige me with the loan of the cat. Dick Whittington, you know. When you set out to become a Lord Mayor, a cat is essential.'

'I'm sorry, sir, but the cat is not available at the present moment.'

'How is that?'

'A family of eight, sir. Arrived this morning.'

'You don't say so. I thought its name was Peter.'

'So it is, sir. A great surprise to all of us.'

'A case of careless christening and the deceitful sex, eh? Well, well, I shall have to go catless. Pack up those things at once, will you?'

'Very good, sir.'

Rogers hesitated, then advanced a little farther into the room.

'You'll excuse the liberty, sir, but if I was you, I shouldn't take too much notice of anything Mr Rowland said this morning. He was at one of those city dinners last night, and –'

'Say no more,' said George. 'I understand.'

'And being inclined to gout –'

'I know, I know. Rather a strenuous evening for you, Rogers, with two of us, eh? But I've set my heart on distinguishing myself at Rowland's Castle – the cradle of my historic race – that would go well in a speech, wouldn't it? A wire to me there, or a discreet advertisement in the morning papers, will recall me at any time if a fricassée of veal is in preparation. And now – to Waterloo! – as Wellington said on the eve of the historic battle.'

Waterloo Station was not at its brightest and best that afternoon. Mr Rowland eventually discovered a train that would take him to his destination, but it was an undistinguished train, an unimposing train – a train that nobody seemed anxious to travel by. Mr Rowland had a first-class carriage to himself, up in the front of the train. A fog was descending in an indeterminate way over the metropolis, now it lifted, now it descended. The platform was deserted, and only the asthmatic breathing of the engine broke the silence.

And then, all of a sudden, things began to happen with bewildering rapidity.

A girl happened first. She wrenched open the door and jumped in, rousing Mr Rowland from something perilously near a nap, exclaiming as she did so: 'Oh! hide me – oh! please hide me.'

George was essentially a man of action – his not to reason why, his but to do and die, etc. There is only one place to hide in a railway carriage – under the seat. In seven seconds the girl was bestowed there, and

George's suit-case, negligently standing on end, covered her retreat. None too soon. An infuriated face appeared at the carriage window.

'My niece! You have her here. I want my niece.'

George, a little breathless, was reclining in the corner, deep in the sporting column of the evening paper, one-thirty edition. He laid it aside with the air of a man recalling himself from far away.

'I beg your pardon, sir?' he said politely.

'My niece – what have you done with her?'

Acting on the policy that attack is always better than defence, George leaped into action.

'What the devil do you mean?' he cried, with a very creditable imitation of his own uncle's manner.

The other paused a minute, taken aback by this sudden fierceness. He was a fat man, still panting a little as though he had run some way. His hair was cut *en brosse*, and he had a moustache of the Hohenzollern persuasion. His accents were decidedly guttural, and the stiffness of his carriage denoted that he was more at home in uniform than out of it. George had the true-born Briton's prejudice against foreigners – and an especial distaste for German-looking foreigners.

'What the devil do you mean, sir?' he repeated angrily.

'She came in here,' said the other. 'I saw her. What have you done with her?'

George flung aside the paper and thrust his head and shoulders through the window.

'So that's it, is it?' he roared. 'Blackmail. But you've tried it on the wrong person. I read all about you in the *Daily Mail* this morning. Here, guard, guard!'

Already attracted from afar by the altercation, that functionary came hurrying up.

'Here, guard,' said Mr Rowland, with that air of authority which the lower classes so adore. 'This fellow is annoying me. I'll give him in charge for attempted blackmail if necessary. Pretends I've got his niece hidden in here. There's a regular gang of these foreigners trying this sort of thing on. It ought to be stopped. Take him away, will you? Here's my card if you want it.'

The guard looked from one to the other. His mind was soon made up. His training led him to despise foreigners, and to respect and admire well-dressed gentlemen who travelled first class.

He laid his hand on the shoulder of the intruder.

'Here,' he said, 'you come out of this.'

At this crisis the stranger's English failed him, and he plunged into passionate profanity in his native tongue.

'That's enough of that,' said the guard. 'Stand away, will you? She's due out.'

Flags were waved and whistles were blown. With an unwilling jerk the train drew out of the station.

George remained at his observation post until they were clear of the platform. Then he drew in his head, and picking up the suit-case tossed it into the rack.

'It's quite all right. You can come out,' he said reassuringly.

The girl crawled out.

'Oh!' she gasped. 'How can I thank you?'

'That's quite all right. It's been a pleasure, I assure you,' returned George nonchalantly.

He smiled at her reassuringly. There was a slightly puzzled look in her eyes. She seemed to be missing something to which she was accustomed. At that moment, she caught sight of herself in the narrow glass opposite, and gave a heartfelt gasp.

Whether the carriage cleaners do, or do not, sweep under the seats every day is doubtful. Appearances were against their doing so, but it may be that every particle of dirt and smoke finds its way there like a homing bird. George had hardly had time to take in the girl's appearance, so sudden had been her arrival, and so brief the space of time before she crawled into hiding, but it was certainly a trim and well-dressed young woman who had disappeared under the seat. Now her little red hat was crushed and dented, and her face was disfigured with long streaks of dirt.

'Oh!' said the girl.

She fumbled for her bag. George, with the tact of a true gentleman, looked fixedly out of the window and admired the streets of London south of the Thames.

'How can I thank you?' said the girl again.

Taking this as a hint that conversation might now be resumed, George withdrew his gaze, and made another polite disclaimer, but this time with a good deal of added warmth in his manner.

The girl was absolutely lovely! Never before, George told himself, had he seen such a lovely girl. The *empressement* of his manner became even more marked.

'I think it was simply splendid of you,' said the girl with enthusiasm.

'Not at all. Easiest thing in the world. Only too pleased been of use,' mumbled George.

'Splendid,' she reiterated emphatically.

It is undoubtedly pleasant to have the loveliest girl you have even seen gazing into your eyes and telling you how splendid you are. George enjoyed it as much as anyone could.

Then there came a rather difficult silence. It seemed to dawn upon the girl that further explanation might be expected. She flushed a little.

'The awkward part of it is,' she said nervously, 'that I'm afraid I can't explain.'

She looked at him with a piteous air of uncertainty.

'You can't explain?'

'No.'

'How perfectly splendid!' said Mr Rowland with enthusiasm.

'I beg your pardon?'

'I said, How perfectly splendid. Just like one of those books that keep you up all night. The heroine always says "I can't explain" in the first chapter. She explains in the last, of course, and there's never any real reason why she shouldn't have done so in the beginning – except that it would spoil the story. I can't tell you how pleased I am to be mixed up in a real mystery – I didn't know there were such things. I hope it's got something to do with secret documents of immense importance, and the Balkan express. I dote upon the Balkan express.'

The girl stared at him with wide, suspicious eyes.

'What makes you say the Balkan express?' she asked sharply.

'I hope I haven't been indiscreet,' George hastened to put in. 'Your uncle travelled by it, perhaps.'

'My uncle –' She paused, then began again. 'My uncle –'

'Quite so,' said George sympathetically. 'I've got an uncle myself. Nobody should be held responsible for their uncles. Nature's little throw-backs – that's how I look at it.'

The girl began to laugh suddenly. When she spoke George was aware of the slight foreign inflection in her voice. At first he had taken her to be English.

'What a refreshing and unusual person you are, Mr –'

'Rowland. George to my friends.'

'My name is Elizabeth –'

She stopped abruptly.

'I like the name of Elizabeth,' said George, to cover her momentary confusion. 'They don't call you Bessie, or anything horrible like that, I hope?'

She shook her head.

'Well,' said George, 'now that we know each other, we'd better get down to business. If you'll stand up, Elizabeth, I'll brush down the back of your coat.'

She stood up obediently, and George was as good as his word.

'Thank you, Mr Rowland.'

'George. George to my friends, remember. And you can't come into my nice empty carriage, roll under the seat, induce me to tell lies to your uncle, and then refuse to be friends, can you?'

'Thank you, George.'

'That's better.'

'Do I look quite all right now?' asked Elizabeth, trying to see over her left shoulder.

'You look – oh! you look – you look all right,' said George, curbing himself sternly.

'It was all so sudden, you see,' explained the girl.

'It must have been.'

'He saw us in the taxi, and then at the station I just bolted in here knowing he was close behind me. Where is this train going to, by the way?'

'Rowland's Castle,' said George firmly.

The girl looked puzzled.

'Rowland's Castle?'

'Not at once, of course. Only after a good deal of stopping and slow going. But I confidently expect to be there before midnight. The old South-Western was a very reliable line – slow but sure – and I'm sure the Southern Railway is keeping up the old traditions.'

'I don't know that I want to go to Rowland's Castle,' said Elizabeth doubtfully.

'You hurt me. It's a delightful spot.'

'Have you ever been there?'

'Not exactly. But there are lots of other places you can go to, if you don't fancy Rowland's Castle. There's Woking, and Weybridge, and Wimbledon. The train is sure to stop at one or other of them.'

'I see,' said the girl. 'Yes, I can get out there, and perhaps motor back to London. That would be the best plan, I think.'

Even as she spoke, the train began to slow up. Mr Rowland gazed at her with appealing eyes.

'If I can do anything –'

'No, indeed. You've done a lot already.'

There was a pause, then the girl broke out suddenly:

'I – I wish I could explain. I –'

'For heaven's sake don't do that! It would spoil everything. But look here, isn't there anything that I could do? Carry the secret papers to Vienna – or something of that kind? There always are secret papers. Do give me a chance.'

The train had stopped. Elizabeth jumped quickly out on to the platform. She turned and spoke to him through the window.

'Are you in earnest? Would you really do something for us – for me?'

'I'd do anything in the world for you, Elizabeth.'

'Even if I could give you no reasons?'

'Rotten things, reasons!'

'Even if it were – dangerous?'

'The more danger, the better.'

She hesitated a minute then seemed to make up her mind.

'Lean out of the window. Look down the platform as though you weren't really looking.' Mr Rowland endeavoured to comply with this somewhat difficult recommendation. 'Do you see that man getting in – with a small dark beard – light overcoat? Follow him, see what he does and where he goes.'

'Is that all?' asked Mr Rowland. 'What do I –?'

She interrupted him.

'Further instructions will be sent to you. Watch him – and guard this.' She thrust a small sealed packet into his hand. 'Guard it with your life. It's the key to everything.'

The train went on. Mr Rowland remained staring out of the window, watching Elizabeth's tall, graceful figure threading its way down the platform. In his hand he clutched the small sealed packet.

The rest of his journey was both monotonous and uneventful. The train was a slow one. It stopped everywhere. At every station, George's head shot out of the window, in case his quarry should alight. Occasionally he strolled up and down the platform when the wait promised to be a long one, and reassured himself that the man was still there.

The eventual destination of the train was Portsmouth, and it was there that the black-bearded traveller alighted. He made his way to a small second-class hotel where he booked a room. Mr Rowland also booked a room.

The rooms were in the same corridor, two doors from each other. The arrangement seemed satisfactory to George. He was a complete novice in the art of shadowing, but was anxious to acquit himself well, and justify Elizabeth's trust in him.

At dinner George was given a table not far from that of his quarry. The room was not full, and the majority of the diners George put down as commercial travellers, quiet respectable men who ate their food with appetite. Only one man attracted his special notice, a small man with ginger hair and moustache and a suggestion of horsiness in his apparel. He seemed to be interested in George also, and suggested a drink and a game of billiards when the meal had come to a close. But George had just espied the black-bearded man putting on his hat and overcoat, and declined politely. In another minute he was out in the street, gaining fresh insight into the difficult art of shadowing. The chase was a long and a weary one – and in the end it seemed to lead nowhere. After twisting and turning through the streets of Portsmouth for about four miles, the man returned to the hotel, George hard upon his heels. A faint doubt assailed the latter. Was it possible that the man was aware of his presence? As he debated this point, standing in the hall, the outer door was pushed open, and the little ginger man entered. Evidently he, too, had been out for a stroll.

George was suddenly aware that the beauteous damsel in the office was addressing him.

'Mr Rowland, isn't it? Two gentlemen have called to see you. Two foreign gentlemen. They are in the little room at the end of the passage.'

Somewhat astonished, George sought the room in question. Two men who were sitting there, rose to their feet and bowed punctiliously.

'Mr Rowland? I have no doubt, sir, that you can guess our identity.'

George gazed from one to the other of them. The spokesman was the elder of the two, a grey-haired, pompous gentleman who spoke excellent English. The other was a tall, somewhat pimply young man, with a blond Teutonic cast of countenance which was not rendered more attractive by the fierce scowl which he wore at the present moment.

Somewhat relieved to find that neither of his visitors was the old gentleman he had encountered at Waterloo, George assumed his most debonair manner.

'Pray sit down, gentlemen. I'm delighted to make your acquaintance. How about a drink?'

The elder man held up a protesting hand.

'Thank you, Lord Rowland – not for us. We have but a few brief moments – just time for you to answer a question.'

'It's very kind of you to elect me to the peerage,' said George. 'I'm sorry you won't have a drink. And what is this momentous question?'

'Lord Rowland, you left London in company with a certain lady. You arrived here alone. Where is the lady?'

George rose to his feet.

'I fail to understand the question,' he said coldly, speaking as much like the hero of a novel as he could. 'I have the honour to wish you good-evening, gentlemen.'

'But you do understand it. You understand it perfectly,' cried the younger man, breaking out suddenly. 'What have you done with Alexa?'

'Be calm, sir,' murmured the other. 'I beg of you to be calm.'

'I can assure you,' said George, 'that I know no lady of that name. There is some mistake.'

The older man was eyeing him keenly.

'That can hardly be,' he said drily. 'I took the liberty of examining the

hotel register. You entered yourself as Mr G Rowland of Rowland's
Castle.'

George was forced to blush.

'A – a little joke of mine,' he explained feebly.

'A somewhat poor subterfuge. Come, let us not beat about the bush.
Where is Her Highness?'

'If you mean Elizabeth –'

With a howl of rage the young man flung himself forward again.

'Insolent pig-dog! To speak of her thus.'

'I am referring,' said the other slowly, 'as you very well know, to the
Grand Duchess Anastasia Sophia Alexandra Marie Helena Olga Elizabeth of Catonia.'

'Oh!' said Mr Rowland helplessly.

He tried to recall all that he had ever known of Catonia. It was, as far
as he remembered, a small Balkan kingdom, and he seemed to remember something about a revolution having occurred there. He rallied himself
with an effort.

'Evidently we mean the same person,' he said cheerfully, 'only *I* call
her Elizabeth.'

'You will give me satisfaction for that,' snarled the younger man. 'We
will fight.'

'Fight?'

'A duel.'

'I never fight duels,' said Mr Rowland firmly.

'Why not?' demanded the other unpleasantly.

'I'm too afraid of getting hurt.'

'Aha! is that so? Then I will at least pull your nose for you.'

The younger man advanced fiercely. Exactly what happened was difficult to see, but he described a sudden semi-circle in the air and fell to
the ground with a heavy thud. He picked himself up in a dazed manner.
Mr Rowland was smiling pleasantly.

'As I was saying,' he remarked, 'I'm always afraid of getting hurt.
That's why I thought it well to learn jujitsu.'

There was a pause. The two foreigners looked doubtfully at this
amiable looking young man, as though they suddenly realized that some
dangerous quality lurked behind the pleasant nonchalance of his manner.
The younger Teuton was white with passion.

'You will repent this,' he hissed.

The older man retained his dignity.

'That is your last word, Lord Rowland? You refuse to tell us Her Highness's whereabouts?'

'I am unaware of them myself.'

'You can hardly expect me to believe that.'

'I am afraid you are of an unbelieving nature, sir.'

The other merely shook his head, and murmuring: 'This is not the end. You will hear from us again,' the two men took their leave.

George passed his hand over his brow. Events were proceeding at a bewildering rate. He was evidently mixed up in a first-class European scandal.

'It might even mean another war,' said George hopefully, as he hunted round to see what had become of the man with the black beard.

To his great relief, he discovered him sitting in a corner of the commercial-room. George sat down in another corner. In about three minutes the black-bearded man got up and went up to bed. George followed and saw him go into his room and close the door. George heaved a sigh of relief.

'I need a night's rest,' he murmured. 'Need it badly.'

Then a dire thought struck him. Supposing the black-bearded man had realized that George was on his trail? Supposing that he should slip away during the night whilst George himself was sleeping the sleep of the just? A few minutes' reflection suggested to Mr Rowland a way of dealing with his difficulty. He unravelled one of his socks till he got a good length of neutral-coloured wool, then creeping quietly out of his room, he pasted one end of the wool to the farther side of the stranger's door with stamp paper, carrying the wool across it and along to his own room. There he hung the end with a small silver bell – a relic of last night's entertainment. He surveyed these arrangements with a good deal of satisfaction. Should the black-bearded man attempt to leave his room George would be instantly warned by the ringing of the bell.

This matter disposed of, George lost no time in seeking his couch. The small packet he placed carefully under his pillow. As he did so, he fell into a momentary brown study. His thoughts could have been translated thus:

'Anastasia Sophia Marie Alexandra Olga Elizabeth. Hang it all, I've missed out one. I wonder now –'

He was unable to go to sleep immediately, being tantalized with his failure to grasp the situation. What was it all about? What was the connection between the escaping Grand Duchess, the sealed packet and the black-bearded man? What was the Grand Duchess escaping from? Were the foreigners aware that the sealed packet was in his possession? What was it likely to contain?

Pondering these matters, with an irritated sense that he was no nearer the solution, Mr Rowland fell asleep.

He was awakened by the faint jangle of a bell. Not one of those men who awake to instant action, it took him just a minute and a half to realize the situation. Then he jumped up, thrust on some slippers, and, opening the door with the utmost caution, slipped out into the corridor. A faint moving patch of shadow at the far end of the passage showed him the direction taken by his quarry. Moving as noiselessly as possible, Mr Rowland followed the trail. He was just in time to see the black-bearded man disappear into a bathroom. That was puzzling, particularly so as there was a bathroom just opposite his own room. Moving up close to the door, which was ajar, George peered through the crack. The man was on his knees by the side of the bath, doing something to the skirting board immediately behind it. He remained there for about five minutes, then he rose to his feet, and George beat a prudent retreat. Safe in the shadow of his own door, he watched the other pass and regain his own room.

'Good,' said George to himself. 'The mystery of the bathroom will be investigated tomorrow morning.'

He got into bed and slipped his hand under the pillow to assure himself that the precious packet was still there. In another minute, he was scattering the bedclothes in a panic. The packet was gone!

It was a sadly chastened George who sat consuming eggs and bacon the following morning. He had failed Elizabeth. He had allowed the precious packet she had entrusted to his charge to be taken from him, and the 'Mystery of the Bathroom' was miserably inadequate. Yes, undoubtedly George had made a mutt of himself.

After breakfast he strolled upstairs again. A chambermaid was standing in the passage looking perplexed.

'Anything wrong, my dear?' said George kindly.

'It's the gentleman here, sir. He asked to be called at half-past eight, and I can't get any answer and the door's locked.'

'You don't say so,' said George.

An uneasy feeling rose in his own breast. He hurried into his room. Whatever plans he was forming were instantly brushed aside by a most unexpected sight. There on the dressing-table was the little packet which had been stolen from him the night before!

George picked it up and examined it. Yes, it was undoubtedly the same. But the seals had been broken. After a minute's hesitation, he unwrapped it. If other people had seen its contents there was no reason why he should not see them also. Besides, it was possible that the contents had been abstracted. The unwound paper revealed a small cardboard box, such as jewellers use. George opened it. Inside, nestling on a bed of cotton wool, was a plain gold wedding ring.

He picked it up and examined it. There was no inscription inside –

nothing whatever to make it out from any other wedding ring. George dropped his head into his hands with a groan.

'Lunacy,' he murmured. 'That's what it is. Stark staring lunacy. There's no sense anywhere.'

Suddenly he remembered the chambermaid's statement, and at the same time he observed that there was a broad parapet outside the window. It was not a feat he would ordinarily have attempted, but he was so aflame with curiosity and anger that he was in the mood to make light of difficulties. He sprang upon the window sill. A few seconds later he was peering in at the window of the room occupied by the black-bearded man. The window was open and the room was empty. A little further along was a fire escape. It was clear how the quarry had taken his departure.

George jumped in through the window. The missing man's effects were still scattered about. There might be some clue amongst them to shed light on George's perplexities. He began to hunt about, starting with the contents of a battered kit-bag.

It was a sound that arrested his search – a very slight sound, but a sound indubitably in the room. George's glance leapt to the big wardrobe. He sprang up and wrenched open the door. As he did so, a man jumped out from it and went rolling over the floor locked in George's embrace. He was no mean antagonist. All George's special tricks availed very little. They fell apart at length in sheer exhaustion, and for the first time George saw who his adversary was. It was the little man with the ginger moustache.

'Who the devil are you?' demanded George.

For answer the other drew out a card and handed it to him. George read it aloud.

'Detective-Inspector Jarrold, Scotland Yard.'

'That's right, sir. And you'd do well to tell me all you know about this business.'

'I would, would I?' said George thoughtfully. 'Do you know, Inspector, I believe you're right. Shall we adjourn to a more cheerful spot?'

In a quiet corner of the bar George unfolded his soul. Inspector Jarrold listened sympathetically.

'Very puzzling, as you say, sir,' he remarked when George had finished. 'There's a lot as I can't make head or tail of myself, but there's one or two points I can clear up for you. I was here after Mardenberg (your black-bearded friend) and your turning up and watching him the way you did made me suspicious. I couldn't place you. I slipped into your room last night when you were out of it, and it was I who sneaked the little packet from under your pillow. When I opened it and found it wasn't what I was after, I took the first opportunity of returning it to your room.'

'That makes things a little clearer certainly,' said George thoughtfully. 'I seem to have made rather an ass of myself all through.'

'I wouldn't say that, sir. You did uncommon well for a beginner. You say you visited the bathroom this morning and took away what was concealed behind the skirting board?'

'Yes. But it's only a rotten love letter,' said George gloomily. 'Dash it all, I didn't mean to go nosing out the poor fellow's private life.'

'Would you mind letting me see it, sir?'

George took a folded letter from his pocket and passed it to the inspector. The latter unfolded it.

'As you say, sir. But I rather fancy that if you drew lines from one dotted *i* to another, you'd get a different result. Why, bless you, sir, this is a plan of the Portsmouth harbour defences.'

'What?'

'Yes. We've had our eye on the gentleman for some time. But he was too sharp for us. Got a woman to do most of the dirty work.'

'A woman?' said George, in a faint voice. 'What was her name?'

'She goes by a good many, sir. Most usually known as Betty Brighteyes. A remarkably good-looking young woman she is.'

'Betty – Brighteyes,' said George. 'Thank you, Inspector.'

'Excuse me, sir, but you're not looking well.'

'I'm not well. I'm very ill. In fact, I think I'd better take the first train back to town.'

The Inspector looked at his watch.

'That will be a slow train, I'm afraid, sir. Better wait for the express.'

'It doesn't matter,' said George gloomily. 'No train could be slower than the one I came down by yesterday.'

Seated once more in a first-class carriage, George leisurely perused the day's news. Suddenly he sat bolt upright and stared at the sheet in front of him.

'A romantic wedding took place yesterday in London when Lord Roland Gaigh, second son of the Marquis of Axminster, was married to the Grand Duchess Anastasia of Catonia. The ceremony was kept a profound secret. The Grand Duchess has been living in Paris with her uncle since the upheaval in Catonia. She met Lord Roland when he was secretary to the British Embassy in Catonia and their attachment dates from that time.'

'Well, I'm –'

Mr Rowland could not think of anything strong enough to express his feelings. He continued to stare into space. The train stopped at a small station and a lady got in. She sat down opposite him.

'Good-morning, George,' she said sweetly.

'Good heavens!' cried George. 'Elizabeth!'

She smiled at him. She was, if possible, lovelier than ever.

'Look here,' cried George, clutching his head. 'For God's sake tell me. Are you the Grand Duchess Anastasia, or are you Betty Brighteyes?'

She stared at him.

'I'm not either. I'm Elizabeth Gaigh. I can tell you all about it now. And I've got to apologize too. You see, Roland (that's my brother) has always been in love with Alexa –'

'Meaning the Grand Duchess?'

'Yes, that's what the family call her. Well, as I say, Roland was always in love with her, and she with him. And then the revolution came, and Alexa was in Paris, and they were just going to fix it up when old Stürm, the chancellor, came along and insisted on carrying off Alexa and forcing her to marry Prince Karl, her cousin, a horrid pimply person –'

'I fancy I've met him,' said George.

'Whom she simply hates. And old Prince Usric, her uncle, forbade her to see Roland again. So she ran away to England, and I came up to town and met her, and we wired to Roland who was in Scotland. And just at the very last minute, when we were driving to the Registry Office in a taxi, whom should we meet in another taxi face to face, but old Prince Usric. Of course he followed us, and we were at our wits' end what to do because he'd have made the most fearful scene, and, anyway, he is her guardian. Then I had the brilliant idea of changing places. You can practically see nothing of a girl nowadays but the tip of her nose. I put on Alexa's red hat and brown wrap coat, and she put on my grey. Then we told the taxi to go to Waterloo, and I skipped out there and hurried into the station. Old Osric followed the red hat all right, without a thought for the other occupant of the taxi sitting huddled up inside, but of course it wouldn't do for him to see my face. So I just bolted into your carriage and threw myself on your mercy.'

'I've got that all right,' said George. 'It's the rest of it.'

'I know. That's what I've got to apologize about. I hope you won't be awfully cross. You see, you looked so keen on its being a real mystery – like in books, that I really couldn't resist the temptation. I picked out a rather sinister looking man on the platform and told you to follow him. And then I thrust the parcel on you.'

'Containing a wedding ring.'

'Yes. Alexa and I bought that, because Roland wasn't due to arrive from Scotland until just before the wedding. And of course I knew that by the time I got to London they wouldn't want it – they would have had to use a curtain ring or something.'

'I see,' said George. 'It's like all these things – so simple when you know! Allow me, Elizabeth.'

He stripped off her left glove, and uttered a sigh of relief at the sight of the bare third finger.

'That's all right,' he remarked. 'That ring won't be wasted after all.'

'Oh!' cried Elizabeth; 'but I don't know anthing about you.'

'You know how nice I am,' said George. 'By the way, it has just occurred to me, you are the Lady Elizabeth Gaigh, of course.'

'Oh! George, are you a snob?'

'As a matter of fact, I am, rather. My best dream was one where King George borrowed half a crown from me to see him over the week-end. But I was thinking of my uncle – the one from whom I am estranged. He's a frightful snob. When he knows I'm going to marry you, and that we'll have a title in the family, he'll make me a partner at once!'

'Oh! George, is he very rich?'

'Elizabeth, are you mercenary?'

'Very. I adore spending money. But I was thinking of Father. Five daughters, full of beauty and blue blood. He's just yearning for a rich son-in-law.'

'H'm,' said George. 'It will be one of those marriages made in Heaven and approved on earth. Shall we live at Rowland's Castle? They'd be sure to make me Lord Mayor with you for a wife. Oh! Elizabeth, darling, it's probably contravening the company's by-laws, but I simply must kiss you!'

3

While the Light Lasts

'While the Light Lasts' was first published
in *Novel Magazine*, April 1924.

The Ford car bumped from rut to rut, and the hot African sun poured down unmercifully. On either side of the so-called road stretched an unbroken line of trees and scrub, rising and falling in gently undulating lines as far as the eye could reach, the colouring a soft, deep yellow-green, the whole effect languorous and strangely quiet. Few birds stirred the slumbering silence. Once a snake wriggled across the road in front of the car, escaping the driver's efforts at destruction with sinuous ease. Once a native stepped out from the bush, dignified and upright, behind him a woman with an infant bound closely to her broad back and a complete household equipment, including a frying pan, balanced magnificently on her head.

All these things George Crozier had not failed to point out to his wife, who had answered him with a monosyllabic lack of attention which irritated him.

'Thinking of that fellow,' he deduced wrathfully. It was thus that he was wont to allude in his own mind to Deirdre Crozier's first husband, killed in the first year of the War. Killed, too, in the campaign against German West Africa. Natural she should, perhaps – he stole a glance at her, her fairness, the pink and white smoothness of her cheek; the rounded lines of her figure – rather more rounded perhaps than they had been in those far-off days when she had passively permitted him to become engaged to her, and then, in that first emotional scare of war, had abruptly cast him aside and made a war wedding of it with that lean, sunburnt boy lover of hers, Tim Nugent.

Well, well, the fellow was dead – gallantly dead – and he, George Crozier, had married the girl he had always meant to marry. She was fond of him, too; how could she help it when he was ready to gratify her every wish and had the money to do it, too! He reflected with some complacency on his last gift to her, at Kimberley, where, owing to his friendship with some of the directors of De Beers, he had been able to purchase a diamond which, in the ordinary way, would not have been in the market, a stone not remarkable as to size, but of a very exquisite and rare shade, a peculiar deep amber, almost old gold, a diamond such as you might not find in a hundred years. And the look in her eyes when he gave it to her! Women were all the same about diamonds.

The necessity of holding on with both hands to prevent himself being jerked out brought George Crozier back to the realities. He cried out for perhaps the fourteenth time, with the pardonable irritation of a man who owns two Rolls-Royce cars and who has exercised his stud on the highways of civilization: 'Good Lord, what a car! What a road!' He went on angrily: 'Where the devil is this tobacco estate, anyway? It's over an hour since we left Bulawayo.'

'Lost in Rhodesia,' said Deirdre lightly between two involuntary leaps into the air.

But the coffee-coloured driver, appealed to, responded with the cheering news that their destination was just round the next bend of the road.

The manager of the estate, Mr Walters, was waiting on the stoep to receive them with the touch of deference due to George Crozier's prominence in Union Tobacco. He introduced his daughter-in-law, who shepherded Deirdre through the cool, dark inner hall to a bedroom beyond, where she could remove the veil with which she was always careful to shield her complexion when motoring. As she unfastened the pins in her usual leisurely, graceful fashion, Deirdre's eyes swept round the whitewashed ugliness of the bare room. No luxuries here, and Deirdre, who loved comfort as a cat loves cream, shivered a little. On the wall a text confronted her. 'What shall it profit a man if he gain the whole world and lose his own soul?' it demanded of all and sundry, and Deirdre, pleasantly conscious that the question had nothing to do with her, turned to accompany her shy and rather silent guide. She noted, but not in the least maliciously, the spreading hips and the unbecoming cheap cotton gown. And with a glow of quiet appreciation her eyes dropped to the exquisite, costly simplicity of her own French white linen. Beautiful clothes, especially when worn by herself, roused in her the joy of the artist.

The two men were waiting for her.

'It won't bore you to come round, too, Mrs Crozier?'

'Not at all. I've never been over a tobacco factory.'

They stepped out into the still Rhodesian afternoon.

'These are the seedlings here; we plant them out as required. You see —'

The manager's voice droned on, interpolated by her husband's sharp staccato questions – output, stamp duty, problems of coloured labour. She ceased to listen.

This was Rhodesia, this was the land Tim had loved, where he and she were to have gone together after the War was over. If he had not been killed! As always, the bitterness of revolt surged up in her at that thought. Two short months – that was all they had had. Two months of happiness – if that mingled rapture and pain were happiness. Was love ever happiness? Did not a thousand tortures beset the lover's heart? She had lived intensely in that short space, but had she ever known the peace, the leisure, the quiet contentment of her present life? And for the first time she admitted, somewhat unwillingly, that perhaps all had been for the best.

'I wouldn't have liked living out here. I mightn't have been able to make Tim happy. I might have disappointed him. George loves me, and I'm very fond of him, and he's very, very good to me. Why, look at that diamond he bought me only the other day.' And, thinking of it, her eyelids dropped a little in pure pleasure.

'This is where we thread the leaves.' Walters led the way into a low, long shed. On the floor were vast heaps of green leaves, and white-clad black 'boys' squatted round them, picking and rejecting with deft fingers, sorting them into sizes, and stringing them by means of primitive needles on a long line of string. They worked with a cheerful leisureliness, jesting amongst themselves, and showing their white teeth as they laughed.

'Now, out here –'

They passed through the shed into the daylight again, where the lines of leaves hung drying in the sun. Deirdre sniffed delicately at the faint, almost imperceptible fragrance that filled the air.

Walters led the way into other sheds where the tobacco, kissed by the sun into faint yellow discoloration, underwent its further treatment. Dark here, with the brown swinging masses above, ready to fall to powder at a rough touch. The fragrance was stronger, almost overpowering it seemed to Deirdre, and suddenly a sort of terror came upon her, a fear of she knew not what, that drove her from that menacing, scented obscurity out into the sunlight. Crozier noted her pallor.

'What's the matter, my dear, don't you feel well? The sun, perhaps. Better not come with us round the plantations? Eh?'

Walters was solicitous. Mrs Crozier had better go back to the house and rest. He called to a man a little distance away.

'Mr Arden – Mrs Crozier. Mrs Crozier's feeling a little done up with the heat, Arden. Just take her back to the house, will you?'

The momentary feeling of dizziness was passing. Deirdre walked by Arden's side. She had as yet hardly glanced at him.

'Deirdre!'

Her heart gave a leap, and then stood still. Only one person had ever spoken her name like that, with the faint stress on the first syllable that made of it a caress.

She turned and stared at the man by her side. He was burnt almost black by the sun, he walked with a limp, and on the cheek nearer hers was a long scar which altered his expression, but she knew him.

'Tim!'

For an eternity, it seemed to her, they gazed at each other, mute and trembling, and then, without knowing how or why, they were in each other's arms. Time rolled back for them. Then they drew apart again, and Deirdre, conscious as she put it of the idiocy of the question, said:

'Then you're not dead?'

'No, they must have mistaken another chap for me. I was badly knocked on the head, but I came to and managed to crawl into the bush. After that I don't know what happened for months and months, but a friendly tribe looked after me, and at last I got my proper wits again and managed to get back to civilization.' He paused. 'I found you'd been married six months.'

Deirdre cried out:

'Oh, Tim, understand, please understand! It was so awful, the loneliness – and the poverty. I didn't mind being poor with you, but when I was alone I hadn't the nerve to stand up against the sordidness of it all.'

'It's all right, Deirdre; I did understand. I know you always have had a hankering after the flesh-pots. I took you from them once – but the second time, well – my nerve failed. I was pretty badly broken up, you see, could hardly walk without a crutch, and then there was this scar.'

She interrupted him passionately.

'Do you think I would have cared for that?'

'No, I know you wouldn't. I was a fool. Some women did mind, you know. I made up my mind I'd manage to get a glimpse of you. If you looked happy, if I thought you were contented to be with Crozier – why, then I'd remain dead. I did see you. You were just getting into a big car. You had on some lovely sable furs – things I'd never be able to give you if I worked my fingers to the bone – and – well – you seemed happy enough. I hadn't the same strength and courage, the same belief in myself, that I'd had before the War. All I could see was myself, broken and useless, barely able to earn enough to keep you – and you looked so beautiful, Deirdre, such a queen amongst women, so worthy to have furs and jewels and lovely clothes and all the hundred and one luxuries Crozier could give you. That – and – well, the pain – of seeing you together, decided me. Everyone believed me dead. I would stay dead.'

'The pain!' repeated Deirdre in a low voice.

'Well, damn it all, Deirdre, it hurt! It isn't that I blame you. I don't. But it hurt.'

They were both silent. Then Tim raised her face to his and kissed it with a new tenderness.

'But that's all over now, sweetheart. The only thing to decide is how we're going to break it to Crozier.'

'Oh!' She drew herself away abruptly. 'I hadn't thought –' She broke off as Crozier and the manager appeared round the angle of the path. With a swift turn of the head she whispered:

'Do nothing now. Leave it to me. I must prepare him. Where could I meet you tomorrow?'

Nugent reflected.

'I could come in to Bulawayo. How about the Café near the Standard Bank? At three o'clock it would be pretty empty.'

Deirdre gave a brief nod of assent before turning her back on him and joining the other two men. Tim Nugent looked after her with a faint frown. Something in her manner puzzled him.

Deirdre was very silent during the drive home. Sheltering behind the fiction of a 'touch of the sun', she deliberated on her course of action. How should she tell him? How would he take it? A strange lassitude seemed to possess her, and a growing desire to postpone the revelation as long as might be. Tomorrow would be soon enough. There would be plenty of time before three o'clock.

The hotel was uncomfortable. Their room was on the ground floor, looking out on to an inner court. Deirdre stood that evening sniffing the stale air and glancing distastefully at the tawdry furniture. Her mind flew to the easy luxury of Monkton Court amidst the Surrey pinewoods. When her maid left her at last, she went slowly to her jewel case. In the palm of her hand the golden diamond returned her stare.

With an almost violent gesture she returned it to the case and slammed down the lid. Tomorrow morning she would tell George.

She slept badly. It was stifling beneath the heavy folds of the mosquito netting. The throbbing darkness was punctuated by the ubiquitous *ping* she had learnt to dread. She awoke white and listless. Impossible to start a scene so early in the day!

She lay in the small, close room all the morning, resting. Lunchtime came upon her with a sense of shock. As they sat drinking coffee, George Crozier proposed a drive to the Matopos.

'Plenty of time if we start at once.'

Deirdre shook her head, pleading a headache, and she thought to herself: 'That settles it. I can't rush the thing. After all, what does a day more or less matter? I'll explain to Tim.'

She waved goodbye to Crozier as he rattled off in the battered Ford. Then, glancing at her watch, she walked slowly to the meeting place.

The Café was deserted at this hour. They sat down at a little table and ordered the inevitable tea that South Africa drinks at all hours of the day and night. Neither of them said a word till the waitress brought it and withdrew to her fastness behind some pink curtains. Then Deirdre looked up and started as she met the intense watchfulness in his eyes.

'Deirdre, have you told him?'

She shook her head, moistening her lips, seeking for words that would not come.

'Why not?'

'I haven't had a chance; there hasn't been time.'

Even to herself the words sounded halting and unconvincing.

'It's not that. There's something else. I suspected it yesterday. I'm sure of it today. Deirdre, what is it?'

She shook her head dumbly.

'There's some reason why you don't want to leave George Crozier, why you don't want to come back to me. What is it?'

It was true. As he said it she knew it, knew it with sudden scorching shame, but knew it beyond any possibility of doubt. And still his eyes searched her.

'It isn't that you love him! You don't. But there's something.'

She thought: 'In another moment he'll see! Oh, God, don't let him!'

Suddenly his face whitened.

'Deirdre – is it – is it that there's going to be a – child?'

In a flash she saw the chance he offered her. A wonderful way! Slowly, almost without her own volition, she bowed her head.

She heard his quick breathing, then his voice, rather high and hard.

'That – alters things. I didn't know. We've got to find a different way out.' He leant across the table and caught both her hands in his. 'Deirdre, my darling, never think – never dream that you were in any way to blame. Whatever happens, remember that. I should have claimed you when I came back to England. I funked it, so it's up to me to do what I can to put things straight now. You see? Whatever happens, don't fret, darling. Nothing has been your fault.'

He lifted first one hand, then the other to his lips. Then she was alone, staring at the untasted tea. And, strangely enough, it was only one thing that she saw – a gaudily illuminated text hanging on a whitewashed wall. The words seemed to spring out from it and hurl themselves at her. 'What shall it profit a man –' She got up, paid for her tea and went out.

On his return George Crozier was met by a request that his wife might not be disturbed. Her headache, the maid said, was very bad.

It was nine o'clock the next morning when he entered her bedroom, his face rather grave. Deirdre was sitting up in bed. She looked white and haggard, but her eyes shone.

'George, I've got something to tell you, something rather terrible –'

He interrupted her brusquely.

'So you've heard. I was afraid it might upset you.'

'*Upset* me?'

'Yes. You talked to the poor young fellow that day.'

He saw her hand steal to her heart, her eyelids flicker, then she said in a low, quick voice that somehow frightened him:

'I've heard nothing. Tell me quickly.'

'I thought –'

'Tell me!'

'Out at that tobacco estate. Chap shot himself. Badly broken up in the War, nerves all to pieces, I suppose. There's no other reason to account for it.'

'He shot himself – in that dark shed where the tobacco was hanging.' She spoke with certainty, her eyes like a sleep-walker's as she saw before her in the odorous darkness a figure lying there, revolver in hand.

'Why, to be sure; that's where you were taken queer yesterday. Odd thing, that!'

Deirdre did not answer. She saw another picture – a table with tea things on it, and a woman bowing her head in acceptance of a lie.

'Well, well, the War has a lot to answer for,' said Crozier, and stretched out his hand for a match, lighting his pipe with careful puffs.

His wife's cry startled him.

'Ah! don't, don't! I can't bear the smell!'

He stared at her in kindly astonishment.

'My dear girl, you mustn't be nervy. After all, you can't escape from the smell of tobacco. You'll meet it everywhere.'

'Yes, everywhere!' She smiled a slow, twisted smile, and murmured some words that he did not catch, words that she had chosen for the original obituary notice of Tim Nugent's death. 'While the light lasts I shall remember, and in the darkness I shall not forget.'

Her eyes widened as they followed the ascending spiral of smoke, and she repeated in a low, monotonous voice: 'Everywhere, everywhere.'

The Red Signal

'The Red Signal' was first published in *Grand Magazine*, June 1924.

'No, but how too thrilling,' said pretty Mrs Eversleigh, opening her lovely, but slightly vacant eyes very wide. 'They always say women have a sixth sense; do you think it's true, Sir Alington?'

The famous alienist smiled sardonically. He had an unbounded contempt for the foolish pretty type, such as his fellow guest. Alington West was the supreme authority on mental disease, and he was fully alive to his own position and importance. A slightly pompous man of full figure.

'A great deal of nonsense is talked, I know that, Mrs Eversleigh. What does the term mean – a sixth sense?'

'You scientific men are always so severe. And it really is extraordinary the way one seems to positively know things sometimes – just know them, feel them, I mean – quite uncanny – it really is. Claire knows what I mean, don't you, Claire?'

She appealed to her hostess with a slight pout, and a tilted shoulder.

Claire Trent did not reply at once. It was a small dinner party, she and her husband, Violet Eversleigh, Sir Alington West, and his nephew, Dermot West, who was an old friend of Jack Trent's. Jack Trent himself, a somewhat heavy florid man, with a good-humoured smile, and a pleasant lazy laugh, took up the thread.

'Bunkum, Violet! Your best friend is killed in a railway accident. Straight away you remember that you dreamt of a black cat last Tuesday – marvellous, you felt all along that something was going to happen!'

'Oh, no, Jack, you're mixing up premonitions with intuition now. Come, now, Sir Alington, you must admit that premonitions are real?'

'To a certain extent, perhaps,' admitted the physician cautiously. 'But coincidence accounts for a good deal, and then there is the invariable tendency to make the most of a story afterwards – you've always got to take that into account.'

'I don't think there is any such thing as premonition,' said Claire Trent, rather abruptly. 'Or intuition, or a sixth sense, or any of the things we talk about so glibly. We go through life like a train rushing through the darkness to an unknown destination.'

'That's hardly a good simile, Mrs Trent,' said Dermot West, lifting his head for the first time and taking part in the discussion. There was a curious glitter in the clear grey eyes that shone out rather oddly from the deeply tanned face. 'You've forgotten the signals, you see.'

'The signals?'

'Yes, green if its all right, and red – for danger!'

'Red – for danger – how thrilling!' breathed Violet Eversleigh.

Dermot turned from her rather impatiently.

'That's just a way of describing it, of course. Danger ahead! The red signal! Look out!'

Trent stared at him curiously.

'You speak as though it were an actual experience, Dermot, old boy.'

'So it is – has been, I mean.'

'Give us the yarn.'

'I can give you one instance. Out in Mesopotamia – just after the Armistice, I came into my tent one evening with the feeling strong upon me. Danger! Look out! Hadn't the ghost of a notion what it was all about. I made a round of the camp, fussed unnecessarily, took all precautions against an attack by hostile Arabs. Then I went back to my tent. As soon as I got inside, the feeling popped up again stronger than ever. Danger! In the end, I took a blanket outside, rolled myself up in it and slept there.'

'Well?'

'The next morning, when I went inside the tent, first thing I saw was a great knife arrangement – about half a yard long – struck down through my bunk, just where I would have lain. I soon found out about it – one of the Arab servants. His son had been shot as a spy. What have you got to say to that, Uncle Alington, as an example of what I call the red signal?'

The specialist smiled non-committally.

'A very interesting story, my dear Dermot.'

'But not one that you would accept unreservedly?'

'Yes, yes, I have no doubt that you had the premonition of danger, just as you state. But it is the origin of the premonition I dispute. According to you, it came from without, impressed by some outside source upon your mentality. But nowadays we find that nearly everything comes from within – from our subconscious self.'

'Good old subconscious,' cried Jack Trent. 'It's the jack-of-all-trades nowadays.'

Sir Alington continued without heeding the interruption.

'I suggest that by some glance or look this Arab had betrayed himself. Your conscious self did not notice or remember, but with your subconscious self it was otherwise. The subconscious never forgets. We believe, too, that it can reason and deduce quite independently of the higher or conscious will. Your subconscious self, then, believed that an attempt might be made to assassinate you, and succeeded in forcing its fear upon your conscious realization.'

'That sounds very convincing, I admit,' said Dermot smiling.

'But not nearly so exciting,' pouted Mrs Eversleigh.

'It is also possible that you may have been subconsciously aware of the hate felt by the man towards you. What in the old days used to be called telepathy certainly exists, though the conditions governing it are very little understood.'

'Have there been any other instances?' asked Claire of Dermot.

'Oh! yes, but nothing very pictorial – and I suppose they could all be explained under the heading of coincidence. I refused an invitation to a country house once, for no other reason than the hoisting of the "red signal". The place was burnt out during the week. By the way, Uncle Alington, where does the subconscious come in there?'

'I'm afraid it doesn't,' said Alington, smiling.

'But you've got an equally good explanation. Come, now. No need to be tactful with near relatives.'

'Well, then, nephew, I venture to suggest that you refused the invitation for the ordinary reason that you didn't much want to go, and that after the fire, you suggested to yourself that you had had a warning of danger, which explanation you now believe implicitly.'

'It's hopeless,' laughed Dermot. 'It's heads you win, tails I lose.'

'Never mind, Mr West,' cried Violet Eversleigh. 'I believe in your Red Signal implicitly. Is the time in Mesopotamia the last time you had it?'

'Yes – until –'

'I beg your pardon?'

'Nothing.'

Dermot sat silent. The words which had nearly left his lips were: 'Yes, *until tonight.*' They had come quite unbidden to his lips, voicing a thought which had as yet not been consciously realized, but he was aware at once that they were true. The Red Signal was looming up out of the darkness. Danger! Danger at hand!

But why? What conceivable danger could there be here? Here in the house of his friends? At least – well, yes, there was that kind of danger. He looked at Claire Trent – her whiteness, her slenderness, the exquisite droop of her golden head. But that danger had been there for some time

– it was never likely to get acute. For Jack Trent was his best friend, and more than his best friend, the man who had saved his life in Flanders and had been recommended for the VC for doing so. A good fellow, Jack, one of the best. Damned bad luck that he should have fallen in love with Jack's wife. He'd get over it some day, he supposed. A thing couldn't go on hurting like this for ever. One could starve it out – that was it, starve it out. It was not as though she would ever guess – and if she did guess, there was no danger of her caring. A statue, a beautiful statue, a thing of gold and ivory and pale pink coral . . . a toy for a king, not a real woman . . .

Claire . . . the very thought of her name, uttered silently, hurt him . . . He must get over it. He'd cared for women before . . . 'But not like this!' said something. 'Not like this.' Well, there it was. No danger there – heartache, yes, but not danger. Not the danger of the Red Signal. That was for something else.

He looked round the table and it struck him for the first time that it was rather an unusual little gathering. His uncle, for instance, seldom dined out in this small, informal way. It was not as though the Trents were old friends; until this evening Dermot had not been aware that he knew them at all.

To be sure, there was an excuse. A rather notorious medium was coming after dinner to give a *seance*. Sir Alington professed to be mildly interested in spiritualism. Yes, that was an excuse, certainly.

The word forced itself on his notice. An *excuse*. Was the *seance* just an excuse to make the specialist's presence at dinner natural? If so, what was the real object of his being here? A host of details came rushing into Dermot's mind, trifles unnoticed at the time, or, as his uncle would have said, unnoticed by the conscious mind.

The great physician had looked oddly, very oddly, at Claire more than once. He seemed to be watching her. She was uneasy under his scrutiny. She made little twitching motions with her hands. She was nervous, horribly nervous, and was it, could it be, *frightened*? Why was she frightened?

With a jerk, he came back to the conversation round the table. Mrs Eversleigh had got the great man talking upon his own subject.

'My dear lady,' he was saying, 'what *is* madness? I can assure you that the more we study the subject, the more difficult we find it to pronounce. We all practise a certain amount of self-deception, and when we carry it so far as to believe we are the Czar of Russia, we are shut up or restrained. But there is a long road before we reach that point. At what particular spot on it shall we erect a post and say, "On this side sanity, on the other madness?" It can't be done, you know. And I will tell you this, if the man suffering from a delusion happened to hold his tongue about it, in all probability we should never be able to distinguish him from a normal individual. The extraordinary sanity of the insane is a most interesting subject.'

Sir Alington sipped his wine with appreciation, and beamed upon the company.

'I've always heard they are very cunning,' remarked Mrs Eversleigh. 'Loonies, I mean.'

'Remarkably so. And suppression of one's particular delusion has a disastrous effect very often. All suppressions are dangerous, as psycho-analysis has taught us. The man who has a harmless eccentricity, and can indulge it as such, seldom goes over the border line. But the man' – he paused – 'or woman who is to all appearance perfectly normal may be in reality a poignant source of danger to the community.'

His gaze travelled gently down the table to Claire, and then back again. He sipped his wine once more.

A horrible fear shook Dermot. Was *that* what he meant? Was *that* what he was driving at? Impossible, but –

'And all from suppressing oneself,' sighed Mrs Eversleigh. 'I quite see that one should be very careful always to – to express one's personality. The dangers of the other are frightful.'

'My dear Mrs Eversleigh,' expostulated the physician. 'You have quite misunderstood me. The cause of the mischief is in the physical matter of the brain – sometimes arising from some outward agency such as a blow; sometimes, alas, congenital.'

'Heredity is so sad,' sighed the lady vaguely. 'Consumption and all that.'

'Tuberculosis is not hereditary,' said Sir Alington drily.

'Isn't it? I always thought it was. But madness is! How dreadful. What else?'

'Gout,' said Sir Alington smiling. 'And colour blindness – the latter is rather interesting. It is transmitted direct to males, but is latent in females. So, while there are many colourblind men, for a woman to be colour-blind, it must have been latent in her mother as well as present in her father – rather an unusual state of things to occur. That is what is called sex-limited heredity.'

'How interesting. But madness is not like that, is it?'

'Madness can be handed down to men or women equally,' said the physician gravely.

Claire rose suddenly, pushing back her chair so abruptly that it over-turned and fell to the ground. She was very pale and the nervous motions of her fingers were very apparent.

'You – you will not be long, will you?' she begged. 'Mrs Thompson will be here in a few minutes now.'

'One glass of port, and I will be with you, for one,' declared Sir Alington. 'To see this wonderful Mrs Thompson's performance is what I have come for, is it not? Ha, ha! Not that I needed any inducement.' He bowed.

Claire gave a faint smile of acknowledgment and passed out of the room, her hand on Mrs Eversleigh's shoulder.

'Afraid I've been talking shop,' remarked the physician as he resumed his seat. 'Forgive me, my dear fellow.'

'Not at all,' said Trent perfunctorily.

He looked strained and worried. For the first time Dermot felt an outsider in the company of his friend. Between these two was a secret that even an old friend might not share. And yet the whole thing was fantastic and incredible. What had he to go upon? Nothing but a couple of glances and a woman's nervousness.

They lingered over their wine but a very short time, and arrived up in the drawing-room just as Mrs Thompson was announced.

The medium was a plump middle-aged woman, atrociously dressed in magenta velvet, with a loud rather common voice.

'Hope I'm not late, Mrs Trent,' she said cheerily. 'You did say nine o'clock, didn't you?'

'You are quite punctual, Mrs Thompson,' said Claire in her sweet, slight husky voice. 'This is our little circle.'

No further introductions were made, as was evidently the custom. The medium swept them all with a shrewd, penetrating eye.

'I hope we shall get some good results,' she remarked briskly. 'I can't tell you how I hate it when I go out and I can't give satisfaction, so to speak. It just makes me mad. But I think Shiromako (my Japanese control, you know) will be able to get through all right tonight. I'm feeling ever so fit, and I refused the welsh rabbit, fond of toasted cheese though I am.'

Dermot listened, half amused, half disgusted. How prosaic the whole thing was! And yet, was he not judging foolishly? Everything, after all, was natural – the powers claimed by mediums were natural powers, as yet imperfectly understood. A great surgeon might be wary of indigestion on the eve of a delicate operation. Why not Mrs Thompson?

Chairs were arranged in a circle, lights so that they could conveniently be raised or lowered. Dermot noticed that there was no question of *tests*, or of Sir Alington satisfying himself as to the conditions of the *seance*. No, this business of Mrs Thompson was only a blind. Sir Alington was here for quite another purpose. Claire's mother, Dermot remembered, had died abroad. There had been some mystery about her . . . Hereditary . . .

With a jerk he forced his mind back to the surroundings of the moment.

Everyone took their places, and the lights were turned out, all but a small red-shaded one on a far table.

For a while nothing was heard but the low even breathing of the medium. Gradually it grew more and more stertorous. Then, with a suddenness that made Dermot jump, a loud rap came from the far end of the room. It was repeated from the other side. Then a perfect crescendo of raps was heard. They died away, and a sudden high peal of mocking laughter rang through the room. Then silence, broken by a voice utterly unlike that of Mrs Thompson, a high-pitched quaintly inflected voice.

'I am here, gentlemen,' it said. 'Yess, I am here. You wish to ask me things?'

'Who are you? Shiromako?'

'Yess. I Shiromako. I pass over long time ago. I work. I very happy.'

Further details of Shiromako's life followed. It was all very flat and uninteresting, and Dermot had heard it often before. Everyone was happy, very happy. Messages were given from vaguely described relatives, the description being so loosely worded as to fit almost any contingency. An elderly lady, the mother of someone present, held the floor for some time, imparting copy book maxims with an air of refreshing novelty hardly borne out by her subject matter.

'Someone else want to get through now,' announced Shiromako. 'Got a very important message for one of the gentlemen.'

There was a pause, and then a new voice spoke, prefacing its remark with an evil demoniacal chuckle.

'Ha, ha! Ha, ha, ha! Better not go home. Better not go home. Take my advice.'

'Who are you speaking to?' asked Trent.

'One of you three. I shouldn't go home if I were him. Danger! Blood! Not very much blood – quite enough. No, don't go home.' The voice grew fainter. '*Don't go home!*'

It died away completely. Dermot felt his blood tingling. He was convinced that the warning was meant for him. Somehow or other, there was danger abroad tonight.

There was a sigh from the medium, and then a groan. She was coming round. The lights were turned on, and presently she sat upright, her eyes blinking a little.

'Go off well, my dear? I hope so.'

'Very good indeed, thank you, Mrs Thompson.'

'Shiromako, I suppose?'

'Yes, and others.'

Mrs Thompson yawned.

'I'm dead beat. Absolutely down and out. Does fairly take it out of you. Well, I'm glad it was a success. I was a bit afraid it mightn't be – afraid something disagreeable might happen. There's a queer feel about this room tonight.'

She glanced over each ample shoulder in turn, and then shrugged them uncomfortably.

'I don't like it,' she said. 'Any sudden deaths among any of you people lately?'

'What do you mean – among us?'

'Near relatives – dear friends? No? Well, if I wanted to be melodramatic, I'd say there was death in the air tonight. There, it's only my nonsense. Goodbye, Mrs Trent. I'm glad you've been satisfied.'

Mrs Thompson in her magenta velvet gown went out.

'I hope you've been interested, Sir Alington,' murmured Claire.

'A most interesting evening, my dear lady. Many thanks for the opportunity. Let me wish you good night. You are all going to a dance, are you not?'

'Won't you come with us?'

'No, no. I make it a rule to be in bed by half past eleven. Good night. Good night, Mrs Eversleigh. Ah! Dermot, I rather want to have a word with you. Can you come with me now? You can rejoin the others at the Grafton Galleries.'

'Certainly, uncle. I'll meet you there then, Trent.'

Very few words were exchanged between uncle and nephew during the short drive to Harley Street. Sir Alington made a semi-apology for dragging Dermot away, and assured him that he would only detain him a few minutes.

'Shall I keep the car for you, my boy?' he asked, as they alighted.

'Oh, don't bother, uncle. I'll pick up a taxi.'

'Very good. I don't like to keep Charlson up later than I can help. Good night, Charlson. Now where the devil did I put my key?'

The car glided away as Sir Alington stood on the steps vainly searching his pockets.

'Must have left it in my other coat,' he said at length. 'Ring the bell, will you? Johnson is still up, I dare say.'

The imperturbable Johnson did indeed open the door within sixty seconds.

'Mislaid my key, Johnson,' explained Sir Alington. 'Bring a couple of whiskies and sodas into the library, will you?'

'Very good, Sir Alington.'

The physician strode on into the library and turned on the lights. He motioned to Dermot to close the door behind him after entering.

'I won't keep you long, Dermot, but there's just something I want to say to you. Is it my fancy, or have you a certain – *tendresse*, shall we say, for Mrs Jack Trent?'

The blood rushed to Dermot's face.

'Jack Trent is my best friend.'

'Pardon me, but that is hardly answering my question. I dare say that you consider my views on divorce and such matters highly puritanical, but I must remind you that you are my only near relative and that you are my heir.'

'There is no question of a divorce,' said Dermot angrily.

'There certainly is not, for a reason which I understand perhaps better than you do. That particular reason I cannot give you now, but I do wish to warn you. Claire Trent is not for you.'

The young man faced his uncle's gaze steadily.

'I do understand – and permit me to say, perhaps better than you think. I know the reason for your presence at dinner tonight.'

'Eh?' The physician was clearly startled. 'How did you know that?'

'Call it a guess, sir. I am right, am I not, when I say that you were there in your – professional capacity.'

Sir Alington strode up and down.

'You are quite right, Dermot. I could not, of course, have told you so myself, though I am afraid it will soon be common property.'

Dermot's heart contracted.

'You mean that you have – made up your mind?'

'Yes, there is insanity in the family – on the mother's side. A sad case – a very sad case.'

'I can't believe it, sir.'

'I dare say not. To the layman there are few if any signs apparent.'

'And to the expert?'

'The evidence is conclusive. In such a case, the patient must be placed under restraint as soon as possible.'

'My God!' breathed Dermot. 'But you can't shut anyone up for nothing at all.'

'My dear Dermot! Cases are only placed under restraint when their being at large would result in danger to the community.

'Very grave danger. In all probability a peculiar form of homicidal mania. It was so in the mother's case.'

Dermot turned away with a groan, burying his face in his hands. Claire – white and golden Claire!

'In the circumstances,' continued the physician comfortably, 'I felt it incumbent on me to warn you.'

'Claire,' murmured Dermot. 'My poor Claire.'

'Yes, indeed, we must all pity her.'

Suddenly Dermot raised his head.

'I don't believe it.'

'What?'

'I say I don't believe it. Doctors make mistakes. Everyone knows that. And they're always keen on their own speciality.'

'My dear Dermot,' cried Sir Alington angrily.

'I tell you I don't believe it – and anyway, even if it is so, I don't care. I love Claire. If she will come with me, I shall take her away – far away – out of the reach of meddling physicians. I shall guard her, care for her, shelter her with my love.'

'You will do nothing of the sort. Are you mad?'

Dermot laughed scornfully.

'*You* would say so, I dare say.'

'Understand me, Dermot.' Sir Alington's face was red with suppressed passion. 'If you do this thing – this shameful thing – it is the end. I shall withdraw the allowance I am now making you, and I shall make a new will leaving all I possess to various hospitals.'

'Do as you please with your damned money,' said Dermot in a low voice. 'I shall have the woman I love.'

'A woman who –'

'Say a word against her, and, by God! I'll kill you!' cried Dermot.

A slight clink of glasses made them both swing round. Unheard by them in the heat of their argument, Johnson had entered with a tray of glasses. His face was the imperturbable one of the good servant, but Dermot wondered how much he had overheard.

'That'll do, Johnson,' said Sir Alington curtly. 'You can go to bed.'

'Thank you, sir. Good night, sir.'

Johnson withdrew.

The two men looked at each other. The momentary interruption had calmed the storm.

'Uncle,' said Dermot. 'I shouldn't have spoken to you as I did. I can quite see that from your point of view you are perfectly right. But I have loved Claire Trent for a long time. The fact that Jack Trent is my best friend has hitherto stood in the way of my ever speaking of love to Claire herself. But in these circumstances that fact no longer counts. The idea that any monetary conditions can deter me is absurd. I think we've both said all there is to be said. Good night.'

'Dermot –'

'It is really no good arguing further. Good night, Uncle Alington. I'm sorry, but there it is.'

He went out quickly, shutting the door behind him. The hall was in darkness. He passed through it, opened the front door and emerged into the street, banging the door behind him.

A taxi had just deposited a fare at a house farther along the street and Dermot hailed it, and drove to the Grafton Galleries.

In the door of the ballroom he stood for a minute bewildered, his head spinning. The raucous jazz music, the smiling women – it was as though he had stepped into another world.

Had he dreamt it all? Impossible that that grim conversation with his uncle should have really taken place. There was Claire floating past, like a lily in her white and silver gown that fitted sheathlike to her slenderness. She smiled at him, her face calm and serene. Surely it was all a dream.

The dance had stopped. Presently she was near him, smiling up into his face. As in a dream he asked her to dance. She was in his arms now, the raucous melodies had begun again.

He felt her flag a little.

'Tired? Do you want to stop?'

'If you don't mind. Can we go somewhere where we can talk? There is something I want to say to you.'

Not a dream. He came back to earth with a bump. Could he ever have thought her face calm and serene? It was haunted with anxiety, with dread. How much did she know?

He found a quiet corner, and they sat down side by side.

'Well,' he said, assuming a lightness he did not feel. 'You said you had something you wanted to say to me?'

'Yes.' Her eyes were cast down. She was playing nervously with the tassel of her gown. 'It's difficult – rather.'

'Tell me, Claire.'

'It's just this. I want you to – to go away for a time.'

He was astonished. Whatever he had expected, it was not this.

'You want me to go away? Why?'

'It's best to be honest, isn't it? I – I know that you are a – a gentleman and my friend. I want you to go away because I – I have let myself get fond of you.'

'Claire.'

Her words left him dumb – tongue-tied.

'Please do not think that I am conceited enough to fancy that you – that you would ever be likely to fall in love with me. It is only that – I am not very happy – and – oh! I would rather you went away.'

'Claire, don't you know that I have cared – cared damnably – ever since I met you?'

She lifted startled eyes to his face.

'You cared? You have cared a long time?'

'Since the beginning.'

'Oh!' she cried. 'Why didn't you tell me? Then? When I could have come to you! Why tell me now when it's too late. No, I'm mad – I don't know what I'm saying. I could never have come to you.'

'Claire, what did you mean when you said "now that it's too late?" Is it – is it because of my uncle? What he knows? What he thinks?'

She nodded dumbly, the tears running down her face.

'Listen, Claire, you're not to believe all that. You're not to think about it. Instead you will come away with me. We'll go to the South Seas, to islands like green jewels. You will be happy there, and I will look after you – keep you safe for always.'

His arms went round her. He drew her to him, felt her tremble at his touch. Then suddenly she wrenched herself free.

'Oh, no, please. Can't you see? I couldn't now. It would be ugly – ugly – ugly. All along I've wanted to be good – and now – it would be ugly as well.'

He hesitated, baffled by her words. She looked at him appealingly.

'Please,' she said. 'I want to be good . . .'

Without a word, Dermot got up and left her. For the moment he was touched and racked by her words beyond argument. He went for his hat and coat, running into Trent as he did so.

'Hallo, Dermot, you're off early.'

'Yes, I'm not in the mood for dancing tonight.'

'It's a rotten night,' said Trent gloomily. 'But you haven't got my worries.'

Dermot had a sudden panic that Trent might be going to confide in him. Not that – anything but that!

'Well, so long,' he said hurriedly. 'I'm off home.'

'Home, eh? What about the warning of the spirits?'

'I'll risk that. Good night, Jack.'

Dermot's flat was not far away. He walked there, feeling the need of the cool night air to calm his fevered brain.

He let himself in with his key and switched on the light in the bedroom.

And all at once, for the second time that night, the feeling that he had designated by the title of the Red Signal surged over him. So overpowering was it that for the moment it swept even Claire from his mind.

Danger! He was in danger. At this very moment, in this very room, he was in danger.

He tried in vain to ridicule himself free of the fear. Perhaps his efforts were secretly half hearted. So far, the Red Signal had given him timely warning which had enabled him to avoid disaster. Smiling a little at his own superstition, he made a careful tour of the flat. It was possible that some malefactor had got in and was lying concealed there. But his search revealed nothing. His man Milson, was away, and the flat was absolutely empty.

He returned to his bedroom and undressed slowly, frowning to himself. The sense of danger was acute as ever. He went to a drawer to get out a handkerchief, and suddenly stood stock still. There was an unfamiliar lump in the middle of the drawer – something hard.

His quick nervous fingers tore aside the handkerchiefs and took out the object concealed beneath them. It was a revolver.

With the utmost astonishment Dermot examined it keenly. It was of a somewhat unfamiliar pattern, and one shot had been fired from it lately. Beyond that, he could make nothing of it. Someone had placed it in that drawer that very evening. It had not been there when he dressed for dinner – he was sure of that.

He was about to replace it in the drawer, when he was startled by a bell ringing. It rang again and again, sounding unusually loud in the quietness of the empty flat.

Who could it be coming to the front door at this hour? And only one answer came to the question – an answer instinctive and persistent.

'Danger – danger – danger . . .'

Led by some instinct for which he did not account, Dermot switched off his light, slipped on an overcoat that lay across a chair, and opened the hall door.

Two men stood outside. Beyond them Dermot caught sight of a blue uniform. A policeman!

'Mr West?' asked the foremost of the two men.

It seemed to Dermot that ages elapsed before he answered. In reality it was only a few seconds before he replied in a very fair imitation of his man's expressionless voice:

'Mr West hasn't come in yet. What do you want with him at this time of night?'

'Hasn't come in yet, eh? Very well, then, I think we'd better come in and wait for him.'

'No, you don't.'

'See here, my man, my name is Inspector Verall of Scotland Yard, and I've got a warrant for the arrest of your master. You can see it if you like.'

Dermot perused the proffered paper, or pretended to do so, asking in a dazed voice:

'What for? What's he done?'

'Murder. Sir Alington West of Harley Street.'

His brain in a whirl, Dermot fell back before his redoubtable visitors.

He went into the sitting-room and switched on the light. The inspector followed him.

'Have a search round,' he directed the other man. Then he turned to Dermot.

'You stay here, my man. No slipping off to warn your master. What's your name, by the way?'

'Milson, sir.'

'What time do you expect your master in, Milson?'

'I don't know, sir, he was going to a dance, I believe. At the Grafton Galleries.'

'He left there just under an hour ago. Sure he's not been back here?'

'I don't think so, sir. I fancy I should have heard him come in.'

At this moment the second man came in from the adjoining room. In his hand he carried the revolver. He took it across to the inspector in some excitement. An expression of satisfaction flitted across the latter's face.

'That settles it,' he remarked. 'Must have slipped in and out without your hearing him. He's hooked it by now. I'd better be off. Cawley, you stay here, in case he should come back again, and you keep an eye on this fellow. He may know more about his master than he pretends.'

The inspector bustled off. Dermot endeavoured to get at the details of the affair from Cawley, who was quite ready to be talkative.

'Pretty clear case,' he vouchsafed. 'The murder was discovered almost immediately. Johnson, the manservant, had only just gone up to bed when he fancied he heard a shot, and came down again. Found Sir Alington dead, shot through the heart. He rang us up at once and we came along and heard his story.'

'Which made it a pretty clear case?' ventured Dermot.

'Absolutely. This young West came in with his uncle and they were quarrelling when Johnson brought in the drinks. The old boy was threatening to make a new will, and your master was talking about shooting him. Not five minutes later the shot was heard. Oh! yes, clear enough. Silly young fool.'

Clear enough indeed. Dermot's heart sank as he realized the overwhelming nature of the evidence against him. Danger indeed – horrible danger! And no way out save that of flight. He set his wits to work. Presently he suggested making a cup of tea. Cawley assented readily enough. He had already searched the flat and knew there was no back entrance.

Dermot was permitted to depart to the kitchen. Once there he put the kettle on, and chinked cups and saucers industriously. Then he stole swiftly to the window and lifted the sash. The flat was on the second floor, and outside the window was a small wire lift used by tradesmen which ran up and down on its steel cable.

Like a flash Dermot was outside the window and swinging himself down the wire rope. It cut into his hands, making them bleed, but he went on desperately.

A few minutes later he was emerging cautiously from the back of the block. Turning the corner, he cannoned into a figure standing by the sidewalk. To his utter amazement he recognized Jack Trent. Trent was fully alive to the perils of the situation.

'My God! Dermot! Quick, don't hang about here.'

Taking him by the arm, he led him down a by-street then down another. A lonely taxi was sighted and hailed and they jumped in, Trent giving the man his own address.

'Safest place for the moment. There we can decide what to do next to put those fools off the track. I came round here hoping to be able to warn you before the police got here, but I was too late.'

'I didn't even know that you had heard of it. Jack, you don't believe –'

'Of course not, old fellow, not for one minute. I know you far too well. All the same, it's a nasty business for you. They came round asking questions – what time you got to the Grafton Galleries, when you left, etc. Dermot, who could have done the old boy in?'

'I can't imagine. Whoever did it put the revolver in my drawer, I suppose. Must have been watching us pretty closely.'

'That *seance* business was damned funny. "*Don't go home.*" Meant for poor old West. He did go home, and got shot.'

'It applies to me to,' said Dermot. 'I went home and found a planted revolver and a police inspector.'

'Well, I hope it doesn't get me too,' said Trent. 'Here we are.'

He paid the taxi, opened the door with his latch-key, and guided Dermot up the dark stairs to his den, which was a small room on the first floor.

He threw open the door and Dermot walked in, whilst Trent switched on the light, and then came to join him.

'Pretty safe here for the time being,' he remarked. 'Now we can get our heads together and decide what is best to be done.'

'I've made a fool of myself,' said Dermot suddenly. 'I ought to have faced it out. I see more clearly now. The whole thing's a plot. What the devil are you laughing at?'

For Trent was leaning back in his chair, shaking with unrestrained mirth. There was something horrible in the sound – something horrible, too, about the man altogether. There was a curious light in his eyes.

'A damned clever plot,' he gasped out. 'Dermot, my boy, you're done for.'

He drew the telephone towards him.

'What are you going to do?' asked Dermot.

'Ring up Scotland Yard. Tell 'em their bird's here – safe under lock and key. Yes, I locked the door when I came in and the key's in my pocket. No good looking at that other door behind me. That leads into Claire's room, and she always locks it on her side. She's afraid of me, you know. Been afraid of me a long time. She always knows when I'm thinking about that knife – a long sharp knife. No, you don't –'

Dermot had been about to make a rush at him, but the other had suddenly produced an ugly-looking revolver.

'That's the second of them,' chuckled Trent. 'I put the first of them in your drawer – after shooting old West with it – What are you looking at over my head? That door? It's no use, even if Claire was to open it – and she might to *you* – I'd shoot you before you got there. Not in the heart – not to kill, just wing you, so that you couldn't get away. I'm a jolly good shot, you know. I saved your life once. More fool I. No, no, I want you hanged – yes, hanged. It isn't you I want the knife for. It's Claire – pretty Claire, so white and soft. Old West knew. That's what he was here for tonight, to see if I was mad or not. He wanted to shut me up – so that I shouldn't get Claire with the knife. I was very cunning. I took his latchkey and yours too. I slipped away from the dance as soon as I got there. I saw you come out from his house, and I went in. I shot him and came away at once. Then I went to your place and left the revolver. I was at the Grafton Galleries again almost as soon as you were, and I put the latchkey back in your coat pocket when I was saying good night to you. I don't mind telling you all this. There's no one else to hear, and when you're being hanged I'd like you to know I did it . . . God, how it makes me laugh! What are you thinking of? What the devil are you looking at?'

'I'm thinking of some words you quoted just now. You'd have done better, Trent, not to come home.'

'What do you mean?'

'Look behind you!' Trent spun round. In the doorway of the communicating room stood Claire – and Inspector Verall . . .

Trent was quick. The revolver spoke just once – and found its mark. He fell forward across the table. The inspector sprang to his side, as Dermot stared at Claire in a dream. Thoughts flashed through his brain disjointedly. His uncle – their quarrel – the colossal misunderstanding –

the divorce laws of England which would never free Claire from an insane husband – 'we must all pity her' – the plot between her and Sir Alington the cunning of Trent had seen through – her cry to him, 'Ugly – ugly – ugly!' Yes, but now –

The inspector straightened up again.

'Dead,' he said vexedly.

'Yes,' Dermot heard himself saying, 'he was always a good shot . . .'

The Mystery of the Blue Jar

'The Mystery of the Blue Jar' was first published in
Grand Magazine, July 1924.

Jack Hartington surveyed his topped drive ruefully. Standing by the ball, he looked back to the tee, measuring the distance. His face was eloquent of the disgusted contempt which he felt. With a sigh he drew out his iron, executed two vicious swings with it, annihilating in turn a dandelion and a tuft of grass, and then addressed himself firmly to the ball.

It is hard when you are twenty-four years of age, and your one ambition in life is to reduce your handicap at golf, to be forced to give time and attention to the problem of earning your living. Five and a half days out of the seven saw Jack imprisoned in a kind of mahogany tomb in the city. Saturday afternoon and Sunday were religiously devoted to the real business of life, and in an excess of zeal he had taken rooms at the small hotel near Stourton Heath links, and rose daily at the hour of six a.m. to get in an hour's practice before catching the 8.46 to town.

The only disadvantage to the plan was that he seemed constitutionally unable to hit anything at that hour in the morning. A foozled iron succeeded a muffed drive. His mashie shots ran merrily along the ground, and four putts seemed to be the minimum on any green.

Jack sighed, grasped his iron firmly and repeated to himself the magic words, 'Left arm right through, and don't look up.'

He swung back – and then stopped, petrified, as a shrill cry rent the silence of the summer's morning.

'Murder,' it called. 'Help! Murder!'

It was a woman's voice, and it died away at the end into a sort of gurgling sigh.

Jack flung down his club and ran in the direction of the sound. It had come from somewhere quite near at hand. This particular part of the course was quite wild country, and there were few houses about. In fact, there was only one near at hand, a small picturesque cottage, which Jack had often noticed for its air of old world daintiness. It was towards this cottage that he ran. It was hidden from him by a heather-covered slope, but he rounded this and in less than a minute was standing with his hand on the small latched gate.

There was a girl standing in the garden, and for a moment Jack jumped to the natural conclusion that it was she who had uttered the cry for help. But he quickly changed his mind.

She had a little basket in her hand, half full of weeds, and had evidently just straightened herself up from weeding a wide border of pansies. Her eyes, Jack noticed, were just like pansies themselves, velvety and soft and dark, and more violet than blue. She was like a pansy altogether, in her straight purple linen gown.

The girl was looking at Jack with an expression midway between annoyance and surprise.

'I beg your pardon,' said the young man. 'But did you cry out just now?'

'I? No, indeed.'

Her surprise was so genuine that Jack felt confused. Her voice was very soft and pretty with slight foreign inflection.

'But you must have heard it,' he exclaimed. 'It came from somewhere just near here.'

She stared at him.

'I heard nothing at all.'

Jack in his turn stared at her. It was perfectly incredible that she should not have heard that agonized appeal for help. And yet her calmness was so evident that he could not believe she was lying to him.

'It came from somewhere close at hand,' he insisted.

She was looking at him suspiciously now.

'What did it say?' she asked.

'Murder – help! Murder!'

'Murder – help! Murder,' repeated the girl. 'Somebody has played a trick on you, Monsieur. Who could be murdered here?'

Jack looked about him with a confused idea of discovering a dead body upon a garden path. Yet he was still perfectly sure that the cry he had heard was real and not a product of his imagination. He looked up at the cottage windows. Everything seemed perfectly still and peaceful.

'Do you want to search our house?' asked the girl drily.

She was so clearly sceptical that Jack's confusion grew deeper than ever. He turned away.

'I'm sorry,' he said. 'It must have come from higher up in the woods.'

He raised his cap and retreated. Glancing back over his shoulder, he saw that the girl had calmly resumed her weeding.

For some time he hunted through the woods, but could find no sign of anything unusual having occurred. Yet he was as positive as ever that he had really heard the cry. In the end, he gave up the search and hurried home to bolt his breakfast and catch the 8.46 by the usual narrow margin of a second or so. His conscience pricked him a little as he sat in the train. Ought he not to have immediately reported what he had heard to the police? That he had not done so was solely owing to the pansy girl's incredulity. She had clearly suspected him of romancing – possibly the police might do the same. *Was* he absolutely certain that he had heard the cry?

By now he was not nearly so positive as he had been – the natural result of trying to recapture a lost sensation. Was it some bird's cry in the distance that he had twisted into the semblance of a woman's voice?

But he rejected the suggestion angrily. It was a woman's voice, and he had heard it. He remembered looking at his watch just before the cry had come. As nearly as possible it must have been five and twenty minutes past seven when he had heard the call. That might be a fact useful to the police if – if anything should be discovered.

Going home that evening, he scanned the evening papers anxiously to see if there were any mention of a crime having been committed. But there was nothing, and he hardly knew whether to be relieved or disappointed.

The following morning was wet – so wet that even the most ardent golfer might have his enthusiasm damped. Jack rose at the last possible moment, gulped his breakfast, ran for the train and again eagerly scanned the papers. Still no mention of any gruesome discovery having been made. The evening papers told the same tale.

'Queer,' said Jack to himself, 'but there it is. Probably some blinking little boys having a game together up in the woods.'

He was out early the following morning. As he passed the cottage, he noted out of the tail of his eye that the girl was out in the garden again weeding. Evidently a habit of hers. He did a particularly good approach shot, and hoped that she had noticed it. As he teed up on the next tee, he glanced at his watch.

'Just five and twenty past seven,' he murmured. 'I wonder –'

The words were frozen on his lips. From behind him came the same cry which had so startled him before. A woman's voice, in dire distress.

'Murder – help! Murder!'

Jack raced back. The pansy girl was standing by the gate. She looked startled, and Jack ran up to her triumphantly, crying out:

'You heard it this time, anyway.'

Her eyes were wide with some emotion he could not fathom but he noticed that she shrank back from him as he approached, and even glanced back at the house, as though she meditated running to it for shelter.

She shook her head, staring at him.

'I heard nothing at all,' she said wonderingly.

It was as though she had struck him a blow between the eyes. Her sincerity was so evident that he could not disbelieve her. Yet he couldn't have imagined it – he couldn't – he couldn't –

He heard her voice speaking gently – almost with sympathy.

'You have had the shellshock, yes?'

In a flash he understood her look of fear, her glance back at the house. She thought that he suffered from delusions . . .

And then, like a douche of cold water, came the horrible thought, was she right? *Did* he suffer from delusions? Obsessed by the horror of the thought, he turned and stumbled away without vouchsafing a word. The girl watched him go, sighed, shook her head, and bent down to her weeding again.

Jack endeavoured to reason matters out with himself. 'If I hear the damned thing again at twenty-five minutes past seven,' he said to himself, 'it's clear that I've got hold of a hallucination of some sort. But I won't hear it.'

He was nervous all that day, and went to bed early determined to put the matter to the proof the following morning.

As was perhaps natural in such a case, he remained awake half the night, and finally overslept himself. It was twenty past seven by the time he was clear of the hotel and running towards the links. He realized that he would not be able to get to the fatal spot by twenty-five past, but surely, if the voice was a hallucination pure and simple, he would hear it anywhere. He ran on, his eyes fixed on the hands of his watch.

Twenty-five past. From far off came the echo of a woman's voice, calling. The words could not be distinguished, but he was convinced that it was the same cry he had heard before, and that it came from the same spot, somewhere in the neighbourhood of the cottage.

Strangely enough, that fact reassured him. It might, after all, be a hoax. Unlikely as it seemed, the girl herself might be playing a trick on him. He set his shoulders resolutely, and took out a club from his golf bag. He would play the few holes up to the cottage.

The girl was in the garden as usual. She looked up this morning, and when he raised his cap to her, said good morning rather shyly . . . She looked, he thought, lovelier than ever.

'Nice day, isn't it?' Jack called out cheerily, cursing the unavoidable banality of the observation.

'Yes, indeed, it is lovely.'

'Good for the garden, I expect?'

The girl smiled a little, disclosing a fascinating dimple.

'Alas, no! For my flowers the rain is needed. See, they are all dried up.'

Jack accepted the invitation of her gesture, and came up to the low hedge dividing the garden from the course, looking over it into the garden.

'They seem all right,' he remarked awkwardly, conscious as he spoke of the girl's slightly pitying glance running over him.

'The sun is good, is it not?' she said. 'For the flowers one can always water them. But the sun gives strength and repairs the health. Monsieur is much better today, I can see.'

Her encouraging tone annoyed Jack intensely.

'Curse it all,' he said to himself. 'I believe she's trying to cure me by suggestion.'

'I'm perfectly well,' he said.

'That is good then,' returned the girl quickly and soothingly.

Jack had the irritating feeling that she didn't believe him.

He played a few more holes and hurried back to breakfast. As he ate it, he was conscious, not for the first time, of the close scrutiny of a man who sat at the table next to him. He was a man of middle age, with a powerful forceful face. He had a small dark beard and very piercing grey eyes, and an ease and assurance of manner which placed him among the higher ranks of the professional classes. His name, Jack knew, was Lavington, and he had heard vague rumours as to his being a well-known medical specialist, but as Jack was not a frequenter of Harley Street, the name had conveyed little or nothing to him.

But this morning he was very conscious of the quiet observation under which he was being kept, and it frightened him a little. Was his secret written plainly in his face for all to see? Did this man, by reason of his professional calling, know that there was something amiss in the hidden grey matter?

Jack shivered at the thought. Was it true? Was he really going mad? Was the whole thing a hallucination, or was it a gigantic hoax?

And suddenly a very simple way of testing the solution occurred to him. He had hitherto been alone on his round. Supposing someone else was with him? Then one out of three things might happen. The voice might be silent. They might both hear it. Or – he only might hear it.

That evening he proceeded to carry his plan into effect. Lavington was the man he wanted with him. They fell into conversation easily enough – the older man might have been waiting for such an opening. It was clear that for some reason or other Jack interested him. The latter was able to come quite easily and naturally to the suggestion that they might play a few holes together before breakfast. The arrangement was made for the following morning.

They started out a little before seven. It was a perfect day, still and cloudless, but not too warm. The doctor was playing well, Jack wretchedly. His whole mind was intent on the forthcoming crisis. He kept glancing surreptitiously at his watch. They reached the seventh tee, between which and the hole the cottage was situated, about twenty past seven.

The girl, as usual, was in the garden as they passed. She did not look up.

Two balls lay on the green, Jack's near the hole, the doctor's some little distance away.

'I've got this for it,' said Lavington. 'I must go for it, I suppose.'

He bent down, judging the line he should take. Jack stood rigid, his eyes glued to his watch. It was exactly twenty-five minutes past seven.

The ball ran swiftly along the grass, stopped on the edge of the hole, hesitated and dropped in.

'Good putt,' said Jack. His voice sounded hoarse and unlike himself . . . He shoved his wrist watch farther up his arm with a sigh of over-whelming relief. Nothing had happened. The spell was broken.

'If you don't mind waiting a minute,' he said, 'I think I'll have a pipe.'

They paused a while on the eighth tee. Jack filled and lit the pipe with fingers that trembled a little in spite of himself. An enormous weight seemed to have lifted from his mind.

'Lord, what a good day it is,' he remarked, staring at the prospect ahead of him with great contentment. 'Go on, Lavington, your swipe.'

And then it came. Just at the very instant the doctor was hitting. A woman's voice, high and agonized.

'Murder – Help! Murder!'

The pipe fell from Jack's nerveless hand, as he spun round in the direction of the sound, and then, remembering, gazed breathlessly at his companion.

Lavington was looking down the course, shading his eyes.

'A bit short – just cleared the bunker, though, I think.'

He had heard nothing.

The world seemed to spin round with Jack. He took a step or two, lurching heavily. When he recovered himself, he was lying on the short turf, and Lavington was bending over him.

'There, take it easy now, take it easy.'

'What did I do?'

'You fainted, young man – or gave a very good try at it.'

'My God!' said Jack, and groaned.

'What's the trouble? Something on your mind?'

'I'll tell you in one minute, but I'd like to ask you something first.'

The doctor lit his own pipe and settled himself on the bank.

'Ask anything you like,' he said comfortably.

'You've been watching me for the last day or two. Why?'

Lavington's eyes twinkled a little.

'That's rather an awkward question. A cat can look at a king, you know.'

'Don't put me off. I'm earnest. Why was it? I've a vital reason for asking.'

Lavington's face grew serious.

'I'll answer you quite honestly. I recognized in you all the signs of a man labouring under a sense of acute strain, and it intrigued me what that strain could be.'

'I can tell you that easily enough,' said Jack bitterly. 'I'm going mad.'

He stopped dramatically, but his statement not seeming to arouse the interest and consternation he expected, he repeated it.

'I tell you I'm going mad.'

'Very curious,' murmured Lavington. 'Very curious indeed.'

Jack felt indignant.

'I suppose that's all it does seem to you. Doctors are so damned callous.'

'Come, come my young friend, you're talking at random. To begin with, although I have taken my degree, I do not practise medicine. Strictly speaking, I am not a doctor – not a doctor of the body, that is.'

Jack looked at him keenly.

'Or the mind?'

'Yes, in a sense, but more truly I call myself a doctor of the soul.'

'Oh!'

'I perceive the disparagement in your tone, and yet we must use some word to denote the active principle which can be separated and exist independently of its fleshy home, the body. You've got to come to terms with the soul, you know, young man, it isn't just a religious term invented by clergymen. But we'll call it the mind, or the subconscious self, or any term that suits you better. You took offence at my tone just now, but I can assure you that it really did strike me as very curious that such a well-balanced and perfectly normal young man as yourself should suffer from the delusion that he was going out of his mind.'

'I'm out of my mind all right. Absolutely balmy.'

'You will forgive me for saying so, but I don't believe it.'

'I suffer from delusions.'

'After dinner?'

'No, in the morning.'

'Can't be done,' said the doctor, relighting his pipe which had gone out.

'I tell you I hear things that no one else hears.'

'One man in a thousand can see the moons of Jupiter. Because the other nine hundred and ninety nine can't see them there's no reason to doubt that the moons of Jupiter exist, and certainly no reason for calling the thousandth man a lunatic.'

'The moons of Jupiter are a proved scientific fact.'

'It's quite possible that the delusions of today may be the proved scientific facts of tomorrow.'

In spite of himself, Lavington's matter-of-fact manner was having its effect upon Jack. He felt immeasurably soothed and cheered. The doctor looked at him attentively for a minute or two and then nodded.

'That's better,' he said. 'The trouble with you young fellows is that you're so cocksure nothing can exist outside your own philosophy that you get the wind up when something occurs to jolt you out of that opinion. Let's hear your grounds for believing that you're going mad, and we'll decide whether or not to lock you up afterwards.'

As faithfully as he could, Jack narrated the whole series of occurrences.

'But what I can't understand,' he ended, 'is why this morning it should come at half past seven – five minutes late.'

Lavington thought for a minute or two. Then –

'What's the time now by your watch?' he asked.

'Quarter to eight,' replied Jack, consulting it.

'That's simple enough, then. Mine says twenty to eight. Your watch is five minutes fast. That's a very interesting and important point – to me. In fact, it's invaluable.'

'In what way?'

Jack was beginning to get interested.

'Well, the obvious explanation is that on the first morning you *did* hear some such cry – may have been a joke, may not. On the following mornings, you suggestioned yourself to hear it at exactly the same time.'

'I'm sure I didn't.'

'Not consciously, of course, but the subconscious plays us some funny tricks, you know. But anyway, that explanation won't wash. If it was a case of suggestion, you would have heard the cry at twenty-five minutes past seven by your watch, and you could never have heard it when the time, as you thought, was past.'

'Well, then?'

'Well – it's obvious, isn't it? This cry for help occupies a perfectly definite place and time in space. The place is the vicinity of that cottage and the time is twenty-five minutes past seven.'

'Yes, but why should *I* be the one to hear it? I don't believe in ghosts and all that spook stuff – spirits rapping and all the rest of it. Why should I hear the damned thing?'

'Ah! that we can't tell at present. It's a curious thing that many of the best mediums are made out of confirmed sceptics. It isn't the people who are interested in occult phenomena who get the manifestations. Some people see and hear things that other people don't – we don't know why, and nine times out of ten they don't want to see or hear them, and are convinced that they are suffering from delusions – just as you were. It's like electricity. Some substances are good conductors, others are non-conductors, and for a long time we didn't know why, and had to be content just to accept the fact. Nowadays we do know why. Some day, no doubt, we shall know why you hear this thing and I and the girl don't. Everything's governed by natural law, you know – there's no such thing really as the supernatural. Finding out the laws that govern so called psychic phenomena is going to be a tough job – but every little helps.'

'But what am I going to *do?*' asked Jack.

Lavington chuckled.

'Practical, I see. Well, my young friend, you are going to have a good breakfast and get off to the city without worrying your head further about things you don't understand. I, on the other hand, am going to poke about, and see what I can find out about that cottage back there. That's where the mystery centres, I dare swear.'

Jack rose to his feet.

'Right, sir, I'm on, but, I say –'

'Yes?'

Jack flushed awkwardly.

'I'm sure the girl's all right,' he muttered.

Lavington looked amused.

'You didn't tell me she was a pretty girl! Well, cheer up, I think the mystery started before her time.'

Jack arrived home that evening in a perfect fever of curiosity. He was by now pinning his faith blindly to Lavington. The doctor had accepted the matter so naturally, had been so matter-of-fact and unperturbed by it, that Jack was impressed.

He found his new friend waiting for him in the hall when he came down for dinner, and the doctor suggested that they should dine together at the same table.

'Any news, sir?' asked Jack anxiously.

'I've collected the life history of Heather Cottage all right. It was tenanted first by an old gardener and his wife. The old man died, and the old woman went to her daughter. Then a builder got hold of it, and modernized it with great success, selling it to a city gentleman who used it for weekends. About a year ago, he sold it to some people called Turner – Mr and Mrs Turner. They seem to have been rather a curious couple from all I can make out. He was an Englishman, his wife was popularly supposed to be partly Russian, and was a very handsome exotic-looking woman. They lived very quietly, seeing no one, and hardly ever going outside the cottage garden. The local rumour goes that they were afraid of something – but I don't think we ought to rely on that.

'And then suddenly one day they departed, cleared out one morning early, and never came back. The agents here got a letter from Mr Turner, written from London, instructing him to sell up the place as quickly as possible. The furniture was sold off, and the house itself was sold to a Mr Mauleverer. He only actually lived in it a fortnight – then he advertised it to be let furnished. The people who have it now are a comsumptive French professor and his daughter. They have been there just ten days.'

Jack digested this in silence.

'I don't see that that gets us any forrader,' he said at last. 'Do you?'

'I rather want to know more about the Turners,' said Lavington quietly. 'They left very early in the morning, you remember. As far as I can make out, nobody actually saw them go. Mr Turner has been seen since – but I can't find anybody who has seen Mrs Turner.

Jack paled.

'It can't be – you don't mean –'

'Don't excite yourself, young man. The influence of anyone at the point of death – and especially of violent death – upon their surroundings is very strong. Those surroundings might conceivably absorb that influence, transmitting it in turn to a suitably tuned receiver – in this case yourself.'

'But why me?' murmured Jack rebelliously. 'Why not someone who could do some good?'

'You are regarding the force as intelligent and purposeful, instead of blind and mechanical. I do not believe myself in earthbound spirits, haunting a spot for one particular purpose. But the thing I have seen, again and again, until I can hardly believe it to be pure coincidence, is a kind of blind groping towards justice – a subterranean moving of blind forces, always working obscurely towards that end . . .'

He shook himself – as though casting off some obsession that pre-occupied him, and turned to Jack with a ready smile.

'Let us banish the subject – for tonight at all events,' he suggested.

Jack agreed readily enough, but did not find it so easy to banish the subject from his own mind.

During the weekend, he made vigorous inquiries of his own, but succeeded in eliciting little more than the doctor had done. He had definitely given up playing golf before breakfast.

The next link in the chain came from an unexpected quarter. On getting back one day, Jack was informed that a young lady was waiting to see him. To his intense surprise it proved to be the girl of the garden – the pansy girl, as he always called her in his own mind. She was very nervous and confused.

'You will forgive me, Monsieur, for coming to seek you like this? But there is something I want to tell you – I –'

She looked round uncertainly.

'Come in here,' said Jack promptly, leading the way into the now deserted 'Ladies' Drawing-room' of the hotel, a dreary apartment, with a good deal of red plush about it. 'Now, sit down, Miss, Miss –'

'Marchaud, Monsieur, Felise Marchaud.'

'Sit down, Mademoiselle Marchaud, and tell me all about it.'

Felise sat down obediently. She was dressed in dark green today, and the beauty and charm of the proud little face was more evident than ever. Jack's heart beat faster as he sat down beside her.

'It is like this,' explained Felise. 'We have been here but a short time, and from the beginning we hear the house – our so sweet little house – is haunted. No servant will stay in it. That does not matter so much – me, I can do the *menage* and cook easily enough.'

'Angel,' thought the infatuated young man. 'She's wonderful.'

But he maintained an outward semblance of businesslike attention.

'This talk of ghosts, I think it is all folly – that is until four days ago. Monsieur, four nights running, I have had the same dream. A lady stands there – she is beautiful, tall and very fair. In her hands she holds a blue china jar. She is distressed – very distressed, and continually she holds out the jar to me, as though imploring me to do something with it – but alas! she cannot speak, and I – I do not know what she asks. That was the dream for the first two nights – but the night before last, there was more of it. She and the blue jar faded away, and suddenly I heard her voice crying out – I know it is her voice, you comprehend – and, oh! Monsieur, the words she says are those you spoke to me that morning. "Murder – Help! Murder!" I awoke in terror. I say to myself – it is a nightmare, the words you heard are an accident. But last night the dream came again. Monsieur, what is it? You too have heard. What shall we do?'

Felise's face was terrified. Her small hands clasped themselves together, and she gazed appealingly at Jack. The latter affected an unconcern he did not feel.

'That's all right, Mademoiselle Marchaud. You mustn't worry. I tell you what I'd like you to do, if you don't mind, repeat the whole story to a friend of mine who is staying here, a Dr Lavington.'

Felise signified her willingness to adopt this course, and Jack went off in search of Lavington. He returned with him a few minutes later.

Lavington gave the girl a keen scrutiny as he acknowledged Jack's hurried introductions. With a few reassuring words, he soon put the girl at her ease, and he, in his turn, listened attentively to her story.

'Very curious,' he said, when she had finished. 'You have told your father of this?'

Felise shook her head.

'I have not liked to worry him. He is very ill still' – her eyes filled with tears – 'I keep from him anything that might excite or agitate him.'

'I understand,' said Lavington kindly. 'And I am glad you came to us, Mademoiselle Marchaud. Hartington here, as you know, had an experience something similar to yours. I think I may say that we are well on the track now. There is nothing else that you can think of?'

Felise gave a quick movement.

'Of course! How stupid I am. It is the point of the whole story. Look, Monsieur, at what I found at the back of one of the cupboards where it had slipped behind the shelf.'

She held out to them a dirty piece of drawing-paper on which was executed roughly in water colours a sketch of a woman. It was a mere daub, but the likeness was probably good enough. It represented a tall fair woman, with something subtly un-English about her face. She was standing by a table on which was standing a blue china jar.

'I only found it this morning,' explained Felise. 'Monsieur le docteur, that is the face of the woman I saw in my dream, and that is the identical blue jar.'

'Extraordinary,' commented Lavington. 'The key to the mystery is evidently the blue jar. It looks like a Chinese jar to me, probably an old one. It seems to have a curious raised pattern over it.'

'It is Chinese,' declared Jack. 'I have seen an exactly similar one in my uncle's collection – he is a great collector of Chinese porcelain, you know, and I remember noticing a jar just like this a short time ago.'

'The Chinese jar,' mused Lavington. He remained a minute or two lost in thought, then raised his head suddenly, a curious light shining in his eyes. 'Hartington, how long has your uncle had that jar?'

'How long? I really don't know.'

'Think. Did he buy it lately?'

'I don't know – yes, I believe he did, now I come to think of it. I'm not very interested in porcelain myself, but I remember his showing me his "recent acquisitions," and this was one of them.'

'Less than two months ago? The Turners left Heather Cottage just two months ago.'

'Yes, I believe it was.'

'Your uncle attends country sales sometimes?'

'He's always tooling round to sales.'

'Then there is no inherent improbability in our assuming that he bought this particular piece of porcelain at the sale of the Turners' things. A curious coincidence – or perhaps what I call the groping of blind justice. Hartington, you must find out from your uncle at once where he bought this jar.'

Jack's face fell.

'I'm afraid that's impossible. Uncle George is away on the Continent. I don't even know where to write to him.'

'How long will he be away?'

'Three weeks to a month at least.'

There was a silence. Felise sat looking anxiously from one man to the other.

'Is there nothing that we can do?' she asked timidly.

'Yes, there is one thing,' said Lavington, in a tone of suppressed excitement. 'It is unusual, perhaps, but I believe that it will succeed. Hartington, you must get hold of that jar. Bring it down here, and, if Mademoiselle permits, we will spend a night at Heather Cottage, taking the blue jar with us.'

Jack felt his skin creep uncomfortably.

'What do you think will happen?' he asked uneasily.

'I have not the slightest idea – but I honestly believe that the mystery will be solved and the ghost laid. Quite possibly there may be a false bottom to the jar and something is concealed inside it. If no phenomenon occurs, we must use our own ingenuity.'

Felise clasped her hands.

'It is a wonderful idea,' she exclaimed.

Her eyes were alight with enthusiasm. Jack did not feel nearly so enthusiastic – in fact, he was inwardly funking it badly, but nothing would have induced him to admit the fact before Felise. The doctor acted as though his suggestion were the most natural one in the world.

'When can you get the jar?' asked Felise, turning to Jack.

'Tomorrow,' said the latter, unwillingly.

He had to go through with it now, but the memory of the frenzied cry for help that had haunted him each morning was something to be ruthlessly thrust down and not thought about more than could be helped.

He went to his uncle's house the following evening, and took away the jar in question. He was more than ever convinced when he saw it again that it was the identical one pictured in the water colour sketch, but carefully as he looked it over he could see no sign that it contained a secret receptacle of any kind.

It was eleven o'clock when he and Lavington arrived at Heather Cottage. Felise was on the look-out for them, and opened the door softly before they had time to knock.

'Come in,' she whispered. 'My father is asleep upstairs, and we must not wake him. I have made coffee for you in here.'

She led the way into the small cosy sitting room. A spirit lamp stood in the grate, and bending over it, she brewed them both some fragrant coffee.

Then Jack unfastened the Chinese jar from its many wrappings. Felise gasped as her eyes fell on it.

'But yes, but yes,' she cried eagerly. 'That is it – I would know it anywhere.'

Meanwhile Lavington was making his own preparations. He removed all the ornaments from a small table and set it in the middle of the room. Round it he placed three chairs. Then, taking the blue jar from Jack, he placed it in the centre of the table.

'Now,' he said, 'we are ready. Turn off the lights, and let us sit round the table in the darkness.'

The others obeyed him. Lavington's voice spoke again out of the darkness.

'Think of nothing – or of everything. Do not force the mind. It is possible that one of us has mediumistic powers. If so, that person will go into a trance. Remember, there is nothing to fear. Cast out fear from your hearts, and drift – drift –'

His voice died away and there was silence. Minute by minute, the silence seemed to grow more pregnant with possibilities. It was all very well for Lavington to say 'Cast out fear.' It was not fear that Jack felt – it was panic. And he was almost certain that Felise felt the same way. Suddenly he heard her voice, low and terrified.

'Something terrible is going to happen. I feel it.'

'Cast out fear,' said Lavington. 'Do not fight against the influence.'

The darkness seemed to get darker and the silence more acute. And nearer and nearer came that indefinable sense of menace.

Jack felt himself choking – stifling – the evil thing was very near . . .

And then the moment of conflict passed. He was drifting, drifting down stream – his lids closed – peace – darkness . . .

*   *   *

Jack stirred slightly. His head was heavy – heavy as lead. Where was he?

Sunshine . . . birds . . . He lay staring up at the sky.

Then it all came back to him. The sitting. The little room. Felise and the doctor. What had happened?

He sat up, his head throbbing unpleasantly, and looked round him. He was lying in a little copse not far from the cottage. No one else was near him. He took out his watch. To his amazement it registered half past twelve.

Jack struggled to his feet, and ran as fast as he could in the direction of the cottage. They must have been alarmed by his failure to come out of the trance, and carried him out into the open air.

Arrived at the cottage, he knocked loudly on the door. But there was no answer, and no signs of life about it. They must have gone off to get help. Or else – Jack felt an indefinable fear invade him. What had happened last night?

He made his way back to the hotel as quickly as possible. He was about to make some inquiries at the office, when he was diverted by a colossal punch in the ribs which nearly knocked him off his feet. Turning in some indignation, he beheld a white-haired old gentleman wheezing with mirth.

'Didn't expect me, my boy. Didn't expect me, hey?' said this individual.

'Why, Uncle George, I thought you were miles away – in Italy somewhere.'

'Ah! but I wasn't. Landed at Dover last night. Thought I'd motor up to town and stop here to see you on the way. And what did I find. Out all night, hey? Nice goings on –'

'Uncle George,' Jack checked him firmly. 'I've got the most extraordinary story to tell you. I dare say you won't believe it.'

'I dare say I shan't,' laughed the old man. 'But do your best, my boy.'

'But I must have something to eat,' continued Jack. 'I'm famished.'

He led the way to the dining-room, and over a substantial repast, he narrated the whole story.

'And God knows what's become of them,' he ended.

His uncle seemed on the verge of apoplexy.

'The jar,' he managed to ejaculate at last. 'THE BLUE JAR! What's become of that?'

Jack stared at him in non-comprehension, but submerged in the torrent of words that followed he began to understand.

It came with a rush: 'Ming – unique – gem of my collection – worth ten thousand pounds at least – offer from Hoggenheimer, the American millionaire – only one of its kind in the world – Confound it, sir, what have you done with my BLUE JAR?'

Jack rushed from the room. He must find Lavington. The young lady at the office eyed him coldly.

'Dr Lavington left late last night – by motor. He left a note for you.'

Jack tore it open. It was short and to the point.

MY DEAR YOUNG FRIEND,

Is the day of the supernatural over? Not quite – especially when tricked out in new scientific language. Kindest regards from Felise, invalid father, and myself. We have twelve hours start, which ought to be ample.

Yours ever,

AMBROSE LAVINGTON,

Doctor of the Soul.

Jane in Search of a Job

'Jane in Search of a Job' was first published
in *Grand Magazine*, August 1924.

Jane Cleveland rustled the pages of the *Daily Leader* and sighed. A deep sigh that came from the innermost recesses of her being. She looked with distaste at the marble-topped table, the poached egg on toast which reposed on it, and the small pot of tea. Not because she was not hungry. That was far from being the case. Jane was extremely hungry. At that moment she felt like consuming a pound and a half of well-cooked beefsteak, with chip potatoes, and possibly French beans. The whole washed down with some more exciting vintage than tea.

But young women whose exchequers are in a parlous condition cannot be choosers. Jane was lucky to be able to order a poached egg and a pot of tea. It seemed unlikely that she would be able to do so tomorrow. That is unless –

She turned once more to the advertisement columns of the *Daily Leader*. To put it plainly, Jane was out of a job, and the position was becoming acute. Already the genteel lady who presided over the shabby boarding-house was looking askance at this particular young woman.

'And yet,' said Jane to herself, throwing up her chin indignantly, which was a habit of hers, 'and yet I'm intelligent and good-looking and well educated. What more does anyone want?'

According to the *Daily Leader*, they seemed to want shorthand typists of vast experience, managers for business houses with a little capital to invest, ladies to share in the profits of poultry farming (here again a little capital was required), and innumerable cooks, housemaids and parlour-maids – particularly parlourmaids.

'I wouldn't mind being a parlourmaid,' said Jane to herself. 'But there again, no one would take me without experience. I could go somewhere,

I dare say, as a Willing Young Girl – but they don't pay willing young girls anything to speak of.'

She sighed again, propped the paper up in front of her, and attacked the poached egg with all the vigour of healthy youth.

When the last mouthful had been despatched, she turned the paper, and studied the Agony and Personal column whilst she drank her tea. The Agony column was always the last hope.

Had she but possessed a couple of thousand pounds, the thing would have been easy enough. There were at least seven unique opportunities – all yielding not less than three thousand a year. Jane's lip curled a little.

'If I had two thousand pounds,' she murmured, 'it wouldn't be easy to separate me from it.'

She cast her eyes rapidly down to the bottom of the column and ascended with the ease born of long practice.

There was the lady who gave such wonderful prices for cast-off clothing. 'Ladies' wardrobes inspected at their own dwellings.' There were gentlemen who bought anything – but principally teeth. There were ladies of title going abroad who would dispose of their furs at a ridiculous figure. There was the distressed clergyman and the hard-working widow, and the disabled officer, all needing sums varying from fifty pounds to two thousand. And then suddenly Jane came to an abrupt halt. She put down her teacup and read the advertisement through again.

'There's a catch in it, of course,' she murmured. 'There always is a catch in these sort of things. I shall have to be careful. But still –'

The advertisement which so intrigued Jane Cleveland ran as follows:

If a young lady of twenty-five to thirty years of age, eyes dark blue, very fair hair, black lashes and brows, straight nose, slim figure, height five feet seven inches, good mimic and able to speak French, will call at 7 Endersleigh Street, between 5 and 6 p.m., she will hear of something to her advantage.

'Guileless Gwendolen, or why girls go wrong,' murmured Jane. 'I shall certainly have to be careful. But there are too many specifications, really, for that sort of thing. I wonder now . . . Let us overhaul the catalogue.'

She proceeded to do so.

'Twenty-five to thirty – I'm twenty-six. Eyes dark blue, that's right. Hair very fair – black lashes and brows – all OK. Straight nose? Ye-es – straight enough, anyway. It doesn't hook or turn up. And I've got a slim figure – slim even for nowadays. I'm only five feet six inches – but I could wear high heels. I *am* a good mimic – nothing wonderful, but I can copy people's voices, and I speak French like an angel or a

Frenchwoman. In fact, I'm absolutely the goods. They ought to tumble over themselves with delight when I turn up. Jane Cleveland, go in and win.'

Resolutely Jane tore out the advertisement and placed it in her handbag. Then she demanded her bill, with a new briskness in her voice.

At ten minutes to five Jane was reconnoitring in the neighbourhood of Endersleigh Street. Endersleigh Street itself is a small street sandwiched between two larger streets in the neighbourhood of Oxford Circus. It is drab, but respectable.

No. 7 seemed in no way different from the neighbouring houses. It was composed like they were of offices. But looking up at it, it dawned upon Jane for the first time that she was not the only blue-eyed, fair-haired, straight-nosed, slim-figured girl of between twenty-five and thirty years of age. London was evidently full of such girls, and forty or fifty of them at least were grouped outside No. 7 Endersleigh Street.

'Competition,' said Jane. 'I'd better join the queue quickly.'

She did so, just as three more girls turned the corner of the street. Others followed them. Jane amused herself by taking stock of her immediate neighbours. In each case she managed to find something wrong – fair eyelashes instead of dark, eyes more grey than blue, fair hair that owed its fairness to art and not to Nature, interesting variations in noses, and figures that only an all-embracing charity could have described as slim. Jane's spirits rose.

'I believe I've got as good an all-round chance as anyone,' she murmured to herself. 'I wonder what it's all about? A beauty chorus, I hope.'

The queue was moving slowly but steadily forward. Presently a second stream of girls began, issuing from inside the house. Some of them tossed their heads, some of them smirked.

'Rejected,' said Jane, with glee. 'I hope to goodness they won't be full up before I get in.'

And still the queue of girls moved forwards. There were anxious glances in tiny mirrors, and a frenzied powdering of noses. Lipsticks were brandished freely.

'I wish I had a smarter hat,' said Jane to herself sadly.

At last it was her turn. Inside the door of the house was a glass door at one side, with the legend, Messrs. Cuthbertsons, inscribed on it. It was through this glass door that the applicants were passing one by one. Jane's turn came. She drew a deep breath and entered.

Inside was an outer office, obviously intended for clerks. At the end was another glass door. Jane was directed to pass through this, and did so. She found herself in a smaller room. There was a big desk in it, and behind the desk was a keen-eyed man of middle age with a thick rather foreign-looking moustache. His glance swept over Jane, then he pointed to a door on the left.

'Wait in there, please,' he said crisply.

Jane obeyed. The apartment she entered was already occupied. Five girls sat there, all very upright and all glaring at each other. It was clear to Jane that she had been included amongst the likely candidates, and her spirits rose. Nevertheless, she was forced to admit that these five girls were equally eligible with herself as far as the terms of the advertisement went.

The time passed. Streams of girls were evidently passing through the inner office. Most of them were dismissed through another door giving on the corridor, but every now and then a recruit arrived to swell the select assembly. At half-past six there were fourteen girls assembled there.

Jane heard a murmur of voices from the inner office, and then the foreign-looking gentleman, whom she had nicknamed in her mind 'the Colonel' owing to the military character of his moustache, appeared in the doorway.

'I will see you ladies one at a time, if you please,' he announced. 'In the order in which you arrived, please.'

Jane was, of course, the sixth on the list. Twenty minutes elapsed before she was called in. 'The Colonel' was standing with his hands behind his back. He put her through a rapid catechism, tested her knowledge of French, and measured her height.

'It is possible, mademoiselle,' he said in French, 'that you may suit. I do not know. But it is possible.'

'What is this post, if I may ask?' said Jane bluntly.

He shrugged his shoulders.

'That I cannot tell you as yet. If you are chosen – then you shall know.'

'This seems very mysterious,' objected Jane. 'I couldn't possibly take up anything without knowing all about it. Is it connected with the stage, may I ask?'

'The stage? Indeed, no.'

'Oh!' said Jane, rather taken aback.

He was looking at her keenly.

'You have intelligence, yes? And discretion?'

'I've quantities of intelligence and discretion,' said Jane calmly. 'What about the pay?'

'The pay will amount to two thousand pounds – for a fortnight's work.'

'Oh!' said Jane faintly.

She was too taken aback by the munificence of the sum named to recover all at once.

The Colonel resumed speaking.

'One other young lady I have already selected. You and she are equally suitable. There may be others I have not yet seen. I will give you instruction as to your further proceedings. You know Harridge's Hotel?'

Jane gasped. Who in England did not know Harridge's Hotel? That famous hostelry situated modestly in a bystreet of Mayfair, where notabilities and royalties arrived and departed as a matter of course. Only this morning Jane had read of the arrival of the Grand Duchess Pauline of Ostrova. She had come over to open a big bazaar in aid of Russian refugees, and was, of course, staying at Harridge's.

'Yes,' said Jane, in answer to the Colonel's question.

'Very good. Go there. Ask for Count Streptitch. Send up your card – you have a card?'

Jane produced one. The Colonel took it from her and inscribed in the corner a minute P. He handed the card back to her.

'That ensures that the count will see you. He will understand that you come from me. The final decision lies with him – and another. If he considers you suitable, he will explain matters to you, and you can accept or decline his proposal. Is that satisfactory?'

'Perfectly satisfactory,' said Jane.

'So far,' she murmured to herself as she emerged into the street, 'I can't see the catch. And yet, there must be one. There's no such thing as money for nothing. It must be crime! There's nothing else left.'

Her spirits rose. In moderation Jane did not object to crime. The papers had been full lately of the exploits of various girl bandits. Jane had seriously thought of becoming one if all else failed.

She entered the exclusive portals of Harridge's with slight trepidation. More than ever, she wished that she had a new hat.

But she walked bravely up to the bureau and produced her card, and asked for Count Streptitch without a shade of hesitation in her manner. She fancied that the clerk looked at her rather curiously. He took the card, however, and gave it to a small page boy with some low-voiced instructions which Jane did not catch. Presently the page returned, and Jane was invited to accompany him. They went up in the lift and along a corridor to some big double doors where the page knocked. A moment later Jane found herself in a big room, facing a tall thin man with a fair beard, who was holding her card in a languid white hand.

'Miss Jane Cleveland,' he read slowly. 'I am Count Streptitch.'

His lips parted suddenly in what was presumably intended to be a smile, disclosing two rows of white even teeth. But no effect of merriment was obtained.

'I understand that you applied in answer to our advertisement,' continued the count. 'The good Colonel Kranin sent you on here.'

'He *was* a colonel,' thought Jane, pleased with her perspicacity, but she merely bowed her head.

'You will pardon me if I ask you a few questions?'

He did not wait for a reply, but proceeded to put Jane through a catechism very similar to that of Colonel Kranin. Her replies seemed to satisfy him. He nodded his head once or twice.

'I will ask you now, mademoiselle, to walk to the door and back again slowly.'

'Perhaps they want me to be a mannequin,' thought Jane, as she complied. 'But they wouldn't pay two thousand pounds to a mannequin. Still, I suppose I'd better not ask questions yet awhile.'

Count Streptitch was frowning. He tapped on the table with his white fingers. Suddenly he rose, and opening the door of an adjoining room, he spoke to someone inside.

He returned to his seat, and a short middle-aged lady came through the door, closing it behind her. She was plump and extremely ugly, but had nevertheless the air of being a person of importance.

'Well, Anna Michaelovna,' said the count. 'What do you think of her?'

The lady looked Jane up and down much as though the girl had been a wax-work at a show. She made no pretence of any greeting.

'She might do,' she said at length. 'Of actual likeness in the real sense of the word, there is very little. But the figure and the colouring are very good, better than any of the others. What do you think of it, Feodor Alexandrovitch?'

'I agree with you, Anna Michaelovna.'

'Does she speak French?'

'Her French is excellent.'

Jane felt more and more of a dummy. Neither of these strange people appeared to remember that she was a human being.

'But will she be discreet?' asked the lady, frowning heavily at the girl.

'This is the Princess Poporensky,' said Count Streptitch to Jane in French. 'She asks whether you can be discreet?'

Jane addressed her reply to the princess.

'Until I have had the position explained to me, I can hardly make promises.'

'It is just what she says there, the little one,' remarked the lady. 'I think she is intelligent, Feodor Alexandrovitch – more intelligent than the others. Tell me, little one, have you also courage?'

'I don't know,' said Jane, puzzled. 'I don't particularly like being hurt, but I can bear it.'

'Ah! that is not what I mean. You do not mind danger, no?'

'Oh!' said Jane. 'Danger! That's all right. I like danger.'

'And you are poor? You would like to earn much money?'

'Try me,' said Jane with something approaching enthusiasm.

Count Streptitch and Princess Poporensky exchanged glances. Then, simultaneously, they nodded.

'Shall I explain matters, Anna Michaelovna?' the former asked.

The princess shook her head.

'Her Highness wishes to do that herself.'

'It is unnecessary – and unwise.'

'Nevertheless those are her commands. I was to bring the girl in as soon as you had done with her.'

Streptitch shrugged his shoulders. Clearly he was not pleased. Equally clearly he had no intention of disobeying the edict. He turned to Jane.

'The Princess Poporensky will present you to Her Highness the Grand Duchess Pauline. Do not be alarmed.'

Jane was not in the least alarmed. She was delighted at the idea of being presented to a real live grand duchess. There was nothing of the Socialist about Jane. For the moment she had even ceased to worry about her hat.

The Princess Poporensky led the way, waddling along with a gait that she managed to invest with a certain dignity in spite of adverse circumstances. They passed through the adjoining room, which was a kind of antechamber, and the princess knocked upon a door in the farther wall. A voice from inside replied and the princess opened the door and passed in, Jane close upon her heels.

'Let me present to you, madame,' said the princess in a solemn voice, 'Miss Jane Cleveland.'

A young woman who had been sitting in a big armchair at the other end of the room jumped up and ran forward. She stared fixedly at Jane for a minute or two, and then laughed merrily.

'But this is splendid, Anna,' she replied. 'I never imagined we should succeed so well. Come, let us see ourselves side by side.'

Taking Jane's arm, she drew the girl across the room, pausing before a full-length mirror which hung on the wall.

'You see?' she cried delightedly. 'It is a perfect match!'

Already, with her first glance at the Grand Duchess Pauline, Jane had begun to understand. The Grand Duchess was a young woman perhaps a year or two older than Jane. She had the same shade of fair hair, and the same slim figure. She was, perhaps, a shade taller. Now that they stood side by side, the likeness was very apparent. Detail for detail, the colouring was almost exactly the same.

The Grand Duchess clapped her hands. She seemed an extremely cheerful young woman.

'Nothing could be better,' she declared. 'You must congratulate Feodor Alexandrovitch for me, Anna. He has indeed done well.'

'As yet, madame,' murmured the princess, in a low voice, 'this young woman does not know what is required of her.'

'True,' said the Grand Duchess, becoming somewhat calmer in manner. 'I forgot. Well, I will enlighten her. Leave us together, Anna Michaelovna.'

'But, madame –'

'Leave us alone, I say.'

She stamped her foot angrily. With considerable reluctance Anna Michaelovna left the room. The Grand Duchess sat down and motioned to Jane to do the same.

'They are tiresome, these old women,' remarked Pauline. 'But one has to have them. Anna Michaelovna is better than most. Now then, Miss – ah, yes, Miss Jane Cleveland. I like the name. I like you too. You are sympathetic. I can tell at once if people are sympathetic.'

'That's very clever of you, ma'am,' said Jane, speaking for the first time.

'I am clever,' said Pauline calmly. 'Come now, I will explain things to you. Not that there is much to explain. You know the history of Ostrova. Practically all of my family are dead – massacred by the Communists. I am, perhaps, the last of my line. I am a woman, I cannot sit upon the throne. You think they would let me be. But no, wherever I go attempts are made to assassinate me. Absurd, is it not? These vodka-soaked brutes never have any sense of proportion.'

'I see,' said Jane, feeling that something was required of her.

'For the most part I live in retirement – where I can take precautions, but now and then I have to take part in public ceremonies. While I am here, for instance, I have to attend several semi-public functions. Also in Paris on my way back. I have an estate in Hungary, you know. The sport there is magnificent.'

'Is it really?' said Jane.

'Superb. I adore sport. Also – I ought not to tell you this, but I shall because your face is so sympathetic – there are plans being made there – very quietly, you understand. Altogether it is very important that I should not be assassinated during the next two weeks.'

'But surely the police –' began Jane.

'The police? Oh, yes, they are very good, I believe. And we too – we have our spies. It is possible that I shall be forewarned when the attempt is to take place. But then, again, I might not.'

She shrugged her shoulders.

'I begin to understand,' said Jane slowly. 'You want me to take your place?'

'Only on certain occasions,' said the Grand Duchess eagerly. 'You must be somewhere at hand, you understand? I may require you twice, three times, four times in the next fortnight. Each time it will be upon the occasion of some public function. Naturally in intimacy of any kind, you could not represent me.'

'Of course not,' agreed Jane.

'You will do very well indeed. It was clever of Feodor Alexandrovitch to think of an advertisement, was it not?'

'Supposing,' said Jane, 'that I get assassinated?'

The Grand Duchess shrugged her shoulders.

'There is the risk, of course, but according to our own secret information, they want to kidnap me, not kill me outright. But I will be quite honest – it is always possible that they might throw a bomb.'

'I see,' said Jane.

She tried to imitate the light-hearted manner of Pauline. She wanted very much to come to the question of money, but did not quite see how best to introduce the subject. But Pauline saved her the trouble.

'We will pay you well, of course,' she said carelessly. 'I cannot remember now exactly how much Feodor Alexandrovitch suggested. We were speaking in francs or kronen.'

'Colonel Kranin,' said Jane, 'said something about two thousand pounds.'

'That was it,' said Pauline, brightening. 'I remember now. It is enough, I hope? Or would you rather have three thousand?'

'Well,' said Jane, 'if it's all the same to you, I'd rather have three thousand.'

'You are business-like, I see,' said the Grand Duchess kindly. 'I wish I was. But I have no idea of money at all. What I want I have to have, that is all.'

It seemed to Jane a simple but admirable attitude of mind.

'And of course, as you say, there is danger,' Pauline continued thoughtfully. 'Although you do not look to me as though you minded danger. I do not myself. I hope you do not think that it is because I am a coward that I want you to take my place? You see, it is most important for Ostrova that I should marry and have at least two sons. After that, it does not matter what happens to me.'

'I see,' said Jane.

'And you accept?'

'Yes,' said Jane resolutely. 'I accept.'

Pauline clapped her hands vehemently several times. Princess Poporensky appeared immediately.

'I have told her all, Anna,' announced the Grand Duchess. 'She will do what we want, and she is to have three thousand pounds. Tell Feodor to make a note of it. She is really very like me, is she not? I think she is better looking, though.'

The princess waddled out of the room, and returned with Count Streptitch.

'We have arranged everything, Feodor Alexandrovitch,' the Grand Duchess said.

He bowed.

'Can she play her part, I wonder?' he queried, eyeing Jane doubtfully.

'I'll show you,' said the girl suddenly. 'You permit, ma'am?' she said to the Grand Duchess.

The latter nodded delightedly.

Jane stood up.

'But this is splendid, Anna,' she said. 'I never imagined we should succeed so well. Come, let us see ourselves, side by side.'

And, as Pauline had done, she drew the other girl to the glass.

'You see? A perfect match!'

Words, manner and gesture, it was an excellent imitation of Pauline's greeting. The princess nodded her head, and uttered a grunt of approbation.

'It is good, that,' she declared. 'It would deceive most people.'

'You are very clever,' said Pauline appreciatively. 'I could not imitate anyone else to save my life.'

Jane believed her. It had already struck her that Pauline was a young woman who was very much herself.

'Anna will arrange details with you,' said the Grand Duchess. 'Take her into my bedroom, Anna, and try some of my clothes on her.'

She nodded a gracious farewell, and Jane was convoyed away by the Princess Poporensky.

'This is what Her Highness will wear to open the bazaar,' explained the old lady, holding up a daring creation of white and black. 'This is in three days' time. It may be necessary for you to take her place there. We do not know. We have not yet received information.'

At Anna's bidding, Jane slipped off her own shabby garments, and tried on the frock. It fitted her perfectly. The other nodded approvingly.

'It is almost perfect – just a shade long on you, because you are an inch or so shorter than Her Highness.'

'That is easily remedied,' said Jane quickly. 'The Grand Duchess wears low-heeled shoes, I noticed. If I wear the same kind of shoes, but with high heels, it will adjust things nicely.'

Anna Michaelovna showed her the shoes that the Grand Duchess usually wore with the dress. Lizard skin with a strap across. Jane memorized them, and arranged to get a pair just like them, but with different heels.

'It would be well,' said Anna Michaelovna, 'for you to have a dress of distinctive colour and material quite unlike Her Highness's. Then in case it becomes necessary for you to change places at a moment's notice, the substitution is less likely to be noticed.'

Jane thought a minute.

'What about a flame-red marocain? And I might, perhaps, have plain glass pince-nez. That alters the appearance very much.'

Both suggestions were approved, and they went into further details.

Jane left the hotel with bank-notes for a hundred pounds in her purse, and instructions to purchase the necessary outfit and engage rooms at the Blitz Hotel as Miss Montresor of New York.

On the second day after this, Count Streptitch called upon her there.

'A transformation indeed,' he said, as he bowed.

Jane made him a mock bow in return. She was enjoying the new clothes and the luxury of her life very much.

'All this is very nice,' she sighed. 'But I suppose that your visit means I must get busy and earn my money.'

'That is so. We have received information. It seems possible that an attempt will be made to kidnap Her Highness on the way home from the bazaar. That is to take place, as you know, at Orion House, which is about ten miles out of London. Her Highness will be forced to attend the bazaar in person, as the Countess of Anchester, who is promoting it, knows her personally. But the following is the plan I have concocted.'

Jane listened attentively as he outlined it to her.

She asked a few questions, and finally declared that she understood perfectly the part that she had to play.

The next day dawned bright and clear – a perfect day for one of the great events of the London Season, the bazaar at Orion House, promoted by the Countess of Anchester in aid of Ostrovian refugees in this country.

Having regard to the uncertainty of the English climate, the bazaar itself took place within the spacious rooms of Orion House, which has been for five hundred years in the possession of the Earls of Anchester. Various collections had been loaned, and a charming idea was the gift by a hundred society women of one pearl each taken from their own necklaces, each pearl to be sold by auction on the second day. There were also numerous sideshows and attractions in the grounds.

Jane was there early in the rôle of Miss Montresor. She wore a dress of flame-coloured marocain, and a small red cloche hat. On her feet were high-heeled lizard-skin shoes.

The arrival of the Grand Duchess Pauline was a great event. She was escorted to the platform and duly presented with a bouquet of roses by a small child. She made a short but charming speech and declared the bazaar open. Count Streptitch and Princess Poporensky were in attendance upon her.

She wore the dress that Jane had seen, white with a bold design of black, and her hat was a small cloche of black with a profusion of white ospreys hanging over the brim and a tiny lace veil coming half-way down the face. Jane smiled to herself.

The Grand Duchess went round the bazaar, visiting every stall, making a few purchases, and being uniformly gracious. Then she prepared to depart.

Jane was prompt to take up her cue. She requested a word with the Princess Poporensky and asked to be presented to the Grand Duchess.

'Ah, yes!' said Pauline, in a clear voice. 'Miss Montresor, I remember the name. She is an American journalist, I believe. She has done much for our cause. I should be glad to give her a short interview for her paper. Is there anywhere where we could be undisturbed?'

A small anteroom was immediately placed at the Grand Duchess's disposal, and Count Streptitch was despatched to bring in Miss Montresor. As soon as he had done so, and withdrawn again, the Princess Poporensky remaining in attendance, a rapid exchange of garments took place.

Three minutes later, the door opened and the Grand Duchess emerged, her bouquet of roses held up to her face.

Bowing graciously, and uttering a few words of farewell to Lady Anchester in French, she passed out and entered her car which was waiting. Princess Poporensky took her place beside her, and the car drove off.

'Well,' said Jane, 'that's that. I wonder how Miss Montresor's getting on.'

'No one will notice her. She can slip out quietly.'

'That's true,' said Jane. 'I did it nicely, didn't I?'

'You acted your part with great distinction.'

'Why isn't the count with us?'

'He was forced to remain. Someone must watch over the safety of Her Highness.'

'I hope nobody's going to throw bombs,' said Jane apprehensively. 'Hi! we're turning off the main road. Why's that?'

Gathering speed, the car was shooting down a side road.

Jane jumped up and put her head out of the window, remonstrating with the driver. He only laughed and increased his speed. Jane sank back into her seat again.

'Your spies were right,' she said, with a laugh. 'We're for it all right. I suppose the longer I keep it up, the safer it is for the Grand Duchess. At all events we must give her time to return to London safely.'

At the prospect of danger, Jane's spirits rose. She had not relished the prospect of a bomb, but this type of adventure appealed to her sporting instincts.

Suddenly, with a grinding of brakes, the car pulled up in its own length. A man jumped on the step. In his hand was a revolver.

'Put your hands up,' he snarled.

The Princess Poporensky's hands rose swiftly, but Jane merely looked at him disdainfully, and kept her hands on her lap.

'Ask him the meaning of this outrage,' she said in French to her companion.

But before the latter had time to say a word, the man broke in. He poured out a torrent of words in some foreign language.

Not understanding a single thing, Jane merely shrugged her shoulders and said nothing. The chauffeur had got down from his seat and joined the other man.

'Will the illustrious lady be pleased to descend?' he asked, with a grin.

Raising the flowers to her face again, Jane stepped out of the car. The Princess Poporensky followed her.

'Will the illustrious lady come this way?'

Jane took no notice of the man's mock insolent manner, but of her own accord she walked towards a low-built, rambling house which stood about a hundred yards away from where the car had stopped. The road had been a *cul-de-sac* ending in the gateway and drive which led to this apparently untenanted building.

The man, still brandishing his pistol, came close behind the two women. As they passed up the steps, he brushed past them and flung open a door on the left. It was an empty room, into which a table and two chairs had evidently been brought.

Jane passed in and sat down. Anna Michaelovna followed her. The man banged the door and turned the key.

Jane walked to the window and looked out.

'I could jump out, of course,' she remarked. 'But I shouldn't get far. No, we'll just have to stay here for the present and make the best of it. I wonder if they'll bring us anything to eat?'

About half an hour later her question was answered.

A big bowl of steaming soup was brought in and placed on the table in front of her. Also two pieces of dry bread.

'No luxury for aristocrats evidently,' remarked Jane cheerily as the door was shut and locked again. 'Will you start, or shall I?'

The Princess Poporensky waved the mere idea of food aside with horror.

'How could I eat? Who knows what danger my mistress might not be in?'

'She's all right,' said Jane. 'It's myself I'm worrying about. You know these people won't be at all pleased when they find they have got hold of the wrong person. In fact, they may be very unpleasant. I shall keep up the haughty Grand Duchess stunt as long as I can, and do a bunk if the opportunity offers.'

The Princess Poporensky offered no reply.

Jane, who was hungry, drank up all the soup. It had a curious taste, but was hot and savoury.

Afterwards she felt rather sleepy. The Princess Poporensky seemed to be weeping quietly. Jane arranged herself on her uncomfortable chair in the least uncomfortable way, and allowed her head to droop.

She slept.

Jane awoke with a start. She had an idea that she had been a very long time asleep. Her head felt heavy and uncomfortable.

And then suddenly she saw something that jerked her faculties wide awake again.

She was wearing the flame-coloured marocain frock.

She sat up and looked around her. Yes, she was still in the room in the empty house. Everything was exactly as it had been when she went to sleep, except for two facts. The first was that the Princess Poporensky was no longer sitting on the other chair. The second was her own inexplicable change of costume.

'I can't have dreamt it,' said Jane. 'Because if I'd dreamt it, I shouldn't be here.'

She looked across at the window and registered a second significant fact. When she had gone to sleep the sun had been pouring through the window. Now the house threw a sharp shadow on the sunlit drive.

'The house faces west,' she reflected. 'It was afternoon when I went to sleep. Therefore it must be tomorrow morning now. Therefore that soup was drugged. Therefore – oh, I don't know. It all seems mad.'

She got up and went to the door. It was unlocked. She explored the house. It was silent and empty.

Jane put her hand to her aching head and tried to think.

And then she caught sight of a torn newspaper lying by the front door. It had glaring headlines which caught her eye.

'American Girl Bandit in England,' she read. 'The Girl in the Red Dress. Sensational hold-up at Orion House Bazaar.'

Jane staggered out into the sunlight. Sitting on the steps she read, her eyes growing bigger and bigger. The facts were short and succinct.

Just after the departure of the Grand Duchess Pauline, three men and a girl in a red dress had produced revolvers and successfully held up the crowd. They had annexed the hundred pearls and made a getaway in a fast racing car. Up to now, they had not been traced.

In the stop press (it was a late evening paper) were a few words to the effect that the 'girl bandit in the red dress' had been staying at the Blitz as a Miss Montresor of New York.

'I'm dished,' said Jane. 'Absolutely dished. I always knew there was a catch in it.'

And then she started. A strange sound had smote the air. The voice of a man, uttering one word at frequent intervals.

'Damn,' it said. 'Damn.' And yet again, 'Damn!'

Jane thrilled to the sound. It expressed so exactly her own feelings. She ran down the steps. By the corner of them lay a young man. He was endeavouring to raise his head from the ground. His face struck Jane as one of the nicest faces she had ever seen. It was freckled and slightly quizzical in expression.

'Damn my head,' said the young man. 'Damn it. I —'

He broke off and stared at Jane.

'I must be dreaming,' he said faintly.

'That's what I said,' said Jane. 'But we're not. What's the matter with your head?'

'Somebody hit me on it. Fortunately it's a thick one.'

He pulled himself into a sitting position, and made a wry face.

'My brain will begin to function shortly, I expect. I'm still in the same old spot, I see.'

'How did you get here?' asked Jane curiously.

'That's a long story. By the way, you're not the Grand Duchess What's-her-name, are you?'

'I'm not. I'm plain Jane Cleveland.'

'You're not plain anyway,' said the young man, looking at her with frank admiration.

Jane blushed.

'I ought to get you some water or something, oughtn't I?' she asked uncertainly.

'I believe it is customary,' agreed the young man. 'All the same, I'd rather have whisky if you can find it.'

Jane was unable to find any whisky. The young man took a deep draught of water, and announced himself better.

'Shall I relate my adventures, or will you relate yours?' he asked.

'You first.'

'There's nothing much to mine. I happened to notice that the Grand Duchess went into that room with low-heeled shoes on and came out with high-heeled ones. It struck me as rather odd. I don't like things to be odd.

'I followed the car on my motor bicycle, I saw you taken into the house. About ten minutes later a big racing car came tearing up. A girl in red got out and three men. She had low-heeled shoes on, all right. They went into the house. Presently low heels came out dressed in black and white, and went off in the first car, with an old pussy and a tall man with a fair beard. The others went off in the racing car. I thought they'd all gone, and was just trying to get in at that window and rescue you when someone hit me on the head from behind. That's all. Now for your turn.'

Jane related her adventures.

'And it's awfully lucky for me that you did follow,' she ended. 'Do you see what an awful hole I should have been in otherwise? The Grand Duchess would have had a perfect alibi. She left the bazaar before the hold-up began, and arrived in London in her car. Would anybody ever have believed my fantastic improbable story?'

'Not on your life,' said the young man with conviction.

They had been so absorbed in their respective narratives that they had been quite oblivious of their surroundings. They looked up now with a slight start to see a tall sad-faced man leaning against the house. He nodded at them.

'Very interesting,' he commented.

'Who are you?' demanded Jane.

The sad-faced man's eyes twinkled a little.

'Detective-Inspector Farrell,' he said gently. 'I've been very interested in hearing your story and this young lady's. We might have found a little difficulty in believing hers, but for one or two things.'

'For instance?'

'Well, you see, we heard this morning that the real Grand Duchess had eloped with a chauffeur in Paris.'

Jane gasped.

'And then we knew that this American "girl bandit" had come to this country, and we expected a coup of some kind. We'll have laid hands on them very soon, I can promise you that. Excuse me a minute, will you?'

He ran up the steps into the house.

'Well!' said Jane. She put a lot of force into the expression.

'I think it was awfully clever of you to notice those shoes,' she said suddenly.

'Not at all,' said the young man. 'I was brought up in the boot trade. My father's a sort of boot king. He wanted me to go into the trade – marry and settle down. All that sort of thing. Nobody in particular – just the principle of the thing. But I wanted to be an artist.' He sighed.

'I'm so sorry,' said Jane kindly.

'I've been trying for six years. There's no blinking it. I'm a rotten painter. I've a good mind to chuck it and go home like the prodigal son. There's a good billet waiting for me.'

'A job is the great thing,' agreed Jane wistfully. 'Do you think you could get me one trying on boots somewhere?'

'I could give you a better one than that – if you'd take it.'

'Oh, what?'

'Never mind now. I'll tell you later. You know, until yesterday I never saw a girl I felt I could marry.'

'Yesterday?'

'At the bazaar. And then I saw her – the one and only Her!'

He looked very hard at Jane.

'How beautiful the delphiniums are,' said Jane hurriedly, with very pink cheeks.

'They're lupins,' said the young man.

'It doesn't matter,' said Jane.

'Not a bit,' he agreed. And he drew a little nearer.

Mr Eastwood's Adventure

'Mr Eastwood's Adventure' was first published as 'The Mystery of the Second Cucumber' in *The Novel Magazine*, August 1924. It also appeared later as 'The Mystery of the Spanish Shawl'.

Mr Eastwood looked at the ceiling. Then he looked down at the floor. From the floor his gaze travelled slowly up the right-hand wall. Then, with a sudden stern effort, he focused his gaze once more upon the typewriter before him.

The virgin white of the sheet of paper was defaced by a title written in capital letters.

'THE MYSTERY OF THE SECOND CUCUMBER,' so it ran. A pleasing title. Anthony Eastwood felt that anyone reading that title would be at once intrigued and arrested by it. 'The Mystery of the Second Cucumber,' they would say. 'What *can* that be about? A *cucumber*? The second *cucumber*? I must certainly read that story.' And they would be thrilled and charmed by the consummate ease with which this master of detective fiction had woven an exciting plot round this simple vegetable.

That was all very well. Anthony Eastwood knew as well as anyone what the story ought to be like – the bother was that somehow or other he couldn't get on with it. The two essentials for a story were a title and a plot – the rest was mere spade-work, sometimes the title led to a plot all by itself, as it were, and then all was plain sailing – but in this case the title continued to adorn the top of the page, and not the vestige of a plot was forthcoming.

Again Anthony Eastwood's gaze sought inspiration from the ceiling, the floor, and the wallpaper, and still nothing materialized.

'I shall call the heroine Sonia,' said Anthony, to urge himself on. 'Sonia or possibly Dolores – she shall have a skin of ivory pallor – the kind that's not due to ill-health, and eyes like fathomless pools. The hero shall be called George, or possibly John – something short and British. Then the gardener – I suppose there will have to be a gardener, we've got to drag that beastly cucumber in somehow or other – the gardener might be Scottish, and amusingly pessimistic about the early frost.'

This method sometimes worked, but it didn't seem to be going to this morning. Although Anthony could see Sonia and George and the comic gardener quite clearly, they didn't show any willingness to be active and do things.

'I could make it a banana, of course,' thought Anthony desperately. 'Or a lettuce, or a Brussels sprout – Brussels sprout, now, how about that? Really a cryptogram for *Brussels* – stolen bearer bonds – sinister Belgian Baron.'

For a moment a gleam of light seemed to show, but it died down again. The Belgian Baron wouldn't materialize, and Anthony suddenly remembered that early frosts and cucumbers were incompatible, which seemed to put the lid on the amusing remarks of the Scottish gardener.

'Oh! Damn!' said Mr Eastwood.

He rose and seized the *Daily Mail*. It was just possible that someone or other had been done to death in such a way as to lend inspiration to a perspiring author. But the news this morning was mainly political and foreign. Mr Eastwood cast down the paper in disgust.

Next, seizing a novel from the table, he closed his eyes and dabbed his finger down on one of the pages. The word thus indicated by Fate was 'sheep'. Immediately, with startling brilliance, a whole story unrolled itself in Mr Eastwood's brain. Lovely girl – lover killed in the war, her brain unhinged, tends sheep on the Scottish mountains – mystic meeting with dead lover, final effect of sheep and moonlight like Academy picture with girl lying dead in the snow, and *two trails of footsteps* . . .

It was a beautiful story. Anthony came out of its conception with a sigh and a sad shake of the head. He knew only too well the editor in question did not want that kind of story – beautiful though it might be. The kind of story he wanted, and insisted on having (and incidentally paid handsomely for getting), was all about mysterious dark women, stabbed to the heart, a young hero unjustly suspected, and the sudden unravelling of the mystery and fixing of the guilt on the least likely person, by the means of wholly inadequate clues – in fact, 'THE MYSTERY OF THE SECOND CUCUMBER.'

'Although,' reflected Anthony, 'ten to one, he'll alter the title and call it something rotten, like "*Murder Most Foul*" without so much as asking me! Oh, curse that telephone.'

He strode angrily to it, and took down the receiver. Twice already in the last hour he had been summoned to it – once for a wrong number, and once to be roped in for dinner by a skittish society dame whom he hated bitterly, but who had been too pertinacious to defeat.

'Hallo!' he growled into the receiver.

A woman's voice answered him, a soft caressing voice with a trace of foreign accent.

'Is that you, beloved?' it said softly.

'Well – er – I don't know,' said Mr Eastwood cautiously. 'Who's speaking?'

'It is I. Carmen. Listen, beloved. I am pursued – in danger – you must come at once. It is life or death now.'

'I beg your pardon,' said Mr Eastwood politely. 'I'm afraid you've got the wrong –'

She broke in before he could complete the sentence.

'*Madre de Dios!* They are coming. If they find out what I am doing, they will kill me. Do not fail me. Come at once. It is death for me if you don't come. You know, 320 Kirk Street. The word is cucumber . . . Hush . . .'

He heard the faint click as she hung up the receiver at the other end.

'Well, I'm damned,' said Mr Eastwood, very much astonished.

He crossed over to his tobacco jar, and filled his pipe carefully.

'I suppose,' he mused, 'that that was some curious effect of my subconscious self. She can't have *said* cucumber. The whole thing is very extraordinary. Did she say cucumber, or didn't she?'

He strolled up and down, irresolutely.

'320 Kirk Street. I wonder what it's all about? She'll be expecting the other man to turn up. I wish I could have explained. 320 Kirk Street. The word is cucumber – oh, impossible, absurd – hallucination of a busy brain.'

He glanced malevolently at the typewriter.

'What good are you, I should like to know? I've been looking at you all the morning, and a lot of good it's done me. An author should get his plot from life – from life, do you hear? I'm going out to get one now.'

He clapped a hat on his head, gazed affectionately at his priceless collection of old enamels, and left the flat.

Kirk Street, as most Londoners know, is a long, straggling thoroughfare, chiefly devoted to antique shops, where all kinds of spurious goods are offered at fancy prices. There are also old brass shops, glass shops, decayed second-hand shops and second-hand clothes dealers.

No. 320 was devoted to the sale of old glass. Glass-ware of all kinds filled it to overflowing. It was necessary for Anthony to move gingerly as he advanced up a centre aisle flanked by wine glasses and with lustres and chandeliers swaying and twinkling over his head. A very old lady was sitting at the back of the shop. She had a budding moustache that many an undergraduate might have envied, and a truculent manner.

She looked at Anthony and said, 'Well?' in a forbidding voice.

Anthony was a young man somewhat easily discomposed. He immediately inquired the price of some hock glasses.

'Forty-five shillings for half a dozen.'

'Oh, really,' said Anthony. 'Rather nice, aren't they? How much are these things?'

'Beautiful, they are, old Waterford. Let you have the pair for eighteen guineas.'

Mr Eastwood felt that he was laying up trouble for himself. In another minute he would be buying something, hypnotized by this fierce old woman's eye. And yet he could not bring himself to leave the shop.

'What about that?' he asked, and pointed to a chandelier.

'Thirty-five guineas.'

'Ah!' said Mr Eastwood regretfully. 'That's rather more than I can afford.'

'What do you want?' asked the old lady. 'Something for a wedding present?'

'That's it,' said Anthony, snatching at the explanation. 'But they're very difficult to suit.'

'Ah, well,' said the lady, rising with an air of determination. 'A nice piece of old glass comes amiss to nobody. I've got a couple of old decanters here – and there's a nice little liqueur set, just the thing for a bride –'

For the next ten minutes Anthony endured agonies. The lady had him firmly in hand. Every conceivable specimen of the glass-maker's art was paraded before his eyes. He became desperate.

'Beautiful, beautiful,' he exclaimed in a perfunctory manner, as he put down a large goblet that was being forced on his attention. Then blurted out hurriedly, 'I say, are you on the telephone here?'

'No, we're not. There's a call office at the post office just opposite. Now, what do you say, the goblet – or these fine old rummers?'

Not being a woman, Anthony was quite unversed in the gentle art of getting out of a shop without buying anything.

'I'd better have the liqueur set,' he said gloomily.

It seemed the smallest thing. He was terrified of being landed with the chandelier.

With bitterness in his heart he paid for his purchase. And then, as the old lady was wrapping up the parcel, courage suddenly returned to him. After all, she would only think him eccentric, and, anyway, what the devil did it matter what she thought?

'Cucumber,' he said, clearly and firmly.

The old crone paused abruptly in her wrapping operations.

'Eh? What did you say?'

'Nothing,' lied Anthony defiantly.

'Oh! I thought you said cucumber.'

'So I did,' said Anthony defiantly.

'Well,' said the old lady. 'Why ever didn't you say that before? Wasting my time. Through that door there and upstairs. She's waiting for you.'

As though in a dream, Anthony passed through the door indicated, and climbed some extremely dirty stairs. At the top of them a door stood ajar displaying a tiny sitting-room.

Sitting on a chair, her eyes fixed on the door, and an expression of eager expectancy on her face, was a girl.

Such a girl! She really had the ivory pallor that Anthony had so often written about. And her eyes! Such eyes! She was not English, that could be seen at a glance. She had a foreign exotic quality which showed itself even in the costly simplicity of her dress.

Anthony paused in the doorway, somewhat abashed. The moment of explanations seemed to have arrived. But with a cry of delight the girl rose and flew into his arms.

'You have come,' she cried. 'You have come. Oh, the saints and the Holy Madonna be praised.'

Anthony, never one to miss opportunities, echoed her fervently. She drew away at last, and looked up in his face with a charming shyness.

'I should never have known you,' she declared. 'Indeed I should not.'

'Wouldn't you?' said Anthony feebly.

'No, even your eyes seem different – and you are ten times handsomer than I ever thought you would be.'

'Am I?'

To himself Anthony was saying, 'Keep calm, my boy, keep calm. The situation is developing very nicely, but don't lose your head.'

'I may kiss you again, yes?'

'Of course you can,' said Anthony heartily. 'As often as you like.'

There was a very pleasant interlude.

'I wonder who the devil I am?' thought Anthony. 'I hope to goodness the real fellow won't turn up. What a perfect darling she is.'

Suddenly the girl drew away from him, and a momentary terror showed in her face.

'You were not followed here?'

'Lord, no.'

'Ah, but they are very cunning. You do not know them as well as I do. Boris, he is a fiend.'

'I'll soon settle Boris for you.'

'You are a lion – yes, but a lion. As for them, they are *canaille* – all of them. Listen, *I have it!* They would have killed me had they known. I was afraid – I did not know what to do, and then I thought of you . . . Hush, what was that?'

It was a sound in the shop below. Motioning to him to remain where he was, she tiptoed out on to the stairs. She returned with a white face and staring eyes.

'*Madre de Dios!* It is the police. They are coming up here. You have a knife? A revolver? Which?'

'My dear girl, you don't expect me seriously to murder a policeman?'

'Oh, but you are mad – mad! They will take you away and hang you by the neck until you're dead.'

'They'll *what?*' said Mr Eastwood, with a very unpleasant feeling going up and down his spine.

Steps sounded on the stair.

'Here they come,' whispered the girl. 'Deny everything. It is the only hope.'

'That's easy enough,' admitted Mr Eastwood, *sotto voce*.

In another minute two men had entered the room. They were in plain clothes, but they had an official bearing that spoke of long training. The smaller of the two, a little dark man with quiet grey eyes, was the spokesman.

'I arrest you, Conrad Fleckman,' he said, 'for the murder of Anna Rosenburg. Anything you say will be used in evidence against you. Here is my warrant and you will do well to come quietly.'

A half-strangled scream burst from the girl's lips. Anthony stepped forward with a composed smile.

'You are making a mistake, officer,' he said pleasantly. 'My name is Anthony Eastwood.'

The two detectives seemed completely unimpressed by his statement.

'We'll see about that later,' said one of them, the one who had not spoken before. 'In the meantime, you come along with us.'

'Conrad,' wailed the girl. 'Conrad, do not let them take you.'

Anthony looked at the detectives.

'You will permit me, I am sure, to say goodbye to this young lady?'

With more decency of feeling than he had expected, the two men moved towards the door. Anthony drew the girl into the corner by the window, and spoke to her in a rapid undertone.

'Listen to me. What I said was true. I am not Conrad Fleckman. When you rang up this morning, they must have given you the wrong number. My name is Anthony Eastwood. I came in answer to your appeal because – well, I came.'

She stared at him incredulously.

'You are not Conrad Fleckman?'

'No.'

'Oh!' she cried, with a deep accent of distress. 'And I kissed you!'

'That's all right,' Mr Eastwood assured her. 'The early Christians made a practice of that sort of thing. Jolly sensible. Now look here, I'll tool off with these people. I shall soon prove my identity. In the meantime, they won't worry you, and you can warn this precious Conrad of yours. Afterwards –'

'Yes?'

'Well – just this. My telephone number is North-western 1743 – and mind they don't give you the wrong one.'

She gave him an enchanting glance, half-tears, half a smile.

'I shall not forget – indeed, I shall not forget.'

'That's all right then. Goodbye. I say –'

'Yes?'

'Talking of the early Christians – once more wouldn't matter, would it?'

She flung her arms round his neck. Her lips just touched his.

'I do like you – yes, I do like you. You will remember that, whatever happens, won't you?'

Anthony disengaged himself reluctantly and approached his captors.

'I am ready to come with you. You don't want to detain this young lady, I suppose?'

'No, sir, that will be quite all right,' said the small man civilly.

'Decent fellows, these Scotland Yard men,' thought Anthony to himself, as he followed them down the narrow stairway.

There was no sign of the old woman in the shop, but Anthony caught a heavy breathing from a door at the rear, and guessed that she stood behind it, cautiously observing events.

Once out in the dinginess of Kirk Street, Anthony drew a long breath, and addressed the smaller of the two men.

'Now then, inspector – you are an inspector, I suppose?'

'Yes, sir. Detective-Inspector Verrall. This is Detective-Sergeant Carter.'

'Well, Inspector Verrall, the time has come to talk sense – and to listen to it too. I'm not Conrad What's-his-name. My name is Anthony Eastwood, as I told you, and I am a writer by profession. If you will accompany me to my flat, I think that I shall be able to satisfy you of my identity.'

Something in the matter-of-fact way Anthony spoke seemed to impress the detectives. For the first time an expression of doubt passed over Verrall's face.

Carter, apparently, was harder to convince.

'I dare say,' he sneered. 'But you'll remember the young lady was calling you "Conrad" all right.'

'Ah! that's another matter. I don't mind admitting to you both that for – er – reasons of my own, I was passing myself off upon that lady as a person called Conrad. A private matter, you understand.'

'Likely story, isn't it?' observed Carter. 'No, sir, you come along with us. Hail that taxi, Joe.'

A passing taxi was stopped, and the three men got inside. Anthony made a last attempt, addressing himself to Verrall as the more easily convinced of the two.

'Look here, my dear inspector, what harm is it going to do you to come along to my flat and see if I'm speaking the truth? You can keep the taxi if you like – there's a generous offer! It won't make five minutes' difference either way.'

Verrall looked at him searchingly.

'I'll do it,' he said suddenly. 'Strange as it appears, I believe you're speaking the truth. We don't want to make fools of ourselves at the station by arresting the wrong man. What's the address?'

'Forty-eight Brandenburg Mansions.'

Verrall leant out and shouted the address to the taxi-driver. All three sat in silence until they arrived at their destination, when Carter sprang out, and Verrall motioned to Anthony to follow him.

'No need for any unpleasantness,' he explained, as he, too, descended. 'We'll go in friendly like, as though Mr Eastwood was bringing a couple of pals home.'

Anthony felt extremely grateful for the suggestion, and his opinion of the Criminal Investigation Department rose every minute.

In the hall-way they were fortunate enough to meet Rogers, the porter. Anthony stopped.

'Ah! Good-evening, Rogers,' he remarked casually.

'Good-evening, Mr Eastwood,' replied the porter respectfully.

He was attached to Anthony, who set an example of liberality not always followed by his neighbours.

Anthony paused with his foot on the bottom step of the stairs.

'By the way, Rogers,' he said casually. 'How long have I been living here? I was just having a little discussion about it with these friends of mine.'

'Let me see, sir, it must be getting on for close on four years now.'

'Just what I thought.'

Anthony flung a glance of triumph at the two detectives. Carter grunted, but Verrall was smiling broadly.

'Good, but not good enough, sir,' he remarked. 'Shall we go up?'

Anthony opened the door of the flat with his latch-key. He was thankful to remember that Seamark, his man, was out. The fewer witnesses of this catastrophe the better.

The typewriter was as he had left it. Carter strode across to the table and read the headline on the paper.

'THE MYSTERY OF THE SECOND CUCUMBER'

he announced in a gloomy voice.

'A story of mine,' explained Anthony nonchalantly.

'That's another good point, sir,' said Verrall, nodding his head, his eyes twinkling. 'By the way, sir, what was it about? What *was* the mystery of the second cucumber?'

'Ah, there you have me,' said Anthony. 'It's that second cucumber that's been at the bottom of all this trouble.'

Carter was looking at him intently. Suddenly he shook his head and tapped his forehead significantly.

'Balmy, poor young fellow,' he murmured in an audible aside.

'Now, gentlemen,' said Mr Eastwood briskly. 'To business. Here are letters addressed to me, my bank-book, communications from editors. What more do you want?'

Verrall examined the papers that Anthony thrust upon him.

'Speaking for myself, sir,' he said respectfully, 'I want nothing more. I'm quite convinced. But I can't take the responsibility of releasing you upon myself. You see, although it seems positive that you have been residing here as Mr Eastwood for some years, yet it is possible that Conrad Fleckman and Anthony Eastwood are one and the same person. I must make a thorough search of the flat, take your fingerprints, and telephone to headquarters.'

'That seems a comprehensive programme,' remarked Anthony. 'I can assure you that you're welcome to any guilty secrets of mine you may lay your hands on.'

The inspector grinned. For a detective, he was a singularly human person.

'Will you go into the little end room, sir, with Carter, whilst I'm getting busy?'

'All right,' said Anthony unwillingly. 'I suppose it couldn't be the other way about, could it?'

'Meaning?'

'That you and I and a couple of whiskies and sodas should occupy the end room whilst our friend, the Sergeant, does the heavy searching.'

'If you prefer it, sir?'

'I do prefer it.'

They left Carter investigating the contents of the desk with business-like dexterity. As they passed out of the room, they heard him take down the telephone and call up Scotland Yard.

'This isn't so bad,' said Anthony, settling himself with a whisky and soda by his side, having hospitably attended to the wants of Inspector Verrall. 'Shall I drink first, just to show you that the whisky isn't poisoned?'

The inspector smiled.

'Very irregular, all this,' he remarked. 'But we know a thing or two in our profession. I realized right from the start that we'd made a mistake. But of course one had to observe all the usual forms. You can't get away from red tape, can you, sir?'

'I suppose not,' said Anthony regretfully. 'The sergeant doesn't seem very matey yet, though, does he?'

'Ah, he's a fine man, Detective-Sergeant Carter. You wouldn't find it easy to put anything over on him.'

'I've noticed that,' said Anthony.

'By the way, inspector,' he added, 'is there any objection to my hearing something about myself?'

'In what way, sir?'

'Come now, don't you realize that I'm devoured by curiosity? Who was Anna Rosenburg, and why did I murder her?'

'You'll read all about it in the newspapers tomorrow, sir.'

'Tomorrow I may be Myself with Yesterday's ten thousand years,' quoted Anthony. 'I really think you might satisfy my perfectly legitimate curiosity, inspector. Cast aside your official reticence, and tell me all.'

'It's quite irregular, sir.'

'My dear inspector, when we are becoming such fast friends?'

'Well, sir, Anna Rosenburg was a German-Jewess who lived at Hampstead. With no visible means of livelihood, she grew yearly richer and richer.'

'I'm just the opposite,' commented Anthony. 'I have a visible means of livelihood and I get yearly poorer and poorer. Perhaps I should do better if I lived in Hampstead. I've always heard Hampstead is very bracing.'

'At one time,' continued Verrall, 'she was a secondhand clothes dealer –'

'That explains it,' interrupted Anthony. 'I remember selling my uniform after the war – not khaki, the other stuff. The whole flat was full of red trousers and gold lace, spread out to best advantage. A fat man in a check suit arrived in a Rolls-Royce with a factotum complete with bag. He bid one pound ten for the lot. In the end I threw in a hunting coat and some

Zeiss glasses to make up the two pounds, at a given signal the factotum opened the bag and shovelled the goods inside, and the fat man tendered me a ten-pound note and asked me for change.'

'About ten years ago,' continued the inspector, 'there were several Spanish political refugees in London – amongst them a certain Don Fernando Ferrarez with his young wife and child. They were very poor, and the wife was ill. Anna Rosenburg visited the place where they were lodging and asked if they had anything to sell. Don Fernando was out, and his wife decided to part with a very wonderful Spanish shawl, embroidered in a marvellous manner, which had been one of her husband's last presents to her before flying from Spain. When Don Fernando returned, he flew into a terrible rage on hearing the shawl had been sold, and tried vainly to recover it. When he at last succeeded in finding the second-hand clothes woman in question, she declared that she had resold the shawl to a woman whose name she did not know. Don Fernando was in despair. Two months later he was stabbed in the street and died as a result of his wounds. From that time onward, Anna Rosenburg seemed suspiciously flush of money. In the ten years that followed, her house was burgled no less than eight times. Four of the attempts were frustrated and nothing was taken, on the other four occasions, an embroidered shawl of some kind was amongst the booty.'

The inspector paused, and then went on in obedience to an urgent gesture from Anthony.

'A week ago, Carmen Ferrarez, the young daughter of Don Fernando, arrived in this country from a convent in France. Her first action was to seek out Anna Rosenburg at Hampstead. There she is reported to have had a violent scene with the old woman, and her words at leaving were overheard by one of the servants.

'"You have it still," she cried. "All these years you have grown rich on it – but I say to you solemnly that in the end it will bring you bad luck. You have no moral right to it, and the day will come when you will wish you had never seen the Shawl of the Thousand Flowers."

'Three days after that, Carmen Ferrarez disappeared mysteriously from the hotel where she was staying. In her room was found a name and address – the name of Conrad Fleckman, and also a note from a man purporting to be an antique dealer asking if she were disposed to part with a certain embroidered shawl which he believed she had in her possession. The address given on the note was a false one.

'It is clear that the shawl is the centre of the whole mystery. Yesterday morning Conrad Fleckman called upon Anna Rosenburg. She was shut up with him for an hour or more, and when he left she was obliged to go to bed, so white and shaken was she by the interview. But she gave orders that if he came to see her again he was always to be admitted. Last night she got up and went out about nine o'clock, and did not return. She was found this morning in the house occupied by Conrad Fleckman, stabbed through the heart. On the floor beside her was – what do you think?'

'The shawl?' breathed Anthony. 'The Shawl of a Thousand Flowers.'

'Something far more gruesome than that. Something which explained the whole mysterious business of the shawl and made its hidden value clear . . . Excuse me, I fancy that's the chief –'

There had indeed been a ring at the bell. Anthony contained his impatience as best he could and waited for the inspector to return. He was pretty well at ease about his own position now. As soon as they took the fingerprints they would realise their mistake.

And then, perhaps, Carmen would ring up . . .

The Shawl of a Thousand Flowers! What a strange story – just the kind of story to make an appropriate setting for the girl's exquisite dark beauty.

Carmen Ferrarez . . .

He jerked himself back from day dreaming. What a time that inspector fellow was. He rose and pulled the door open. The flat was strangely silent. Could they have gone? Surely not without a word to him.

He strode out into the next room. It was empty – so was the sitting-room. Strangely empty! It had a bare dishevelled appearance. Good heavens! His enamels – the silver!

He rushed wildly through the flat. It was the same tale everywhere. The place had been denuded. Every single thing of value, and Anthony had a very pretty collector's taste in small things, had been taken.

With a groan Anthony staggered to a chair, his head in his hands. He was aroused by the ringing of the front door bell. He opened it to confront Rogers.

'You'll excuse me, sir,' said Rogers. 'But the gentlemen fancied you might be wanting something.'

'The gentlemen?'

'Those two friends of yours, sir. I helped them with the packing as best I could. Very fortunately I happened to have them two good cases in the basement.' His eyes dropped to the floor. 'I've swept up the straw as best I could, sir.'

'You packed the things in here?' groaned Anthony.

'Yes, sir. Was that not your wishes, sir? It was the tall gentleman told me to do so, sir, and seeing as you were busy talking to the other gentleman in the little end room, I didn't like to disturb you.'

'I wasn't talking to him,' said Anthony. 'He was talking to me – curse him.'

Rogers coughed.

'I'm sure I'm very sorry for the necessity, sir,' he murmured.

'Necessity?'

'Of parting with your little treasures, sir.'

'Eh? Oh, yes. Ha, ha!' He gave a mirthless laugh. 'They've driven off by now, I suppose. Those – those friends of mine, I mean?'

'Oh, yes, sir, some time ago. I put the cases on the taxi and the tall gentleman went upstairs again, and then they both came running down and drove off at once . . . Excuse me, sir, but is anything wrong, sir?'

Rogers might well ask. The hollow groan which Anthony emitted would have aroused surmise anywhere.

'Everything is wrong, thank you, Rogers. But I see clearly that you were not to blame. Leave me, I would commune a while with my telephone.'

Five minutes later saw Anthony pouring his tale into the ears of Inspector Driver, who sat opposite to him, note-book in hand. An unsympathetic man, Inspector Driver, and not (Anthony reflected) nearly so like a real inspector! Distinctly stagey, in fact. Another striking example of the superiority of Art over Nature.

Anthony reached the end of his tale. The inspector shut up his note-book.

'Well?' said Anthony anxiously.

'Clear as paint,' said the inspector. 'It's the Patterson gang. They've done a lot of smart work lately. Big fair man, small dark man, and the girl.'

'The girl?'

'Yes, dark and mighty good looking. Acts as a decoy usually.'

'A – a Spanish girl?'

'She might call herself that. She was born in Hampstead.'

'I *said* it was a bracing place,' murmured Anthony.

'Yes, it's clear enough,' said the inspector, rising to depart. 'She got you on the phone and pitched you a tale – she guessed you'd come along all right. Then she goes along to old Mother Gibson's who isn't above accepting a tip for the use of her room for them as finds it awkward to meet in public – lovers, you understand, nothing criminal. You fall for it all right, they get you back here, and while one of them pitches you a tale, the other gets away with the swag. It's the Pattersons all right – just their touch.'

'And my things?' said Anthony anxiously.

'We'll do what we can, sir. But the Pattersons are uncommon sharp.'

'They seem to be,' said Anthony bitterly.

The inspector departed, and scarcely had he gone before there came

a ring at the door. Anthony opened it. A small boy stood there, holding
a package.

'Parcel for you, sir.'

Anthony took it with some surprise. He was not expecting a parcel of
any kind. Returning to the sitting-room with it, he cut the string.

It was the liqueur set!

'Damn!' said Anthony.

Then he noticed that at the bottom of one of the glasses there was a
tiny artificial rose. His mind flew back to the upper room in Kirk Street.

'I do like you – yes, I do like you. You will remember that whatever
happens, won't you?'

That was what she had said. *Whatever happens* . . . Did she mean –
Anthony took hold of himself sternly.

'This won't do,' he admonished himself.

His eye fell on the typewriter, and he sat down with a resolute face.

THE MYSTERY OF THE SECOND CUCUMBER

His face grew dreamy again. The Shawl of a Thousand Flowers. What
was it that was found on the floor beside the dead body? The gruesome
thing that explained the whole mystery?

Nothing, of course, since it was only a trumped-up tale to hold his
attention, and the teller had used the old Arabian Nights' trick of breaking off at the most interesting point. But couldn't there be a gruesome
thing that explained the whole mystery? couldn't there now? If one gave
one's mind to it?

Anthony tore the sheet of paper from his typewriter and substituted
another. He typed a headline:

THE MYSTERY OF THE SPANISH SHAWL

He surveyed it for a moment or two in silence.

Then he began to type rapidly . . .

Philomel Cottage

'Philomel Cottage' was first published
in *Grand Magazine*, November 1924.

'Goodbye, darling.'

'Goodbye, sweetheart.'

Alix Martin stood leaning over the small rustic gate, watching the retreating figure of her husband as he walked down the road in the direction of the village.

Presently he turned a bend and was lost to sight, but Alix still stayed in the same position, absentmindedly smoothing a lock of the rich brown hair which had blown across her face, her eyes far away and dreamy.

Alix Martin was not beautiful, nor even, strictly speaking, pretty. But her face, the face of a woman no longer in her first youth, was irradiated and softened until her former colleagues of the old office days would hardly have recognized her. Miss Alex King had been a trim businesslike young woman, efficient, slightly brusque in manner, obviously capable and matter-of-fact.

Alix had graduated in a hard school. For fifteen years, from the age of eighteen until she was thirty-three, she had kept herself (and for seven years of the time an invalid mother) by her work as a shorthand typist. It was the struggle for existence which had hardened the soft lines of her girlish face.

True, there had been romance – of a kind – Dick Windyford, a fellow-clerk. Very much of a woman at heart, Alix had always known without seeming to know that he cared. Outwardly they had been friends, nothing more. Out of his slender salary Dick had been hard put to it to provide for the schooling of a younger brother. For the moment he could not think of marriage.

And then suddenly deliverance from daily toil had come to the girl in the most unexpected manner. A distant cousin had died, leaving her money to Alix – a few thousand pounds, enough to bring in a couple of hundred a year. To Alix it was freedom, life, independence. Now she and Dick need wait no longer.

But Dick reacted unexpectedly. He had never directly spoken of his love to Alix; now he seemed less inclined to do so than ever. He avoided her, became morose and gloomy. Alix was quick to realize the truth. She had become a woman of means. Delicacy and pride stood in the way of Dick's asking her to be his wife.

She liked him none the worse for it, and was indeed deliberating as to whether she herself might not take the first step, when for the second time the unexpected descended upon her.

She met Gerald Martin at a friend's house. He fell violently in love with her and within a week they were engaged. Alix, who had always considered herself 'not the falling-in-love kind', was swept clean off her feet.

Unwittingly she had found the way to arouse her former lover. Dick Windyford had come to her stammering with rage and anger.

'The man's a perfect stranger to you! You know nothing about him!'

'I know that I love him.'

'How can you know – in a week?'

'It doesn't take everyone eleven years to find out that they're in love with a girl,' cried Alix angrily.

His face went white.

'I've cared for you ever since I met you. I thought that you cared also.'

Alix was truthful.

'I thought so too,' she admitted. 'But that was because I didn't know what love was.'

Then Dick had burst out again. Prayers, entreaties, even threats – threats against the man who had supplanted him. It was amazing to Alix to see the volcano that existed beneath the reserved exterior of the man she had thought she knew so well.

Her thoughts went back to that interview now, on this sunny morning, as she leant on the gate of the cottage. She had been married a month, and she was idyllically happy. Yet, in the momentary absence of the husband who was everything to her, a tinge of anxiety invaded her perfect happiness. And the cause of that anxiety was Dick Windyford.

Three times since her marriage she had dreamed the same dream. The environment differed, but the main facts were always the same. *She saw her husband lying dead and Dick Windyford standing over him, and she knew clearly and distinctly that his was the hand which had dealt the fatal blow.*

But horrible though that was, there was something more horrible still – horrible, that was, on awakening, for in the dream it seemed perfectly natural and inevitable. *She, Alix Martin, was glad that her husband was dead*; she stretched out grateful hands to the murderer, sometimes she thanked him. The dream always ended the same way, with herself clasped in Dick Windyford's arms.

She had said nothing of this dream to her husband, but secretly it had perturbed her more than she liked to admit. Was it a warning – a warning against Dick Windyford?

Alix was roused from her thoughts by the sharp ringing of the telephone bell from within the house. She entered the cottage and picked up the receiver. Suddenly she swayed, and put out a hand against the wall.

'Who did you say was speaking?'

'Why, Alix, what's the matter with your voice? I wouldn't have known it. It's Dick.'

'Oh!' said Alix. 'Oh! Where – where are you?'

'At the Traveller's Arms – that's the right name, isn't it? Or don't you even know of the existence of your village pub? I'm on my holiday – doing a bit of fishing here. Any objection to my looking you two good people up this evening after dinner?'

'No,' said Alix sharply. 'You mustn't come.'

There was a pause, and then Dick's voice, with a subtle alteration in it, spoke again.

'I beg your pardon,' he said formally. 'Of course I won't bother you –'

Alix broke in hastily. He must think her behaviour too extraordinary. It *was* extraordinary. Her nerves must be all to pieces.

'I only meant that we were – engaged tonight,' she explained, trying to make her voice sound as natural as possible. 'Won't you – won't you come to dinner tomorrow night?'

But Dick evidently noticed the lack of cordiality in her tone.

'Thanks very much,' he said, in the same formal voice, 'but I may be moving on any time. Depends if a pal of mine turns up or not. Goodbye, Alix.' He paused, and then added hastily, in a different tone: 'Best of luck to you, my dear.'

Alix hung up the receiver with a feeling of relief.

'He mustn't come here,' she repeated to herself. 'He mustn't come here. Oh, what a fool I am! To imagine myself into a state like this. All the same, I'm glad he's not coming.'

She caught up a rustic rush hat from a table, and passed out into the garden again, pausing to look up at the name carved over the porch: Philomel Cottage.

'Isn't it a very fanciful name?' she had said to Gerald once before they were married. He had laughed.

'You little Cockney,' he had said, affectionately. 'I don't believe you have ever heard a nightingale. I'm glad you haven't. Nightingales should sing only for lovers. We'll hear them together on a summer's evening outside our own home.'

And at the remembrance of how they had indeed heard them, Alix, standing in the doorway of her home, blushed happily.

It was Gerald who had found Philomel Cottage. He had come to Alix bursting with excitement. He had found the very spot for them – unique – a gem – the chance of a lifetime. And when Alix had seen it she too was captivated. It was true that the situation was rather lonely – they were two miles from the nearest village – but the cottage itself was so exqui-site with its old-world appearance, and its solid comfort of bathrooms, hot-water system, electric light, and telephone, that she fell a victim to its charm immediately. And then a hitch occurred. The owner, a rich man who had made it his whim, declined to let it. He would only sell.

Gerald Martin, though possessed of a good income, was unable to touch his capital. He could raise at most a thousand pounds. The owner was asking three. But Alix, who had set her heart on the place, came to the rescue. Her own capital was easily realized, being in bearer bonds. She would contribute half of it to the purchase of the home. So Philomel Cottage became their very own, and never for a minute had Alix regret-ted the choice. It was true that servants did not appreciate the rural solitude – indeed, at the moment they had none at all – but Alix, who had been starved of domestic life, thoroughly enjoyed cooking dainty little meals and looking after the house.

The garden, which was magnificently stocked with flowers, was attended by an old man from the village who came twice a week.

As she rounded the corner of the house, Alix was surprised to see the old gardener in question busy over the flower-beds. She was surprised because his days for work were Mondays and Fridays, and today was Wednesday.

'Why, George, what are you doing here?' she asked, as she came towards him.

The old man straightened up with a chuckle, touching the brim of an aged cap.

'I thought as how you'd be surprised, ma'am. But 'tis this way. There be a fête over to Squire's on Friday, and I sez to myself, I sez, neither Mr Martin nor yet his good lady won't take it amiss if I comes for once on a Wednesday instead of a Friday.'

'That's quite all right,' said Alix. 'I hope you'll enjoy yourself at the fête.'

'I reckon to,' said George simply. 'It's a fine thing to be able to eat your fill and know all the time as it's not you as is paying for it. Squire allus has a proper sit-down tea for 'is tenants. Then I thought too, ma'am, as I might as well see you before you goes away so as to learn your wishes for the borders. You have no idea when you'll be back, ma'am, I suppose?'

'But I'm not going away.'

George stared.

'Bain't you going to Lunnon tomorrow?'

'No. What put such an idea into your head?'

George jerked his head over his shoulder.

'Met Maister down to village yesterday. He told me you was both going away to Lunnon tomorrow, and it was uncertain when you'd be back again.'

'Nonsense,' said Alix, laughing. 'You must have misunderstood him.'

All the same, she wondered exactly what it could have been that Gerald had said to lead the old man into such a curious mistake. Going to London? She never wanted to go to London again.

'I hate London,' she said suddenly and harshly.

'Ah!' said George placidly. 'I must have been mistook somehow, and yet he said it plain enough, it seemed to me. I'm glad you're stopping on here. I don't hold with all this gallivanting about, and I don't think nothing of Lunnon. *I've* never needed to go there. Too many moty cars – that's the trouble nowadays. Once people have got a moty car, blessed if they can stay still anywheres. Mr Ames, wot used to have this house – nice peaceful sort of gentleman he was until he bought one of them things. Hadn't had it a month before he put up this cottage for sale. A tidy lot he'd spent on it too, with taps in all the bedrooms, and the electric light and all. "You'll never see your money back," I sez to him. "But," he sez to me, "I'll get every penny of two thousand pounds for this house." And, sure enough, he did.'

'He got three thousand,' said Alix, smiling.

'Two thousand,' repeated George. 'The sum he was asking was talked of at the time.'

'It really was three thousand,' said Alix.

'Ladies never understand figures,' said George, unconvinced. 'You'll not tell me that Mr Ames had the face to stand up to you and say three thousand brazen-like in a loud voice?'

'He didn't say it to me,' said Alix; 'he said it to my husband.'

George stooped again to his flower-bed.

'The price was two thousand,' he said obstinately.

Alix did not trouble to argue with him. Moving to one of the farther beds, she began to pick an armful of flowers.

As she moved with her fragrant posy towards the house, Alix noticed a small dark-green object peeping from between some leaves in one of the beds. She stooped and picked it up, recognizing it for her husband's pocket diary.

She opened it, scanning the entries with some amusement. Almost from the beginning of their married life she had realized that the impulsive and emotional Gerald had the uncharacteristic virtues of neatness and method. He was extremely fussy about meals being punctual, and always planned his day ahead with the accuracy of a timetable.

Looking through the diary, she was amused to notice the entry on the date of May 14th: 'Marry Alix St Peter's 2.30.'

'The big silly,' murmured Alix to herself, turning the pages. Suddenly she stopped.

'"Wednesday, June 18th" – why, that's today.'

In the space for that day was written in Gerald's neat, precise hand: '9 p.m.' Nothing else. What had Gerald planned to do at 9 p.m.? Alix wondered. She smiled to herself as she realized that had this been a story, like those she had so often read, the diary would doubtless have furnished her with some sensational revelation. It would have had in it for certain the name of another woman. She fluttered the back pages idly. There were dates, appointments, cryptic references to business deals, but only one woman's name – her own.

Yet as she slipped the book into her pocket and went on with her flowers to the house, she was aware of a vague uneasiness. Those words of Dick Windyford's recurred to her almost as though he had been at her elbow repeating them: 'The man's a perfect stranger to you. You know nothing about him.'

It was true. What did she know about him? After all, Gerald was forty. In forty years there must have been women in his life . . .

Alix shook herself impatiently. She must not give way to these thoughts. She had a far more instant preoccupation to deal with. Should she, or should she not, tell her husband that Dick Windyford had rung her up?

There was the possibility to be considered that Gerald might have already run across him in the village. But in that case he would be sure to mention it to her immediately upon his return, and matters would be taken out of her hands. Otherwise – what? Alix was aware of a distinct desire to say nothing about it.

If she told him, he was sure to suggest asking Dick Windyford to Philomel Cottage. Then she would have to explain that Dick had proposed himself, and that she had made an excuse to prevent his coming. And when he asked her why she had done so, what could she say? Tell him her dream? But he would only laugh – or worse, see that she attached an importance to it which he did not.

In the end, rather shamefacedly, Alix decided to say nothing. It was the first secret she had ever kept from her husband, and the consciousness of it made her feel ill at ease.

When she heard Gerald returning from the village shortly before lunch, she hurried into the kitchen and pretended to be busy with the cooking so as to hide her confusion.

It was evident at once that Gerald had seen nothing of Dick Windyford. Alix felt at once relieved and embarrassed. She was definitely committed now to a policy of concealment.

It was not until after their simple evening meal, when they were sitting in the oak-benched living-room with the windows thrown open to let in the sweet night air scented with the perfume of the mauve and white stocks outside, that Alix remembered the pocket diary.

'Here's something you've been watering the flowers with,' she said, and threw it into his lap.

'Dropped it in the border, did I?'

'Yes; I know all your secrets now.'

'Not guilty,' said Gerald, shaking his head.

'What about your assignation at nine o'clock tonight?'

'Oh! that –' he seemed taken aback for a moment, then he smiled as though something afforded him particular amusement. 'It's an assignation with a particularly nice girl, Alix. She's got brown hair and blue eyes, and she's very like you.'

'I don't understand,' said Alix, with mock severity. 'You're evading the point.'

'No, I'm not. As a matter of fact, that's a reminder that I'm going to develop some negatives tonight, and I want you to help me.'

Gerald Martin was an enthusiastic photographer. He had a somewhat old-fashioned camera, but with an excellent lens, and he developed his own plates in a small cellar which he had had fitted up as a dark-room.

'And it must be done at nine o'clock precisely,' said Alix teasingly.

Gerald looked a little vexed.

'My dear girl,' he said, with a shade of testiness in his manner, 'one should always plan a thing for a definite time. Then one gets through one's work properly.'

Alix sat for a minute or two in silence, watching her husband as he lay in his chair smoking, his dark head flung back and the clear-cut lines of his clean-shaven face showing up against the sombre background. And suddenly, from some unknown source, a wave of panic surged over her, so that she cried out before she could stop herself, 'Oh, Gerald, I wish I knew more about you!'

Her husband turned an astonished face upon her.

'But, my dear Alix, you do know all about me. I've told you of my boyhood in Northumberland, of my life in South Africa, and these last ten years in Canada which have brought me success.'

'Oh! business!' said Alix scornfully.

Gerald laughed suddenly.

'I know what you mean – love affairs. You women are all the same. Nothing interests you but the personal element.'

Alix felt her throat go dry, as she muttered indistinctly: 'Well, but there must have been – love affairs. I mean – if I only knew –'

There was silence again for a minute or two. Gerald Martin was frowning, a look of indecision on his face. When he spoke it was gravely, without a trace of his former bantering manner.

'Do you think it wise, Alix – this – Bluebeard's chamber business? There have been women in my life; yes, I don't deny it. You wouldn't believe me if I denied it. But I can swear to you truthfully that not one of them meant anything to me.'

There was a ring of sincerity in his voice which comforted the listening wife.

'Satisfied, Alix?' he asked, with a smile. Then he looked at her with a shade of curiosity.

'What has turned your mind on to these unpleasant subjects, tonight of all nights?'

Alix got up, and began to walk about restlessly.

'Oh, I don't know,' she said. 'I've been nervy all day.'

'That's odd,' said Gerald, in a low voice, as though speaking to himself. 'That's very odd.'

'Why it it odd?'

'Oh, my dear girl, don't flash out at me so. I only said it was odd, because, as a rule, you're so sweet and serene.'

Alix forced a smile.

'Everything's conspired to annoy me today,' she confessed. 'Even old George had got some ridiculous idea into his head that we were going away to London. He said you had told him so.'

'Where did you see him?' asked Gerald sharply.

'He came to work today instead of Friday.'

'Damned old fool,' said Gerald angrily.

Alix stared in surprise. Her husband's face was convulsed with rage. She had never seen him so angry. Seeing her astonishment Gerald made an effort to regain control of himself.

'Well, he *is* a damned old fool,' he protested.

'What can you have said to make him think that?'

'I? I never said anything. At least – oh, yes, I remember; I made some weak joke about being "off to London in the morning," and I suppose he took it seriously. Or else he didn't hear properly. You undeceived him, of course?'

He waited anxiously for her reply.

'Of course, but he's the sort of old man who if once he gets an idea in his head – well, it isn't so easy to get it out again.'

Then she told him of George's insistence on the sum asked for the cottage.

Gerald was silent for a minute or two, then he said slowly:

'Ames was willing to take two thousand in cash and the remaining thousand on mortgage. That's the origin of that mistake, I fancy.'

'Very likely,' agreed Alix.

Then she looked up at the clock, and pointed to it with a mischievous finger.

'We ought to be getting down to it, Gerald. Five minutes behind schedule.'

A very peculiar smile came over Gerald Martin's face.

'I've changed my mind,' he said quietly; 'I shan't do any photography tonight.'

A woman's mind is a curious thing. When she went to bed that Wednesday night Alix's mind was contented and at rest. Her momentarily assailed happiness reasserted itself, triumphant as of yore.

But by the evening of the following day she realized that some subtle forces were at work undermining it. Dick Windyford had not rung up again, nevertheless she felt what she supposed to be his influence at work. Again and again those words of his recurred to her: '*The man's a perfect stranger. You know nothing about him.*' And with them came the memory of her husband's face, photographed clearly on her brain, as he said, 'Do you think it wise, Alix, this – Bluebeard's chamber business?' Why had he said that?

There had been warning in them – a hint of menace. It was as though he had said in effect: 'You had better not pry into my life, Alix. You may get a nasty shock if you do.'

By Friday morning Alix had convinced herself that there *had* been a woman in Gerald's life – a Bluebeard's chamber that he had sedulously sought to conceal from her. Her jealousy, slow to awaken, was now rampant.

Was it a woman he had been going to meet that night at 9 p.m.? Was his story of photographs to develop a lie invented upon the spur of the moment?

Three days ago she would have sworn that she knew her husband through and through. Now it seemed to her that he was a stranger of whom she knew nothing. She remembered his unreasonable anger against old George, so at variance with his usual good-tempered manner. A small thing, perhaps, but it showed her that she did not really know the man who was her husband.

There were several little things required on Friday from the village. In the afternoon Alix suggested that she should go for them whilst Gerald remained in the garden; but somewhat to her surprise he opposed this plan vehemently, and insisted on going himself whilst she remained at home. Alix was forced to give way to him, but his insistence surprised and alarmed her. Why was he so anxious to prevent her going to the village?

Suddenly an explanation suggested itself to her which made the whole thing clear. Was it not possible that, whilst saying nothing to her, Gerald had indeed come across Dick Windyford? Her own jealousy, entirely dormant at the time of their marriage, had only developed afterwards. Might it not be the same with Gerald? Might he not be anxious to prevent her seeing Dick Windyford again? This explanation was so consistent with the facts, and so comforting to Alix's perturbed mind, that she embraced it eagerly.

Yet when tea-time had come and passed she was restless and ill at ease. She was struggling with a temptation that had assailed her ever since Gerald's departure. Finally, pacifying her conscience with the assurance that the room did need a thorough tidying, she went upstairs to her husband's dressing-room. She took a duster with her to keep up the pretence of housewifery.

'If I were only sure,' she repeated to herself. 'If I could only be *sure*.'

In vain she told herself that anything compromising would have been destroyed ages ago. Against that she argued that men do sometimes keep the most damning piece of evidence through an exaggerated sentimentality.

In the end Alix succumbed. Her cheeks burning with the shame of her action, she hunted breathlessly through packets of letters and documents, turned out the drawers, even went through the pockets of her husband's clothes. Only two drawers eluded her; the lower drawer of the chest of drawers and the small right-hand drawer of the writing-desk were both locked. But Alix was by now lost to all shame. In one of these drawers she was convinced that she would find evidence of this imaginary woman of the past who obsessed her.

She remembered that Gerald had left his keys lying carelessly on the sideboard downstairs. She fetched them and tried them one by one. The third key fitted the writing-table drawer. Alix pulled it open eagerly. There was a cheque-book and a wallet well stuffed with notes, and at the back of the drawer a packet of letters tied up with a piece of tape.

Her breath coming unevenly, Alix untied the tape. Then a deep burning blush overspread her face, and she dropped the letters back into the drawer, closing and relocking it. For the letters were her own, written to Gerald Martin before she married him.

She turned now to the chest of drawers, more with a wish to feel that she had left nothing undone than from any expectation of finding what she sought.

To her annoyance none of the keys on Gerald's bunch fitted the drawer in question. Not to be defeated, Alix went into the other rooms and brought back a selection of keys with her. To her satisfaction the key of the spare room wardrobe also fitted the chest of drawers. She unlocked the drawer and pulled it open. But there was nothing in it but a roll of newspaper clippings already dirty and discoloured with age.

Alix breathed a sigh of relief. Nevertheless, she glanced at the clippings, curious to know what subject had interested Gerald so much that he had taken the trouble to keep the dusty roll. They were nearly all American papers, dated some seven years ago, and dealing with the trial of the notorious swindler and bigamist, Charles Lemaitre. Lemaitre had been suspected of doing away with his women victims. A skeleton had been found beneath the floor of one of the houses he had rented, and most of the women he had 'married' had never been heard of again.

He had defended himself from the charges with consummate skill, aided by some of the best legal talent in the United States. The Scottish verdict of 'Not Proven' might perhaps have stated the case best. In its absence, he was found Not Guilty on the capital charge, though sentenced to a long term of imprisonment on the other charges preferred against him.

Alix remembered the excitement caused by the case at the time, and also the sensation aroused by the escape of Lemaitre some three years later. He had never been recaptured. The personality of the man and his extraordinary power over women had been discussed at great length in the English papers at the time, together with an account of his excitability in court, his passionate protestations, and his occasional sudden physical collapses, due to the fact that he had a weak heart, though the ignorant accredited it to his dramatic powers.

There was a picture of him in one of the clippings Alix held, and she studied it with some interest – a long-bearded, scholarly-looking gentleman.

Who was it the face reminded her of? Suddenly, with a shock, she realized that it was Gerald himself. The eyes and brow bore a strong resemblance to his. Perhaps he had kept the cutting for that reason. Her eyes went on to the paragraph beside the picture. Certain dates, it seemed, had been entered in the accused's pocket-book, and it was contended that these were dates when he had done away with his victims. Then a woman gave evidence and identified the prisoner positively by the fact that he had a mole on his left wrist, just below the palm of the hand.

Alix dropped the papers and swayed as she stood. *On his left wrist, just below the palm, her husband had a small scar . . .*

The room whirled round her. Afterwards it struck her as strange that she should have leaped at once to such absolute certainty. Gerald Martin was Charles Lemaitre! She knew it, and accepted it in a flash. Disjointed fragments whirled through her brain, like pieces of a jigsaw puzzle fitting into place.

The money paid for the house – her money – her money only; the bearer bonds she had entrusted to his keeping. Even her dream appeared in its true significance. Deep down in her, her subconscious self had always feared Gerald Martin and wished to escape from him. And it was to Dick Windyford this self of hers had looked for help. That, too, was why she was able to accept the truth too easily, without doubt or hesitation. She was to have been another of Lemaitre's victims. Very soon, perhaps . . .

A half-cry escaped her as she remembered something. *Wednesday, 9 p.m.* The cellar, with the flagstones that were so easily raised! Once before he had buried one of his victims in a cellar. It had been all planned for Wednesday night. But to write it down beforehand in that methodical manner – insanity! No, it was logical. Gerald always made a memorandum of his engagements; murder was to him a business proposition like any other.

But what had saved her? What could possibly have saved her? Had he relented at the last minute? No. In a flash the answer came to her – *old George.*

She understood now her husband's uncontrollable anger. Doubtless he had paved the way by telling everyone he met that they were going to London the next day. Then George had come to work unexpectedly, had mentioned London to her, and she had contradicted the story. Too risky to do away with her that night, with old George repeating that conversation. But what an escape! If she had not happened to mention that trivial matter – Alix shuddered.

And then she stayed motionless as though frozen to stone. She had heard the creak of the gate into the road. *Her husband had returned.*

For a moment Alix stayed as though petrified, then she crept on tiptoe to the window, looking out from behind the shelter of the curtain.

Yes, it was her husband. He was smiling to himself and humming a little tune. In his hand he held an object which almost made the terrified girl's heart stop beating. It was a brand-new spade.

Alix leaped to a knowledge born of instinct. *It was to be tonight . . .*

But there was still a chance. Gerald, humming his little tune, went round to the back of the house.

Without hesitating a moment, she ran down the stairs and out of the cottage. But just as she emerged from the door, her husband came round the other side of the house.

'Hallo,' he said, 'where are you running off to in such a hurry?'

Alix strove desperately to appear calm and as usual. Her chance was gone for the moment, but if she was careful not to arouse his suspicions, it would come again later. Even now, perhaps . . .

'I was going to walk to the end of the lane and back,' she said in a voice that sounded weak and uncertain in her own ears.

'Right,' said Gerald. 'I'll come with you.'

'No – please, Gerald. I'm – nervy, headachy – I'd rather go alone.'

He looked at her attentively. She fancied a momentary suspicion gleamed in his eye.

'What's the matter with you, Alix? You're pale – trembling.'

'Nothing.' She forced herself to be brusque – smiling. 'I've got a headache, that's all. A walk will do me good.'

'Well, it's no good your saying you don't want me,' declared Gerald, with his easy laugh. 'I'm coming, whether you want me or not.'

She dared not protest further. If he suspected that she *knew* . . .

With an effort she managed to regain something of her normal manner. Yet she had an uneasy feeling that he looked at her sideways every now and then, as though not quite satisfied. She felt that his suspicions were not completely allayed.

When they returned to the house he insisted on her lying down, and brought some eau-de-Cologne to bathe her temples. He was, as ever, the devoted husband. Alix felt herself as helpless as though bound hand and foot in a trap.

Not for a minute would he leave her alone. He went with her into the kitchen and helped her to bring in the simple cold dishes she had already prepared. Supper was a meal that choked her, yet she forced herself to eat, and even to appear gay and natural. She knew now that she was fighting for her life. She was alone with this man, miles from help, absolutely at his mercy. Her only chance was so to lull his suspicions that he would leave her alone for a few moments – long enough for her to get to the telephone in the hall and summon assistance. That was her only hope now.

A momentary hope flashed over her as she remembered how he had abandoned his plan before. Suppose she told him that Dick Windyford was coming up to see them that evening?

The words trembled on her lips – then she rejected them hastily. This man would not be baulked a second time. There was a determination, an elation, underneath his calm bearing that sickened her. She would only precipitate the crime. He would murder her there and then, and calmly ring up Dick Windyford with a tale of having been suddenly called away. Oh! if only Dick Windyford were coming to the house this evening! If Dick . . .

A sudden idea flashed into her mind. She looked sharply sideways at her husband as though she feared that he might read her mind. With the forming of a plan, her courage was reinforced. She became so completely natural in manner that she marvelled at herself.

She made the coffee and took it out to the porch where they often sat on fine evenings.

'By the way,' said Gerald suddenly, 'we'll do those photographs later.'

Alix felt a shiver run through her, but she replied nonchalantly, 'Can't you manage alone? I'm rather tired tonight.'

'It won't take long.' He smiled to himself. 'And I can promise you you won't be tired afterwards.'

The words seemed to amuse him. Alix shuddered. Now or never was the time to carry out her plan.

She rose to her feet.

'I'm just going to telephone to the butcher,' she announced nonchalantly. 'Don't you bother to move.'

'To the butcher? At this time of night?'

'His shop's shut, of course, silly. But he's in his house all right. And tomorrow's Saturday, and I want him to bring me some veal cutlets early, before someone else grabs them off him. The old dear will do anything for me.'

She passed quickly into the house, closing the door behind her. She heard Gerald say, 'Don't shut the door,' and was quick with her light reply, 'It keeps the moths out. I hate moths. Are you afraid I'm going to make love to the butcher, silly?'

Once inside, she snatched down the telephone receiver and gave the number of the Traveller's Arms. She was put through at once.

'Mr Windyford? Is he still there? Can I speak to him?'

Then her heart gave a sickening thump. The door was pushed open and her husband came into the hall.

'Do go away, Gerald,' she said pettishly. 'I hate anyone listening when I'm telephoning.'

He merely laughed and threw himself into a chair.

'Sure it really is the butcher you're telephoning to?' he quizzed.

Alix was in despair. Her plan had failed. In a minute Dick Windyford would come to the phone. Should she risk all and cry out an appeal for help?

And then, as she nervously depressed and released the little key in the receiver she was holding, which permits the voice to be heard or not heard at the other end, another plan flashed into her head.

'It will be difficult,' she thought to herself. 'It means keeping my head, and thinking of the right words, and not faltering for a moment, but I believe I could do it. I *must* do it.'

And at that minute she heard Dick Windyford's voice at the other end of the phone.

Alix drew a deep breath. Then she depressed the key firmly and spoke.

'*Mrs Martin speaking – from Philomel Cottage. Please come* (she released the key) tomorrow morning with six nice veal cutlets (she depressed the key again). *It's very important* (she released the key). Thank you so much, Mr Hexworthy: you won't mind my ringing you up so late. I hope, but those veal cutlets are really a matter of (she depressed the key again) *life or death* (she released it). Very well – tomorrow morning (she depressed it) *as soon as possible.*'

She replaced the receiver on the hook and turned to face her husband, breathing hard.

'So that's how you talk to your butcher, is it?' said Gerald.

'It's the feminine touch,' said Alix lightly.

She was simmering with excitement. He had suspected nothing. Dick, even if he didn't understand, would come.

She passed into the sitting-room and switched on the electric light. Gerald followed her.

'You seem very full of spirits now?' he said, watching her curiously.

'Yes,' said Alix. 'My headache's gone.'

She sat down in her usual seat and smiled at her husband as he sank into his own chair opposite her. She was saved. It was only five and twenty past eight. Long before nine o'clock Dick would have arrived.

'I didn't think much of that coffee you gave me,' complained Gerald. 'It tasted very bitter.'

'It's a new kind I was trying. We won't have it again if you don't like it, dear.'

Alix took up a piece of needlework and began to stitch. Gerald read a few pages of his book. Then he glanced up at the clock and tossed the book away.

'Half-past eight. Time to go down to the cellar and start work.'

The sewing slipped from Alix's fingers.

'Oh, not yet. Let us wait until nine o'clock.'

'No, my girl – half-past eight. That's the time I fixed. You'll be able to get to bed all the earlier.'

'But I'd rather wait until nine.'

'You know when I fix a time I always stick to it. Come along, Alix. I'm not going to wait a minute longer.'

Alix looked up at him, and in spite of herself she felt a wave of terror slide over her. The mask had been lifted. Gerald's hands were twitching, his eyes were shining with excitement, he was continually passing his tongue over his dry lips. He no longer cared to conceal his excitement.

Alix thought, 'It's true – *he can't wait* – he's like a madman.'

He strode over to her, and jerked her on to her feet with a hand on her shoulder.

'Come on, my girl – or I'll carry you there.'

His tone was gay, but there was an undisguised ferocity behind it that appalled her. With a supreme effort she jerked herself free and clung cowering against the wall. She was powerless. She couldn't get away – she couldn't do anything – and he was coming towards her.

'Now, Alix –'

'No – no.'

She screamed, her hands held out impotently to ward him off.

'Gerald – stop – I've got something to tell you, something to confess –'

He did stop.

'To confess?' he said curiously.

'Yes, to confess.' She had used the words at random, but she went on desperately, seeking to hold his arrested attention.

A look of contempt swept over his face.

'A former lover, I suppose,' he sneered.

'No,' said Alix. 'Something else. You'd call it, I expect – yes, you'd call it a crime.'

And at once she saw that she had struck the right note. Again his attention was arrested, held. Seeing that, her nerve came back to her. She felt mistress of the situation once more.

'You had better sit down again,' she said quietly.

She herself crossed the room to her old chair and sat down. She even stooped and picked up her needlework. But behind her calmness she was thinking and inventing feverishly: for the story she invented must hold his interest until help arrived.

'I told you,' she said slowly, 'that I had been a shorthand-typist for fifteen years. That was not entirely true. There were two intervals. The first occurred when I was twenty-two. I came across a man, an elderly man with a little property. He fell in love with me and asked me to marry him. I accepted. We were married.' She paused. 'I induced him to insure his life in my favour.'

She saw a sudden keen interest spring up in her husband's face, and went on with renewed assurance:

'During the war I worked for a time in a hospital dispensary. There I had the handling of all kinds of rare drugs and poisons.'

She paused reflectively. He was keenly interested now, not a doubt of it. The murderer is bound to have an interest in murder. She had gambled on that, and succeeded. She stole a glance at the clock. It was five and twenty to nine.

'There is one poison – it is a little white powder. A pinch of it means death. You know something about poisons perhaps?'

She put the question in some trepidation. If he did, she would have to be careful.

'No,' said Gerald: 'I know very little about them.'

She drew a breath of relief.

'You have heard of hyoscine, of course? This is a drug that acts much the same way, but is absolutely untraceable. Any doctor would give a certificate of heart failure. I stole a small quantity of this drug and kept it by me.'

She paused, marshalling her forces.

'Go on,' said Gerald.

'No. I'm afraid. I can't tell you. Another time.'

'Now,' he said impatiently. 'I want to hear.'

'We had been married a month. I was very good to my elderly husband, very kind and devoted. He spoke in praise of me to all the neighbours. Everyone knew what a devoted wife I was. I always made his coffee myself every evening. One evening, when we were alone together, I put a pinch of the deadly alkaloid in his cup –'

Alix paused, and carefully re-threaded her needle. She, who had never acted in her life, rivalled the greatest actress in the world at this moment. She was actually living the part of the cold-blooded poisoner.

'It was very peaceful. I sat watching him. Once he gasped a little and asked for air. I opened the window. Then he said he could not move from his chair. *Presently he died.*'

She stopped, smiling. It was a quarter to nine. Surely they would come soon.

'How much,' said Gerald, 'was the insurance money?'

'About two thousand pounds. I speculated with it, and lost it. I went back to my office work. But I never meant to remain there long. Then I met another man. I had stuck to my maiden name at the office. He didn't know I had been married before. He was a younger man, rather good-looking, and quite well-off. We were married quietly in Sussex. He didn't want to insure his life, but of course he made a will in my favour. He liked me to make his coffee myself just as my first husband had done.'

Alix smiled reflectively, and added simply, 'I make very good coffee.'

Then she went on:

'I had several friends in the village where we were living. They were very sorry for me, with my husband dying suddenly of heart failure one evening after dinner. I didn't quite like the doctor. I don't think he suspected me, but he was certainly very surprised at my husband's sudden death. I don't quite know why I drifted back to the office again. Habit, I suppose. My second husband left about four thousand pounds. I didn't speculate with it this time; I invested it. Then, you see –'

But she was interrupted. Gerald Martin, his face suffused with blood, half-choking, was pointing a shaking forefinger at her.

'The coffee – my God! the coffee!'

She stared at him.

'I understand now why it was bitter. You devil! You've been up to your tricks again.'

His hands gripped the arms of his chair. He was ready to spring upon her.

'You've poisoned me.'

Alix had retreated from him to the fireplace. Now, terrified, she opened her lips to deny – and then paused. In another minute he would spring upon her. She summoned all her strength. Her eyes held his steadily, compellingly.

'Yes,' she said. 'I poisoned you. Already the poison is working. At the minute you can't move from your chair – you can't move –'

If she could keep him there – even a few minutes . . .

Ah! what was that? Footsteps on the road. The creak of the gate. Then footsteps on the path outside. The outer door opening.

'*You can't move*,' she said again.

Then she slipped past him and fled headlong from the room to fall fainting into Dick Windyford's arms.

'My God! Alix,' he cried.

Then he turned to the man with him, a tall stalwart figure in policeman's uniform.

'Go and see what's been happening in that room.'

He laid Alix carefully down on a couch and bent over her.

'My little girl,' he murmured. 'My poor little girl. What have they been doing to you?'

Her eyelids fluttered and her lips just murmured his name.

Dick was aroused by the policeman's touching him on the arm.

'There's nothing in that room, sir, but a man sitting in a chair. Looks as though he'd had some kind of bad fright, and –'

'Yes?'

'Well, sir, he's – dead.'

They were startled by hearing Alix's voice. She spoke as though in some kind of dream, her eyes still closed.

'*And presently*,' she said, almost as though she were quoting from something, '*he died –*'

The Manhood of
Edward Robinson

'The Manhood of Edward Robinson' was first published as
'The Day of His Dreams' in *Grand Magazine*, December 1924.

'With a swing of his mighty arms, Bill lifted her right off her feet, crushing her to his breast. With a deep sigh she yielded her lips in such a kiss as he had never dreamed of –'

With a sigh, Mr Edward Robinson put down *When Love is King* and stared out of the window of the underground train. They were running through Stamford Brook. Edward Robinson was thinking about Bill. Bill was the real hundred per cent he-man beloved of lady novelists. Edward envied him his muscles, his rugged good looks and his terrific passions. He picked up the book again and read the description of the proud Marchesa Bianca (she who had yielded her lips). So ravishing was her beauty, the intoxication of her was so great, that strong men went down before her like ninepins, faint and helpless with love.

'Of course,' said Edward to himself, 'it's all bosh, this sort of stuff. All bosh, it is. And yet, I wonder –'

His eyes looked wistful. Was there such a thing as a world of romance and adventure somewhere? Were there women whose beauty intoxicated? Was there such a thing as love that devoured one like a flame?

'This is real life, this is,' said Edward. 'I've got to go on the same just like all the other chaps.'

On the whole, he supposed, he ought to consider himself a lucky young man. He had an excellent berth – a clerkship in a flourishing concern. He had good health, no one dependent upon him, and he was engaged to Maud.

But the mere thought of Maud brought a shadow over his face.

Though he would never have admitted it, he was afraid of Maud. He loved her – yes – he still remembered the thrill with which he had admired the back of her white neck rising out of the cheap four and elevenpenny blouse on the first occasion they had met. He had sat behind her at the cinema, and the friend he was with had known her and had introduced them. No doubt about it, Maud was very superior. She was good looking and clever and very lady-like, and she was always right about everything. The kind of girl, everyone said, who would make such an excellent wife.

Edward wondered whether the Marchesa Bianca would have made an excellent wife. Somehow, he doubted it. He couldn't picture the voluptuous Bianca, with her red lips and her swaying form, tamely sewing on buttons, say, for the virile Bill. No, Bianca was Romance, and this was real life. He and Maud would be very happy together. She had so much common sense . . .

But all the same, he wished that she wasn't quite so – well, sharp in manner. So prone to "jump upon him".

It was, of course, her prudence and her common sense which made her do so. Maud was very sensible. And, as a rule, Edward was very sensible too, but sometimes – He had wanted to get married this Christmas, for instance. Maud had pointed out how much more prudent it would be to wait a while – a year or two, perhaps. His salary was not large. He had wanted to give her an expensive ring – she had been horror stricken, and had forced him to take it back and exchange it for a cheaper one. Her qualities were all excellent qualities, but sometimes Edward wished that she had more faults and less virtues. It was her virtues that drove him to desperate deeds.

For instance –

A blush of guilt overspread his face. He had got to tell her – and tell her soon. His secret guilt was already making him behave strangely. Tomorrow was the first of three days holiday, Christmas Eve, Christmas Day and Boxing Day. She had suggested that he should come round and spend the day with her people, and in a clumsy foolish manner, a manner that could not fail to arouse her suspicions, he had managed to get out of it – had told a long, lying story about a pal of his in the country with whom he had promised to spend the day.

And there was no pal in the country. There was only his guilty secret.

Three months ago, Edward Robinson, in company with a few hundred thousand other young men, had gone in for a competition in one of the weekly papers. Twelve girls' names had to be arranged in order of popularity. Edward had had a brilliant idea. His own preference was sure to be wrong – he had noticed that in several similar competitions. He wrote down the twelve names arranged in his own order of merit, then he wrote them down again this time placing one from the top and one from the bottom of the list alternately.

When the result was announced, Edward had got eight right out of the twelve, and was awarded the first prize of £500. This result, which might easily be ascribed to luck, Edward persisted in regarding as the direct outcome of his 'system.' He was inordinately proud of himself.

The next thing was, what do do with the £500? He knew very well what Maud would say. Invest it. A nice little nest egg for the future. And, of course, Maud would be quite right, he knew that. But to win money as the result of a competition is an entirely different feeling from anything else in the world.

Had the money been left to him as a legacy, Edward would have invested it religiously in Conversion Loan or Savings Certificates as a matter of course. But money that one has achieved by a mere stroke of the pen, by a lucky and unbelievable chance, comes under the same heading as a child's sixpence – 'for your very own – to spend as you like'.

And in a certain rich shop which he passed daily on his way to the office, was the unbelievable dream, a small two-seater car, with a long shining nose, and the price clearly displayed on it – £465.

'If I were rich,' Edward had said to it, day after day. 'If I were rich, I'd have you.'

And now he was – if not rich – at least possessed of a lump sum of money sufficient to realize his dream. That car, that shining alluring piece of loveliness, was his if he cared to pay the price.

He had meant to tell Maud about the money. Once he had told her, he would have secured himself against temptation. In face of Maud's horror and disapproval, he would never have the courage to persist in his madness. But, as it chanced, it was Maud herself who clinched the matter. He had taken her to the cinema – and to the best seats in the house. She had pointed out to him, kindly but firmly, the criminal folly of his behaviour – wasting good money – three and sixpence against two and fourpence, when one saw just as well from the latter places.

Edward took her reproaches in sullen silence. Maud felt contentedly that she was making an impression. Edward could not be allowed to continue in these extravagant ways. She loved Edward, but she realized that he was weak – hers the task of being ever at hand to influence him in the way he should go. She observed his worm-like demeanour with satisfaction.

Edward was indeed worm-like. Like worms, he turned. He remained crushed by her words, but it was at that precise minute that he made up his mind to buy the car.

'Damn it,' said Edward to himself. 'For once in my life, I'll do what I like. Maud can go hang!'

And the very next morning he had walked into that palace of plate glass, with its lordly inmates in their glory of gleaming enamel and shimmering metal, and with an insouciance that surprised himself, he bought the car. It was the easiest thing in the world, buying a car!

It had been his for four days now. He had gone about, outwardly calm, but inwardly bathed in ecstasy. And to Maud he had as yet breathed no word. For four days, in his luncheon hour, he had received instruction in the handling of the lovely creature. He was an apt pupil.

Tomorrow, Christmas Eve, he was to take her out into the country. He had lied to Maud, and he would lie again if need be. He was enslaved body and soul by his new possession. It stood to him for Romance, for Adventure, for all the things that he had longed for and had never had. Tomorrow, he and his mistress would take the road together. They would rush through the keen cold air, leaving the throb and fret of London far behind – out into the wide clear spaces . . .

At this moment, Edward, though he did not know it, was very near to being a poet.

Tomorrow –

He looked down at the book in his hand – *When Love is King*. He laughed and stuffed it into his pocket. The car, and the red lips of the Marchesa Bianca, and the amazing prowess of Bill seemed all mixed up together. Tomorrow –

The weather, usually a sorry jade to those who count upon her, was kindly disposed towards Edward. She gave him the day of his dreams, a day of glittering frost, and pale-blue sky, and a primrose-yellow sun.

So, in a mood of high adventure, of dare-devil wickedness, Edward drove out of London. There was trouble at Hyde Park Corner, and a sad *contretemps* at Putney Bridge, there was much protesting of gears, and a frequent jarring of brakes, and much abuse was freely showered upon Edward by the drivers of other vehicles. But for a novice he did not acquit himself so badly, and presently he came out on to one of those fair wide roads that are the joy of the motorist. There was little congestion on this particular road today. Edward drove on and on, drunk with his mastery over this creature of the gleaming sides, speeding through the cold white world with the elation of a god.

It was a delirious day. He stopped for lunch at an old-fashioned inn, and again later for tea. Then reluctantly he turned homewards – back again to London, to Maud, to the inevitable explanation, recriminations . . .

He shook off the thought with a sigh. Let tomorrow look after itself. He still had today. And what could be more fascinating than this? Rushing through the darkness with the headlights searching out the way in front. Why, this was the best of all!

He judged that he had no time to stop anywhere for dinner. This driving through the darkness was a ticklish business. It was going to take longer to get back to London than he had thought. It was just eight o'clock when he passed through Hindhead and came out upon the rim of the Devil's Punch Bowl. There was moonlight, and the snow that had fallen two days ago was still unmelted.

He stopped the car and stood staring. What did it matter if he didn't get back to London until midnight? What did it matter if he never got back? He wasn't going to tear himself away from this at once.

He got out of the car, and approached the edge. There was a path winding down temptingly near him. Edward yielded to the spell. For the next half-hour he wandered deliriously in a snowbound world. Never had he imagined anything quite like this. And it was his, his very own, given to him by his shining mistress who waited for him faithfully on the road above.

He climbed up again, got into the car and drove off, still a little dizzy from that discovery of sheer beauty which comes to the most prosaic men once in a while.

Then, with a sigh, he came to himself, and thrust his hand into the pocket of the car where he had stuffed an additional muffler earlier in the day.

But the muffler was no longer there. The pocket was empty. No, not completely empty – there was something scratchy and hard – like pebbles.

Edward thrust his hand deep down. In another minute he was staring like a man bereft of his senses. The object that he held in his hand, dangling from his fingers, with the moonlight striking a hundred fires from it, was a diamond necklace.

Edward stared and stared. But there was no doubting possible. A diamond necklace worth probably thousands of pounds (for the stones were large ones) had been casually reposing in the side-pocket of the car.

But who had put it there? It had certainly not been there when he started from town. Someone must have come along when he was walking about in the snow, and deliberately thrust it in. But why? Why choose *his* car? Had the owner of the necklace made a mistake? Or was it – could it possibly be *a stolen* necklace?

And then, as all these thoughts went whirling through his brain, Edward suddenly stiffened and went cold all over. *This was not his car.*

It was very like it, yes. It was the same brilliant shade of scarlet – red as the Marchesa Bianca's lips – it had the same long and gleaming nose, but by a thousand small signs, Edward realized that it was not his car.

Its shining newness was scarred here and there, it bore signs, faint but unmistakeable, of wear and tear. In that case . . .

Edward, without more ado, made haste to turn the car. Turning was not his strong point. With the car in reverse, he invariably lost his head and twisted the wheel the wrong way. Also, he frequently became entangled between the accelerator and the foot brake with disastrous results. In the end, however, he succeeded, and straight away the car began purring up the hill again.

Edward remembered that there had been another car standing some little distance away. He had not noticed it particularly at the time. He had returned from his walk by a different path from that by which he had gone down into the hollow. This second path had brought him out on the road immediately behind, as he had thought, his own car. It must really have been the other one.

In about ten minutes he was once more at the spot where he had halted. But there was now no car at all by the roadside. Whoever had owned this car must now have gone off in Edward's – he also, perhaps, misled by the resemblance.

Edward took out the diamond necklace from his pocket and let it run through his fingers perplexedly.

What to do next? Run on to the nearest police station? Explain the circumstances, hand over the necklace, and give the number of his own car.

By the by, what was the number of his car? Edward thought and thought, but for the life of him he couldn't remember. He felt a cold sinking sensation. He was going to look the most utter fool at the police station. There was an eight in it, that was all that he could remember. Of course, it didn't really matter – at least . . . He looked uncomfortably at the diamonds. Supposing they should think – oh, but they wouldn't – and yet again they might – that he had stolen the car and the diamonds? Because, after all, when one came to think of it, would anyone in their senses thrust a valuable diamond necklace carelessly into the open pocket of a car?

Edward got out and went round to the back of the motor. Its number was XR10061. Beyond the fact that that was certainly not the number of his car, it conveyed nothing to him. Then he set to work systematically to search all the pockets. In the one where he had found the diamonds he made a discovery – a small scrap of paper with some words pencilled on it. By the light of the headlights, Edward read them easily enough.

'*Meet me, Greane, corner of Salter's Lane, ten o'clock.*'

He remembered the name Greane. He had seen it on a sign-post earlier in the day. In a minute, his mind was made up. He would go to this village, Greane, find Salter's Lane, meet the person who had written the note, and explain the circumstances. That would be much better than looking a fool in the local police station.

He started off almost happily. After all, this was an adventure. This was the sort of thing that didn't happen every day. The diamond necklace made it exciting and mysterious.

He had some little difficulty in finding Greane, and still more difficulty in finding Salter's Lane, but after knocking up two cottages, he succeeded.

Still, it was a few minutes after the appointed hour when he drove cautiously along a narrow road, keeping a sharp look-out on the left-hand side where he had been told Salter's Lane branched off.

He came upon it quite suddenly round a bend, and even as he drew up, a figure came forward out of the darkness.

'At last!' a girl's voice cried. 'What an age you've been, Gerald!'

As she spoke, the girl stepped right into the glare of the headlights, and Edward caught his breath. She was the most glorious creature he had ever seen.

She was quite young, with hair black as night, and wonderful scarlet lips. The heavy cloak that she wore swung open, and Edward saw that she was in full evening dress – a kind of flame-coloured sheath, outlining her perfect body. Round her neck was a row of exquisite pearls.

Suddenly the girl started.

'Why,' she cried; 'it isn't Gerald.'

'No,' said Edward hastily. 'I must explain.' He took the diamond necklace from his pocket and held it out to her. 'My name is Edward –'

He got no further, for the girl clapped her hands and broke in:

'Edward, of course! I am so glad. But that idiot Jimmy told me over the phone that he was sending Gerald along with the car. It's awfully sporting of you to come. I've been dying to meet you. Remember I haven't seen you since I was six years old. I see you've got the necklace all right. Shove it in your pocket again. The village policeman might come along and see it. Brrr, it's cold as ice waiting here! Let me get in.'

As though in a dream Edward opened the door, and she sprang lightly in beside him. Her furs swept his cheek, and an elusive scent, like that of violets after rain, assailed his nostrils.

He had no plan, no definite thought even. In a minute, without conscious volition, he had yielded himself to the adventure. She had called him Edward – what matter if he were the wrong Edward? She would find him out soon enough. In the meantime, let the game go on. He let in the clutch and they glided off.

Presently the girl laughed. Her laugh was just as wonderful as the rest of her.

'It's easy to see you don't know much about cars. I suppose they don't have them out there?'

'I wonder where "out there" is?' thought Edward. Aloud he said, 'Not much.'

'Better let me drive,' said the girl. 'It's tricky work finding your way round these lanes until we get on the main road again.'

He relinquished his place to her gladly. Presently they were humming through the night at a pace and with a recklessness that secretly appalled Edward. She turned her head towards him.

'I like pace. Do you? You know – you're not a bit like Gerald. No one would ever take you to be brothers. You're not a bit like what I imagined, either.'

'I suppose,' said Edward, 'that I'm so completely ordinary. Is that it?'

'Not ordinary – different. I can't make you out. How's poor old Jimmy? Very fed up, I suppose?'

'Oh, Jimmy's all right,' said Edward.

'It's easy enough to say that – but it's rough luck on him having a sprained ankle. Did he tell you the whole story?'

'Not a word. I'm completely in the dark. I wish you'd enlighten me.'

'Oh, the thing worked like a dream. Jimmy went in at the front door, togged up in his girl's clothes. I gave him a minute or two, and then shinned up to the window. Agnes Larella's maid was there laying out Agnes's dress and jewels, and all the rest. Then there was a great yell downstairs, and the squib went off, and everyone shouted fire. The maid dashed out, and I hopped in, helped myself to the necklace, and was out and down in a flash, and out of the place by the back way across the Punch Bowl. I shoved the necklace and the notice where to pick me up in the pocket of the car in passing. Then I joined Louise at the hotel, having shed my snow boots of course. Perfect alibi for me. She'd no idea I'd been out at all.'

'And what about Jimmy?'

'Well, you know more about that than I do.'

'He didn't tell me anything,' said Edward easily.

'Well, in the general rag, he caught his foot in his skirt and managed to sprain it. They had to carry him to the car, and the Larellas' chauffeur drove him home. Just fancy if the chauffeur had happened to put his hand in the pocket!'

Edward laughed with her, but his mind was busy. He understood the position more or less now. The name of Larella was vaguely familiar to him – it was a name that spelt wealth. This girl, and an unknown man called Jimmy, had conspired together to steal the necklace, and had succeeded. Owing to his sprained ankle and the presence of the Larellas' chauffeur

Jimmy had not been able to look in the pocket of the car before telephoning to the girl – probably had had no wish to do so. But it was almost certain that the other unknown 'Gerald' would do so at any early opportunity. And in it, he would find Edward's muffler!

'Good going,' said the girl.

A tram flashed past them, they were on the outskirts of London. They flashed in and out of the traffic. Edward's heart stood in his mouth. She was a wonderful driver, this girl, but she took risks!

Quarter of an hour later they drew up before an imposing house in a frigid square.

'We can shed some of our clothing here,' said the girl, 'before we go on to Ritson's.'

'Ritson's?' queried Edward. He mentioned the famous night-club almost reverently.

'Yes, didn't Gerald tell you?'

'He did not,' said Edward grimly. 'What about my clothes?'

She frowned.

'Didn't they tell you *anything*? We'll rig you up somehow. We've got to carry this through.'

A stately butler opened the door and stood aside to let them enter.

'Mr Gerald Champneys rang up, your ladyship. He was very anxious to speak to you, but he wouldn't leave a message.'

'I bet he was anxious to speak to her,' said Edward to himself. 'At any rate, I know my full name now. Edward Champneys. But who is she? Your ladyship, they called her. What does she want to steal a necklace for? Bridge debts?'

In the *feuilletons* which he occasionally read, the beautiful and titled heroine was always driven desperate by bridge debts.

Edward was led away by the stately butler, and delivered over to a smooth-mannered valet. A quarter of an hour later he rejoined his hostess in the hall, exquisitely attired in evening clothes made in Savile Row which fitted him to a nicety.

Heavens! What a night!

They drove in the car to the famous Ritson's. In common with everyone else Edward had read scandalous paragraphs concerning Ritson's. Anyone who was anyone turned up at Ritson's sooner or later. Edward's only fear was that someone who knew the real Edward Champneys might turn up. He consoled himself by the reflection that the real man had evidently been out of England for some years.

Sitting at a little table against the wall, they sipped cocktails. Cocktails! To the simple Edward they represented the quintessence of the fast life. The girl, wrapped in a wonderful embroidered shawl, sipped nonchalantly. Suddenly she dropped the shawl from her shoulders and rose.

'Let's dance.'

Now the one thing that Edward could do to perfection was to dance. When he and Maud took the floor together at the Palais de Danse, lesser lights stood still and watched in admiration.

'I nearly forgot,' said the girl suddenly. 'The necklace?'

She held out her hand. Edward, completely bewildered, drew it from his pocket and gave it to her. To his utter amazement, she coolly clasped it round her neck. Then she smiled up at him intoxicatingly.

'Now,' she said softly, 'we'll dance.'

They danced. And in all Ritson's nothing more perfect could be seen.

Then, as at length they returned to their table, an old gentleman with a would-be rakish air accosted Edward's companion.

'Ah! Lady Noreen, always dancing! Yes, yes. Is Captain Folliot here tonight?'

'Jimmy's taken a toss – racked his ankle.'

'You don't say so? How did that happen?'

'No details as yet.'

She laughed and passed on.

Edward followed, his brain in a whirl. He knew now. Lady Noreen Eliot, the famous Lady Noreen herself, perhaps the most talked of girl in England. Celebrated for her beauty, for her daring – the leader of that set known as the Bright Young People. Her engagement to Captain James Folliot, V.C., of the Household Calvalry, had been recently announced.

But the necklace? He still couldn't understand the necklace. He must risk giving himself away, but know he must.

As they sat down again, he pointed to it.

'Why that, Noreen?' he said. 'Tell me why?'

She smiled dreamily, her eyes far away, the spell of the dance still holding her.

'It's difficult for you to understand, I suppose. One gets so tired of the same thing – always the same thing. Treasure hunts were all very well for a while, but one gets used to everything. "Burglaries" were my idea. Fifty pounds entrance fee, and lots to be drawn. This is the third. Jimmy and I drew Agnes Larella. You know the rules? Burglary to be carried out within three days and the loot to be worn for at least an hour in a public place, or you forfeit your stake and a hundred-pound fine. It's rough luck on Jimmy spraining his ankle, but we'll scoop the pool all right.'

'I see,' said Edward, drawing a deep breath. 'I see.'

Noreen rose suddenly, pulling her shawl round her.

'Drive me somewhere in the car. Down to the docks. Somewhere horrible and exciting. Wait a minute –' She reached up and unclasped the diamonds from her neck. 'You'd better take these again. I don't want to be murdered for them.'

They went out of Ritson's together. The car stood in a small by-street, narrow and dark. As they turned the corner towards it, another car drew up to the curb, and a young man sprang out.

'Thank the Lord, Noreen, I've got hold of you at last,' he cried. 'There's the devil to pay. That ass Jimmy got off with the wrong car. God knows where those diamonds are at this minute. We're in the devil of a mess.'

Lady Noreen stared at him.

'What do you mean? We've got the diamonds – at least Edward has.'

'Edward?'

'Yes.' She made a slight gesture to indicate the figure by her side.

'It's I who am in the devil of a mess,' thought Edward. 'Ten to one this is brother Gerald.'

The young man stared at him.

'What do you mean?' he said slowly. 'Edward's in Scotland.'

'Oh!' cried the girl. She stared at Edward. 'Oh!'

Her colour came and went.

'So you,' she said, in a low voice, 'are the real thing?'

It took Edward just one minute to grasp the situation. There was awe in the girl's eyes – was it, could it be – admiration? Should he explain? Nothing so tame! He would play up to the end.

He bowed ceremoniously.

'I have to thank you, Lady Noreen,' he said, in the best highwayman manner, 'for a most delightful evening.'

One quick look he cast at the car from which the other had just alighted. A scarlet car with a shining bonnet. His car!

'And I will wish you good-evening.'

One quick spring and he was inside, his foot on the clutch. The car started forward. Gerald stood paralysed, but the girl was quicker. As the car slid past she leapt for it, alighting on the running board.

The car swerved, shot blindly round the corner and pulled up. Noreen, still panting from her spring, laid her hand on Edward's arm.

'You must give it me – oh, you must give it me. I've got to return it to Agnes Larella. Be a sport – we've had a good evening together – we've danced – we've been – pals. Won't you give it to me? To *me*?'

A woman who intoxicated you with her beauty. There were such women then . . .

Also, Edward was only too anxious to get rid of the necklace. It was a heaven-sent opportunity for a *beau geste*.

He took it from his pocket and dropped it into her outstretched hand.

'We've been – pals,' he said.

'Ah!' Her eyes smouldered – lit up.

Then surprisingly she bent her head to him. For a moment he held her, her lips against his . . .

Then she jumped off. The scarlet car sped forward with a great leap.

Romance!

Adventure!

At twelve o'clock on Christmas Day, Edward Robinson strode into the tiny drawing-room of a house in Clapham with the customary greeting of 'Merry Christmas'.

Maud, who was rearranging a piece of holly, greeted him coldly.

'Have a good day in the country with that friend of yours?' she inquired.

'Look here,' said Edward. 'That was a lie I told you. I won a competition – £500, and I bought a car with it. I didn't tell you because I knew you'd kick up a row about it. That's the first thing. I've bought the car and there's nothing more to be said about it. The second thing is this – I'm not going to hang about for years. My prospects are quite good enough and I mean to marry you next month. See?'

'Oh!' said Maud faintly.

Was this – could this be – *Edward* speaking in this masterful fashion?

'Will you?' said Edward. 'Yes or no?'

She gazed at him, fascinated. There was awe and admiration in her eyes, and the sight of that look was intoxicating to Edward. Gone was that patient motherliness which had roused him to exasperation.

So had the Lady Noreen looked at him last night. But the Lady Noreen had receded far away, right into the region of Romance, side by side with the Marchesa Bianca. This was the Real Thing. This was his woman.

'Yes or no?' he repeated, and drew a step nearer.

'Ye – ye-es,' faltered Maud. 'But, oh, Edward, what has happened to you? You're quite different today.'

'Yes,' said Edward. 'For twenty-four hours I've been a man instead of a worm – and, by God, it pays!'

He caught her in his arms almost as Bill the superman might have done.

'Do you love me, Maud? Tell me, do you love me?'

'Oh, Edward!' breathed Maud. 'I adore you . . .'

10

The Witness for the Prosecution

'The Witness for the Prosecution' was first published in the USA as 'Traitor Hands' in *Flynn's Weekly*, 31 January 1925.

Mr Mayherne adjusted his pince-nez and cleared his throat with a little dry-as-dust cough that was wholly typical of him. Then he looked again at the man opposite him, the man charged with wilful murder.

Mr Mayherne was a small man precise in manner, neatly, not to say foppishly dressed, with a pair of very shrewd and piercing grey eyes. By no means a fool. Indeed, as a solicitor, Mr Mayherne's reputation stood very high. His voice, when he spoke to his client, was dry but not unsympathetic.

'I must impress upon you again that you are in very grave danger, and that the utmost frankness is necessary.'

Leonard Vole, who had been staring in a dazed fashion at the blank wall in front of him, transferred his glance to the solicitor.

'I know,' he said hopelessly. 'You keep telling me so. But I can't seem to realize yet that I'm charged with murder – *murder*. And such a dastardly crime too.'

Mr Mayherne was practical, not emotional. He coughed again, took off his pince-nez, polished them carefully, and replaced them on his nose. Then he said:

'Yes, yes, yes. Now, my dear Mr Vole, we're going to make a determined effort to get you off – and we shall succeed – we shall succeed. But I must have all the facts. I must know just how damaging the case against you is likely to be. Then we can fix upon the best line of defence.'

Still the young man looked at him in the same dazed, hopeless fashion. To Mr Mayherne the case had seemed black enough, and the guilt of the prisoner assured. Now, for the first time, he felt a doubt.

'You think I'm guilty,' said Leonard Vole, in a low voice. 'But, by God, I swear I'm not! It looks pretty black against me, I know that. I'm like a man caught in a net – the meshes of it all round me, entangling me whichever way I turn. But I didn't do it, Mr Mayherne, I didn't do it!'

In such a position a man was bound to protest his innocence. Mr Mayherne knew that. Yet, in spite of himself, he was impressed. It might be, after all, that Leonard Vole was innocent.

'You are right, Mr Vole,' he said gravely. 'The case does look very black against you. Nevertheless, I accept your assurance. Now, let us get to facts. I want you to tell me in your own words exactly how you came to make the acquaintance of Miss Emily French.'

'It was one day in Oxford Street. I saw an elderly lady crossing the road. She was carrying a lot of parcels. In the middle of the street she dropped them, tried to recover them, found a bus was almost on top of her and just managed to reach the kerb safely, dazed and bewildered by people having shouted at her. I recovered the parcels, wiped the mud off them as best I could, retied the string of one, and returned them to her.'

'There was no question of your having saved her life?'

'Oh! dear me, no. All I did was to perform a common act of courtesy. She was extremely grateful, thanked me warmly, and said something about my manners not being those of most of the younger generation – I can't remember the exact words. Then I lifted my hat and went on. I never expected to see her again. But life is full of coincidences. That very evening I came across her at a party at a friend's house. She recognized me at once and asked that I should be introduced to her. I then found out that she was a Miss Emily French and that she lived at Cricklewood. I talked to her for some time. She was, I imagine, an old lady who took sudden violent fancies to people. She took one to me on the strength of a perfectly simple action which anyone might have performed. On leaving, she shook me warmly by the hand, and asked me to come and see her. I replied, of course, that I should be very pleased to do so, and she then urged me to name a day. I did not want particularly to go, but it would have seemed churlish to refuse, so I fixed on the following Saturday. After she had gone, I learned something about her from my friends. That she was rich, eccentric, lived alone with one maid and owned no less than eight cats.'

'I see,' said Mr Mayherne. 'The question of her being well off came up as early as that?'

'If you mean that I inquired –' began Leonard Vole hotly, but Mr Mayherne stilled him with a gesture.

'I have to look at the case as it will be presented by the other side. An ordinary observer would not have supposed Miss French to be a lady of means. She lived poorly, almost humbly. Unless you had been told the contrary, you would in all probability have considered her to be in poor circumstances – at any rate to begin with. Who was it exactly who told you that she was well off?'

'My friend, George Harvey, at whose house the party took place.'

'Is he likely to remember having done so?'

'I really don't know. Of course it is some time ago now.'

'Quite so, Mr Vole. You see, the first aim of the prosecution will be to establish that you were in low water financially – that is true, is it not?'

Leonard Vole flushed.

'Yes,' he said, in a low voice. 'I'd been having a run of infernal bad luck just then.'

'Quite so,' said Mr Mayherne again. 'That being, as I say, in low water financially, you met this rich old lady and cultivated her acquaintance assiduously. Now if we are in a position to say that you had no idea she was well off, and that you visited her out of pure kindness of heart –'

'Which is the case.'

'I dare say. I am not disputing the point. I am looking at it from the outside point of view. A great deal depends on the memory of Mr Harvey. Is he likely to remember that conversation or is he not? Could he be confused by counsel into believing that it took place later?'

Leonard Vole reflected for some minutes. Then he said steadily enough, but with a rather paler face:

'I do not think that that line would be successful, Mr Mayherne. Several of those present heard his remark, and one or two of them chaffed me about my conquest of a rich old lady.'

The solicitor endeavoured to hide his disappointment with a wave of the hand.

'Unfortunately,' he said. 'But I congratulate you upon your plain speaking, Mr Vole. It is to you I look to guide me. Your judgement is quite right. To persist in the line I spoke of would have been disastrous. We must leave that point. You made the acquaintance of Miss French, you called upon her, the acquaintanceship progressed. We want a clear reason for all this. Why did you, a young man of thirty-three, good-looking, fond of sport, popular with your friends, devote so much time to an elderly woman with whom you could hardly have anything in common?'

Leonard Vole flung out his hands in a nervous gesture.

'I can't tell you – I really can't tell you. After the first visit, she pressed me to come again, spoke of being lonely and unhappy. She made it difficult for me to refuse. She showed so plainly her fondness and affection for me that I was placed in an awkward position. You see, Mr Mayherne, I've got a weak nature – I drift – I'm one of those people who can't say "No." And believe me or not, as you like, after the third or fourth visit I paid her I found myself getting genuinely fond of the old thing. My mother died when I was young, an aunt brought me up, and she too died before I was fifteen. If I told you that I genuinely enjoyed being mothered and pampered, I dare say you'd only laugh.'

Mr Mayherne did not laugh. Instead he took off his pince-nez again and polished them, always a sign with him that he was thinking deeply.

'I accept your explanation, Mr Vole,' he said at last. 'I believe it to be psychologically probable. Whether a jury would take that view of it is another matter. Please continue your narrative. When was it that Miss French first asked you to look into her business affairs?'

'After my third or fourth visit to her. She understood very little of money matters, and was worried about some investments.'

Mr Mayherne looked up sharply.

'Be careful, Mr Vole. The maid, Janet Mackenzie, declares that her mistress was a good woman of business and transacted all her own affairs, and this is borne out by the testimony of her bankers.'

'I can't help that,' said Vole earnestly. 'That's what she said to me.'

Mr Mayherne looked at him for a moment or two in silence. Though he had no intention of saying so, his belief in Leonard Vole's innocence was at that moment strengthened. He knew something of the mentality of elderly ladies. He saw Miss French, infatuated with the good-looking young man, hunting about for pretexts that should bring him to the house. What more likely than that she should plead ignorance of business, and beg him to help her with her money affairs? She was enough of a woman of the world to realize that any man is slightly flattered by such an admission of his superiority. Leonard Vole had been flattered. Perhaps, too, she had not been averse to letting this young man know that she was wealthy. Emily French had been a strong-willed old woman, willing to pay her price for what she wanted. All this passed rapidly through Mr Mayherne's mind, but he gave no indication of it, and asked instead a further question.

'And you did handle her affairs for her at her request?'

'I did.'

'Mr Vole,' said the solicitor, 'I am going to ask you a very serious question, and one to which it is vital I should have a truthful answer. You were in low water financially. You had the handling of an old lady's affairs – an old lady who, according to her own statement, knew little or nothing of business. Did you at any time, or in any manner, convert to your own use the securities which you handled? Did you engage in any transaction for your own pecuniary advantage which will not bear the light of day?' He quelled the other's response. 'Wait a minute before you answer. There are two courses open to us. Either we can make a feature of your probity and honesty in conducting her affairs whilst pointing out how unlikely it is that you would commit murder to obtain money which you might have obtained by such infinitely easier means. If, on the other hand, there is anything in your dealings which the prosecution will get hold of – if, to put it baldly, it can be proved that you swindled the old lady in any way, we must take the line that you had no motive for the murder, since she was already a profitable source of income to you. You perceive the distinction. Now, I beg of you, take your time before you reply.'

But Leonard Vole took no time at all.

'My dealings with Miss French's affairs are all perfectly fair and above board. I acted for her interests to the very best of my ability, as anyone will find who looks into the matter.'

'Thank you,' said Mr Mayherne. 'You relieve my mind very much. I pay you the compliment of believing that you are far too clever to lie to me over such an important matter.'

'Surely,' said Vole eagerly, 'the strongest point in my favour is the lack of motive. Granted that I cultivated the acquaintanceship of a rich old lady in the hope of getting money out of her – that, I gather, is the substance of what you have been saying – surely her death frustrates all my hopes?'

The solicitor looked at him steadily. Then, very deliberately, he repeated his unconscious trick with his pince-nez. It was not until they were firmly replaced on his nose that he spoke.

'Are you not aware, Mr Vole, Miss French left a will under which you are the principal beneficiary?'

'What?' The prisoner sprang to his feet. His dismay was obvious and unforced. 'My God! What are you saying? She left her money to me?'

Mr Mayherne nodded slowly. Vole sank down again, his head in his hands.

'You pretend you know nothing of this will?'

'Pretend? There's no pretence about it. I knew nothing about it.'

'What would you say if I told you that the maid, Janet Mackenzie, swears that you *did* know? That her mistress told her distinctly that she had consulted you in the matter, and told you of her intentions?'

'Say? That she's lying! No, I go too fast. Janet is an elderly woman. She was a faithful watchdog to her mistress, and she didn't like me. She was jealous and suspicious. I should say that Miss French confided her intentions to Janet, and that Janet either mistook something she said, or else was convinced in her own mind that I had persuaded the old lady into doing it. I dare say that she believes herself now that Miss French actually told her so.'

'You don't think she dislikes you enough to lie deliberately about the matter?'

Leonard Vole looked shocked and startled.

'No, indeed! Why should she?'

'I don't know,' said Mr Mayherne thoughtfully. 'But she's very bitter against you.'

The wretched young man groaned again.

'I'm beginning to see,' he muttered. 'It's frightful. I made up to her, that's what they'll say, I got her to make a will leaving her money to me, and then I go there that night, and there's nobody in the house – they find her the next day – oh! my God, it's awful!'

'You are wrong about there being nobody in the house,' said Mr Mayherne. 'Janet, as you remember, was to go out for the evening. She went, but about half past nine she returned to fetch the pattern of a blouse sleeve which she had promised to a friend. She let herself in by the back door, went upstairs and fetched it, and went out again. She heard voices in the sitting-room, though she could not distinguish what they said, but she will swear that one of them was Miss French's and one was a man's.'

'At half past nine,' said Leonard Vole. 'At half past nine . . .' He sprang to his feet. 'But then I'm saved – saved –'

'What do you mean, saved?' cried Mr Mayherne, astonished.

'*By half past nine I was at home again!* My wife can prove that. I left Miss French about five minutes to nine. I arrived home about twenty past nine. My wife was there waiting for me. Oh! thank God – thank God! And bless Janet Mackenzie's sleeve pattern.'

In his exuberance, he hardly noticed that the grave expression of the solicitor's face had not altered. But the latter's words brought him down to earth with a bump.

'Who, then, in your opinion, murdered Miss French?'

'Why, a burglar, of course, as was thought at first. The window was forced, you remember. She was killed with a heavy blow from a crowbar, and the crowbar was found lying on the floor beside the body. And several articles were missing. But for Janet's absurd suspicions and dislike of me, the police would never have swerved from the right track.'

'That will hardly do, Mr Vole,' said the solicitor. 'The things that were missing were mere trifles of no value, taken as a blind. And the marks on the window were not all conclusive. Besides, think for yourself. You say you were no longer in the house by half past nine. Who, then, was the man Janet heard talking to Miss French in the sitting-room? She would hardly be having an amicable conversation with a burglar?'

'No,' said Vole. 'No –' He looked puzzled and discouraged. 'But anyway,' he added with reviving spirit, 'it lets me out. I've got an *alibi*. You must see Romaine – my wife – at once.'

'Certainly,' acquiesced the lawyer. 'I should already have seen Mrs

Vole but for her being absent when you were arrested. I wired to Scotland at once, and I understand that she arrives back tonight. I am going to call upon her immediately I leave here.'

Vole nodded, a great expression of satisfaction settling down over his face.

'Yes, Romaine will tell you. My God! it's a lucky chance that.'

'Excuse me, Mr Vole, but you are very fond of your wife?'

'Of course.'

'And she of you?'

'Romaine is devoted to me. She'd do anything in the world for me.'

He spoke enthusiastically, but the solicitor's heart sank a little lower. The testimony of a devoted wife – would it gain credence?

'Was there anyone else who saw you return at nine-twenty? A maid, for instance?'

'We have no maid.'

'Did you meet anyone in the street on the way back?'

'Nobody I knew. I rode part of the way in a bus. The conductor might remember.'

Mr Mayherne shook his head doubtfully.

'There is no one, then, who can confirm your wife's testimony?'

'No. But it isn't necessary, surely?'

'I dare say not. I dare say not,' said Mr Mayherne hastily. 'Now there's just one thing more. Did Miss French know that you were a married man?'

'Oh, yes.'

'Yet you never took your wife to see her. Why was that?'

For the first time, Leonard Vole's answer came halting and uncertain. 'Well – I don't know.'

'Are you aware that Janet Mackenzie says her mistress believed you to be single, and contemplated marrying you in the future?'

Vole laughed.

'Absurd! There was forty years difference in age between us.'

'It has been done,' said the solicitor drily. 'The fact remains. Your wife never met Miss French?'

'No –' Again the constraint.

'You will permit me to say,' said the lawyer, 'that I hardly understand your attitude in the matter.'

Vole flushed, hesitated, and then spoke.

'I'll make a clean breast of it. I was hard up, as you know. I hoped that Miss French might lend me some money. She was fond of me, but she wasn't at all interested in the struggles of a young couple. Early on, I found that she had taken it for granted that my wife and I didn't get on – were living apart. Mr Mayherne – I wanted the money – for Romaine's sake. I said nothing, and allowed the old lady to think what she chose. She spoke of my being an adopted son for her. There was never any question of marriage – that must be just Janet's imagination.'

'And that is all?'

'Yes – that is all.'

Was there just a shade of hesitation in the words? The lawyer fancied so. He rose and held out his hand.

'Goodbye, Mr Vole.' He looked into the haggard young face and spoke with an unusual impulse. 'I believe in your innocence in spite of the multitude of facts arrayed against you. I hope to prove it and vindicate you completely.'

Vole smiled back at him.

'You'll find the alibi is all right,' he said cheerfully.

Again he hardly noticed that the other did not respond.

'The whole thing hinges a good deal on the testimony of Janet Mackenzie,' said Mr Mayherne. 'She hates you. That much is clear.'

'She can hardly hate me,' protested the young man.

The solicitor shook his head as he went out.

'Now for Mrs Vole,' he said to himself.

He was seriously disturbed by the way the thing was shaping.

The Voles lived in a small shabby house near Paddington Green. It was to this house that Mr Mayherne went.

In answer to his ring, a big slatternly woman, obviously a charwoman, answered the door.

'Mrs Vole? Has she returned yet?'

'Got back an hour ago. But I dunno if you can see her.'

'If you will take my card to her,' said Mr Mayherne quietly, 'I am quite sure that she will do so.'

The woman looked at him doubtfully, wiped her hand on her apron and took the card. Then she closed the door in his face and left him on the step outside.

In a few minutes, however, she returned with a slightly altered manner.

'Come inside, please.'

She ushered him into a tiny drawing-room. Mr Mayherne, examining a drawing on the wall, stared up suddenly to face a tall pale woman who had entered so quietly that he had not heard her.

'Mr Mayherne? You are my husband's solicitor, are you not? You have come from him? Will you please sit down?'

Until she spoke he had not realized that she was not English. Now, observing her more closely, he noticed the high cheekbones, the dense blue-black of the hair, and an occasional very slight movement of the hands that was distinctly foreign. A strange woman, very quiet. So quiet as to make one uneasy. From the very first Mr Mayherne was conscious that he was up against something that he did not understand.

'Now, my dear Mrs Vole,' he began, 'you must not give way –'

He stopped. It was so very obvious that Romaine Vole had not the slightest intention of giving way. She was perfectly calm and composed.

'Will you please tell me all about it?' she said. 'I must know everything. Do not think to spare me. I want to know the worst.' She hesitated, then repeated in a lower tone, with a curious emphasis which the lawyer did not understand: 'I want to know the worst.'

Mr Mayherne went over his interview with Leonard Vole. She listened attentively, nodding her head now and then.

'I see,' she said, when he had finished. 'He wants me to say that he came in at twenty minutes past nine that night?'

'He did come in at that time?' said Mr Mayherne sharply.

'That is not the point,' she said coldly. 'Will my saying so acquit him? Will they believe me?'

Mr Mayherne was taken aback. She had gone so quickly to the core of the matter.

'That is what I want to know,' she said. 'Will it be enough? Is there anyone else who can support my evidence?'

There was a suppressed eagerness in her manner that made him vaguely uneasy.

'So far there is no one else,' he said reluctantly.

'I see,' said Romaine Vole.

She sat for a minute or two perfectly still. A little smile played over her lips.

The lawyer's feeling of alarm grew stronger and stronger.

'Mrs Vole –' he began. 'I know what you must feel –'

'Do you?' she said. 'I wonder.'

'In the circumstances –'

'In the circumstances – I intend to play a lone hand.'

He looked at her in dismay.

'But, my dear Mrs Vole – you are overwrought. Being so devoted to your husband –'

'I beg your pardon?'

The sharpness of her voice made him start. He repeated in a hesitating manner:

'Being so devoted to your husband –'

Romaine Vole nodded slowly, the same strange smile on her lips.

'Did he tell you that I was devoted to him?' she asked softly. 'Ah! yes, I can see he did. How stupid men are! Stupid – stupid – stupid –'

She rose suddenly to her feet. All the intense emotion that the lawyer had been conscious of in the atmosphere was now concentrated in her tone.

'I hate him, I tell you! I hate him. I hate him, I hate him! I would like to see him hanged by the neck till he is dead.'

The lawyer recoiled before her and the smouldering passion in her eyes.

She advanced a step nearer, and continued vehemently:

'Perhaps I *shall* see it. Supposing I tell you that he did not come in that night at twenty past nine, but at twenty past *ten*? You say that he tells you he knew nothing about the money coming to him. Supposing I tell you he knew all about it, and counted on it, and committed murder to get it? Supposing I tell you that he admitted to me that night when he came in what he had done? That there was blood on his coat? What then? Supposing that I stand up in court and say all these things?'

Her eyes seemed to challenge him. With an effort, he concealed his growing dismay, and endeavoured to speak in a rational tone.

'You cannot be asked to give evidence against your own husband —'

'He is not my husband!'

The words came out so quickly that he fancied he had misunderstood her.

'I beg your pardon? I —'

'He is not my husband.'

The silence was so intense that you could have heard a pin drop.

'I was an actress in Vienna. My husband is alive but in a madhouse. So we could not marry. I am glad now.'

She nodded defiantly.

'I should like you to tell me one thing,' said Mr Mayherne. He contrived to appear as cool and unemotional as ever. 'Why are you so bitter against Leonard Vole?'

She shook her head, smiling a little.

'Yes, you would like to know. But I shall not tell you. I will keep my secret . . .'

Mr Mayherne gave his dry little cough and rose.

'There seems no point in prolonging this interview,' he remarked. 'You will hear from me again after I have communicated with my client.'

She came closer to him, looking into his eyes with her own wonderful dark ones.

'Tell me,' she said, 'did you believe – honestly – that he was innocent when you came here today?'

'I did,' said Mr Mayherne.

'You poor little man,' she laughed.

'And I believe so still,' finished the lawyer. 'Good evening, madam.'

He went out of the room, taking with him the memory of her startled face.

'This is going to be the devil of a business,' said Mr Mayherne to himself as he strode along the street.

Extraordinary, the whole thing. An extraordinary woman. A very dangerous woman. Women were the devil when they got their knife into you.

What was to be done? That wretched young man hadn't a leg to stand upon. Of course, possibly he did commit the crime . . .

'No,' said Mr Mayherne to himself. 'No – there's almost too much evidence against him. I don't believe this woman. She was trumping up the whole story. But she'll never bring it into court.'

He wished he felt more conviction on the point.

The police court proceedings were brief and dramatic. The principal witnesses for the prosecution were Janet Mackenzie, maid to the dead woman, and Romaine Heilger, Austrian subject, the mistress of the prisoner.

Mr Mayherne sat in the court and listened to the damning story that the latter told. It was on the lines she had indicated to him in their interview.

The prisoner reserved his defence and was committed for trial.

Mr Mayherne was at his wits' end. The case against Leonard Vole was black beyond words. Even the famous KC who was engaged for the defence held out little hope.

'If we can shake that Austrian woman's testimony, we might do something,' he said dubiously. 'But it's a bad business.'

Mr Mayherne had concentrated his energies on one single point. Assuming Leonard Vole to be speaking the truth, and to have left the murdered woman's house at nine o'clock, who was the man whom Janet heard talking to Miss French at half past nine?

The only ray of light was in the shape of a scapegrace nephew who had in bygone days cajoled and threatened his aunt out of various sums of money. Janet Mackenzie, the solicitor learned, had always been attached to this young man, and had never ceased urging his claims upon her mistress. It certainly seemed possible that it was this nephew who had been with Miss French after Leonard Vole left, especially as he was not to be found in any of his old haunts.

In all other directions, the lawyer's researches had been negative in their result. No one had seen Leonard Vole entering his own house, or leaving that of Miss French. No one had seen any other man enter or leave the house in Cricklewood. All inquiries drew blank.

It was the eve of the trial when Mr Mayherne received the letter which was to lead his thoughts in an entirely new direction.

It came by the six o'clock post. An illiterate scrawl, written on common paper and enclosed in a dirty envelope with the stamp stuck on crooked.

Mr Mayherne read it through once or twice before he grasped its meaning.

> *Dear Mister*
> *Youre the lawyer chap wot acks for the young feller. if you want that painted foreign hussy showd up for wot she is an her pack of lies you come to 16 Shaw's Rents Stepney tonight. It ul cawst you 2 hundred quid Arsk for Missis Mogson.*

The solicitor read and re-read this strange epistle. It might, of course, be a hoax, but when he thought it over, he became increasingly convinced that it was genuine, and also convinced that it was the one hope for the prisoner. The evidence of Romaine Heilger damned him completely, and the line the defence meant to pursue, the line that the evidence of a woman who had admittedly lived an immoral life was not to be trusted, was at best a weak one.

Mr Mayherne's mind was made up. It was his duty to save his client at all costs. He must go to Shaw's Rents.

He had some difficulty in finding the place, a ramshackle building in an evil-smelling slum, but at last he did so, and on inquiry for Mrs Mogson was sent up to a room on the third floor. On this door he knocked and getting no answer, knocked again.

At this second knock, he heard a shuffling sound inside, and presently the door was opened cautiously half an inch and a bent figure peered out.

Suddenly the woman, for it was a woman, gave a chuckle and opened the door wider.

'So it's you, dearie,' she said, in a wheezy voice. 'Nobody with you, is there? No playing tricks? That's right. You can come in – you can come in.'

With some reluctance the lawyer stepped across the threshold into the small dirty room, with its flickering gas jet. There was an untidy unmade bed in a corner, a plain deal table and two rickety chairs. For the first time Mr Mayherne had a full view of the tenant of this unsavoury apartment. She was a woman of middle age, bent in figure, with a mass of untidy grey hair and a scarf wound tightly round her face. She saw him looking at this and laughed again, the same curious toneless chuckle.

'Wondering why I hide my beauty, dear? He, he, he. Afraid it may tempt you, eh? But you shall see – you shall see.'

She drew aside the scarf and the lawyer recoiled involuntarily before the almost formless blur of scarlet. She replaced the scarf again.

'So you're not wanting to kiss me, dearie? He, he, I don't wonder. And yet I was a pretty girl once – not so long ago as you'd think, either. Vitriol, dearie, vitriol – that's what did that. Ah! but I'll be even with em –'

She burst into a hideous torrent of profanity which Mr Mayherne tried vainly to quell. She fell silent at last, her hands clenching and unclenching themselves nervously.

'Enough of that,' said the lawyer sternly. 'I've come here because I have reason to believe you can give me information which will clear my client, Leonard Vole. Is that the case?'

Her eye leered at him cunningly.

'What about the money, dearie?' she wheezed. 'Two hundred quid, you remember.'

'It is your duty to give evidence, and you can be called upon to do so.'

'That won't do, dearie. I'm an old woman, and I know nothing. But you give me two hundred quid, and perhaps I can give you a hint or two. See?'

'What kind of hint?'

'What should you say to a letter? A letter from *her*. Never mind now how I got hold of it. That's my business. It'll do the trick. But I want my two hundred quid.'

Mr Mayherne looked at her coldly, and made up his mind.

'I'll give you ten pounds, nothing more. And only that if this letter is what you say it is.'

'Ten pounds?' She screamed and raved at him.

'Twenty,' said Mr Mayherne, 'and that's my last word.'

He rose as if to go. Then, watching her closely, he drew out a pocket book, and counted out twenty one-pound notes.

'You see,' he said. 'That is all I have with me. You can take it or leave it.'

But already he knew that the sight of the money was too much for her. She cursed and raved impotently, but at last she gave in. Going over to the bed, she drew something out from beneath the tattered mattress.

'Here you are, damn you!' she snarled. 'It's the top one you want.'

It was a bundle of letters that she threw to him, and Mr Mayherne untied them and scanned them in his usual cool, methodical manner. The woman, watching him eagerly, could gain no clue from his impassive face.

He read each letter through, then returned again to the top one and read it a second time. Then he tied the whole bundle up again carefully.

They were love letters, written by Romaine Heilger, and the man they were written to was not Leonard Vole. The top letter was dated the day of the latter's arrest.

'I spoke true, dearie, didn't I?' whined the woman. 'It'll do for her, that letter?'

Mr Mayherne put the letters in his pocket, then he asked a question. 'How did you get hold of this correspondence?'

'That's telling,' she said with a leer. 'But I know something more. I heard in court what that hussy said. Find out where *she* was at twenty past ten, the time she says she was at home. Ask at the Lion Road Cinema. They'll remember – a fine upstanding girl like that – curse her!'

'Who is the man?' asked Mr Mayherne. 'There's only a Christian name here.'

The other's voice grew thick and hoarse, her hands clenched and unclenched. Finally she lifted one to her face.

'He's the man that did this to me. Many years ago now. She took him away from me – a chit of a girl she was then. And when I went after him – and went for him too – he threw the cursed stuff at me! And she laughed – damn her! I've had it in for her for years. Followed her, I have, spied upon her. And now I've got her! She'll suffer for this, won't she, Mr Lawyer? She'll suffer?'

'She will probably be sentenced to a term of imprisonment for perjury,' said Mr Mayherne quietly.

'Shut away – that's what I want. You're going, are you? Where's my money? Where's that good money?'

Without a word, Mr Mayherne put down the notes on the table. Then, drawing a deep breath, he turned and left the squalid room. Looking back, he saw the old woman crooning over the money.

He wasted no time. He found the cinema in Lion Road easily enough, and, shown a photograph of Romaine Heilger, the commissionaire recognized her at once. She had arrived at the cinema with a man some time after ten o'clock on the evening in question. He had not noticed her escort particularly, but he remembered the lady who had spoken to him about the picture that was showing. They stayed until the end, about an hour later.

Mr Mayherne was satisfied. Romaine Heilger's evidence was a tissue of lies from beginning to end. She had evolved it out of her passionate hatred. The lawyer wondered whether he would ever know what lay behind that hatred. What had Leonard Vole done to her? He had seemed dumbfounded when the solicitor had reported her attitude to him. He had declared earnestly that such a thing was incredible – yet it had seemed to Mr Mayherne that after the first astonishment his protests had lacked sincerity.

He *did* know. Mr Mayherne was convinced of it. He knew, but had no intention of revealing the fact. The secret between those two remained a secret. Mr Mayherne wondered if some day he should come to learn what it was.

The solicitor glanced at his watch. It was late, but time was everything. He hailed a taxi and gave an address.

'Sir Charles must know of this at once,' he murmured to himself as he got in. The trial of Leonard Vole for the murder of Emily French aroused widespread interest. In the first place the prisoner was young and good-looking, then he was accused of a particularly dastardly crime, and there was the further interest of Romaine Heilger, the principal witness for the prosecution. There had been pictures of her in many papers, and several fictitious stories as to her origin and history.

The proceedings opened quietly enough. Various technical evidence came first. Then Janet Mackenzie was called. She told substantially the same story as before. In cross-examination counsel for the defence succeeded in getting her to contradict herself once or twice over her account of Vole's association with Miss French, he emphasized the fact that though she had heard a man's voice in the sitting-room that night, there was nothing to show that it was Vole who was there, and he managed to drive home a feeling that jealousy and dislike of the prisoner were at the bottom of a good deal of her evidence.

Then the next witness was called.

'Your name is Romaine Heilger?'

'Yes.'

'You are an Austrian subject?'

'Yes.'

'For the last three years you have lived with the prisoner and passed yourself off as his wife?'

Just for a moment Romaine Heilger's eye met those of the man in the dock. Her expression held something curious and unfathomable.

'Yes.'

The questions went on. Word by word the damning facts came out. On the night in question the prisoner had taken out a crowbar with him. He had returned at twenty minutes past ten, and had confessed to having killed the old lady. His cuffs had been stained with blood, and he had burned them in the kitchen stove. He had terrorized her into silence by means of threats.

As the story proceeded, the feeling of the court which had, to begin with, been slightly favourable to the prisoner, now set dead against him. He himself sat with downcast head and moody air, as though he knew he were doomed.

Yet it might have been noted that her own counsel sought to restrain Romaine's animosity. He would have preferred her to be a more unbiased witness.

Formidable and ponderous, counsel for the defence arose.

He put it to her that her story was a malicious fabrication from start to finish, that she had not even been in her own house at the time in question, that she was in love with another man and was deliberately seeking to send Vole to his death for a crime he did not commit.

Romaine denied these allegations with superb insolence.

Then came the surprising denouement, the production of the letter. It was read aloud in court in the midst of a breathless stillness.

Max, beloved, the Fates have delivered him into our hands! He has been arrested for murder – but, yes, the murder of an old lady! Leonard who would not hurt a fly! At last I shall have my revenge. The poor chicken! I shall say that he came in that night with blood upon him – that he confessed to me. I shall hang him, Max – and when he hangs he will know and realize that it was Romaine who sent him to his death. And then – happiness, Beloved! Happiness at last!

There were experts present ready to swear that the handwriting was that of Romaine Heilger, but they were not needed. Confronted with the letter, Romaine broke down utterly and confessed everything. Leonard Vole had returned to the house at the time he said, twenty past nine. She had invented the whole story to ruin him.

With the collapse of Romaine Heilger, the case for the Crown collapsed also. Sir Charles called his few witnesses, the prisoner himself went into the box and told his story in a manly straightforward manner, unshaken by cross-examination.

The prosecution endeavoured to rally, but without great success. The judge's summing up was not wholly favourable to the prisoner, but a reaction had set in and the jury needed little time to consider their verdict.

'We find the prisoner not guilty.'

Leonard Vole was free!

Little Mr Mayherne hurried from his seat. He must congratulate his client.

He found himself polishing his pince-nez vigorously, and checked himself. His wife had told him only the night before that he was getting a habit of it. Curious things habits. People themselves never knew they had them.

An interesting case – a very interesting case. That woman, now, Romaine Heilger.

The case was dominated for him still by the exotic figure of Romaine Heilger. She had seemed a pale quiet woman in the house at Paddington, but in court she had flamed out against the sober background. She had flaunted herself like a tropical flower.

If he closed his eyes he could see her now, tall and vehement, her exquisite body bent forward a little, her right hand clenching and unclenching itself unconsciously all the time. Curious things, habits. That gesture of hers with the hand was her habit, he supposed. Yet he had seen someone else do it quite lately. Who was it now? Quite lately –

He drew in his breath with a gasp as it came back to him. *The woman in Shaw's Rents* . . .

He stood still, his head whirling. It was impossible – impossible – Yet, Romaine Heilger was an actress.

The KC came up behind him and clapped him on the shoulder.

'Congratulated our man yet? He's had a narrow shave, you know. Come along and see him.'

But the little lawyer shook off the other's hand.

He wanted one thing only – to see Romaine Heilger face to face.

He did not see her until some time later, and the place of their meeting is not relevant.

'So you guessed,' she said, when he had told her all that was in his mind. 'The face? Oh! that was easy enough, and the light of that gas jet was too bad for you to see the makeup.'

'But why – why –'

'Why did I play a lone hand?' She smiled a little, remembering the last time she had used the words.

'Such an elaborate comedy!'

'My friend – I had to save him. The evidence of a woman devoted to him would not have been enough – you hinted as much yourself. But I know something of the psychology of crowds. Let my evidence be wrung from me, as an admission, damning me in the eyes of the law, and a reaction in favour of the prisoner would immediately set in.'

'And the bundle of letters?'

'One alone, the vital one, might have seemed like a – what do you call it? – put-up job.'

'Then the man called Max?'

'Never existed, my friend.'

'I still think,' said little Mr Mayherne, in an aggrieved manner, 'that we could have got him off by the – er – normal procedure.'

'I dared not risk it. You see, you *thought* he was innocent –'

'And you *knew* it? I see,' said little Mr Mayherne.

'My dear Mr Mayherne,' said Romaine, 'you do not see at all. I knew – he was guilty!'

Wireless

'Wireless' was first published in the
Sunday Chronicle Annual 1925, September 1925.

'Above all, avoid worry and excitement,' said Dr Meynell, in the comfortable fashion affected by doctors.

Mrs Harter, as is often the case with people hearing these soothing but meaningless words, seemed more doubtful than relieved.

'There is a certain cardiac weakness,' continued the doctor fluently, 'but nothing to be alarmed about. I can assure you of that.

'All the same,' he added, 'it might be as well to have a lift installed. Eh? What about it?'

Mrs Harter looked worried.

Dr Meynell, on the contrary, looked pleased with himself. The reason he liked attending rich patients rather than poor ones was that he could exercise his active imagination in prescribing for their ailments.

'Yes, a lift,' said Dr Meynell, trying to think of something else even more dashing – and failing. 'Then we shall avoid all undue exertion. Daily exercise on the level on a fine day, but avoid walking up hills. And above all,' he added happily, 'plenty of distraction for the mind. Don't dwell on your health.'

To the old lady's nephew, Charles Ridgeway, the doctor was slightly more explicit.

'Do not misunderstand me,' he said. 'Your aunt may live for years, probably will. At the same time shock or over-exertion might carry her off like that!' He snapped his fingers. 'She must lead a very quiet life. No exertion. No fatigue. But, of course, she must not be allowed to brood. She must be kept cheerful and the mind well distracted.'

'Distracted,' said Charles Ridgeway thoughtfully.

Charles was a thoughtful young man. He was also a young man who believed in furthering his own inclinations whenever possible.

That evening he suggested the installation of a wireless set.

Mrs Harter, already seriously upset at the thought of the lift, was disturbed and unwilling. Charles was fluent and persuasive.

'I do not know that I care for these new-fangled things.' said Mrs Harter piteously. 'The waves, you know – the electric waves. They might affect me.'

Charles in a superior and kindly fashion pointed out the futility of this idea.

Mrs Harter, whose knowledge of the subject was of the vaguest, but who was tenacious of her own opinion, remained unconvinced.

'All that electricity,' she murmured timorously. 'You may say what you like, Charles, but some people *are* affected by electricity. I always have a terrible headache before a thunderstorm. I know that.'

She nodded her head triumphantly.

Charles was a patient young man. He was also persistent.

'My dear Aunt Mary,' he said, 'let me make the thing clear to you.'

He was something of an authority on the subject. He delivered now quite a lecture on the theme; warming to his task, he spoke of bright-emitter valves, of dull-emitter valves, of high frequency and low frequency, of amplification and of condensers.

Mrs Harter, submerged in a sea of words that she did not understand, surrendered.

'Of course, Charles,' she murmured, 'if you really think –'

'My dear Aunt Mary,' said Charles enthusiastically. 'It is the very thing for you, to keep you from moping and all that.'

The lift prescribed by Dr Meynell was installed shortly afterwards and was very nearly the death of Mrs Harter since, like many other old ladies, she had a rooted objection to strange men in the house. She suspected them one and all of having designs on her old silver.

After the lift the wireless set arrived. Mrs Harter was left to contemplate the, to her, repellent object – a large ungainly-looking box, studded with knobs.

It took all Charles' enthusiasm to reconcile her to it.

Charles was in his element, he turned knobs, discoursing eloquently the while.

Mrs Harter sat in her high-backed chair, patient and polite, with a rooted conviction in her own mind that these new fangled notions were neither more nor less than unmitigated nuisances.

'Listen, Aunt Mary, we are on to Berlin, isn't that splendid? Can you hear the fellow?'

'I can't hear anything except a good deal of buzzing and clicking,' said Mrs Harter.

Charles continued to twirl knobs. 'Brussels,' he announced with enthusiasm.

'Is it really?' said Mrs Harter with no more than a trace of interest.

Charles again turned knobs and an unearthly howl echoed forth into the room.

'Now we seem to be on to the Dogs' Home,' said Mrs Harter, who was an old lady with a certain amount of spirit.

'Ha, ha!' said Charles, 'you will have your joke, won't you, Aunt Mary? Very good that!'

Mrs Harter could not help smiling at him. She was very fond of Charles. For some years a niece, Miriam Harter, had lived with her. She had intended to make the girl her heiress, but Miriam had not been a success. She was impatient and obviously bored by her aunt's society. She was always out, 'gadding about' as Mrs Harter called it. In the end, she had entangled herself with a young man of whom her aunt thoroughly disapproved. Miriam had been returned to her mother with a curt note much as if she had been goods on approval. She had married the young man in question and Mrs Harter usually sent her a handkerchief case or a table-centre at Christmas.

Having found nieces disappointing, Mrs Harter turned her attention to nephews. Charles, from the first, had been an unqualified success. He was always pleasantly deferential to his aunt, and listened with an appearance of intense interest to the reminiscences of her youth. In this he was a great contrast to Miriam, who had been frankly bored and showed it. Charles was never bored, he was always good-tempered, always gay. He told his aunt many times a day that she was a perfectly marvellous old lady.

Highly satisfied with her new acquisition, Mrs Harter had written to her lawyer with instructions as to the making of a new will. This was sent to her, duly approved by her and signed.

And now even in the matter of the wireless, Charles was soon proved to have won fresh laurels.

Mrs Harter, at first antagonistic, became tolerant and finally fascinated. She enjoyed it very much better when Charles went out. The trouble with Charles was that he could not leave the thing alone. Mrs Harter would be seated in her chair comfortably listening to a symphony concert or a lecture on Lucrezia Borgia or Pond Life, quite happy and at peace with the world. Not so Charles. The harmony would be shattered by discordant shrieks while he enthusiastically attempted to get foreign stations. But on those evenings when Charles was dining out with friends Mrs Harter enjoyed the wireless very much indeed. She would turn on two switches, sit in her high-backed chair and enjoy the programme of the evening.

It was about three months after the wireless had been installed that the first eerie happening occurred. Charles was absent at a bridge party.

The programme for that evening was a ballad concert. A well-known soprano was singing 'Annie Laurie,' and in the middle of 'Annie Laurie' a strange thing happened. There was a sudden break, the music ceased for a moment, the buzzing, clicking noise continued and then that too died away. There was dead silence, and then very faintly a low buzzing sound was heard.

Mrs Harter got the impression, why she did not know, that the machine was tuned into somewhere very far away, and then clearly and distinctly a voice spoke, a man's voice with a faint Irish accent.

'*Mary* – can you hear me, Mary? It is Patrick speaking . . . I am coming for you soon. You will be ready, won't you, Mary?'

Then, almost immediately, the strains of 'Annie Laurie' once more filled the room. Mrs Harter sat rigid in her chair, her hands clenched on each arm of it. Had she been dreaming? Patrick! Patrick's voice! Patrick's voice in this very room, speaking to her. No, it must be a dream, a hallucination perhaps. She must just have dropped off to sleep for a minute or two. A curious thing to have dreamed – that her dead husband's voice should speak to her over the ether. It frightened her just a little. What were the words he had said?

'*I am coming for you soon, Mary. You will be ready, won't you?*'

Was it, could it be a premonition? Cardiac weakness. Her heart. After all, she was getting on in years.

'It's a warning – that's what it is,' said Mrs Harter, rising slowly and painfully from her chair, and added characteristically:

'All that money wasted on putting in a lift!'

She said nothing of her experience to anyone, but for the next day or two she was thoughtful and a little pre-occupied.

And then came the second occasion. Again she was alone in the room. The wireless, which had been playing an orchestral selection, died away with the same suddenness as before. Again there was silence, the sense of distance, and finally Patrick's voice not as it had been in life – but a voice rarefied, far away, with a strange unearthly quality. *Patrick speaking to you, Mary, I will be coming for you very soon now . . .*'

Then click, buzz, and the orchestral selection was in full swing again.

Mrs Harter glanced at the clock. No, she had not been asleep this time. Awake and in full possession of her faculties, she had heard Patrick's voice speaking. It was no hallucination, she was sure of that. In a confused way she tried to think over all that Charles had explained to her of the theory of ether waves.

Could it be Patrick had *really* spoken to her? That his actual voice had been wafted through space? There were missing wave lengths or something of that kind. She remembered Charles speaking of 'gaps in the scale'. Perhaps the missing waves explained all the so-called psychological phenomena? No, there was nothing inherently impossible in the idea. Patrick had spoken to her. He had availed himself of modern science to prepare her for what must soon be coming.

Mrs Harter rang the bell for her maid, Elizabeth.

Elizabeth was a tall gaunt woman of sixty. Beneath an unbending exterior she concealed a wealth of affection and tenderness for her mistress.

'Elizabeth,' said Mrs Harter when her faithful retainer had appeared, 'you remember what I told you? The top left-hand drawer of my bureau. It is locked, the long key with the white label. Everything is there ready.'

'Ready, ma'am?'

'For my burial,' snorted Mrs Harter. 'You know perfectly well what I mean, Elizabeth. You helped me to put the things there yourself.'

Elizabeth's face began to work strangely.

'Oh, ma'am,' she wailed, 'don't dwell on such things. I thought you was a sight better.'

'We have all got to go sometime or another,' said Mrs Harter practically. 'I am over my three score years and ten, Elizabeth. There, there, don't make a fool of yourself. If you must cry, go and cry somewhere else.'

Elizabeth retired, still sniffing.

Mrs Harter looked after her with a good deal of affection.

'Silly old fool, but faithful,' she said, 'very faithful. Let me see, was it a hundred pounds or only fifty I left her? It ought to be a hundred. She has been with me a long time.'

The point worried the old lady and the next day she sat down and wrote to her lawyer asking if he would send her will so that she might look over it. It was that same day that Charles startled her by something he said at lunch.

'By the way, Aunt Mary,' he said, 'who is that funny old josser up in the spare room? The picture over the mantelpiece, I mean. The old johnny with the beaver and side whiskers?'

Mrs Harter looked at him austerely.

'That is your Uncle Patrick as a young man,' she said.

'Oh, I say, Aunt Mary, I am awfully sorry. I didn't mean to be rude.'

Mrs Harter accepted the apology with a dignified bend of the head.

Charles went on rather uncertainly:

'I just wondered. You see –'

He stopped undecidedly and Mrs Harter said sharply:

'Well? What were you going to say?'

'Nothing,' said Charles hastily. 'Nothing that makes sense, I mean.'

For the moment the old lady said nothing more, but later that day, when they were alone together, she returned to the subject.

'I wish you would tell me, Charles, what it was made you ask me about that picture of your uncle.'

Charles looked embarrassed.

'I told you, Aunt Mary. It was nothing but a silly fancy of mine – quite absurd.'

'Charles,' said Mrs Harter in her most autocratic voice, 'I insist upon knowing.'

'Well, my dear aunt, if you will have it, I fancied I saw him – the man in the picture, I mean – looking out of the end window when I was coming up the drive last night. Some effect of the light, I suppose. I wondered who on earth he could be, the face was so – early Victorian, if you know what I mean. And then Elizabeth said there was no one, no visitor or stranger in the house, and later in the evening I happened to drift into the spare room, and there was the picture over the mantelpiece. My man to the life! It is quite easily explained, really, I expect. Subconscious and all that. Must have noticed the picture before without realizing that I had noticed it, and then just fancied the face at the window.'

'The end window?' said Mrs Harter sharply.

'Yes, why?'

'Nothing,' said Mrs Harter.

But she was startled all the same. That room had been her husband's dressing-room.

That same evening, Charles again being absent, Mrs Harter sat listening to the wireless with feverish impatience. If for the third time she heard the mysterious voice, it would prove to her finally and without a shadow of doubt that she was really in communication with some other world.

Although her heart beat faster, she was not surprised when the same break occurred, and after the usual interval of deathly silence the faint far-away Irish voice spoke once more.

'*Mary* – you are prepared now . . . On Friday I shall come for you . . . Friday at half past nine . . . Do not be afraid – there will be no pain . . . Be ready . . .'

Then almost cutting short the last word, the music of the orchestra broke out again, clamorous and discordant.

Mrs Harter sat very still for a minute or two. Her face had gone white and she looked blue and pinched round the lips.

Presently she got up and sat down at her writing desk. In a somewhat shaky hand she wrote the following lines:

Tonight, at 9.15, I have distinctly heard the voice of my dead husband.
He told me that he would come for me on Friday night at 9.30. If I
should die on that day and at that hour I should like the facts made
known so as to prove beyond question the possibility of communicating
with the spirit world.
Mary Harter.

Mrs Harter read over what she had written, enclosed it in an envelope
and addressed the envelope. Then she rang the bell which was promptly
answered by Elizabeth. Mrs Harter got up from her desk and gave the
note she had just written to the old woman.

'Elizabeth,' she said, 'if I should die on Friday night I should like that
note given to Dr Meynell. No,' – as Elizabeth appeared to be about to
protest – 'do not argue with me. You have often told me you believe in
premonitions. I have a premonition now. There is one thing more. I have
left you in my will £50. I should like you to have £100. If I am not able
to go to the bank myself before I die Mr Charles will see to it.'

As before, Mrs Harter cut short Elizabeth's tearful protests. In
pursuance of her determination, the old lady spoke to her nephew on the
subject the following morning.

'Remember, Charles, that if anything should happen to me, Elizabeth
is to have an extra £50.'

'You are very gloomy these days, Aunt Mary,' said Charles cheerfully.
'What is going to happen to you? According to Dr Meynell, we shall be
celebrating your hundredth birthday in twenty years or so!'

Mrs Harter smiled affectionately at him but did not answer. After a
minute or two she said:

'What are you doing on Friday evening, Charles?'

Charles looked a trifle surprised.

'As a matter of fact, the Ewings asked me to go in and play bridge,
but if you would rather I stayed at home –'

'No,' said Mrs Harter with determination. 'Certainly not. I mean it,
Charles. On that night of all nights I should much rather be alone.'

Charles looked at her curiously, but Mrs Harter vouchsafed no further
information. She was an old lady of courage and determination. She felt
that she must go through with her strange experience singlehanded.

Friday evening found the house very silent. Mrs Harter sat as usual
in her straight-backed chair drawn up to the fireplace. All her preparations were made. That morning she had been to the bank, had drawn out
£50 in notes and had handed them over to Elizabeth despite the latter's
tearful protests. She had sorted and arranged all her personal belongings

and had labelled one or two pieces of jewellery with the names of friends or relations. She had also written out a list of instructions for Charles. The Worcester tea service was to go to Cousin Emma. The Sèvres jars to young William, and so on.

Now she looked at the long envelope she held in her hand and drew from it a folded document. This was her will sent to her by Mr Hopkinson in accordance with her instructions. She had already read it carefully, but now she looked over it once more to refresh her memory. It was a short, concise document. A bequest of £50 to Elizabeth Marshall in consideration of faithful service, two bequests of £500 to a sister and a first cousin, and the remainder to her beloved nephew Charles Ridgeway.

Mrs Harter nodded her head several times. Charles would be a very rich man when she was dead. Well, he had been a dear good boy to her. Always kind, always affectionate, and with a merry tongue which never failed to please her.

She looked at the clock. Three minutes to the half hour. Well she was ready. And she was calm – quite calm. Although she repeated these last words to herself several times, her heart beat strangely and unevenly. She hardly realized it herself, but she was strung up to a fine point of overwrought nerves.

Half past nine. The wireless was switched on. What would she hear? A familiar voice announcing the weather forecast or that far-away voice belonging to a man who had died twenty-five years before?

But she heard neither. Instead there came a familiar sound, a sound she knew well but which tonight made her feel as though an icy hand were laid on her heart. A fumbling at the door . . .

It came again. And then a cold blast seemed to sweep though the room. Mrs Harter had now no doubt what her sensations were. She was afraid . . . She was more than afraid – she was terrified . . .

And suddenly there came to her the thought: Twenty-five years is a long *time*. *Patrick is a stranger to me now.*

Terror! That was what was invading her.

A soft step outside the door – a soft halting footstep. Then the door swung silently open . . .

Mrs Harter staggered to her feet, swaying slightly from side to side, her eyes fixed on the doorway, something slipped from her fingers into the grate.

She gave a strangled cry which died in her throat. In the dim light of the doorway stood a familiar figure with chestnut beard and whiskers and an old-fashioned Victorian coat.

Patrick had come for her!

Her heart gave one terrified leap and stood still. She slipped to the ground in a huddled heap.

There Elizabeth found her, an hour later.

Dr Meynell was called at once and Charles Ridgeway was hastily recalled from his bridge party. But nothing could be done. Mrs Harter had gone beyond human aid.

It was not until two days later that Elizabeth remembered the note given to her by her mistress. Dr Meynell read it with great interest and showed it to Charles Ridgeway.

'A very curious coincidence,' he said. 'It seems clear that your aunt had been having hallucinations about her dead husband's voice. She must have strung herself up to such a point that the excitement was fatal and when the time actually came she died of the shock.'

'Auto-suggestion?' said Charles.

'Something of the sort. I will let you know the result of the autopsy as soon as possible, though I have no doubt of it myself.' In the circumstances an autopsy was desirable, though purely as a matter of form.

Charles nodded comprehendingly.

On the preceding night, when the household was in bed, he had removed a certain wire which ran from the back of the wireless cabinet to his bedroom on the floor above. Also, since the evening had been a chilly one, he had asked Elizabeth to light a fire in his room, and in that fire he had burned a chestnut beard and whiskers. Some Victorian clothing belonging to his late uncle he replaced in the camphor-scented chest in the attic.

As far as he could see, he was perfectly safe. His plan, the shadowy outline of which had first formed in his brain when Doctor Meynell had told him that his aunt might with due care live for many years, had succeeded admirably. A sudden shock, Dr Meynell had said. Charles, that affectionate young man, beloved of old ladies, smiled to himself.

When the doctor departed, Charles went about his duties mechanically. Certain funeral arrangements had to be finally settled. Relatives coming from a distance had to have trains looked out for them. In one or two cases they would have to stay the night. Charles went about it all efficiently and methodically, to the accompaniment of an undercurrent of his own thoughts.

A very good stroke of business! That was the burden of them. Nobody, least of all his dead aunt, had known in what perilous straits Charles stood. His activities, carefully concealed from the world, had landed him where the shadow of a prison loomed ahead.

Exposure and ruin had stared him in the face unless he could in a few short months raise a considerable sum of money. Well – that was all right now. Charles smiled to himself. Thanks to – yes, call it a practical joke – nothing criminal about *that* – he was saved. He was now a very rich man. He had no anxieties on the subject, for Mrs Harter had never made any secret of her intentions.

Chiming in very appositely with these thoughts, Elizabeth put her head round the door and informed him that Mr Hopkinson was here and would like to see him.

About time, too, Charles thought. Repressing a tendency to whistle, he composed his face to one of suitable gravity and repaired to the library. There he greeted the precise old gentleman who had been for over a quarter of a century the late Mrs Harter's legal adviser.

The lawyer seated himself at Charles' invitation and with a dry cough entered upon business matters.

'I did not quite understand your letter to me, Mr Ridgeway. You seemed to be under the impression that the late Mrs Harter's will was in our keeping?'

Charles stared at him.

'But surely – I've heard my aunt say as much.'

'Oh! quite so, quite so. It *was* in our keeping.'

'*Was?*'

'That is what I said. Mrs Harter wrote to us, asking that it might be forwarded to her on Tuesday last.'

An uneasy feeling crept over Charles. He felt a far-off premonition of unpleasantness.

'Doubtless it will come to light amongst her papers,' continued the lawyer smoothly.

Charles said nothing. He was afraid to trust his tongue. He had already been through Mrs Harter's papers pretty thoroughly, well enough to be quite certain that no will was amongst them. In a minute or two, when he had regained control of himself, he said so. His voice sounded unreal to himself, and he had a sensation as of cold water trickling down his back.

'Has anyone been through her personal effects?' asked the lawyer.

Charles replied that her own maid, Elizabeth, had done so. At Mr Hopkinson's suggestion, Elizabeth was sent for. She came promptly, grim and upright, and answered the questions put to her.

She had been through all her mistress's clothes and personal belongings. She was quite sure that there had been no legal document such as a will amongst them. She knew what the will looked like – her mistress had had it in her hand only the morning of her death.

'You are sure of that?' asked the lawyer sharply.

'Yes, sir. She told me so, and she made me take fifty pounds in notes. The will was in a long blue envelope.'

'Quite right,' said Mr Hopkinson.

'Now I come to think of it,' continued Elizabeth, 'that same blue envelope was lying on this table the morning after – but empty. I laid it on the desk.'

'I remember seeing it there,' said Charles.

He got up and went over to the desk. In a minute or two he turned round with an envelope in his hand which he handed to Mr Hopkinson. The latter examined it and nodded his head.

'That is the envelope in which I despatched the will on Tuesday last.'

Both men looked hard at Elizabeth.

'Is there anything more, sir?' she inquired respectfully.

'Not at present, thank you.'

Elizabeth went towards the door.

'One minute,' said the lawyer. 'Was there a fire in the grate that evening?'

'Yes, sir, there was always a fire.'

'Thank you, that will do.'

Elizabeth went out. Charles leaned forward, resting a shaking hand on the table.

'What do you think? What are you driving at?'

Mr Hopkinson shook his head.

'We must still hope the will may turn up. If it does not –'

'Well, if it does not?'

'I am afraid there is only one conclusion possible. Your aunt sent for that will in order to destroy it. Not wishing Elizabeth to lose by that, she gave her the amount of her legacy in cash.'

'But why?' cried Charles wildly. 'Why?'

Mr Hopkinson coughed. A dry cough.

'You have had no – er – disagreement with your aunt, Mr Ridgeway?' he murmured.

Charles gasped.

'No, indeed,' he cried warmly. 'We were on the kindest, most affectionate terms, right up to the end.'

'Ah!' said Mr Hopkinson, not looking at him.

It came to Charles with a shock that the lawyer did not believe him. Who knew what this dry old stick might not have heard? Rumours of Charles' doings might have come round to him. What more natural than that he should suppose that these same rumours had come to Mrs Harter, and the aunt and nephew should have had an altercation on the subject?

But it wasn't so! Charles knew one of the bitterest moments of his career. His lies had been believed. Now that he spoke the truth, belief was withheld. The irony of it!

Of course his aunt had never burnt the will! Of course –

His thoughts came to a sudden check. What was that picture rising before his eyes? An old lady with one hand clasped to her heart . . . something slipping . . . a paper . . . falling on the red-hot embers . . .

Charles' face grew livid. He heard a hoarse voice – his own – asking: 'If that will's never found –?'

'There is a former will of Mrs Harter's still extant. Dated September 1920. By it Mrs Harter leaves everything to her niece, Miriam Harter, now Miriam Robinson.'

What was the old fool saying? Miriam? Miriam with her nondescript husband, and her four whining brats. All his cleverness – for Miriam!

The telephone rang sharply at his elbow. He took up the receiver. It was the doctor's voice, hearty and kindly.

'That you Ridgeway? Thought you'd like to know. The autopsy's just concluded. Cause of death as I surmised. But as a matter of fact the cardiac trouble was much more serious than I suspected when she was alive. With the utmost care, she couldn't have lived longer than two months at the outside. Thought you'd like to know. Might console you more or less.'

'Excuse me,' said Charles, 'would you mind saying that again?'

'She couldn't have lived longer than two months,' said the doctor in a slightly louder tone. 'All things work out for the best, you know, my dear fellow –'

But Charles had slammed back the receiver on its hook. He was conscious of the lawyer's voice speaking from a long way off.

'Dear me, Mr Ridgeway, are you ill?'

Damn them all! The smug-faced lawyer. That poisonous old ass Meynell. No hope in front of him – only the shadow of the prison wall . . .

He felt that Somebody had been playing with him – playing with him like a cat with a mouse. Somebody must be laughing . . .

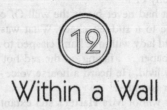

Within a Wall

'Within a Wall' was first published in *Royal Magazine*, October 1925.

It was Mrs Lemprière who discovered the existence of Jane Haworth. It would be, of course. Somebody once said that Mrs Lemprière was easily the most hated woman in London, but that, I think, is an exaggeration. She has certainly a knack of tumbling on the one thing you wish to keep quiet about, and she does it with real genius. It is always an accident.

In this case we had been having tea in Alan Everard's studio. He gave these teas occasionally, and used to stand about in corners, wearing very old clothes, rattling the coppers in his trouser pockets and looking profoundly miserable.

I do not suppose anyone will dispute Everard's claim to genius at this date. His two most famous pictures, *Colour*, and *The Connoisseur*, which belong to his early period, before he became a fashionable portrait painter, were purchased by the nation last year, and for once the choice went unchallenged. But at the date of which I speak, Everard was only beginning to come into his own, and we were free to consider that we had discovered him.

It was his wife who organized these parties. Everard's attitude to her was a peculiar one. That he adored her was evident, and only to be expected. Adoration was Isobel's due. But he seemed always to feel himself slightly in her debt. He assented to anything she wished, not so much through tenderness as through an unalterable conviction that she had a right to her own way. I suppose that was natural enough, too, when one comes to think of it.

For Isobel Loring had been really very celebrated. When she came out she had been *the* débutante of the season. She had everything except money; beauty, position, breeding, brains. Nobody expected her to marry for love. She wasn't that kind of girl. In her second season she had three strings to her bow, the heir to a dukedom, a rising politician, and a South

African millionaire. And then, to everyone's surprise, she married Alan Everard – a struggling young painter whom no one had ever heard of.

It is a tribute to her personality, I think, that everyone went on calling her Isobel Loring. Nobody ever alluded to her as Isobel Everard. It would be: 'I saw Isobel Loring this morning. Yes – with her husband, young Everard, the painter fellow.'

People said Isobel had 'done for herself'. It would, I think, have 'done' for most men to be known as 'Isobel Loring's husband'. But Everard was different. Isobel's talent for success hadn't failed her after all. Alan Everard painted *Colour*.

I suppose everyone knows the picture: a stretch of road with a trench dug down it, the turned earth, reddish in colour, a shining length of brown glazed drainpipe and the huge navvy, resting for a minute on his spade – a Herculean figure in stained corduroys with a scarlet neckerchief. His eyes look out at you from the canvas, without intelligence, without hope, but with a dumb unconscious pleading, the eyes of a magnificent brute beast. It is a flaming thing – a symphony of orange and red. A lot has been written about its symbolism, about what it is meant to express. Alan Everard himself says he didn't mean it to express anything. He was, he said, nauseated by having had to look at a lot of pictures of Venetian sunsets, and a sudden longing for a riot of purely English colour assailed him.

After that, Everard gave the world that epic painting of a public house – *Romance*; the black street with rain falling – the half-open door, the lights and shining glasses, the little foxy-faced man passing through the doorway, small, mean, insignificant, with lips parted and eyes eager, passing in to forget.

On the strength of these two pictures Everard was acclaimed as a painter of 'working men'. He had his niche. But he refused to stay in it. His third and most brilliant work, a full-length portrait of Sir Rufus Herschman. The famous scientist is painted against a background of retorts and crucibles and laboratory shelves. The whole has what may be called a Cubist effect, but the lines of perspective run strangely.

And now he had completed his fourth work – a portrait of his wife. We had been invited to see and criticize. Everard himself scowled and looked out of the window; Isobel Loring moved amongst the guests, talking technique with unerring accuracy.

We made comments. We had to. We praised the painting of the pink satin. The treatment of that, we said, was really marvellous. Nobody had painted satin in quite that way before.

Mrs Lemprière, who is one of the most intelligent art critics I know, took me aside almost at once.

'Georgie,' she said, 'what has he done to himself? The thing's dead. It's smooth. It's – oh! it's damnable.'

'Portrait of a Lady in Pink Satin?' I suggested.

'Exactly. And yet the technique's perfect. And the care! There's enough work there for sixteen pictures.'

'Too much work?' I suggested.

'Perhaps that's it. If there ever was anything there, he's killed it. An extremely beautiful woman in a pink satin dress. Why not a coloured photograph?'

'Why not?' I agreed. 'Do you suppose he knows?' 'Don't you see the man's on edge? It comes, I daresay, of mixing up sentiment and business. He's put his whole soul into painting Isobel, because she is Isobel, and in sparing her, he's lost her. He's been too kind. You've got to – to destroy the flesh before you can get at the soul sometimes.'

I nodded reflectively. Sir Rufus Herschman had not been flattered physically, but Everard had succeeded in putting on the canvas a personality that was unforgettable.

'And Isobel's got such a very forceful personality,' continued Mrs Lemprière.

'Perhaps Everard can't paint women,' I said.

'Perhaps not,' said Mrs Lemprière thoughtfully. 'Yes, that may be the explanation.'

And it was then, with her usual genius for accuracy, that she pulled out a canvas that was leaning with its face to the wall. There were about eight of them, stacked carelessly. It was pure chance that Mrs Lemprière selected the one she did – but as I said before, these things happen with Mrs Lemprière.

'Ah!' said Mrs Lemprière as she turned it to the light.

It was unfinished, a mere rough sketch. The woman, or girl – she was not, I thought, more than twenty-five or six – was leaning forward, her chin on her hand. Two things struck me at once: the extraordinary vitality of the picture and the amazing cruelty of it. Everard had painted with a vindictive brush. The attitude even was a cruel one – it had brought out every awkwardness, every sharp angle, every crudity. It was a study in brown – brown dress, brown background, brown eyes – wistful, eager eyes. Eagerness was, indeed, the prevailing note of it.

Mrs Lemprière looked at it for some minutes in silence. Then she called to Everard.

'Alan,' she said. 'Come here. Who's this?'

Everard came over obediently. I saw the sudden flash of annoyance that he could not quite hide.

'That's only a daub,' he said. 'I don't suppose I shall ever finish it.'

'Who is she?' said Mrs Lemprière.

Everard was clearly unwilling to answer, and his unwillingness was as meat and drink to Mrs Lemprière, who always believes the worst on principle.

'A friend of mine. A Miss Jane Haworth.'

'I've never met her here,' said Mrs Lemprière.

'She doesn't come to these shows.' He paused a minute, then added: 'She's Winnie's godmother.'

Winnie was his little daughter, aged five.

'Really?' said Mrs Lemprière. 'Where does she live?'

'Battersea. A flat.'

'Really,' said Mrs Lemprière again, and then added: 'And what has she ever done to you?'

'To me?'

'To you. To make you so – ruthless.'

'Oh, that!' he laughed. 'Well, you know, she's not a beauty. I can't make her one out of friendship, can I?'

'You've done the opposite,' said Mrs Lemprière. 'You've caught hold of every defect of hers and exaggerated it and twisted it. You've tried to make her ridiculous – but you haven't succeeded, my child. That portrait, if you finish it, will live.'

Everard looked annoyed.

'It's not bad,' he said lightly, 'for a sketch, that is. But, of course, it's not a patch on Isobel's portrait. That's far and away the best thing I've ever done.'

He said the last words defiantly and aggressively. Neither of us answered.

'Far and away the best thing,' he repeated.

Some of the others had drawn near us. They, too, caught sight of the sketch. There were exclamations, comments. The atmosphere began to brighten up.

It was in this way that I first heard of Jane Haworth. Later, I was to meet her – twice. I was to hear details of her life from one of her most intimate friends. I was to learn much from Alan Everard himself. Now that they are both dead, I think it is time to contradict some of the stories Mrs Lemprière is busily spreading abroad. Call some of my story invention if you will – it is not far from the truth.

When the guests had left, Alan Everard turned the portrait of Jane Haworth with its face to the wall again. Isobel came down the room and stood beside him.

'A success, do you think?' she asked thoughtfully. 'Or – not quite a success?'

'The portrait?' he asked quickly.

'No, silly, the party. Of course the portrait's a success.'

'It's the best thing I've done,' Everard declared aggressively.

'We're getting on,' said Isobel. 'Lady Charmington wants you to paint her.'

'Oh, Lord!' He frowned. 'I'm not a fashionable portrait painter, you know.'

'You will be. You'll get to the top of the tree.'

'That's not the tree I want to get to the top of.'

'But, Alan dear, that's the way to make mints of money.'

'Who wants mints of money?'

'Perhaps I do,' she said smiling.

At once he felt apologetic, ashamed. If she had not married him she could have had her mints of money. And she needed it. A certain amount of luxury was her proper setting.

'We've not done so badly just lately,' he said wistfully.

'No, indeed; but the bills are coming in rather fast.'

Bills – always bills!

He walked up and down.

'Oh, hang it! I don't want to paint Lady Charmington,' he burst out, rather like a petulant child.

Isobel smiled a little. She stood by the fire without moving. Alan stopped his restless pacing and came nearer to her. What was there in her, in her stillness, her inertia, that drew him – drew him like a magnet? How beautiful she was – her arms like sculptured white marble, the pure gold of her hair, her lips – red full lips.

He kissed them – felt them fasten on his own. Did anything else matter? What was there in Isobel that soothed you, that took all your cares from you? She drew you into her own beautiful inertia and held you there, quiet and content. Poppy and mandragora; you drifted there, on a dark lake, asleep.

'I'll do Lady Charmington,' he said presently. 'What does it matter? I shall be bored – but after all, painters must eat. There's Mr Pots the painter, Mrs Pots the painter's wife, and Miss Pots the painter's daughter – all needing sustenance.'

'Absurd boy!' said Isobel. 'Talking of our daughter – you ought to go and see Jane some time. She was here yesterday, and said she hadn't seen you for months.'

'Jane was here?'

'Yes – to see Winnie.'

Alan brushed Winnie aside.

'Did she see the picture of you?'

'Yes.'

'What did she think of it?'

'She said it was splendid.'

'Oh!'

He frowned, lost in thought.

'Mrs Lemprière suspects you of a guilty passion for Jane, I think,' remarked Isobel. 'Her nose twitched a good deal.'

'That woman!' said Alan, with deep disgust. 'That woman! What wouldn't she think? What doesn't she think?'

'Well, *I* don't think,' said Isobel, smiling. 'So go and see Jane soon.'

Alan looked across at her. She was sitting now on a low couch by the fire. Her face was half turned away, the smile still lingered on her lips. And at that moment he felt bewildered, confused, as though a mist had formed round him, and, suddenly parting, had given him a glimpse into a strange country.

Something said to him: 'Why does she want you to go and see Jane? There's a reason.' Because with Isobel, there was bound to be a reason. There was no impulse in Isobel, only calculation.

'Do you like Jane?' he asked suddenly.

'She's a dear,' said Isobel.

'Yes, but do you really like her?'

'Of course. She's so devoted to Winnie. By the way, she wants to carry Winnie off to the seaside next week. You don't mind, do you? It will leave us free for Scotland.'

'It will be extraordinarily convenient.'

It would, indeed, be just that. Extraordinarily convenient. He looked across at Isobel with a sudden suspicion. Had she *asked* Jane? Jane was so easily imposed upon.

Isobel got up and went out of the room, humming to herself. Oh, well, it didn't matter. Anyway, he would go and see Jane.

Jane Haworth lived at the top of a block of mansion flats overlooking Battersea Park. When Everard had climbed four flights of stairs and pressed the bell, he felt annoyed with Jane. Why couldn't she live somewhere more get-at-able? When, not having obtained an answer, he had pressed the bell three times, his annoyance had grown greater. Why couldn't she keep someone capable of answering the door?

Suddenly it opened, and Jane herself stood in the doorway. She was flushed.

'Where's Alice?' asked Everard, without any attempt at greeting.

'Well, I'm afraid – I mean – she's not well today.'

'Drunk, you mean?' said Everard grimly.

What a pity that Jane was such an inveterate liar.

'I suppose that's it,' said Jane reluctantly.

'Let me see her.'

He strode into the flat. Jane followed him with disarming meekness. He found the delinquent Alice in the kitchen. There was no doubt whatever as to her condition. He followed Jane into the sitting-room in grim silence.

'You'll have to get rid of that woman,' he said. 'I told you so before.'

'I know you did, Alan, but I can't do that. You forget, her husband's in prison.'

'Where he ought to be,' said Everard. 'How often has that woman been drunk in the three months you've had her?'

'Not so very many times; three or four perhaps. She gets depressed, you know.'

'Three or four! Nine or ten would be nearer the mark. How does she cook? Rottenly. Is she the least assistance or comfort to you in this flat? None whatever. For God's sake, get rid of her tomorrow morning and engage a girl who is of some use.'

Jane looked at him unhappily.

'You won't,' said Everard gloomily, sinking into a big armchair. 'You're such an impossibly sentimental creature. What's this I hear about your taking Winnie to the seaside? Who suggested it, you or Isobel?'

Jane said very quickly: 'I did, of course.'

'Jane,' said Everard, 'if you would only learn to speak the truth, I should be quite fond of you. Sit down, and for goodness' sake don't tell any more lies for at least ten minutes.'

'Oh, Alan!' said Jane, and sat down.

The painter examined her critically for a minute or two. Mrs Lemprière – that woman – had been quite right. He had been cruel in his handling of Jane. Jane was almost, if not quite, beautiful. The long lines of her body were pure Greek. It was that eager anxiety of hers to please that made her awkward. He had seized on that – exaggerated it – had sharpened the line of her slightly pointed chin, flung her body into an ugly poise.

Why? Why was it impossible for him to be five minutes in the room with Jane without feeling violent irritation against her rising up in him? Say what you would, Jane was a dear, but irritating. He was never soothed and at peace with her as he was with Isobel. And yet Jane was so anxious to please, so willing to agree with all he said, but alas! so transparently unable to conceal her real feelings.

He looked round the room. Typically Jane. Some lovely things, pure gems, that piece of Battersea enamel, for instance, and there next to it, an atrocity of a vase hand-painted with roses.

He picked the latter up.

'Would you be very angry, Jane, if I pitched this out of the window?'

'Oh! Alan, you mustn't.'

'What do you want with all this trash? You've plenty of taste if you care to use it. Mixing things up!'

'I know, Alan. It isn't that I don't *know*. But people give me things. That vase – Miss Bates brought it back from Margate – and she's so poor, and has to scrape, and it must have cost her quite a lot – for her, you know, and she thought I'd be so pleased. I simply had to put it in a good place.'

Everard said nothing. He went on looking round the room. There were one or two etchings on the walls – there were also a number of photographs of babies. Babies, whatever their mothers may think, do not always photograph well. Any of Jane's friends who acquired babies hurried to send photographs of them to her, expecting these tokens to be cherished. Jane had duly cherished them.

'Who's this little horror?' asked Everard, inspecting a pudgy addition with a squint. 'I've not seen him before.'

'It's a her,' said Jane. 'Mary Carrington's new baby.'

'Poor Mary Carrington,' said Everard. 'I suppose you'll pretend that you like having that atrocious infant squinting at you all day?'

Jane's chin shot out.

'She's a lovely baby. Mary is a very old friend of mine.'

'Loyal Jane,' said Everard smiling at her. 'So Isobel landed you with Winnie, did she?'

'Well, she did say you wanted to go to Scotland, and I jumped at it. You will let me have Winnie, won't you? I've been wondering if you would let her come to me for ages, but I haven't liked to ask.'

'Oh, you can have her – but it's awfully good of you.'

'Then that's all right,' said Jane happily.

Everard lit a cigarette.

'Isobel show you the new portrait?' he asked rather indistinctly.

'She did.'

'What did you think of it?'

Jane's answer came quickly – too quickly:

'It's perfectly splendid. Absolutely splendid.'

Alan sprang suddenly to his feet. The hand that held the cigarette shook.

'Damn you, Jane, don't lie to me!'

'But, Alan, I'm sure, it *is* perfectly splendid.'

'Haven't you learnt by now, Jane, that I know every tone of your voice? You lie to me like a hatter so as not to hurt my feelings, I suppose. Why can't you be honest? Do you think I want you to tell me a thing is splendid when I know as well as you do that it's not? The damned thing's dead – dead. There's no life in it – nothing behind, nothing but surface, damned smooth surface. I've cheated myself all along – yes, even this afternoon. I came along to you to find out. Isobel doesn't know. But you know, you always do know. I knew you'd tell me it was good – you've no moral sense about that sort of thing. But I can tell by the tone of your voice. When I showed you *Romance* you didn't say anything at all – you held your breath and gave a sort of gasp.'

'Alan . . .'

Everard gave her no chance to speak. Jane was producing the effect upon him he knew so well. Strange that so gentle a creature could stir him to such furious anger.

'You think I've lost the power, perhaps,' he said angrily, 'but I haven't. I can do work every bit as good as *Romance* – better, perhaps. I'll show you, Jane Haworth.'

He fairly rushed out of the flat. Walking rapidly, he crossed through the Park and over Albert Bridge. He was still tingling all over with irritation and baffled rage. Jane, indeed! What did *she* know about painting? What was *her* opinion worth? Why should he care? But he did care. He wanted to paint something that would make Jane gasp. Her mouth would open just a little, and her cheeks would flush red. She would look first at the picture and then at him. She wouldn't say anything at all probably.

In the middle of the bridge he saw the picture he was going to paint. It came to him from nowhere at all, out of the blue. He saw it, there in the air, or was it in his head?

A little, dingy curio shop, rather dark and musty-looking. Behind the counter a Jew – a small Jew with cunning eyes. In front of him the customer, a big man, sleek, well fed, opulent, bloated, a great jowl on him. Above them, on a shelf, a bust of white marble. The light there, on the boy's marble face, the deathless beauty of old Greece, scornful, unheeding of sale and barter. The Jew, the rich collector, the Greek boy's head. He saw them all.

'*The Connoisseur*, that's what I'll call it,' muttered Alan Everard, stepping off the kerb and just missing being annihilated by a passing bus. 'Yes, *The Connoisseur*. I'll *show* Jane.'

When he arrived home, he passed straight into the studio. Isobel found him there, sorting out canvases.

'Alan, don't forget we're dining with the Marches –'

Everard shook his head impatiently.

'Damn the Marches. I'm going to work. I've got hold of something, but I must get it fixed – fixed at once on the canvas before it goes. Ring them up. Tell them I'm dead.'

Isobel looked at him thoughtfully for a moment or two, and then went out. She understood the art of living with a genius very thoroughly. She went to the telephone and made some plausible excuse.

She looked round her, yawning a little. Then she sat down at her desk and began to write.

> '*Dear Jane,*
>
> *Many thanks for your cheque received today. You are good to your godchild. A hundred pounds will do all sorts of things. Children are a terrible expense. You are so fond of Winnie that I felt I was not doing wrong in coming to you for help. Alan, like all geniuses, can only work at what he wants to work at – and unfortunately that doesn't always keep the pot boiling. Hope to see you soon.*
>
> *Yours, Isobel*'

When *The Connoisseur* was finished, some months later, Alan invited Jane to come and see it. The thing was not quite as he had conceived it – that was impossible to hope for – but it was near enough. He felt the glow of the creator. He had made this thing and it was good.

Jane did not this time tell him it was splendid. The colour crept into her cheeks and her lips parted. She looked at Alan, and he saw in her eyes that which he wished to see. Jane knew.

He walked on air. He had shown Jane!

The picture off his mind, he began to notice his immediate surroundings once more.

Winnie had benefited enormously from her fortnight at the seaside, but it struck him that her clothes were very shabby. He said so to Isobel.

'Alan! You who never notice anything! But I like children to be simply dressed – I hate them all fussed up.'

'There's a difference between simplicity and darns and patches.'

Isobel said nothing, but she got Winnie a new frock.

Two days later Alan was struggling with income tax returns. His own pass book lay in front of him. He was hunting through Isobel's desk for hers when Winnie danced into the room with a disreputable doll.

'Daddy, I've got a riddle. Can you guess it? "Within a wall as white as milk, within a curtain soft as silk, bathed in a sea of crystal clear, a golden apple doth appear." Guess what that is?'

'Your mother,' said Alan absently. He was still hunting.

'Daddy!' Winnie gave a scream of laughter. 'It's an *egg*. Why did you think it was mummy?'

Alan smiled too.

'I wasn't really listening,' he said. 'And the words sounded like mummy, somehow.'

A wall as white as milk. A curtain. Crystal. The golden apple. Yes, it did suggest Isobel to him. Curious things, words.

He had found the pass book now. He ordered Winnie peremptorily from the room. Ten minutes later he looked up, startled by a sharp exclamation.

'Alan!'

'Hullo, Isobel. I didn't hear you come in. Look here, I can't make out these items in your pass book.'

'What business had you to touch my pass book?'

He stared at her, astonished. She was angry. He had never seen her angry before.

'I had no idea you would mind.'

'I do mind – very much indeed. You have no business to touch my things.'

Alan suddenly became angry too.

'I apologize. But since I have touched your things, perhaps you will explain one or two entries that puzzle me. As far as I can see, nearly five hundred pounds has been paid into your account this year which I cannot check. Where does it come from?'

Isobel had recovered her temper. She sank into a chair.

'You needn't be so solemn about it, Alan,' she said lightly. 'It isn't the wages of sin, or anything like that.'

'Where did this money come from?'

'From a woman. A friend of yours. It's not mine at all. It's for Winnie.'

'Winnie? Do you mean – this money came from Jane?'

Isobel nodded.

'She's devoted to the child – can't do enough for her.'

'Yes, but – surely the money ought to have been invested for Winnie.'

'Oh! it isn't that sort of thing at all. It's for current expenses, clothes and all that.'

Alan said nothing. He was thinking of Winnie's frocks – all darns and patches.

'Your account's overdrawn, too, Isobel?'

'Is it? That's always happening to me.'

'Yes, but that five hundred –'

'My dear Alan, I've spent it on Winnie in the way that seemed best to me. I can assure you Jane is quite satisfied.'

Alan was *not* satisfied. Yet such was the power of Isobel's calm that he said nothing more. After all, Isobel was careless in money matters. She hadn't meant to use for herself money given to her for the child. A receipted bill came that day addressed by a mistake to Mr Everard. It was from a dressmaker in Hanover Square and was for two hundred odd pounds. He gave it to Isobel without a word. She glanced over it, smiled, and said:

'Poor boy, I suppose it seems an awful lot to you, but one really *must* be more or less clothed.'

The next day he went to see Jane.

Jane was irritating and elusive as usual. He wasn't to bother. Winnie was her godchild. Women understood these things, men didn't. Of course she didn't want Winnie to have five hundred pounds' worth of frocks. Would he please leave it to her and Isobel? They understood each other perfectly.

Alan went away in a state of growing dissatisfaction. He knew perfectly well that he had shirked the one question he really wished to ask. He wanted to say: 'Has Isobel ever asked you for money for Winnie?' He didn't say it because he was afraid that Jane might not lie well enough to deceive him.

But he was worried. Jane was poor. He knew she was poor. She mustn't – mustn't denude herself. He made up his mind to speak to Isobel. Isobel was calm and reassuring. Of course she wouldn't let Jane spend more than she could afford.

A month later Jane died.

It was influenza, followed by pneumonia. She made Alan Everard her executor and left all she had to Winnie. But it wasn't very much.

It was Alan's task to go through Jane's papers. She left a record there that was clear to follow – numerous evidences of acts of kindness, begging letters, grateful letters.

And lastly, he found her diary. With it was a scrap of paper:

'To be read after my death by Alan Everard. He has often reproached me with not speaking the truth. The truth is all here.'

So he came to know at last, finding the one place where Jane had dared to be honest. It was a record, very simple and unforced, of her love for him.

There was very little sentiment about it – no fine language. But there was no blinking of facts.

'I know you are often irritated by me,' she had written. 'Everything I do or say seems to make you angry sometimes. I do not know why this should be, for I try so hard to please you; but I do believe, all the same, that I mean something real to you. One isn't angry with the people who don't count.'

It was not Jane's fault that Alan found other matters. Jane was loyal – but she was also untidy; she filled her drawers too full. She had, shortly before her death, burnt carefully all Isobel's letters. The one Alan found was wedged behind a drawer. When he had read it, the meaning of certain cabalistic signs on the counterfoils of Jane's cheque book became clear to him. In this particular letter Isobel had hardly troubled to keep up the pretence of the money being required for Winnie.

Alan sat in front of the desk staring with unseeing eyes out of the window for a long time. Finally he slipped the cheque book into his pocket and left the flat. He walked back to Chelsea, conscious of an anger that grew rapidly stronger.

Isobel was out when he got back, and he was sorry. He had so clearly in his mind what he wanted to say. Instead, he went up to the studio and pulled out the unfinished portrait of Jane. He set it on an easel near the portrait of Isobel in pink satin.

The Lemprière woman had been right; there was life in Jane's portrait. He looked at her, the eager eyes, the beauty that he had tried so unsuccessfully to deny her. That was Jane – the aliveness, more than anything else, was Jane. She was, he thought, the most alive person he had ever met, so much so, that even now he could not think of her as dead.

And he thought of his other pictures – *Colour*, *Romance*, Sir Rufus Herschman. They had all, in a way, been pictures of Jane. She had kindled the spark for each one of them – had sent him away fuming and fretting – to *show* her! And now? Jane was dead. Would he ever paint a picture – a real picture – again? He looked again at the eager face on the canvas. Perhaps, Jane wasn't very far away.

A sound made him wheel round. Isobel had come into the studio. She was dressed for dinner in a straight white gown that showed up the pure gold of her hair.

She stopped dead and checked the words on her lips. Eyeing him warily, she went over to the divan and sat down. She had every appearance of calm.

Alan took the cheque book from his pocket.

'I've been going through Jane's papers.'

'Yes?'

He tried to imitate her calm, to keep his voice from shaking.

'For the last four years she's been supplying you with money.'

'Yes. For Winnie.'

'No, not for Winnie,' shouted Everard. 'You pretended, both of you, that it was for Winnie, but you both knew that that wasn't so. Do you realize that Jane has been selling her securities, living from hand to mouth, to supply you with clothes – clothes that you didn't really need?'

Isobel never took her eyes from his face. She settled her body more comfortably on the cushions as a white Persian cat might do.

'I can't help it if Jane denuded herself more than she should have done,' she said. 'I supposed she could afford the money. She was always crazy about you – I could see that, of course. Some wives would have kicked up a fuss about the way you were always rushing off to see her, and spending hours there. I didn't.'

'No,' said Alan, very white in the face. 'You made her pay instead.'

'You are saying very offensive things, Alan. Be careful.'

'Aren't they true? Why did you find it so easy to get money out of Jane?'

'Not for love of me, certainly. It must have been for love of you.'

'That's just what it was,' said Alan simply. 'She paid for my freedom – freedom to work in my own way. So long as you had a sufficiency of money, you'd leave me alone – not badger me to paint a crowd of awful women.'

Isobel said nothing.

'Well?' cried Alan angrily.

Her quiescence infuriated him.

Isobel was looking at the floor. Presently she raised her head and said quietly:

'Come here, Alan.'

She touched the divan at her side. Uneasily, unwillingly, he came and sat there, not looking at her. But he knew that he was afraid.

'Alan,' said Isobel presently.

'Well?'

He was irritable, nervous.

'All that you say may be true. It doesn't matter. I'm like that. I want things – clothes, money, *you. Jane's dead*, Alan.'

'What do you mean?'

'Jane's dead. You belong to me altogether now. You never did before – not quite.'

He looked at her – saw the light in her eyes, acquisitive, possessive – was revolted, yet fascinated.

'Now you shall be all mine.'

He understood Isobel then as he had never understood her before.

'You want me as a slave? I'm to paint what you tell me to paint, live as you tell me to live, be dragged at your chariot wheels.'

'Put it like that if you please. What are words?'

He felt her arms round his neck, white, smooth, firm as a wall. Words danced through his brain. 'A wall as white as milk.' Already he was inside the wall. Could he still escape? Did he want to escape?

He heard her voice close against his ear – poppy and mandragora.

'What else is there to live for? Isn't this enough? Love – happiness – success – love –'

The wall was growing up all round him now – 'the curtain soft as silk', the curtain wrapping him round, stifling him a little, but so soft, so sweet! Now they were drifting together, at peace, out on the crystal sea. The wall was very high now, shutting out all those other things – those dangerous, disturbing things that hurt – that always hurt. Out on the sea of crystal, the golden apple between their hands.

The light faded from Jane's picture.

The Listerdale Mystery

'The Listerdale Mystery' was first published as 'The Benevolent Butler'
in *Grand Magazine*, December 1925.

Mrs St Vincent was adding up figures. Once or twice she sighed, and
her hand stole to her aching forehead. She had always disliked arithmetic.
It was unfortunate that nowadays her life should seem to be composed
entirely of one particular kind of sum, the ceaseless adding together of
small necessary items of expenditure making a total that never failed to
surprise and alarm her.

Surely it couldn't come to *that!* She went back over the figures. She
had made a trifling error in the pence, but otherwise the figures were
correct.

Mrs St Vincent sighed again. Her headache by now was very bad
indeed. She looked up as the door opened and her daughter Barbara
came into the room. Barbara St Vincent was a very pretty girl, she had
her mother's delicate features, and the same proud turn of the head, but
her eyes were dark instead of blue, and she had a different mouth, a sulky
red mouth not without attraction.

'Oh! Mother,' she cried. 'Still juggling with those horrid old accounts?
Throw them all into the fire.'

'We must know where we are,' said Mrs St Vincent uncertainly.

The girl shrugged her shoulders.

'We're always in the same boat,' she said drily. 'Damned hard up.
Down to the last penny as usual.'

Mrs St Vincent sighed.

'I wish –' she began, and then stopped.

'I must find something to do,' said Barbara in hard tones. 'And find
it quickly. After all, I have taken that shorthand and typing course. So
have about one million other girls from all I can see! "What experience?"

"None, but –" "Oh! thank you, good-morning. We'll let you know." But they never do! I must find some other kind of a job – *any* job.'

'Not yet, dear,' pleaded her mother. 'Wait a little longer.'

Barbara went to the window and stood looking out with unseeing eyes that took no note of the dingy line of houses opposite.

'Sometimes,' she said slowly, 'I'm sorry Cousin Amy took me with her to Egypt last winter. Oh! I know I had fun – about the only fun I've ever had or am likely to have in my life. I *did* enjoy myself – enjoyed myself thoroughly. But it was very unsettling. I mean – coming back to *this*.'

She swept a hand round the room. Mrs St Vincent followed it with her eyes and winced. The room was typical of cheap furnished lodgings. A dusty aspidistra, showily ornamental furniture, a gaudy wallpaper faded in patches. There were signs that the personality of the tenants had struggled with that of the landlady; one or two pieces of good china, much cracked and mended, so that their saleable value was *nil*, a piece of embroidery thrown over the back of the sofa, a water colour sketch of a young girl in the fashion of twenty years ago; near enough still to Mrs St Vincent not to be mistaken.

'It wouldn't matter,' continued Barbara, 'if we'd never known anything else. But to think of Ansteys –'

She broke off, not trusting herself to speak of that dearly loved home which had belonged to the St Vincent family for centuries and which was now in the hands of strangers.

'If only father – hadn't speculated – and borrowed –'

'My dear,' said Mrs St Vincent, 'your father was never, in any sense of the word, a business man.'

She said it with a graceful kind of finality, and Barbara came over and gave her an aimless sort of kiss, as she murmured, 'Poor old Mums. I won't say anything.'

Mrs St Vincent took up her pen again, and bent over her desk. Barbara went back to the window. Presently the girl said:

'Mother. I heard from – from Jim Masterton this morning. He wants to come over and see me.'

Mrs St Vincent laid down her pen and looked up sharply.

'Here?' she exclaimed.

'Well, we can't ask him to dinner at the Ritz very well,' sneered Barbara.

Her mother looked unhappy. Again she looked round the room with innate distaste.

'You're right,' said Barbara. 'It's a disgusting place. Genteel poverty! Sounds all right – a white-washed cottage, in the country, shabby chintzes of good design, bowls of roses, crown Derby tea service that you wash up yourself. That's what it's like in books. In real life, with a son starting on the bottom rung of office life, it means London. Frowsy landladies, dirty children on the stairs, fellow-lodgers who always seem to be half-castes, haddocks for breakfasts that aren't quite – quite and so on.'

'If only –' began Mrs St Vincent. 'But, really, I'm beginning to be afraid we can't afford even this room much longer.'

'That means a bed-sitting room – horror! – for you and me,' said Barbara. 'And a cupboard under the tiles for Rupert. And when Jim comes to call, I'll receive him in that dreadful room downstairs with tabbies all round the walls knitting, and staring at us, and coughing that dreadful kind of gulping cough they have!'

There was a pause.

'Barbara,' said Mrs St Vincent at last. 'Do you – I mean – would you –?'

She stopped, flushing a little.

'You needn't be delicate, Mother,' said Barbara. 'Nobody is nowadays. Marry Jim, I suppose you mean? I would like a shot if he asked me. But I'm so awfully afraid he won't.'

'Oh, Barbara, dear.'

'Well, it's one thing seeing me out there with Cousin Amy, moving (as they say in novelettes) in the best society. He *did* take a fancy to me. Now he'll come here and see me in *this*! And he's a funny creature, you know, fastidious and old-fashioned. I – I rather like him for that. It reminds me of Ansteys and the village – everything a hundred years behind the times, but so – so – oh! I don't know – so fragrant. Like lavender!'

She laughed, half-ashamed of her eagerness. Mrs St Vincent spoke with a kind of earnest simplicity.

'I should like you to marry Jim Masterton,' she said. 'He is – one of us. He is very well off, also, but that I don't mind about so much.'

'I do,' said Barbara. 'I'm sick of being hard up.'

'But, Barbara, it isn't –'

'Only for that? No. I do really. I – oh! Mother, can't you *see* I do?'

Mrs St Vincent looked very unhappy.

'I wish he could see you in your proper setting, darling,' she said wistfully.

'Oh, well!' said Barbara. 'Why worry? We might as well try and be cheerful about things. Sorry I've had such a grouch. Cheer up, darling.'

She bent over her mother, kissed her forehead lightly, and went out. Mrs St Vincent, relinquishing all attempts at finance, sat down on the uncomfortable sofa. Her thoughts ran round in circles like squirrels in a cage.

'One may say what one likes, appearances *do* put a man off. Not later – not if they were really engaged. He'd know then what a sweet, dear girl she is. But it's so easy for young people to take the tone of their surroundings. Rupert, now, he's quite different from what he used to be. Not that I want my children to be stuck up. That's not it a bit. But I should hate it if Rupert got engaged to that dreadful girl in the tobacconist's. I daresay she may be a very nice girl, really. But she's not our kind. It's all so difficult. Poor little Babs. If I could do anything – anything. But where's the money to come from? We've sold everything to give Rupert his start. We really can't even afford this.'

To distract herself Mrs St Vincent picked up the *Morning Post*, and glanced down the advertisements on the front page. Most of them she knew by heart. People who wanted capital, people who had capital and were anxious to dispose of it on note of hand alone, people who wanted to buy teeth (she always wondered why), people who wanted to sell furs and gowns and who had optimistic ideas on the subject of price.

Suddenly she stiffened to attention. Again and again she read the printed words.

'To gentle people only. Small house in Westminster, exquisitely furnished, offered to those who would really care for it. Rent purely nominal. No agents.'

A very ordinary advertisement. She had read many the same or – well, nearly the same. Nominal rent, that was where the trap lay.

Yet, since she was restless and anxious to escape from her thoughts she put on her hat straight away, and took a convenient bus to the address given in the advertisement.

It proved to be that of a firm of house-agents. Not a new bustling firm – a rather decrepit, old-fashioned place. Rather timidly she produced the advertisement, which she had torn out, and asked for particulars.

The white-haired old gentleman who was attending to her stroked his chin thoughtfully.

'Perfectly. Yes, perfectly, madam. That house, the house mentioned in the advertisement is No 7 Cheviot Place. You would like an order?'

'I should like to know the rent first?' said Mrs St Vincent.

'Ah! the rent. The exact figure is not settled, but I can assure you that it is purely nominal.'

'Ideas of what is purely nominal can vary,' said Mrs St Vincent.

The old gentleman permitted himself to chuckle a little.

'Yes, that's an old trick – an old trick. But you can take my word for it, it isn't so in this case. Two or three guineas a week, perhaps, not more.'

Mrs St Vincent decided to have the order. Not, of course, that there was any real likelihood of her being able to afford the place. But, after all, she might just *see* it. There must be some grave disadvantage attaching to it, to be offered at such a price.

But her heart gave a little throb as she looked up at the outside of 7 Cheviot Place. A gem of a house. Queen Anne, and in perfect condition! A butler answered the door, he had grey hair and little side-whiskers, and the meditative calm of an archbishop. A kindly archbishop, Mrs St Vincent thought.

He accepted the order with a benevolent air.

'Certainly, madam. I will show you over. The house is ready for occupation.'

He went before her, opening doors, announcing rooms.

'The drawing-room, the white study, a powder closet through here, madam.'

It was perfect – a dream. The furniture all of the period, each piece with signs of wear, but polished with loving care. The loose rugs were of beautiful dim old colours. In each room were bowls of fresh flowers. The back of the house looked over the Green Park. The whole place radiated an old-world charm.

The tears came into Mrs St Vincent's eyes, and she fought them back with difficulty. So had Ansteys looked – Ansteys . . .

She wondered whether the butler had noticed her emotion. If so, he was too much the perfectly trained servant to show it. She liked these old servants, one felt safe with them, at ease. They were like friends.

'It is a beautiful house,' she said softly. 'Very beautiful. I am glad to have seen it.'

'Is it for yourself alone, madam?'

'For myself and my son and daughter. But I'm afraid –'

She broke off. She wanted it so dreadfully – so dreadfully.

She felt instinctively that the butler understood. He did not look at her, as he said in a detached impersonal way:

'I happen to be aware, madam, that the owner requires above all, suitable tenants. The rent is of no importance to him. He wants the house to be tenanted by someone who will really care for and appreciate it.'

'I should appreciate it,' said Mrs St Vincent in a low voice.

She turned to go.

'Thank you for showing me over,' she said courteously.

'Not at all, madam.'

He stood in the doorway, very correct and upright as she walked away down the street. She thought to herself: 'He knows. He's sorry for me. He's one of the old lot too. He'd like *me* to have it – not a labour member, or a button manufacturer! We're dying out, our sort, but we band together.'

In the end she decided not to go back to the agents. What was the good? She could afford the rent – but there were servants to be considered. There would have to be servants in a house like that.

The next morning a letter lay by her plate. It was from the house-agents. It offered her the tenancy of 7 Cheviot Place for six months at two guineas a week, and went on: 'You have, I presume, taken into consideration the fact that the servants are remaining at the landlord's expense? It is really a unique offer.'

It was. So startled was she by it, that she read the letter out. A fire of questions followed and she described her visit of yesterday.

'Secretive little Mums!' cried Barbara. 'Is it really so lovely?'

Rupert cleared his throat, and began a judicial cross-questioning.

'There's something behind all this. It's fishy if you ask me. Decidedly fishy.'

'So's my egg,' said Barbara wrinkling her nose. 'Ugh! Why should there be something behind it? That's just like you, Rupert, always making mysteries out of nothing. It's those dreadful detective stories you're always reading.'

'The rent's a joke,' said Rupert. 'In the city,' he added importantly, 'one gets wise to all sorts of queer things. I tell you, there's something very fishy about this business.'

'Nonsense,' said Barbara. 'House belongs to a man with lots of money, he's fond of it, and he wants it lived in by decent people whilst he's away. Something of that kind. Money's probably no object to him.'

'What did you say the address was?' asked Rupert of his mother.

'Seven Cheviot Place.'

'Whew!' He pushed back his chair. 'I say, this is exciting. That's the house Lord Listerdale disappeared from.'

'Are you sure?' asked Mrs St Vincent doubtfully.

'Positive. He's got a lot of other houses all over London, but this is the one he lived in. He walked out of it one evening saying he was going to his club, and nobody ever saw him again. Supposed to have done a bunk to East Africa or somewhere like that, but nobody knows why. Depend upon it, he was murdered in that house. You say there's a lot of panelling?'

'Ye-es,' said Mrs St Vincent faintly: 'but –'

Rupert gave her no time. He went on with immense enthusiasm.

'Panelling! There you are. Sure to be a secret recess somewhere. Body's been stuffed in there and has been there ever since. Perhaps it was embalmed first.'

'Rupert, dear, don't talk nonsense,' said his mother.

'Don't be a double-dyed idiot,' said Barbara. 'You've been taking that peroxide blonde to the pictures too much.'

Rupert rose with dignity – such dignity as his lanky and awkward age allowed, and delivered a final ultimatum.

'You take that house, Mums. *I'll* ferret out the mystery. You see if I don't.'

Rupert departed hurriedly, in fear of being late at the office.

The eyes of the two women met.

'Could we, Mother?' murmured Barbara tremulously. 'Oh! if we could.'

'The servants,' said Mrs St Vincent pathetically, 'would *eat*, you know. I mean, of course, one would want them to – but that's the drawback. One can so easily – just do without things – when it's only oneself.'

She looked piteously at Barbara, and the girl nodded.

'We must think it over,' said the mother.

But in reality her mind was made up. She had seen the sparkle in the girl's eyes. She thought to herself: 'Jim Masterton *must* see her in proper surroundings. This is a chance – a wonderful chance. I must take it.'

She sat down and wrote to the agents accepting their offer.

'Quentin, where did the lilies come from? I really can't buy expensive flowers.'

'They were sent up from King's Cheviot, madam. It has always been the custom here.'

The butler withdrew. Mrs St Vincent heaved a sigh of relief. What would she do without Quentin? He made everything so *easy*. She thought to herself, 'It's too good to last. I shall wake up soon, I know I shall, and find it's been all a dream. I'm so *happy* here – two months already, and it's passed like a flash.'

Life indeed had been astonishingly pleasant. Quentin, the butler, had displayed himself the autocrat of 7 Cheviot Place. 'If you will leave everything to me, madam,' he had said respectfully. 'You will find it the best way.'

Each week, he brought her the housekeeping books, their totals astonishingly low. There were only two other servants, a cook and a housemaid. They were pleasant in manner, and efficient in their duties, but it was Quentin who ran the house. Game and poultry appeared on the table sometimes, causing Mrs St Vincent solicitude. Quentin reassured her. Sent up from Lord Listerdale's country seat, King's Cheviot, or from his Yorkshire moor. 'It has always been the custom, madam.'

Privately Mrs St Vincent doubted whether the absent Lord Listerdale would agree with those words. She was inclined to suspect Quentin of usurping his master's authority. It was clear that he had taken a fancy to them, and that in his eyes nothing was too good for them.

Her curiosity aroused by Rupert's declaration, Mrs St Vincent had make a tentative reference to Lord Listerdale when she next interviewed the house-agent. The white-haired old gentleman had responded immediately.

Yes, Lord Listerdale was in East Africa, had been there for the last eighteen months.

'Our client is rather an eccentric man,' he had said, smiling broadly. 'He left London in a most unconventional manner, as you may perhaps remember? Not a word to anyone. The newspapers got hold of it. There were actually inquiries on foot at Scotland Yard. Luckily news was received from Lord Listerdale himself from East Africa. He invested his cousin, Colonel Carfax, with power of attorney. It is the latter who conducts all Lord Listerdale's affairs. Yes, rather eccentric, I fear. He has always been a great traveller in the wilds – it is quite on the cards that he may not return for years to England, though he is getting on in years.'

'Surely he is not so very old,' said Mrs St Vincent, with a sudden memory of a bluff, bearded face, rather like an Elizabethan sailor, which she had once noticed in an illustrated magazine.

'Middle-aged,' said the white-haired gentleman. 'Fifty-three, according to Debrett.'

This conversation Mrs St Vincent had retailed to Rupert with the intention of rebuking that young gentleman.

Rupert, however, was undismayed.

'It looks fishier than ever to me,' he had declared. 'Who's this Colonel Carfax? Probably comes into the title if anything happens to Listerdale. The letter from East Africa was probably forged. In three years, or whatever it is, this Carfax will presume death, and take the title. Meantime, he's got all the handling of the estate. Very fishy, I call it.'

He had condescended graciously to approve the house. In his leisure moments he was inclined to tap the panelling and make elaborate measurements for the possible location of a secret room, but little by little his interest in the mystery of Lord Listerdale abated. He was also less enthusiastic on the subject of the tobacconist's daughter. Atmosphere tells.

To Barbara the house had brought great satisfaction. Jim Masterton had come home, and was a frequent visitor. He and Mrs St Vincent got on splendidly together, and he said something to Barbara one day that startled her.

'This house is a wonderful setting for your mother, you know.'

'For *Mother*?'

'Yes. It was made for her! She belongs to it in an extraordinary way. You know there's something queer about this house altogether, something uncanny and haunting.'

'Don't get like Rupert,' Barbara implored him. 'He is convinced that the wicked Colonel Carfax murdered Lord Listerdale and hid his body under the floor.'

Masterton laughed.

'I admire Rupert's detective zeal. No, I didn't mean anything of *that* kind. But there's something in the air, some atmosphere that one doesn't quite understand.'

They had been three months in Cheviot Place when Barbara came to her mother with a radiant face.

'Jim and I – we're engaged. Yes – last night. Oh, Mother! It all seems like a fairy tale come true.'

'Oh, my dear! I'm so glad – so glad.'

Mother and daughter clasped each other close.

'You know Jim's almost as much in love with you as he is with me,' said Barbara at last, with a mischievous laugh.

Mrs St Vincent blushed very prettily.

'He is,' persisted the girl. 'You thought this house would make such a beautiful setting for me, and all the time it's really a setting for *you*. Rupert and I don't quite belong here. You do.'

'Don't talk nonsense, darling.'

'It's not nonsense. There's a flavour of enchanted castle about it, with you as an enchanted princess and Quentin as – as – oh! a benevolent magician.'

Mrs St Vincent laughed and admitted the last item.

Rupert received the news of his sister's engagement very calmly.

'I thought there was something of the kind in the wind,' he observed sapiently.

He and his mother were dining alone together; Barbara was out with Jim.

Quentin placed the port in front of him, and withdrew noiselessly.

'That's a rum old bird,' said Rupert, nodding towards the closed door. 'There's something odd about him, you know, something –'

'Not fishy?' interrupted Mrs St Vincent, with a faint smile.

'Why, Mother, how did you know what I was going to say?' demanded Rupert in all seriousness.

'It's rather a word of yours, darling. You think everything is fishy. I suppose you have an idea that it was Quentin who did away with Lord Listerdale and put him under the floor?'

'Behind the panelling,' corrected Rupert. 'You always get things a little bit wrong, Mother. No, I've inquired about that. Quentin was down at King's Cheviot at the time.'

Mrs St Vincent smiled at him, as she rose from table and went up to the drawing-room. In some ways Rupert was a long time growing up.

Yet a sudden wonder swept over her for the first time as to Lord Listerdale's reasons for leaving England so abruptly. There must be something behind it, to account for that sudden decision. She was still thinking the matter over when Quentin came in with the coffee tray, and she spoke out impulsively.

'You have been with Lord Listerdale a long time, haven't you, Quentin?'

'Yes, madam; since I was a lad of twenty-one. That was in the late Lord's time. I started as third footman.'

'You must know Lord Listerdale very well. What kind of a man is he?'

The butler turned the tray a little, so that she could help herself to sugar more conveniently, as he replied in even unemotional tones:

'Lord Listerdale was a very selfish gentleman, madam: with no consideration for others.'

He removed the tray and bore it from the room. Mrs St Vincent sat with her coffee cup in her hand, and a puzzled frown on her face. Something struck her as odd in the speech apart from the views it expressed. In another minute it flashed home to her.

Quentin had used the word '*was*' not '*is*'. But then, he must think – must believe – She pulled herself up. She was as bad as Rupert! But a very definite uneasiness assailed her. Afterwards she dated her first suspicions from that moment.

With Barbara's happiness and future assured, she had time to think her own thoughts, and against her will, they began to centre round the mystery of Lord Listerdale. What was the real story? Whatever it was Quentin knew something about it. Those had been odd words of his – 'a very selfish gentleman – no consideration for others.' What lay behind them? He had spoken as a judge might speak, detachedly and impartially.

Was Quentin involved in Lord Listerdale's disappearance? Had he taken an active part in any tragedy there might have been? After all, ridiculous as Rupert's assumption had seemed at the time, that single letter with its power of attorney coming from East Africa was – well, open to suspicion.

But try as she would, she could not believe any real evil of Quentin. Quentin, she told herself over and over again, was *good* – she used the word as simply as a child might have done. Quentin was *good*. But he knew something!

She never spoke with him again of his master. The subject was apparently forgotten. Rupert and Barbara had other things to think of, and there were no further discussions.

It was towards the end of August that her vague surmises crystallized into realities. Rupert had gone for a fortnight's holiday with a friend who had a motor-cycle and trailer. It was some ten days after his departure that Mrs St Vincent was startled to see him rush into the room where she sat writing.

'Rupert!' she exclaimed.

'I know, Mother. You didn't expect to see me for another three days. But something's happened. Anderson – my pal, you know – didn't much care where he went, so I suggested having a look in at King's Cheviot –'

'King's Cheviot? But why –?'

'You know perfectly well, Mother, that I've always scented something fishy about things here. Well, I had a look at the old place – it's let, you know – nothing there. Not that I actually expected to find anything – I was just nosing round, so to speak.'

Yes, she thought. Rupert was very like a dog at this moment. Hunting in circles for something vague and undefined, led by instinct, busy and happy.

'It was when we were passing through a village about eight or nine miles away that it happened – that I saw him, I mean.'

'Saw whom?'

'Quentin – just going into a little cottage. Something fishy here, I said to myself, and we stopped the bus, and I went back. I rapped on the door and he himself opened it.'

'But I don't understand. Quentin hasn't been away –'

'I'm coming to that, Mother. If you'd only listen, and not interrupt. It was Quentin, and it wasn't Quentin, if you know what I mean.'

Mrs St Vincent clearly did not know, so he elucidated matters further.

'It was Quentin all right, but it wasn't *our* Quentin. It was the real man.'

'Rupert!'

'You listen. I was taken in myself at first, and said: "It is Quentin, isn't it?" And the old johnny said: "Quite right, sir, that is my name. What can I do for you?" And then I saw that it wasn't our man, though it was precious like him, voice and all. I asked a few questions, and it all came out. The old chap hadn't an idea of anything fishy being on. He'd been butler to Lord Listerdale all right, and was retired on a pension and given this cottage just about the time that Lord Listerdale was supposed to have gone off to Africa. You see where that leads us. This man's an impostor – he's playing the part of Quentin for purposes of his own. My theory is that he came up to town that evening, pretending to be the butler from King's Cheviot, got an interview with Lord Listerdale, killed him and hid his body behind the panelling. It's an old house, there's sure to be a secret recess –'

'Oh, don't let's go into all that again,' interrupted Mrs St Vincent wildly. 'I can't bear it. Why should he – that's what I want to know – why? *If* he did such a thing – which I don't believe for one minute, mind you – what was the *reason* for it all?'

'You're right,' said Rupert. 'Motive – that's important. Now I've made inquiries. Lord Listerdale had a lot of house property. In the last two days I've discovered that practically every one of these houses of his has been let in the last eighteen months to people like ourselves for a merely nominal rent – *and with the proviso that the servants should remain*. And in every case Quentin himself – the man calling himself Quentin, I mean – has been there for part of the time as butler. That looks as though there were something – jewels, or papers – secreted in one of Lord Listerdale's houses, and the gang doesn't know which. I'm assuming a gang, but of course this fellow Quentin may be in it single-handed. There's a –'

Mrs St Vincent interrupted him with a certain amount of determination:

'Rupert! Do stop talking for one minute. You're making my head spin. Anyway, what you are saying is nonsense – about gangs and hidden papers.'

'There's another theory,' admitted Rupert. 'This Quentin may be someone that Lord Listerdale has injured. The real butler told me a long story about a man called Samuel Lowe – an under-gardener he was, and about the same height and build as Quentin himself. He'd got a grudge against Listerdale –'

Mrs St Vincent started.

'With no consideration for others.' The words came back to her mind in their passionless, measured accents. Inadequate words, but what might they not stand for?

In her absorption she hardly listened to Rupert. He made a rapid explanation of something that she did not take in, and went hurriedly from the room.

Then she woke up. Where had Rupert gone? What was he going to do? She had not caught his last words. Perhaps he was going for the police. In that case . . .

She rose abruptly and rang the bell. With his usual promptness, Quentin answered it.

'You rang, madam?'

'Yes. Come in, please, and shut the door.'

The butler obeyed, and Mrs St Vincent was silent a moment whilst she studied him with earnest eyes.

She thought: 'He's been kind to me – nobody knows how kind. The children wouldn't understand. This wild story of Rupert's may be all nonsense – on the other hand, there may – yes, there may – be something in it. Why should one judge? One can't *know*. The rights and wrongs of it, I mean . . . And I'd stake my life – yes, I would! – on his being a good man.'

Flushed and tremulous, she spoke.

'Quentin, Mr Rupert has just got back. He has been down to King's Cheviot – to a village near there –'

She stopped, noticing the quick start he was not able to conceal.

'He has – seen someone,' she went on in measured accents.

She thought to herself: 'There – he's warned. At any rate, he's warned.'

After that first quick start, Quentin had resumed his unruffled demeanour, but his eyes were fixed on her face, watchful and keen, with something in them she had not seen there before. They were, for the first time, the eyes of a man and not of a servant.

He hesitated for a minute, then said in a voice which also had subtly changed:

'Why do you tell me this, Mrs St Vincent?'

Before she could answer, the door flew open and Rupert strode into the room. With him was a dignified middle-aged man with little side-whiskers and the air of a benevolent archbishop. *Quentin!*

'Here he is,' said Rupert. 'The real Quentin. I had him outside in the taxi. Now, Quentin, look at this man and tell me – is he Samuel Lowe?'

It was for Rupert a triumphant moment. But it was short-lived, almost at once he scented something wrong. For while the real Quentin was looking abashed and highly uncomfortable the second Quentin was smiling, a broad smile of undisguised enjoyment.

He slapped his embarrassed duplicate on the back.

'It's all right, Quentin. Got to let the cat out of the bag some time, I suppose. You can tell 'em who I am.'

The dignified stranger drew himself up.

'This, sir,' he announced, in a reproachful tone, 'is my master, Lord Listerdale, sir.'

The next minute beheld many things. First, the complete collapse of the cocksure Rupert. Before he knew what was happening, his mouth still open from the shock of the discovery, he found himself being gently manoeuvred towards the door, a friendly voice that was, and yet was not, familiar in his ear.

'It's quite all right, my boy. No bones broken. But I want a word with your mother. Very good work of yours, to ferret me out like this.'

He was outside on the landing gazing at the shut door. The real Quentin was standing by his side, a gentle stream of explanation flowing from his lips. Inside the room Lord Listerdale was confronting Mrs St Vincent.

'Let me explain – if I can! I've been a selfish devil all my life – the fact came home to me one day. I thought I'd try a little altruism for a change, and being a fantastic kind of fool, I started my career fantastically. I'd sent subscriptions to odd things, but I felt the need of doing something – well, something *personal*. I've been sorry always for the class that can't beg, that must suffer in silence – poor gentlefolk. I have a lot of house property. I conceived the idea of leasing these houses to people who – well, needed and appreciated them. Young couples with their way to make, widows with sons and daughters starting in the world. Quentin has been more than butler to me, he's a friend. With his consent and assistance I borrowed his personality. I've always had a talent for acting. The idea came to me on my way to the club one night, and I went straight off to talk it over with Quentin. When I found they were making a fuss about my disappearance, I arranged that a letter should come from me in East Africa. In it, I gave full instructions to my cousin, Maurice Carfax. And – well, that's the long and short of it.'

He broke off rather lamely, with an appealing glance at Mrs St Vincent. She stood very straight, and her eyes met his steadily.

'It was a kind plan,' she said. 'A very unusual one, and one that does you credit. I am – most grateful. But – of course, you understand that we cannot stay?'

'I expected that,' he said. 'Your pride won't let you accept what you'd probably style "charity".'

'Isn't that what it is?' she asked steadily.

'No,' he answered. 'Because I ask something in exchange.'

'Something?'

'Everything.' His voice rang out, the voice of one accustomed to dominate.

'When I was twenty-three,' he went on, 'I married the girl I loved. She died a year later. Since then I have been very lonely. I have wished very much I could find a certain lady – the lady of my dreams . . .'

'Am I that?' she asked, very low. 'I am so old – so faded.'

He laughed.

'Old? You are younger than either of your children. Now I am old, if you like.'

But her laugh rang out in turn. A soft ripple of amusement.

'You? You are a boy still. A boy who loves to dress up.'

She held out her hands and he caught them in his.

The Fourth Man

'The Fourth Man' was first published in
Pearson's Magazine, December 1925.

Canon Parfitt panted a little. Running for trains was not much of a business for a man of his age. For one thing his figure was not what it was and with the loss of his slender silhouette went an increasing tendency to be short of breath. This tendency the Canon himself always referred to, with dignity, as '*My heart*, you know!'

He sank into the corner of the first-class carriage with a sigh of relief. The warmth of the heated carriage was most agreeable to him. Outside the snow was falling. Lucky to get a corner seat on a long night journey. Miserable business if you didn't. There ought to be a sleeper on this train.

The other three corners were already occupied, and noting this fact Canon Parfitt became aware that the man in the far corner was smiling at him in gentle recognition. He was a clean-shaven man with a quizzical face and hair just turning grey on the temples. His profession was so clearly the law that no one could have mistaken him for anything else for a moment. Sir George Durand was, indeed, a very famous lawyer.

'Well, Parfitt,' he remarked genially, 'you had a run for it, didn't you?'

'Very bad for my heart, I'm afraid,' said the Canon. 'Quite a coincidence meeting you, Sir George. Are you going far north?'

'Newcastle,' said Sir George laconically. 'By the way,' he added, 'do you know Dr Campbell Clark?'

The man sitting on the same side of the carriage as the Canon inclined his head pleasantly.

'We met on the platform,' continued the lawyer. 'Another coincidence.'

Canon Parfitt looked at Dr Campbell Clark with a good deal of interest. It was a name of which he had often heard. Dr Clark was in the forefront as a physician and mental specialist, and his last book, *The Problem of the Unconscious Mind*, had been the most discussed book of the year.

Canon Parfitt saw a square jaw, very steady blue eyes and reddish hair untouched by grey, but thinning rapidly. And he received also the impression of a very forceful personality.

By a perfectly natural association of ideas the Canon looked across to the seat opposite him, half-expecting to receive a glance of recognition there also, but the fourth occupant of the carriage proved to be a total stranger – a foreigner, the Canon fancied. He was a slight dark man, rather insignificant in appearance. Huddled in a big overcoat, he appeared to be fast asleep.

'Canon Parfitt of Bradchester?' inquired Dr Campbell Clark in a pleasant voice.

The Canon looked flattered. Those 'scientific sermons' of his had really made a great hit – especially since the Press had taken them up. Well, that was what the Church needed – good modern up-to-date stuff.

'I have read your book with great interest, Dr Campbell Clark,' he said. 'Though it's a bit technical here and there for me to follow.'

Durand broke in.

'Are you for talking or sleeping, Canon?' he asked. 'I'll confess at once that I suffer from insomnia and that therefore I'm in favour of the former.'

'Oh! certainly. By all means,' said the Canon. 'I seldom sleep on these night journeys, and the book I have with me is a very dull one.'

'We are at any rate a representative gathering,' remarked the doctor with a smile. 'The Church, the Law, the Medical Profession.'

'Not much we couldn't give an opinion on between us, eh?' laughed Durand. 'The Church for the spiritual view, myself for the purely worldly and legal view, and you, doctor, with widest field of all, ranging from the purely pathological to the super-psychological! Between us three we should cover any ground pretty completely, I fancy.'

'Not so completely as you imagine, I think,' said Dr Clark. 'There's another point of view, you know, that you left out, and that's rather an important one.'

'Meaning?' queried the lawyer.

'The point of view of the Man in the Street.'

'Is that so important? Isn't the Man in the Street usually wrong?'

'Oh! almost always. But he has the thing that all expert opinion must lack – the personal point of view. In the end, you know, you can't get away from personal relationships. I've found that in my profession. For every patient who comes to me genuinely ill, at least five come who have nothing whatever the matter with them except an inability to live happily with the inmates of the same house. They call it everything – from housemaid's knee to writer's cramp, but it's all the same thing, the raw surface produced by mind rubbing against mind.'

'You have a lot of patients with "nerves", I suppose,' the Canon remarked disparagingly. His own nerves were excellent.

'Ah! and what do you mean by that?' The other swung round on him, quick as a flash. 'Nerves! People use that word and laugh after it, just as you did. "Nothing the matter with so and so," they say. "Just nerves." But, good God, man, you've got the crux of everything there! You can get at a mere bodily ailment and heal it. But at this day we know very little more about the obscure causes of the hundred and one forms of nervous disease than we did in – well, the reign of Queen Elizabeth!'

'Dear me,' said Canon Parfitt, a little bewildered by this onslaught. 'Is that so?'

'Mind you, it's a sign of grace,' Dr Campbell Clark went on. 'In the old days we considered man a simple animal, body and soul – with stress laid on the former.'

'Body, soul and spirit,' corrected the clergyman mildly.

'Spirit?' The doctor smiled oddly. 'What do you parsons mean exactly by spirit? You've never been very clear about it, you know. All down the ages you've funked an exact definition.'

The Canon cleared his throat in preparation for speech, but to his chagrin he was given no opportunity. The doctor went on.

'Are we even sure the word is spirit – might it not be *spirits?*'

'Spirits?' Sir George Durand questioned, his eyebrows raised quizzically.

'Yes.' Campbell Clark's gaze transferred itself to him. He leaned forward and tapped the other man lightly on the breast. 'Are you so sure,' he said gravely, 'that there is only one occupant of this structure – for that is all it is, you know – this desirable residence to be let furnished – for seven, twenty-one, forty-one, seventy-one – whatever it may be! – years? And in the end the tenant moves his things out – little by little – and then goes out of the house altogether – and down comes the house, a mass of ruin and decay. You're the master of the house – we'll admit that, but aren't you ever conscious of the presence of others – soft-footed servants, hardly noticed, except for the work they do – work that you're not conscious of having done? Or friends – moods that take hold of you and make you, for the time being, a "different man" as the saying goes? You're the king of the castle, right enough, but be very sure the "dirty rascal" is there too.'

'My dear Clark,' drawled the lawyer. 'You make me positively uncomfortable. Is my mind really a battleground of conflicting personalities? Is that Science's latest?'

It was the doctor's turn to shrug his shoulders.

'Your body is,' he said drily. 'If the body, why not the mind?'

'Very interesting,' said Canon Parfitt. 'Ah! Wonderful science – wonderful science.'

And inwardly he thought to himself: 'I can get a most interesting sermon out of that idea.'

But Dr Campbell Clark had leant back in his seat, his momentary excitement spent.

'As a matter of fact,' he remarked in a dry professional manner, 'it is a case of dual personality that takes me to Newcastle tonight. Very interesting case. Neurotic subject, of course. But quite genuine.'

'Dual personality,' said Sir George Durand thoughtfully. 'It's not so very rare, I believe. There's loss of memory as well, isn't there? I know the matter cropped up in a case in the Probate Court the other day.'

Dr Clark nodded.

'The classic case, of course,' he said, 'was that of Felicie Bault. You may remember hearing of it?'

'Of course,' said Canon Parfitt. 'I remember reading about it in the papers – but quite a long time ago – seven years at least.'

Dr Campbell Clark nodded.

'That girl became one of the most famous figures in France. Scientists from all over the world came to see her. She had no less than four distinct personalities. They were known as Felicie 1, Felicie 2, Felicie 3, etc.'

'Wasn't there some suggestion of deliberate trickery?' asked Sir George alertly.

'The personalities of Felicie 3 and Felicie 4 were a little open to doubt,' admitted the doctor. 'But the main facts remain. Felicie Bault was a Brittany peasant girl. She was the third of a family of five; the daughter of a drunken father and a mentally defective mother. In one of his drinking bouts the father strangled the mother and was, if I remember rightly, transported for life. Felicie was then five years of age. Some charitable people interested themselves in the children and Felicie was brought up and educated by an English maiden lady who had a kind of home for destitute children. She could make very little of Felicie, however. She describes the girl as abnormally slow and stupid, only taught to read and write with the greatest difficulty and clumsy with her hands. This lady, Miss Slater, tried to fit the girl for domestic service, and did indeed find her several places when she was of an age to take them. But she never stayed long anywhere owing to her stupidity and also her intense laziness.'

The doctor paused for a minute, and the Canon, re-crossing his legs, and arranging his travelling rug more closely round him, was suddenly aware that the man opposite him had moved very slightly. His eyes, which had formerly been shut, were now open, and something in them, something mocking and indefinable, startled the worthy Canon. It was as though the man were listening and gloating secretly over what he heard.

'There is a photograph taken of Felicie Bault at the age of seventeen,' continued the doctor. 'It shows her as a loutish peasant girl, heavy of build. There is nothing in that picture to indicate that she was soon to be one of the most famous persons in France.

'Five years later, when she was 22, Felicie Bault had a severe nervous illness, and on recovery the strange phenomena began to manifest themselves. The following are facts attested to by many eminent scientists. The personality called Felicie 1 was undistinguishable from the Felicie Bault of the last twenty-two years. Felicie 1 wrote French badly and haltingly, she spoke no foreign languages and was unable to play the piano. Felicie 2, on the contrary, spoke Italian fluently and German moderately. Her handwriting was quite dissimilar to that of Felicie 1, and she wrote fluent and expressive French. She could discuss politics and art and she was passionately fond of playing the piano. Felicie 3 had many points in common with Felicie 2. She was intelligent and apparently well educated, but in moral character she was a total contrast. She appeared, in fact, an utterly depraved creature – but depraved in a Parisian and not a provincial way. She knew all the Paris *argot*, and the expressions of the chic *demi monde*. Her language was filthy and she would rail against religion and so-called "good people" in the most blasphemous terms. Finally there was Felicie 4 – a dreamy, almost half-witted creature, distinctly pious and professedly clairvoyant, but this fourth personality was very unsatisfactory and elusive and has been sometimes thought to be a deliberate trickery on the part of Felicie 3 – a kind of joke played by her on a credulous public. I may say that (with the possible exception of Felicie 4) each personality was distinct and separate and had no knowledge of the others. Felicie 2 was undoubtedly the most predominant and would last sometimes for a fortnight at a time, then Felicie 1 would appear abruptly for a day or two. After that, perhaps Felicie 3 or 4, but the two latter seldom remained in command for more than a few hours. Each change was accompanied by severe headache and heavy sleep, and in each case there was complete loss of memory of the other states, the personality in question taking up life where she had left it, unconscious of the passage of time.'

'Remarkable,' murmured the Canon. 'Very remarkable. As yet we know next to nothing of the marvels of the universe.'

'We know that there are some very astute impostors in it,' remarked the lawyer drily.

'The case of Felicie Bault was investigated by lawyers as well as by doctors and scientists,' said Dr Campbell Clark quickly. 'Maitre Quim-bellier, you remember, made the most thorough investigation and confirmed the views of the scientists. And after all, why should it surprise us so much? We come across the double-yolked egg, do we not? And the twin banana? Why not the double soul – in the single body?'

'The double soul?' protested the Canon.

Dr Campbell Clark turned his piercing blue eyes on him.

'What else can we call it? That is to say – if the personality is the soul?'

'It is a good thing such a state of affairs is only in the nature of a "freak",' remarked Sir George. 'If the case were common, it would give rise to pretty complications.'

'The condition is, of course, quite abnormal,' agreed the doctor. 'It was a great pity that a longer study could not have been made, but all that was put an end to by Felicie's unexpected death.'

'There was something queer about that, if I remember rightly,' said the lawyer slowly.

Dr Campbell Clark nodded.

'A most unaccountable business. The girl was found one morning dead in bed. She had clearly been strangled. But to everyone's stupefaction it was presently proved beyond doubt that she had actually strangled herself. The marks on her neck were those of her own fingers. A method of suicide which, though not physically impossible, must have necessitated terrific muscular strength and almost superhuman will power. What had driven the girl to such straits has never been found out. Of course her mental balance must always have been precarious. Still, there it is. The curtain has been rung down for ever on the mystery of Felicie Bault.'

It was then that the man in the far corner laughed.

The other three men jumped as though shot. They had totally forgotten the existence of the fourth amongst them. As they stared towards the place where he sat, still huddled in his overcoat, he laughed again.

'You must excuse me, gentlemen,' he said, in perfect English that had, nevertheless, a foreign flavour.

He sat up, displaying a pale face with a small jet-black moustache.

'Yes, you must excuse me,' he said, with a mock bow. 'But really! in science, is the last word ever said?'

'You know something of the case we have been discussing?' asked the doctor courteously.

'Of the case? No. But I knew her.'

'Felicie Bault?'

'Yes. And Annette Ravel also. You have not heard of Annette Ravel, I see? And yet the story of the one is the story of the other. Believe me, you know nothing of Felicie Bault if you do not also know the history of Annette Ravel.'

He drew out his watch and looked at it.

'Just half an hour before the next stop. I have time to tell you the story – that is, if you care to hear it?'

'Please tell it to us,' said the doctor quietly.

'Delighted,' said the Canon. 'Delighted.'

Sir George Durand merely composed himself in an attitude of keen attention.

'My name, gentlemen,' began their strange travelling companion, 'is Raoul Letardeau. You have spoken just now of an English lady, Miss Slater, who interested herself in works of charity. I was born in that Brittany fishing village and when my parents were both killed in a railway accident it was Miss Slater who came to the rescue and saved me from the equivalent of your English workhouse. There were some twenty children under her care, girls and boys. Amongst these children were Felicie Bault and Annette Ravel. If I cannot make you understand the personality of Annette, gentlemen, you will understand nothing. She was the child of what you call a "fille de joie" who had died of consumption abandoned by her lover. The mother had been a dancer, and Annette, too, had the desire to dance. When I saw her first she was eleven years old, a little shrimp of a thing with eyes that alternately mocked and promised – a little creature all fire and life. And at once – yes, at once – she made me her slave. It was "Raoul, do this for me." "Raoul, do that for me." And me, I obeyed. Already I worshipped her, and she knew it.

'We would go down to the shore together, we three – for Felicie would come with us. And there Annette would pull off her shoes and stockings and dance on the sand. And then when she sank down breathless, she would tell us of what she meant to do and to be.

'"See you, I shall be famous. Yes, exceedingly famous. I will have hundreds and thousands of silk stockings – the finest silk. And I shall live in an exquisite apartment. All my lovers shall be young and handsome as well as being rich. And when I dance all Paris shall come to see me. They will yell and call and shout and go mad over my dancing. And in the winters I shall not dance. I shall go south to the sunlight. There are villas there with orange trees. I shall have one of them. I shall lie in the sun on silk cushions, eating oranges. As for you, Raoul, I will never forget you, however rich and famous I shall be. I will protect you and advance your career. Felicie here shall be my maid – no, her hands are too clumsy. Look at them, how large and coarse they are."

'Felicie would grow angry at that. And then Annette would go on teasing her.

"'She is so ladylike, Felicie – so elegant, so refined. She is a princess in disguise – ha, ha.'

"'My father and mother were married, which is more than yours were,' Felicie would growl out spitefully.

"'Yes, and your father killed your mother. A pretty thing, to be a murderer's daughter.'

"'Your father left your mother to rot,' Felicie would rejoin.

"'Ah! yes.' Annette became thoughtful. "*Pauvre Maman*. One must keep strong and well. It is everything to keep strong and well.'

"'I am as strong as a horse,' Felicie boasted.

'And indeed she was. She had twice the strength of any other girl in the Home. And she was never ill.

'But she was stupid, you comprehend, stupid like a brute beast. I often wondered why she followed Annette round as she did. It was, with her, a kind of fascination. Sometimes, I think, she actually hated Annette, and indeed Annette was not kind to her. She jeered at her slowness and stupidity, and baited her in front of the others. I have seen Felicie grow quite white with rage. Sometimes I have thought that she would fasten her fingers round Annette's neck and choke the life out of her. She was not nimble-witted enough to reply to Annette's taunts, but she did learn in time to make one retort which never failed. That was a reference to her own health and strength. She had learned (what I had always known) that Annette envied her her strong physique, and she struck instinctively at the weak spot in her enemy's armour.

'One day Annette came to me in great glee.

"'Raoul,' she said. "We shall have fun today with that stupid Felicie. We shall die of laughing.'

"'What are you going to do?'

"'Come behind the little shed, and I will tell you.'

'It seemed that Annette had got hold of some book. Part of it she did not understand, and indeed the whole thing was much over her head. It was an early work on hypnotism.

"'A bright object, they say. The brass knob of my bed, it twirls round. I made Felicie look at it last night. 'Look at it steadily,' I said. 'Do not take your eyes off it.' And then I twirled it. Raoul, I was frightened. Her eyes looked so queer – so queer. 'Felicie, you will do what I say always,' I said. 'I will do what you say always, Annette,' she answered. And then – and then – I said: 'Tomorrow you will bring a tallow candle out into the playground at twelve o'clock and start to eat it. And if anyone asks you, you will say that is it the best *galette* you ever tasted.' Oh! Raoul, think of it!'

"'But she'll never do such a thing,' I objected.

'"The book says so. Not that I can quite believe it – but, oh! Raoul, if the book is all true, how we shall amuse ourselves!"

'I, too, thought the idea very funny. We passed word round to the comrades and at twelve o'clock we were all in the playground. Punctual to the minute, out came Felicie with a stump of candle in her hand. Will you believe me, Messieurs, she began solemnly to nibble at it? We were all in hysterics! Every now and then one or other of the children would go up to her and say solemnly: "It is good, what you eat there, eh, Felicie?" And she would answer: "But, yes, it is the best *galette* I ever tasted." And then we would shriek with laughter. We laughed at last so loud that the noise seemed to wake up Felicie to a realization of what she was doing. She blinked her eyes in a puzzled way, looked at the candle, then at us. She passed her hand over her forehead.

'"But what is it that I do here?" she muttered.

'"You are eating a candle," we screamed.

'"*I* made you do it. *I* made you do it," cried Annette, dancing about. 'Felicie stared for a moment. Then she went slowly up to Annette.

'"So it is you – it is you who have made me ridiculous? I seem to remember. Ah! I will kill you for this."

'She spoke in a very quiet tone, but Annette rushed suddenly away and hid behind me.

'"Save me, Raoul! I am afraid of Felicie. It was only a joke, Felicie. Only a joke."

'"I do not like these jokes," said Felicie. "You understand? I hate you. I hate you all."

'She suddenly burst out crying and rushed away.

'Annette was, I think, scared by the result of her experiment, and did not try to repeat it. But from that day on, her ascendency over Felicie seemed to grow stronger.

'Felicie, I now believe, always hated her, but nevertheless she could not keep away from her. She used to follow Annette around like a dog.

'Soon after that, Messieurs, employment was found for me, and I only came to the Home for occasional holidays. Annette's desire to become a dancer was not taken seriously, but she developed a very pretty singing voice as she grew older and Miss Slater consented to her being trained as a singer.

'She was not lazy, Annette. She worked feverishly, without rest. Miss Slater was obliged to prevent her doing too much. She spoke to me once about her.

'"You have always been fond of Annette," she said. "Persuade her not to work too hard. She has a little cough lately that I do not like."

'My work took me far afield soon afterwards. I received one or two letters from Annette at first, but then came silence. For five years after that I was abroad.

'Quite by chance, when I returned to Paris, my attention was caught by a poster advertising Annette Ravelli with a picture of the lady. I recognized her at once. That night I went to the theatre in question. Annette sang in French and Italian. On the stage she was wonderful. Afterwards I went to her dressingroom. She received me at once.

'"Why, Raoul," she cried, stretching out her whitened hands to me. "This is splendid. Where have you been all these years?"

'I would have told her, but she did not really want to listen.'

'"You see, I have very nearly arrived!"

'She waved a triumphant hand round the room filled with bouquets.

'"The good Miss Slater must be proud of your success."

'"That old one? No, indeed. She designed me, you know, for the Conservatoire. Decorous concert singing. But me, I am an artist. It is here, on the variety stage, that I can express myself."

'Just then a handsome middle-aged man came in. He was very distinguished. By his manner I soon saw that he was Annette's protector. He looked sideways at me, and Annette explained.

'"A friend of my infancy. He passes through Paris, sees my picture on a poster *et voila!*"

'The man was then very affable and courteous. In my presence he produced a ruby and diamond bracelet and clasped it on Annette's wrist. As I rose to go, she threw me a glance of triumph and a whisper.

'"I arrive, do I not? You see? All the world is before me."

'But as I left the room, I heard her cough, a sharp dry cough. I knew what it meant, that cough. It was the legacy of her consumptive mother.

'I saw her next two years later. She had gone for refuge to Miss Slater. Her career had broken down. She was in a state of advanced consumption for which the doctors said nothing could be done.

'Ah! I shall never forget her as I saw her then! She was lying in a kind of shelter in the garden. She was kept out-doors night and day. Her cheeks were hollow and flushed, her eyes bright and feverish and she coughed repeatedly.

'She greeted me with a kind of desperation that startled me.

'"It is good to see you, Raoul. You know what they say – that I may not get well? They say it behind my back, you understand. To me they are soothing and consolatory. But it is not true, Raoul, it is not true! I shall not permit myself to die. Die? With beautiful life stretching in front of me? It is the will to live that matters. All the great doctors say that nowadays. I am not one of the feeble ones who let go. Already I feel myself infinitely better – infinitely better, do you hear?"

'She raised herself on her elbow to drive her words home, then fell back, attacked by a fit of coughing that racked her thin body.

'"The cough – it is nothing," she gasped. "And haemorrhages do not frighten me. I shall surprise the doctors. It is the will that counts. Remember, Raoul, I am going to live."

'It was pitiful, you understand, pitiful.

'Just then, Felicie Bault came out with a tray. A glass of hot milk. She gave it to Annette and watched her drink it with an expression that I could not fathom. There was a kind of smug satisfaction in it.

'Annette too caught the look. She flung the glass down angrily, so that it smashed to bits.

'"You see her? That is how she always looks at me. She is glad I am going to die! Yes, she gloats over it. She who is well and strong. Look at her, never a day's illness, that one! And all for nothing. What good is that great carcass of hers to her? What can she make of it?"

'Felicie stooped and picked up the broken fragments of glass.

'"I do not mind what she says," she observed in a sing-song voice. "What does it matter? I am a respectable girl, I am. As for her. She will be knowing the fires of Purgatory before very long. I am a Christian, I say nothing."

'"You hate me," cried Annette. "You have always hated me. Ah! but I can charm you, all the same. I can make you do what I want. See now, if I ask you to, you would go down on your knees before me now on the grass."

'"You are absurd," said Felicie uneasily.

'"But, yes, you will do it. You will. To please me. Down on your knees. I ask it of you, I, Annette. Down on your knees, Felicie."

'Whether it was the wonderful pleading in the voice, or some deeper motive, Felicie obeyed. She sank slowly to her knees, her arms spread wide, her face vacant and stupid.

'Annette flung her head back and laughed – peal upon peal of laughter.

'"Look at her, with her stupid face! How ridiculous she looks. You can get up now, Felicie, thank you! It is of no use to scowl at me. I am your mistress. You have to do what I say."

'She lay back on her pillows exhausted. Felicie picked up the tray and moved slowly away. Once she looked back over her shoulder, and the smouldering resentment in her eyes startled me.

'I was not there when Annette died. But it was terrible, it seems. She clung to life. She fought against death like a madwoman. Again and again she gasped out: "I will not die – do you hear me? I will not die. I will live – live –"

'Miss Slater told me all this when I came to see her six months later.

'"My poor Raoul," she said kindly. "You loved her, did you not?"

'"Always – always. But of what use could I be to her? Let us not talk of it. She is dead – she so brilliant, so full of burning life . . ."

'Miss Slater was a sympathetic woman. She went on to talk of other things. She was very worried about Felicie, so she told me. The girl had had a queer sort of nervous breakdown, and ever since she had been very strange in manner.

'"You know," said Miss Slater, after a momentary hesitation, "that she is learning the piano?"

'I did not know it, and was very much surprised to hear it. Felicie – learning the piano! I would have declared the girl would not know one note from another.

'"She has talent, they say," continued Miss Slater. "I can't understand it. I have always put her down as – well, Raoul, you know yourself, she was always a stupid girl."

'I nodded.

'"She is so strange in her manner sometimes – I really don't know what to make of it."

'A few minutes later I entered the Salle de Lecture. Felicie was playing the piano. She was playing the air that I had heard Annette sing in Paris. You understand, Messieurs, it gave me quite a turn. And then, hearing me, she broke off suddenly and looked round at me, her eyes full of mockery and intelligence. For a moment I thought – Well, I will not tell you what I thought.

'"Tiens!" she said. "So it is you – *Monsieur* Raoul."

'I cannot describe the way she said it. To Annette I had never ceased to be Raoul. But Felicie, since we had met as grown-ups, always addressed me as *Monsieur* Raoul. But the way she said it now was different – as though the *Monsieur*, slightly stressed, was somehow very amusing.

'"Why, Felicie," I stammered. "You look quite different today."

'"Do I?" she said reflectively. "It is odd, that. But do not be so solemn, Raoul – decidedly I shall call you Raoul – did we not play together as children? – Life was made for laughter. Let us talk of the poor Annette – she who is dead and buried. Is she in Purgatory, I wonder, or where?"

'And she hummed a snatch of song – untunefully enough, but the words caught my attention.

'"Felicie," I cried. "You speak Italian?"

'"Why not, Raoul? I am not as stupid as I pretend to be, perhaps." She laughed at my mystification.

'"I don't understand –" I began.

'"But I will tell you. I am a very fine actress, though no one suspects it. I can play many parts – and play them very well."

'She laughed again and ran quickly out of the room before I could stop her.

'I saw her again before I left. She was asleep in an armchair. She was snoring heavily. I stood and watched her, fascinated, yet repelled. Suddenly she woke with a start. Her eyes, dull and lifeless, met mine.

"'Monsieur Raoul," she muttered mechanically.

"'Yes, Felicie, I am going now. Will you play to me again before I go?"

"'I? Play? You are laughing at me, Monsieur Raoul."

"'Don't you remember playing to me this morning?"

'She shook her head.

"'I play? How can a poor girl like me play?"

'She paused for a minute as though in thought, then beckoned me nearer.

"'Monsieur Raoul, there are strange things going on in this house! They play tricks upon you. They alter the clocks. Yes, yes, I know what I am saying. And it is all her doing."

"'Whose doing?" I asked, startled.

"'That Annette's. That wicked one's. When she was alive she always tormented me. Now that she is dead, she comes back from the dead to torment me."

'I stared at Felicie. I could see now that she was in an extremity of terror, her eyes staring from her head.

"'She is bad, that one. She is bad, I tell you. She would take the bread from your mouth, the clothes from your back, *the soul from your body* . . ."

'She clutched me suddenly.

"'I am afraid, I tell you – afraid. I hear her voice – not in my ear – no, not in my ear. Here, in my head –" She tapped her forehead. "She will drive me away – drive me away altogether, and then what shall I do, what will become of me?"

'Her voice rose almost to a shriek. She had in her eyes the look of the terrified brute beast at bay . . .

'Suddenly she smiled, a peasant smile, full of cunning, with something in it that made me shiver.

"'If it should come to it, Monsieur Raoul, I am very strong with my hands – very strong with my hands."

'I had never noticed her hands particularly before. I looked at them now and shuddered in spite of myself. Squat brutal fingers, and as Felicie had said, terribly strong . . . I cannot explain to you the nausea that swept over me. With hands such as these her father must have strangled her mother . . .

'That was the last time I ever saw Felicie Bault. Immediately afterwards

I went abroad – to South America. I returned from there two years after her death. Something I had read in the newspapers of her life and sudden death. I have heard fuller details tonight – from you – gentlemen! Felicie 3 and Felicie 4 – I wonder? She was a good actress, you know!'

The train suddenly slackened speed. The man in the corner sat erect and buttoned his overcoat more closely.

'What is your theory?' asked the lawyer, leaning forward.

'I can hardly believe –' began Canon Parfitt, and stopped.

The doctor said nothing. He was gazing steadily at Raoul Lepardeau.

'*The clothes from your back, the soul from your body*,' quoted the Frenchman lightly. He stood up. 'I say to you, Messieurs, that the history of Felicie Bault is the history of Annette Ravel. You did not know her, gentlemen. I did. *She was very fond of life* . . .'

His hand on the door, ready to spring out, he turned suddenly and bending down tapped Canon Parfitt on the chest.

'M. le docteur over there, he said just now, that all *this*' – his hand smote the Canon's stomach, and the Canon winced – 'was only a residence. Tell me, if you find a burglar in your house what do you do? Shoot him, do you not?'

'No,' cried the Canon. 'No, indeed – I mean – not in this country.'

But he spoke the last words to empty air. The carriage door banged.

The clergyman, the lawyer and the doctor were alone. The fourth corner was vacant.

15

The House of Dreams

'The House of Dreams' was first published in *The Sovereign Magazine*, January 1926. According to Agatha Christie's autobiography, it was a revised version of the unpublished 'The House of Beauty', written before the First World War and 'the first thing I ever wrote that showed any kind of promise'.

This is the story of John Segrave – of his life, which was unsatisfactory; of his love, which was unsatisfied; of his dreams, and of his death; and if in the two latter he found what was denied in the two former, then his life may, after all, be taken as a success. Who knows?

John Segrave came of a family which had been slowly going downhill for the last century. They had been landowners since the days of Elizabeth, but their last piece of property was sold. It was thought well that one of the sons at least should acquire the useful art of money making. It was an unconscious irony of Fate that John should be the one chosen.

With his strangely sensitive mouth, and the long dark blue slits of eyes that suggested an elf or a faun, something wild and of the woods, it was incongruous that he should be offered up, a sacrifice on the altar of Finance. The smell of the earth, the taste of the sea salt on one's lips, and the free sky above one's head – these were the things beloved by John Segrave, to which he was to bid farewell.

At the age of eighteen he became a junior clerk in a big business house. Seven years later he was still a clerk, not quite so junior, but with status otherwise unchanged. The faculty for 'getting on in the world' had been omitted from his make-up. He was punctual, industrious, plodding – a clerk and nothing but a clerk.

And yet he might have been – what? He could hardly answer that question himself, but he could not rid himself of the conviction that somewhere there was a life in which he could have – counted. There was power in him, swiftness of vision, a something of which his fellow toilers had never had a glimpse. They liked him. He was popular because of his air of careless friendship, and they never appreciated the fact that he barred them but by that same manner from any real intimacy.

The dream came to him suddenly. It was no childish fantasy growing and developing through the years. It came on a midsummer night, or rather early morning, and he woke from it tingling all over, striving to hold it to him as it fled, slipping from his clutch in the elusive way dreams have.

Desperately he clung to it. It must not go – it must not – he must remember the house. It was *the* House, of course! The House he knew so well. Was it a real house, or did he merely know it in dreams? He didn't remember – but he certainly knew it – knew it very well.

The faint grey light of the early morning was stealing into the room. The stillness was extraordinary. At four-thirty a.m. London, weary London, found her brief instant of peace.

John Segrave lay quiet, wrapped in the joy, the exquisite wonder and beauty of his dream. How clever it had been of him to remember it! A dream flitted so quickly as a rule, ran past you just as with waking consciousness your clumsy fingers sought to stop and hold it. But he had been too quick for this dream! He had seized it as it was slipping swiftly by him.

It was really a most remarkable dream! There was the house and – his thoughts were brought up with a jerk, for when he came to think of it, he couldn't remember anything but the house. And suddenly, with a tinge of disappointment, he recognized that, after all, the house was quite strange to him. He hadn't even dreamed of it before.

It was a white house, standing on high ground. There were trees near it, blue hills in the distance, but its peculiar charm was independent of surroundings for (and this was the point, the climax of the dream) it was a beautiful, a strangely beautiful house. His pulses quickened as he remembered anew the strange beauty of the house.

The outside of it, of course, for he hadn't been inside. There had been no question of that – no question of it whatsoever.

Then, as the dingy outlines of his bed-sitting-room began to take shape in the growing light, he experienced the disillusion of the dreamer. Perhaps, after all, his dream hadn't been so very wonderful – or had the wonderful, the explanatory part, slipped past him, and laughed at his ineffectual clutching hands? A white house, standing on high ground – there wasn't much there to get excited about, surely? It was rather a big house, he remembered, with a lot of windows in it, and the blinds were all down, not because the people were away (he was sure of that), but because it was so early that no one was up yet.

Then he laughed at the absurdity of his imaginings, and remembered that he was to dine with Mr Wetterman that night.

Maisie Wetterman was Rudolf Wetterman's only daughter, and she had been accustomed all her life to having exactly what she wanted. Paying a visit to her father's office one day, she had noticed John Segrave. He had brought in some letters that her father had asked for. When he had departed again, she asked her father about him. Wetterman was communicative.

'One of Sir Edward Segrave's sons. Fine old family, but on its last legs. This boy will never set the Thames on fire. I like him all right, but there's nothing to him. No punch of any kind.'

Maisie was, perhaps, indifferent to punch. It was a quality valued more by her parent than herself. Anyway, a fortnight later she persuaded her father to ask John Segrave to dinner. It was an intimate dinner, herself and her father, John Segrave, and a girl friend who was staying with her.

The girl friend was moved to make a few remarks.

'On approval, I suppose, Maisie? Later, father will do it up in a nice little parcel and bring it home from the city as a present to his dear little daughter, duly bought and paid for.'

'Allegra! You are the limit.'

Allegra Kerr laughed.

'You do take fancies, you know, Maisie. I like that hat – I must have it! If hats, why not husbands?'

'Don't be absurd. I've hardly spoken to him yet.'

'No. But you've made up your mind,' said the other girl. 'What's the attraction, Maisie?'

'I don't know,' said Maisie Wetterman slowly. 'He's – different.'

'Different?'

'Yes. I can't explain. He's good looking, you know, in a queer sort of way, but it's not that. He's a way of not seeing you're there. Really, I don't believe he as much as glanced at me that day in father's office.'

Allegra laughed.

'That's an old trick. Rather an astute young man, I should say.'

'Allegra, you're hateful!'

'Cheer up, darling. Father will buy a woolly lamb for his little Maisiekins.'

'I don't want it to be like that.'

'Love with a capital L. Is that it?'

'Why shouldn't he fall in love with me?'

'No reason at all. I expect he will.'

Allegra smiled as she spoke, and let her glance sweep over the other.

Maisie Wetterman was short – inclined to be plump – she had dark hair, well shingled and artistically waved. Her naturally good complexion was enhanced by the latest colours in powder and lipstick. She had a good mouth and teeth, dark eyes, rather small and twinkly, and a jaw and chin slightly on the heavy side. She was beautifully dressed.

'Yes,' said Allegra, finishing her scrutiny. 'I've no doubt he will. The whole effect is really very good, Maisie.'

Her friend looked at her doubtfully.

'I mean it,' said Allegra. 'I mean it – honour bright. But just supposing, for the sake of argument, that he shouldn't. Fall in love, I mean. Suppose his affection was to become sincere, but platonic. What then?'

'I may not like him at all when I know him better.'

'Quite so. On the other hand you may like him very much indeed. And in that latter case –'

Maisie shrugged her shoulders.

'I should hope I've too much pride –'

Allegra interrupted.

'Pride comes in handy for masking one's feelings – it doesn't stop you from feeling them.'

'Well,' said Maisie, flushed. 'I don't see why I shouldn't say it. I *am* a very good match. I mean – from his point of view, father's daughter and everything.'

'Partnership in the offing, et cetera,' said Allegra. 'Yes, Maisie. You're father's daughter, all right. I'm awfully pleased. I do like my friends to run true to type.'

The faint mockery of her tone made the other uneasy.

'You are hateful, Allegra.'

'But stimulating, darling. That's why you have me here. I'm a student of history, you know, and it always intrigued me why the court jester was permitted and encouraged. Now that I'm one myself, I see the point. It's rather a good rôle, you see, I had to do something. There was I, proud and penniless like the heroine of a novelette, well born and badly educated. *"What to do, girl? God wot,"* saith she. The poor relation type of girl, all willingness to do without a fire in her room and content to do odd jobs and "help dear Cousin So-and-So", I observed to be at a premium. Nobody really wants her – except those people who can't keep their servants, and they treat her like a galley slave.

'So I became the court fool. Insolence, plain speaking, a dash of wit now and again (not too much lest I should have to live up to it), and behind it all, a very shrewd observation of human nature. People rather like being told how horrible they really are. That's why they flock to popular preachers. It's been a great success. I'm always overwhelmed with invitations. I can live on my friends with the greatest ease, and I'm careful to make no pretence of gratitude.'

'There's no one quite like you, Allegra. You don't mind in the least what you say.'

'That's where you're wrong. I mind very much – I take care and thought about the matter. My seeming outspokenness is always calculated. I've got to be careful. This job has got to carry me on to old age.'

'Why not marry? I know heaps of people have asked you.'

Allegra's face grew suddenly hard.

'I can never marry.'

'Because –' Maisie left the sentence unfinished, looking at her friend. The latter gave a short nod of assent.

Footsteps were heard on the stairs. The butler threw open the door and announced:

'Mr Segrave.'

John came in without any particular enthusiasm. He couldn't imagine why the old boy had asked him. If he could have got out of it he would have done so. The house depressed him, with its solid magnificence and the soft pile of its carpet.

A girl came forward and shook hands with him. He remembered vaguely having seen her one day in her father's office.

'How do you do, Mr Segrave? Mr Segrave – Miss Kerr.'

Then he woke. Who was she? Where did she come from? From the flame-coloured draperies that floated round her, to the tiny Mercury wings on her small Greek head, she was a being transitory and fugitive, standing out against the dull background with an effect of unreality.

Rudolf Wetterman came in, his broad expanse of gleaming shirt-front creaking as he walked. They went down informally to dinner.

Allegra Kerr talked to her host. John Segrave had to devote himself to Maisie. But his whole mind was on the girl on the other side of him. She was marvellously effective. Her effectiveness was, he thought, more studied than natural. But behind all that, there lay something else. Flickering fire, fitful, capricious, like the will-o'-the-wisps that of old lured men into the marshes.

At last he got a chance to speak to her. Maisie was giving her father a message from some friend she had met that day. Now that the moment had come, he was tongue-tied. His glance pleaded with her dumbly.

'Dinner-table topics,' she said lightly. 'Shall we start with the theatres, or with one of those innumerable openings beginning, "Do you like –?"'

John laughed.

'And if we find we both like dogs and dislike sandy cats, it will form what is called a "bond" between us?'

'Assuredly,' said Allegra gravely.

'It is, I think, a pity to begin with a catechism.'

'Yet it puts conversation within the reach of all.'

'True, but with disastrous results.'

'It is useful to know the rules – if only to break them.'

John smiled at her.

'I take it, then, that you and I will indulge our personal vagaries. Even though we display thereby the genius that is akin to madness.'

With a sharp unguarded movement, the girl's hand swept a wineglass off the table. There was the tinkle of broken glass. Maisie and her father stopped speaking.

'I'm so sorry, Mr Wetterman. I'm throwing glasses on the floor.'

'My dear Allegra, it doesn't matter at all, not at all.'

Beneath his breath John Segrave said quickly:

'Broken glass. That's bad luck. I wish – it hadn't happened.'

'Don't worry. How does it go? "Ill luck thou canst not bring where ill luck has its home."'

She turned once more to Wetterman. John, resuming conversation with Maisie, tried to place the quotation. He got it at last. They were the words used by Sieglinde in the Walküre when Sigmund offers to leave the house.

He thought: 'Did she mean –?'

But Maisie was asking his opinion of the latest Revue. Soon he had admitted that he was fond of music.

'After dinner,' said Maisie, 'we'll make Allegra play for us.'

They all went up to the drawing-room together. Secretly, Wetterman considered it a barbarous custom. He liked the ponderous gravity of the wine passing round, the handed cigars. But perhaps it was as well tonight. He didn't know what on earth he could find to say to young Segrave. Maisie was too bad with her whims. It wasn't as though the fellow were good looking – really good looking – and certainly he wasn't amusing. He was glad when Maisie asked Allegra Kerr to play. They'd get through the evening sooner. The young idiot didn't even play Bridge.

Allegra played well, though without the sure touch of a professional. She played modern music, Debussy and Strauss, a little Scriabin. Then she dropped into the first movement of Beethoven's *Pathétique*, that expression of a grief that is infinite, a sorrow that is endless and vast as the ages, but in which from end to end breathes the spirit that will not accept defeat. In the solemnity of undying woe, it moves with the rhythm of the conqueror to its final doom.

Towards the end she faltered, her fingers struck a discord, and she broke off abruptly. She looked across at Maisie and laughed mockingly.

'You see,' she said. 'They won't let me.'

Then, without waiting for a reply to her somewhat enigmatical remark, she plunged into a strange haunting melody, a thing of weird harmonies and curious measured rhythm, quite unlike anything Segrave had ever heard before. It was delicate as the flight of a bird, poised, hovering – suddenly, without the least warning, it turned into a mere discordant jangle of notes, and Allegra rose laughing from the piano.

In spite of her laugh, she looked disturbed and almost frightened. She sat down by Maisie, and John heard the latter say in a low tone to her:

'You shouldn't do it. You really shouldn't do it.'

'What was the last thing?' John asked eagerly.

'Something of my own.'

She spoke sharply and curtly. Wetterman changed the subject.

That night John Segrave dreamt again of the House.

John was unhappy. His life was irksome to him as never before. Up to now he had accepted it patiently – a disagreeable necessity, but one which left his inner freedom essentially untouched. Now all that was changed. The outer world and the inner intermingled.

He did not disguise to himself the reason for the change. He had fallen in love at first sight with Allegra Kerr. What was he going to do about it?

He had been too bewildered that first night to make any plans. He had not even tried to see her again. A little later, when Maisie Wetterman asked him down to her father's place in the country for a weekend, he went eagerly, but he was disappointed, for Allegra was not there.

He mentioned her once, tentatively, to Maisie, and she told him that Allegra was up in Scotland paying a visit. He left it at that. He would have liked to go on talking about her, but the words seemed to stick in his throat.

Maisie was puzzled by him that weekend. He didn't appear to see – well, to see what was so plainly to be seen. She was a direct young woman in her methods, but directness was lost upon John. He thought her kind, but a little overpowering.

Yet the Fates were stronger than Maisie. They willed that John should see Allegra again.

They met in the park one Sunday afternoon. He had seen her from far off, and his heart thumped against the side of his ribs. Supposing she should have forgotten him –

But she had not forgotten. She stopped and spoke. In a few minutes they were walking side by side, striking out across the grass. He was ridiculously happy.

He said suddenly and unexpectedly:

'Do you believe in dreams?'

'I believe in nightmares.'

The harshness of her voice startled him.

'Nightmares,' he said stupidly. 'I didn't mean nightmares.'

Allegra looked at him.

'No,' she said. 'There have been no nightmares in your life. I can see that.'

Her voice was gentle – different.

He told her then of his dream of the white house, stammering a little. He had had it now six – no, seven times. Always the same. It was beautiful – so beautiful!

He went on.

'You see – it's to do with *you* – in some way. I had it first the night before I met you.'

'To do with me?' She laughed – a short bitter laugh. 'Oh, no, that's impossible. The house was beautiful.'

'So are you,' said John Segrave.

Allegra flushed a little with annoyance.

'I'm sorry – I was stupid. I seemed to ask for a compliment, didn't I? But I didn't really mean that at all. The outside of me is all right, I know.'

'I haven't seen the inside of the house yet,' said John Segrave. 'When I do I know it will be quite as beautiful as the outside.'

He spoke slowly and gravely, giving the words a meaning that she chose to ignore.

'There is something more I want to tell you – if you will listen.'

'I will listen,' said Allegra.

'I am chucking up this job of mine. I ought to have done it long ago – I see that now. I have been content to drift along knowing I was an utter failure, without caring much, just living from day to day. A man shouldn't do that. It's a man's business to find something he can do and make a success of it. I'm chucking this, and taking on something else – quite a different sort of thing. It's a kind of expedition in West Africa – I can't tell you the details. They're not supposed to be known; but if it comes off – well, I shall be a rich man.'

'So you, too, count success in terms of money?'

'Money,' said John Segrave, 'means just one thing to me – you! When I come back –' he paused.

She bent her head. Her face had grown very pale.

'I won't pretend to misunderstand. That's why I must tell you now, once and for all: *I shall never marry.*'

He stayed a little while considering, then he said very gently:

'Can't you tell me why?'

'I could, but more than anything in the world I do not want to tell you.'

Again he was silent, then he looked up suddenly and a singularly attractive smile illumined his faun's face.

'I see,' he said. 'So you won't let me come inside the House – not even to peep in for a second? The blinds are to stay down.'

Allegra leaned forward and laid her hand on his.

'I will tell you this much. You dream of your House. But I – don't dream. My dreams are nightmares!'

And on that she left him, abruptly, disconcertingly.

That night, once more, he dreamed. Of late, he had realized that the House was most certainly tenanted. He had seen a hand draw aside the blinds, had caught glimpses of moving figures within.

Tonight the House seemed fairer than it had ever done before. Its white walls shone in the sunlight. The peace and the beauty of it were complete.

Then, suddenly, he became aware of a fuller ripple of the waves of joy. Someone was coming to the window. He knew it. A hand, the same hand that he had seen before, laid hold of the blind, drawing it back. In a minute he would see . . .

He was awake – still quivering with the horror, the unutterable loathing of the *Thing* that had looked out at him from the window of the House.

It was a Thing utterly and wholly horrible, a Thing so vile and loathsome that the mere remembrance of it made him feel sick. And he knew that the most unutterably and horribly vile thing about it was its presence in that House – the House of Beauty.

For where that Thing abode was horror – horror that rose up and slew the peace and the serenity which were the birthright of the House. The beauty, the wonderful immortal beauty of the House was destroyed for ever, for within its holy consecrated walls there dwelt the Shadow of an Unclean Thing!

If ever again he should dream of the House, Segrave knew he would awake at once with a start of terror, lest from its white beauty that Thing might suddenly look out at him.

The following evening, when he left the office, he went straight to the Wettermans' house. He must see Allegra Kerr. Maisie would tell him where she was to be found.

He never noticed the eager light that flashed into Maisie's eyes as he was shown in, and she jumped up to greet him. He stammered out his request at once, with her hand still in his.

'Miss Kerr. I met her yesterday, but I don't know where she's staying.'

He did not feel Maisie's hand grow limp in his as she withdrew it. The sudden coldness of her voice told him nothing.

'Allegra is here – staying with us. But I'm afraid you can't see her.'

'But –'

'You see, her mother died this morning. We've just had the news.'

'Oh!' He was taken aback.

'It is all very sad,' said Maisie. She hesitated just a minute, then went on. 'You see, she died in – well, practically an asylum. There's insanity in the family. The grandfather shot himself, and one of Allegra's aunts is a hopeless imbecile, and another drowned herself.'

John Segrave made an inarticulate sound.

'I thought I ought to tell you,' said Maisie virtuously. 'We're such friends, aren't we? And of course Allegra is very attractive. Lots of people have asked her to marry them, but naturally she won't marry at all – she couldn't, could she?'

'She's all right,' said Segrave. 'There's nothing wrong with *her*.'

His voice sounded hoarse and unnatural in his own ears.

'One never knows, her mother was quite all right when she was young. And she wasn't just – peculiar, you know. She was quite raving mad. It's a dreadful thing – insanity.'

'Yes,' he said, 'it's a most awful Thing.'

He knew now what it was that had looked at him from the window of the House.

Maisie was still talking on. He interrupted her brusquely.

'I really came to say goodbye – and to thank you for all your kindness.'

'You're not – going away?'

There was alarm in her voice.

He smiled sideways at her – a crooked smile, pathetic and attractive.

'Yes,' he said. 'To Africa.'

'Africa!'

Maisie echoed the word blankly. Before she could pull herself together he had shaken her by the hand and gone. She was left standing there, her hands clenched by her sides, an angry spot of colour in each cheek.

Below, on the doorstep, John Segrave came face to face with Allegra coming in from the street. She was in black, her face white and lifeless. She took one glance at him then drew him into a small morning room.

'Maisie told you,' she said. 'You *know*?'

He nodded.

'But what does it matter? *You're* all right. It – it leaves some people out.'

She looked at him sombrely, mournfully.

'You *are* all right,' he repeated.

'I don't know,' she almost whispered it. 'I don't know. I told you –

about my dreams. And when I play – when I'm at the piano – *those others* come and take hold of my hands.'

He was staring at her – paralysed. For one instant, as she spoke, something looked out from her eyes. It was gone in a flash – but he knew it. It was the Thing that had looked out from the House.

She caught his momentary recoil.

'You see,' she whispered. 'You see – but I wish Maisie hadn't told you. It takes everything from you.'

'Everything?'

'Yes. There won't even be the dreams left. For now – you'll never dare to dream of the House again.'

The West African sun poured down, and the heat was intense.

John Segrave continued to moan.

'I can't find it. I can't find it.'

The little English doctor with the red head and the tremendous jaw, scowled down upon his patient in that bullying manner which he had made his own.

'He's always saying that. What does he mean?'

'He speaks, I think, of a house, monsieur.' The soft-voiced Sister of Charity from the Roman Catholic Mission spoke with her gentle detachment, as she too looked down on the stricken man.

'A house, eh? Well, he's got to get it out of his head, or we shan't pull him through. It's on his mind. Segrave! Segrave!'

The wandering attention was fixed. The eyes rested with recognition on the doctor's face.

'Look here, you're going to pull through. I'm going to pull you through. But you've got to stop worrying about this house. It can't run away, you know. So don't bother about looking for it now.'

'All right.' He seemed obedient. 'I suppose it can't very well run away if it's never been there at all.'

'Of course not!' The doctor laughed his cheery laugh. 'Now you'll be all right in no time.' And with a boisterous bluntness of manner he took his departure.

Segrave lay thinking. The fever had abated for the moment, and he could think clearly and lucidly. He *must* find that House.

For ten years he had dreaded finding it – the thought that he might come upon it unawares had been his greatest terror. And then, he remembered, when his fears were quite lulled to rest, one day *it* had found *him*. He recalled clearly his first haunting terror, and then his sudden, his exquisite, relief. For, after all, the House was empty!

Quite empty and exquisitely peaceful. It was as he remembered it ten years before. He had not forgotten. There was a huge black furniture van moving slowly away from the House. The last tenant, of course, moving out with his goods. He went up to the men in charge of the van and spoke to them. There was something rather sinister about that van, it was so very black. The horses were black, too, with freely flowing manes and tails, and the men all wore black clothes and gloves. It all reminded him of something else, something that he couldn't remember.

Yes, he had been quite right. The last tenant was moving out, as his lease was up. The House was to stand empty for the present, until the owner came back from abroad.

And waking, he had been full of the peaceful beauty of the empty House.

A month after that, he had received a letter from Maisie (she wrote to him perseveringly, once a month). In it she told him that Allegra Kerr had died in the same home as her mother, and wasn't it dreadfully sad? Though of course a merciful release.

It had really been very odd indeed. Coming after his dream like that. He didn't quite understand it all. But it was odd.

And the worst of it was that he'd never been able to find the House since. Somehow, he'd forgotten the way.

The fever began to take hold of him once more. He tossed restlessly. Of course, he'd forgotten, the House was on high ground! He must climb to get there. But it was hot work climbing cliffs – dreadfully hot. Up, up, up – oh! he had slipped! He must start again from the bottom. Up, up, up – days passed, weeks – he wasn't sure that years didn't go by! And he was still climbing.

Once he heard the doctor's voice. But he couldn't stop climbing to listen. Besides the doctor would tell him to leave off looking for the House. *He* thought it was an ordinary house. He didn't know.

He remembered suddenly that he must be calm, very calm. You couldn't find the House unless you were very calm. It was no use looking for the House in a hurry, or being excited.

If he could only keep calm! But it was so hot! Hot? It was *cold* – yes, cold. These weren't cliffs, they were icebergs – jagged cold, icebergs.

He was so tired. He wouldn't go on looking – it was no good. Ah! here was a lane – that was better than icebergs, anyway. How pleasant and shady it was in the cool, green lane. And those trees – they were splendid! They were rather like – what? He couldn't remember, but it didn't matter.

Ah! here were flowers. All golden and blue! How lovely it all was – and how strangely familiar. Of course, he had been here before. There, through the trees, was the gleam of the House, standing on the high ground. How beautiful it was. The green lane and the trees and the flowers were as nothing to the paramount, the all-satisfying, beauty of the House.

He hastened his steps. To think that he had never yet been inside! How unbelievably stupid of him – when he had the key in his pocket all the time!

And of course the beauty of the exterior was as nothing to the beauty that lay within – especially now that the owner had come back from abroad. He mounted the steps to the great door.

Cruel strong hands were dragging him back! They fought him, dragging him to and fro, backwards and forwards.

The doctor was shaking him, roaring in his ear. 'Hold on, man, you can. Don't let go. Don't let go.' His eyes were alight with the fierceness of one who sees an enemy. Segrave wondered who the Enemy was. The black-robed nun was praying. That, too, was strange.

And all *he* wanted was to be left alone. To go back to the House. For every minute the House was growing fainter.

That, of course, was because the doctor was so strong. He wasn't strong enough to fight the doctor. If he only could.

But stop! There was another way – the way dreams went in the moment of waking. No strength could stop *them* – they just flitted past. The doctor's hands wouldn't be able to hold him if he slipped – just slipped!

Yes, that was the way! The white walls were visible once more, the doctor's voice was fainter, his hands were barely felt. He knew now how dreams laugh when they give you the slip!

He was at the door of the House. The exquisite stillness was unbroken. He put the key in the lock and turned it.

Just a moment he waited, to realize to the full the perfect, the ineffable, the all-satisfying completeness of joy.

Then – he passed over the Threshold.

16

S.O.S.

'S.O.S.' was first published in *Grand Magazine*, February 1926.

'Ah!' said Mr Dinsmead appreciatively.

He stepped back and surveyed the round table with approval. The firelight gleamed on the coarse white tablecloth, the knives and forks, and the other table appointments.

'Is – is everything ready?' asked Mrs Dinsmead hesitatingly. She was a little faded woman, with a colourless face, meagre hair scraped back from her forehead, and a perpetually nervous manner.

'Everything's ready,' said her husband with a kind of ferocious geniality.

He was a big man, with stooping shoulders, and a broad red face. He had little pig's eyes that twinkled under his bushy brows, and a big jowl devoid of hair.

'Lemonade?' suggested Mrs Dinsmead, almost in a whisper.

Her husband shook his head.

'Tea. Much better in every way. Look at the weather, streaming and blowing. A nice cup of hot tea is what's needed for supper on an evening like this.'

He winked facetiously, then fell to surveying the table again.

'A good dish of eggs, cold corned beef, and bread and cheese. That's my order for supper. So come along and get it ready, Mother. Charlotte's in the kitchen waiting to give you a hand.'

Mrs Dinsmead rose, carefully winding up the ball of her knitting.

'She's grown a very good-looking girl,' she murmured. 'Sweetly pretty, I say.'

'Ah!' said Mr Dinsmead. 'The mortal image of her Ma! So go along with you, and don't let's waste any more time.'

He strolled about the room humming to himself for a minute or two. Once he approached the window and looked out.

'Wild weather,' he murmured to himself. 'Not much likelihood of our having visitors tonight.'

Then he too left the room.

About ten minutes later Mrs Dinsmead entered bearing a dish of fried eggs. Her two daughters followed, bringing in the rest of the provisions. Mr Dinsmead and his son Johnnie brought up the rear. The former seated himself at the head of the table.

'And for what we are to receive, etcetera,' he remarked humorously. 'And blessings on the man who first thought of tinned foods. What would we do, I should like to know, miles from anywhere, if we hadn't a tin now and then to fall back upon when the butcher forgets his weekly call?'

He proceeded to carve corned beef dexterously.

'I wonder who ever thought of building a house like this, miles from anywhere,' said his daughter Magdalen pettishly. 'We never see a soul.'

'No,' said her father. 'Never a soul.'

'I can't think what made you take it, Father,' said Charlotte.

'Can't you, my girl? Well, I had my reasons – I had my reasons.'

His eyes sought his wife's furtively, but she frowned.

'And haunted too,' said Charlotte. 'I wouldn't sleep alone here for anything.'

'Pack of nonsense,' said her father. 'Never seen anything, have you? Come now.'

'Not *seen* anything perhaps, but –'

'But what?'

Charlotte did not reply, but she shivered a little. A great surge of rain came driving against the window-pane, and Mrs Dinsmead dropped a spoon with a tinkle on the tray.

'Not nervous are you, Mother?' said Mr Dinsmead. 'It's a wild night, that's all. Don't you worry, we're safe here by our fireside, and not a soul from outside likely to disturb us. Why, it would be a miracle if anyone did. And miracles don't happen. No,' he added as though to himself, with a kind of peculiar satisfaction. 'Miracles don't happen.'

As the words left his lips there came a sudden knocking at the door. Mr Dinsmead stayed as though petrified.

'Whatever's that?' he muttered. His jaw fell.

Mrs Dinsmead gave a little whimpering cry and pulled her shawl up round her. The colour came into Magdalen's face and she leant forward and spoke to her father.

'The miracle has happened,' she said. 'You'd better go and let whoever it is in.'

Twenty minutes earlier Mortimer Cleveland had stood in the driving rain and mist surveying his car. It was really cursed bad luck. Two punctures within ten minutes of each other, and here he was, stranded miles from anywhere, in the midst of these bare Wiltshire downs with night coming on, and no prospect of shelter. Serve him right for trying to take a short-cut. If only he had stuck to the main road! Now he was lost on what seemed a mere cart-track, and no idea if there were even a village anywhere near.

He looked round him perplexedly, and his eye was caught by a gleam of light on the hillside above him. A second later the mist obscured it once more, but, waiting patiently, he presently got a second glimpse of it. After a moment's cogitation, he left the car and struck up the side of the hill.

Soon he was out of the mist, and he recognized the light as shining from the lighted window of a small cottage. Here, at any rate, was shelter. Mortimer Cleveland quickened his pace, bending his head to meet the furious onslaught of wind and rain which seemed to be trying its best to drive him back.

Cleveland was in his own way something of a celebrity though doubtless the majority of folks would have displayed complete ignorance of his name and achievements. He was an authority on mental science and had written two excellent text books on the subconscious. He was also a member of the Psychical Research Society and a student of the occult in so far as it affected his own conclusions and line of research.

He was by nature peculiarly susceptible to atmosphere, and by deliberate training he had increased his own natural gift. When he had at last reached the cottage and rapped at the door, he was conscious of an excitement, a quickening of interest, as though all his faculties had suddenly been sharpened.

The murmur of voices within had been plainly audible to him. Upon his knock there came a sudden silence, then the sound of a chair being pushed back along the floor. In another minute the door was flung open by a boy of about fifteen. Cleveland looked straight over his shoulder upon the scene within.

It reminded him of an interior by some Dutch Master. A round table spread for a meal, a family party sitting round it, one or two flickering candles and the firelight's glow over all. The father, a big man, sat one side of the table, a little grey woman with a frightened face sat opposite him. Facing the door, looking straight at Cleveland, was a girl. Her startled eyes looked straight into his, her hand with a cup in it was arrested half-way to her lips.

She was, Cleveland saw at once, a beautiful girl of an extremely uncommon type. Her hair, red gold, stood out round her face like a mist, her eyes, very far apart, were a pure grey. She had the mouth and chin of an early Italian Madonna.

There was a moment's dead silence. Then Cleveland stepped into the room and explained his predicament. He brought his trite story to a close, and there was another pause harder to understand. At last, as though with an effort, the father rose.

'Come in, sir – Mr Cleveland, did you say?'

'That is my name,' said Mortimer, smiling.

'Ah! yes. Come in, Mr Cleveland. Not weather for a dog outside, is it? Come in by the fire. Shut the door, can't you, Johnnie? Don't stand there half the night.'

Cleveland came forward and sat on a wooden stool by the fire. The boy Johnnie shut the door.

'Dinsmead, that's my name,' said the other man. He was all geniality now. 'This is the Missus, and these are my two daughters, Charlotte and Magdalen.'

For the first time, Cleveland saw the face of the girl who had been sitting with her back to him, and saw that, in a totally different way, she was quite as beautiful as her sister. Very dark, with a face of marble pallor, a delicate aquiline nose, and a grave mouth. It was a kind of frozen beauty, austere and almost forbidding. She acknowledged her father's introduction by bending her head, and she looked at him with an intent gaze that was searching in character. It was as though she were summing him up, weighing him in the balance of her young judgement.

'A drop of something to drink, eh, Mr Cleveland?'

'Thank you,' said Mortimer. 'A cup of tea will meet the case admirably.'

Mr Dinsmead hesitated a minute, then he picked up the five cups, one after another, from the table and emptied them into a slop bowl.

'This tea's cold,' he said brusquely. 'Make us some more will you, Mother?'

Mrs Dinsmead got up quickly and hurried off with the teapot. Mortimer had an idea that she was glad to get out of the room.

The fresh tea soon came, and the unexpected guest was plied with viands.

Mr Dinsmead talked and talked. He was expansive, genial, loquacious. He told the stranger all about himself. He'd lately retired from the building trade – yes, made quite a good thing of it. He and the Missus thought they'd like a bit of country air – never lived in the country before. Wrong time of year to choose, of course, October and November, but they didn't want to wait. 'Life's uncertain, you know, sir.' So they had taken this cottage. Eight miles from anywhere, and nineteen miles from anything you could call a town. No, they didn't complain. The girls found it a bit dull, but he and mother enjoyed the quiet.

So he talked on, leaving Mortimer almost hypnotized by the easy flow.

Nothing here, surely, but rather commonplace domesticity. And yet, at that first glimpse of the interior, he had diagnosed something else, some tension, some strain, emanating from one of those five people – he didn't know which. Mere foolishness, his nerves were all awry! They were all startled by his sudden appearance – that was all.

He broached the question of a night's lodging, and was met with a ready response.

'You'll have to stop with us, Mr Cleveland. Nothing else for miles around. We can give you a bedroom, and though my pyjamas may be a bit roomy, why, they're better than nothing, and your own clothes will be dry by morning.'

'It's very good of you.'

'Not at all,' said the other genially. 'As I said just now, one couldn't turn away a dog on a night like this. Magdalen, Charlotte, go up and see to the room.'

The two girls left the room. Presently Mortimer heard them moving about overhead.

'I can quite understand that two attractive young ladies like your daughters might find it dull here,' said Cleveland.

'Good lookers, aren't they?' said Mr Dinsmead with fatherly pride. 'Not much like their mother or myself. We're a homely pair, but much attached to each other. I'll tell you that, Mr Cleveland. Eh, Maggie, isn't that so?'

Mrs Dinsmead smiled primly. She had started knitting again. The needles clicked busily. She was a fast knitter.

Presently the room was announced ready, and Mortimer, expressing thanks once more, declared his intention of turning in.

'Did you put a hot-water bottle in the bed?' demanded Mrs Dinsmead, suddenly mindful of her house pride.

'Yes, Mother, two.'

'That's right,' said Dinsmead. 'Go up with him, girls, and see that there's nothing else he wants.'

Magdalen went over to the window and saw that the fastenings were secure. Charlotte cast a final eye over the washstand appointments. Then they both lingered by the door.

'Good night, Mr Cleveland. You are sure there is everything?'

'Yes, thank you, Miss Magdalen. I am ashamed to have given you both so much trouble. Good night.'

'Good night.'

They went out, shutting the door behind them. Mortimer Cleveland was alone. He undressed slowly and thoughtfully. When he had donned Mr Dinsmead's pink pyjamas he gathered up his own wet clothes and put them outside the door as his host had bade him. From downstairs he could hear the rumble of Dinsmead's voice.

What a talker the man was! Altogether an odd personality – but indeed there was something odd about the whole family, or was it his imagination?

He went slowly back into his room and shut the door. He stood by the bed lost in thought. And then he started –

The mahogany table by the bed was smothered in dust. Written in the dust were three letters, clearly visible, *SOS*.

Mortimer stared as if he could hardly believe his eyes. It was confirmation of all his vague surmises and forebodings. He was right, then. Something was wrong in this house.

SOS. A call for help. But whose finger had written it in the dust? Magdalen's or Charlotte's? They had both stood there, he remembered, for a moment or two, before going out of the room. Whose hand had secretly dropped to the table and traced out those three letters?

The faces of the two girls came up before him. Magdalen's, dark and aloof, and Charlotte's, as he had seen it first, wide-eyed, startled, with an unfathomable something in her glance . . .

He went again to the door and opened it. The boom of Mr Dinsmead's voice was no longer to be heard. The house was silent.

He thought to himself.

'I can do nothing tonight. Tomorrow – well. We shall see.'

Cleveland woke early. He went down through the living-room, and out into the garden. The morning was fresh and beautiful after the rain. Someone else was up early, too. At the bottom of the garden, Charlotte was leaning on the fence staring out over the Downs. His pulse quickened a little as he went down to join her. All along he had been secretly convinced that it was Charlotte who had written the message. As he came up to her, she turned and wished him 'Good morning'. Her eyes were direct and childlike, with no hint of a secret understanding in them.

'A very good morning,' said Mortimer, smiling. 'The weather this morning is a contrast to last night.'

'It is indeed.'

Mortimer broke off a twig from a tree near by. With it he began idly to draw on the smooth, sandy patch at his feet. He traced an S, then an O, then an S, watching the girl narrowly as he did so. But again he could detect no gleam of comprehension.

'Do you know what these letters represent?' he said abruptly.

Charlotte frowned a little. 'Aren't they what boats – liners, send out when they are in distress?' she asked.

Mortimer nodded. 'Someone wrote that on the table by my bed last night,' he said quietly. 'I thought perhaps *you* might have done so.'

She looked at him in wide-eyed astonishment.

'I? Oh, no.'

He was wrong then. A sharp pang of disappointment shot through him. He had been so sure – so sure. It was not often that his intuitions led him astray.

'You are quite certain?' he persisted.

'Oh, yes.'

They turned and went slowly together toward the house. Charlotte seemed preoccupied about something. She replied at random to the few observations he made. Suddenly she burst out in a low, hurried voice:

'It – it's odd your asking about those letters, SOS. I didn't write them, of course, but – I so easily might have done.'

He stopped and looked at her, and she went on quickly:

'It sounds silly, I know, but I have been so frightened, so dreadfully frightened, and when you came in last night, it seemed like an – an answer to something.'

'What are you frightened of?' he asked quickly.

'I don't know.'

'You don't know.'

'I think – it's the house. Ever since we came here it has been growing and growing. Everyone seems different somehow. Father, Mother, and Magdalen, they all seem different.'

Mortimer did not speak at once, and before he could do so, Charlotte went on again.

'You know this house is supposed to be haunted?'

'What?' All his interest was quickened.

'Yes, a man murdered his wife in it, oh, some years ago now. We only found out about it after we got here. Father says ghosts are all nonsense, but I – don't know.'

Mortimer was thinking rapidly.

'Tell me,' he said in a businesslike tone, 'was this murder committed in the room I had last night?'

'I don't know anything about that,' said Charlotte.

'I wonder now,' said Mortimer half to himself, 'yes, that may be it.'

Charlotte looked at him uncomprehendingly.

'Miss Dinmead,' said Mortimer, gently, 'have you ever had any reason to believe that you are mediumistic?'

She stared at him.

'I think you know that you *did* write SOS last night,' he said quietly. 'Oh! quite unconsciously, of course. A crime stains the atmosphere, so to speak. A sensitive mind such as yours might be acted upon in such a manner. You have been reproducing the sensations and impressions of the victim. Many years ago *she* may have written SOS on that table, and you unconsciously reproduced her act last night.'

Charlotte's face brightened.

'I see,' she said. 'You think that is the explanation?'

A voice called her from the house, and she went in leaving Mortimer to pace up and down the garden path. Was he satisfied with his own explanation? Did it cover the facts as he knew them? Did it account for the tension he had felt on entering the house last night?

Perhaps, and yet he still had the odd feeling that his sudden appearance had produced something very like consternation, he thought to himself:

'I must not be carried away by the psychic explanation, it might account for Charlotte – but not for the others. My coming has upset them horribly, all except Johnnie. What ever it is that's the matter, Johnnie is out of it.'

He was quite sure of that, strange that he should be so positive, but there it was.

At that minute, Johnnie himself came out of the cottage and approached the guest.

'Breakfast's ready,' he said awkwardly. 'Will you come in?'

Mortimer noticed that the lad's fingers were much stained. Johnnie felt his glance and laughed ruefully.

'I'm always messing about with chemicals, you know,' he said. 'It makes Dad awfully wild sometimes. He wants me to go into building, but I want to do chemistry and research work.'

Mr Dinsmead appeared at the window ahead of them, broad, jovial, smiling, and at sight of him all Mortimer's distrust and antagonism reawakened. Mrs Dinsmead was already seated at the table. She wished him 'Good morning' in her colourless voice, and he had again the impression that for some reason or other, she was afraid of him.

Magdalen came in last. She gave him a brief nod and took her seat opposite him.

'Did you sleep well?' she asked abruptly. 'Was your bed comfortable?'

She looked at him very earnestly, and when he replied courteously in the affirmative he noticed something very like a flicker of disappointment pass over her face. What had she expected him to say, he wondered?

He turned to his host.

'This lad of yours is interested in chemistry, it seems?' he said pleasantly.

There was a crash. Mrs Dinsmead had dropped her tea cup.

'Now then, Maggie, now then,' said her husband.

It seemed to Mortimer that there was admonition, warning, in his voice. He turned to his guest and spoke fluently of the advantages of the building trade, and of not letting young boys get above themselves.

After breakfast, he went out in the garden by himself, and smoked. The time was clearly at hand when he must leave the cottage. A night's shelter was one thing, to prolong it was difficult without an excuse, and what possible excuse could he offer? And yet he was singularly loath to depart.

Turning the thing over and over in his mind, he took a path that led round the other side of the house. His shoes were soled with crepe rubber, and made little or no noise. He was passing the kitchen window, when he heard Dinsmead's words from within, and the words attracted his attention immediately.

'It's a fair lump of money, it is.'

Mrs Dinsmead's voice answered. It was too faint in tone for Mortimer to hear the words, but Dinsmead replied:

'Nigh on £60,000, the lawyer said.'

Mortimer had no intention of eavesdropping, but he retraced his steps very thoughtfully. The mention of money seemed to crystallize the situation. Somewhere or other there was a question of £60,000 – it made the thing clearer – and uglier.

Magdalen came out of the house, but her father's voice called her almost immediately, and she went in again. Presently Dinsmead himself joined his guest.

'Rare good morning,' he said genially. 'I hope your car will be none the worse.'

'Wants to find out when I'm going,' thought Mortimer to himself.

Aloud he thanked Mr Dinsmead once more for his timely hospitality.

'Not at all, not at all,' said the other.

Magdalen and Charlotte came together out of the house, and strolled arm in arm to a rustic seat some little distance away. The dark head and the golden one made a pleasant contrast together, and on an impulse Mortimer said:

'Your daughters are very unalike, Mr Dinsmead.'

The other who was just lighting his pipe gave a sharp jerk of the wrist, and dropped the match.

'Do you think so?' he asked. 'Yes, well, I suppose they are.'

Mortimer had a flash of intuition.

'But of course they are not both your daughters,' he said smoothly.

He saw Dinsmead look at him, hesitate for a moment, and then make up his mind.

'That's very clever of you, sir,' he said. 'No, one of them is a foundling, we took her in as a baby and we have brought her up as our own. She herself has not the least idea of the truth, but she'll have to know soon.' He sighed.

'A question of inheritance?' suggested Mortimer quietly.

The other flashed a suspicious look at him.

Then he seemed to decide that frankness was best; his manner became almost aggressively frank and open.

'It's odd that you should say that, sir.'

'A case of telepathy, eh?' said Mortimer, and smiled.

'It is like this, sir. We took her in to oblige the mother – for a consideration, as at the time I was just starting in the building trade. A few months ago I noticed an advertisement in the papers, and it seemed to me that the child in question must be our Magdalen. I went to see the lawyers, and there has been a lot of talk one way and another. They were suspicious – naturally, as you might say, but everything is cleared up now. I am taking the girl herself to London next week, she doesn't know anything about it so far. Her father, it seems, was one of these rich Jewish gentlemen. He only learnt of the child's existence a few months before his death. He set agents on to try and trace her, and left all his money to her when she should be found.'

Mortimer listened with close attention. He had no reason to doubt Mr Dinsmead's story. It explained Magdalen's dark beauty; explained too, perhaps, her aloof manner. Nevertheless, though the story itself might be true, something lay behind it undivulged.

But Mortimer had no intention of rousing the other's suspicions. Instead, he must go out of his way to allay them.

'A very interesting story, Mr Dinsmead,' he said. 'I congratulate Miss Magdalen. An heiress and a beauty, she has a great time ahead of her.'

'She has that,' agreed her father warmly, 'and she's a rare good girl too, Mr Cleveland.'

There was every evidence of hearty warmth in his manner.

'Well,' said Mortimer, 'I must be pushing along now, I suppose. I have got to thank you once more, Mr Dinsmead, for your singularly well-timed hospitality.'

Accompanied by his host, he went into the house to bid farewell to Mrs Dinsmead. She was standing by the window with her back to them, and did not hear them enter. At her husband's jovial: 'Here's Mr Cleveland come to say goodbye,' she started nervously and swung round, dropping something which she held in her hand. Mortimer picked it up for her. It was a miniature of Charlotte done in the style of some twenty-five years ago. Mortimer repeated to her the thanks he had already proffered to her husband. He noticed again her look of fear and the furtive glances that she shot at him from beneath her eyelids.

The two girls were not in evidence, but it was not part of Mortimer's policy to seem anxious to see them; also he had his own idea, which was shortly to prove correct.

He had gone about half a mile from the house on his way down to where he had left the car the night before, when the bushes on the side of the path were thrust aside, and Magdalen came out on the track ahead of him.

'I had to see you,' she said.

'I expected you,' said Mortimer. 'It was you who wrote SOS on the table in my room last night, wasn't it?'

Magdalen nodded.

'Why?' asked Mortimer gently.

The girl turned aside and began pulling off leaves from a bush.

'I don't know,' she said, 'honestly, I don't know.'

'Tell me,' said Mortimer.

Magdalen drew a deep breath.

'I am a practical person,' she said, 'not the kind of person who imagines things or fancies them. You, I know, believe in ghosts and spirits. I don't, and when I tell you that there is something very wrong in that house,' she pointed up the hill, 'I mean that there is something tangibly wrong; it's not just an echo of the past. It has been coming on ever since we've been there. Every day it grows worse, Father is different, Mother is different, Charlotte is different.'

Mortimer interposed. 'Is Johnnie different?' he asked.

Magdalen looked at him, a dawning appreciation in her eyes. 'No,' she said, 'now I come to think of it. Johnnie is not different. He is the only one who's – who's untouched by it all. He was untouched last night at tea.'

'And you?' asked Mortimer.

'I was afraid – horribly afraid, just like a child – without knowing what it was I was afraid of. And father was – queer, there's no other word for it, queer. He talked about miracles and then I prayed – actually prayed for a miracle, and *you* knocked on the door.'

She stopped abruptly, staring at him.

'I seem mad to you, I suppose,' she said defiantly.

'No,' said Mortimer, 'on the contrary you seem extremely sane. All sane people have a premonition of danger if it is near them.'

'You don't understand,' said Magdalen. 'I was not afraid – for myself.'

'For whom, then?'

But again Magdalen shook her head in a puzzled fashion. 'I don't know.'

She went on:

'I wrote SOS on an impulse. I had an idea – absurd, no doubt, that they would not let me speak to you – the rest of them, I mean. I don't know what it was I meant to ask you to do. I don't know now.'

'Never mind,' said Mortimer. 'I shall do it.'

'What can you do?'

Mortimer smiled a little.

'I can think.'

She looked at him doubtfully.

'Yes,' said Mortimer, 'a lot can be done that way, more than you would ever believe. Tell me, was there any chance word or phrase that attracted your attention just before the meal last evening?'

Magdalen frowned. 'I don't think so,' she said. 'At least I heard Father say something to Mother about Charlotte being the living image of her, and he laughed in a very queer way, but – there's nothing odd in that, is there?'

'No,' said Mortimer slowly, 'except that Charlotte is not like your mother.'

He remained lost in thought for a minute or two, then looked up to find Magdalen watching him uncertainly.

'Go home, child,' he said, 'and don't worry; leave it in my hands.'

She went obediently up the path towards the cottage. Mortimer strolled on a little further, then threw himself down on the green turf. He closed his eyes, detached himself from conscious thought or effort, and let a series of pictures flit at will across his mind.

Johnnie! He always came back to Johnnie. Johnnie, completely innocent, utterly free from all the network of suspicion and intrigue, but nevertheless the pivot round which everything turned. He remembered the crash of Mrs Dinsmead's cup on her saucer at breakfast that morning. What had caused her agitation? A chance reference on his part to the lad's fondness for chemicals? At the moment he had not been conscious of Mr Dinsmead, but he saw him now clearly, as he sat, his teacup poised half way to his lips.

That took him back to Charlotte, as he had seen her when the door opened last night. She had sat staring at him over the rim of her teacup. And swiftly on that followed another memory. Mr Dinsmead emptying teacups one after the other, and saying 'this tea is cold'.

He remembered the steam that went up. Surely the tea had not been so very cold after all?

Something began to stir in his brain. A memory of something read not so very long ago, within a month perhaps. Some account of a whole family poisoned by a lad's carelessness. A packet of arsenic left in the larder had all dripped through on the bread below. He had read it in the paper. Probably Mr Dinsmead had read it too.

Things began to grow clearer . . .

Half an hour later, Mortimer Cleveland rose briskly to his feet.

It was evening once more in the cottage. The eggs were poached tonight and there was a tin of brawn. Presently Mrs Dinsmead came in from the kitchen bearing the big teapot. The family took their places round the table.

'A contrast to last night's weather,' said Mrs Dinsmead, glancing towards the window.

'Yes,' said Mr Dinsmead, 'it's so still tonight that you could hear a pin drop. Now then, Mother, pour out, will you?'

Mrs Dinsmead filled the cups and handed them round the table. Then, as she put the teapot down, she gave a sudden little cry and pressed her hand to her heart. Mr Dinsmead swung round his chair, following the direction of her terrified eyes. Mortimer Cleveland was standing in the doorway.

He came forward. His manner was pleasant and apologetic.

'I'm afraid I startled you,' he said. 'I had to come back for something.'

'Back for something,' cried Mr Dinsmead. His face was purple, his veins swelling. 'Back for what, I should like to know?'

'Some tea,' said Mortimer.

With a swift gesture he took something from his pocket, and, taking up one of the teacups from the table, emptied some of its contents into a little test-tube he held in his left hand.

'What – what are you doing?' gasped Mr Dinsmead. His face had gone chalky-white, the purple dying out as if by magic. Mrs Dinsmead gave a thin, high, frightened cry.

'You read the papers, I think, Mr Dinsmead? I am sure you do. Sometimes one reads accounts of a whole family being poisoned, some of them recover, some do not. In this case, *one would not*. The first explanation would be the tinned brawn you were eating, but supposing the doctor to be a suspicious man, not easily taken in by the tinned food theory? There is a packet of arsenic in your larder. On the shelf below it is a packet of tea. There is a convenient hole in the top shelf, what more natural to suppose then that the arsenic found its way into the tea by accident? Your son Johnnie might be blamed for carelessness, nothing more.'

'I – I don't know what you mean,' gasped Dinsmead.

'I think you do,' Mortimer took up a second teacup and filled a second test-tube. He fixed a red label to one and a blue label to the other.

'The red-labelled one,' he said, 'contains tea from your daughter Charlotte's cup, the other from your daughter Magdalen's. I am prepared to swear that in the first I shall find four or five times the amount of arsenic than in the latter.'

'You are mad,' said Dinsmead.

'Oh! dear me, no. I am nothing of the kind. You told me today, Mr Dinsmead, that Magdalen *is* your daughter. Charlotte was the child you adopted, the child who was so like her mother that when I held a miniature of that mother in my hand today I mistook it for one of Charlotte herself. Your own daughter was to inherit the fortune, and since it might be impossible to keep your supposed daughter Charlotte out of sight, and someone who knew the mother might have realized the truth of the resemblance, you decided on, well – a pinch of white arsenic at the bottom of a teacup.'

Mrs Dinsmead gave a sudden high cackle, rocking herself to and fro in violent hysterics.

'Tea,' she squeaked, 'that's what he said, tea, not lemonade.'

'Hold your tongue, can't you?' roared her husband wrathfully.

Mortimer saw Charlotte looking at him, wide-eyed, wondering, across the table. Then he felt a hand on his arm, and Magdalen dragged him out of earshot.

'Those,' she pointed at the phials – 'Daddy. You won't –'

Mortimer laid his hand on her shoulder. 'My child,' he said, 'you don't believe in the past. I do. I believe in the atmosphere of this house. If he had not come to it, perhaps – I say *perhaps* – your father might not have conceived the plan he did. I keep these two test-tubes to safeguard Charlotte now and in the future. Apart from that, I shall do nothing, in gratitude, if you will, to that hand that wrote SOS.'

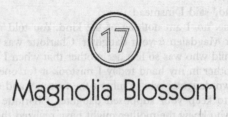

Magnolia Blossom

'Magnolia Blossom' was first published in *Royal Magazine*, March 1926.

Vincent Easton was waiting under the clock at Victoria Station. Now and then he glanced up at it uneasily. He thought to himself: 'How many other men have waited here for a woman who didn't come?'

A sharp pang shot through him. Supposing that Theo didn't come, that she had changed her mind? Women did that sort of thing. Was he sure of her – had he ever been sure of her? Did he really know anything at all about her? Hadn't she puzzled him from the first? There had seemed to be two women – the lovely, laughing creature who was Richard Darrell's wife, and the other – silent, mysterious, who had walked by his side in the garden of Haymer's Close. Like a magnolia flower – that was how he thought of her – perhaps because it was under the magnolia tree that they had tasted their first rapturous, incredulous kiss. The air had been sweet with the scent of magnolia bloom, and one or two petals, velvety-soft and fragrant, had floated down, resting on that upturned face that was as creamy and as soft and as silent as they. Magnolia blossom – exotic, fragrant, mysterious.

That had been a fortnight ago – the second day he had met her. And now he was waiting for her to come to him forever. Again incredulity shot through him. She wouldn't come. How could he ever have believed it? It would be giving up so much. The beautiful Mrs Darrell couldn't do this sort of thing quietly. It was bound to be a nine days' wonder, a far-reaching scandal that would never quite be forgotten. There were better, more expedient ways of doing these things – a discreet divorce, for instance.

But they had never thought of that for a moment – at least he had not. Had she, he wondered? He had never known anything of her thoughts. He had asked her to come away with him almost timorously – for after all, what was he? Nobody in particular – one of a thousand orange growers in the Transvaal. What a life to take her to – after the brilliance of London!

And yet, since he wanted her so desperately, he must needs ask.

She had consented very quietly, with no hesitations or protests, as though it were the simplest thing in the world that he was asking her.

'Tomorrow?' he had said, amazed, almost unbelieving.

And she had promised in that soft, broken voice that was so different from the laughing brilliance of her social manner. He had compared her to a diamond when he first saw her – a thing of flashing fire, reflecting light from a hundred facets. But at that first touch, that first kiss, she had changed miraculously to the clouded softness of a pearl – a pearl like a magnolia blossom, creamy-pink.

She had promised. And now he was waiting for her to fulfil that promise.

He looked again at the clock. If she did not come soon, they would miss the train.

Sharply a wave of reaction set in. She wouldn't come! Of course she wouldn't come. Fool that he had been ever to expect it! What were promises? He would find a letter when he got back to his rooms – explaining, protesting, saying all the things that women do when they are excusing themselves for lack of courage.

He felt anger – anger and the bitterness of frustration.

Then he saw her coming towards him down the platform, a faint smile on her face. She walked slowly, without haste or fluster, as one who had all eternity before her. She was in black – soft black that clung, with a little black hat that framed the wonderful creamy pallor of her face.

He found himself grasping her hand, muttering stupidly:

'So you've come – you have come. After all!'

'Of course.'

How calm her voice sounded! How calm!

'I thought you wouldn't,' he said, releasing her hand and breathing hard.

Her eyes opened – wide, beautiful eyes. There was wonder in them, the simple wonder of a child.

'Why?'

He didn't answer. Instead he turned aside and requisitioned a passing porter. They had not much time. The next few minutes were all bustle and confusion. Then they were sitting in their reserved compartment and the drab houses of southern London were drifting by them.

Theodora Darrell was sitting opposite him. At last she was his. And he knew now how incredulous, up to the very last minute, he had been. He had not dared to let himself believe. That magical, elusive quality about her had frightened him. It had seemed impossible that she should ever belong to him.

Now the suspense was over. The irrevocable step was taken. He looked across at her. She lay back in the corner, quite still. The faint smile lingered on her lips, her eyes were cast down, the long, black lashes swept the creamy curve of her cheek.

He thought: 'What's in her mind now? What is she thinking of? Me? Her husband? What does she think about him anyway? Did she care for him once? Or did she never care? Does she hate him, or is she indifferent to him?' And with a pang the thought swept through him: 'I don't know. I never shall know. I love her, and I don't know anything about her — what she thinks or what she feels.'

His mind circled round the thought of Theodora Darrell's husband. He had known plenty of married women who were only too ready to talk about their husbands — of how they were misunderstood by them, of how their finer feelings were ignored. Vincent Easton reflected cynically that it was one of the best-known opening gambits.

But except casually, Theo had never spoken of Richard Darrell. Easton knew of him what everybody knew. He was a popular man, handsome, with an engaging, carefree manner. Everybody liked Darrell. His wife always seemed on excellent terms with him. But that proved nothing, Vincent reflected. Theo was well-bred — she would not air her grievances in public.

And between them, no word had passed. From that second evening of their meeting, when they had walked together in the garden, silent, their shoulders touching, and he had felt the faint tremor that shook her at his touch, there had been no explainings, no defining of the position. She had returned his kisses, a dumb, trembling creature, shorn of all that hard brilliance which, together with her cream-and-rose beauty, had made her famous. Never once had she spoken of her husband. Vincent had been thankful for that at the time. He had been glad to be spared the arguments of a woman who wished to assure herself and her lover that they were justified in yielding to their love.

Yet now the tacit conspiracy of silence worried him. He had again that panic-stricken sense of knowing nothing about this strange creature who was willingly linking her life to his. He was afraid.

In the impulse to reassure himself, he bent forward and laid a hand on the black-clad knee opposite him. He felt once again the faint tremor that shook her, and he reached up for her hand. Bending forward, he kissed the palm, a long, lingering kiss. He felt the response of her fingers on his and, looking up, met her eyes, and was content.

He leaned back in his seat. For the moment, he wanted no more. They were together. She was his. And presently he said in a light, almost bantering tone:

'You're very silent?'

'Am I?'

'Yes.' He waited a minute, then said in a graver tone: 'You're sure you don't – regret?'

Her eyes opened wide at that. 'Oh, no!'

He did not doubt the reply. There was an assurance of sincerity behind it.

'What are you thinking about? I want to know.'

In a low voice she answered: 'I think I'm afraid.'

'Afraid?'

'Of happiness.'

He moved over beside her then, held her to him and kissed the softness of her face and neck.

'I love you,' he said. 'I love you – love you.'

Her answer was in the clinging of her body, the abandon of her lips.

Then he moved back to his own corner. He picked up a magazine and so did she. Every now and then, over the top of the magazines, their eyes met. Then they smiled.

They arrived at Dover just after five. They were to spend the night there, and cross to the Continent on the following day. Theo entered their sitting room in the hotel with Vincent close behind her. He had a couple of evening papers in his hand which he threw down on the table. Two of the hotel servants brought in the luggage and withdrew.

Theo turned from the window where she had been standing looking out. In another minute they were in each other's arms.

There was a discreet tap on the door and they drew apart again.

'Damn it all,' said Vincent, 'it doesn't seem as though we were ever going to be alone.'

Theo smiled. 'It doesn't look like it,' she said softly. Sitting down on the sofa, she picked up one of the papers.

The knock proved to be a waiter bearing tea. He laid it on the table, drawing the latter up to the sofa on which Theo was sitting, cast a deft glance round, inquired if there were anything further, and withdrew.

Vincent, who had gone into the adjoining room, came back into the sitting room.

'Now for tea,' he said cheerily, but stopped suddenly in the middle of the room. 'Anything wrong?' he asked.

Theo was sitting bolt upright on the sofa. She was staring in front of her with dazed eyes, and her face had gone deathly white.

Vincent took a quick step towards her.

'What is it, sweetheart?'

For answer she held out the paper to him, her finger pointing to the headline.

Vincent took the paper from her. 'FAILURE OF HOBSON, JEKYLL AND LUCAS,' he read. The name of the big city firm conveyed nothing to him at the moment, though he had an irritating conviction in the back of his mind that it ought to do so. He looked inquiringly at Theo.

'Richard is Hobson, Jekyll and Lucas,' she explained.

'Your husband?'

'Yes.'

Vincent returned to the paper and read the bald information it conveyed carefully. Phrases such as 'sudden crash', 'serious revelations to follow', 'other houses affected' struck him disagreeably.

Roused by a movement, he looked up. Theo was adjusting her little black hat in front of the mirror. She turned at the movement he made. Her eyes looked steadily into his.

'Vincent – I must go to Richard.'

He sprang up.

'Theo – don't be absurd.'

She repeated mechanically:

'I must go to Richard.'

'But, my dear –'

She made a gesture towards the paper on the floor.

'That means ruin – bankruptcy. I can't choose this day of all others to leave him.'

'You had left him before you heard of this. Be reasonable!'

She shook her head mournfully.

'You don't understand. I must go to Richard.'

And from that he could not move her. Strange that a creature so soft, so pliant, could be so unyielding. After the first, she did not argue. She let him say what he had to say unhindered. He held her in his arms, seeking to break her will by enslaving her senses, but though her soft mouth returned his kisses, he felt in her something aloof and invincible that withstood all his pleadings.

He let her go at last, sick and weary of the vain endeavour. From pleading he had turned to bitterness, reproaching her with never having loved him. That, too, she took in silence, without protest, her face, dumb and pitiful, giving the lie to his words. Rage mastered him in the end; he hurled at her every cruel word he could think of, seeking only to bruise and batter her to her knees.

At last the words gave out; there was nothing more to say. He sat, his head in his hands, staring down at the red pile carpet. By the door, Theodora stood, a black shadow with a white face.

It was all over.

She said quietly: 'Goodbye, Vincent.'

He did not answer.

The door opened – and shut again.

The Darrells lived in a house in Chelsea – an intriguing, old-world house, standing in a little garden of its own. Up the front of the house grew a magnolia tree, smutty, dirty, begrimed, but still a magnolia.

Theo looked up at it, as she stood on the doorstep some three hours later. A sudden smile twisted her mouth in pain.

She went straight to the study at the back of the house. A man was pacing up and down in the room – a young man, with a handsome face and a haggard expression.

He gave an ejaculation of relief as she came in.

'Thank God you've turned up, Theo. They said you'd taken your luggage with you and gone off out of town somewhere.'

'I heard the news and came back.'

Richard Darrell put an arm about her and drew her to the couch. They sat down upon it side by side. Theo drew herself free of the encircling arm in what seemed a perfectly natural manner.

'How bad is it, Richard?' she asked quietly.

'Just as bad as it can be – and that's saying a lot.'

'Tell me!'

He began to walk up and down again as he talked. Theo sat and watched him. He was not to know that every now and then the room went dim, and his voice faded from her hearing, while another room in a hotel at Dover came clearly before her eyes.

Nevertheless she managed to listen intelligently enough. He came back and sat down on the couch by her.

'Fortunately,' he ended, 'they can't touch your marriage settlement. The house is yours also.'

Theo nodded thoughtfully.

'We shall have that at any rate,' she said. 'Then things will not be too bad? It means a fresh start, that is all.'

'Oh! Quite so. Yes.'

But his voice did not ring true, and Theo thought suddenly: 'There's something else. He hasn't told me everything.'

'There's nothing more, Richard?' she said gently. 'Nothing worse?'

He hesitated for just half a second, then: 'Worse? What should there be?'

'I don't know,' said Theo.

'It'll be all right,' said Richard, speaking more as though to reassure himself than Theo. 'Of course, it'll be all right.'

He flung an arm about her suddenly.

'I'm glad you're here,' he said. 'It'll be all right now that you're here. Whatever else happens, I've got you, haven't I?'

She said gently: 'Yes, you've got me.' And this time she left his arm round her.

He kissed her and held her close to him, as though in some strange way he derived comfort from her nearness.

'I've got you, Theo,' he said again presently, and she answered as before: 'Yes, Richard.'

He slipped from the couch to the floor at her feet.

'I'm tired out,' he said fretfully. 'My God, it's been a day. Awful! I don't know what I should do if you weren't here. After all, one's wife is one's wife, isn't she?'

She did not speak, only bowed her head in assent.

He laid his head on her lap. The sigh he gave was like that of a tired child.

Theo thought again: 'There's something he hasn't told me. What is it?'

Mechanically her hand dropped to his smooth, dark head, and she stroked it gently, as a mother might comfort a child.

Richard murmured vaguely:

'It'll be all right now you're here. You won't let me down.'

His breathing grew slow and even. He slept. Her hand still smoothed his head.

But her eyes looked steadily into the darkness in front of her, seeing nothing.

'Don't you think, Richard,' said Theodora, 'that you'd better tell me everything?'

It was three days later. They were in the drawing room before dinner.

Richard started, and flushed.

'I don't know what you mean,' he parried.

'Don't you?'

He shot a quick glance at her.

'Of course there are – well – details.'

'I ought to know everything, don't you think, if I am to help?'

He looked at her strangely.

'What makes you think I want you to help?'

She was a little astonished.

'My dear Richard, I'm your wife.'

He smiled suddenly, the old, attractive, carefree smile.

'So you are, Theo. And a very good-looking wife, too. I never could stand ugly women.'

He began walking up and down the room, as was his custom when something was worrying him.

'I won't deny you're right in a way,' he said presently. 'There is something.'

He broke off.

'Yes?'

'It's so damned hard to explain things of this kind to women. They get hold of the wrong end of the stick – fancy a thing is – well, what it isn't.'

Theo said nothing.

'You see,' went on Richard, 'the law's one thing, and right and wrong are quite another. I may do a thing that's perfectly right and honest, but the law wouldn't take the same view of it. Nine times out of ten, everything pans out all right, and the tenth time you – well, hit a snag.'

Theo began to understand. She thought to herself: 'Why am I not surprised? Did I always know, deep down, that he wasn't straight?'

Richard went on talking. He explained himself at unnecessary lengths. Theo was content for him to cloak the actual details of the affair in this mantle of verbosity. The matter concerned a large tract of South African property. Exactly what Richard had done, she was not concerned to know. Morally, he assured her, everything was fair and above board; legally – well, there it was; no getting away from the fact, he had rendered himself liable to criminal prosecution.

He kept shooting quick glances at his wife as he talked. He was nervous and uncomfortable. And still he excused himself and tried to explain away that which a child might have seen in its naked truth. Then finally in a burst of justification, he broke down. Perhaps Theo's eyes, momentarily scornful, had something to do with it. He sank down in a chair by the fireplace, his head in his hands.

'There it is, Theo,' he said brokenly, 'What are you going to do about it?'

She came over to him with scarcely a moment's pause and, kneeling down by the chair, put her face against his.

'What can be done, Richard? What can we do?'

He caught her to him.

'You mean it? You'll stick to me?'

'Of course. My dear, of course.'

He said, moved to sincerity in spite of himself: 'I'm a thief, Theo. That's what it means, shorn of fine language – just a thief.'

'Then I'm a thief's wife, Richard. We'll sink or swim together.'

They were silent for a little while. Presently Richard recovered something of his jaunty manner.

'You know, Theo, I've got a plan, but we'll talk of that later. It's just on dinnertime. We must go and change. Put on that creamy thingummybob of yours, you know – the Caillot model.'

Theo raised her eyebrows quizzically.

'For an evening at home?'

'Yes, yes, I know. But I like it. Put it on, there's a good girl. It cheers me up to see you looking your best.'

Theo came down to dinner in the Caillot. It was a creation in creamy brocade, with a faint pattern of gold running through it and an undernote of pale pink to give warmth to the cream. It was cut daringly low in the back, and nothing could have been better designed to show off the dazzling whiteness of Theo's neck and shoulders. She was truly now a magnolia flower.

Richard's eye rested upon her in warm approval. 'Good girl. You know, you look simply stunning in that dress.'

They went in to dinner. Throughout the evening Richard was nervous and unlike himself, joking and laughing about nothing at all, as if in a vain attempt to shake off his cares. Several times Theo tried to lead him back to the subject they had been discussing before, but he edged away from it.

Then suddenly, as she rose to go to bed, he came to the point.

'No, don't go yet. I've got something to say. You know, about this miserable business.'

She sat down again.

He began talking rapidly. With a bit of luck, the whole thing could be hushed up. He had covered his tracks fairly well. So long as certain papers didn't get into the receiver's hands –

He stopped significantly.

'Papers?' asked Theo perplexedly. 'You mean you will destroy them?'

Richard made a grimace.

'I'd destroy them fast enough if I could get hold of them. That's the devil of it all!'

'Who has them, then?'

'A man we both know – Vincent Easton.'

A very faint exclamation escaped Theo. She forced it back, but Richard had noticed it.

'I've suspected he knew something of the business all along. That's why I've asked him here a good bit. You may remember that I asked you to be nice to him?'

'I remember,' said Theo.

'Somehow I never seem to have got on really friendly terms with him. Don't know why. But he likes you. I should say he likes you a good deal.'

Theo said in a very clear voice: 'He does.'

'Ah!' said Richard appreciatively. 'That's good. Now you see what I'm driving at. I'm convinced that if you went to Vincent Easton and asked him to give you those papers, he wouldn't refuse. Pretty woman, you know – all that sort of thing.'

'I can't do that,' said Theo quickly.

'Nonsense.'

'It's out of the question.'

The red came slowly out in blotches on Richard's face. She saw that he was angry.

'My dear girl, I don't think you quite realize the position. If this comes out, I'm liable to go to prison. It's ruin – disgrace.'

'Vincent Easton will not use those papers against you. I am sure of that.'

'That's not quite the point. He mayn't realize that they incriminate me. It's only taken in conjunction with – with my affairs – with the figures they're bound to find. Oh! I can't go into details. He'll ruin me without knowing what he's doing unless somebody puts the position before him.'

'You can do that yourself, surely. Write to him.'

'A fat lot of good that would be! No, Theo, we've only got one hope. You're the trump card. You're my wife. You must help me. Go to Easton tonight –'

A cry broke from Theo.

'Not tonight. Tomorrow perhaps.'

'My God, Theo, can't you realize things? Tomorrow may be too late. If you could go now – at once – to Easton's rooms.' He saw her flinch, and tried to reassure her. 'I know, my dear girl, I know. It's a beastly thing to do. But it's life or death. Theo, you won't fail me? You said you'd do anything to help me –'

Theo heard herself speaking in a hard, dry voice. 'Not this thing. There are reasons.'

'It's life or death, Theo. I mean it. See here.'

He snapped open a drawer of the desk and took out a revolver. If there was something theatrical about that action, it escaped her notice.

'It's that or shooting myself. I can't face the racket. If you won't do as I ask, I'll be a dead man before morning. I swear to you solemnly that that's the truth.'

Theo gave a low cry. 'No, Richard, not that!'

'Then help me.'

He flung the revolver down on the table and knelt by her side. 'Theo my darling – if you love me – if you've ever loved me – do this for me. You're my wife, Theo, I've no one else to turn to.'

On and on his voice went, murmuring, pleading. And at last Theo heard her own voice saying: 'Very well – yes.'

Richard took her to the door and put her into a taxi.

'Theo!'

Vincent Easton sprang up in incredulous delight. She stood in the doorway. Her wrap of white ermine was hanging from her shoulders. Never, Easton thought, had she looked so beautiful.

'You've come after all.'

She put out a hand to stop him as he came towards her.

'No, Vincent, this isn't what you think.'

She spoke in a low, hurried voice.

'I'm here from my husband. He thinks there are some papers which may – do him harm. I have come to ask you to give them to me.'

Vincent stood very still, looking at her. Then he gave a short laugh.

'So that's it, is it? I thought Hobson, Jekyll and Lucas sounded familiar the other day, but I couldn't place them at the minute. Didn't know your husband was connected with the firm. Things have been going wrong there for some time. I was commissioned to look into the matter. I suspected some underling. Never thought of the man at the top.'

Theo said nothing. Vincent looked at her curiously.

'It makes no difference to you, this?' he asked. 'That – well, to put it plainly, that your husband's a swindler?'

She shook her head.

'It beats me,' said Vincent. Then he added quietly: 'Will you wait a minute or two? I will get the papers.'

Theo sat down in a chair. He went into the other room. Presently he returned and delivered a small package into her hand.

'Thank you,' said Theo. 'Have you a match?'

Taking the matchbox he proffered, she knelt down by the fireplace. When the papers were reduced to a pile of ashes, she stood up.

'Thank you,' she said again.

'Not at all,' he answered formally. 'Let me get you a taxi.'

He put her into it, saw her drive away. A strange, formal little interview. After the first, they had not even dared look at each other. Well, that was that, the end. He would go away, abroad, try and forget.

Theo leaned her head out of the window and spoke to the taxi driver. She could not go back at once to the house in Chelsea. She must have a breathing space. Seeing Vincent again had shaken her horribly. If only – if only. But she pulled herself up. Love for her husband she had none – but she owed him loyalty. He was down, she must stick by him. Whatever else he might have done, he loved her; his offence had been committed against society, not against her.

The taxi meandered on through the wide streets of Hampstead. They came out on the heath, and a breath of cool, invigorating air fanned Theo's cheeks. She had herself in hand again now. The taxi sped back towards Chelsea.

Richard came out to meet her in the hall.

'Well,' he demanded, 'you've been a long time.'

'Have I?'

'Yes – a very long time. Is it – all right?'

He followed her, a cunning look in his eyes. His hands were shaking.

'It's – it's all right, eh?' he said again.

'I burnt them myself.'

'Oh!'

She went on into the study, sinking into a big armchair. Her face was dead white and her whole body drooped with fatigue. She thought to herself: 'If only I could go to sleep now and never, never wake up again!'

Richard was watching her. His glance, shy, furtive, kept coming and going. She noticed nothing. She was beyond noticing.

'It went off quite all right, eh?'

'I've told you so.'

'You're sure they were the right papers? Did you look?'

'No.'

'But then –'

'I'm sure, I tell you. Don't bother me, Richard. I can't bear any more tonight.'

Richard shifted nervously.

'No, no. I see.'

He fidgeted about the room. Presently he came over to her, laid a hand on her shoulder. She shook it off.

'Don't touch me.' She tried to laugh. 'I'm sorry, Richard. My nerves are on edge. I feel I can't bear to be touched.'

'I know. I understand.'

Again he wandered up and down.

'Theo,' he burst out suddenly. 'I'm damned sorry.'

'What?' She looked up, vaguely startled.

'I oughtn't to have let you go there at this time of night. I never dreamed that you'd be subjected to any – unpleasantness.'

'Unpleasantness?' She laughed. The word seemed to amuse her. 'You don't know! Oh, Richard, you don't know!'

'I don't know what?'

She said very gravely, looking straight in front of her: 'What this night has cost me.'

'My God! Theo! I never meant – You – you did that, for me? The swine! Theo – Theo – I couldn't have known. I couldn't have guessed. My God!'

He was kneeling by her now stammering, his arms round her, and she turned and looked at him with faint surprise, as though his words had at last really penetrated to her attention.

'I – I never meant –'

'You never meant what, Richard?'

Her voice startled him.

'Tell me. What was it that you never meant?'

'Theo, don't let us speak of it. I don't want to know. I want never to think of it.'

She was staring at him, wide awake now, with every faculty alert. Her words came clear and distinct:

'You never meant – What do you think happened?'

'It didn't happen, Theo. Let's say it didn't happen.'

And still she stared, till the truth began to come to her.

'You think that –'

'I don't want –'

She interrupted him: 'You think that Vincent Easton asked a price for those letters? You think that I – paid him?'

Richard said weakly and unconvincingly: 'I – I never dreamed he was that kind of man.'

'Didn't you?' She looked at him searchingly. His eyes fell before hers. 'Why did you ask me to put on this dress this evening? Why did you send me there alone at this time of night? You guessed he – cared for me. You wanted to save your skin – save it at any cost – even at the cost of my honour.' She got up.

'I see now. You meant that from the beginning – or at least you saw it as a possibility, and it didn't deter you.'

'Theo –'

'You can't deny it. Richard, I thought I knew all there was to know about you years ago. I've known almost from the first that you weren't straight as regards the world. But I thought you were straight with me.'

'Theo –'

'Can you deny what I've just been saying?'

He was silent, in spite of himself.

'Listen, Richard. There is something I must tell you. Three days ago when this blow fell on you, the servants told you I was away – gone to the country. That was only partly true. I had gone away with Vincent Easton –'

Richard made an inarticulate sound. She held out a hand to stop him.

'Wait. We were at Dover. I saw a paper – I realized what had happened. Then, as you know, I came back.'

She paused.

Richard caught her by the wrist. His eyes burnt into hers.

'You came back – in time?'

Theo gave a short, bitter laugh.

'Yes, I came back, as you say, "in time", Richard.'

Her husband relinquished his hold on her arm. He stood by the mantelpiece, his head thrown back. He looked handsome and rather noble.

'In that case,' he said, 'I can forgive.'

'I cannot.'

The two words came crisply. They had the semblance and the effect of a bomb in the quiet room. Richard started forward, staring, his jaw dropped with an almost ludicrous effect.

'You – er – what did you say, Theo?'

'I said I cannot forgive! In leaving you for another man. I sinned – not technically, perhaps, but in intention, which is the same thing. But if I sinned, I sinned through love. You, too, have not been faithful to me since our marriage. Oh, yes, I know. That I forgave, because I really believed in your love for me. But the thing you have done tonight is different. It is an ugly thing, Richard – a thing no woman should forgive. You sold me, your own wife, to purchase safety!'

She picked up her wrap and turned towards the door.

'Theo,' he stammered out, 'where are you going?'

She looked back over her shoulder at him.

'We all have to pay in this life, Richard. For my sin I must pay in loneliness. For yours – well, you gambled with the thing you love, and you have lost it!'

'You are going?'

She drew a long breath.

'To freedom. There is nothing to bind me here.'

He heard the door shut. Ages passed, or was it a few minutes? Something fluttered down outside the window – the last of the magnolia petals, soft, fragrant.

The Lonely God

'The Lonely God' was first published in *Royal Magazine*, July 1926.

He stood on a shelf in the British Museum, alone and forlorn amongst a company of obviously more important deities. Ranged round the four walls, these greater personages all seemed to display an overwhelming sense of their own superiority. The pedestal of each was duly inscribed with the land and race that had been proud to possess him. There was no doubt of their position; they were divinities of importance and recognized as such.

Only the little god in the corner was aloof and remote from their company. Roughly hewn out of grey stone, his features almost totally obliterated by time and exposure, he sat there in isolation, his elbows on his knees, and his head buried in his hands; a lonely little god in a strange country.

There was no inscription to tell the land whence he came. He was indeed lost, without honour or renown, a pathetic little figure very far from home. No one noticed him, no one stopped to look at him. Why should they? He was so insignificant, a block of grey stone in a corner. On either side of him were two Mexican gods worn smooth with age, placid idols with folded hands, and cruel mouths curved in a smile that showed openly their contempt of humanity. There was also a rotund, violently self-assertive little god, with a clenched fist, who evidently suffered from a swollen sense of his own importance, but passers-by stopped to give him a glance sometimes, even if it was only to laugh at the contrast of his absurd pomposity with the smiling indifference of his Mexican companions.

And the little lost god sat on there hopelessly, his head in his hands, as he had sat year in and year out, till one day the impossible happened, and he found – a worshipper.

* * *

'Any letters for me?'

The hall porter removed a packet of letters from a pigeon-hole, gave a cursory glance through them, and said in a wooden voice:

'Nothing for you, sir.'

Frank Oliver sighed as he walked out of the club again. There was no particular reason why there should have been anything for him. Very few people wrote to him. Ever since he had returned from Burma in the spring, he had become conscious of a growing and increasing loneliness.

Frank Oliver was a man just over forty, and the last eighteen years of his life had been spent in various parts of the globe, with brief furloughs in England. Now that he had retired and come home to live for good, he realized for the first time how very much alone in the world he was.

True, there was his sister Greta, married to a Yorkshire clergyman, very busy with parochial duties and the bringing up of a family of small children. Greta was naturally very fond of her only brother, but equally naturally she had very little time to give him. Then there was his old friend Tom Hurley. Tom was married to a nice, bright, cheerful girl, very energetic and practical, of whom Frank was secretly afraid. She told him brightly that he must not be a crabbed old bachelor, and was always producing 'nice girls'. Frank Oliver found that he never had anything to say to these 'nice girls'; they persevered with him for a while, then gave him up as hopeless.

And yet he was not really unsociable. He had a great longing for companionship and sympathy, and ever since he had been back in England he had become aware of a growing discouragement. He had been away too long, he was out of tune with the times. He spent long, aimless days wandering about, wondering what on earth he was to do with himself next.

It was on one of these days that he strolled into the British Museum. He was interested in Asiatic curiosities, and so it was that he chanced upon the lonely god. Its charm held him at once. Here was something vaguely akin to himself; here, too, was someone lost and astray in a strange land. He became in the habit of paying frequent visits to the Museum, just to glance in on the little grey stone figure, in its obscure place on the high shelf.

'Rough luck on the little chap,' he thought to himself. 'Probably had a lot of fuss made about him once, kow-towing and offerings and all the rest of it.'

He had begun to feel such a proprietary right in his little friend (it really almost amounted to a sense of actual ownership) that he was inclined to be resentful when he found that the little god had made a second conquest. *He* had discovered the lonely god; nobody else, he felt, had a right to interfere.

But after the first flash of indignation, he was forced to smile at himself. For this second worshipper was such a little bit of a thing, such a ridiculous, pathetic creature, in a shabby black coat and skirt that had seen its best days. She was young, a little over twenty he should judge, with fair hair and blue eyes, and a wistful droop to her mouth.

Her hat especially appealed to his chivalry. She had evidently trimmed it herself, and it made such a brave attempt to be smart that its failure was pathetic. She was obviously a lady, though a poverty-stricken one, and he immediately decided in his own mind that she was a governess and alone in the world.

He soon found out that her days for visiting the god were Tuesdays and Fridays, and she always arrived at ten o'clock, as soon as the Museum was open. At first he disliked her intrusion, but little by little it began to form one of the principal interests of his monotonous life. Indeed, the fellow devotee was fast ousting the object of devotion from his position of pre-eminence. The days that he did not see the 'Little Lonely Lady', as he called her to himself, were blank.

Perhaps she, too, was equally interested in him, though she endeavoured to conceal the fact with studious unconcern. But little by little a sense of fellowship was slowly growing between them, though as yet they had exchanged no spoken word. The truth of the matter was, the man was too shy! He argued to himself that very likely she had not even noticed him (some inner sense gave the lie to that instantly), that she would consider it a great impertinence, and, finally, that he had not the least idea what to say.

But Fate, or the little god, was kind and sent him an inspiration – or what he regarded as such. With infinite delight in his own cunning, he purchased a woman's handkerchief, a frail little affair of cambric and lace which he almost feared to touch, and, thus armed, he followed her as she departed and stopped her in the Egyptian room.

'Excuse me, but is this yours?' He tried to speak with airy unconcern, and signally failed.

The Lonely Lady took it, and made a pretence of examining it with minute care.

'No, it is not mine.' She handed it back, and added, with what he felt guiltily was a suspicious glance: 'It's quite a new one. The price is still on it.'

But he was unwilling to admit that he had been found out. He started on an over-plausible flow of explanation.

'You see, I picked it up under that big case. It was just by the farthest leg of it.' He derived great relief from this detailed account. 'So, as you had been standing there, I thought it must be yours and came after you with it.'

She said again: 'No, it isn't mine,' and added, as if with a sense of ungraciousness, 'thank you.'

The conversation came to an awkward standstill. The girl stood there, pink and embarrassed, evidently uncertain how to retreat with dignity.

He made a desperate effort to take advantage of his opportunity.

'I – I didn't know there was anyone else in London who cared for our little lonely god till you came.'

She answered eagerly, forgetting her reserve:

'Do *you* call him that too?'

Apparently, if she had noticed his pronoun, she did not resent it. She had been startled into sympathy, and his quiet 'Of course!' seemed the most natural rejoinder in the world.

Again there was a silence, but this time it was a silence born of understanding.

It was the Lonely Lady who broke it in a sudden remembrance of the conventionalities.

She drew herself up to her full height, and with an almost ridiculous assumption of dignity for so small a person, she observed in chilling accents:

'I must be going now. Good morning.' And with a slight, stiff inclination of her head, she walked away, holding herself very erect.

By all acknowledged standards Frank Oliver ought to have felt rebuffed, but it is a regrettable sign of his rapid advance in depravity that he merely murmured to himself: 'Little darling!'

He was soon to repent of his temerity, however. For ten days his little lady never came near the Museum. He was in despair! He had frightened her away! She would never come back! He was a brute, a villain! He would never see her again!

In his distress he haunted the British Museum all day long. She might merely have changed her time of coming. He soon began to know the adjacent rooms by heart, and he contracted a lasting hatred of mummies. The guardian policeman observed him with suspicion when he spent three hours poring over Assyrian hieroglyphics, and the contemplation of endless vases of all ages nearly drove him mad with boredom.

But one day his patience was rewarded. She came again, rather pinker than usual, and trying hard to appear self-possessed.

He greeted her with cheerful friendliness.

'Good morning. It is ages since you've been here.'

'Good morning.'

She let the words slip out with icy frigidity, and coldly ignored the end part of his sentence.

But he was desperate.

'Look here!' He stood confronting her with pleading eyes that reminded her irresistibly of a large, faithful dog. 'Won't you be friends? I'm all alone in London – all alone in the world, and I believe you are, too. We ought to be friends. Besides, our little god has introduced us.'

She looked up half doubtfully, but there was a faint smile quivering at the corners of her mouth.

'Has he?'

'Of course!'

It was the second time he had used this extremely positive form of assurance, and now, as before, it did not fail of its effect, for after a minute or two the girl said, in that slightly royal manner of hers:

'Very well.'

'That's splendid,' he replied gruffly, but there was something in his voice as he said it that made the girl glance at him swiftly, with a sharp impulse of pity.

And so the queer friendship began. Twice a week they met, at the shrine of a little heathen idol. At first they confined their conversation solely to him. He was, as it were, at once a palliation of, and an excuse for, their friendship. The question of his origin was widely discussed. The man insisted on attributing to him the most bloodthirsty characteristics. He depicted him as the terror and dread of his native land, insatiable for human sacrifice, and bowed down to by his people in fear and trembling. In the contrast between his former greatness and his present insignificance there lay, according to the man, all the pathos of the situation.

The Lonely Lady would have none of this theory. He was essentially a kind little god, she insisted. She doubted whether he had ever been very powerful. If he had been so, she argued, he would not now be lost and friendless, and, anyway, he was a dear little god, and she loved him, and she hated to think of him sitting there day after day with all those other horrid, supercilious things jeering at him, because you could see they did! After this vehement outburst the little lady was quite out of breath.

That topic exhausted, they naturally began to talk of themselves. He found out that his surmise was correct. She was a nursery governess to a family of children who lived at Hampstead. He conceived an instant dislike of these children; of Ted, who was five and really not *naughty*, only mischievous; of the twins who *were* rather trying, and of Molly, who wouldn't do anything she was told, but was such a dear you couldn't be cross with her!

'Those children bully you,' he said grimly and accusingly to her.

'They do not,' she retorted with spirit. 'I am extremely stern with them.'

'Oh! Ye gods!' he laughed. But she made him apologize humbly for his scepticism.

She was an orphan she told him, quite alone in the world.

Gradually he told her something of his own life: of his official life, which had been painstaking and mildly successful; and of his unofficial pastime, which was the spoiling of yards of canvas.

'Of course, I don't know anything about it,' he explained. 'But I have always felt I could paint something some day. I can sketch pretty decently, but I'd like to do a real picture of something. A chap who knew once told me that my technique wasn't bad.'

She was interested, pressed for details.

'I am sure you paint awfully well.' He shook his head.

'No, I've begun several things lately and chucked them up in despair. I always thought that, when I had the time, it would be plain sailing. I have been storing up that idea for years, but now, like everything else, I suppose, I've left it too late.'

'Nothing's too late – ever,' said the little lady, with the vehement earnestness of the very young.

He smiled down on her. 'You think not, child? It's too late for some things for me.'

And the little lady laughed at him and nick-named him Methuselah.

They were beginning to feel curiously at home in the British Museum. The solid and sympathetic policeman who patrolled the galleries was a man of tact, and on the appearance of the couple he usually found that his onerous duties of guardianship were urgently needed in the adjoining Assyrian room.

One day the man took a bold step. He invited her out to tea!

At first she demurred.

'I have no time. I am not free. I can come some mornings because the children have French lessons.'

'Nonsense,' said the man, 'You could manage one day. Kill off an aunt or a second cousin or something, but *come*. We'll go to a little ABC shop near here, and have buns for tea! I know you must love buns!'

'Yes, the penny kind with currants!'

'And a lovely glaze on top –'

'They are such plump, dear things –'

'There is something,' Frank Oliver said solemnly, 'infinitely comforting about a bun!'

So it was arranged, and the little governess came, wearing quite an expensive hothouse rose in her belt in honour of the occasion.

He had noticed that, of late, she had a strained, worried look, and it was more apparent than ever this afternoon as she poured out the tea at the little marble-topped table.

'Children been bothering you?' he asked solicitously.

She shook her head. She had seemed curiously disinclined to talk about the children lately.

'*They're* all right. I never mind them.'

'Don't you?'

His sympathetic tone seemed to distress her unwarrantably.

'Oh, no. It was never that. But – but, indeed, I was lonely. I was indeed!'
Her tone was almost pleading.

He said quickly, touched: 'Yes, yes, child, I know – I know.'

After a minute's pause he remarked in a cheerful tone: 'Do you know, you haven't even asked my name yet?'

She held up a protesting hand.

'Please, I don't want to know it. And don't ask mine. Let us be just two lonely people who've come together and made friends. It makes it so much more wonderful – and – and different.'

He said slowly and thoughtfully: 'Very well. In an otherwise lonely world we'll be two people who have just each other.'

It was a little different from her way of putting it, and she seemed to find it difficult to go on with the conversation. Instead, she bent lower and lower over her plate, till only the crown of her hat was visible.

'That's rather a nice hat,' he said by way of restoring her equanimity.

'I trimmed it myself,' she informed him proudly.

'I thought so the moment I saw it,' he answered, saying the wrong thing with cheerful ignorance.

'I'm afraid it is not as fashionable as I meant it to be!'

'I think it's a perfectly lovely hat,' he said loyally.

Again constraint settled down upon them. Frank Oliver broke the silence bravely.

'Little Lady, I didn't mean to tell you yet, but I can't help it. I love you. I want you. I loved you from the first moment I saw you standing there in your little black suit. Dearest, if two lonely people were together – why – there would be no more loneliness. And I'd work, oh! how I'd work! I'd paint you. I could, I know I could. Oh! my little girl, I can't live without you. I can't indeed –'

His little lady was looking at him very steadily. But what she said was quite the last thing he expected her to say. Very quietly and distinctly she said: 'You *bought* that handkerchief!'

He was amazed at this proof of feminine perspicacity, and still more amazed at her remembering it against him now. Surely, after this lapse of time, it might have been forgiven him.

'Yes, I did,' he acknowledged humbly. 'I wanted an excuse to speak to you. Are you very angry?' He waited meekly for her words of condemnation.

'I think it was sweet of you!' cried the little lady with vehemence. 'Just sweet of you!' Her voice ended uncertainly.

Frank Oliver went on in his gruff tone:

'Tell me, child, is it impossible? I know I'm an ugly, rough old fellow . . .'

The Lonely Lady interrupted him.

'No, you're not! I wouldn't have you different, not in any way. I love you just as you are, do you understand? Not because I'm sorry for you, not because I'm alone in the world and want someone to be fond of me and take care of me – but because you're just – *you*. Now do you understand?'

'Is it true?' he asked half in a whisper.

And she answered steadily: 'Yes, it's true –' The wonder of it overpowered them.

At last he said whimsically: 'So we've fallen upon heaven, dearest!'

'In an ABC shop,' she answered in a voice that held tears and laughter.

But terrestrial heavens are short-lived. The little lady started up with an exclamation.

'I'd no idea how late it was! I must go at once.'

'I'll see you home.'

'No, no, *no!*'

He was forced to yield to her insistence, and merely accompanied her as far as the Tube station.

'Goodbye, dearest.' She clung to his hand with an intensity that he remembered afterwards.

'Only goodbye till tomorrow,' he answered cheerfully. 'Ten o'clock as usual, and we'll tell each other our names and our histories, and be frightfully practical and prosaic.'

'Goodbye to – heaven, though,' she whispered.

'It will be with us always, sweetheart!'

She smiled back at him, but with that same sad appeal that disquieted him and which he could not fathom. Then the relentless lift dragged her down out of sight.

*   *   *

He was strangely disturbed by those last words of hers, but he put them resolutely out of his mind and substituted radiant anticipations of tomorrow in their stead.

At ten o'clock he was there, in the accustomed place. For the first time he noticed how malevolently the other idols looked down upon him. It almost seemed as if they were possessed of some secret evil knowledge affecting him, over which they were gloating. He was uneasily aware of their dislike.

The little lady was late. Why didn't she come? The atmosphere of this place was getting on his nerves. Never had his own little friend (*their* god) seemed so hopelessly impotent as today. A helpless lump of stone, hugging his own despair!

His cogitations were interrupted by a small, sharp-faced boy who had stepped up to him, and was earnestly scrutinizing him from head to foot. Apparently satisfied with the result of his observations, he held out a letter.

'For me?'

It had no superscription. He took it, and the sharp boy decamped with extraordinary rapidity.

Frank Oliver read the letter slowly and unbelievingly. It was quite short.

Dearest,
I can never marry you. Please forget that I ever came into your life at all, and try to forgive me if I have hurt you. Don't try to find me, because it will be no good. It is really 'goodbye'.
The Lonely Lady

There was a postscript which had evidently been scribbled at the last moment:

I do love you. I do indeed.

And that little impulsive postscript was all the comfort he had in the weeks that followed. Needless to say, he disobeyed her injunction 'not to try to find her', but all in vain. She had vanished completely, and he had no clue to trace her by. He advertised despairingly, imploring her in veiled terms at least to explain the mystery, but blank silence rewarded his efforts. She was gone, never to return.

And then it was that for the first time in his life he really began to paint. His technique had always been good. Now craftsmanship and inspiration went hand in hand.

The picture that made his name and brought him renown was accepted and hung in the Academy, and was accounted to be *the* picture of the year, no less for the exquisite treatment of the subject than for the masterly workmanship and technique. A certain amount of mystery, too, rendered it more interesting to the general outside public.

His inspiration had come quite by chance. A fairy story in a magazine had taken a hold on his imagination.

It was the story of a fortunate Princess who had always had everything she wanted. Did she express a wish? It was instantly gratified. A desire? It was granted. She had a devoted father and mother, great riches, beautiful clothes and jewels, slaves to wait upon her and fulfil her lightest whim, laughing maidens to bear her company, all that the heart of a Princess could desire. The handsomest and richest Princes paid her court and sued in vain for her hand, and were willing to kill any number of dragons to prove their devotion. And yet, the loneliness of the Princess was greater than that of the poorest beggar in the land.

He read no more. The ultimate fate of the Princess interested him not at all. A picture had risen up before him of the pleasure-laden Princess with the sad, solitary soul, surfeited with happiness, suffocated with luxury, starving in the Palace of Plenty.

He began painting with furious energy. The fierce joy of creation possessed him.

He represented the Princess surrounded by her court, reclining on a divan. A riot of Eastern colour pervaded the picture. The Princess wore a marvellous gown of strange-coloured embroideries; her golden hair fell round her, and on her head was a heavy jewelled circlet. Her maidens surrounded her, and Princes knelt at her feet bearing rich gifts. The whole scene was one of luxury and richness.

But the face of the Princess was turned away; she was oblivious of the laughter and mirth around her. Her gaze was fixed on a dark and shadowy corner where stood a seemingly incongruous object: a little grey stone idol with its head buried in its hand in a quaint abandonment of despair.

Was it so incongruous? The eyes of the young Princess rested on it with a strange sympathy, as though a dawning sense of her own isolation drew her glance irresistibly. They were akin, these two. The world was at her feet – yet she was alone: a Lonely Princess looking at a lonely little god.

All London talked of this picture, and Greta wrote a few hurried words of congratulation from Yorkshire, and Tom Hurley's wife besought Frank Oliver to 'come for a weekend and meet a really delightful girl, a great admirer of your work'. Frank Oliver laughed once sardonically, and threw the letter into the fire. Success had come – but what was the use of it? He only wanted one thing – that little lonely lady who had gone out of his life for ever.

It was Ascot Cup Day, and the policeman on duty in a certain section of the British Museum rubbed his eyes and wondered if he were dreaming, for one does not expect to see there an Ascot vision, in a lace frock and a marvellous hat, a veritable nymph as imagined by a Parisian genius. The policeman stared in rapturous admiration.

The lonely god was not perhaps so surprised. He may have been in his way a powerful little god; at any rate, here was one worshipper brought back to the fold.

The Little Lonely Lady was staring up at him, and her lips moved in a rapid whisper.

'Dear little god, oh! dear little god, please help me! Oh, please do help me!'

Perhaps the little god was flattered. Perhaps, if he was indeed the ferocious, unappeasable deity Frank Oliver had imagined him, the long weary years and the march of civilization had softened his cold, stone heart. Perhaps the Lonely Lady had been right all along and he was really a kind little god. Perhaps it was merely a coincidence. However that may be, it was at that very moment that Frank Oliver walked slowly and sadly through the door of the Assyrian room.

He raised his head and saw the Parisian nymph.

In another moment his arm was round her, and she was stammering out rapid, broken words.

'I was so lonely – *you* know, you must have read that story I wrote; you couldn't have painted that picture unless you had, and unless you had understood. The Princess was I; I had everything, and yet I was lonely beyond words. One day I was going to a fortune-teller's, and I borrowed my maid's clothes. I came in here on the way and saw you looking at the little god. That's how it all began. I pretended – oh! it was hateful of me, and I went on pretending, and afterwards I didn't dare confess that I had told you such dreadful lies. I thought you would be disgusted at the way I had deceived you. I couldn't bear you to find out, so I went away. Then I wrote that story, and yesterday I saw your picture. It *was* your picture, wasn't it?'

Only the gods really know the word 'ingratitude'. It is to be presumed that the lonely little god knew the black ingratitude of human nature. As a divinity he had unique opportunities of observing it, yet in the hour of trial he who had had sacrifices innumerable offered to him, made sacrifice in his turn. He sacrificed his only two worshippers in a strange land,

and it showed him to be a great little god in his way, since he sacrificed all that he had.

Through the chinks in his fingers he watched them go, hand in hand, without a backward glance, two happy people who had found heaven and had no need of him any longer.

What was he, after all, but a very lonely little god in a strange land?

The Rajah's Emerald

'The Rajah's Emerald' was first published
in *Red Magazine*, 30 July 1926.

With a serious effort James Bond bent his attention once more on the little yellow book in his hand. On its outside the book bore the simple but pleasing legend, 'Do you want your salary increased by £300 per annum?' Its price was one shilling. James had just finished reading two pages of crisp paragraphs instructing him to look his boss in the face, to cultivate a dynamic personality, and to radiate an atmosphere of efficiency. He had now arrived at a subtler matter, 'There is a time for frankness, there is a time for discretion,' the little yellow book informed him. 'A strong man does not always blurt out *all* he knows.' James let the little book close, and raising his head, gazed out over a blue expanse of ocean. A horrible suspicion assailed him, that he was *not* a strong man. A strong man would have been in command of the present situation, not a victim to it. For the sixtieth time that morning James rehearsed his wrongs.

This was his holiday. His holiday? Ha, ha! Sardonic laughter. Who had persuaded him to come to that fashionable seaside resort, Kimpton-on-Sea? Grace. Who had urged him into an expenditure of more than he could afford? Grace. And he had fallen in with the plan eagerly. She had got him here, and what was the result? Whilst he was staying in an obscure boarding-house about a mile and a half from the sea-front, Grace who should have been in a similar boarding-house (not the same one – the proprieties of James's circle were very strict) had flagrantly deserted him, and was staying at no less than the Esplanade Hotel upon the sea-front.

It seemed that she had friends there. Friends! Again James laughed sardonically. His mind went back over the last three years of his leisurely courtship of Grace. Extremely pleased she had been when he first singled her out for notice. That was before she had risen to heights of glory in the millinery salon at Messrs Bartles in the High Street. In those early days it had been James who gave himself airs, now alas! the boot was on the other leg. Grace was what is technically known as 'earning good money'. It had made her uppish. Yes, that was it, thoroughly uppish. A confused fragment out of a poetry book came back to James's mind, something about 'thanking heaven fasting, for a good man's love'. But there was nothing of that kind of thing observable about Grace. Well fed on an Esplanade Hotel breakfast, she was ignoring a good man's love utterly. She was indeed accepting the attentions of a poisonous idiot called Claud Sopworth, a man, James felt convinced, of no moral worth whatsoever.

James ground a heel into the the earth, and scowled darkly at the horizon. Kimpton-on-Sea. What had possessed him to come to such a place? It was pre-eminently a resort of the rich and fashionable, it possessed two large hotels, and several miles of picturesque bungalows belonging to fashionable actresses, rich Jews and those members of the English aristocracy who had married wealthy wives. The rent, furnished, of the smallest bungalow was twenty-five guineas a week. Imagination boggled at what the rent of the large ones might amount to. There was one of these palaces immediately behind James's seat. It belonged to that famous sportsman Lord Edward Campion, and there were staying there at the moment a houseful of distinguished guests including the Rajah of Maraputna, whose wealth was fabulous. James had read all about him in the local weekly newspaper that morning; the extent of his Indian possessions, his palaces, his wonderful collection of jewels, with a special mention of one famous emerald which the papers declared enthusiastically was the size of a pigeon's egg. James, being town bred, was somewhat hazy about the size of a pigeon's egg, but the impression left on his mind was good.

'If I had an emerald like that,' said James, scowling at the horizon again, 'I'd show Grace.'

The sentiment was vague, but the enunciation of it made James feel better. Laughing voices hailed him from behind, and he turned abruptly to confront Grace. With her was Clara Sopworth, Alice Sopworth, Dorothy Sopworth and – alas! Claud Sopworth. The girls were arm-in-arm and giggling.

'Why, you are quite a stranger,' cried Grace archly.

'Yes,' said James.

He could, he felt, have found a more telling retort. You cannot convey the impression of a dynamic personality by the use of the one word 'yes'. He looked with intense loathing at Claud Sopworth. Claud Sopworth was almost as beautifully dressed as the hero of a musical comedy. James longed passionately for the moment when an enthusiastic beach dog should plant wet, sandy forefeet on the unsullied whiteness of Claud's flannel trousers. He himself wore a serviceable pair of dark-grey flannel trousers which had seen better days.

'Isn't the air beau-tiful?' said Clara, sniffing it appreciatively. 'Quite sets you up, doesn't it?'

She giggled.

'It's ozone,' said Alice Sopworth. 'It's as good as a tonic, you know.' And she giggled also.

James thought:

'I should like to knock their silly heads together. What is the sense of laughing all the time? They are not saying anything funny.'

The immaculate Claud murmured languidly:

'Shall we have a bathe, or is it too much of a fag?'

The idea of bathing was accepted shrilly. James fell into line with them. He even managed, with a certain amount of cunning, to draw Grace a little behind the others.

'Look here!' he complained, 'I am hardly seeing anything of you.'

'Well, I am sure we are all together now,' said Grace, 'and you can come and lunch with us at the hotel, at least –'

She looked dubiously at James's legs.

'What is the matter?' demanded James ferociously. 'Not smart enough for you, I suppose?'

'I do think, dear, you might take a little more pains,' said Grace. 'Everyone is so fearfully smart here. Look at Claud Sopworth!'

'I have looked at him,' said James grimly. 'I have never seen a man who looked a more complete ass than he does.'

Grace drew herself up.

'There is no need to criticize my friends, James, it's not manners. He's dressed just like any other gentleman at the hotel is dressed.'

'Bah!' said James. 'Do you know what I read the other day in "Society Snippets"? Why, that the Duke of – the Duke of, I can't remember, but one duke, anyway, was the worst dressed man in England, there!'

'I dare say,' said Grace, 'but then, you see, he is a duke.'

'Well?' demanded James. 'What is wrong with my being a duke some day? At least, well, not perhaps a duke, but a peer.'

He slapped the yellow book in his pocket, and recited to her a long list of peers of the realm who had started life much more obscurely than James Bond. Grace merely giggled.

'Don't be so soft, James,' she said. 'Fancy you Earl of Kimpton-on-Sea!'

James gazed at her in mingled rage and despair. The air of Kimpton-on-Sea had certainly gone to Grace's head.

The beach at Kimpton is a long, straight stretch of sand. A row of bathing-huts and boxes stretched evenly along it for about a mile and a half. The party had just stopped before a row of six huts all labelled imposingly, 'For visitors to the Esplanade Hotel only.'

'Here we are,' said Grace brightly; 'but I'm afraid you can't come in with us, James, you'll have to go along to the public tents over there. We'll meet you in the sea. So long!'

'So long!' said James, and he strode off in the direction indicated.

Twelve dilapidated tents stood solemnly confronting the ocean. An aged mariner guarded them, a roll of blue paper in his hand. He accepted a coin of the realm from James, tore him off a blue ticket from his roll, threw him over a towel, and jerked one thumb over his shoulder.

'Take your turn,' he said huskily.

It was then that James awoke to the fact of competition. Others besides himself had conceived the idea of entering the sea. Not only was each tent occupied, but outside each tent was a determined-looking crowd of people glaring at each other. James attached himself to the smallest group and waited. The strings of the tent parted, and a beautiful young woman, sparsely clad, emerged on the scene settling her bathing-cap with the air of one who had the whole morning to waste. She strolled down to the water's edge, and sat down dreamily on the sands.

'That's no good,' said James to himself, and attached himself forthwith to another group.

After waiting five minutes, sounds of activity were apparent in the second tent. With heavings and strainings, the flaps parted asunder and four children and a father and mother emerged. The tent being so small, it had something of the appearance of a conjuring trick. On the instant two women sprang forward each grasping one flap of the tent.

'Excuse me,' said the first young woman, panting a little.

'Excuse *me*,' said the other young woman, glaring.

'I would have you know I was here quite ten minutes before you were,' said the first young woman rapidly.

'I have been here a good quarter of an hour, as anyone will tell you,' said the second young woman defiantly.

'Now then, now then,' said the aged mariner, drawing near.

Both young women spoke to him shrilly. When they had finished, he jerked his thumb at the second young woman, and said briefly:

'It's yours.'

Then he departed, deaf to remonstrances. He neither knew nor cared which had been there first, but his decision, as they say in newspaper competitions, was final. The despairing James caught at his arm.

'Look here! I say!'

'Well, mister?'

'How long is it going to be before I get a tent?'

The aged mariner threw a dispassionate glance over the waiting throng.

'Might be an hour, might be an hour and a half, I can't say.'

At that moment James espied Grace and the Sopworth girls running lightly down the sands towards the sea.

'Damn!' said James to himself. 'Oh, damn!'

He plucked once more at the aged mariner.

'Can't I get a tent anywhere else? What about one of these huts along here? They all seem empty.'

'The huts,' said the ancient mariner with dignity, 'are private.'

Having uttered this rebuke, he passed on. With a bitter feeling of having been tricked, James detached himself from the waiting groups, and strode savagely down the beach. It was the limit! It was the absolute, complete limit! He glared savagely at the trim bathing-boxes he passed. In that moment from being an Independent Liberal, he became a red-hot Socialist. Why should the rich have bathing-boxes and be able to bathe any minute they chose without waiting in a crowd? 'This system of ours,' said James vaguely, 'is all *wrong*.'

From the sea came the coquettish screams of the splashed. Grace's voice! And above her squeaks, the inane 'Ha, ha, ha,' of Claud Sopworth.

'Damn!' said James, grinding his teeth, a thing which he had never before attempted, only read about in works of fiction.

He came to a stop, twirling his stick savagely, and turning his back firmly on the sea. Instead, he gazed with concentrated hatred upon Eagle's Nest, Buena Vista, and Mon Desir. It was the custom of the inhabitants of Kimpton-on-Sea to label their bathing-huts with fancy names. Eagle's Nest merely struck James as being silly, and Buena Vista was beyond his linguistic accomplishments. But his knowledge of French was sufficient to make him realize the appositeness of the third name.

'Mong Desire,' said James. 'I should jolly well think it was.'

And on that moment he saw that while the doors of the other bathing-huts were tightly closed, that of Mon Desir was ajar. James looked thoughtfully up and down the beach, this particular spot was mainly occupied by mothers of large families, busily engaged in superintending their offspring. It was only ten o'clock, too early as yet for the aristocracy of Kimpton-on-Sea to have come down to bathe.

'Eating quails and mushrooms in their beds as likely as not, brought to them on trays by powdered footmen, pah! Not one of them will be down here before twelve o'clock,' thought James.

He looked again towards the sea. With the obedience of a well-trained leitmotif, the shrill scream of Grace rose upon the air. It was followed by the 'Ha, ha, ha,' of Claud Sopworth.

'I will,' said James between his teeth.

He pushed open the door of Mon Desir and entered. For the moment he had a fright, as he caught sight of sundry garments hanging from pegs, but he was quickly reassured. The hut was partitioned into two, on the right-hand side, a girl's yellow sweater, a battered panama hat and a pair of beach shoes were depending from a peg. On the left-hand side an old pair of grey flannel trousers, a pullover, and a sou'wester proclaimed the fact that the sexes were segregated. James hastily transferred himself to the gentlemen's part of the hut, and undressed rapidly. Three minutes later, he was in the sea puffing and snorting importantly, doing extremely short bursts of professional-looking swimming – head under the water, arms lashing the sea – that style.

'Oh, there you are!' cried Grace. 'I was afraid you wouldn't be in for ages with all that crowd of people waiting there.'

'Really?' said James.

He thought with affectionate loyalty of the yellow book. 'The strong man can on occasions be discreet.' For the moment his temper was quite restored. He was able to say pleasantly but firmly to Claud Sopworth, who was teaching Grace the overarm stroke:

'No, no, old man, you have got it all wrong. I'll show her.'

And such was the assurance of his tone, that Claud withdrew discomfited. The only pity of it was, that his triumph was short-lived. The temperature of our English waters is not such as to induce bathers to remain in them for any length of time. Grace and the Sopworth girls were already displaying blue chins and chattering teeth. They raced up the beach, and James pursued his solitary way back to Mon Desir. As he towelled himself vigorously and slipped his shirt over his head, he was pleased with himself. He had, he felt, displayed a dynamic personality.

And then suddenly he stood still, frozen with terror. Girlish voices sounded from outside, and voices quite different from those of Grace and her friends. A moment later he had realized the truth, the rightful owners of Mon Desir were arriving. It is possible that if James had been fully dressed, he would have waited their advent in a dignified manner, and attempted an explanation. As it was he acted on panic. The windows of Mon Desir were modestly screened by dark green curtains. James flung himself on the door and held the knob in a desperate clutch. Hands tried ineffectually to turn it from outside.

'It's locked after all,' said a girl's voice. 'I thought Peg said it was open.'

'No, Woggle said so.'

'Woggle is the limit,' said the other girl. 'How perfectly foul, we shall have to go back for the key.'

James heard their footsteps retreating. He drew a long, deep breath.

In desperate haste he huddled on the rest of his garments. Two minutes later saw him strolling negligently down the beach with an almost aggressive air of innocence. Grace and the Sopworth girls joined him on the beach a quarter of an hour later. The rest of the morning passed agreeably in stone throwing, writing in the sand and light badinage. Then Claud glanced at his watch.

'Lunch-time,' he observed. 'We'd better be strolling back.'

'I'm terribly hungry,' said Alice Sopworth.

All the other girls said that they were terribly hungry too.

'Are you coming, James?' asked Grace.

Doubtless James was unduly touchy. He chose to take offence at her tone.

'Not if my clothes are not good enough for you,' he said bitterly. 'Perhaps, as you are so particular, I'd better not come.'

That was Grace's cue for murmured protestations, but the seaside air had affected Grace unfavourably. She merely replied:

'Very well. Just as you like, see you this afternoon then.'

James was left dumbfounded.

'Well!' he said, staring after the retreating group. 'Well, of all the –'

He strolled moodily into the town. There were two cafés in Kimpton-on-Sea, they are both hot, noisy and overcrowded. It was the affair of the bathing-huts once more, James had to wait his turn. He had to wait longer than his turn, an unscrupulous matron who had just arrived forestalling him when a vacant seat did present itself. At last he was seated at a small table. Close to his left ear three raggedly bobbed maidens were making a determined hash of Italian opera. Fortunately James was not musical. He studied the bill of fare dispassionately, his hands thrust deep into his pockets. He thought to himself:

'Whatever I ask for it's sure to be "off". That's the kind of fellow I am.'

His right hand, groping in the recesses of his pocket, touched an unfamiliar object. It felt like a pebble, a large round pebble.

'What on earth did I want to put a stone in my pocket for?' thought James.

His fingers closed round it. A waitress drifted up to him.

'Fried plaice and chipped potatoes, please,' said James.

'Fried plaice is "off",' murmured the waitress, her eyes fixed dreamily on the ceiling.

'Then I'll have curried beef,' said James.

'Curried beef is "off".'

'Is there anything on this beastly menu that isn't "off"?' demanded James.

The waitress looked pained, and placed a pale-grey forefinger against haricot mutton. James resigned himself to the inevitable and ordered haricot mutton. His mind still seething with resentment against the ways of cafés, he drew his hand out of his pocket, the stone still in it. Unclosing his fingers, he looked absent-mindedly at the object in his palm. Then with a shock all lesser matters passed from his mind, and he stared with all his eyes. The thing he held was not a pebble, it was – he could hardly doubt it – an emerald, an enormous green emerald. James stared at it horror-stricken. No, it couldn't be an emerald, it must be coloured glass. There couldn't be an emerald of that size, unless – printed words danced before James's eyes, 'The Rajah of Maraputna – famous emerald the size of a pigeon's egg.' Was it – could it be – *that* emerald at which he was now looking? The waitress returned with the haricot mutton, and James closed his fingers spasmodically. Hot and cold shivers chased themselves up and down his spine. He had the sense of being caught in a terrible dilemma. If this was the emerald – but was it? Could it be? He unclosed his fingers and peeped anxiously. James was no expert on precious stones, but the depth and the glow of the jewel convinced him this was the real thing. He put both elbows on the table and leaned forward staring with unseeing eyes at the haricot mutton slowly congealing on the dish in front of him. He had got to think this out. If this was the Rajah's emerald, what was he going to do about it? The word 'police' flashed into his mind. If you found anything of value you took it to the police station. Upon this axiom had James been brought up.

Yes, but – how on earth had the emerald got into his trouser pocket? That was doubtless the question the police would ask. It was an awkward question, and it was moreover a question to which he had at the moment no answer. How had the emerald got into his trouser pocket? He looked despairingly down at his legs, and as he did so a misgiving shot through him. He looked more closely. One pair of old grey flannel trousers is very much like another pair of old grey flannel trousers, but all the same, James had an instinctive feeling that these were not his trousers after all. He sat back in his chair stunned with the force of the discovery. He saw now what had happened, in the hurry of getting out of the bathing-hut, he had taken the wrong trousers. He had hung his own, he remembered, on an adjacent peg to the old pair hanging there. Yes, that explained matters so far, he had taken the wrong trousers. But all the same, what on earth was an emerald worth hundreds and thousands of pounds doing there? The more he thought about it, the more curious it seemed. He could, of course, explain to the police –

It was awkward, no doubt about it, it was decidedly awkward. One would have to mention the fact that one had deliberately entered someone else's bathing-hut. It was not, of course, a serious offence, but it started him off wrong.

'Can I bring you anything else, sir?'

It was the waitress again. She was looking pointedly at the untouched haricot mutton. James hastily dumped some of it on his plate and asked for his bill. Having obtained it, he paid and went out. As he stood undecidedly in the street, a poster opposite caught his eye. The adjacent town of Harchester possessed an evening paper, and it was the contents bill of this paper that James was looking at. It announced a simple, sensational fact: 'The Rajah's Emerald Stolen.' 'My God,' said James faintly, and leaned against a pillar. Pulling himself together he fished out a penny and purchased a copy of the paper. He was not long in finding what he sought. Sensational items of local news were few and far between. Large headlines adorned the front page. 'Sensational Burglary at Lord Edward Campion's. Theft of Famous Historical Emerald. Rajah of Maraputna's Terrible Loss.' The facts were few and simple. Lord Edward Campion had entertained several friends the evening before. Wishing to show the stone to one of the ladies present, the Rajah had gone to fetch it and had found it missing. The police had been called in. So far no clue had been obtained. James let the paper fall to the ground. It was still not clear to him how the emerald had come to be reposing in the pocket of an old pair of flannel trousers in a bathing-hut, but it was borne in upon him every minute that the police would certainly regard his own story as suspicious. What on earth was he to do? Here he was, standing in the principal street of Kimpton-on-Sea with stolen booty worth a king's ransom reposing idly in his pocket, whilst the entire police force of the district were busily searching for just that same booty. There were two courses open to him. Course number one, to go straight to the police station and tell his story – but it must be admitted that James funked that course badly. Course number two, somehow or other to get rid of the emerald. It occurred to him to do it up in a neat little parcel and post it back to the Rajah. Then he shook his head, he had read too many detective stories for that sort of thing. He knew how your super-sleuth could get busy with a magnifying glass and every kind of patent device. Any detective worth his salt would get busy on James's parcel and would in half an hour or so have discovered the sender's profession, age, habits and personal appearance. After that it would be a mere matter of hours before he was tracked down.

It was then that a scheme of dazzling simplicity suggested itself to James. It was the luncheon hour, the beach would be comparatively deserted, he would return to Mon Desir, hang up the trousers where he had found them, and regain his own garments. He started briskly towards the beach.

Nevertheless, his conscience pricked him slightly. The emerald *ought* to be returned to the Rajah. He conceived the idea that he might perhaps do a little detective work – once, that is, that he had regained his own trousers and replaced the others. In pursuance of this idea, he directed his steps towards the aged mariner, whom he rightly regarded as being an exhaustible source of Kimpton information.

'Excuse me!' said James politely; 'but I belive a friend of mine has a hut on this beach, Mr Charles Lampton. It is called Mon Desir, I fancy.'

The aged mariner was sitting very squarely in a chair, a pipe in his mouth, gazing out to sea. He shifted his pipe a little, and replied without removing his gaze from the horizon:

'Mon Desir belongs to his lordship, Lord Edward Campion, every-one knows that. I never heard of Mr Charles Lampton, he must be a newcomer.'

'Thank you,' said James, and withdrew.

The information staggered him. Surely the Rajah could not himself have slipped the stone into the pocket and forgotten it. James shook his head, the theory did not satisfy him, but evidently some member of the house-party must be the thief. The situation reminded James of some of his favourite works of fiction.

Nevertheless, his own purpose remained unaltered. All fell out easily enough. The beach was, as he hoped it would be, practically deserted. More fortunate still, the door of Mon Desir remained ajar. To slip in was the work of a moment, Edward was just lifting his own trousers from the hook, when a voice behind him made him spin round suddenly.

'So I have caught you, my man!' said the voice.

James stared open-mouthed. In the doorway of Mon Desir stood a stranger; a well-dressed man of about forty years of age, his face keen and hawk-like.

'So I have caught you!' the stranger repeated.

'Who – who are you?' stammered James.

'Detective-Inspector Merrilees from the Yard,' said the other crisply. 'And I will trouble you to hand over that emerald.'

'The – the emerald?'

James was seeking to gain time.

'That's what I said, didn't I?' said Inspector Merrilees.

He had a crisp, business-like enunciation. James tried to pull himself together.

'I don't know what you are talking about,' he said with an assumption of dignity.

'Oh, yes, my lad, I think you do.'

'The whole thing,' said James, 'is a mistake. I can explain it quite easily –' He paused.

A look of weariness had settled on the face of the other.

'They always say that,' murmured the Scotland Yard man dryly. 'I suppose you picked it up as you were strolling along the beach, eh? That is the sort of explanation.'

It did indeed bear a resemblance to it, James recognized the fact, but still he tried to gain time.

'How do I know you are what you say you are?' he demanded weakly.

Merrilees flapped back his coat for a moment, showing a badge. Edward stared at him with eyes that popped out of his head.

'And now,' said the other almost genially, 'you see what you are up against! You are a novice – I can tell that. Your first job, isn't it?'

James nodded.

'I thought as much. Now, my boy, are you going to hand over that emerald, or have I got to search you?'

James found his voice.

'I – I haven't got it on me,' he declared.

He was thinking desperately.

'Left it at your lodgings?' queried Merrilees.

James nodded.

'Very well, then,' said the detective, 'we will go there together.'

He slipped his arm through James's.

'I am taking no chances of your getting away from me,' he said gently. 'We will go to your lodgings, and you will hand that stone over to me.'

James spoke unsteadily.

'If I do, will you let me go?' he asked tremulously.

Merrilees appeared embarrassed.

'We know just how that stone was taken,' he explained, 'and about the lady involved, and, of course, as far as that goes – well, the Rajah wants it hushed up. You know what these native rulers are?'

James, who knew nothing whatsoever about native rulers, except for one *cause célèbre*, nodded his head with an appearance of eager comprehension.

'It will be most irregular, of course,' said the detective; 'but you *may* get off scot-free.'

Again James nodded. They had walked the length of the Esplanade, and were now turning into the town. James intimated the direction, but the other man never relinquished his sharp grip on James's arm.

Suddenly James hesitated and half-spoke. Merrilees looked up sharply, and then laughed. They were just passing the police station, and he noticed James's agonized glances at it.

'I am giving you a chance first,' he said good-humouredly.

It was at that moment that things began to happen. A loud bellow broke from James, he clutched the other's arm, and yelled at the top of his voice:

'Help! thief. Help! thief.'

A crowd surrounded them in less than a minute. Merrilees was trying to wrench his arm from James's grasp.

'I charge this man,' cried James. 'I charge this man, he picked my pocket.'

'What are you talking about, you fool?' cried the other.

A constable took charge of matters. Mr Merrilees and James were escorted into the police station. James reiterated his complaint.

'This man has just picked my pocket,' he declared excitedly. 'He has got my note-case in his right-hand pocket, there!'

'The man is mad,' grumbled the other. 'You can look for yourself, inspector, and see if he is telling the truth.'

At a sign from the inspector, the constable slipped his hand deferentially into Merrilees's pocket. He drew something out and held it up with a gasp of astonishment.

'My God!' said the inspector, startled out of professional decorum. 'It must be the Rajah's emerald.'

Merrilees looked more incredulous than anyone else.

'This is monstrous,' he spluttered; 'monstrous. The man must have put it into my pocket himself as we were walking along together. It's a plant.'

The forceful personality of Merrilees caused the inspector to waver. His suspicions swung round to James. He whispered something to the constable, and the latter went out.

'Now then, gentlemen,' said the inspector, 'let me have your statements please, one at a time.'

'Certainly,' said James. 'I was walking along the beach, when I met this gentleman, and he pretended he was acquainted with me. I could not remember having met him before, but I was too polite to say so. We walked along together. I had my suspicions of him, and just when we got opposite the police station, I found his hand in my pocket. I held on to him and shouted for help.'

The inspector transferred his glance to Merrilees.

'And now you, sir.'

Merrilees seemed a little embarrassed.

'The story is very nearly right,' he said slowly; 'but not quite. It was not I who scraped acquaintance with him, but he who scraped acquaintance with me. Doubtless he was trying to get rid of the emerald, and slipped it into my pocket while we were talking.'

The inspector stopped writing.

'Ah!' he said impartially. 'Well, there will be a gentleman here in a minute who will help us to get to the bottom of the case.'

Merrilees frowned.

'It is really impossible for me to wait,' he murmured, pulling out his watch. 'I have an appointment. Surely, inspector, you can't be so ridiculous as to suppose I'd steal the emerald and walk along with it in my pocket?'

'It is not likely, sir, I agree,' the inspector replied. 'But you will have to wait just a matter of five or ten minutes till we get this thing cleared up. Ah! here is his lordship.'

A tall man of forty strode into the room. He was wearing a pair of dilapidated trousers and an old sweater.

'Now then, inspector, what is all this?' he said. 'You have got hold of the emerald, you say? That's splendid, very smart work. Who are these people you have got here?'

His eyes ranged over James and came to rest on Merrilees. The forceful personality of the latter seemed to dwindle and shrink.

'Why – Jones!' exclaimed Lord Edward Campion.

'You recognize this man, Lord Edward?' asked the inspector sharply.

'Certainly I do,' said Lord Edward dryly. 'He is my valet, came to me a month ago. The fellow they sent down from London was on to him at once, but there was not a trace of the emerald anywhere among his belongings.'

'He was carrying it in his coat pocket,' the inspector declared. 'This gentleman put us on to him.' He indicated James.

In another minute James was being warmly congratulated and shaken by the hand.

'My dear fellow,' said Lord Edward Campion. 'So you suspected him all along, you say?'

'Yes,' said James. 'I had to trump up the story about my pocket being picked to get him into the police station.'

'Well, it is splendid,' said Lord Edward, 'absolutely splendid. You must come back and lunch with us, that is if you haven't lunched. It is late, I know, getting on for two o'clock.'

'No,' said James; 'I haven't lunched – but –'

'Not a word, not a word,' said Lord Edward. 'The Rajah, you know, will want to thank you for getting back his emerald for him. Not that I have quite got the hang of the story yet.'

They were out of the police station by now, standing on the steps.

'As a matter of fact,' said James, 'I think I should like to tell you the true story.'

He did so. His lordship was very much entertained.

'Best thing I ever heard in my life,' he declared. 'I see it all now. Jones must have hurried down to the bathing-hut as soon as he had pinched the thing, knowing that the police would make a thorough search of the house. That old pair of trousers I sometimes put on for going out fishing, nobody was likely to touch them, and he could recover the jewel at his leisure. Must have been a shock to him when he came today to find it gone. As soon as you appeared, he realized that you were the person who had removed the stone. I still don't quite see how you managed to see through that detective pose of his, though!'

'A strong man,' thought James to himself, 'knows when to be frank and when to be discreet.'

He smiled deprecatingly whilst his fingers passed gently over the inside of his coat lapel feeling the small silver badge of that little-known club, the Merton Park Super Cycling Club. An astonishing coincidence that the man Jones should also be a member, but there it was!

'Hallo, James!'

He turned. Grace and the Sopworth girls were calling to him from the other side of the road. He turned to Lord Edward.

'Excuse me a moment?'

He crossed the road to them.

'We are going to the pictures,' said Grace. 'Thought you might like to come.'

'I am sorry,' said James. 'I am just going back to lunch with Lord Edward Campion. Yes, that man over there in the comfortable old clothes. He wants me to meet the Rajah of Maraputna.'

He raised his hat politely and rejoined Lord Edward.

Swan Song

'Swan Song' was first published
in *Grand Magazine*, September 1926.

It was eleven o'clock on a May morning in London. Mr Cowan was looking out of the window, behind him was the somewhat ornate splendour of a sitting-room in a suite at the Ritz Hotel. The suite in question had been reserved for Mme Paula Nazorkoff, the famous operatic star, who had just arrived in London. Mr Cowan, who was Madame's principal man of business, was awaiting an interview with the lady. He turned his head suddenly as the door opened, but it was only Miss Read, Mme Nazorkoff's secretary, a pale girl with an efficient mïanner.

'Oh, so it's you, my dear,' said Mr Cowan. 'Madame not up yet, eh?' Miss Read shook her head.

'She told me to come round at ten o'clock,' Mr Cowan said. 'I have been waiting an hour.'

He displayed neither resentment nor surprise. Mr Cowan was indeed accustomed to the vagaries of the artistic temperament. He was a tall man, clean-shaven, with a frame rather too well covered, and clothes that were rather too faultless. His hair was very black and shining, and his teeth were aggressively white. When he spoke, he had a way of slurring his 's's' which was not quite a lisp, but came perilously near to it. It required no stretch of imagination to realize that his father's name had probably been Cohen. At that minute a door at the other side of the room opened, and a trim, French girl hurried through.

'Madame getting up?' inquired Cowan hopefully. 'Tell us the news, Elise.' Elise immediately elevated both hands to heaven.

'Madame she is like seventeen devils this morning, nothing pleases her! The beautiful yellow roses which monsieur sent to her last night, she says they are all very well for New York, but that it is *imbecile* to send them to her in London. In London, she says, red roses are the only things possible, and straight away she opens the door, and precipitates the yellow roses into the passage, where they descend upon a monsieur, *très comme il faut*, a military gentleman, I think, and he is justly indignant, that one!'

Cowan raised his eyebrows, but displayed no other signs of emotion. Then he took from his pocket a small memorandum book and pencilled in it the words 'red roses'.

Elise hurried out through the other door, and Cowan turned once more to the window. Vera Read sat down at the desk, and began opening letters and sorting them. Ten minutes passed in silence, and then the door of the bedroom burst open, and Paula Nazorkoff flamed into the room. Her immediate effect upon it was to make it seem smaller, Vera Read appeared more colourless, and Cowan retreated into a mere figure in the background.

'Ah, ha! My children,' said the prima donna, 'am I not punctual?'

She was a tall woman, and for a singer not unduly fat. Her arms and legs were still slender, and her neck was a beautiful column. Her hair, which was coiled in a great roll half-way down her neck, was of a dark, glowing red. If it owed some at least of its colour to henna, the result was none the less effective. She was not a young woman, forty at least, but the lines of her face were still lovely, though the skin was loosened and wrinkled round the flashing, dark eyes. She had the laugh of a child, the digestion of an ostrich, and the temper of a fiend, and she was acknowledged to be the greatest dramatic soprano of her day. She turned directly upon Cowan.

'Have you done as I asked you? Have you taken that abominable English piano away, and thrown it into the Thames?'

'I have got another for you,' said Cowan, and gestured towards where it stood in the corner.

Nazorkoff rushed across to it, and lifted the lid.

'An Erard,' she said, 'that is better. Now let us see.'

The beautiful soprano voice rang out in an arpeggio, then it ran lightly up and down the scale twice, then took a soft little run up to a high note, held it, its volume swelling louder and louder, then softened again till it died away in nothingness.

'Ah!' said Paula Nazorkoff in naïve satisfaction. 'What a beautiful voice I have! Even in London I have a beautiful voice.'

'That is so,' agreed Cowan in hearty congratulation. 'And you bet London is going to fall for you all right, just as New York did.'

'You think so?' queried the singer.

There was a slight smile on her lips, and it was evident that for her the question was a mere commonplace.

'Sure thing,' said Cowan.

Paula Nazorkoff closed the piano lid down and walked across to the table, with that slow undulating walk that proved so effective on the stage.

'Well, well,' she said, 'let us get to business. You have all the arrangements there, my friend?'

Cowan took some papers out of the portfolio he had laid on a chair.

'Nothing has been altered much,' he remarked. 'You will sing five times at Covent Garden, three times in *Tosca*, twice in *Aida*.'

'*Aida!* Pah,' said the prima donna; 'it will be unutterable boredom. *Tosca*, that is different.'

'Ah, yes,' said Cowan. '*Tosca* is *your* part.'

Paula Nazorkoff drew herself up.

'I am the greatest Tosca in the world,' she said simply.

'That is so,' agreed Cowan. 'No one can touch you.'

'Roscari will sing "Scarpia", I suppose?'

Cowan nodded.

'And Emile Lippi.'

'What?' shrieked Nazorkoff. 'Lippi, that hideous little barking frog, croak – croak – croak. I will not sing with him, I will bite him, I will scratch his face.'

'Now, now,' said Cowan soothingly.

'He does not sing, I tell you, he is a mongrel dog who barks.'

'Well, we'll see, we'll see,' said Cowan.

He was too wise ever to argue with temperamental singers.

'The Cavardossi?' demanded Nazorkoff.

'The American tenor, Hensdale.'

The other nodded.

'He is a nice little boy, he sings prettily.'

'And Barrère is to sing it once, I believe.'

'He is an artist,' said Madame generously. 'But to let that croaking frog Lippi be Scarpia! Bah – I'll not sing with him.'

'You leave it to me,' said Cowan soothingly.

He cleared his throat, and took up a fresh set of papers.

'I am arranging for a special concert at the Albert Hall.'

Nazorkoff made a grimace.

'I know, I know,' said Cowan; 'but everybody does it.'

'I will be good,' said Nazorkoff, 'and it will be filled to the ceiling, and I shall have much money. *Ecco!*68'

Again Cowan shuffled papers.

'Now here is quite a different proposition,' he said, 'from Lady Rustonbury. She wants you to go down and sing.'

'Rustonbury?'

The prima donna's brow contracted as if in the effort to recollect something.

'I have read that name lately, very lately. It is a town – or a village, isn't it?'

'That's right, pretty little place in Hertfordshire. As for Lord Ruston-bury's place, Rustonbury Castle, it's a real dandy old feudal seat, ghosts and family pictures, and secret staircases, and a slap-up private theatre. Rolling in money they are, and always giving some private show. She suggests that we give a complete opera, preferably *Butterfly*.'

'*Butterfly?*'

Cowan nodded.

'And they are prepared to pay. We'll have to square Covent Garden, of course, but even after that it will be well worth your while financially. In all probability, royalty will be present. It will be a slap-up advertise-ment.'

Madame raised her still beautiful chin.

'Do I need advertisement?' she demanded proudly.

'You can't have too much of a good thing,' said Cowan, unabashed.

'Rustonbury,' murmured the singer, 'where did I see –?'

She sprang up suddenly, and running to the centre table, began turning over the pages of an illustrated paper which lay there. There was a sudden pause as her hand stopped, hovering over one of the pages, then she let the periodical slip to the floor and returned slowly to her seat. With one of her swift changes of mood, she seemed now an entirely different personality. Her manner was very quiet, almost austere.

'Make all arrangements for Rustonbury, I would like to sing there, but there is one condition – the opera must be *Tosca*.'

Cowan looked doubtful.

'That will be rather difficult – for a private show, you know, scenery and all that.'

'*Tosca* or nothing.'

Cowan looked at her very closely. What he saw seemed to convince him, he gave a brief nod and rose to his feet.

'I will see what I can arrange,' he said quietly.

Nazorkoff rose too. She seemed more anxious than was usual, with her, to explain her decision.

'It is my greatest rôle, Cowan. I can sing that part as no other woman has ever sung it.'

'It is a fine part,' said Cowan. 'Jeritza made a great hit in it last year.'

'Jeritza!' cried the other, a flush mounting in her cheeks. She proceeded to give him at great length her opinion of Jeritza.

Cowan, who was used to listening to singers' opinions of other singers, abstracted his attention till the tirade was over; he then said obstinately:

'Anyway, she sings "Vissi D'Arte" lying on her stomach.'

'And why not?' demanded Nazorkoff. 'What is there to prevent her? I will sing it on my back with my legs waving in the air.'

Cowan shook his head with perfect seriousness.

'I don't believe that would go down any,' he informed her. 'All the same, that sort of thing takes on, you know.'

'No one can sing "Vissi D'Arte" as I can,' said Nazorkoff confidently. 'I sing it in the voice of the convent – as the good nuns taught me to sing years and years ago. In the voice of a choir boy or an angel, without feeling, without passion.'

'I know,' said Cowan heartily. 'I have heard you, you are wonderful.'

'That is art,' said the prima donna, 'to pay the price, to suffer, to endure, and in the end not only to have all knowledge, but also the power to go back, right back to the beginning and recapture the lost beauty of the heart of a child.'

Cowan looked at her curiously. She was staring past him with a strange, blank look in her eyes, and something about that look of hers gave him a creepy feeling. Her lips just parted, and she whispered a few words softly to herself. He only just caught them.

'At last,' she murmured. 'At last – *after all these years.*'

Lady Rustonbury was both an ambitious and an artistic woman, she ran the two qualities in harness with complete success. She had the good fortune to have a husband who cared for neither ambition nor art and who therefore did not hamper her in any way. The Earl of Rustonbury was a large, square man, with an interest in horseflesh and in nothing else. He admired his wife, and was proud of her, and was glad that his great wealth enabled her to indulge all her schemes. The private theatre had been built less than a hundred years ago by his grandfather. It was Lady Rustonbury's chief toy – she had already given an Ibsen drama in it, and a play of the ultra new school, all divorce and drugs, also a poetical fantasy with Cubist scenery. The forthcoming performance of *Tosca* had created wide-spread interest. Lady Rustonbury was entertaining a very distinguished houseparty for it, and all London that counted was motoring down to attend.

Mme Nazorkoff and her company had arrived just before luncheon. The new young American tenor, Hensdale, was to sing 'Cavaradossi', and Roscari, the famous Italian baritone, was to be Scarpia. The expense of the production had been enormous, but nobody cared about that. Paula Nazorkoff was in the best of humours, she was charming, gracious, her most delightful and cosmopolitan self. Cowan was agreeably surprised, and prayed that this state of things might continue.

After luncheon the company went out to the theatre, and inspected the scenery and various appointments. The orchestra was under the direction of Mr Samuel Ridge, one of England's most famous conductors. Everything seemed to be going without a hitch, and strangely enough, that fact worried Mr Cowan. He was more at home in an atmosphere of trouble, this unusual peace disturbed him.

'Everything is going a darned sight too smoothly,' murmured Mr Cowan to himself. 'Madame is like a cat that has been fed on cream, it's too good to last, something is bound to happen.'

Perhaps as the result of his long contact with the operatic world, Mr Cowan had developed the sixth sense, certainly his prognostications were justified. It was just before seven o'clock that evening when the French maid, Elise, came running to him in great distress.

'Ah, Mr Cowan, come quickly, I beg of you come quickly.'

'What's the matter?' demanded Cowan anxiously. 'Madame got her back up about anything – ructions, eh, is that it?'

'No, no, it is not Madame, it is Signor Roscari, he is ill, he is dying!'

'Dying? Oh, come now.'

Cowan hurried after her as she led the way to the stricken Italian's bedroom. The little man was lying on his bed, or rather jerking himself all over it in a series of contortions that would have been humorous had they been less grave. Paula Nazorkoff was bending over him; she greeted Cowan imperiously.

'Ah! there you are. Our poor Roscari, he suffers horribly. Doubtless he has eaten something.'

'I am dying,' groaned the little man. 'The pain – it is terrible. Ow!'

He contorted himself again, clasping both hands to his stomach, and rolling about on the bed.

'We must send for a doctor,' said Cowan.

Paula arrested him as he was about to move to the door.

'The doctor is already on his way, he will do all that can be done for the poor suffering one, that is arranged for, but never never will Roscari be able to sing tonight.'

'I shall never sing again, I am dying,' groaned the Italian.

'No, no, you are not dying,' said Paula. 'It is but an indigestion, but all the same, impossible that you should sing.'

'I have been poisoned.'

'Yes, it is the ptomaine without doubt,' said Paula. 'Stay with him, Elise, till the doctor comes.'

The singer swept Cowan with her from the room.

'What are we to do?' she demanded.

Cowan shook his head hopelessly. The hour was so far advanced that it would not be possible to get anyone from London to take Roscari's place. Lady Rustonbury, who had just been informed of her guest's illness, came hurrying along the corridor to join them. Her principal concern, like Paula Nazorkoff's, was the success of *Tosca*.

'If there were only someone near at hand,' groaned the prima donna.

'Ah!' Lady Rustonbury gave a sudden cry. 'Of course! Bréon.'

'Bréon?'

'Yes, Edouard Bréon, you know, the famous French baritone. He lives near here, there was a picture of his house in this week's *Country Homes*. He is the very man.'

'It is an answer from heaven,' cried Nazorkoff. 'Bréon as Scarpia, I remember him well, it was one of his greatest rôles. But he has retired, has he not?'

'I will get him,' said Lady Rustonbury. 'Leave it to me.'

And being a woman of decision, she straightway ordered out the *Hispano Suiza*. Ten minutes later, M. Edouard Bréon's country retreat was invaded by an agitated countess. Lady Rustonbury, once she had made her mind up, was a very determined woman, and doubtless M. Bréon realized that there was nothing for it but to submit. Himself a man of very humble origin, he had climbed to the top of his profession, and had consorted on equal terms with dukes and princes, and the fact never failed to gratify him. Yet, since his retirement to this old-world English spot, he had known discontent. He missed the life of adulation and applause, and the English county had not been as prompt to recognize him as he thought they should have been. So he was greatly flattered and charmed by Lady Rustonbury's request.

'I will do my poor best,' he said, smiling. 'As you know, I have not sung in public for a long time now. I do not even take pupils, only one or two as a great favour. But there – since Signor Roscari is unfortunately indisposed –'

'It was a terrible blow,' said Lady Rustonbury.

'Not that he is really a singer,' said Bréon.

He told her at some length why this was so. There had been, it seemed, no baritone of distinction since Edouard Bréon retired.

'Mme Nazorkoff is singing "Tosca",' said Lady Rustonbury. 'You know her, I dare say?'

'I have never met her,' said Bréon. 'I heard her sing once in New York. A great artist – she has a sense of drama.'

Lady Rustonbury felt relieved – one never knew with these singers – they had such queer jealousies and antipathies.

She re-entered the hall at the castle some twenty minutes later waving a triumphant hand.

'I have got him,' she cried, laughing. 'Dear M. Bréon has really been too kind, I shall never forget it.'

Everyone crowded round the Frenchman, and their gratitude and appreciation were as incense to him. Edouard Bréon, though now close on sixty, was still a fine-looking man, big and dark, with a magnetic personality.

'Let me see,' said Lady Rustonbury. 'Where is Madame –? Oh! there she is.'

Paula Nazorkoff had taken no part in the general welcoming of the Frenchman. She had remained quietly sitting in a high oak chair in the shadow of the fireplace. There was, of course, no fire, for the evening was a warm one and the singer was slowly fanning herself with an immense palm-leaf fan. So aloof and detached was she, that Lady Rustonbury feared she had taken offence.

'M. Bréon.' She led him up to the singer. 'You have never yet met Madame Nazorkoff, you say.'

With a last wave, almost a flourish, of the palm leaf, Paula Nazorkoff laid it down, and stretched out her hand to the Frenchman. He took it and bowed low over it, and a faint sigh escaped from the prima donna's lips.

'Madame,' said Bréon, 'we have never sung together. That is the penalty of my age! But Fate has been kind to me, and come to my rescue.'

Paula laughed softly.

'You are too kind, M. Bréon. When I was still but a poor little unknown singer, I have sat at your feet. Your "Rigoletto" – what art, what perfection! No one could touch you.'

'Alas!' said Bréon, pretending to sigh. 'My day is over. Scarpia, Rigoletto, Radames, Sharpless, how many times have I not sung them, and now – no more!'

'Yes – tonight.'

'True, Madame – I forgot. Tonight.'

'You have sung with many "Toscas",' said Nazorkoff arrogantly; 'but never with me!'

The Frenchman bowed.

'It will be an honour,' he said softly. 'It is a great part, Madame.'

'It needs not only a singer, but an actress,' put in Lady Rustonbury.

'That is true,' Bréon agreed. 'I remember when I was a young man in Italy, going to a little out of the way theatre in Milan. My seat cost me only a couple of lira, but I heard as good singing that night as I have heard in the Metropolitan Opera House in New York. Quite a young girl sang "Tosca", she sang it like an angel. Never shall I forget her voice in "Vissi D'Arte", the clearness of it, the purity. But the dramatic force, that was lacking.'

Nazorkoff nodded.

'That comes later,' she said quietly.

'True. This young girl – Bianca Capelli, her name was – I interested myself in her career. Through me she had the chance of big engagements, but she was foolish – regrettably foolish.'

He shrugged his shoulders.

'How was she foolish?'

It was Lady Rustonbury's twenty-four-year-old daughter, Blanche Amery, who spoke. A slender girl with wide blue eyes.

The Frenchman turned to her at once politely.

'Alas! Mademoiselle, she had embroiled herself with some low fellow, a ruffian, a member of the Camorra. He got into trouble with the police, was condemned to death; she came to me begging me to do something to save her lover.'

Blanche Amery was staring at him.

'And did you?' she asked breathlessly.

'Me, Mademoiselle, what could I do? A stranger in the country.'

'You might have had influence?' suggested Nazorkoff, in her low vibrant voice.

'If I had, I doubt whether I should have exerted it. The man was not worth it. I did what I could for the girl.'

He smiled a little, and his smile suddenly struck the English girl as having something peculiarly disagreeable about it. She felt that, at that moment, his words fell far short of representing his thoughts.

'You did what you could,' said Nazorkoff. 'That was kind of you, and she was grateful, eh?'

The Frenchman shrugged his shoulders.

'The man was executed,' he said, 'and the girl entered a convent. Eh, *voilà!* The world has lost a singer.'

Nazorkoff gave a low laugh.

'We Russians are more fickle,' she said lightly.

Blanche Amery happened to be watching Cowan just as the singer spoke, and she saw his quick look of astonishment, and his lips that half-opened and then shut tight in obedience to some warning glance from Paula.

The butler appeared in the doorway.

'Dinner,' said Lady Rustonbury, rising. 'You poor things, I am so sorry for you, it must be dreadful always to have to starve yourself before singing. But there will be a very good supper afterwards.'

'We shall look forward to it,' said Paula Nazorkoff. She laughed softly. '*Afterwards!*'

Inside the theatre, the first act of *Tosca* had just drawn to a close. The audience stirred, spoke to each other. The royalties, charming and gracious, sat in the three velvet chairs in the front row. Everyone was whispering and murmuring to each other, there was a general feeling that in the first act Nazorkoff had hardly lived up to her great reputation. Most of the audience did not realize that in this the singer showed her art, in the first act she was saving her voice and herself. She made of La Tosca a light, frivolous figure, toying with love, coquettishly jealous and exciting. Bréon, though the glory of his voice was past its prime, still struck a magnificent figure as the cynical Scarpia. There was no hint of the decrepit roué in his conception of the part. He made of Scarpia a handsome, almost benign figure, with just a hint of the subtle malevolence that underlay the outward seeming. In the last passage, with the organ and the procession, when Scarpia stands lost in thought, gloating over his plan to secure Tosca, Bréon had displayed a wonderful art. Now the curtain rose up on the second act, the scene in Scarpia's apartments.

This time, when Tosca entered, the art of Nazorkoff at once became apparent. Here was a woman in deadly terror playing her part with the assurance of a fine actress. Her easy greeting of Scarpia, her nonchalance, her smiling replies to him! In this scene, Paula Nazorkoff acted with her eyes, she carried herself with deadly quietness, with an impassive, smiling face. Only her eyes that kept darting glances at Scarpia betrayed her true feelings. And so the story went on, the torture scene, the breaking down of Tosca's composure, and her utter abandonment when she fell at Scarpia's feet imploring him vainly for mercy. Old Lord Leconmere, a connoisseur of music, moved appreciatively, and a foreign ambassador sitting next to him murmured:

'She surpasses herself, Nazorkoff, tonight. There is no other woman on the stage who can let herself go as she does.'

Leconmere nodded.

And now Scarpia has named his price, and Tosca, horrified, flies from him to the window. Then comes the beat of drums from afar, and Tosca flings herself wearily down on the sofa. Scarpia standing over her, recites how his people are raising up the gallows – and then silence, and again the far-off beat of drums. Nazorkoff lay prone on the sofa, her head hanging downwards almost touching the floor, masked by her hair. Then, in exquisite contrast to the passion and stress of the last twenty minutes, her voice rang out, high and clear, the voice, as she had told Cowan, of a choir boy or an angel.

'Vissi d'arte, vissi d'arte, no feci mai male ad anima viva. Con man furtiva quante miserie conobbi, aiutai.'

It was the voice of a wondering, puzzled child. Then she is once more kneeling and imploring, till the instant when Spoletta enters. Tosca, exhausted, gives in, and Scarpia utters his fateful words of double-edged meaning. Spoletta departs once more. Then comes the dramatic moment, whe Tosca, raising a glass of wine in her trembling hand, catches sight of the knife on the table, and slips it behind her.

Bréon rose up, handsome, saturnine, inflamed with passion. '*Tosca, finalmente mia!*' The lightning stabs with the knife, and Tosca's hiss of vengeance:

'*Questo e il bacio di Tosca!*' ('It is thus that Tosca kisses.')

Never had Nazorkoff shown such an appreciation of Tosca's act of vengeance. That last fierce whispered '*Muori dannato*,' and then in a strange, quiet voice that filled the theatre:

'*Or gli perdono!*' ('Now I forgive him!')

The soft death tune began as Tosca set about her ceremonial, placing the candles each side of his head, the crucifix on his breast, her last pause in the doorway looking back, the roll of distant drums, and the curtain fell.

This time real enthusiasm broke out in the audience, but it was short-lived. Someone hurried out from behind the wings, and spoke to Lord Rustonbury. He rose, and after a minute or two's consultation, turned and beckoned to Sir Donald Calthorp, who was an eminent physician. Almost immediately the truth spread through the audience. Something had happened, an accident, someone was badly hurt. One of the singers appeared before the curtain and explained that M Bréon had unfortunately met with an accident – the opera could not proceed. Again the rumour went round, Bréon had been stabbed, Nazorkoff had lost her head, she had lived in her part so completely that she had actually stabbed the man who was acting with her. Lord Leconmere, talking to his ambassador friend, felt a touch on his arm, and turned to look into Blanche Amery's eyes.

'It was not an accident,' the girl was saying. 'I am sure it was not an accident. Didn't you hear, just before dinner, that story he was telling about the girl in Italy? That girl was Paula Nazorkoff. Just after, she said something about being Russian, and I saw Mr Cowan look amazed. She may have taken a Russian name, but he knows well enough that she is Italian.'

'My dear Blanche,' said Lord Leconmere.

'I tell you I am sure of it. She had a picture paper in her bedroom opened at the page showing M Bréon in his English country home. She knew before she came down here. I believe she gave something to that poor little Italian man to make him ill.'

'But why?' cried Lord Leconmere. 'Why?'

'Don't you see? It's the story of Tosca all over again. He wanted her in Italy, but she was faithful to her lover, and she went to him to try to get him to save her lover, and he pretended he would. Instead he let him die. And now at last her revenge has come. Didn't you hear the way she hissed "*I am Tosca*"? And I saw Bréon's face when she said it, *he knew then* – he recognized her!'

In her dressing-room, Paula Nazorkoff sat motionless, a white ermine cloak held round her. There was a knock at the door.

'Come in,' said the prima donna.

Elise entered. She was sobbing.

'Madame, Madame, he is dead! And –'

'Yes?'

'Madame, how can I tell you? There are two gentlemen of the police there, they want to speak to you.'

Paula Nazorkoff rose to her full height.

'I will go to them,' she said quietly.

She untwisted a collar of pearls from her neck, and put them into the French girl's hands.

'Those are for you, Elise, you have been a good girl. I shall not need them now where I am going. You understand, Elise? *I shall not sing "Tosca" again.*'

She stood a moment by the door, her eyes sweeping over the dressing-room, as though she looked back over the past thirty years of her career.

Then softly between her teeth, she murmured the last line of another opera:

'*La commedia e finita!*'

The Last Séance

'The Last Séance' was first published in the USA in *Ghost Stories*
magazine, November 1926, and as 'The Stolen Ghost' in
The Sovereign Magazine, March 1927.

Raoul Daubreuil crossed the Seine humming a little tune to himself. He was a good-looking young Frenchman of about thirty-two, with a fresh-coloured face and a little black moustache. By profession he was an engineer. In due course he reached the Cardonet and turned in at the door of No. 17. The concierge looked out from her lair and gave him a grudging 'Good morning,' to which he replied cheerfully. Then he mounted the stairs to the apartment on the third floor. As he stood there waiting for his ring at the bell to be answered he hummed once more his little tune. Raoul Daubreuil was feeling particularly cheerful this morning. The door was opened by an elderly Frenchwoman whose wrinkled face broke into smiles when she saw who the visitor was.

'Good morning, Monsieur.'

'Good morning, Elise,' said Raoul.

He passed into the vestibule, pulling off his gloves as he did so.

'Madame expects me, does she not?' he asked over his shoulder.

'Ah, yes, indeed, Monsieur.'

Elise shut the front door and turned towards him.

'If Monsieur will pass into the little *salon* Madame will be with him in a few minutes. At the moment she reposes herself.'

Raoul looked up sharply.

'Is she not well?'

'*Well!*'

Elise gave a snort. She passed in front of Raoul and opened the door of the little *salon* for him. He went in and she followed him.

'*Well!*' she continued. 'How could she be well, poor lamb? *Séances, séances*, and always *séances*! It is not right – not natural, not what the good

God intended for us. For me, I say straight out, it is trafficking with the devil.'

Raoul patted her on the shoulder reassuringly.

'There, there, Elise,' he said soothingly, 'do not excite yourself, and do not be too ready to see the devil in everything you do not understand.'

Elise shook her head doubtingly.

'Ah, well,' she grumbled under her breath, 'Monsieur may say what he pleases, I don't like it. Look at Madame, every day she gets whiter and thinner, and the headaches!'

She held up her hands.

'Ah, no, it is not good, all this spirit business. Spirits indeed! All the good spirits are in Paradise, and the others are in Purgatory.'

'Your view of the life after death is refeshingly simple, Elise,' said Raoul as he dropped into the chair.

The old woman drew herself up.

'I am a good Catholic, Monsieur.'

She crossed herself, went towards the door, then paused, her hand on the handle.

'Afterwards when you are married, Monsieur,' she said pleadingly, 'it will not continue – all this?'

Raoul smiled at her affectionately.

'You are a good faithful creature, Elise,' he said, 'and devoted to your mistress. Have no fear, once she is my wife, all this "spirit business" as you call it, will cease. For Madame Daubreuil there will be no more *séances*.'

Elise's face broke into smiles.

'Is it true what you say?' she asked eagerly.

The other nodded gravely.

'Yes,' he said, speaking almost more to himself than to her. 'Yes, all this must end. Simone has a wonderful gift and she has used it freely, but now she has done her part. As you have justly observed, Elise, day by day she gets whiter and thinner. The life of a medium is a particularly trying and arduous one, involving a terrible nervous strain. All the same, Elise, your mistress is the most wonderful medium in Paris – more, in France. People from all over the world come to her because they know that with her there is no trickery, no deceit.'

Elise gave a snort of contempt.

'Deceit! Ah, no, indeed. Madame could not deceive a newborn babe if she tried.'

'She is an angel,' said the young Frenchman with fervour. 'And I – I shall do everything a man can to make her happy. You believe that?'

Elise drew herself up, and spoke with a certain simple dignity.

'I have served Madame for many years, Monsieur. With all respect I may say that I love her. If I did not believe that you adored her as she deserves to be adored – *eh bien*, Monsieur! I should be willing to tear you limb from limb.'

Raoul laughed.

'Bravo, Elise! you are a faithful friend, and you must approve of me now that I have told you Madame is going to give up the spirits.'

He expected the old woman to receive this pleasantry with a laugh, but somewhat to his surprise she remained grave.

'Supposing, Monsieur,' she said hesitatingly, 'the spirits will not give *her* up?'

Raoul stared at her.

'Eh! What do you mean?'

'I said,' repeated Elise, 'supposing the spirits will not give *her* up?'

'I thought you didn't believe in the spirits, Elise?'

'No more I do,' said Elise stubbornly. 'It is foolish to believe in them. All the same –'

'Well?'

'It is difficult for me to explain, Monsieur. You see, me, I always thought that these mediums, as they call themselves, were just clever cheats who imposed on the poor souls who had lost their dear ones. But Madame is not like that. Madame is good. Madame is honest and –'

She lowered her voice and spoke in a tone of awe.

'*Things happen.* It is no trickery, things happen, and that is why I am afraid. For I am sure of this, Monsieur, it is not right. It is against nature and le bon Dieu, and *somebody will have to pay.*'

Raoul got up from his chair and came and patted her on the shoulder.

'Calm yourself, my good Elise,' he said, smiling. 'See, I will give you some good news. Today is the last of these *séances*; after today there will be no more.'

'There *is* one today then?' asked the old woman suspiciously.

'The last, Elise, the last.'

Elise shook her head disconsolately.

'Madame is not fit –' she began.

But her words were interrupted, the door opened and a tall, fair woman came in. She was slender and graceful, with the face of a Botticelli Madonna. Raoul's face lighted up, and Elise withdrew quickly and discreetly.

'Simone!'

He took both her long, white hands in his and kissed each in turn. She murmured his name very softly.

'Raoul, my dear one.'

Again he kissed her hands and then looked intently into her face.

'Simone, how pale you are! Elise told me you were resting; you are not ill, my well-beloved?'

'No, not ill –' she hesitated.

He led her over to the sofa and sat down on it beside her.

'But tell me then.'

The medium smiled faintly.

'You will think me foolish,' she murmured.

'I? Think you foolish? Never.'

Simone withdrew her hand from his grasp. She sat perfectly still for a moment or two gazing down at the carpet. Then she spoke in a low, hurried voice.

'I am afraid, Raoul.'

He waited for a minute or two expecting her to go on, but as she did not he said encouragingly:

'Yes, afraid of what?'

'Just afraid – that is all.'

'But –'

He looked at her in perplexity, and she answered the look quickly.

'Yes, it is absurd, isn't it, and yet I feel just that. Afraid, nothing more. I don't know what of, or why, but all the time I am possessed with the idea that something terrible – terrible, is going to happen to me . . .'

She stared out in front of her. Raoul put an arm gently round her.

'My dearest,' he said, 'come, you must not give way. I know what it is, the strain, Simone, the strain of a medium's life. All you need is rest – rest and quiet.'

She looked at him gratefully.

'Yes, Raoul, you are right. That is what I need, rest and quiet.'

She closed her eyes and leant back a little against his arm.

'And happiness,' murmured Raoul in her ear.

His arm drew her closer. Simone, her eyes still closed, drew a deep breath.

'Yes,' she murmured, 'yes. When your arms are round me I feel safe. I forget my life – the terrible life – of a medium. You know much, Raoul, but even you do not know all it means.'

He felt her body grow rigid in his embrace. Her eyes opened again, staring in front of her.

'One sits in the cabinet in the darkness, waiting, and the darkness is terrible, Raoul, for it is the darkness of emptiness, of nothingness. Deliberately one gives oneself up to be lost in it. After that one knows nothing, one feels nothing, but at last there comes the slow, painful return, the awakening out of sleep, but so tired – so terribly tired.'

'I know,' murmured Raoul, 'I know.'

'So tired,' murmured Simone again.

Her whole body seemed to droop as she repeated the words.

'But you are wonderful, Simone.'

He took her hands in his, trying to rouse her to share his enthusiasm.

'You are unique – the greatest medium the world has ever known.'

She shook her head, smiling a little at that.

'Yes, yes,' Raoul insisted.

He drew two letters from his pocket.

'See here, from Professor Roche of the *Salpêtrière*, and this one from Dr Genir at Nancy, both imploring that you will continue to sit for them occasionally.'

'Ah, no!'

Simone sprang to her feet.

'I will not, I will not. It is to be all finished – all done with. You promised me, Raoul.'

Raoul stared at her in astonishment as she stood wavering, facing him almost like a creature at bay. He got up and took her hand.

'Yes, yes,' he said. 'Certainly it is finished, that is understood. But I am so proud of you, Simone, that is why I mentioned those letters.'

She threw him a swift sideways glance of suspicion.

'It is not that you will ever want me to sit again?'

'No, no,' said Raoul, 'unless perhaps you yourself would care to, just occasionally for these old friends –'

But she interrupted him, speaking excitedly.

'No, no, never again. There is a danger. I tell you, I can feel it, great danger.'

She clasped her hands on her forehead a minute, then walked across to the window.

'Promise me never again,' she said in a quieter voice over her shoulder.

Raoul followed her and put his arms round her shoulders.

'My dear one,' he said tenderly, 'I promise you after today you shall never sit again.'

He felt the sudden start she gave.

'Today,' she murmured. 'Ah, yes – I had forgotten Madame Exe.'

Raoul looked at his watch.

'She is due any minute now; but perhaps, Simone, if you do not feel well –'

Simone hardly seemed to be listening to him; she was following out her own train of thought.

'She is – a strange woman, Raoul, a very strange woman. Do you know I – I have almost a horror of her.'

'Simone!'

There was reproach in his voice, and she was quick to feel it.

'Yes, yes, I know, you are like all Frenchmen, Raoul. To you a mother is sacred and it is unkind of me to feel like that about her when she grieves so for her lost child. But – I cannot explain it, she is so big and black, and her hands – have you ever noticed her hands, Raoul? Great big strong hands, as strong as a man's. Ah!'

She gave a little shiver and closed her eyes. Raoul withdrew his arm and spoke almost coldly.

'I really cannot understand you, Simone. Surely you, a woman, should have nothing but sympathy for another woman, a mother bereft of her only child.'

Simone made a gesture of impatience.

'Ah, it is you who do not understand, my friend! One cannot help these things. The first moment I saw her I felt –'

She flung her hands out.

'*Fear!* You remember, it was a long time before I would consent to sit for her? I felt sure in some way she would bring me misfortune.'

Raoul shrugged his shoulders.

'Whereas, in actual fact, she brought you the exact opposite,' he said drily. 'All the sittings have been attended with marked success. The spirit of the little Amelie was able to control you at once, and the materializations have really been striking. Professor Roche ought really to have been present at the last one.'

'Materializations,' said Simone in a low voice. 'Tell me, Raoul (you know that I know nothing of what takes place while I am in the trance), are the materializations really so wonderful?'

He nodded enthusiastically.

'At the first few sittings the figure of the child was visible in a kind of nebulous haze,' he explained, 'but at the last *seance* –'

'Yes?'

He spoke very softly.

'Simone, the child that stood there was an actual living child of flesh and blood. I even touched her – but seeing that the touch was acutely painful to you, I would not permit Madame Exe to do the same. I was afraid that her self-control might break down, and that some harm to you might result.'

Simone turned away again towards the window.

'I was terribly exhausted when I woke,' she murmured. 'Raoul, are you sure – are you really sure that all this is *right*? You know what dear old Elise thinks, that I am trafficking with the devil?'

She laughed rather uncertainly.

'You know what I believe,' said Raoul gravely. 'In the handling of the unknown there must always be danger, but the cause is a noble one, for it is the cause of Science. All over the world there have been martyrs to Science, pioneers who have paid the price so that others may follow safely in their footsteps. For ten years now you have worked for Science at the cost of a terrific nervous strain. Now your part is done, from today onward you are free to be happy.'

She smiled at him affectionately, her calm restored. Then she glanced quickly up at the clock.

'Madame Exe is late,' she murmured. 'She may not come.'

'I think she will,' said Raoul. 'Your clock is a little fast, Simone.'

Simone moved about the room, rearranging an ornament here and there.

'I wonder who she is, this Madame Exe?' she observed. 'Where she comes from, who her people are? It is strange that we know nothing about her.'

Raoul shrugged his shoulders.

'Most people remain incognito if possible when they come to a medium,' he observed. 'It is an elementary precaution.'

'I suppose so,' agreed Simone listlessly.

A little china vase she was holding slipped from her fingers and broke to pieces on the tiles of the fireplace. She turned sharply on Raoul.

'You see,' she murmured, 'I am not myself. Raoul, would you think me very – very cowardly if I told Madame Exe I could not sit today?'

His look of pained astonishment made her redden.

'You promised, Simone –' he began gently.

She backed against the wall.

'I won't do it, Raoul. I won't do it.'

And again that glance of his, tenderly reproachful, made her wince.

'It is not of the money I am thinking, Simone, though you must realize that the money this woman has offered you for the last sitting is enormous – simply enormous.'

She interrupted him defiantly.

'There are things that matter more than money.'

'Certainly there are,' he agreed warmly. 'That is just what I am saying. Consider – this woman is a mother, a mother who has lost her only child. If you are not really ill, if it is only a whim on your part – you can deny a rich woman a caprice, can you deny a mother one last sight of her child?'

The medium flung her hands out despairingly in front of her.

'Oh, you torture me,' she murmured. 'All the same you are right. I will do as you wish, but I know now what I am afraid of – it is the word "mother".'

'Simone!'

'There are certain primitive elementary forces, Raoul. Most of them have been destroyed by civilization, but motherhood stands where it stood at the beginning. Animals – human beings, they are all the same. A mother's love for her child is like nothing else in the world. It knows no law, no pity, it dares all things and crushes down remorselessly all that stands in its path.'

She stopped, panting a little, then turned to him with a quick, disarming smile.

'I am foolish today, Raoul. I know it.'

He took her hand in his.

'Lie down for a minute or two,' he urged. 'Rest till she comes.'

'Very well.' She smiled at him and left the room.

Raoul remained for a minute or two lost in thought, then he strode to the door, opened it, and crossed the little hall. He went into a room the other side of it, a sitting room very much like the one he had left, but at one end was an alcove with a big armchair set in it. Heavy black velvet curtains were arranged so as to pull across the alcove. Elise was busy arranging the room. Close to the alcove she had set two chairs and a small round table. On the table was a tambourine, a horn, and some paper and pencils.

'The last time,' murmured Elise with grim satisfaction. 'Ah, Monsieur, I wish it were over and done with.'

The sharp ting of an electric bell sounded.

'There she is, the great gendarme of a woman,' continued the old servant. 'Why can't she go and pray decently for her little one's soul in a church, and burn a candle to Our Blessed Lady? Does not the good God know what is best for us?'

'Answer the bell, Elise,' said Raoul peremptorily.

She threw him a look, but obeyed. In a minute or two she returned ushering in the visitor.

'I will tell my mistress you are here, Madame.'

Raoul came forward to shake hands with Madame Exe. Simone's words floated back to his memory.

'So big and so black.'

She *was* a big woman, and the heavy black of French mourning seemed almost exaggerated in her case. Her voice when she spoke was very deep.

'I fear I am a little late, Monsieur.'

'A few moments only,' said Raoul, smiling. 'Madame Simone is lying down. I am sorry to say she is far from well, very nervous and overwrought.'

Her hand, which she was just withdrawing, closed on his suddenly like a vice.

'But she will sit?' she demanded sharply.

'Oh, yes, Madame.'

Madame Exe gave a sigh of relief, and sank into a chair, loosening one of the heavy black veils that floated round her.

'Ah, Monsieur!' she murmured, 'you cannot imagine, you cannot conceive the wonder and the joy of these *séances* to me! My little one! My Amelie! To see her, to hear her, even – perhaps – yes, perhaps to be even able to – stretch out my hand and touch her.'

Raoul spoke quickly and peremptorily.

'Madame Exe – how can I explain? – on no account must you do anything except under my express directions, otherwise there is the gravest danger.'

'Danger to me?'

'No, Madame,' said Raoul, 'to the medium. You must understand that the phenomena that occur are explained by Science in a certain way. I will put the matter very simply, using no technical terms. A spirit, to manifest itself, has to use the actual physical substance of the medium. You have seen the vapour of fluid issuing from the lips of the medium. This finally condenses and is built up into the physical semblance of the spirit's dead body. But this ectoplasm we believe to be the actual substance of the medium. We hope to prove this some day by careful weighing and testing – but the great difficulty is the danger and pain which attends the medium on any handling of the phenomena. Were anyone to seize hold of the materialization roughly the death of the medium might result.'

Madame Exe had listened to him with close attention.

'That is very interesting, Monsieur. Tell me, shall not a time come when the materialization shall advance so far that it shall be capable of detachment from its parent, the medium?'

'That is a fantastic speculation, Madame.'

She persisted.

'But, on the facts, not impossible?'

'Quite impossible today.'

'But perhaps in the future?'

He was saved from answering, for at that moment Simone entered. She looked languid and pale, but had evidently regained entire control of herself. She came forward and shook hands with Madame Exe, though Raoul noticed the faint shiver that passed through her as she did so.

'I regret, Madame, to hear that you are indisposed,' said Madame Exe.

'It is nothing,' said Simone rather brusquely. 'Shall we begin?'

She went to the alcove and sat down in the arm-chair. Suddenly Raoul in his turn felt a wave of fear pass over him.

'You are not strong enough,' he exclaimed. 'We had better cancel the *seance*. Madame Exe will understand.'

'Monsieur!'

Madame Exe rose indignantly.

'Yes, yes, it is better not, I am sure of it.'

'Madame Simone promised me one last sitting.'

'That is so,' agreed Simone quietly, 'and I am prepared to carry out my promise.'

'I hold you to it, Madame,' said the other woman.

'I do not break my word,' said Simone coldly. 'Do not fear, Raoul,' she added gently, 'after all, it is for the last time – the last time, thank God.'

At a sign from her Raoul drew the heavy black curtains across the alcove. He also pulled the curtains of the window so that the room was in semi-obscurity. He indicated one of the chairs to Madame Exe and prepared himself to take the other. Madame Exe, however, hesitated.

'You will pardon me, Monsieur, but – you understand I believe absolutely in your integrity and in that of Madame Simone. All the same, so that my testimony may be the more valuable, I took the liberty of bringing this with me.'

From her handbag she drew a length of fine cord.

'Madame!' cried Raoul. 'This is an insult!'

'A precaution.'

'I repeat it is an insult.'

'I don't understand your objection, Monsieur,' said Madame Exe coldly. 'If there is no trickery you have nothing to fear.'

Raoul laughed scornfully.

'I can assure you that I have nothing to fear, Madame. Bind me hand and foot if you will.'

His speech did not produce the effect he hoped, for Madame Exe merely murmured unemotionally:

'Thank you, Monsieur,' and advanced upon him with her roll of cord.

Suddenly Simone from behind the curtain gave a cry.

'No, no, Raoul, don't let her do it.'

Madame Exe laughed derisively.

'Madame is afraid,' she observed sarcastically.

'Yes, I am afraid.'

'Remember what you are saying, Simone,' cried Raoul. 'Madame Exe is apparently under the impression that we are charlatans.'

'I must make sure,' said Madame Exe grimly.

She went methodically about her task, binding Raoul securely to his chair.

'I must congratulate you on your knots, Madame,' he observed ironically when she had finished. 'Are you satisfied now?'

Madame Exe did not reply. She walked round the room examining
the panelling of the walls closely. Then she locked the door leading into
the hall, and, removing the key, returned to her chair.

'Now,' she said in an indescribable voice, 'I am ready.'

The minutes passed. From behind the curtain the sound of Simone's
breathing became heavier and more stertorous. Then it died away altogether,
to be succeeded by a series of moans. Then again there was silence for a
little while, broken by the sudden clattering of the tambourine. The horn
was caught up from the table and dashed to the ground. Ironic laughter was
heard. The curtains of the alcove seemed to have been pulled back a little,
the medium's figure was just visible through the opening, her head fallen
forward on her breast. Suddenly Madame Exe drew in her breath sharply.
A ribbon-like stream of mist was issuing from the medium's mouth. It
condensed and began gradually to assume a shape, the shape of a little child.

'Amelie! My little Amelie!'

The hoarse whisper came from Madame Exe. The hazy figure
condensed still further. Raoul stared almost incredulously. Never had
there been a more successful materialization. Now, surely it was a real
child, a real flesh and blood child standing there.

'*Maman!*'

The soft childish voice spoke.

'My child!' cried Madame Exe. 'My child!'

She half rose from her seat.

'Be careful, Madame,' cried Raoul warningly.

The materialization came hesitatingly through the curtains. It was a
child. She stood there, her arms held out.

'*Maman!*'

'Ah!' cried Madame Exe.

Again she half rose from her seat.

'Madame,' cried Raoul, alarmed, 'the medium –'

'I must touch her,' cried Madame Exe hoarsely.

She moved a step forward.

'For God's sake, Madame, control yourself,' cried Raoul.

He was really alarmed now.

'Sit down at once.'

'My little one, I must touch her.'

'Madame, I command you, sit down!'

He was writhing desperately in his bonds, but Madame Exe had done
her work well; he was helpless. A terrible sense of impending disaster
swept over him.

'In the name of God, Madame, sit down!' he shouted. 'Remember the medium.'

Madame Exe turned on him with a harsh laugh.

'What do I care for your medium?' she cried. 'I want my child.'

'You are mad!'

'My child, I tell you. Mine! My own! My own flesh and blood! My little one come back to me from the dead, alive and breathing.'

Raoul opened his lips, but no words would come. She was terrible, this woman! Remorseless, savage, absorbed by her own passion. The baby lips parted, and for the third time the word echoed:

'*Maman!*'

'Come then, my little one,' cried Madame Exe.

With a sharp gesture she caught up the child in her arms. From behind the curtains came a long-drawn scream of utter anguish.

'Simone!' cried Raoul. 'Simone!'

He was aware vaguely of Madame Exe rushing past him, of the unlocking of the door, of the retreating footsteps down the stairs.

From behind the curtains there still sounded the terrible high long-drawn scream – such a scream as Raoul had never heard. It died away with a horrible kind of gurgle. Then there came the thud of a body falling . . .

Raoul was working like a maniac to free himself from his bonds. In his frenzy he accomplished the impossible, snapping the cord by sheer strength. As he struggled to his feet, Elise rushed in crying 'Madame!'

'Simone!' cried Raoul.

Together they rushed forward and pulled the curtain.

Raoul staggered back.

'My God!' he murmured. 'Red – all red . . .'

Elise's voice came beside him harsh and shaking.

'So Madame is dead. It is ended. But tell me, Monsieur, what has happened. *Why is Madame all shrunken away* – why is she half her usual size? What has been happening here?'

'I do not know,' said Raoul.

His voice rose to a scream.

'I do not know. I do not know. But I think – I am going mad . . . Simone! Simone!'

The Edge

'The Edge' was first published in
Pearson's Magazine, February 1927.

Clare Halliwell walked down the short path that led from her cottage door to the gate. On her arm was a basket, and in the basket was a bottle of soup, some homemade jelly and a few grapes. There were not many poor people in the small village of Daymer's End, but such as there were were assiduously looked after, and Clare was one of the most efficient of the parish workers.

Clare Halliwell was thirty-two. She had an upright carriage, a healthy colour and nice brown eyes. She was not beautiful, but she looked fresh and pleasant and very English. Everybody liked her, and said she was a good sort. Since her mother's death, two years ago, she had lived alone in the cottage with her dog, Rover. She kept poultry and was fond of animals and of a healthy outdoor life.

As she unlatched the gate, a two-seater car swept past, and the driver, a girl in a red hat, waved a greeting. Clare responded, but for a moment her lips tightened. She felt that pang at her heart which always came when she saw Vivien Lee. Gerald's wife!

Medenham Grange, which lay just a mile outside the village, had belonged to the Lees for many generations. Sir Gerald Lee, the present owner of the Grange, was a man old for his years and considered by many stiff in manner. His pomposity really covered a good deal of shyness. He and Clare had played together as children. Later they had been friends, and a closer and dearer tie had been confidently expected by many – including, it may be said, Clare herself. There was no hurry, of course – but some day . . . She left it so in her own mind. Some day.

And then, just a year ago, the village had been startled by the news of Sir Gerald's marriage to a Miss Harper – a girl nobody had ever heard of!

The new Lady Lee had not been popular in the village. She took not the faintest interest in parochial matters, was bored by hunting, and loathed the country and outdoor sports. Many of the wiseacres shook their heads and wondered how it would end. It was easy to see where Sir Gerald's infatuation had come in. Vivien was a beauty. From head to foot she was a complete contrast to Clare Halliwell, small, elfin, dainty, with golden-red hair that curled enchantingly over her pretty ears, and big violet eyes that could shoot a sideways glance of provocation to the manner born.

Gerald Lee, in his simple man's way, had been anxious that his wife and Clare should be great friends. Clare was often asked to dine at the Grange, and Vivien made a pretty pretence of affectionate intimacy whenever they met. Hence that gay salutation of hers this morning.

Clare walked on and did her errand. The Vicar was also visiting the old woman in question and he and Clare walked a few yards together afterwards before their ways parted. They stood still for a minute discussing parish affairs.

'Jones has broken out again, I'm afraid,' said the Vicar. 'And I had such hopes after he had volunteered, of his own accord, to take the pledge.'

'Disgusting,' said Clare crisply.

'It seems so to us,' said Mr Wilmot, 'but we must remember that it is very hard to put ourselves in his place and realize his temptation. The desire for drink is unaccountable to us, but we all have our own temptations, and thus we can understand.'

'I suppose we have,' said Clare uncertainly.

The Vicar glanced at her.

'Some of us have the good fortune to be very little tempted,' he said gently. 'But even to those people their hour comes. Watch and pray, remember, that ye enter not into temptation.'

Then bidding her goodbye, he walked briskly away. Clare went on thoughtfully, and presently she almost bumped into Sir Gerald Lee.

'Hullo, Clare. I was hoping to run across you. You look jolly fit. What a colour you've got.'

The colour had not been there a minute before. Lee went on:

'As I say, I was hoping to run across you. Vivien's got to go off to Bournemouth for the weekend. Her mother's not well. Can you dine with us Tuesday instead of tonight?'

'Oh, yes! Tuesday will suit me just as well.'

'That's all right, then. Splendid. I must hurry along.'

Clare went home to find her one faithful domestic standing on the doorstep looking out for her.

'There you are, Miss. Such a to-do. They've brought Rover home. He went off on his own this morning, and a car ran clean over him.'

Clare hurried to the dog's side. She adored animals, and Rover was her especial darling. She felt his legs one by one, and then ran her hands over his body. He groaned once or twice and licked her hand.

'If there's any serious injury, it's internal,' she said at last. 'No bones seem to be broken.'

'Shall we get the vet to see him, Miss?'

Clare shook her head. She had little faith in the local vet.

'We'll wait until tomorrow. He doesn't seem to be in great pain, and his gums are a good colour, so there can't be much internal bleeding. Tomorrow, if I don't like the look of him, I'll take him over to Skippington in the car and let Reeves have a look at him. He's far and away the best man.'

On the following day, Rover seemed weaker, and Clare duly carried out her project. The small town of Skippington was about forty miles away, a long run, but Reeves, the vet there, was celebrated for many miles round.

He diagnosed certain internal injuries, but held out good hopes of recovery, and Clare went away quite content to leave Rover in his charge.

There was only one hotel of any pretensions in Skippington, the *County Arms*. It was mainly frequented by commercial travellers, for there was no good hunting country near Skippington, and it was off the track of the main roads for motorists.

Lunch was not served till one o'clock, and as it wanted a few minutes of that hour, Clare amused herself by glancing over the entries in the open visitors' book.

Suddenly she gave a stifled exclamation. Surely she knew that handwriting, with its loops and whirls and flourishes? She had always considered it unmistakable. Even now she could have sworn – but of course it was clearly impossible. Vivien Lee was at Bournemouth. The entry itself showed it to be impossible: *Mr and Mrs Cyril Brown. London.*

But in spite of herself her eyes strayed back again and again to that curly writing, and on an impulse she could not quite define she asked abruptly of the woman in the office:

'Mrs Cyril Brown? I wonder if that is the same one I know?'

'A small lady? Reddish hair? Very pretty. She came in a red two-seater car, madam. A Peugeot, I believe.'

Then it was! A coincidence would be too remarkable. As if in a dream, she heard the woman go on:

'They were here just over a month ago for a weekend, and liked it so much that they have come again. Newly married, I should fancy.'

Clare heard herself saying: 'Thank you. I don't think that could be my friend.'

Her voice sounded different, as though it belonged to someone else. Presently she was sitting in the dining-room, quietly eating cold roast beef, her mind a maze of conflicting thought and emotions.

She had no doubts whatever. She had summed Vivien up pretty correctly on their first meeting. Vivien was that kind. She wondered vaguely who the man was. Someone Vivien had known before her marriage? Very likely – it didn't matter – nothing mattered, but Gerald.

What was she – Clare – to do about Gerald? He ought to know – surely he ought to know. It was clearly her duty to tell him. She had discovered Vivien's secret by accident, but she must lose no time in acquainting Gerald with the facts. She was Gerald's friend, not Vivien's.

But somehow or other she felt uncomfortable. Her conscience was not satisfied. On the face of it, her reasoning was good, but duty and inclination jumped suspiciously together. She admitted to herself that she disliked Vivien. Besides, if Gerald Lee were to divorce his wife – and Clare had no doubts at all that that was exactly what he would do, he was a man with an almost fanatical view of his own honour – then – well, the way would lie open for Gerald to come to her. Put like that, she shrank back fastidiously. Her own proposed action seemed naked and ugly.

The personal element entered in too much. She could not be sure of her own motives. Clare was essentially a high-minded, conscientious woman. She strove now very earnestly to see where her duty lay. She wished, as she had always wished, to do right. What was right in this case? What was wrong?

By a pure accident she had come into possession of facts that affected vitally the man she loved and the woman whom she disliked and – yes, one might as well be frank – of whom she was bitterly jealous. She could ruin that woman. Was she justified in doing so?

Clare had always held herself aloof from the back-biting and scandal which is an inevitable part of village life. She hated to feel that she now resembled one of those human ghouls she had always professed to despise.

Suddenly the Vicar's words that morning flashed across her mind:

'*Even to those people their hour comes.*'

Was this *her* hour? Was this *her* temptation? Had it come insidiously disguised as a duty? She was Clare Halliwell, a Christian, in love and charity with all men – and women. If she were to tell Gerald, she must be quite sure that only impersonal motives guided her. For the present she would say nothing.

She paid her bill for luncheon and drove away, feeling an indescribable lightening of spirit. Indeed, she felt happier than she had done for a long time. She felt glad that she had had the strength to resist temptation, to do nothing mean or unworthy. Just for a second it flashed across her mind that it might be a sense of power that had so lightened her spirits, but she dismissed the idea as fantastic.

By Tuesday night she was strengthened in her resolve. The revelation could not come through her. She must keep silence. Her own secret love for Gerald made speech impossible. Rather a high-minded view to take? Perhaps; but it was the only one possible for her.

She arrived at the Grange in her own little car. Sir Gerald's chauffeur was at the front door to drive it round to the garage after she had alighted, as the night was a wet one. He had just driven off when Clare remembered some books which she had borrowed and had brought with her to return. She called out, but the man did not hear her. The butler ran out after the car.

So, for a minute or two, Clare was alone in the hall, close to the door of the drawing-room which the butler had just unlatched prior to announcing her. Those inside the room, however, knew nothing of her arrival, and so it was that Vivien's voice, high pitched – not quite the voice of a lady – rang out clearly and distinctly.

'Oh, we're only waiting for Clare Halliwell. You must know her – lives in the village – supposed to be one of the local belles, but frightfully unattractive really. She tried her best to catch Gerald, but he wasn't having any.

'Oh, yes, darling' – this in answer to a murmured protest from her husband. 'She did – you mayn't be aware of the fact – but she did her very utmost. Poor old Clare! A good sort, but such a dump!'

Clare's face went dead white, her hands, hanging against her sides, clenched themselves in anger such as she had never known before. At that moment she could have murdered Vivien Lee. It was only by a supreme physical effort that she regained control of herself. That, and the half-formed thought that she held it in her power to punish Vivien for those cruel words.

The butler had returned with the books. He opened the door, announced her, and in another moment she was greeting a roomful of people in her usual pleasant manner.

Vivien, exquisitely dressed in some dark wine colour that showed off her white fragility, was particularly affectionate and gushing. They didn't see half enough of Clare. She, Vivien, was going to learn golf, and Clare must come out with her on the links.

Gerald was very attentive and kind. Though he had no suspicion that she had overheard his wife's words, he had some vague idea of making up for them. He was very fond of Clare, and he wished Vivien wouldn't say the things she did. He and Clare had been friends, nothing more – and if there was an uneasy suspicion at the back of his mind that he was shirking the truth in that last statement, he put it away from him.

After dinner the talk fell on dogs, and Clare recounted Rover's accident. She purposely waited for a lull in the conversation to say:

'. . . so, on Saturday, I took him to Skippington.'

She heard the sudden rattle of Vivien Lee's coffee-cup on the saucer, but she did not look at her – yet.

'To see that man, Reeves?'

'Yes. He'll be all right, I think. I had lunch at the *County Arms* afterwards. Rather a decent little pub.' She turned now to Vivien. 'Have you ever stayed there?'

If she had had any doubts, they were swept aside. Vivien's answer came quick – in stammering haste.

'I? Oh! N-no, no.'

Fear was in her eyes. They were wide and dark with it, as they met Clare's. Clare's eyes told nothing. They were calm, scrutinizing. No one could have dreamt of the keen pleasure that they veiled. At that moment Clare almost forgave Vivien for the words she had overheard earlier in the evening. She tasted in that moment a fullness of power that almost made her head reel. She held Vivien Lee in the hollow of her hand.

The following day, she received a note from the other woman. Would Clare come up and have tea with her quietly that afternoon? Clare refused.

Then Vivien called on her. Twice she came at hours when Clare was almost certain to be at home. On the first occasion, Clare really was out; on the second, she slipped out by the back way when she saw Vivien coming up the path.

'She's not sure yet whether I know or not,' she said to herself. 'She wants to find out without committing herself. But she shan't – not until I'm ready.'

Clare hardly knew herself what she was waiting for. She had decided to keep silence – that was the only straight and honourable course. She felt an additional glow of virtue when she remembered the extreme provocation she had received. After overhearing the way Vivien talked of her behind her back, a weaker character, she felt, might have abandoned her good resolutions.

She went twice to church on Sunday. First to early Communion, from which she came out strengthened and uplifted. No personal feelings should weigh with her – nothing mean or petty. She went again to morning service. Mr Wilmot preached on the famous prayer of the Pharisee. He sketched the life of that man, a good man, pillar of the church. And he pictured the slow, creeping blight of spiritual pride that distorted and soiled all that he was.

Clare did not listen very attentively. Vivien was in the big square pew of the Lee family, and Clare knew by instinct that the other intended to get hold of her afterwards.

So it fell out. Vivien attached herself to Clare, walked home with her, and asked if she might come in. Clare, of course, assented. They sat in Clare's little sitting-room, bright with flowers and old-fashioned chintzes. Vivien's talk was desultory and jerky.

'I was at Bournemouth, you know, last weekend,' she remarked presently.

'Gerald told me so,' said Clare.

They looked at each other. Vivien appeared almost plain today. Her face had a sharp, foxy look that robbed it of much of its charm.

'When you were at Skippington –' began Vivien.

'When I was at Skippington?' echoed Clare politely.

'You were speaking about some little hotel there.'

'The *County Arms*. Yes. You didn't know it, you said?'

'I – I have been there once.'

'Oh!'

She had only to keep still and wait. Vivien was quite unfitted to bear a strain of any kind. Already she was breaking down under it. Suddenly she leant forward and spoke vehemently.

'You don't like me. You never have. You've always hated me. You're enjoying yourself now, playing with me like a cat with a mouse. You're cruel – cruel. That's why I'm afraid of you, because deep down you're cruel.'

'Really, Vivien!' said Clare sharply.

'You *know*, don't you? Yes, I can see that you know. You knew that night – when you spoke about Skippington. You've found out somehow. Well, I want to know what you are going to do about it? What are you going to do?'

Clare did not reply for a minute, and Vivien sprang to her feet.

'What are you going to do? I must know. You're not going to deny that you know all about it?'

'I do not propose to deny anything,' said Clare coldly.

'You saw me there that day?'

'No. I saw your handwriting in the book – Mr and Mrs Cyril Brown.' Vivien flushed darkly.

'Since then,' continued Clare quietly, 'I have made inquiries. I find that you were not at Bournemouth that weekend. Your mother never sent for you. Exactly the same thing happened about six weeks previously.'

Vivien sank down again on the sofa. She burst into furious crying, the crying of a frightened child.

'What are you going to do?' she gasped. 'Are you going to tell Gerald?'

'I don't know yet,' said Clare.

She felt calm, omnipotent.

Vivien sat up, pushing the red curls back from her forehead.

'Would you like to hear all about it?'

'It would be as well, I think.'

Vivien poured out the whole story. There was no reticence in her. Cyril 'Brown' was Cyril Haviland, a young engineer to whom she had previously been engaged. His health failed, and he lost his job, whereupon he made no bones about jilting the penniless Vivien and marrying a rich widow many years older than himself. Soon afterwards Vivien married Gerald Lee.

She had met Cyril again by chance. That was the first of many meetings. Cyril, backed by his wife's money, was prospering in his career, and becoming a well-known figure. It was a sordid story, a story of backstairs meeting, of ceaseless lying and intrigue.

'I love him so,' Vivien repeated again and again, with a sudden moan, and each time the words made Clare feel physically sick.

At last the stammering recital came to an end. Vivien muttered a shamefaced: 'Well?'

'What am I going to do?' asked Clare. 'I can't tell you. I must have time to think.'

'You won't give me away to Gerald?'

'It may be my duty to do so.'

'No, no.' Vivien's voice rose to a hysterical shriek. 'He'll divorce me. He won't listen to a word. He'll find out from that hotel, and Cyril will be dragged into it. And then his wife will divorce him. Everything will go – his career, his health – he'll be penniless again. He'd never forgive me – never.'

'If you'll excuse my saying so,' said Clare, 'I don't think much of this Cyril of yours.'

Vivien paid no attention.

'I tell you he'll hate me – hate me. I can't bear it. Don't tell Gerald. I'll do anything you like, but don't tell Gerald.'

'I must have time to decide,' said Clare gravely. 'I can't promise anything off-hand. In the meantime, you and Cyril mustn't meet again.'

'No, no, we won't. I swear it.'

'When I know what's the right thing to do,' said Clare, 'I'll let you know.'

She got up. Vivien went out of the house in a furtive, slinking way, glancing back over her shoulder.

Clare wrinkled her nose in disgust. A beastly affair. Would Vivien keep her promise not to see Cyril? Probably not. She was weak – rotten all through.

That afternoon Clare went for a long walk. There was a path which led along the downs. On the left the green hills sloped gently down to the sea far below, while the path wound steadily upward. This walk was known locally as the Edge. Though safe enough if you kept to the path, it was dangerous to wander from it. Those insidious gentle slopes were dangerous. Clare had lost a dog there once. The animal had gone racing over the smooth grass, gaining momentum, had been unable to stop and had gone over the edge of the cliff to be dashed to pieces on the sharp rocks below.

The afternoon was clear and beautiful. From far below there came the ripple of the sea, a soothing murmur. Clare sat down on the short green turf and stared out over the blue water. She must face this thing clearly. What did she mean to do?

She thought of Vivien with a kind of disgust. How the girl had crumpled up, how abjectly she had surrendered! Clare felt a rising contempt. She had no pluck – no grit.

Nevertheless, much as she disliked Vivien, Clare decided that she would continue to spare her for the present. When she got home she wrote a note to her, saying that although she could make no definite promise for the future, she had decided to keep silence for the present.

Life went on much the same in Daymer's End. It was noticed locally that Lady Lee was looking far from well. On the other hand, Clare Halliwell bloomed. Her eyes were brighter, she carried her head higher, and there was a new confidence and assurance in her manner. She and Lady Lee often met, and it was noticed on these occasions that the younger woman watched the older with a flattering attention to her slightest word.

Sometimes Miss Halliwell would make remarks that seemed a little ambiguous – not entirely relevant to the matter in hand. She would suddenly say that she had changed her mind about many things lately – that it was curious how a little thing might alter one's point of view entirely. One was apt to give way too much to pity – and that was really quite wrong.

When she said things of that kind she usually looked at Lady Lee in a peculiar way, and the latter would suddenly grow quite white, and look almost terrified.

But as the year drew on, these little subtleties became less apparent. Clare continued to make the same remarks, but Lady Lee seemed less affected by them. She began to recover her looks and spirits. Her old gay manner returned.

* * *

One morning, when she was taking her dog for a walk, Clare met Gerald in a lane. The latter's spaniel fraternized with Rover, while his master talked to Clare.

'Heard our news?' he said buoyantly. 'I expect Vivien's told you.'

'What sort of news? Vivien hasn't mentioned anything in particular.'

'We're going abroad – for a year – perhaps longer. Vivien's fed up with this place. She never has cared for it, you know.' He sighed, for a moment or two he looked downcast. Gerald Lee was very proud of his home. 'Anyway, I've promised her a change. I've taken a villa near Algiers. A wonderful place, by all accounts.' He laughed a little self-consciously. 'Quite a second honeymoon, eh?'

For a minute or two Clare could not speak. Something seemed to be rising up in her throat and suffocating her. She could see the white walls of the villa, the orange trees, smell the soft perfumed breath of the South. A second honeymoon!

They were going to escape. Vivien no longer believed in her threats. She was going away, care-free, gay, happy.

Clare heard her own voice, a little hoarse in timbre, saying the appropriate things. How lovely! She envied them!

Mercifully at that moment Rover and the spaniel decided to disagree. In the scuffle that ensued further conversation was out of the question.

That afternoon Clare sat down and wrote a note to Vivien. She asked her to meet her on the Edge the following day, as she had something very important to say to her.

The next morning dawned bright and cloudless. Clare walked up the steep path of the Edge with a lightened heart. What a perfect day! She was glad that she had decided to say what had to be said out in the open, under the blue sky, instead of in her stuffy little sitting-room. She was sorry for Vivien, very sorry indeed, but the thing had got to be done.

She saw a yellow dot, like some yellow flower higher up by the side of the path. As she came nearer it resolved itself into the figure of Vivien, dressed in a yellow knitted frock, sitting on the short turf, her hands clasped round her knees.

'Good morning,' said Clare. 'Isn't it a perfect morning?'

'Is it?' said Vivien. 'I haven't noticed. What was it you wanted to say to me?'

Clare dropped down on the grass beside her.

'I'm quite out of breath,' she said apologetically. 'It's a steep pull up here.'

'Damn you!' cried Vivien shrilly. 'Why can't you say it, you smooth-faced devil, instead of torturing me?'

Clare looked shocked, and Vivien hastily recanted.

'I didn't mean that. I'm sorry, Clare. I am indeed. Only – my nerves are all to pieces, and your sitting here and talking about the weather – well, it got me all rattled.'

'You'll have a nervous breakdown if you're not careful,' said Clare coldly.

Vivien gave a short laugh.

'Go over the edge? No – I'm not that kind. I'll never be a loony. Now tell me – what's all this about?'

Clare was silent for a moment, then she spoke, looking not at Vivien, but steadily out over the sea.

'I thought it only fair to warn you that I can no longer keep silence about – about what happened last year.'

'You mean – you'll go to Gerald with the whole story?'

'Unless you'll tell him yourself. That would be infinitely the better way.'

Vivien laughed sharply.

'You know well enough I haven't got the pluck to do that.'

Clare did not contradict the assertion. She had had proof before of Vivien's utterly craven temper.

'It would be infinitely better,' she repeated.

Again Vivien gave that short, ugly laugh.

'It's your precious conscience, I suppose, that drives you to do this?' she sneered.

'I dare say it seems very strange to you,' said Clare quietly. 'But it honestly is that.'

Vivien's white, set face stared into hers.

'My God!' she said. 'I really believe you mean it, too. You actually think that's the reason.'

'It *is* the reason.'

'No, it isn't. If so, you'd have done it before – long ago. Why didn't you? No, don't answer. I'll tell you. You got more pleasure out of holding it over me – that's why. You liked to keep me on tenterhooks, and make me wince and squirm. You'd say things – diabolical things – just to torment me and keep me perpetually on the jump. And so they did for a bit – till I got used to them.'

'You got to feel secure,' said Clare.

'You saw that, didn't you? But even then, you held back, enjoying your sense of power. But now we're going away, escaping from you, perhaps even going to be happy – you couldn't stick that at any price. So your convenient conscience wakes up!'

She stopped, panting. Clare said, still very quietly:

'I can't prevent your saying all these fantastical things; but I can assure you they're not true.'

Vivien turned suddenly and caught her by the hand.

'Clare – for God's sake! I've been straight – I've done what you said. I've not seen Cyril again – I swear it.'

'That's nothing to do with it.'

'Clare – haven't you any pity – any kindness? I'll go down on my knees to you.'

'Tell Gerald yourself. If you tell him, he may forgive you.'

Vivien laughed scornfully.

'You know Gerald better than that. He'll be rabid – vindictive. He'll make me suffer – he'll make Cyril suffer. That's what I can't bear. Listen, Clare – he's doing so well. He's invented something – machinery, I don't understand about it, but it may be a wonderful success. He's working it out now – his wife supplies the money for it, of course. But she's suspicious – jealous. If she finds out, and she will find out if Gerald starts proceedings for divorce – she'll chuck Cyril – his work, everything. Cyril will be ruined.'

'I'm not thinking of Cyril,' said Clare. 'I'm thinking of Gerald. Why don't you think a little of him, too?'

'Gerald! I don't care that –' she snapped her fingers 'for Gerald. I never have. We might as well have the truth now we're at it. But I do care for Cyril. I'm a rotter, through and through, I admit it. I dare say he's a rotter, too. But my feeling for him – that *isn't* rotten. I'd die for him, do you hear? I'd die for him!'

'That is easily said,' said Clare derisively.

'You think I'm not in earnest? Listen, if you go on with this beastly business, I'll kill myself. Sooner than have Cyril brought into it and ruined, I'd do that.'

Clare remained unimpressed.

'You don't believe me?' said Vivien, panting.

'Suicide needs a lot of courage.'

Vivien flinched back as though she had been struck.

'You've got me there. Yes, I've no pluck. If there were an easy way –'

'There's an easy way in front of you,' said Clare. 'You've only got to run straight down that green slope. It would be all over in a couple of minutes. Remember that child last year.'

'Yes,' said Vivien thoughtfully. 'That would be easy – quite easy – if one really wanted to –'

Clare laughed.

Vivien turned to her.

'Let's have this out once more. Can't you see that by keeping silence as long as you have, you've – you've no right to go back on it now? I'll not see Cyril again. I'll be a good wife to Gerald – I swear I will. Or I'll go away and never see him again? Whichever you like. Clare –'

Clare got up.

'I advise you,' she said, 'to tell your husband yourself . . . otherwise – I shall.'

'I see,' said Vivien softly. 'Well, I can't let Cyril suffer . . .'

She got up, stood still as though considering for a minute or two, then ran lightly down to the path, but instead of stopping, crossed it and went down the slope. Once she half turned her head and waved a hand gaily to Clare, then she ran on gaily, lightly, as a child might run, out of sight . . .

Clare stood petrified. Suddenly she heard cries, shouts, a clamour of voices. Then – silence.

She picked her way stiffly down to the path. About a hundred yards away a party of people coming up it had stopped. They were staring and pointing. Clare ran down and joined them.

'Yes, Miss, someone's fallen over the cliff. Two men have gone down – to see.'

She waited. Was it an hour, or eternity, or only a few minutes?

A man came toiling up the ascent. It was the Vicar in his shirt sleeves. His coat had been taken off to cover what lay below.

'Horrible,' he said, his face was very white. 'Mercifully death must have been instantaneous.'

He saw Clare, and came over to her.

'This must have been a terrible shock to you. You were taking a walk together, I understand?'

Clare heard herself answering mechanically.

Yes. They had just parted. No, Lady Lee's manner had been quite normal. One of the group interposed the information that the lady was laughing and waving her hand. A terribly dangerous place – there ought to be a railing along the path.

The Vicar's voice rose again.

'An accident – yes, clearly an accident.'

And then suddenly Clare laughed – a hoarse, raucous laugh that echoed along the cliff.

'*That's a damned lie*,' she said. '*I killed her*.'

She felt someone patting her shoulder, a voice spoke soothingly.

'There, there. It's all right. You'll be all right presently.'

But Clare was not all right presently. She was never all right again. She persisted in the delusion – certainly a delusion, since at least eight persons had witnessed the scene – that she had killed Vivien Lee.

She was very miserable till Nurse Lauriston came to take charge. Nurse Lauriston was very successful with mental cases.

'Humour them, poor things,' she would say comfortably.

So she told Clare that she was a wardress from Pentonville Prison. Clare's sentence, she said, had been commuted to penal servitude for life. A room was fitted up as a cell.

'And now, I think, we shall be quite happy and comfortable,' said Nurse Lauriston to the doctor. 'Round-bladed knives if you like, doctor, but I don't think there's the least fear of suicide. She's not the type. Too self-centred. Funny how those are often the ones who go over the edge most easily.'

The Tuesday Night Club

'The Tuesday Night Club' was first published in *Royal Magazine*, December 1927, and in the USA as 'The Solving Six' in *Detective Story Magazine*, 2 June 1928. This was Miss Marple's debut, a full two years before her first appearance in a full-length novel, *The Murder at the Vicarage* (Collins, 1930).

'Unsolved mysteries.'

Raymond West blew out a cloud of smoke and repeated the words with a kind of deliberate self-conscious pleasure.

'Unsolved mysteries.'

He looked round him with satisfaction. The room was an old one with broad black beams across the ceiling and it was furnished with good old furniture that belonged to it. Hence Raymond West's approving glance. By profession he was a writer and he liked the atmosphere to be flawless. His Aunt Jane's house always pleased him as the right setting for her personality. He looked across the hearth to where she sat erect in the big grandfather chair. Miss Marple wore a black brocade dress, very much pinched in round the waist. Mechlin lace was arranged in a cascade down the front of the bodice. She had on black lace mittens, and a black lace cap surmounted the piled-up masses of her snowy hair. She was knitting – something white and soft and fleecy. Her faded blue eyes, benignant and kindly, surveyed her nephew and her nephew's guests with gentle pleasure. They rested first on Raymond himself, self-consciously debonair, then on Joyce Lemprière, the artist, with her close-cropped black head and queer hazel-green eyes, then on that well-groomed man of the world, Sir Henry Clithering. There were two other people in the room, Dr Pender, the elderly clergyman of the parish, and Mr Petherick, the solicitor, a dried-up little man with eyeglasses which he looked over and not through. Miss Marple gave a brief moment of attention to all these people and returned to her knitting with a gentle smile upon her lips.

Mr Petherick gave the dry little cough with which he usually prefaced his remarks.

'What is that you say, Raymond? Unsolved mysteries? Ha – and what about them?'

'Nothing about them,' said Joyce Lemprière. 'Raymond just likes the sound of the words and of himself saying them.'

Raymond West threw her a glance of reproach at which she threw back her head and laughed.

'He is a humbug, isn't he, Miss Marple?' she demanded. 'You know that, I am sure.'

Miss Marple smiled gently at her but made no reply.

'Life itself is an unsolved mystery,' said the clergyman gravely.

Raymond sat up in his chair and flung away his cigarette with an impulsive gesture.

'That's not what I mean. I was not talking philosophy,' he said. 'I was thinking of actual bare prosaic facts, things that have happened and that no one has ever explained.'

'I know just the sort of thing you mean, dear,' said Miss Marple. 'For instance Mrs Carruthers had a very strange experience yesterday morning. She bought two gills of picked shrimps at Elliot's. She called at two other shops and when she got home she found she had not got the shrimps with her. She went back to the two shops she had visited but these shrimps had completely disappeared. Now that seems to me very remarkable.'

'A very fishy story,' said Sir Henry Clithering gravely.

'There are, of course, all kinds of possible explanations,' said Miss Marple, her cheeks growing slightly pinker with excitement. 'For instance, somebody else –'

'My dear Aunt,' said Raymond West with some amusement, 'I didn't mean that sort of village incident. I was thinking of murders and disappearances – the kind of thing that Sir Henry could tell us about by the hour if he liked.'

'But I never talk shop,' said Sir Henry modestly. 'No, I never talk shop.'

Sir Henry Clithering had been until lately Commissioner of Scotland Yard.

'I suppose there are a lot of murders and things that never are solved by the police,' said Joyce Lemprière.

'That is an admitted fact, I believe,' said Mr Petherick.

'I wonder,' said Raymond West, 'what class of brain really succeeds best in unravelling a mystery? One always feels that the average police detective must be hampered by lack of imagination.'

'That is the layman's point of view,' said Sir Henry dryly.

'You really want a committee,' said Joyce, smiling. 'For psychology and imagination go to the writer –'

She made an ironical bow to Raymond but he remained serious.

'The art of writing gives one an insight into human nature,' he said gravely. 'One sees, perhaps, motives that the ordinary person would pass by.'

'I know, dear,' said Miss Marple, 'that your books are very clever. But do you think that people are really so unpleasant as you make them out to be?'

'My dear Aunt,' said Raymond gently, 'keep your beliefs. Heaven forbid that *I* should in any way shatter them.'

'I mean,' said Miss Marple, puckering her brow a little as she counted the stitches in her knitting, 'that so many people seem to me not to be either bad or good, but simply, you know, very silly.'

Mr Petherick gave his dry little cough again.

'Don't you think, Raymond,' he said, 'that you attach too much weight to imagination? Imagination is a very dangerous thing, as we lawyers know only too well. To be able to sift evidence impartially, to take the facts and look at them as facts – that seems to me the only logical method of arriving at the truth. I may add that in my experience it is the only one that succeeds.'

'Bah!' cried Joyce, flinging back her black head indignantly. 'I bet I could beat you all at this game. I am not only a woman – and say what you like, women have an intuition that is denied to men – I am an artist as well. I see things that you don't. And then, too, as an artist I have knocked about among all sorts and conditions of people. I know life as darling Miss Marple here cannot possibly know it.'

'I don't know about that, dear,' said Miss Marple. 'Very painful and distressing things happen in villages sometimes.'

'May I speak?' said Dr Pender smiling. 'It is the fashion nowadays to decry the clergy, I know, but we hear things, we know a side of human character which is a sealed book to the outside world.'

'Well,' said Joyce, 'it seems to me we are a pretty representative gathering. How would it be if we formed a Club? What is today? Tuesday? We will call it The Tuesday Night Club. It is to meet every week, and each member in turn has to propound a problem. Some mystery of which they have personal knowledge, and to which, of course, they know the answer. Let me see, how many are we? One, two, three, four, five. We ought really to be six.'

'You have forgotten me, dear,' said Miss Marple, smiling brightly.

Joyce was slightly taken aback, but she concealed the fact quickly.

'That would be lovely, Miss Marple,' she said. 'I didn't think you would care to play.'

'I think it would be very interesting,' said Miss Marple, 'especially with so many clever gentlemen present. I am afraid I am not clever myself, but living all these years in St Mary Mead does give one an insight into human nature.'

'I am sure your co-operation will be very valuable,' said Sir Henry, courteously.

'Who is going to start?' said Joyce.

'I think there is no doubt as to that,' said Dr Pender, 'when we have the great good fortune to have such a distinguished man as Sir Henry staying with us –'

He left his sentence unfinished, making a courtly bow in the direction of Sir Henry.

The latter was silent for a minute or two. At last he sighed and recrossed his legs and began:

'It is a little difficult for me to select just the kind of thing you want, but I think, as it happens, I know of an instance which fits these conditions very aptly. You may have seen some mention of the case in the papers of a year ago. It was laid aside at the time as an unsolved mystery, but, as it happens, the solution came into my hands not very many days ago.

'The facts are very simple. Three people sat down to a supper consisting, amongst other things, of tinned lobster. Later in the night, all three were taken ill, and a doctor was hastily summoned. Two of the people recovered, the third one died.'

'Ah!' said Raymond approvingly.

'As I say, the facts as such were very simple. Death was considered to be due to ptomaine poisoning, a certificate was given to that effect, and the victim was duly buried. But things did not rest at that.'

Miss Marple nodded her head.

'There was talk, I suppose,' she said, 'there usually is.'

'And now I must describe the actors in this little drama. I will call the husband and wife Mr and Mrs Jones, and the wife's companion Miss Clark. Mr Jones was a traveller for a firm of manufacturing chemists. He was a good-looking man in a kind of coarse, florid way, aged about fifty. His wife was a rather commonplace woman, of about forty-five. The companion, Miss Clark, was a woman of sixty, a stout cheery woman with a beaming rubicund face. None of them, you might say, very interesting.

'Now the beginning of the troubles arose in a very curious way. Mr Jones had been staying the previous night at a small commercial hotel in Birmingham. It happened that the blotting paper in the blotting book had been put in fresh that day, and the chambermaid, having apparently nothing better to do, amused herself by studying the blotter in the mirror just after Mr Jones had been writing a letter there. A few days later there was a report in the papers of the death of Mrs Jones as the result of eating tinned lobster, and the chambermaid then imparted to her fellow servants the words that she had deciphered on the blotting pad. They were as follows: *Entirely dependent on my wife . . . when she is dead I will . . . hundreds and thousands . . .*

'You may remember that there had recently been a case of a wife being poisoned by her husband. It needed very little to fire the imagination of these maids. Mr Jones had planned to do away with his wife and inherit hundreds of thousands of pounds! As it happened one of the maids had relations living in the small market town where the Joneses resided. She wrote to them, and they in return wrote to her. Mr Jones, it seemed, had been very attentive to the local doctor's daughter, a good-looking young woman of thirty-three. Scandal began to hum. The Home Secretary was petitioned. Numerous anonymous letters poured into Scotland Yard all accusing Mr Jones of having murdered his wife. Now I may say that not for one moment did we think there was anything in it except idle village talk and gossip. Nevertheless, to quiet public opinion an exhumation order was granted. It was one of these cases of popular superstition based on nothing solid whatever, which proved to be so surprisingly justified. As a result of the autopsy sufficient arsenic was found to make it quite clear that the deceased lady had died of arsenical poisoning. It was for Scotland Yard working with the local authorities to prove how that arsenic had been administered, and by whom.'

'Ah!' said Joyce. 'I like this. This is the real stuff.'

'Suspicion naturally fell on the husband. He benefited by his wife's death. Not to the extent of the hundreds of thousands romantically imagined by the hotel chambermaid, but to the very solid amount of £8000. He had no money of his own apart from what he earned, and he was a man of somewhat extravagant habits with a partiality for the society of women. We investigated as delicately as possible the rumour of his attachment to the doctor's daughter; but while it seemed clear that there had been a strong friendship between them at one time, there had been a most abrupt break two months previously, and they did not appear to have seen each other since. The doctor himself, an elderly man of a straightforward and unsuspicious type, was dumbfounded at the result of the autopsy. He had been called in about midnight to find all three people suffering. He had realized immediately the serious condition of Mrs Jones, and had sent back to his dispensary for some opium pills, to allay the pain. In spite of all his efforts, however, she succumbed, but not for a moment did he suspect that anything was amiss. He was convinced that her death was due to a form of botulism. Supper that night had consisted of tinned lobster and salad, trifle and bread and cheese. Unfortunately none of the lobster remained – it had all been eaten and the tin thrown away. He had interrogated the young maid, Gladys Linch. She was terribly upset, very tearful and agitated, and he found it hard to get her to keep to the point, but she declared again and again that the tin had not been distended in any way and that the lobster had appeared to her in a perfectly good condition.

'Such were the facts we had to go upon. If Jones had feloniously administered arsenic to his wife, it seemed clear that it could not have been done in any of the things eaten at supper, as all three persons had partaken of the meal. Also – another point – Jones himself had returned from Birmingham just as supper was being brought in to table, so that he would have had no opportunity of doctoring any of the food beforehand.'

'What about the companion?' asked Joyce – 'the stout woman with the good-humoured face.'

Sir Henry nodded.

'We did not neglect Miss Clark, I can assure you. But it seemed doubtful what motive she could have had for the crime. Mrs Jones left her no legacy of any kind and the net result of her employer's death was that she had to seek for another situation.'

'That seems to leave her out of it,' said Joyce thoughtfully.

'Now one of my inspectors soon discovered a significant fact,' went on Sir Henry. 'After supper on that evening Mr Jones had gone down to the kitchen and had demanded a bowl of cornflour for his wife who had complained of not feeling well. He had waited in the kitchen until Gladys Linch prepared it, and then carried it up to his wife's room himself. That, I admit, seemed to clinch the case.'

The lawyer nodded.

'Motive,' he said, ticking the points off on his fingers. 'Opportunity. As a traveller for a firm of druggists, easy access to the poison.'

'And a man of weak moral fibre,' said the clergyman.

Raymond West was staring at Sir Henry.

'There is a catch in this somewhere,' he said. 'Why did you not arrest him?'

Sir Henry smiled rather wryly.

'That is the unfortunate part of the case. So far all had gone swimmingly, but now we come to the snags. Jones was not arrested because on interrogating Miss Clark she told us that the whole of the bowl of cornflour was drunk not by Mrs Jones but by her.

'Yes, it seems that she went to Mrs Jones's room as was her custom.

Mrs Jones was sitting up in bed and the bowl of cornflour was beside her.

"'I am not feeling a bit well, Milly," she said. "Serves me right, I suppose, for touching lobster at night. I asked Albert to get me a bowl of cornflour, but now that I have got it I don't seem to fancy it."

"'A pity," commented Miss Clark – "it is nicely made too, no lumps. Gladys is really quite a nice cook. Very few girls nowadays seem to be able to make a bowl of cornflour nicely. I declare I quite fancy it myself, I am that hungry."

"'I should think you were with your foolish ways," said Mrs Jones.

'I must explain,' broke off Sir Henry, 'that Miss Clark, alarmed at her increasing stoutness, was doing a course of what is popularly known as "banting".

"'It is not good for you, Milly, it really isn't," urged Mrs Jones. "If the Lord made you stout he meant you to be stout. You drink up that bowl of cornflour. It will do you all the good in the world."

'And straight away Miss Clark set to and did in actual fact finish the bowl. So, you see, that knocked our case against the husband to pieces. Asked for an explanation of the words on the blotting book Jones gave one readily enough. The letter, he explained, was in answer to one written from his brother in Australia who had applied to him for money. He had written, pointing out that he was entirely dependent on his wife. When his wife was dead he would have control of money and would assist his brother if possible. He regretted his inability to help but pointed out that there were hundreds and thousands of people in the world in the same unfortunate plight.'

'And so the case fell to pieces?' said Dr Pender.

'And so the case fell to pieces,' said Sir Henry gravely. 'We could not take the risk of arresting Jones with nothing to go upon.'

There was a silence and then Joyce said, 'And that is all, is it?'

'That is the case as it has stood for the last year. The true solution is now in the hands of Scotland Yard, and in two or three days' time you will probably read of it in the newspapers.'

'The true solution,' said Joyce thoughtfully. 'I wonder. Let's all think for five minutes and then speak.'

Raymond West nodded and noted the time on his watch. When the five minutes were up he looked over at Dr Pender.

'Will you speak first?' he said.

The old man shook his head. 'I confess,' he said, 'that I am utterly baffled. I can but think that the husband in some way must be the guilty party, but how he did it I cannot imagine. I can only suggest that he must have given her the poison in some way that has not yet been discovered, although how in that case it should have come to light after all this time I cannot imagine.'

'Joyce?'

'The companion!' said Joyce decidedly. 'The companion every time! How do we know what motive she may have had? Just because she was old and stout and ugly it doesn't follow that she wasn't in love with Jones herself. She may have hated the wife for some other reason. Think of being a companion – always having to be pleasant and agree and stifle yourself and bottle yourself up. One day she couldn't bear it any longer and then she killed her. She probably put the arsenic in the bowl of cornflour and all that story about eating it herself is a lie.'

'Mr Petherick?'

The lawyer joined the tips of his fingers together professionally. 'I should hardly like to say. On the facts I should hardly like to say.'

'But you have got to, Mr Petherick,' said Joyce. 'You can't reserve judgement and say "without prejudice", and be legal. You have got to play the game.'

'On the facts,' said Mr Petherick, 'there seems nothing to be said. It is my private opinion, having seen, alas, too many cases of this kind, that the husband was guilty. The only explanation that will cover the facts seems to be that Miss Clark for some reason or other deliberately sheltered him. There may have been some financial arrangement made between them. He might realize that he would be suspected, and she, seeing only a future of poverty before her, may have agreed to tell the story of drinking the cornflour in return for a substantial sum to be paid to her privately. If that was the case it was of course most irregular. Most irregular indeed.'

'I disagree with you all,' said Raymond. 'You have forgotten the one important factor in the case. *The doctor's daughter.* I will give you my reading of the case. The tinned lobster was bad. It accounted for the poisoning symptoms. The doctor was sent for. He finds Mrs Jones, who has eaten more lobster than the others, in great pain, and he sends, as you told us, for some opium pills. He does not go himself, he sends. Who will give the messenger the opium pills? Clearly his daughter. Very likely she dispenses his medicines for him. She is in love with Jones and at this moment all the worst instincts in her nature rise and she realizes that the means to procure his freedom are in her hands. The pills she sends contain pure white arsenic. That is my solution.'

'And now, Sir Henry, tell us,' said Joyce eagerly.

'One moment,' said Sir Henry. 'Miss Marple has not yet spoken.'

Miss Marple was shaking her head sadly.

'Dear, dear,' she said. 'I have dropped another stitch. I have been so interested in the story. A sad case, a very sad case. It reminds me of old

Mr Hargraves who lived up at the Mount. His wife never had the least suspicion – until he died, leaving all his money to a woman he had been living with and by whom he had five children. She had at one time been their housemaid. Such a nice girl, Mrs Hargraves always said – thoroughly to be relied upon to turn the mattresses every day – except Fridays, of course. And there was old Hargraves keeping this woman in a house in the neighbouring town and continuing to be a Churchwarden and to hand round the plate every Sunday.'

'My dear Aunt Jane,' said Raymond with some impatience. 'What has dead and gone Hargraves got to do with the case?'

'This story made me think of him at once,' said Miss Marple. 'The facts are so very alike, aren't they? I suppose the poor girl has confessed now and that is how you know, Sir Henry.'

'What girl?' said Raymond. 'My dear Aunt, what *are* you talking about?'

'That poor girl, Gladys Linch, of course – the one who was so terribly agitated when the doctor spoke to her – and well she might be, poor thing. I hope that wicked Jones is hanged, I am sure, making that poor girl a murderess. I suppose they will hang her too, poor thing.'

'I think, Miss Marple, that you are under a slight misapprehension,' began Mr Petherick.

But Miss Marple shook her head obstinately and looked across at Sir Henry.

'I am right, am I not? It seems so clear to me. The hundreds and thousands – and the trifle – I mean, one cannot miss it.'

'What about the trifle and the hundreds and thousands?' cried Raymond.

His aunt turned to him.

'Cooks nearly always put hundreds and thousands on trifle, dear,' she said. 'Those little pink and white sugar things. Of course when I heard that they had trifle for supper and that the husband had been writing to someone about hundreds and thousands, I naturally connected the two things together. That is where the arsenic was – in the hundreds and thousands. He left it with the girl and told her to put it on the trifle.'

'But that is impossible,' said Joyce quickly. 'They all ate the trifle.'

'Oh, no,' said Miss Marple. 'The companion was banting, you remember. You never eat anything like trifle if you are banting; and I expect Jones just scraped the hundreds and thousands off his share and left them at the side of his plate. It was a clever idea, but a very wicked one.'

The eyes of the others were all fixed upon Sir Henry.

'It is a very curious thing,' he said slowly, 'but Miss Marple happens to have hit upon the truth. Jones had got Gladys Linch into trouble, as the saying goes. She was nearly desperate. He wanted his wife out of the way and promised to marry Gladys when his wife was dead. He doctored the hundreds and thousands and gave them to her with instructions how to use them. Gladys Linch died a week ago. Her child died at birth and Jones had deserted her for another woman. When she was dying she confessed the truth.'

There was a few moments' silence and then Raymond said:

'Well, Aunt Jane, this is one up to you. I can't think how on earth you managed to hit upon the truth. I should never have thought of the little maid in the kitchen being connected with the case.'

'No, dear,' said Miss Marple, 'but you don't know as much of life as I do. A man of that Jones's type – coarse and jovial. As soon as I heard there was a pretty young girl in the house I felt sure that he would not have left her alone. It is all very distressing and painful, and not a very nice thing to talk about. I can't tell you the shock it was to Mrs Hargraves, and a nine days' wonder in the village.'

The Idol House of Astarte

'The Idol House of Astarte' was first published in *Royal Magazine*, January 1928, and in the USA as 'The Solving Six and the Evil Hour' in *Detective Story Magazine*, 9 June 1928.

'And now, Dr Pender, what are you going to tell us?'

The old clergyman smiled gently.

'My life has been passed in quiet places,' he said. 'Very few eventful happenings have come my way. Yet once, when I was a young man, I had one very strange and tragic experience.'

'Ah!' said Joyce Lemprière encouragingly.

'I have never forgotten it,' continued the clergyman. 'It made a profound impression on me at the time, and to this day by a slight effort of memory I can feel again the awe and horror of that terrible moment when I saw a man stricken to death by apparently no mortal agency.'

'You make me feel quite creepy, Pender,' complained Sir Henry.

'It made me feel creepy, as you call it,' replied the other. 'Since then I have never laughed at the people who use the word atmosphere. There is such a thing. There are certain places imbued and saturated with good or evil influences which can make their power felt.'

'That house, The Larches, is a very unhappy one,' remarked Miss Marple. 'Old Mr Smithers lost all his money and had to leave it, then the Carslakes took it and Johnny Carslake fell downstairs and broke his leg and Mrs Carslake had to go away to the south of France for her health, and now the Burdens have got it and I hear that poor Mr Burden has got to have an operation almost immediately.'

'There is, I think, rather too much superstition about such matters,' said Mr Petherick. 'A lot of damage is done to property by foolish reports heedlessly circulated.'

'I have known one or two "ghosts" that have had a very robust personality,' remarked Sir Henry with a chuckle.

'I think,' said Raymond, 'we should allow Dr Pender to go on with his story.'

Joyce got up and switched off the two lamps, leaving the room lit only by the flickering firelight.

'Atmosphere,' she said. 'Now we can get along.'

Dr Pender smiled at her, and leaning back in his chair and taking off his pince-nez, he began his story in a gentle reminiscent voice.

'I don't know whether any of you know Dartmoor at all. The place I am telling you about is situated on the borders of Dartmoor. It was a very charming property, though it had been on the market without finding a purchaser for several years. The situation was perhaps a little bleak in winter, but the views were magnificent and there were certain curious and original features about the property itself. It was bought by a man called Haydon – Sir Richard Haydon. I had known him in his college days, and though I had lost sight of him for some years, the old ties of friendship still held, and I accepted with pleasure his invitation to go down to Silent Grove, as his new purchase was called.

'The house party was not a very large one. There was Richard Haydon himself, and his cousin, Elliot Haydon. There was a Lady Mannering with a pale, rather inconspicuous daughter called Violet. There was a Captain Rogers and his wife, hard riding, weatherbeaten people, who lived only for horses and hunting. There was also a young Dr Symonds and there was Miss Diana Ashley. I knew something about the last named. Her picture was very often in the Society papers and she was one of the notorious beauties of the Season. Her appearance was indeed very striking. She was dark and tall, with a beautiful skin of an even tint of pale cream, and her half closed dark eyes set slantways in her head gave her a curiously piquant oriental appearance. She had, too, a wonderful speaking voice, deep-toned and bell-like.

'I saw at once that my friend Richard Haydon was very much attracted by her, and I guessed that the whole party was merely arranged as a setting for her. Of her own feelings I was not so sure. She was capricious in her favours. One day talking to Richard and excluding everyone else from her notice, and another day she would favour his cousin, Elliot, and appear hardly to notice that such a person as Richard existed, and then again she would bestow the most bewitching smiles upon the quiet and retiring Dr Symonds.

'On the morning after my arrival our host showed us all over the place. The house itself was unremarkable, a good solid house built of Devonshire granite. Built to withstand time and exposure. It was unromantic but very comfortable. From the windows of it one looked out over the panorama of the Moor, vast rolling hills crowned with weather-beaten Tors.

'On the slopes of the Tor nearest to us were various hut circles, relics of the bygone days of the late Stone Age. On another hill was a barrow which had recently been excavated, and in which certain bronze implements had been found. Haydon was by way of being interested in antiquarian matters and he talked to us with a great deal of energy and enthusiasm. This particular spot, he explained, was particularly rich in relics of the past.

'Neolithic hut dwellers, Druids, Romans, and even traces of the early Phoenicians were to be found.

'"But this place is the most interesting of all," he said "You know its name – Silent Grove. Well, it is easy enough to see what it takes its name from."

'He pointed with his hand. That particular part of the country was bare enough – rocks, heather and bracken, but about a hundred yards from the house there was a densely planted grove of trees.

'"That is a relic of very early days," said Haydon, "The trees have died and been replanted, but on the whole it has been kept very much as it used to be – perhaps in the time of the Phoenician settlers. Come and look at it."

'We all followed him. As we entered the grove of trees a curious oppression came over me. I think it was the silence. No birds seemed to nest in these trees. There was a feeling about it of desolation and horror. I saw Haydon looking at me with a curious smile.

'"Any feeling about this place, Pender?" he asked me. "Antagonism now? Or uneasiness?"

'"I don't like it," I said quietly.

'"You are within your rights. This was a stronghold of one of the ancient enemies of your faith. This is the Grove of Astarte."

'"Astarte?"

'"Astarte, or Ishtar, or Ashtoreth, or whatever you choose to call her. I prefer the Phoenician name of Astarte. There is, I believe, one known Grove of Astarte in this country – in the North on the Wall. I have no evidence, but I like to believe that we have a true and authentic Grove of Astarte here. Here, within this dense circle of trees, sacred rites were performed."

'"Sacred rites," murmured Diana Ashley. Her eyes had a dreamy faraway look. "What were they, I wonder?"

'"Not very reputable by all accounts," said Captain Rogers with a loud unmeaning laugh. "Rather hot stuff, I imagine."

'Haydon paid no attention to him.

'"In the centre of the Grove there should be a Temple," he said. "I can't run to Temples, but I have indulged in a little fancy of my own."

'We had at that moment stepped out into a little clearing in the centre of the trees. In the middle of it was something not unlike a summerhouse made of stone. Diana Ashley looked inquiringly at Haydon.

'"I call it The Idol House," he said. "It is the Idol House of Astarte."

'He led the way up to it. Inside, on a rude ebony pillar, there reposed a curious little image representing a woman with crescent horns, seated on a lion.

'"Astarte of the Phoenicians," said Haydon, "the Goddess of the Moon."

'"The Goddess of the Mooon," cried Diana. "Oh, do let us have a wild orgy tonight. Fancy dress. And we will come out here in the moonlight and celebrate the rites of Astarte."

'I made a sudden movement and Elliot Haydon, Richard's cousin, turned quickly to me.

'"You don't like all this, do you, Padre?" he said.

'"No," I said gravely. "I don't."

'He looked at me curiously. "But it is only tomfoolery. Dick can't know that this really is a sacred grove. It is just a fancy of his; he likes to play with the idea. And anyway, if it were –"

'"If it were?"

'"Well –" he laughed uncomfortably. "You don't believe in that sort of thing, do you? You, a parson."

'"I am not sure that as a parson I ought not to believe in it."

'"But that sort of thing is all finished and done with."

'"I am not so sure," I said musingly. "I only know this: I am not as a rule a sensitive man to atmosphere, but ever since I entered this grove of trees I have felt a curious impression and sense of evil and menace all round me."

'He glanced uneasily over his shoulder.

'"Yes," he said, "it is – it is queer, somehow. I know what you mean but I suppose it is only our imagination makes us feel like that. What do you say, Symonds?"

'The doctor was silent a minute or two before he replied. Then he said quietly:

'"I don't like it. I can't tell you why. But somehow or other, I don't like it."

'At that moment Violet Mannering came across to me.

'"I hate this place," she cried. "I hate it. Do let's get out of it."

'We moved away and the others followed us. Only Diana Ashley lingered. I turned my head over my shoulder and saw her standing in front of the Idol House gazing earnestly at the image within it.

'The day was an unusually hot and beautiful one and Diana Ashley's suggestion of a Fancy Dress party that evening was received with general favour. The usual laughing and whispering and frenzied secret sewing took place and when we all made our appearance for dinner there were the usual outcries of merriment. Rogers and his wife were Neolithic hut dwellers – explaining the sudden lack of hearth rugs. Richard Haydon called himself a Phoenician sailor, and his cousin was a Brigand Chief, Dr Symonds was a chef, Lady Mannering was a hospital nurse, and her daughter was a Circassian slave. I myself was arrayed somewhat too warmly as a monk. Diana Ashley came down last and was somewhat of a disappointment to all of us, being wrapped in a shapeless black domino.

"'The Unknown,' she declared airily. "That is what I am. Now for goodness' sake let's go in to dinner."

'After dinner we went outside. It was a lovely night, warm and soft, and the moon was rising.

'We wandered about and chatted and the time passed quickly enough. It must have been an hour later when we realized that Diana Ashley was not with us.

"'Surely she has not gone to bed," said Richard Haydon.

'Violet Mannering shook her head.

"'Oh, no," she said. "I saw her going off in that direction about a quarter of an hour ago." She pointed as she spoke towards the grove of trees that showed black and shadowy in the moonlight.

"'I wonder what she is up to," said Richard Haydon, "some devilment, I swear. Let's go and see."

'We all trooped off together, somewhat curious as to what Miss Ashley had been up to. Yet I, for one, felt a curious reluctance to enter that dark foreboding belt of trees. Something stronger than myself seemed to be holding me back and urging me not to enter. I felt more definitely convinced than ever of the essential evilness of the spot. I think that some of the others experienced the same sensations that I did, though they would have been loath to admit it. The trees were so closely planted that the moonlight could not penetrate. There were a dozen soft sounds all round us, whisperings and sighings. The feeling was eerie in the extreme, and by common consent we all kept close together.

'Suddenly we came out into the open clearing in the middle of the grove and stood rooted to the spot in amazement, for there, on the threshold of the Idol House, stood a shimmering figure wrapped tightly round in diaphanous gauze and with two crescent horns rising from the dark masses of her hair.

"'My God!" said Richard Haydon, and the sweat sprang out on his brow.

'But Violet Mannering was sharper.

'"Why, it's Diana," she exclaimed. "What has she done to herself? Oh, she looks quite different somehow!"'

'The figure in the doorway raised her hands. She took a step forward and chanted in a high sweet voice.

'"I am the Priestess of Astarte," she crooned. "Beware how you approach me, for I hold death in my hand."

'"Don't do it, dear," protested Lady Mannering. "You give us the creeps, you really do."

'Haydon sprang forward towards her.

'"My God, Diana!" he cried. "You are wonderful."

'My eyes were accustomed to the moonlight now and I could see more plainly. She did, indeed, as Violet had said, look quite different. Her face was more definitely oriental, and her eyes more of slits with something cruel in their gleam, and the strange smile on her lips was one that I had never seen there before.

'"Beware," she cried warningly. "Do not approach the Goddess. If anyone lays a hand on me it is death."

'"You are wonderful, Diana," cried Haydon, "but do stop it. Somehow or other I – I don't like it."

'He was moving towards her across the grass and she flung out a hand towards him.

'"Stop," she cried. "One step nearer and I will smite you with the magic of Astarte."

'Richard Haydon laughed and quickened his pace, when all at once a curious thing happened. He hesitated for a moment, then seemed to stumble and fall headlong.

'He did not get up again, but lay where he had fallen prone on the ground.

'Suddenly Diana began to laugh hysterically. It was a strange horrible sound breaking the silence of the glade.

'With an oath Elliot sprang forward.

'"I can't stand this," he cried, "get up, Dick, get up, man."

'But still Richard Haydon lay where he had fallen. Elliot Haydon reached his side, knelt by him and turned him gently over. He bent over him, peering in his face.

'Then he rose sharply to his feet and stood swaying a little.

'"Doctor," he said. "Doctor, for God's sake come. I – I think he is dead."

'Symonds ran forward and Elliot rejoined us walking very slowly. He was looking down at his hands in a way I didn't understand.

'At that moment there was a wild scream from Diana.

"'I have killed him," she cried. "Oh, my God! I didn't mean to, but I have killed him."

'And she fainted dead away, falling in a crumpled heap on the grass.

'There was a cry from Mrs Rogers.

"'Oh, do let us get away from this dreadful place," she wailed, "anything might happen to us here. Oh, it's awful!"

'Elliot got hold of me by the shoulder.

"'It can't be, man," he murmured. "I tell you it can't *be*. A man cannot be killed like that. It is – it's against Nature."

'I tried to soothe him.

"'There is some explanation," I said. "Your cousin must have had some unsuspected weakness of the heart. The shock and excitement –"

'He interrupted me.

"'You don't understand," he said. He held up his hands for me to see and I noticed a red stain on them.

"'Dick didn't die of shock, he was stabbed – stabbed to the heart, and *there is no weapon*."

'I stared at him incredulously. At that moment Symonds rose from his examination of the body and came towards us. He was pale and shaking all over.

"'Are we all mad?" he said. "What is this place – that things like this can happen in it?"

"'Then it is true," I said.

'He nodded.

"'The wound is such as would be made by a long thin dagger, but – there is no dagger there."

'We all looked at each other.

"'But it must be there," cried Elliot Haydon. "It must have dropped out. It must be on the ground somewhere. Let us look."

'We peered about vainly on the ground. Violet Mannering said suddenly:

"'Diana had something in her hand. A kind of dagger. I saw it. I saw it glitter when she threatened him."

'Elliot Haydon shook his head.

"'He never even got within three yards of her," he objected.

'Lady Mannering was bending over the prostrate girl on the ground.

"'There is nothing in her hand now," she announced, "and I can't see anything on the ground. Are you sure you saw it, Violet? I didn't."

'Dr Symonds came over to the girl.

"'We must get her to the house," he said. "Rogers, will you help?"

'Between us we carried the unconscious girl back to the house. Then we returned and fetched the body of Sir Richard.'

Dr Pender broke off apologetically and looked round.

'One would know better nowadays,' he said, 'owing to the prevalence of detective fiction. Every street boy knows that a body must be left where it is found. But in these days we had not the same knowledge, and accordingly we carried the body of Richard Haydon back to his bedroom in the square granite house and the butler was despatched on a bicycle in search of the police – a ride of some twelve miles.

'It was then that Elliot Haydon drew me aside.

'"Look here," he said. "I am going back to the grove. That weapon has got to be found."

'"If there was a weapon," I said doubtfully.

'He seized my arm and shook it fiercely. "You have got that superstitious stuff into your head. You think his death was supernatural; well, I am going back to the grove to find out."

'I was curiously averse to his doing so. I did my utmost to dissuade him, but without result. The mere idea of that thick circle of trees was abhorrent to me and I felt a strong premonition of further disaster. But Elliot was entirely pig-headed. He was, I think, scared himself, but would not admit it. He went off fully armed with determination to get to the bottom of the mystery.

'It was a very dreadful night, none of us could sleep, or attempt to do so. The police, when they arrived, were frankly incredulous of the whole thing. They evinced a strong desire to cross-examine Miss Ashley, but there they had to reckon with Dr Symonds, who opposed the idea vehemently. Miss Ashley had come out of her faint or trance and he had given her a long sleeping draught. She was on no account to be disturbed until the following day.

'It was not until about seven o'clock in the morning that anyone thought about Elliot Haydon, and then Symonds suddenly asked where he was. I explained what Elliot had done and Symonds's grave face grew a shade graver. "I wish he hadn't. It is – it is foolhardy," he said.

'"You don't think any harm can have happened to him?"

'"I hope not. I think, Padre, that you and I had better go and see."

'I knew he was right, but it took all the courage in my command to nerve myself for the task. We set out together and entered once more that ill-fated grove of trees. We called him twice and got no reply. In a minute or two we came into the clearing, which looked pale and ghostly in the early morning light. Symonds clutched my arm and I uttered a muttered exclamation. Last night when we had seen it in the moonlight there had been the body of a man lying face downwards on the grass. Now in the early morning light the same sight met our eyes. Elliot Haydon was lying on the exact spot where his cousin had been.

'"My God!" said Symonds. "*It has got him too!*"

'We ran together over the grass. Elliot Haydon was unconscious but breathing feebly and this time there was no doubt of what had caused the tragedy. A long thin bronze weapon remained in the wound.

'"Got him through the shoulder, not through the heart. That is lucky," commented the doctor. "On my soul, I don't know what to think. At any rate he is not dead and he will be able to tell us what happened."

'But that was just what Elliot Haydon was not able to do. His description was vague in the extreme. He had hunted about vainly for the dagger and at last giving up the search had taken up a stand near the Idol House. It was then that he became increasingly certain that someone was watching him from the belt of trees. He fought against this impression but was not able to shake it off. He described a cold strange wind that began to blow. It seemed to come not from the trees but from the interior of the Idol House. He turned round, peering inside it. He saw the small figure of the Goddess and he felt he was under an optical delusion. The figure seemed to grow larger and larger. Then he suddenly received something that felt like a blow between his temples which sent him reeling back, and as he fell he was conscious of a sharp burning pain in his left shoulder.

'The dagger was identified this time as being the identical one which had been dug up in the barrow on the hill, and which had been bought by Richard Haydon. Where he had kept it, in the house or in the Idol House in the grove, none seemed to know.

'The police were of the opinion, and always will be, that he was deliberately stabbed by Miss Ashley, but in view of our combined evidence that she was never within three yards of him, they could not hope to support the charge against her. So the thing has been and remains a mystery.'

There was a silence.

'There doesn't seem anything to say,' said Joyce Lemprière at length. 'It is all so horrible – and uncanny. Have you no explanation for yourself, Dr Pender?'

The old man nodded. 'Yes,' he said. 'I have an explanation – a kind of explanation, that is. Rather a curious one – but to my mind it still leaves certain factors unaccounted for.'

'I have been to séances,' said Joyce, 'and you may say what you like, very queer things can happen. I suppose one can explain it by some kind of hypnotism. The girl really turned herself into a Priestess of Astarte, and I suppose somehow or other she must have stabbed him. Perhaps she threw the dagger that Miss Mannering saw in her hand.'

'Or it might have been a javelin,' suggested Raymond West. 'After all, moonlight is not very strong. She might have had a kind of spear in her hand and stabbed him at a distance, and then I suppose mass hypnotism comes into account. I mean, you were all prepared to see him stricken down by supernatural means and so you saw it like that.'

'I have seen many wonderful things done with weapons and knives at music halls,' said Sir Henry. 'I suppose it is possible that a man could have been con-cealed in the belt of trees, and that he might from there have thrown a knife or a dagger with sufficient accuracy – agreeing, of course, that he was a professional. I admit that that seems rather far-fetched, but it seems the only really feasible theory. You remember that the other man was distinctly under the impression that there was someone in the grove of trees watching him. As to Miss Mannering saying that Miss Ashley had a dagger in her hand and the others saying she hadn't, that doesn't surprise me. If you had had my experience you would know that five persons' account of the same thing will differ so widely as to be almost incredible.'

Mr Petherick coughed.

'But in all these theories we seem to be overlooking one essential fact,' he remarked. 'What became of the weapon? Miss Ashley could hardly get rid of a javelin standing as she was in the middle of an open space; and if a hidden murderer had thrown a dagger, then the dagger would still have been in the wound when the man was turned over. We must, I think, discard all far-fetched theories and confine ourselves to sober fact.'

'And where does sober fact lead us?'

'Well, one thing seems quite clear. No one was near the man when he was stricken down, so the only person who *could* have stabbed him was he himself. Suicide, in fact.'

'But why on earth should he wish to commit suicide?' asked Raymond West incredulously.

The lawyer coughed again. 'Ah, that is a question of theory once more,' he said. 'At the moment I am not concerned with theories. It seems to me, excluding the supernatural in which I do not for one moment believe, that that was the only way things could have happened. He stabbed himself, and as he fell his arms flew out, wrenching the dagger from the wound and flinging it far into the zone of the trees. That is, I think, although somewhat unlikely, a possible happening.'

'I don't like to say, I am sure,' said Miss Marple. 'It all perplexes me very much indeed. But curious things do happen. At Lady Sharpley's garden party last year the man who was arranging the clock golf tripped over one of the numbers – quite unconscious he was – and didn't come round for about five minutes.'

'Yes, dear Aunt,' said Raymond gently, 'but he wasn't stabbed, was he?'

'Of course not, dear,' said Miss Marple. 'That is what I am telling you. Of course there is only one way that poor Sir Richard could have been stabbed, but I do wish I knew what caused him to stumble in the first place. Of course, it might have been a tree root. He would be looking at the girl, of course, and when it is moonlight one does trip over things.'

'You say that there is only one way that Sir Richard could have been stabbed, Miss Marple,' said the clergyman, looking at her curiously.

'It is very sad and I don't like to think of it. He was a right-handed man, was he not? I mean to stab himself in the left shoulder he must have been. I was always so sorry for poor Jack Baynes in the War. He shot himself in the foot, you remember, after very severe fighting at Arras. He told me about it when I went to see him in hospital, and very ashamed of it he was. I don't expect this poor man, Elliot Haydon, profited much by his wicked crime.'

'Elliot Haydon,' cried Raymond. 'You think he did it?'

'I don't see how anyone else could have done it,' said Miss Marple, opening her eyes in gentle surprise. 'I mean if, as Mr Petherick so wisely says, one looks at the facts and disregards all that atmosphere of heathen goddesses which I don't think is very nice. He went up to him first and turned him over, and of course to do that he would have to have had his back to them all, and being dressed as a brigand chief he would be sure to have a weapon of some kind in his belt. I remember dancing with a man dressed as a brigand chief when I was a young girl. He had five kinds of knives and daggers, and I can't tell you how awkward and uncomfortable it was for his partner.'

All eyes were turned towards Dr Pender.

'I knew the truth,' said he, 'five years after that tragedy occurred. It came in the shape of a letter written to me by Elliot Haydon. He said in it that he fancied that I had always suspected him. He said it was a sudden temptation. He too loved Diana Ashley, but he was only a poor struggling barrister. With Richard out of the way and inheriting his title and estates, he saw a wonderful prospect opening up before him. The dagger had jerked out of his belt as he knelt down by his cousin, and almost before he had time to think he drove it in and returned it to his belt again. He stabbed himself later in order to divert suspicion. He wrote to me on the eve of starting on an expedition to the South Pole in case, as he said, he should never come back. I do not think that he meant to come back, and I know that, as Miss Marple has said, his crime profited him nothing. "For five years," he wrote, "I have lived in Hell. I hope, at least, that I may expiate my crime by dying honourably."'

There was a pause.

'And he did die honourably,' said Sir Henry. 'You have changed the names in your story, Dr Pender, but I think I recognize the man you mean.'

'As I said,' went on the old clergyman, 'I do not think that explanation quite covers the facts. I still think there was an evil influence in that grove, an influence that directed Elliot Haydon's action. Even to this day I can never think without a shudder of The Idol House of Astarte.'

Ingots of Gold

'Ingots of Gold' was first published in *Royal Magazine*, February 1928, and in the USA as 'The Solving Six and the Golden Grave' in *Detective Story Magazine*, 16 June 1928.

'I do not know that the story that I am going to tell you is a fair one,' said Raymond West, 'because I can't give you the solution of it. Yet the facts were so interesting and so curious that I should like to propound it to you as a problem. And perhaps between us we may arrive at some logical conclusion.

'The date of these happenings was two years ago, when I went down to spend Whitsuntide with a man called John Newman, in Cornwall.'

'Cornwall?' said Joyce Lemprière sharply.

'Yes. Why?'

'Nothing. Only it's odd. My story is about a place in Cornwall, too – a little fishing village called Rathole. Don't tell me yours is the same?'

'No. My village is called Polperran. It is situated on the west coast of Cornwall; a very wild and rocky spot. I had been introduced a few weeks previously and had found him a most interesting companion. A man of intelligence and independent means, he was possessed of a romantic imagination. As a result of his latest hobby he had taken the lease of Pol House. He was an authority on Elizabethan times, and he described to me in vivid and graphic language the rout of the Spanish Armada. So enthusiastic was he that one could almost imagine that he had been an eyewitness at the scene. Is there anything in reincarnation? I wonder – I very much wonder.'

'You are so romantic, Raymond dear,' said Miss Marple, looking benignantly at him.

'Romantic is the last thing that I am,' said Raymond West, slightly annoyed. 'But this fellow Newman was chock-full of it, and he interested me for that reason as a curious survival of the past. It appears that a certain ship belonging to the Armada, and known to contain a vast amount of treasure in the form of gold from the Spanish Main, was wrecked off the coast of Cornwall on the famous and treacherous Serpent Rocks. For some years, so Newman told me, attempts had been made to salve the ship and recover the treasure. I believe such stories are not uncommon, though the number of mythical treasure ships is largely in excess of the genuine ones. A company had been formed, but had gone bankrupt, and Newman had been able to buy the rights of the thing – or whatever you call it – for a mere song. He waxed very enthusiastic about it all. According to him it was merely a question of the latest scientific, up-to-date machinery. The gold was there, and he had no doubt whatever that it could be recovered.

'It occurred to me as I listened to him how often things happen that way. A rich man such as Newman succeeds almost without effort, and yet in all probability the actual value in money of his find would mean little to him. I must say that his ardour infected me. I saw galleons drifting up the coast, flying before the storm, beaten and broken on the black rocks. The mere word galleon has a romantic sound. The phrase "Spanish Gold" thrills the schoolboy – and the grown-up man also. Moreover, I was working at the time upon a novel, some scenes of which were laid in the sixteenth century, and I saw the prospect of getting valuable local colour from my host.

'I set off that Friday morning from Paddington in high spirits, and looking forward to my trip. The carriage was empty except for one man, who sat facing me in the opposite corner. He was a tall, soldierly-looking man, and I could not rid myself of the impression that somewhere or other I had seen him before. I cudgelled my brains for some time in vain; but at last I had it. My travelling companion was Inspector Badgworth, and I had run across him when I was doing a series of articles on the Everson disappearance case.

'I recalled myself to his notice, and we were soon chatting pleasantly enough. When I told him I was going to Polperran he remarked that that was a rum coincidence, because he himself was also bound for that place. I did not like to seem inquisitive, so was careful not to ask him what took him there. Instead, I spoke of my own interest in the place, and mentioned the wrecked Spanish galleon. To my surprise the Inspector seemed to know all about it. "That will be the *Juan Fernandez*," he said. "Your friend won't be the first who has sunk money trying to get money out of her. It is a romantic notion."

'"And probably the whole story is a myth," I said. "No ship was ever wrecked there at all."

'"Oh, the ship was sunk there right enough," said the Inspector –

"along with a good company of others. You would be surprised if you knew how many wrecks there are on that part of the coast. As a matter of fact, that is what takes me down there now. That is where the *Otranto* was wrecked six months ago."

"'I remember reading about it," I said. "No lives were lost, I think?"

"'No lives were lost," said the Inspector; "but something else was lost. It is not generally known, but the *Otranto* was carrying bullion."

"'Yes?" I said, much interested.

"'Naturally we have had divers at work on salvage operations, but – *the gold has gone, Mr West.*"

"'Gone!" I said, staring at him. "How can it have gone?"

"'That is the question," said the Inspector. "The rocks tore a gaping hole in her strongroom. It was easy enough for the divers to get in that way, but they found the strongroom empty. The question is, was the gold stolen before the wreck or afterwards? Was it ever in the strongroom at all?"

"'It seems a curious case," I said.

"'It is a very curious case, when you consider what bullion is. Not a diamond necklace that you could put into your pocket. When you think how cumbersome it is and how bulky – well, the whole thing seems absolutely impossible. There may have been some hocus-pocus before the ship sailed; but if not, it must have been removed within the last six months – and I am going down to look into the matter."

'I found Newman waiting to meet me at the station. He apologized for the absence of his car, which had gone to Truro for some necessary repairs. Instead, he met me with a farm lorry belonging to the property.

'I swung myself up beside him, and we wound carefully in and out of the narrow streets of the fishing village. We went up a steep ascent, with a gradient, I should say, of one in five, ran a little distance along a winding lane, and turned in at the granite-pillared gates of Pol House.

'The place was a charming one; it was situated high up the cliffs, with a good view out to sea. Part of it was some three or four hundred years old, and a modern wing had been added. Behind it farming land of about seven or eight acres ran inland.

"'Welcome to Pol House," said Newman. "And to the Sign of the Golden Galleon." And he pointed to where, over the front door, hung a perfect reproduction of a Spanish galleon with all sails set.

'My first evening was a most charming and instructive one. My host showed me the old manuscripts relating to the *Juan Fernandez*. He unrolled charts for me and indicated positions on them with dotted lines, and he produced plans of diving apparatus, which, I may say, mystified me utterly and completely.

'I told him of my meeting with Inspector Badgworth, in which he was much interested.

'"They are a queer people round this coast," he said reflectively. "Smuggling and wrecking is in their blood. When a ship goes down on their coast they cannot help regarding it as lawful plunder meant for their pockets. There is a fellow here I should like you to see. He is an interesting survival."

'Next day dawned bright and clear. I was taken down into Polperran and there introduced to Newman's diver, a man called Higgins. He was a wooden-faced individual, extremely taciturn, and his contributions to the conversation were mostly monosyllables. After a discussion between them on highly technical matters, we adjourned to the Three Anchors. A tankard of beer somewhat loosened the worthy fellow's tongue.

'"Detective gentleman from London has come down," he grunted. "They do say that that ship that went down there last November was carrying a mortal lot of gold. Well, she wasn't the first to go down, and she won't be the last."

'"Hear, hear," chimed in the landlord of the Three Anchors. "That is a true word you say there, Bill Higgins."

'"I reckon it is, Mr Kelvin," said Higgins.

'I looked with some curiosity at the landlord. He was a remarkable-looking man, dark and swarthy, with curiously broad shoulders. His eyes were bloodshot, and he had a curiously furtive way of avoiding one's glance. I suspected that this was the man of whom Newman had spoken, saying he was an interesting survival.

'"We don't want interfering foreigners on this coast," he said, somewhat truculently.

'"Meaning the police?" asked Newman, smiling.

'"Meaning the police – *and others*," said Kelvin significantly. "And don't you forget it, mister."

'"Do you know, Newman, that sounded to me very like a threat," I said as we climbed the hill homewards.

'My friend laughed.

'"Nonsense; I don't do the folk down here any harm."

'I shook my head doubtfully. There was something sinister and uncivilized about Kelvin. I felt that his mind might run in strange, unrecognized channels.

'I think I date the beginning of my uneasiness from that moment. I had slept well enough that first night, but the next night my sleep was troubled and broken. Sunday dawned, dark and sullen, with an overcast sky and the threatenings of thunder in the air. I am always a bad hand at hiding my feelings, and Newman noticed the change in me.

"'What is the matter with you, West? You are a bundle of nerves this morning.'

"'I don't know,' I confessed, 'but I have got a horrible feeling of foreboding.'

"'It's the weather.'

"'Yes, perhaps.'

'I said no more. In the afternoon we went out in Newman's motor boat, but the rain came on with such vigour that we were glad to return to shore and change into dry clothing.

'And that evening my uneasiness increased. Outside the storm howled and roared. Towards ten o'clock the tempest calmed down. Newman looked out of the window.

"'It is clearing,' he said. 'I shouldn't wonder if it was a perfectly fine night in another half-hour. If so, I shall go out for a stroll.'

'I yawned. 'I am frightfully sleepy,' I said. 'I didn't get much sleep last night. I think that tonight I shall turn in early.'

'This I did. On the previous night I had slept little. Tonight I slept heavily. Yet my slumbers were not restful. I was still oppressed with an awful foreboding of evil. I had terrible dreams. I dreamt of dreadful abysses and vast chasms, amongst which I was wandering, knowing that a slip of the foot meant death. I waked to find the hands of my clock pointing to eight o'clock. My head was aching badly, and the terror of my night's dreams was still upon me.

'So strongly was this so that when I went to the window and drew it up I started back with a fresh feeling of terror, for the first thing I saw, or thought I saw – was a man digging an open grave.

'It took me a minute or two to pull myself together; then I realized that the grave-digger was Newman's gardener, and the "grave" was destined to accommodate three new rose trees which were lying on the turf waiting for the moment they should be securely planted in the earth.

'The gardener looked up and saw me and touched his hat.

"'Good morning, sir. Nice morning, sir.'

"'I suppose it is,' I said doubtfully, still unable to shake off completely the depression of my spirits.

'However, as the gardener had said, it was certainly a nice morning. The sun was shining and the sky a clear pale blue that promised fine weather for the day. I went down to breakfast whistling a tune. Newman had no maids living in the house. Two middle-aged sisters, who lived in a farm-house near by, came daily to attend to his simple wants. One of them was placing the coffee-pot on the table as I entered the room.

"'Good morning, Elizabeth,' I said. 'Mr Newman not down yet?'

'"He must have been out very early, sir," she replied. "He wasn't in the house when we arrived."

'Instantly my uneasiness returned. On the two previous mornings Newman had come down to breakfast somewhat late; and I didn't fancy that at any time he was an early riser. Moved by those forebodings, I ran up to his bedroom. It was empty, and, moreover, his bed had not been slept in. A brief examination of his room showed me two other things. If Newman had gone out for a stroll he must have gone out in his evening clothes, for they were missing.

'I was sure now that my premonition of evil was justified. Newman had gone, as he had said he would do, for an evening stroll. For some reason or other he had not returned. Why? Had he met with an accident? Fallen over the cliffs? A search must be made at once.

'In a few hours I had collected a large band of helpers, and together we hunted in every direction along the cliffs and on the rocks below. But there was no sign of Newman.

'In the end, in despair, I sought out Inspector Badgworth. His face grew very grave.

'"It looks to me as if there has been foul play," he said. "There are some not over-scrupulous customers in these parts. Have you seen Kelvin, the landlord of the Three Anchors?"

'I said that I had seen him.

'"Did you know he did a turn in gaol four years ago? Assault and battery."

'"It doesn't surprise me," I said.

'"The general opinion in this place seems to be that your friend is a bit too fond of nosing his way into things that do not concern him. I hope he has come to no serious harm."

'The search was continued with redoubled vigour. It was not until late that afternoon that our efforts were rewarded. We discovered Newman in a deep ditch in a corner of his own property. His hands and feet were securely fastened with rope, and a handkerchief had been thrust into his mouth and secured there so as to prevent him crying out.

'He was terribly exhausted and in great pain; but after some frictioning of his wrists and ankles, and a long draught from a whisky flask, he was able to give his account of what had occurred.

'The weather having cleared, he had gone out for a stroll about eleven o'clock. His way had taken him some distance along the cliffs to a spot commonly known as Smugglers' Cove, owing to the large number of caves to be found there. Here he had noticed some men landing something from a small boat, and had strolled down to see what was going on. Whatever the stuff was it seemed to be a great weight, and it was being carried into one of the farthermost caves.

'With no real suspicion of anything being amiss, nevertheless Newman had wondered. He had drawn quite near them without being observed. Suddenly there was a cry of alarm, and immediately two powerful seafaring men had set upon him and rendered him unconscious. When next he came to himself he found himself lying on a motor vehicle of some kind, which was proceeding, with many bumps and bangs, as far as he could guess, up the lane which led from the coast to the village. To his great surprise, the lorry turned in at the gate of his own house. There, after a whispered conversation between the men, they at length drew him forth and flung him into a ditch at a spot where the depth of it rendered discovery unlikely for some time. Then the lorry drove on, and, he thought, passed out through another gate some quarter of a mile nearer the village. He could give no description of his assailants except that they were certainly seafaring men and, by their speech, Cornishmen.

'Inspector Badgworth was very interested.

'"Depend upon it that is where the stuff has been hidden," he cried. "Somehow or other it has been salvaged from the wreck and has been stored in some lonely cave somewhere. It is known that we have searched all the caves in Smugglers' Cove, and that we are now going farther afield, and they have evidently been moving the stuff at night to a cave that has been already searched and is not likely to be searched again. Unfortunately they have had at least eighteen hours to dispose of the stuff. If they got Mr Newman last night I doubt if we will find any of it there by now."

'The Inspector hurried off to make a search. He found definite evidence that the bullion had been stored as supposed, but the gold had been once more removed, and there was no clue as to its fresh hiding-place.

'One clue there was, however, and the Inspector himself pointed it out to me the following morning.

'"That lane is very little used by motor vehicles," he said, "and in one or two places we get the traces of the tyres very clearly. There is a three-cornered piece out of one tyre, leaving a mark which is quite unmistakable. It shows going into the gate; here and there is a faint mark of it going out of the other gate, so there is not much doubt that it is the right vehicle we are after. Now, why did they take it out through the farther gate? It seems quite clear to me that the lorry came from the village. Now, there aren't many people who own a lorry in the village – not more than two or three at most. Kelvin, the landlord of the Three Anchors, has one."

'"What was Kelvin's original profession?" asked Newman.

'"It is curious that you should ask me that, Mr Newman. In his young days Kelvin was a professional diver."

'Newman and I looked at each other. The puzzle seemed to be fitting itself together piece by piece.

'"You didn't recognize Kelvin as one of the men on the beach?" asked the Inspector.

'Newman shook his head.

'"I am afraid I can't say anything as to that," he said regretfully. "I really hadn't time to see anything."

'The Inspector very kindly allowed me to accompany him to the Three Anchors. The garage was up a side street. The big doors were closed, but by going up a little alley at the side we found a small door that led into it, and the door was open. A very brief examination of the tyres sufficed for the Inspector. "We have got him, by Jove!" he exclaimed. "Here is the mark as large as life on the rear left wheel. Now, Mr Kelvin, I don't think you will be clever enough to wriggle out of this."'

Raymond West came to a halt.

'Well?' said Joyce. 'So far I don't see anything to make a problem about – unless they never found the gold.'

'They never found the gold certainly,' said Raymond. 'And they never got Kelvin either. I expect he was too clever for them, but I don't quite see how he worked it. He was duly arrested – on the evidence of the tyre mark. But an extraordinary hitch arose. Just opposite the big doors of the garage was a cottage rented for the summer by a lady artist.'

'Oh, these lady artists!' said Joyce, laughing.

'As you say, "Oh, these lady artists!" This particular one had been ill for some weeks, and, in consequence, had two hospital nurses attending her. The nurse who was on night duty had pulled her armchair up to the window, where the blind was up. She declared that the motor lorry could not have left the garage opposite without her seeing it, and she swore that in actual fact it never left the garage that night.'

'I don't think that is much of a problem,' said Joyce. 'The nurse went to sleep, of course. They always do.'

'That has – er – been known to happen,' said Mr Petherick, judiciously; 'but it seems to me that we are accepting facts without sufficient examination. Before accepting the testimony of the hospital nurse, we should inquire very closely into her bona fides. The alibi coming with such suspicious promptness is inclined to raise doubts in one's mind.'

'There is also the lady artist's testimony,' said Raymond. 'She declared that she was in pain, and awake most of the night, and that she would certainly have heard the lorry, it being an unusual noise, and the night being very quiet after the storm.'

'H'm,' said the clergyman, 'that is certainly an additional fact. Had Kelvin himself any alibi?'

'He declared that he was at home and in bed from ten o'clock onwards, but he could produce no witnesses in support of that statement.'

'The nurse went to sleep,' said Joyce, 'and so did the patient. Ill people always think they have never slept a wink all night.'

Raymond West looked inquiringly at Dr Pender.

'Do you know, I feel very sorry for that man Kelvin. It seems to me very much a case of "Give a dog a bad name." Kelvin had been in prison. Apart from the tyre mark, which certainly seems too remarkable to be coincidence, there doesn't seem to be much against him except his unfortunate record.'

'You, Sir Henry?'

Sir Henry shook his head.

'As it happens,' he said, smiling, 'I know something about this case. So clearly I mustn't speak.'

'Well, go on, Aunt Jane; haven't you got anything to say?'

'In a minute, dear,' said Miss Marple. 'I am afraid I have counted wrong. Two purl, three plain, slip one, two purl – yes, that's right. What did you say, dear?'

'What is your opinion?'

'You wouldn't like my opinion, dear. Young people never do, I notice. It is better to say nothing.'

'Nonsense, Aunt Jane; out with it.'

'Well, dear Raymond,' said Miss Marple, laying down her knitting and looking across at her nephew. 'I do think you should be more careful how you choose your friends. You are so credulous, dear, so easily gulled. I suppose it is being a writer and having so much imagination. All that story about a Spanish galleon! If you were older and had more experience of life you would have been on your guard at once. A man you had known only a few weeks, too!'

Sir Henry suddenly gave vent to a great roar of laughter and slapped his knee.

'Got you this time, Raymond,' he said. 'Miss Marple, you are wonderful. Your friend Newman, my boy, has another name – several other names in fact. At the present moment he is not in Cornwall but in Devonshire – Dartmoor, to be exact – a convict in Princetown prison. We didn't catch him over the stolen bullion business, but over the rifling of the strongroom of one of the London banks. Then we looked up his past record and we found a good portion of the gold stolen buried in the garden at Pol House. It was rather a neat idea. All along that Cornish coast there are stories of wrecked galleons full of gold. It accounted for the diver and it would account later for the gold. But a scapegoat was needed, and Kelvin was ideal for the purpose. Newman played his little comedy very well, and our friend Raymond, with his celebrity as a writer, made an unimpeachable witness.'

'But the tyre mark?' objected Joyce.

'Oh, I saw that at once, dear, although I know nothing about motors,' said Miss Marple. 'People change a wheel, you know – I have often seen them doing it – and, of course, they could take a wheel off Kelvin's lorry and take it out through the small door into the alley and put it on to Mr Newman's lorry and take the lorry out of one gate down to the beach, fill it up with the gold and bring it up through the other gate, and then they must have taken the wheel back and put it back on Mr Kelvin's lorry while, I suppose, someone else was tying up Mr Newman in a ditch. Very uncomfortable for him and probably longer before he was found than he expected. I suppose the man who called himself the gardener attended to that side of the business.'

'Why do you say, "called himself the gardener," Aunt Jane?' asked Raymond curiously.

'Well, he can't have been a real gardener, can he?' said Miss Marple. 'Gardeners don't work on Whit Monday. Everybody knows that.'

She smiled and folded up her knitting.

'It was really that little fact that put me on the right scent,' she said. She looked across at Raymond.

'When you are a householder, dear, and have a garden of your own, you will know these little things.'

The Bloodstained Pavement

'The Blood-Stained Pavement' was first published in
Royal Magazine, March 1928, and in the USA as 'Drip! Drip!'
in *Detective Story Magazine*, 23 June 1928.

'It's curious,' said Joyce Lemprière, 'but I hardly like telling you my story.
It happened a long time ago – five years ago to be exact – but it's sort
of haunted me ever since. The smiling, bright, top part of it – and the
hidden gruesomeness underneath. And the queer thing is that the sketch
I painted at the time has become tinged with the same atmosphere. When
you look at it first it is just a rough sketch of a little steep Cornish street
with the sunlight on it. But if you look long enough at it something sinister creeps in. I have never sold it but I never look at it. It lives in the
studio in a corner with its face to the wall.

'The name of the place was Rathole. It is a queer little Cornish fishing
village, very picturesque – too picturesque perhaps. There is rather too
much of the atmosphere of "Ye Olde Cornish Tea House" about it. It
has shops with bobbed-headed girls in smocks doing hand-illuminated
mottoes on parchment. It is pretty and it is quaint, but it is very self-
consciously so.'

'Don't I know,' said Raymond West, groaning. 'The curse of the charabanc, I suppose. No matter how narrow the lanes leading down to them
no picturesque village is safe.'

Joyce nodded.

'They are narrow lanes that lead down to Rathole and very steep, like
the side of a house. Well, to get on with my story. I had come down to
Cornwall for a fortnight, to sketch. There is an old inn in Rathole, The
Polharwith Arms. It was supposed to be the only house left standing by the
Spaniards when they shelled the place in fifteen hundred and something.'

'Not shelled,' said Raymond West, frowning. 'Do try to be historically
accurate, Joyce.'

'Well, at all events they landed guns somewhere along the coast and they fired them and the houses fell down. Anyway that is not the point. The inn was a wonderful old place with a kind of porch in front built on four pillars. I got a very good pitch and was just settling down to work when a car came creeping and twisting down the hill. Of course, it *would* stop before the inn – just where it was most awkward for me. The people got out – a man and a woman – I didn't notice them particularly. She had a kind of mauve linen dress on and a mauve hat.

'Presently the man came out again and to my great thankfulness drove the car down to the quay and left it there. He strolled back past me towards the inn. Just at that moment another beastly car came twisting down, and a woman got out of it dressed in the brightest chintz frock I have ever seen, scarlet poinsettias, I think they were, and she had on one of those big native straw hats – Cuban, aren't they? – in very bright scarlet.

'This woman didn't stop in front of the inn but drove the car farther down the street towards the other one. Then she got out and the man seeing her gave an astonished shout. "Carol," he cried, "in the name of all that is wonderful. Fancy meeting you in this out-of-the-way spot. I haven't seen you for years. Hello, there's Margery – my wife, you know. You must come and meet her."

'They went up the street towards the inn side by side, and I saw the other woman had just come out of the door and was moving down towards them. I had had just a glimpse of the woman called Carol as she passed by me. Just enough to see a very white powdered chin and a flaming scarlet mouth and I wondered – I just wondered – if Margery would be so very pleased to meet her. I hadn't seen Margery near to, but in the distance she looked dowdy and extra prim and proper.

'Well, of course, it was not any of my business but you get very queer little glimpses of life sometimes, and you can't help speculating about them. From where they were standing I could just catch fragments of their conversation that floated down to me. They were talking about bathing. The husband, whose name seemed to be Denis, wanted to take a boat and row round the coast. There was a famous cave well worth seeing, so he said, about a mile along. Carol wanted to see the cave too but suggested walking along the cliffs and seeing it from the land side. She said she hated boats. In the end they fixed it that way. Carol was to go along the cliff path and meet them at the cave, and Denis and Margery would take a boat and row round.

'Hearing them talk about bathing made me want to bathe too. It was a very hot morning and I wasn't doing particularly good work. Also, I fancied that the afternoon sunlight would be far more attractive in effect.

So I packed up my things and went off to a little beach that I knew of – it was quite the opposite direction from the cave, and was rather a discovery of mine. I had a ripping bathe there and I lunched off a tinned tongue and two tomatoes, and I came back in the afternoon full of confidence and enthusiasm to get on with my sketch.

'The whole of Rathole seemed to be asleep. I had been right about the afternoon sunlight, the shadows were far more telling. The Polharwith Arms was the principal note of my sketch. A ray of sunlight came slanting obliquely down and hit the ground in front of it and had rather a curious effect. I gathered that the bathing party had returned safely, because two bathing dresses, a scarlet one and a dark blue one, were hanging from the balcony, drying in the sun.

'Something had gone a bit wrong with one corner of my sketch and I bent over it for some moments doing something to put it right. When I looked up again there was a figure leaning against one of the pillars of The Polharwith Arms, who seemed to have appeared there by magic. He was dressed in seafaring clothes and was, I suppose, a fisherman. But he had a long dark beard, and if I had been looking for a model for a wicked Spanish captain I couldn't have imagined anyone better. I got to work with feverish haste before he should move away, though from his attitude he looked as though he was pefectly prepared to prop up the pillars through all eternity.

'He did move, however, but luckily not until I had got what I wanted. He came over to me and he began to talk. Oh, how that man talked.

'"Rathole," he said, "was a very interesting place."

'I knew that already but although I said so that didn't save me. I had the whole history of the shelling – I mean the destroying – of the village, and how the landlord of the Polharwith Arms was the last man to be killed. Run through on his own threshold by a Spanish captain's sword, and of how his blood spurted out on the pavement and no one could wash out the stain for a hundred years.

'It all fitted in very well with the languorous drowsy feeling of the afternoon. The man's voice was very suave and yet at the same time there was an undercurrent in it of something rather frightening. He was very obsequious in his manner, yet I felt underneath he was cruel. He made me understand the Inquisition and the terrors of all the things the Spaniards did better than I have ever done before.

'All the time he was talking to me I went on painting, and suddenly I realized that in the excitement of listening to his story I had painted in something that was not there. On that white square of pavement where the sun fell before the door of The Polharwith Arms, I had painted in bloodstains. It seemed extraordinary that the mind could play such tricks with the hand, but as I looked over towards the inn again I got a second shock. My hand had only painted what my eyes saw – drops of blood on the white pavement.

'I stared for a minute or two. Then I shut my eyes, said to myself, "Don't be so stupid, there's nothing there, really," then I opened them again, but the bloodstains were still there.

'I suddenly felt I couldn't stand it. I interrupted the fisherman's flood of language.

'"Tell me," I said, "my eyesight is not very good. Are those bloodstains on that pavement over there?"

'He looked at me indulgently and kindly.

'"No bloodstains in these days, lady. What I am telling you about is nearly five hundred years ago."

'"Yes," I said, "but now – on the pavement" – the words died away in my throat. I *knew* – *I knew* that he wouldn't see what I was seeing. I got up and with shaking hands began to put my things together. As I did so the young man who had come in the car that morning came out of the inn door. He looked up and down the street perplexedly. On the balcony above his wife came out and collected the bathing things. He walked down towards the car but suddenly swerved and came across the road towards the fisherman.

'"Tell me, my man," he said. "You don't know whether the lady who came in that second car there has got back yet?"

'"Lady in a dress with flowers all over it? No, sir, I haven't seen her. She went along the cliff towards the cave this morning."

'"I know, I know. We all bathed there together, and then she left us to walk home and I have not seen her since. It can't have taken her all this time. The cliffs round here are not dangerous, are they?"

'"It depends, sir, on the way you go. The best way is to take a man what knows the place with you."

'He very clearly meant himself and was beginning to enlarge on the theme, but the young man cut him short unceremoniously and ran back towards the inn calling up to his wife on the balcony.

'"I say, Margery, Carol hasn't come back yet. Odd, isn't it?"

'I didn't hear Margery's reply, but her husband went on. "Well, we can't wait any longer. We have got to push on to Penrithar. Are you ready? I will turn the car."

'He did as he had said, and presently the two of them drove off together. Meanwhile I had deliberately been nerving myself to prove how ridiculous my fancies were. When the car had gone I went over to the inn and examined the pavement closely. Of course there were no bloodstains there. No, all along it had been the result of my distorted imagination.

Yet, somehow, it seemed to make the thing more frightening. It was while I was standing there that I heard the fisherman's voice.

'He was looking at me curiously. "You thought you saw bloodstains here, eh, lady?"

'I nodded.

'"That is very curious, that is very curious. We have got a superstition here, lady. If anyone sees those bloodstains —"

'He paused.

'"Well?" I said.

'He went on in his soft voice, Cornish in intonation, but unconsciously smooth and well-bred in its pronunciation, and completely free from Cornish turns of speech.

'"They do say, lady, that if anyone sees those bloodstains that there will be a death within twenty-four hours."

'Creepy! It gave me a nasty feeling all down my spine.

'He went on persuasively. "There is a very interesting tablet in the church, lady, about a death —"

'"No thanks," I said decisively, and I turned sharply on my heel and walked up the street towards the cottage where I was lodging. Just as I got there I saw in the distance the woman called Carol coming along the cliff path. She was hurrying. Against the grey of the rocks she looked like some poisonous scarlet flower. Her hat was the colour of blood . . .

'I shook myself. Really, I had blood on the brain.

'Later I heard the sound of her car. I wondered whether she too was going to Penrithar; but she took the road to the left in the opposite direction. I watched the car crawl up the hill and disappear, and I breathed somehow more easily. Rathole seemed its quiet sleepy self once more.'

'If that is all,' said Raymond West as Joyce came to a stop, 'I will give my verdict at once. Indigestion, spots before the eyes after meals.'

'It isn't all,' said Joyce. 'You have got to hear the sequel. I read it in the paper two days later under the heading of "Sea Bathing Fatality". It told how Mrs Dacre, the wife of Captain Denis Dacre, was unfortunately drowned at Landeer Cove, just a little farther along the coast. She and her husband were staying at the time at the hotel there, and had declared their intention of bathing, but a cold wind sprang up. Captain Dacre had declared it was too cold, so he and some other people in the hotel had gone off to the golf links near by. Mrs Dacre, however, had said it was not too cold for her and she went off alone down to the cove. As she didn't return her husband became alarmed, and in company with his friends went down to the beach. They found her clothes lying beside a rock, but no trace of the unfortunate lady. Her body was not found until nearly a week later when it was washed ashore at a point some distance down the coast. There was a bad blow on her head which had occurred before death, and the theory was that she must have dived into the sea and hit her head on a rock. As far as I could make out her death would have occurred just twenty-four hours after the time I saw the bloodstains.'

'I protest,' said Sir Henry. 'This is not a problem – this is a ghost story. Miss Lemprière is evidently a medium.'

Mr Petherick gave his usual cough.

'One point strikes me –' he said, 'that blow on the head. We must not, I think, exclude the possibility of foul play. But I do not see that we have any data to go upon. Miss Lemprière's hallucination, or vision, is interesting certainly, but I do not see clearly the point on which she wishes us to pronounce.'

'Indigestion and coincidence,' said Raymond, 'and anyway you can't be sure that they were the same people. Besides, the curse, or whatever it was, would only apply to the actual inhabitants of Rathole.'

'I feel,' said Sir Henry, 'that the sinister seafaring man has something to do with this tale. But I agree with Mr Petherick, Miss Lemprière has given us very little data.'

Joyce turned to Dr Pender who smilingly shook his head.

'It is a most interesting story,' he said, 'but I am afraid I agree with Sir Henry and Mr Petherick that there is very little data to go upon.'

Joyce then looked curiously at Miss Marple, who smiled back at her.

'I, too, think you are just a little unfair, Joyce dear,' she said. 'Of course, it is different for me. I mean, we, being women, appreciate the point about clothes. I don't think it is a fair problem to put to a man. It must have meant a lot of rapid changing. What a wicked woman! And a still more wicked man.'

Joyce stared at her.

'Aunt Jane,' she said. 'Miss Marple, I mean, I believe – I do really believe you know the truth.'

'Well, dear,' said Miss Marple, 'it is much easier for me sitting here quietly than it was for you – and being an artist you are so susceptible to atmosphere, aren't you? Sitting here with one's knitting, one just sees the facts. Bloodstains dropped on the pavement from the bathing dress hanging above, and being a red bathing dress, of course, the criminals themselves did not realize it was bloodstained. Poor thing, poor young thing!'

'Excuse me, Miss Marple,' said Sir Henry, 'but you do know that I am entirely in the dark still. You and Miss Lemprière seem to know what you are talking about, but we men are still in utter darkness.'

'I will tell you the end of the story now,' said Joyce. 'It was a year later. I was at a little east coast seaside resort, and I was sketching, when suddenly

I had that queer feeling one has of something having happened before. There were two people, a man and a woman, on the pavement in front of me, and they were greeting a third person, a woman dressed in a scarlet poinsettia chintz dress. "Carol, by all that is wonderful! Fancy meeting you after all these years. You don't know my wife? Joan, this is an old friend of mine, Miss Harding."

'I recognized the man at once. It was the same Denis I had seen at Rathole. The wife was different – that is, she was a Joan instead of a Margery; but she was the same type, young and rather dowdy and very inconspicuous. I thought for a minute I was going mad. They began to talk of going bathing. I will tell you what I did. I marched straight then and there to the police station. I thought they would probably think I was off my head, but I didn't care. And as it happened everything was quite all right. There was a man from Scotland Yard there, and he had come down just about this very thing. It seems – oh, it's horrible to talk about – that the police had got suspicions of Denis Dacre. That wasn't his real name – he took different names on different occasions. He got to know girls, usually quiet inconspicuous girls without many relatives or friends, he married them and insured their lives for large sums and then – oh, it's horrible! The woman called Carol was his real wife, and they always carried out the same plan. That is really how they came to catch him. The insurance companies became suspicious. He would come to some quiet seaside place with his new wife, then the other woman would turn up and they would all go bathing together. Then the wife would be murdered and Carol would put on her clothes and go back in the boat with him. Then they would leave the place, wherever it was, after inquiring for the supposed Carol and when they got outside the village Carol would hastily change back into her own flamboyant clothes and her vivid make-up and would go back there and drive off in her own car. They would find out which way the current was flowing and the supposed death would take place at the next bathing place along the coast that way. Carol would play the part of the wife and would go down to some lonely beach and would leave the wife's clothes there by a rock and depart in her flowery chintz dress to wait quietly until her husband could rejoin her.

'I suppose when they killed poor Margery some of the blood must have spurted over Carol's bathing suit, and being a red one they didn't notice it, as Miss Marple says. But when they hung it over the balcony it dripped. Ugh!' she gave a shiver. 'I can see it still.'

'Of course,' said Sir Henry, 'I remember very well now. Davis was the man's real name. It had quite slipped my memory that one of his many aliases was Dacre. They were an extraordinarily cunning pair. It always seemed so amazing to me that no one spotted the change of identity. I suppose, as Miss Marple says, clothes are more easily identified than faces; but it was a very clever scheme, for although we suspected Davis it was not easy to bring the crime home to him as he always seemed to have an unimpeachable alibi.'

'Aunt Jane,' said Raymond, looking at her curiously, 'how do you do it? You have lived such a peaceful life and yet nothing seems to surprise you.'

'I always find one thing very like another in this world,' said Miss Marple. 'There was Mrs Green, you know, she buried five children – and every one of them insured. Well, naturally, one began to get suspicious.'

She shook her head.

'There is a great deal of wickedness in village life. I hope you dear young people will never realize how very wicked the world is.'

Motive v. Opportunity

'Motive v. Opportunity' was first published in *Royal Magazine*,
April 1928, and in the USA as 'Where's the Catch?' in
Detective Story Magazine, 30 June 1928.

Mr Petherick cleared his throat rather more importantly than usual.

'I am afraid my little problem will seem rather tame to you all,' he said apologetically, 'after the sensational stories we have been hearing. There is no bloodshed in mine, but it seems to me an interesting and rather ingenious little problem, and fortunately I am in the position to know the right answer to it.'

'It isn't terribly legal, is it?' asked Joyce Lemprière. 'I mean points of law and lots of Barnaby *v* Skinner in the year 1881, and things like that.'

Mr Petherick beamed appreciatively at her over his eyeglasses.

'No, no, my dear young lady. You need have no fears on that score. The story I am about to tell is a perfectly simple and straightforward one and can be followed by any layman.'

'No legal quibbles, now,' said Miss Marple, shaking a knitting needle at him.

'Certainly not,' said Mr Petherick.

'Ah well, I am not so sure, but let's hear the story.'

'It concerns a former client of mine. I will call him Mr Clode – Simon Clode. He was a man of considerable wealth and lived in a large house not very far from here. He had had one son killed in the War and this son had left one child, a little girl. Her mother had died at her birth, and on her father's death she had come to live with her grandfather who at once became passionately attached to her. Little Chris could do anything she liked with her grandfather. I have never seen a man more completely wrapped up in a child, and I cannot describe to you his grief and despair when, at the age of eleven, the child contracted pneumonia and died.

'Poor Simon Clode was inconsolable. A brother of his had recently died in poor circumstances and Simon Clode had generously offered a home to his brother's children – two girls, Grace and Mary, and a boy, George. But though kind and generous to his nephew and nieces, the old man never expended on them any of the love and devotion he had accorded to his little grandchild. Employment was found for George Clode in a bank near by, and Grace married a clever young research chemist of the name of Philip Garrod. Mary, who was a quiet, self-contained girl, lived at home and looked after her uncle. She was, I think, fond of him in her quiet undemonstrative way. And to all appearances things went on very peacefully. I may say that after the death of little Christobel, Simon Clode came to me and instructed me to draw up a new will. By this will, his fortune, a very considerable one, was divided equally between his nephew and nieces, a third share to each.

'Time went on. Chancing to meet George Clode one day I inquired for his uncle, whom I had not seen for some time. To my surprise George's face clouded over. "I wish you could put some sense into Uncle Simon," he said ruefully. His honest but not very brilliant countenance looked puzzled and worried. "This spirit business is getting worse and worse."

'"What spirit business?" I asked, very much surprised.

'Then George told me the whole story. How Mr Clode had gradually got interested in the subject and how on the top of this interest he had chanced to meet an American medium, a Mrs Eurydice Spragg. This woman, whom George did not hesitate to characterize as an out and out swindler, had gained an immense ascendancy over Simon Clode. She was practically always in the house and many séances were held in which the spirit of Christobel manifested itself to the doting grandfather.

'I may say here and now that I do not belong to the ranks of those who cover spiritualism with ridicule and scorn. I am, as I have told you, a believer in evidence. And I think that when we have an impartial mind and weigh the evidence in favour of spiritualism there remains much that cannot be put down to fraud or lightly set aside. Therefore, as I say, I am neither a believer nor an unbeliever. There is certain testimony with which one cannot afford to disagree.

'On the other hand, spiritualism lends itself very easily to fraud and imposture, and from all young George Clode told me about this Mrs Eurydice Spragg I felt more and more convinced that Simon Clode was in bad hands and that Mrs Spragg was probably an imposter of the worst type. The old man, shrewd as he was in practical matters, would be easily imposed on where his love for his dead grandchild was concerned.

'Turning things over in my mind I felt more and more uneasy. I was fond of the young Clodes, Mary and George, and I realized that this Mrs Spragg and her influence over their uncle might lead to trouble in the future.

'At the earliest opportunity I made a pretext for calling on Simon Clode. I found Mrs Spragg installed as an honoured and friendly guest. As soon as I saw her my worst apprehensions were fulfilled. She was a stout woman of middle age, dressed in a flamboyant style. Very full of cant phrases about "Our dear ones who have passed over," and other things of the kind.

'Her husband was also staying in the house, Mr Absalom Spragg, a thin lank man with a melancholy expression and extremely furtive eyes. As soon as I could, I got Simon Clode to myself and sounded him tactfully on the subject. He was full of enthusiasm. Eurydice Spragg was wonderful! She had been sent to him directly in answer to a prayer! She cared nothing for money, the joy of helping a heart in affliction was enough for her. She had quite a mother's feeling for little Chris. He was beginning to regard her almost as a daughter. Then he went on to give me details – how he had heard his Chris's voice speaking – how she was well and happy with her father and mother. He went on to tell other sentiments expressed by the child, which in my remembrance of little Christobel seemed to me highly unlikely. She laid stress on the fact that "Father and Mother loved dear Mrs Spragg".

'"But, of course," he broke off, "you are a scoffer, Petherick."

'"No, I am not a scoffer. Very far from it. Some of the men who have written on the subject are men whose testimony I would accept unhesitatingly, and I should accord any medium recommended by them respect and credence. I presume that this Mrs Spragg is well vouched for?"

'Simon went into ecstasies over Mrs Spragg. She had been sent to him by Heaven. He had come across her at the watering place where he had spent two months in the summer. A chance meeting, with what a wonderful result!

'I went away very dissatisfied. My worst fears were realized, but I did not see what I could do. After a good deal of thought and deliberation I wrote to Philip Garrod who had, as I mentioned, just married the eldest Clode girl, Grace. I set the case before him – of course, in the most carefully guarded language. I pointed out the danger of such a woman gaining ascendancy over the old man's mind. And I suggested that Mr Clode should be brought into contact if possible with some reputable spiritualistic circles. This, I thought, would not be a difficult matter for Philip Garrod to arrange.

'Garrod was prompt to act. He realized, which I did not, that Simon Clode's health was in a very precarious condition, and as a practical man he had no intention of letting his wife or her sister and brother be despoiled of the inheritance which was so rightly theirs. He came down the following week, bringing with him as a guest no other than the famous

Professor Longman. Longman was a scientist of the first order, a man whose association with spiritualism compelled the latter to be treated with respect. Not only a brilliant scientist; he was a man of the utmost uprightness and probity.

'The result of the visit was most unfortunate. Longman, it seemed, had said very little while he was there. Two séances were held – under what conditions I do not know. Longman was non-committal all the time he was in the house, but after his departure he wrote a letter to Philip Garrod. In it he admitted that he had not been able to detect Mrs Spragg in fraud, nevertheless his private opinion was that the phenomena were not genuine. Mr Garrod, he said, was at liberty to show this letter to his uncle if he thought fit, and he suggested that he himself should put Mr Clode in touch with a medium of perfect integrity.

'Philip Garrod had taken this letter straight to his uncle, but the result was not what he had anticipated. The old man flew into a towering rage. It was all a plot to discredit Mrs Spragg who was a maligned and injured saint! She had told him already what bitter jealousy there was of her in this country. He pointed out that Longman was forced to say he had not detected fraud. Eurydice Spragg had come to him in the darkest hour of his life, had given him help and comfort, and he was prepared to espouse her cause even if it meant quarrelling with every member of his family. She was more to him than anyone else in the world.

'Philip Garrod was turned out of the house with scant ceremony; but as a result of his rage Clode's own health took a decided turn for the worse. For the last month he had kept to his bed pretty continuously, and now there seemed every possibility of his being a bedridden invalid until such time as death should release him. Two days after Philip's departure I received an urgent summons and went hurriedly over. Clode was in bed and looked even to my layman's eye very ill indeed. He was gasping for breath.

'"This is the end of me," he said. "I feel it. Don't argue with me, Petherick. But before I die I am going to do my duty by the one human being who has done more for me than anyone else in the world. I want to make a fresh will."

'"Certainly," I said, "if you will give me your instructions now I will draft out a will and send it to you."

'"That won't do," he said. "Why, man, I might not live through the night. I have written out what I want here," he fumbled under his pillow, "and you can tell me if it is right."

'He produced a sheet of paper with a few words roughly scribbled on it in pencil. It was quite simple and clear. He left £5000 to each of his nieces and nephew, and the residue of his vast property outright to Eurydice Spragg "in gratitude and admiration".

'I didn't like it, but there it was. There was no question of unsound mind, the old man was as sane as anybody.

'He rang the bell for two of the servants. They came promptly. The housemaid, Emma Gaunt, was a tall middle-aged woman who had been in service there for many years and who had nursed Clode devotedly. With her came the cook, a fresh buxom young woman of thirty. Simon Clode glared at them both from under his bushy eyebrows.

'"I want you to witness my will. Emma, get me my fountain pen."

'Emma went over obediently to the desk.

'"Not that left-hand drawer, girl," said old Simon irritably. "Don't you know it is in the right-hand one?"

'"No, it is here, sir," said Emma, producing it.

'"Then you must have put it away wrong last time," grumbled the old man. "I can't stand things not being kept in their proper places."

'Still grumbling he took the pen from her and copied his own rough draught, amended by me, on to a fresh piece of paper. Then he signed his name. Emma Gaunt and the cook, Lucy David, also signed. I folded the will up and put it into a long blue envelope. It was necessarily, you understand, written on an ordinary piece of paper.

'Just as the servants were turning to leave the room Clode lay back on the pillows with a gasp and a distorted face. I bent over him anxiously and Emma Gaunt came quickly back. However, the old man recovered and smiled weakly.

'"It is all right, Petherick, don't be alarmed. At any rate I shall die easy now having done what I wanted to."

'Emma Gaunt looked inquiringly at me as if to know whether she could leave the room. I nodded reassuringly and she went out – first stopping to pick up the blue envelope which I had let slip to the ground in my moment of anxiety. She handed it to me and I slipped it into my coat pocket and then she went out.

'"You are annoyed, Petherick," said Simon Clode. "You are prejudiced, like everybody else."

'"It is not a question of prejudice," I said. "Mrs Spragg may be all that she claims to be. I should see no objection to you leaving her a small legacy as a memento of gratitude; but I tell you frankly, Clode, that to disinherit your own flesh and blood in favour of a stranger is wrong."

'With that I turned to depart. I had done what I could and made my protest.

'Mary Clode came out of the drawing-room and met me in the hall.

'"You will have tea before you go, won't you? Come in here," and she led me into the drawing-room.

'A fire was burning on the hearth and the room looked cosy and cheerful. She relieved me of my overcoat just as her brother, George, came into the room. He took it from her and laid it across a chair at the far end of the room, then he came back to the fireside where we drank tea. During the meal a question arose about some point concerning the estate. Simon Clode said he didn't want to be bothered with it and had left it to George to decide. George was rather nervous about trusting to his own judgment. At my suggestion, we adjourned to the study after tea and I looked over the papers in question. Mary Clode accompanied us.

'A quarter of an hour later I prepared to take my departure. Remembering that I had left my overcoat in the drawing-room, I went there to fetch it. The only occupant of the room was Mrs Spragg, who was kneeling by the chair on which the overcoat lay. She seemed to be doing something rather unnecessary to the cretonne cover. She rose with a very red face as we entered.

'"That cover never did sit right," she complained. "My! I could make a better fit myself."

'I took up my overcoat and put it on. As I did so I noticed that the envelope containing the will had fallen out of the pocket and was lying on the floor. I replaced it in my pocket, said goodbye, and took my departure.

'On arrival at my office, I will describe my next actions carefully. I removed my overcoat and took the will from the pocket. I had it in my hand and was standing by the table when my clerk came in. Somebody wished to speak to me on the telephone, and the extension to my desk was out of order. I accordingly accompanied him to the outer office and remained there for about five minutes engaged in conversation over the telephone.

'When I emerged, I found my clerk waiting for me.

'"Mr Spragg has called to see you, sir. I showed him into your office."

'I went there to find Mr Spragg sitting by the table. He rose and greeted me in a somewhat unctuous manner, then proceeded to a long discursive speech. In the main it seemed to be an uneasy justification of himself and his wife. He was afraid people were saying etc., etc. His wife had been known from her babyhood upwards for the pureness of her heart and her motives . . . and so on and so on. I was, I am afraid, rather curt with him. In the end I think he realized that his visit was not being a success and he left somewhat abruptly. I then remembered that I had left the will lying on the table. I took it, sealed the envelope, and wrote on it and put it away in the safe.

'Now I come to the crux of my story. Two months later Mr Simon Clode died. I will not go into long-winded discussions, I will just state the bare facts. *When the sealed envelope containing the will was opened it was found to contain a sheet of blank paper.'*

He paused, looking round the circle of interested faces. He smiled himself with a certain enjoyment.

'You appreciate the point, of course? For two months the sealed envelope had lain in my safe. It could not have been tampered with then. No, the time limit was a very short one. Between the moment the will was signed and my locking it away in the safe. Now who had had the opportunity, and to whose interests would it be to do so?

'I will recapitulate the vital points in a brief summary: The will was signed by Mr Clode, placed by me in an envelope – so far so good. It was then put by me in my overcoat pocket. That overcoat was taken from me by Mary and handed by her to George, who was in full sight of me whilst handling the coat. During the time that I was in the study Mrs Eurydice Spragg would have had plenty of time to extract the envelope from the coat pocket and read its contents and, as a matter of fact, finding the envelope on the ground and not in the pocket seemed to point to her having done so. But here we come to a curious point: she had the *opportunity* of substituting the blank paper, but no *motive*. The will was in her favour, and by substituting a blank piece of paper she despoiled herself of the heritage she had been so anxious to gain. The same applied to Mr Spragg. He, too, had the opportunity. He was left alone with the document in question for some two or three minutes in my office. But again, it was not to his advantage to do so. So we are faced with this curious problem: the two people who had the *opportunity* of substituting a blank piece of paper had no *motive* for doing so, and the two people who had a *motive* had no *opportunity*. By the way, I would not exclude the housemaid, Emma Gaunt, from suspicion. She was devoted to her young master and mistress and detested the Spraggs. She would, I feel sure, have been quite equal to attempting the substitution if she had thought of it. But although she actually handled the envelope when she picked it up from the floor and handed it to me, she certainly had no opportunity of tampering with its contents and she could not have substituted another envelope by some sleight of hand (of which anyway she would not be capable) because the envelope in question was brought into the house by me and no one there would be likely to have a duplicate.'

He looked round, beaming on the assembly.

'Now, there is my little problem. I have, I hope, stated it clearly. I should be interested to hear your views.'

To everyone's astonishment Miss Marple gave vent to a long and prolonged chuckle. Something seemed to be amusing her immensely.

'What *is* the matter, Aunt Jane? Can't we share the joke?' said Raymond.

'I was thinking of little Tommy Symonds, a naughty little boy, I am afraid, but sometimes very amusing. One of those children with innocent childlike faces who are always up to some mischief or other. I was thinking how last week in Sunday School he said, "Teacher, do you say yolk of eggs *is* white or yolk of eggs *are* white?" And Miss Durston explained that anyone would say "yolks of eggs *are* white, or yolk of egg *is* white" – and naughty Tommy said: "Well, *I* should say yolk of egg is yellow!" Very naughty of him, of course, and as old as the hills. I knew that one as a child.'

'Very funny, my dear Aunt Jane,' Raymond said gently, 'but surely that has nothing to do with the very interesting story that Mr Petherick has been telling us.'

'Oh yes, it has,' said Miss Marple. 'It is a catch! And so is Mr Petherick's story a catch. So like a lawyer! Ah, my dear old friend!' She shook a reproving head at him.

'I wonder if you really know,' said the lawyer with a twinkle.

Miss Marple wrote a few words on a piece of paper, folded them up and passed them across to him.

Mr Petherick unfolded the paper, read what was written on it and looked across at her appreciatively.

'My dear friend,' he said, 'is there anything you do not know?'

'I knew that as a child,' said Miss Marple. 'Played with it too.'

'I feel rather out of this,' said Sir Henry. 'I feel sure that Mr Petherick has some clever legal legerdemain up his sleeve.'

'Not at all,' said Mr Petherick. 'Not at all. It is a perfectly fair straightforward proposition. You must not pay any attention to Miss Marple. She has her own way of looking at things.'

'We *should* be able to arrive at the truth,' said Raymond West a trifle vexedly. 'The facts certainly seem plain enough. Five persons actually touched that envelope. The Spraggs clearly could have meddled with it but equally clearly they did not do so. There remains the other three. Now, when one sees the marvellous ways that conjurers have of doing a thing before one's eyes, it seems to me that the paper could have been extracted and another substituted by George Clode during the time he was carrying the overcoat to the far end of the room.'

'Well, *I* think it was the girl,' said Joyce. 'I think the housemaid ran down and told her what was happening and she got hold of another blue envelope and just substituted the one for the other.'

Sir Henry shook his head. 'I disagree with you both,' he said slowly. 'These sort of things are done by conjurers, and they are done on the stage and in novels, but I think they would be impossible to do in real life, especially under the shrewd eyes of a man like my friend Mr Petherick here.

But I have an idea – it is only an idea and nothing more. We know that Professor Longman had just been down for a visit and that he said very little. It is only reasonable to suppose that the Spraggs may have been very anxious as to the result of that visit. If Simon Clode did not take them into his confidence, which is quite probable, they may have viewed his sending for Mr Petherick from quite another angle. They may have believed that Mr Clode had already made a will which benefited Eurydice Spragg and that this new one might be made for the express purpose of cutting her out as a result of Professor Longman's revelations, or alternatively, as you lawyers say, Philip Garrod had impressed on his uncle the claims of his own flesh and blood. In that case, suppose Mrs Spragg prepared to effect a substitution. This she does, but Mr Petherick coming in at an unfortunate moment she had no time to read the real document and hastily destroys it by fire in case the lawyer should discover his loss.'

Joyce shook her head very decidedly.

'She would never burn it without reading it.'

'The solution is rather a weak one,' admitted Sir Henry. 'I suppose – er – Mr Petherick did not assist Providence himself.'

The suggestion was only a laughing one, but the little lawyer drew himself up in offended dignity.

'A most improper suggestion,' he said with some asperity.

'What does Dr Pender say?' asked Sir Henry.

'I cannot say I have any very clear ideas. I think the substitution must have been effected by either Mrs Spragg or her husband, possibly for the motive that Sir Henry suggests. If she did not read the will until after Mr Petherick had departed, she would then be in somewhat of a dilemma, since she could not own up to her action in the matter. Possibly she would place it among Mr Clode's papers where she thought it would be found after his death. But why it wasn't found I don't know. It *might* be a mere speculation this – that Emma Gaunt came across it – and out of misplaced devotion to her employers – deliberately destroyed it.'

'I think Dr Pender's solution is the best of all,' said Joyce. 'Is it right, Mr Petherick?'

The lawyer shook his head.

'I will go on where I left off. I was dumbfounded and quite as much at sea as all of you are. I don't think I should ever have guessed the truth – probably not – but I was enlightened. It was cleverly done too.

'I went and dined with Philip Garrod about a month later and in the course of our after-dinner conversation he mentioned an interesting case that had recently come to his notice.'

'"I should like to tell you about it, Petherick, in confidence, of course."

'"Quite so," I replied.

"'A friend of mine who had expectations from one of his relatives was greatly distressed to find that that relative had thoughts of benefiting a totally unworthy person. My friend, I am afraid, is a trifle unscrupulous in his methods. There was a maid in the house who was greatly devoted to the interests of what I may call the legitimate party. My friend gave her very simple instructions. He gave her a fountain pen, duly filled. She was to place this in a drawer in the writing table in her master's room, but not the usual drawer where the pen was generally kept. If her master asked her to witness his signature to any document and asked her to bring him his pen, she was to bring him not the right one, but this one which was an exact duplicate of it. That was all she had to do. He gave her no other information. She was a devoted creature and she carried out his instructions faithfully.'"

'He broke off and said:

"'I hope I am not boring you, Petherick.'"

"'Not at all,' I said. 'I am keenly interested.'"

'Our eyes met.

"'My friend is, of course, not known to you,' he said.

"'Of course not,' I replied.

"'Then that is all right,' said Philip Garrod.

'He paused then said smilingly, "You see the point? The pen was filled with what is commonly known as Evanescent Ink – a solution of starch in water to which a few drops of iodine has been added. This makes a deep blue-black fluid, but the writing disappears entirely in four or five days."'

Miss Marple chuckled.

'Disappearing ink,' she said. 'I know it. Many is the time I have played with it as a child.'

And she beamed round on them all, pausing to shake a finger once more at Mr Petherick.

'But all the same it's a catch, Mr Petherick,' she said. 'Just like a lawyer.'

The Thumb Mark of St Peter

'The Thumb Mark of St Peter' was first published in *Royal Magazine*,
May 1928, and in the USA as 'The Thumb-Mark of St Peter' in
Detective Story Magazine, 7 July 1928.

'And now, Aunt Jane, it is up to you,' said Raymond West.

'Yes, Aunt Jane, we are expecting something really spicy,' chimed in
Joyce Lemprière.

'Now, you are laughing at me, my dears,' said Miss Marple placidly.
'You think that because I have lived in this out-of-the-way spot all my
life I am not likely to have had any very interesting experiences.'

'God forbid that I should ever regard village life as peaceful and
uneventful,' said Raymond with fervour. 'Not after the horrible revelations we have heard from you! The cosmopolitan world seems a mild and
peaceful place compared with St Mary Mead.'

'Well, my dear,' said Miss Marple, 'human nature is much the same
everywhere, and, of course, one has opportunities of observing it at close
quarters in a village.'

'You really are unique, Aunt Jane,' cried Joyce. 'I hope you don't mind
me calling you Aunt Jane?' she added. 'I don't know why I do it.'

'Don't you, my dear?' said Miss Marple.

She looked up for a moment or two with something quizzical in her
glance, which made the blood flame to the girl's cheeks. Raymond West
fidgeted and cleared his throat in a somewhat embarrassed manner.

Miss Marple looked at them both and smiled again, and bent her
attention once more to her knitting.

'It is true, of course, that I have lived what is called a very uneventful
life, but I have had a lot of experience in solving different little problems
that have arisen. Some of them have been really quite ingenious, but it
would be no good telling them to you, because they are about such unimportant things that you would not be interested – just things like: Who

cut the meshes of Mrs Jones's string bag? and why Mrs Sims only wore her new fur coat once. Very interesting things, really, to any student of human nature. No, the only experience I can remember that would be of interest to you is the one about my poor niece Mabel's husband.

'It is about ten or fifteen years ago now, and happily it is all over and done with, and everyone has forgotten about it. People's memories are very short – a lucky thing, I always think.'

Miss Marple paused and murmured to herself:

'I must just count this row. The decreasing is a little awkward. One, two, three, four, five, and then three purl; that is right. Now, what was I saying? Oh, yes, about poor Mabel.

'Mabel was my niece. A nice girl, really a very nice girl, but just a trifle what one might call *silly*. Rather fond of being melodramatic and of saying a great deal more than she meant whenever she was upset. She married a Mr Denman when she was twenty-two, and I am afraid it was not a very happy marriage. I had hoped very much that the attachment would not come to anything, for Mr Denman was a man of very violent temper – not the kind of man who would be patient with Mabel's foibles – and I also learned that there was insanity in his family. However, girls were just as obstinate then as they are now, and as they always will be. And Mabel married him.

'I didn't see very much of her after her marriage. She came to stay with me once or twice, and they asked me there several times, but, as a matter of fact, I am not very fond of staying in other people's houses, and I always managed to make some excuse. They had been married ten years when Mr Denman died suddenly. There were no children, and he left all his money to Mabel. I wrote, of course, and offered to come to Mabel if she wanted me; but she wrote back a very sensible letter, and I gathered that she was not altogether overwhelmed by grief. I thought that was only natural, because I knew they had not been getting on together for some time. It was not until about three months afterwards that I got a most hysterical letter from Mabel, begging me to come to her, and saying that things were going from bad to worse, and she couldn't stand it much longer.

'So, of course,' continued Miss Marple, 'I put Clara on board wages and sent the plate and the King Charles tankard to the bank, and I went off at once. I found Mabel in a very nervous state. The house, Myrtle Dene, was a fairly large one, very comfortably furnished. There was a cook and a house-parlourmaid as well as a nurse-attendant to look after old Mr Denman, Mabel's husband's father, who was what is called "not quite right in the head". Quite peaceful and well behaved, but distinctly odd at times. As I say, there was insanity in the family.

'I was really shocked to see the change in Mabel. She was a mass of nerves, twitching all over, yet I had the greatest difficulty in making her tell me what the trouble was. I got at it, as one always does get at these things, indirectly. I asked her about some friends of hers she was always mentioning in her letters, the Gallaghers. She said, to my surprise, that she hardly ever saw them nowadays. Other friends whom I mentioned elicited the same remark. I spoke to her then of the folly of shutting herself up and brooding, and especially of the silliness of cutting herself adrift from her friends. Then she came bursting out with the truth.

'"It is not my doing, it is theirs. There is not a soul in the place who will speak to me now. When I go down the High Street they all get out of the way so that they shan't have to meet me or speak to me. I am like a kind of leper. It is awful, and I can't bear it any longer. I shall have to sell the house and go abroad. Yet why should I be driven away from a home like this? I have done nothing."

'I was more disturbed than I can tell you. I was knitting a comforter for old Mrs Hay at the time, and in my perturbation I dropped two stitches and never discovered it until long after.

'"My dear Mabel," I said, "you amaze me. But what is the cause of all this?"

'Even as a child Mabel was always difficult. I had the greatest difficulty in getting her to give me a straightforward answer to my question. She would only say vague things about wicked talk and idle people who had nothing better to do than gossip, and people who put ideas into other people's heads.

'"That is all quite clear to me," I said. "There is evidently some story being circulated about you. But what that story is you must know as well as anyone. And you are going to tell me."

'"It is so wicked," moaned Mabel.

'"Of course it is wicked," I said briskly. "There is nothing that you can tell me about people's minds that would astonish or surprise me. Now, Mabel, will you tell me in plain English what people are saying about you?"

'Then it all came out.

'It seemed that Geoffrey Denman's death, being quite sudden and unexpected, gave rise to various rumours. In fact – and in plain English as I had put it to her – people were saying that she had poisoned her husband.

'Now, as I expect you know, there is nothing more cruel than talk, and there is nothing more difficult to combat. When people say things behind your back there is nothing you can refute or deny, and the rumours go on growing and growing, and no one can stop them. I was quite certain of one thing: Mabel was quite incapable of poisoning anyone. And I didn't see why life should be ruined for her and her home made unbearable just because in all probability she had been doing something silly and foolish.

'"There is no smoke without fire," I said. "Now, Mabel, you have got to tell me what started people off on this tack. There must have been something."

'Mabel was very incoherent, and declared there was nothing – nothing at all, except, of course, that Geoffrey's death had been very sudden. He had seemed quite well at supper that evening, and had taken violently ill in the night. The doctor had been sent for, but the poor man had died a few minutes after the doctor's arrival. Death had been thought to be the result of eating poisoned mushrooms.

'"Well," I said, "I suppose a sudden death of that kind might start tongues wagging, but surely not without some additional facts. Did you have a quarrel with Geoffrey or anything of that kind?"

'She admitted that she had had a quarrel with him on the preceding morning at breakfast time.

'"And the servants heard it, I suppose?" I asked.

'"They weren't in the room."

'"No, my dear," I said, "but they probably were fairly near the door outside."

'I knew the carrying power of Mabel's high-pitched hysterical voice only too well. Geoffrey Denman, too, was a man given to raising his voice loudly when angry.

'"What did you quarrel about?" I asked.

'"Oh, the usual things. It was always the same things over and over again. Some little thing would start us off, and then Geoffrey became impossible and said abominable things, and I told him what I thought of him."

'"There had been a lot of quarrelling, then?" I asked.

'"It wasn't my fault –"

'"My dear child," I said, "it doesn't matter whose fault it was. That is not what we are discussing. In a place like this everybody's private affairs are more or less public property. You and your husband were always quarrelling. You had a particularly bad quarrel one morning, and that night your husband died suddenly and mysteriously. Is that all, or is there anything else?"

'"I don't know what you mean by anything else," said Mabel sullenly.

'"Just what I say, my dear. If you have done anything silly, don't for Heaven's sake keep it back now. I only want to do what I can to help you."

'"Nothing and nobody can help me," said Mabel wildly, "except death."

'"Have a little more faith in Providence, dear," I said. "Now then, Mabel, I know perfectly well there *is* something else that you are keeping back."

'I always did know, even when she was a child, when she was not telling me the whole truth. It took a long time, but I got it out at last. She had gone down to the chemist's that morning and had bought some arsenic. She had had, of course, to sign the book for it. Naturally, the chemist had talked.

'"Who is your doctor?" I asked.

'"Dr Rawlinson."

'I knew him by sight. Mabel had pointed him out to me the other day. To put it in perfectly plain language he was what I would describe as an old dodderer. I have had too much experience of life to believe in the infallibility of doctors. Some of them are clever men and some of them are not, and half the time the best of them don't know what is the matter with you. I have no truck with doctors and their medicines myself.

'I thought things over, and then I put my bonnet on and went to call on Dr Rawlinson. He was just what I had thought him – a nice old man, kindly, vague, and so short-sighted as to be pitiful, slightly deaf, and, withal, touchy and sensitive to the last degree. He was on his high horse at once when I mentioned Geoffrey Denman's death, talked for a long time about various kinds of fungi, edible and otherwise. He had questioned the cook, and she had admitted that one or two of the mushrooms cooked had been "a little queer", but as the shop had sent them she thought they must be all right. The more she had thought about them since, the more she was convinced that their appearance was unusual.

'"She would be," I said. "They would start by being quite like mushrooms in appearance, and they would end by being orange with purple spots. There is nothing that class cannot remember if it tries."

'I gathered that Denman had been past speech when the doctor got to him. He was incapable of swallowing, and had died within a few minutes. The doctor seemed perfectly satisfied with the certificate he had given. But how much of that was obstinacy and how much of it was genuine belief I could not be sure.

'I went straight home and asked Mabel quite frankly why she had bought arsenic.

'"You must have had some idea in your mind," I pointed out.

'Mabel burst into tears. "I wanted to make away with myself," she moaned. "I was too unhappy. I thought I would end it all."

'"Have you the arsenic still?" I asked.

'"No, I threw it away."

'I sat there turning things over and over in my mind.

"'What happened when he was taken ill? Did he call you?"

"'No." She shook her head. "He rang the bell violently. He must have rung several times. At last Dorothy, the house-parlourmaid, heard it, and she waked the cook up, and they came down. When Dorothy saw him she was frightened. He was rambling and delirious. She left the cook with him and came rushing to me. I got up and went to him. Of course I saw at once he was dreadfully ill. Unfortunately Brewster, who looks after old Mr Denman, was away for the night, so there was no one who knew what to do. I sent Dorothy off for the doctor, and cook and I stayed with him, but after a few minutes I couldn't bear it any longer; it was too dreadful. I ran away back to my room and locked the door."

"'Very selfish and unkind of you," I said; "and no doubt that conduct of yours has done nothing to help you since, you may be sure of that. Cook will have repeated it everywhere. Well, well, this is a bad business."

'Next I spoke to the servants. The cook wanted to tell me about the mushrooms, but I stopped her. I was tired of these mushrooms. Instead, I questioned both of them very closely about their master's condition on that night. They both agreed that he seemed to be in great agony, that he was unable to swallow, and he could only speak in a strangled voice, and when he did speak it was only rambling – nothing sensible.

"'What did he say when he was rambling?" I asked curiously.

"'Something about some fish, wasn't it?" turning to the other.

'Dorothy agreed.

"'A heap of fish," she said; "some nonsense like that. I could see at once he wasn't in his right mind, poor gentleman."

'There didn't seem to be any sense to be made out of that. As a last resource I went up to see Brewster, who was a gaunt, middle-aged woman of about fifty.

"'It is a pity that I wasn't here that night," she said. "Nobody seems to have tried to do anything for him until the doctor came."

"'I suppose he was delirious," I said doubtfully; "but that is not a symptom of ptomaine poisoning, is it?"

"'It depends," said Brewster.

'I asked her how her patient was getting on.

'She shook her head.

"'He is pretty bad," she said.

"'Weak?"

"'Oh no, he is strong enough physically – all but his eyesight. That is failing badly. He may outlive all of us, but his mind is failing very fast now. I have already told both Mr and Mrs Denman that he ought to be in an institution, but Mrs Denman wouldn't hear of it at any price."

'I will say for Mabel that she always had a kindly heart.

'Well, there the thing was. I thought it over in every aspect, and at last I decided that there was only one thing to be done. In view of the rumours that were going about, permission must be applied for to exhume the body, and a proper post-mortem must be made and lying tongues quietened once and for all. Mabel, of course, made a fuss, mostly on sentimental grounds – disturbing the dead man in his peaceful grave, etc., etc. – but I was firm.

'I won't make a long story of this part of it. We got the order and they did the autopsy, or whatever they call it, but the result was not so satisfactory as it might have been. There was no trace of arsenic – that was all to the good – but the actual words of the report were *that there was nothing to show by what means deceased had come to his death*.

'So, you see, that didn't lead us out of trouble altogether. People went on talking – about rare poisons impossible to detect, and rubbish of that sort. I had seen the pathologist who had done the post-mortem, and I had asked him several questions, though he tried his best to get out of answering most of them; but I got out of him that he considered it highly unlikely that the poisoned mushrooms were the cause of death. An idea was simmering in my mind, and I asked him what poison, if any, could have been employed to obtain that result. He made a long explanation to me, most of which, I must admit, I did not follow, but it amounted to this: That death might have been due to some strong vegetable alkaloid.

'The idea I had was this: Supposing the taint of insanity was in Geoffrey Denman's blood also, might he not have made away with himself? He had, at one period of his life, studied medicine, and he would have a good knowledge of poisons and their effects.

'I didn't think it sounded very likely, but it was the only thing I could think of. And I was nearly at my wits' end, I can tell you. Now, I dare say you modern young people will laugh, but when I am in really bad trouble I always say a little prayer to myself – anywhere, when I am walking along the street, or at a bazaar. And I always get an answer. It may be some trifling thing, apparently quite unconnected with the subject, but there it is. I had that text pinned over my bed when I was a little girl: *Ask and you shall receive*. On the morning that I am telling you about, I was walking along the High Street, and I was praying hard. I shut my eyes, and when I opened them, what do you think was the first thing that I saw?'

Five faces with varying degrees of interest were turned to Miss Marple. It may be safely assumed, however, that no one would have guessed the answer to the question right.

'I saw,' said Miss Marple impressively, '*the window of the fishmonger's shop*. There was only one thing in it, *a fresh haddock*.'

She looked round triumphantly.

'Oh, my God!' said Raymond West. 'An answer to prayer – a fresh haddock!'

'Yes, Raymond,' said Miss Marple severely, 'and there is no need to be profane about it. The hand of God is everywhere. The first thing I saw were the black spots – the marks of St Peter's thumb. That is the legend, you know. St Peter's thumb. And that brought things home to me. I needed faith, the ever true faith of St Peter. I connected the two things together, faith – and fish.'

Sir Henry blew his nose rather hurriedly. Joyce bit her lip.

'Now what did that bring to my mind? Of course, both the cook and house-parlourmaid mentioned fish as being one of the things spoken of by the dying man. I was convinced, absolutely convinced, that there was some solution of the mystery to be found in these words. I went home determined to get to the bottom of the matter.'

She paused.

'Has it ever occurred to you,' the old lady went on, 'how much we go by what is called, I believe, the context? There is a place on Dartmoor called Grey Wethers. If you were talking to a farmer there and mentioned Grey Wethers, he would probably conclude that you were speaking of these stone circles, yet it is possible that you might be speaking of the atmosphere; and in the same way, if you were meaning the stone circles, an outsider, hearing a fragment of the conversation, might think you meant the weather. So when we repeat a conversation, we don't, as a rule, repeat the actual words; we put in some other words that seem to us to mean exactly the same thing.

'I saw both the cook and Dorothy separately. I asked the cook if she was quite sure that her master had really mentioned a heap of fish. She said she was quite sure.

'"Were these his exact words," I asked, "or did he mention some particular kind of fish?"

'"That's it," said the cook; "it was some particular kind of fish, but I can't remember what now. A heap of – now what was it? Not any of the fish you send to table. Would it be a perch now – or pike? No. It didn't begin with a P."

'Dorothy also recalled that her master had mentioned some special kind of fish. "Some outlandish kind of fish it was," she said.

'"A pile of – now what was it?"

'"Did he say heap or pile?" I asked.

'"I think he said pile. But there, I really can't be sure – it's so hard to remember the actual words, isn't it, Miss, especially when they don't seem to make sense. But now I come to think of it, I am pretty sure that it was a pile, and the fish began with C; but it wasn't a cod or a crayfish."

'The next part is where I am really proud of myself,' said Miss Marple, 'because, of course, I don't know anything about drugs – nasty, dangerous things I call them. I have got an old recipe of my grandmother's for tansy tea that is worth any amount of your drugs. But I knew that there were several medical volumes in the house, and in one of them there was an index of drugs. You see, my idea was that Geoffrey had taken some particular poison, and was trying to say the name of it.

'Well, I looked down the list of H's, beginning He. Nothing there that sounded likely; then I began on the P's, and almost at once I came to – what do you think?'

She looked round, postponing her moment of triumph.

'Pilocarpine. Can't you understand a man who could hardly speak trying to drag that word out? What would that sound like to a cook who had never heard the word? Wouldn't it convey the impression "pile of carp"?'

'By Jove!' said Sir Henry.

'I should never have hit upon that,' said Dr Pender.

'Most interesting,' said Mr Petherick. 'Really most interesting.'

'I turned quickly to the page indicated in the index. I read about pilocarpine and its effect on the eyes and other things that didn't seem to have any bearing on the case, but at last I came to a most significant phrase: *Has been tried with success as an antidote for atropine poisoning.*

'I can't tell you the light that dawned upon me then. I never had thought it likely that Geoffrey Denman would commit suicide. No, this new solution was not only possible, but I was absolutely sure it was the correct one, because all the pieces fitted in logically.'

'I am not going to try to guess,' said Raymond. 'Go on, Aunt Jane, and tell us what was so startlingly clear to you.'

'I don't know anything about medicine, of course,' said Miss Marple, 'but I did happen to know this, that when my eyesight was failing, the doctor ordered me drops with atropine sulphate in them. I went straight upstairs to old Mr Denman's room. I didn't beat about the bush.

'"Mr Denman," I said, "I know everything. Why did you poison your son?"

'He looked at me for a minute or two – rather a handsome old man he was, in his way – and then he burst out laughing. It was one of the most vicious laughs I have ever heard. I can assure you it made my flesh creep. I had only heard anything like it once before, when poor Mrs Jones went off her head.

'"Yes," he said, "I got even with Geoffrey. I was too clever for Geoffrey. He was going to put me away, was he? Have me shut up in an asylum? I heard them talking about it. Mabel is a good girl – Mabel stuck up for me, but I knew she wouldn't be able to stand up against Geoffrey. In the end he would have his own way; he always did. But I settled him – I settled my kind, loving son! Ha, ha! I crept down in the night. It was quite easy. Brewster was away. My dear son was asleep; he had a glass of water by the side of his bed; he always woke up in the middle of the night and drank it off. I poured it away – ha, ha! – and I emptied the bottle of eyedrops into the glass. He would wake up and swill it down before he knew what it was. There was only a tablespoonful of it – quite enough, quite enough. And so he did! They came to me in the morning and broke it to me very gently. They were afraid it would upset me. Ha! Ha! Ha! Ha! Ha!"

'Well,' said Miss Marple, 'that is the end of the story. Of course, the poor old man was put in an asylum. He wasn't really responsible for what he had done, and the truth was known, and everyone was sorry for Mabel and could not do enough to make up to her for the unjust suspicions they had had. But if it hadn't been for Geoffrey realizing what the stuff was he had swallowed and trying to get everybody to get hold of the antidote without delay, it might never have been found out. I believe there are very definite symptoms with atropine – dilated pupils of the eyes, and all that; but, of course, as I have said, Dr Rawlinson was very short-sighted, poor old man. And in the same medical book which I went on reading – and some of it was *most* interesting – it gave the symptoms of ptomaine poisoning and atropine, and they are not unlike. But I can assure you I have never seen a pile of fresh haddock without thinking of the thumb mark of St Peter.'

There was a very long pause.

'My dear friend,' said Mr Petherick. 'My very dear friend, you really are amazing.'

'I shall recommend Scotland Yard to come to you for advice,' said Sir Henry.

'Well, at all events, Aunt Jane,' said Raymond, 'there is one thing that you don't know.'

'Oh, yes, I do, dear,' said Miss Marple. 'It happened just before dinner, didn't it? When you took Joyce out to admire the sunset. It is a very favourite place, that. There by the jasmine hedge. That is where the milkman asked Annie if he could put up the banns.'

'Dash it all, Aunt Jane,' said Raymond, 'don't spoil all the romance. Joyce and I aren't like the milkman and Annie.'

'That is where you make a mistake, dear,' said Miss Marple. 'Everybody is very much alike, really. But fortunately, perhaps, they don't realize it.'

29

A Fruitful Sunday

'A Fruitful Sunday' was first published in
the *Daily Mail*, 11 August 1928.

'Well, really, I call this too delightful,' said Miss Dorothy Pratt for the fourth time. 'How I wish the old cat could see me now. She and her Janes!'

The 'old cat' thus scathingly alluded to was Miss Pratt's highly estimable employer, Mrs Mackenzie Jones, who had strong views upon the Christian names suitable for parlourmaids and had repudiated Dorothy in favour of Miss Pratt's despised second name of Jane.

Miss Pratt's companion did not reply at once – for the best of reasons. When you have just purchased a Baby Austin, fourth hand, for the sum of twenty pounds, and are taking it out for the second time only, your whole attention is necessarily focused on the difficult task of using both hands and feet as the emergencies of the moment dictate.

'Er – ah!' said Mr Edward Palgrove and negotiated a crisis with a horrible grinding sound that would have set a true motorist's teeth on edge.

'Well, you don't talk to a girl much,' complained Dorothy.

Mr Palgrove was saved from having to respond as at that moment he was roundly and soundly cursed by the driver of a motor omnibus.

'Well, of all the impudence,' said Miss Pratt, tossing her head.

'I only wish *he* had this foot-brake,' said her swain bitterly.

'Is there anything wrong with it?'

'You can put your foot on it till kingdom comes,' said Mr Palgrove. 'But nothing happens.'

'Oh, well, Ted, you can't expect everything for twenty pounds. After all, here we are, in a real car, on Sunday afternoon going out of town the same as everybody else.'

More grinding and crashing sounds.

'Ah,' said Ted, flushed with triumph. 'That was a better change.'

'You do drive something beautiful,' said Dorothy admiringly.

Emboldened by feminine appreciation, Mr Palgrove attempted a dash across Hammersmith Broadway, and was severely spoken to by a policeman.

'Well, I never,' said Dorothy, as they proceeded towards Hammersmith Bridge in a chastened fashion. 'I don't know what the police are coming to. You'd think they'd be a bit more civil spoken seeing the way they've been shown up lately.'

'Anyway, I didn't want to go along this road,' said Edward sadly. 'I wanted to go down the Great West Road and do a bust.'

'And be caught in a trap as likely as not,' said Dorothy. 'That's what happened to the master the other day. Five pounds and costs.'

'The police aren't so dusty after all,' said Edward generously. 'They pitch into the rich all right. No favour. It makes me mad to think of these swells who can walk into a place and buy a couple of Rolls-Royces without turning a hair. There's no sense in it. I'm as good as they are.'

'And the jewellery,' said Dorothy, sighing. 'Those shops in Bond Street. Diamonds and pearls and I don't know what! And me with a string of Woolworth pearls.'

She brooded sadly upon the subject. Edward was able once more to give his full attention to his driving. They managed to get through Richmond without mishap. The altercation with the policeman had shaken Edward's nerve. He now took the line of least resistance, following blindly behind any car in front whenever a choice of thoroughfares presented itself.

In this way he presently found himself following a shady country lane which many an experienced motorist would have given his soul to find.

'Rather clever turning off the way I did,' said Edward, taking all the credit to himself.

'Sweetly pretty, I call it,' said Miss Pratt. 'And I do declare, there's a man with fruit to sell.'

Sure enough, at a convenient corner, was a small wicker table with baskets of fruit on it, and the legend eat more fruit displayed on a banner.

'How much?' said Edward apprehensively when frenzied pulling of the hand-brake had produced the desired result.

'Lovely strawberries,' said the man in charge.

He was an unprepossessing-looking individual with a leer.

'Just the thing for the lady. Ripe fruit, fresh picked. Cherries too. Genuine English. Have a basket of cherries, lady?'

'They do look nice ones,' said Dorothy.

'Lovely, that's what they are,' said the man hoarsely. 'Bring you luck, lady, that basket will.' He at last condescended to reply to Edward. 'Two shillings, sir, and dirt cheap. You'd say so if you knew what was inside the basket.'

'They look awfully nice,' said Dorothy.

Edward sighed and paid over two shillings. His mind was obsessed by calculation. Tea later, petrol – this Sunday motoring business wasn't what you'd call *cheap*. That was the worst of taking girls out! They always wanted everything they saw.

'Thank you, sir,' said the unprepossessing-looking one. 'You've got more than your money's worth in that basket of cherries.'

Edward shoved his foot savagely down and the Baby Austin leaped at the cherry vendor after the manner of an infuriated Alsatian.

'Sorry,' said Edward. 'I forgot she was in gear.'

'You ought to be careful, dear,' said Dorothy. 'You might have hurt him.'

Edward did not reply. Another half-mile brought them to an ideal spot by the banks of a stream. The Austin was left by the side of the road and Edward and Dorothy sat affectionately upon the river bank and munched cherries. A Sunday paper lay unheeded at their feet.

'What's the news?' said Edward at last, stretching himself flat on his back and tilting his hat to shade his eyes.

Dorothy glanced over the headlines.

'The Woeful Wife. Extraordinary story. Twenty-eight people drowned last week. Reported death of Airman. Startling Jewel Robbery. Ruby Necklace worth fifty thousand pounds missing. Oh, Ted! Fifty thousand pounds. Just fancy!' She went on reading. 'The necklace is composed of twenty-one stones set in platinum and was sent by registered post from Paris. On arrival, the packet was found to contain a few pebbles and the jewels were missing.'

'Pinched in the post,' said Edward. 'The posts in France are awful, I believe.'

'I'd like to see a necklace like that,' said Dorothy. 'All glowing like blood – pigeon's blood, that's what they call the colour. I wonder what it would feel like to have a thing like that hanging round your neck.'

'Well, *you're* never likely to know, my girl,' said Edward facetiously.

Dorothy tossed her head.

'Why not, I should like to know. It's amazing the way girls can get on in the world. I might go on the stage.'

'Girls that behave themselves don't get anywhere,' said Edward discouragingly.

Dorothy opened her mouth to reply, checked herself, and murmured, 'Pass me the cherries.'

'I've been eating more than you have,' she remarked. 'I'll divide up what's left and – why, whatever's this at the bottom of the basket?'

She drew it out as she spoke – a long glittering chain of blood-red stones.

They both stared at it in amazement.

'In the basket, did you say?' said Edward at last.

Dorothy nodded.

'Right at the bottom – under the fruit.'

Again they stared at each other.

'How did it get there, do you think?'

'I can't imagine. It's odd, Ted, just after reading that bit in the paper – about the rubies.'

Edward laughed.

'You don't imagine you're holding fifty thousand pounds in your hand, do you?'

'I just said it was odd. Rubies set in platinum. Platinum is that sort of dull silvery stuff – like this. Don't they sparkle and aren't they a lovely colour? I wonder how many of them there are?' She counted. 'I say, Ted, there are twenty-one exactly.'

'No!'

'Yes. The same number as the paper said. Oh, Ted, you don't think –'

'It could be.' But he spoke irresolutely. 'There's some sort of way you can tell – scratching them on glass.'

'That's diamonds. But you know, Ted, that was a very odd-looking man – the man with the fruit – a nasty-looking man. And he was funny about it – said we'd got more than our money's worth in the basket.'

'Yes, but look here, Dorothy, what would he want to hand us over fifty thousand pounds for?'

Miss Pratt shook her head, discouraged.

'It doesn't seem to make sense,' she admitted. 'Unless the police were after him.'

'The police?' Edward paled slightly.

'Yes. It goes on to say in the paper – "the police have a clue."'

Cold shivers ran down Edward's spine.

'I don't like this, Dorothy. Supposing the police get after *us*.'

Dorothy stared at him with her mouth open.

'But we haven't done anything, Ted. We found it in the basket.'

'And that'll sound a silly sort of story to tell! It isn't likely.'

'It isn't very,' admitted Dorothy. 'Oh, Ted, do you really think it is it? It's like a fairy story!'

'I don't think it sounds like a fairy story,' said Edward. 'It sounds to me more like the kind of story where the hero goes to Dartmoor unjustly accused for fourteen years.'

But Dorothy was not listening. She had clasped the necklace round her neck and was judging the effect in a small mirror taken from her handbag.

'The same as a duchess might wear,' she murmured ecstatically.

'I won't believe it,' said Edward violently. 'They're imitation. They *must* be imitation.'

'Yes, dear,' said Dorothy, still intent on her reflection in the mirror. 'Very likely.'

'Anything else would be too much of a – a coincidence.'

'Pigeon's blood,' murmured Dorothy.

'It's absurd. That's what I say. Absurd. Look here, Dorothy, are you listening to what I say, or are you not?'

Dorothy put away the mirror. She turned to him, one hand on the rubies round her neck.

'How do I look?' she asked.

Edward stared at her, his grievance forgotten. He had never seen Dorothy quite like this. There was a triumph about her, a kind of regal beauty that was completely new to him. The belief that she had jewels round her neck worth fifty thousand pounds had made of Dorothy Pratt a new woman. She looked insolently serene, a kind of Cleopatra and Semiramis and Zenobia rolled into one.

'You look – you look – stunning,' said Edward humbly.

Dorothy laughed, and her laugh, too, was entirely different.

'Look here,' said Edward. 'We've got to do something. We must take them to a police station or something.'

'Nonsense,' said Dorothy. 'You said yourself just now that they wouldn't believe you. You'll probably be sent to prison for stealing them.'

'But – but what else can we do?'

'Keep them,' said the new Dorothy Pratt.

Edward stared at her.

'Keep them? You're mad.'

'We found them, didn't we? Why should we think they're valuable. We'll keep them and I shall wear them.'

'And the police will pinch *you*.'

Dorothy considered this for a minute or two.

'All right,' she said. 'We'll sell them. And you can buy a Rolls-Royce, or two Rolls-Royces, and I'll buy a diamond head-thing and some rings.'

Still Edward stared. Dorothy showed impatience.

'You've got your chance now – it's up to you to take it. We didn't steal the thing – I wouldn't hold with that. It's come to us and it's probably the only chance we'll ever have of getting all the things we want. Haven't you got any spunk at all, Edward Palgrove?'

Edward found his voice.

'Sell it, you say? That wouldn't be so jolly easy. Any jeweller would want to know where I got the blooming thing.'

'You don't take it to a jeweller. Don't you ever read detective stories, Ted? You take it to a "fence", of course.'

'And how should I know any fences? I've been brought up respectable.'

'Men ought to know everything,' said Dorothy. 'That's what they're for.'

He looked at her. She was serene and unyielding.

'I wouldn't have believed it of you,' he said weakly.

'I thought you had more spirit.'

There was a pause. Then Dorothy rose to her feet.

'Well,' she said lightly. 'We'd best be getting home.'

'Wearing that thing round your neck?'

Dorothy removed the necklace, looked at it reverently and dropped it into her handbag.

'Look here,' said Edward. 'You give that to me.'

'No.'

'Yes, you do. I've been brought up honest, my girl.'

'Well, you can go on being honest. You need have nothing to do with it.'

'Oh, hand it over,' said Edward recklessly. 'I'll do it. I'll find a fence. As you say, it's the only chance we shall ever have. We came by it honest – bought it for two shillings. It's no more than what gentlemen do in antique shops every day of their life and are proud of it.'

'That's it!' said Dorothy. 'Oh, Edward, you're splendid!'

She handed over the necklace and he dropped it into his pocket. He felt worked up, exalted, the very devil of a fellow! In this mood he started the Austin. They were both too excited to remember tea. They drove back to London in silence. Once at a cross-roads, a policeman stepped towards the car, and Edward's heart missed a beat. By a miracle, they reached home without mishap.

Edward's last words to Dorothy were imbued with the adventurous spirit.

'We'll go through with this. Fifty thousand pounds! It's worth it!'

He dreamt that night of broad arrows and Dartmoor, and rose early, haggard and unrefreshed. He had to set about finding a fence – and how to do it he had not the remotest idea!

His work at the office was slovenly and brought down upon him two sharp rebukes before lunch.

How did one find a 'fence'? Whitechapel, he fancied, was the correct neighbourhood – or was it Stepney?

On his return to the office a call came through for him on the telephone. Dorothy's voice spoke – tragic and tearful.

'Is that you, Ted? I'm using the telephone, but she may come in any minute, and I'll have to stop. Ted, you haven't done anything, have you?'

Edward replied in the negative.

'Well, look here, Ted, you mustn't. I've been lying awake all night. It's been awful. Thinking of how it says in the Bible you mustn't steal. I must have been mad yesterday – I really must. You won't do anything, will you, Ted, dear?'

Did a feeling of relief steal over Mr Palgrove? Possibly it did – but he wasn't going to admit any such thing.

'When I say I'm going through with a thing, I go through with it,' he said in a voice such as might belong to a strong superman with eyes of steel.

'Oh, but, Ted, dear, you mustn't. Oh, Lord, she's coming. Look here, Ted, she's going out to dinner tonight. I can slip out and meet you. Don't do anything till you've seen me. Eight o'clock. Wait for me round the corner.' Her voice changed to a seraphic murmur. 'Yes, ma'am, I think it was a wrong number. It was Bloomsbury 0234 they wanted.'

As Edward left the office at six o'clock, a huge headline caught his eye.

JEWEL ROBBERY. LATEST DEVELOPMENTS

Hurriedly he extended a penny. Safely ensconced in the Tube, having dexterously managed to gain a seat, he eagerly perused the printed sheet. He found what he sought easily enough.

A suppressed whistle escaped him.

'Well – I'm –'

And then another adjacent paragraph caught his eye. He read it through and let the paper slip to the floor unheeded.

Precisely at eight o'clock, he was waiting at the rendezvous. A breathless Dorothy, looking pale but pretty, came hurrying along to join him.

'You haven't done anything, Ted?'

'I haven't done anything.' He took the ruby chain from his pocket. 'You can put it on.'

'But, Ted –'

'The police have got the rubies all right – and the man who pinched them. And now read this!'

He thrust a newspaper paragraph under her nose. Dorothy read:

NEW ADVERTISING STUNT

A clever new advertising dodge is being adopted by the All-English Fivepenny Fair who intend to challenge the famous Woolworths. Baskets of fruit were sold yesterday and will be on sale every

Sunday. Out of every fifty baskets, one will contain an imitation necklace in different coloured stones. These necklaces are really wonderful value for the money. Great excitement and merriment was caused by them yesterday and EAT MORE FRUIT will have a great vogue next Sunday. We congratulate the Fivepenny Fair on their resource and wish them all good luck in their campaign of Buy British Goods.

'Well –' said Dorothy.

And after a pause: 'Well!'

'Yes,' said Edward. 'I felt the same.'

A passing man thrust a paper into his hand.

'Take one, brother,' he said.

'*The price of a virtuous woman is far above rubies.*'

'There!' said Edward. 'I hope that cheers you up.'

'I don't know,' said Dorothy doubtfully. 'I don't exactly want to *look* like a good woman.'

'You don't,' said Edward. 'That's why the man gave me that paper. With those rubies round your neck you don't look one little bit like a good woman.'

Dorothy laughed.

'You're rather a dear, Ted,' she said. 'Come on, let's go to the pictures.'

The Golden Ball

'The Golden Ball' was first published as 'Playing the Innocent'
in the *Daily Mail*, 5 August 1929.

George Dundas stood in the City of London meditating.

All about him toilers and money-makers surged and flowed like an enveloping tide. But George, beautifully dressed, his trousers exquisitely creased, took no heed of them. He was busy thinking what to do next.

Something had occurred! Between George and his rich uncle (Ephraim Leadbetter of the firm of Leadbetter and Gilling) there had been what is called in a lower walk of life 'words'. To be strictly accurate the words had been almost entirely on Mr Leadbetter's side. They had flowed from his lips in a steady stream of bitter indignation, and the fact that they consisted almost entirely of repetition did not seem to have worried him. To say a thing once beautifully and then let it alone was not one of Mr Leadbetter's mottos.

The theme was a simple one – the criminal folly and wickedness of a young man, who has his way to make, taking a day off in the middle of the week without even asking leave. Mr Leadbetter, when he had said everything he could think of and several things twice, paused for breath and asked George what he meant by it.

George replied simply that he had felt he wanted a day off. A holiday, in fact.

And what, Mr Leadbetter wanted to know, were Saturday afternoon and Sunday? To say nothing of Whitsuntide, not long past, and August Bank Holiday to come?

George said he didn't care for Saturday afternoons, Sundays or Bank Holidays. He meant a real day, when it might be possible to find some spot where half London was not assembled already.

Mr Leadbetter then said that he had done his best by his dead sister's son – nobody could say he hadn't given him a chance. But it was plain that it was no use. And in future George could have five real days with Saturday and Sunday added to do with as he liked.

'The golden ball of opportunity has been thrown up for you, my boy,' said Mr Leadbetter in a last touch of poetical fancy. 'And you have failed to grasp it.'

George said it seemed to him that that was just what he *had* done, and Mr Leadbetter dropped poetry for wrath and told him to get out.

Hence George – meditating. Would his uncle relent or would he not? Had he any secret affection for George, or merely a cold distaste?

It was just at that moment that a voice – a most unlikely voice – said, 'Hallo!'

A scarlet touring car with an immense long bonnet had drawn up to the curb beside him. At the wheel was that beautiful and popular society girl, Mary Montresor. (The description is that of the illustrated papers who produced a portrait of her at least four times a month.) She was smiling at George in an accomplished manner.

'I never knew a man could look so like an island,' said Mary Montresor. 'Would you like to get in?'

'I should love it above all things,' said George with no hesitation, and stepped in beside her.

They proceeded slowly because the traffic forbade anything else.

'I'm tired of the city,' said Mary Montresor. 'I came to see what it was like. I shall go back to London.'

Without presuming to correct her geography, George said it was a splendid idea. They proceeded sometimes slowly, sometimes with wild bursts of speed when Mary Montresor saw a chance of cutting in. It seemed to George that she was somewhat optimistic in the latter view, but he reflected that one could only die once. He thought it best, however, to essay no conversation. He preferred his fair driver to keep strictly to the job in hand.

It was she who reopened the conversation, choosing the moment when they were doing a wild sweep round Hyde Park Corner.

'How would you like to marry me?' she inquired casually.

George gave a gasp, but that may have been due to a large bus that seemed to spell certain destruction. He prided himself on his quickness in response.

'I should love it,' he replied easily.

'Well,' said Mary Montresor, vaguely. 'Perhaps you may some day.'

They turned into the straight without accident, and at that moment George perceived large new bills at Hyde Park Corner tube station. Sandwiched between GRAVE POLITICAL SITUATION and COLONEL IN

DOCK, one said SOCIETY GIRL TO MARRY DUKE and the other DUKE OF EDGEHILL AND MISS MONTRESOR.

'What's this about the Duke of Edgehill?' demanded George sternly.

'Me and Bingo? We're engaged.'

'But then – what you said just now –'

'Oh, *that*,' said Mary Montresor. 'You see, I haven't made up my mind who I shall actually *marry*.'

'Then why did you get engaged to him?'

'Just to see if I could. Everybody seemed to think it would be frightfully difficult, and it wasn't a bit!'

'Very rough luck on – er – Bingo,' said George, mastering his embarrassment at calling a real live duke by a nickname.

'Not at all,' said Mary Montresor. 'It will be good for Bingo if anything *could* do him good – which I doubt.'

George made another discovery – again aided by a convenient poster.

'Why, of course, it's cup day at Ascot. I should have thought that was the one place you were simply bound to be today.'

Mary Montresor sighed.

'I wanted a holiday,' she said plaintively.

'Why, so did I,' said George, delighted. 'And as a result my uncle has kicked me out to starve.'

'Then in case we marry,' said Mary, 'my twenty thousand a year may come in useful?'

'It will certainly provide us with a few home comforts,' said George.

'Talking of homes,' said Mary, 'let's go in the country and find a home we would like to live in.'

It seemed a simple and charming plan. They negotiated Putney Bridge, reached the Kingston by-pass and with a sigh of satisfaction Mary pressed her foot down on the accelerator. They got into the country very quickly. It was half an hour later that with a sudden exclamation Mary shot out a dramatic hand and pointed.

On the brow of a hill in front of them there nestled a house of what house-agents describe (but seldom truthfully) as 'old-world' charm. Imagine the description of most houses in the country really come true for once, and you get an idea of this house.

Mary drew up outside a white gate.

'We'll leave the car and go up and look at it. It's our house!'

'Decidedly, it's our house,' agreed George. 'But just for the moment other people seem to be living in it.'

Mary dismissed the other people with a wave of her hand. They walked up the winding drive together. The house appeared even more desirable at close quarters.

'We'll go and peep in at all the windows,' said Mary.

George demurred.

'Do you think the other people –?'

'I shan't consider them. It's our house – they're only living in it by a sort of accident. Besides, it's a lovely day and they're sure to be out. And if anyone does catch us, I shall say – I shall say – that I thought it was Mrs – Mrs Pardonstenger's house, and that I *am* so sorry I made a mistake.'

'Well, that ought to be safe enough,' said George reflectively.

They looked in through windows. The house was delightfully furnished. They had just got to the study when footsteps crunched on the gravel behind them and they turned to face a most irreproachable butler.

'Oh!' said Mary. And then putting on her most enchanting smile, she said, 'Is Mrs Pardonstenger in? I was looking to see if she was in the study.'

'Mrs Pardonstenger is at home, madam,' said the butler. 'Will you come this way, please.'

They did the only thing they could. They followed him. George was calculating what the odds against this happening could possibly be. With a name like Pardonstenger he came to the conclusion it was about one in twenty thousand. His companion whispered, 'Leave it to me. It will be all right.'

George was only too pleased to leave it to her. The situation, he considered, called for feminine finesse.

They were shown into a drawing-room. No sooner had the butler left the room than the door almost immediately reopened and a big florid lady with peroxide hair came in expectantly.

Mary Montresor made a movement towards her, then paused in well-simulated surprise.

'Why!' she exclaimed. 'It *isn't* Amy! What an extraordinary thing!'

'It *is* an extraordinary thing,' said a grim voice.

A man had entered behind Mrs Pardonstenger, an enormous man with a bulldog face and a sinister frown. George thought he had never seen such an unpleasant brute. The man closed the door and stood with his back against it.

'A very extraordinary thing,' he repeated sneeringly. 'But I fancy we understand your little game!' He suddenly produced what seemed an outsize in revolvers. 'Hands up. Hands up, I say. Frisk 'em, Bella.'

George in reading detective stories had often wondered what it meant to be frisked. Now he knew. Bella (alias Mrs P.) satisfied herself that neither he nor Mary concealed any lethal weapons on their persons.

'Thought you were mighty clever, didn't you?' sneered the man.

'Coming here like this and playing the innocents. You've made a mistake this time – a bad mistake. In fact, I very much doubt whether your friends and relations will ever see you again. Ah! you would, would you?' as George made a movement. 'None of your games. I'd shoot you as soon as look at you.'

'Be careful, George,' quavered Mary.

'I shall,' said George with feeling. 'Very careful.'

'And now march,' said the man. 'Open the door, Bella. Keep your hands above your heads, you two. The lady first – that's right. I'll come behind you both. Across the hall. Upstairs . . .'

They obeyed. What else could they do? Mary mounted the stairs, her hands held high. George followed. Behind them came the huge ruffian, revolver in hand.

Mary reached the top of the staircase and turned the corner. At the same moment, without the least warning, George lunged out in a fierce backward kick. He caught the man full in the middle and he capsized backwards down the stairs. In a moment George had turned and leaped down after him, kneeling on his chest. With his right hand, he picked up the revolver which had fallen from the other's hand as he fell.

Bella gave a scream and retreated through a baize door. Mary came running down the stairs, her face as white as paper.

'George, you haven't killed him?'

The man was lying absolutely still. George bent over him.

'I don't think I've killed him,' he said regretfully. 'But he's certainly taken the count all right.'

'Thank God.' She was breathing rapidly.

'Pretty neat,' said George with permissible self-admiration. 'Many a lesson to be learnt from a jolly old mule. Eh, what?'

Mary pulled at his hand.

'Come away,' she cried feverishly. 'Come away quick.'

'If we had something to tie this fellow up with,' said George, intent on his own plans. 'I suppose you couldn't find a bit of rope or cord anywhere?'

'No, I couldn't,' said Mary. 'And come away, please – please – I'm so frightened.'

'You needn't be frightened,' said George with manly arrogance. '*I'm* here.'

'Darling George, please – for my sake. I don't want to be mixed up in this. *Please* let's go.'

The exquisite way in which she breathed the words 'for my sake' shook George's resolution. He allowed himself to be led forth from the house and hurried down the drive to the waiting car. Mary said faintly: 'You drive. I don't feel I can.' George took command of the wheel.

'But we've got to see this thing through,' he said. 'Heaven knows what blackguardism that nasty looking fellow is up to. I won't bring the police into it if you don't want me to – but I'll have a try on my own. I ought to be able to get on their track all right.'

'No, George, I don't want you to.'

'We have a first-class adventure like this, and you want me to back out of it? Not on my life.'

'I'd no idea you were so bloodthirsty,' said Mary tearfully.

'I'm not bloodthirsty. I didn't begin it. The damned cheek of the fellow – threatening us with an outsize revolver. By the way – why on earth didn't that revolver go off when I kicked him downstairs?'

He stopped the car and fished the revolver out of the side-pocket of the car where he had placed it. After examining it, he whistled.

'Well, I'm damned! The thing isn't loaded. If I'd known that –' He paused, wrapped in thought. 'Mary, this is a very curious business.'

'I know it is. That's why I'm begging you to leave it alone.'

'Never,' said George firmly.

Mary uttered a heartrending sigh.

'I see,' she said, 'that I shall have to tell you. And the worst of it is that I haven't the least idea how you'll take it.'

'What do you mean – tell me?'

'You see, it's like this.' She paused. 'I feel girls should stick together nowadays – they should insist on knowing something about the men they meet.'

'Well?' said George, utterly fogged.

'And the most important thing to a girl is how a man will behave in an emergency – has he got presence of mind – courage – quick wittedness? That's the kind of thing you can hardly ever know – until it's too late. An emergency mightn't arise until you'd been married for years. All you do know about a man is how he dances and if he's good at getting taxis on a wet night.'

'Both very useful accomplishments,' George pointed out.

'Yes, but one wants to feel a man is a man.'

'The great wide-open spaces where men *are* men.' George quoted absently.

'Exactly. But we have no wide-open spaces in England. So one has to create a situation artificially. That's what I did.'

'Do you mean –?'

'I do mean. That house, as it happens, actually *is* my house. We came to it by design – not by chance. And the man – that man that you nearly killed –'

'Yes?'

'He's Rube Wallace – the film actor. He does prize-fighters, you know. The dearest and gentlest of men. I engaged him. Bella's his wife. That's why I was so terrified that you'd killed him. Of course the revolver wasn't loaded. It's a stage property. Oh, George, are you very angry?'

'Am I the first person you have – er – tried this test on?'

'Oh, no. There have been – let me see – nine and a half!'

'Who was the half?' inquired George with curiosity.

'Bingo,' replied Mary coldly.

'Did any of them think of kicking like a mule?'

'No – they didn't. Some tried to bluster and some gave in at once, but they all allowed themselves to be marched upstairs and tied up, and gagged. Then, of course, I managed to work myself loose from my bonds – like in books – and I freed them and we got away – finding the house empty.'

'And nobody thought of the mule trick or anything like it?'

'No.'

'In that case,' said George graciously, 'I forgive you.'

'Thank you, George,' said Mary meekly.

'In fact,' said George, 'the only question that arises is: where do we go now? I'm not sure if it's Lambeth Palace or Doctor's Commons, wherever that is.'

'What *are* you talking about?'

'The licence. A special licence, I think, is indicated. You're too fond of getting engaged to one man and then immediately asking another one to marry you.'

'I didn't ask you to marry me!'

'You did. At Hyde Park Corner. Not a place I should choose for a proposal myself, but everyone has their idiosyncrasies in these matters.'

'I did nothing of the kind. I just asked, as a joke, whether you would care to marry me? It wasn't intended seriously.'

'If I were to take counsel's opinion, I am sure that he would say it constituted a genuine proposal. Besides, you know you want to marry me.'

'I don't.'

'Not after nine and a half failures? Fancy what a feeling of security it will give you to go through life with a man who can extricate you from any dangerous situation.'

Mary appeared to weaken slightly at this telling argument. But she said firmly: 'I wouldn't marry any man unless he went on his knees to me.'

George looked at her. She was adorable. But George had other characteristics of the mule beside its kick. He said with equal firmness:

'To go on one's knees to any woman is degrading. I will not do it.'

Mary said with enchanting wistfulness: 'What a pity.'

They drove back to London. George was stern and silent. Mary's face was hidden by the brim of her hat. As they passed Hyde Park Corner, she murmured softly:

'Couldn't you go on your knees to me?'

George said firmly: 'No.'

He felt he was being a superman. She admired him for his attitude. But unluckily he suspected her of mulish tendencies herself. He drew up suddenly.

'Excuse me,' he said.

He jumped out of the car, retraced his steps to a fruit barrow they had just passed and returned so quickly that the policeman who was bearing down upon them to ask what they meant by it, had not had time to arrive.

George drove on, lightly tossing an apple into Mary's lap.

'Eat more fruit,' he said. 'Also symbolical.'

'Symbolical?'

'Yes. Originally Eve gave Adam an apple. Nowadays Adam gives Eve one. See?'

'Yes,' said Mary rather doubtfully.

'Where shall I drive you?' inquired George formally.

'Home, please.'

He drove to Grosvenor Square. His face was absolutely impassive. He jumped out and came round to help her out. She made a last appeal.

'Darling George – couldn't you? Just to please me?'

'Never,' said George.

And at that moment it happened. He slipped, tried to recover his balance and failed. He was kneeling in the mud before her. Mary gave a squeal of joy and clapped her hands.

'Darling George! Now I will marry you. You can go straight to Lambeth Palace and fix up with the Archbishop of Canterbury about it.'

'I didn't mean to,' said George hotly. 'It was a bl – er – a banana skin.' He held the offender up reproachfully.

'Never mind,' said Mary. 'It happened. When we quarrel and you throw it in my teeth that I proposed to you, I can retort that you had to go on your knees to me before I would marry you. And all because of that blessed banana skin! It *was* a blessed banana skin you were going to say?'

'Something of the sort,' said George.

At five-thirty that afternoon, Mr Leadbetter was informed that his nephew had called and would like to see him.

'Called to eat humble pie,' said Mr Leadbetter to himself. 'I dare say I was rather hard on the lad, but it was for his own good.'

And he gave orders that George should be admitted.

George came in airily.

'I want a few words with you, uncle,' he said. 'You did me a grave injustice this morning. I should like to know whether, at my age, you could have gone out into the street, disowned by your relatives, and between the hours of eleven-fifteen and five-thirty acquire an income of twenty thousand a year. This is what I have done!'

'You're mad, boy.'

'Not mad, resourceful! I am going to marry a young, rich, beautiful society girl. One, moreover, who is throwing over a duke for my sake.'

'Marrying a girl for her money? I'd not have thought it of you.'

'And you'd have been right. I would never have dared to ask her if she hadn't – very fortunately – asked me. She retracted afterwards, but I made her change her mind. And do you know, uncle, how all this was done? By a judicious expenditure of twopence and a grasping of the golden ball of opportunity.'

'Why the tuppence?' asked Mr Leadbetter, financially interested.

'One banana – off a barrow. Not everyone would have thought of that banana. Where do you get a marriage licence? Is it Doctor's Commons or Lambeth Palace?'

Accident

'Accident' was first published as 'The Uncrossed Path' in
The Sunday Dispatch, 22 September 1929.

'. . . And I tell you this – it's the same woman – not a doubt of it!'

Captain Haydock looked into the eager, vehement face of his friend
and sighed. He wished Evans would not be so positive and so jubilant.
In the course of a career spent at sea, the old sea captain had learned to
leave things that did not concern him well alone. His friend, Evans, late
C.I.D. Inspector, had a different philosophy of life. 'Acting on information received –' had been his motto in early days, and he had improved
upon it to the extent of finding out his own information. Inspector Evans
had been a very smart, wide-awake officer, and had justly earned the
promotion which had been his. Even now, when he had retired from the
force, and had settled down in the country cottage of his dreams, his
professional instinct was still active.

'Don't often forget a face,' he reiterated complacently. 'Mrs Anthony
– yes, it's Mrs Anthony right enough. When you said Mrs Merrowdene
– I knew her at once.'

Captain Haydock stirred uneasily. The Merrowdenes were his nearest
neighbours, barring Evans himself, and this identifying of Mrs Merrowdene with a former heroine of a *cause célèbre* distressed him.

'It's a long time ago,' he said rather weakly.

'Nine years,' said Evans, accurately as ever. 'Nine years and three
months. You remember the case?'

'In a vague sort of way.'

'Anthony turned out to be an arsenic eater,' said Evans, 'so they acquitted her.'

'Well, why shouldn't they?'

'No reason in the world. Only verdict they could give on the evidence.
Absolutely correct.'

'Then that's all right,' said Haydock. 'And I don't see what we're bothering about.'

'Who's bothering?'

'I thought you were.'

'Not at all.'

'The thing's over and done with,' summed up the captain. 'If Mrs Merrowdene at one time of her life was unfortunate enough to be tried and acquitted for murder –'

'It's not usually considered unfortunate to be acquitted,' put in Evans.

'You know what I mean,' said Captain Haydock irritably. 'If the poor lady has been through that harrowing experience, it's no business of ours to rake it up, is it?'

Evans did not answer.

'Come now, Evans. The lady was innocent – you've just said so.'

'I didn't say she was innocent. I said she was acquitted.'

'It's the same thing.'

'Not always.'

Captain Haydock, who had commenced to tap his pipe out against the side of his chair, stopped, and sat up with a very alert expression.

'Hallo – allo – allo,' he said. 'The wind's in that quarter, is it? You think she wasn't innocent?'

'I wouldn't say that. I just – don't know. Anthony was in the habit of taking arsenic. His wife got it for him. One day, by mistake, he takes far too much. Was the mistake his or his wife's? Nobody could tell, and the jury very properly gave her the benefit of the doubt. That's all quite right and I'm not finding fault with it. All the same – I'd like to *know*.'

Captain Haydock transferred his attention to his pipe once more.

'Well,' he said comfortably. 'It's none of our business.'

'I'm not so sure . . .'

'But surely –'

'Listen to me a minute. This man, Merrowdene – in his laboratory this evening, fiddling round with tests – you remember –'

'Yes. He mentioned Marsh's test for arsenic. Said *you* would know all about it – it was in *your* line – and chuckled. He wouldn't have said that if he'd thought for one moment –'

Evans interrupted him.

'You mean he wouldn't have said that if he *knew*. They've been married how long – six years you told me? I bet you anything he has no idea his wife is the once notorious Mrs Anthony.'

'And he will certainly not know it from me,' said Captain Haydock stiffly.

Evans paid no attention, but went on:

'You interrupted me just now. After Marsh's test, Merrowdene heated a substance in a test-tube, the metallic residue he dissolved in water and then precipitated it by adding silver nitrate. That was a test for chlorates. A neat unassuming little test. But I chanced to read these words in a book that stood open on the table:

H_2SO_4 *decomposes chlorates with evolution of* CL_4O_2. *If heated, violent explosions occur; the mixture ought therefore to be kept cool and only very small quantities used.*'

Haydock stared at his friend.

'Well, what about it?'

'Just this. In my profession we've got tests too – tests for murder. There's adding up the facts – weighing them, dissecting the residue when you've allowed for prejudice and the general inaccuracy of witnesses. But there's another test of murder – one that is fairly accurate, but rather – dangerous! *A murderer is seldom content with one crime.* Give him time, and a lack of suspicion, and he'll commit another. You catch a man – has he murdered his wife or hasn't he? – perhaps the case isn't very black against him. Look into his past – if you find that he's had several wives – and that they've all died shall we say – rather curiously? – then you *know*! I'm not speaking *legally*, you understand. I'm speaking of *moral* certainty. Once you *know*, you can go ahead looking for evidence.'

'Well?'

'I'm coming to the point. That's all right if there *is* a past to look into. But suppose you catch your murderer at his or her first crime? Then that test will be one from which you get no reaction. But suppose the prisoner acquitted – starting life under another name. Will or will not the murderer repeat the crime?'

'That's a horrible idea!'

'Do you still say it's none of our business?'

'Yes, I do. You've no reason to think that Mrs Merrowdene is anything but a perfectly innocent woman.'

The ex-inspector was silent for a moment. Then he said slowly:

'I told you that we looked into her past and found nothing. That's not quite true. There was a stepfather. As a girl of eighteen she had a fancy for some young man – and her stepfather exerted his authority to keep them apart. She and her stepfather went for a walk along a rather dangerous part of the cliff. There was an accident – the stepfather went too near the edge – it gave way, and he went over and was killed.'

'You don't think –'

'It was an accident. *Accident!* Anthony's over-dose of arsenic was an accident. She'd never have been tried if it hadn't transpired that there was another man – he sheered off, by the way. Looked as though he weren't satisfied even if the jury were. I tell you, Haydock, where that woman is concerned I'm afraid of another – accident!'

The old captain shrugged his shoulders.

'It's been nine years since that affair. Why should there be another "accident", as you call it, now?'

'I didn't say now. I said some day or other. If the necessary motive arose.'

Captain Haydock shrugged his shoulders.

'Well, I don't know how you're going to guard against that.'

'Neither do I,' said Evans ruefully.

'I should leave well alone,' said Captain Haydock. 'No good ever came of butting into other people's affairs.'

But that advice was not palatable to the ex-inspector. He was a man of patience but determination. Taking leave of his friend, he sauntered down to the village, revolving in his mind the possibilities of some kind of successful action.

Turning into the post office to buy some stamps, he ran into the object of his solicitude, George Merrowdene. The ex-chemistry professor was a small dreamy-looking man, gentle and kindly in manner, and usually completely absent-minded. He recognized the other and greeted him amicably, stooping to recover the letters that the impact had caused him to drop on the ground. Evans stooped also and, more rapid in his movements than the other, secured them first, handing them back to their owner with an apology.

He glanced down at them in doing so, and the address on the topmost suddenly awakened all his suspicions anew. It bore the name of a well-known insurance firm.

Instantly his mind was made up. The guileless George Merrowdene hardly realized how it came about that he and the ex-inspector were strolling down the village together, and still less could he have said how it came about that the conversation should come round to the subject of life insurance.

Evans had no difficulty in attaining his object. Merrowdene of his own accord volunteered the information that he had just insured his life for his wife's benefit, and asked Evans's opinion of the company in question.

'I made some rather unwise investments,' he explained. 'As a result my income has diminished. If anything were to happen to me, my wife would be left very badly off. This insurance will put things right.'

'She didn't object to the idea?' inquired Evans casually. 'Some ladies do, you know. Feel it's unlucky – that sort of thing.'

'Oh, Margaret is very practical,' said Merrowdene, smiling. 'Not at all superstitious. In fact, I believe it was her idea originally. She didn't like my being so worried.'

Evans had got the information he wanted. He left the other shortly afterwards, and his lips were set in a grim line. The late Mr Anthony had insured his life in his wife's favour a few weeks before his death.

Accustomed to rely on his instincts, he was perfectly sure in his own mind. But how to act was another matter. He wanted, not to arrest a criminal red-handed, but to prevent a crime being committed, and that was a very different and a very much more difficult thing.

All day he was very thoughtful. There was a Primrose League Fête that afternoon held in the grounds of the local squire, and he went to it, indulging in the penny dip, guessing the weight of a pig, and shying at coconuts all with the same look of abstracted concentration on his face. He even indulged in half a crown's worth of Zara, the Crystal Gazer, smiling a little to himself as he did so, remembering his own activities against fortune-tellers in his official days.

He did not pay very much heed to her sing-song droning voice – till the end of a sentence held his attention.

'. . . And you will very shortly – very shortly indeed – be engaged on a matter of life or death . . . Life or death to one person.'

'Eh – what's that?' he asked abruptly.

'A decision – you have a decision to make. You must be very careful – very, very careful . . . If you were to make a mistake – the smallest mistake –'

'Yes?'

The fortune-teller shivered. Inspector Evans knew it was all nonsense, but he was nevertheless impressed.

'I warn you – *you must not make a mistake*. If you do, I see the result clearly – a death . . .'

Odd, damned odd. A death. Fancy her lighting upon that!

'If I make a mistake a death will result? Is that it?'

'Yes.'

'In that case,' said Evans, rising to his feet and handing over half a crown, 'I mustn't make a mistake, eh?'

He spoke lightly enough, but as he went out of the tent, his jaw set determinedly. Easy to say – not so easy to be sure of doing. He mustn't make a slip. A life, a vulnerable human life depended on it.

And there was no one to help him. He looked across at the figure of his friend Haydock in the distance. No help there. 'Leave things alone,' was Haydock's motto. And that wouldn't do here.

Haydock was talking to a woman. She moved away from him and

came towards Evans and the inspector recognized her. It was Mrs Merrowdene. On an impulse he put himself deliberately in her path.

Mrs Merrowdene was rather a fine-looking woman. She had a broad serene brow, very beautiful brown eyes, and a placid expression. She had the look of an Italian madonna which she heightened by parting her hair in the middle and looping it over her ears. She had a deep rather sleepy voice.

She smiled up at Evans, a contented welcoming smile.

'I thought it was you, Mrs Anthony – I mean Mrs Merrowdene,' he said glibly.

He made the slip deliberately, watching her without seeming to do so. He saw her eyes widen, heard the quick intake of her breath. But her eyes did not falter. She gazed at him steadily and proudly.

'I was looking for my husband,' she said quietly. 'Have you seen him anywhere about?'

'He was over in that direction when I last saw him.'

They went side by side in the direction indicated, chatting quietly and pleasantly. The inspector felt his admiration mounting. What a woman! What self-command. What wonderful poise. A remarkable woman – and a very dangerous one. He felt sure – a very dangerous one.

He still felt very uneasy, though he was satisfied with his initial step. He had let her know that he recognized her. That would put her on her guard. She would not dare attempt anything rash. There was the question of Merrowdene. If he could be warned . . .

They found the little man absently contemplating a china doll which had fallen to his share in the penny dip. His wife suggested going home and he agreed eagerly. Mrs Merrowdene turned to the inspector:

'Won't you come back with us and have a quiet cup of tea, Mr Evans?'

Was there a faint note of challenge in her voice? He thought there was.

'Thank you, Mrs Merrowdene. I should like to very much.'

They walked there, talking together of pleasant ordinary things. The sun shone, a breeze blew gently, everything around them was pleasant and ordinary.

Their maid was out at the fête, Mrs Merrowdene explained, when they arrived at the charming old-world cottage. She went into her room to remove her hat, returning to set out tea and boil the kettle on a little silver lamp. From a shelf near the fireplace she took three small bowls and saucers.

'We have some very special Chinese tea,' she explained. 'And we always drink it in the Chinese manner – out of bowls, not cups.'

She broke off, peered into a bowl and exchanged it for another with an exclamation of annoyance.

'George – it's too bad of you. You've been taking these bowls again.'

'I'm sorry, dear,' said the professor apologetically. 'They're such a convenient size. The ones I ordered haven't come.'

'One of these days you'll poison us all,' said his wife with a half-laugh. 'Mary finds them in the laboratory and brings them back here, and never troubles to wash them out unless they've anything very noticeable in them. Why, you were using one of them for potassium cyanide the other day. Really, George, it's frightfully dangerous.'

Merrowdene looked a little irritated.

'Mary's no business to remove things from the laboratory. She's not to touch anything there.'

'But we often leave our teacups there after tea. How is she to know? Be reasonable, dear.'

The professor went into his laboratory, murmuring to himself, and with a smile Mrs Merrowdene poured boiling water on the tea and blew out the flame of the little silver lamp.

Evans was puzzled. Yet a glimmering of light penetrated to him. For some reason or other, Mrs Merrowdene was showing her hand. Was this to be the 'accident'? Was she speaking of all this so as deliberately to prepare her alibi beforehand? So that when, one day, the 'accident' happened, he would be forced to give evidence in her favour. Stupid of her, if so, because before that –

Suddenly he drew in his breath. She had poured the tea into the three bowls. One she set before him, one before herself, the other she placed on a little table by the fire near the chair her husband usually sat in, and it was as she placed this last one on the table that a little strange smile curved round her lips. It was the smile that did it.

He knew!

A remarkable woman – a dangerous woman. No waiting – no preparation. This afternoon – this very afternoon – with him here as witness. The boldness of it took his breath away.

It was clever – it was damnably clever. He would be able to prove nothing. She counted on his not suspecting – simply because it was 'so soon'. A woman of lightning rapidity of thought and action.

He drew a deep breath and leaned forward.

'Mrs Merrowdene, I'm a man of queer whims. Will you be very kind and indulge me in one of them?'

She looked inquiring but unsuspicious.

He rose, took the bowl from in front of her and crossed to the little table where he substituted it for the other. This other he brought back and placed in front of her.

'I want to see you drink this.'

Her eyes met his. They were steady, unfathomable. The colour slowly drained from her face.

She stretched out her hand, raised the cup. He held his breath. Supposing all along he had made a mistake.

She raised it to her lips – at the last moment, with a shudder, she leant forward and quickly poured it into a pot containing a fern. Then she sat back and gazed at him defiantly.

He drew a long sigh of relief, and sat down again.

'Well?' she said.

Her voice had altered. It was slightly mocking – defiant.

He answered her soberly and quietly:

'You are a very clever woman, Mrs Merrowdene. I think you understand me. There must be no – repetition. You know what I mean?'

'I know what you mean.'

Her voice was even, devoid of expression. He nodded his head, satisfied. She was a clever woman, and she didn't want to be hanged.

'To your long life and to that of your husband,' he said significantly, and raised his tea to his lips.

Then his face changed. It contorted horribly . . . he tried to rise – to cry out . . . His body stiffened – his face went purple. He fell back sprawling over his chair – his limbs convulsed.

Mrs Merrowdene leaned forward, watching him. A little smile crossed her lips. She spoke to him – very softly and gently.

'You made a mistake, Mr Evans. You thought I wanted to kill George . . . How stupid of you – how very stupid.'

She sat there a minute longer looking at the dead man, the third man who had threatened to cross her path and separate her from the man she loved.

Her smile broadened. She looked more than ever like a madonna. Then she raised her voice and called:

'George, George! . . . Oh, do come here! I'm afraid there's been the most dreadful accident . . . Poor Mr Evans . . .'

Next to a Dog

'Next to a Dog' was first published in
Grand Magazine, September 1929.

The ladylike woman behind the Registry Office table cleared her throat and peered across at the girl who sat opposite.

'Then you refuse to consider the post? It only came in this morning. A very nice part of Italy, I believe, a widower with a little boy of three and an elderly lady, his mother or aunt.'

Joyce Lambert shook her head.

'I can't go out of England,' she said in a tired voice; 'there are reasons. If only you could find me a daily post?'

Her voice shook slightly – ever so slightly, for she had it well under control. Her dark blue eyes looked appealingly at the woman opposite her.

'It's very difficult, Mrs Lambert. The only kind of daily governess required is one who has full qualifications. You have none. I have hundreds on my books – literally hundreds.' She paused. 'You have someone at home you can't leave?'

Joyce nodded.

'A child?'

'No, not a child.' And a faint smile flickered across her face.

'Well, it is very unfortunate. I will do my best, of course, but –'

The interview was clearly at an end. Joyce rose. She was biting her lip to keep the tears from springing to her eyes as she emerged from the frowsy office into the street.

'You mustn't,' she admonished herself sternly. 'Don't be a snivelling little idiot. You're panicking – that's what you're doing – panicking. No good ever came of giving way to panic. It's quite early in the day still and lots of things may happen. Aunt Mary ought to be good for a fortnight anyway. Come on, girl, step out, and don't keep your well-to-do relations waiting.'

She walked down Edgware Road, across the park, and then down to

Victoria Street, where she turned into the Army and Navy Stores. She went to the lounge and sat down glancing at her watch. It was just half past one. Five minutes sped by and then an elderly lady with her arms full of parcels bore down upon her.

'Ah! There you are, Joyce. I'm a few minutes late, I'm afraid. The service is not as good as it used to be in the luncheon room. You've had lunch, of course?'

Joyce hesitated a minute or two, then she said quietly: 'Yes, thank you.'

'I always have mine at half past twelve,' said Aunt Mary, settling herself comfortably with her parcels. 'Less rush and a clearer atmosphere. The curried eggs here are excellent.'

'Are they?' said Joyce faintly. She felt that she could hardly bear to think of curried eggs – the hot steam rising from them – the delicious smell! She wrenched her thoughts resolutely aside.

'You look peaky, child,' said Aunt Mary, who was herself of a comfortable figure. 'Don't go in for this modern fad of eating no meat. All fal-de-lal. A good slice off the joint never did anyone any harm.'

Joyce stopped herself from saying, 'It wouldn't do me any harm now.' If only Aunt Mary would stop talking about food. To raise your hopes by asking you to meet her at half past one and then to talk of curried eggs and slices of roast meat – oh! cruel – cruel.

'Well, my dear,' said Aunt Mary. 'I got your letter – and it was very nice of you to take me at my word. I said I'd be pleased to see you anytime and so I should have been – but as it happens, I've just had an extremely good offer to let the house. Quite too good to be missed, and bringing their own plate and linen. Five months. They come in on Thursday and I go to Harrogate. My rheumatism's been troubling me lately.'

'I see,' said Joyce. 'I'm so sorry.'

'So it'll have to be for another time. Always pleased to see you, my dear.'

'Thank you, Aunt Mary.'

'You know, you do look peaky,' said Aunt Mary, considering her attentively. 'You're thin, too; no flesh on your bones, and what's happened to your pretty colour? You always had a nice healthy colour. Mind you take plenty of exercise.'

'I'm taking plenty of exercise today,' said Joyce grimly. She rose. 'Well Aunt Mary, I must be getting along.'

Back again – through St James's Park this time, and so on through Berkeley Square and across Oxford Street and up Edgware Road, past Praed Street to the point where the Edgware Road begins to think of becoming something else. Then aside, through a series of dirty little streets till one particular dingy house was reached.

Joyce inserted her latchkey and entered a small frowsy hall. She ran
up the stairs till she reached the top landing. A door faced her and from
the bottom of this door a snuffling noise proceeded succeeded in a second
by a series of joyful whines and yelps.

'Yes, Terry darling – it's Missus come home.'

As the door opened, a white body precipitated itself upon the girl –
an aged wire-haired terrier very shaggy as to coat and suspiciously bleary
as to eyes. Joyce gathered him up in her arms and sat down on the floor.

'Terry darling! Darling, darling Terry. Love your Missus, Terry; love
your Missus a lot!'

And Terry obeyed, his eager tongue worked busily, he licked her face,
her ears, her neck and all the time his stump of a tail wagged furiously.

'Terry darling, what are we going to do? What's going to become of
us? Oh! Terry darling, I'm so tired.'

'Now then, miss,' said a tart voice behind her. 'If you'll give over
hugging and kissing that dog, here's a cup of nice hot tea for you.'

'Oh! Mrs Barnes, how good of you.'

Joyce scrambled to her feet. Mrs Barnes was a big, formidable-looking
woman. Beneath the exterior of a dragon she concealed an unexpectedly
warm heart.

'A cup of hot tea never did anyone any harm,' enunciated Mrs Barnes,
voicing the universal sentiment of her class.

Joyce sipped gratefully. Her landlady eyed her covertly.

'Any luck, miss – ma'am, I should say?'

Joyce shook her head, her face clouded over.

'Ah!' said Mrs Barnes with a sigh. 'Well, it doesn't seem to be what
you might call a lucky day.'

Joyce looked up sharply.

'Oh, Mrs Barnes – you don't mean –'

Mrs Barnes was nodding gloomily.

'Yes – it's Barnes. Out of work again. What we're going to do, I'm sure
I don't know.'

'Oh, Mrs Barnes – I must – I mean you'll want –'

'Now don't you fret, my dear. I'm not denying but that I'd be glad if
you'd found something – but if you haven't – you haven't. Have you
finished that tea? I'll take the cup.'

'Not quite.'

'Ah!' said Mrs Barnes accusingly. 'You're going to give what's left to
that dratted dog – I know you.'

'Oh, please, Mrs Barnes. Just a little drop. You don't mind really, do
you?'

'It wouldn't be any use if I did. You're crazy about that cantankerous brute. Yes, that's what I say – and that's what he is. As near as nothing bit me this morning, he did.'

'Oh, no, Mrs Barnes! Terry wouldn't do such a thing.'

'Growled at me – showed his teeth. I was just trying to see if there was anything could be done to those shoes of yours.'

'He doesn't like anyone touching my things. He thinks he ought to guard them.'

'Well, what does he want to think for? It isn't a dog's business to think. He'd be well enough in his proper place, tied up in the yard to keep off burglars. All this cuddling! He ought to be put away, miss – that's what I say.'

'No, no, no. Never. Never!'

'Please yourself,' said Mrs Barnes. She took the cup from the table, retrieved the saucer from the floor where Terry had just finished his share, and stalked from the room.

'Terry,' said Joyce. 'Come here and talk to me. What are we going to do, my sweet?'

She settled herself in the rickety armchair, with Terry on her knees. She threw off her hat and leaned back. She put one of Terry's paws on each side of her neck and kissed him lovingly on his nose and between his eyes. Then she began talking to him in a soft low voice, twisting his ears gently between her fingers.

'What are we going to do about Mrs Barnes, Terry? We owe her four weeks – and she's such a lamb, Terry – such a lamb. She'd never turn us out. But we can't take advantage of her being a lamb, Terry. We can't do that. Why does Barnes want to be out of work? I hate Barnes. He's always getting drunk. And if you're always getting drunk, you are usually out of work. But I don't get drunk, Terry, and yet I'm out of work.

'I can't leave you, darling. I can't leave you. There's not even anyone I could leave you with – nobody who'd be good to you. You're getting old, Terry – twelve years old – and nobody wants an old dog who's rather blind and a little deaf and a little – yes, just a little – bad-tempered. You're sweet to me, darling, but you're not sweet to everyone, are you? You growl. It's because you know the world's turning against you. We've just got each other, haven't we, darling?'

Terry licked her cheek delicately.

'Talk to me, darling.'

Terry gave a long lingering groan – almost a sigh, then he nuzzled his nose in behind Joyce's ear.

'You trust me, don't you, angel? You know I'd never leave you. But what are we going to do? We're right down to it now, Terry.'

She settled back further in the chair, her eyes half closed.

'Do you remember, Terry, all the happy times we used to have? You and I and Michael and Daddy. Oh, Michael – Michael! It was his first leave, and he wanted to give me a present before he went back to France. And I told him not to be extravagant. And then we were down in the country – and it was all a surprise. He told me to look out of the window, and there you were, dancing up the path on a long lead. The funny little man who brought you, a little man who smelt of dogs. How he talked. "The goods, that's what he is. Look at him, ma'am, ain't he a picture? I said to myself, as soon as the lady and gentleman see him they'll say: 'That dog's the goods!'"'

'He kept on saying that – and we called you that for quite a long time – the Goods! Oh, Terry, you were such a darling of a puppy, with your little head on one side, wagging your absurd tail! And Michael went away to France and I had you – the darlingest dog in the world. You read all Michael's letters with me, didn't you? You'd sniff them, and I'd say – "From Master," and you'd understand. We were so happy – so happy. You and Michael and I. And now Michael's dead, and you're old, and I – I'm so tired of being brave.'

Terry licked her.

'You were there when the telegram came. If it hadn't been for you, Terry – if I hadn't had you to hold on to . . .'

She stayed silent for some minutes.

'And we've been together ever since – been through all the ups and downs together – there have been a lot of downs, haven't there? And now we've come right up against it. There are only Michael's aunts, and they think I'm all right. They don't know he gambled that money away. We must never tell anyone that. *I* don't care – why shouldn't he? Everyone has to have some fault. He loved us both, Terry, and that's all that matters. His own relations were always inclined to be down on him and to say nasty things. We're not going to give them the chance. But I wish I had some relations of my own. It's very awkward having no relations at all.

'I'm so tired, Terry – and remarkably hungry. I can't believe I'm only twenty-nine – I feel sixty-nine. I'm not really brave – I only pretend to be. And I'm getting awfully mean ideas. I walked all the way to Ealing yesterday to see Cousin Charlotte Green. I thought if I got there at half past twelve she'd be sure to ask me to stop to lunch. And then when I got to the house, I felt it was too cadging for anything. I just couldn't. So I walked all the way back. And that's foolish. You should be a determined cadger or else not even think of it. I don't think I'm a strong character.'

Terry groaned again and put a black nose into Joyce's eye.

'You've got a lovely nose still, Terry – all cold like ice cream. Oh, I do

love you so! I can't part from you. I can't have you "put away", I can't
. . . I can't . . . I can't . . .'

The warm tongue licked eagerly.

'You understand so, my sweet. You'd do anything to help Missus,
wouldn't you?'

Terry clambered down and went unsteadily to a corner. He came back
holding a battered bowl between his teeth.

Joyce was midway between tears and laughter.

'Was he doing his only trick? The only thing he could think of to help
Missus. Oh, Terry – Terry – nobody shall part us! I'd do anything. Would
I, though? One says that – and then when you're shown the thing, you
say, "I didn't mean anything like *that*." Would I do anything?'

She got down on the floor beside the dog.

'You see, Terry, it's like this. Nursery governesses can't have dogs, and
companions to elderly ladies can't have dogs. Only married women can
have dogs, Terry – little fluffy expensive dogs that they take shopping
with them – and if one preferred an old blind terrier – well, why not?'

She stopped frowning and at that minute there was a double knock
from below.

'The post. I wonder.'

She jumped up and hurried down the stairs, returning with a letter.
'It might be. If only . . .'

She tore it open.

Dear Madam,
We have inspected the picture and our opinion is that it is not a genuine
Cuyp and that its value is practically nil.
Yours truly,
Sloane & Ryder

Joyce stood holding it. When she spoke, her voice had changed.

'That's that,' she said. 'The last hope gone. But we won't be parted.
There's a way – and it won't be cadging. Terry darling, I'm going out.
I'll be back soon.'

Joyce hurried down the stairs to where the telephone stood in a dark
corner. There she asked for a certain number. A man's voice answered
her, its tone changing as he realized her identity.

'Joyce, my dear girl. Come out and have some dinner and dance tonight.'

'I can't,' said Joyce lightly. 'Nothing fit to wear.'

And she smiled grimly as she thought of the empty pegs in the flimsy
cupboard.

'How would it be if I came along and saw you now? What's the address? Good Lord, where's that? Rather come off your high horse, haven't you?'

'Completely.'

'Well, you're frank about it. So long.'

Arthur Halliday's car drew up outside the house about three quarters of an hour later. An awestruck Mrs Barnes conducted him upstairs.

'My dear girl – what an awful hole. What on earth has got you into this mess?'

'Pride and a few other unprofitable emotions.'

She spoke lightly enough; her eyes looked at the man opposite her sardonically.

Many people called Halliday handsome. He was a big man with square shoulders, fair, with small, very pale blue eyes and a heavy chin.

He sat down on the rickety chair she indicated.

'Well,' he said thoughtfully. 'I should say you'd had your lesson. I say – will that brute bite?'

'No, no, he's all right. I've trained him to be rather a – a watchdog.'

Halliday was looking her up and down.

'Going to climb down, Joyce,' he said softly. 'Is that it?'

Joyce nodded.

'I told you before, my dear girl. I always get what I want in the end. I knew you'd come in time to see which way your bread was buttered.'

'It's lucky for me you haven't changed your mind,' said Joyce.

He looked at her suspiciously. With Joyce you never knew quite what she was driving at.

'You'll marry me?'

She nodded. 'As soon as you please.'

'The sooner, the better, in fact.' He laughed, looking round the room. Joyce flushed.

'By the way, there's a condition.'

'A condition?' He looked suspicious again.

'My dog. He must come with me.'

'This old scarecrow? You can have any kind of a dog you choose. Don't spare expense.'

'I want Terry.'

'Oh! All right, please yourself.'

Joyce was staring at him.

'You do know – don't you – that I don't love you? Not in the least.'

'I'm not worrying about that. I'm not thin-skinned. But no hanky-panky, my girl. If you marry me, you play fair.'

The colour flashed into Joyce's cheeks.

'You will have your money's worth,' she said.

'What about a kiss now?'

He advanced upon her. She waited, smiling. He took her in his arms, kissing her face, her lips, her neck. She neither stiffened nor drew back. He released her at last.

'I'll get you a ring,' he said. 'What would you like, diamonds or pearls?'

'A ruby,' said Joyce. 'The largest ruby possible – the colour of blood.'

'That's an odd idea.'

'I should like it to be a contrast to the little half hoop of pearls that was all that Michael could afford to give me.'

'Better luck this time, eh?'

'You put things wonderfully, Arthur.'

Halliday went out chuckling.

'Terry,' said Joyce. 'Lick me – lick hard – all over my face and my neck – particularly my neck.'

And as Terry obeyed, she murmured reflectively:

'Thinking of something else very hard – that's the only way. You'd never guess what I thought of – jam – jam in a grocer's shop. I said it over to myself. Strawberry, blackcurrant, raspberry, damson. And perhaps, Terry, he'll get tired of me fairly soon. I hope so, don't you? They say men do when they're married to you. But Michael wouldn't have tired of me – never – never – never – Oh! Michael . . .'

Joyce rose the next morning with a heart like lead. She gave a deep sigh and immediately Terry, who slept on her bed, had moved up and was kissing her affectionately.

'Oh, darling – darling! We've got to go through with it. But if only something would happen. Terry darling, can't you help Missus? You would if you could, I know.'

Mrs Barnes brought up some tea and bread and butter and was heartily congratulatory.

'There now, ma'am, to think of you going to marry that gentleman. It was a Rolls he came in. It was indeed. It quite sobered Barnes up to think of one of them Rolls standing outside our door. Why, I declare that dog's sitting out on the window sill.'

'He likes the sun,' said Joyce. 'But it's rather dangerous. Terry, come in.'

'I'd have the poor dear put out of his misery if I was you,' said Mrs Barnes, 'and get your gentleman to buy you one of them plumy dogs as ladies carry in their muffs.'

Joyce smiled and called again to Terry. The dog rose awkwardly and just at that moment the noise of a dog fight rose from the street below. Terry craned his neck forward and added some brisk barking. The window sill was old and rotten. It tilted and Terry, too old and stiff to regain his balance, fell.

With a wild cry, Joyce ran down the stairs and out of the front door. In a few seconds she was kneeling by Terry's side. He was whining piti-fully and his position showed her that he was badly hurt. She bent over him.

'Terry – Terry darling – darling, darling, darling –'

Very feebly, he tried to wag his tail.

'Terry boy – Missus will make you better – darling boy –'

A crowd, mainly composed of small boys, was pushing round.

'Fell from the window, 'e did.'

'My, 'e looks bad.'

'Broke 'is back as likely as not.'

Joyce paid no heed.

'Mrs Barnes, where's the nearest vet?'

'There's Jobling – round in Mere Street – if you could get him there.'

'A taxi.'

'Allow me.'

It was the pleasant voice of an elderly man who had just alighted from a taxi. He knelt down by Terry and lifted the upper lip, then passed his hand down the dog's body.

'I'm afraid he may be bleeding internally,' he said. 'There don't seem to be any bones broken. We'd better get him along to the vet's.'

Between them, he and Joyce lifted the dog. Terry gave a yelp of pain. His teeth met in Joyce's arm.

'Terry – it's all right – all right, old man.'

They got him into the taxi and drove off. Joyce wrapped a handker-chief round her arm in an absent-minded way. Terry, distressed, tried to lick it.

'I know, darling; I know. You didn't mean to hurt me. It's all right. It's all right, Terry.'

She stroked his head. The man opposite watched her but said nothing.

They arrived at the vet's fairly quickly and found him in. He was a red-faced man with an unsympathetic manner.

He handled Terry none too gently while Joyce stood by, agonized. The tears were running down her face. She kept on talking in a low, reassuring voice.

'It's all right, darling. It's all right . . .'

The vet straightened himself.

'Impossible to say exactly. I must make a proper examination. You must leave him here.'

'Oh! I can't.'

'I'm afraid you must. I must take him below. I'll telephone you in – say – half an hour.'

Sick at heart, Joyce gave in. She kissed Terry on his nose. Blind with tears, she stumbled down the steps. The man who had helped her was still there. She had forgotten him.

'The taxi's still here. I'll take you back.' She shook her head.

'I'd rather walk.'

'I'll walk with you.'

He paid off the taxi. She was hardly conscious of him as he walked quietly by her side without speaking. When they arrived at Mrs Barnes', he spoke.

'Your wrist. You must see to it.'

She looked down at it.

'Oh! That's all right.'

'It wants properly washing and tying up. I'll come in with you.'

He went with her up the stairs. She let him wash the place and bind it up with a clean handkerchief. She only said one thing.

'Terry didn't mean to do it. He would never, *never* mean to do it. He just didn't realize it was me. He must have been in dreadful pain.'

'I'm afraid so, yes.'

'And perhaps they're hurting him dreadfully now?'

'I'm sure that everything that can be done for him is being done. When the vet rings up, you can go and get him and nurse him here.'

'Yes, of course.'

The man paused, then moved towards the door.

'I hope it will be all right,' he said awkwardly. 'Goodbye.'

'Goodbye.'

Two or three minutes later it occurred to her that he had been kind and that she had never thanked him.

Mrs Barnes appeared, cup in hand.

'Now, my poor lamb, a cup of hot tea. You're all to pieces, I can see that.'

'Thank you, Mrs Barnes, but I don't want any tea.'

'It would do you good, dearie. Don't take on so now. The doggie will be all right and even if he isn't that gentleman of yours will give you a pretty new dog –'

'Don't, Mrs Barnes. Don't. Please, if you don't mind, I'd rather be left alone.'

'Well, I never – there's the telephone.'

Joyce sped down to it like an arrow. She lifted the receiver. Mrs Barnes panted down after her. She heard Joyce say, 'Yes – speaking. What? Oh! Oh! Yes. Yes, thank you.'

She put back the receiver. The face she turned to Mrs Barnes startled that good woman. It seemed devoid of any life or expression.

'Terry's dead, Mrs Barnes,' she said. 'He died alone there without me.'

She went upstairs and, going into her room, shut the door very decisively.

'Well, I never,' said Mrs Barnes to the hall wallpaper.

Five minutes later she poked her head into the room. Joyce was sitting bolt upright in a chair. She was not crying.

'It's your gentleman, miss. Shall I send him up?'

A sudden light came into Joyce's eyes.

'Yes, please. I'd like to see him.'

Halliday came in boisterously.

'Well, here we are. I haven't lost much time, have I? I'm prepared to carry you off from this dreadful place here and now. You can't stay here. Come on, get your things on.'

'There's no need, Arthur.'

'No need? What do you mean?'

'Terry's dead. I don't need to marry you now.'

'What are you talking about?'

'My dog – Terry. He's dead. I was only marrying you so that we could be together.'

Halliday stared at her, his face growing redder and redder. 'You're mad.'

'I dare say. People who love dogs are.'

'You seriously tell me that you were only marrying me because – Oh, it's absurd!'

'Why did you think I was marrying you? You knew I hated you.'

'You were marrying me because I could give you a jolly good time – and so I can.'

'To my mind,' said Joyce, 'that is a much more revolting motive than mine. Anyway, it's off. I'm not marrying you!'

'Do you realize that you are treating me damned badly?'

She looked at him coolly but with such a blaze in her eyes that he drew back before it.

'I don't think so. I've heard you talk about getting a kick out of life. That's what you got out of me – and my dislike of you heightened it. You knew I hated you and you enjoyed it. When I let you kiss me yesterday, you were disappointed because I didn't flinch or wince. There's something brutal in you, Arthur, something cruel – something that likes hurting . . . Nobody could treat you as badly as you deserve. And now do you mind getting out of my room? I want it to myself.'

He spluttered a little.

'Wh – what are you going to do? You've no money.'

'That's my business. Please go.'

'You little devil. You absolutely maddening little devil. You haven't done with me yet.'

Joyce laughed.

The laugh routed him as nothing else had done. It was so unexpected. He went awkwardly down the stairs and drove away.

Joyce heaved a sigh. She pulled on her shabby black felt hat and in her turn went out. She walked along the streets mechanically, neither thinking nor feeling. Somewhere at the back of her mind there was pain – pain that she would presently feel, but for the moment everything was mercifully dulled.

She passed the Registry Office and hesitated.

'I must do something. There's the river, of course. I've often thought of that. Just finish everything. But it's so cold and wet. I don't think I'm brave enough. I'm not brave really.'

She turned into the Registry Office.

'Good morning, Mrs Lambert. I'm afraid we've no daily post.'

'It doesn't matter,' said Joyce. 'I can take any kind of post now. My friend, whom I lived with, has – gone away.'

'Then you'd consider going abroad?'

Joyce nodded.

'Yes, as far away as possible.'

'Mr Allaby is here now, as it happens, interviewing candidates. I'll send you in to him.'

In another minute Joyce was sitting in a cubicle answering questions. Something about her interlocutor seemed vaguely familiar to her, but she could not place him. And then suddenly her mind awoke a little, aware that the last question was faintly out of the ordinary.

'Do you get on well with old ladies?' Mr Allaby was asking.

Joyce smiled in spite of herself.

'I think so.'

'You see my aunt, who lives with me, is rather difficult. She is very fond of me and she is a great dear really, but I fancy that a young woman might find her rather difficult sometimes.'

'I think I'm patient and good-tempered,' said Joyce, 'and I have always got on with elderly people very well.'

'You would have to do certain things for my aunt and otherwise you would have the charge of my little boy, who is three. His mother died a year ago.'

'I see.'

There was a pause.

'Then if you think you would like the post, we will consider that settled. We travel out next week. I will let you know the exact date, and I expect you would like a small advance of salary to fit yourself out.'

'Thank you very much. That would be very kind of you.'

They had both risen. Suddenly Mr Allaby said awkwardly:

'I – hate to butt in – I mean I wish – I would like to know – I mean, is your dog all right?'

For the first time Joyce looked at him. The colour came into her face, her blue eyes deepened almost to black. She looked straight at him. She had thought him elderly, but he was not so very old. Hair turning grey, a pleasant weatherbeaten face, rather stooping shoulders, eyes that were brown and something of the shy kindliness of a dog's. He looked a little like a dog, Joyce thought.

'Oh, it's *you*,' she said. 'I thought afterwards – I never thanked you.'

'No need. Didn't expect it. Knew what you were feeling like. What about the poor old chap?'

The tears came into Joyce's eyes. They streamed down her cheeks. Nothing on earth could have kept them back.

'He's dead.'

'Oh!'

He said nothing else, but to Joyce that Oh! was one of the most comforting things she had ever heard. There was everything in it that couldn't be put into words.

After a minute or two he said jerkily:

'Matter of fact, I had a dog. Died two years ago. Was with a crowd of people at the time who couldn't understand making heavy weather about it. Pretty rotten to have to carry on as though nothing had happened.'

Joyce nodded.

'I *know* –' said Mr Allaby.

He took her hand, squeezed it hard and dropped it. He went out of the little cubicle. Joyce followed in a minute or two and fixed up various details with the ladylike person. When she arrived home. Mrs Barnes met her on the doorstep with that relish in gloom typical of her class.

'They've sent the poor little doggie's body home,' she announced. 'It's up in your room. I was saying to Barnes, and he's ready to dig a nice little hole in the back garden –'

Sing a Song of Sixpence

'Sing a Song of Sixpence' was first published in *Holly Leaves* (published by Illustrated Sporting and Dramatic News), 2 December 1929.

Sir Edward Palliser, K.C., lived at No 9 Queen Anne's Close. Queen Anne's Close is a *cul-de-sac*. In the very heart of Westminster it manages to have a peaceful old-world atmosphere far removed from the turmoil of the twentieth century. It suited Sir Edward Palliser admirably.

Sir Edward had been one of the most eminent criminal barristers of his day and now that he no longer practised at the Bar he had amused himself by amassing a very fine criminological library. He was also the author of a volume of Reminiscences of Eminent Criminals.

On this particular evening Sir Edward was sitting in front of his library fire sipping some very excellent black coffee, and shaking his head over a volume of Lombroso. Such ingenious theories and so completely out of date.

The door opened almost noiselessly and his well-trained man-servant approached over the thick pile carpet, and murmured discreetly:

'A young lady wishes to see you, sir.'

'A young lady?'

Sir Edward was surprised. Here was something quite out of the usual course of events. Then he reflected that it might be his niece, Ethel – but no, in that case Armour would have said so.

He inquired cautiously.

'The lady did not give her name?'

'No, sir, but she said she was quite sure you would wish to see her.'

'Show her in,' said Sir Edward Palliser. He felt pleasurably intrigued.

A tall, dark girl of close on thirty, wearing a black coat and skirt, well cut, and a little black hat, came to Sir Edward with outstretched hand and a look of eager recognition on her face. Armour withdrew, closing the door noiselessly behind him.

'Sir Edward – you do know me, don't you? I'm Magdalen Vaughan.'

'Why, of course.' He pressed the outstretched hand warmly.

He remembered her perfectly now. That trip home from America on the *Siluric*! This charming child – for she had been little more than a child. He had made love to her, he remembered, in a discreet elderly man-of-the-world fashion. She had been so adorably young – so eager – so full of admiration and hero worship – just made to captivate the heart of a man nearing sixty. The remembrance brought additional warmth into the pressure of his hand.

'This is most delightful of you. Sit down, won't you.' He arranged an armchair for her, talking easily and evenly, wondering all the time why she had come. When at last he brought the easy flow of small talk to an end, there was a silence.

Her hand closed and unclosed on the arm of the chair, she moistened her lips. Suddenly she spoke – abruptly.

'Sir Edward – I want you to help me.'

He was surprised and murmured mechanically:

'Yes?'

She went on, speaking more intensely:

'You said that if ever I needed help – that if there was anything in the world you could do for me – you would do it.'

Yes, he *had* said that. It was the sort of thing one did say – particularly at the moment of parting. He could recall the break in his voice – the way he had raised her hand to his lips.

'*If there is ever anything I can do – remember, I mean it . . .*'

Yes, one said that sort of thing . . . But very, very rarely did one have to fulfil one's words! And certainly not after – how many? – nine or ten years. He flashed a quick glance at her – she was still a very good-looking girl, but she had lost what had been to him her charm – that look of dewy untouched youth. It was a more interesting face now, perhaps – a younger man might have thought so – but Sir Edward was far from feeling the tide of warmth and emotion that had been his at the end of that Atlantic voyage.

His face became legal and cautious. He said in a rather brisk way:

'Certainly, my dear young lady. I shall be delighted to do anything in my power – though I doubt if I can be very helpful to anyone in these days.'

If he was preparing his way of retreat she did not notice it. She was of the type that can only see one thing at a time and what she was seeing at this moment was her own need. She took Sir Edward's willingness to help for granted.

'We are in terrible trouble, Sir Edward.'

'*We*? You are married?'

'No – I meant my brother and I. Oh! and William and Emily too, for that matter. But I must explain. I have – I had an aunt – Miss Crabtree. You may have read about her in the papers. It was horrible. She was killed – murdered.'

'Ah!' A flash of interest lit up Sir Edward's face. 'About a month ago, wasn't it?'

The girl nodded.

'Rather less than that – three weeks.'

'Yes, I remember. She was hit on the head in her own house. They didn't get the fellow who did it.'

Again Magdalen Vaughan nodded.

'They didn't get the man – I don't believe they ever will get the man. You see – there mightn't be any man to get.'

'What?'

'Yes – it's awful. Nothing's come out about it in the papers. But that's what the police think. They *know* nobody came to the house that night.'

'You mean –?'

'That it's one of us four. It *must* be. They don't know which – and *we* don't know which . . . *We don't know*. And we sit there every day looking at each other surreptitiously and wondering. Oh! if only it could have been someone from outside – but I don't see how it can . . .'

Sir Edward stared at her, his interest arising.

'You mean that the members of the family are under suspicion?'

'Yes, that's what I mean. The police haven't said so, of course. They've been quite polite and nice. But they've ransacked the house, they've questioned us all, and Martha again and again . . . And because they don't know which, they're holding their hand. I'm so frightened – so horribly frightened . . .'

'My dear child. Come now, surely now, surely you are exaggerating.'

'I'm not. It's one of us four – it must be.'

'Who are the four to whom you refer?'

Magdalen sat up straight and spoke more composedly.

'There's myself and Matthew. Aunt Lily was our great aunt. She was my grandmother's sister. We've lived with her ever since we were fourteen (we're twins, you know). Then there was William Crabtree. He was her nephew – her brother's child. He lived there too, with his wife Emily.'

'She supported them?'

'More or less. He has a little money of his own, but he's not strong and has to live at home. He's a quiet, dreamy sort of man. I'm sure it would have been impossible for him to have – oh! – it's awful of me to think of it even!'

'I am still very far from understanding the position. Perhaps you would not mind running over the facts – if it does not distress you too much.'

'Oh! no – I want to tell you. And it's all quite clear in my mind still – horribly clear. We'd had tea, you understand, and we'd all gone off to do things of our own. I to do some dressmaking. Matthew to type an article – he does a little journalism; William to do his stamps. Emily hadn't been down to tea. She'd taken a headache powder and was lying down. So there we were, all of us, busy and occupied. And when Martha went in to lay supper at half-past seven, there Aunt Lily was – dead. Her head – oh! it's horrible – all crushed in.'

'The weapon was found, I think?'

'Yes. It was a heavy paper-weight that always lay on the table by the door. The police tested it for fingerprints, but there were none. It had been wiped clean.'

'And your first surmise?'

'We thought of course it was a burglar. There were two or three drawers of the bureau pulled out, as though a thief had been looking for something. Of course we thought it was a burglar! And then the police came – and they said she had been dead at least an hour, and asked Martha who had been to the house, and Martha said nobody. And all the windows were fastened on the inside, and there seemed no signs of anything having been tampered with. And then they began to ask us questions . . .'

She stopped. Her breast heaved. Her eyes, frightened and imploring, sought Sir Edward's in search of reassurance.

'For instance, who benefited by your aunt's death?'

'That's simple. We all benefit equally. She left her money to be divided in equal shares among the four of us.'

'And what was the value of her estate?'

'The lawyer told us it will come to about eighty thousand pounds after the death duties are paid.'

Sir Edward opened his eyes in some slight surprise.

'That is quite a considerable sum. You knew, I suppose, the total of your aunt's fortune?'

Magdalen shook her head.

'No – it came quite as a surprise to us. Aunt Lily was always terribly careful about money. She kept just the one servant and always talked a lot about economy.'

Sir Edward nodded thoughtfully. Magdalen leaned forward a little in her chair.

'You will help me – you will?'

Her words came to Sir Edward as an unpleasant shock just at the moment when he was becoming interested in her story for its own sake.

'My dear young lady – what can I possibly do? If you want good legal advice, I can give you the name –'

She interrupted him.

'Oh! I don't want that sort of thing! I want you to help me person-ally – as a friend.'

'That's very charming of you, but –'

'I want you to come to our house. I want you to ask questions. I want you to see and judge for yourself.'

'But my dear young –'

'Remember, you promised. Anywhere – any time – you said, if I wanted help . . .'

Her eyes, pleading yet confident, looked into his. He felt ashamed and strangely touched. That terrific sincerity of hers, that absolute belief in an idle promise, ten years old, as a sacred binding thing. How many men had not said those self-same words – a *cliché* almost! – and how few of them had ever been called upon to make good.

He said rather weakly: 'I'm sure there are many people who could advise you better than I could.'

'I've got lots of friends – naturally.' (He was amused by the naïve self-assurance of that.) 'But you see, none of them are clever. Not like you. You're used to questioning people. And with all your experience you must *know*.'

'Know what?'

'Whether they're innocent or guilty.'

He smiled rather grimly to himself. He flattered himself that on the whole he usually *had* known! Though, on many occasions, his private opinion had not been that of the jury.

Magdalen pushed back her hat from her forehead with a nervous gesture, looked round the room, and said:

'How quiet it is here. Don't you sometimes long for some noise?'

The *cul-de-sac*! All unwittingly her words, spoken at random, touched him on the raw. A *cul-de-sac*. Yes, but there was always a way out – the way you had come – the way back into the world . . . Something impetu-ous and youthful stirred in him. Her simple trust appealed to the best side of his nature – and the condition of her problem appealed to some-thing else – the innate criminologist in him. He wanted to see these people of whom she spoke. He wanted to form his own judgement.

He said: 'If you are really convinced I can be of any use . . . Mind, I guarantee nothing.'

He expected her to be overwhelmed with delight, but she took it very calmly.

'I knew you would do it. I've always thought of you as a real friend. Will you come back with me now?'

'No. I think if I pay you a visit tomorrow it will be more satisfactory. Will you give me the name and address of Miss Crabtree's lawyer? I may want to ask him a few questions.'

She wrote it down and handed it to him. Then she got up and said rather shyly:

'I – I'm really most awfully grateful. Goodbye.'

'And your own address?'

'How stupid of me. 18 Palatine Walk, Chelsea.'

It was three o'clock on the following afternoon when Sir Edward Palliser approached 18 Palatine Walk with a sober, measured tread. In the interval he had found out several things. He had paid a visit that morning to Scotland Yard, where the Assistant Commissioner was an old friend of his, and he had also had an interview with the late Miss Crabtree's lawyer. As a result he had a clearer vision of the circumstances. Miss Crabtree's arrangements in regard to money had been somewhat peculiar. She never made use of a cheque-book. Instead she was in the habit of writing to her lawyer and asking him to have a certain sum in five-pound notes waiting for her. It was nearly always the same sum. Three hundred pounds four times a year. She came to fetch it herself in a four-wheeler which she regarded as the only safe means of conveyance. At other times she never left the house.

At Scotland Yard Sir Edward learned that the question of finance had been gone into very carefully. Miss Crabtree had been almost due for her next instalment of money. Presumably the previous three hundred had been spent – or almost spent. But this was exactly the point that had not been easy to ascertain. By checking the household expenditure, it was soon evident that Miss Crabtree's expenditure per quarter fell a good deal short of three hundred pounds. On the other hand she was in the habit of sending five-pound notes away to needy friends or relatives. Whether there had been much or little money in the house at the time of her death was a debatable point. None had been found.

It was this particular point which Sir Edward was revolving in his mind as he approached Palatine Walk.

The door of the house (which was a non-basement one) was opened to him by a small elderly woman with an alert gaze. He was shown into a big double room on the left of the small hallway and there Magdalen came to him. More clearly than before, he saw the traces of nervous strain in her face.

'You told me to ask questions, and I have come to do so,' said Sir Edward, smiling as he shook hands. 'First of all I want to know who last saw your aunt and exactly what time that was?'

'It was after tea – five o'clock. Martha was the last person with her. She had been paying the books that afternoon, and brought Aunt Lily the change and the accounts.'

'You trust Martha?'

'Oh, absolutely. She was with Aunt Lily for – oh! thirty years, I suppose. She's honest as the day.'

Sir Edward nodded.

'Another question. Why did your cousin, Mrs Crabtree, take a headache powder?'

'Well, because she had a headache.'

'Naturally, but was there any particular reason why she *should* have a headache?'

'Well, yes, in a way. There was rather a scene at lunch. Emily is very excitable and highly strung. She and Aunt Lily used to have rows sometimes.'

'And they had one at lunch?'

'Yes. Aunt Lily was rather trying about little things. It all started out of nothing – and then they were at it hammer and tongs – with Emily saying all sorts of things she couldn't possibly have meant – that she'd leave the house and never come back – that she was grudged every mouthful she ate – oh! all sorts of silly things. And Aunt Lily said the sooner she and her husband packed their boxes and went the better. But it all meant nothing, really.'

'Because Mr and Mrs Crabtree couldn't afford to pack up and go?'

'Oh, not only that. William was fond of Aunt Emily. He really was.'

'It wasn't a day of quarrels by any chance?'

Magdalen's colour heightened.

'You mean me? The fuss about my wanting to be a mannequin?'

'Your aunt wouldn't agree?'

'No.'

'Why did you want to be a mannequin, Miss Magdalen? Does the life strike you as a very attractive one?'

'No, but anything would be better than going on living here.'

'Yes, then. But now you will have a comfortable income, won't you?'

'Oh! yes, it's quite different *now*.'

She made the admission with the utmost simplicity.

He smiled but pursued the subject no further. Instead he said: 'And your brother? Did he have a quarrel too?'

'Matthew? Oh, no.'

'Then no one can say he had a motive for wishing his aunt out of the way.'

He was quick to seize on the momentary dismay that showed in her face.

'I forgot,' he said casually. 'He owed a good deal of money, didn't he?'

'Yes; poor old Matthew.'

'Still, that will be all right now.'

'Yes –' She sighed. 'It *is* a relief.'

And still she saw nothing! He changed the subject hastily.

'Your cousins and your brother are at home?'

'Yes; I told them you were coming. They are all so anxious to help. Oh, Sir Edward – I feel, somehow, that you are going to find out that everything is all right – that none of us had anything to do with it – that, after all, it *was* an outsider.'

'I can't do miracles. I may be able to find out the truth, but I can't make the truth be what you want it to be.'

'Can't you? I feel that you could do anything – anything.'

She left the room. He thought, disturbed, 'What did she mean by that? Does she want me to suggest a line of defence? For whom?'

His meditations were interrupted by the entrance of a man about fifty years of age. He had a naturally powerful frame, but stooped slightly. His clothes were untidy and his hair carelessly brushed. He looked good-natured but vague.

'Sir Edward Palliser? Oh, how do you do. Magdalen sent me along. It's very good of you, I'm sure, to wish to help us. Though I don't think anything will ever be really discovered. I mean, they won't catch the fellow.'

'You think it was a burglar then – someone from outside?'

'Well, it must have been. It couldn't be one of the family. These fellows are very clever nowadays, they climb like cats and they get in and out as they like.'

'Where were you, Mr Crabtree, when the tragedy occurred?'

'I was busy with my stamps – in my little sitting-room upstairs.'

'You didn't hear anything?'

'No – but then I never do hear anything when I'm absorbed. Very foolish of me, but there it is.'

'Is the sitting-room you refer to over this room?'

'No, it's at the back.'

Again the door opened. A small fair woman entered. Her hands were twitching nervously. She looked fretful and excited.

'William, why didn't you wait for me? I said "wait".'

'Sorry, my dear, I forgot. Sir Edward Palliser – my wife.'

'How do you do, Mrs Crabtree? I hope you don't mind my coming here to ask a few questions. I know how anxious you must all be to have things cleared up.'

'Naturally. But I can't tell you anything – can I, William? I was asleep – on my bed – I only woke up when Martha screamed.'

Her hands continued to twitch.

'Where is your room, Mrs Crabtree?'

'It's over this. But I didn't hear anything – how could I? I was asleep.'

He could get nothing out of her but that. She knew nothing – she had heard nothing – she had been asleep. She reiterated it with the obstinacy of a frightened woman. Yet Sir Edward knew very well that it might easily be – probably was – the bare truth.

He excused himself at last – said he would like to put a few questions to Martha. William Crabtree volunteered to take him to the kitchen. In the hall, Sir Edward nearly collided with a tall dark young man who was striding towards the front door.

'Mr Matthew Vaughan?'

'Yes – but look here, I can't wait. I've got an appointment.'

'Matthew!' It was his sister's voice from the stairs. 'Oh! Matthew, you promised –'

'I know, sis. But I can't. Got to meet a fellow. And, anyway, what's the good of talking about the damned thing over and over again. We have enough of that with the police. I'm fed up with the whole show.'

The front door banged. Mr Matthew Vaughan had made his exit.

Sir Edward was introduced into the kitchen. Martha was ironing. She paused, iron in hand. Sir Edward shut the door behind him.

'Miss Vaughan has asked me to help her,' he said. 'I hope you won't object to my asking you a few questions.'

She looked at him, then shook her head.

'None of them did it, sir. I know what you're thinking, but it isn't so. As nice a set of ladies and gentlemen as you could wish to see.'

'I've no doubt of it. But their niceness isn't what we call evidence, you know.'

'Perhaps not, sir. The law's a funny thing. But there is evidence – as you call it, sir. None of them could have done it without *my* knowing.'

'But surely –'

'I know what I'm talking about sir. There, listen to that –'

'That' was a creaking sound above their heads.

'The stairs, sir. Every time anyone goes up or down, the stairs creak something awful. It doesn't matter how quiet you go. Mrs Crabtree, she was lying on her bed, and Mr Crabtree was fiddling about with them wretched stamps of his, and Miss Magdalen she was up above again working her machine, and if any one of those three had come down the stairs I should have known it. And they didn't!'

She spoke with a positive assurance which impressed the barrister. He thought: 'A good witness. She'd carry weight.'

'You mightn't have noticed.'

'Yes, I would. I'd have noticed without noticing, so to speak. Like you notice when a door shuts and somebody goes out.'

Sir Edward shifted his ground.

'That is three of them acounted for, but there is a fourth. Was Mr Matthew Vaughan upstairs also?'

'No, but he was in the little room downstairs. Next door. And he was typewriting. You can hear it plain in here. His machine never stopped for a moment. Not for a moment, sir, I can swear to it. A nasty irritating tap tapping noise it is, too.'

Sir Edward paused a minute.

'It was you who found her, wasn't it?'

'Yes, sir, it was. Lying there with blood on her poor hair. And no one hearing a sound on account of the tap-tapping of Mr Matthew's type-writer.'

'I understand you are positive that no one came into the house?'

'How could they, sir, without my knowing? The bell rings in here. And there's only the one door.'

He looked at her straight in the face.

'You were attached to Miss Crabtree?'

A warm glow – genuine – unmistakable – came into her face.

'Yes, indeed, I was, sir. But for Miss Crabtree – well, I'm getting on and I don't mind speaking of it now. I got into trouble, sir, when I was a girl, and Miss Crabtree stood by me – took me back into her service, she did, when it was all over. I'd have died for her – I would indeed.'

Sir Edward knew sincerity when he heard it. Martha was sincere.

'As far as you know, no one came to the door –?'

'No one could have come.'

'I said *as far as you* know. But if Miss Crabtree had been expecting someone – if she opened the door to that someone herself . . .'

'Oh!' Martha seemed taken aback.

'That's possible, I suppose?' Sir Edward urged.

'It's possible – yes – but it isn't very likely. I mean . . .'

She was clearly taken aback. She couldn't deny and yet she wanted to do so. Why? Because she knew that the truth lay elsewhere. Was that it? The four people in the house – one of them guilty? Did Martha want to shield that guilty party? *Had* the stairs creaked? Had someone come stealthily down and did Martha know who that someone was?

She herself was honest – Sir Edward was convinced of that.

He pressed his point, watching her.

'Miss Crabtree might have done that, I suppose? The window of that room faces the street. She might have seen whoever it was she was waiting for from the window and gone out into the hall and let him – or her – in. She might even have wished that no one should see the person.'

Martha looked troubled. She said at last reluctantly:

'Yes, you may be right, sir. I never thought of that. That she was expecting a gentleman – yes, it well might be.'

It was though she began to perceive advantages in the idea.

'You were the last person to see her, were you not?'

'Yes, sir. After I'd cleared away the tea. I took the receipted books to her and the change from the money she'd given me.'

'Had she given the money to you in five-pound notes?'

'A five-pound note, sir,' said Martha in a shocked voice. 'The book never came up as high as five pounds. I'm very careful.'

'Where did she keep her money?'

'I don't rightly know, sir. I should say that she carried it about with her – in her black velvet bag. But of course she may have kept it in one of the drawers in her bedroom that were locked. She was very fond of locking up things, though prone to lose her keys.'

Sir Edward nodded.

'You don't know how much money she had – in five-pound notes, I mean?'

'No, sir, I couldn't say what the exact amount was.'

'And she said nothing to you that could lead you to believe that she was expecting anybody?'

'No, sir.'

'You're quite sure? What exactly did she say?'

'Well,' Martha considered, 'she said the butcher was nothing more than a rogue and a cheat, and she said I'd had in a quarter of a pound of tea more than I ought, and she said Mrs Crabtree was full of nonsense for not liking to eat margarine, and she didn't like one of the sixpences I'd brought her back – one of the new ones with oak leaves on it – she said it was bad, and I had a lot of trouble to convince her. And she said – oh, that the fishmonger had sent haddocks instead of whitings, and had I told him about it, and I said I had – and, really, I think that's all, sir.'

Martha's speech had made the deceased lady loom clear to Sir Edward as a detailed description would never have done. He said casually:

'Rather a difficult mistress to please, eh?'

'A bit fussy, but there, poor dear, she didn't often get out, and staying cooped up she had to have something to amuse herself like. She was pernickety but kind hearted – never a beggar sent away from the door without something. Fussy she may have been, but a real charitable lady.'

'I am glad, Martha, that she leaves one person to regret her.'

The old servant caught her breath.

'You mean – oh, but they were all fond of her – really – underneath. They all had words with her now and again, but it didn't mean anything.'

Sir Edward lifted his head. There was a creak above.

'That's Miss Magdalen coming down.'

'How do you know?' he shot at her.

The old woman flushed. 'I know her step,' she muttered.

Sir Edward left the kitchen rapidly. Martha had been right. Magdalen had just reached the bottom stair. She looked at him hopefully.

'Not very far on as yet,' said Sir Edward, answering her look, and added, 'You don't happen to know what letters your aunt received on the day of her death?'

'They are all together. The police have been through them, of course.'

She led the way to the big double drawing-room, and unlocking a drawer took out a large black velvet bag with an old-fashioned silver clasp.

'This is Aunt's bag. Everything is in here just as it was on the day of her death. I've kept it like that.'

Sir Edward thanked her and proceeded to turn out the contents of the bag on the table. It was, he fancied, a fair specimen of an eccentric elderly lady's handbag.

There was some odd silver change, two ginger nuts, three newspaper cuttings about Joanna Southcott's box, a trashy printed poem about the unemployed, an *Old Moore's Almanack*, a large piece of camphor, some spectacles and three letters. A spidery one from someone called 'Cousin Lucy', a bill for mending a watch, and an appeal from a charitable institution.

Sir Edward went through everything very carefully, then repacked the bag and handed it to Magdalen with a sigh.

'Thank you, Miss Magdalen. I'm afraid there isn't much there.'

He rose, observed that from the window you commanded a good view of the front door steps, then took Magdalen's hand in his.

'You are going?'

'Yes.'

'But it's – it's going to be all right?'

'Nobody connected with the law ever commits himself to a rash statement like that,' said Sir Edward solemnly, and made his escape.

He walked along the street lost in thought. The puzzle was there under his hand – and he had not solved it. It needed something – some little thing. Just to point the way.

A hand fell on his shoulder and he started. It was Matthew Vaughan, somewhat out of breath.

'I've been chasing you, Sir Edward. I want to apologize. For my rotten manners half an hour ago. But I've not got the best temper in the world, I'm afraid. It's awfully good of you to bother about this business. Please ask me whatever you like. If there's anything I can do to help –'

Suddenly Sir Edward stiffened. His glance was fixed – not on Matthew – but across the street. Somewhat bewildered, Matthew repeated:

'If there's anything I can do to help –'

'You have already done it, my dear young man,' said Sir Edward. 'By stopping me at this particular spot and so fixing my attention on something I might otherwise have missed.'

He pointed across the street to a small restaurant opposite.

'*The Four and Twenty Blackbirds?*' asked Matthew in a puzzled voice.

'Exactly.'

'It's an odd name – but you get quite decent food there, I believe.'

'I shall not take the risk of experimenting,' said Sir Edward. 'Being further from my nursery days than you are, my friend, I probably remember my nursery rhymes better. There is a classic that runs thus, if I remember rightly: *Sing a song of sixpence, a pocket full of rye, Four and twenty blackbirds, baked in a pie* – and so on. The rest of it does not concern us.'

He wheeled round sharply.

'Where are you going?' asked Matthew Vaughan.

'Back to your house, my friend.'

They walked there in silence, Matthew Vaughan shooting puzzled glances at his companion. Sir Edward entered, strode to a drawer, lifted out a velvet bag and opened it. He looked at Matthew and the young man reluctantly left the room.

Sir Edward tumbled out the silver change on the table. Then he nodded. His memory had not been at fault.

He got up and rang the bell, slipping something into the palm of his hand as he did so.

Martha answered the bell.

'You told me, Martha, if I remember rightly, that you had a slight altercation with your late mistress over one of the new sixpences.'

'Yes, sir.'

'Ah! but the curious thing is, Martha, that among this loose change, there is no new sixpence. There are two sixpences, but they are both old ones.'

She stared at him in a puzzled fashion.

'You see what that means? *Someone did come to the house that evening*

– someone to whom your mistress gave sixpence . . . I think she gave it him in exchange for this . . .'

With a swift movement, he shot his hand forward, holding out the doggerel verse about unemployment.

One glance at her face was enough.

'The game is up, Martha – you see, I know. You may as well tell me everything.'

She sank down on a chair – the tears raced down her face.

'It's true – it's true – the bell didn't ring properly – I wasn't sure, and then I thought I'd better go and see. I got to the door just as he struck her down. The roll of five-pound notes was on the table in front of her – it was the sight of them as made him do it – that and thinking she was alone in the house as she'd let him in. I couldn't scream. I was too paralysed and then he turned – and I saw it was my boy . . .

'Oh, he's been a bad one always. I gave him all the money I could. He's been in gaol twice. He must have come around to see me, and then Miss Crabtree, seeing as I didn't answer the door, went to answer it herself, and he was taken aback and pulled out one of those unemployment leaflets, and the mistress being kind of charitable, told him to come in and got out a sixpence. And all the time that roll of notes was lying on the table where it had been when I was giving her the change. And the devil got into my Ben and he got behind her and struck her down.'

'And then?' asked Sir Edward.

'Oh, sir, what could I do? My own flesh and blood. His father was a bad one, and Ben takes after him – but he was my own son. I hustled him out, and I went back to the kitchen and I went to lay for supper at the usual time. Do you think it was very wicked of me, sir? I tried to tell you no lies when you was asking me questions.'

Sir Edward rose.

'My poor woman,' he said with feeling in his voice, 'I am very sorry for you. All the same, the law will have to take its course, you know.'

'He's fled the country, sir. I don't know where he is.'

'There's a chance, then, that he may escape the gallows, but don't build upon it. Will you send Miss Magdalen to me.'

'Oh, Sir Edward. How wonderful of you – how wonderful you are,' said Magdalen when he had finished his brief recital. 'You've saved us all. How can I ever thank you?'

Sir Edward smiled down at her and patted her hand gently. He was very much the great man. Little Magdalen had been very charming on the *Siluric*. That bloom of seventeen – wonderful! She had completely lost it now, of course.

'Next time you need a friend –' he said.

'I'll come straight to you.'

'No, no,' cried Sir Edward in alarm. 'That's just what I don't want you to do. Go to a younger man.'

He extricated himself with dexterity from the grateful household and hailing a taxi sank into it with a sigh of relief.

Even the charm of a dewy seventeen seemed doubtful.

It could not really compare with a really well-stocked library on criminology.

The taxi turned into Queen Anne's Close.

His *cul-de-sac*.

The Blue Geranium

'The Blue Geranium' was first published in
The Christmas Story-Teller, December 1929.

'When I was down here last year –' said Sir Henry Clithering, and
stopped.

His hostess, Mrs Bantry, looked at him curiously.

The Ex-Commissioner of Scotland Yard was staying with old friends
of his, Colonel and Mrs Bantry, who lived near St Mary Mead.

Mrs Bantry, pen in hand, had just asked his advice as to who should
be invited to make a sixth guest at dinner that evening.

'Yes?' said Mrs Bantry encouragingly. 'When you were here last year?'

'Tell me,' said Sir Henry, 'do you know a Miss Marple?'

Mrs Bantry was surprised. It was the last thing she had expected.

'Know Miss Marple? Who doesn't! The typical old maid of fiction.
Quite a dear, but hopelessly behind the times. Do you mean you would
like me to ask *her* to dinner?'

'You are surprised?'

'A little, I must confess. I should hardly have thought you – but
perhaps there's an explanation?'

'The explanation is simple enough. When I was down here last year we
got into the habit of discussing unsolved mysteries – there were five or six
of us – Raymond West, the novelist, started it. We each supplied a story to
which we knew the answer, but nobody else did. It was supposed to be an
exercise in the deductive faculties – to see who could get nearest the truth.'

'Well?'

'Like in the old story – we hardly realized that Miss Marple was
playing; but we were very polite about it – didn't want to hurt the old
dear's feelings. And now comes the cream of the jest. The old lady outdid
us every time!'

'What?'

'I assure you – straight to the truth like a homing pigeon.'

'But how extraordinary! Why, dear old Miss Marple has hardly ever been out of St Mary Mead.'

'Ah! But according to her, that has given her unlimited opportunities of observing human nature – under the microscope as it were.'

'I suppose there's something in that,' conceded Mrs Bantry. 'One would at least know the petty side of people. But I don't think we have any really exciting criminals in our midst. I think we must try her with Arthur's ghost story after dinner. I'd be thankful if she'd find a solution to that.'

'I didn't know that Arthur believed in ghosts?'

'Oh! he doesn't. That's what worries him so. And it happened to a friend of his, George Pritchard – a most prosaic person. It's really rather tragic for poor George. Either this extraordinary story is true – or else –'

'Or else what?'

Mrs Bantry did not answer. After a minute or two she said irrelevantly:

'You know, I like George – everyone does. One can't believe that he – but people do do such extraordinary things.'

Sir Henry nodded. He knew, better than Mrs Bantry, the extraordinary things that people did.

So it came about that that evening Mrs Bantry looked round her dinner table (shivering a little as she did so, because the dining-room, like most English dining-rooms, was extremely cold) and fixed her gaze on the very upright old lady sitting on her husband's right. Miss Marple wore black lace mittens; an old lace fichu was draped round her shoulders and another piece of lace surmounted her white hair. She was talking animatedly to the elderly doctor, Dr Lloyd, about the Workhouse and the suspected shortcomings of the District Nurse.

Mrs Bantry marvelled anew. She even wondered whether Sir Henry had been making an elaborate joke – but there seemed no point in that. Incredible that what he had said could be really true.

Her glance went on and rested affectionately on her red-faced broad-shouldered husband as he sat talking horses to Jane Helier, the beautiful and popular actress. Jane, more beautiful (if that were possible) off the stage than on, opened enormous blue eyes and murmured at discreet intervals: 'Really?' 'Oh fancy!' 'How extra-ordinary!' She knew nothing whatever about horses and cared less.

'Arthur,' said Mrs Bantry, 'you're boring poor Jane to distraction. Leave horses alone and tell her your ghost story instead. You know . . . George Pritchard.'

'Eh, Dolly? Oh! but I don't know –'

'Sir Henry wants to hear it too. I was telling him something about it this morning. It would be interesting to hear what everyone has to say about it.'

'Oh do!' said Jane. 'I love ghost stories.'

'Well –' Colonel Bantry hesitated. 'I've never believed much in the supernatural. But this –

'I don't think any of you know George Pritchard. He's one of the best. His wife – well, she's dead now, poor woman. I'll just say this much: she didn't give George any too easy a time when she was alive. She was one of those semi-invalids – I believe she had really something wrong with her, but whatever it was she played it for all it was worth. She was capricious, exacting, unreasonable. She complained from morning to night. George was expected to wait on her hand and foot, and every thing he did was always wrong and he got cursed for it. Most men, I'm fully convinced, would have hit her over the head with a hatchet long ago. Eh, Dolly, isn't that so?'

'She was a dreadful woman,' said Mrs Bantry with conviction. 'If George Pritchard had brained her with a hatchet, and there had been any woman on the jury, he would have been triumphantly acquitted.'

'I don't quite know how this business started. George was rather vague about it. I gather Mrs Pritchard had always had a weakness for fortune tellers, palmists, clairvoyantes – anything of that sort. George didn't mind. If she found amusement in it well and good. But he refused to go into rhapsodies himself, and that was another grievance.

'A succession of hospital nurses was always passing through the house, Mrs Pritchard usually becoming dissatisfied with them after a few weeks. One young nurse had been very keen on this fortune telling stunt, and for a time Mrs Pritchard had been very fond of her. Then she suddenly fell out with her and insisted on her going. She had back another nurse who had been with her previously – an older woman, experienced and tactful in dealing with a neurotic patient. Nurse Copling, according to George, was a very good sort – a sensible woman to talk to. She put up with Mrs Pritchard's tantrums and nervestorms with complete indifference.

'Mrs Pritchard always lunched upstairs, and it was usual at lunch time for George and the nurse to come to some arrangement for the afternoon. Strictly speaking, the nurse went off from two to four, but "to oblige" as the phrase goes, she would sometimes take her time off after tea if George wanted to be free for the afternoon. On this occasion, she mentioned that she was going to see a sister at Golders Green and might be a little late returning. George's face fell, for he had arranged to play a round of golf. Nurse Copling, however, reassured him.

"'We'll neither of us be missed, Mr Pritchard." A twinkle came into her eye. "Mrs Pritchard's going to have more exciting company than ours."

"'Who's that?"

"'Wait a minute," Nurse Copling's eyes twinkled more than ever. "Let me get it right. *Zarida, Psychic Reader of the Future.*"

"'Oh Lord!" groaned George. "That's a new one, isn't it?"

"'Quite new. I believe my predecessor, Nurse Carstairs, sent her along. Mrs Pritchard hasn't seen her yet. She made me write, fixing an appointment for this afternoon."

"'Well, at any rate, I shall get my golf," said George, and he went off with the kindliest feelings towards Zarida, the Reader of the Future.

'On his return to the house, he found Mrs Pritchard in a state of great agitation. She was, as usual, lying on her invalid couch, and she had a bottle of smelling salts in her hand which she sniffed at frequent intervals.

"'George," she exclaimed. "What did I tell you about this house? The moment I came into it, I *felt* there was something wrong! Didn't I tell you so at the time?"

'Repressing his desire to reply, "You always do," George said, "No, I can't say I remember it."

"'You never do remember anything that has to do with me. Men are all extraordinarily callous – but I really believe that you are even more insensitive than most."

"'Oh, come now, Mary dear, that's not fair."

"'Well, as I was telling you, this woman *knew* at once! She – she actually blenched – if you know what I mean – as she came in at the door, and she said: "There is evil here – evil and danger. I feel it.'"

'Very unwisely George laughed.

"'Well, you have had your money's worth this afternoon."

'His wife closed her eyes and took a long sniff from her smelling bottle.

"'How you hate me! You would jeer and laugh if I were dying."

'George protested and after a minute or two she went on.

"'You may laugh, but I shall tell you the whole thing. This house is definitely dangerous to me – the woman said so."

'George's formerly kind feeling towards Zarida underwent a change. He knew his wife was perfectly capable of insisting on moving to a new house if the caprice got hold of her.

"'What else did she say?" he asked.

"'She couldn't tell me very much. She was so upset. One thing she did say. I had some violets in a glass. She pointed at them and cried out:

"'Take those away. No blue flowers – never have blue flowers. *Blue flowers are fatal to you – remember that.*'"

"'And you know," added Mrs Pritchard, "I always have told you that blue as a colour is repellent to me. I feel a natural instinctive sort of warning against."

'George was much too wise to remark that he had never heard her say so before. Instead he asked what the mysterious Zarida was like. Mrs Pritchard entered with gusto upon a description.

"'Black hair in coiled knobs over her ears – her eyes were half closed – great black rims round them – she had a black veil over her mouth and chin – and she spoke in a kind of singing voice with a marked foreign accent – Spanish, I think –"

"'In fact all the usual stock-in-trade," said George cheerfully.

'His wife immediately closed her eyes.

"'I feel extremely ill," she said. "Ring for nurse. Unkindness upsets me, as you know only too well."

'It was two days later that Nurse Copling came to George with a grave face.

"'Will you come to Mrs Pritchard, please. She has had a letter which upsets her greatly."

'He found his wife with the letter in her hand. She held it out to him.

"'Read it," she said.

'George read it. It was on heavily scented paper, and the writing was big and black.

'*I have seen the future. Be warned before it is too late. Beware of the Full Moon. The Blue Primrose means Warning; the Blue Hollyhock means Danger; the Blue Geranium means Death . . .*

'Just about to burst out laughing, George caught Nurse Copling's eye. She made a quick warning gesture. He said rather awkwardly, "The woman's probably trying to frighten you, Mary. Anyway there aren't such things as blue primroses and blue geraniums."

'But Mrs Pritchard began to cry and say her days were numbered. Nurse Copling came out with George upon the landing.

"'Of all the silly tomfoolery," he burst out.

"'I suppose it is."

'Something in the nurse's tone struck him, and he stared at her in amazement.

"'Surely, nurse, you don't believe –"

"'No, no, Mr Pritchard. I don't believe in reading the future – that's nonsense. What puzzles me is the *meaning* of this. Fortune-tellers are usually out for what they can get. But this woman seems to be frightening Mrs Pritchard with no advantage to herself. I can't see the point. There's another thing –"

"'Yes?"

'"Mrs Pritchard says that something about Zarida was faintly familiar to her."

'"Well?"

'"Well, I don't like it, Mr Pritchard, that's all."

'"I didn't know you were so superstitious, nurse."

'"I'm not superstitious; but I know when a thing is fishy."

'It was about four days after this that the first incident happened. To explain it to you, I shall have to describe Mrs Pritchard's room –'

'You'd better let me do that,' interrupted Mrs Bantry. 'It was papered with one of those new wallpapers where you apply clumps of flowers to make a kind of herbaceous border. The effect is almost like being in a garden – though, of course, the flowers are all wrong. I mean they simply couldn't be in bloom all at the same time –'

'Don't let a passion for horticultural accuracy run away with you, Dolly,' said her husband. 'We all know you're an enthusiastic gardener.'

'Well, it *is* absurd,' protested Mrs Bantry. 'To have bluebells and daffodils and lupins and hollyhocks and Michaelmas daisies all grouped together.'

'Most unscientific,' said Sir Henry. 'But to proceed with the story.'

'Well, among these massed flowers were primroses, clumps of yellow and pink primroses and – oh go on, Arthur, this is your story –'

Colonel Bantry took up the tale.

'Mrs Pritchard rang her bell violently one morning. The household came running – thought she was in extremis; not at all. She was violently excited and pointing at the wallpaper; and there sure enough was *one blue primrose* in the midst of the others . . .'

'Oh!' said Miss Helier, 'how creepy!'

'The question was: Hadn't the blue primrose always been there? That was George's suggestion and the nurse's. But Mrs Pritchard wouldn't have it at any price. She had never noticed it till that very morning and the night before had been full moon. She was very upset about it.'

'I met George Pritchard that same day and he told me about it,' said Mrs Bantry. 'I went to see Mrs Pritchard and did my best to ridicule the whole thing; but without success. I came away really concerned, and I remember I met Jean Instow and told her about it. Jean is a queer girl. She said, "So she's really upset about it?" I told her that I thought the woman was perfectly capable of dying of fright – she was really abnormally superstitious.

'I remember Jean rather startled me with what she said next. She said, "Well, that might be all for the best, mightn't it?" And she said it so coolly, in so matter-of-fact a tone that I was really – well, shocked. Of course I know it's done nowadays – to be brutal and outspoken; but

I never get used to it. Jean smiled at me rather oddly and said, "You don't like my saying that – but it's true. What use is Mrs Pritchard's life to her? None at all; and it's hell for George Pritchard. To have his wife frightened out of existence would be the best thing that could happen to him." I said, "George is most awfully good to her always." And she said, "Yes, he deserves a reward, poor dear. He's a very attractive person, George Pritchard. The last nurse thought so – the pretty one – what was her name? Carstairs. That was the cause of the row between her and Mrs P."

'Now I didn't like hearing Jean say that. Of course one had *wondered* –' Mrs Bantry paused significantly.

'Yes, dear,' said Miss Marple placidly. 'One always does. Is Miss Instow a pretty girl? I suppose she plays golf?'

'Yes. She's good at all games. And she's nice-looking, attractive-looking, very fair with a healthy skin, and nice steady blue eyes. Of course we always have felt that she and George Pritchard – I mean if things had been different – they are so well suited to one another.'

'And they were friends?' asked Miss Marple.

'Oh yes. Great friends.'

'Do you think, Dolly,' said Colonel Bantry plaintively, 'that I might be allowed to go on with my story?'

'Arthur,' said Mrs Bantry resignedly, 'wants to get back to his ghosts.'

'I had the rest of the story from George himself,' went on the Colonel. 'There's no doubt that Mrs Pritchard got the wind up badly towards the end of the next month. She marked off on a calendar the day when the moon would be full, and on that night she had both the nurse and then George into her room and made them study the wallpaper carefully. There were pink hollyhocks and red ones, but there were no blue amongst them. Then when George left the room she locked the door –'

'And in the morning there was a large blue hollyhock,' said Miss Helier joyfully.

'Quite right,' said Colonel Bantry. 'Or at any rate, nearly right. One flower of a hollyhock just above her head had turned blue. It staggered George; and of course the more it staggered him the more he refused to take the thing seriously. He insisted that the whole thing was some kind of practical joke. He ignored the evidence of the locked door and the fact that Mrs Pritchard discovered the change before anyone – even Nurse Copling – was admitted.

'It staggered George; and it made him unreasonable. His wife wanted to leave the house, and he wouldn't let her. He was inclined to believe in the supernatural for the first time, but he wasn't going to admit it. He usually gave in to his wife, but this time he wouldn't. Mary was not to make a fool of herself, he said. The whole thing was the most infernal nonsense.

'And so the next month sped away. Mrs Pritchard made less protest than one would have imagined. I think she was superstitious enough to believe that she couldn't escape her fate. She repeated again and again: "The blue primrose – warning. The blue hollyhock – danger. The blue geranium – *death*." And she would lie looking at the clump of pinky-red geraniums nearest her bed.

'The whole business was pretty nervy. Even the nurse caught the infection. She came to George two days before full moon and begged him to take Mrs Pritchard away. George was angry.

'"If all the flowers on that damned wall turned into blue devils it couldn't kill anyone!" he shouted.

'"It might. Shock has killed people before now."

'"Nonsense," said George.

'George has always been a shade pig-headed. You can't drive him. I believe he had a secret idea that his wife worked the change herself and that it was all some morbid hysterical plan of hers.

'Well, the fatal night came. Mrs Pritchard locked the door as usual. She was very calm – in almost an exalted state of mind. The nurse was worried by her state – wanted to give her a stimulant, an injection of strychnine, but Mrs Pritchard refused. In a way, I believe, she was enjoying herself. George said she was.'

'I think that's quite possible,' said Mrs Bantry. 'There must have been a strange sort of glamour about the whole thing.'

'There was no violent ringing of a bell the next morning. Mrs Pritchard usually woke about eight. When, at eight-thirty, there was no sign from her, nurse rapped loudly on the door. Getting no reply, she fetched George, and insisted on the door being broken open. They did so with the help of a chisel.

'One look at the still figure on the bed was enough for Nurse Copling. She sent George to telephone for the doctor, but it was too late. Mrs Pritchard, he said, must have been dead at least eight hours. Her smelling salts lay by her hand on the bed, *and on the wall beside her one of the pinky-red geraniums was a bright deep blue.*'

'Horrible,' said Miss Helier with a shiver.

Sir Henry was frowning.

'No additional details?'

Colonel Bantry shook his head, but Mrs Bantry spoke quickly.

'The gas.'

'What about the gas?' asked Sir Henry.

'When the doctor arrived there was a slight smell of gas, and sure enough he found the gas ring in the fireplace very slightly turned on; but so little it couldn't have mattered.'

'Did Mr Pritchard and the nurse not notice it when they first went in?'

'The nurse said she did notice a slight smell. George said he didn't notice gas, but something made him feel very queer and overcome; but he put that down to shock – and probably it was. At any rate there was no question of gas poisoning. The smell was scarcely noticeable.'

'And that's the end of the story?'

'No, it isn't. One way and another, there was a lot of talk. The servants, you see, had overheard things – had heard, for instance, Mrs Pritchard telling her husband that he hated her and would jeer if she were dying. And also more recent remarks. She had said one day, apropos of his refusing to leave the house: "Very well, when I am dead, I hope everyone will realize that you have killed me." And as ill luck would have it, he had been mixing some weed killer for the garden paths the day before. One of the younger servants had seen him and had afterwards seen him taking up a glass of hot milk for his wife.

'The talk spread and grew. The doctor had given a certificate – I don't know exactly in what terms – shock, syncope, heart failure, probably some medical terms meaning nothing much. However the poor lady had not been a month in her grave before an exhumation order was applied for and granted.'

'And the result of the autopsy was nil, I remember,' said Sir Henry gravely. 'A case, for once, of smoke without fire.'

'The whole thing is really very curious,' said Mrs Bantry. 'That fortune-teller, for instance – Zarida. At the address where she was supposed to be, no one had ever heard of any such person!'

'She appeared once – out of the blue,' said her husband, 'and then utterly vanished. Out of the *blue* – that's rather good!'

'And what is more,' continued Mrs Bantry, 'little Nurse Carstairs, who was supposed to have recommended her, had never even heard of her.'

They looked at each other.

'It's a mysterious story,' said Dr Lloyd. 'One can make guesses; but to guess –'

He shook his head.

'Has Mr Pritchard married Miss Instow?' asked Miss Marple in her gentle voice.

'Now why do you ask that?' inquired Sir Henry.

Miss Marple opened gentle blue eyes.

'It seems to me so important,' she said. 'Have they married?'

Colonel Bantry shook his head.

'We – well, we expected something of the kind – but it's eighteen months now. I don't believe they even see much of each other.'

'That is important,' said Miss Marple. 'Very important.'

'Then you think the same as I do,' said Mrs Bantry. 'You think –'

'Now, Dolly,' said her husband. 'It's unjustifiable – what you're going to say. You can't go about accusing people without a shadow of proof.'

'Don't be so – so manly, Arthur. Men are always afraid to say *anything*. Anyway, this is all between ourselves. It's just a wild fantastic idea of mine that possibly – only *possibly* – Jean Instow disguised herself as a fortune-teller. Mind you, she may have done it for a joke. I don't for a minute think that she meant any harm; but if she did do it, and if Mrs Pritchard was foolish enough to die of fright – well, that's what Miss Marple meant, wasn't it?'

'No, dear, not quite,' said Miss Marple. 'You see, if I were going to kill anyone – which, of course, I wouldn't dream of doing for a minute, because it would be very wicked, and besides I don't like killing – not even wasps, though I know it has to be, and I'm sure the gardener does it as humanely as possible. Let me see, what was I saying?'

'If you wished to kill anyone,' prompted Sir Henry.

'Oh yes. Well, if I did, I shouldn't be at all satisfied to trust to *fright*. I know one reads of people dying of it, but it seems a very uncertain sort of thing, and the most nervous people are far more brave than one really thinks they are. I should like something definite and certain, and make a thoroughly good plan about it.'

'Miss Marple,' said Sir Henry, 'you frighten me. I hope you will never wish to remove me. Your plans would be too good.'

Miss Marple looked at him reproachfully.

'I thought I had made it clear that I would never contemplate such wickedness,' she said. 'No, I was trying to put myself in the place of – er – a certain person.'

'Do you mean George Pritchard?' asked Colonel Bantry. 'I'll never believe it of George – though – mind you, even the nurse believes it. I went and saw her about a month afterwards, at the time of the exhumation. She didn't know how it was done – in fact, she wouldn't say anything at all – but it was clear enough that she believed George to be in some way responsible for his wife's death. She was convinced of it.'

'Well,' said Dr Lloyd, 'perhaps she wasn't so far wrong. And mind you, a nurse often *knows*. She can't say – she's got no proof – but she *knows*.'

Sir Henry leant forward.

'Come now, Miss Marple,' he said persuasively. 'You're lost in a daydream. Won't you tell us all about it?'

Miss Marple started and turned pink.

'I beg your pardon,' she said. 'I was just thinking about our District Nurse. A most difficult problem.'

'More difficult than the problem of the blue geranium?'

'It really depends on the primroses,' said Miss Marple. 'I mean, Mrs Bantry said they were yellow and pink. If it was a pink primrose that turned blue, of course, that fits in perfectly. But if it happened to be a yellow one –'

'It was a pink one,' said Mrs Bantry.

She stared. They all stared at Miss Marple.

'Then that seems to settle it,' said Miss Marple. She shook her head regretfully. 'And the wasp season and everything. And of course the gas.'

'It reminds you, I suppose, of countless village tragedies?' said Sir Henry.

'Not tragedies,' said Miss Marple. 'And certainly nothing criminal. But it does remind me a little of the trouble we are having with the District Nurse. After all, nurses are human beings, and what with having to be so correct in their behaviour and wearing those uncomfortable collars and being so thrown with the family – well, can you wonder that things sometimes happen?'

A glimmer of light broke upon Sir Henry.

'You mean Nurse Carstairs?'

'Oh no. Not Nurse Carstairs. Nurse *Copling*. You see, she had been there before, and very much thrown with Mr Pritchard, who you say is an attractive man. I dare say she thought, poor thing – well, we needn't go into that. I don't suppose she knew about Miss Instow, and of course afterwards, when she found out, it turned her against him and she tried to do all the harm she could. Of course the letter really gave her away, didn't it?'

'What letter?'

'Well, she wrote to the fortune-teller at Mrs Pritchard's request, and the fortune-teller came, apparently in answer to the letter. But later it was discovered that there never had been such a person at that address. So that shows that Nurse Copling was in it. She only pretended to write – so what could be more likely than that *she* was the fortune-teller herself?'

'I never saw the point about the letter,' said Sir Henry. 'That's a most important point, of course.'

'Rather a bold step to take,' said Miss Marple, 'because Mrs Pritchard might have recognized her in spite of the disguise – though of course if she had, the nurse could have pretended it was a joke.'

'What did you mean,' said Sir Henry, 'when you said that if you were a certain person you would not have trusted to fright?'

'One couldn't be *sure* that way,' said Miss Marple. 'No, I think that the warnings and the blue flowers were, if I may use a military term,' she laughed self-consciously – '*just camouflage.*'

'And the real thing?'

'I know,' said Miss Marple apologetically, 'that I've got wasps on the brain. Poor things, destroyed in their thousands – and usually on such a beautiful summer's day. But I remember thinking, when I saw the gardener shaking up the cyanide of potassium in a bottle with water, how like smelling-salts it looked. And if it were put in a smelling-salt bottle and substituted for the real one – well, the poor lady was in the habit of using her smelling-salts. Indeed you said they were found by her hand. Then, of course, while Mr Pritchard went to telephone to the doctor, the nurse would change it for the real bottle, and she'd just turn on the gas a little bit to mask any smell of almonds and in case anyone felt queer, and I always have heard that cyanide leaves no trace if you wait long enough. But, of course I may be wrong, and it may have been something entirely different in the bottle; but that doesn't really matter, does it?'

Miss Marple paused, a little out of breath.

Jane Helier leant forward and said, 'But the blue geranium, and the other flowers?'

'Nurses always have litmus paper, don't they?' said Miss Marple, 'for – well, for testing. Not a very pleasant subject. We won't dwell on it. I have done a little nursing myself.' She grew delicately pink. 'Blue turns red with acids, and red turns blue with alkalis. So easy to paste some red litmus over a red flower – near the bed, of course. And then, when the poor lady used her smelling-salts, the strong ammonia fumes would turn it blue. Really most ingenious. Of course, the geranium wasn't blue when they first broke into the room – nobody noticed it till afterwards. When nurse changed the bottles, she held the Sal Ammoniac against the wallpaper for a minute, I expect.'

'You might have been there, Miss Marple,' said Sir Henry.

'What worries me,' said Miss Marple, 'is poor Mr Pritchard and that nice girl, Miss Instow. Probably both suspecting each other and keeping apart – and life so very short.'

She shook her head.

'You needn't worry,' said Sir Henry. 'As a matter of fact I have something up my sleeve. A nurse has been arrested on a charge of murdering an elderly patient who had left her a legacy. It was done with cyanide of potassium substituted for smelling-salts. Nurse Copling trying the same trick again. Miss Instow and Mr Pritchard need have no doubts as to the truth.'

'Now isn't that nice?' cried Miss Marple. 'I don't mean about the new murder, of course. That's very sad, and shows how much wickedness there is in the world, and that if once you give way – which reminds me I *must* finish my little conversation with Dr Lloyd about the village nurse.'

The Companion

'The Companion' was first published as 'The Resurrection of Amy Durrant' in *Storyteller*, February 1930, and then in the USA as 'Companions' in *Pictorial Review*, March 1930.

'Now, Dr Lloyd,' said Miss Helier. 'Don't *you* know any creepy stories?'

She smiled at him – the smile that nightly bewitched the theatre-going public. Jane Helier was sometimes called the most beautiful woman in England, and jealous members of her own profession were in the habit of saying to each other: 'Of course Jane's not an *artist*. She can't *act* – if you know what I mean. It's those eyes!'

And those 'eyes' were at this minute fixed appealingly on the grizzled elderly bachelor doctor who, for the last five years, had ministered to the ailments of the village of St Mary Mead.

With an unconscious gesture, the doctor pulled down his waistcoat (inclined of late to be uncomfortably tight) and racked his brains hastily, so as not to disappoint the lovely creature who addressed him so confidently.

'I feel,' said Jane dreamily, 'that I would like to wallow in crime this evening.'

'Splendid,' said Colonel Bantry, her host. 'Splendid, splendid.' And he laughed a loud hearty military laugh. 'Eh, Dolly?'

His wife, hastily recalled to the exigencies of social life (she had been planning her spring border) agreed enthusiastically.

'Of course it's splendid,' she said heartily but vaguely. 'I always thought so.'

'Did you, my dear?' said old Miss Marple, and her eyes twinkled a little.

'We don't get much in the creepy line – and still less in the criminal line – in St Mary Mead, you know, Miss Helier,' said Dr Lloyd.

'You surprise me,' said Sir Henry Clithering. The ex-Commissioner of Scotland Yard turned to Miss Marple. 'I always understood from our friend here that St Mary Mead is a positive hotbed of crime and vice.'

'Oh, Sir Henry!' protested Miss Marple, a spot of colour coming into her cheeks. 'I'm sure I never said anything of the kind. The only thing I ever said was that human nature is much the same in a village as anywhere else, only one has opportunities and leisure for seeing it at closer quarters.'

'But *you* haven't always lived here,' said Jane Helier, still addressing the doctor. 'You've been in all sorts of queer places all over the world – places where things *happen!*'

'That is so, of course,' said Dr Lloyd, still thinking desperately. 'Yes, of course . . . Yes . . . Ah! I have it!'

He sank back with a sigh of relief.

'It is some years ago now – I had almost forgotten. But the facts were really very strange – very strange indeed. And the final coincidence which put the clue into my hand was strange also.'

Miss Helier drew her chair a little nearer to him, applied some lipstick and waited expectantly. The others also turned interested faces towards him.

'I don't know whether any of you know the Canary Islands,' began the doctor.

'They must be wonderful,' said Jane Helier. 'They're in the South Seas, aren't they? Or is it the Mediterranean?'

'I've called in there on my way to South Africa,' said the Colonel. 'The Peak of Tenerife is a fine sight with the setting sun on it.'

'The incident I am describing happened in the island of Grand Canary, not Tenerife. It is a good many years ago now. I had had a breakdown in health and was forced to give up my practice in England and go abroad. I practised in Las Palmas, which is the principal town of Grand Canary. In many ways I enjoyed the life out there very much. The climate was mild and sunny, there was excellent surf bathing (and I am an enthusiastic bather) and the sea life of the port attracted me. Ships from all over the world put in at Las Palmas. I used to walk along the mole every morning far more interested than any member of the fair sex could be in a street of hat shops.

'As I say, ships from all over the world put in at Las Palmas. Sometimes they stay a few hours, sometimes a day or two. In the principal hotel there, the Metropole, you will see people of all races and nationalities – birds of passage. Even the people going to Tenerife usually come here and stay a few days before crossing to the other island.

'My story begins there, in the Metropole Hotel, one Thursday evening in January. There was a dance going on and I and a friend had been sitting at a small table watching the scene. There were a fair sprinkling of English and other nationalities, but the majority of the dancers were Spanish; and when the orchestra struck up a tango, only half a dozen couples of the latter nationality took the floor. They all danced well and we looked on and admired. One woman in particular excited our lively admiration. Tall, beautiful and sinuous, she moved with the grace of a half-tamed leopardess. There was something dangerous about her. I said as much to my friend and he agreed.

"'Women like that,' he said, "are bound to have a history. Life will not pass them by."

"'Beauty is perhaps a dangerous possession," I said.

"'It's not only beauty," he insisted. "There is something else. Look at her again. Things are bound to happen to that woman, or because of her. As I said, life will not pass her by. Strange and exciting events will surround her. You've only got to look at her to know it."

'He paused and then added with a smile:

"'Just as you've only got to look at those two women over there, and know that nothing out of the way could ever happen to either of them! They are made for a safe and uneventful existence."

'I followed his eyes. The two women he referred to were travellers who had just arrived – a Holland Lloyd boat had put into port that evening, and the passengers were just beginning to arrive.

'As I looked at them I saw at once what my friend meant. They were two English ladies – the thoroughly nice travelling English that you do find abroad. Their ages, I should say, were round about forty. One was fair and a little – just a little – too plump; the other was dark and a little – again just a little – inclined to scragginess. They were what is called well-preserved, quietly and inconspicuously dressed in well-cut tweeds, and innocent of any kind of make-up. They had that air of quiet assurance which is the birthright of well-bred Englishwomen. There was nothing remarkable about either of them. They were like thousands of their sisters. They would doubtless see what they wished to see, assisted by Baedeker, and be blind to everything else. They would use the English library and attend the English Church in any place they happened to be, and it was quite likely that one or both of them sketched a little. And as my friend said, nothing exciting or remarkable would ever happen to either of them, though they might quite likely travel half over the world. I looked from them back to our sinuous Spanish woman with her half-closed smouldering eyes and I smiled.'

'Poor things,' said Jane Helier with a sigh. 'But I do think it's so silly of people not to make the most of themselves. That woman in Bond Street – Valentine – is really wonderful. Audrey Denman goes to her; and have you seen her in "The Downward Step"? As the schoolgirl in the first act she's really marvel- lous. And yet Audrey is fifty if she's a day. As a matter of fact I happen to know she's really nearer sixty.'

'Go on,' said Mrs Bantry to Dr Lloyd. 'I love stories about sinuous Spanish dancers. It makes me forget how old and fat I am.'

'I'm sorry,' said Dr Lloyd apologetically. 'But you see, as a matter of fact, this story isn't about the Spanish woman.'

'It isn't?'

'No. As it happens my friend and I were wrong. Nothing in the least exciting happened to the Spanish beauty. She married a clerk in a shipping office, and by the time I left the island she had had five children and was getting very fat.'

'Just like that girl of Israel Peters,' commented Miss Marple. 'The one who went on the stage and had such good legs that they made her principal boy in the pantomime. Everyone said she'd come to no good, but she married a commercial traveller and settled down splendidly.'

'The village parallel,' murmured Sir Henry softly.

'No,' went on the doctor. 'My story is about the two English ladies.'

'Something happened to them?' breathed Miss Helier.

'Something happened to them – and the very next day, too.'

'Yes?' said Mrs Bantry encouragingly.

'Just for curiosity, as I went out that evening I glanced at the hotel register. I found the names easily enough. Miss Mary Barton and Miss Amy Durrant of Little Paddocks, Caughton Weir, Bucks. I little thought then how soon I was to encounter the owners of those names again – and under what tragic circumstances.

'The following day I had arranged to go for a picnic with some friends. We were to motor across the island, taking our lunch, to a place called (as far as I remember – it is so long ago) Las Nieves, a well-sheltered bay where we could bathe if we felt inclined. This programme we duly carried out, except that we were somewhat late in starting, so that we stopped on the way and picnicked, going on to Las Nieves afterwards for a bathe before tea.

'As we approached the beach, we were at once aware of a tremendous commotion. The whole population of the small village seemed to be gathered on the shore. As soon as they saw us they rushed towards the car and began explaining excitedly. Our Spanish not being very good, it took me a few minutes to understand, but at last I got it.

'Two of the mad English ladies had gone in to bathe, and one had swum out too far and got into difficulties. The other had gone after her and had tried to bring her in, but her strength in turn had failed and she too would have drowned had not a man rowed out in a boat and brought in rescuer and rescued – the latter beyond help.

'As soon as I got the hang of things I pushed the crowd aside and hurried down the beach. I did not at first recognize the two women. The plump figure in the black stockinet costume and the tight green rubber bathing cap awoke no chord of recognition as she looked up anxiously. She was kneeling beside the body of her friend, making somewhat amateurish attempts at artificial respiration. When I told her that I was a doctor she gave a sigh of relief, and I ordered her off at once to one of the cottages for a rub down and dry clothing. One of the ladies in my party went with her. I myself worked unavailingly on the body of the drowned woman in vain. Life was only too clearly extinct, and in the end I had reluctantly to give in.

'I rejoined the others in the small fisherman's cottage and there I had to break the sad news. The survivor was attired now in her own clothes, and I immediately recognized her as one of the two arrivals of the night before. She received the sad news fairly calmly, and it was evidently the horror of the whole thing that struck her more than any great personal feeling.

'"Poor Amy," she said. "Poor, poor Amy. She had been looking forward to the bathing here so much. And she was a good swimmer too. I can't understand it. What do you think it can have been, doctor?"

'"Possibly cramp. Will you tell me exactly what happened?"

'"We had both been swimming about for some time – twenty minutes, I should say. Then I thought I would go in, but Amy said she was going to swim out once more. She did so, and suddenly I heard her call and realized she was crying for help. I swam out as fast as I could. She was still afloat when I got to her, but she clutched at me wildly and we both went under. If it hadn't been for that man coming out with his boat I should have been drowned too."

'"That has happened fairly often," I said. "To save anyone from drowning is not an easy affair."

'"It seems so awful," continued Miss Barton. "We only arrived yesterday, and were so delighting in the sunshine and our little holiday. And now this – this terrible tragedy occurs."

'I asked her then for particulars about the dead woman, explaining that I would do everything I could for her, but that the Spanish authorities would require full information. This she gave me readily enough.

'The dead woman, Miss Amy Durrant, was her companion and had come to her about five months previously. They had got on very well together, but Miss Durrant had spoken very little about her people. She had been left an orphan at an early age and had been brought up by an uncle and had earned her own living since she was twenty-one.

'And so that was that,' went on the doctor. He paused and said again, but this time with a certain finality in his voice, 'And so that was that.'

'I don't understand,' said Jane Helier. 'Is that all? I mean, it's very tragic, I suppose, but it isn't – well, it isn't what I call *creepy*.'

'I think there's more to follow,' said Sir Henry.

'Yes,' said Dr Lloyd, 'there's more to follow. You see, right at the time there was one queer thing. Of course I asked questions of the fishermen, etc., as to what they'd seen. They were eye-witnesses. And one woman had rather a funny story. I didn't pay any attention to it at the time, but it came back to me afterwards. She insisted, you see, that Miss Durrant wasn't in difficulties when she called out. The other swam out to her and, according to this woman, deliberately held Miss Durrant's head under water. I didn't, as I say, pay much attention. It was such a fantastic story, and these things look so differently from the shore. Miss Barton might have tried to make her friend lose consciousness, realizing that the latter's panic-stricken clutching would drown them both. You see, according to the Spanish woman's story, it looked as though – well, as though Miss Barton was deliberately trying to drown her companion.

'As I say, I paid very little attention to this story at the time. It came back to me later. Our great difficulty was to find out anything about this woman, Amy Durrant. She didn't seem to have any relations. Miss Barton and I went through her things together. We found one address and wrote there, but it proved to be simply a room she had taken in which to keep her things. The landlady knew nothing, had only seen her when she took the room. Miss Durrant had remarked at the time that she always liked to have one place she could call her own to which she could return at any moment. There were one or two nice pieces of old furniture and some bound numbers of Academy pictures, and a trunk full of pieces of material bought at sales, but no personal belongings. She had mentioned to the landlady that her father and mother had died in India when she was a child and that she had been brought up by an uncle who was a clergyman, but she did not say if he was her father's or her mother's brother, so the name was no guide.

'It wasn't exactly mysterious, it was just unsatisfactory. There must be many lonely women, proud and reticent, in just that position. There were a couple of photographs amongst her belongings in Las Palmas – rather old and faded and they had been cut to fit the frames they were in, so that there was no photographer's name upon them, and there was an old daguerreotype which might have been her mother or more probably her grandmother.

'Miss Barton had had two references with her. One she had forgotten, the other name she recollected after an effort. It proved to be that of a lady who was now abroad, having gone to Australia. She was written to. Her answer, of course, was a long time in coming, and I may say that when it did arrive there was no particular help to be gained from it. She said Miss Durrant had been with her as companion and had been most efficient and that she was a very charming woman, but that she knew nothing of her private affairs or relations.

'So there it was – as I say, nothing unusual, really. It was just the two things together that aroused my uneasiness. This Amy Durrant of whom no one knew anything, and the Spanish woman's queer story. Yes, and I'll add a third thing: When I was first bending over the body and Miss Barton was walking away towards the huts, she looked back. Looked back with an expression on her face that I can only describe as one of poignant anxiety – a kind of anguished uncertainty that imprinted itself on my brain.

'It didn't strike me as anything unusual at the time. I put it down to her terrible distress over her friend. But, you see, later I realized that they weren't on those terms. There was no devoted attachment between them, no terrible grief. Miss Barton was fond of Amy Durrant and shocked by her death – that was all.

'But, then, why that terrible poignant anxiety? That was the question that kept coming back to me. I had not been mistaken in that look. And almost against my will, an answer began to shape itself in my mind. Supposing the Spanish woman's story were true; supposing that Mary Barton wilfully and in cold blood tried to drown Amy Durrant. She succeeds in holding her under water whilst pretending to be saving her. She is rescued by a boat. They are on a lonely beach far from anywhere. And then I appear – the last thing she expects. A doctor! And an English doctor! She knows well enough that people who have been under water far longer than Amy Durrant have been revived by artificial respiration. But she has to play her part – to go off leaving me alone with her victim. And as she turns for one last look, a terrible poignant anxiety shows in her face. Will Amy Durrant come back to life *and tell what she knows?*'

'Oh!' said Jane Helier. 'I'm thrilled now.'

'Viewed in that aspect the whole business seemed more sinister, and the personality of Amy Durrant became more mysterious. Who was Amy Durrant? Why should she, an insignificant paid companion, be murdered by her employer? What story lay behind that fatal bathing expedition? She had entered Mary Barton's employment only a few months before. Mary Barton had brought her abroad, and the very day after they landed the tragedy had occurred. And they were both nice, commonplace, refined Englishwomen! The whole thing was fantastic, and I told myself so. I had been letting my imagination run away with me.'

'You didn't do anything, then?' asked Miss Helier.

'My dear young lady, what could I do? There was no evidence. The majority of the eye-witnesses told the same story as Miss Barton. I had built up my own suspicions out of a fleeting expression which I might possibly have imagined. The only thing I could and did do was to see that the widest inquiries were made for the relations of Amy Durrant. The next time I was in England I even went and saw the landlady of her room, with the results I have told you.'

'But you felt there was something wrong,' said Miss Marple.

Dr Lloyd nodded.

'Half the time I was ashamed of myself for thinking so. Who was I to go suspecting this nice, pleasant-mannered English lady of a foul and cold-blooded crime? I did my best to be as cordial as possible to her during the short time she stayed on the island. I helped her with the Spanish authorities. I did everything I could do as an Englishman to help a compatriot in a foreign country; and yet I am convinced that she knew I suspected and disliked her.'

'How long did she stay out there?' asked Miss Marple.

'I think it was about a fortnight. Miss Durrant was buried there, and it must have been about ten days later when she took a boat back to England. The shock had upset her so much that she felt she couldn't spend the winter there as she had planned. That's what she said.'

'Did it seem to have upset her?' asked Miss Marple.

The doctor hesitated.

'Well, I don't know that it affected her appearance at all,' he said cautiously.

'She didn't, for instance, grow fatter?' asked Miss Marple.

'Do you know – it's a curious thing your saying that. Now I come to think back, I believe you're right. She – yes, she did seem, if anything, to be putting on weight.'

'How horrible,' said Jane Helier with a shudder. 'It's like – it's like fattening on your victim's blood.'

'And yet, in another way, I may be doing her an injustice,' went on Dr Lloyd. 'She certainly said something before she left, which pointed in an entirely different direction. There may be, I think there are, consciences which work very slowly – which take some time to awaken to the enormity of the deed committed.

'It was the evening before her departure from the Canaries. She had asked me to go and see her, and had thanked me very warmly for all I had done to help her. I, of course, made light of the matter, said I had only done what was natural under the circumstances, and so on. There was a pause after that, and then she suddenly asked me a question.'

"'Do you think,' she asked, "that one is ever justified in taking the law into one's own hands?"

'I replied that that was rather a difficult question, but that on the whole, I thought not. The law was the law, and we had to abide by it.

"'Even when it is powerless?"

"'I don't quite understand."

"'It's difficult to explain; but one might do something that is considered definitely wrong – that is considered a crime, even, for a good and sufficient reason."

'I replied drily that possibly several criminals had thought that in their time, and she shrank back.

"'But that's horrible," she murmured. "Horrible."

'And then with a change of tone she asked me to give her something to make her sleep. She had not been able to sleep properly since – she hesitated – since that terrible shock.

"'You're sure it is that? There is nothing worrying you? Nothing on your mind?"

"'On my mind? What should be on my mind?"

'She spoke fiercely and suspiciously.

"'Worry is a cause of sleeplessness sometimes," I said lightly.

'She seemed to brood for a moment.

"'Do you mean worrying over the future, or worrying over the past, which can't be altered?"

"'Either."

"'Only it wouldn't be any good worrying over the past. You couldn't bring back – Oh! what's the use! One mustn't think. One must not think."

'I prescribed her a mild sleeping draught and made my adieu. As I went away I wondered not a little over the words she had spoken. "You couldn't bring back –" What? Or *who*?

'I think that last interview prepared me in a way for what was to come. I didn't expect it, of course, but when it happened, I wasn't surprised. Because, you see, Mary Barton struck me all along as a conscientious woman – not a weak sinner, but a woman with convictions, who would act up to them, and who would not relent as long as she still believed in them. I fancied that in the last conversation we had she was beginning to doubt her own convictions. I know her words suggested to me that she was feeling the first faint beginnings of that terrible soul-searcher – remorse.

'The thing happened in Cornwall, in a small watering-place, rather deserted at that season of the year. It must have been – let me see – late March. I read about it in the papers. A lady had been staying at a small hotel there – a Miss Barton. She had been very odd and peculiar in her manner. That had been noticed by all. At night she would walk up and down her room, muttering to herself, and not allowing the people on either side of her to sleep. She had called on the vicar one day and had told him that she had a communication of the gravest importance to make to him. She had, she said, committed a crime. Then, instead of proceeding, she had stood up abruptly and said she would call another day. The vicar put her down as being slightly mental, and did not take her self-accusation seriously.

'The very next morning she was found to be missing from her room. A note was left addressed to the coroner. It ran as follows:

'I tried to speak to the vicar yesterday, to confess all, but was not allowed. She would not let me. I can make amends only one way – a life for a life; and my life must go the same way as hers did. I, too, must drown in the deep sea. I believed I was justified. I see now that that was not so. If I desire Amy's forgiveness I must go to her. Let no one be blamed for my death – Mary Barton.

'Her clothes were found lying on the beach in a secluded cove nearby, and it seemed clear that she had undressed there and swum resolutely out to sea where the current was known to be dangerous, sweeping one down the coast.

'The body was not recovered, but after a time leave was given to presume death. She was a rich woman, her estate being proved at a hundred thousand pounds. Since she died intestate it all went to her next of kin – a family of cousins in Australia. The papers made discreet references to the tragedy in the Canary Islands, putting forward the theory that the death of Miss Durrant had unhinged her friend's brain. At the inquest the usual verdict of *Suicide whilst temporarily insane* was returned.

'And so the curtain falls on the tragedy of Amy Durrant and Mary Barton.'

There was a long pause and then Jane Helier gave a great gasp.

'Oh, but you mustn't stop there – just at the most interesting part. Go on.'

'But you see, Miss Helier, this isn't a serial story. This is real life; and real life stops just where it chooses.'

'But I don't want it to,' said Jane. 'I want to know.'

'This is where we use our brains, Miss Helier,' explained Sir Henry. 'Why did Mary Barton kill her companion? That's the problem Dr Lloyd has set us.'

'Oh, well,' said Miss Helier, 'she might have killed her for lots of reasons. I mean – oh, I don't know. She might have got on her nerves, or else she got jealous, although Dr Lloyd doesn't mention any men, but still on the boat out – well, you know what everyone says about boats and sea voyages.'

Miss Helier paused, slightly out of breath, and it was borne in upon her audience that the outside of Jane's charming head was distinctly superior to the inside.

'I would like to have a lot of guesses,' said Mrs Bantry. 'But I suppose I must confine myself to one. Well, I think that Miss Barton's father made all his money out of ruining Amy Durrant's father, so Amy determined to have her revenge. Oh, no, that's the wrong way round. How tiresome! Why does the rich employer kill the humble companion? I've got it. Miss Barton had a young brother who shot himself for love of Amy Durrant. Miss Barton waits her time. Amy comes down in the world. Miss B. engages her as companion and takes her to the Canaries and accomplishes her revenge. How's that?'

'Excellent,' said Sir Henry. 'Only we don't know that Miss Barton ever had a young brother.'

'We deduce that,' said Mrs Bantry. 'Unless she had a young brother there's no motive. So she must have had a young brother. Do you see, Watson?'

'That's all very fine, Dolly,' said her husband. 'But it's only a guess.'

'Of course it is,' said Mrs Bantry. 'That's all we can do – guess. We haven't got any clues. Go on, dear, have a guess yourself.'

'Upon my word, I don't know what to say. But I think there's something in Miss Helier's suggestion that they fell out about a man. Look here, Dolly, it was probably some high church parson. They both embroidered him a cope or something, and he wore the Durrant woman's first. Depend upon it, it was something like that. Look how she went off to a parson at the end. These women all lose their heads over a good-looking clergyman. You hear of it over and over again.'

'I think I must try to make my explanation a little more subtle,' said Sir Henry, 'though I admit it's only a guess. I suggest that Miss Barton was always mentally unhinged. There are more cases like that than you would imagine. Her mania grew stronger and she began to believe it her duty to rid the world of certain persons – possibly what is termed unfortunate females. Nothing much is known about Miss Durrant's past. So very possibly she *had* a past – an "unfortunate" one. Miss Barton learns of this and decides on extermination. Later, the righteousness of her act begins to trouble her and she is overcome by remorse. Her end shows her to be completely unhinged. Now, do say you agree with me, Miss Marple.'

'I'm afraid I don't, Sir Henry,' said Miss Marple, smiling apologetically. 'I think her end shows her to have been a very clever and resourceful woman.'

Jane Helier interrupted with a little scream.

'Oh! I've been so stupid. May I guess again? Of course it must have been that. Blackmail! The companion woman was blackmailing her. Only I don't see why Miss Marple says it was clever of her to kill herself. I can't see that at all.'

'Ah!' said Sir Henry. 'You see, Miss Marple knew a case just like it in St Mary Mead.'

'You always laugh at me, Sir Henry,' said Miss Marple reproachfully. 'I must confess it does remind me, just a little, of old Mrs Trout. She drew the old age pension, you know, for three old women who were dead, in different parishes.'

'It sounds a most complicated and resourceful crime,' said Sir Henry. 'But it doesn't seem to me to throw any light upon our present problem.'

'Of course not,' said Miss Marple. 'It wouldn't – to you. But some of the families were very poor, and the old age pension was a great boon to the children. I know it's difficult for anyone outside to understand. But what I really meant was that the whole thing hinged upon one old woman being so like any other old woman.'

'Eh?' said Sir Henry, mystified.

'I always explain things so badly. What I mean is that when Dr Lloyd described the two ladies first, he didn't know which was which, and I don't suppose anyone else in the hotel did. They would have, of course, after a day or so, but the very next day one of the two was drowned, and if the one who was left said she was Miss Barton, I don't suppose it would ever occur to anyone that she mightn't be.'

'You think – Oh! I see,' said Sir Henry slowly.

'It's the only natural way of thinking of it. Dear Mrs Bantry began that way just now. Why *should* the rich employer kill the humble companion? It's so much more likely to be the other way about. I mean – that's the way things happen.'

'Is it?' said Sir Henry. 'You shock me.'

'But of course,' went on Miss Marple, 'she would have to wear Miss Barton's clothes, and they would probably be a little tight on her, so that her general appearance would look as though she had got a little fatter. That's why I asked that question. A gentleman would be sure to think it was the lady who had got fatter, and not the clothes that had got smaller – though that isn't quite the right way of putting it.'

'But if Amy Durrant killed Miss Barton, what did she gain by it?' asked Mrs Bantry. 'She couldn't keep up the deception for ever.'

'She only kept it up for another month or so,' pointed out Miss Marple. 'And during that time I expect she travelled, keeping away from anyone who might know her. That's what I meant by saying that one lady of a certain age looks so like another. I don't suppose the different photograph on her passport was ever noticed – you know what passports are. And then in March, she went down to this Cornish place and began to act queerly and draw attention to herself so that when people found her clothes on the beach and read her last letter they shouldn't think of the commonsense conclusion.'

'Which was?' asked Sir Henry.

'No *body*,' said Miss Marple firmly. 'That's the thing that would stare you in the face, if there weren't such a lot of red herrings to draw you off the trail – including the suggestion of foul play and remorse. *No body*. That was the real significant fact.'

'Do you mean –' said Mrs Bantry – 'do you mean that there wasn't any remorse? That there wasn't – that she didn't drown herself?'

'Not she!' said Miss Marple. 'It's just Mrs Trout over again. Mrs Trout was very good at red herrings, but she met her match in me. And I can see through your remorse-driven Miss Barton. Drown herself? Went off to Australia, if I'm any good at guessing.'

'You are, Miss Marple,' said Dr Lloyd. 'Undoubtedly you are. Now it again took me quite by surprise. Why, you could have knocked me down with a feather that day in Melbourne.'

'Was that what you spoke of as a final coincidence?'

Dr Lloyd nodded.

'Yes, it was rather rough luck on Miss Barton – or Miss Amy Durrant – whatever you like to call her. I became a ship's doctor for a while, and landing in Melbourne, the first person I saw as I walked down the street was the lady I thought had been drowned in Cornwall. She saw the game was up as far as I was concerned, and she did the bold thing – took me into her confidence. A curious woman, completely lacking, I suppose, in some moral sense. She was the eldest of a family of nine, all wretchedly poor. They had applied once for help to their rich cousin in England and been repulsed, Miss Barton having quarrelled with their father. Money was wanted desperately, for the three youngest children were delicate and wanted expensive medical treatment. Amy Barton then and there seems to have decided on her plan of cold-blooded murder. She set out for England, working her passage over as a children's nurse. She obtained the situation of companion to Miss Barton, calling herself Amy Durrant. She engaged a room and put some furniture into it so as to create more of a personality for herself. The drowning plan was a sudden inspiration. She had been waiting for some opportunity to present itself. Then she staged the final scene of the drama and returned to Australia, and in due time she and her brothers and sisters inherited Miss Barton's money as next of kin.'

'A very bold and perfect crime,' said Sir Henry. 'Almost *the* perfect crime. If it had been Miss Barton who had died in the Canaries, suspicion might attach to Amy Durrant and her connection with the Barton family might have been discovered; but the change of identity and the double crime, as you may call it, effectually did away with that. Yes, almost the perfect crime.'

'What happened to her?' asked Mrs Bantry. 'What did you do in the matter, Dr Lloyd?'

'I was in a very curious position, Mrs Bantry. Of evidence as the law understands it, I still have very little. Also, there were certain signs, plain to me as a medical man, that though strong and vigorous in appearance, the lady was not long for this world. I went home with her and saw the rest of the family – a charming family, devoted to their eldest sister and without an idea in their heads that she might prove to have committed a crime. Why bring sorrow on them when I could prove nothing? The lady's admission to me was unheard by anyone else. I let Nature take its course. Miss Amy Barton died six months after my meeting with her. I have often wondered if she was cheerful and unrepentant up to the last.'

'Surely not,' said Mrs Bantry.

'I expect so,' said Miss Marple. 'Mrs Trout was.'

Jane Helier gave herself a little shake.

'Well,' she said. 'It's very, very thrilling. I don't quite understand now who drowned which. And how does this Mrs Trout come into it?'

'She doesn't, my dear,' said Miss Marple. 'She was only a person – not a very nice person – in the village.'

'Oh!' said Jane. 'In the village. But nothing ever happens in a village, does it?' She sighed. 'I'm sure I shouldn't have any brains at all if I lived in a village.'

The Four Suspects

'The Four Suspects' was first published in the USA as 'Four Suspects' in *Pictorial Review*, January 1930, and then in *Storyteller*, April 1930.

The conversation hovered round undiscovered and unpunished crimes. Everyone in turn vouchsafed their opinion: Colonel Bantry, his plump amiable wife, Jane Helier, Dr Lloyd, and even old Miss Marple. The one person who did not speak was the one best fitted in most people's opinion to do so. Sir Henry Clithering, ex-Commissioner of Scotland Yard, sat silent, twisting his moustache – or rather stroking it – and half smiling, as though at some inward thought that amused him.

'Sir Henry,' said Mrs Bantry at last. 'If you don't say something I shall scream. Are there a lot of crimes that go unpunished, or are there not?'

'You're thinking of newspaper headlines, Mrs Bantry. Scotland Yard at fault again. And a list of unsolved mysteries to follow.'

'Which really, I suppose, form a very small percentage of the whole?' said Dr Lloyd.

'Yes; that is so. The hundreds of crimes that are solved and the perpetrators punished are seldom heralded and sung. But that isn't quite the point at issue, is it? When you talk of *undiscovered* crimes and *unsolved* crimes, you are talking of two different things. In the first category come all the crimes that Scotland Yard never hears about, the crimes that no one even knows have been committed.'

'But I suppose there aren't very many of those?' said Mrs Bantry.

'Aren't there?'

'Sir Henry! You don't mean there *are*?'

'I should think,' said Miss Marple thoughtfully, 'that there must be a very large number.'

The charming old lady, with her old-world unruffled air, made her statement in a tone of the utmost placidity.

'My dear Miss Marple,' said Colonel Bantry.

'Of course,' said Miss Marple, 'a lot of people are stupid. And stupid people get found out, whatever they do. But there are quite a number of people who aren't stupid, and one shudders to think of what they might accomplish unless they had very strongly rooted principles.'

'Yes,' said Sir Henry, 'there are a lot of people who aren't stupid. How often does some crime come to light simply by reason of a bit of unmitigated bungling, and each time one asks oneself the question: If this hadn't been bungled, would anyone ever have known?'

'But that's very serious, Clithering,' said Colonel Bantry. 'Very serious, indeed.'

'Is it?'

'What do you mean! It is! Of course it's serious.'

'You say crime goes unpunished; but does it? Unpunished by the law perhaps; but cause and effect works outside the law. To say that every crime brings its own punishment is by way of being a platitude, and yet in my opinion nothing can be truer.'

'Perhaps, perhaps,' said Colonel Bantry. 'But that doesn't alter the seriousness – the – er – seriousness –' He paused, rather at a loss.

Sir Henry Clithering smiled.

'Ninety-nine people out of a hundred are doubtless of your way of thinking,' he said. 'But you know, it isn't really guilt that is important – it's innocence. That's the thing that nobody will realize.'

'I don't understand,' said Jane Helier.

'I do,' said Miss Marple. 'When Mrs Trent found half a crown missing from her bag, the person it affected most was the daily woman, Mrs Arthur. Of course the Trents thought it was her, but being kindly people and knowing she had a large family and a husband who drinks, well – they naturally didn't want to go to extremes. But they felt differently towards her, and they didn't leave her in charge of the house when they went away, which made a great difference to her; and other people began to get a feeling about her too. And then it suddenly came out that it was the governess. Mrs Trent saw her through a door reflected in a mirror. The purest chance – though I prefer to call it Providence. And that, I think, is what Sir Henry means. Most people would be only interested in who took the money, and it turned out to be the most unlikely person – just like in detective stories! But the real person it was life and death to was poor Mrs Arthur, who had done nothing. That's what you mean, isn't it, Sir Henry?'

'Yes, Miss Marple, you've hit off my meaning exactly. Your charwoman person was lucky in the instance you relate. Her innocence was shown. But some people may go through a lifetime crushed by the weight of a suspicion that is really unjustified.'

'Are you thinking of some particular instance, Sir Henry?' asked Mrs Bantry shrewdly.

'As a matter of fact, Mrs Bantry, I am. A very curious case. A case where we believe murder to have been committed, but with no possible chance of ever proving it.'

'Poison, I suppose,' breathed Jane. 'Something untraceable.'

Dr Lloyd moved restlessly and Sir Henry shook his head.

'No, dear lady. *Not* the secret arrow poison of the South American Indians! I wish it *were* something of that kind. We have to deal with something much more prosaic – so prosaic, in fact, that there is no hope of bringing the deed home to its perpetrator. An old gentleman who fell downstairs and broke his neck; one of those regrettable accidents which happen every day.'

'But what happened really?'

'Who can say?' Sir Henry shrugged his shoulders. 'A push from behind? A piece of cotton or string tied across the top of the stairs and carefully removed afterwards? That we shall never know.'

'But you do think that it – well, wasn't an accident? Now why?' asked the doctor.

'That's rather a long story, but – well, yes, we're pretty sure. As I said there's no chance of being able to bring the deed home to anyone – the evidence would be too flimsy. But there's the other aspect of the case – the one I was speaking about. You see, there were four people who might have done the trick. One's guilty; *but the other three are innocent*. And unless the truth is found out, those three are going to remain under the terrible shadow of doubt.'

'I think,' said Mrs Bantry, 'that you'd better tell us your long story.'

'I needn't make it so very long after all,' said Sir Henry. 'I can at any rate condense the beginning. That deals with a German secret society – the Schwartze Hand – something after the lines of the Camorra or what is most people's idea of the Camorra. A scheme of blackmail and terrorization. The thing started quite suddenly after the War, and spread to an amazing extent. Numberless people were victimized by it. The authorities were not successful in coping with it, for its secrets were jealously guarded, and it was almost impossible to find anyone who could be induced to betray them.

'Nothing much was ever known about it in England, but in Germany it was having a most paralysing effect. It was finally broken up and dispersed through the efforts of one man, a Dr Rosen, who had at one time been very prominent in Secret Service work. He became a member, penetrated its inmost circle, and was, as I say, instrumental in bringing about its downfall.

'But he was, in consequence, a marked man, and it was deemed wise that he should leave Germany – at any rate for a time. He came to England, and we had letters about him from the police in Berlin. He came and had a personal interview with me. His point of view was both dispassionate and resigned. He had no doubts of what the future held for him.

'"They will get me, Sir Henry," he said. "Not a doubt of it." He was a big man with a fine head, and a very deep voice, with only a slight guttural intonation to tell of his nationality. "That is a foregone conclusion. It does not matter, I am prepared. I faced the risk when I undertook this business. I have done what I set out to do. The organization can never be got together again. But there are many members of it at liberty, and they will take the only revenge they can – my life. It is simply a question of time; but I am anxious that that time should be as long as possible. You see, I am collecting and editing some very interesting material – the result of my life's work. I should like, if possible, to be able to complete my task."

'He spoke very simply, with a certain grandeur which I could not but admire. I told him we would take all precautions, but he waved my words aside.

'"Some day, sooner or later, they will get me," he repeated. "When that day comes, do not distress yourself. You will, I have no doubt, have done all that is possible."

'He then proceeded to outline his plans which were simple enough. He proposed to take a small cottage in the country where he could live quietly and go on with his work. In the end he selected a village in Somerset – King's Gnaton, which was seven miles from a railway station, and singularly untouched by civilization. He bought a very charming cottage, had various improvements and alterations made, and settled down there most contentedly. His household consisted of his niece, Greta, a secretary, an old German servant who had served him faithfully for nearly forty years, and an outside handyman and gardener who was a native of King's Gnaton.'

'The four suspects,' said Dr Lloyd softly.

'Exactly. The four suspects. There is not much more to tell. Life went on peacefully at King's Gnaton for five months and then the blow fell. Dr Rosen fell down the stairs one morning and was found dead about half an hour later. At the time the accident must have taken place, Gertrud was in her kitchen with the door closed and heard nothing – so *she* says. Fräulein Greta was in the garden planting some bulbs – again, so *she* says. The gardener, Dobbs, was in the small potting shed having his elevenses – so *he* says; and the secretary was out for a walk, and once more there is only his own word for it. No one has an alibi – no one can corroborate anyone else's story. But one thing *is* certain. No one from outside could have done it, for a stranger in the little village of King's Gnaton would be noticed without fail. Both the back and the front doors were locked, each member of the household having their own key. So you see it narrows down to those four. And yet each one seems to be above suspicion. Greta, his own brother's child. Gertrud, with forty years of faithful service. Dobbs, who has never been out of King's Gnaton. And Charles Templeton, the secretary –'

'Yes,' said Colonel Bantry, 'what about him? He seems the suspicious person to my mind. What do you know about him?'

'It is what I knew about him that put him completely out of court – at any rate at the time,' said Sir Henry gravely. 'You see, Charles Templeton was one of my own men.'

'Oh!' said Colonel Bantry, considerably taken aback.

'Yes. I wanted to have someone on the spot, and at the same time I didn't want to cause talk in the village. Rosen really needed a secretary. I put Templeton on the job. He's a gentleman, he speaks German fluently, and he's altogether a very able fellow.'

'But, then, which do you suspect?' asked Mrs Bantry in a bewildered tone. 'They all seem so – well, impossible.'

'Yes, so it appears. But you can look at the thing from another angle. Fräulein Greta was his niece and a very lovely girl, but the War has shown us time and again that brother can turn against sister, or father against son and so on, and the loveliest and gentlest of young girls did some of the most amazing things. The same thing applies to Gertrud, and who knows what other forces might be at work in her case. A quarrel, perhaps, with her master, a growing resentment all the more lasting because of the long faithful years behind her. Elderly women of that class can be amazingly bitter sometimes. And Dobbs? Was he right outside it because he had no connection with the family? Money will do much. In some way Dobbs might have been approached and bought.

'For one thing seems certain: Some message or some order must have come from outside. Otherwise why five months' immunity? No, the agents of the society must have been at work. Not yet sure of Rosen's perfidy, they delayed till the betrayal had been traced to him beyond any possible doubt. And then, all doubts set aside, they must have sent their message to the spy within the gates – the message that said, "Kill".'

'How nasty!' said Jane Helier, and shuddered.

'But how did the message come? That was the point I tried to elucidate – the one hope of solving my problem. One of those four people must have been approached or communicated with in some way. There would be no delay – I knew that – as soon as the command came, it would be carried out. That was a peculiarity of the Schwartze Hand.

'I went into the question, went into it in a way that will probably strike you as being ridiculously meticulous. Who had come to the cottage that morning? I eliminated nobody. Here is the list.'

He took an envelope from his pocket and selected a paper from its contents.

'*The butcher*, bringing some neck of mutton. Investigated and found correct.

'*The grocer's assistant*, bringing a packet of cornflour, two pounds of sugar, a pound of butter, and a pound of coffee. Also investigated and found correct.

'*The postman*, bringing two circulars for Fräulein Rosen, a local letter for Gertrud, three letters for Dr Rosen, one with a foreign stamp and two letters for Mr Templeton, one also with a foreign stamp.'

Sir Henry paused and then took a sheaf of documents from the envelope.

'It may interest you to see these for yourself. They were handed me by the various people concerned, or collected from the waste-paper basket. I need hardly say they've been tested by experts for invisible ink, etc. No excitement of that kind is possible.'

Everyone crowded round to look. The catalogues were respectively from a nurseryman and from a prominent London fur establishment. The two bills addressed to Dr Rosen were a local one for seeds for the garden and one from a London stationery firm. The letter addressed to him ran as follows:

My Dear Rosen – Just back from Dr Helmuth Spath's. I saw Edgar Jackson the other day. He and Amos Perry have just come back from Tsingtau. In all Honesty I can't say I envy them the trip. Let me have news of you soon. As I said before: Beware of a certain person. You know who I mean, though you don't agree. –
Yours, Georgine.

'Mr Templeton's mail consisted of this bill, which as you see, is an account rendered from his tailor, and a letter from a friend in Germany,' went on Sir Henry. 'The latter, unfortunately, he tore up whilst out on his walk. Finally we have the letter received by Gertrud.'

Dear Mrs Swartz, – We're hoping as how you be able to come the social on friday evening, the vicar says has he hopes you will – one and all being welcome. The resipy for the ham was very good, and I thanks you

*for it. Hoping as this finds you well and that we shall see you friday I
remain. – Yours faithfully, Emma Greene.*

Dr Lloyd smiled a little over this and so did Mrs Bantry.

'I think the last letter can be put out of court,' said Dr Lloyd.

'I thought the same,' said Sir Henry; 'but I took the precaution of veri-
fying that there was a Mrs Greene and a Church Social. One can't be
too careful, you know.'

'That's what our friend Miss Marple always says,' said Dr Lloyd,
smiling. 'You're lost in a daydream, Miss Marple. What are you thinking
out?'

Miss Marple gave a start.

'So stupid of me,' she said. 'I was just wondering why the word
Honesty in Dr Rosen's letter was spelt with a capital H.'

Mrs Bantry picked it up.

'So it is,' she said. '*Oh!*'

'Yes, dear,' said Miss Marple. 'I thought you'd notice!'

'There's a definite warning in that letter,' said Colonel Bantry. 'That's
the first thing caught my attention. I notice more than you'd think. Yes,
a definite warning – against whom?'

'There's rather a curious point about that letter,' said Sir Henry.
'According to Templeton, Dr Rosen opened the letter at breakfast and
tossed it across to him saying he didn't know who the fellow was from
Adam.'

'But it wasn't a fellow,' said Jane Helier. 'It was signed "Georgina".'

'It's difficult to say which it is,' said Dr Lloyd. 'It might be Georgey;
but it certainly looks more like Georgina. Only it strikes me that the
writing is a man's.'

'You know, that's interesting,' said Colonel Bantry. 'His tossing it across
the table like that and pretending he knew nothing about it. Wanted to
watch somebody's face. Whose face – the girl's? or the man's?'

'Or even the cook's?' suggested Mrs Bantry. 'She might have been in
the room bringing in the breakfast. But what I don't see is . . . it's most
peculiar –'

She frowned over the letter. Miss Marple drew closer to her. Miss
Marple's finger went out and touched the sheet of paper. They murmured
together.

'But why did the secretary tear up the other letter?' asked Jane Helier
suddenly. 'It seems – oh! I don't know – it seems queer. Why should he
have letters from Germany? Although, of course, if he's above suspicion,
as you say –'

'But Sir Henry didn't say that,' said Miss Marple quickly, looking up from her murmured conference with Mrs Bantry. 'He said *four* suspects. So that shows that he includes Mr Templeton. I'm right, am I not, Sir Henry?'

'Yes, Miss Marple. I have learned one thing through bitter experience. Never say to yourself that *anyone* is above suspicion. I gave you reasons just now why three of these people might after all be guilty, unlikely as it seemed. I did not at that time apply the same process to Charles Templeton. But I came to it at last through pursuing the rule I have just mentioned. And I was forced to recognize this: That every army and every navy and every police force has a certain number of traitors within its ranks, much as we hate to admit the idea. And I examined dispassionately the case against Charles Templeton.

'I asked myself very much the same questions as Miss Helier has just asked. Why should he, alone of all the house, not be able to produce the letter he had received – a letter, moreover, with a German stamp on it. Why should he have letters from Germany?

'The last question was an innocent one, and I actually put it to him. His reply came simply enough. His mother's sister was married to a German. The letter had been from a German girl cousin. So I learned something I did not know before – that Charles Templeton had relations with people in Germany. And that put him definitely on the list of suspects – very much so. He is my own man – a lad I have always liked and trusted; but in common justice and fairness I must admit that he heads that list.

'But there it is – I do not know! I do not *know* . . . And in all probability I never shall know. It is not a question of punishing a murderer. It is a question that to me seems a hundred times more important. It is the blighting, perhaps, of an honourable man's whole career . . . because of suspicion – a suspicion that I dare not disregard.'

Miss Marple coughed and said gently:

'Then, Sir Henry, if I understand you rightly, it is this young Mr Templeton only who is so much on your mind?'

'Yes, in a sense. It should, in theory, be the same for all four, but that is not actually the case. Dobbs, for instance – suspicion may attach to him in my mind, but it will not actually affect his career. Nobody in the village has ever had any idea that old Dr Rosen's death was anything but an accident. Gertrud is slightly more affected. It must make, for instance, a difference in Fräulein Rosen's attitude toward her. But that, possibly, is not of great importance to her.

'As for Greta Rosen – well, here we come to the crux of the matter. Greta is a very pretty girl and Charles Templeton is a good-looking young man, and for five months they were thrown together with no outer distractions. The inevitable happened. They fell in love with each other – even if they did not come to the point of admitting the fact in words.

'And then the catastrophe happens. It is three months ago now and a day or two after I returned, Greta Rosen came to see me. She had sold the cottage and was returning to Germany, having finally settled up her uncle's affairs. She came to me personally, although she knew I had retired, because it was really about a personal matter she wanted to see me. She beat about the bush a little, but at last it all came out. What did I think? That letter with the German stamp – she had worried about it and worried about it – the one Charles had torn up. Was it all right? Surely it *must* be all right. Of course she believed his story, but – oh! if she only *knew*! If she knew – for certain.

'You see? The same feeling: the wish to trust – but the horrible lurking suspicion, thrust resolutely to the back of the mind, but persisting nevertheless. I spoke to her with absolute frankness, and asked her to do the same. I asked her whether she had been on the point of caring for Charles, and he for her.

'"I think so," she said. "Oh, yes, I know it was so. We were so happy. Every day passed so contentedly. We knew – we both knew. There was no hurry – there was all the time in the world. Some day he would tell me he loved me, and I should tell him that I too – Ah! But you can guess! And now it is all changed. A black cloud has come between us – we are constrained, when we meet we do not know what to say. It is, perhaps, the same with him as with me . . . We are each saying to ourselves, 'If I were *sure*!' That is why, Sir Henry, I beg of you to say to me, 'You may be sure, whoever killed your uncle, it was not Charles Templeton!' Say it to me! Oh, say it to me! I beg – I beg!"

'And, damn it all,' said Sir Henry, bringing down his fist with a bang on the table, 'I couldn't say it to her. They'll drift farther and farther apart, those two – with suspicion like a ghost between them – a ghost that can't be laid.'

He leant back in his chair, his face looked tired and grey. He shook his head once or twice despondently.

'And there's nothing more can be done, unless –' He sat up straight again and a tiny whimsical smile crossed his face – 'unless Miss Marple can help us. Can't you, Miss Marple? I've a feeling that letter might be in your line, you know. The one about the Church Social. Doesn't it remind you of something or someone that makes everything perfectly plain? Can't you do something to help two helpless young people who want to be happy?'

Behind the whimsicality there was something earnest in his appeal. He had come to think very highly of the mental powers of this frail old-fashioned maiden lady. He looked across at her with something very like hope in his eyes.

Miss Marple coughed and smoothed her lace.

'It does remind me a little of Annie Poultny,' she admitted. 'Of course the letter is perfectly plain – both to Mrs Bantry and myself. I don't mean the Church Social letter, but the other one. You living so much in London and not being a gardener, Sir Henry, would not have been likely to notice.'

'Eh?' said Sir Henry. 'Notice what?'

Mrs Bantry reached out a hand and selected a catalogue. She opened it and read aloud with gusto:

'Dr Helmuth Spath. Pure lilac, a wonderfully fine flower, carried on exceptionally long and stiff stem. Splendid for cutting and garden decoration. A novelty of striking beauty.

'Edgar Jackson. Beautifully shaped chrysanthemum-like flower of a distinct brick-red colour.

'Amos Perry. Brilliant red, highly decorative.

'Tsingtau. Brilliant orange-red, showy garden plant and lasting cut flower.

'Honesty –'

'With a capital H, you remember,' murmured Miss Marple.

'Honesty. Rose and white shades, enormous perfect shaped flower.'

Mrs Bantry flung down the catalogue, and said with immense explosive force:

'Dahlias!'

'And their initial letters spell "death",' explained Miss Marple.

'But the letter came to Dr Rosen himself,' objected Sir Henry.

'That was the clever part of it,' said Miss Marple. 'That and the warning in it. What would he do, getting a letter from someone he didn't know, full of names he didn't know. Why, of course, toss it over to his secretary.'

'Then, after all –'

'Oh, no!' said Miss Marple. 'Not the secretary. Why, that's what makes it so perfectly clear that it wasn't him. He'd never have let that letter be found if so. And equally he'd never have destroyed a letter to himself with a German stamp on it. Really, his innocence is – if you'll allow me to use the word – just shining.'

'Then who –'

'Well, it seems almost certain – as certain as anything can be in this world. There was another person at the breakfast table, and she would – quite naturally under the circumstances – put out her hand for the letter and read it. And that would be that. You remember that she got a gardening catalogue by the same post –'

'Greta Rosen,' said Sir Henry, slowly. 'Then her visit to me –'

'Gentlemen never see through these things,' said Miss Marple. 'And I'm afraid they often think we old women are – well, cats, to see things the way we do. But there it is. One does know a great deal about one's own sex, unfortunately. I've no doubt there was a barrier between them. The young man felt a sudden inexplicable repulsion. He suspected, purely through instinct, and couldn't hide the suspicion. And I really think that the girl's visit to you was just pure *spite*. She was safe enough really; but she just went out of her way to fix your suspicions definitely on poor Mr Templeton. You weren't nearly so sure about him until after her visit.'

'I'm sure it was nothing that she said –' began Sir Henry.

'Gentlemen,' said Miss Marple calmly, 'never see through these things.'

'And that girl –' he stopped. 'She commits a cold-blooded murder and gets off scot-free!'

'Oh! no, Sir Henry,' said Miss Marple. 'Not scot-free. Neither you nor I believe that. Remember what you said not long ago. No. Greta Rosen will not escape punishment. To begin with, she must be in with a very queer set of people – blackmailers and terrorists – associates who will do her no good, and will probably bring her to a miserable end. As you say, one mustn't waste thoughts on the guilty – it's the innocent who matter. Mr Templeton, who I dare say will marry that German cousin, his tearing up her letter looks – well, it looks *suspicious* – using the word in quite a different sense from the one we've been using all the evening. A little as though he were afraid of the other girl noticing or asking to see it? Yes, I think there must have been some little romance there. And then there's Dobbs – though, as you say, I dare say it won't matter much to him. His elevenses are probably all he thinks about. And then there's that poor old Gertrud – the one who reminded me of Annie Poultny. Poor Annie Poultny. Fifty years' faithful service and suspected of making away with Miss Lamb's will, though nothing could be proved. Almost broke the poor creature's faithful heart; and then after she was dead it came to light in the secret drawer of the tea caddy where old Miss Lamb had put it herself for safety. But too late then for poor Annie.

'That's what worries me so about that poor old German woman. When one is old, one becomes embittered very easily. I felt much more sorry for her than for Mr Templeton, who is young and good-looking and evidently a favourite with the ladies. You will write to her, won't you, Sir Henry, and just tell her that her innocence is established beyond doubt? Her dear old master dead, and she no doubt brooding and feeling herself suspected of . . . Oh! It won't bear thinking about!'

'I will write, Miss Marple,' said Sir Henry. He looked at her curiously.

'You know, I shall never quite understand you. Your outlook is always a different one from what I expect.'

'My outlook, I am afraid, is a very petty one,' said Miss Marple humbly. 'I hardly ever go out of St Mary Mead.'

'And yet you have solved what may be called an International mystery,' said Sir Henry. 'For you *have* solved it. I am convinced of that.'

Miss Marple blushed, then bridled a little.

'I was, I think, well educated for the standard of my day. My sister and I had a German governess – a Fräulein. A very sentimental creature. She taught us the language of flowers – a forgotten study nowadays, but most charming. A yellow tulip, for instance, means Hopeless Love, whilst a China Aster means I die of Jealousy at your feet. That letter was signed Georgine, which I seem to remember is Dahlia in German, and that of course made the whole thing perfectly clear. I wish I could remember the meaning of Dahlia, but alas, that eludes me. My memory is not what it was.'

'At any rate it didn't mean death.'

'No, indeed. Horrible, is it not? There are very sad things in the world.'

'There are,' said Mrs Bantry with a sigh. 'It's lucky one has flowers and one's friends.'

'She puts us last, you observe,' said Dr Lloyd.

'A man used to send me purple orchids every night to the theatre,' said Jane dreamily.

'"I await your favours," – that's what that means,' said Miss Marple brightly.

Sir Henry gave a peculiar sort of cough and turned his head away.

Miss Marple gave a sudden exclamation.

'I've remembered. Dahlias mean "Treachery and Misrepresentation."'

'Wonderful,' said Sir Henry. 'Absolutely wonderful.'

And he sighed.

A Christmas Tragedy

'A Christmas Tragedy' was first published as
'The Hat and the Alibi' in *Storyteller*, January 1930.

'I have a complaint to make,' said Sir Henry Clithering. His eyes twinkled gently as he looked round at the assembled company. Colonel Bantry, his legs stretched out, was frowning at the mantelpiece as though it were a delinquent soldier on parade, his wife was surreptitiously glancing at a catalogue of bulbs which had come by the late post, Dr Lloyd was gazing with frank admiration at Jane Helier, and that beautiful young actress herself was thoughtfully regarding her pink polished nails. Only that elderly, spinster lady, Miss Marple, was sitting bolt upright, and her faded blue eyes met Sir Henry's with an answering twinkle.

'A complaint?' she murmured.

'A very serious complaint. We are a company of six, three representatives of each sex, and I protest on behalf of the downtrodden males. We have had three stories told tonight – and told by the three men! I protest that the ladies have not done their fair share.'

'Oh!' said Mrs Bantry with indignation. 'I'm sure we have. We've listened with the most intelligent appreciation. We've displayed the true womanly attitude – not wishing to thrust ourselves in the limelight!'

'It's an excellent excuse,' said Sir Henry; 'but it won't do. And there's a very good precedent in the Arabian Nights! So, forward, Scheherazade.'

'Meaning me?' said Mrs Bantry. 'But I don't know anything to tell. I've never been surrounded by blood or mystery.'

'I don't absolutely insist upon blood,' said Sir Henry. 'But I'm sure one of you three ladies has got a pet mystery. Come now, Miss Marple – the "Curious Coincidence of the Charwoman" or the "Mystery of the Mothers' Meeting". Don't disappoint me in St Mary Mead.'

Miss Marple shook her head.

'Nothing that would interest you, Sir Henry. We have our little mysteries, of course – there was that gill of picked shrimps that disappeared so incomprehensibly; but that wouldn't interest you because it all turned out to be so trivial, though throwing a considerable light on human nature.'

'You have taught me to dote on human nature,' said Sir Henry solemnly.

'What about you, Miss Helier?' asked Colonel Bantry. 'You must have had some interesting experiences.'

'Yes, indeed,' said Dr Lloyd.

'Me?' said Jane. 'You mean – you want me to tell you something that happened to me?'

'Or to one of your friends,' amended Sir Henry.

'Oh!' said Jane vaguely. 'I don't think anything has ever happened to me – I mean not that kind of thing. Flowers, of course, and queer messages – but that's just men, isn't it? I don't think' – she paused and appeared lost in thought.

'I see we shall have to have that epic of the shrimps,' said Sir Henry. 'Now then, Miss Marple.'

'You're so fond of your joke, Sir Henry. The shrimps are only nonsense; but now I come to think of it, I *do* remember one incident – at least not exactly an incident, something very much more serious – a tragedy. And I was, in a way, mixed up in it; and for what I did, I have never had any regrets – no, no regrets at all. But it didn't happen in St Mary Mead.'

'That disappoints me,' said Sir Henry. 'But I will endeavour to bear up. I knew we should not rely upon you in vain.'

He settled himself in the attitude of a listener. Miss Marple grew slightly pink.

'I hope I shall be able to tell it properly,' she said anxiously. 'I fear I am very inclined to become *rambling*. One wanders from the point – altogether without knowing that one is doing so. And it is so hard to remember each fact in its proper order. You must all bear with me if I tell my story badly. It happened a very long time ago now.

'As I say, it was not connected with St Mary Mead. As a matter of fact, it had to do with a Hydro –'

'Do you mean a seaplane?' asked Jane with wide eyes.

'You wouldn't know, dear,' said Mrs Bantry, and explained. Her husband added his quota:

'Beastly places – absolutely beastly! Got to get up early and drink filthy-tasting water. Lot of old women sitting about. Ill-natured tittle tattle. God, when I think –'

'Now, Arthur,' said Mrs Bantry placidly. 'You know it did you all the good in the world.'

'Lot of old women sitting round talking scandal,' grunted Colonel Bantry.

'That I am afraid is true,' said Miss Marple. 'I myself –'

'My dear Miss Marple,' cried the Colonel, horrified. 'I didn't mean for one moment –'

With pink cheeks and a little gesture of the hand, Miss Marple stopped him.

'But it is *true*, Colonel Bantry. Only I should just like to say this. Let me recollect my thoughts. Yes. Talking scandal, as you say – well, it *is* done a good deal. And people are very down on it – especially young people. My nephew, who writes books – and very clever ones, I believe – has said some most *scathing* things about taking people's characters away without any kind of proof – and how wicked it is, and all that. But what I say is that none of these young people ever stop to *think*. They really don't examine the facts. Surely the whole crux of the matter is this: *How often is tittle tattle*, as you call it, *true*! And I think if, as I say, they really examined the facts they would find that it was true nine times out of ten! That's really just what makes people so annoyed about it.'

'The inspired guess,' said Sir Henry.

'No, not that, not that at all! It's really a matter of practice and experience. An Egyptologist, so I've heard, if you show him one of those curious little beetles, can tell you by the look and the feel of the thing what date bc it is, or if it's a Birmingham imitation. And he can't always give a definite rule for doing so. He just *knows*. His life has been spent handling such things.

'And that's what I'm trying to say (very badly, I know). What my nephew calls "superfluous women" have a lot of time on their hands, and their chief interest is usually *people*. And so, you see, they get to be what one might call *experts*. Now young people nowadays – they talk very freely about things that weren't mentioned in my young days, but on the other hand their minds are terribly innocent. They believe in everyone and everything. And if one tries to warn them, ever so gently, they tell one that one has a Victorian mind – and that, they say, is like a *sink*.'

'After all,' said Sir Henry, 'what is wrong with a *sink*?'

'Exactly,' said Miss Marple eagerly. 'It's the most necessary thing in any house; but, of course, not romantic. Now I must confess that I have my *feelings*, like everyone else, and I have sometimes been cruelly hurt by unthinking remarks. I know gentlemen are not interested in domestic matters, but I must just mention my maid Ethel – a very good-looking girl and obliging in every way. Now I realized as soon as I saw her that she was the same type as Annie Webb and poor Mrs Bruitt's girl. If the opportunity arose *mine* and *thine* would mean nothing to her. So I let her go at the month and I gave her a written reference saying she was honest and sober, but privately I warned old Mrs Edwards against taking her; and my nephew, Raymond, was exceedingly angry and said he had never heard of anything so wicked – yes, *wicked*. Well, she went to Lady Ashton, whom I felt no obligation to warn – and what happened? All the lace cut off her underclothes and two diamond brooches taken – and the girl departed in the middle of the night and never heard of since!'

Miss Marple paused, drew a long breath, and then went on.

'You'll be saying this has nothing to do with what went on at Keston Spa Hydro – but it has in a way. It explains why I felt no doubt in my mind the first moment I saw the Sanders together that he meant to do away with her.'

'Eh?' said Sir Henry, leaning forward.

Miss Marple turned a placid face to him.

'As I say, Sir Henry, I felt no doubt in my own mind. Mr Sanders was a big, good-looking, florid-faced man, very hearty in his manner and popular with all. And nobody could have been pleasanter to his wife than he was. But I knew! He meant to make away with her.'

'My dear Miss Marple –'

'Yes, I know. That's what my nephew, Raymond West, would say. He'd tell me I hadn't a shadow of proof. But I remember Walter Hones, who kept the Green Man. Walking home with his wife one night she fell into the river – and *he* collected the insurance money! And one or two other people that are walking about scot-free to this day – one indeed in our own class of life. Went to Switzerland for a summer holiday climbing with his wife. I warned her not to go – the poor dear didn't get angry with me as she might have done – she only laughed. It seemed to her funny that a queer old thing like me should say such things about her Harry. Well, well, there was an accident – and Harry is married to another woman now. But what could I *do*? I *knew*, but there was no proof.'

'Oh! Miss Marple,' cried Mrs Bantry. 'You don't really mean –'

'My dear, these things are very common – very common indeed. And gentlemen are especially tempted, being so much the stronger. So easy if a thing looks like an accident. As I say, I knew at once with the Sanders. It was on a tram. It was full inside and I had had to go on top. We all three got up to get off and Mr Sanders lost his balance and fell right against his wife, sending her headfirst down the stairs. Fortunately the conductor was a very strong young man and caught her.'

'But surely that must have been an accident.'

'Of course it was an accident – nothing could have looked more acci-dental! But Mr Sanders had been in the Merchant Service, so he told me, and a man who can keep his balance on a nasty tilting boat doesn't lose it on top of a tram if an old woman like me doesn't. Don't tell me!'

'At any rate we can take it that you made up your mind, Miss Marple,' said Sir Henry. 'Made it up then and there.'

The old lady nodded.

'I was sure enough, and another incident in crossing the street not long afterwards made me surer still. Now I ask you, what could I do, Sir Henry? Here was a nice contented happy little married woman shortly going to be murdered.'

'My dear lady, you take my breath away.'

'That's because, like most people nowadays, you won't face facts. You prefer to think such a thing couldn't be. But it was so, and I knew it. But one is so sadly handicapped! I couldn't, for instance, go to the police. And to warn the young woman would, I could see, be useless. She was devoted to the man. I just made it my business to find out as much as I could about them. One has a lot of opportunities doing one's needlework round the fire. Mrs Sanders (Gladys, her name was) was only too willing to talk. It seems they had not been married very long. Her husband had some property that was coming to him, but for the moment they were very badly off. In fact, they were living on her little income. One has heard that tale before. She bemoaned the fact that she could not touch the capital. It seems that somebody had had some sense somewhere! But the money was hers to will away – I found that out. And she and her husband had made wills in favour of each other directly after their marriage. Very touching. Of course, when Jack's affairs came right – That was the burden all day long, and in the meantime they were very hard up indeed – actually had a room on the top floor, all among the servants – and so dangerous in case of fire, though, as it happened, there was a fire escape just outside their window. I inquired carefully if there was a balcony – dangerous things, balconies. One push – you know!

'I made her promise not to go out on the balcony; I said I'd had a dream. That impressed her – one can do a lot with superstition some-times. She was a fair girl, rather washed-out complexion, and an untidy roll of hair on her neck. Very credulous. She repeated what I had said to her husband, and I noticed him looking at me in a curious way once or twice. *He* wasn't credulous; and he knew I'd been on that tram.

'But I was very worried – terribly worried – because I couldn't see how to circumvent him. I could prevent anything happening at the Hydro, just by saying a few words to show him I suspected. But that only meant his putting off his plan till later. No, I began to believe that the only policy was a bold one – somehow or other to lay a trap for him. If I could induce him to attempt her life in a way of my own choosing – well, then he would be unmasked, and she would be forced to face the truth however much of a shock it was to her.'

'You take my breath away,' said Dr Lloyd. 'What conceivable plan could you adopt?'

'I'd have found one – never fear,' said Miss Marple. 'But the man was too clever for me. He didn't wait. He thought I might suspect, and so he struck before I could be sure. He knew I would suspect an accident. So he made it murder.'

A little gasp went round the circle. Miss Marple nodded and set her lips grimly together.

'I'm afraid I've put that rather abruptly. I must try and tell you exactly what occurred. I've always felt very bitterly about it – it seems to me that I ought, somehow, to have prevented it. But doubtless Providence knew best. I did what I could at all events.

'There was what I can only describe as a curiously eerie feeling in the air. There seemed to be something weighing on us all. A feeling of misfortune. To begin with, there was George, the hall porter. Had been there for years and knew everybody. Bronchitis and pneumonia, and passed away on the fourth day. Terribly sad. A real blow to everybody. And four days before Christmas too. And then one of the housemaids – such a nice girl – a septic finger, actually died in twenty-four hours.

'I was in the drawing-room with Miss Trollope and old Mrs Carpenter, and Mrs Carpenter was being positively ghoulish – relishing it all, you know.

'"Mark my words," she said. "*This isn't the end.* You know the saying? *Never two without three.* I've proved it true time and again. There'll be another death. Not a doubt of it. And we shan't have long to wait. *Never two without three.*"

'As she said the last words, nodding her head and clicking her knitting needles, I just chanced to look up and there was Mr Sanders standing in the doorway. Just for a minute he was off guard, and I saw the look in his face as plain as plain. I shall believe till my dying day that it was that ghoulish Mrs Carpenter's words that put the whole thing into his head. I saw his mind working.

'He came forward into the room smiling in his genial way.

'"Any Christmas shopping I can do for you ladies?" he asked. "I'm going down to Keston presently."

'He stayed a minute or two, laughing and talking, and then went out. As I tell you, I was troubled, and I said straight away:

'"Where's Mrs Sanders? Does anyone know?"

'Mrs Trollope said she'd gone out to some friends of hers, the Mortimers, to play bridge, and that eased my mind for the moment. But

I was still very worried and most uncertain as to what to do. About half an hour later I went up to my room. I met Dr Coles, my doctor, there, coming down the stairs as I was going up, and as I happened to want to consult him about my rheumatism, I took him into my room with me then and there. He mentioned to me then (in confidence, he said) about the death of the poor girl Mary. The manager didn't want the news to get about, he said, so would I keep it to myself. Of course I didn't tell him that we'd all been discussing nothing else for the last hour – ever since the poor girl breathed her last. These things are always known at once, and a man of his experience should know that well enough; but Dr Coles always was a simple unsuspicious fellow who believed what he wanted to believe and that's just what alarmed me a minute later. He said as he was leaving that Sanders had asked him to have a look at his wife. It seemed she'd been seedy of late – indigestion, etc.

'*Now that very self-same day Gladys Sanders had said to me that she'd got a wonderful digestion and was thankful for it.*

'You see? All my suspicions of that man came back a hundredfold. He was preparing the way – for what? Dr Coles left before I could make up my mind whether to speak to him or not – though really if I had spoken I shouldn't have known what to say. As I came out of my room, the man himself – Sanders – came down the stairs from the floor above. He was dressed to go out and he asked me again if he could do anything for me in the town. It was all I could do to be civil to the man! I went straight into the lounge and ordered tea. It was just on half past five, I remember.

'Now I'm very anxious to put clearly what happened next. I was still in the lounge at a quarter to seven when Mr Sanders came in. There were two gentlemen with him and all three of them were inclined to be a little on the lively side. Mr Sanders left his two friends and came right over to where I was sitting with Miss Trollope. He explained that he wanted our advice about a Christmas present he was giving his wife. It was an evening bag.

'"And you see, ladies," he said. "I'm only a rough sailorman. What do I know about such things? I've had three sent to me on approval and I want an expert opinion on them."

'We said, of course, that we would be delighted to help him, and he asked if we'd mind coming upstairs, as his wife might come in any minute if he brought the things down. So we went up with him. I shall never forget what happened next – I can feel my little fingers tingling now.

'Mr Sanders opened the door of the bedroom and switched on the light. I don't know which of us saw it first . . .

'*Mrs Sanders was lying on the floor, face downwards – dead.*

'I got to her first. I knelt down and took her hand and felt for the pulse, but it was useless, the arm itself was cold and stiff. Just by her head was a stocking filled with sand – the weapon she had been struck down with. Miss Trollope, silly creature, was moaning and moaning by the door and holding her head. Sanders gave a great cry of "My wife, my wife," and rushed to her. I stopped him touching her. You see, I was sure at the moment he had done it, and there might have been something that he wanted to take away or hide.

"'Nothing must be touched," I said. "Pull yourself together, Mr Sanders. Miss Trollope, please go down and fetch the manager."

'I stayed there, kneeling by the body. I wasn't going to leave Sanders alone with it. And yet I was forced to admit that if the man was acting, he was acting marvellously. He looked dazed and bewildered and scared out of his wits.

'The manager was with us in no time. He made a quick inspection of the room then turned us all out and locked the door, the key of which he took. Then he went off and telephoned to the police. It seemed a positive age before they came (we learnt afterwards that the line was out of order). The manager had to send a messenger to the police station, and the Hydro is right out of the town, up on the edge of the moor; and Mrs Carpenter tried us all very severely. She was so pleased at her prophecy of "Never two without three" coming true so quickly. Sanders, I hear, wandered out into the grounds, clutching his head and groaning and displaying every sign of grief.

'However, the police came at last. They went upstairs with the manager and Mr Sanders. Later they sent down for me. I went up. The Inspector was there, sitting at a table writing. He was an intelligent-looking man and I liked him.

"'Miss Jane Marple?" he said.

"'Yes."

"'I understand, Madam, that you were present when the body of the deceased was found?"

'I said I was and I described exactly what had occurred. I think it was a relief to the poor man to find someone who could answer his questions coherently, having previously had to deal with Sanders and Emily Trollope, who, I gather, was completely demoralized – she would be, the silly creature! I remember my dear mother teaching me that a gentlewoman should always be able to control herself in public, however much she may give way in private.'

'An admirable maxim,' said Sir Henry gravely.

'When I had finished the Inspector said:

"'Thank you, Madam. Now I'm afraid I must ask you just to look at the body once more. Is that exactly the position in which it was lying when you entered the room? It hasn't been moved in any way?"

'I explained that I had prevented Mr Sanders from doing so, and the Inspector nodded approval.

"'The gentleman seems terribly upset," he remarked.

"'He seems so – yes," I replied.

'I don't think I put any special emphasis on the "seems", but the Inspector looked at me rather keenly.

"'So we can take it that the body is exactly as it was when found?" he said.

"'Except for the hat, yes," I replied.

'The Inspector looked up sharply.

"'What do you mean – the hat?"

'I explained that the hat had been on poor Gladys's head, whereas now it was lying beside her. I thought, of course, that the police had done this. The Inspector, however, denied it emphatically. Nothing had, as yet, been moved or touched. He stood looking down at that poor prone figure with a puzzled frown. Gladys was dressed in her outdoor clothes – a big dark-red tweed coat with a grey fur collar. The hat, a cheap affair of red felt, lay just by her head.

'The Inspector stood for some minutes in silence, frowning to himself. Then an idea struck him.

"'Can you, by any chance, remember, Madam, whether there were earrings in the ears, or whether the deceased habitually wore earrings?"

'Now fortunately I am in the habit of observing closely. I remembered that there had been a glint of pearls just below the hat brim, though I had paid no particular notice to it at the time. I was able to answer his first question in the affirmative.

"'Then that settles it. The lady's jewel case was rifled – not that she had anything much of value, I understand – and the rings were taken from her fingers. The murderer must have forgotten the earrings, and come back for them after the murder was discovered. A cool customer! Or perhaps –" He stared round the room and said slowly, "He may have been concealed here in this room – all the time."

'But I negatived that idea. I myself, I explained, had looked under the bed. And the manager had opened the doors of the wardrobe. There was nowhere else where a man could hide. It is true the hat cupboard was locked in the middle of the wardrobe, but as that was only a shallow affair with shelves, no one could have been concealed there.

'The Inspector nodded his head slowly whilst I explained all this.

"'I'll take your word for it, Madam," he said. "In that case, as I said before, he must have come back. A very cool customer."

'"But the manager locked the door and took the key!"

'"That's nothing. The balcony and the fire escape – that's the way the thief came. Why, as likely as not, you actually disturbed him at work. He slips out of the window, and when you've all gone, back he comes and goes on with his business."

'"You are sure," I said, "that there *was* a thief?"

'He said drily:

'"Well, it looks like it, doesn't it?"

'But something in his tone satisfied me. I felt that he wouldn't take Mr Sanders in the rôle of the bereaved widower too seriously.

'You see, I admit it frankly. I was absolutely under the opinion of what I believe our neighbours, the French, call the *idée fixe*. I knew that that man, Sanders, intended his wife to die. What I didn't allow for was that strange and fantastic thing, coincidence. My views about Mr Sanders were – I was sure of it – absolutely right and *true*. The man was a scoundrel. But although his hypocritical assumptions of grief didn't deceive me for a minute, I do remember feeling at the time that his *surprise* and *bewilderment* were marvellously well done. They seemed absolutely *natural* – if you know what I mean. I must admit that after my conversation with the Inspector, a curious feeling of doubt crept over me. Because if Sanders had done this dreadful thing, I couldn't imagine any conceivable reason why he should creep back by means of the fire escape and take the earrings from his wife's ears. It wouldn't have been a *sensible* thing to do, and Sanders was such a very sensible man – that's just why I always felt he was so dangerous.'

Miss Marple looked round at her audience.

'You see, perhaps, what I am coming to? It is, so often, the unexpected that happens in this world. I was so *sure*, and that, I think, was what blinded me. The result came as a shock to me. *For it was proved, beyond any possible doubt, that Mr Sanders could not possibly have committed the crime . . .*'

A surprised gasp came from Mrs Bantry. Miss Marple turned to her.

'I know, my dear, that isn't what you expected when I began this story. It wasn't what I expected either. But facts are facts, and if one is proved to be wrong, one must just be humble about it and start again. That Mr Sanders was a murderer at heart I knew – and nothing ever occurred to upset that firm conviction of mine.

'And now, I expect, you would like to hear the actual facts themselves. Mrs Sanders, as you know, spent the afternoon playing bridge with some friends, the Mortimers. She left them at about a quarter past six. From her friends' house to the Hydro was about a quarter of an hour's walk – less if one hurried. She must have come in then about six-thirty. No one saw her come in, so she must have entered by the side door and hurried straight up to her room. There she changed (the fawn coat and skirt she wore to the bridge party were hanging up in the cupboard) and was evidently preparing to go out again, when the blow fell. Quite possibly, they say, she never even knew who struck her. The sandbag, I understand, is a very efficient weapon. That looks as though the attackers were concealed in the room, possibly in one of the big wardrobe cupboards – the one she didn't open.

'Now as to the movements of Mr Sanders. He went out, as I have said, at about five-thirty – or a little after. He did some shopping at a couple of shops and at about six o'clock he entered the Grand Spa Hotel where he encountered two friends – the same with whom he returned to the Hydro later. They played billiards and, I gather, had a good many whiskies and sodas together. These two men (Hitchcock and Spender, their names were) were actually with him the whole time from six o'clock onwards. They walked back to the Hydro with him and he only left them to come across to me and Miss Trollope. That, as I told you, was about a quarter to seven – at which time his wife must have been already dead.

'I must tell you that I talked myself to these two friends of his. I did not like them. They were neither pleasant nor gentlemanly men, but I was quite certain of one thing, that they were speaking the absolute truth when they said that Sanders had been the whole time in their company.

'There was just one other little point that came up. It seems that while bridge was going on Mrs Sanders was called to the telephone. A Mr Littleworth wanted to speak to her. She seemed both excited and pleased about something – and incidentally made one or two bad mistakes. She left rather earlier than they had expected her to do.

'Mr Sanders was asked whether he knew the name of Littleworth as being one of his wife's friends, but he declared he had never heard of anyone of that name. And to me that seems borne out by his wife's attitude – she too, did not seem to know the name of Littleworth. Nevertheless she came back from the telephone smiling and blushing, so it looks as though whoever it was did not give his real name, and that in itself has a suspicious aspect, does it not?

'Anyway, that is the problem that was left. The burglar story, which seems unlikely – or the alternative theory that Mrs Sanders was preparing to go out and meet somebody. Did that somebody come to her room by means of the fire escape? Was there a quarrel? Or did he treacherously attack her?'

Miss Marple stopped.

'Well?' said Sir Henry. 'What is the answer?'

'I wondered if any of you could guess.'

'I'm never good at guessing,' said Mrs Bantry. 'It seems a pity that Sanders had such a wonderful alibi; but if it satisfied you it must have been all right.'

Jane Helier moved her beautiful head and asked a question.

'Why,' she said, 'was the hat cupboard locked?'

'How very clever of you, my dear,' said Miss Marple, beaming. 'That's just what I wondered myself. Though the explanation was quite simple. In it were a pair of embroidered slippers and some pocket handkerchiefs that the poor girl was embroidering for her husband for Christmas. That's why she locked the cupboard. The key was found in her handbag.'

'Oh!' said Jane. 'Then it isn't very interesting after all.'

'Oh! but it is,' said Miss Marple. 'It's just the one really interesting thing – the thing that made all the murderer's plans go wrong.'

Everyone stared at the old lady.

'I didn't see it myself for two days,' said Miss Marple. 'I puzzled and puzzled – and then suddenly there it was, all clear. I went to the Inspector and asked him to try something and he did.'

'What did you ask him to try?'

'*I asked him to fit that hat on the poor girl's head* – and of course he couldn't. It wouldn't go on. *It wasn't her hat, you see.*'

Mrs Bantry stared.

'But it was on her head to begin with?'

'Not on *her* head –'

Miss Marple stopped a moment to let her words sink in, and then went on.

'We took it for granted that it was poor Gladys's body there; but we never looked at the face. She was face downwards, remember, and the hat hid everything.'

'But she *was* killed?'

'Yes, later. At the moment that we were telephoning to the police, Gladys Sanders was alive and well.'

'You mean it was someone pretending to be her? But surely when you touched her –'

'It was a dead body, right enough,' said Miss Marple gravely.

'But, dash it all,' said Colonel Bantry, 'you can't get hold of dead bodies right and left. What did they do with the – the first corpse afterwards?'

'He put it back,' said Miss Marple. 'It was a wicked idea – but a very clever one. It was our talk in the drawing-room that put it into his head. The body of poor Mary, the housemaid – why not use it? Remember, the Sanders' room was up amongst the servants' quarters. Mary's room was two doors off. The undertakers wouldn't come till after dark – he counted on that. He carried the body along the balcony (it was dark at five), dressed it in one of his wife's dresses and her big red coat. And then he found the hat cupboard locked! There was only one thing to be done, he fetched one of the poor girl's own hats. No one would notice. He put the sandbag down beside her. Then he went off to establish his alibi.

'He telephoned to his wife – calling himself Mr Littleworth. I don't know what he said to her – she was a credulous girl, as I said just now. But he got her to leave the bridge party early and not to go back to the Hydro, and arranged with her to meet him in the grounds of the Hydro near the fire escape at seven o'clock. He probably told her he had some surprise for her.

'He returns to the Hydro with his friends and arranges that Miss Trollope and I shall discover the crime with him. He even pretends to turn the body over – and I stop him! Then the police are sent for, and he staggers out into the grounds.

'Nobody asked him for an alibi *after* the crime. He meets his wife, takes her up the fire escape, they enter their room. Perhaps he has already told her some story about the body. She stoops over it, and he picks up his sandbag and strikes . . . Oh, dear! It makes me sick to think of, even now! Then quickly he strips off her coat and skirt, hangs them up, and dresses her in the clothes from the other body.

'*But the hat won't go on.* Mary's head is shingled – Gladys Sanders, as I say, had a great bun of hair. He is forced to leave it beside the body and hope no one will notice. Then he carries poor Mary's body back to her own room and arranges it decorously once more.'

'It seems incredible,' said Dr Lloyd. 'The risks he took. The police might have arrived too soon.'

'You remember the line was out of order,' said Miss Marple. 'That was a piece of *his* work. He couldn't afford to have the police on the spot too soon. When they did come, they spent some time in the manager's office before going up to the bedroom. That was the weakest point – the chance that someone might notice the difference between a body that had been dead two hours and one that had been dead just over half an hour; but he counted on the fact that the people who first discovered the crime would have no expert knowledge.'

Dr Lloyd nodded.

'The crime would be supposed to have been committed about a quarter to seven or thereabouts, I suppose,' he said. 'It was actually committed at seven or a few minutes after. When the police surgeon examined the body it would be about half past seven at the earliest. He couldn't possibly tell.'

'I am the person who should have known,' said Miss Marple. 'I felt the poor girl's hand and it was icy cold. Yet a short time later the Inspector spoke as though the murder must have been committed just before we arrived – and I saw nothing!'

'I think you saw a good deal, Miss Marple,' said Sir Henry. 'The case was before my time. I don't even remember hearing of it. What happened?'

'Sanders was hanged,' said Miss Marple crisply. 'And a good job too. I have never regretted my part in bringing that man to justice. I've no patience with modern humanitarian scruples about capital punishment.'

Her stern face softened.

'But I have often reproached myself bitterly with failing to save the life of that poor girl. But who would have listened to an old woman jumping to conclusions? Well, well – who knows? Perhaps it was better for her to die while life was still happy than it would have been for her to live on, unhappy and disillusioned, in a world that would have seemed suddenly horrible. She loved that scoundrel and trusted him. She never found him out.'

'Well, then,' said Jane Helier, 'she was all right. Quite all right. I wish –' she stopped.

Miss Marple looked at the famous, the beautiful, the successful Jane Helier and nodded her head gently.

'I see, my dear,' she said very gently. 'I see.'

The Herb of Death

'The Herb of Death' was first published in *Storyteller*, March 1930.

'Now then, Mrs B.,' said Sir Henry Clithering encouragingly.

Mrs Bantry, his hostess, looked at him in cold reproof.

'I've told you before that I will *not* be called Mrs B. It's not dignified.'

'Scheherazade, then.'

'And even less am I Sche – what's her name! I never can tell a story properly, ask Arthur if you don't believe me.'

'You're quite good at the facts, Dolly,' said Colonel Bantry, 'but poor at the embroidery.'

'That's just it,' said Mrs Bantry. She flapped the bulb catalogue she was holding on the table in front of her. 'I've been listening to you all and I don't know how you do it. "He said, she said, you wondered, they thought, everyone implied" – well, I just couldn't and there it is! And besides I don't know anything to tell a story about.'

'We can't believe that, Mrs Bantry,' said Dr Lloyd. He shook his grey head in mocking disbelief.

Old Miss Marple said in her gentle voice: 'Surely dear –'

Mrs Bantry continued obstinately to shake her head.

'You don't know how banal my life is. What with the servants and the difficulties of getting scullery maids, and just going to town for clothes, and dentists, and Ascot (which Arthur hates) and then the garden –'

'Ah!' said Dr Lloyd. 'The garden. We all know where your heart lies, Mrs Bantry.'

'It must be nice to have a garden,' said Jane Helier, the beautiful young actress. 'That is, if you hadn't got to dig, or to get your hands messed up. I'm ever so fond of flowers.'

'The garden,' said Sir Henry. 'Can't we take that as a starting point? Come, Mrs B. The poisoned bulb, the deadly daffodils, the herb of death!'

'Now it's odd your saying that,' said Mrs Bantry. 'You've just reminded me. Arthur, do you remember that business at Clodderham Court? You know. Old Sir Ambrose Bercy. Do you remember what a courtly charming old man we thought him?'

'Why, of course. Yes, that *was* a strange business. Go ahead, Dolly.'

'You'd better tell it, dear.'

'Nonsense. Go ahead. Must paddle your own canoe. I did my bit just now.'

Mrs Bantry drew a deep breath. She clasped her hands and her face registered complete mental anguish. She spoke rapidly and fluently.

'Well, there's really not much to tell. The Herb of Death – that's what put it into my head, though in my own mind I call it *sage and onions*.'

'Sage and onions?' asked Dr Lloyd.

Mrs Bantry nodded.

'That was how it happened you see,' she explained. 'We were staying, Arthur and I, with Sir Ambrose Bercy at Clodderham Court, and one day, by mistake (though very stupidly, I've always thought) a lot of foxglove leaves were picked with the sage. The ducks for dinner that night were stuffed with it and everyone was very ill, and one poor girl – Sir Ambrose's ward – died of it.'

She stopped.

'Dear, dear,' said Miss Marple, 'how very tragic.'

'Wasn't it?'

'Well,' said Sir Henry, 'what next?'

'There isn't any next,' said Mrs Bantry, 'that's all.'

Everyone gasped. Though warned beforehand, they had not expected quite such brevity as this.

'But, my dear lady,' remonstrated Sir Henry, 'it can't be all. What you have related is a tragic occurrence, but not in any sense of the word a problem.'

'Well, of course there's some more,' said Mrs Bantry. 'But if I were to tell you it, you'd know what it was.'

She looked defiantly round the assembly and said plaintively:

'I told you I couldn't dress things up and make it sound properly like a story ought to do.'

'Ah ha!' said Sir Henry. He sat up in his chair and adjusted an eyeglass. 'Really, you know, Scheherazade, this is most refreshing. Our ingenuity is challenged. I'm not so sure you haven't done it on purpose – to stimulate our curiosity. A few brisk rounds of "Twenty Questions" is indicated, I think. Miss Marple, will you begin?'

'I'd like to know something about the cook,' said Miss Marple. 'She must have been a very stupid woman, or else very inexperienced.'

'She was just very stupid,' said Mrs Bantry. 'She cried a great deal afterwards and said the leaves had been picked and brought in to her as sage, and how was she to know?'

'Not one who thought for herself,' said Miss Marple.

'Probably an elderly woman and, I dare say, a very good cook?'

'Oh! excellent,' said Mrs Bantry.

'Your turn, Miss Helier,' said Sir Henry.

'Oh! You mean – to ask a question?' There was a pause while Jane pondered. Finally she said helplessly, 'Really – I don't know what to ask.'

Her beautiful eyes looked appealingly at Sir Henry.

'Why not dramatis personae, Miss Helier?' he suggested smiling.

Jane still looked puzzled.

'Characters in order of their appearance,' said Sir Henry gently.

'Oh, yes,' said Jane. 'That's a good idea.'

Mrs Bantry began briskly to tick people off on her fingers.

'Sir Ambrose – Sylvia Keene (that's the girl who died) – a friend of hers who was staying there, Maud Wye, one of those dark ugly girls who manage to make an effort somehow – I never know how they do it. Then there was a Mr Curle who had come down to discuss books with Sir Ambrose – you know, rare books – queer old things in Latin – all musty parchment. There was Jerry Lorimer – he was a kind of next door neighbour. His place, Fairlies, joined Sir Ambrose's estate. And there was Mrs Carpenter, one of those middle-aged pussies who always seem to manage to dig themselves in comfortably somewhere. She was by way of being *dame de compagnie* to Sylvia, I suppose.'

'If it is my turn,' said Sir Henry, 'and I suppose it is, as I'm sitting next to Miss Helier, I want a good deal. I want a short verbal portrait, please, Mrs Bantry, of all the foregoing.'

'Oh!' Mrs Bantry hesitated.

'Sir Ambrose now,' continued Sir Henry. 'Start with him. What was he like?'

'Oh! he was a very distinguished-looking old man – and not so very old really – not more than sixty, I suppose. But he was very delicate – he had a weak heart, could never go upstairs – he had to have a lift put in, and so that made him seem older than he was. Very charming manners – *courtly* – that's the word that describes him best. You never saw him ruffled or upset. He had beautiful white hair and a particularly charming voice.'

'Good,' said Sir Henry. 'I see Sir Ambrose. Now the girl Sylvia – what did you say her name was?'

'Sylvia Keene. She was pretty – really *very* pretty. Fair-haired, you know, and a lovely skin. Not, perhaps, very clever. In fact, rather stupid.'

'Oh! come, Dolly,' protested her husband.

'Arthur, of course, wouldn't think so,' said Mrs Bantry drily. 'But she *was* stupid – she really never said anything worth listening to.'

'One of the most graceful creatures I ever saw,' said Colonel Bantry warmly. 'See her playing tennis – charming, simply charming. And she was full of fun – most amusing little thing. And such a pretty way with her. I bet the young fellows all thought so.'

'That's just where you're wrong,' said Mrs Bantry. 'Youth, as such, has no charms for young men nowadays. It's only old buffers like you, Arthur, who sit maundering on about young girls.'

'Being young's no good,' said Jane. 'You've got to have SA.'

'What,' said Miss Marple, 'is SA?'

'Sex appeal,' said Jane.

'Ah! yes,' said Miss Marple. 'What in my day they used to call "having the come hither in your eye".'

'Not a bad description,' said Sir Henry. 'The *dame de compagnie* you described, I think, as a pussy, Mrs Bantry?'

'I didn't mean a *cat*, you know,' said Mrs Bantry. 'It's quite different. Just a big soft white purry person. Always very sweet. That's what Adelaide Carpenter was like.'

'What sort of aged woman?'

'Oh! I should say fortyish. She'd been there some time – ever since Sylvia was eleven, I believe. A very tactful person. One of those widows left in unfortunate circumstances with plenty of aristocratic relations, but no ready cash. I didn't like her myself – but then I never do like people with very white long hands. And I don't like pussies.'

'Mr Curle?'

'Oh! one of those elderly stooping men. There are so many of them about, you'd hardly know one from the other. He showed enthusiasm when talking about his musty books, but not at any other time. I don't think Sir Ambrose knew him very well.'

'And Jerry next door?'

'A really charming boy. He was engaged to Sylvia. That's what made it so sad.'

'Now I wonder –' began Miss Marple, and then stopped.

'What?'

'Nothing, dear.'

Sir Henry looked at the old lady curiously. Then he said thoughtfully:

'So this young couple were engaged. Had they been engaged long?'

'About a year. Sir Ambrose had opposed the engagement on the plea that Sylvia was too young. But after a year's engagement he had given in and the marriage was to have taken place quite soon.'

'Ah! Had the young lady any property?'

'Next to nothing – a bare hundred or two a year.'

'No rat in that hole, Clithering,' said Colonel Bantry, and laughed.

'It's the doctor's turn to ask a question,' said Sir Henry. 'I stand down.'

'My curiosity is mainly professional,' said Dr Lloyd. 'I should like to know what medical evidence was given at the inquest – that is, if our hostess remembers, or, indeed, if she knows.'

'I know roughly,' said Mrs Bantry. 'It was poisoning by digitalin – is that right?'

Dr Lloyd nodded.

'The active principle of the foxglove – digitalis – acts on the heart. Indeed, it is a very valuable drug in some forms of heart trouble. A very curious case altogther. I would never have believed that eating a preparation of foxglove leaves could possibly result fatally. These ideas of eating poisonous leaves and berries are very much exaggerated. Very few people realize that the vital principle, or alkaloid, has to be extracted with much care and preparation.'

'Mrs MacArthur sent some special bulbs round to Mrs Toomie the other day,' said Miss Marple. 'And Mrs Toomie's cook mistook them for onions, and all the Toomies were very ill indeed.'

'But they didn't die of it,' said Dr Lloyd.

'No. They didn't die of it,' admitted Miss Marple.

'A girl I knew died of ptomaine poisoning,' said Jane Helier.

'We must get on with investigating the crime,' said Sir Henry.

'Crime?' said Jane, startled. 'I thought it was an accident.'

'If it were an accident,' said Sir Henry gently, 'I do not think Mrs Bantry would have told us this story. No, as I read it, this was an accident only in appearance – behind it is something more sinister. I remember a case – various guests in a house party were chatting after dinner. The walls were adorned with all kinds of old-fashioned weapons. Entirely as a joke one of the party seized an ancient horse pistol and pointed it at another man, pretending to fire it. The pistol was loaded and went off, killing the man. We had to ascertain in that case, first, who had secretly prepared and loaded that pistol, and secondly who had so led and directed the conversation that that final bit of horseplay resulted – for the man who had fired the pistol was entirely innocent!

'It seems to me we have much the same problem here. Those digitalin leaves were deliberately mixed with the sage, knowing what the result would be. Since we exonerate the cook – we do exonerate the cook, don't we? – the question arises: Who picked the leaves and delivered them to the kitchen?'

'That's easily answered,' said Mrs Bantry. 'At least the last part of it is. It was Sylvia herself who took the leaves to the kitchen. It was part of her daily job to gather things like salad or herbs, bunches of young carrots – all the sort of things that gardeners never pick right. They hate giving you anything young and tender – they wait for them to be fine specimens. Sylvia and Mrs Carpenter used to see to a lot of these things themselves. And there was foxglove actually growing all amongst the sage in one corner, so the mistake was quite natural.'

'But did Sylvia actually pick them herself?'

'That, nobody ever knew. It was assumed so.'

'Assumptions,' said Sir Henry, 'are dangerous things.'

'But I do know that Mrs Carpenter didn't pick them,' said Mrs Bantry. 'Because, as it happened, she was walking with me on the terrace that morning. We went out there after breakfast. It was unusually nice and warm for early spring. Sylvia went alone down into the garden, but later I saw her walking arm-in-arm with Maud Wye.'

'So they were great friends, were they?' asked Miss Marple.

'Yes,' said Mrs Bantry. She seemed as though about to say something, but did not do so.

'Had she been staying there long?' asked Miss Marple.

'About a fortnight,' said Mrs Bantry.

There was a note of trouble in her voice.

'You didn't like Miss Wye?' suggested Sir Henry.

'I did. That's just it. I did.'

The trouble in her voice had grown to distress.

'You're keeping something back, Mrs Bantry,' said Sir Henry accusingly.

'I wondered just now,' said Miss Marple, 'but I didn't like to go on.'

'When did you wonder?'

'When you said that the young people were engaged. You said that that was what made it so sad. But, if you know what I mean, your voice didn't sound right when you said it – not convincing, you know.'

'What a dreadful person you are,' said Mrs Bantry. 'You always seem to *know*. Yes, I was thinking of something. But I don't really know whether I ought to say it or not.'

'You must say it,' said Sir Henry. 'Whatever your scruples, it mustn't be kept back.'

'Well, it was just this,' said Mrs Bantry. 'One evening – in fact the very evening before the tragedy – I happened to go out on the terrace before dinner. The window in the drawing-room was open. And as it chanced I saw Jerry Lorimer and Maud Wye. He was – well – kissing her. Of course I didn't know whether it was just a sort of chance affair, or whether – well, I mean, one can't *tell*. I knew Sir Ambrose never had really liked Jerry Lorimer – so perhaps he knew he was that kind of young man. But one thing I *am* sure of: that girl, Maud Wye, was *really* fond of him. You'd only to see her looking at him when she was off guard. And I think, too, they were really better suited than he and Sylvia were.'

'I am going to ask a question quickly, before Miss Marple can,' said Sir Henry. 'I want to know whether, after the tragedy, Jerry Lorimer married Maud Wye?'

'Yes,' said Mrs Bantry. 'He did. Six months afterwards.'

'Oh! Scheherezade, Scheherezade,' said Sir Henry. 'To think of the way you told us this story at first! Bare bones indeed – and to think of the amount of flesh we're finding on them now.'

'Don't speak so ghoulishly,' said Mrs Bantry. 'And don't use the word flesh. Vegetarians always do. They say, "I never eat flesh" in a way that puts you right off your little beefsteak. Mr Curle was a vegetarian. He used to eat some peculiar stuff that looked like bran for breakfast. Those elderly stooping men with beards are often faddy. They have patent kinds of underwear, too.'

'What on earth, Dolly,' said her husband, 'do you know about Mr Curle's underwear?'

'Nothing,' said Mrs Bantry with dignity. 'I was just making a guess.'

'I'll amend my former statement,' said Sir Henry. 'I'll say instead that the dramatis personae in your problem are very interesting. I'm beginning to see them all – eh, Miss Marple?'

'Human nature is always interesting, Sir Henry. And it's curious to see how certain types always tend to act in exactly the same way.'

'Two women and a man,' said Sir Henry. 'The old eternal human triangle. Is that the base of our problem here? I rather fancy it is.'

Dr Lloyd cleared his throat.

'I've been thinking,' he said rather diffidently. 'Do you say, Mrs Bantry, that you yourself were ill?'

'Was I not! So was Arthur! So was everyone!'

'That's just it – everyone,' said the doctor. 'You see what I mean? In Sir Henry's story which he told us just now, one man shot another – he didn't have to shoot the whole room full.'

'I don't understand,' said Jane. 'Who shot who?'

'I'm saying that whoever planned this thing went about it very curiously, either with a blind belief in chance, or else with an absolutely reckless disregard for human life. I can hardly believe there is a man capable of deliberately poisoning eight people with the object of removing one amongst them.'

'I see your point,' said Sir Henry, thoughtfully. 'I confess I ought to have thought of that.'

'And mightn't he have poisoned himself too?' asked Jane.

'Was anyone absent from dinner that night?' asked Miss Marple.

Mrs Bantry shook her head.

'Everyone was there.'

'Except Mr Lorimer, I suppose, my dear. He wasn't staying in the house, was he?'

'No; but he was dining there that evening,' said Mrs Bantry.

'Oh!' said Miss Marple in a changed voice. 'That makes all the difference in the world.'

She frowned vexedly to herself.

'I've been very stupid,' she murmured. 'Very stupid indeed.'

'I confess your point worries me, Lloyd,' said Sir Henry.

'How ensure that the girl, and the girl only, should get a fatal dose?'

'You can't,' said the doctor. 'That brings me to the point I'm going to make. *Supposing the girl was not the intended victim after all?*'

'What?'

'In all cases of food poisoning, the result is very uncertain. Several people share a dish. What happens? One or two are slightly ill, two more, say, are seriously indisposed, one dies. That's the way of it – there's no certainty anywhere. But there are cases where another factor might enter in. Digitalin is a drug that acts directly on the heart – as I've told you it's prescribed in certain cases. *Now, there was one person in that house who suffered from a heart complaint.* Suppose he was the victim selected? What would not be fatal to the rest *would* be fatal to him – or so the murderer might reasonably suppose. That the thing turned out differently is only a proof of what I was saying just now – the uncertainty and unreliability of the effects of drugs on human beings.'

'Sir Ambrose,' said Sir Henry, 'you think *he* was the person aimed at? Yes, yes – and the girl's death was a mistake.'

'Who got his money after he was dead?' asked Jane.

'A very sound question, Miss Helier. One of the first we always ask in my late profession,' said Sir Henry.

'Sir Ambrose had a son,' said Mrs Bantry slowly. 'He had quarrelled with him many years previously. The boy was wild, I believe. Still, it was not in Sir Ambrose's power to disinherit him – Clodderham Court was entailed. Martin Bercy succeeded to the title and estate. There was, however, a good deal of other property that Sir Ambrose could leave as he chose, and that he left to his ward Sylvia. I know this because Sir Ambrose died less than a year after the events I am telling you of, and he had not troubled to make a new will after Sylvia's death. I think the money went to the Crown – or perhaps it was to his son as next of kin – I don't really remember.'

'So it was only to the interest of a son who wasn't there and the girl who died herself to make away with him,' said Sir Henry thoughtfully. 'That doesn't seem very promising.'

'Didn't the other woman get anything?' asked Jane. 'The one Mrs Bantry calls the Pussy woman.'

'She wasn't mentioned in the will,' said Mrs Bantry.

'Miss Marple, you're not listening,' said Sir Henry. 'You're somewhere far away.'

'I was thinking of old Mr Badger, the chemist,' said Miss Marple. 'He had a very young housekeeper – young enough to be not only his daughter, but his grand-daughter. Not a word to anyone, and his family, a lot of nephews and nieces, full of expectations. And when he died, would you believe it, he'd been secretly married to her for two years? Of course Mr Badger was a chemist, and a very rude, common old man as well, and Sir Ambrose Bercy was a very courtly gentleman, so Mrs Bantry says, but for all that human nature is much the same everywhere.'

There was a pause. Sir Henry looked very hard at Miss Marple who looked back at him with gently quizzical blue eyes. Jane Helier broke the silence.

'Was this Mrs Carpenter good-looking?' she asked.

'Yes, in a very quiet way. Nothing startling.'

'She had a very sympathetic voice,' said Colonel Bantry.

'Purring – that's what I call it,' said Mrs Bantry. 'Purring!'

'You'll be called a cat yourself one of these days, Dolly.'

'I like being a cat in my home circle,' said Mrs Bantry. 'I don't much like women anyway, and you know it. I like men and flowers.'

'Excellent taste,' said Sir Henry. 'Especially in putting men first.'

'That was tact,' said Mrs Bantry. 'Well, now, what about my little problem? I've been quite fair, I think. Arthur, don't you think I've been fair?'

'Yes, my dear. I don't think there'll be any inquiry into the running by the stewards of the Jockey Club.'

'First boy,' said Mrs Bantry, pointing a finger at Sir Henry.

'I'm going to be long-winded. Because, you see, I haven't really got any feeling of certainty about the matter. First, Sir Ambrose. Well, he wouldn't take such an original method of committing suicide – and on the other hand he certainly had nothing to gain by the death of his ward. Exit Sir Ambrose. Mr Curle. No motive for death of girl. If Sir Ambrose was intended victim, he might possibly have purloined a rare manuscript or two that no one else would miss. Very thin and most unlikely. So I think, that in spite of Mrs Bantry's suspicions as to his underclothing, Mr Curle is cleared. Miss Wye. Motive for death of Sir Ambrose – none. Motive for death of Sylvia pretty strong. She wanted Sylvia's young man, and wanted him rather badly – from Mrs Bantry's account. She was with Sylvia that morning in the garden, so had opportunity to pick leaves. No, we can't dismiss Miss Wye so easily. Young Lorimer. He's got a motive in either case. If he gets rid of his sweetheart, he can marry the other girl. Still it seems a bit drastic to kill her – what's a broken engagement these days? If Sir Ambrose dies, he will marry a rich girl instead of a poor one. That might be important or not – depends on his financial position. If I find that his estate was heavily mortgaged and that Mrs Bantry has deliberately withheld that fact from us, I shall claim a foul. Now Mrs Carpenter. You know, I have suspicions of Mrs Carpenter. Those white hands, for one thing, and her excellent alibi at the time the herbs were picked – I always distrust alibis. And I've got another reason for suspecting her which I will keep to myself. Still, on the whole, if I've got to plump, I shall plump for Miss Maude Wye, because there's more evidence against her than anyone else.'

'Next boy,' said Mrs Bantry, and pointed at Dr Lloyd.

'I think you're wrong, Clithering, in sticking to the theory that the girl's death was meant. I am convinced that the murderer intended to do away with Sir Ambrose. I don't think that young Lorimer had the necessary knowledge. I am inclined to believe that Mrs Carpenter was the guilty party. She had been a long time with the family, knew all about the state of Sir Ambrose's health, and could easily arrange for this girl Sylvia (who, you said yourself, was rather stupid) to pick the right leaves. Motive, I confess, I don't see; but I hazard the guess that Sir Ambrose had at one time made a will in which she was mentioned. That's the best I can do.'

Mrs Bantry's pointing finger went on to Jane Helier.

'I don't know what to say,' said Jane, 'except this: Why shouldn't the girl herself have done it? She took the leaves into the kitchen after all. And you say Sir Ambrose had been sticking out against her marriage. If he died, she'd get the money and be able to marry at once. She'd know just as much about Sir Ambrose's health as Mrs Carpenter would.'

Mrs Bantry's finger came slowly round to Miss Marple.

'Now then, School Marm,' she said.

'Sir Henry has put it all very clearly – very clearly indeed,' said Miss Marple. 'And Dr Lloyd was so right in what he said. Between them they seem to have made things so very clear. Only I don't think Dr Lloyd quite realized one aspect of what he said. You see, not being Sir Ambrose's medical adviser, he couldn't know just what kind of heart trouble Sir Ambrose had, could he?'

'I don't quite see what you mean, Miss Marple,' said Dr Lloyd.

'You're assuming – aren't you? – that Sir Ambrose had the kind of heart that digitalin would affect adversely? But there's nothing to prove that that's so. It might be just the other way about.'

'The other way about?'

'Yes, you did say that it was often prescribed for heart trouble?'

'Even then, Miss Marple, I don't see what that leads to?'

'Well, it would mean that he would have digitalin in his possession quite naturally – without having to account for it. What I am trying to say (I always express myself so badly) is this: Supposing you wanted to poison anyone with a fatal dose of digitalin. Wouldn't the simplest and easiest way be to arrange for everyone to be poisoned – actually by digitalin leaves? It wouldn't be fatal in anyone else's case, of course, but no one would be surprised at one victim because, as Dr Lloyd said, these things are so uncertain. No one would be likely to ask whether the girl had actually had a fatal dose of infusion of digitalis or something of that kind. He might have put it in a cocktail, or in her coffee or even made her drink it quite simply as a tonic.'

'You mean Sir Ambrose poisoned his ward, the charming girl whom he loved?'

'That's just it,' said Miss Marple. 'Like Mr Badger and his young housekeeper. Don't tell me it's absurd for a man of sixty to fall in love with a girl of twenty. It happens every day – and I dare say with an old autocrat like Sir Ambrose, it might take him queerly. These things become a madness sometimes. He couldn't bear the thought of her getting married – did his best to oppose it – and failed. His mad jealousy became so great that he preferred killing her to letting her go to young Lorimer. He must have thought of it some time beforehand, because that foxglove seed would have to be sown among the sage. He'd pick it himself when the time came, and send her into the kitchen with it. It's horrible to think of, but I suppose we must take as merciful a view of it as we can. Gentlemen of that age are sometimes very peculiar indeed where young girls are concerned. Our last organist – but there, I mustn't talk scandal.'

'Mrs Bantry,' said Sir Henry. 'Is this so?'

Mrs Bantry nodded.

'Yes. I'd no idea of it – never dreamed of the thing being anything but an accident. Then, after Sir Ambrose's death, I got a letter. He had left directions to send it to me. He told me the truth in it. I don't know why – but he and I always got on very well together.'

In the momentary silence, she seemed to feel an unspoken criticism and went on hastily:

'You think I'm betraying a confidence – but that isn't so. I've changed all the names. He wasn't really called Sir Ambrose Bercy. Didn't you see how Arthur stared stupidly when I said that name to him? He didn't understand at first. I've changed everything. It's like they say in magazines and in the beginning of books: "All the characters in this story are purely fictitious." You never know who they really are.'

The Affair at the Bungalow

'The Affair at the Bungalow' was first published
in *Storyteller*, May 1930.

'I've thought of something,' said Jane Helier.

Her beautiful face was lit up with the confident smile of a child expecting approbation. It was a smile such as moved audiences nightly in London, and which had made the fortunes of photographers.

'It happened,' she went on carefully, 'to a friend of mine.'

Everyone made encouraging but slightly hypocritical noises. Colonel Bantry, Mrs Bantry, Sir Henry Clithering, Dr Lloyd and old Miss Marple were one and all convinced that Jane's 'friend' was Jane herself. She would have been quite incapable of remembering or taking an interest in anything affecting anyone else.

'My friend,' went on Jane, '(I won't mention her name) was an actress – a very well-known actress.'

No one expressed surprise. Sir Henry Clithering thought to himself: 'Now I wonder how many sentences it will be before she forgets to keep up the fiction, and says "I" instead of "She"?'

'My friend was on tour in the provinces – this was a year or two ago. I suppose I'd better not give the name of the place. It was a riverside town not very far from London. I'll call it –'

She paused, her brows perplexed in thought. The invention of even a simple name appeared to be too much for her. Sir Henry came to the rescue.

'Shall we call it Riverbury?' he suggested gravely.

'Oh, yes, that would do splendidly. Riverbury, I'll remember that. Well, as I say, this – my friend – was at Riverbury with her company, and a very curious thing happened.'

She puckered her brows again.

'It's very difficult,' she said plaintively, 'to say just what you want. One gets things mixed up and tells the wrong things first.'

'You're doing it beautifully,' said Dr Lloyd encouragingly. 'Go on.'

'Well, this curious thing happened. My friend was sent for to the police station. And she went. It seemed there had been a burglary at a riverside bungalow and they'd arrested a young man, and he told a very odd story. And so they sent for her.

'She'd never been to a police station before, but they were very nice to her – very nice indeed.'

'They would be, I'm sure,' said Sir Henry.

'The sergeant – I think it was a sergeant – or it may have been an inspector – gave her a chair and explained things, and of course I saw at once that it was some mistake –'

'Aha,' thought Sir Henry. 'I. Here we are. I thought as much.'

'My friend said so,' continued Jane, serenely unconscious of her self-betrayal. 'She explained she had been rehearsing with her understudy at the hotel and that she'd never even heard of this Mr Faulkener. And the sergeant said, "Miss Hel –"'

She stopped and flushed.

'Miss Helman,' suggested Sir Henry with a twinkle.

'Yes – yes, that would do. Thank you. He said, "Well, Miss Helman, I felt it must be some mistake, knowing that you were stopping at the Bridge Hotel," and he said would I have any objection to confronting – or was it being confronted? I can't remember.'

'It doesn't really matter,' said Sir Henry reassuringly.

'Anyway, with the young man. So I said, "Of course not." And they brought him and said, "This is Miss Helier," and – Oh!' Jane broke off open-mouthed.

'Never mind, my dear,' said Miss Marple consolingly. 'We were bound to guess, you know. And you haven't given us the name of the place or anything that really matters.'

'Well,' said Jane. 'I did mean to tell it as though it happened to someone else. But it is difficult, isn't it! I mean one forgets so.'

Everyone assured her that it was very difficult, and soothed and reassured, she went on with her slightly involved narrative.

'He was a nice-looking man – quite a nice-looking man. Young, with reddish hair. His mouth just opened when he saw me. And the sergeant said, "Is this the lady?" And he said, "No, indeed it isn't. What an ass I have been." And I smiled at him and said it didn't matter.'

'I can picture the scene,' said Sir Henry.

Jane Helier frowned.

'Let me see – how had I better go on?'

'Supposing you tell us what it was all about, dear,' said Miss Marple, so mildly that no one could suspect her of irony. 'I mean what the young man's mistake was, and about the burglary.'

'Oh, yes,' said Jane. 'Well, you see, this young man – Leslie Faulkener, his name was – had written a play. He'd written several plays, as a matter of fact, though none of them had ever been taken. And he had sent this particular play to me to read. I didn't know about it, because of course I have hundreds of plays sent to me and I read very few of them myself – only the ones I know something about. Anyway, there it was, and it seems that Mr Faulkener got a letter from me – only it turned out not to be really from me – you understand –'

She paused anxiously, and they assured her that they understood.

'Saying that I'd read the play, and liked it very much and would he come down and talk it over with me. And it gave the address – The Bungalow, Riverbury. So Mr Faulkener was frightfully pleased and he came down and arrived at this place – The Bungalow. A parlourmaid opened the door, and he asked for Miss Helier, and she said Miss Helier was in and expecting him and showed him into the drawing-room, and there a woman came to him. And he accepted her as me as a matter of course – which seems queer because after all he had seen me act and my photographs are very well known, aren't they?'

'Over the length and breadth of England,' said Mrs Bantry promptly. 'But there's often a lot of difference between a photograph and its original, my dear Jane. And there's a great deal of difference between behind the footlights and off the stage. It's not every actress who stands the test as well as you do, remember.'

'Well,' said Jane slightly mollified, 'that may be so. Anyway, he described this woman as tall and fair with big blue eyes and very good-looking, so I suppose it must have been near enough. He certainly had no suspicions. She sat down and began talking about his play and said she was anxious to do it. Whilst they were talking cocktails were brought in and Mr Faulkener had one as a matter of course. Well – that's all he remembers – having this cocktail. When he woke up, or came to himself, or whatever you call it – he was lying out in the road, by the hedge, of course, so that there would be no danger of his being run over. He felt very queer and shaky – so much so that he just got up and staggered along the road not quite knowing where he was going. He said if he'd had his sense about him he'd have gone back to The Bungalow and tried to find out what had happened. But he felt just stupid and mazed and walked along without quite knowing what he was doing. He was just more or less coming to himself when the police arrested him.'

'Why did the police arrest him?' asked Dr Lloyd.

'Oh! didn't I tell you?' said Jane opening her eyes very wide. 'How very stupid I am. The burglary.'

'You mentioned a burglary – but you didn't say where or what or why,' said Mrs Bantry.

'Well, this bungalow – the one he went to, of course – it wasn't mine at all. It belonged to a man whose name was –'

Again Jane furrowed her brows.

'Do you want me to be godfather again?' asked Sir Henry. 'Pseudonyms supplied free of charge. Describe the tenant and I'll do the naming.'

'It was taken by a rich city man – a knight.'

'Sir Herman Cohen,' suggested Sir Henry.

'That will do beautifully. He took it for a lady – she was the wife of an actor, and she was also an actress herself.'

'We'll call the actor Claud Leason,' said Sir Henry, 'and the lady would be known by her stage name, I suppose, so we'll call her Miss Mary Kerr.'

'I think you're awfully clever,' said Jane. 'I don't know how you think of these things so easily. Well, you see this was a sort of week-end cottage for Sir Herman – did you say Herman? – and the lady. And, of course, his wife knew nothing about it.'

'Which is so often the case,' said Sir Henry.

'And he'd given this actress woman a good deal of jewellery including some very fine emeralds.'

'Ah!' said Dr Lloyd. 'Now we're getting at it.'

'This jewellery was at the bungalow, just locked up in a jewel case. The police said it was very careless – anyone might have taken it.'

'You see, Dolly,' said Colonel Bantry. 'What do I always tell you?'

'Well, in my experience,' said Mrs Bantry, 'it's always the people who are so dreadfully careful who lose things. I don't lock mine up in a jewel case – I keep it in a drawer loose, under my stockings. I dare say if – what's her name? – Mary Kerr had done the same, it would never have been stolen.'

'It would,' said Jane, 'because all the drawers were burst open, and the contents strewn about.'

'Then they weren't really looking for jewels,' said Mrs Bantry. 'They were looking for secret papers. That's what always happens in books.'

'I don't know about secret papers,' said Jane doubtfully. 'I never heard of any.'

'Don't be distracted, Miss Helier,' said Colonel Bantry. 'Dolly's wild red-herrings are not to be taken seriously.'

'About the burglary,' said Sir Henry.

'Yes. Well, the police were rung up by someone who said she was Miss Mary Kerr. She said the bungalow had been burgled and described a young man with red hair who had called there that morning. Her maid had thought there was something odd about him and had refused him admittance, but later they had seen him getting out through a window. She described the man so accurately that the police arrested him only an hour later and then he told his story and showed them the letter from me. And as I told you, they fetched me and when he saw me he said what I told you – that it hadn't been me at all!'

'A very curious story,' said Dr Lloyd. 'Did Mr Faulkener know this Miss Kerr?'

'No, he didn't – or he said he didn't. But I haven't told you the most curious part yet. The police went to the bungalow of course, and they found everything as described – drawers pulled out and jewels gone, but the whole place was empty. It wasn't till some hours later that Mary Kerr came back, and when she did she said she'd never rung them up at all and this was the first she'd heard of it. It seemed that she had had a wire that morning from a manager offering her a most important part and making an appointment, so she had naturally rushed up to town to keep it. When she got there, she found that the whole thing was a hoax. No telegram had ever been sent.'

'A common enough ruse to get her out of the way,' commented Sir Henry. 'What about the servants?'

'The same sort of thing happened there. There was only one, and she was rung up on the telephone – apparently by Mary Kerr, who said she had left a most important thing behind. She directed the maid to bring up a certain handbag which was in the drawer of her bedroom. She was to catch the first train. The maid did so, of course locking up the house; but when she arrived at Miss Kerr's club, where she had been told to meet her mistress, she waited there in vain.'

'H'm,' said Sir Henry. 'I begin to see. The house was left empty, and to make an entry by one of the windows would present few difficulties, I should imagine. But I don't quite see where Mr Faulkener comes in. Who did ring up the police, if it wasn't Miss Kerr?'

'That's what nobody knew or ever found out.'

'Curious,' said Sir Henry. 'Did the young man turn out to be genuinely the person he said he was?'

'Oh, yes, that part of it was all right. He'd even got the letter which was supposed to be written by me. It wasn't the least bit like my handwriting – but then, of course, he couldn't be supposed to know that.'

'Well, let's state the position clearly,' said Sir Henry. 'Correct me if I go wrong. The lady and the maid are decoyed from the house. This young man is decoyed down there by means of a bogus letter – colour being lent to this last by the fact that you actually are performing at Riverbury that week. The young man is doped, and the police are rung up and have their suspicions directed against him. A burglary actually has taken place. I presume the jewels were taken?'

'Oh, yes.'

'Were they ever recovered?'

'No, never. I think, as a matter of fact, Sir Herman tried to hush things up all he knew how. But he couldn't manage it, and I rather fancy his wife started divorce proceedings in consequence. Still, I don't really know about that.'

'What happened to Mr Leslie Faulkener?'

'He was released in the end. The police said they hadn't really got enough against him. Don't you think the whole thing was rather odd?'

'Distinctly odd. The first question is whose story to believe? In telling it, Miss Helier, I noticed that you incline towards believing Mr Faulkener. Have you any reason for doing so beyond your own instinct in the matter?'

'No-no,' said Jane unwillingly. 'I suppose I haven't. But he was so very nice, and so apologetic for having mistaken anyone else for me, that I feel sure he *must* have been telling the truth.'

'I see,' said Sir Henry smiling. 'But you must admit that he could have invented the story quite easily. He could write the letter purporting to be from you himself. He could also dope himself after successfully committing the burglary. But I confess I don't see where the *point* of all that would be. Easier to enter the house, help himself, and disappear quietly – unless just possibly he was observed by someone in the neighbourhood and knew himself to have been observed. Then he might hastily concoct this plan for diverting suspicion from himself and accounting for his presence in the neighbourhood.'

'Was he well off?' asked Miss Marple.

'I don't think so,' said Jane. 'No, I believe he was rather hard up.'

'The whole thing seems curious,' said Dr Lloyd. 'I must confess that if we accept the young man's story as true, it seems to make the case very much more difficult. Why should the unknown woman who pretended to be Miss Helier drag this unknown man into the affair? Why should she stage such an elaborate comedy?'

'Tell me, Jane,' said Mrs Bantry. 'Did young Faulkener ever come face to face with Mary Kerr at any stage of the proceedings?'

'I don't quite know,' said Jane slowly, as she puzzled her brows in remembrance.

'Because if he didn't the case is solved!' said Mrs Bantry. 'I'm sure

I'm right. What is easier than to pretend you're called up to town? You telephone to your maid from Paddington or whatever station you arrive at, and as she comes up to town, you go down again. The young man calls by appointment, he's doped, you set the stage for the burglary, over-doing it as much as possible. You telephone the police, give a description of your scapegoat, and off you go to town again. Then you arrive home by a later train and do the surprised innocent.'

'But why should she steal her own jewels, Dolly?'

'They always do,' said Mrs Bantry. 'And anyway, I can think of hundreds of reasons. She may have wanted money at once – old Sir Herman wouldn't give her the cash, perhaps, so she pretends the jewels are stolen and then sells them secretly. Or she may have been being black-mailed by someone who threatened to tell her husband or Sir Herman's wife. Or she may have already sold the jewels and Sir Herman was getting ratty and asking to see them, so she had to do something about it. That's done a good deal in books. Or perhaps she was going to have them reset and she'd got paste replicas. Or – here's a very good idea – and not so much done in books – she pretends they are stolen, gets in an awful state and he gives her a fresh lot. So she gets two lots instead of one. That kind of woman, I am sure, is most frightfully artful.'

'You are clever, Dolly,' said Jane admiringly. 'I never thought of that.'

'You may be clever, but she doesn't say you're right,' said Colonel Bantry. 'I incline to suspicion of the city gentleman. He'd know the sort of telegram to get the lady out of the way, and he could manage the rest easily enough with the help of a new lady friend. Nobody seems to have thought of asking *him* for an alibi.'

'What do you think, Miss Marple?' asked Jane, turning towards the old lady who had sat silent, a puzzled frown on her face.

'My dear, I really don't know what to say. Sir Henry will laugh, but I recall no village parallel to help me this time. Of course there are several questions that suggest themselves. For instance, the servant question. In – ahem – an irregular ménage of the kind you describe, the servant employed would doubtless be perfectly aware of the state of things, and a really nice girl would not take such a place – her mother wouldn't let her for a minute. So I think we can assume that the maid was *not* a really trustworthy character. She may have been in league with the thieves. She would leave the house open for them and actually go to London as though sure of the pretence telephone message so as to divert suspicion from herself. I must confess that that seems the most probable solution. Only if ordinary thieves were concerned it seems very odd. It seems to argue more knowledge than a maidservant was likely to have.'

Miss Marple paused and then went on dreamily:

'I can't help feeling that there was some – well, what I must describe as personal feeling about the whole thing. Supposing somebody had a spite, for instance? A young actress that he hadn't treated well? Don't you think that that would explain things better? A deliberate attempt to get him into trouble. That's what it looks like. And yet – that's not entirely satisfactory . . .'

'Why, doctor, you haven't said anything,' said Jane. 'I'd forgotten you.'

'I'm always getting forgotten,' said the grizzled doctor sadly. 'I must have a very inconspicuous personality.'

'Oh, no!' said Jane. 'Do tell us what you think.'

'I'm rather in the position of agreeing with everyone's solutions – and yet with none of them. I myself have a far-fetched and probably totally erroneous theory that the wife may have had something to do with it. Sir Herman's wife, I mean. I've no grounds for thinking so – only you would be surprised if you knew the extraordinary – really *very* extraordinary things that a wronged wife will take it into her head to do.'

'Oh! Dr Lloyd,' cried Miss Marple excitedly. 'How clever of you. And I never thought of poor Mrs Pebmarsh.'

Jane stared at her.

'Mrs Pebmarsh? Who is Mrs Pebmarsh?'

'Well –' Miss Marple hesitated. 'I don't know that she really comes in. She's a laundress. And she stole an opal pin that was pinned into a blouse and put it in another woman's house.'

Jane looked more fogged than ever.

'And that makes it all perfectly clear to you, Miss Marple?' said Sir Henry, with his twinkle.

But to his surprise Miss Marple shook her head.

'No, I'm afraid it doesn't. I must confess myself completely at a loss. What I do realize is that women must stick together – one should, in an emergency, stand by one's own sex. I think that's the moral of the story Miss Helier has told us.'

'I must confess that that particular ethical significance of the mystery has escaped me,' said Sir Henry gravely. 'Perhaps I shall see the significance of your point more clearly when Miss Helier has revealed the solution.'

'Eh?' said Jane looking rather bewildered.

'I was observing that, in childish language, we "give it up". You and you alone, Miss Helier, have had the high honour of presenting such an absolutely baffling mystery that even Miss Marple has to confess herself defeated.'

'You all give it up?' asked Jane.

'Yes.' After a minute's silence during which he waited for the others to speak, Sir Henry constituted himself spokesman once more. 'That is to say we stand or fall by the sketchy solutions we have tentatively advanced. One each for the mere men, two for Miss Marple, and a round dozen from Mrs B.'

'It was not a dozen,' said Mrs Bantry. 'They were variations on a main theme. And how often am I to tell you that I will *not* be called Mrs B?'

'So you all give it up,' said Jane thoughtfully. 'That's very interesting.'

She leaned back in her chair and began to polish her nails rather absent-mindedly.

'Well,' said Mrs Bantry. 'Come on, Jane. What is the solution?'

'The solution?'

'Yes. What really happened?'

Jane stared at her.

'I haven't the least idea.'

'*What?*'

'I've always wondered. I thought you were all so clever one of you would be able to tell *me*.'

Everybody harboured feelings of annoyance. It was all very well for Jane to be so beautiful – but at this moment everyone felt that stupidity could be carried too far. Even the most transcendent loveliness could not excuse it.

'You mean the truth was never discovered?' said Sir Henry.

'No. That's why, as I say, I did think you would be able to tell *me*.'

Jane sounded injured. It was plain that she felt she had a grievance.

'Well – I'm – I'm –' said Colonel Bantry, words failing him.

'You are the most aggravating girl, Jane,' said his wife. 'Anyway, I'm sure and always will be that I was right. If you just tell us the proper names of the people, I shall be *quite* sure.'

'I don't think I could do that,' said Jane slowly.

'No, dear,' said Miss Marple. 'Miss Helier couldn't do that.'

'Of course she could,' said Mrs Bantry. 'Don't be so high-minded, Jane. We older folk must have a bit of scandal. At any rate tell us who the city magnate was.'

But Jane shook her head, and Miss Marple, in her old-fashioned way, continued to support the girl.

'It must have been a very distressing business,' she said.

'No,' said Jane truthfully. 'I think – I think I rather enjoyed it.'

'Well, perhaps you did,' said Miss Marple. 'I suppose it was a break in the monotony. What play were you acting in?'

'*Smith*.'

'Oh, yes. That's one of Mr Somerset Maugham's, isn't it? All his are very clever, I think. I've seen them nearly all.'

'You're reviving it to go on tour next autumn, aren't you?' asked Mrs Bantry.

Jane nodded.

'Well,' said Miss Marple rising. 'I must go home. Such late hours! But we've had a very entertaining evening. Most unusually so. I think Miss Helier's story wins the prize. Don't you agree?'

'I'm sorry you're angry with me,' said Jane. 'About not knowing the end, I mean. I suppose I should have said so sooner.'

Her tone sounded wistful. Dr Lloyd rose gallantly to the occasion.

'My dear young lady, why should you? You gave us a very pretty problem to sharpen our wits on. I am only sorry we could none of us solve it convincingly.'

'Speak for yourself,' said Mrs Bantry. 'I *did* solve it. I'm convinced I am right.'

'Do you know, I really believe you are,' said Jane. 'What you said sounded so probable.'

'Which of her seven solutions do you refer to?' asked Sir Henry teasingly.

Dr Lloyd gallantly assisted Miss Marple to put on her goloshes. 'Just in case,' as the old lady explained. The doctor was to be her escort to her old-world cottage. Wrapped in several woollen shawls, Miss Marple wished everyone good night once more. She came to Jane Helier last and leaning forward, she murmured something in the actress's ear. A startled 'Oh!' burst from Jane – so loud as to cause the others to turn their heads.

Smiling and nodding, Miss Marple made her exit, Jane Helier staring after her.

'Are you coming to bed, Jane?' asked Mrs Bantry. 'What's the matter with you? You're staring as though you'd seen a ghost.'

With a deep sigh Jane came to herself, shed a beautiful and bewildering smile on the two men and followed her hostess up the staircase. Mrs Bantry came into the girl's room with her.

'Your fire's nearly out,' said Mrs Bantry, giving it a vicious and ineffectual poke. 'They can't have made it up properly. How stupid housemaids are. Still, I suppose we are rather late tonight. Why, it's actually past one o'clock!'

'Do you think there are many people like her?' asked Jane Helier.

She was sitting on the side of the bed apparently wrapped in thought.

'Like the housemaid?'

'No. Like that funny old woman – what's her name – Marple?'

'Oh! I don't know. I suppose she's a fairly common type in a small village.'

'Oh dear,' said Jane. 'I don't know what to do.'

She sighed deeply.

'What's the matter?'

'I'm worried.'

'What about?'

'Dolly,' Jane Helier was portentously solemn. 'Do you know what that queer old lady whispered to me before she went out of the door tonight?'

'No. What?'

'She said: "*I shouldn't do it if I were you, my dear. Never put yourself too much in another woman's power, even if you do think she's your friend at the moment.*" You know, Dolly, that's awfully true.'

'The maxim? Yes, perhaps it is. But I don't see the application.'

'I suppose you can't ever really trust a woman. And I should be in her power. I never thought of that.'

'What woman are you talking about?'

'Netta Greene, my understudy.'

'What on earth does Miss Marple know about your understudy?'

'I suppose she guessed – but I can't see how.'

'Jane, will you kindly tell me at once what you are talking about?'

'The story. The one I told. Oh, Dolly, that woman, you know – the one that took Claud from me?'

Mrs Bantry nodded, casting her mind back rapidly to the first of Jane's unfortunate marriages – to Claud Averbury, the actor.

'He married her; and I could have told him how it would be. Claud doesn't know, but she's carrying on with Sir Joseph Salmon – week-ends with him at the bungalow I told you about. I wanted her shown up – I would like everyone to know the sort of woman she was. And you see, with a burglary, everything would be bound to come out.'

'Jane!' gasped Mrs Bantry. 'Did *you* engineer this story you've been telling us?'

Jane nodded.

'That's why I chose *Smith*. I wear parlourmaid's kit in it, you know. So I should have it handy. And when they sent for me to the police station it's the easiest thing in the world to say I was rehearsing my part with my understudy at the hotel. Really, of course, we would be at the bungalow. I just have to open the door and bring in the cocktails, and Netta to pretend to be me. He'd never see *her* again, of course, so there would be no fear of his recognizing her. And I can make myself look quite different as a parlourmaid; and besides, one doesn't look at parlourmaids as though they were people. We planned to drag him out into the road afterwards, bag the jewel case, telephone the police and get back to the hotel. I shouldn't like the poor young man to suffer, but Sir Henry didn't seem to think he would, did he? And she'd be in the papers and everything – and Claud would see what she was really like.'

Mrs Bantry sat down and groaned.

'Oh! my poor head. And all the time – Jane Helier, you deceitful girl! Telling us that story the way you did!'

'I *am* a good actress,' said Jane complacently. 'I always have been, whatever people choose to say. I didn't give myself away once, did I?'

'Miss Marple was right,' murmured Mrs Bantry. 'The personal element. Oh, yes, the personal element. Jane, my good child, do you realize that theft is theft, and you might have been sent to prison?'

'Well, none of you guessed,' said Jane. 'Except Miss Marple.' The worried expression returned to her face. 'Dolly, do you *really* think there are many like her?'

'Frankly, I don't,' said Mrs Bantry.

Jane sighed again.

'Still, one had better not risk it. And of course I should be in Netta's power – that's true enough. She might turn against me or blackmail me or anything. She helped me think out the details and she professed to be devoted to me, but one never *does* know with women. No, I think Miss Marple was right. I had better not risk it.'

'But, my dear, you have risked it.'

'Oh, no.' Jane opened her blue eyes very wide. 'Don't you understand? *None of this has happened yet*! I was – well, trying it on the dog, so to speak.'

'I don't profess to understand your theatrical slang,' said Mrs Bantry with dignity. 'Do you mean this is a future project – not a past deed?'

'I was going to do it this autumn – in September. I don't know what to do now.'

'And Jane Marple guessed – actually guessed the truth and never told us,' said Mrs Bantry wrathfully.

'I think that was why she said that – about women sticking together. She wouldn't give me away before the men. That was nice of her. I don't mind *your* knowing, Dolly.'

'Well, give the idea up, Jane. I beg of you.'

'I think I shall,' murmured Miss Helier. 'There might be other Miss Marples . . .'

Manx Gold

'Manx Gold' was first published in *The Daily Dispatch* between 23–28 May 1930 as a treasure hunt to promote tourism in the Isle of Man.

> *Old Mylecharane liv'd up on the broo.*
> *Where Jurby slopes down to the wold,*
> *His croft was all golden with cushag and furze,*
> *His daughter was fair to behold.*
>
> *'O father, they say you've plenty of store,*
> *But hidden all out of the way.*
> *No gold can I see, but its glint on the gorse;*
> *Then what have you done with it, pray?'*
>
> *'My gold is locked up in a coffer of oak,*
> *Which I dropped in the tide and it sank,*
> *And there it lies fixed like an anchor of hope,*
> *All bright and as safe as the bank.'*

'I like that song,' I said appreciatively, as Fenella finished.

'You should do,' said Fenella. 'It's about our ancestor, yours and mine. Uncle Myles's grandfather. He made a fortune out of smuggling and hid it somewhere, and no one ever knew where.'

Ancestry is Fenella's strong point. She takes an interest in all her forebears. My tendencies are strictly modern. The difficult present and the uncertain future absorb all my energy. But I like hearing Fenella singing old Manx ballads.

Fenella is very charming. She is my first cousin and also, from time to time, my fiancée. In moods of financial optimism we are engaged. When a corresponding wave of pessimism sweeps over us and we realize that we shall not be able to marry for at least ten years, we break it off.

'Didn't anyone ever try to find the treasure?' I inquired.

'Of course. But they never did.'

'Perhaps they didn't look scientifically.'

'Uncle Myles had a jolly good try,' said Fenella. 'He said anyone with intelligence ought to be able to solve a little problem like that.'

That sounded to me very like our Uncle Myles, a cranky and eccentric old gentleman, who lived in the Isle of Man, and who was much given to didactic pronouncements.

It was at that moment that the post came – and the letter!

'Good Heavens,' cried Fenella. 'Talk of the devil – I mean angels – Uncle Myles is dead!'

Both she and I had only seen our eccentric relative on two occasions, so we could neither of us pretend to a very deep grief. The letter was from a firm of lawyers in Douglas, and it informed us that under the will of Mr Myles Mylecharane, deceased, Fenella and I were joint inheritors of his estate, which consisted of a house near Douglas, and an infinitesimal income. Enclosed was a sealed envelope, which Mr Mylecharane had directed should be forwarded to Fenella at his death. This letter we opened and read its surprising contents. I reproduce it in full, since it was a truly characteristic document.

'*My dear Fenella and Juan (for I take it that where one of you is the other will not be far away! Or so gossip has whispered), You may remember having heard me say that anyone displaying a little intelligence could easily find the treasure concealed by my amiable scoundrel of a grandfather. I displayed that intelligence – and my reward was four chests of solid gold – quite like a fairy story, is it not?*

Of living relations I have only four, you two, my nephew Ewan Corjeag, whom I have always heard is a thoroughly bad lot, and a cousin, a Doctor Fayll, of whom I have heard very little, and that little not always good.

My estate proper I am leaving to you and Fenella, but I feel a certain obligation laid upon me with regard to this 'treasure' which has fallen to my lot solely through my own ingenuity. My amiable ancestor would not, I feel, be satisfied for me to pass it on tamely by inheritance. So I, in my turn, have devised a little problem.

There are still four 'chests' of treasure (though in a more modern form than gold ingots or coins) and there are to be four competitors – my four living relations. It would be fairest to assign one 'chest' to each – but the world, my children, is not fair. The race is to the swiftest – and often to the most unscrupulous!

Who am I to go against Nature? You must pit your wits against the other two. There will be, I fear, very little chance for you. Goodness and innocence are seldom rewarded in this world. So strongly do I feel this that I have deliberately cheated (unfairness again, you notice!). This letter goes to you twenty-four hours in advance of the letters to the other two. Thus you will have a very good chance of securing the first "treasure" – twenty-four hours' start, if you have any brains at all, ought to be sufficient.

The clues for finding this treasure are to be found at my house in Douglas. The clues for the second "treasure" will not be released till the first treasure is found. In the second and succeeding cases, therefore, you will all start even. You have my good wishes for success, and nothing would please me better than for you to acquire all four "chests", but for the reasons which I have already stated I think that most unlikely. Remember that no scruples will stand in dear Ewan's way. Do not make the mistake of trusting him in any respect. As to Dr Richard Fayll, I know little about him, but he is, I fancy, a dark horse.

Good luck to you both, but with little hopes of your success,
Your affectionate Uncle,
Myles Mylecharane'

As we reached the signature, Fenella made a leap from my side.

'What is it?' I cried.

Fenella was rapidly turning the pages of an ABC.

'We must get to the Isle of Man as soon as possible,' she cried. 'How dare he say we were good and innocent and stupid? I'll show him! Juan, we're going to find all four of these "chests" and get married and live happily ever afterwards, with Rolls-Royces and footmen and marble baths. But we *must* get to the Isle of Man at once.'

It was twenty-four hours later. We had arrived in Douglas, interviewed the lawyers, and were now at Maughold House facing Mrs Skillicorn, our late Uncle's housekeeper, a somewhat formidable woman who nevertheless relented a little before Fenella's eagerness.

'Queer ways he had,' she said. 'Liked to set everyone puzzling and contriving.'

'But the clues,' cried Fenella. 'The clues?'

Deliberately, as she did everything, Mrs Skillicorn left the room. She returned after an absence of some minutes and held out a folded piece of paper.

We unfolded it eagerly. It contained a doggerel rhyme in my Uncle's crabbed handwriting.

Four points of the compass so there be
S., and W., N. and E.
East winds are bad for man and beast.
Go south and west and
North not east.

'Oh!' said Fenella, blankly.

'Oh!' said I, with much the same intonation.

Mrs Skillicorn smiled on us with gloomy relish.

'Not much sense to it, is there?' she said helpfully.

'It – I don't see how to begin,' said Fenella, piteously.

'Beginning,' I said, with a cheerfulness I did not feel, 'is always the difficulty. Once we get going –'

Mrs Skillicorn smiled more grimly than ever. She was a depressing woman.

'Can't you help us?' asked Fenella, coaxingly.

'I know nothing about the silly business. Didn't confide in me, your uncle didn't. I have told him to put his money in the bank, and no nonsense. I never knew what he was up to.'

'He never went out with any chests – or anything of that kind?'

'That he didn't.'

'You don't know when he hid the stuff – whether it was lately or long ago?'

Mrs Skillicorn shook her head.

'Well,' I said, trying to rally. 'There are two possibilities. Either the treasure is hidden here, in the actual grounds, or else it may be hidden anywhere on the Island. It depends on the bulk, of course.'

A sudden brain-wave occurred to Fenella.

'You haven't noticed anything missing?' she said. 'Among my Uncle's things, I mean?'

'Why, now, it's odd your saying that –'

'You have, then?'

'As I say, it's odd your saying that. Snuffboxes – there's at least four of them I can't lay my hand on anywhere.'

'Four of them!' cried Fenella, 'that must be it! We're on the track. Let's go out in the garden and look about.'

'There's nothing there,' said Mrs Skillicorn. 'I'd know if there were. Your Uncle couldn't have buried anything in the garden without my knowing about it.'

'Points of the compass are mentioned,' I said. 'The first thing we need is a map of the Island.'

'There's one on that desk,' said Mrs Skillicorn.

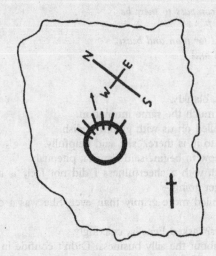

Fenella unfolded it eagerly. Something fluttered out as she did so. I caught it.

'Hullo,' I said. 'This looks like a further clue.'

We both went over it eagerly.

It appeared to be a rude kind of map. There was a cross on it and a circle and a pointing arrow, and directions were roughly indicated, but it was hardly illuminating. We studied it in silence.

'It's not very illuminating, is it?' said Fenella.

'Naturally it wants puzzling over,' I said. 'We can't expect it to leap to the eye.'

Mrs Skillicorn interrupted with a suggestion of supper, to which we agreed thankfully.

'And could we have some coffee?' said Fenella. 'Lots of it – very black.'

Mrs Skillicorn provided us with an excellent meal, and at its conclusion a large jug of coffee made its appearance.

'And now,' said Fenella, 'we must get down to it.'

'The first thing,' I said, 'is direction. This seems to point clearly to the north-east of the Island.'

'It seems so. Let's look at the map.'

We studied the map attentively.

'It all depends on how you take the thing,' said Fenella. 'Does the cross represent the treasure? Or is it something like a church? There really ought to be rules!'

'That would make it too easy.'

'I suppose it would. Why are there little lines one side of the circle and not the other.'

'I don't know.'

'Are there any more maps anywhere?'

We were sitting in the library. There were several excellent maps. There were also various guide books descriptive of the Island. There was a book on folklore. There was a book on the history of the Island. We read them all.

And at last we formed a possible theory.

'It does seem to fit,' said Fenella at last. 'I mean the two together is a likely conjunction which doesn't seem to occur anywhere else.'

'It's worth trying, anyhow,' I said. 'I don't think we can do anything more tonight. Tomorrow, first thing, we'll hire a car and go off and try our luck.'

'It's tomorrow now,' said Fenella. 'Half-past two! Just fancy!'

Early morning saw us on the road. We had hired a car for a week, arranging to drive it ourselves. Fenella's spirits rose as we sped along the excellent road, mile after mile.

'If only it wasn't for the other two, what fun this would be,' she said. 'This is where the Derby was originally run, wasn't it? Before it was changed to Epsom. How queer that is to think of!'

I drew her attention to a farmhouse.

'That must be where there is said to be a secret passage running under the sea to that island.'

'What fun! I love secret passages, don't you? Oh! Juan, we're getting quite near now. I'm terribly excited. If we should be right!'

Five minutes later we abandoned the car.

'Everything's in the right position,' said Fenella, tremulously.

We walked on.

'Six of them – that's right. Now between these two. Have you got the compass?'

Five minutes later, we were standing facing each other, an incredulous joy on our faces – and on my outstretched palm lay an antique snuffbox.

We had been successful!

On our return to Maughold House, Mrs Skillicorn met us with the information that two gentlemen had arrived. One had departed again, but the other was in the library.

A tall, fair man, with a florid face, rose smilingly from an armchair as we entered the room.

'Mr Faraker and Miss Mylecharane? Delighted to meet you. I am your distant cousin, Dr Fayll. Amusing game all this, isn't it?'

His manner was urbane and pleasant, but I took an immediate dislike to him. I felt that in some way the man was dangerous. His pleasant manner was, somehow, *too* pleasant, and his eyes never met yours fairly.

'I'm afraid we've got bad news for you,' I said. 'Miss Mylecharane and myself have already discovered the first "treasure".'

He took it very well.

'Too bad – too bad. Posts from here must be odd. Barford and I started at once.'

We did not dare to confess the perfidy of Uncle Myles.

'Anyway, we shall all start fair for the second round,' said Fenella.

'Splendid. What about getting down to the clues right away? Your excellent Mrs – er – Skillicorn holds them, I believe?'

'That wouldn't be fair to Mr Corjeag,' said Fenella, quickly. 'We must wait for him.'

'True, true – I had forgotten. We must get in touch with him as quickly as possible. I will see to that – you two must be tired out and want to rest.'

Thereupon he took his departure. Ewan Corjeag must have been unexpectedly difficult to find, for it was not till nearly eleven o'clock that night that Dr Fayll rang up. He suggested that he and Ewan should come over to Maughold House at ten o'clock the following morning, when Mrs Skillicorn could hand us out the clues.

'That will do splendidly,' said Fenella. 'Ten o'clock tomorrow.'

We retired to bed tired but happy.

The following morning we were aroused by Mrs Skillicorn, completely shaken out of her usual pessimistic calm.

'Whatever do you think?' she panted. 'The house has been broken into.'

'Burglars?' I exclaimed, incredulously. 'Has anything been taken?'

'Not a thing – and that's the odd part of it! No doubt they were after the silver – but the door being locked on the outside they couldn't get any further.'

Fenella and I accompanied her to the scene of the outrage, which happened to be in her own sitting-room. The window there had undeniably been forced, yet nothing seemed to have been taken. It was all rather curious.

'I don't see what they can have been looking for?' said Fenella.

'It's not as though there were a "treasure chest" hidden in the house,' I agreed facetiously. Suddenly an idea flashed into my mind. I turned to Mrs Skillicorn. 'The clues – the clues you were to give us this morning?'

'Why to be sure – they're in that top drawer.' She went across to it. 'Why – I do declare – there's nothing here! They're gone!'

'Not burglars,' I said. 'Our esteemed relations!' And I remember Uncle Myles's warning on the subject of unscrupulous dealing. Clearly he had known what he was talking about. A dirty trick!

'Hush,' said Fenella, suddenly, holding up a finger. 'What was that?'

The sound she had caught came plainly to our ears. It was a groan and it came from outside. We went to the window and leaned out. There was a shrubbery growing against this side of the house and we could see nothing; but the groan came again, and we could see that the bushes seemed to have been disturbed and trampled.

We hurried down and out round the house. The first thing we found was a fallen ladder, showing how the thieves had reached the window. A few steps further brought us to where a man was lying.

He was a youngish man, dark, and he was evidently badly injured, for his head was lying in a pool of blood. I knelt down beside him.

'We must get a doctor at once. I'm afraid he's dying.'

The gardener was sent off hurriedly. I slipped my hand into his breast pocket and brought out a pocket book. On it were the initials EC.

'Ewan Corjeag,' said Fenella.

The man's eyes opened. He said, faintly: 'Fell from ladder . . .' then lost consciousness again.

Close by his head was a large jagged stone stained with blood.

'It's clear enough,' I said. 'The ladder slipped and he fell, striking his head on this stone. I'm afraid it's done for him, poor fellow.'

'So you think that was it?' said Fenella, in an odd tone of voice.

But at that moment the doctor arrived. He held out little hope of recovery. Ewan Corjeag was moved into the house and a nurse was sent for to take charge of him. Nothing could be done, and he would die a couple of hours later.

We had been sent for and were standing by his bed. His eyes opened and flickered.

'We are your cousins Juan and Fenella,' I said. 'Is there anything we can do?'

He made a faint negative motion of the head. A whisper came from his lips. I bent to catch it.

'Do you want the clue? I'm done. Don't let Fayll do you down.'

'Yes,' said Fenella. 'Tell me.'

Something like a grin came over his face.

'*D'ye ken –*' he began.

Then suddenly his head fell over sideways and he died.

*   *   *

'I don't like it,' said Fenella, suddenly.

'What don't you like?'

'Listen, Juan. Ewan stole those clues – he admits falling from the ladder. *Then where are they?* We've seen all the contents of his pockets. There were three sealed envelopes, so Mrs Skillicorn says. Those sealed envelopes aren't there.'

'What do you think, then?'

'I think there was someone else there, someone who jerked away the ladder so that he fell. And that stone – he never fell on it – it was brought from some distance away – I've found the mark. He was deliberately bashed on the head with it.'

'But Fenella – that's murder!'

'Yes,' said Fenella, very white. 'It's murder. Remember, Dr Fayll never turned up at ten o'clock this morning. Where is he?'

'You think he's the murderer?'

'Yes. You know – this treasure – it's a lot of money, Juan.'

'And we've no idea where to look for him,' I said. 'A pity Corjeag couldn't have finished what he was going to say.'

'There's one thing might help. This was in his hand.'

She handed me a torn snap-shot.

'Suppose it's a clue. The murderer snatched it away and never noticed he'd left a corner of it behind. If we were to find the other half –'

'To do that,' I said, 'we must find the second treasure. Let's look at this thing.'

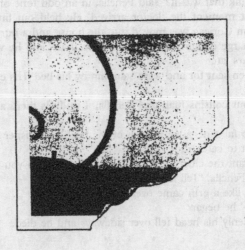

'H'm,' I said, 'there's nothing much to go by. That seems a kind of tower in the middle of the circle, but it would be very hard to identify.'

Fenella nodded.

'Dr Fayll has the important half. He knows where to look. We've got to find that man, Juan, and watch him. Of course, we won't let him see we suspect.'

'I wonder whereabouts in the Island he is this minute. If we only knew –'

My mind went back to the dying man. Suddenly, I sat up excitedly.

'Fenella,' I said, 'Corjeag wasn't Scotch?'

'No, of course not.'

'Well, then, don't you see? What he meant, I mean?'

'No?'

I scribbled something on a piece of paper and tossed it to her.

'What's this?'

'The name of a firm that might help us.'

'Bellman and True. Who are they? Lawyers?'

'No – they're more in our line – private detectives.'

And I proceeded to explain.

'Dr Fayll to see you,' said Mrs Skillicorn.

We looked at each other. Twenty-four hours had elapsed. We had returned from our quest successful for the second time. Not wishing to draw attention to ourselves, we had journeyed in the Snaefell – a charabanc.

'I wonder if he knows we saw him in the distance?' murmured Fenella.

'It's extraordinary. If it hadn't been for the hint that photograph gave us –'

'Hush – and do be careful, Juan. He must be simply furious at our having outwitted him, in spite of everything.'

No trace of it appeared in the doctor's manner, however. He entered the room his urbane and charming self, and I felt my faith in Fenella's theory dwindling.

'What a shocking tragedy!' he said. 'Poor Corjeag. I suppose he was – well – trying to steal a march on us. Retribution was swift. Well, well – we scarcely knew him, poor fellow. You must have wondered why I didn't turn up this morning as arranged. I got a fake message – Corjeag's doing, I suppose – it sent me off on a wild-goose chase right across the Island. And now you two have romped home again. How do you do it?'

There was a note of really eager inquiry in his voice which did not escape me.

'Cousin Ewan was fortunately able to speak just before he died,' said Fenella.

I was watching the man, and I could swear I saw alarm leap into his eyes at her words.

'Eh – eh? What's that?' he said.

'He was just able to give us a clue as to the whereabouts of the treasure,' explained Fenella.

'Oh! I see – I see. I've been clean out of things – though, curiously enough, I myself was in that part of the Island. You may have seen me strolling round.'

'We were so busy,' said Fenella, apologetically.

'Of course, of course. You must have run across the thing more or less by accident. Lucky young people, aren't you? Well, what's the next programme? Will Mrs Skillicorn oblige us with the new clues?'

But it seemed that this third set of clues had been deposited with the lawyers, and we all three repaired to the lawyer's office, where the sealed envelopes were handed over to us.

The contents were simple. A map with a certain area marked off on it, and a paper of directions attached.

In '85, this place made history.
Ten paces from the landmark to
The east, then an equal ten
Paces north. Stand there
Looking east. Two trees are in the
Line of vision. One of them
Was sacred in this island. Draw
A circle five feet from
The Spanish chestnut and,
With head bent, walk round. Look well. You'll find.

'Looks as though we were going to tread on each other's toes a bit today,' commented the doctor.

True to my policy of apparent friendliness, I offered him a lift in our car, which he accepted. We had lunch at Port Erin, and then started on our search.

I had debated in my own mind the reason of my uncle's depositing this particular set of clues with his lawyer. Had he foreseen the possibility of a theft? And had he determined that not more than one set of clues should fall into the thief's possession?

The treasure hunt this afternoon was not without its humour. The area of search was limited, and we were continually in sight of each other. We eyed each other suspiciously, each trying to determine whether the other was farther on or had had a brain-wave.

'This is all part of Uncle Myles's plan,' said Fenella. 'He wanted us to watch each other and go through all the agonies of thinking the other person was getting there.'

'Come,' I said. 'Let's get down to it scientifically. We've got one definite clue to start on. "*In '85 this place made history.*" Look up the reference books we've got with us and see if we can't hunt that down. Once we get that –'

'He's looking in that hedge,' interrupted Fenella. 'Oh! I can't bear it. If he's got it –'

'Attend to me,' I said firmly. 'There's really only one way to go about it – the proper way.'

'There are so few trees on the Island that it would be much simpler just to look for a chestnut tree!' said Fenella.

I pass over the next hour. We grew hot and despondent – and all the time we were tortured with fear that Fayll might be succeeding whilst we failed.

'I remember once reading in a detective story,' I said, 'how a fellow stuck a paper of writing in a bath of acid – and all sorts of other words came out.'

'Do you think – but we haven't got a bath of acid!'

'I don't think Uncle Myles could expect expert chemical knowledge. But there's common-or-garden heat –'

We slipped round the corner of a hedge and in a minute or two I had kindled a few twigs. I held the paper as close to the blaze as I dared. Almost at once I was rewarded by seeing characters begin to appear at the foot of the sheet. There were just two words.

'Kirkhill Station,' read out Fenella.

Just at that moment Fayll came round the corner. Whether he had heard or not we had no means of judging. He showed nothing.

'But, Juan,' said Fenella, when he moved away, 'there isn't a Kirkhill Station!' She held out the map as she spoke.

'No,' I said, examining it, 'but look here.'

And with a pencil I drew a line on it.

'Of course! And somewhere on that line –'

'Exactly.'

'But I wish we knew the exact spot.'

It was then that my second brain-wave came to me.

'We do!' I cried, and, seizing the pencil again, I said: 'Look!'

Fenella uttered a cry.

'How idiotic!' she cried. 'And how marvellous! What a sell! Really, Uncle Myles was a most ingenious old gentleman!'

The time had come for the last clue. This, the lawyer had informed us, was not in his keeping. It was to be posted to us on receipt of a post-card sent by him. He would impart no further information.

Nothing arrived, however, on the morning it should have done, and Fenella and I went through agonies, believing that Fayll had managed somehow to intercept our letter. The next day, however, our fears were calmed and the mystery explained when we received the following illiterate scrawl:

> *Dear Sir or Madam,*
> *Escuse delay but have been all sixes and sevens but i do now as mr Mylecharane axed me to and send you the piece of riting wot as been in my family many long years the wot he wanted it for i do not know. thanking you i am*
> *Mary Kerruish'*

'Post mark – Bride,' I remarked. 'Now for the "piece of riting handed down in my family"!'

Upon a rock, a sign you'll see.
O, Tell me what the point of
That may be? Well, firstly, (A). Near
By you'll find, quite suddenly, the light
You seek. Then (B). A house. A
Cottage with a thatch and wall.
A meandering lane near by. That's all.

'It's very unfair to begin with a rock,' said Fenella. 'There are rocks everywhere. How can you tell which one has the sign on it?'

'If we could settle on the district,' I said, 'it ought to be fairly easy to find the rock. It must have a mark on it pointing in a certain direction, and in that direction there will be something hidden which will throw light on the finding of the treasure.'

'I think you're right,' said Fenella.

'That's A. The new clue will give us a hint where B, the cottage, is to be found. The treasure itself is hidden down a lane alongside the cottage. But clearly we've got to find A first.'

Owing to the difficulty of the initial step, Uncle Myles's last problem proved a real teaser. To Fenella falls the distinction of unravelling it – and even then she did not accomplish it for nearly a week. Now and then we had come across Fayll in our search of rocky districts, but the area was a wide one.

When we finally made our discovery it was late in the evening. Too late, I said, to start off to the place indicated. Fenella disagreed.

'Supposing Fayll finds it, too,' she said. 'And we wait till tomorrow and he starts off tonight. How we should kick ourselves!'

Suddenly, a marvellous idea occurred to me.

'Fenella,' I said, 'do you still believe that Fayll murdered Ewan Corjeag?'

'I do.'

'Then I think that now we've got our chance to bring the crime home to him.'

'That man makes me shiver. He's bad all through. Tell me.'

'Advertise the fact that we've found A. Then start off. Ten to one he'll follow us. It's a lonely place – just what would suit his book. He'll come out in the open if we pretend to find the treasure.'

'And then?'

'And then,' I said, 'he'll have a little surprise.'

It was close on midnight. We had left the car some distance away and were creeping along by the side of a wall. Fenella had a powerful flashlight which she was using. I myself carried a revolver. I was taking no chances.

Suddenly, with a low cry, Fenella stopped.

'Look, Juan,' she cried. 'We've got it. At last.'

For a moment I was off my guard. Led by instinct I whirled round – but too late. Fayll stood six paces away and his revolver covered us both.

'Good evening,' he said. 'This trick is mine. You'll hand over that treasure, if you please.'

'Would you like me also to hand over something else?' I asked. 'Half a snap-shot torn from a dying man's hand? *You have the other half, I think.*'

His hand wavered.

'What are you talking about?' he growled.

'The truth's known,' I said. 'You and Corjeag were there together. You pulled away the ladder and crashed his head with that stone. The police are cleverer than you imagine, Dr Fayll.'

'They know, do they? Then, by Heaven, I'll swing for three murders instead of one!'

'Drop, Fenella,' I screamed. And at the same minute his revolver barked loudly.

We had both dropped in the heather, and before he could fire again uniformed men sprang out from behind the wall where they had been hiding. A moment later Fayll had been handcuffed and led away.

I caught Fenella in my arms.

'I knew I was right,' she said tremulously.

'Darling!' I cried, 'it was too risky. He might have shot you.'

'But he didn't,' said Fenella. 'And we know where the treasure is.'

'Do we?'

'I do. See –' she scribbled a word. 'We'll look for it tomorrow. There can't be many hiding places there, I should say.'

It was just noon when:

'Eureka!' said Fenella, softly. 'The fourth snuffbox. We've got them all. Uncle Myles would be pleased. And now –'

'Now,' I said, 'we can be married and live together happily ever afterwards.'

'We'll live in the Isle of Man,' said Fenella.

'On Manx Gold,' I said, and laughed aloud for sheer happiness.

Death by Drowning

'Death by Drowning' was first published in
Nash's Pall Mall, November 1931.

Sir Henry Clithering, Ex-Commissioner of Scotland Yard, was staying with his friends the Bantrys at their place near the little village of St Mary Mead.

On Saturday morning, coming down to breakfast at the pleasant guestly hour of ten-fifteen, he almost collided with his hostess, Mrs Bantry, in the doorway of the breakfast room. She was rushing from the room, evidently in a condition of some excitement and distress.

Colonel Bantry was sitting at the table, his face rather redder than usual.

"Morning, Clithering,' he said. 'Nice day. Help yourself.'

Sir Henry obeyed. As he took his seat, a plate of kidneys and bacon in front of him, his host went on:

'Dolly's a bit upset this morning.'

'Yes – er – I rather thought so,' said Sir Henry mildly.

He wondered a little. His hostess was of a placid disposition, little given to moods or excitement. As far as Sir Henry knew, she felt keenly on one subject only – gardening.

'Yes,' said Colonel Bantry. 'Bit of news we got this morning upset her. Girl in the village – Emmott's daughter – Emmott who keeps the Blue Boar.'

'Oh, yes, of course.'

'Ye-es,' said Colonel Bantry ruminatively. 'Pretty girl. Got herself into trouble. Usual story. I've been arguing with Dolly about that. Foolish of me. Women never see sense. Dolly was all up in arms for the girl – you know what women are – men are brutes – all the rest of it, etcetera. But it's not so simple as all that – not in these days. Girls know what they're about. Fellow who seduces a girl's not necessarily a villain. Fifty-fifty as often as not. I rather liked young Sandford myself. A young ass rather than a Don Juan, I should have said.'

'It is this man Sandford who got the girl into trouble?'

'So it seems. Of course I don't know anything personally,' said the Colonel cautiously. 'It's all gossip and chat. You know what this place is! As I say, I *know* nothing. And I'm not like Dolly – leaping to conclusions, flinging accusations all over the place. Damn it all, one ought to be careful in what one says. You know – inquest and all that.'

'Inquest?'

Colonel Bantry stared.

'Yes. Didn't I tell you? Girl drowned herself. That's what all the pother's about.'

'That's a nasty business,' said Sir Henry.

'Of course it is. Don't like to think of it myself. Poor pretty little devil. Her father's a hard man by all accounts. I suppose she just felt she couldn't face the music.'

He paused.

'That's what's upset Dolly so.'

'Where did she drown herself?'

'In the river. Just below the mill it runs pretty fast. There's a footpath and a bridge across. They think she threw herself off that. Well, well, it doesn't bear thinking about.'

And with a portentous rustle, Colonel Bantry opened his newspaper and proceeded to distract his mind from painful matters by an absorption in the newest iniquities of the government.

Sir Henry was only mildly interested by the village tragedy. After breakfast, he established himself on a comfortable chair on the lawn, tilted his hat over his eyes and contemplated life from a peaceful angle.

It was about half past eleven when a neat parlourmaid tripped across the lawn.

'If you please, sir, Miss Marple has called, and would like to see you.'

'Miss Marple?'

Sir Henry sat up and straightened his hat. The name surprised him. He remembered Miss Marple very well – her gentle quiet old-maidish ways, her amazing penetration. He remembered a dozen unsolved and hypothetical cases – and how in each case this typical 'old maid of the village' had leaped unerringly to the right solution of the mystery. Sir Henry had a very deep respect for Miss Marple. He wondered what had brought her to see him.

Miss Marple was sitting in the drawing-room – very upright as always, a gaily coloured marketing basket of foreign extraction beside her. Her cheeks were rather pink and she seemed flustered.

'Sir Henry – I am so glad. So fortunate to find you. I just happened to hear that you were staying down here . . . I do hope you will forgive me . . .'

'This is a great pleasure,' said Sir Henry, taking her hand. 'I'm afraid Mrs Bantry's out.'

'Yes,' said Miss Marple. 'I saw her talking to Footit, the butcher, as I passed. Henry Footit was run over yesterday – that was his dog. One of those smooth-haired fox terriers, rather stout and quarrelsome, that butchers always seem to have.'

'Yes,' said Sir Henry helpfully.

'I was glad to get here when she wasn't at home,' continued Miss Marple. 'Because it was you I wanted to see. About this sad affair.'

'Henry Footit?' asked Sir Henry, slightly bewildered.

Miss Marple threw him a reproachful glance.

'No, no. Rose Emmott, of course. You've heard?'

Sir Henry nodded.

'Bantry was telling me. Very sad.'

He was a little puzzled. He could not conceive why Miss Marple should want to see him about Rose Emmott.

Miss Marple sat down again. Sir Henry also sat. When the old lady spoke her manner had changed. It was grave, and had a certain dignity.

'You may remember, Sir Henry, that on one or two occasions we played what was really a pleasant kind of game. Propounding mysteries and giving solutions. You were kind enough to say that I – that I did not do too badly.'

'You beat us all,' said Sir Henry warmly. 'You displayed an absolute genius for getting to the truth. And you always instanced, I remember, some village parallel which had supplied you with the clue.'

He smiled as he spoke, but Miss Marple did not smile. She remained very grave.

'What you said has emboldened me to come to you now. I feel that if I say something to you – at least you will not laugh at me.'

He realized suddenly that she was in deadly earnest.

'Certainly, I will not laugh,' he said gently.

'Sir Henry – this girl – Rose Emmott. She did not drown herself – *she was murdered* . . . And I know who murdered her.'

Sir Henry was silent with sheer astonishment for quite three seconds. Miss Marple's voice had been perfectly quiet and unexcited. She might have been making the most ordinary statement in the world for all the emotion she showed.

'This is a very serious statement to make, Miss Marple,' said Sir Henry when he had recovered his breath.

She nodded her head gently several times.

'I know — I know — that is why I have come to you.'

'But, my dear lady, I am not the person to come to. I am merely a private individual nowadays. If you have knowledge of the kind you claim, you must go to the police.'

'I don't think I can do that,' said Miss Marple.

'But why not?'

'Because, you see, I haven't got any — what you call *knowledge*.'

'You mean it's only a guess on your part?'

'You can call it that, if you like, but it's not really that at all. I *know*. I'm in a position to know; but if I gave my reasons for knowing to Inspector Drewitt — well, he'd simply laugh. And really, I don't know that I'd blame him. It's very difficult to understand what you might call specialized knowledge.'

'Such as?' suggested Sir Henry.

Miss Marple smiled a little.

'If I were to tell you that I know because of a man called Peasegood leaving turnips instead of carrots when he came round with a cart and sold vegetables to my niece several years ago —'

She stopped eloquently.

'A very appropriate name for the trade,' murmured Sir Henry. 'You mean that you are simply judging from the facts in a parallel case.'

'I know human nature,' said Miss Marple. 'It's impossible not to know human nature living in a village all these years. The question is, do you believe me, or don't you?'

She looked at him very straight. The pink flush had heightened on her cheeks. Her eyes met his steadily without wavering.

Sir Henry was a man with a very vast experience of life. He made his decisions quickly without beating about the bush. Unlikely and fantastic as Miss Marple's statement might seem, he was instantly aware that he accepted it.

'I *do* believe you, Miss Marple. But I do not see what you want me to do in the matter, or why you have come to me.'

'I have thought and thought about it,' said Miss Marple. 'As I said, it would be useless going to the police without any facts. I have no facts. What I would ask you to do is to interest yourself in the matter — Inspector Drewitt would be most flattered, I am sure. And, of course, if the matter went farther, Colonel Melchett, the Chief Constable, I am sure, would be wax in your hands.'

She looked at him appealingly.

'And what data are you going to give me to work upon?'

'I thought,' said Miss Marple, 'of writing a name — *the* name — on a piece of paper and giving it to you. Then if, on investigation, you decided that the – the *person* – is not involved in any way – well, I shall have been quite wrong.'

She paused and then added with a slight shiver. 'It would be so dreadful – so very dreadful – if an innocent person were to be hanged.'

'What on earth –' cried Sir Henry, startled.

She turned a distressed face upon him.

'I may be wrong about that – though I don't think so. Inspector Drewitt, you see, is really an intelligent man. But a mediocre amount of intelligence is sometimes most dangerous. It does not take one far enough.'

Sir Henry looked at her curiously.

Fumbling a little, Miss Marple opened a small reticule, took out a little notebook, tore out a leaf, carefully wrote a name on it and folding it in two, handed it to Sir Henry.

He opened it and read the name. It conveyed nothing to him, but his eyebrows lifted a little. He looked across at Miss Marple and tucked the piece of paper in his pocket.

'Well, well,' he said. 'Rather an extraordinary business, this. I've never done anything like it before. But I'm going to back my judgment – of *you*, Miss Marple.'

Sir Henry was sitting in a room with Colonel Melchett, the Chief Constable of the county, and Inspector Drewitt.

The Chief Constable was a little man of aggressively military demeanour. The Inspector was big and broad and eminently sensible.

'I really do feel I'm butting in,' said Sir Henry with his pleasant smile. 'I can't really tell you why I'm doing it.' (Strict truth this!)

'My dear fellow, we're charmed. It's a great compliment.'

'Honoured, Sir Henry,' said the Inspector.

The Chief Constable was thinking: 'Bored to death, poor fellow, at the Bantrys. The old man abusing the government and the old woman babbling on about bulbs.'

The Inspector was thinking: 'Pity we're not up against a real teaser. One of the best brains in England, I've heard it said. Pity it's all such plain sailing.'

Aloud, the Chief Constable said:

'I'm afraid it's all very sordid and straightforward. First idea was that the girl had pitched herself in. She was in the family way, you understand. However, our doctor, Haydock, is a careful fellow. He noticed the bruises on each arm – upper arm. Caused before death. Just where a fellow would have taken her by the arms and flung her in.'

'Would that require much strength?'

'I think not. There would be no struggle – the girl would be taken unawares. It's a footbridge of slippery wood. Easiest thing in the world to pitch her over – there's no handrail that side.'

'You know for a fact that the tragedy occurred there?'

'Yes. We've got a boy – Jimmy Brown – aged twelve. He was in the woods on the other side. He heard a kind of scream from the bridge and a splash. It was dusk you know – difficult to see anything. Presently he saw something white floating down in the water and he ran and got help. They got her out, but it was too late to revive her.'

Sir Henry nodded.

'The boy saw no one on the bridge?'

'No. But, as I tell you, it was dusk, and there's mist always hanging about there. I'm going to question him as to whether he saw anyone about just afterwards or just before. You see he naturally assumed that the girl had thrown herself over. Everybody did to start with.'

'Still, we've got the note,' said Inspector Drewitt. He turned to Sir Henry.

'Note in the dead girl's pocket, sir. Written with a kind of artist's pencil it was, and all of a sop though the paper was we managed to read it.'

'And what did it say?'

'It was from young Sandford. "All right," that's how it ran. "I'll meet you at the bridge at eight-thirty. – R.S." Well, it was near as might be to eight-thirty – a few minutes after – when Jimmy Brown heard the cry and the splash.'

'I don't know whether you've met Sandford at all?' went on Colonel Melchett. 'He's been down here about a month. One of these modern day young architects who build peculiar houses. He's doing a house for Allington. God knows what it's going to be like – full of new-fangled stuff, I suppose. Glass dinner table and surgical chairs made of steel and webbing. Well, that's neither here nor there, but it shows the kind of chap Sandford is. Bolshie, you know – no morals.'

'Seduction,' said Sir Henry mildly, 'is quite an old-established crime though it does not, of course, date back so far as murder.'

Colonel Melchett stared.

'Oh! yes,' he said. 'Quite. Quite.'

'Well, Sir Henry,' said Drewitt, 'there it is – an ugly business, but plain. This young Sandford gets the girl into trouble. Then he's all for clearing off back to London. He's got a girl there – nice young lady – he's engaged to be married to her. Well, naturally this business, if she gets to hear of it, may cook his goose good and proper. He meets Rose at the bridge – it's a misty evening, no one about – he catches her by the shoulders and pitches her in. A proper young swine – and deserves what's coming to him. That's my opinion.'

Sir Henry was silent for a minute or two. He perceived a strong undercurrent of local prejudice. A new-fangled architect was not likely to be popular in the conservative village of St Mary Mead.

'There is no doubt, I suppose, that this man, Sandford, was actually the father of the coming child?' he asked.

'He's the father all right,' said Drewitt. 'Rose Emmott let out as much to her father. She thought he'd marry her. Marry her! Not he!'

'Dear me,' thought Sir Henry. 'I seem to be back in mid-Victorian melodrama. Unsuspecting girl, the villain from London, the stern father, the betrayal – we only need the faithful village lover. Yes, I think it's time I asked about him.'

And aloud he said:

'Hadn't the girl a young man of her own down here?'

'You mean Joe Ellis?' said the Inspector. 'Good fellow Joe. Carpentering's his trade. Ah! If she'd stuck to Joe –'

Colonel Melchett nodded approval.

'Stick to your own class,' he snapped.

'How did Joe Ellis take this affair?' asked Sir Henry.

'Nobody knew how he was taking it,' said the Inspector. 'He's a quiet fellow, is Joe. Close. Anything Rose did was right in his eyes. She had him on a string all right. Just hoped she'd come back to him some day – that was his attitude, I reckon.'

'I'd like to see him,' said Sir Henry.

'Oh! We're going to look him up,' said Colonel Melchett. 'We're not neglecting any line. I thought myself we'd see Emmott first, then Sandford, and then we can go on and see Ellis. That suits you, Clithering?'

Sir Henry said it would suit him admirably.

They found Tom Emmott at the Blue Boar. He was a big burly man of middle age with a shifty eye and a truculent jaw.

'Glad to see you, gentlemen – good morning, Colonel. Come in here and we can be private. Can I offer you anything, gentlemen? No? It's as you please. You've come about this business of my poor girl. Ah! She was a good girl, Rose was. Always was a good girl – till this bloody swine – beg pardon, but that's what he is – till he came along. Promised her marriage, he did. But I'll have the law on him. Drove her to it, he did. Murdering swine. Bringing disgrace on all of us. My poor girl.'

'Your daughter distinctly told you that Mr Sandford was responsible for her condition?' asked Melchett crisply.

'She did. In this very room she did.'

'And what did you say to her?' asked Sir Henry.

'Say to her?' The man seemed momentarily taken aback.

'Yes. You didn't, for example, threaten to turn her out of the house.'

'I was a bit upset – that's only natural. I'm sure you'll agree that's only natural. But, of course, I didn't turn her out of the house. I wouldn't do such a thing.' He assumed virtuous indignation. 'No. What's the law for – that's what I say. What's the law for? He'd got to do the right by her. And if he didn't, by God, he'd got to pay.'

He brought down his fist on the table.

'What time did you last see your daughter?' asked Melchett.

'Yesterday – tea time.'

'What was her manner then?'

'Well, much as usual. I didn't notice anything. If I'd known –'

'But you didn't know,' said the Inspector drily.

They took their leave.

'Emmott hardly creates a favourable impression,' said Sir Henry thoughtfully.

'Bit of a blackguard,' said Melchett. 'He'd have bled Sandford all right if he'd had the chance.'

Their next call was on the architect. Rex Sandford was very unlike the picture Sir Henry had unconsciously formed of him. He was a tall young man, very fair and very thin. His eyes were blue and dreamy, his hair was untidy and rather too long. His speech was a little too ladylike.

Colonel Melchett introduced himself and his companions. Then passing straight to the object of his visit, he invited the architect to make a statement as to his movements on the previous evening.

'You understand,' he said warningly. 'I have no power to compel a statement from you and any statement you make may be used in evidence against you. I want the position to be quite clear to you.'

'I – I don't understand,' said Sandford.

'You understand that the girl Rose Emmott was drowned last night?'

'I know. Oh! it's too, too distressing. Really, I haven't slept a wink. I've been incapable of any work today. I feel responsible – terribly responsible.'

He ran his hands through his hair, making it untidier still.

'I never meant any harm,' he said piteously. 'I never thought. I never dreamt she'd take it that way.'

He sat down at a table and buried his face in his hands.

'Do I understand you to say, Mr Sandford, that you refuse to make a statement as to where you were last night at eight-thirty?'

'No, no – certainly not. I was out. I went for a walk.'

'You went to meet Miss Emmott?'

'No. I went by myself. Through the woods. A long way.'

'Then how do you account for this note, sir, which was found in the dead girl's pocket?'

And Inspector Drewitt read it unemotionally aloud.

'Now, sir,' he finished. 'Do you deny that you wrote that?'

'No – no. You're right. I did write it. Rose asked me to meet her. She insisted. I didn't know what to do. So I wrote that note.'

'Ah, that's better,' said the Inspector.

'But I didn't go!' Sandford's voice rose high and excited. 'I didn't go! I felt it would be much better not. I was returning to town tomorrow. I felt it would be better not – not to meet. I intended to write from London and – and make – some arrangement.'

'You are aware, sir, that this girl was going to have a child, and that she had named you as its father?'

Sandford groaned, but did not answer.

'Was that statement true, sir?'

Sandford buried his face deeper.

'I suppose so,' he said in a muffled voice.

'Ah!' Inspector Drewitt could not disguise the satisfaction. 'Now about this "walk" of yours. Is there anyone who saw you last night?'

'I don't know. I don't think so. As far as I can remember, I didn't meet anybody.'

'That's a pity.'

'What do you mean?' Sandford stared wildly at him. 'What does it matter whether I was out for a walk or not? What difference does that make to Rose drowning herself?'

'Ah!' said the Inspector. 'But you see, *she didn't*. She was thrown in deliberately, Mr Sandford.'

'She was –' It took him a minute or two to take in all the horror of it. 'My God! Then –'

He dropped into a chair.

Colonel Melchett made a move to depart.

'You understand, Sandford,' he said. 'You are on no account to leave this house.'

The three men left together. The Inspector and the Chief Constable exchanged glances.

'That's enough, I think, sir,' said the Inspector.

'Yes. Get a warrant made out and arrest him.'

'Excuse me,' said Sir Henry, 'I've forgotten my gloves.'

He re-entered the house rapidly. Sandford was sitting just as they had left him, staring dazedly in front of him.

'I have come back,' said Sir Henry, 'to tell you that I personally, am anxious to do all I can to assist you. The motive of my interest in you I am not at liberty to reveal. But I am going to ask you, if you will, to tell me as briefly as possible exactly what passed between you and this girl Rose.'

'She was very pretty,' said Sandford. 'Very pretty and very alluring. And – and she made a dead seat at me. Before God, that's true. She wouldn't let me alone. And it was lonely down here, and nobody liked me much, and – and, as I say she was amazingly pretty and she seemed to know her way about and all that –' His voice died away. He looked up. 'And then this happened. She wanted me to marry her. I didn't know what to do. I'm engaged to a girl in London. If she ever gets to hear of this – and she will, of course – well, it's all up. She won't understand. How could she? And I'm a rotter, of course. As I say, I didn't know what to do. I avoided seeing Rose again. I thought I'd get back to town – see my lawyer – make arrangements about money and so forth, for her. God, what a fool I've been! And it's all so clear – the case against me. But they've made a mistake. She *must* have done it herself.'

'Did she ever threaten to take her life?'

Sandford shook his head.

'Never. I shouldn't have said she was that sort.'

'What about a man called Joe Ellis?'

'The carpenter fellow? Good old village stock. Dull fellow – but crazy about Rose.'

'He might have been jealous?' suggested Sir Henry.

'I suppose he was a bit – but he's the bovine kind. He'd suffer in silence.'

'Well,' said Sir Henry. 'I must be going.'

He rejoined the others.

'You know, Melchett,' he said, 'I feel we ought to have a look at this other fellow – Ellis – before we do anything drastic. Pity if you made an arrest that turned out to be a mistake. After all, jealousy is a pretty good motive for murder – and a pretty common one, too.'

'That's true enough,' said the Inspector. 'But Joe Ellis isn't that kind. He wouldn't hurt a fly. Why, nobody's ever seen him out of temper. Still, I agree we'd better just ask him where he was last night. He'll be at home now. He lodges with Mrs Bartlett – very decent soul – a widow, she takes in a bit of washing.'

The little cottage to which they bent their footsteps was spotlessly clean and neat. A big stout woman of middle age opened the door to them. She had a pleasant face and blue eyes.

'Good morning, Mrs Bartlett,' said the Inspector. 'Is Joe Ellis here?'

'Came back not ten minutes ago,' said Mrs Bartlett. 'Step inside, will you, please, sirs.'

Wiping her hands on her apron she led them into a tiny front parlour with stuffed birds, china dogs, a sofa and several useless pieces of furniture.

She hurriedly arranged seats for them, picked up a whatnot bodily to make further room and went out calling:

'Joe, there's three gentlemen want to see you.'

A voice from the back kitchen replied:

'I'll be there when I've cleaned myself.'

Mrs Bartlett smiled.

'Come in, Mrs Bartlett,' said Colonel Melchett. 'Sit down.'

'Oh, no, sir, I couldn't think of it.'

Mrs Bartlett was shocked at the idea.

'You find Joe Ellis a good lodger?' inquired Melchett in a seemingly careless tone.

'Couldn't have a better, sir. A real steady young fellow. Never touches a drop of drink. Takes a pride in his work. And always kind and helpful about the house. He put up those shelves for me, and he's fixed a new dresser in the kitchen. And any little thing that wants doing in the house – why, Joe does it as a matter of course, and won't hardly take thanks for it. Ah! there aren't many young fellows like Joe, sir.'

'Some girl will be lucky some day,' said Melchett carelessly. 'He was rather sweet on that poor girl, Rose Emmott, wasn't he?'

Mrs Bartlett sighed.

'It made me tired, it did. Him worshipping the ground she trod on and her not caring a snap of the fingers for him.'

'Where does Joe spend his evenings, Mrs Bartlett?'

'Here, sir, usually. He does some odd piece of work in the evenings, sometimes, and he's trying to learn book-keeping by correspondence.'

'Ah! really. Was he in yesterday evening?'

'Yes, sir.'

'You're sure, Mrs Bartlett?' said Sir Henry sharply.

She turned to him.

'Quite sure, sir.'

'He didn't go out, for instance, somewhere about eight to eight-thirty?'

'Oh, no.' Mrs Barlett laughed. 'He was fixing the kitchen dresser for me nearly all the evening, and I was helping him.'

Sir Henry looked at her smiling assured face and felt his first pang of doubt.

A moment later Ellis himself entered the room.

He was a tall broad-shouldered young man, very good-looking in a rustic way. He had shy, blue eyes and a good-tempered smile. Altogether an amiable young giant.

Melchett opened the conversation. Mrs Bartlett withdrew to the kitchen.

'We are investigating the death of Rose Emmott. You knew her, Ellis.'

'Yes.' He hesitated, then muttered, 'Hoped to marry her one day. Poor lass.'

'You have heard of what her condition was?'

'Yes.' A spark of anger showed in his eyes. 'Let her down, he did. But 'twere for the best. She wouldn't have been happy married to him. I reckoned she'd come to me when this happened. I'd have looked after her.'

'In spite of –'

"'Tweren't her fault. He led her astray with fine promises and all. Oh! she told me about it. She'd no call to drown herself. He weren't worth it.'

'Where were you, Ellis, last night at eight-thirty?'

Was it Sir Henry's fancy, or was there really a shade of constraint in the ready – almost too ready – reply.

'I was here. Fixing up a contraption in the kitchen for Mrs B. You ask her. She'll tell you.'

'He was too quick with that,' thought Sir Henry. 'He's a slow-thinking man. That popped out so pat that I suspect he'd got it ready beforehand.'

Then he told himself that it was imagination. He was imagining things – yes, even imagining an apprehensive glint in those blue eyes.

A few more questions and answers and they left. Sir Henry made an excuse to go to the kitchen. Mrs Bartlett was busy at the stove. She looked up with a pleasant smile. A new dresser was fixed against the wall. It was not quite finished. Some tools lay about and some pieces of wood.

'That's what Ellis was at work on last night?' said Sir Henry.

'Yes, sir, it's a nice bit of work, isn't it? He's a very clever carpenter, Joe is.'

No apprehensive gleam in her eye – no embarrassment.

But Ellis – had he imagined it? No, there *had* been something.

'I must tackle him,' thought Sir Henry.

Turning to leave the kitchen, he collided with a perambulator.

'Not woken the baby up, I hope,' he said.

Mrs Bartlett's laugh rang out.

'Oh, no, sir. I've no children – more's the pity. That's what I take the laundry on, sir.'

'Oh! I see –'

He paused then said on an impulse:

'Mrs Bartlett. You knew Rose Emmott. Tell me what you really thought of her.'

She looked at him curiously.

'Well, sir, I thought she was flighty. But she's dead – and I don't like to speak ill of the dead.'

'But I have a reason – a very good reason for asking.'

He spoke persuasively.

She seemed to consider, studying him attentively. Finally she made up her mind.

'She was a bad lot, sir,' she said quietly. 'I wouldn't say so before Joe. She took *him* in good and proper. That kind can – more's the pity. You know how it is, sir.'

Yes, Sir Henry knew. The Joe Ellises of the world were peculiarly vulnerable. They trusted blindly. But for that very cause the shock of discovery might be greater.

He left the cottage baffled and perplexed. He was up against a blank wall. Joe Ellis had been working indoors all yesterday evening. Mrs Bartlett had actually been there watching him. Could one possibly get round that? There was nothing to set against it – except possibly that suspicious readiness in replying on Joe Ellis's part – that suggestion of having a story pat.

'Well,' said Melchett, 'that seems to make the matter quite clear, eh?'

'It does, sir,' agreed the Inspector. 'Sandford's our man. Not a leg to stand upon. The thing's as plain as daylight. It's my opinion as the girl and her father were out to – well – practically blackmail him. He's no money to speak of – he didn't want the matter to get to his young lady's ears. He was desperate and he acted accordingly. What do you say, sir?' he added, addressing Sir Henry deferentially.

'It seems so,' admitted Sir Henry. 'And yet – I can hardly picture Sandford committing any violent action.'

But he knew as he spoke that that objection was hardly valid. The meekest animal, when cornered, is capable of amazing actions.

'I should like to see the boy, though,' he said suddenly. 'The one who heard the cry.'

Jimmy Brown proved to be an intelligent lad, rather small for his age, with a sharp, rather cunning face. He was eager to be questioned and was rather disappointed when checked in his dramatic tale of what he had heard on the fatal night.

'You were on the other side of the bridge, I understand,' said Sir Henry. 'Across the river from the village. Did you see anyone on that side as you came over the bridge?'

'There was someone walking up in the woods. Mr Sandford, I think it was, the architecting gentleman who's building the queer house.'

The three men exchanged glances.

'That was about ten minutes or so before you heard the cry?'

The boy nodded.

'Did you see anyone else – on the village side of the river?'

'A man came along the path that side. Going slow and whistling he was. Might have been Joe Ellis.'

'You couldn't possibly have seen who it was,' said the Inspector sharply. 'What with the mist and its being dusk.'

'It's on account of the whistle,' said the boy. 'Joe Ellis always whistles the same tune – "I wanner be happy" – it's the only tune he knows.'

He spoke with the scorn of the modernist for the old-fashioned.

'Anyone might whistle a tune,' said Melchett. 'Was he going towards the bridge?'

'No. Other way – to village.'

'I don't think we need concern ourselves with this unknown man,' said Melchett. 'You heard the cry and the splash and a few minutes later you saw the body floating downstream and you ran for help, going back to the bridge, crossing it, and making straight for the village. You didn't see anyone near the bridge as you ran for help?'

'I think as there were two men with a wheelbarrow on the river path; but they were some way away and I couldn't tell if they were going or coming and Mr Giles's place was nearest – so I ran there.'

'You did well, my boy,' said Melchett. 'You acted very creditably and with presence of mind. You're a scout, aren't you?'

'Yes, sir.'

'Very good. Very good indeed.'

Sir Henry was silent – thinking. He took a slip of paper from his pocket, looked at it, shook his head. It didn't seem possible – and yet –

He decided to pay a call on Miss Marple.

She received him in her pretty, slightly overcrowded old-style drawing-room.

'I've come to report progress,' said Sir Henry. 'I'm afraid that from our point of view things aren't going well. They are going to arrest Sandford. And I must say I think they are justified.'

'You have found nothing in – what shall I say – support of my theory, then?' She looked perplexed – anxious. 'Perhaps I have been wrong – quite wrong. You have such wide experience – you would surely detect it if it were so.'

'For one thing,' said Sir Henry, 'I can hardly believe it. And for another we are up against an unbreakable alibi. Joe Ellis was fixing shelves in the kitchen all the evening and Mrs Bartlett was watching him do it.'

Miss Marple leaned forward, taking in a quick breath.

'But that can't be so,' she said. 'It was Friday night.'

'Friday night?'

'Yes – Friday night. On Friday evenings Mrs Bartlett takes the laundry she has done round to the different people.'

Sir Henry leaned back in his chair. He remembered the boy Jimmy's story of the whistling man and — yes — it would all fit in.

He rose, taking Miss Marple warmly by the hand.

'I think I see my way,' he said. 'At least I can try . . .'

Five minutes later he was back at Mrs Bartlett's cottage and facing Joe Ellis in the little parlour among the china dogs.

'You lied to us, Ellis, about last night,' he said crisply. 'You were not in the kitchen here fixing the dresser between eight and eight-thirty. You were seen walking along the path by the river towards the bridge a few minutes before Rose Emmott was murdered.'

The man gasped.

'She weren't murdered — she weren't. I had naught to do with it. She threw herself in, she did. She was desperate like. I wouldn't have harmed a hair on her head, I wouldn't.'

'Then why did you lie as to where you were?' asked Sir Henry keenly.

The man's eyes shifted and lowered uncomfortably.

'I was scared. Mrs B. saw me around there and when we heard just afterwards what had happened — well, she thought it might look bad for me. I fixed I'd say I was working here, and she agreed to back me up. She's a rare one, she is. She's always been good to me.'

Without a word Sir Henry left the room and walked into the kitchen. Mrs Bartlett was washing up at the sink.

'Mrs Bartlett,' he said, 'I know everything. I think you'd better confess — that is, unless you want Joe Ellis hanged for something he didn't do . . . No. I see you don't want that. I'll tell you what happened. You were out taking the laundry home. You came across Rose Emmott. You thought she'd given Joe the chuck and was taking up with this stranger. Now she was in trouble — Joe was prepared to come to the rescue — marry her if need be, and if she'd have him. He's lived in your house for four years. You've fallen in love with him. You want him for yourself. You hated this girl — you couldn't bear that this worthless little slut should take your man from you. You're a strong woman, Mrs Bartlett. You caught the girl by the shoulders and shoved her over into the stream. A few minutes later you met Joe Ellis. The boy Jimmy saw you together in the distance — but in the darkness and the mist he assumed the perambulator was a wheelbarrow and two men wheeling it. You persuaded Joe that he might be suspected and you concocted what was supposed to be an alibi for him, but which was really an alibi for *you*. Now then, I'm right, am I not?'

He held his breath. He had staked all on this throw.

She stood before him rubbing her hands on her apron, slowly making up her mind.

'It's just as you say, sir,' she said at last, in her quiet subdued voice (a dangerous voice, Sir Henry suddenly felt it to be). 'I don't know what came over me. Shameless — that's what she was. It just came over me — she shan't take Joe from me. I haven't had a happy life, sir. My husband, he was a poor lot — an invalid and cross-grained. I nursed and looked after him true. And then Joe came here to lodge. I'm not such an old woman, sir, in spite of my grey hair. I'm just forty, sir. Joe's one in a thousand. I'd have done anything for him — anything at all. He was like a little child, sir, so gentle and believing. He was mine, sir, to look after and see to. And this — this —' She swallowed — checked her emotion. Even at this moment she was a strong woman. She stood up straight and looked at Sir Henry curiously. 'I'm ready to come, sir. I never thought anyone would find out. I don't know how you knew, sir — I don't, I'm sure.'

Sir Henry shook his head gently.

'It was not I who knew,' he said — and he thought of the piece of paper still reposing in his pocket with the words on it written in neat old-fashioned handwriting.

'Mrs Bartlett, with whom Joe Ellis lodges at 2 Mill Cottages.'

Miss Marple had been right again.

The Hound of Death

'The Hound of Death' was first published in the hardback
The Hound of Death and Other Stories (Odhams Press, 1933).
No previous appearances have been found.

It was from William P. Ryan, American newspaper correspondent, that I
first heard of the affair. I was dining with him in London on the eve of
his return to New York and happened to mention that on the morrow I
was going down to Folbridge.

He looked up and said sharply: 'Folbridge, Cornwall?'

Now only about one person in a thousand knows that there is a
Folbridge in Cornwall. They always take it for granted that the Folbridge,
Hampshire, is meant. So Ryan's knowledge aroused my curiosity.

'Yes,' I said. 'Do you know it?'

He merely replied that he was darned. He then asked if I happened
to know a house called Trearne down there.

My interest increased.

'Very well indeed. In fact, it's to Trearne I'm going. It's my sister's
house.'

'Well,' said William P. Ryan. 'If that doesn't beat the band!'

I suggested that he should cease making cryptic remarks and explain
himself.

'Well,' he said. 'To do that I shall have to go back to an experience of
mine at the beginning of the war.'

I sighed. The events which I am relating to took place in 1921. To be
reminded of the war was the last thing any man wanted. We were, thank
God, beginning to forget . . . Besides, William P. Ryan on his war experiences was apt, as I knew, to be unbelievably long-winded.

But there was no stopping him now.

'At the start of the war, as I dare say you know, I was in Belgium for
my paper – moving about some. Well, there's a little village – I'll call it

X. A one horse place if there ever was one, but there's quite a big convent there. Nuns in white what do you call 'em – I don't know the name of the order. Anyway, it doesn't matter. Well, this little burgh was right in the way of the German advance. The Uhlans arrived –'

I shifted uneasily. William P. Ryan lifted a hand reassuringly.

'It's all right,' he said. 'This isn't a German atrocity story. It might have been, perhaps, but it isn't. As a matter of fact, the boot's on the other leg. The Huns made for that convent – they got there and the whole thing blew up.'

'Oh!' I said, rather startled.

'Odd business, wasn't it? Of course, off hand, I should say the Huns had been celebrating and had monkeyed round with their own explosives. But is seems they hadn't anything of that kind with them. They weren't the high explosive johnnies. Well, then, I ask you, what should a pack of nuns know about high explosive? Some nuns, I should say!'

'It is odd,' I agreed.

'I was interested in hearing the peasants' account of the matter. They'd got it all cut and dried. According to them it was a slap-up one hundred per cent efficient first-class modern miracle. It seems one of the nuns had got something of a reputation – a budding saint – went into trances and saw visions. And according to them she worked the stunt. She called down the lightning to blast the impious Hun – and it blasted him all right – and everything else within range. A pretty efficient miracle, that!

'I never really got at the truth of the matter – hadn't time. But miracles were all the rage just then – angels at Mons and all that. I wrote up the thing, put in a bit of sob stuff, and pulled the religious stop out well, and sent it to my paper. It went down very well in the States. They were liking that kind of thing just then.

'But (I don't know if you'll understand this) in writing, I got kinder interested. I felt I'd like to know what really had happened. There was nothing to see at the spot itself. Two walls still left standing, and on one of them was a black powder mark that was the exact shape of a great hound.

'The peasants round about were scared to death of that mark. They called it the Hound of Death and they wouldn't pass that way after dark.

'Superstition's always interesting. I felt I'd like to see the lady who worked the stunt. She hadn't perished, it seemed. She'd gone to England with a batch of other refugees. I took the trouble to trace her. I found she'd been sent to Trearne, Folbridge, Cornwall.'

I nodded.

'My sister took in a lot of Belgian refugees the beginning of the war. About twenty.'

'Well, I always meant, if I had time, to look up the lady. I wanted to hear her own account of the disaster. Then, what with being busy and one thing and another, it slipped my memory. Cornwall's a bit out of the way anyhow. In fact, I'd forgotten the whole thing till your mentioning Folbridge just now brought it back.'

'I must ask my sister,' I said. 'She may have heard something about it. Of course, the Belgians have all been repatriated long ago.'

'Naturally. All the same, in case your sister does know anything I'll be glad if you pass it on to me.'

'Of course I will,' I said heartily.

And that was that.

It was the second day after my arrival at Trearne that the story recurred to me. My sister and I were having tea on the terrace.

'Kitty,' I said, 'didn't you have a nun among your Belgians?'

'You don't mean Sister Marie Angelique, do you?'

'Possibly I do,' I said cautiously. 'Tell me about her.'

'Oh! my dear, she was the most uncanny creature. She's still here, you know.'

'What? In the house?'

'No, no, in the village. Dr Rose – you remember Dr Rose?'

I shook my head.

'I remember an old man of about eighty-three.'

'Dr Laird. Oh! he died. Dr Rose has only been here a few years. He's quite young and very keen on new ideas. He took the most enormous interest in Sister Marie Angelique. She has hallucinations and things, you know, and apparently is most frightfully interesting from a medical point of view. Poor thing, she'd nowhere to go – and really was in my opinion quite potty – only impressive, if you know what I mean – well, as I say, she'd nowhere to go, and Dr Rose very kindly fixed her up in the village. I believe he's writing a monograph or whatever it is that doctors write, about her.'

She paused and then said:

'But what do you know about her?'

'I heard a rather curious story.'

I passed on the story as I had received it from Ryan. Kitty was very much interested.

'She looks the sort of person who could blast you – if you know what I mean,' she said.

'I really think,' I said, my curiosity heightened, 'that I must see this young woman.'

'Do. I'd like to know what you think of her. Go and see Dr Rose first. Why not walk down to the village after tea?'

I accepted the suggestion.

I found Dr Rose at home and introduced myself. He seemed a pleasant young man, yet there was something about his personality that rather repelled me. It was too forceful to be altogether agreeable.

The moment I mentioned Sister Marie Angelique he stiffened to attention. He was evidently keenly interested. I gave him Ryan's account of the matter.

'Ah!' he said thoughtfully. 'That explains a great deal.'

He looked up quickly at me and went on.

'The case is really an extraordinarily interesting one. The woman arrived here having evidently suffered some severe mental shock. She was in a state of great mental excitement also. She was given to hallucinations of a most startling character. Her personality is most unusual. Perhaps you would like to come with me and call upon her. She is really well worth seeing.'

I agreed readily.

We set out together. Our objective was a small cottage on the outskirts of the village. Folbridge is a most picturesque place. It lies at the mouth of the river Fol mostly on the east bank, the west bank is too precipitous for building, though a few cottages do cling to the cliffside there. The doctor's own cottage was perched on the extreme edge of the cliff on the west side. From it you looked down on the big waves lashing against the black rocks.

The little cottage to which we were now proceeding lay inland out of the sight of the sea.

'The district nurse lives here,' explained Dr Rose. 'I have arranged for Sister Marie Angelique to board with her. It is just as well that she should be under skilled supervision.'

'Is she quite normal in her manner?' I asked curiously.

'You can judge for yourself in a minute,' he replied, smiling.

The district nurse, a dumpy pleasant little body, was just setting out on her bicycle when we arrived.

'Good evening, nurse, how's your patient?' called out the doctor.

'She's much as usual, doctor. Just sitting there with her hands folded and her mind far away. Often enough she'll not answer when I speak to her, though for the matter of that it's little enough English she understands even now.'

Rose nodded, and as the nurse bicycled away, he went up to the cottage door, rapped sharply and entered.

Sister Marie Angelique was lying in a long chair near the window. She turned her head as we entered.

It was a strange face – pale, transparent looking, with enormous eyes. There seemed to be an infinitude of tragedy in those eyes.

'Good evening, my sister,' said the doctor in French.

'Good evening, M. le docteur.'

'Permit me to introduce a friend, Mr Anstruther.'

I bowed and she inclined her head with a faint smile.

'And how are you today?' inquired the doctor, sitting down beside her.

'I am much the same as usual.' She paused and then went on. 'Nothing seems real to me. Are they days that pass – or months – or years? I hardly know. Only my dreams seem real to me.'

'You still dream a lot, then?'

'Always – always – and, you understand? – the dreams seem more real than life.'

'You dream of your own country – of Belgium?'

She shook her head.

'No. I dream of a country that never existed – never. But you know this, M. le docteur. I have told you many times.' She stopped and then said abruptly: 'But perhaps this gentleman is also a doctor – a doctor perhaps for the diseases of the brain?'

'No, no.' Rose said reassuring, but as he smiled I noticed how extraordinarily pointed his canine teeth were, and it occurred to me that there was something wolf-like about the man. He went on:

'I thought you might be interested to meet Mr Anstruther. He knows something of Belgium. He has lately been hearing news of your convent.'

Her eyes turned to me. A faint flush crept into her cheeks.

'It's nothing, really,' I hastened to explain. 'But I was dining the other evening with a friend who was describing the ruined walls of the convent to me.'

'So it is ruined!'

It was a soft exclamation, uttered more to herself than to us. Then looking at me once more she asked hesitatingly: 'Tell me, Monsieur, did your friend say how – in what way – it was ruined?'

'It was blown up,' I said, and added: 'The peasants are afraid to pass that way at night.'

'Why are they afraid?'

'Because of a black mark on a ruined wall. They have a superstitious fear of it.'

She leaned forward.

'Tell me, Monsieur – quick – quick – tell me! What is that mark like?'

'It has the shape of a huge hound,' I answered. 'The peasants call it the Hound of Death.'

'Ah!'

A shrill cry burst from her lips.

'It is true then – it is true. All that I remember is true. It is not some black nightmare. It happened! It happened!'

'What happened, my sister?' asked the doctor in a low voice.

She turned to him eagerly.

'*I remembered.* There on the steps, I remembered. I remembered the way of it. I used the power as we used to use it. I stood on the altar steps and I bade them to come no farther. I told them to depart in peace. They would not listen, they came on although I warned them. And so –' She leaned forward and made a curious gesture. 'And so I loosed the Hound of Death on them . . .'

She lay back on her chair shivering all over, her eyes closed.

The doctor rose, fetched a glass from a cupboard, half-filled it with water, added a drop or two from a little bottle which he produced from his pocket, then took the glass to her.

'Drink this,' he said authoritatively.

She obeyed – mechanically as it seemed. Her eyes looked far away as though they contemplated some inner vision of her own.

'But then it is all true,' she said. 'Everything. The City of the Circles, the People of the Crystal – everything. It is all true.'

'It would seem so,' said Rose.

His voice was low and soothing, clearly designed to encourage and not to disturb her train of thought.

'Tell me about the City,' he said. 'The City of Circles, I think you said?'

She answered absently and mechanically.

'Yes – there were three circles. The first circle for the chosen, the second for the priestesses and the outer circle for the priests.'

'And in the centre?'

She drew her breath sharply and her voice sank to a tone of indescribable awe.

'The House of the Crystal . . .'

As she breathed the words, her right hand went to her forehead and her finger traced some figure there.

Her figure seemed to grow more rigid, her eyes closed, she swayed a little – then suddenly she sat upright with a jerk, as though she had suddenly awakened.

'What is it?' she said confusedly. 'What have I been saying?'

'It is nothing,' said Rose. 'You are tired. You want to rest. We will leave you.'

She seemed a little dazed as we took our departure.

'Well,' said Rose when we were outside. 'What do you think of it?'

He shot a sharp glance sideways at me.

'I suppose her mind must be totally unhinged,' I said slowly.

'It struck you like that?'

'No – as a matter of fact, she was – well, curiously convincing. When listening to her I had the impression that she actually had done what she claimed to do – worked a kind of gigantic miracle. Her belief that she did so seems genuine enough. That is why –'

'That is why you say her mind must be unhinged. Quite so. But now approach the matter from another angle. Supposing that she did actually work that miracle – supposing that she did, personally, destroy a building and several hundred human beings.'

'By the mere exercise of will?' I said with a smile.

'I should not put it quite like that. You will agree that one person could destroy a multitude by touching a switch which controlled a system of mines.'

'Yes, but that is mechanical.'

'True, that is mechanical, but it is, in essence, the harnessing and controlling of natural forces. The thunder-storm and the power house are, fundamentally, the same thing.'

'Yes, but to control the thunderstorm we have to use mechanical means.' Rose smiled.

'I am going off at a tangent now. There is a substance called wintergreen. It occurs in nature in vegetable form. It can also be built up by man synthetically and chemically in the laboratory.'

'Well?'

'My point is that there are often two ways of arriving at the same result. Ours is, admittedly, the synthetic way. There might be another. The extraordinary results arrived at by Indian fakirs for instance, cannot be explained away in any easy fashion. The things we call supernatural is only the natural of which the laws are not yet understood.'

'You mean?' I asked, fascinated.

'That I cannot entirely dismiss the possibility that a human being *might* be able to tap some vast destructive force and use it to further his or her ends. The means by which this was accomplished might seem to us supernatural – but would not be so in reality.'

I stared at him.

He laughed.

'It's a speculation, that's all,' he said lightly. 'Tell me, did you notice a gesture she made when she mentioned the House of the Crystal?'

'She put her hand to her forehead.'

'Exactly. And traced a circle there. Very much as a Catholic makes the sign of the cross. Now, I will tell you something rather interesting, Mr Anstruther. The word crystal having occurred so often in my patient's rambling, I tried an experiment. I borrowed a crystal from someone and produced it unexpectedly one day to test my patient's reaction to it.'

'Well?'

'Well, the result was very curious and suggestive. Her whole body stiffened. She stared at it as though unable to believe her eyes. Then she slid to her knees in front of it, murmured a few words – and fainted.'

'What were the few words?'

'Very curious ones. She said: "*The Crystal! Then the Faith still lives!*"'

'Extraordinary!'

'Suggestive, is it not? Now the next curious thing. When she came round from her faint she had forgotten the whole thing. I showed her the crystal and asked her if she knew what it was. She replied that she supposed it was a crystal such as fortune tellers used. I asked her if she had ever seen one before? She replied: "Never, M. le docteur." But I saw a puzzled look in her eyes. "What troubles you, my sister?" I asked. She replied: "Because it is so strange. I have never seen a crystal before and yet – it seems to me that I know it well. There is something – if only I could remember . . ." The effort at memory was obviously so distressing to her that I forbade her to think any more. That was two weeks ago. I have purposely been biding my time. Tomorrow, I shall proceed to a further experiment.'

'With the crystal?'

'With the crystal. I shall get her to gaze into it. I think the result ought to be interesting.'

'What do you expect to get hold of?' I asked curiously.

The words were idle ones but they had an unlooked-for result. Rose stiffened, flushed, and his manner when he spoke changed insensibly. It was more formal, more professional.

'Light on certain mental disorders imperfectly understood. Sister Marie Angelique is a most interesting study.'

So Rose's interest was purely professional? I wondered.

'Do you mind if I come along too?' I asked.

It may have been my fancy, but I thought he hesitated before he replied. I had a sudden intuition that he did not want me.

'Certainly. I can see no objection.'

He added: 'I suppose you're not going to be down here very long?'

'Only till the day after tomorrow.'

I fancied that the answer pleased him. His brow cleared and he began talking of some recent experiments carried out on guinea pigs.

I met the doctor by appointment the following afternoon, and we went together to Sister Marie Angelique. Today, the doctor was all geniality.

He was anxious, I thought, to efface the impression he had made the day before.

'You must not take what I said too seriously,' he observed, laughing. 'I shouldn't like you to believe me a dabbler in occult sciences. The worst of me is I have an infernal weakness for making out a case.'

'Really?'

'Yes, and the more fantastic it is, the better I like it.'

He laughed as a man laughs at an amusing weakness.

When we arrived at the cottage, the district nurse had something she wanted to consult Rose about, so I was left with Sister Marie Angelique.

I saw her scrutinizing me closely. Presently she spoke.

'The good nurse here, she tells me that you are the brother of the kind lady at the big house where I was brought when I came from Belgium?'

'Yes,' I said.

'She was very kind to me. She is good.'

She was silent, as though following out some train of thought. Then she said:

'M. le docteur, he too is a good man?'

I was a little embarrassed.

'Why, yes. I mean – I think so.'

'Ah!' She paused and then said: 'Certainly he has been very kind to me.'

'I'm sure he has.'

She looked up at me sharply.

'Monsieur – you – you who speak to me now – do you believe that I am mad?'

'Why, my sister, such an idea never –'

She shook her head slowly – interrupting my protest.

'Am I mad? I do not know – the things I remember – the things I forget . . .'

She sighed, and at that moment Rose entered the room.

He greeted her cheerily and explained what he wanted her to do.

'Certain people, you see, have a gift for seeing things in a crystal. I fancy you might have such a gift, my sister.'

She looked distressed.

'No, no, I cannot do that. To try to read the future – that is sinful.'

Rose was taken aback. It was the nun's point of view for which he had not allowed. He changed his ground cleverly.

'One should not look into the future. You are quite right. But to look into the past – that is different.'

'The past?'

'Yes – there are many strange things in the past. Flashes come back to one – they are seen for a moment – then gone again. Do not seek to see anything in the crystal since that is not allowed you. Just take it in your hands – so. Look into it – look deep. Yes – deeper – deeper still. You remember, do you not? You remember. You hear me speaking to you. You can answer my questions. Can you not hear me?'

Sister Marie Angelique had taken the crystal as bidden, handling it with a curious reverence. Then, as she gazed into it, her eyes became blank and unseeing, her head drooped. She seemed to sleep.

Gently the doctor took the crystal from her and put it on the table. He raised the corner of her eyelid. Then he came and sat by me.

'We must wait till she wakes. It won't be long, I fancy.'

He was right. At the end of five minutes, Sister Marie Angelique stirred. Her eyes opened dreamily.

'Where am I?'

'You are here – at home. You have had a little sleep. You have dreamt, have you not?'

She nodded.

'Yes, I have dreamt.'

'You have dreamt of the Crystal?'

'Yes.'

'Tell us about it.'

'You will think me mad, M. le docteur. For see you, in my dream, the Crystal was a holy emblem. I even figured to myself a second Christ, a Teacher of the Crystal who died for his faith, his followers hunted down – persecuted . . . But the faith endured.

'Yes – for fifteen thousand full moons – I mean, for fifteen thousand years.'

'How long was a full moon?'

'Thirteen ordinary moons. Yes, it was in the fifteen thousandth full moon – of course, I was a Priestess of the Fifth Sign in the House of the Crystal. It was in the first days of the coming of the Sixth Sign . . .'

Her brows drew together, a look of fear passed over her face.

'Too soon,' she murmured. 'Too soon. A mistake . . . Ah! yes, I remember! The Sixth Sign . . .'

She half sprang to her feet, then dropped back, passing her hand over her face and murmuring:

'But what am I saying? I am raving. These things never happened.'

'Now don't distress yourself.'

But she was looking at him in anguished perplexity.

'M. le docteur, I do not understand. Why should I have these dreams – these fancies? I was only sixteen when I entered the religious life. I have never travelled. Yet I dream of cities, of strange people, of strange customs. Why?' She pressed both hands to her head.

'Have you ever been hypnotized, my sister? Or been in a state of trance?'

'I have never been hypnotized, M. le docteur. For the other, when at prayer in the chapel, my spirit has often been caught up from my body, and I have been as one dead for many hours. It was undoubtedly a blessed state, the Reverend Mother said – a state of grace. Ah! yes,' she caught her breath. '*I remember, we too called it a state of grace.*'

'I would like to try an experiment, my sister.' Rose spoke in a matter-of-fact voice. 'It may dispel those painful half-recollections. I will ask you to gaze once more in the crystal. I will then say a certain word to you. You will answer another. We will continue in this way until you become tired. Concentrate your thoughts on the crystal, not upon the words.'

As I once more unwrapped the crystal and gave it into Sister Marie Angelique's hands, I noticed the reverent way her hands touched it. Reposing on the black velvet, it lay between her slim palms. Her wonderful deep eyes gazed into it. There was a short silence, and then the doctor said:

'*Hound.*'

Immediately Sister Marie Angelique answered '*Death.*'

I do not propose to give a full account of the experiment. Many unimportant and meaningless words were purposely introduced by the doctor. Other words he repeated several times, sometimes getting the same answer to them, sometimes a different one.

That evening in the doctor's little cottage on the cliffs we discussed the result of the experiment.

He cleared his throat, and drew his note-book closer to him.

'These results are very interesting – very curious. In answer to the words "Sixth Sign," we get variously *Destruction, Purple, Hound, Power*, then again *Destruction*, and finally *Power*. Later, as you may have noticed, I reversed the method, with the following results. In answer to *Destruction*, I get *Hound*; to *Purple, Power*; to *Hound, Death*, again, and to *Power*, *Hound*. That all holds together, but on a second repetition of *Destruction*, I get *Sea*, which appears utterly irrelevant. To the words "Fifth Sign," I get *Blue, Thoughts, Bird, Blue* again, and finally the rather suggestive phrase *Opening of mind to mind*. From the fact that "Fourth Sign" elicits the word *Yellow*, and later *Light*, and that "First Sign" is answered by *Blood*, I deduce that each Sign had a particular colour, and possibly a particular symbol, that of the Fifth Sign being a *bird*, and that of the Sixth a *hound*. However, I surmise that the Fifth Sign represented what is familiarly known as telepathy – the opening of mind to mind. The Sixth Sign undoubtedly stands for the Power of Destruction.'

'What is the meaning of *Sea*?'

'That I confess I cannot explain. I introduced the word later and got the ordinary answer of *Boat*. To "Seventh Sign" I got first *Life*, the second time *Love*. To "Eighth Sign," I got the answer *None*. I take it therefore that Seven was the sum and number of the signs.'

'But the Seventh was not achieved,' I said on a sudden inspiration. 'Since through the Sixth came *Destruction*!'

'Ah! You think so? But we are taking these – mad ramblings very seriously. They are really only interesting from a medical point of view.'

'Surely they will attract the attention of psychic investigators.'

The doctor's eyes narrowed. 'My dear sir, I have no intention of making them public.'

'Then your interest?'

'Is purely personal. I shall make notes on the case, of course.'

'I see.' But for the first time I felt, like the blind man, that I didn't see at all. I rose to my feet.

'Well, I'll wish you good night, doctor. I'm off to town again tomorrow.'

'Ah!' I fancied there was satisfaction, relief perhaps, behind the exclamation.

'I wish you good luck with your investigations,' I continued lightly. 'Don't loose the Hound of Death on me next time we meet!'

His hand was in mine as I spoke, and I felt the start it gave. He recovered himself quickly. His lips drew back from his long pointed teeth in a smile.

'For a man who loved power, what a power that would be!' he said. 'To hold every human being's life in the hollow of your hand!'

And his smile broadened.

That was the end of my direct connection with the affair.

Later, the doctor's note-book and diary came into my hands. I will reproduce the few scant entries in it here, though you will understand that it did not really come into my possession until some time afterwards.

Aug. 5th. Have discovered that by 'the Chosen,' Sister M.A. means those who reproduced the race. Apparently they were held in the highest honour, and exalted above the Priesthood. Contrast this with early Christians.

Aug. 7th. Persuaded Sister M.A. to let me hypnotize her. Succeeded in inducing hypnoptic sleep and trance, but no *rapport* established.

Aug. 9th. Have there been civilizations in the past to which ours is as nothing? Strange if it should be so, and I the only man with the clue to it . . .

Aug. 12th. Sister M.A. not at all amenable to suggestion when hypnotized. Yet state of trance easily induced. Cannot understand it.

Aug. 13th. Sister M.A. mentioned today that in 'state of grace' the 'gate must be closed, lest another should command the body'. Interesting – but baffling.

Aug. 18th. So the First Sign is none other than . . . (*words erased here*) . . . then how many centuries will it take to reach the Sixth? But if there should be a short-cut to Power . . .

Aug. 20th. Have arranged for M.A. to come here with Nurse. Have told her it is necessary to keep patient under morphia. Am I mad? Or shall I be the Superman, with the Power of Death in my hands?

(*Here the entries cease*)

It was, I think, on August 29th that I received the letter. It was directed to me, care of my sister-in-law, in a sloping foreign handwriting. I opened it with some curiosity. It ran as follows:

Cher Monsieur,
I have seen you but twice, but I have felt I could trust you. Whether my dreams are real or not, they have grown clearer of late . . . And, Monsieur, one thing at all events, the Hound of Death is no dream . . . In the days I told you of (Whether they are real or not, I do not know) He who was Guardian of the Crystal revealed the Sixth Sign to the people too soon . . . Evil entered into their hearts. They had the power to slay at will – and they slew without justice – in anger. They were drunk with the lust of Power. When we saw this, We who were yet pure, we knew that once again we should not complete the Circle and come to the Sign of Everlasting Life. He who would have been the next Guardian of the Crystal was bidden to act. That the old might die, and the new, after endless ages, might come again, he loosed the Hound of Death upon the sea (being careful not to close the circle), and the sea rose up in the shape of a Hound and swallowed the land utterly . . .

Once before I remembered this – on the altar steps in Belgium . . .

The Dr Rose, he is of the Brotherhood. He knows the First Sign, and the form of the Second, though its meaning is hidden to all save a chosen few. He would learn of me the Sixth. I have withstood him so far –

but I grow weak, Monsieur, it is not well that a man should come to power before his time. Many centuries must go by ere the world is ready to have the power of death delivered into its hand . . . I beseech you, Monsieur, you who love goodness and truth, to help me . . . before it is too late.

Your sister in Christ,
Marie Angelique

I let the paper fall. The solid earth beneath me seemed a little less solid than usual. Then I began to rally. The poor woman's belief, genuine enough, had almost affected me! One thing was clear. Dr Rose, in his zeal for a case, was grossly abusing his professional standing. I would run down and –

Suddenly I noticed a letter from Kitty amongst my other correspondence. I tore it open.

'Such an awful thing has happened,' I read. 'You remember Dr Rose's little cottage on the cliff? It was swept away by a landslide last night, the doctor and that poor nun, Sister Marie Angelique, were killed. The *debris* on the beach is too awful – all piled up in a fantastic mass – from a distance it looks like a great *hound* . . .'

The letter dropped from my hand.

The other facts may be coincidence. A Mr Rose, whom I discovered to be a wealthy relative of the doctor's, died suddenly that same night – it was said struck by lightning. As far as was known no thunderstorm had occurred in the neighbourhood, but one or two people declared they had heard one peal of thunder. He had an electric burn on him 'of a curious shape.' His will left everything to his nephew, Dr Rose.

Now, supposing that Dr Rose succeeded in obtaining the secret of the sixth Sign from Sister Marie Angelique. I had always felt him to be an unscrupulous man – he would not shrink at taking his uncle's life if he were sure it could not be brought home to him. But one sentence of Sister Marie Angelique's letter rings in my brain . . . 'being careful not to close the Circle . . .' Dr Rose did not exercise that care – was perhaps unaware of the steps to take, or even of the need for them. So the Force he employed returned, completing its circuit . . .

But of course it is all nonsense! Everything can be accounted for quite naturally. That the doctor believed in Sister Marie Angelique's hallucinations merely proves that *his* mind, too, was slightly unbalanced.

Yet sometimes I dream of a continent under the seas where men once lived and attained to a degree of civilization far ahead of ours . . .

Or did Sister Marie Angelique remember *backwards* – as some say is possible – and is this City of the Circles in the future and not in the past?

Nonsense – of course the whole thing was merely hallucination!

The Gipsy

'The Gipsy' was first published in the hardback *The Hound of Death and Other Stories* (Odhams Press, 1933).
No previous appearances have been found.

Macfarlane had often noticed that his friend, Dickie Carpenter, had a strange aversion to gipsies. He had never known the reason for it. But when Dickie's engagement to Esther Lawes was broken off, there was a momentary tearing down of reserves between the two men.

Macfarlane had been engaged to the younger sister, Rachel, for about a year. He had known both the Lawes girls since they were children. Slow and cautious in all things, he had been unwilling to admit to himself the growing attraction that Rachel's childlike face and honest brown eyes had for him. Not a beauty like Esther, no! But unutterably truer and sweeter. With Dickie's engagement to the elder sister, the bond between the two men seemed to be drawn closer.

And now, after a few brief weeks, that engagement was off again, and Dickie, simple Dickie, hard hit. So far in his young life all had gone so smoothly. His career in the Navy had been well chosen. His craving for the sea was inborn. There was something of the Viking about him, primitive and direct, a nature on which subtleties of thought were wasted. He belonged to that inarticulate order of young Englishmen who dislike any form of emotion, and who find it peculiarly hard to explain their mental processes in words.

Macfarlane, that dour Scot, with a Celtic imagination hidden away somewhere, listened and smoked while his friend floundered along in a sea of words. He had known an unburdening was coming. But he had expected the subject matter to be different. To begin with, anyway, there was no mention of Esther Lawes. Only, it seemed, the story of a childish terror.

'It all started with a dream I had when I was a kid. Not a nightmare exactly. She – the gipsy, you know – would just come into any old dream – even a good dream (or a kid's idea of what's good – a party and crackers and things). I'd be enjoying myself no end, and then I'd feel, I'd *know*, that if I looked up, *she'd* be there, standing as she always stood, watching me . . . With sad eyes, you know, as though she understood something that I didn't . . . Can't explain why it rattled me so – but it did! Every time! I used to wake up howling with terror, and my old nurse used to say: "There! Master Dickie's had one of his gipsy dreams again!"'

'Ever been frightened by real gipsies?'

'Never saw one till later. That was queer, too. I was chasing a pup of mine. He'd run away. I got through the garden door, and along one of the forest paths. We lived in the New Forest then, you know. I came to a sort of clearing at the end, with a wooden bridge over a stream. And just beside it a gipsy was standing – with a red handkerchief over her head – just the same as in my dream. And at once I was frightened! She looked at me, you know . . . Just the same look – as though she knew something I didn't, and was sorry about it . . . And then she said quite quietly, nodding her head at me: "*I shouldn't go that way, if I were you.*" I can't tell you why, but it frightened me to death. I dashed past her on to the bridge. I suppose it was rotten. Anyway, it gave way, and I was chucked into the stream. It was running pretty fast, and I was nearly drowned. Beastly to be nearly drowned. I've never forgotten it. And I felt it had all to do with the gipsy . . .'

'Actually, though, she warned you against it?'

'I suppose you could put it like that,' Dickie paused, then went on: 'I've told you about this dream of mine, not because it has anything to do with what happened after (at least, I suppose it hasn't), but because it's the jumping off point, as it were. You'll understand now what I mean by the "gipsy feeling." So I'll go on to that first night at the Lawes'. I'd just come back from the west coast then. It was awfully rum to be in England again. The Lawes were old friends of my people's. I hadn't seen the girls since I was about seven, but young Arthur was a great pal of mine, and after he died, Esther used to write to me, and send me out papers. Awfully jolly letters, she wrote! Cheered me up no end. I always wished I was a better hand at writing back. I was awfully keen to see her. It seemed odd to know a girl quite well from her letters, and not otherwise. Well, I went down to the Lawes' place first thing. Esther was away when I arrived, but was expected back that evening. I sat next to Rachel at dinner, and as I looked up and down the long table a queer feeling came over me. I felt someone was watching me, and it made me uncomfortable. Then I saw her –'

'Saw who –'

'Mrs Haworth – what I'm telling you about.'

It was on the tip of Macfarlane's tongue to say: 'I thought you were telling me about Esther Lawes.' But he remained silent, and Dickie went on.

'There was something about her quite different from all the rest. She was sitting next to old Lawes – listening to him very gravely with her head bent down. She had some of that red tulle stuff round her neck. It had got torn, I think, anyway it stood up behind her head like little tongues of flame . . . I said to Rachel: "Who's that woman over there. Dark – with a red scarf?"

'"Do you mean Alistair Haworth? She's got a red scarf. But she's fair. *Very* fair."

'So she was, you know. Her hair was a lovely pale shining yellow. Yet I could have sworn positively she was dark. Queer what tricks one's eyes play on one . . . After dinner, Rachel introduced us, and we walked up and down in the garden. We talked about reincarnation . . .'

'Rather out of your line, Dickie!'

'I suppose it is. I remember saying that it seemed to be a jolly sensible way of accounting for how one seems to know some people right off – as if you'd met them before. She said: "You mean lovers . . ." There was something queer about the way she said it – something soft and eager. It reminded me of something – but I couldn't remember what. We went on jawing a bit, and then old Lawes called us from the terrace – said Esther had come, and wanted to see me. Mrs Haworth put her hand on my arm and said: "You're going in?" "Yes," I said. "I suppose we'd better," and then – then –'

'Well?'

'It sounds such rot. Mrs Haworth said: "*I shouldn't go in if I were you . . .*"' He paused. 'It frightened me, you know. It frightened me badly. That's why I told you about the dream . . . Because, you see, she said it just the same way – quietly, as though she knew something I didn't. It wasn't just a pretty woman who wanted to keep me out in the garden with her. Her voice was just kind – and very sorry. Almost as though she knew what was to come . . . I suppose it was rude, but I turned and left her – almost ran to the house. It seemed like safety. I knew then that I'd been afraid of her from the first. It was a relief to see old Lawes. Esther was there beside him . . .' He hesitated a minute and then muttered rather obscurely: 'There was no question – the moment I saw her. I knew I'd got it in the neck.'

Macfarlane's mind flew swiftly to Esther Lawes. He had once heard her summed up as 'Six foot one of Jewish perfection.' A shrewd portrait, he thought, as he remembered her unusual height and the long slenderness of her, the marble whiteness of her face with its delicate down-drooping nose, and the black splendour of hair and eyes. Yes, he did not wonder that the boyish simplicity of Dickie had capitulated. Esther could never have made his own pulses beat one jot faster, but he admitted her magnificence.

'And then,' continued Dickie, 'we got engaged.'

'At once?'

'Well, after about a week. It took her about a fortnight after that to find out that she didn't care after all . . .' He gave a short bitter laugh.

'It was the last evening before I went back to the old ship. I was coming back from the village through the woods – and then I saw *her* – Mrs Haworth, I mean. She had on a red tam-o'-shanter, and – just for a minute, you know – it made me jump! I've told you about my dream, so you'll understand . . . Then we walked along a bit. Not that there was a word Esther couldn't have heard, you know . . .'

'No?' Macfarlane looked at his friend curiously. Strange how people told you things of which they themselves were unconscious!

'And then, when I was turning to go back to the house, she stopped me. She said: "You'll be home soon enough. *I shouldn't go back too soon if I were you* . . ." And then *I knew* – that there was something beastly waiting for me . . . and . . . as soon as I got back Esther met me, and told me – that she'd found out she didn't really care . . .'

Macfarlane grunted sympathetically. 'And Mrs Haworth?' he asked.

'I never saw her again – until tonight.'

'Tonight?'

'Yes. At the doctor johnny's nursing home. They had a look at my leg, the one that got messed up in that torpedo business. It's worried me a bit lately. The old chap advised an operation – it'll be quite a simple thing. Then as I left the place, I ran into a girl in a red jumper over her nurse's things, and she said: "*I wouldn't have that operation, if I were* you . . ." Then I saw it was Mrs Haworth. She passed on so quickly I couldn't stop her. I met another nurse, and asked about her. But she said there wasn't anyone of that name in the home . . . . Queer . . .'

'Sure it was her?'

'Oh! yes, you see – she's very beautiful . . .' He paused, and then added: 'I shall have the old op, of course – but – but in case my number *should* be up –'

'Rot!'

'Of course it's rot. But all the same I'm glad I told you about this gipsy business . . . You know, there's more of it if only I could remember . . .'

* * *

Macfarlane walked up the steep moorland road. He turned in at the gate of the house near the crest of the hill. Setting his jaw squarely, he pulled the bell.

'Is Mrs Haworth in?'

'Yes, sir. I'll tell her.' The maid left him in a low long room, with windows that gave on the wildness of the moorland. He frowned a little. Was he making a colossal ass of himself?

Then he started. A low voice was singing overhead:

> *The gipsy woman*
> *Lives on the moor –'*

The voice broke off. Macfarlane's heart beat a shade faster. The door opened.

The bewildering, almost Scandinavian fairness of her came as a shock. In spite of Dickie's description, he had imagined her gipsy dark . . . And he suddenly remembered Dickie's words, and the peculiar tone of them. '*You see, she's very beautiful . . .*' Perfect unquestionable beauty is rare, and perfect unquestionable beauty was what Alistair Haworth possessed.

He caught himself up, and advanced towards her. 'I'm afraid you don't know me from Adam. I got your address from the Lawes. But – I'm a friend of Dickie Carpenter's.'

She looked at him closely for a minute or two. Then she said: 'I was going out. Up on the moor. Will you come too?'

She pushed open the window, and stepped out on the hillside. He followed her. A heavy, rather foolish-looking man was sitting in a basket-chair smoking.

'My husband! We're going out on the moor, Maurice. And then Mr Macfarlane will come back to lunch with us. You will, won't you?'

'Thanks very much.' He followed her easy stride up the hill, and thought to himself: 'Why? Why, on God's earth, marry *that?*'

Alistair made her way to some rocks. 'We'll sit here. And you shall tell me – what you came to tell me.'

'You knew?'

'I always know when bad things are coming. It is bad, isn't it? About Dickie?'

'He underwent a slight operation – quite successfully. But his heart must have been weak. He died under the anaesthetic.'

What he expected to see on her face, he scarcely knew – hardly that look of utter eternal weariness . . . He heard her murmur: 'Again – to wait – so long – so long . . .' She looked up: 'Yes, what were you going to say?'

'Only this. Someone warned him against this operation. A nurse. He thought it was you. Was it?'

She shook her head. 'No, it wasn't me. But I've got a cousin who is a nurse. She's rather like me in a dim light. I dare say that was it.' She looked up at him again. 'It doesn't matter, does it?' And then suddenly her eyes widened. She drew in her breath. 'Oh!' she said. 'Oh! How funny! You don't understand . . .'

Macfarlane was puzzled. She was still staring at him.

'I thought you did . . . You *should* do. You look as though you'd got it, too . . .'

'Got what?'

'The gift – curse – call it what you like. I believe you have. Look hard at that hollow in the rocks. Don't think of anything, just look . . . Ah!' she marked his slight start. 'Well – you saw something?'

'It must have been imagination. Just for a second I saw it full of blood!'

She nodded. 'I knew you had it. That's the place where the old sun-worshippers sacrificed victims. I knew that before anyone told me. And there are times when I know just how they felt about it – almost as though I'd been there myself . . . And there's something about the moor that makes me feel as though I were coming back home . . . Of course it's natural that I should have the gift. I'm a Ferguesson. There's second sight in the family. And my mother was a medium until my father married her. Cristing was her name. She was rather celebrated.'

'Do you mean by "the gift" the power of being able to see things before they happen?'

'Yes, forwards or backwards – it's all the same. For instance, I saw you wondering why I married Maurice – oh! yes, you did! – It's simply because I've always known that there's something dreadful hanging over him . . . I wanted to save him from it . . . Women are like that. With my gift, I ought to be able to prevent it happening . . . if one ever can . . . I couldn't help Dickie. And Dickie wouldn't understand . . . He was afraid. He was very young.'

'Twenty-two.'

'And I'm thirty. But I didn't mean that. There are so many ways of being divided, length and height and breadth . . . but to be divided by time is the worst way of all . . .' She fell into a long brooding silence.

The low peal of a gong from the house below roused them.

At lunch, Macfarlane watched Maurice Haworth. He was undoubtedly madly in love with his wife. There was the unquestioning happy fondness of a dog in his eyes. Macfarlane marked also the tenderness of her response, with its hint of maternity. After lunch he took his leave.

'I'm staying down at the inn for a day or so. May I come and see you again? Tomorrow, perhaps?'

'Of course. But –'

'But what –'

She brushed her hand quickly across her eyes. 'I don't know. I – I fancied that we shouldn't meet again – that's all . . . Good-bye.'

He went down the road slowly. In spite of himself, a cold hand seemed tightening round his heart. Nothing in her words, of course, but –

A motor swept round the corner. He flattened himself against the hedge . . . only just in time. A curious greyish pallor crept across his face . . .

'Good Lord, my nerves are in a rotten state,' muttered Macfarlane, as he awoke the following morning. He reviewed the events of the afternoon before dispassionately. The motor, the short-cut to the inn and the sudden mist that had made him lose his way with the knowledge that a dangerous bog was no distance off. Then the chimney pot that had fallen off the inn, and the smell of burning in the night which he had traced to a cinder on his hearthrug. Nothing in it at all! Nothing at all – but for her words, and that deep unacknowledged certainty in his heart that she *knew* . . .

He flung off his bedclothes with sudden energy. He must go up and see her first thing. That would break the spell. That is, *if he got there safely* . . . Lord, what a fool he was!

He could eat little breakfast. Ten o'clock saw him starting up the road. At ten-thirty his hand was on the bell. Then, and not till then, he permitted himself to draw a long breath of relief.

'Is Mr Haworth in?'

It was the same elderly woman who had opened the door before. But her face was different – ravaged with grief.

'Oh! sir, oh! sir, you haven't heard then?'

'Heard what?'

'Miss Alistair, the pretty lamb. It was her tonic. She took it every night. The poor captain is beside himself, he's nearly mad. He took the wrong bottle off the shelf in the dark . . . They sent for the doctor, but he was too late –'

And swiftly there recurred to Macfarlane the words: *I've always known there was something dreadful hanging over him. I ought to be able to prevent it happening* – if one ever can –' Ah! but one couldn't cheat Fate . . . Strange fatality of vision that had destroyed where it sought to save . . .

The old servant went on: 'My pretty lamb! So sweet and gentle she was, and so sorry for anything in trouble. Couldn't bear anyone to be hurt.' She hesitated, then added: 'Would you like to go up and see her, sir? I think, from what she said, that you must have known her long ago. A *very* long time ago, she said . . .'

Macfarlane followed the old woman up the stairs, into the room over the drawing-room where he had heard the voice singing the day before. There was stained glass at the top of the windows. It threw a red light on the head of the bed . . . *A gipsy with a red handkerchief over her head* . . . Nonsense, his nerves were playing tricks again. He took a long last look at Alistair Haworth.

'There's a lady to see you, sir.'

'Eh?' Macfarlane looked at the landlady abstractedly. 'Oh! I beg your pardon, Mrs Rowse, I've been seeing ghosts.'

'Not really, sir? There's queer things to be seen on the moor after nightfall, I know. There's the white lady, and the Devil's blacksmith, and the sailor and the gipsy –'

'What's that? A sailor and a gipsy?'

'So they say, sir. It was quite a tale in my young days. Crossed in love they were, a while back . . . But they've not walked for many a long day now.'

'No? I wonder if perhaps – they will again now . . .'

'Lor! sir, what things you do say! About that young lady –'

'What young lady?'

'The one that's waiting to see you. She's in the parlour. Miss Lawes, she said her name was.'

'Oh!'

Rachel! He felt a curious feeling of contraction, a shifting of perspective. He had been peeping through at another world. He had forgotten Rachel, for Rachel belonged to this life only . . . Again that curious shifting of perspective, that slipping back to a world of three dimensions only.

He opened the parlour door. Rachel – with her honest brown eyes. And suddenly, like a man awakening from a dream, a warm rush of glad reality swept over him. He was alive – alive! He thought: 'There's only one life one can be *sure* about! This one!'

'Rachel!' he said, and, lifting her chin, he kissed her lips.

The Lamp

'The Lamp' was first published in the hardback *The Hound
of Death and Other Stories* (Odhams Press, 1933).
No previous appearances have been found.

It was undoubtedly an old house. The whole square was old, with that
disapproving dignified old age often met with in a cathedral town. But
No. 19 gave the impression of an elder among elders; it had a veritable
patriarchal solemnity; it towered greyest of the grey, haughtiest of the
haughty, chillest of the chill. Austere, forbidding, and stamped with that
particular desolation attaching to all houses that have been long
untenanted, it reigned above the other dwellings.

In any other town it would have been freely labelled 'haunted,' but
Weyminster was averse from ghosts and considered them hardly
respectable except at the appanage of a 'county family'. So No. 19 was
never alluded to as a haunted house; but nevertheless it remained, year
after year, To be Let or Sold.

Mrs Lancaster looked at the house with approval as she drove up with
the talkative house agent, who was in an unusually hilarious mood at the
idea of getting No. 19 off his books. He inserted the key in the door
without ceasing his appreciative comments.

'How long has the house been empty?' inquired Mrs Lancaster, cutting
short his flow of language rather brusquely.

Mr Raddish (of Raddish and Foplow) became slightly confused.

'E – er – some time,' he remarked blandly.

'So I should think,' said Mrs Lancaster drily.

The dimly lighted hall was chill with a sinister chill. A more imaginative woman might have shivered, but this woman happened to be
eminently practical. She was tall with much dark brown hair just tinged
with grey and rather cold blue eyes.

She went over the house from attic to cellar, asking a pertinent question from time to time. The inspection over, she came back into one of the front rooms looking out on the square and faced the agent with a resolute mien.

'What is the matter with the house?'

Mr Raddish was taken by surprise.

'Of course, an unfurnished house is always a little gloomy,' he parried feebly.

'Nonsense,' said Mrs Lancaster. 'The rent is ridiculously low for such a house – purely nominal. There must be some reason for it. I suppose the house is haunted?'

Mr Raddish gave a nervous little start but said nothing.

Mrs Lancaster eyed him keenly. After a few moments she spoke again.

'Of course that is all nonsense, I don't believe in ghosts or anything of that sort, and personally it is no deterrent to my taking the house; but servants, unfortunately, are very credulous and easily frightened. It would be kind of you to tell me exactly what – what thing *is* supposed to haunt this place.'

'I – er – really don't know,' stammered the house agent.

'I am sure you must,' said the lady quietly. 'I cannot take the house without knowing. What was it? A murder?'

'Oh! no,' cried Mr Raddish, shocked by the idea of anything so alien to the respectability of the square. 'It's – it's only a child.'

'A child?'

'Yes.'

'I don't know the story exactly,' he continued reluctantly. 'Of course, there are all kinds of different versions, but I believe that about thirty years ago a man going by the name of Williams took No. 19. Nothing was known of him; he kept no servants; he had no friends; he seldom went out in the day time. He had one child, a little boy. After he had been there about two months, he went up to London, and had barely set foot in the metropolis before he was recognized as being a man "wanted" by the police on some charge – exactly what, I do not know. But it must have been a grave one, because, sooner than give himself up he shot himself. Meanwhile, the child lived on here, alone in the house. He had food for a little time, and he waited day after day for his father's return. Unfortunately, it had been impressed upon him that he was never under any circumstances to go out of the house or speak to anyone. He was a weak, ailing, little creature, and did not dream of disobeying this command. In the night, the neighbours, not knowing that his father had gone away, often heard him sobbing in the awful loneliness and desolation of the empty house.'

Mr Raddish paused.

'And – er – the child starved to death,' he concluded, in the same tones as he might have announced that it had just begun to rain.

'And it is the child's ghost that is supposed to haunt the place?' asked Mrs Lancaster.

'It is nothing of consequence really,' Mr Raddish hastened to assure her. 'There's nothing *seen*, not *seen*, only people say, ridiculous, of course, but they do say they hear – the child – crying, you know.'

Mrs Lancaster moved towards the front door.

'I like the house very much,' she said. 'I shall get nothing as good for the price. I will think it over and let you know.'

'It really looks very cheerful, doesn't it, Papa?'

Mrs Lancaster surveyed her new domain with approval. Gay rugs, well-polished furniture, and many knick-knacks, had quite transformed the gloomy aspect of No. 19.

She spoke to a thin, bent old man with stooping shoulders and a delicate mystical face. Mr Winburn did not resemble his daughter; indeed no greater contrast could be imagined than that presented by her resolute practicalness and his dreamy abstraction.

'Yes,' he answered with a smile, 'no one would dream the house was haunted.'

'Papa, don't talk nonsense! On our first day too.'

Mr Winburn smiled.

'Very well, my dear, we will agree that there are no such things as ghosts.'

'And please,' continued Mrs Lancaster, 'don't say a word before Geoff. He's so imaginative.'

Geoff was Mrs Lancaster's little boy. The family consisted of Mr Winburn, his widowed daughter, and Geoffrey.

Rain had begun to beat against the window – pitter-patter, pitter-patter.

'Listen,' said Mr Winburn. 'Is it not like little footsteps?'

'It is more like rain,' said Mrs Lancaster, with a smile.

'But *that, that* is a footstep,' cried her father, bending forward to listen.

Mrs Lancaster laughed outright.

Mr Winburn was obliged to laugh too. They were having tea in the hall, and he had been sitting with his back to the staircase. He now turned his chair round to face it.

Little Geoffrey was coming down, rather slowly and sedately, with a child's awe of a strange place. The stairs were of polished oak, uncarpeted. He came across and stood by his mother. Mr Winburn gave a slight start. As the child was crossing the floor, he distincty heard another pair of footsteps on the stairs, as of someone following Geoffrey. Dragging footsteps, curiously painful they were. Then he shrugged his shoulders incredulously. 'The rain, no doubt,' he thought.

'I'm looking at the spongecakes,' remarked Geoff with the admirably detached air of one who points out an interesting fact.

His mother hastened to comply with the hint.

'Well, Sonny, how do you like your new home?' she asked.

'Lots,' replied Geoffrey with his mouth generously filled. 'Pounds and pounds and pounds.' After this last assertion, which was evidently expressive of the deepest contentment, he relapsed into silence, only anxious to remove the spongecake from the sight of man in the least time possible.

Having bolted the last mouthful, he burst forth into speech.

'Oh! Mummy, there's attics here, Jane says; and can I go at once and eggzplore them? And there might be a secret door, Jane says there isn't, but I think there must be, and, anyhow, I know there'll be *pipes, water pipes* (with a face full of ecstasy) and can I play with them, and, oh! can I go and see the Boi-i-ler?' He spun out the last word with such evident rapture that his grandfather felt ashamed to reflect that this peerless delight of childhood only conjured up to his imagination the picture of hot water that wasn't hot, and heavy and numerous plumber's bills.

'We'll see about the attics tomorrow, darling,' said Mrs Lancaster. 'Suppose you fetch your bricks and build a nice house, or an engine.'

'Don't want to build an 'ouse.'

'*House*.'

'House, or h'engine h'either.'

'Build a boiler,' suggested his grandfather.

Geoffrey brightened.

'With pipes?'

'Yes, lots of pipes.'

Geoffrey ran away happily to fetch his bricks.

The rain was still falling. Mr Winburn listened. Yes, it must have been the rain he had heard; but it did sound like footsteps.

He had a queer dream that night.

He dreamt that he was walking through a town, a great city it seemed to him. But it was a children's city; there were no grown-up people there, nothing but children, crowds of them. In his dream they all rushed to the stranger crying: 'Have you brought him?' It seemed that he understood what they meant and shook his head sadly. When they saw this, the children turned away and began to cry, sobbing bitterly.

The city and the children faded away and he awoke to find himself in bed, but the sobbing was still in his ears. Though wide awake, he heard it distinctly; and he remembered that Geoffrey slept on the floor below, while this sound of a child's sorrow descended from above. He sat up and struck a match. Instantly the sobbing ceased.

Mr Winburn did not tell his daughter of the dream or its sequel. That it was no trick of his imagination, he was convinced; indeed soon afterwards he heard it again in the day time. The wind was howling in the chimney but *this* was a separate sound – distinct, unmistakable; pitiful little heartbroken sobs.

He found out too, that he was not the only one to hear them. He overheard the housemaid saying to the parlour maid that she 'didn't think as that there nurse was kind to Master Geoffrey, she'd 'eard 'im crying 'is little 'eart out only that morning.' Geoffrey had come down to breakfast and lunch beaming with health and happiness; and Mr Winburn knew that it was not Geoff who had been crying, but that other child whose dragging footsteps had startled him more than once.

Mrs Lancaster alone never heard anything. Her ears were not perhaps attuned to catch sounds from another world.

Yet one day she also received a shock.

'Mummy,' said Geoff plaintively. 'I wish you'd let me play with that little boy.'

Mrs Lancaster looked up from her writing-table with a smile.

'What little boy, dear?'

'I don't know his name. He was in a attic, sitting on the floor crying, but he ran away when he saw me. I suppose he was *shy* (with slight contempt), not like a *big* boy, and then, when I was in the nursery building, I saw him standing in the door watching me build, and he looked so awful lonely and as though he wanted to play wiv me. I said: "Come and build a h'engine," but he didn't say nothing, just looked as – as though he saw a lot of chocolates, and his Mummy had told him not to touch them.' Geoff sighed, sad personal reminiscences evidently recurring to him. 'But when I asked Jane who he was and told her I wanted to play wiv him, she said there wasn't no little boy in the 'ouse and not to tell naughty stories. I don't love Jane at all.'

Mrs Lancaster got up.

'Jane was right. There was no little boy.'

'But I saw him. Oh! Mummy, do let me play wiv him, he did look so awful lonely and unhappy. I *do* want to do something to "make him better".'

Mrs Lancaster was about to speak again, but her father shook his head.

'Geoff,' he said very gently, 'that poor little boy *is* lonely, and perhaps you may do something to comfort him; but you must find out how by yourself – like a puzzle – do you see?'

'Is it because I am getting *big* I must do it all my lone?'

'Yes, because you are getting big.'

As the boy left the room, Mrs Lancaster turned to her father impatiently.

'Papa, this is absurd. To encourage the boy to believe the servants' idle tales!'

'No servant has told the child anything,' said the old man gently. 'He's seen – what I *hear*, what I could see perhaps if I were his age.'

'But it's such nonsense! Why don't I see it or hear it?'

Mr Winburn smiled, a curiously tired smile, but did not reply.

'Why?' repeated his daughter. 'And why did you tell him he could help the – the – thing. It's – it's all so impossible.'

The old man looked at her with his thoughtful glance.

'Why not?' he said. 'Do you remember these words:

"What Lamp has Destiny to guide
Her little Children stumbling in the Dark?
'A Blind Understanding,' Heaven replied."

'Geoffrey has that – a blind understanding. All children possess it. It is only as we grow older that we lose it, that we cast it away from us. Sometimes, when we are quite old, a faint gleam comes back to us, but the Lamp burns brightest in childhood. That is why I think Geoffrey may help.'

'I don't understand,' murmured Mrs Lancaster feebly.

'No more do I. That – that child is in trouble and wants – to be set free. But how? I do not know, but – it's awful to think of it – sobbing its heart out – a *child*.'

A month after this conversation Geoffrey fell very ill. The east wind had been severe, and he was not a strong child. The doctor shook his head and said that it was a grave case. To Mr Winburn he divulged more and confessed that the case was quite hopeless. 'The child would never have lived to grow up, under any circumstances,' he added.

'There has been serious lung trouble for a long time.'

It was when nursing Geoff that Mrs Lancaster became aware of that – other child. At first the sobs were an indistinguishable part of the wind, but gradually they became more distinct, more unmistakable. Finally she heard them in moments of dead calm: a child's sobs – dull, hopeless, heartbroken.

Geoff grew steadily worse and in his delirium he spoke of the 'little boy' again and again. 'I do want to help him get away, I do!' he cried.

Succeeding the delirium there came a state of lethargy. Geoffrey lay very still, hardly breathing, sunk in oblivion. There was nothing to do but wait and watch. Then there came a still night, clear and calm, without one breath of wind.

Suddenly the child stirred. His eyes opened. He looked past his mother toward the open door. He tried to speak and she bent down to catch the half breathed words.

'All right, I'm comin',' he whispered; then he sank back.

The mother felt suddenly terrified, she crossed the room to her father. Somewhere near them the other child was laughing. Joyful, contented, triumphant and silvery laughter echoed through the room.

'I'm frightened; I'm frightened,' she moaned.

He put his arm round her protectingly. A sudden gust of wind made them both start, but it passed swiftly and left the air quiet as before.

The laughter had ceased and there crept to them a faint sound, so faint as hardly to be heard, but growing louder till they could distinguish it. Footsteps – light footsteps, swiftly departing.

Pitter-patter, pitter-patter, they ran – those well-known halting little feet. Yet – surely – now *other* footsteps suddenly mingled with them, moving with a quicker and a lighter tread.

With one accord they hastened to the door.

Down, down, down, past the door, close to them, pitter-patter, pitter-patter, went the unseen feet of the little children *together*.

Mrs Lancaster looked up wildly.

'There are *two* of them – *two!*'

Grey with sudden fear, she turned towards the cot in the corner, but her father restrained her gently, and pointed away.

'There,' he said simply.

Pitter-patter, pitter-patter – fainter and fainter.

And then – silence.

The Strange Case of
Sir Arthur Carmichael

'The Strange Case of Sir Arthur Carmichael' was first published in the
hardback *The Hound of Death and Other Stories* (Odhams Press, 1933).
No previous appearances have been found.

(Taken from the notes of the late Dr Edward Carstairs, M.D. the eminent
psychologist.)

I am perfectly aware that there are two distinct ways of looking at the
strange and tragic events which I have set down here. My own opinion
has never wavered. I have been persuaded to write the story out in full,
and indeed I believe it to be due to science that such strange and inexplicable facts should not be buried in oblivion.

It was a wire from my friend, Dr Settle, that first introduced me to
the matter. Beyond mentioning the name Carmichael, the wire was not
explicit, but in obedience to it I took the 12.20 train from Paddington
to Wolden, in Hertfordshire.

The name of Carmichael was not unfamiliar to me. I had been slightly
acquainted with the late Sir William Carmichael of Wolden, though I had
seen nothing of him for the last eleven years. He had, I knew, one son,
the present baronet, who must now be a young man of about twenty-
three. I remembered vaguely having heard some rumours about Sir
William's second marriage, but could recall nothing definite unless it were
a vague impression detrimental to the second Lady Carmichael.

Settle met me at the station.

'Good of you to come,' he said as he wrung my hand.

'Not at all. I understand this is something in my line?'

'Very much so.'

'A mental case, then?' I hazarded. 'Possessing some unusual features?'

We had collected my luggage by this time and were seated in a dogcart driving away from the station in the direction of Wolden, which lay about three miles away. Settle did not answer for a minute or two. Then he burst out suddenly.

'The whole thing's incomprehensible! Here is a young man, twenty-three years of age, thoroughly normal in every respect. A pleasant amiable boy, with no more than his fair share of conceit, not brilliant intellectually perhaps, but an excellent type of the ordinary upperclass young Englishman. Goes to bed in his usual health one evening, and is found the next morning wandering about the village in a semi-idiotic condition, incapable of recognizing his nearest and dearest.'

'Ah!' I said, stimulated. This case promised to be interesting. 'Complete loss of memory? And this occurred –?'

'Yesterday morning. The 9th of August.'

'And there has been nothing – no shock that you know of – to account for this state?'

'Nothing.'

I had a sudden suspicion.

'Are you keeping anything back?'

'N – no.'

His hesitation confirmed my suspicion.

'I must know everything.'

'It's nothing to do with Arthur. It's to do with – with the house.'

'With the house,' I repeated, astonished.

'You've had a great deal to do with that sort of thing, haven't you, Carstairs? You've "tested" so-called haunted houses. What's your opinion of the whole thing?'

'In nine cases out of ten, fraud,' I replied. 'But the tenth – well, I have come across phenomena that are absolutely unexplainable from the ordinary materialistic standpoint. I am a believer in the occult.'

Settle nodded. We were just turning in at the Park gates. He pointed with his whip at a low-lying white mansion on the side of a hill.

'That's the house,' he said. 'And – there's *something* in that house, something uncanny – horrible. We all feel it . . . And I'm not a superstitious man . . .'

'What form does it take?' I asked.

He looked straight in front of him. 'I'd rather you knew nothing. You see, if you – coming here unbiased – knowing nothing about it – see it too – well –'

'Yes,' I said, 'it's better so. But I should be glad if you will tell me a little more about the family.'

'Sir William,' said Settle, 'was twice married. Arthur is the child of his first wife. Nine years ago he married again, and the present Lady Carmichael is something of a mystery. She is only half English, and, I suspect, has Asiatic blood in her veins.'

He paused.

'Settle,' I said, 'you don't like Lady Carmichael.'

He admitted it frankly. 'No, I don't. There has always seemed to be something sinister about her. Well, to continue, by his second wife Sir William had another child, also a boy, who is now eight years old. Sir William died three years ago, and Arthur came into the title and place. His stepmother and half brother continued to live with him at Wolden. The estate, I must tell you, is very much impoverished. Nearly the whole of Sir Arthur's income goes to keeping it up. A few hundreds a year was all Sir William could leave his wife, but fortunately Arthur has always got on splendidly with his stepmother, and has been only too delighted to have her live with him. Now –'

'Yes?'

'Two months ago Arthur became engaged to a charming girl, a Miss Phyllis Patterson.' He added, lowering his voice with a touch of emotion: 'They were to have been married next month. She is staying here now. You can imagine her distress –'

I bowed my head silently.

We were driving up close to the house now. On our right the green lawn sloped gently away. And suddenly I saw a most charming picture. A young girl was coming slowly across the lawn to the house. She wore no hat, and the sunlight enhanced the gleam of her glorious golden hair. She carried a great basket of roses, and a beautiful grey Persian cat twined itself lovingly round her feet as she walked.

I looked at Settle interrogatively.

'That is Miss Patterson,' he said.

'Poor girl,' I said, 'poor girl. What a picture she makes with the roses and her grey cat.'

I heard a faint sound and looked quickly round at my friend. The reins had slipped out of his fingers, and his face was quite white.

'What's the matter?' I exclaimed.

He recovered himself with an effort.

In a few moments more we had arrived, and I was following him into the green drawing-room, where tea was laid out.

A middle-aged but still beautiful woman rose as we entered and came forward with an outstretched hand.

'This is my friend, Dr Carstairs, Lady Carmichael.'

I cannot explain the instinctive wave of repulsion that swept over me as I took the proffered hand of this charming and stately woman who moved with the dark and languorous grace that recalled Settle's surmise of Oriental blood.

'It is very good of you to come, Dr Carstairs,' she said in a low musical voice, 'and to try and help us in our great trouble.'

I made some trivial reply and she handed me my tea.

In a few minutes the girl I had seen on the lawn outside entered the room. The cat was no longer with her, but she still carried the basket of roses in her hand. Settle introduced me and she came forward impulsively.

'Oh! Dr Carstairs, Dr Settle has told us so much about you. I have a feeling that you will be able to do something for poor Arthur.'

Miss Patterson was certainly a very lovely girl, though her cheeks were pale, and her frank eyes were outlined with dark circles.

'My dear young lady,' I said reassuringly, 'indeed you must not despair. These cases of lost memory, or secondary personality, are often of very short duration. At any minute the patient may return to his full powers.'

She shook her head. 'I can't believe in this being a second personality,' she said. '*This* isn't Arthur at all. It is *no* personality of his. It isn't *him*. I –'

'Phyllis, dear,' said Lady Carmichael's soft voice, 'here is your tea.'

And something in the expression of her eyes as they rested on the girl told me that Lady Carmichael had little love for her prospective daughter-in-law.

Miss Patterson declined the tea, and I said, to ease the conversation: 'Isn't the pussy cat going to have a saucer of milk?'

She looked at me rather strangely.

'The – pussy cat?'

'Yes, your companion of a few moments ago in the garden –'

I was interrupted by a crash. Lady Carmichael had upset the tea kettle, and the hot water was pouring all over the floor. I remedied the matter, and Phyllis Patterson looked questioningly at Settle. He rose.

'Would you like to see your patient now, Carstairs?'

I followed him at once. Miss Patterson came with us. We went upstairs and Settle took a key from his pocket.

'He sometimes has a fit of wandering,' he explained. 'So I usually lock the door when I'm away from the house.'

He turned the key in the lock and went in.

The young man was sitting on the window seat where the last rays of the westerly sun struck broad and yellow. He sat curiously still, rather hunched together, with every muscle relaxed. I thought at first that he was quite unaware of our presence until I suddenly saw that, under immovable lids, he was watching us closely. His eyes dropped as they met mine, and he blinked. But he did not move.

'Come, Arthur,' said Settle cheerfully. 'Miss Patterson and a friend of mine have come to see you.'

But the young fellow in the window seat only blinked. Yet a moment or two later I saw him watching us again – furtively and secretly.

'Want your tea?' asked Settle, still loudly and cheerfully, as though talking to a child.

He set on the table a cup full of milk. I lifted my eyebrows in surprise, and Settle smiled.

'Funny thing,' he said, 'the only drink he'll touch is milk.'

In a moment or two, without undue haste, Sir Arthur uncoiled himself, limb by limb, from his huddled position, and walked slowly over to the table. I recognized suddenly that his movements were absolutely silent, his feet made no sound as they trod. Just as he reached the table he gave a tremendous stretch, poised on one leg forward, the other stretching out behind him. He prolonged this exercise to its utmost extent, and then yawned. Never have I seen such a yawn! It seemed to swallow up his entire face.

He now turned his attention to the milk, bending down to the table until his lips touched the fluid.

Settle answered my inquiring look.

'Won't make use of his hands at all. Seems to have returned to a primitive state. Odd, isn't it?'

I felt Phyllis Patterson shrink against me a little, and I laid my hand soothingly on her arm.

The milk was finished at last, and Arthur Carmichael stretched himself once more, and then with the same quiet noiseless footsteps he regained the window seat, where he sat, huddled up as before, blinking at us.

Miss Patterson drew us out into the corridor. She was trembling all over.

'Oh! Dr Carstairs,' she cried. 'It *isn't* him – that thing in there isn't Arthur! I should feel – I should know –'

I shook my head sadly.

'The brain can play strange tricks, Miss Patterson.'

I confess that I was puzzled by the case. It presented unusual features. Though I had never seen young Carmichael before there was something about his peculiar manner of walking, and the way he blinked, that reminded me of someone or something that I could not quite place.

Our dinner that night was a quiet affair, the burden of conversation being sustained by Lady Carmichael and myself. When the ladies had withdrawn Settle asked me my impression of my hostess.

'I must confess,' I said, 'that for no cause or reason I dislike her intensely. You are quite right, she has Eastern blood, and, I should say, possesses marked occult powers. She is a woman of extraordinary magnetic force.'

Settle seemed on the point of saying something, but checked himself and merely remarked after a minute or two: 'She is absolutely devoted to her little son.'

We sat in the green drawing-room again after dinner. We had just finished coffee and were conversing rather stiffly on the topics of the day when the cat began to miaow piteously for admission outside the door. No one took any notice, and, as I am fond of animals, after a moment or two I rose.

'May I let the poor thing in?' I asked Lady Carmichael.

Her face seemed very white, I thought, but she made a faint gesture of the head which I took as assent and, going to the door, I opened it. But the corridor outside was quite empty.

'Strange,' I said, 'I could have sworn I heard a cat.'

As I came back to my chair I noticed they were all watching me intently. It somehow made me feel a little uncomfortable.

We retired to bed early. Settle accompanied me to my room.

'Got everything you want?' he asked, looking around.

'Yes, thanks.'

He still lingered rather awkwardly as though there was something he wanted to say but could not quite get out.

'By the way,' I remarked, 'you said there was something uncanny about this house? As yet it seems most normal.'

'You call it a cheerful house?'

'Hardly that, under the circumstances. It is obviously under the shadow of a great sorrow. But as regards any abnormal influence, I should give it a clean bill of health.'

'Good night,' said Settle abruptly. 'And pleasant dreams.'

Dream I certainly did. Miss Patterson's grey cat seemed to have impressed itself upon my brain. All night long, it seemed to me, I dreamt of the wretched animal.

Awaking with a start, I suddenly realized what had brought the cat so forcibly into my thoughts. The creature was miaowing persistently outside my door. Impossible to sleep with that racket going on. I lit my candle and went to the door. But the passage outside my room was empty, though the miaowing still continued. A new idea struck me. The unfortunate animal was shut up somewhere, unable to get out. To the left was the end of the passage, where Lady Carmichael's room was situated. I turned therefore to the right and had taken but a few paces when the noise broke out again from behind me. I turned sharply and the sound came again, this time distinctly on the *right* of me.

Something, probably a draught in the corridor, made me shiver, and I went sharply back to my room. Everything was silent now, and I was soon asleep once more – to wake to another glorious summer's day.

As I was dressing I saw from my window the disturber of my night's rest. The grey cat was creeping slowly and stealthily across the lawn. I judged its object of attack to be a small flock of birds who were busy chirruping and preening themselves not far away.

And then a very curious thing happened. The cat came straight on and passed through the midst of the birds, its fur almost brushing against them – and the birds did not fly away. I could not understand it – the thing seemed incomprehensible.

So vividly did it impress me that I could not refrain from mentioning it at breakfast.

'Do you know?' I said to Lady Carmichael, 'that you have a very unusual cat?'

I heard the quick rattle of a cup on a saucer, and I saw Phyllis Patterson, her lips parted and her breath coming quickly, gazing earnestly at me.

There was a moment's silence, and then Lady Carmichael said in a distinctly disagreeable manner: 'I think you must have made a mistake. There is no cat here. I have never had a cat.'

It was evident that I had managed to put my foot in it badly, so I hastily changed the subject.

But the matter puzzled me. Why had Lady Carmichael declared there was no cat in the house? Was it perhaps Miss Patterson's, and its presence concealed from the mistress of the house? Lady Carmichael might have one of those strange antipathies to cats which are so often met with nowadays. It hardly seemed a plausible explanation, but I was forced to rest content with it for the moment.

Our patient was still in the same condition. This time I made a thorough examination and was able to study him more closely than the night before. At my suggestion it was arranged that he should spend as much time with the family as possible. I hoped not only to have a better opportunity of observing him when he was off his guard, but the ordinary everyday routine might awaken some gleam of intelligence. His demeanour, however, remained unchanged. He was quiet and docile, seemed vacant, but was in point of fact, intensely and rather slyly watchful. One thing certainly came as a surprise to me, the intense affection he displayed towards his stepmother. Miss Patterson he ignored completely, but he always managed to sit as near Lady Carmichael as possible, and once I saw him rub his head against her shoulder in a dumb expression of love.

I was worried about the case. I could not but feel that there was some clue to the whole matter which had so far escaped me.

'This is a very strange case,' I said to Settle.

'Yes,' said he, 'it's very – suggestive.'

He looked at me rather furtively, I thought.

'Tell me,' he said. 'He doesn't – remind you of anything?'

The words struck me disagreeably, reminding me of my impression of the day before.

'Remind me of what?' I asked.

He shook his head.

'Perhaps it's my fancy,' he muttered. 'Just my fancy.'

And he would say no more on the matter.

Altogether there was mystery shrouding the affair. I was still obsessed with that baffling feeling of having missed the clue that should elucidate it to me. And concerning a lesser matter there was also mystery. I mean that trifling affair of the grey cat. For some reason or other the thing was getting on my nerves. I dreamed of cats – I continually fancied I heard him. Now and then in the distance I caught a glimpse of the beautiful animal. And the fact that there was some mystery connected with it fretted me unbearably. On a sudden impulse I applied one afternoon to the footman for information.

'Can you tell me anything,' I said, 'about the cat I see?'

'The cat, sir?' He appeared politely surprised.

'Wasn't there – isn't there – a cat?'

'Her ladyship *had* a cat, sir. A great pet. Had to be put away though. A great pity, as it was a beautiful animal.'

'A grey cat?' I asked slowly.

'Yes, sir. A Persian.'

'And you say it was destroyed?'

'Yes, sir.'

'You're quite sure it was destroyed?'

'Oh! quite sure, sir. Her ladyship wouldn't have him sent to the vet – but did it herself. A little less than a week ago now. He's buried out there under the copper beech, sir.' And he went out of the room, leaving me to my meditations.

Why had Lady Carmichael affirmed so positively that she had never had a cat?

I felt an intuition that this trifling affair of the cat was in some way significant. I found Settle and took him aside.

'Settle,' I said. 'I want to ask you a question. Have you, or have you not, both seen and heard a cat in this house?'

He did not seem surprised at the question. Rather did he seem to have been expecting it.

'I've heard it,' he said. 'I've not seen it.'

'But the first day,' I cried. 'On the lawn with Miss Patterson!'

He looked at me very steadily.

'I saw Miss Patterson walking across the lawn. Nothing else.'

I began to understand. 'Then,' I said, 'the cat –?'

He nodded.

'I wanted to see if you – unprejudiced – would hear what we all hear . . . ?'

'You all hear it then?'

He nodded again.

'It's strange,' I murmured thoughtfully. 'I never heard of a cat haunting a place before.'

I told him what I had learnt from the footman, and he expressed surprise.

'That's news to me. I didn't know that.'

'But what does it mean?' I asked helplessly.

He shook his head. 'Heaven only knows! But I'll tell you, Carstairs – I'm afraid. The – thing's voice sounds – menacing.'

'Menacing?' I said sharply. 'To whom?'

He spread out his hands. 'I can't say.'

It was not till that evening after dinner that I realized the meaning of his words. We were sitting in the green drawing-room, as on the night of my arrival, when it came – the loud insistent miaowing of a cat outside the door. But this time it was unmistakably angry in its tone – a fierce cat yowl, long-drawn and menacing. And then as it ceased the brass hook outside the door was rattled violently as by a cat's paw.

Settle started up.

'I swear that's real,' he cried.

He rushed to the door and flung it open.

There was nothing there.

He came back mopping his brow. Phyllis was pale and trembling, Lady Carmichael deathly white. Only Arthur, squatting contentedly like a child, his head against his stepmother's knee, was calm and undisturbed.

Miss Patterson laid her hand on my arm and we went upstairs.

'Oh! Dr Carstairs,' she cried. 'What is it? What does it all mean?'

'We don't know yet, my dear young lady,' I said. 'But I mean to find out. But you mustn't be afraid. I am convinced there is no danger to you personally.'

She looked at me doubtfully. 'You think that?'

'I am sure of it,' I answered firmly. I remembered the loving way the grey cat had twined itself round her feet, and I had no misgivings. The menace was not for her.

I was some time dropping off to sleep, but at length I fell into an uneasy slumber from which I awoke with a sense of shock. I heard a scratching sputtering noise as of something being violently ripped or torn. I sprang out of bed and rushed out into the passage. At the same moment Settle burst out of his room opposite. The sound came from our left.

'You hear it, Carstairs?' he cried. 'You hear it?'

We came swiftly up to Lady Carmichael's door. Nothing had passed us, but the noise had ceased. Our candles glittered blankly on the shiny panels of Lady Carmichael's door. We stared at one another.

'You know what it was?' he half whispered.

I nodded. 'A cat's claws ripping and tearing something.' I shivered a little. Suddenly I gave an exclamation and lowered the candle I held.

'Look here, Settle.'

'Here' was a chair that rested against the wall – and the seat of it was ripped and torn in long strips . . .

We examined it closely. He looked at me and I nodded.

'Cat's claws,' he said, drawing in his breath sharply. 'Unmistakable.' His eyes went from the chair to the closed door. 'That's the person who is menaced. Lady Carmichael!'

I slept no more that night. Things had come to a pass where something must be done. As far as I knew there was only one person who had the key to the situation. I suspected Lady Carmichael of knowing more than she chose to tell.

She was deathly pale when she came down the next morning, and only toyed with the food on her plate. I was sure that only an iron determination kept her from breaking down. After breakfast I requested a few words with her. I went straight to the point.

'Lady Carmichael,' I said. 'I have reason to believe that you are in very grave danger.'

'Indeed?' She braved it out with wonderful unconcern.

'There is in this house,' I continued, 'A Thing – a Presence – that is obviously hostile to you.'

'What nonsense,' she murmured scornfully. 'As if I believed in any rubbish of that kind.'

'The chair outside your door,' I remarked drily, 'was ripped to ribbons last night.'

'Indeed?' With raised eyebrows she pretended surprise, but I saw that I had told her nothing she did not know. 'Some stupid practical joke, I suppose.'

'It was not that,' I replied with some feeling. 'And I want you to tell me – for your own sake –' I paused.

'Tell you what?' she queried.

'Anything that can throw light on the matter,' I said gravely.

She laughed.

'I know nothing,' she said. 'Absolutely nothing.'

And no warnings of danger could induce her to relax the statement. Yet I was convinced that she *did* know a great deal more than any of us, and held some clue to the affair of which we were absolutely ignorant. But I saw that it was quite impossible to make her speak.

I determined, however, to take every precaution that I could, convinced as I was that she was menaced by a very real and immediate danger. Before she went to her room the following night Settle and I made a thorough examination of it. We had agreed that we would take it in turns to watch the passage.

I took the first watch, which passed without incident, and at three o'clock Settle relieved me. I was tired after my sleepless night the day before, and dropped off at once. And I had a very curious dream.

I dreamed that the grey cat was sitting at the foot of my bed and that its eyes were fixed on mine with a curious pleading. Then, with the ease of dreams, I knew that the creature wanted me to follow it. I did so, and it led me down the great staircase and right to the opposite wing of the house to a room which was obviously the library. It paused there at one side of the room and raised its front paws till they rested on one of the lower shelves of books, while it gazed at me once more with that same moving look of appeal.

Then – cat and library faded, and I awoke to find that morning had come.

Settle's watch had passed without incident, but he was keenly interested to hear of my dream. At my request he took me to the library, which coincided in every particular with my vision of it. I could even point out the exact spot where the animal had given me that last sad look.

We both stood there in silent perplexity. Suddenly an idea occurred to me, and I stooped to read the title of the book in that exact place. I noticed that there was a gap in the line.

'Some book has been taken out of here,' I said to Settle.

He stooped also to the shelf.

'Hallo,' he said. 'There's a nail at the back here that has torn off a fragment of the missing volume.'

He detached the little scrap of paper with care. It was not more than an inch square – but on it were printed two significant words: 'The cat . . .'

'This thing gives me the creeps,' said Settle. 'It's simply horribly uncanny.'

'I'd give anything to know,' I said, 'what book it is that is missing from here. Do you think there is any way of finding out?'

'May be a catalogue somewhere. Perhaps Lady Carmichael –'

I shook my head.

'Lady Carmichael will tell you nothing.'

'You think so?'

'I am sure of it. While we are guessing and feeling about in the dark Lady Carmichael *knows*. And for reasons of her own she will say nothing. She prefers to run a most horrible risk sooner than break silence.'

The day passed with an uneventfulness that reminded me of the calm before a storm. And I had a strange feeling that the problem was near solution. I was groping about in the dark, but soon I should see. The facts were all there, ready, waiting for the little flash of illumination that should weld them together and show out their significance.

And come it did! In the strangest way!

It was when we were all sitting together in the green drawing-room as usual after dinner. We had been very silent. So noiseless indeed was the room that a little mouse ran across the floor – and in an instant the thing happened.

With one long spring Arthur Carmichael leapt from his chair. His quivering body was swift as an arrow on the mouse's track. It had disappeared behind the wainscoting, and there he crouched – watchful – his body still trembling with eagerness.

It was horrible! I have never known such a paralysing moment. I was no longer puzzled as to that something that Arthur Carmichael reminded me of with his stealthy feet and watching eyes. And in a flash an explanation, wild, incredible, unbelievable, swept into my mind. I rejected it as impossible – unthinkable! But I could not dismiss it from my thoughts.

I hardly remember what happened next. The whole thing seemed blurred and unreal. I know that somehow we got upstairs and said our good nights briefly, almost with a dread of meeting each other's eyes, lest we should see there some confirmation of our own fears.

Settle established himself outside Lady Carmichael's door to take the first watch, arranging to call me at 3 a.m. I had no special fears for Lady Carmichael; I was too taken up with my fantastic impossible theory. I told myself it was impossible – but my mind returned to it, fascinated.

And then suddenly the stillness of the night was disturbed. Settle's voice rose in a shout, calling me. I rushed out to the corridor.

He was hammering and pounding with all his might on Lady Carmichael's door.

'Devil take the woman!' he cried. 'She's locked it!'

'But –'

'It's in there, man! In with her! Can't you hear it?'

From behind the locked door a long-drawn cat yowl sounded fiercely. And then following it a horrible scream – and another . . . I recognized Lady Carmichael's voice.

'The door!' I yelled. 'We must break it in. In another minute we shall be too late.'

We set our shoulders against it, and heaved with all our might. It gave with a crash – and we almost fell into the room.

Lady Carmichael lay on the bed bathed in blood. I have seldom seen a more horrible sight. Her heart was still beating, but her injuries were terrible, for the skin of the throat was all ripped and torn . . . Shuddering, I whispered: 'The Claws . . .' A thrill of superstitious horror ran over me.

I dressed and bandaged the wounds carefully and suggested to Settle that the exact nature of the injuries had better be kept secret, especially from Miss Patterson. I wrote out a telegram for a hospital nurse, to be despatched as soon as the telegraph office was open.

The dawn was now stealing in at the window. I looked out on the lawn below.

'Get dressed and come out,' I said abruptly to Settle. 'Lady Carmichael will be all right now.'

He was soon ready, and we went out into the garden together.

'What are you going to do?'

'Dig up the cat's body,' I said briefly. 'I must be sure –'

I found a spade in a toolshed and we set to work beneath the large copper beech tree. At last our digging was rewarded. It was not a pleasant job. The animal had been dead a week. But I saw what I wanted to see.

'That's the cat,' I said. 'The identical cat I saw the first day I came here.'

Settle sniffed. An odour of bitter almonds was still perceptible.

'Prussic acid,' he said.

I nodded.

'What are you thinking?' he asked curiously.

'What you think too!'

My surmise was no new one to him – it had passed through his brain also, I could see.

'It's impossible,' he murmured. 'Impossible! It's against all science – all nature . . .' His voice tailed off in a shudder. 'That mouse last night,' he said. 'But – oh! it couldn't be!'

'Lady Carmichael,' I said, 'is a very strange woman. She has occult powers – hypnotic powers. Her forebears came from the East. Can we know what use she might have made of these powers over a weak lovable nature such as Arthur Carmichael's? And remember, Settle, if Arthur Carmichael remains a hopeless imbecile, devoted to her, the whole property is practically hers and her son's – whom you have told me she adores. And Arthur was going to be married!'

'But what are we going to do, Carstairs?'

'There's nothing to be done,' I said. 'We'll do our best though to stand between Lady Carmichael and vengeance.'

Lady Carmichael improved slowly. Her injuries healed themselves as well as could be expected – the scars of that terrible assault she would probably bear to the end of her life.

I had never felt more helpless. The power that defeated us was still at large, undefeated, and though quiescent for the minute we could hardly regard it as doing otherwise than biding its time. I was determined upon one thing. As soon as Lady Carmichael was well enough to be moved she must be taken away from Wolden. There was just a chance that the terrible manifestation might be unable to follow her. So the days went on.

I had fixed September 18th as the date of Lady Carmichael's removal. It was on the morning of the 14th when the unexpected crisis arose.

I was in the library discussing details of Lady Carmichael's case with Settle when an agitated housemaid rushed into the room.

'Oh! sir,' she cried. 'Be quick! Mr Arthur – he's fallen into the pond. He stepped on the punt and it pushed off with him, and he overbalanced and fell in! I saw it from the window.'

I waited for no more, but ran straight out of the room followed by Settle. Phyllis was just outside and had heard the maid's story. She ran with us.

'But you needn't be afraid,' she cried. 'Arthur is a magnificent swimmer.'

I felt forebodings, however, and redoubled my pace. The surface of the pond was unruffled. The empty punt floated lazily about – but of Arthur there was no sign.

Settle pulled off his coat and his boots. 'I'm going in,' he said. 'You take the boathook and fish about from the other punt. It's not very deep.'

Very long the time seemed as we searched vainly. Minute followed minute. And then, just as we were despairing, we found him, and bore the apparently lifeless body of Arthur Carmichael to shore.

As long as I live I shall never forget the hopeless agony of Phyllis's face.

'Not – not –' her lips refused to frame the dreadful word.

'No, no, my dear,' I cried. 'We'll bring him round, never fear.'

But inwardly I had little hope. He had been under water for half an hour. I sent off Settle to the house for hot blankets and other necessaries, and began myself to apply artificial respiration.

We worked vigorously with him for over an hour but there was no sign of life. I motioned to Settle to take my place again, and I approached Phyllis.

'I'm afraid,' I said gently, 'that it is no good. Arthur is beyond our help.'

She stayed quite still for a moment and then suddenly flung herself down on the lifeless body.

'Arthur!' she cried desperately. 'Arthur! Come back to me! Arthur – come back – come back!'

Her voice echoed away into silence. Suddenly I touched Settle's arm. 'Look!' I said.

A faint tinge of colour crept into the drowned man's face. I felt his heart.

'Go on with the respiration,' I cried. 'He's coming round!'

The moments seemed to fly now. In a marvellously short time his eyes opened.

Then suddenly I realized a difference. *These were intelligent eyes, human eyes . . .*

They rested on Phyllis.

'Hallo! Phil,' he said weakly. 'Is it you? I thought you weren't coming until tomorrow.'

She could not yet trust herself to speak but she smiled at him. He looked round with increasing bewilderment.

'But, I say, where am I? And – how rotten I feel! What's the matter with me? Hallo, Dr Settle!'

'You've been nearly drowned – that's what's the matter,' returned Settle grimly.

Sir Arthur made a grimace.

'I've always heard it was beastly coming back afterwards! But how did it happen? Was I walking in my sleep?'

Settle shook his head.

'We must get him to the house,' I said, stepping forward.

He stared at me, and Phyllis introduced me. 'Dr Carstairs, who is staying here.'

We supported him between us and started for the house. He looked up suddenly as though struck by an idea.

'I say, doctor, this won't knock me up for the 12th, will it?'

'The 12th?' I said slowly, 'you mean the 12th of August?'

'Yes – next Friday.'

'Today is the 14th of September,' said Settle abruptly. His bewilderment was evident.

'But – but I thought it was the 8th of August? I must have been ill then?'

Phyllis interposed rather quickly in her gentle voice.

'Yes,' she said, 'you've been very ill.'

He frowned. 'I can't understand it. I was perfectly all right when I went to bed last night – at least of course it wasn't really last night. I had dreams though. I remember, dreams . . .' His brow furrowed itself still more as he strove to remember. 'Something – what was it? Something dreadful – someone had done it to me – and I was angry – desperate . . . And then I dreamed I was a cat – yes, a cat! Funny, wasn't it? But it wasn't a funny dream. It was more – horrible! But I can't remember. It all goes when I think.'

I laid my hand on his shoulder. 'Don't try to think, Sir Arthur,' I said gravely. 'Be content – to forget.'

He looked at me in a puzzled way and nodded. I heard Phyllis draw a breath of relief. We had reached the house.

'By the way,' said Sir Arthur suddenly, 'where's the mater?'

'She has been – ill,' said Phyllis after a momentary pause.

'Oh! poor old mater!' His voice rang with genuine concern. 'Where is she? In her room?'

'Yes,' I said, 'but you had better not disturb –'

The words froze on my lips. The door of the drawing-room opened and Lady Carmichael, wrapped in a dressing-gown, came out into the hall.

Her eyes were fixed on Arthur, and if ever I have seen a look of absolute guilt-stricken terror I saw it then. Her face was hardly human in its frenzied terror. Her hand went to her throat.

Arthur advanced towards her with boyish affection.

'Hello, mater! So you've been knocked up too? I say, I'm awfully sorry.'

She shrank back before him, her eyes dilating. Then suddenly, with a shriek of a doomed soul, she fell backwards through the open door.

I rushed and bent over her, then beckoned to Settle.

'Hush,' I said. 'Take him upstairs quietly and then come down again. Lady Carmichael is dead.'

He returned in a few minutes.

'What was it?' he asked. 'What caused it?'

'Shock,' I said grimly. 'The shock of seeing Arthur Carmichael, restored to life! Or you may call it, as I prefer to, the judgment of God!'

'You mean –' he hesitated.

I looked at him in the eyes so that he understood.

'A life for a life,' I said significantly.

'But –'

Oh! I know that a strange and unforeseen accident permitted the spirit of Arthur Carmichael to return to his body. But, nevertheless, Arthur Carmichael was murdered.'

He looked at me half fearfully. 'With prussic acid?' he asked in a low tone.

'Yes,' I answered. 'With prussic acid.'

Settle and I have never spoken our belief. It is not one likely to be credited. According to the orthodox point of view Arthur Carmichael merely suffered from loss of memory, Lady Carmichael lacerated her own throat in a temporary fit of mania, and the apparition of the Grey Cat was mere imagination.

But there are two facts that to my mind are unmistakable. One is the ripped chair in the corridor. The other is even more significant. A catalogue of the library was found, and after exhaustive search it was proved that the missing volume was an ancient and curious work on the possibilities of the metamorphosis of human beings into animals!

One thing more. I am thankful to say that Arthur knows nothing. Phyllis has locked the secret of those weeks in her own heart, and she will never, I am sure, reveal them to the husband she loves so dearly, and who came back across the barrier of the grave at the call of her voice.

The Call of Wings

'The Call of Wings' was first published in the hardback *The Hound of Death and Other Stories* (Odhams Press, 1933).
No previous appearances have been found.

Silas Hamer heard it first on a wintry night in February. He and Dick Borrow had walked from a dinner given by Bernard Seldon, the nerve specialist. Borrow had been unusually silent, and Silas Hamer asked him with some curiosity what he was thinking about. Borrow's answer was unexpected.

'I was thinking, that of all these men tonight, only two amongst them could lay claim to happiness. And that these two, strangely enough, were you and I!'

The word 'strangely' was apposite, for no two men could be more dissimilar than Richard Borrow, the hard working East-end parson, and Silas Hamer, the sleek complacent man whose millions were a matter of household knowledge.

'It's odd, you know,' mused Borrow, 'I believe you're the only contented millionaire I've ever met.'

Hamer was silent a moment. When he spoke his tone had altered.

'I used to be a wretched shivering little newspaper boy. I wanted then – what I've got now! – the comfort and the luxury of money, not its power. I wanted money, not to wield as a force, but to spend lavishly – on myself! I'm frank about it, you see. Money can't buy everything, they say. Very true. But it can buy everything I want – therefore I'm satisfied. I'm a materialist, Borrow, out and out a materialist!'

The broad glare of the lighted thoroughfare confirmed this confession of faith. The sleek lines of Silas Hamer's body were amplified by the heavy fur-lined coat, and the white light emphasized the thick rolls of flesh beneath his chin. In contrast to him walked Dick Borrow, with the thin ascetic face and the star-gazing fanatical eyes.

'It's *you*,' said Hamer with emphasis, 'that I can't understand.'
Borrow smiled.

I live in the midst of misery, want, starvation – all the ills of the flesh! And a predominant Vision upholds me. It's not easy to understand unless you believe in Visions, which I gather you don't.'

'I don't believe,' said Silas Hamer stolidly, 'in anything I can't see, hear and touch.'

'Quite so. That's the difference between us. Well, good bye, the earth now swallows me up!'

They had reached the doorway of a lighted tube station, which was Borrow's route home.

Hamer proceeded alone. He was glad he had sent away the car tonight and elected to walk home. The air was keen and frosty, his senses were delightfully conscious of the enveloping warmth of the fur-lined coat.

He paused for an instant on the kerbstone before crossing the road. A great motor bus was heavily ploughing its way towards him. Hamer, with the feeling of infinite leisure, waited for it to pass. If he were to cross in front of it he would have to hurry – and hurry was distasteful to him.

By his side a battered derelict of the human race rolled drunkenly off the pavement. Hamer was aware of a shout, an ineffectual swerve of the motor bus, and then – he was looking stupidly, with a gradually awakening horror, at a limp inert heap of rags in the middle of the road.

A crowd gathered magically, with a couple of policemen and the bus driver as its nucleus. But Hamer's eyes were riveted in horrified fascination on that lifeless bundle that had once been a man – a man like himself! He shuddered as at some menace.

'Dahn't yer blime yerself, guv'nor,' remarked a rough-looking man at his side. 'Yer couldn't 'a done nothin'. 'E was done for anyways.'

Hamer stared at him. The idea that it was possible in any way to save the man had quite honestly never occurred to him. He scouted the notion now as an absurdity. Why if he had been so foolish, he might at this moment . . . His thoughts broke off abruptly, and he walked away from the crowd. He felt himself shaking with a nameless unquenchable dread. He was forced to admit to himself that he was *afraid* – horribly afraid – of Death . . . Death that came with dreadful swiftness and remorseless certainty to rich and poor alike . . .

He walked faster, but the new fear was still with him, enveloping him in its cold and chilling grasp.

He wondered at himself, for he knew that by nature he was no coward. Five years ago, he reflected, this fear would not have attacked him. For then Life had not been so sweet . . . Yes, that was it; love of Life was the key to the mystery. The zest of living was at its height for him; it knew but one menace, Death, the destroyer!

He turned out of the lighted thoroughfare. A narrow passageway, between high walls, offered a short-cut to the Square where his house, famous for its art treasures, was situated.

The noise of the street behind him lessened and faded, the soft thud of his own footsteps was the only sound to be heard.

And then out of the gloom in front of him came another sound. Sitting against the wall was a man playing the flute. One of the enormous tribe of street musicians, of course, but why had he chosen such a peculiar spot? Surely at this time of night the police – Hamer's reflections were interrupted suddenly as he realized with a shock that the man had no legs. A pair of crutches rested against the wall beside him. Hamer saw now that it was not a flute he was playing but a strange instrument whose notes were much higher and clearer than those of a flute.

The man played on. He took no notice of Hamer's approach. His head was flung far back on his shoulders, as though uplifted in the joy of his own music, and the notes poured out clearly and joyously, rising higher and higher . . .

It was a strange tune – strictly speaking, it was not a tune at all, but a single phrase, not unlike the slow turn given out by the violins of *Rienzi*, repeated again and again, passing from key to key, from harmony to harmony, but always rising and attaining each time to a greater and more boundless freedom.

It was unlike anything Hamer had ever heard. There was something strange about it, something inspiring – and uplifting . . . it . . . He caught frantically with both hands to a projection in the wall beside him. He was conscious of one thing only – *that he must keep down* – at all costs he must *keep down* . . .

He suddenly realized that the music had stopped. The legless man was reaching out for his crutches. And here was he, Silas Hamer, clutching like a lunatic at a stone buttress, for the simple reason that he had had the utterly preposterous notion – absurd on the face of it! – that he was rising from the ground – that the music was carrying him upwards . . .

He laughed. What a wholly mad idea! Of course his feet had never left the earth for a moment, but what a strange hallucination! The quick tap-tapping of wood on the pavement told him that the cripple was moving away. He looked after him until the man's figure was swallowed up in the gloom. An odd fellow!

He proceeded on his way more slowly; he could not efface from his mind the memory of that strange impossible sensation when the ground had failed beneath his feet . . .

And then on an impulse he turned and followed hurriedly in the direction the other had taken. The man could not have gone far – he would soon overtake him.

He shouted as soon as he caught sight of the maimed figure swinging itself slowly along.

'Hi! One minute.'

The man stopped and stood motionless until Hamer came abreast of him. A lamp burned just over his head and revealed every feature. Silas Hamer caught his breath in involuntary surprise. The man possessed the most singularly beautiful head he had ever seen. He might have been any age; assuredly he was not a boy, yet youth was the most predominant characteristic – youth and vigour in passionate intensity!

Hamer found an odd difficulty in beginning his conversation.

'Look here,' he said awkwardly, 'I want to know what was that thing you were playing just now?'

The man smiled . . . With his smile the world seemed suddenly to leap into joyousness . . .

'It was an old tune – a very old tune . . . Years old – centuries old.'

He spoke with an odd purity and distinctness of enunciation, giving equal value to each syllable. He was clearly not an Englishman, yet Hamer was puzzled as to his nationality.

'You're not English? Where do you come from?'

Again the broad joyful smile.

'From over the sea, sir. I came – a long time ago – a very long time ago.'

'You must have had a bad accident. Was it lately?'

'Some time now, sir.'

'Rough luck to lose both legs.'

'It was well,' said the man very calmly. He turned his eyes with a strange solemnity on his interlocutor. 'They were evil.'

Hamer dropped a shilling in his hand and turned away. He was puzzled and vaguely disquieted. 'They were evil!' What a strange thing to say! Evidently an operation for some form of disease, but – how odd it had sounded.

Hamer went home thoughtful. He tried in vain to dismiss the incident from his mind. Lying in bed, with the first incipient sensation of drowsiness stealing over him, he heard a neighbouring clock strike one. One clear stroke and then silence – silence that was broken by a faint familiar sound . . . Recognition came leaping. Hamer felt his heart beating quickly. It was the man in the passageway playing, somewhere not far distant . . .

The notes came gladly, the slow turn with its joyful call, the same haunting little phrase . . . 'It's uncanny,' murmured Hamer, 'it's uncanny. It's got wings to it . . .'

Clearer and clearer, higher and higher – each wave rising above the last, and catching *him* up with it. This time he did not struggle, he let himself go . . . Up – up . . . The waves of sound were carrying him higher and higher . . . Triumphant and free, they swept on.

Higher and higher . . . They had passed the limits of human sound now, but they still continued – rising, ever rising . . . Would they reach the final goal, the full perfection of height?

Rising . . .

Something was pulling – pulling him downwards. Something big and heavy and insistent. It pulled remorselessly – pulled him back, and down . . . down . . .

He lay in bed gazing at the window opposite. Then, breathing heavily and painfully, he stretched an arm out of bed. The movement seemed curiously cumbrous to him. The softness of the bed was oppressive, oppressive too were the heavy curtains over the window that blocked out the light and air. The ceiling seemed to press down upon him. He felt stifled and choked. He moved slightly under the bed clothes, and the weight of his body seemed to him the most oppressive of all . . .

'I want your advice, Seldon.'

Seldon pushed back his chair an inch or so from the table. He had been wondering what was the object of this tête-à-tête dinner. He had seen little of Hamer since the winter, and he was aware tonight of some indefinable change in his friend.

'It's just this,' said the millionaire. 'I'm worried about myself.'

Seldon smiled as he looked across the table.

'You're looking in the pink of condition.'

'It's not that.' Hamer paused a minute, then added quietly. 'I'm afraid I'm going mad.'

The nerve specialist glanced up with a sudden keen interest. He poured himself out a glass of port with a rather slow movement, and then said quietly, but with a sharp glance at the other man: 'What makes you think that?'

'Something that's happened to me. Something inexplicable, unbelievable. It can't be true, so I must be going mad.'

'Take your time,' said Seldon, 'and tell me about it.'

'I don't believe in the supernatural,' began Hamer. 'I never have. But this thing . . . Well, I'd better tell you the whole story from the beginning. It began last winter one evening after I had dined with you.'

Then briefly and concisely he narrated the events of his walk home and the strange sequel.

'That was the beginning of it all. I can't explain it to you properly – the feeling, I mean – but it was wonderful! Unlike anything I've ever felt or dreamed. Well, it's gone on ever since. Not every night, just now and then. The music, the feeling of being uplifted, the soaring flight . . . and then the terrible drag, the pull back to earth, and afterwards the pain, the actual physical pain of the awakening. It's like coming down from a high mountain – you know the pains in the ears one gets? Well, this is the same thing, but intensified – and with it goes the awful sense of *weight* – of being hemmed in, stifled . . .'

He broke off and there was a pause.

'Already the servants think I'm mad. I couldn't bear the roof and the walls – I've had a place arranged up at the top of the house, open to the sky, with no furniture or carpets, or any stifling things . . . But even then the houses all round are nearly as bad. It's open country I want, some-where where one can breathe . . .' He looked across at Seldon. 'Well, what do you say? Can you explain it?'

'H'm,' said Seldon. 'Plenty of explanations. You've been hypnotized, or you've hynotized yourself. Your nerves have gone wrong. Or it may be merely a dream.'

Hamer shook his head. 'None of those explanations will do.'

'And there are others,' said Seldon slowly, 'but they're not generally admitted.'

'*You* are prepared to admit them?'

'On the whole, yes! There's a great deal we can't understand which can't possibly be explained normally. We've any amount to find out still, and I for one believe in keeping an open mind.'

'What do you advise me to do?' asked Hamer after a silence.

Seldon leaned forward briskly. 'One of several things. Go away from London, seek out your "open country". The dreams may cease.'

'I can't do that,' said Hamer quickly. 'It's come to this, that I can't do without them. I don't want to do without them.'

'Ah! I guessed as much. Another alternative, find this fellow, this cripple. You're endowing him now with all sorts of supernatural attributes. Talk to him. Break the spell.'

Hamer shook his head again.

'Why not?'

'I'm afraid,' said Hamer simply.

Seldon made a gesture of impatience. 'Don't believe in it all so blindly! This tune now, the medium that starts it all, what is it like?'

Hamer hummed it, and Seldon listened with a puzzled frown.

'Rather like a bit out of the Overture to *Rienzi*. There *is* something uplifting about it – it has wings. But I'm not carried off the earth! Now, these flights of yours, are they all exactly the same?'

'No, no.' Hamer leaned forward eagerly. 'They develop. Each time I see a little more. It's difficult to explain. You see, I'm always conscious of reaching a certain point – the music carries me there – not direct, but a succession of *waves*, each reaching higher than the last, until the highest point where one can go no further. I stay there until I'm dragged back. It isn't a place, it's more a *state*. Well, not just at first, but after a little while, I began to understand that there were other things all round me waiting until I was able to perceive them. Think of a kitten. It has eyes, but at first it can't see with them. It's blind and has to learn to see. Well, that was what it was to me. Mortal eyes and ears were no good to me, but there was something corresponding to them that hadn't yet been developed – something that wasn't *bodily* at all. And little by little that grew . . . there were sensations of light . . . then of sound . . . then of colour . . . All very vague and unformulated. It was more the knowledge of things than seeing or hearing them. First it was light, a light that grew stronger and clearer . . . then sand, great stretches of reddish sand . . . and here and there straight long lines of water like canals –'

Seldon drew in his breath sharply. '*Canals!* That's interesting. Go on.'

'But these things didn't matter – they didn't count any longer. The real things were the things I couldn't see yet – but I heard them . . . . It was a sound like the rushing of wings . . . somehow, I can't explain why, it was glorious! There's nothing like it here. And then came another glory – *I saw them* – the Wings! Oh, Seldon, the Wings!'

'But what were they? Men – angels – birds?'

'I don't know. I couldn't see – not yet. But the colour of them! *Wing colour* – we haven't got it here – it's a wonderful colour.'

'Wing colour?' repeated Seldon. 'What's it like?' Hamer flung up his hands impatiently. 'How can I tell you? Explain the colour blue to a blind person! It's a colour you've never seen – Wing colour!'

'Well?'

'Well? That's all. That's as far as I've got. But each time the coming back has been worse – more painful. I can't understand that. I'm convinced my body never leaves the bed. In this place I get to I'm convinced I've got no *physical* presence. Why should it hurt so confoundly then?'

Seldon shook his head in silence.

'It's something awful – the coming back. The *pull* of it – then the pain, pain in every limb and every nerve, and my ears feel as though they were bursting. Then everything *presses* so, the weight of it all, the dreadful sense of imprisonment. I want light, air, space – above all *space* to breathe in! And I want freedom.'

'And what,' asked Seldon, 'of all the other things that used to mean so much to you?'

'That's the worst of it. I care for them still as much as, if not more than, ever. And these things, comfort, luxury, pleasure, seem to pull opposite ways to the Wings. It's a perpetual struggle between them – and I can't see how it's going to end.'

Seldon sat silent. The strange tale he had been listening to was fantastic enough in all truth. Was it all a delusion, a wild hallucination – or could it by any possibility be true? And if so, why *Hamer*, of all men . . . ? Surely the materialist, the man who loved the flesh and denied the spirit, was the last man to see the sights of another world.

Across the table Hamer watched him anxiously.

'I suppose,' said Seldon slowly, 'that you can only wait. Wait and see what happens.'

'I can't! I tell you I can't! Your saying that shows you don't understand. It's tearing me in two, this awful struggle – this killing long-drawn-out fight between – between –' He hesitated.

'The flesh and the spirit?' suggested Seldon.

Hamer stared heavily in front of him. 'I suppose one might call it that. Anyway, it's unbearable . . . I can't get free . . .'

Again Bernard Seldon shook his head. He was caught up in the grip of the inexplicable. He made one more suggestion.

'If I were you,' he advised, 'I would get hold of that cripple.'

But as he went home he muttered to himself: '*Canals* – I wonder.'

Silas Hamer went out of the house the following morning with a new determination in his step. He had decided to take Seldon's advice and find the legless man. Yet inwardly he was convinced that his search would be in vain and that the man would have vanished as completely as though the earth had swallowed him up.

The dark buildings on either side of the passageway shut out the sunlight and left it dark and mysterious. Only in one place, half-way up it, there was a break in the wall, and through it there fell a shaft of golden light that illuminated with radiance a figure sitting on the ground. A figure – yes, it was the man!

The instrument of pipes leaned against the wall beside his crutches, and he was covering the paving stones with designs in coloured chalk. Two were completed, sylvan scenes of marvellous beauty and delicacy, swaying trees and a leaping brook that seemed alive.

And again Hamer doubted. Was this man a mere street musician, a pavement artist? Or was he something more . . .

Suddenly the millionaire's self-control broke down, and he cried fiercely and angrily: 'Who are you? For God's sake, who are you?'

The man's eyes met his, smiling.

'Why don't you answer? Speak, man, speak!'

Then he noticed that the man was drawing with incredible rapidity on a bare slab of stone. Hamer followed the movement with his eyes . . . A few bold strokes, and giant trees took form. Then, seated on a boulder . . . a man . . . playing an instrument of pipes. A man with a strangely beautiful face – *and goat's legs* . . .

The cripple's hand made a swift movement. The man still sat on the rock, but the goat's legs were gone. Again his eyes met Hamer's.

'They were evil,' he said.

Hamer stared, fascinated. For the face before him was the face of the picture, but strangely and incredibly beautified . . . Purified from all but an intense and exquisite joy of living.

Hamer turned and almost fled down the passageway into the bright sunlight, repeating to himself incessantly: 'It's impossible. Impossible . . . I'm mad – dreaming!' But the face haunted him – the face of Pan . . .

He went into the Park and sat on a chair. It was a deserted hour. A few nursemaids with their charges sat in the shade of the trees, and dotted here and there in the stretches of green, like islands in a sea, lay the recumbent forms of men . . .

The words 'a wretched tramp' were to Hamer an epitome of misery. But suddenly, today, he envied them . . .

They seemed to him of all created beings the only free ones. The earth beneath them, the sky above them, the world to wander in . . . they were not hemmed in or chained.

Like a flash it came to him that that which bound him so remorselessly was the thing he had worshipped and prized above all others – wealth! He had thought it the strongest thing on earth, and now, wrapped round by its golden strength, he saw the truth of his words. It was his money that held him in bondage . . .

But was it? Was that really it? Was there a deeper and more pointed truth that he had not seen? Was it the money or was it his own love of the money? He was bound in fetters of his own making; not wealth itself, but love of wealth was the chain.

He knew now clearly the two forces that were tearing at him, the warm composite strength of materialism that enclosed and surrounded him, and, opposed to it, the clear imperative call – he named it to himself the Call of the Wings.

And while the one fought and clung the other scorned war and would not stoop to struggle. It only called – called unceasingly . . . He heard it so clearly that it almost spoke in words.

'You cannot make terms with me,' it seemed to say.

'For I am above all other things. If you follow my call you must give up all else and cut away the forces that hold you. For only the Free shall follow where I lead . . .'

'I can't,' cried Hamer. 'I can't . . .'

A few people turned to look at the big man who sat talking to himself.

So sacrifice was being asked of him, the sacrifice of that which was most dear to him, that which was part of himself.

Part of himself – he remembered the man without legs . . .

'What in the name of Fortune brings you here?' asked Borrow.

Indeed the East-end mission was an unfamiliar background to Hamer.

'I've listened to a good many sermons,' said the millionaire, 'all saying what could be done if you people had funds. I've come to tell you this: you can have funds.'

'Very good of you,' answered Borrow, with some surprise. 'A big subscription, eh?'

Hamer smiled dryly. 'I should say so. Just every penny I've got.'

'*What?*'

Hamer rapped out details in a brisk businesslike manner. Borrow's head was whirling.

'You – you mean to say that you're making over your entire fortune to be devoted to the relief of the poor in the East-end with myself appointed as trustee?'

'That's it.'

'But why – *why?*'

'I can't explain,' said Hamer slowly. 'Remember our talk about vision last February? Well, a vision has got hold of me.'

'It's splendid!' Borrow leaned forward, his eyes gleaming.

'There's nothing particularly splendid about it,' said Hamer grimly. 'I don't care a button about poverty in the East-end. All they want is grit! *I* was poor enough – and I got out of it. But I've got to get rid of the money, and these tom-fool societies shan't get hold of it. You're a man I can trust. Feed bodies or souls with it – preferably the former. I've been hungry, but you can do as you like.'

'There's never been such a thing known,' stammered Borrow.

'The whole thing's done and finished with,' continued Hamer. 'The lawyers have fixed it up at last, and I've signed everything. I can tell you

I've been busy this last fortnight. It's almost as difficult getting rid of a fortune as making one.'

'But you – you've kept *something*?'

'Not a penny,' said Hamer cheerfully. 'At least – that's not quite true. I've just two pence in my pocket.' He laughed.

He said goodbye to his bewildered friend, and walked out of the mission into the narrow evil-smelling streets. The words he had said so gaily just now came back to him with an aching sense of loss. 'Not a penny!' Of all his vast wealth he had kept nothing. He was afraid now – afraid of poverty and hunger and cold. Sacrifice had no sweetness for him.

Yet behind it all he was conscious that the weight and menace of things had lifted, he was no longer oppressed and bound down. The severing of the chain had seared and torn him, but the vision of freedom was there to strengthen him. His material needs might dim the Call, but they could not deaden it, for he knew it to be a thing of immortality that could not die.

There was a touch of autumn in the air, and the wind blew chill. He felt the cold and shivered, and then, too, he was hungry – he had forgotten to have any lunch. It brought the future very near to him. It was incredible that he should have given it all up; the ease, the comfort, the warmth! His body cried out impotently . . . And then once again there came to him a glad and uplifting sense of freedom.

Hamer hesitated. He was near the Tube station. He had twopence in his pocket. The idea came to him to journey by it to the Park where he had watched the recumbent idlers a fortnight ago. Beyond this whim he did not plan for the future. He believed honestly enough now that he was mad – sane people did not act as he had done. Yet, if so, madness was a wonderful and amazing thing.

Yes, he would go now to the open country of the Park, and there was a special significance to him in reaching it by Tube. For the Tube represented to him all the horrors of buried, shut-in life . . . He would ascend from its imprisonment free to the wide green and the trees that concealed the menace of the pressing houses.

The lift bore him swiftly and relentlessly downward. The air was heavy and lifeless. He stood at the extreme end of the platform, away from the mass of people. On his left was the opening of the tunnel from which the train, snakelike, would presently emerge. He felt the whole place to be subtly evil. There was no one near him but a hunched-up lad sitting on a seat, sunk, it seemed, in a drunken stupor.

In the distance came the faint menacing roar of the train. The lad rose from his seat and shuffled unsteadily to Hamer's side, where he stood on the edge of the platform peering into the tunnel.

Then – it happened so quickly as to be almost incredible – he lost his balance and fell . . .

A hundred thoughts rushed simultaneously to Hamer's brain. He saw a huddled heap run over by a motor bus, and heard a hoarse voice saying: 'Dahn't yer blime yerself, guv'nor. Yer couldn't 'a done nothin'.' And with that came the knowledge that *this* life could only be saved, if it were saved, by himself. There was no one else near, and the train was close . . . It all passed through his mind with lightning rapidity. He experienced a curious calm lucidity of thought.

He had one short second in which to decide, and he knew in that moment that his fear of Death was unabated. He was horribly afraid. And then the train, rushing round the curve of the tunnel, powerless to pull up in time.

Swiftly Hamer caught up the lad in his arms. No natural gallant impulse swayed him, his shivering flesh was but obeying the command of the alien spirit that called for sacrifice. With a last effort he flung the lad forward on to the platform, falling himself . . .

Then suddenly his Fear died. The material world held him down no longer. He was free of his shackles. He fancied for a moment that he heard the joyous piping of Pan. Then – nearer and louder – swallowing up all else – came the glad rushing of innumerable Wings . . . enveloping and encircling him . . .

In a Glass Darkly

'In a Glass Darkly' was first published in the USA in *Collier's*, July 1934, and then in *Woman's Journal*, December 1934. However, its very first public airing was on 6 April 1934 when Agatha Christie read the story on BBC Radio's National Programme. No recording of this 15-minute performance is known to exist.

'I've no explanation of this story. I've no theories about the why and wherefore of it. It's just a thing – that happened.

All the same, I sometimes wonder how things would have gone if I'd noticed at the time just that one essential detail that I never appreciated until so many years afterwards. If I *had* noticed it – well, I suppose the course of three lives would have been entirely altered. Somehow – that's a very frightening thought.

For the beginning of it all, I've got to go back to the summer of 1914 – just before the war – when I went down to Badgeworthy with Neil Carslake. Neil was, I suppose, about my best friend. I'd known his brother Alan too, but not so well. Sylvia, their sister, I'd never met. She was two years younger than Alan and three years younger than Neil. Twice, while we were at school together, I'd been going to spend part of the holidays with Neil at Badgeworthy and twice something had intervened. So it came about that I was twenty-three when I first saw Neil and Alan's home.

We were to be quite a big party there. Neil's sister Sylvia had just got engaged to a fellow called Charles Crawley. He was, so Neil said, a good deal older than she was, but a thoroughly decent chap and quite reasonably well-off.

We arrived, I remember, about seven o'clock in the evening. Everyone had gone to his room to dress for dinner. Neil took me to mine. Badgeworthy was an attractive, rambling old house. It had been added to freely in the last three centuries and was full of little steps up and down, and unexpected staircases. It was the sort of house in which it's not easy to find your way about. I remember Neil promised to come and fetch me on his way down to dinner. I was feeling a little shy at the prospect of meeting his people for the first time. I remember saying with a laugh that it was the kind of house one expected to meet ghosts in the passages, and he said carelessly that he believed the place was said to be haunted but that none of them had ever seen anything, and he didn't even know what form the ghost was supposed to take.

Then he hurried away and I set to work to dive into my suitcases for my evening clothes. The Carslakes weren't well-off; they clung on to their old home, but there were no menservants to unpack for you or valet you.

Well, I'd just got to the stage of tying my tie. I was standing in front of the glass. I could see my own face and shoulders and behind them the wall of the room – a plain stretch of wall just broken in the middle by a door – and just as I finally settled my tie I noticed that the door was opening.

I don't know why I didn't turn around – I think that would have been the natural thing to do; anyway, I didn't. I just watched the door swing slowly open – and as it swung I saw into the room beyond.

It was a bedroom – a larger room than mine – with two bedsteads in it, and suddenly I caught my breath.

For at the foot of one of those beds was a girl and round her neck were a pair of man's hands and the man was slowly forcing her backwards and squeezing her throat as he did so, so that the girl was being slowly suffocated.

There wasn't the least possibility of a mistake. What I saw was perfectly clear. What was being done was murder.

I could see the girl's face clearly, her vivid golden hair, the agonized terror of her beautiful face, slowly suffusing with blood. Of the man I could see his back, his hands, and a scar that ran down the left side of his face towards his neck.

It's taken some time to tell, but in reality only a moment or two passed while I stared dumbfounded. Then I wheeled round to the rescue . . .

And on the wall behind me, the wall reflected in the glass, there was only a Victorian mahogany wardrobe. No door open – no scene of violence. I swung back to the mirror. The mirror reflected only the wardrobe . . .

I passed my hands across my eyes. Then I sprang across the room and tried to pull forward the wardrobe and at that moment Neil entered by the other door from the passage and asked me what the hell I was trying to do.

He must have thought me slightly barmy as I turned on him and demanded whether there was a door behind the wardrobe. He said, yes, there was a door, it led into the next room. I asked him who was occupying the next room and he said people called Oldham – a Major Oldham and his wife. I asked him then if Mrs Oldham had very fair hair and when he replied dryly that she was dark I began to realize that I was probably making a fool of myself. I pulled myself together, made some lame explanation and we went downstairs together. I told myself that I must have had some kind of hallucination – and felt generally rather ashamed and a bit of an ass.

And then – and then – Neil said, 'My sister Sylvia,' and I was looking into the lovely face of the girl I had just seen being suffocated to death . . . and I was introduced to her fiancé, a tall dark man *with a scar down the left side of his face.*

Well – that's that. I'd like you to think and say what you'd have done in my place. Here was the girl – the identical girl – and here was the man I'd seen throttling her – and they were to be married in about a month's time . . .

Had I – or had I not – had a prophetic vision of the future? Would Sylvia and her husband come down here to stay some time in the future, and be given that room (the best spare room) and would that scene I'd witnessed take place in grim reality?

What was I to do about it? *Could* I do anything? Would anyone – Neil – or the girl herself – would they believe me?

I turned the whole business over and over in my mind the week I was down there. To speak or not to speak? And almost at once another complication set in. You see, I fell in love with Sylvia Carslake the first moment I saw her . . . I wanted her more than anything on earth . . . And in a way that tied my hands.

And yet, if I didn't say anything, Sylvia would marry Charles Crawley and Crawley would kill her . . .

And so, the day before I left, I blurted it all out to her. I said I expect she'd think me touched in the intellect or something, but I swore solemnly that I'd seen the thing just as I told it to her and that I felt if she was determined to marry Crawley, I ought to tell her my strange experience.

She listened very quietly. There was something in her eyes I didn't understand. She wasn't angry at all. When I'd finished, she just thanked me gravely. I kept repeating like an idiot, 'I *did* see it. I really did see it,' and she said, 'I'm sure you did if you say so. I believe you.'

Well, the upshot was that I went off not knowing whether I'd done right or been a fool, and a week later Sylvia broke off her engagement to Charles Crawley.

After that the war happened, and there wasn't much leisure for thinking of anything else. Once or twice when I was on leave, I came across Sylvia, but as far as possible I avoided her.

I loved her and wanted her just as badly as ever, but I felt somehow that it wouldn't be playing the game. It was owing to me that she'd broken off her engagement to Crawley, and I kept saying to myself that I could only justify the action I had taken by making my attitude a purely disinterested one.

Then, in 1916, Neil was killed and it fell to me to tell Sylvia about his last moments. We couldn't remain on formal footing after that. Sylvia had adored Neil and he had been my best friend. She was sweet – adorably sweet in her grief. I just managed to hold my tongue and went out again praying that a bullet might end the whole miserable business. Life without Sylvia wasn't worth living.

But there was no bullet with my name on it. One nearly got me below the right ear and one was deflected by a cigarette case in my pocket, but I came through unscathed. Charles Crawley was killed in action at the beginning of 1918.

Somehow that made a difference. I came home in the autumn of 1918 just before the Armistice and I went straight to Sylvia and told her that I loved her. I hadn't much hope that she'd care for me straight away, and you could have knocked me down with a feather when she asked me why I hadn't told her sooner. I stammered out something about Crawley and she said, 'But why did you think I broke it off with him?' and then she told me that she'd fallen in love with me just as I'd done with her – from the very first minute.

I said I thought she'd broken off her engagement because of the story I told her and she laughed scornfully and said that if you loved a man you wouldn't be as cowardly as that, and we went over that old vision of mine again and agreed that it was queer, but nothing more.

'Well, there's nothing much to tell for some time after that. Sylvia and I were married and we were very happy. But I realized, as soon as she was really mine, that I wasn't cut out for the best kind of husband. I loved Sylvia devotedly, but I was jealous, absurdly jealous of anyone she so much as smiled at. It amused her at first, I think she even rather like it. It proved, at least, how devoted I was.

As for me, I realized quite fully and unmistakably that I was not only making a fool of myself, but that I was endangering all the peace and happiness of our life together. I knew, I say, but I couldn't change. Every time Sylvia got a letter she didn't show to me I wondered who it was from. If she laughed and talked with any man, I found myself getting sulky and watchful.

At first, as I say, Sylvia laughed at me. She thought it a huge joke. Then she didn't think the joke so funny. Finally she didn't think it a joke at all –

And slowly, she began to draw away from me. Not in any physical sense, but she withdrew her secret mind from me. I no longer knew what her thoughts were. She was kind – but sadly, as though from a long distance.

Little by little I realized that she no longer loved me. Her love had died and it was I who had killed it . . .

The next step was inevitable, I found myself waiting for it – dreading it . . .

Then Derek Wainwright came into our lives. He had everything that I hadn't. He had brains and a witty tongue. He was good-looking, too, and – I'm forced to admit it – a thoroughly good chap. As soon as I saw him I said to myself, 'This is just the man for Sylvia . . .'

She fought against it. I know she struggled . . . but I gave her no help. I couldn't. I was entrenched in my gloomy, sullen reserve. I was suffering like hell – and I couldn't stretch out a finger to save myself. I didn't help her. I made things worse. I let loose at her one day – a string of savage, unwarranted abuse. I was nearly mad with jealousy and misery. The things I said were cruel and untrue and I knew while I was saying them how cruel and how untrue they were. And yet I took a savage pleasure in saying them . . .

I remember how Sylvia flushed and shrank . . .

I drove her to the edge of endurance.

I remember she said, 'This can't go on . . .'

When I came home that night the house was empty – empty. There was a note – quite in the traditional fashion.

In it she said that she was leaving me – for good. She was going down to Badgeworthy for a day or two. After that she was going to the one person who loved her and needed her. I was to take that as final.

I suppose that up to then I hadn't really believed my own suspicions. This confirmation in black and white of my worst fears sent me raving mad. I went down to Badgeworthy after her as fast as the car would take me.

She had just changed her frock for dinner, I remember, when I burst into the room. I can see her face – startled – beautiful – afraid.

I said, 'No one but me shall ever have you. No one.'

And I caught her throat in my hands and gripped it and bent her backwards.

Suddenly I saw our reflection in the mirror. Sylvia choking and myself strangling her, and the scar on my cheek where the bullet grazed it under the right ear.

No – I didn't kill her. That sudden revelation paralysed me and I loosened my grasp and let her slip on to the floor . . .

And then I broke down – and she comforted me . . . Yes, she comforted me.

I told her everything and she told me that by the phrase 'the one person who loved and needed her' she had meant her brother Alan . . . We saw into each other's hearts that night, and I don't think, from that moment, that we ever drifted away from each other again . . .

It's a sobering thought to go through life with – that, but for the grace of God and a mirror, one might be a murderer . . .

One thing did die that night – the devil of jealousy that had possessed me so long . . .

But I wonder sometimes – suppose I hadn't made that initial mistake – the scar on the *left* cheek – when really it was the *right* – reversed by the mirror . . . Should I have been so sure the man was Charles Crawley? Would I have warned Sylvia? Would she be married to me – or to him?

Or are the past and the future all one?

I'm a simple fellow – and I can't pretend to understand these things – but I saw what I saw – and because of what I saw, Sylvia and I are together in the old-fashioned words – till death do us part. And perhaps beyond . . .'

Miss Marple Tells a Story

'Miss Marple Tells a Story' was first published as 'Behind Closed Doors' in *Home Journal*, 25 May 1935.

I don't think I've ever told you, my dears – you, Raymond, and you, Joan, about the rather curious little business that happened some years ago now. I don't want to seem *vain* in any way – of course I know that in comparison with you young people I'm not clever at all – Raymond writes those very modern books all about rather unpleasant young men and women – and Joan paints those very remarkable pictures of square people with curious bulges on them – very clever of you, my dear, but as Raymond always says (only quite kindly, because he is the kindest of nephews) I am hopelessly Victorian. I admire Mr Alma-Tadema and Mr Frederic Leighton and I suppose to you they seem hopelessly *vieux jeu*. Now let me see, what was I saying? Oh, yes – that I didn't want to appear vain – but I couldn't help being just a teeny weeny bit pleased with myself, because, just by applying a little common sense, I believe I really did solve a problem that had baffled cleverer heads than mine. Though really I should have thought the whole thing was *obvious* from the beginning . . .

Well, I'll tell you my little story, and if you think I'm inclined to be conceited about it, you must remember that I did at least help a fellow creature who was in very grave distress.

The first I knew of this business was one evening about nine o'clock when Gwen – (you remember Gwen? My little maid with red hair) well – Gwen came in and told me that Mr Petherick and a gentleman had called to see me. Gwen had shown them into the drawing-room – quite rightly. I was sitting in the dining-room because in early spring I think it is so wasteful to have two fires going.

I directed Gwen to bring in the cherry brandy and some glasses and I hurried into the drawing-room. I don't know whether you remember

Mr Petherick? He died two years ago, but he had been a friend of mine for many years as well as attending to all my legal business. A very shrewd man and a really clever solicitor. His son does my business for me now – a very nice lad and very up to date – but somehow I don't feel quite the *confidence* I had with Mr Petherick.

I explained to Mr Petherick about the fires and he said at once that he and his friend would come into the dining-room – and then he introduced his friend – a Mr Rhodes. He was a youngish man – not much over forty – and I saw at once there was something very wrong. His manner was most *peculiar*. One might have called it *rude* if one hadn't realized that the poor fellow was suffering from *strain*.

When we were settled in the dining-room and Gwen had brought the cherry brandy, Mr Petherick explained the reason for his visit.

'Miss Marple,' he said, 'you must forgive an old friend for taking a liberty. What I have come here for is a consultation.'

I couldn't understand at all what he meant, and he went on:

'In a case of illness one likes two points of view – that of the specialist and that of the family physician. It is the fashion to regard the former as of more value, but I am not sure that I agree. The specialist has experience only in his own subject – the family doctor has, perhaps, less knowledge – but a wider experience.'

I knew just what he meant, because a young niece of mine not long before had hurried her child off to a very well-known specialist in skin diseases without consulting her own doctor whom she considered an old dodderer, and the specialist had ordered some very expensive treatment, and later found that all the child was suffering from was a rather unusual form of measles.

I just mention this – though I have a horror of *digressing* – to show that I appreciate Mr Petherick's point – but I still hadn't any idea what he was driving at.

'If Mr Rhodes is ill –' I said, and stopped – because the poor man gave a most dreadful laugh.

He said: 'I expect to die of a broken neck in a few months' time.'

And then it all came out. There had been a case of murder lately in Barnchester – a town about twenty miles away. I'm afraid I hadn't paid much attention to it at the time, because we had been having a lot of excitement in the village about our district nurse, and outside occurrences like an earthquake in India and a murder in Barnchester, although of course far more important really – had given way to our own little local excitements. I'm afraid villages are like that. Still, I *did* remember having read about a woman having been stabbed in a hotel, though I hadn't remembered her name. But now it seemed that this woman had been Mr

Rhodes's wife – and as if that wasn't bad enough – he was actually under suspicion of having murdered her himself.

All this Mr Petherick explained to me very clearly, saying that, although the Coroner's jury had brought in a verdict of murder by a person or persons unknown, Mr Rhodes had reason to believe that he would probably be arrested within a day or two, and that he had come to Mr Petherick and placed himself in his hands. Mr Petherick went on to say that they had that afternoon consulted Sir Malcolm Olde, K.C., and that in the event of the case coming to trial Sir Malcolm had been briefed to defend Mr Rhodes.

Sir Malcolm was a young man, Mr Petherick said, very up to date in his methods, and he had indicated a certain line of defence. But with that line of defence Mr Petherick was not entirely satisfied.

'You see, my dear lady,' he said, 'it is tainted with what I call the specialist's point of view. Give Sir Malcolm a case and he sees only one point – the most likely line of defence. But even the best line of defence may ignore completely what is, to my mind, the vital point. It takes no account of what actually happened.'

Then he went on to say some very kind and flattering things about my acumen and judgement and my knowledge of human nature, and asked permission to tell me the story of the case in the hopes that I might be able to suggest some explanation.

I could see that Mr Rhodes was highly sceptical of my being of any use and he was annoyed at being brought here. But Mr Petherick took no notice and proceeded to give me the facts of what occurred on the night of March 8th.

Mr and Mrs Rhodes had been staying at the Crown Hotel in Barnchester. Mrs Rhodes who (so I gathered from Mr Petherick's careful language) was perhaps just a shade of a hypochondriac, had retired to bed immediately after dinner. She and her husband occupied adjoining rooms with a connecting door. Mr Rhodes, who is writing a book on prehistoric flints, settled down to work in the adjoining room. At eleven o'clock he tidied up his papers and prepared to go to bed. Before doing so, he just glanced into his wife's room to make sure that there was nothing she wanted. He discovered the electric light on and his wife lying in bed stabbed through the heart. She had been dead at least an hour – probably longer. The following were the points made. There was another door in Mrs Rhodes's room leading into the corridor. This door was locked and bolted on the inside. The only window in the room was closed and latched. According to Mr Rhodes nobody had passed through the room in which he was sitting except a chambermaid bringing hot-water bottles. The weapon found in the wound was a stiletto dagger which had been lying on Mrs Rhodes's dressing-table. She was in the habit of using it as a paper knife. There were no fingerprints on it.

The situation boiled down to this – no one but Mr Rhodes and the chambermaid had entered the victim's room.

I enquired about the chambermaid.

'That was our first line of enquiry,' said Mr Petherick. 'Mary Hill is a local woman. She had been chambermaid at the Crown for ten years. There seems absolutely no reason why she should commit a sudden assault on a guest. She is, in any case, extraordinarily stupid, almost half-witted. Her story has never varied. She brought Mrs Rhodes her hot-water bottle and says the lady was drowsy – just dropping off to sleep. Frankly, I cannot believe, and I am sure no jury would believe, that she committed the crime.'

Mr Petherick went on to mention a few additional details. At the head of the staircase in the Crown Hotel is a kind of miniature lounge where people sometimes sit and have coffee. A passage goes off to the right and the last door in it is the door into the room occupied by Mr Rhodes. The passage then turns sharply to the right again and the first door round the corner is the door into Mrs Rhodes's room. As it happened, both these doors could be seen by witnesses. The first door – that into Mr Rhodes's room, which I will call A, could be seen by four people, two commercial travellers and an elderly married couple who were having coffee. According to them nobody went in or out of door A except Mr Rhodes and the chambermaid. As to the other door in the passage B, there was an electrician at work there and he also swears that nobody entered or left door B except the chambermaid.

It was certainly a very curious and interesting case. On the face of it, it looked as though Mr Rhodes *must* have murdered his wife. But I could see that Mr Petherick was quite convinced of his client's innocence and Mr Petherick was a very shrewd man.

At the inquest Mr Rhodes had told a hesitating and rambling story about some woman who had written threatening letters to his wife. His story, I gathered, had been unconvincing in the extreme. Appealed to by Mr Petherick, he explained himself.

'Frankly,' he said, 'I never believed it. I thought Amy had made most of it up.'

Mrs Rhodes, I gathered, was one of those romantic liars who go through life embroidering everything that happens to them. The amount of adventures that, according to her own account, happened to her in a year was simply incredible. If she slipped on a bit of banana peel it was a case of near escape from death. If a lampshade caught fire she was rescued from a burning building at the hazard of her life. Her husband got into the habit of discounting her statements. Her tale as to some woman whose child she had injured in a motor accident and who had vowed vengeance on her – well – Mr Rhodes had simply not taken any notice of it. The incident had happened before he married his wife and although she had read him letters couched in crazy language, he had suspected her of composing them herself. She had actually done such a thing once or twice before. She was a woman of hysterical tendencies who craved ceaselessly for excitement.

Now, all that seemed to me very natural – indeed, we have a young woman in the village who does much the same thing. The danger with such people is that when anything at all extraordinary really does happen to them, nobody believes they are speaking the truth. It seemed to me that that was what had happened in this case. The police, I gathered, merely believed that Mr Rhodes was making up this unconvincing tale in order to avert suspicion from himself.

I asked if there had been any women staying by themselves in the hotel. It seemed there were two – a Mrs Granby, an Anglo-Indian widow, and a Miss Carruthers, rather a horsey spinster who dropped her g's. Mr Petherick added that the most minute enquiries had failed to elicit anyone who had seen either of them near the scene of the crime and there was nothing to connect either of them with it in any way. I asked him to describe their personal appearance. He said that Mrs Granby had reddish hair rather untidily done, was sallow-faced and about fifty years of age. Her clothes were rather picturesque, being made mostly of native silk, etc. Miss Carruthers was about forty, wore pince-nez, had close-cropped hair like a man and wore mannish coats and skirts.

'Dear me,' I said, 'that makes it very difficult.'

Mr Petherick looked enquiringly at me, but I didn't want to say any more just then, so I asked what Sir Malcolm Olde had said.

Sir Malcolm was confident of being able to call conflicting medical testimony and to suggest some way of getting over the fingerprint difficulty. I asked Mr Rhodes what he thought and he said all doctors were fools but he himself couldn't really believe that his wife had killed herself. 'She wasn't that kind of woman,' he said simply – and I believed him. Hysterical people don't usually commit suicide.

I thought a minute and then I asked if the door from Mrs Rhodes's room led straight into the corridor. Mr Rhodes said no – there was a little hallway with a bathroom and lavatory. It was the door from the bedroom to the hallway that was locked and bolted on the inside.

'In that case,' I said, 'the whole thing seems remarkably simple.'

And really, you know, it *did* . . . the simplest thing in the world. And yet no one seemed to have seen it that way.

Both Mr Petherick and Mr Rhodes were staring at me so that I felt quite embarrassed.

'Perhaps,' said Mr Rhodes, 'Miss Marple hasn't quite appreciated the difficulties.'

'Yes,' I said, 'I think I have. There are four possibilities. Either Mrs Rhodes was killed by her husband, or by the chambermaid, or she committed suicide, or she was killed by an outsider whom nobody saw enter or leave.'

'And that's impossible,' Mr Rhodes broke in. 'Nobody could come in or go out through my room without my seeing them, and even if anyone did manage to come in through my wife's room without the electrician seeing them, how the devil could they get out again leaving the door locked and bolted on the inside?'

Mr Petherick looked at me and said: 'Well, Miss Marple?' in an encouraging manner.

'I should like,' I said, 'to ask a question. Mr Rhodes, what did the chambermaid look like?'

He said he wasn't sure – she was tallish, he thought – he didn't remember if she was fair or dark. I turned to Mr Petherick and asked the same question.

He said she was of medium height, had fairish hair and blue eyes and rather a high colour.

Mr Rhodes said: 'You are a better observer than I am, Petherick.'

I ventured to disagree. I then asked Mr Rhodes if he could describe the maid in my house. Neither he nor Mr Petherick could do so.

'Don't you see what that means?' I said. 'You both came here full of your own affairs and the person who let you in was only a *parlourmaid*. The same applies to Mr Rhodes at the hotel. He saw her uniform and her apron. He was engrossed by his work. But Mr Petherick has interviewed the same woman in a different capacity. He has looked at her as a *person*.

'That's what the woman who did the murder counted upon.'

As they still didn't see, I had to explain.

'I think,' I said, 'that this is how it went. The chambermaid came in by door A, passed through Mr Rhodes's room into Mrs Rhodes's room with the hot-water bottle and went out through the hallway into passage B. X – as I will call our murderess – came in by door B into the little hallway, concealed herself in – well, in a certain apartment, ahem – and waited until the chambermaid had passed out. Then she entered Mrs Rhodes's room, took the stiletto from the dressing table (she had doubtless explored the room earlier in the day), went up to the bed, stabbed the dozing woman, wiped the handle of the stiletto, locked and bolted the door by which she had entered, and then passed out through the room where Mr Rhodes was working.'

Mr Rhodes cried out: 'But I should have *seen* her. The electrician would have seen her go in.'

'No,' I said. 'That's where you're wrong. You wouldn't see her – *not if she were dressed as a chambermaid.*' I let it sink in, then I went on, 'You were engrossed in your work – out of the tail of your eye you saw a chambermaid come in, go into your wife's room, come back and go out. It was the same *dress* – but not the same woman. That's what the people having coffee saw – a chambermaid go in and a chambermaid come out. The electrician did the same. I dare say if a chambermaid were very pretty a gentleman might notice her face – human nature being what it is – but if she were just an ordinary middle-aged woman – well – it would be the chambermaid's *dress* you would see – not the woman herself.'

Mr Rhodes cried: 'Who was she?'

'Well,' I said, 'that is going to be a little difficult. It must be either Mrs Granby or Miss Carruthers. Mrs Granby sounds as though she might wear a wig normally – so she could wear her own hair as a chambermaid. On the other hand, Miss Carruthers with her close-cropped mannish head might easily put on a wig to play her part. I dare say you will find out easily enough which of them it is. Personally, I incline myself to think it will be Miss Carruthers.'

And really, my dears, that is the end of the story. Carruthers was a false name, but she was the woman all right. There was insanity in her family. Mrs Rhodes, who was a most reckless and dangerous driver, had run over her little girl, and it had driven the poor woman off her head. She concealed her madness very cunningly except for writing distinctly insane latters to her intended victim. She had been following her about for some time, and she laid her plans very cleverly. The false hair and maid's dress she posted in a parcel first thing the next morning. When taxed with the truth she broke down and confessed at once. The poor thing is in Broadmoor now. Completely unbalanced of course, but a very cleverly planned crime.

Mr Petherick came to me afterwards and brought me a very nice letter from Mr Rhodes – really, it made me blush. Then my old friend said to me: 'Just one thing – why did you think it was more likely to be Carruthers than Granby? You'd never seen either of them.'

'Well,' I said. 'It was the g's. You said she dropped her g's. Now, that's done by a lot of hunting people in books, but I don't know many people who do it in reality – and certainly no one under sixty. You said this woman was forty. Those dropped g's sounded to me like a woman who was playing a part and over-doing it.'

I shan't tell you what Mr Petherick said to that – but he was very complimentary – and I really couldn't help feeling just a teeny weeny bit pleased with myself.

And it's extraordinary how things turn out for the best in this world. Mr Rhodes has married again – such a nice, sensible girl – and they've got a dear little baby and – what do you think? – they asked me to be godmother. Wasn't it nice of them?

Now I do hope you don't think I've been running on too long . . .

Strange Jest

'Strange Jest' was first published in the USA in *This Week*, 2 November 1941, and then as 'A Case of Buried Treasure' in *Strand Magazine*, July 1944 (sic).

'And this,' said Jane Helier, completing her introductions, 'is Miss Marple!'

Being an actress, she was able to make her point. It was clearly the climax, the triumphant finale! Her tone was equally compounded of reverent awe and triumph.

The odd part of it was that the object thus proudly proclaimed was merely a gentle, fussy-looking, elderly spinster. In the eyes of the two young people who had just, by Jane's good offices, made her acquaintance, there showed incredulity and a tinge of dismay. They were nice-looking people; the girl, Charmian Stroud, slim and dark – the man, Edward Rossiter, a fair-haired, amiable young giant.

Charmian said a little breathlessly. 'Oh! We're awfully pleased to meet you.' But there was doubt in her eyes. She flung a quick, questioning glance at Jane Helier.

'Darling,' said Jane, answering the glance, 'she's absolutely *marvellous*. Leave it all to her. I told you I'd get her here and I have.' She added to Miss Marple, '*You'll* fix it for them, I know. It will be easy for *you*.'

Miss Marple turned her placid, china-blue eyes towards Mr Rossiter. 'Won't you tell me,' she said, 'what all this is about?'

'Jane's a friend of ours,' Charmian broke in impatiently. 'Edward and I are in rather a fix. Jane said if we would come to her party, she'd introduce us to someone who was – who would – who could –'

Edward came to the rescue. 'Jane tells us you're the last word in sleuths, Miss Marple!'

The old lady's eyes twinkled, but she protested modestly. 'Oh, no, no! Nothing of the kind. It's just that living in a village as I do, one gets to know so much about human nature. But really you have made me quite curious. Do tell me your problem.'

'I'm afraid it's terribly hackneyed – just buried treasure,' said Edward.

'Indeed? But that sounds most exciting!'

'I know. Like *Treasure Island*. But our problem lacks the usual romantic touches. No point on a chart indicated by a skull and crossbones, no directions like "four paces to the left, west by north". It's horribly prosaic – just where we ought to dig.'

'Have you tried at all?'

'I should say we'd dug about two solid square acres! The whole place is ready to be turned into a market garden. We're just discussing whether to grow vegetable marrows or potatoes.'

Charmian said rather abruptly, 'May we really tell you all about it?'

'But, of course, my dear.'

'Then let's find a peaceful spot. Come on, Edward.' She led the way out of the overcrowded and smoke-laden room, and they went up the stairs, to a small sitting-room on the second floor.

When they were seated, Charmian began abruptly. 'Well, here goes! The story starts with Uncle Mathew, uncle – or rather, great-great-uncle – to both of us. He was incredibly ancient. Edward and I were his only relations. He was fond of us and always declared that when he died he would leave his money between us. Well, he died last March and left everything he had to be divided equally between Edward and myself. What I've just said sounds rather callous – I don't mean that it was right that he died – actually we were very fond of him. But he'd been ill for some time.

'The point is that the "everything" he left turned out to be practically nothing at all. And that, frankly, was a bit of a blow to us both, wasn't it, Edward?'

The amiable Edward agreed. 'You see,' he said, 'we'd counted on it a bit. I mean, when you know a good bit of money is coming to you, you don't – well – buckle down and try to make it yourself. I'm in the army – not got anything to speak of outside my pay – and Charmian herself hasn't got a bean. She works as a stage manager in a repertory theatre – quite interesting, and she enjoys it – but no money in it. We'd counted on getting married, but weren't worried about the money side of it because we both knew we'd be jolly well off some day.'

'And now, you see, we're not!' said Charmian. 'What's more, Ansteys – that's the family place, and Edward and I both love it – will probably have to be sold. And Edward and I feel we just can't bear that! But if we don't find Uncle Mathew's money, we shall have to sell.'

Edward said, 'You know, Charmian, we still haven't come to the vital point.'

'Well, you talk, then.'

Edward turned to Miss Marple. 'It's like this, you see. As Uncle Mathew grew older, he got more and more suspicious. He didn't trust anybody.'

'Very wise of him,' said Miss Marple. 'The depravity of human nature is unbelievable.'

'Well, you may be right. Anyway, Uncle Mathew thought so. He had a friend who lost his money in a bank, and another friend who was ruined by an absconding solicitor, and he lost some money himself in a fraudulent company. He got so that he used to hold forth at great length that the only safe and sane thing to do was to convert your money into solid bullion and bury it.'

'Ah,' said Miss Marple. 'I begin to see.'

'Yes. Friends argued with him, pointed out that he'd get no interest that way, but he held that that didn't really matter. The bulk of your money, he said, should be "kept in a box under the bed or buried in the garden". Those were his words.'

Charmian went on. 'And when he died, he left hardly anything at all in securities, though he was very rich. So we think that that's what he must have done.'

Edward explained. 'We found that he had sold securities and drawn out large sums of money from time to time, and nobody knows what he did with them. But it seems probable that he lived up to his principles, and that he did buy gold and bury it.'

'He didn't say anything before he died? Leave any paper? No letter?'

'That's the maddening part of it. He didn't. He'd been unconscious for some days, but he rallied before he died. He looked at us both and chuckled – a faint, weak little chuckle. He said, "*You'll* be all right, my pretty pair of doves." And then he tapped his eye – his right eye – and winked at us. And then – he died. Poor old Uncle Mathew.'

'He tapped his eye,' said Miss Marple thoughtfully.

Edward said eagerly. 'Does that convey anything to you? It made me think of an Arsene Lupin story where there was something hidden in a man's glass eye. But Uncle Mathew didn't have a glass eye.'

Miss Marple shook her head. 'No – I can't think of anything at the moment.'

Charmian said disappointedly, 'Jane told us you'd say *at once* where to dig!'

Miss Marple smiled. 'I'm not quite a conjurer, you know. I didn't know your uncle, or what sort of man he was, and I don't know the house or the grounds.'

Charmian said, 'If you did know them?'

'Well, it must be quite simple, really, mustn't it?' said Miss Marple.

'Simple!' said Charmian. 'You come down to Ansteys and see if it's simple!'

It is possible that she did not mean the invitation to be taken seriously, but Miss Marple said briskly, 'Well, really, my dear, that's very kind of you. I've always wanted to have the chance of looking for buried treasure. And,' she added, looking at them with a beaming, late-Victorian smile, 'with a love interest, too!'

'You see!' said Charmian, gesturing dramatically.

They had just completed a grand tour of Ansteys. They had been round the kitchen garden – heavily trenched. They had been through the little woods, where every important tree had been dug round, and had gazed sadly on the pitted surface of the once smooth lawn. They had been up to the attic, where old trunks and chests had been rifled of their contents. They had been down to the cellars, where flagstones had been heaved unwillingly from their sockets. They had measured and tapped walls, and Miss Marple had been shown every antique piece of furniture that contained or could be suspected of containing a secret drawer.

On a table in the morning-room there was a heap of papers – all the papers that the late Mathew Stroud had left. Not one had been destroyed, and Charmian and Edward were wont to return to them again and again, earnestly perusing bills, invitations, and business correspondence in the hope of spotting a hitherto unnoticed clue.

'Can you think of anywhere we haven't looked?' demanded Charmian hopefully.

Miss Marple shook her head. 'You seem to have been very thorough, my dear. Perhaps, if I may say so, just a little *too* thorough. I always think, you know, that one should have a plan. It's like my friend, Mrs Eldritch, she had such a nice little maid, polished linoleum beautifully, but she was so thorough that she polished the bathroom floor too much, and as Mrs Eldritch was stepping out of the bath the cork mat slipped from under her, and she had a very nasty fall and actually broke her leg! Most awkward, because the bathroom door was locked, of course, and the gardener had to get a ladder and come in through the window – terribly distressing to Mrs Eldritch, who had always been a very modest woman.'

Edward moved restlessly.

Miss Marple said quickly, 'Please forgive me. So apt, I know, to fly off at a tangent. But one thing does remind one of another. And sometimes that is helpful. All I was trying to say was that perhaps if we tried to sharpen our wits and think of a likely place –'

Edward said crossly, 'You think of one, Miss Marple. Charmian's brains and mine are now only beautiful blanks!'

'Dear, dear. Of course – most tiring for you. If you don't mind I'll just look through all this.' She indicated the papers on the table. 'That is, if there's nothing private – I don't want to appear to pry.'

'Oh, that's all right. But I'm afraid you won't find anything.'

She sat down by the table and methodically worked through the sheaf of documents. As she replaced each one, she sorted them automatically into tidy little heaps. When she had finished she sat staring in front of her for some minutes.

Edward asked, not without a touch of malice, 'Well, Miss Marple?'

Miss Marple came to herself with a little start. 'I beg your pardon. Most helpful.'

'You've found something relevant?'

'Oh, no, nothing like that, but I do believe I know what sort of man your Uncle Mathew was. Rather like my own Uncle Henry, I think. Fond of rather obvious jokes. A bachelor, evidently – I wonder why – perhaps an early disappointment? Methodical up to a point, but not very fond of being tied up – so few bachelors are!'

Behind Miss Marple's back, Charmian made a sign to Edward. It said, *She's ga-ga.*

Miss Marple was continuing happily to talk of her deceased Uncle Henry. 'Very fond of puns, he was. And to some people, puns are most annoying. A mere play upon words may be very irritating. He was a suspicious man, too. Always was convinced the servants were robbing him. And sometimes, of course, they were, but not always. It grew upon him, poor man. Towards the end he suspected them of tampering with his food, and finally refused to eat anything but boiled eggs! Said nobody could tamper with the inside of a boiled egg. Dear Uncle Henry, he used to be such a merry soul at one time – very fond of his coffee after dinner. He always used to say, "This coffee is very Moorish," meaning, you know, that he'd like a little more.'

Edward felt that if he heard any more about Uncle Henry he'd go mad.

'Fond of young people, too,' went on Miss Marple, 'but inclined to tease them a little, if you know what I mean. Used to put bags of sweets where a child just couldn't reach them.'

Casting politeness aside, Charmian said, 'I think he sounds horrible!'

'Oh, no, dear, just an old bachelor, you know, and not used to children. And he wasn't at all stupid, really. He used to keep a good deal of money in the house, and he had a safe put in. Made a great fuss about it – and how very secure it was. As a result of his talking so much, burglars broke in one night and actually cut a hole in the safe with a chemical device.'

'Served him right,' said Edward.

'Oh, but there was nothing in the safe,' said Miss Marple. 'You see, he really kept the money somewhere else – behind some volumes of sermons in the library, as a matter of fact. He said people never took a book of that kind out of the shelf!'

Edward interrupted excitedly. 'I say, that's an idea. What about the library?'

But Charmian shook a scornful head. 'Do you think I hadn't thought of that? I went through all the books Tuesday of last week, when you went off to Portsmouth. Took them all out, shook them. Nothing there.'

Edward sighed. Then, rousing himself, he endeavoured to rid himself tactfully of their disappointing guest. 'It's been awfully good of you to come down as you have and try to help us. Sorry it's been all a wash-out. Feel we trespassed a lot on your time. However – I'll get the car out, and you'll be able to catch the three-thirty –'

'Oh,' said Miss Marple, 'but we've got to find the money, haven't we? You mustn't give up, Mr Rossiter. "If at first you don't succeed, try, try, try again."'

'You mean you're going to – go on trying?'

'Strictly speaking,' said Miss Marple, 'I haven't begun yet. "First catch your hare –" as Mrs Beaton says in her cookery book – a wonderful book but terribly expensive; most of the recipes begin, "Take a quart of cream and a dozen eggs." Let me see, where was I? Oh, yes. Well, we have, so to speak, caught our hare – the hare being, of course, your Uncle Mathew, and we've only got to decide now where he would have hidden the money. It ought to be quite simple.'

'Simple?' demanded Charmian.

'Oh, yes, dear. I'm sure he would have done the obvious thing. A secret drawer – that's my solution.'

Edward said dryly, 'You couldn't put bars of gold in a secret drawer.'

'No, no, of course not. But there's no reason to believe the money is in gold.'

'He always used to say –'

'So did my Uncle Henry about his safe! So I should strongly suspect that that was just a blind. Diamonds – now they could be in a secret drawer quite easily.'

'But we've looked in all the secret drawers. We had a cabinetmaker over to examine the furniture.'

'Did you, dear? That was clever of you. I should suggest your uncle's own desk would be the most likely. Was it the tall escritoire against the wall there?'

'Yes. And I'll show you.' Charmian went over to it. She took down the flap. Inside were pigeonholes and little drawers. She opened a small door in the centre and touched a spring inside the left-hand drawer. The bottom of the centre recess clicked and slid forward. Charmian drew it out, revealing a shallow well beneath. It was empty.

'Now isn't that a coincidence?' exclaimed Miss Marple. 'Uncle Henry had a desk just like this, only his was burr walnut and this is mahogany.'

'At any rate,' said Charmian, 'there's nothing there, as you can see.'

'I expect,' said Miss Marple, 'your cabinetmaker was a young man. He didn't know everything. People were very artful when they made hiding-places in those days. There's such a thing as a secret inside a secret.'

She extracted a hairpin from her neat bun of grey hair. Straightening it out, she stuck the point into what appeared to be a tiny wormhole in one side of the secret recess. With a little difficulty she pulled out a small drawer. In it was a bundle of faded letters and a folded paper.

Edward and Charmian pounced on the find together. With trembling fingers Edward unfolded the paper. He dropped it with an exclamation of disgust.

'A damned cookery recipe. Baked ham!'

Charmian was untying a ribbon that held the letters together. She drew one out and glanced at it. 'Love letters!'

Miss Marple reacted with Victorian gusto. 'How interesting! Perhaps the reason your uncle never married.'

Charmian read aloud:

'"*My ever dear Mathew, I must confess that the time seems long indeed since I received your last letter. I try to occupy myself with the various tasks allotted to me, and often say to myself that I am indeed fortunate to see so much of the globe, though little did I think when I went to America that I should voyage off to these far islands!*"'

Charmain broke off. 'Where is it from? Oh! Hawaii!' She went on:

'"*Alas, these natives are still far from seeing the light. They are in an unclothed and savage state and spend most of their time swimming and dancing, adorning themselves with garlands of flowers. Mr Gray has made some converts but it is uphill work, and he and Mrs Gray get sadly discouraged. I try to do all I can to cheer and encourage him, but I, too, am often sad for a reason you can guess, dear Mathew. Alas, absence is a severe trial for a loving heart. Your renewed vows and protestations of affection cheered me greatly. Now and always you have my*"'

*faithful and devoted heart, dear Mathew, and I remain – Your true love,
Betty Martin.*

*"'PS – I address my letter under cover to our mutual friend, Matilda
Graves, as usual. I hope heaven will pardon this little subterfuge.'"*

Edward whistled. 'A female missionary! So that was Uncle Mathew's
romance. I wonder why they never married?'

'She seems to have gone all over the world,' said Charmian, looking
through the letters. 'Mauritius – all sorts of places. Probably died of yellow
fever or something.'

A gentle chuckle made them start. Miss Marple was apparently much
amused. 'Well, well,' she said. 'Fancy that, now!'

She was reading the recipe for baked ham. Seeing their enquiring
glances, she read out: '"Baked ham with spinach. Take a nice piece of
gammon, stuff with cloves, and cover with brown sugar. Bake in a slow
oven. Serve with a border of pureed spinach." What do you think of that,
now?'

'I think it sounds filthy,' said Edward.

'No, no, actually it would be very good – but what do you think of
the whole thing?'

A sudden ray of light illuminated Edward's face. 'Do you think it's a
code – cryptogram of some kind?' He seized it. 'Look here, Charmian,
it might be, you know! No reason to put a cooking-recipe in a secret
drawer otherwise.'

'Exactly,' said Miss Marple. 'Very, very significant.'

Charmian said, 'I know what it might be – invisible ink! Let's heat it.
Turn on the electric fire.'

Edward did so, but no signs of writing appeared under the treatment.

Miss Marple coughed. 'I really think, you know, that you're making it
rather *too* difficult. The recipe is only an indication, so to speak. It is, I
think, the letters that are significant.'

'The letters?'

'Especially,' said Miss Marple, 'the signature.'

But Edward hardly heard her. He called excitedly, 'Charmian! Come
here! She's right. See – the envelopes are old, right enough, but the letters
themselves were written much later.'

'Exactly,' said Miss Marple.

'They're only fake old. I bet anything old Uncle Mat faked them
himself –'

'Precisely,' said Miss Marple.

'The whole thing's a sell. There never was a female missionary. It must
be a code.'

'My dear, dear children – there's really no need to make it all so difficult. Your uncle was really a very simple man. He had to have his little joke, that was all.'

For the first time they gave her their full attention.

'Just exactly what do you mean, Miss Marple?' asked Charmian.

'I mean, dear, that you're actually holding the money in your hand this minute.'

Charmian stared down.

'The signature, dear. That gives the whole thing away. The recipe is just an indication. Shorn of all the cloves and brown sugar and the rest of it, what is it *actually?* Why, gammon and spinach to be sure! *Gammon and spinach!* Meaning – nonsense! So it's clear that it's the letters that are important. And then, if you take into consideration what your uncle did just before he died. He tapped his eye, you said. Well, there you are – that gives you the clue, you see.'

Charmian said, 'Are we mad, or are you?'

'Surely, my dear, you must have heard the expression meaning that something is not a true picture, or has it quite died out nowadays? "All my eye and Betty Martin."'

Edward gasped, his eyes falling to the letter in his hand. 'Betty Martin –'

'Of course, Mr Rossiter. As you have just said, there isn't – there wasn't any such person. The letters were written by your uncle, and I dare say he got a lot of fun out of writing them! As you say, the writing on the envelopes is much older – in fact, the envelope couldn't belong to the letters, anyway, because the postmark of one you are holding is eighteen fifty-one.'

She paused. She made it very emphatic. 'Eighteen fifty-one. And that explains everything, doesn't it?'

'Not to me,' said Edward.

'Well, of course,' said Miss Marple, 'I dare say it wouldn't to me if it weren't for my great-nephew Lionel. Such a dear little boy and a passionate stamp collector. Knows all about stamps. It was he who told me about the rare and expensive stamps and that a wonderful new find had come up for auction. And I actually remember his mentioning one stamp – an eighteen fifty-one *blue two-cent*. It realized something like twenty-five thousand dollars, I believe. Fancy! I should imagine that the other stamps are something also rare and expensive. No doubt your uncle bought through dealers and was careful to "cover his tracks", as they say in detective stories.'

Edward groaned. He sat down and buried his face in his hands.

'What's the matter?' demanded Charmian.

'Nothing. It's only the awful thought that, but for Miss Marple, we might have burned these letters in a decent, gentlemanly way!'

'Ah,' said Miss Marple, 'that's just what these old gentlemen who are fond of their jokes never realize. Uncle Henry, I remember, sent a favourite niece a five-pound note for a Christmas present. He put it in a Christmas card, gummed the card together, and wrote on it, "Love and best wishes. Afraid this is all I can manage this year."'

'She, poor girl, was annoyed at what she thought was his meanness and threw it all straight into the fire; then, of course, he had to give her another.'

Edward's feelings towards Uncle Henry had suffered an abrupt and complete change.

'Miss Marple,' he said, 'I'm going to get a bottle of champagne. We'll all drink the health of your Uncle Henry.'

Tape-Measure Murder

'Tape-Measure Murder' was first published in the USA in *This Week*, 16 November 1941, and then as 'The Case of the Retired Jeweller' in *Strand Magazine*, February 1942.

Miss Politt took hold of the knocker and rapped politely on the cottage door. After a discreet interval she knocked again. The parcel under her left arm shifted a little as she did so, and she readjusted it. Inside the parcel was Mrs Spenlow's new green winter dress, ready for fitting. From Miss Politt's left hand dangled a bag of black silk, containing a tape measure, a pincushion, and a large, practical pair of scissors.

Miss Politt was tall and gaunt, with a sharp nose, pursed lips, and meagre iron-grey hair. She hesitated before using the knocker for the third time. Glancing down the street, she saw a figure rapidly approaching. Miss Hartnell, jolly, weather-beaten, fifty-five, shouted out in her usual loud bass voice, 'Good afternoon, Miss Politt!'

The dressmaker answered, 'Good afternoon, Miss Hartnell.' Her voice was excessively thin and genteel in its accents. She had started life as a lady's maid. 'Excuse me,' she went on, 'but do you happen to know if by any chance Mrs Spenlow isn't at home?'

'Not the least idea,' said Miss Hartnell.

'It's rather awkward, you see. I was to fit on Mrs Spenlow's new dress this afternoon. Three-thirty, she said.'

Miss Hartnell consulted her wrist watch. 'It's a little past the half-hour now.'

'Yes. I have knocked three times, but there doesn't seem to be any answer, so I was wondering if perhaps Mrs Spenlow might have gone out and forgotten. She doesn't forget appointments as a rule, and she wants the dress to wear the day after tomorrow.'

Miss Hartnell entered the gate and walked up the path to join Miss Politt outside the door of Laburnum Cottage.

'Why doesn't Gladys answer the door?' she demanded. 'Oh, no, of course, it's Thursday – Gladys's day out. I expect Mrs Spenlow has fallen asleep. I don't expect you've made enough noise with this thing.'

Seizing the knocker, she executed a deafening *rat-a-tat-tat*, and in addition thumped upon the panels of the door. She also called out in a stentorian voice, 'What ho, within there!'

There was no response.

Miss Politt murmured, 'Oh, I think Mrs Spenlow must have forgotten and gone out, I'll call round some other time.' She began edging away down the path.

'Nonsense,' said Miss Hartnell firmly. 'She can't have gone out. I'd have met her. I'll just take a look through the windows and see if I can find any signs of life.'

She laughed in her usual hearty manner, to indicate that it was a joke, and applied a perfunctory glance to the nearest window-pane – perfunctory because she knew quite well that the front room was seldom used, Mr and Mrs Spenlow preferring the small back sitting-room.

Perfunctory as it was, though, it succeeded in its object. Miss Hartnell, it is true, saw no signs of life. On the contrary, she saw, through the window, Mrs Spenlow lying on the hearthrug – dead.

'Of course,' said Miss Hartnell, telling the story afterwards, 'I managed to keep my head. That Politt creature wouldn't have had the least idea of what to do. "Got to keep our heads," I said to her. "*You* stay here, and I'll go for Constable Palk." She said something about not wanting to be left, but I paid no attention at all. One has to be firm with that sort of person. I've always found they enjoy making a fuss. So I was just going off when, at that very moment, Mr Spenlow came round the corner of the house.'

Here Miss Hartnell made a significant pause. It enabled her audience to ask breathlessly, 'Tell me, how did he *look*?'

Miss Hartnell would then go on, 'Frankly, *I* suspected something at once! He was *far* too calm. He didn't seem surprised in the least. And you may say what you like, it isn't natural for a man to hear that his wife is dead and display no emotion whatever.'

Everybody agreed with this statement.

The police agreed with it, too. So suspicious did they consider Mr Spenlow's detachment, that they lost no time in ascertaining how that gentleman was situated as a result of his wife's death. When they discovered that Mrs Spenlow had been the monied partner, and that her money went to her husband under a will made soon after their marriage, they were more suspicious than ever.

Miss Marple, that sweet-faced – and, some said, vinegar-tongued –

elderly spinster who lived in the house next to the rectory, was interviewed very early – within half an hour of the discovery of the crime. She was approached by Police Constable Palk, importantly thumbing a notebook. 'If you don't mind, ma'am, I've a few questions to ask you.'

Miss Marple said, 'In connection with the murder of Mrs Spenlow?'

Palk was startled. 'May I ask, madam, how you got to know of it?'

'The fish,' said Miss Marple.

The reply was perfectly intelligible to Constable Palk. He assumed correctly that the fishmonger's boy had brought it, together with Miss Marple's evening meal.

Miss Marple continued gently. 'Lying on the floor in the sitting-room, strangled – possibly by a very narrow belt. But whatever it was, it was taken away.'

Palk's face was wrathful. 'How that young Fred gets to know everything –'

Miss Marple cut him short adroitly. She said, 'There's a pin in your tunic.'

Constable Palk looked down, startled. He said, 'They do say, "See a pin and pick it up, all the day you'll have good luck."'

'I hope that will come true. Now what is it you want me to tell you?'

Constable Palk cleared his throat, looked important, and consulted his notebook. 'Statement was made to me by Mr Arthur Spenlow, husband of the deceased. Mr Spenlow says that at two-thirty, as far as he can say, he was rung up by Miss Marple, and asked if he would come over at a quarter past three as she was anxious to consult him about something. Now, ma'am, is that true?'

'Certainly not,' said Miss Marple.

'You did not ring up Mr Spenlow at two-thirty?'

'Neither at two-thirty nor any other time.'

'Ah,' said Constable Palk, and sucked his moustache with a good deal of satisfaction.

'What else did Mr Spenlow say?'

'Mr Spenlow's statement was that he came over here as requested, leaving his own house at ten minutes past three; that on arrival here he was informed by the maid-servant that Miss Marple was "not at 'ome".'

'That part of it is true,' said Miss Marple. 'He did come here, but I was at a meeting at the Women's Institute.'

'Ah,' said Constable Palk again.

Miss Marple exclaimed, 'Do tell me, Constable, do you suspect Mr Spenlow?'

'It's not for me to say at this stage, but it looks to me as though somebody, naming no names, has been trying to be artful.'

Miss Marple said thoughtfully, 'Mr Spenlow?'

She liked Mr Spenlow. He was a small, spare man, stiff and conventional in speech, the acme of respectability. It seemed odd that he should have come to live in the country, he had so clearly lived in towns all his life. To Miss Marple he confided the reason. He said, 'I have always intended, ever since I was a small boy, to live in the country some day and have a garden of my own. I have always been very much attached to flowers. My wife, you know, kept a flower shop. That's where I saw her first.'

A dry statement, but it opened up a vista of romance. A younger, prettier Mrs Spenlow, seen against a background of flowers.

Mr Spenlow, however, really knew nothing about flowers. He had no idea of seeds, of cuttings, of bedding out, of annuals or perennials. He had only a vision – a vision of a small cottage garden thickly planted with sweet-smelling, brightly coloured blossoms. He had asked, almost pathetically, for instruction, and had noted down Miss Marple's replies to questions in a little book.

He was a man of quiet method. It was, perhaps, because of this trait, that the police were interested in him when his wife was found murdered. With patience and perseverance they learned a good deal about the late Mrs Spenlow – and soon all St Mary Mead knew it, too.

The late Mrs Spenlow had begun life as a between-maid in a large house. She had left that position to marry the second gardener, and with him had started a flower shop in London. The shop had prospered. Not so the gardener, who before long had sickened and died.

His widow carried on the shop and enlarged it in an ambitious way. She had continued to prosper. Then she had sold the business at a handsome price and embarked upon matrimony for the second time – with Mr Spenlow, a middle-aged jeweller who had inherited a small and struggling business. Not long afterwards, they had sold the business and came down to St Mary Mead.

Mrs Spenlow was a well-to-do woman. The profits from her florist's establishment she had invested – 'under spirit guidance', as she explained to all and sundry. The spirits had advised her with unexpected acumen.

All her investments had prospered, some in quite a sensational fashion. Instead, however, of this increasing her belief in spiritualism, Mrs Spenlow basely deserted mediums and sittings, and made a brief but wholehearted plunge into an obscure religion with Indian affinities which was based on various forms of deep breathing. When, however, she arrived at St Mary Mead, she had relapsed into a period of orthodox Church-of-England beliefs. She was a good deal at the vicarage, and attended church services with assiduity. She patronized the village shops, took an interest in the local happenings, and played village bridge.

A humdrum, everyday life. And – suddenly – murder.

Colonel Melchett, the chief constable, had summoned Inspector Slack.

Slack was a positive type of man. When he had made up his mind, he was sure. He was quite sure now. 'Husband did it, sir,' he said.

'You think so?'

'Quite sure of it. You've only got to look at him. Guilty as hell. Never showed a sign of grief or emotion. He came back to the house knowing she was dead.'

'Wouldn't he at least have tried to act the part of the distracted husband?'

'Not him, sir. Too pleased with himself. Some gentlemen can't act. Too stiff.'

'Any other woman in his life?' Colonel Melchett asked.

'Haven't been able to find any trace of one. Of course, he's the artful kind. He'd cover his tracks. As I see it, he was just fed up with his wife. She'd got the money, and I should say was a trying woman to live with – always taking up with some "ism" or other. He cold-bloodedly decided to do away with her and live comfortably on his own.'

'Yes, that could be the case, I suppose.'

'Depend upon it, that was it. Made his plans careful. Pretended to get a phone call –'

Melchett interrupted him. 'No call been traced?'

'No, sir. That means either that he lied, or that the call was put through from a public telephone booth. The only two public phones in the village are at the station and the post office. Post office it certainly wasn't. Mrs Blade sees everyone who comes in. Station it might be. Train arrives at two twenty-seven and there's a bit of a bustle then. But the main thing is *he* says it was Miss Marple who called him up, and that certainly isn't true. The call didn't come from her house, and she herself was away at the Institute.'

'You're not overlooking the possibility that the husband was deliberately got out of the way – by someone who wanted to murder Mrs Spenlow?'

'You're thinking of young Ted Gerard, aren't you, sir? I've been working on him – what we're up against there is lack of motive. He doesn't stand to gain anything.'

'He's an undesirable character, though. Quite a pretty little spot of embezzlement to his credit.'

'I'm not saying he isn't a wrong 'un. Still, he did go to his boss and own up to that embezzlement. And his employers weren't wise to it.'

'An Oxford Grouper,' said Melchett.

'Yes, sir. Became a convert and went off to do the straight thing and own up to having pinched money. I'm not saying, mind you, that it mayn't have been astuteness. He may have thought he was suspected and decided to gamble on honest repentance.'

'You have a sceptical mind, Slack,' said Colonel Melchett. 'By the way, have you talked to Miss Marple at all?'

'What's *she* got to do with it, sir?'

'Oh, nothing. But she hears things, you know. Why don't you go and have a chat with her? She's a very sharp old lady.'

Slack changed the subject. 'One thing I've been meaning to ask you, sir. That domestic-service job where the deceased started her career – Sir Robert Abercrombie's place. That's where that jewel robbery was – emeralds – worth a packet. Never got them. I've been looking it up – must have happened when the Spenlow woman was there, though she'd have been quite a girl at the time. Don't think she was mixed up in it, do you, sir? Spenlow, you know, was one of those little tuppenny-ha'penny jewellers – just the chap for a fence.'

Melchett shook his head. 'Don't think there's anything in that. She didn't even know Spenlow at the time. I remember the case. Opinion in police circles was that a son of the house was mixed up in it – Jim Abercrombie – awful young waster. Had a pile of debts, and just after the robbery they were all paid off – some rich woman, so they said, but I don't know – Old Abercrombie hedged a bit about the case – tried to call the police off.'

'It was just an idea, sir,' said Slack.

Miss Marple received Inspector Slack with gratification, especially when she heard that he had been sent by Colonel Melchett.

'Now, really, that is very kind of Colonel Melchett. I didn't know he remembered me.'

'He remembers you, all right. Told me that what you didn't know of what goes on in St Mary Mead isn't worth knowing.'

'Too kind of him, but really I don't know anything at all. About this murder, I mean.'

'You know what the talk about it is.'

'Oh, of course – but it wouldn't do, would it, to repeat just idle talk?'

Slack said, with an attempt at geniality, 'This isn't an official conversation, you know. It's in confidence, so to speak.'

'You mean you really want to know what people are saying? Whether there's any truth in it or not?'

'That's the idea.'

'Well, of course, there's been a great deal of talk and speculation. And there are really two distinct camps, if you understand me. To begin with, there are the people who think that the husband did it. A husband or a wife is, in a way, the natural person to suspect, don't you think so?'

'Maybe,' said the inspector cautiously.

'Such close quarters, you know. Then, so often, the money angle. I hear that it was Mrs Spenlow who had the money, and therefore Mr Spenlow does benefit by her death. In this wicked world I'm afraid the most uncharitable assumptions are often justified.'

'He comes into a tidy sum, all right.'

'Just so. It would seem quite plausible, wouldn't it, for him to strangle her, leave the house by the back, come across the fields to my house, ask for me and pretend he'd had a telephone call from me, then go back and find his wife murdered in his absence – hoping, of course, that the crime would be put down to some tramp or burglar.'

The inspector nodded. 'What with the money angle – and if they'd been on bad terms lately –'

But Miss Marple interrupted him. 'Oh, but they hadn't.'

'You know that for a fact?'

'Everyone would have known if they'd quarrelled! The maid, Gladys Brent – she'd have soon spread it round the village.'

The inspector said feebly, 'She mightn't have known –' and received a pitying smile in reply.

Miss Marple went on. 'And then there's the other school of thought. Ted Gerard. A good-looking young man. I'm afraid, you know, that good looks are inclined to influence one more than they should. Our last curate but one – quite a magical effect! All the girls came to church – evening service as well as morning. And many older women became unusually active in parish work – and the slippers and scarfs that were made for him! Quite embarrassing for the poor young man.

'But let me see, where was I? Oh, yes, this young man, Ted Gerard. Of course, there has been talk about him. He's come down to see her so often. Though Mrs Spenlow told me herself that he was a member of what I think they call the Oxford Group. A religious movement. They are quite sincere and very earnest, I believe, and Mrs Spenlow was impressed by it all.'

Miss Marple took a breath and went on. 'And I'm sure there was no reason to believe that there was anything more in it than that, but you know what people are. Quite a lot of people are convinced that Mrs Spenlow was infatuated with the young man, and that she'd lent him quite a lot of money. And it's perfectly true that he was actually seen at the station that day. In the train – the two twenty-seven down train. But of course it would be quite easy, wouldn't it, to slip out of the other side of the train and go through the cutting and over the fence and round by the hedge and never come out of the station entrance at all. So that he need not have been seen going to the cottage. And, of course, people do think that what Mrs Spenlow was wearing was rather peculiar.'

'Peculiar?'

'A kimono. Not a dress.' Miss Marple blushed. 'That sort of thing, you know, is, perhaps, rather suggestive to some people.'

'You think it was suggestive?'

'Oh, no, *I* don't think so, I think it was perfectly natural.'

'You think it was natural?'

'Under the circumstances, yes.' Miss Marple's glance was cool and reflective.

Inspector Slack said, 'It might give us another motive for the husband. Jealousy.'

'Oh, no, Mr Spenlow would never be jealous. He's not the sort of man who notices things. If his wife had gone away and left a note on the pincushion, it would be the first he'd know of anything of that kind.'

Inspector Slack was puzzled by the intent way she was looking at him. He had an idea that all her conversation was intended to hint at something he didn't understand. She said now, with some emphasis, 'Didn't *you* find any clues, Inspector – on the spot?'

'People don't leave fingerprints and cigarette ash nowadays, Miss Marple.'

'But this, I think,' she suggested, 'was an old-fashioned crime –'

Slack said sharply, 'Now what do you mean by that?'

Miss Marple remarked slowly, 'I think, you know, that Constable Palk could help you. He was the first person on the – on the "scene of the crime", as they say.'

Mr Spenlow was sitting in a deck chair. He looked bewildered. He said, in his thin, precise voice, 'I may, of course, be imagining what occurred. My hearing is not as good as it was. But I distinctly think I heard a small boy call after me, "Yah, who's a Crippen?" It – it conveyed the impression to me that he was of the opinion that I had – had killed my dear wife.'

Miss Marple, gently snipping off a dead rose head, said, 'That was the impression he meant to convey, no doubt.'

'But what could possibly have put such an idea into a child's head?'

Miss Marple coughed. 'Listening, no doubt, to the opinions of his elders.'

'You – you really mean that other people think that, also?'

'Quite half the people in St Mary Mead.'

'But – my dear lady – what can possibly have given rise to such an idea? I was sincerely attached to my wife. She did not, alas, take to living in the country as much as I had hoped she would do, but perfect agreement on every subject is an impossible idea. I assure you I feel her loss very keenly.'

'Probably. But if you will excuse my saying so, you don't sound as though you do.'

Mr Spenlow drew his meagre frame up to its full height. 'My dear lady, many years ago I read of a certain Chinese philosopher who, when his dearly loved wife was taken from him, continued calmly to beat a gong in the street – a customary Chinese pastime, I presume – exactly as usual. The people of the city were much impressed by his fortitude.'

'But,' said Miss Marple, 'the people of St Mary Mead react rather differently. Chinese philosophy does not appeal to them.'

'But you understand?'

Miss Marple nodded. 'My Uncle Henry,' she explained, 'was a man of unusual self-control. His motto was "Never display emotion". He, too, was very fond of flowers.'

'I was thinking,' said Mr Spenlow with something like eagerness, 'that I might, perhaps, have a pergola on the west side of the cottage. Pink roses and, perhaps, wisteria. And there is a white starry flower, whose name for the moment escapes me –'

In the tone in which she spoke to her grandnephew, aged three, Miss Marple said, 'I have a very nice catalogue here, with pictures. Perhaps you would like to look through it – I have to go up to the village.'

Leaving Mr Spenlow sitting happily in the garden with his catalogue, Miss Marple went up to her room, hastily rolled up a dress in a piece of brown paper, and, leaving the house, walked briskly up to the post office. Miss Politt, the dressmaker, lived in the rooms over the post office.

But Miss Marple did not at once go through the door and up the stairs. It was just two-thirty, and, a minute late, the Much Benham bus drew up outside the post office door. It was one of the events of the day in St Mary Mead. The postmistress hurried out with parcels, parcels connected with the shop side of her business, for the post office also dealt in sweets, cheap books, and children's toys.

For some four minutes Miss Marple was alone in the post office.

Not till the postmistress returned to her post did Miss Marple go upstairs and explain to Miss Politt that she wanted her old grey crepe altered and made more fashionable if that were possible. Miss Politt promised to see what she could do.

★   ★   ★

The chief constable was rather astonished when Miss Marple's name was brought to him. She came in with many apologies. 'So sorry – so very sorry to disturb you. You are so busy, I know, but then you have always been so very kind, Colonel Melchett, and I felt I would rather come to you instead of Inspector Slack. For one thing, you know, I should hate Constable Palk to get into any trouble. Strictly speaking, I suppose he shouldn't have touched anything at all.'

Colonel Melchett was slightly bewildered. He said, 'Palk? That's the St Mary Mead constable, isn't it? What has he been doing?'

'He picked up a pin, you know. It was in his tunic. And it occurred to me at the time that it was quite probable he had actually picked it up in Mrs Spenlow's house.'

'Quite, quite. But after all, you know, what's a pin? Matter of fact he did pick the pin up just by Mrs Spenlow's body. Came and told Slack about it yesterday – you put him up to that, I gather? Oughtn't to have touched anything, of course, but as I said, what's a pin? It was only a common pin. Sort of thing any woman might use.'

'Oh, no, Colonel Melchett, that's where you're wrong. To a man's eye, perhaps, it looked like an ordinary pin, but it wasn't. It was a special pin, a very thin pin, the kind you buy by the box, the kind used mostly by dressmakers.'

Melchett stared at her, a faint light of comprehension breaking in on him. Miss Marple nodded her head several times, eagerly.

'Yes, of course. It seems to me so obvious. She was in her kimono because she was going to try on her new dress, and she went into the front room, and Miss Politt just said something about measurements and put the tape measure round her neck – and then all she'd have to do was to cross it and pull – quite easy, so I've heard. And then, of course, she'd go outside and pull the door to and stand there knocking as though she'd just arrived. But the pin shows she'd *already been in the house*.'

'And it was Miss Politt who telephoned to Spenlow?'

'Yes. From the post office at two-thirty – just when the bus comes and the post office would be empty.'

Colonel Melchett said, 'But my dear Miss Marple, why? In heaven's name, why? You can't have a murder without a motive.'

'Well, I think, you know, Colonel Melchett, from all I've heard, that the crime dates from a long time back. It reminds me, you know, of my two cousins, Antony and Gordon. Whatever Antony did always went right for him, and with poor Gordon it was just the other way about. Race horses went lame, and stocks went down, and property depreciated. As I see it, the two women were in it together.'

'In what?'

'The robbery. Long ago. Very valuable emeralds, so I've heard. The lady's maid and the tweeny. Because one thing hasn't been explained – how, when the tweeny married the gardener, did they have enough money to set up a flower shop?

'The answer is, it was her share of the – the swag, I think is the right expression. Everything she did turned out well. Money made money. But the other one, the lady's maid, must have been unlucky. She came down to being just a village dressmaker. Then they met again. Quite all right at first, I expect, until Mr Ted Gerard came on the scene.

'Mrs Spenlow, you see, was already suffering from conscience, and was inclined to be emotionally religious. This young man no doubt urged her to "face up" and to "come clean" and I dare say she was strung up to do it. But Miss Politt didn't see it that way. All she saw was that she might go to prison for a robbery she had committed years ago. So she made up her mind to put a stop to it all. I'm afraid, you know, that she was always rather a wicked woman. I don't believe she'd have turned a hair if that nice, stupid Mr Spenlow had been hanged.'

Colonel Melchett said slowly, 'We can – er – verify your theory – up to a point. The identity of the Politt woman with the lady's maid at the Abercrombies', but –'

Miss Marple reassured him. 'It will be all quite easy. She's the kind of woman who will break down at once when she's taxed with the truth. And then, you see, I've got her tape measure. I – er – abstracted it yesterday when I was trying on. When she misses it and thinks the police have got it – well, she's quite an ignorant woman and she'll think it will prove the case against her in some way.'

She smiled at him encouragingly. 'You'll have no trouble, I can assure you.' It was the tone in which his favourite aunt had once assured him that he could not fail to pass his entrance examination into Sandhurst.

And he had passed.

The Case of the Caretaker

'The Case of the Caretaker' was first published in *Strand Magazine*, January 1942, and then in the USA in *Chicago Sunday Tribune*, 5 July 1942.

'Well,' demanded Doctor Haydock of his patient. 'And how goes it today?'

Miss Marple smiled at him wanly from pillows.

'I suppose, really, that I'm better,' she admitted, 'but I feel so terribly depressed. I can't help feeling how much better it would have been if I had died. After all, I'm an old woman. Nobody wants me or cares about me.'

Doctor Haydock interrupted with his usual brusqueness. 'Yes, yes, typical after-reaction of this type of flu. What you need is something to take you out of yourself. A mental tonic.'

Miss Marple sighed and shook her head.

'And what's more,' continued Doctor Haydock, 'I've brought my medicine with me!'

He tossed a long envelope on to the bed.

'Just the thing for you. The kind of puzzle that is right up your street.'

'A puzzle?' Miss Marple looked interested.

'Literary effort of mine,' said the doctor, blushing a little. 'Tried to make a regular story of it. "He said," "she said," "the girl thought," etc. Facts of the story are true.'

'But why a puzzle?' asked Miss Marple.

Doctor Haydock grinned. 'Because the interpretation is up to you. I want to see if you're as clever as you always make out.'

With that Parthian shot he departed.

Miss Marple picked up the manuscript and began to read.

'And where is the bride?' asked Miss Harmon genially.

The village was all agog to see the rich and beautiful young wife that Harry Laxton had brought back from abroad. There was a general indulgent feeling that Harry – wicked young scapegrace – had had all the luck. Everyone had always felt indulgent towards Harry. Even the owners of windows that had suffered from his indiscriminate use of a catapult had found their indignation dissipated by young Harry's abject expression of regret. He had broken windows, robbed orchards, poached rabbits, and later had run into debt, got entangled with the local tobacconist's daughter – been disentangled and sent off to Africa – and the village as represented by various ageing spinsters had murmured indulgently. 'Ah, well! Wild oats! He'll settle down!'

And now, sure enough, the prodigal had returned – not in affliction, but in triumph. Harry Laxton had 'made good' as the saying goes. He had pulled himself together, worked hard, and had finally met and successfully wooed a young Anglo-French girl who was the possessor of a considerable fortune.

Harry might have lived in London, or purchased an estate in some fashionable hunting county, but he preferred to come back to the part of the world that was home to him. And there, in the most romantic way, he purchased the derelict estate in the dower house of which he had passed his childhood.

Kingsdean House had been unoccupied for nearly seventy years. It had gradually fallen into decay and abandon. An elderly caretaker and his wife lived in the one habitable corner of it. It was a vast, unprepossessing grandiose mansion, the gardens overgrown with rank vegetation and the trees hemming it in like some gloomy enchanter's den.

The dower house was a pleasant, unpretentious house and had been let for a long term of years to Major Laxton, Harry's father. As a boy, Harry had roamed over the Kingsdean estate and knew every inch of the tangled woods, and the old house itself had always fascinated him.

Major Laxton had died some years ago, so it might have been thought that Harry would have had no ties to bring him back – nevertheless it was to the home of his boyhood that Harry brought his bride. The ruined old Kingsdean House was pulled down. An army of builders and contractors swooped down upon the place, and in almost a miraculously short space of time – so marvellously does wealth tell – the new house rose white and gleaming among the trees.

Next came a posse of gardeners and after them a procession of furniture vans.

The house was ready. Servants arrived. Lastly, a costly limousine deposited Harry and Mrs Harry at the front door.

The village rushed to call, and Mrs Price, who owned the largest house, and who considered herself to lead society in the place, sent out cards of invitation for a party 'to meet the bride'.

It was a great event. Several ladies had new frocks for the occasion. Everyone was excited, curious, anxious to see this fabulous creature. They said it was all so like a fairy story!

Miss Harmon, weather-beaten, hearty spinster, threw out her question as she squeezed her way through the crowded drawing-room door. Little Miss Brent, a thin, acidulated spinster, fluttered out information.

'Oh, my dear, quite charming. Such pretty manners. And quite young. Really, you know, it makes one feel quite envious to see someone who has everything like that. Good looks and money and breeding – most distinguished, nothing in the least common about her – and dear Harry so devoted!'

'Ah,' said Miss Harmon, 'it's early days yet!'

Miss Brent's thin nose quivered appreciatively. 'Oh, my dear, do you really think –'

'We all know what Harry is,' said Miss Harmon.

'We know what he was! But I expect now –'

'Ah,' said Miss Harmon, 'men are always the same. Once a gay deceiver, always a gay deceiver. I know them.'

'Dear, dear. Poor young thing.' *Miss Brent looked much happier.* 'Yes, I expect she'll have trouble with him. Someone ought really to warn her. I wonder if she's heard anything of the old story?'

'It seems so very unfair,' said Miss Brent, 'that she should know nothing. So awkward. Especially with only the one chemist's shop in the village.'

For the erstwhile tobacconist's daughter was now married to Mr Edge, the chemist.

'It would be so much nicer,' said Miss Brent, 'if Mrs Laxton were to deal with Boots in Much Benham.'

'I dare say,' said Miss Harmon, 'that Harry Laxton will suggest that himself.'

And again a significant look passed between them.

'But I certainly think,' said Miss Harmon, 'that she ought to know.'

'Beasts!' said Clarice Vane indignantly to her uncle, Doctor Haydock. 'Absolute beasts some people are.'

He looked at her curiously.

She was a tall, dark girl, handsome, warm-hearted and impulsive. Her big brown eyes were alight now with indignation as she said, 'All these cats – saying things – hinting things.'

'About Harry Laxton?'

'Yes, about his affair with the tobacconist's daughter.'

'Oh, that!' *The doctor shrugged his shoulders.* 'A great many young men have affairs of that kind.'

'Of course they do. And it's all over. So why harp on it? And bring it up years after? It's like ghouls feasting on dead bodies.'

'I dare say, my dear, it does seem like that to you. But you see, they have very little to talk about down here, and so I'm afraid they do tend to dwell upon past scandals. But I'm curious to know why it upsets you so much?'

Clarice Vane bit her lip and flushed. She said, in a curiously muffled voice. 'They – they look so happy. The Laxtons, I mean. They're young and in love, and it's all so lovely for them. I hate to think of it being spoiled by whispers and hints and innuendoes and general beastliness.'

'H'm. I see.'

Clarice went on. 'He was talking to me just now. He's so happy and eager and excited and – yes, thrilled – at having got his heart's desire and rebuilt Kingsdean. He's like a child about it all. And she – well, I don't suppose anything has ever gone wrong in her whole life. She's always had everything. You've seen her. What did you think of her?'

The doctor did not answer at once. For other people, Louise Laxton might be an object of envy. A spoiled darling of fortune. To him she had brought only the refrain of a popular song heard many years ago, Poor little rich girl –

A small, delicate figure, with flaxen hair curled rather stiffly round her face and big, wistful blue eyes.

Louise was drooping a little. The long stream of congratulations had tired her. She was hoping it might soon be time to go. Perhaps, even now, Harry might say so. She looked at him sideways. So tall and broad-shouldered with his eager pleasure in this horrible, dull party.

Poor little rich girl –

'Ooph!' It was a sigh of relief.

Harry turned to look at his wife amusedly. They were driving away from the party.

She said, 'Darling, what a frightful party!'

Harry laughed. 'Yes, pretty terrible. Never mind, my sweet. It had to be done, you know. All these old pussies knew me when I lived here as a boy. They'd have been terribly disappointed not to have got a look at you close up.'

Louise made a grimace. She said, 'Shall we have to see a lot of them?'

'What? Oh, no. They'll come and make ceremonious calls with card cases, and you'll return the calls and then you needn't bother any more. You can have your own friends down or whatever you like.'

Louise said, after a minute or two, 'Isn't there anyone amusing living down here?'

'Oh, yes. There's the County, you know. Though you may find them a bit dull, too. Mostly interested in bulbs and dogs and horses. You'll ride, of course. You'll enjoy that. There's a horse over at Eglinton I'd like you to see. A beautiful animal, perfectly trained, no vice in him but plenty of spirit.'

The car slowed down to take the turn into the gates of Kingsdean. Harry wrenched the wheel and swore as a grotesque figure sprang up in the middle of the road and he only just managed to avoid it. It stood there, shaking a fist and shouting after them.

Louise clutched his arm. 'Who's that – that horrible old woman?'

Harry's brow was black. 'That's old Murgatroyd. She and her husband were caretakers in the old house. They were there for nearly thirty years.'

'Why does she shake her fist at you?'

Harry's face got red. 'She – well, she resented the house being pulled down. And she got the sack, of course. Her husband's been dead two years. They say she got a bit queer after he died.'

'Is she – she isn't – starving?'

Louise's ideas were vague and somewhat melodramatic. Riches prevented you coming into contact with reality.

Harry was outraged. 'Good Lord, Louise, what an idea! I pensioned her off, of course – and handsomely, too! Found her a new cottage and everything.'

Louise asked, bewildered, 'Then why does she mind?'

Harry was frowning, his brows drawn together. 'Oh, how should I know? Craziness! She loved the house.'

'But it was a ruin, wasn't it?'

'Of course it was – crumbling to pieces – roof leaking – more or less unsafe. All the same I suppose it meant something to her. She'd been there a long time. Oh, I don't know! The old devil's cracked, I think.'

Louise said uneasily, 'She – I think she cursed us. Oh, Harry, I wish she hadn't.'

It seemed to Louise that her new home was tainted and poisoned by the malevolent figure of one crazy old woman. When she went out in the car, when she rode, when she walked out with the dogs, there was always the same figure waiting. Crouched down on herself, a battered hat over wisps of iron-grey hair, and the slow muttering of imprecations.

Louise came to believe that Harry was right – the old woman was mad. Nevertheless that did not make things easier. Mrs Murgatroyd never actually came to the house, nor did she use definite threats, nor offer violence. Her squatting figure remained always just outside the gates. To appeal to the police would have been useless and, in any case,

Harry Laxton was averse to that course of action. It would, he said, arouse local sympathy for the old brute. He took the matter more easily than Louise did.

'Don't worry about it, darling. She'll get tired of this silly cursing business. Probably she's only trying it on.'

'She isn't, Harry. She – she hates us! I can feel it. She – she's ill-wishing us.'

'She's not a witch, darling, although she may look like one! Don't be morbid about it all.'

Louise was silent. Now that the first excitement of settling in was over, she felt curiously lonely and at a loose end. She had been used to life in London and the Riviera. She had no knowledge of or taste for English country life. She was ignorant of gardening, except for the final act of 'doing the flowers'. She did not really care for dogs. She was bored by such neighbours as she met. She enjoyed riding best, sometimes with Harry, sometimes, when he was busy about the estate, by herself. She hacked through the woods and lanes, enjoying the easy paces of the beautiful horse that Harry had bought for her. Yet even Prince Hal, most sensitive of chestnut steeds, was wont to shy and snort as he carried his mistress past the huddled figure of a malevolent old woman.

One day Louise took her courage in both hands. She was out walking. She had passed Mrs Murgatroyd, pretending not to notice her, but suddenly she swerved back and went right up to her. She said, a little breathlessly, 'What is it? What's the matter? What do you want?'

The old woman blinked at her. She had a cunning, dark gypsy face, with wisps of iron-grey hair, and bleared, suspicious eyes. Louise wondered if she drank.

She spoke in a whining and yet threatening voice. 'What do I want, you ask? What, indeed! That which has been took away from me. Who turned me out of Kingsdean House? I'd lived there, girl and woman, for near on forty years. It was a black deed to turn me out and it's black bad luck it'll bring to you and him!'

Louise said, 'You've got a very nice cottage and –'

She broke off. The old woman's arms flew up. She screamed, 'What's the good of that to me? It's my own place I want and my own fire as I sat beside all them years. And as for you and him, I'm telling you there will be no happiness for you in your new fine house. It's the black sorrow will be upon you! Sorrow and death and my curse. May your fair face rot.'

Louise turned away and broke into a little stumbling run. She thought, I must get away from here! We must sell the house! We must go away.

At the moment, such a solution seemed easy to her. But Harry's utter incomprehension took her back. He exclaimed, 'Leave here? Sell the house? Because of a crazy old woman's threats? You must be mad.'

'No, I'm not. But she – she frightens me, I know something will happen.'

Harry Laxton said grimly, 'Leave Mrs Murgatroyd to me. I'll settle her!'

A friendship had sprung up between Clarice Vane and young Mrs Laxton. The two girls were much of an age, though dissimilar both in character and in tastes. In Clarice's company, Louise found reassurance. Clarice was so self-reliant, so sure of herself. Louise mentioned the matter of Mrs Murgatroyd and her threats, but Clarice seemed to regard the matter as more annoying than frightening.

'It's so stupid, that sort of thing,' she said. 'And really very annoying for you.'

'You know, Clarice, I – I feel quite frightened sometimes. My heart gives the most awful jumps.'

'Nonsense, you mustn't let a silly thing like that get you down. She'll soon tire of it.'

She was silent for a minute or two. Clarice said, 'What's the matter?'

Louise paused for a minute, then her answer came with a rush. 'I hate this place! I hate being here. The woods and this house, and the awful silence at night, and the queer noise owls make. Oh, and the people and everything.'

'The people. What people?'

'The people in the village. Those prying, gossiping old maids.'

Clarice said sharply, 'What have they been saying?'

'I don't know. Nothing particular. But they've got nasty minds. When you've talked to them you feel you wouldn't trust anybody – not anybody at all.'

Clarice said harshly, 'Forget them. They've nothing to do but gossip. And most of the muck they talk they just invent.'

Louise said, 'I wish we'd never come here. But Harry adores it so.' Her voice softened.

Clarice thought, How she adores him. She said abruptly, 'I must go now.'

'I'll send you back in the car. Come again soon.'

Clarice nodded. Louise felt comforted by her new friend's visit. Harry was pleased to find her more cheerful and from then on urged her to have Clarice often to the house.

Then one day he said, 'Good news for you, darling.'

'Oh, what?'

'I've fixed the Murgatroyd. She's got a son in America, you know. Well, I've arranged for her to go out and join him. I'll pay her passage.'

'Oh, Harry, how wonderful. I believe I might get to like Kingsdean after all.'

'Get to like it? Why, it's the most wonderful place in the world!'

Louise gave a little shiver. She could not rid herself of her superstitious fear so easily.

If the ladies of St Mary Mead had hoped for the pleasure of imparting information about her husband's past to the bride, this pleasure was denied them by Harry Laxton's own prompt action.

Miss Harmon and Clarice Vane were both in Mr Edge's shop, the one buying mothballs and the other a packet of boracic, when Harry Laxton and his wife came in.

After greeting the two ladies, Harry turned to the counter and was just demanding a toothbrush when he stopped in mid-speech and exclaimed heartily, 'Well, well, just see who's here! Bella, I do declare.'

Mrs Edge, who had hurried out from the back parlour to attend to the congestion of business, beamed back cheerfully at him, showing her big white teeth. She had been a dark, handsome girl and was still a reasonably handsome woman, though she had put on weight, and the lines of her face had coarsened; but her large brown eyes were full of warmth as she answered, 'Bella, it is, Mr Harry, and pleased to see you after all these years.'

Harry turned to his wife. 'Bella's an old flame of mine, Louise,' he said. 'Head-over-heels in love with her, wasn't I, Bella?'

'That's what you say,' said Mrs Edge.

Louise laughed. She said, 'My husband's very happy seeing all his old friends again.'

'Ah,' said Mrs Edge, 'we haven't forgotten you, Mr Harry. Seems like a fairy tale to think of you married and building up a new house instead of that ruined old Kingsdean House.'

'You look very well and blooming,' said Harry, and Mrs Edge laughed and said there was nothing wrong with her and what about that toothbrush?

Clarice, watching the baffled look on Miss Harmon's face, said to herself exultantly, Oh, well done, Harry. You've spiked their guns.

Doctor Haydock said abruptly to his niece, 'What's all this nonsense about old Mrs Murgatroyd hanging about Kingsdean and shaking her fist and cursing the new regime?'

'It isn't nonsense. It's quite true. It's upset Louise a good deal.'

'Tell her she needn't worry – when the Murgatroyds were caretakers they never stopped grumbling about the place – they only stayed because Murgatroyd drank and couldn't get another job.'

'I'll tell her,' said Clarice doubtfully, 'but I don't think she'll believe you. The old woman fairly screams with rage.'

'Always used to be fond of Harry as a boy. I can't understand it.'

Clarice said, 'Oh, well – they'll be rid of her soon. Harry's paying her passage to America.'

Three days later, Louise was thrown from her horse and killed.

Two men in a baker's van were witnesses of the accident. They saw Louise ride out of the gates, saw the old woman spring up and stand in the road waving her arms and shouting, saw the horse start, swerve, and then bolt madly down the road, flinging Louise Laxton over his head.

One of them stood over the unconscious figure, not knowing what to do, while the other rushed to the house to get help.

Harry Laxton came running out, his face ghastly. They took off a door of the van and carried her on it to the house. She died without regaining consciousness and before the doctor arrived.

(End of Doctor Haydock's manuscript.)

When Doctor Haydock arrived the following day, he was pleased to note that there was a pink flush in Miss Marple's cheek and decidedly more animation in her manner.

'Well,' he said, 'what's the verdict?'

'What's the problem, Doctor Haydock?' countered Miss Marple.

'Oh, my dear lady, do I have to tell you that?'

'I suppose,' said Miss Marple, 'that it's the curious conduct of the caretaker. Why did she behave in that very odd way? People do mind being turned out of their old homes. But it wasn't her home. In fact, she used to complain and grumble while she was there. Yes, it certainly looks very fishy. What became of her, by the way?'

'Did a bunk to Liverpool. The accident scared her. Thought she'd wait there for her boat.'

'All very convenient for somebody,' said Miss Marple. 'Yes, I think the "Problem of the Caretaker's Conduct" can be solved easily enough. Bribery, was it not?'

'That's your solution?'

'Well, if it wasn't natural for her to behave in that way, she must have been "putting on an act" as people say, and that means that somebody paid her to do what she did.'

'And you know who that somebody was?'

'Oh, I think so. Money again, I'm afraid. And I've always noticed that gentlemen always tend to admire the same type.'

'Now I'm out of my depth.'

'No, no, it all hangs together. Harry Laxton admired Bella Edge, a dark, vivacious type. Your niece Clarice was the same. But the poor little wife was quite a different type – fair-haired and clinging – not his type at all. So he must have married her for her money. And murdered her for her money, too!'

'You use the word "murder"?'

'Well, he sounds the right type. Attractive to women and quite unscrupulous. I suppose he wanted to keep his wife's money and marry your niece. He may have been seen talking to Mrs Edge. But I don't fancy he was attached to her any more. Though I dare say he made the poor woman think he was, for ends of his own. He soon had her well under his thumb, I fancy.'

'How exactly did he murder her, do you think?'

Miss Marple stared ahead of her for some minutes with dreamy blue eyes.

'It was very well timed – with the baker's van as witness. They could see the old woman and, of course, they'd put down the horse's fright to that. But I should imagine, myself, that an air gun, or perhaps a catapult. Yes, just as the horse came through the gates. The horse bolted, of course, and Mrs Laxton was thrown.'

She paused, frowning.

'The fall might have killed her. But he couldn't be sure of that. And he seems the sort of man who would lay his plans carefully and leave nothing to chance. After all, Mrs Edge could get him something suitable without her husband knowing. Otherwise, why would Harry bother with her? Yes, I think he had some powerful drug handy, that could be administered before you arrived. After all, if a woman is thrown from her horse and has serious injuries and dies without recovering consciousness, well – a doctor wouldn't normally be suspicious, would he? He'd put it down to shock or something.'

Doctor Haydock nodded.

'Why did you suspect?' asked Miss Marple.

'It wasn't any particular cleverness on my part,' said Doctor Haydock. 'It was just the trite, well-known fact that a murderer is so pleased with his cleverness that he doesn't take proper precautions. I was just saying a few consolatory words to the bereaved husband – and feeling damned sorry for the fellow, too – when he flung himself down on the settee to do a bit of play-acting and a hypodermic syringe fell out of his pocket.

'He snatched it up and looked so scared that I began to think. Harry Laxton didn't drug; he was in perfect health; what was he doing with a hypodermic syringe? I did the autopsy with a view to certain possibilities. I found strophanthin. The rest was easy. There was strophanthin in Laxton's possession, and Bella Edge, questioned by the police, broke down and admitted to having got it for him. And finally old Mrs Murgatroyd confessed that it was Harry Laxton who had put her up to the cursing stunt.'

'And your niece got over it?'

'Yes, she was attracted by the fellow, but it hadn't gone far.'

The doctor picked up his manuscript.

'Full marks to you, Miss Marple – and full marks to me for my prescription. You're looking almost yourself again.'

The Case of the Perfect Maid

'The Case of the Perfect Maid' was first published as 'The Perfect Maid' in
Strand Magazine, April 1942, and then in the USA as 'The Maid Who
Disappeared' in the *Chicago Sunday Tribune,* 13 September 1942.

'Oh, if you please, madam, could I speak to you a moment?'

It might be thought that this request was in the nature of an absurdity, since Edna, Miss Marple's little maid, was actually speaking to her mistress at the moment.

Recognizing the idiom, however, Miss Marple said promptly, 'Certainly, Edna, come in and shut the door. What is it?'

Obediently shutting the door, Edna advanced into the room, pleated the corner of her apron between her fingers, and swallowed once or twice.

'Yes, Edna?' said Miss Marple encouragingly.

'Oh, please, ma'am, it's my cousin, Gladdie.'

'Dear me,' said Miss Marple, her mind leaping to the worst – and, alas, the most usual conclusion. 'Not – not in trouble?'

Edna hastened to reassure her. 'Oh, no, ma'am, nothing of that kind. Gladdie's not that kind of girl. It's just that she's upset. You see, she's lost her place.'

'Dear me, I am sorry to hear that. She was at Old Hall, wasn't she, with the Miss – Misses – Skinner?'

'Yes, ma'am, that's right, ma'am. And Gladdie's very upset about it – very upset indeed.'

'Gladys has changed places rather often before, though, hasn't she?'

'Oh, yes, ma'am. She's always one for a change, Gladdie is. She never seems to get really settled, if you know what I mean. But she's always been the one to give the notice, you see!'

'And this time it's the other way round?' asked Miss Marple dryly.

'Yes, ma'am, and it's upset Gladdie something awful.'

Miss Marple looked slightly surprised. Her recollection of Gladys, who had occasionally come to drink tea in the kitchen on her 'days out', was a stout, giggling girl of unshakably equable temperament.

Edna went on. 'You see, ma'am, it's the way it happened – the way Miss Skinner looked.'

'How,' enquired Miss Marple patiently, 'did Miss Skinner look?'

This time Edna got well away with her news bulletin.

'Oh, ma'am, it was ever such a shock to Gladdie. You see, one of Miss Emily's brooches was missing, and such a hue and cry for it as never was, and of course nobody likes a thing like that to happen; it's upsetting, ma'am, if you know what I mean. And Gladdie's helped search everywhere, and there was Miss Lavinia saying she was going to the police about it, and then it turned up again, pushed right to the back of a drawer in the dressing-table, and very thankful Gladdie was.

'And the very next day as ever was a plate got broken, and Miss Lavinia she bounced out right away and told Gladdie to take a month's notice. And what Gladdie feels is it couldn't have been the plate and that Miss Lavinia was just making an excuse of that, and that it must be because of the brooch and they think as she took it and put it back when the police was mentioned, and Gladdie wouldn't do such a thing, not never she wouldn't, and what she feels is as it will get round and tell against her and it's a very serious thing for a girl, as you know, ma'am.'

Miss Marple nodded. Though having no particular liking for the bouncing, self-opinionated Gladys, she was quite sure of the girl's intrinsic honesty and could well imagine that the affair must have upset her.

Edna said wistfully, 'I suppose, ma'am, there isn't anything you could do about it? Gladdie's in ever such a taking.'

'Tell her not to be silly,' said Miss Marple crisply. 'If she didn't take the brooch – which I'm sure she didn't – then she has no cause to be upset.'

'It'll get about,' said Edna dismally.

Miss Marple said, 'I – er – am going up that way this afternoon. I'll have a word with the Misses Skinner.'

'Oh, thank you, madam,' said Edna.

Old Hall was a big Victorian house surrounded by woods and park land. Since it had been proved unlettable and unsaleable as it was, an enterprising speculator had divided it into four flats with a central hot-water system, and the use of 'the grounds' to be held in common by the tenants. The experiment had been satisfactory. A rich and eccentric old lady and her maid occupied one flat. The old lady had a passion for birds and entertained a feathered gathering to meals every day. A retired Indian judge and his wife rented a second. A very young couple, recently married, occupied the third, and the fourth had been taken only two months ago by two maiden ladies of the name of Skinner. The four sets of tenants were only on the most distant terms with each other, since none of them had anything in common. The landlord had been heard to say that this was an excellent thing. What he dreaded were friendships followed by estrangements and subsequent complaints to him.

Miss Marple was acquainted with all the tenants, though she knew none of them well. The elder Miss Skinner, Miss Lavinia, was what might be termed the working member of the firm, Miss Emily, the younger, spent most of her time in bed suffering from various complaints which, in the opinion of St Mary Mead, were largely imaginary. Only Miss Lavinia believed devoutly in her sister's martyrdom and patience under affliction, and willingly ran errands and trotted up and down to the village for things that 'my sister had suddenly fancied'.

It was the view of St Mary Mead that if Miss Emily suffered half as much as she said she did, she would have sent for Doctor Haydock long ago. But Miss Emily, when this was hinted to her, shut her eyes in a superior way and murmured that her case was not a simple one – the best specialists in London had been baffled by it – and that a wonderful new man had put her on a most revolutionary course of treatment and that she really hoped her health would improve under it. No humdrum GP could possibly understand her case.

'And it's my opinion,' said the outspoken Miss Hartnell, 'that she's very wise not to send for him. Dear Doctor Haydock, in that breezy manner of his, would tell her that there was nothing the matter with her and to get up and not make a fuss! Do her a lot of good!'

Failing such arbitrary treatment, however, Miss Emily continued to lie on sofas, to surround herself with strange little pill boxes, and to reject nearly everything that had been cooked for her and ask for something else – usually something difficult and inconvenient to get.

The door was opened to Miss Marple by 'Gladdie', looking more depressed than Miss Marple had ever thought possible. In the sitting-room (a quarter of the late drawing-room, which had been partitioned into a dining-room, drawing-room, bathroom, and housemaid's cupboard), Miss Lavinia rose to greet Miss Marple.

Lavinia Skinner was a tall, gaunt, bony female of fifty. She had a gruff voice and an abrupt manner.

'Nice to see you,' she said. 'Emily's lying down – feeling low today, poor dear. Hope she'll see you, it would cheer her up, but there are times when she doesn't feel up to seeing anybody. Poor dear, she's wonderfully patient.'

Miss Marple responded politely. Servants were the main topic of conversation in St Mary Mead, so it was not difficult to lead the conversation in that direction. Miss Marple said she had heard that that nice girl, Gladys Holmes, was leaving.

Miss Lavinia nodded. 'Wednesday week. Broke things, you know. Can't have that.'

Miss Marple sighed and said we all had to put up with things nowadays. It was so difficult to get girls to come to the country. Did Miss Skinner really think it was wise to part with Gladys?

'Know it's difficult to get servants,' admitted Miss Lavinia. 'The Devereuxs haven't got anybody – but then, I don't wonder – always quarrelling, jazz on all night – meals any time – that girl knows nothing of housekeeping. I pity her husband! Then the Larkins have just lost their maid. Of course, what with the judge's Indian temper and his wanting chota hazri, as he calls it, at six in the morning and Mrs Larkin always fussing, I don't wonder at that, either. Mrs Carmichael's Janet is a fixture of course – though in my opinion she's the most disagreeable woman, and absolutely bullies the old lady.'

'Then don't you think you might reconsider your decision about Gladys? She really is a nice girl. I know all her family; very honest and superior.'

Miss Lavinia shook her head.

'I've got my reasons,' she said importantly.

Miss Marple murmured, 'You missed a brooch, I understand –'

'Now, who has been talking? I suppose the girl has. Quite frankly, I'm almost certain she took it. And then got frightened and put it back – but, of course, one can't say anything unless one is sure.' She changed the subject. 'Do come and see Emily, Miss Marple. I'm sure it would do her good.'

Miss Marple followed meekly to where Miss Lavinia knocked on a door, was bidden enter, and ushered her guest into the best room in the flat, most of the light of which was excluded by half-drawn blinds. Miss Emily was lying in bed, apparently enjoying the half-gloom and her own indefinite sufferings.

The dim light showed her to be a thin, indecisive-looking creature, with a good deal of greyish-yellow hair untidily wound around her head and erupting into curls, the whole thing looking like a bird's nest of which no self-respecting bird could be proud. There was a smell in the room of Eau de Cologne, stale biscuits, and camphor.

With half-closed eyes and a thin, weak voice, Emily Skinner explained that this was 'one of her bad days'.

'The worst of ill health is,' said Miss Emily in a melancholy tone, 'that one knows what a burden one is to everyone around one.

'Lavinia is very good to me. Lavvie dear, I do so hate giving trouble but if my hot-water bottle could only be filled in the way I like it – too full it weighs on me so – on the other hand, if it is not sufficiently filled, it gets cold immediately!'

'I'm sorry, dear. Give it to me. I will empty a little out.'

'Perhaps, if you're doing that, it might be refilled. There are no rusks in the house, I suppose – no, no, it doesn't matter. I can do without. Some weak tea and a slice of lemon – no lemons? No, really, I couldn't drink tea without lemon. I think the milk was slightly turned this morning. It has put me against milk in my tea. It doesn't matter. I can do without my tea. Only I do feel so weak. Oysters, they say, are nourishing. I wonder if I could fancy a few? No, no, too much bother to get hold of them so late in the day. I can fast until tomorrow.'

Lavinia left the room murmuring something incoherent about bicycling down to the village.

Miss Emily smiled feebly at her guest and remarked that she did hate giving anyone any trouble.

Miss Marple told Edna that evening that she was afraid her embassy had met with no success.

She was rather troubled to find that rumours as to Gladys's dishonesty were already going around the village.

In the post office, Miss Wetherby tackled her. 'My dear Jane, they gave her a written reference saying she was willing and sober and respectable, but saying nothing about honesty. That seems to me most significant! I hear there was some trouble about a brooch. I think there must be something in it, you know, because one doesn't let a servant go nowadays unless it's something rather grave. They'll find it most difficult to get anyone else. Girls simply will not go to Old Hall. They're nervous coming home on their days out. You'll see, the Skinners won't find anyone else, and then, perhaps, that dreadful hypochondriac sister will have to get up and do something!'

Great was the chagrin of the village when it was made known that the Misses Skinner had engaged, from an agency, a new maid who, by all accounts, was a perfect paragon.

'A three-years' reference recommending her most warmly, she prefers the country, and actually asks less wages than Gladys. I really feel we have been most fortunate.'

'Well, really,' said Miss Marple, to whom these details were imparted by Miss Lavinia in the fishmonger's shop. 'It does seem too good to be true.'

It then became the opinion of St Mary Mead that the paragon would cry off at the last minute and fail to arrive.

None of these prognostications came true, however, and the village was able to observe the domestic treasure, by name, Mary Higgins, driving through the village in Reed's taxi to Old Hall. It had to be admitted that her appearance was good. A most respectable-looking woman, very neatly dressed.

When Miss Marple next visited Old Hall, on the occasion of recruiting stall-holders for the vicarage fete, Mary Higgins opened the door. She was certainly a most superior-looking maid, at a guess forty years of age, with neat black hair, rosy cheeks, a plump figure discreetly arrayed in black with a white apron and cap – 'quite the good, old-fashioned type of servant,' as Miss Marple explained afterwards, and with the proper, inaudible respectful voice, so different from the loud but adenoidal accents of Gladys.

Miss Lavinia was looking far less harassed than usual and, although she regretted that she could not take a stall owing to her preoccupation with her sister, she nevertheless tendered a handsome monetary contribution, and promised to produce a consignment of pen-wipers and babies' socks.

Miss Marple commented on her air of well-being.

'I really feel I owe a great deal to Mary, I am so thankful I had the resolution to get rid of that other girl. Mary is really invaluable. Cooks nicely and waits beautifully and keeps our little flat scrupulously clean – mattresses turned over every day. And she is really wonderful with Emily!'

Miss Marple hastily enquired after Emily.

'Oh, poor dear, she has been very much under the weather lately. She can't help it, of course, but it really makes things a little difficult sometimes. Wanting certain things cooked and then, when they come, saying she can't eat now – and then wanting them again half an hour later and everything spoiled and having to be done again. It makes, of course, a lot of work – but fortunately Mary does not seem to mind at all. She's used to waiting on invalids, she says, and understands them. It is such a comfort.'

'Dear me,' said Miss Marple. 'You are fortunate.'

'Yes, indeed. I really feel Mary has been sent to us as an answer to prayer.'

'She sounds to me,' said Miss Marple, 'almost too good to be true. I should – well, I should be a little careful if I were you.'

Lavinia Skinner failed to perceive the point of this remark. She said, 'Oh! I assure you I do all I can to make her comfortable. I don't know what I should do if she left.'

'I don't expect she'll leave until she's ready to leave,' said Miss Marple and stared very hard at her hostess.

Miss Lavinia said, 'If one has no domestic worries, it takes such a load off one's mind, doesn't it? How is your little Edna shaping?'

'She's doing quite nicely. Not much head, of course. Not like your Mary. Still, I do know all about Edna because she's a village girl.'

As she went out into the hall she heard the invalid's voice fretfully raised. 'This compress has been allowed to get quite dry – Doctor Allerton particularly said moisture continually renewed. There, there, leave it. I want a cup of tea and a boiled egg – boiled only three minutes and a half, remember, and send Miss Lavinia to me.'

The efficient Mary emerged from the bedroom and, saying to Lavinia, 'Miss Emily is asking for you, madam,' proceeded to open the door for Miss Marple, helping her into her coat and handing her her umbrella in the most irreproachable fashion.

Miss Marple took the umbrella, dropped it, tried to pick it up, and dropped her bag, which flew open. Mary politely retrieved various odds and ends – a handkerchief, an engagement book, an old-fashioned leather purse, two shillings, three pennies, and a striped piece of peppermint rock.

Miss Marple received the last with some signs of confusion.

'Oh, dear, that must have been Mrs Clement's little boy. He was sucking it, I remember, and he took my bag to play with. He must have put it inside. It's terribly sticky, isn't it?'

'Shall I take it, madam?'

'Oh, would you? Thank you so much.'

Mary stooped to retrieve the last item, a small mirror, upon recovering which Miss Marple exclaimed fervently, 'How lucky, now, that that isn't broken.'

She thereupon departed, Mary standing politely by the door holding a piece of striped rock with a completely expressionless face.

For ten days longer St Mary Mead had to endure hearing of the excellencies of Miss Lavinia's and Miss Emily's treasure.

On the eleventh day, the village awoke to its big thrill.

Mary, the paragon, was missing! Her bed had not been slept in, and the front door was found ajar. She had slipped out quietly during the night.

And not Mary alone was missing! Two brooches and five rings of Miss Lavinia's; three rings, a pendant, a bracelet, and four brooches of Miss Emily's were missing, also!

It was the beginning of a chapter of catastrophe.

Young Mrs Devereux had lost her diamonds which she kept in an unlocked drawer and also some valuable furs given to her as a wedding present. The judge and his wife also had had jewellery taken and a certain amount of money. Mrs Carmichael was the greatest sufferer. Not only had she some very valuable jewels but she also kept in the flat a large sum of money which had gone. It had been Janet's evening out, and her mistress was in the habit of walking round the gardens at dusk calling to the birds and scattering crumbs. It seemed clear that Mary, the perfect maid, had had keys to fit all the flats!

There was, it must be confessed, a certain amount of ill-natured pleasure in St Mary Mead. Miss Lavinia had boasted so much of her marvellous Mary.

'And all the time, my dear, just a common thief!'

Interesting revelations followed. Not only had Mary disappeared into the blue, but the agency who had provided her and vouched for her credentials was alarmed to find that the Mary Higgins who had applied to them and whose references they had taken up had, to all intents and purposes, never existed. It was the name of a bona fide servant who had lived with the bona fide sister of a dean, but the real Mary Higgins was existing peacefully in a place in Cornwall.

'Damned clever, the whole thing,' Inspector Slack was forced to admit. 'And, if you ask me, that woman works with a gang. There was a case of much the same kind in Northumberland a year ago. Stuff was never traced, and they never caught her. However, we'll do better than that in Much Benham!'

Inspector Slack was always a confident man.

Nevertheless, weeks passed, and Mary Higgins remained triumphantly at large. In vain Inspector Slack redoubled that energy that so belied his name.

Miss Lavinia remained tearful. Miss Emily was so upset, and felt so alarmed by her condition that she actually sent for Doctor Haydock.

The whole of the village was terribly anxious to know what he thought of Miss Emily's claims to ill health, but naturally could not ask him. Satisfactory data came to hand on the subject, however, through Mr Meek, the chemist's assistant, who was walking out with Clara, Mrs Price-Ridley's maid. It was then known that Doctor Haydock had prescribed a mixture of asafoetida and valerian which, according to Mr Meek, was the stock remedy for malingerers in the army!

Soon afterwards it was learned that Miss Emily, not relishing the medical attention she had had, was declaring that in the state of her health she felt it her duty to be near the specialist in London who understood her case. It was, she said, only fair to Lavinia.

The flat was put up for subletting.

* * *

It was a few days after that that Miss Marple, rather pink and flustered, called at the police station in Much Benham and asked for Inspector Slack.

Inspector Slack did not like Miss Marple. But he was aware that the Chief Constable, Colonel Melchett, did not share that opinion. Rather grudgingly, therefore, he received her.

'Good afternoon, Miss Marple, what can I do for you?'

'Oh, dear,' said Miss Marple, 'I'm afraid you're in a hurry.'

'Lots of work on,' said Inspector Slack, 'but I can spare a few moments.'

'Oh dear,' said Miss Marple. 'I hope I shall be able to put what I say properly. So difficult, you know, to explain oneself, don't you think? No, perhaps you don't. But you see, not having been educated in the modern style – just a governess, you know, who taught one the dates of the kings of England and general knowledge – Doctor Brewer – three kinds of diseases of wheat – blight, mildew – now what was the third – was it smut?'

'Do you want to talk about smut?' asked Inspector Slack and then blushed.

'Oh, no, no.' Miss Marple hastily disclaimed any wish to talk about smut. 'Just an illustration, you know. And how needles are made, and all that. Discursive, you know, but not teaching one to keep to the point. Which is what I want to do. It's about Miss Skinner's maid, Gladys, you know.'

'Mary Higgins,' said Inspector Slack.

'Oh, yes, the second maid. But it's Gladys Holmes I mean – rather an impertinent girl and far too pleased with herself but really strictly honest, and it's so important that that should be recognized.'

'No charge against her so far as I know,' said the inspector.

'No, I know there isn't a charge – but that makes it worse. Because, you see, people go on thinking things. Oh, dear – I knew I should explain things badly. What I really mean is that the important thing is to find Mary Higgins.'

'Certainly,' said Inspector Slack. 'Have you any ideas on the subject?'

'Well, as a matter of fact, I have,' said Miss Marple. 'May I ask you a question? Are fingerprints of no use to you?'

'Ah,' said Inspector Slack, 'that's where she was a bit too artful for us. Did most of her work in rubber gloves or housemaid's gloves, it seems. And she'd been careful – wiped off everything in her bedroom and on the sink. Couldn't find a single fingerprint in the place!'

'If you did have fingerprints, would it help?'

'It might, madam. They may be known at the Yard. This isn't her first job, I'd say!'

Miss Marple nodded brightly. She opened her bag and extracted a small cardboard box. Inside it, wedged in cotton wool, was a small mirror.

'From my handbag,' said Miss Marple. 'The maid's prints are on it. I think they should be satisfactory – she touched an extremely sticky substance a moment previously.'

Inspector Slack stared. 'Did you get her fingerprints on purpose?'

'Of course.'

'You suspected her then?'

'Well, you know, it did strike me that she was a little too good to be true. I practically told Miss Lavinia so. But she simply wouldn't take the hint! I'm afraid, you know, Inspector, that I don't believe in paragons. Most of us have our faults – and domestic service shows them up very quickly!'

'Well,' said Inspector Slack, recovering his balance, 'I'm obliged to you, I'm sure. We'll send these up to the Yard and see what they have to say.'

He stopped. Miss Marple had put her head a little on one side and was regarding him with a good deal of meaning.

'You wouldn't consider, I suppose, Inspector, looking a little nearer home?'

'What do you mean, Miss Marple?'

'It's very difficult to explain, but when you come across a peculiar thing you notice it. Although, often, peculiar things may be the merest trifles. I've felt that all along, you know; I mean about Gladys and the brooch. She's an honest girl; she didn't take that brooch. Then why did Miss Skinner think she did? Miss Skinner's not a fool; far from it! Why was she so anxious to let a girl go who was a good servant when servants are hard to get? It was peculiar, you know. So I wondered. I wondered a good deal. And I noticed another peculiar thing! Miss Emily's a hypochondriac, but she's the first hypochondriac who hasn't sent for some doctor or other at once. Hypochondriacs love doctors, Miss Emily didn't!'

'What are you suggesting, Miss Marple?'

'Well, I'm suggesting, you know, that Miss Lavinia and Miss Emily are peculiar people. Miss Emily spends nearly all her time in a dark room. And if that hair of hers isn't a wig I – I'll eat my own back switch! And what I say is this – it's perfectly possible for a thin, pale, grey-haired, whining woman to be the same as a black-haired, rosy-cheeked, plump woman. And nobody that I can find ever saw Miss Emily and Mary Higgins at one and the same time.

'Plenty of time to get impressions of all the keys, plenty of time to find out all about the other tenants, and then – get rid of the local girl. Miss Emily takes a brisk walk across country one night and arrives at the station as Mary Higgins next day. And then, at the right moment, Mary Higgins disappears, and off goes the hue and cry after her. I'll tell you where you'll find her, Inspector. On Miss Emily Skinner's sofa! Get her fingerprints if you don't believe me, but you'll find I'm right! A couple of clever thieves, that's what the Skinners are – and no doubt in league with a clever post and rails or fence or whatever you call it. But they won't get away with it this time! I'm not going to have one of our village girls' character for honesty taken away like that! Gladys Holmes is as honest as the day, and everybody's going to know it! Good afternoon!'

Miss Marple had stalked out before Inspector Slack had recovered.

'Whew?' he muttered. 'I wonder if she's right?'

He soon found out that Miss Marple was right again.

Colonel Melchett congratulated Slack on his efficiency, and Miss Marple had Gladys come to tea with Edna and spoke to her seriously on settling down in a good situation when she got one.

Sanctuary

'Sanctuary' was first published in the USA as 'Murder at the Vicarage'
in *This Week*, 12 & 19 September 1954, and then in
Woman's Journal, October 1954.

The vicar's wife came round the corner of the vicarage with her arms
full of chrysanthemums. A good deal of rich garden soil was attached to
her strong brogue shoes and a few fragments of earth were adhering to
her nose, but of that fact she was perfectly unconscious.

She had a slight struggle in opening the vicarage gate which hung,
rustily, half off its hinges. A puff of wind caught at her battered felt hat,
causing it to sit even more rakishly than it had done before. 'Bother!' said
Bunch.

Christened by her optimistic parents Diana, Mrs Harmon had become
Bunch at an early age for somewhat obvious reasons and the name had
stuck to her ever since. Clutching the chrysanthemums, she made her
way through the gate to the churchyard, and so to the church door.

The November air was mild and damp. Clouds scudded across the
sky with patches of blue here and there. Inside, the church was dark and
cold; it was unheated except at service times.

'Brrrrh!' said Bunch expressively. 'I'd better get on with this quickly.
I don't want to die of cold.'

With the quickness born of practice she collected the necessary para-
phernalia: vases, water, flower-holders. 'I wish we had lilies,' thought Bunch
to herself. 'I get so tired of these scraggy chrysanthemums.' Her nimble
fingers arranged the blooms in their holders.

There was nothing particularly original or artistic about the decorations, for Bunch Harmon herself was neither original nor artistic, but it
was a homely and pleasant arrangement. Carrying the vases carefully,
Bunch stepped up the aisle and made her way towards the altar. As she
did so the sun came out.

It shone through the east window of somewhat crude coloured glass, mostly blue and red – the gift of a wealthy Victorian churchgoer. The effect was almost startling in its sudden opulence. 'Like jewels,' thought Bunch. Suddenly she stopped, staring ahead of her. On the chancel steps was a huddled dark form.

Putting down the flowers carefully, Bunch went up to it and bent over it. It was a man lying there, huddled over on himself. Bunch knelt down by him and slowly, carefully, she turned him over. Her fingers went to his pulse – a pulse so feeble and fluttering that it told its own story, as did the almost greenish pallor of his face. There was no doubt, Bunch thought, that the man was dying.

He was a man of about forty-five, dressed in a dark, shabby suit. She laid down the limp hand she had picked up and looked at his other hand. This seemed clenched like a fist on his breast. Looking more closely she saw that the fingers were closed over what seemed to be a large wad or handkerchief which he was holding tightly to his chest. All round the clenched hand there were splashes of a dry brown fluid which, Bunch guessed, was dry blood. Bunch sat back on her heels, frowning.

Up till now the man's eyes had been closed but at this point they suddenly opened and fixed themselves on Bunch's face. They were neither dazed nor wandering. They seemed fully alive and intelligent. His lips moved, and Bunch bent forward to catch the words, or rather the word. It was only one word that he said:

'*Sanctuary.*'

There was, she thought, just a very faint smile as he breathed out this word. There was no mistaking it, for after a moment he said it again, 'Sanctuary . . .'

Then, with a faint, long-drawn-out sigh, his eyes closed again. Once more Bunch's fingers went to his pulse. It was still there, but fainter now and more intermittent. She got up with decision.

'Don't move,' she said, 'or try to move. I'm going for help.'

The man's eyes opened again but he seemed now to be fixing his attention on the coloured light that came through the east window. He murmured something that Bunch could not quite catch. She thought, startled, that it might have been her husband's name.

'Julian?' she said. 'Did you come here to find Julian?' But there was no answer. The man lay with eyes closed, his breathing coming in slow, shallow fashion.

Bunch turned and left the church rapidly. She glanced at her watch and nodded with some satisfaction. Dr Griffiths would still be in his surgery. It was only a couple of minutes' walk from the church. She went in, without waiting to knock or ring, passing through the waiting room and into the doctor's surgery.

'You must come at once,' said Bunch. 'There's a man dying in the church.'

Some minutes later Dr Griffiths rose from his knees after a brief examination.

'Can we move him from here into the vicarage? I can attend to him better there – not that it's any use.'

'Of course,' said Bunch. 'I'll go along and get things ready. I'll get Harper and Jones, shall I? To help you carry him.'

'Thanks. I can telephone from the vicarage for an ambulance, but I'm afraid – by the time it comes . . .' He left the remark unfinished.

Bunch said, 'Internal bleeding?'

Dr Griffiths nodded. He said, 'How on earth did he come here?'

'I think he must have been here all night,' said Bunch, considering. 'Harper unlocks the church in the morning as he goes to work, but he doesn't usually come in.'

It was about five minutes later when Dr Griffiths put down the telephone receiver and came back into the morning-room where the injured man was lying on quickly arranged blankets on the sofa. Bunch was moving a basin of water and clearing up after the doctor's examination.

'Well, that's that,' said Griffiths. 'I've sent for an ambulance and I've notified the police.' He stood, frowning, looking down on the patient who lay with closed eyes. His left hand was plucking in a nervous, spasmodic way at his side.

'He was shot,' said Griffiths. 'Shot at fairly close quarters. He rolled his handkerchief up into a ball and plugged the wound with it so as to stop the bleeding.'

'Could he have gone far after that happened?' Bunch asked.

'Oh, yes, it's quite possible. A mortally wounded man has been known to pick himself up and walk along a street as though nothing had happened, and then suddenly collapse five or ten minutes later. So he needn't have been shot in the church. Oh no. He may have been shot some distance away. Of course, he may have shot himself and then dropped the revolver and staggered blindly towards the church. I don't quite know why he made for the church and not for the vicarage.'

'Oh, I know *that*,' said Bunch. 'He said it: "Sanctuary."'

The doctor stared at her. 'Sanctuary?'

'Here's Julian,' said Bunch, turning her head as she heard her husband's steps in the hall. 'Julian! Come here.'

The Reverend Julian Harmon entered the room. His vague, scholarly manner always made him appear much older than he really was. 'Dear me!' said Julian Harmon, staring in a mild, puzzled manner at the surgical appliances and the prone figure on the sofa.

Bunch explained with her usual economy of words. 'He was in the church, dying. He'd been shot. Do you know him, Julian? I thought he said your name.'

The vicar came up to the sofa and looked down at the dying man. 'Poor fellow,' he said, and shook his head. 'No, I don't know him. I'm almost sure I've never seen him before.'

At that moment the dying man's eyes opened once more. They went from the doctor to Julian Harmon and from him to his wife. The eyes stayed there, staring into Bunch's face. Griffiths stepped forward.

'If you could tell us,' he said urgently.

But with eyes fixed on Bunch, the man said in a weak voice, 'Please – *please* –' And then, with a slight tremor, he died . . .

Sergeant Hayes licked his pencil and turned the page of his notebook. 'So that's all you can tell me, Mrs Harmon?'

'That's all,' said Bunch. 'These are the things out of his coat pockets.'

On a table at Sergeant Hayes's elbow was a wallet, a rather battered old watch with the initials W.S. and the return half of a ticket to London. Nothing more.

'You've found out who he is?' asked Bunch.

'A Mr and Mrs Eccles phoned up the station. He's her brother, it seems. Name of Sandbourne. Been in a low state of health and nerves for some time. He's been getting worse lately. The day before yesterday he walked out and didn't come back. He took a revolver with him.'

'And he came out here and shot himself with it?' said Bunch. 'Why?'

'Well, you see, he'd been depressed . . .'

Bunch interrupted him. 'I don't mean *that*. I mean, why here?'

Since Sergeant Hayes obviously did not know the answer to that one, he replied in an oblique fashion, 'Come out here, he did, on the five-ten bus.'

'Yes,' said Bunch again. 'But *why*?'

'I don't know, Mrs Harmon,' said Sergeant Hayes. 'There's no accounting. If the balance of the mind is disturbed –'

Bunch finished for him. 'They may do it anywhere. But it still seems to me unnecessary to take a bus out to a small country place like this. He didn't know anyone here, did he?'

'Not so far as can be ascertained,' said Sergeant Hayes. He coughed in an apologetic manner and said, as he rose to his feet, 'It may be as Mr and Mrs Eccles will come out and see you, ma'am – if you don't mind, that is.'

'Of course I don't mind,' said Bunch. 'It's very natural. I only wish I had something to tell them.'

'I'll be getting along,' said Sergeant Hayes.

'I'm only so thankful,' said Bunch, going with him to the front door, 'that it wasn't murder.'

A car had driven up at the vicarage gate. Sergeant Hayes, glancing at it, remarked: 'Looks as though that's Mr and Mrs Eccles come here now, ma'am, to talk with you.'

Bunch braced herself to endure what, she felt, might be rather a difficult ordeal. 'However,' she thought, 'I can always call Julian to help me. A clergyman's a great help when people are bereaved.'

Exactly what she had expected Mr and Mrs Eccles to be like, Bunch could not have said, but she was conscious, as she greeted them, of a feeling of surprise. Mr Eccles was a stout florid man whose natural manner would have been cheerful and facetious. Mrs Eccles had a vaguely flashy look about her. She had a small, mean, pursed-up mouth. Her voice was thin and reedy.

'It's been a terrible shock, Mrs Harmon, as you can imagine,' she said.

'Oh, I know,' said Bunch. 'It must have been. Do sit down. Can I offer you – well, perhaps it's a little early for tea –'

Mr Eccles waved a pudgy hand. 'No, no, nothing for us,' he said. 'It's very kind of you, I'm sure. Just wanted to . . . well . . . what poor William said and all that, you know?'

'He's been abroad a long time,' said Mrs Eccles, 'and I think he must have had some very nasty experiences. Very quiet and depressed he's been, ever since he came home. Said the world wasn't fit to live in and there was nothing to look forward to. Poor Bill, he was always moody.'

Bunch stared at them both for a moment or two without speaking.

'Pinched my husband's revolver, he did,' went on Mrs Eccles. 'Without our knowing. Then it seems he come here by bus. I suppose that was nice feeling on his part. He wouldn't have liked to do it in our house.'

'Poor fellow, poor fellow,' said Mr Eccles, with a sigh. 'It doesn't do to judge.'

There was another short pause, and Mr Eccles said, 'Did he leave a message? Any last words, nothing like that?'

His bright, rather pig-like eyes watched Bunch closely. Mrs Eccles, too, leaned forward as though anxious for the reply.

'No,' said Bunch quietly. 'He came into the church when he was dying, for sanctuary.'

Mrs Eccles said in a puzzled voice. 'Sanctuary? I don't think I quite . . .'

Mr Eccles interrupted. 'Holy place, my dear,' he said impatiently. 'That's what the vicar's wife means. It's a sin – suicide, you know. I expect he wanted to make amends.'

'He tried to say something just before he died,' said Bunch. 'He began, "Please," but that's as far as he got.'

Mrs Eccles put her handkerchief to her eyes and sniffed. 'Oh, dear,' she said. 'It's terribly upsetting, isn't it?'

'There, there, Pam,' said her husband. 'Don't take on. These things can't be helped. Poor Willie. Still, he's at peace now. Well, thank you very much, Mrs Harmon. I hope we haven't interrupted you. A vicar's wife is a busy lady, we know that.'

They shook hands with her. Then Eccles turned back suddenly to say, 'Oh yes, there's just one other thing. I think you've got his coat here, haven't you?'

'His coat?' Bunch frowned.

Mrs Eccles said, 'We'd like all his things, you know. Sentimental-like.'

'He had a watch and a wallet and a railway ticket in the pockets,' said Bunch. 'I gave them to Sergeant Hayes.'

'That's all right, then,' said Mr Eccles. 'He'll hand them over to us, I expect. His private papers would be in the wallet.'

'There was a pound note in the wallet,' said Bunch. 'Nothing else.'

'No letters? Nothing like that?'

Bunch shook her head.

'Well, thank you again, Mrs Harmon. The coat he was wearing – perhaps the sergeant's got that too, has he?'

Bunch frowned in an effort of remembrance.

'No,' she said. 'I don't think . . . let me see. The doctor and I took his coat off to examine his wound.' She looked round the room vaguely. 'I must have taken it upstairs with the towels and basin.'

'I wonder now, Mrs Harmon, if you don't mind . . . We'd like his coat, you know, the last thing he wore. Well, the wife feels rather sentimental about it.'

'Of course,' said Bunch. 'Would you like me to have it cleaned first? I'm afraid it's rather – well – stained.'

'Oh, no, no, no, that doesn't matter.'

Bunch frowned. 'Now I wonder where . . . excuse me a moment.' She went upstairs and it was some few minutes before she returned.

'I'm so sorry,' she said breathlessly, 'my daily woman must have put it aside with other clothes that were going to the cleaners. It's taken me quite a long time to find it. Here it is. I'll do it up for you in brown paper.'

Disclaiming their protests she did so; then once more effusively bidding her farewell the Eccleses departed.

Bunch went slowly back across the hall and entered the study. The Reverend Julian Harmon looked up and his brow cleared. He was composing a sermon and was fearing that he'd been led astray by the interest of the political relations between Judaea and Persia, in the reign of Cyrus.

'Yes, dear?' he said hopefully.

'Julian,' said Bunch. 'What's *Sanctuary* exactly?'

Julian Harmon gratefully put aside his sermon paper.

'Well,' he said. 'Sanctuary in Roman and Greek temples applied to the *cella* in which stood the statue of a god. The Latin word for altar "*ara*" also means protection.' He continued learnedly: 'In three hundred and ninety-nine A.D. the right of sanctuary in Christian churches was finally and definitely recognized. The earliest mention of the right of sanctuary in England is in the Code of Laws issued by Ethelbert in A.D. six hundred . . .'

He continued for some time with his exposition but was, as often, disconcerted by his wife's reception of his erudite pronouncement.

'Darling,' she said. 'You *are* sweet.'

Bending over, she kissed him on the tip of his nose. Julian felt rather like a dog who has been congratulated on performing a clever trick.

'The Eccleses have been here,' said Bunch.

The vicar frowned. 'The Eccleses? I don't seem to remember . . .'

'You don't know them. They're the sister and her husband of the man in the church.'

'My dear, you ought to have called me.'

'There wasn't any need,' said Bunch. 'They were not in need of consolation. I wonder now . . .' She frowned. 'If I put a casserole in the oven tomorrow, can you manage, Julian? I think I shall go up to London for the sales.'

'The sails?' Her husband looked at her blankly. 'Do you mean a yacht or a boat or something?'

Bunch laughed. 'No, darling. There's a special white sale at Burrows and Portman's. You know, sheets, table cloths and towels and glass-cloths. I don't know what we do with our glass-cloths, the way they wear through. Besides,' she added thoughtfully, 'I think I ought to go and see Aunt Jane.'

That sweet old lady, Miss Jane Marple, was enjoying the delights of the metropolis for a fortnight, comfortably installed in her nephew's studio flat.

'So kind of dear Raymond,' she murmured. 'He and Joan have gone to America for a fortnight and they insisted I should come up here and enjoy myself. And now, dear Bunch, do tell me what it is that's worrying you.'

Bunch was Miss Marple's favourite godchild, and the old lady looked at her with great affection as Bunch, thrusting her best felt hat farther on the back of her head, started her story.

Bunch's recital was concise and clear. Miss Marple nodded her head as Bunch finished. 'I see,' she said. 'Yes, I see.'

'That's why I felt I had to see you,' said Bunch. 'You see, not being clever –'

'But you *are* clever, my dear.'

'No, I'm not. Not clever like Julian.'

'Julian, of course, has a very solid intellect,' said Miss Marple.

'That's it,' said Bunch. 'Julian's got the intellect, but on the other hand, I've got the *sense*.'

'You have a lot of common sense, Bunch, and you're very intelligent.'

'You see, I don't really know what I ought to do. I can't ask Julian because – well, I mean, Julian's so full of rectitude . . .'

This statement appeared to be perfectly understood by Miss Marple, who said, 'I know what you mean, dear. We women – well, it's different.' She went on. 'You told me what happened, Bunch, but I'd like to know first exactly what you think.'

'It's all wrong,' said Bunch. 'The man who was there in the church, dying, knew all about Sanctuary. He said it just the way Julian would have said it. I mean, he was a well-read, educated man. And if he'd shot himself, he wouldn't drag himself to a church afterwards and say "sanctuary". Sanctuary means that you're pursued, and when you get into a church you're safe. Your pursuers can't touch you. At one time even the law couldn't get at you.'

She looked questioningly at Miss Marple. The latter nodded. Bunch went on, 'Those people, the Eccleses, were quite different. Ignorant and coarse. And there's another thing. That watch – the dead man's watch. It had the initials W.S. on the back of it. But inside – I opened it – in very small lettering there was "To Walter from his father" and a date. *Walter*. But the Eccleses kept talking of him as William or Bill.'

Miss Marple seemed about to speak but Bunch rushed on. 'Oh, I know you're not always called the name you're baptized by. I mean, I can understand that you might be christened William and called "Porgy" or "Carrots" or something. But your sister wouldn't call you William or Bill if your name was Walter.'

'You mean that she wasn't his sister?'

'I'm quite sure she wasn't his sister. They were horrid – both of them. They came to the vicarage to get his things and to find out if he'd said anything before he died. When I said he hadn't I saw it in their faces – relief. I think myself,' finished Bunch, 'it was Eccles who shot him.'

'Murder?' said Miss Marple.

'Yes,' said Bunch. 'Murder. That's why I came to you, darling.'

Bunch's remark might have seemed incongruous to an ignorant listener, but in certain spheres Miss Marple had a reputation for dealing with murder.

'He said "please" to me before he died,' said Bunch. 'He wanted me to do something for him. The awful thing is I've no idea what.'

Miss Marple considered for a moment or two, and then pounced on the point that had already occurred to Bunch. 'But why was he there at all?' she asked.

'You mean,' said Bunch, 'if you wanted sanctuary you might pop into a church anywhere. There's no need to take a bus that only goes four times a day and come out to a lonely spot like ours for it.'

'He must have come there for a purpose,' Miss Marple thought. 'He must have come to see someone. Chipping Cleghorn's not a big place, Bunch. Surely you must have some idea of who it was he came to see?'

Bunch reviewed the inhabitants of her village in her mind before rather doubtfully shaking her head. 'In a way,' she said, 'it could be anybody.'

'He never mentioned a name?'

'He said Julian, or I thought he said Julian. It might have been Julia, I suppose. As far as I know, there isn't any Julia living in Chipping Cleghorn.'

She screwed up her eyes as she thought back to the scene. The man lying there on the chancel steps, the light coming through the window with its jewels of red and blue light.

'Jewels,' said Miss Marple thoughtfully.

'I'm coming now,' said Bunch, 'to the most important thing of all. The reason why I've really come here today. You see, the Eccleses made a great fuss about having his coat. We took it off when the doctor was seeing him. It was an old, shabby sort of coat – there was no reason they should have wanted it. They pretended it was sentimental, but that was nonsense.

'Anyway, I went up to find it, and as I was just going up the stairs I remembered how he'd made a kind of picking gesture with his hand, as though he was fumbling with the coat. So when I got hold of the coat I looked at it very carefully and I saw that in one place the lining had been sewn up again with a different thread. So I unpicked it and I found a little piece of paper inside. I took it out and I sewed it up again properly with thread that matched. I was careful and I don't really think that the Eccleses would know I've done it. I don't *think* so, but I can't be sure. And I took the coat down to them and made some excuse for the delay.'

'The piece of paper?' asked Miss Marple.

Bunch opened her handbag. 'I didn't show it to Julian,' she said, 'because he would have said that I ought to have given it to the Eccleses. But I thought I'd rather bring it to you instead.'

'A cloakroom ticket,' said Miss Marple, looking at it. 'Paddington Station.'

'He had a return ticket to Paddington in his pocket,' said Bunch.

The eyes of the two women met.

'This calls for action,' said Miss Marple briskly. 'But it would be advisable, I think, to be careful. Would you have noticed at all, Bunch dear, whether you were followed when you came to London today?'

'Followed!' exclaimed Bunch. 'You don't think –'

'Well, I think it's *possible*,' said Miss Marple. 'When anything is possible, I think we ought to take precautions.' She rose with a brisk movement. 'You came up here ostensibly, my dear, to go to the sales. I think the right thing to do, therefore, would be for us to *go* to the sales. But before we set out, we might put one or two little arrangements in hand. I don't suppose,' Miss Marple added obscurely, 'that I shall need the old speckled tweed with the beaver collar just at present.'

It was about an hour and a half later that the two ladies, rather the worse for wear and battered in appearance, and both clasping parcels of hardly-won household linen, sat down at a small and sequestered hostelry called the Apple Bough to restore their forces with steak and kidney pudding followed by apple tart and custard.

'Really a prewar quality face towel,' gasped Miss Marple, slightly out of breath. 'With a J on it, too. So fortunate that Raymond's wife's name is Joan. I shall put them aside until I really need them and then they will do for her if I pass on sooner than I expect.'

'I really did need the glass-cloths,' said Bunch. 'And they were very cheap, though not as cheap as the ones that woman with the ginger hair managed to snatch from me.'

A smart young woman with a lavish application of rouge and lipstick entered the Apple Bough at that moment. After looking around vaguely for a moment or two, she hurried to their table. She laid down an envelope by Miss Marple's elbow.

'There you are, miss,' she said briskly.

'Oh, thank you, Gladys,' said Miss Marple. 'Thank you very much. So kind of you.'

'Always pleased to oblige, I'm sure,' said Gladys. 'Ernie always says to me, "Everything what's good you learned from that Miss Marple of yours that you were in service with," and I'm sure I'm always glad to oblige you, miss.'

'Such a dear girl,' said Miss Marple as Gladys departed again. 'Always so willing and so kind.'

She looked inside the envelope and then passed it on to Bunch. 'Now be very careful, dear,' she said. 'By the way, is there still that nice young inspector at Melchester that I remember?'

'I don't know,' said Bunch. 'I expect so.'

'Well, if not,' said Miss Marple thoughtfully. 'I can always ring up the Chief Constable. I *think* he would remember me.'

'Of course he'd remember you,' said Bunch. 'Everybody would remember *you*. You're quite unique.' She rose.

Arrived at Paddington, Bunch went to the luggage office and produced the cloakroom ticket. A moment or two later a rather shabby old suitcase was passed across to her, and carrying this she made her way to the platform.

The journey home was uneventful. Bunch rose as the train approached Chipping Cleghorn and picked up the old suitcase. She had just left her carriage when a man, sprinting along the platform, suddenly seized the suitcase from her hand and rushed off with it.

'Stop!' Bunch yelled. 'Stop him, stop him. He's taken my suitcase.'

The ticket collector who, at this rural station, was a man of somewhat slow processes, had just begun to say, 'Now, look here, you can't do that –' when a smart blow on the chest pushed him aside, and the man with the suitcase rushed out from the station. He made his way towards a waiting car. Tossing the suitcase in, he was about to climb after it, but before he could move a hand fell on his shoulder, and the voice of Police Constable Abel said, 'Now then, what's all this?'

Bunch arrived, panting, from the station. 'He snatched my suitcase. I just got out of the train with it.'

'Nonsense,' said the man. 'I don't know what this lady means. It's my suitcase. I just got out of the train with it.'

He looked at Bunch with a bovine and impartial stare. Nobody would have guessed that Police Constable Abel and Mrs Harmon spent long half-hours in Police Constable Abel's off-time discussing the respective merits of manure and bone meal for rose bushes.

'You say, madam, that this is your suitcase?' said Police Constable Abel.

'Yes,' said Bunch. 'Definitely.'

'And you, sir?'

'I say this suitcase is mine.'

The man was tall, dark and well dressed, with a drawling voice and a superior manner. A feminine voice from inside the car said, 'Of course it's your suitcase, Edwin. I don't know what this woman means.'

'We'll have to get this clear,' said Police Constable Abel. 'If it's your suitcase, madam, what do you say is inside it?'

'Clothes,' said Bunch. 'A long speckled coat with a beaver collar, two wool jumpers and a pair of shoes.'

'Well, that's clear enough,' said Police Constable Abel. He turned to the other.

'I am a theatrical costumer,' said the dark man importantly. 'This suitcase contains theatrical properties which I brought down here for an amateur performance.'

'Right, sir,' said Police Constable Abel. 'Well, we'll just look inside, shall we, and see? We can go along to the police station, or if you're in a hurry we'll take the suitcase back to the station and open it there.'

'It'll suit me,' said the dark man. 'My name is Moss, by the way, Edwin Moss.'

The police constable, holding the suitcase, went back into the station. 'Just taking this into the parcels office, George,' he said to the ticket collector.

Police Constable Abel laid the suitcase on the counter of the parcels office and pushed back the clasp. The case was not locked. Bunch and Mr Edwin Moss stood on either side of him, their eyes regarding each other vengefully.

'Ah!' said Police Constable Abel, as he pushed up the lid.

Inside, neatly folded, was a long rather shabby tweed coat with a beaver fur collar. There were also two wool jumpers and a pair of country shoes.

'Exactly as you say, madam,' said Police Constable Abel, turning to Bunch.

Nobody could have said that Mr Edwin Moss underdid things. His dismay and compunction were magnificent.

'I do apologize,' he said. 'I really *do* apologize. Please believe me, dear lady, when I tell you how very, very sorry I am. Unpardonable – quite unpardonable – my behaviour has been.' He looked at his watch. 'I must rush now. Probably my suitcase has gone on the train.' Raising his hat once more, he said meltingly to Bunch, 'Do, *do* forgive me,' and rushed hurriedly out of the parcels office.

'Are you going to let him get away?' asked Bunch in a conspiratorial whisper to Police Constable Abel.

The latter slowly closed a bovine eye in a wink.

'He won't get too far, ma'am,' he said. 'That's to say he won't get far unobserved, if you take my meaning.'

'Oh,' said Bunch, relieved.

'That old lady's been on the phone,' said Police Constable Abel, 'the one as was down here a few years ago. Bright she is, isn't she? But there's been a lot cooking up all today. Shouldn't wonder if the inspector or sergeant was out to see you about it tomorrow morning.'

*   *   *

It was the inspector who came, the Inspector Craddock whom Miss Marple remembered. He greeted Bunch with a smile as an old friend.

'Crime in Chipping Cleghorn again,' he said cheerfully. 'You don't lack for sensation here, do you, Mrs Harmon?'

'I could do with rather less,' said Bunch. 'Have you come to ask me questions or are you going to tell me things for a change?'

'I'll tell you some things first,' said the inspector. 'To begin with, Mr and Mrs Eccles have been having an eye kept on them for some time. There's reason to believe they've been connected with several robberies in this part of the world. For another thing, although Mrs Eccles *has* a brother called Sandbourne who has recently come back from abroad, the man you found dying in the church yesterday was definitely not Sandbourne.'

'I knew that he wasn't,' said Bunch. 'His name was Walter, to begin with, not William.'

The inspector nodded. 'His name was Walter St John, and he escaped forty-eight hours ago from Charrington Prison.'

'Of course,' said Bunch softly to herself, 'he was being hunted down by the law, and he took sanctuary.' Then she asked, 'What had he done?'

'I'll have to go back rather a long way. It's a complicated story. Several years ago there was a certain dancer doing turns at the music halls. I don't expect you'll have ever heard of her, but she specialized in an Arabian Night turn, "Aladdin in the Cave of Jewels" it was called. She wore bits of rhinestone and not much else.

'She wasn't much of a dancer, I believe, but she was – well – attractive. Anyway, a certain Asiatic royalty fell for her in a big way. Amongst other things he gave her a very magnificent emerald necklace.'

'The historic jewels of a Rajah?' murmured Bunch ecstatically.

Inspector Craddock coughed. 'Well, a rather more modern version, Mrs Harmon. The affair didn't last very long, broke up when our potentate's attention was captured by a certain film star whose demands were not quite so modest.

'Zobeida, to give the dancer her stage name, hung on to the necklace, and in due course it was stolen. It disappeared from her dressing-room at the theatre, and there was a lingering suspicion in the minds of the authorities that she herself might have engineered its disappearance. Such things have been known as a publicity stunt, or indeed from more dishonest motives.

'The necklace was never recovered, but during the course of the investigation the attention of the police was drawn to this man, Walter St John. He was a man of education and breeding who had come down in the world, and who was employed as a working jeweller with a rather obscure firm which was suspected of acting as a fence for jewel robberies.

'There was evidence that this necklace had passed through his hands. It was, however, in connection with the theft of some other jewellery that he was finally brought to trial and convicted and sent to prison. He had not very much longer to serve, so his escape was rather a surprise.'

'But why did he come here?' asked Bunch.

'We'd like to know that very much, Mrs Harmon. Following up his trial, it seems that he went first to London. He didn't visit any of his old associates but he visited an elderly woman, a Mrs Jacobs who had formerly been a theatrical dresser. She won't say a word of what he came for, but according to other lodgers in the house he left carrying a suitcase.'

'I see,' said Bunch. 'He left it in the cloakroom at Paddington and then he came down here.'

'By that time,' said Inspector Craddock, 'Eccles and the man who calls himself Edwin Moss were on his trail. They wanted that suitcase. They saw him get on the bus. They must have driven out in a car ahead of him and been waiting for him when he left the bus.'

'And he was murdered?' said Bunch.

'Yes,' said Craddock. 'He was shot. It was Eccles's revolver, but I rather fancy it was Moss who did the shooting. Now, Mrs Harmon, what we want to know is, where is the suitcase that Walter St John actually deposited at Paddington Station?'

Bunch grinned. 'I expect Aunt Jane's got it by now,' she said. 'Miss Marple, I mean. That was her plan. She sent a former maid of hers with a suitcase packed with her things to the cloakroom at Paddington and we exchanged tickets. I collected her suitcase and brought it down by train. She seemed to expect that an attempt would be made to get it from me.'

It was Inspector Craddock's turn to grin. 'So she said when she rang up. I'm driving up to London to see her. Do you want to come, too, Mrs Harmon?'

'Wel-l,' said Bunch, considering. 'Wel-l, as a matter of fact, it's very fortunate. I had a toothache last night so I really ought to go to London to see the dentist, oughtn't I?'

'Definitely,' said Inspector Craddock . . .

Miss Marple looked from Inspector Craddock's face to the eager face of Bunch Harmon. The suitcase lay on the table. 'Of course, I haven't opened it,' the old lady said. 'I wouldn't dream of doing such a thing till somebody official arrived. Besides,' she added, with a demurely mischievous Victorian smile, 'it's locked.'

'Like to make a guess at what's inside, Miss Marple?' asked the inspector.

'I should imagine, you know,' said Miss Marple, 'that it would be Zobeida's theatrical costumes. Would you like a chisel, Inspector?'

The chisel soon did its work. Both women gave a slight gasp as the lid flew up. The sunlight coming through the window lit up what seemed like an inexhaustible treasure of sparkling jewels, red, blue, green, orange.

'Aladdin's Cave,' said Miss Marple. 'The flashing jewels the girl wore to dance.'

'Ah,' said Inspector Craddock. 'Now, what's so precious about it, do you think, that a man was murdered to get hold of it?'

'She was a shrewd girl, I expect,' said Miss Marple thoughtfully. 'She's dead, isn't she, Inspector?'

'Yes, died three years ago.'

'She had this valuable emerald necklace,' said Miss Marple, musingly. 'Had the stones taken out of their setting and fastened here and there on her theatrical costume, where everyone would take them for merely coloured rhinestones. Then she had a replica made of the real necklace, and that, of course, was what was stolen. No wonder it never came on the market. The thief soon discovered the stones were false.'

'Here is an envelope,' said Bunch, pulling aside some of the glittering stones.

Inspector Craddock took it from her and extracted two official-looking papers from it. He read aloud, '"Marriage Certificate between Walter Edmund St John and Mary Moss." That was Zobeida's real name.'

'So they were married,' said Miss Marple. 'I see.'

'What's the other?' asked Bunch.

'A birth certificate of a daughter, Jewel.'

'Jewel?' cried Bunch. 'Why, of course. Jewel! *Jill!* That's it. I see now why he came to Chipping Cleghorn. *That's* what he was trying to say to me. Jewel. The Mundys, you know. Laburnum Cottage. They look after a little girl for someone. They're devoted to her. She's been like their own granddaughter. Yes, I remember now, her name *was* Jewel, only, of course, they call her Jill.

'Mrs Mundy had a stroke about a week ago, and the old man's been very ill with pneumonia. They were both going to go to the infirmary. I've been trying hard to find a good home for Jill somewhere. I didn't want her taken away to an institution.

'I suppose her father heard about it in prison and he managed to break away and get hold of this suitcase from the old dresser he or his wife left it with. I suppose if the jewels really belonged to her mother, they can be used for the child now.'

'I should imagine so, Mrs Harmon. *If* they're here.'

'Oh, they'll be here all right,' said Miss Marple cheerfully . . .

*   *   *

'Thank goodness you're back, dear,' said the Reverend Julian Harmon, greeting his wife with affection and a sigh of content. 'Mrs Burt always tries to do her best when you're away, but she really gave me some *very* peculiar fish-cakes for lunch. I didn't want to hurt her feelings so I gave them to Tiglath Pileser, but even *he* wouldn't eat them so I had to throw them out of the window.'

'Tiglath Pileser,' said Bunch, stroking the vicarage cat, who was purring against her knee, 'is *very* particular about what fish he eats. I often tell him he's got a proud stomach!'

'And your tooth, dear? Did you have it seen to?'

'Yes,' said Bunch. 'It didn't hurt much, and I went to see Aunt Jane again, too . . .'

'Dear old thing,' said Julian. 'I hope she's not failing at all.'

'Not in the least,' said Bunch, with a grin.

The following morning Bunch took a fresh supply of chrysanthemums to the church. The sun was once more pouring through the east window, and Bunch stood in the jewelled light on the chancel steps. She said very softly under her breath, 'Your little girl will be all right. *I'll* see that she is. I promise.'

Then she tidied up the church, slipped into a pew and knelt for a few moments to say her prayers before returning to the vicarage to attack the piled-up chores of two neglected days.

Greenshaw's Folly

'Greenshaw's Folly' was first published in
the *Daily Mail*, 3–7 December 1956.

The two men rounded the corner of the shrubbery.

'Well, there you are,' said Raymond West. 'That's it.'

Horace Bindler took a deep, appreciative breath.

'But my dear,' he cried, 'how wonderful.' His voice rose in a high screech of 'sthetic delight, then deepened in reverent awe. 'It's unbelievable. Out of this world! A period piece of the best.'

'I thought you'd like it,' said Raymond West, complacently.

'Like it? My dear –' Words failed Horace. He unbuckled the strap of his camera and got busy. 'This will be one of the gems of my collection,' he said happily. 'I do think, don't you, that it's rather amusing to have a collection of monstrosities? The idea came to me one night seven years ago in my bath. My last real gem was in the Campo Santo at Genoa, but I really think this beats it. What's it called?'

'I haven't the least idea,' said Raymond.

'I suppose it's got a name?'

'It must have. But the fact is that it's never referred to round here as anything but Greenshaw's Folly.'

'Greenshaw being the man who built it?'

'Yes. In eighteen-sixty or seventy or thereabouts. The local success story of the time. Barefoot boy who had risen to immense prosperity. Local opinion is divided as to why he built this house, whether it was sheer exuberance of wealth or whether it was done to impress his creditors. If the latter, it didn't impress them. He either went bankrupt or the next thing to it. Hence the name, Greenshaw's Folly.'

Horace's camera clicked. 'There,' he said in a satisfied voice. 'Remind me to show you No. 310 in my collection. A really incredible marble mantelpiece in the Italian manner.' He added, looking at the house, 'I can't conceive of how Mr Greenshaw thought of it all.'

'Rather obvious in some ways,' said Raymond. 'He had visited the châteaux of the Loire, don't you think? Those turrets. And then, rather unfortunately, he seems to have travelled in the Orient. The influence of the Taj Mahal is unmistakable. I rather like the Moorish wing,' he added, 'and the traces of a Venetian palace.'

'One wonders how he ever got hold of an architect to carry out these ideas.'

Raymond shrugged his shoulders.

'No difficulty about that, I expect,' he said. 'Probably the architect retired with a good income for life while poor old Greenshaw went bankrupt.'

'Could we look at it from the other side?' asked Horace, 'or are we trespassing!'

'We're trespassing all right,' said Raymond, 'but I don't think it will matter.'

He turned towards the corner of the house and Horace skipped after him.

'But who lives here, my dear? Orphans or holiday visitors? It can't be a school. No playing-fields or brisk efficiency.'

'Oh, a Greenshaw lives here still,' said Raymond over his shoulder. 'The house itself didn't go in the crash. Old Greenshaw's son inherited it. He was a bit of a miser and lived here in a corner of it. Never spent a penny. Probably never had a penny to spend. His daughter lives here now. Old lady – very eccentric.'

As he spoke Raymond was congratulating himself on having thought of Greenshaw's Folly as a means of entertaining his guest. These literary critics always professed themselves as longing for a week-end in the country, and were wont to find the country extremely boring when they got there. Tomorrow there would be the Sunday papers, and for today Raymond West congratulated himself on suggesting a visit to Greenshaw's Folly to enrich Horace Bindler's well-known collection of monstrosities.

They turned the corner of the house and came out on a neglected lawn. In one corner of it was a large artificial rockery, and bending over it was a figure at sight of which Horace clutched Raymond delightedly by the arm.

'My dear,' he exclaimed, 'do you see what she's got on? A sprigged print dress. Just like a housemaid – when there were housemaids. One of my most cherished memories is staying at a house in the country when I was quite a boy where a real housemaid called you in the morning,

'I know enough law to know that,' said Miss Greenshaw. 'And you two are men of standing.'

She flung down her trowel on her weeding-basket.

'Would you mind coming up to the library with me?'

'Delighted,' said Horace eagerly.

She led the way through french windows and through a vast yellow and gold drawing-room with faded brocade on the walls and dust covers arranged over the furniture, then through a large dim hall, up a staircase and into a room on the first floor.

'My grandfather's library,' she announced.

Horace looked round the room with acute pleasure. It was a room, from his point of view, quite full of monstrosities. The heads of sphinxes appeared on the most unlikely pieces of furniture, there was a colossal bronze representing, he thought, Paul and Virginia, and a vast bronze clock with classical motifs of which he longed to take a photograph.

'A fine lot of books,' said Miss Greenshaw.

Raymond was already looking at the books. From what he could see from a cursory glance there was no book here of any real interest or, indeed, any book which appeared to have been read. They were all superbly bound sets of the classics as supplied ninety years ago for furnishing a gentleman's library. Some novels of a bygone period were included. But they too showed little signs of having been read.

Miss Greenshaw was fumbling in the drawers of a vast desk. Finally she pulled out a parchment document.

'My will,' she explained. 'Got to leave your money to someone – or so they say. If I died without a will I suppose that son of a horse-coper would get it. Handsome fellow, Harry Fletcher, but a rogue if there ever was one. Don't see why *his* son should inherit this place. No,' she went on, as though answering some unspoken objection, 'I've made up my mind. I'm leaving it to Cresswell.'

'Your housekeeper?'

'Yes. I've explained it to her. I make a will leaving her all I've got and then I don't need to pay her any wages. Saves me a lot in current expenses, and it keeps her up to the mark. No giving me notice and walking off at any minute. Very la-di-dah and all that, isn't she? But her father was a working plumber in a very small way. *She's* nothing to give herself airs about.'

She had by now unfolded the parchment. Picking up a pen she dipped it in the inkstand and wrote her signature, Katherine Dorothy Greenshaw.

'That's right,' she said. 'You've seen me sign it, and then you two sign it, and that makes it legal.'

She handed the pen to Raymond West. He hesitated a moment, feeling an unexpected repulsion to what he was asked to do. Then he quickly scrawled the well-known signature, for which his morning's mail usually brought at least six demands a day.

Horace took the pen from him and added his own minute signature. 'That's done,' said Miss Greenshaw.

She moved across to the bookcase and stood looking at them uncertainly, then she opened a glass door, took out a book and slipped the folded parchment inside.

'I've my own places for keeping things,' she said.

'*Lady Audley's Secret*,' Raymond West remarked, catching sight of the title as she replaced the book.

Miss Greenshaw gave another cackle of laughter.

'Best-seller in its day,' she remarked. 'Not like your books, eh?'

She gave Raymond a sudden friendly nudge in the ribs. Raymond was rather surprised that she even knew he wrote books. Although Raymond West was quite a name in literature, he could hardly be described as a best-seller. Though softening a little with the advent of middle-age, his books dealt bleakly with the sordid side of life.

'I wonder,' Horace demanded breathlessly, 'if I might just take a photograph of the clock?'

'By all means,' said Miss Greenshaw. 'It came, I believe, from the Paris exhibition.'

'Very probably,' said Horace. He took his picture.

'This room's not been used much since my grandfather's time,' said Miss Greenshaw. 'This desk's full of old diaries of his. Interesting, I should think. I haven't the eyesight to read them myself. I'd like to get them published, but I suppose one would have to work on them a good deal.'

'You could engage someone to do that,' said Raymond West.

'Could I really? It's an idea, you know. I'll think about it.'

Raymond West glanced at his watch.

'We mustn't trespass on your kindness any longer,' he said.

'Pleased to have seen you,' said Miss Greenshaw graciously. 'Thought you were the policeman when I heard you coming round the corner of the house.'

'Why a policeman?' demanded Horace, who never minded asking questions.

Miss Greenshaw responded unexpectedly.

'If you want to know the time, ask a policeman,' she carolled, and with this example of Victorian wit, nudged Horace in the ribs and roared with laughter.

'It's been a wonderful afternoon,' sighed Horace as they walked home. 'Really, that place has everything. The only thing the library needs is a body. Those old-fashioned detective stories about murder in the library – that's just the kind of library I'm sure the authors had in mind.'

'If you want to discuss murder,' said Raymond, 'you must talk to my Aunt Jane.'

'Your Aunt Jane? Do you mean Miss Marple?' He felt a little at a loss. The charming old-world lady to whom he had been introduced the night before seemed the last person to be mentioned in connection with murder.

'Oh, yes,' said Raymond. 'Murder is a speciality of hers.'

'But my dear, how intriguing. What do you really mean?'

'I mean just that,' said Raymond. He paraphrased: 'Some commit murder, some get mixed up in murders, others have murder thrust upon them. My Aunt Jane comes into the third category.'

'You are joking.'

'Not in the least. I can refer you to the former Commissioner of Scotland Yard, several Chief Constables and one or two hard-working inspectors of the CID.'

Horace said happily that wonders would never cease. Over the tea table they gave Joan West, Raymond's wife, Lou Oxley her niece, and old Miss Marple, a résumé of the afternoon's happenings, recounting in detail everything that Miss Greenshaw had said to them.

'But I do think,' said Horace, 'that there is something a little *sinister* about the whole set-up. That duchess-like creature, the housekeeper – arsenic, perhaps, in the teapot, now that she knows her mistress has made the will in her favour?'

'Tell us, Aunt Jane,' said Raymond. 'Will there be murder or won't there? What do *you* think?'

'I think,' said Miss Marple, winding up her wool with a rather severe air, 'that you shouldn't joke about these things as much as you do, Raymond. Arsenic is, of course, *quite* a possibility. So easy to obtain. Probably present in the toolshed already in the form of weed killer.'

'Oh, really, darling,' said Joan West, affectionately. 'Wouldn't that be rather too obvious?'

'It's all very well to make a will,' said Raymond, 'I don't suppose really the poor old thing has anything to leave except that awful white elephant of a house, and who would want that?'

'A film company possibly,' said Horace, 'or a hotel or an institution?'

'They'd expect to buy it for a song,' said Raymond, but Miss Marple was shaking her head.

'You know, dear Raymond, I cannot agree with you there. About the money, I mean. The grandfather was evidently one of those lavish spenders who make money easily, but can't keep it. He may have gone broke, as you say, but hardly bankrupt or else his son would not have had the house. Now the son, as is so often the case, was an entirely different character to his father. A miser. A man who saved every penny. I should say that in the course of his lifetime he probably put by a very good sum. This Miss Greenshaw appears to have taken after him, to dislike spending money, that is. Yes, I should think it quite likely that she had quite a good sum tucked away.'

'In that case,' said Joan West, 'I wonder now – what about Lou?'

They looked at Lou as she sat, silent, by the fire.

Lou was Joan West's niece. Her marriage had recently, as she herself put it, come unstuck, leaving her with two young children and a bare sufficiency of money to keep them on.

'I mean,' said Joan, 'if this Miss Greenshaw really wants someone to go through diaries and get a book ready for publication . . .'

'It's an idea,' said Raymond.

Lou said in a low voice:

'It's work I could do – and I'd enjoy it.'

'I'll write to her,' said Raymond.

'I wonder,' said Miss Marple thoughtfully, 'what the old lady meant by that remark about a policeman?'

'Oh, it was just a joke.'

'It reminded me,' said Miss Marple, nodding her head vigorously, 'yes, it reminded me very much of Mr Naysmith.'

'Who was Mr Naysmith?' asked Raymond, curiously.

'He kept bees,' said Miss Marple, 'and was very good at doing the acrostics in the Sunday papers. And he liked giving people false impressions just for fun. But sometimes it led to trouble.'

Everybody was silent for a moment, considering Mr Naysmith, but as there did not seem to be any points of resemblance between him and Miss Greenshaw, they decided that dear Aunt Jane was perhaps getting a *little* bit disconnected in her old age.

Horace Bindler went back to London without having collected any more monstrosities and Raymond West wrote a letter to Miss Greenshaw telling her that he knew of a Mrs Louisa Oxley who would be competent to undertake work on the diaries. After a lapse of some days, a letter arrived, written in spidery old-fashioned handwriting, in which Miss Greenshaw declared herself anxious to avail herself of the services of Mrs Oxley, and making an appointment for Mrs Oxley to come and see her.

Lou duly kept the appointment, generous terms were arranged and she started work on the following day.

'I'm awfully grateful to you,' she said to Raymond. 'It will fit in beautifully. I can take the children to school, go on to Greenshaw's Folly and pick them up on my way back. How fantastic the whole set-up is! That old woman has to be seen to be believed.'

On the evening of her first day at work she returned and described her day.

'I've hardly seen the housekeeper,' she said. 'She came in with coffee and biscuits at half past eleven with her mouth pursed up very prunes and prisms, and would hardly speak to me. I think she disapproves deeply of my having been engaged.' She went on, 'It seems there's quite a feud between her and the gardener, Alfred. He's a local boy and fairly lazy, I should imagine, and he and the housekeeper won't speak to each other. Miss Greenshaw said in her rather grand way, "There have always been feuds as far as I can remember between the garden and the house staff. It was so in my grandfather's time. There were three men and a boy in the garden then, and eight maids in the house, but there was always friction."'

On the following day Lou returned with another piece of news.

'Just fancy,' she said, 'I was asked to ring up the nephew this morning.'

'Miss Greenshaw's nephew?'

'Yes. It seems he's an actor playing in the company that's doing a summer season at Boreham on Sea. I rang up the theatre and left a message asking him to lunch tomorrow. Rather fun, really. The old girl didn't want the housekeeper to know. I think Mrs Cresswell has done something that's annoyed her.'

'Tomorrow another instalment of this thrilling serial,' murmured Raymond.

'It's exactly like a serial, isn't it? Reconciliation with the nephew, blood is thicker than water – another will to be made and the old will destroyed.'

'Aunt Jane, you're looking very serious.'

'Was I, my dear? Have you heard any more about the policeman?'

Lou looked bewildered. 'I don't know anything about a policeman.'

'That remark of hers, my dear,' said Miss Marple, 'must have meant *something.*'

Lou arrived at her work the next day in a cheerful mood. She passed through the open front door – the doors and windows of the house were always open. Miss Greenshaw appeared to have no fear of burglars, and was probably justified, as most things in the house weighed several tons and were of no marketable value.

Lou had passed Alfred in the drive. When she first caught sight of him he had been leaning against a tree smoking a cigarette, but as soon as he had caught sight of her he had seized a broom and begun diligently to sweep leaves. An idle young man, she thought, but good looking. His features reminded her of someone. As she passed through the hall on her way upstairs to the library she glanced at the large picture of Nathaniel Greenshaw which presided over the mantelpiece, showing him in the acme of Victorian prosperity, leaning back in a large arm-chair, his hands resting on the gold albert across his capacious stomach. As her glance swept up from the stomach to the face with its heavy jowls, its bushy eyebrows and its flourishing black moustache, the thought occurred to her that Nathaniel Greenshaw must have been handsome as a young man. He had looked, perhaps, a little like Alfred . . .

She went into the library, shut the door behind her, opened her typewriter and got out the diaries from the drawer at the side of the desk. Through the open window she caught a glimpse of Miss Greenshaw in a puce-coloured sprigged print, bending over the rockery, weeding assiduously. They had had two wet days, of which the weeds had taken full advantage.

Lou, a town-bred girl, decided that if she ever had a garden it would never contain a rockery which needed hand weeding. Then she settled down to her work.

When Mrs Cresswell entered the library with the coffee tray at half past eleven, she was clearly in a very bad temper. She banged the tray down on the table, and observed to the universe.

'Company for lunch – and nothing in the house! What am *I* supposed to do, I should like to know? And no sign of Alfred.'

'He was sweeping in the drive when I got here,' Lou offered.

'I dare say. A nice soft job.'

Mrs Cresswell swept out of the room and banged the door behind her. Lou grinned to herself. She wondered what 'the nephew' would be like.

She finished her coffee and settled down to her work again. It was so absorbing that time passed quickly. Nathaniel Greenshaw, when he started to keep a diary, had succumbed to the pleasure of frankness. Trying out a passage relating to the personal charm of a barmaid in the neighbouring town, Lou reflected that a good deal of editing would be necessary.

As she was thinking this, she was startled by a scream from the garden. Jumping up, she ran to the open window. Miss Greenshaw was staggering away from the rockery towards the house. Her hands were clasped to her breast and between them there protruded a feathered shaft that Lou recognized with stupefaction to be the shaft of an arrow.

Miss Greenshaw's head, in its battered straw hat, fell forward on her

breast. She called up to Lou in a failing voice: '. . . shot . . . he shot me
. . . with an arrow . . . get help . . .'

Lou rushed to the door. She turned the handle, but the door would
not open. It took her a moment or two of futile endeavour to realize that
she was locked in. She rushed back to the window.

'I'm locked in.'

Miss Greenshaw, her back towards Lou, and swaying a little on her
feet was calling up to the housekeeper at a window farther along.

'Ring police . . . telephone . . .'

Then, lurching from side to side like a drunkard she disappeared from
Lou's view through the window below into the drawing-room. A moment
later Lou heard a crash of broken china, a heavy fall, and then silence.
Her imagination reconstructed the scene. Miss Greenshaw must have
staggered blindly into a small table with a Sèvres teaset on it.

Desperately Lou pounded on the door, calling and shouting. There
was no creeper or drain-pipe outside the window that could help her to
get out that way.

Tired at last of beating on the door, she returned to the window. From
the window of her sitting-room farther along, the housekeeper's head
appeared.

'Come and let me out, Mrs Oxley. I'm locked in.'

'So am I.'

'Oh dear, isn't it awful? I've telephoned the police. There's an extension in this room, but what I can't understand, Mrs Oxley, is our being
locked in. *I* never heard a key turn, did you?'

'No. I didn't hear anything at all. Oh dear, what shall we do? Perhaps
Alfred might hear us.' Lou shouted at the top of her voice, 'Alfred,
Alfred.'

'Gone to his dinner as likely as not. What time is it?'

Lou glanced at her watch.

'Twenty-five past twelve.'

'He's not supposed to go until half past, but he sneaks off earlier whenever he can.'

'Do you think – do you think –'

Lou meant to ask 'Do you think she's dead?' but the words stuck in
her throat.

There was nothing to do but wait. She sat down on the window-sill.
It seemed an eternity before the stolid helmeted figure of a police constable came round the corner of the house. She leant out of the window
and he looked up at her, shading his eyes with his hand. When he spoke
his voice held reproof.

'What's going on here?' he asked disapprovingly.

From their respective windows, Lou and Mrs Cresswell poured a flood of excited information down on him.

The constable produced a note-book and pencil. 'You ladies ran upstairs and locked yourselves in? Can I have your names, please?'

'No. Somebody else locked us in. Come and let us out.'

The constable said reprovingly, 'All in good time,' and disappeared through the window below.

Once again time seemed infinite. Lou heard the sound of a car arriving, and, after what seemed an hour, but was actually three minutes, first Mrs Cresswell and then Lou, were released by a police sergeant more alert than the original constable.

'Miss Greenshaw?' Lou's voice faltered. 'What – what's happened?'

The sergeant cleared his throat.

'I'm sorry to have to tell you, madam,' he said, 'what I've already told Mrs Cresswell here. Miss Greenshaw is dead.'

'Murdered,' said Mrs Cresswell. 'That's what it is – murder.'

The sergeant said dubiously:

'Could have been an accident – some country lads shooting with bows and arrows.'

Again there was the sound of a car arriving. The sergeant said:

'That'll be the MO,' and started downstairs.

But it was not the MO. As Lou and Mrs Cresswell came down the stairs a young man stepped hesitatingly through the front door and paused, looking round him with a somewhat bewildered air.

Then, speaking in a pleasant voice that in some way seemed familiar to Lou – perhaps it had a family resemblance to Miss Greenshaw's – he asked:

'Excuse me, does – er – does Miss Greenshaw live here?'

'May I have your name if you please,' said the sergeant advancing upon him.

'Fletcher,' said the young man. 'Nat Fletcher. I'm Miss Greenshaw's nephew, as a matter of fact.'

'Indeed, sir, well – I'm sorry – I'm sure –'

'Has anything happened?' asked Nat Fletcher.

'There's been an – accident – your aunt was shot with an arrow – penetrated the jugular vein –'

Mrs Cresswell spoke hysterically and without her usual refinement:

'Your h'aunt's been murdered, that's what's 'appened. Your h'aunt's been murdered.'

Inspector Welch drew his chair a little nearer to the table and let his gaze wander from one to the other of the four people in the room. It was the evening of the same day. He had called at the Wests' house to take Lou Oxley once more over her statement.

'You are sure of the exact words? *Shot – he shot me – with an arrow – get help?*'

Lou nodded.

'And the time?'

'I looked at my watch a minute or two later – it was then twelve twenty-five.'

'Your watch keeps good time?'

'I looked at the clock as well.'

The inspector turned to Raymond West.

'It appears, sir, that about a week ago you and a Mr Horace Bindler were witnesses to Miss Greenshaw's will?'

Briefly, Raymond recounted the events of the afternoon visit that he and Horace Bindler had paid to Greenshaw's Folly.

'This testimony of yours may be important,' said Welch. 'Miss Greenshaw distinctly told you, did she, that her will was being made in favour of Mrs Cresswell, the housekeeper, that she was not paying Mrs Cresswell any wages in view of the expectations Mrs Cresswell had of profiting by her death?'

'That is what she told me – yes.'

'Would you say that Mrs Cresswell was definitely aware of these facts?'

'I should say undoubtedly. Miss Greenshaw made a reference in my presence to beneficiaries not being able to witness a will and Mrs Cresswell clearly understood what she meant by it. Moreover, Miss Greenshaw herself told me that she had come to this arrangement with Mrs Cresswell.'

'So Mrs Cresswell had reason to believe she was an interested party. Motive's clear enough in her case, and I dare say she'd be our chief suspect now if it wasn't for the fact that she was securely locked in her room like Mrs Oxley here, and also that Miss Greenshaw definitely said a *man* shot her –'

'She definitely *was* locked in her room?'

'Oh yes. Sergeant Cayley let her out. It's a big old-fashioned lock with a big old-fashioned key. The key was in the lock and there's not a chance that it could have been turned from inside or any hanky-panky of that kind. No, you can take it definitely that Mrs Cresswell was locked inside that room and couldn't get out. And there were no bows and arrows in the room and Miss Greenshaw couldn't in any case have been shot from a window – the angle forbids it – no, Mrs Cresswell's out of it.'

He paused and went on:

'Would you say that Miss Greenshaw, in your opinion, was a practical joker?'

Miss Marple looked up sharply from her corner.

'So the will wasn't in Mrs Cresswell's favour after all?' she said.

Inspector Welch looked over at her in a rather surprised fashion.

'That's a very clever guess of yours, madam,' he said. 'No. Mrs Cresswell isn't named as beneficiary.'

'Just like Mr Naysmith,' said Miss Marple, nodding her head. 'Miss Greenshaw told Mrs Cresswell she was going to leave her everything and so got out of paying her wages; and then she left her money to somebody else. No doubt she was vastly pleased with herself. No wonder she chortled when she put the will away in *Lady Audley's Secret*.'

'It was lucky Mrs Oxley was able to tell us about the will and where it was put,' said the inspector. 'We might have had a long hunt for it otherwise.'

'A Victorian sense of humour,' murmured Raymond West. 'So she left her money to her nephew after all,' said Lou.

The inspector shook his head.

'No,' he said, 'she didn't leave it to Nat Fletcher. The story goes around here – of course I'm new to the place and I only get the gossip that's second-hand – but it seems that in the old days both Miss Greenshaw and her sister were set on the handsome young riding master, and the sister got him. No, she didn't leave the money to her nephew –' He paused, rubbing his chin, 'She left it to Alfred,' he said.

'Alfred – the gardener?' Joan spoke in a surprised voice.

'Yes, Mrs West. Alfred Pollock.'

'But why?' cried Lou.

Miss Marple coughed and murmured:

'I should imagine, though perhaps I am wrong, that there may have been – what we might call *family* reasons.'

'You could call them that in a way,' agreed the inspector. 'It's quite well known in the village, it seems, that Thomas Pollock, Alfred's grandfather, was one of old Mr Greenshaw's by-blows.'

'Of course,' cried Lou, 'the resemblance! I saw it this morning.'

She remembered how after passing Alfred she had come into the house and looked up at old Greenshaw's portrait.

'I dare say,' said Miss Marple, 'that she thought Alfred Pollock might have a pride in the house, might even want to live in it, whereas her nephew would almost certainly have no use for it whatever and would sell it as soon as he could possibly do so. He's an actor, isn't he? What play exactly is he acting in at present?'

Trust an old lady to wander from the point, thought Inspector Welch, but he replied civilly:

'I believe, madam, they are doing a season of James Barrie's plays.'

'Barrie,' said Miss Marple thoughtfully.

'*What Every Woman Knows*,' said Inspector Welch, and then blushed. 'Name of a play,' he said quickly. 'I'm not much of a theatre-goer myself,' he added, 'but the wife went along and saw it last week. Quite well done, she said it was.'

'Barrie wrote some very charming plays,' said Miss Marple, 'though I must say that when I went with an old friend of mine, General Easterly, to see Barrie's *Little Mary* –' she shook her head sadly, '– neither of us knew where to look.'

The inspector, unacquainted with the play *Little Mary* looked completely fogged. Miss Marple explained:

'When I was a girl, Inspector, nobody ever mentioned the word *stomach*.'

The inspector looked even more at sea. Miss Marple was murmuring titles under her breath.

'*The Admirable Crichton*. Very clever. *Mary Rose* – a charming play. I cried, I remember. *Quality Street* I didn't care for so much. Then there was *A Kiss for Cinderella*. Oh, *of course*.'

Inspector Welch had no time to waste on theatrical discussion. He returned to the matter in hand.

'The question is,' he said, 'did Alfred Pollock know that the old lady had made a will in his favour? Did she tell him?' He added: 'You see – there's an archery club over at Boreham Lovell and *Alfred Pollock's a member*. He's a very good shot indeed with a bow and arrow.'

'Then isn't your case quite clear?' asked Raymond West. 'It would fit in with the doors being locked on the two women – he'd know just where they were in the house.'

The inspector looked at him. He spoke with deep melancholy.

'He's got an alibi,' said the inspector.

'I always think alibis are definitely suspicious.'

'Maybe, sir,' said Inspector Welch. 'You're talking as a writer.'

'I don't write detective stories,' said Raymond West, horrified at the mere idea.

'Easy enough to say that alibis are suspicious,' went on Inspector Welch, 'but unfortunately we've got to deal with facts.'

He sighed.

'We've got three good suspects,' he said. 'Three people who, as it happened, were very close upon the scene at the time. Yet the odd thing is that it looks as though none of the three could have done it. The housekeeper I've already dealt with – the nephew, Nat Fletcher, at the moment Miss Greenshaw was shot, was a couple of miles away filling up his car at a garage and asking his way – as for Alfred Pollock six people will swear that he entered the Dog and Duck at twenty past twelve and was there for an hour having his usual bread and cheese and beer.'

'Deliberately establishing an alibi,' said Raymond West hopefully.

'Maybe,' said Inspector Welch, 'but if so, he *did* establish it.'

There was a long silence. Then Raymond turned his head to where Miss Marple sat upright and thoughtful.

'It's up to you, Aunt Jane,' he said. 'The inspector's baffled, the sergeant's baffled, I'm baffled, Joan's baffled, Lou is baffled. But to you, Aunt Jane, it is crystal clear. Am I right?'

'I wouldn't say that, dear,' said Miss Marple, 'not *crystal* clear, and murder, dear Raymond, isn't a game. I don't suppose poor Miss Greenshaw wanted to die, and it was a particularly brutal murder. Very well planned and quite cold blooded. It's not a thing to make *jokes* about!'

'I'm sorry,' said Raymond, abashed. 'I'm not really as callous as I sound. One treats a thing lightly to take away from the – well, the horror of it.'

'That is, I believe, the modern tendency,' said Miss Marple, 'All these wars, and having to joke about funerals. Yes, perhaps I was thoughtless when I said you were callous.'

'It isn't,' said Joan, 'as though we'd known her at all well.'

'That is *very* true,' said Miss Marple. 'You, dear Joan, did not know her at all. I did not know her at all. Raymond gathered an impression of her from one afternoon's conversation. Lou knew her for two days.'

'Come now, Aunt Jane,' said Raymond, 'tell us your views. You don't mind, Inspector?'

'Not at all,' said the inspector politely.

'Well, my dear, it would seem that we have three people who had, or might have thought they had, a motive to kill the old lady. And three quite simple reasons why none of the three could have done so. The housekeeper could not have done so because she was locked in her room and because Miss Greenshaw definitely stated that a *man* shot her. The gardener could not have done it because he was inside the Dog and Duck at the time the murder was committed, the nephew could not have done it because he was still some distance away in his car at the time of the murder.'

'Very clearly put, madam,' said the inspector.

'And since it seems most unlikely that any outsider should have done it, where, then, are we?'

'That's what the inspector wants to know,' said Raymond West.

'One so often looks at a thing the wrong way round,' said Miss Marple apologetically. 'If we can't alter the movements or the position of those three people, then couldn't we perhaps alter the time of the murder?'

'You mean that both my watch and the clock were wrong?' asked Lou.

'No dear,' said Miss Marple, 'I didn't mean that at all. I mean that the murder didn't occur when you thought it occurred.'

'But I *saw* it,' cried Lou.

'Well, what I have been wondering, my dear, was whether you weren't *meant* to see it. I've been asking myself, you know, whether that wasn't the real reason why you were engaged for this job.'

'What *do* you mean, Aunt Jane?'

'Well, dear, it seems odd. Miss Greenshaw did not like spending money, and yet she engaged you and agreed quite willingly to the terms you asked. It seems to me that perhaps you were meant to be there in that library on the first floor, looking out of the window so that you could be the key witness – someone from outside of irreproachable good faith – to fix a definite time and place for the murder.'

'But you can't mean,' said Lou, incredulously, 'that Miss Greenshaw *intended* to be murdered.'

'What I mean, dear,' said Miss Marple, 'is that you didn't really know Miss Greenshaw. There's no real reason, is there, why the Miss Greenshaw you saw when you went up to the house should be the same Miss Greenshaw that Raymond saw a few days earlier? Oh, yes, I know,' she went on, to prevent Lou's reply, 'she was wearing the peculiar old-fashioned print dress and the strange straw hat, and had unkempt hair. She corresponded exactly to the description Raymond gave us last week-end. But those two women, you know, were much of an age and height and size. The housekeeper, I mean, and Miss Greenshaw.'

'But the housekeeper is fat!' Lou exclaimed. 'She's got an enormous bosom.'

Miss Marple coughed.

'But my dear, surely, nowadays I have seen – er – them myself in shops most indelicately displayed. It is very easy for anyone to have a – a bust – of *any* size and dimension.'

'What are you trying to say?' demanded Raymond.

'I was just thinking, dear, that during the two or three days Lou was working there, one woman could have played the two parts. You said yourself, Lou, that you hardly saw the housekeeper, except for the one moment in the morning when she brought you in the tray with coffee. One sees those clever artists on the stage coming in as different characters with only a minute or two to spare, and I am sure the change could have been effected quite easily. That marquise head-dress could be just a wig slipped on and off.'

'Aunt Jane! Do you mean that Miss Greenshaw was dead before I started work there?'

'Not dead. Kept under drugs, I should say. A very easy job for an unscrupulous woman like the housekeeper to do. Then she made the arrangements with you and got you to telephone to the nephew to ask him to lunch at a definite time. The only person who would have known that this Miss Greenshaw was *not* Miss Greenshaw would have been Alfred. And if you remember, the first two days you were working there it was wet, and Miss Greenshaw stayed in the house. Alfred never came into the house because of his feud with the housekeeper. And on the last morning Alfred was in the drive, while Miss Greenshaw was working on the rockery – I'd like to have a look at that rockery.'

'Do you mean it was Mrs Cresswell who killed Miss Greenshaw?'

'I think that after bringing you your coffee, the woman locked the door on you as she went out, carried the unconscious Miss Greenshaw down to the drawing-room, then assumed her "Miss Greenshaw" disguise and went out to work on the rockery where you could see her from the window. In due course she screamed and came staggering to the house clutching an arrow as though it had penetrated her throat. She called for help and was careful to say "*he* shot me" so as to remove suspicion from the housekeeper. She also called up to the housekeeper's window as though she saw her there. Then, once inside the drawing-room, she threw over a table with porcelain on it – and ran quickly upstairs, put on her marquise wig and was able a few moments later to lean her head out of the window and tell you that she, too, was locked in.'

'But she *was* locked in,' said Lou.

'I know. That is where the policeman comes in.'

'What policeman?'

'Exactly – what policeman? I wonder, Inspector, if you would mind telling me how and when *you* arrived on the scene?'

The inspector looked a little puzzled.

'At twelve twenty-nine we received a telephone call from Mrs Cresswell, housekeeper to Miss Greenshaw, stating that her mistress had been shot. Sergeant Cayley and myself went out there at once in a car and arrived at the house at twelve thirty-five. We found Miss Greenshaw dead and the two ladies locked in their rooms.'

'So, you see, my dear,' said Miss Marple to Lou. 'The police constable *you* saw wasn't a real police constable. You never thought of him again – one doesn't – one just accepts one more uniform as part of the law.'

'But who – why?'

'As to who – well, if they are playing *A Kiss for Cinderella*, a policeman is the principal character. Nat Fletcher would only have to help himself to the costume he wears on the stage. He'd ask his way at a garage being careful to call attention to the time – twelve twenty-five, then drive on quickly, leave his car round a corner, slip on his police uniform and do his "act".'

'But why? – why?'

'*Someone* had to lock the housekeeper's door on the outside, and someone had to drive the arrow through Miss Greenshaw's throat. You can stab anyone with an arrow just as well as by shooting it – but it needs force.'

'You mean they were both in it?'

'Oh yes, I think so. Mother and son as likely as not.'

'But Miss Greenshaw's sister died long ago.'

'Yes, but I've no doubt Mr Fletcher married again. He sounds the sort of man who would, and I think it possible that the child died too, and that this so-called nephew was the second wife's child, and not really a relation at all. The woman got a post as housekeeper and spied out the land. Then he wrote as her nephew and proposed to call upon her – he may have made some joking reference to coming in his policeman's uniform – or asked her over to see the play. But I think she suspected the truth and refused to see him. He would have been her heir if she had died without making a will – but of course once she had made a will in the housekeeper's favour (as they thought) then it was clear sailing.'

'But why use an arrow?' objected Joan. 'So very far fetched.'

'Not far fetched at all, dear. Alfred belonged to an archery club – Alfred was meant to take the blame. The fact that he was in the pub as early as twelve twenty was most unfortunate from their point of view. He always left a little before his proper time and that would have been just right –' she shook her head. 'It really seems all wrong – morally, I mean, that Alfred's laziness should have saved his life.'

The inspector cleared his throat.

'Well, madam, these suggestions of yours are very interesting. I shall have, of course, to investigate –'

Miss Marple and Raymond West stood by the rockery and looked down at that gardening basket full of dying vegetation.

Miss Marple murmured:

'Alyssum, saxifrage, cytisus, thimble campanula . . . Yes, that's all the proof *I* need. Whoever was weeding here yesterday morning was no gardener – she pulled up plants as well as weeds. So now I *know* I'm right. Thank you, dear Raymond, for bringing me here. I wanted to see the place for myself.'

She and Raymond both looked up at the outrageous pile of Greenshaw's Folly.

A cough made them turn. A handsome young man was also looking at the house.

'Plaguey big place,' he said. 'Too big for nowadays – or so they say. I dunno about that. If I won a football pool and made a lot of money, that's the kind of house I'd like to build.'

He smiled bashfully at them.

'Reckon I can say so now – that there house was built by my great-grandfather,' said Alfred Pollock. 'And a fine house it is, for all they call it Greenshaw's Folly!'

The Dressmaker's Doll

'The Dressmaker's Doll' was first published in
Woman's Journal, December 1958.

The doll lay in the big velvet-covered chair. There was not much light
in the room; the London skies were dark. In the gentle, greyish-green
gloom, the sage-green coverings and the curtains and the rugs all blended
with each other. The doll blended, too. She lay long and limp and sprawled
in her green-velvet clothes and her velvet cap and the painted mask of
her face. She was the Puppet Doll, the whim of Rich Women, the doll
who lolls beside the telephone, or among the cushions of the divan. She
sprawled there, eternally limp and yet strangely alive. She looked a deca-
dent product of the twentieth century.

Sybil Fox, hurrying in with some patterns and a sketch, looked at the
doll with a faint feeling of surprise and bewilderment. She wondered –
but whatever she wondered did not get to the front of her mind. Instead,
she thought to herself, 'Now, what's happened to the pattern of the blue
velvet? Wherever have I put it? I'm sure I had it here just now.' She went
out on the landing and called up to the workroom.

'Elspeth, Elspeth, have you the blue pattern up there? Mrs Fellows-
Brown will be here any minute now.'

She went in again, switching on the lights. Again she glanced at the
doll. 'Now where on earth – ah, there it is.' She picked the pattern up
from where it had fallen from her hand. There was the usual creak outside
on the landing as the elevator came to a halt and in a minute or two Mrs
Fellows-Brown, accompanied by her Pekinese, came puffing into the
room rather like a fussy local train arriving at a wayside station.

'It's going to pour,' she said, 'simply *pour*!'

She threw off her gloves and a fur. Alicia Coombe came in. She didn't
always come in nowadays, only when special customers arrived, and Mrs
Fellows-Brown was such a customer.

Elspeth, the forewoman of the workroom, came down with the frock and Sybil pulled it over Mrs Fellows-Brown's head.

'There,' she said, 'I think it's good. Yes, it's definitely a success.'

Mrs Fellows-Brown turned sideways and looked in the mirror.

'I must say,' she said, 'your clothes do *do* something to my behind.'

'You're much thinner than you were three months ago,' Sybil assured her.

'I'm really not,' said Mrs Fellows-Brown, 'though I must say I *look* it in this. There's something about the way you cut, it really does minimize my behind. I almost look as though I hadn't got one – I mean only the usual kind that most people have.' She sighed and gingerly smoothed the troublesome portion of her anatomy. 'It's always been a bit of a trial to me,' she said. 'Of course, for years I could pull it in, you know, by sticking out my front. Well, I can't do that any longer because I've got a stomach now as well as a behind. And I mean – well, you can't pull it in both ways, can you?'

Alicia Coombe said, 'You should see some of my customers!'

Mrs Fellows-Brown experimented to and fro.

'A stomach is worse than a behind,' she said. 'It shows more. Or perhaps you think it does, because, I mean, when you're talking to people you're facing them and that's the moment they can't see your behind but they can notice your stomach. Anyway, I've made it a rule to pull in my stomach and let my behind look after itself.' She craned her neck round still farther, then said suddenly, 'Oh, that doll of yours! She gives me the creeps. How long have you had her?'

Sybil glanced uncertainly at Alicia Coombe, who looked puzzled but vaguely distressed.

'I don't know exactly . . . some time I think – I never *can* remember things. It's awful nowadays – I simply *cannot* remember. Sybil, how long have we had her?'

Sybil said shortly, 'I don't know.'

'Well,' said Mrs Fellows-Brown, 'she gives *me* the creeps. Uncanny! She looks, you know, as though she was watching us all, and perhaps laughing in that velvet sleeve of hers. I'd get rid of her if I were you.' She gave a little shiver, then she plunged once more into dressmaking details. Should she or should she not have the sleeves an inch shorter? And what about the length? When all these important points were settled satisfactorily, Mrs Fellows-Brown resumed her own garments and prepared to leave. As she passed the doll, she turned her head again.

'No,' she said, 'I *don't* like that doll. She looks too much as though she *belonged* here. It isn't healthy.'

'Now what did she mean by that?' demanded Sybil, as Mrs Fellows-Brown departed down the stairs.

Before Alicia Coombe could answer, Mrs Fellows-Brown returned, poking her head round the door.

'Good gracious, I forgot all about Fou-Ling. Where are you, ducksie? Well, I never!'

She stared and the other two women stared, too. The Pekinese was sitting by the green-velvet chair, staring up at the limp doll sprawled on it. There was no expression, either of pleasure or resentment, on his small, pop-eyed face. He was merely looking.

'Come along, mum's darling,' said Mrs Fellows-Brown.

Mum's darling paid no attention whatever.

'He gets more disobedient every day,' said Mrs Fellows-Brown, with the air of one cataloguing a virtue. 'Come *on*, Fou-Ling. Dindins. Luffly liver.'

Fou-Ling turned his head about an inch and a half towards his mistress, then with disdain resumed his appraisal of the doll.

'She's certainly made an impression on him,' said Mrs Fellows-Brown. 'I don't think he's ever noticed her before. *I* haven't either. Was she here last time I came?'

The other two women looked at each other. Sybil now had a frown on her face, and Alicia Coombe said, wrinkling up her forehead, 'I told you – I simply can't remember anything nowadays. How long *have* we had her, Sybil?'

'Where did she come from?' demanded Mrs Fellows-Brown. 'Did you buy her?'

'Oh no.' Somehow Alicia Coombe was shocked at the idea. 'Oh *no*. I suppose – I suppose someone gave her to me.' She shook her head. 'Maddening!' she exclaimed. 'Absolutely maddening, when everything goes out of your head the very moment after it's happened.'

'Now don't be stupid, Fou-Ling,' said Mrs Fellows-Brown sharply. 'Come on. I'll have to pick you up.'

She picked him up. Fou-Ling uttered a short bark of agonized protest. They went out of the room with Fou-Ling's pop-eyed face turned over his fluffy shoulder, still staring with enormous attention at the doll on the chair . . .

'That there doll,' said Mrs Groves, 'fair gives me the creeps, it does.'

Mrs Groves was the cleaner. She had just finished a crablike progress backwards along the floor. Now she was standing up and working slowly round the room with a duster.

'Funny thing,' said Mrs Groves, 'never noticed it really until yesterday. And then it hit me all of a sudden, as you might say.'

'You don't like it?' asked Sybil.

'I tell you, Mrs Fox, it gives me the creeps,' said the cleaning woman.

'It ain't natural, if you know what I mean. All those long hanging legs and the way she's slouched down there and the cunning look she has in her eye. It doesn't look healthy, that's what I say.'

'You've never said anything about her before,' said Sybil.

'I tell you, I never noticed her – not till this morning . . . Of course I know she's been here some time but –' She stopped and a puzzled expression flitted across her face. 'Sort of thing you might dream of at night,' she said, and gathering up various cleaning implements she departed from the fitting-room and walked across the landing to the room on the other side.

Sybil stared at the relaxed doll. An expression of bewilderment was growing on her face. Alicia Coombe entered and Sybil turned sharply.

'Miss Coombe, how long *have* you had this creature?'

'What, the doll? My dear, you know I can't remember things. Yesterday – why, it's too silly! – I was going out to that lecture and I hadn't gone halfway down the street when I suddenly found I couldn't remember where I was going. I thought and I thought. Finally I told myself it *must* be Fortnums. I knew there was something I wanted to get at Fortnums. Well, you won't believe me, it wasn't till I actually got home and was having some tea that I remembered about the lecture. Of course, I've always heard that people go gaga as they get on in life, but it's happening to me much too fast. I've forgotten now where I've put my handbag – and my spectacles, too. Where did I put those spectacles? I had them just now – I was reading something in *The Times*.'

'The spectacles are on the mantelpiece here,' said Sybil, handing them to her. 'How did you get the doll? Who gave her to you?'

'That's a blank, too,' said Alicia Coombe. '*Somebody* gave her to me or sent her to me, I suppose . . . However, she does seem to match the room very well, doesn't she?'

'Rather too well, I think,' said Sybil. 'Funny thing is, *I* can't remember when I first noticed her here.'

'Now don't you get the same way as I am,' Alicia Coombe admonished her. 'After all, you're young still.'

'But really, Miss Coombe, I don't remember. I mean, I looked at her yesterday and thought there was something – well, Mrs Groves is quite right – something creepy about her. And then I thought I'd already thought so, and then I tried to remember when I first thought so, and – well, I just couldn't remember anything! In a way, it was as if I'd never seen her before – only it didn't feel like that. It felt as though she'd been here a long time but I'd only just noticed her.'

'Perhaps she flew in through the window one day on a broomstick,' said Alicia Coombe. 'Anyway, she belongs here now all right.' She looked round. 'You could hardly imagine the room without her, could you?'

'No,' said Sybil, with a slight shiver, 'but I rather wish I could.'

'Could what?'

'Imagine the room without her.'

'Are we all going barmy about this doll?' demanded Alicia Coombe impatiently. 'What's wrong with the poor thing? Looks like a decayed cabbage to me, but perhaps,' she added, 'that's because I haven't got spectacles on.' She put them on her nose and looked firmly at the doll. 'Yes,' she said, 'I see what you mean. She *is* a little creepy . . . Sad-looking but – well, sly and rather determined, too.'

'Funny,' said Sybil, 'Mrs Fellows-Brown taking such a violent dislike to her.'

'She's one who never minds speaking her mind,' said Alicia Coombe.

'But it's odd,' persisted Sybil, 'that this doll should make such an impression on her.'

'Well, people do take dislikes very suddenly sometimes.'

'Perhaps,' said Sybil with a little laugh, 'that doll never *was* here until yesterday . . . Perhaps she just – flew in through the window, as you say, and settled herself here.'

'No,' said Alicia Coombe, 'I'm sure she's been here some time. Perhaps she only became visible yesterday.'

'That's what I feel, too,' said Sybil, 'that she's been here some time . . . but all the same I *don't* remember really seeing her till yesterday.'

'Now, dear,' said Alicia Coombe briskly, 'do stop it. You're making me feel quite peculiar with shivers running up and down my spine. You're not going to work up a great deal of supernatural hoo-hah about that creature, are you?' She picked up the doll, shook it out, rearranged its shoulders, and sat it down again on another chair. Immediately the doll flopped slightly and relaxed.

'It's not a bit lifelike,' said Alicia Coombe, staring at the doll. 'And yet, in a funny way, she does seem alive, doesn't she?'

'Oo, it did give me a turn,' said Mrs Groves, as she went round the showroom, dusting. 'Such a turn as I hardly like to go into the fitting-room any more.'

'What's given you a turn?' demanded Miss Coombe who was sitting at a writing-table in the corner, busy with various accounts. 'This woman,' she added more for her own benefit than that of Mrs Groves, 'thinks she can have two evening dresses, three cocktail dresses, and a suit every year without ever paying me a penny for them! Really, some people!'

'It's that doll,' said Mrs Groves.

'What, our doll again?'

'Yes, sitting up there at the desk, like a human. Oo, it didn't half give me a turn!'

'What are you talking about?'

Alicia Coombe got up, strode across the room, across the landing outside, and into the room opposite – the fitting-room. There was a small Sheraton desk in one corner of it, and there, sitting in a chair drawn up to it, her long floppy arms on the desk, sat the doll.

'Sombody seems to have been having fun,' said Alicia Coombe. 'Fancy sitting her up like that. Really, she looks quite natural.'

Sybil Fox came down the stairs at this moment, carrying a dress that was to be tried on that morning.

'Come here, Sybil. Look at our doll sitting at my private desk and writing letters now.'

The two women looked.

'Really,' said Alicia Coombe, 'it's too ridiculous! I wonder who propped her up there. Did you?'

'No, I didn't,' said Sybil. 'It must have been one of the girls from upstairs.'

'A silly sort of joke, really,' said Alicia Coombe. She picked up the doll from the desk and threw her back on the sofa.

Sybil laid the dress over a chair carefully, then she went out and up the stairs to the workroom.

'You know the doll,' she said, 'the velvet doll in Miss Coombe's room downstairs – in the fitting room?'

The forewoman and three girls looked up.

'Yes, miss, of course we know.'

'Who sat her up at the desk this morning for a joke?'

The three girls looked at her, then Elspeth, the forewoman, said, 'Sat her up at the desk? *I* didn't.'

'Nor did I,' said one of the girls. 'Did you, Marlene?' Marlene shook her head.

'This your bit of fun, Elspeth?'

'No, indeed,' said Elspeth, a stern woman who looked as though her mouth should always be filled with pins. 'I've more to do than going about playing with dolls and sitting them up at desks.'

'Look here,' said Sybil, and to her surprise her voice shook slightly. 'It was – it was quite a good joke, only I'd just like to know who did it.'

The three girls bristled.

'We've told you, Mrs Fox. None of us did it, did we, Marlene?'

'I didn't,' said Marlene, 'and if Nellie and Margaret say they didn't, well then, none of us did.'

'You've heard what *I* had to say,' said Elspeth. 'What's this all about anyway, Mrs Fox?'

'Perhaps it was Mrs Groves?' said Marlene.

Sybil shook her head. 'It wouldn't be Mrs Groves. It gave *her* quite a turn.'

'I'll come down and see for myself,' said Elspeth.

'She's not there now,' said Sybil. 'Miss Coombe took her away from the desk and threw her back on the sofa. Well –' she paused – 'what I mean is, someone must have stuck her up there in the chair at the writing-desk – thinking it was funny. I suppose. And – and I don't see why they won't say so.'

'I've told you twice, Mrs Fox,' said Margaret. 'I don't see why you should go on accusing us of telling lies. None of us would do a silly thing like that.'

'I'm sorry,' said Sybil, 'I didn't mean to upset you. But – but who else could possibly have done it?'

'Perhaps she got up and walked there herself,' said Marlene, and giggled.

For some reason Sybil didn't like the suggestion.

'Oh, it's all a lot of nonsense, anyway,' she said, and went down the stairs again.

Alicia Coombe was humming quite cheerfully. She looked round the room.

'I've lost my spectacles again,' she said, 'but it doesn't really matter. I don't want to see anything this moment. The trouble is, of course, when you're as blind as I am, that when you have lost your spectacles, unless you've got another pair to put on and find them with, well, then you can't find them because you can't see to find them.'

'I'll look round for you,' said Sybil. 'You had them just now.'

'I went into the other room when you went upstairs. I expect I took them back in there.'

She went across to the other room.

'It's such a bother,' said Alicia Coombe. 'I want to get on with these accounts. How can I if I haven't my spectacles?'

'I'll go up and get your second pair from the bedroom,' said Sybil.

'I haven't a second pair at present,' said Alicia Coombe.

'Why, what's happened to them?'

'Well, I think I left them yesterday when I was out at lunch. I've rung up there, and I've rung up the two shops I went into, too.'

'Oh, dear,' said Sybil, 'you'll have to get *three* pairs, I suppose.'

'If I had three pairs of spectacles,' said Alicia Coombe, 'I should spend my whole life looking for one or the other of them. I really think it's best to have only *one*. Then you've *got* to look till you find it.'

'Well, they must be somewhere,' said Sybil. 'You haven't been out of these two rooms. They're cetainly not here, so you must have laid them down in the fitting-room.'

She went back, walking round, looking quite closely. Finally, as a last idea, she took up the doll from the sofa.

'I've got them,' she called.

'Oh, where were they, Sybil?'

'Under our precious doll. I suppose you must have thrown them down when you put her back on the sofa.'

'I didn't. I'm sure I didn't.'

'Oh,' said Sybil with exasperation. 'Then I suppose the doll took them and was hiding them from you!'

'Really, you know,' said Alicia, looking thoughtfully at the doll, 'I wouldn't put it past her. She looks very intelligent, don't you think, Sybil?'

'I don't think I like her face,' said Sybil. 'She looks as though she knew something that we didn't.'

'You don't think she looks sort of sad and sweet?' said Alicia Coombe pleadingly, but without conviction.

'I don't think she's in the least sweet,' said Sybil.

'No . . . perhaps you're right . . . Oh, well, let's get on with things. Lady Lee will be here in another ten minutes. I just want to get these invoices done and posted.'

'Mrs Fox. Mrs Fox?'

'Yes, Margaret?' said Sybil. 'What is it?'

Sybil was busy leaning over a table, cutting a piece of satin material.

'Oh, Mrs Fox, it's that doll again. I took down the brown dress like you said, and there's that doll sitting up at the desk again. And it wasn't me – it wasn't any of us. Please, Mrs Fox, we really wouldn't do such a thing.'

Sybil's scissors slid a little.

'There,' she said angrily, 'look what you've made me do. Oh, well, it'll be all right, I suppose. Now, what's this about the doll?'

'She's sitting at the desk again.'

Sybil went down and walked into the fitting-room. The doll was sitting at the desk exactly as she had sat there before.

'You're very determined, aren't you?' said Sybil, speaking to the doll. She picked her up unceremoniously and put her back on the sofa.

'That's your place, my girl,' she said. 'You stay there.'

She walked across to the other room.

'Miss Coombe.'

'Yes, Sybil?'

'Somebody *is* having a game with us, you know. That doll was sitting at the desk again.'

'Who do you think it is?'

'It must be one of those three upstairs,' said Sybil. 'Thinks it's funny, I suppose. Of course they all swear to high heaven it wasn't them.'

'Who do you think it is – Margaret?'

'No, I don't think it's Margaret. She looked quite queer when she came in and told me. I expect it's that giggling Marlene.'

'Anyway, it's a very silly thing to do.'

'Of course it is – idiotic,' said Sybil. 'However,' she added grimly, 'I'm going to put a stop to it.'

'What are you going to do?'

'You'll see,' said Sybil.

That night when she left, she locked the fitting-room from the outside.

'I'm locking this door,' she said, 'and I'm taking the key with me.'

'Oh, I see,' said Alicia Coombe, with a faint air of amusement. 'You're beginning to think it's me, are you? You think I'm so absent-minded that I go in there and think I'll write at the desk, but instead I pick the doll up and put her there to write for me. Is that the idea? And then I forget all about it?'

'Well, it's a possibility,' Sybil admitted. 'Anyway, I'm going to be quite sure that no silly practical joke is played tonight.'

The following morning, her lips set grimly, the first thing Sybil did on arrival was to unlock the door of the fitting-room and march in. Mrs Groves, with an aggrieved expression and mop and duster in hand, had been waiting on the landing.

'*Now* we'll see!' said Sybil.

Then she drew back with a slight gasp.

The doll was sitting at the desk.

'Coo!' said Mrs Groves behind her. 'It's uncanny! That's what it is. Oh, there, Mrs Fox, you look quite pale, as though you've come over queer. You need a little drop of something. Has Miss Coombe got a drop upstairs, do you know?'

'I'm quite all right,' said Sybil.

She walked over to the doll, lifted her carefully, and crossed the room with her.

'Somebody's been playing a trick on you again,' said Mrs Groves.

'I don't see how they could have played a trick on me this time,' said Sybil slowly. 'I locked that door last night. You know yourself that no one could get in.'

'Somebody's got another key, maybe,' said Mrs Groves helpfully.

'I don't think so,' said Sybil. 'We've never bothered to lock this door before. It's one of those old-fashioned keys and there's only one of them.'

'Perhaps the other key fits it – the one to the door opposite.'

In due course they tried all the keys in the shop, but none fitted the door of the fitting-room.

'It *is* odd, Miss Coombe,' said Sybil later, as they were having lunch together.

Alicia Coombe was looking rather pleased.

'My dear,' she said. 'I think it's simply extraordinary. I think we ought to write to the psychical research people about it. You know, they might send an investigator – a medium or someone – to see if there's anything peculiar about the room.'

'You don't seem to mind at all,' said Sybil.

'Well, I rather enjoy it in a way,' said Alicia Coombe. 'I mean, at my age, it's rather fun when things happen! All the same – no,' she added thoughtfully. 'I don't think I do quite like it. I mean, that doll's getting rather above herself, isn't she?'

On that evening Sybil and Alicia Coombe locked the door once more on the outside.

'I still think,' said Sybil, 'that somebody might be playing a practical joke, though, really, I don't see why . . .'

'Do you think she'll be at the desk again tomorrow morning?' demanded Alicia.

'Yes,' said Sybil, 'I do.'

But they were wrong. The doll was not at the desk. Instead, she was on the window sill, looking out into the street. And again there was an extraordinary naturalness about her position.

'It's all frightfully silly, isn't it?' said Alicia Coombe, as they were snatching a quick cup of tea that afternoon. By common consent they were not having it in the fitting-room, as they usually did, but in Alicia Coombe's own room opposite.

'Silly in what way?'

'Well, I mean, there's nothing you can get hold of. Just a doll that's always in a different place.'

As day followed day it seemed a more and more apt observation. It was not only at night that the doll now moved. At any moment when they came into the fitting-room, after they had been absent even a few minutes, they might find the doll in a different place. They could have left her on the sofa and find her on a chair. Then she'd be on a different chair. Some-times she'd be in the window seat, sometimes at the desk again.

'She just moves about as she likes,' said Alicia Coombe. 'And I think, Sybil, I *think* it's amusing her.'

The two women stood looking down at the inert sprawling figure in its limp, soft velvet, with its painted silk face.

'Some old bits of velvet and silk and a lick of paint, that's all it is,' said Alicia Coombe. Her voice was strained. 'I suppose, you know, we could – er – we could dispose of her.'

'What do you mean, dispose of her?' asked Sybil. Her voice sounded almost shocked.

'Well,' said Alicia Coombe, 'we could put her in the fire, if there was a fire. Burn her, I mean, like a witch . . . Or of course,' she added matter-of-factly, 'we could just put her in the dustbin.'

'I don't think that would do,' said Sybil. 'Somebody would probably take her out of the dustbin and bring her back to us.'

'Or we could send her somewhere,' said Alicia Coombe. 'You know, to one of those societies who are always writing and asking for something – for a sale or a bazaar. I think that's the best idea.'

'I don't know . . .' said Sybil. 'I'd be almost afraid to do that.'

'Afraid?'

'Well, I think she'd come back,' said Sybil.

'You mean, she'd come back *here*?'

'Yes.'

'Like a homing pigeon?'

'Yes, that's what I mean.'

'I suppose we're not going off our heads, are we?' said Alicia Coombe. 'Perhaps I've really gone gaga and perhaps you're just humouring me, is that it?'

'No,' said Sybil. 'But I've got a nasty frightening feeling – a horrid feeling that she's too strong for us.'

'What? That mess of rags?'

'Yes, that horrible limp mess of rags. Because, you see, she's so determined.'

'Determined?'

'To have her own way! I mean, this is *her* room now!'

'Yes,' said Alicia Coombe, looking round, 'it is, isn't it? Of course, it always was, when you come to think of it – the colours and everything . . . I thought she fitted in here, but it's the room that fits her. I must say,' added the dressmaker, with a touch of briskness in her voice, 'it's rather absurd when a doll comes and takes possession of things like this. You know, Mrs Groves won't come in here any longer and clean.'

'Does she say she's frightened of the doll?'

'No. She just makes excuses of some kind or other.' Then Alicia added with a hint of panic, 'What are we going to do, Sybil? It's getting me down, you know. I haven't been able to design anything for weeks.'

'I can't keep my mind on cutting out properly,' Sybil confessed. 'I make all sorts of silly mistakes. Perhaps,' she said uncertainly, 'your idea of writing to the psychical research people might do some good.'

'Just make us look like a couple of fools,' said Alicia Coombe. 'I didn't seriously mean it. No, I suppose we'll just have to go on until –'

'Until what?'

'Oh, I don't know,' said Alicia, and she laughed uncertainly.

On the following day Sybil, when she arrived, found the door of the fitting-room locked.

'Miss Coombe, have you got the key? Did you lock this last night?'

'Yes,' said Alicia Coombe, 'I locked it and it's going to stay locked.'

'What do you mean?'

'I just mean I've given up the room. The doll can have it. We don't need two rooms. We can fit in here.'

'But it's your own private sitting-room.'

'Well, I don't want it any more. I've got a very nice bedroom. I can make a bed-sitting room out of that, can't I?'

'Do you mean you're really not going into that fitting-room ever again?' said Sybil incredulously.

'That's exactly what I mean.'

'But – what about cleaning? It'll get in a terrible state.'

'Let it!' said Alicia Coombe. 'If this place is suffering from some kind of possession by a doll, all right – let her keep possession. And clean the room herself.' And she added, 'She hates us, you know.'

'What do you mean?' said Sybil. 'The doll *hates* us?'

'Yes,' said Alicia. 'Didn't you know? You must have known. You must have seen it when you looked at her.'

'Yes,' said Sybil thoughtfully, 'I suppose I did. I suppose I felt that all along – that she hated us and wanted to get us out of there.'

'She's a malicious little thing,' said Alicia Coombe. 'Anyway, she ought to be satisfied now.'

Things went on rather more peacefully after that. Alicia Coombe announced to her staff that she was giving up the use of the fitting-room for the present – it made too many rooms to dust and clean, she explained.

But it hardly helped her to overhear one of the work girls saying to another on the evening of the same day, 'She really is batty, Miss Coombe is now. I always thought she was a bit queer – the way she lost things and forgot things. But it's really beyond anything now, isn't it? She's got a sort of thing about that doll downstairs.'

'Ooo, you don't think she'll go really bats, do you?' said the other girl. 'That she might knife us or something?'

They passed, chattering, and Alicia sat up indignantly in her chair. Going bats indeed! Then she added ruefully, to herself, 'I suppose, if it wasn't for Sybil, I should think myself that I was going bats. But with me and Sybil and Mrs Groves too, well, it does look as though there was *something* in it. But what I don't see is, how is it going to end?'

Three weeks later, Sybil said to Alicia Coombe, 'We've got to go into that room *sometimes*.'

'Why?'

'Well, I mean, it must be in a filthy state. Moths will be getting into things, and all that. We ought just to dust and sweep it and then lock it up again.'

'I'd much rather keep it shut up and not go back in there,' said Alicia Coombe.

Sybil said, 'Really, you know, you're even more superstitious than I am.'

'I suppose I am,' said Alicia Coombe. 'I was much more ready to believe in all this than you were, but to begin with, you know – I – well, I found it exciting in an odd sort of way. I don't know. I'm just scared, and I'd rather not go into that room again.'

'Well, I want to,' said Sybil, 'and I'm going to.'

'You know what's the matter with you?' said Alicia Coombe. 'You're simply curious, that's all.'

'All right, then I'm curious. I want to see what the doll's done.'

'I still think it's much better to leave her alone,' said Alicia. 'Now we've got out of that room, she's satisfied. You'd better leave her satisfied.' She gave an exasperated sigh. 'What nonsense we are talking!'

'Yes. I know we're talking nonsense, but if you tell me of any way of *not* talking nonsense – come on, now, give me the key.'

'All right, all right.'

'I believe you're afraid I'll let her out or something. I should think she was the kind that could pass through doors or windows.'

Sybil unlocked the door and went in.

'How terribly odd,' she said.

'What's odd?' said Alicia Coombe, peering over her shoulder.

'The room hardly seems dusty at all, does it? You'd think, after being shut up all this time –'

'Yes, it is odd.'

'There she is,' said Sybil.

The doll was on the sofa. She was not lying in her usual limp position. She was sitting upright, a cushion behind her back. She had the air of the mistress of the house, waiting to receive people.

'Well,' said Alicia Coombe, 'she seems at home all right, doesn't she? I almost feel I ought to apologize for coming in.'

'Let's go,' said Sybil.

She backed out; pulling the door to, and locked it again.

The two women gazed at each other.

'I wish I knew,' said Alicia Coombe, 'why it scares us so much . . .'

'My goodness, who wouldn't be scared?'

'Well, I mean, what *happens*, after all? It's nothing really – just a kind of puppet that gets moved around the room. I expect it isn't the puppet itself – it's a poltergeist.'

'Now that *is* a good idea.'

'Yes, but I don't really believe it. I think it's – it's that doll.'

'Are you *sure* you don't know where she really came from?'

'I haven't the faintest idea,' said Alicia. 'And the more I think of it the more I'm perfectly certain that I didn't buy her, and that nobody gave her to me. I think she – well, she just came.'

'Do you think she'll – ever go?'

'Really,' said Alicia, 'I don't see why she should . . . She's got all she wants.'

But it seemed that the doll had not got all she wanted. The next day, when Sybil went into the showroom, she drew in her breath with a sudden gasp. Then she called up the stairs.

'Miss Coombe, Miss Coombe, come down here.'

'What's the matter?'

Alicia Coombe, who had got up late, came down the stairs, hobbling a little precariously for she had rheumatism in her right knee.

'What is the matter with you, Sybil?'

'Look. Look what's happened now.'

They stood in the doorway of the showroom. Sitting on a sofa, sprawled easily over the arm of it, was the doll.

'She's got out,' said Sybil, '*She's got out of that room!* She wants this room as well.'

Alicia Coombe sat down by the door. 'In the end,' she said, 'I suppose she'll want the whole shop.'

'She might,' said Sybil.

'You nasty, sly, malicious brute,' said Alicia, addressing the doll. 'Why do you want to come and pester us so? We don't want you.'

It seemed to her, and to Sybil too, that the doll moved very slightly. It was as though its limbs relaxed still further. A long limp arm was lying on the arm of the sofa and the half-hidden face looked as if it were peering from under the arm. And it was a sly, malicious look.

'Horrible creature,' said Alicia. 'I can't bear it! I can't bear it any longer.'

Suddenly, taking Sybil completely by surprise, she dashed across the room, picked up the doll, ran to the window, opened it, and flung the doll out into the street. There was a gasp and a half cry of fear from Sybil.

'Oh, Alicia, you shouldn't have done that! I'm sure you shouldn't have done that!'

'I had to do something,' said Alicia Coombe. 'I just couldn't stand it any more.'

Sybil joined her at the window. Down below on the pavement the doll lay, loose-limbed, face down.

'You've *killed* her,' said Sybil.

'Don't be absurd . . . How can I kill something that's made of velvet and silk, bits and pieces. It's not real.'

'It's horribly real,' said Sybil.

Alicia caught her breath.

'Good heavens. That child –'

A small ragged girl was standing over the doll on the pavement. She looked up and down the street – a street that was not unduly crowded at this time of the morning though there was some automobile traffic; then, as though satisfied, the child bent, picked up the doll, and ran across the street.

'Stop, stop!' called Alicia.

She turned to Sybil.

'That child mustn't take the doll. She *mustn't*! That doll is dangerous – it's evil. We've got to stop her.'

It was not they who stopped her. It was the traffic. At that moment three taxis came down one way and two tradesmen's vans in the other direction. The child was marooned on an island in the middle of the road. Sybil rushed down the stairs, Alicia Coombe following her. Dodging between a tradesman's van and a private car, Sybil, with Alicia Coombe directly behind her, arrived on the island before the child could get through the traffic on the opposite side.

'You can't take that doll,' said Alicia Coombe. 'Give her back to me.'

The child looked at her. She was a skinny little girl about eight years old, with a slight squint. Her face was defiant.

'Why should I give 'er to you?' she said. 'Pitched her out of the window, you did – I saw you. If you pushed her out of the window you don't want her, so now she's mine.'

'I'll buy you another doll,' said Alicia frantically. 'We'll go to a toy shop – anywhere you like – and I'll buy you the best doll we can find. But give me back this one.'

'Shan't,' said the child.

Her arms went protectingly round the velvet doll.

'You *must* give her back,' said Sybil. 'She isn't yours.'

She stretched out to take the doll from the child and at that moment the child stamped her foot, turned, and screamed at them.

'Shan't! Shan't! Shan't! She's my very own. I love her. *You* don't love her. You hate her. If you didn't hate her you wouldn't have pushed her out of the window. I love her, I tell you, and that's what she wants. She *wants* to be loved.'

And then like an eel, sliding through the vehicles, the child ran across the street, down an alleyway, and out of sight before the two older women could decide to dodge the cars and follow.

'She's gone,' said Alicia.

'She said the doll wanted to be loved,' said Sybil.

'Perhaps,' said Alicia, 'perhaps that's what she wanted all along . . . to be loved . . .'

In the middle of the London traffic the two frightened women stared at each other.

Appendix
Short Story Chronology

This table aims to present all Agatha Christie's short stories published between 1923 and 1971, starting with her series of Hercule Poirot cases for *The Sketch* magazine and ending with her last contributions to the genre, the stories for children in *Star Over Bethlehem* and, finally, *The Harlequin Tea Set*. It should be noted that a number of stories that first appeared in weekly or monthly magazines were subsequently re-worked in book form, where they became simply chapters in a larger work, no longer independent short stories. In *Partners in Crime*, for example, some short stories were subdivided into smaller chapters, while 13 separate stories were re-worked into the episodic novel, *The Big Four*, and are not generally regarded as individual stories in their own right. There are also a handful of stories which were rewritten so substantially that they appear separately in different books, for example *The Mystery of the Baghdad/Spanish Chest*. This all makes counting up the stories very difficult indeed!

However, excluding *The Big Four* (for the reason stated above) and including the published variants, there are a total of 159 stories published in book form in the UK:

Hercule Poirot – 56
Miss Marple – 20
Tommy & Tuppence – 14
Harley Quin – 14
Parker Pyne – 14
Non-series stories – 35
Children's stories – 6

Titles are listed in order of traced first publication date. Actual first publication details are given where known. It is generally assumed that practically everything Christie wrote – novels, short stories, poetry – appeared first in a magazine or newspaper, prior to the hardback edition. However, despite exhaustive research, it has not always been possible to trace a magazine appearance for every story, in which case the first hardback publication is given.

Whilst most stories first appeared in British magazines or newspapers, a number premiered in America, and these are duly noted. Where both 'firsts' were close together, or where a subsequent publication gave rise to an interesting variation in title for the story, both are given.

KARL PIKE
2008

DATE	CHARACTER	STORY (BOOK TITLE)	PUBLICATION	PUBLISHED AS (IF DIFFERENT)	FIRST BOOK APPEARANCE
1923					
Agatha Christie's first batch of 12 published short stories appeared as a series: 'The Grey Cells of M. Poirot I:…					
7 Mar	Poirot	The Affair at the Victory Ball	UK: The Sketch, 1571		Poirot's Early Cases (UK)
Sep			USA: Blue Book Magazine, Vol. 37, No. 6		The Under Dog (US)
14 Mar	Poirot	The Jewel Robbery at the Grand Metropolitan	UK: The Sketch, 1572	The Curious Disappearance of the Opalsen Pearls	Poirot Investigates
Oct			USA: Blue Book Magazine, Vol. 37, No. 6	Mrs Opalsen's Pearls	
21 Mar	Poirot	The King of Clubs	UK: The Sketch, 1573	The Adventure of the King of Clubs	Poirot's Early Cases (UK)
Nov			USA: Blue Book Magazine, Vol. 38, No. 1		The Under Dog (US)
28 Mar	Poirot	The Disappearance of Mr Davenheim	UK: The Sketch, 1574		Poirot Investigates
Dec			USA: Blue Book Magazine, Vol. 38, No. 2	Mr Davenby Disappears	
4 Apr	Poirot	The Plymouth Express	UK: The Sketch, 1575	The Mystery of the Plymouth Express	Poirot's Early Cases (UK)
Jan 1924			USA: Blue Book Magazine, Vol. 38, No. 3	The Plymouth Express Affair	The Under Dog (US)

DATE	CHARACTER	STORY (BOOK TITLE)	PUBLICATION	PUBLISHED AS (IF DIFFERENT)	FIRST BOOK APPEARANCE
11 Apr	Poirot	The Adventure of the Western Star	UK: The Sketch, 1576		Poirot Investigates
Feb 1924			USA: Blue Book Magazine, Vol. 38, No. 4	The Western Star	
18 Apr	Poirot	The Tragedy at Marsdon Manor	UK: The Sketch, 1577		Poirot Investigates
Mar 1924			USA: Blue Book Magazine, Vol. 38, No. 5	The Marsdon Manor Tragedy	
25 Apr	Poirot	The Kidnapped Prime Minister	UK: The Sketch, 1578	The Kidnaped Prime Minister	Poirot Investigates
Jul 1924			USA: Blue Book Magazine, Vol. 39, No. 3		
2 May	Poirot	The Million Dollar Bond Robbery	UK: The Sketch, 1579		Poirot Investigates
Apr 1924			USA: Blue Book Magazine, Vol. 38, No. 6	The Great Bond Robbery	
9 May	Poirot	The Adventure of the Cheap Flat	UK: The Sketch, 1580		Poirot Investigates
May 1924			USA: Blue Book Magazine, Vol. 39, No. 1		
16 May	Poirot	The Mystery of Hunter's Lodge	UK: The Sketch, 1581	The Hunter's Lodge Case	Poirot Investigates
Jun 1924			USA: Blue Book Magazine, Vol. 39, No. 2		

DATE	CHARACTER	STORY (BOOK TITLE)	PUBLICATION	PUBLISHED AS (IF DIFFERENT)	FIRST BOOK APPEARANCE
23 May	Poirot	The Chocolate Box	UK: The Sketch, 1582	The Clue of the Chocolate Box	Poirot's Early Cases (UK)
Feb 1925			USA: Blue Book Magazine, Vol. 40, No. 4		Poirot Investigates (US edition only)
May		The Actress	The Novel Magazine, No. 218	A Trap for the Unwary	While the Light Lasts (UK) The Harlequin Tea Set (US)
...followed by 12 more stories – 'The Grey Cells of M. Poirot II.'					
26 Sep	Poirot	The Adventure of the Egyptian Tomb	UK: The Sketch, 1600		Poirot Investigates
Aug 1924			USA: Blue Book Magazine, Vol. 39, No. 4	The Egyptian Adventure	
3 Oct	Poirot	The Veiled Lady	UK: The Sketch, 1601	The Case of the Veiled Lady	Poirot's Early Cases (UK)
Mar 1925			USA: Blue Book Magazine, Vol. 40, No. 5		Poirot Investigates (US edition only)
10 Oct	Poirot	The Adventure of Johnny Waverly	UK: The Sketch, 1602	The Kidnapping of Johnnie Waverly	Poirot's Early Cases (UK)
Jun 1925			USA: Blue Book Magazine, Vol. 41, No. 2		Three Blind Mice (US)

DATE	CHARACTER	STORY (BOOK TITLE)	PUBLICATION	PUBLISHED AS (IF DIFFERENT)	FIRST BOOK APPEARANCE
17 Oct	Poirot	The Market Basing Mystery	UK: The Sketch, 1603		Poirot's Early Cases (UK)
May 1925			USA: Blue Book Magazine, Vol. 41, No. 1		The Under Dog (US)
24 Oct	Poirot	The Adventure of the Italian Nobleman	UK: The Sketch, 1604		Poirot Investigates
Dec 1924			USA: Blue Book Magazine, Vol. 40, No. 2	The Italian Nobleman	
31 Oct	Poirot	The Case of the Missing Will	UK: The Sketch, 1605		Poirot Investigates
Jan 1925			USA: Blue Book Magazine, Vol. 40, No. 3	The Missing Will	
7 Nov	Poirot	The Submarine Plans	UK: The Sketch, 1606	*Later expanded into*	Poirot's Early Cases (UK)
Jul 1925			USA: Blue Book Magazine, Vol. 41, No. 3	The Incredible Theft (1937)	The Under Dog (US)
14 Nov	Poirot	The Adventure of the Clapham Cook	UK: The Sketch, 1607		Poirot's Early Cases (UK)
Sep 1925			USA: Blue Book Magazine, Vol. 41, No. 5	The Clapham Cook	The Under Dog (US)
21 Nov	Poirot	The Lost Mine	UK: The Sketch, 1608		Poirot's Early Cases (UK)
Apr 1925			USA: Blue Book Magazine, Vol. 40, No. 6		Poirot Investigates (US edition only)
28 Nov	Poirot	The Cornish Mystery	UK: The Sketch, 1609		Poirot's Early Cases (UK)
Oct 1925			USA: Blue Book Magazine, Vol. 41, No. 6		The Under Dog (US)

DATE	CHARACTER	STORY (BOOK TITLE)	PUBLICATION	PUBLISHED AS (IF DIFFERENT)	FIRST BOOK APPEARANCE
5 Dec	Poirot	The Double Clue	UK: The Sketch, 1610		Poirot's Early Cases (UK)
Aug 1925			USA: Blue Book Magazine, Vol. 41, No. 4		Double Sin (US)
Dec	Poirot	The Adventure of the Christmas Pudding *A.k.a.* Christmas Adventure	UK: The Sketch, 1611	*Later expanded into* The Theft of the Royal Ruby (1960)	While the Light Lasts (UK)
12 Dec	Tommy & Tuppence	The Clergyman's Daughter/The Red House	Grand Magazine, No. 226	The First Wish	Partners in Crime
Christmas	Poirot	The Lemesurier Inheritance	UK: The Magpie	The Le Mesurier Inheritance	Poirot's Early Cases (UK)
Nov 1925			USA: Blue Book Magazine, Vol. 42, No. 1		The Under Dog (US)
1924					
This series of 12 stories was subsequently reworked by Agatha Christie into The Big Four (1927), and are therefore not considered to be independent stories. They are included here for the sake of completeness.					
2 Jan	Poirot	The Unexpected Guest	The Sketch, 1614		The Big Four
9 Jan	Poirot	The Adventure of the Dartmoor Bungalow	The Sketch, 1615		The Big Four
16 Jan	Poirot	The Lady on the Stairs	The Sketch, 1616		The Big Four

DATE	CHARACTER	STORY (BOOK TITLE)	PUBLICATION	PUBLISHED AS (IF DIFFERENT)	FIRST BOOK APPEARANCE
23 Jan	Poirot	The Radium Thieves	The Sketch, 1617		The Big Four
30 Jan	Poirot	In the House of the Enemy	The Sketch, 1618		The Big Four
6 Feb	Poirot	The Yellow Jasmine	The Sketch, 1619		The Big Four
13 Feb	Poirot	A Chess Problem	The Sketch, 1620	The Chess Problem	The Big Four
20 Feb	Poirot	The Baited Trap	The Sketch, 1621		The Big Four
27 Feb	Poirot	The Adventure of the Peroxide Blonde	The Sketch, 1622		The Big Four
5 Mar	Poirot	The Terrible Catastrophe	The Sketch, 1619		The Big Four
12 Mar	Poirot	The Dying Chinaman	The Sketch, 1624		The Big Four
19 Mar	Poirot	The Crag in the Dolomites	The Sketch, 1625		The Big Four
Feb		The Girl in the Train	Grand Magazine, No. 228		The Listerdale Mystery (UK) / The Golden Ball (US)
Mar	Mr Quin	The Coming of Mr Quin	Grand Magazine, No. 229	The Passing of Mr Quinn	The Mysterious Mr Quin
Apr		While the Light Lasts	Novel Magazine, No. 229		While the Light Lasts (UK) / The Harlequin Tea Set (US)

DATE	CHARACTER	STORY (BOOK TITLE)	PUBLICATION	PUBLISHED AS (IF DIFFERENT)	FIRST BOOK APPEARANCE
Jun		The Red Signal	Grand Magazine, No. 232		The Hound of Death (UK) The Witness for the Prosecution (US)
Jul		The Mystery of the Blue Jar	Grand Magazine, No. 233		The Hound of Death (UK) The Witness for the Prosecution (US)
Aug		Jane in Search of a Job	Grand Magazine, No. 234		The Listerdale Mystery (UK) The Golden Ball (US)
Aug	Poirot	Mr Eastwood's Adventure *A.k.a.* The Mystery of the Spanish Shawl	The Novel Magazine, No. 233	The Mystery of the Second Cucumber	The Listerdale Mystery (UK) The Witness for the Prosecution (US)
These next 12 stories were subsequently worked into the Tommy & Tuppence book, Partners in Crime (1929):					
24 Sep	Tommy & Tuppence	A Fairy in the Flat/A Pot of Tea	The Sketch, 1652	Publicity	Partners in Crime
1 Oct	Tommy & Tuppence	The Affair of the Pink Pearl	The Sketch, 1653		Partners in Crime
8 Oct	Tommy & Tuppence	Finessing the King/The Gentleman Dressed in Newspaper	The Sketch, 1654	Finessing the King	Partners in Crime

DATE	CHARACTER	STORY (BOOK TITLE)	PUBLICATION	PUBLISHED AS (IF DIFFERENT)	FIRST BOOK APPEARANCE
15 Oct	Tommy & Tuppence	The Case of the Missing Lady	The Sketch, 1655		Partners in Crime
22 Oct	Tommy & Tuppence	The Adventure of the Sinister Stranger	The Sketch, 1656		Partners in Crime
29 Oct	Tommy & Tuppence	The Sunningdale Mystery	The Sketch, 1657	The Sunninghall Mystery	Partners in Crime
5 Nov	Tommy & Tuppence	The House of Lurking Death	The Sketch, 1658		Partners in Crime
12 Nov	Tommy & Tuppence	The Ambassador's Boots	The Sketch, 1659	The Matter of the Ambassador's Boots	Partners in Crime
19 Nov	Tommy & Tuppence	The Crackler	The Sketch, 1660	The Affair of the Forged Notes	Partners in Crime
26 Nov	Tommy & Tuppence	Blindman's Buff	The Sketch, 1661	Blind Man's Buff	Partners in Crime
3 Dec	Tommy & Tuppence	The Man in the Mist	The Sketch, 1662		Partners in Crime
10 Dec	Tommy & Tuppence	The Man Who Was No.16	The Sketch, 1663	The Man Who Was Number Sixteen	Partners in Crime
Oct	Mr Quin	The Shadow on the Glass	Grand Magazine, No. 236		The Mysterious Mr Quin

DATE	CHARACTER	STORY (BOOK TITLE)	PUBLICATION	PUBLISHED AS (IF DIFFERENT)	FIRST BOOK APPEARANCE
Nov		Philomel Cottage	Grand Magazine, No. 237		The Listerdale Mystery (UK) The Witness for the Prosecution (US)
Dec		The Manhood of Edward Robinson	Grand Magazine, No. 238	The Day of His Dreams	The Listerdale Mystery (UK) The Golden Ball (US)
1925					
31 Jan		The Witness for the Prosecution	USA: Flynn's Weekly	Traitor Hands	The Hound of Death (UK) The Witness for the Prosecution (US)
Jun	Mr Quin	The Sign in the Sky	USA: The Police Magazine		The Mysterious Mr Quin
Jul			UK: Grand Magazine, No. 245	A Sign in the Sky	
Sep/Oct		Wireless *A.k.a.* Where There's a Will	Sunday Chronicle Annual 1925		The Hound of Death (UK) The Witness for the Prosecution (US)
Oct		Within a Wall	Royal Magazine, No. 324		While the Light Lasts (UK) The Harlequin Tea Set (US)

DATE	CHARACTER	STORY (BOOK TITLE)	PUBLICATION	PUBLISHED AS (IF DIFFERENT)	FIRST BOOK APPEARANCE
Nov	Mr Quin	At the 'Bells and Motley'	Grand Magazine, No. 249	A Man of Magic	The Mysterious Mr Quin
Dec		The Listerdale Mystery	Grand Magazine, No. 250	The Benevolent Butler	The Listerdale Mystery (UK)
					The Golden Ball (US)
Dec		The Fourth Man	Pearson's Magazine, No. 360		The Hound of Death (UK)
					The Witness for the Prosecution (US)
1926					
Jan		The House of Dreams	The Sovereign Magazine, Vol. 11, No. 74		While the Light Lasts (UK)
					The Harlequin Tea Set (US)
Feb		S.O.S.	Grand Magazine, No. 252		The Hound of Death (UK)
					The Witness for the Prosecution (US)
Mar		Magnolia Blossom	Royal Magazine, No. 329		Problem at Pollensa Bay (UK)
					The Golden Ball (US)
1 Apr	Poirot	The Under Dog	USA: Mystery Magazine, Vol. 8, No. 6		The Adventure of the Christmas Pudding (UK)
					The Under Dog (US)

DATE	CHARACTER	STORY (BOOK TITLE)	PUBLICATION	PUBLISHED AS (IF DIFFERENT)	FIRST BOOK APPEARANCE
Jul		The Lonely God	Royal Magazine, No. 333		While the Light Lasts (UK)
					The Harlequin Tea Set (US)
30 Jul		The Rajah's Emerald	Red Magazine		The Listerdale Mystery (UK)
					The Golden Ball (US)
Sep		Swan Song	Grand Magazine, No. 259		The Listerdale Mystery (UK)
					The Golden Ball (US)
30 Oct	Mr Quin	The Love Detectives	USA: Flynn's Weekly, Vol. 19, No. 3	At the Cross Roads	Problem at Pollensa Bay (UK)
Dec			UK: Storyteller, 236	The Magic of Mr Quin No. 1: At the Cross Roads	Three Blind Mice (US)
Nov		The Last Séance	USA: Ghost Stories magazine		The Hound of Death (UK)
Mar 1927			UK: The Sovereign Magazine, No. 87	The Stolen Ghost	Double Sin (US)
13 Nov	Mr Quin	The Soul of the Croupier	USA: Flynn's Weekly, Vol. 19, No. 5		The Mysterious Mr Quin
Jan 1927			UK: Storyteller magazine, No. 237	The Magic of Mr Quin No. 2: The Soul of the Croupier	

DATE	CHARACTER	STORY (BOOK TITLE)	PUBLICATION	PUBLISHED AS (IF DIFFERENT)	FIRST BOOK APPEARANCE
20 Nov	Mr Quin	The World's End	USA: Flynn's Weekly, Vol. 19, No.6	World's End	The Mysterious Mr Quin
Feb 1927			UK: Storyteller magazine, 238	The Magic of Mr Quin No. 3: The World's End	
4 Dec	Mr Quin	The Voice in the Dark	USA: Flynn's Weekly, Vol. 20, No. 2		The Mysterious Mr Quin
Mar 1927			UK: Storyteller magazine, 239	The Magic of Mr Quin No. 4	
1927					
Feb		The Edge	Pearson's Magazine, Vol. 63, No. 374		While the Light Lasts (UK) The Harlequin Tea Set (US)
Apr	Mr Quin	The Face of Helen	The Storyteller, No. 240	The Magic of Mr Quin No. 5	The Mysterious Mr Quin
May	Mr Quin	Harlequin's Lane	Storyteller, No. 241	The Magic of Mr Quin No. 6	The Mysterious Mr Quin
Dec	Poirot	The Enemy Strikes	USA: Blue Book, Vol. 46, No. 2	Part of the novel The Big Four	The Big Four
Dec	Miss Marple	The Tuesday Night Club	UK: Royal Magazine, No. 350		The Thirteen Problems (UK)
2 Jun 1928			USA: Detective Story Magazine	The Solving Six	The Tuesday Night Club (US)

DATE	CHARACTER	STORY (BOOK TITLE)	PUBLICATION	PUBLISHED AS (IF DIFFERENT)	FIRST BOOK APPEARANCE
1928					
Jan	Miss Marple	The Idol House of Astarte	UK: Royal Magazine, No. 351		The Thirteen Problems (UK)
9 Jun			USA: Detective Story Magazine	The Solving Six and the Evil Hour	The Tuesday Night Club (US)
Feb	Miss Marple	Ingots of Gold	UK: Royal Magazine, No. 352		The Thirteen Problems (UK)
16 Jun			USA: Detective Story Magazine	Solving Six and the Golden Grave	The Tuesday Night Club (US)
Mar	Miss Marple	The Blood-Stained Pavement	UK: Royal Magazine, No. 353		The Thirteen Problems (UK)
23 Jun			USA: Detective Story Magazine	Drip! Drip!	The Tuesday Night Club (US)
Apr	Miss Marple	Motive v. Opportunity	UK: Royal Magazine, No. 354		The Thirteen Problems (UK)
30 Jun			USA: Detective Story Magazine	Where's the Catch?	The Tuesday Night Club (US)
May	Miss Marple	The Thumb Mark of St. Peter	UK: Royal Magazine, No. 35	The Thumb-Mark of St. Peter	The Thirteen Problems (UK)
7 Jul			USA: Detective Story Magazine		The Tuesday Night Club (US)

DATE	CHARACTER	STORY (BOOK TITLE)	PUBLICATION	PUBLISHED AS (IF DIFFERENT)	FIRST BOOK APPEARANCE
11 Aug		A Fruitful Sunday	Daily Mail		Listerdale Mystery (UK)
					The Golden Ball (US)
23 Sep	Poirot	Double Sin	Sunday Dispatch	By Road or Rail	Poirot's Early Cases (UK)
					Double Sin (US)
1 Dec	Tommy & Tuppence	The Unbreakable Alibi	Holly Leaves No. 2880 (pub by Illustrated Sporting and Dramatic News)		Partners in Crime
20 Nov	Poirot	Wasps' Nest	Daily Mail, No. 10164	The Wasps' Nest	Poirot's Early Cases (UK)
					Double Sin (US)
1929					
Jan	Poirot	The Third Floor Flat	UK: Hutchinson's Story Magazine, Vol. 21, No. 1		Poirot's Early Cases (UK)
					Three Blind Mice (US)
5 Jan			USA: Detective Story Magazine, Vol. 106, No.6	In the Third Floor Flat	
Mar	Mr Quin	The Dead Harlequin	Grand Magazine, No. 288		The Mysterious Mr Quin
5 Aug		The Golden Ball	Daily Mail	Playing the Innocent	The Listerdale Mystery (UK)
					The Golden Ball (US)

DATE	CHARACTER	STORY (BOOK TITLE)	PUBLICATION	PUBLISHED AS (IF DIFFERENT)	FIRST BOOK APPEARANCE
22 Sep		Accident	The Sunday Dispatch	The Uncrossed Path	The Listerdale Mystery (UK)
					The Witness for the Prosecution (US)
Sep		Next to a Dog	Grand Magazine, No. 295		Problem at Pollensa Bay (UK)
					The Golden Ball (US)
Oct	Mr Quin	The Man from the Sea	Britannia & Eve, Vol. 1, No. 6		The Mysterious Mr Quin
Dec	Miss Marple	The Blue Geranium	The Christmas Story-Teller, Vol. 46, No. 272)		The Thirteen Problems (UK)
					The Tuesday Night Club (US)
2 Dec		Sing a Song of Sixpence	Holly Leaves No. 2932 (pub by Illustrated Sporting and Dramatic News)		The Listerdale Mystery (UK)
					The Witness for the Prosecution (US)

DATE	CHARACTER	STORY (BOOK TITLE)	PUBLICATION	PUBLISHED AS (IF DIFFERENT)	FIRST BOOK APPEARANCE
			1930		
Jan	Miss Marple	The Four Suspects	USA: Pictorial Review, Vol. 31, No. 4	Four Suspects	The Thirteen Problems (UK)
Apr			UK: Storyteller magazine, No. 276		The Tuesday Night Club (US)
Jan	Miss Marple	A Christmas Tragedy	Storyteller, Vol. 46, No. 273	The Hat and the Alibi	The Thirteen Problems (UK)
					The Tuesday Night Club (US)
Feb	Miss Marple	The Companion	UK: Storyteller, Vol. 46, No. 274	The Resurrection of Amy Durrant	The Thirteen Problems (UK)
Mar			USA: Pictorial Review	Companions	The Tuesday Night Club (US)
Mar	Miss Marple	The Herb of Death	Storyteller, Vol. 46, No. 275		The Thirteen Problems (UK)
					The Tuesday Night Club (US)
Apr	Mr Quin	The Bird with the Broken Wing	The Mysterious Mr Quin (Collins 1930). No pre-hardback appearances found		The Mysterious Mr Quin

DATE	CHARACTER	STORY (BOOK TITLE)	PUBLICATION	PUBLISHED AS (IF DIFFERENT)	FIRST BOOK APPEARANCE
May	Miss Marple	The Affair at the Bungalow	Storyteller, Vol. 46, No. 277		The Thirteen Problems (UK) The Tuesday Night Club (US)
23–28 May		Manx Gold	The Daily Dispatch		While the Light Lasts (UK) The Harlequin Tea Set (US)
1931					
Nov	Miss Marple	Death by Drowning	Nash's Pall Mall, Vol. 88, No. 462		The Thirteen Problems (UK) The Tuesday Night Club (US)
1932					
Jan	Poirot	The Mystery of the Baghdad Chest	UK: Strand Magazine, No. 493	*Later expanded into* The Mystery of the Spanish Chest (1960)	While the Light Lasts (UK)
			USA: Ladies' Home Journal, Vol. 49, No. 1	The Mystery of the Bagdad Chest	The Regatta Mystery (US)
Jun	Poirot	The Second Gong	USA: Ladies' Home Journal, Vol. 49, No 6	*Later expanded into* Dead Man's Mirror (1937)	Problem at Pollensa Bay (UK)
Jul			UK: Strand Magazine, No 499		The Witness for the Prosecution (US)

DATE	CHARACTER	STORY (BOOK TITLE)	PUBLICATION	PUBLISHED AS (IF DIFFERENT)	FIRST BOOK APPEARANCE
Aug	Parker Pyne	The Case of the Rich Woman	USA: Cosmopolitan	The Rich Woman Who Wanted Only To Be Happy	Parker Pyne Investigates (UK)
					Mr Parker Pyne, Detective (US)
Aug	Parker Pyne	The Case of the Distressed Lady	USA: Cosmopolitan	The Pretty Girl Who Wanted a Ring	Parker Pyne Investigates (UK)
22 Oct			UK: Woman's Pictorial	Faked!	Mr Parker Pyne, Detective (US)
Aug	Parker Pyne	The Case of the Discontented Soldier	USA: Cosmopolitan	The Soldier Who Wanted Danger	Parker Pyne Investigates (UK)
15 Oct			UK: Woman's Pictorial	Adventure – By Request	Mr Parker Pyne, Detective (US)
Aug	Parker Pyne	The Case of the Discontented Husband	USA: Cosmopolitan	The Husband Who Wanted To Keep His Wife	Parker Pyne Investigates (UK)
					Mr Parker Pyne, Detective (US)
29 Oct			UK: Woman's Pictorial	His Lady's Affair	
Aug	Parker Pyne	The Case of the City Clerk	USA: Cosmopolitan	The Clerk Who Wanted Excitement	Parker Pyne Investigates (UK)
Nov			UK: Strand Magazine, No. 503	The £10 Adventure	Mr Parker Pyne, Detective (US)

DATE	CHARACTER	STORY (BOOK TITLE)	PUBLICATION	PUBLISHED AS (IF DIFFERENT)	FIRST BOOK APPEARANCE
8 Oct	Parker Pyne	The Case of the Middle-aged Wife	Woman's Pictorial	The Woman Concerned	Parker Pyne Investigates (UK)
					Mr Parker Pyne, Detective (US)
1933					
Feb		The Call of Wings	The Hound of Death (Odhams 1933). No pre-hardback appearances found		The Hound of Death (UK)
					The Golden Ball (US)
		The Gipsy			The Hound of Death (UK)
					The Golden Ball (US)
		The Hound of Death			The Hound of Death (UK)
					The Golden Ball (US)
		The Lamp			The Hound of Death (UK)
					The Golden Ball (US)
		The Strange Case of Sir Arthur Carmichael			The Hound of Death (UK)
					The Golden Ball (US)

DATE	CHARACTER	STORY (BOOK TITLE)	PUBLICATION	PUBLISHED AS (IF DIFFERENT)	FIRST BOOK APPEARANCE
Apr	Parker Pyne	Death on the Nile	USA: Cosmopolitan		Parker Pyne Investigates (UK)
Jul			UK: Nash's Pall Mall, Vol. 91, No. 482		Mr Parker Pyne, Detective (US)
Apr	Parker Pyne	The Oracle at Delphi	USA: Cosmopolitan		Parker Pyne Investigates (UK)
Jul			UK: Nash's Pall Mall, Vol. 91, No. 482		Mr Parker Pyne, Detective (US)
Apr	Parker Pyne	The House at Shiraz	USA: Cosmopolitan		Parker Pyne Investigates (UK)
Jun			UK: Nash's Pall Mall, Vol. 91, No. 481	In the House at Shiraz	Mr Parker Pyne, Detective (US)
Apr	Parker Pyne	Have You Got Everything You Want?	USA: Cosmopolitan		Parker Pyne Investigates (UK)
Jun			UK: Nash's Pall Mall, Vol. 91, No. 481	On the Orient Express	Mr Parker Pyne, Detective (US)
Jun	Parker Pyne	The Gate of Baghdad	Nash's Pall Mall, Vol. 91, No. 481	At the Gate of Baghdad	Parker Pyne Investigates (UK)
					Mr Parker Pyne, Detective (US)

DATE	CHARACTER	STORY (BOOK TITLE)	PUBLICATION	PUBLISHED AS (IF DIFFERENT)	FIRST BOOK APPEARANCE
Jul	Parker Pyne	The Pearl of Price	Nash's Pall Mall, Vol. 91, No. 482	The Pearl	Parker Pyne Investigates (UK)
					Mr Parker Pyne, Detective (US)
1934					
28 Jul		In a Glass Darkly	USA: Collier's, Vol. 94, No. 4		Miss Marple's Final Cases (UK)
Dec			UK: Woman's Journal		The Regatta Mystery (US)
1935					
25 May	Miss Marple	Miss Marple Tells a Story	Home Journal	Behind Closed Doors	Miss Marple's Final Cases (UK)
					The Regatta Mystery (US)
Jun	Poirot	How Does Your Garden Grow?	USA: Ladies' Home Journal, Vol. 52, No. 6		Poirot's Early Cases (UK)
Aug			UK: Strand Magazine, No. 536		The Regatta Mystery (US)
Nov	Parker Pyne	Problem at Pollensa Bay	UK: Strand Magazine, No. 539		Problem at Pollensa Bay (UK)
5 Sep 1936			USA: Liberty	Siren Business	The Regatta Mystery (US)

DATE	CHARACTER	STORY (BOOK TITLE)	PUBLICATION	PUBLISHED AS (IF DIFFERENT)	FIRST BOOK APPEARANCE
			1936		
12 Jan	Poirot	Problem at Sea	USA: This Week		Poirot's Early Cases (UK)
Feb			UK: Strand Magazine, No. 542	Poirot and the Crime in Cabin 66	The Regatta Mystery (US)
2 Feb	Poirot	Triangle at Rhodes	USA: This Week		Murder in the Mews (UK)
May			UK: Strand Magazine, No. 545	Poirot and the Triangle at Rhodes	Dead Man's Mirror (US)
3 May	Poirot / Parker Pyne	The Regatta Mystery	USA: Chicago Tribune		Problem at Pollensa Bay (UK)
Jun			UK: Strand Magazine, No. 546	Poirot and the Regatta Mystery	The Regatta Mystery (US)
Sep/Oct	Poirot	Murder in the Mews	USA: Redbook Magazine, Vol. 67, Nos. 5–6		Murder in the Mews (UK)
Dec			UK: Woman's Journal	Mystery of the Dressing Case	Dead Man's Mirror (US)
			1937		
Mar	Poirot	Dead Man's Mirror	Murder in the Mews (Collins, 1937). No pre-hardback appearance found.	*Expanded version of* The Second Gong (1932)	Murder in the Mews (UK)
					Dead Man's Mirror (US)

DATE	CHARACTER	STORY (BOOK TITLE)	PUBLICATION	PUBLISHED AS (IF DIFFERENT)	FIRST BOOK APPEARANCE
6–12 Apr	Poirot	The Incredible Theft	Daily Express	*Expanded version of* The Submarine Plans (1923). *Adapted by Leslie Stokes as a radio play, broadcast by BBC National Programme, 10 May 1938.*	Murder in the Mews (UK) Dead Man's Mirror (US)
Jul	Poirot	Yellow Iris	UK: Strand Magazine, No. 559	Later expanded into Sparkling Cyanide (Collins 1945)	Problem at Pollensa Bay (UK)
25 Jul			USA: Chicago Tribune		The Regatta Mystery (US)
23 Oct	Poirot	The Dream	USA: Saturday Evening Post, Vol. 210, No. 17		The Adventure of the Christmas Pudding (UK)
Feb 1938			UK: Strand Magazine, No. 566		The Regatta Mystery (US)
1939					
3 Sep	Poirot	The Lernean Hydra	USA: This Week	Invisible Enemy	The Labours of Hercules
Dec			UK: Strand Magazine, No. 588		
10 Sep	Poirot	The Girdle of Hyppolita	USA: This Week	The Disappearance of Winnie King	The Labours of Hercules
Jul 1940			UK: Strand Magazine, No. 595	The Girdle of Hyppolyte	

DATE	CHARACTER	STORY (BOOK TITLE)	PUBLICATION	PUBLISHED AS (IF DIFFERENT)	FIRST BOOK APPEARANCE
17 Sep	Poirot	The Stymphalean Birds	USA: This Week	The Vulture Women	The Labours of Hercules
Apr 1940			UK: Strand Magazine, No. 592	Birds of Ill-Omen	
24 Sep	Poirot	The Cretan Bull	USA: This Week	Midnight Madness	The Labours of Hercules
May 1940			UK: Strand Magazine, No. 593		
Nov	Poirot	The Nemean Lion	UK: Strand Magazine, No. 587		The Labours of Hercules
?			USA: This Week	The Case of the Kidnapped Pekinese	
1940					
Jan	Poirot	The Arcadian Deer	UK: Strand Magazine, No. 589		The Labours of Hercules
19 May			USA: This Week	Vanishing Lady	
Feb	Poirot	The Erymanthian Boar	UK: Strand Magazine, No. 590		The Labours of Hercules
5 May			USA: This Week	Murder Mountain	
Mar	Poirot	The Augean Stables	Strand Magazine, No. 591		The Labours of Hercules

DATE	CHARACTER	STORY (BOOK TITLE)	PUBLICATION	PUBLISHED AS (IF DIFFERENT)	FIRST BOOK APPEARANCE
12 May	Poirot	The Apples of the Hesperides	USA: This Week	The Poison Cup	The Labours of Hercules
Sep			UK: Strand Magazine, No. 597		
26 May	Poirot	The Flock of Geryon	USA: This Week	Weird Monster	The Labours of Hercules
Aug			UK: Strand Magazine, No. 596		
June	Poirot	The Horses of Diomedes	Strand Magazine, No. 594		The Labours of Hercules
?			USA: This Week	The Case of the Drug Peddler	
9 Nov	Poirot	Four-and-Twenty Blackbirds	USA: Collier's, Vol. 106, No.19		The Adventure of the Christmas Pudding (UK)
Mar 1941			UK: Strand Magazine, No. 603	Poirot and the Regular Customer	Three Blind Mice (US)
1941					
2 Nov	Miss Marple	Strange Jest	USA: This Week		Miss Marple's Final Cases (UK)
Jul 1944			UK: Strand Magazine, No. 643	A Case of Buried Treasure	Three Blind Mice (US)
16 Nov	Miss Marple	Tape-Measure Murder	USA: This Week		Miss Marple's Final Cases (UK)
Feb 1942			UK: Strand Magazine, No. 614	The Case of the Retired Jeweller	Three Blind Mice (US)

DATE	CHARACTER	STORY (BOOK TITLE)	PUBLICATION	PUBLISHED AS (IF DIFFERENT)	FIRST BOOK APPEARANCE
			1942		
Jan	Miss Marple	The Case of the Caretaker	UK: Strand Magazine, No. 613		Miss Marple's Final Cases (UK)
5 Jul			USA: Chicago Sunday Tribune		Three Blind Mice (US)
Apr	Miss Marple	The Case of the Perfect Maid	UK: Strand Magazine, No. 616	The Perfect Maid	Miss Marple's Final Cases (UK)
13 Sep			USA: Chicago Sunday Tribune	The Maid Who Disappeared	Three Blind Mice (US)
			1946		
Dec		Star Over Bethlehem	Woman's Journal		Star Over Bethlehem
			1947		
16 Mar	Poirot	The Capture of Cerberus	USA: This Week	Meet Me in Hell	The Labours of Hercules
Sep			UK: The Labours of Hercules (Collins 1947)	*Replacement for original 12th Labour rejected by the Strand Magazine in 1940*	

DATE	CHARACTER	STORY (BOOK TITLE)	PUBLICATION	PUBLISHED AS (IF DIFFERENT)	FIRST BOOK APPEARANCE
1948					
May		Three Blind Mice	USA: Cosmopolitan, No. 743		Three Blind Mice (US)
31 Dec 1948 – 21 Jan 1949			UK: Woman's Own	*In 4 weekly parts. Developed from the radio play of 30 May 1947. Forms the basis of the play The Mousetrap.*	For contractual reasons, this story has never been published in book form in the UK.
1954					
12&19 Sep	Miss Marple	Sanctuary	USA: This Week	Murder at the Vicarage	Miss Marple's Final Cases (UK)
Oct			UK: Woman's Journal		Double Sin (US)
1956					
3–7 Dec	Miss Marple	Greenshaw's Folly	Daily Mail		The Adventure of the Christmas Pudding (UK)
					Double Sin (US)
1958					
Dec		The Dressmaker's Doll	Woman's Journal		Miss Marple's Final Cases (UK)
					Double Sin (US)

DATE	CHARACTER	STORY (BOOK TITLE)	PUBLICATION	PUBLISHED AS (IF DIFFERENT)	FIRST BOOK APPEARANCE
			1960		
17&24 Sep, 1 Oct	Poirot	The Mystery of the Spanish Chest	Woman's Illustrated	*In 3 parts. Expanded version of* The Mystery of the Baghdad Chest (1932)	The Adventure of the Christmas Pudding (UK) The Harlequin Tea Set (US)
25 Sep & 2 Oct	Poirot	The Adventure of the Christmas Pudding	USA: This Week	The Theft of the Royal Ruby, *in 2 parts*	Miss Marple's Final Cases (UK)
24&31 Dec and 7 Jan 1961		A.k.a. The Theft of the Royal Ruby	UK: Woman's Illustrated	*In 3 parts. Expanded version of* Christmas Adventure (1923)	Double Sin (US)
			1965		
Nov		In the Cool of the Evening	Star Over Bethlehem (Collins, 1965)		Star Over Bethlehem
		The Island			Star Over Bethlehem
		The Naughty Donkey			Star Over Bethlehem
		Promotion in the Highest			Star Over Bethlehem
		The Water Bus			Star Over Bethlehem
			1971		
?	Mr Quin	The Harlequin Tea Set	Winter's Crimes, No. 3 (Macmillan)		Problem at Pollensa Bay (UK) The Harlequin Tea Set (US)

ALSO IN THIS SERIES

Agatha Christie

MISS MARPLE Omnibus

VOLUME I

THE BODY IN THE LIBRARY

It's seven in the morning, and the body of a young woman is found in the Bantrys' library. But who is she? And what's the connection with another dead girl? Miss Marple is invited to solve the mystery – before tongues start to wag …

THE MOVING FINGER

The quiet inhabitants of Lymstock are unsettled by a sudden outbreak of hate-mail. But when one of the recipients commits suicide, only Miss Marple questions the coroner's verdict. Is this the work of a poison pen? Or of a poisoner?

A MURDER IS ANNOUNCED

An advertisement in the *Chipping Cleghorn Gazette* announces the time and place of a forthcoming murder. Unable to resist the mysterious invitation, a crowd begins to gather at the appointed time when, without warning, the lights go out …

4.50 FROM PADDINGTON

As two trains run together, side by side, Mrs McGillicuddy watches a murder. Then the other train draws away. With no other witnesses, not even a body, who will take her story seriously? Then she remembers her old friend, Miss Marple …

'Suspense is engendered from the very start, and maintained very skilfully until the final revelation'   Times Literary Supplement

ALSO IN THIS SERIES

Agatha Christie

MISS MARPLE Omnibus

VOLUME II

A CARIBBEAN MYSTERY

As Miss Marple dozes in the West Indian sun, an old soldier talks of elephant-shooting and scandals. Then he dies – and the deceptively frail detective finds herself investigating a most exotic murder …

A POCKET FULL OF RYE

Rex Fortescue, 'king' of a financial empire, was in his counting house; his 'queen' was in the parlour … There are baffling similarities between the rhyme and the crime and it takes all Miss Marple's ingenuity to find them …

THE MIRROR CRACK'D FROM SIDE TO SIDE

Marina Gregg, the famous film actress, witnesses a murder in her country home. But what gave her the expression of frozen terror that only Dolly Bantry saw? Dolly, of course, knows just who can find out: her old friend, Miss Marple …

THEY DO IT WITH MIRRORS

To fulfil a promise to an old schoolfriend, Miss Marple stays in a country house – with 200 juvenile delinquents and seven heirs to an old lady's fortune. One of them is a murderer – with a talent, it seems, for being in two places at once …

'Throws off the false clues and misleading events as only a master of the art can do'
New York Times

'Full of freshness and charm ... Miss Marple is spry, shrewd and compassionate'   *Sunday Telegraph*

Agatha Christie

The
MARY WESTMACOTT
Collection

VOLUME ONE

Agatha Christie is known throughout the world as the Queen of Crime. It was her sharp observations of people's ambitions, relationships and conflicts that added life and sparkle to her ingenious detective novels. When she turned this understanding of human nature away from the crime genre, writing anonymously as Mary Westmacott, she created bittersweet novels, love stories with a jagged edge, as compelling and memorable as the best of her work.

GIANT'S BREAD

When a gifted composer returns home after being reported killed in the war, he finds his wife has already remarried...

UNFINISHED PORTRAIT

On the verge of suicide after a marriage break up, a young novelist unburdens herself on an unsuspecting young man...

ABSENT IN THE SPRING

Unexpectedly stranded in Iraq, a loyal wife and mother tries to come to terms with her husband's love for another woman...

'I've not been so emotionally moved by a story since the memorable *Brief Encounter*. *Absent in the Spring* is a *tour de force* which should be recognized as a classic.' *New York Times*

Agatha Christie

The
MARY WESTMACOTT
Collection

VOLUME TWO

Agatha Christie is known throughout the world as the Queen of Crime. It was her sharp observations of people's ambitions, relationships and conflicts that added life and sparkle to her ingenious detective novels. When she turned this understanding of human nature away from the crime genre, writing anonymously as Mary Westmacott, she created bittersweet novels, love stories with a jagged edge, as compelling and memorable as the best of her work.

THE ROSE AND THE YEW TREE

When an aristocratic young woman falls for a working-class war hero, the price of love proves to be costly for both sides...

A DAUGHTER'S A DAUGHTER

Rejecting personal happiness for the sake of her daughter, a mother later regrets the decision and love turns to bitterness...

THE BURDEN

With childhood jealousy behind them, the growing bond between two sisters becomes dangerously one-sided and destructive...

'Miss Westmacott writes crisply and is always lucid. Much material has been skilfully compressed within little more than 200 pages.' *Times Literary Supplement*

Agatha Christie

HERCULE POIROT:
The Complete Short Stories

At last – the complete collection of over 50 Hercule Poirot short stories in a single volume!

Hercule Poirot had a passion for order, for rational thought, and had a justified confidence in his deductive genius. No matter what the provocation, he always remained calm.

The shrewd little detective with the egg-shaped head and the enormous black moustache was created by one of the world's greatest storytellers, Agatha Christie, who excelled at the art of short story writing. Only she could have devised the cases worthy of Poirot's skill, the ingenious mysteries that challenge the reader as well as the detective.

There is a spectacular diversity in the plots and themes of these cases, ranging from very brief tales to full-length novellas. Violent murders, poisonings, kidnappings and thefts, all are solved or thwarted with Poirot's usual panache – and the characteristic application of his 'little grey cells'.

'Little masterpieces of detection – Poirot and Agatha Christie at their inimitable best.'   *Sunday Express*

Anatoly Marchenko

MY TESTIMONY

Translated by Michael Scammell

First published in Great Britain in 1969 by Pall Mall Press

Penguin Books edition, 1971

Sceptre edition, 1987

Sceptre is an imprint of Hodder and Stoughton Paperbacks, a division of Hodder and Stoughton Limited.

British Library C.I.P.

Marchenko, Anatoly
  My testimony.
  1. Penal colonies – Soviet Union
  2. Forced labor – Soviet Union
  I. Title II. Moi pokazaniia.
  English
  365'.4'0924 HV8959.S65

ISBN 0-340-41724-2

Printed and bound in Great Britain for Hodder and Stoughton Paperbacks, a division of Hodder and Stoughton Limited, Mill Road, Dunton Green, Sevenoaks, Kent TN13 2YA (Editorial Office: 47 Bedford Square, London WC1B 3DP) by Richard Clay Limited, Bungay, Suffolk. Photoset by Rowland Phototypesetting Limited, Bury St Edmunds, Suffolk.

CONTENTS

'Anatoly Marchenko's MY TESTIMONY is one of the most truthful Russian books in existence. Let us remember that the author laid down his life in defence of our right to read it'

Irina Ratushinskaya,
Russian poet and survivor
of Soviet labour camps;
author of NO, I'M NOT AFRAID.

INTRODUCTION

On 27 March 1968, *Literary Gazette* published a long 'Letter to a Reader' by its editor-in-chief, Alexander Chakovsky. A few months previously, in November 1967, Chakovsky had come to London to debate with Malcolm Muggeridge in a BBC television studio the sentence on the Soviet writers Sinyavsky and Daniel. Just as he had then hotly defended the proceedings taken against them, so he now justified in a reply to a Soviet reader the trial in Moscow in January 1968 of two more young Soviet intellectuals, Ginzburg and Galanskov, one of whose offences, in the eyes of their prosecutors, was to have circulated detailed information about the case of Sinyavsky and Daniel. This has now become a familiar pattern in the Soviet Union – one trial inevitably leads to another in a chain reaction of protest and reprisal.

The general policy of the Soviet press has been to ignore the great numbers of written protests (in the form of open letters to the Soviet authorities and newspapers) that circulate in type-script in the country, and Chakovsky's long statement in *Literary Gazette* was the first public response of any importance. While angrily condemning the victims of the trials and those who protest on their behalf, Chakovsky nevertheless affected to be personally in disagreement with the policy of sentencing young rebels to forced labour and suggested, in what was clearly a rhetorical flourish, that they be sent abroad to join the writer Tarsis and thus be maintained at the expense of the foreign tax payer, instead of 'being fed . . . at public expense in [Soviet] prisons or corrective labour colonies'.

The same day that Chakovsky's article appeared in *Literary Gazette*, Anatoly Marchenko, a young worker and the author of the present book, who had been released after six years' hard labour in 1966, wrote an open letter in reply.* It has, needless to say, never been published in the Soviet Union, but it has circulated widely in the country. He pointed out that for the prisoners in the hard labour camps where he and a number of imprisoned intellectuals (including Sinyavsky and Daniel) served their sentences, the daily food ration was 2,400 calories a day – sufficient for a child of seven to eleven, but scarcely enough for an adult expected to do a full day's work. In his book Marchenko goes into much greater detail and shows what a mockery it is to speak of Soviet prisoners being fed 'at public expense'. The camps are in fact maintained at the expense of the prisoners themselves. They are paid a normal wage, of which 50 per cent is deducted for their 'upkeep' and the rest kept in an account from which they are paid only on their release. More than this, the 'public' exploits them in classical Marxist terms, since the State sells at enormous profit the product of their labour (furniture in the case of Marchenko and his fellow prisoners).

It is possible that Chakovsky was genuinely ignorant of these facts. One thing that has definitely not changed since Stalin's time is official reticence, unparalleled in any modern state, about the penal system. In the whole of the Soviet period no figure has ever been given for the number of political prisoners held at any one time in prisons or hard labour camps. Conditions in Soviet penal institutions have always been carefully hidden not only from the outside world, but from the Soviet public too. Occasional glimpses of 'model' prisons (such as the famous Bolshevo near Moscow), accorded to a handful of privileged visitors from abroad, were cynical attempts – often successful – to give the impression that there is not a great deal of difference between a Soviet prison and a sanatorium. After Stalin's death there was for the first time some public admission of the existence of slave labour camps – the vast numbers of people returning from them under amnesty during 1954–6 in any case

---

* For the text of this letter and further material concerning this episode, see Appendix, p. 409.

made further concealment pointless – but there still have not been any official data on the numbers of people involved.

The publication of Solzhenitsyn's *One Day in the Life of Ivan Denisovich* in 1962, which appeared thanks to a squabble between Khrushchev and his colleagues, was the first and only occasion on which something of the truth about conditions in Stalin's camps was allowed to reach Soviet readers. But Solzhenitsyn's even more revealing work on the subject, *The First Circle*, is banned inside Russia and for several years now there has been a party instruction to the censorship forbidding anything on the 'camp theme' to appear in print. There has never been anything at all about the development of the Soviet penal system after Stalin. The importance of Anatoly Marchenko's book is that it is the first detailed and completely unvarnished report on conditions in Soviet camps today by someone who knows them at first hand.

It is therefore now possible for the first time to make some comparisons between the system as it was under Stalin, and as it is today. It immediately becomes apparent that the change is mainly a quantitative one. While the prisoners under Stalin were numbered in millions, they are now numbered in tens (or hundreds?) of thousands. In the absence of official figures, or reliable estimates based on a study of all the materials, it is impossible to be more precise than this. It is quite likely that in the 'peak' years after the war there may have been as many as twenty million people doing forced labour, or condemned to permanent exile in the most remote and inhospitable areas of the country. As Solzhenitsyn shows in *One Day in the Life of Ivan Denisovich* and in *The First Circle*, whole sections of the Soviet populations were automatically suspect and were sent in large numbers, quite indiscriminately, to concentration camps – these included many of the millions of Soviet prisoners of war who returned home (it is a little known fact that about a third of a million stayed in the West, knowing that they would be victimised if they returned home), and people who had lived temporarily under German rule in the occupied territories.

Then there were mass deportations from the Baltic states, the Western Ukraine and the exiling to Siberia and Central Asia of several small peoples *in toto*: the Chechens and Ingush, the Karachai, Balkhars, Kalmyks and the Crimean Tartars (who are still not allowed to go back home, because their lands were given to Ukrainian settlers). As Stalin's paranoia worsened during the years before his death, many non-Russian people living in border areas were also transported to Central Asia or Siberia – this happened, for instance, to the Greek colonies along the Black Sea coast. From the late forties until Stalin's death, a great many Jews were arrested and sent to the camps – in Stalin's eyes, particularly after the creation of the State of Israel, they were a natural fifth column. For most 'political' prisoners during the postwar years maximum sentences of twenty-five years were standard (the much publicised abolition of the death penalty was meant for foreign consumption: in August 1952, all the leading Yiddish-language writers were shot on one day, a fact still not admitted in the Soviet press, even though each of the victims has been posthumously 'rehabilitated').

In all the revelations of recent years attention has been focused on the large camps in Siberia and the Arctic, where prisoners were employed in mining, lumbering and the general economic development of the most inaccessible and the bleakest areas of this great land mass – on the maps Alaska looks like a small, severed rump to it. People died like flies of cold and hunger, and intolerable conditions of work. It is less well known that there was under Stalin an extraordinary system of 'local' forced labour which meant that many, if not all factories and construction sites were run partly by forced labour. As a result of the labour laws passed by Stalin just before the war, workers could be sentenced to short periods (six months or so for a first offence) of forced labour *at their places of work* for being more than twenty minutes late for work, and other infringements of the 'labour code'.

In 1948, on the way to Tolstoy's estate at Yasnaya Polyana, I remember seeing the stockade adjacent to the large steel works in Tula. It was almost as large as the works themselves and at intervals along the high barbed wire fence there were characteristic watch towers, with armed guards looking inwards.

In the same year, going by rail through the industrial suburbs of Tbilisi in Georgia, I noticed several similar prison camps.

It is clear from Marchenko's book that nothing on this scale now exists. There are no longer whole categories of the population behind barbed wire, and although there is still a hard core of 'political' prisoners from Stalin's times, the people now undergoing forced labour have been sentenced individually, not as members of suspect categories, but on specific criminal or 'political' charges.

Since Marchenko himself was sentenced on political grounds, most of what he has to say deals with political prisoners, who now fall into three main groups: intellectuals accused of anti-Soviet propaganda (the cases of only a few of those who stood trial in Moscow, such as Sinyavsky, Daniel, Ginzburg and Galanskov, have become known to the outside world); nationalists, that is people charged with advocating some degree of autonomy (mainly cultural) for non-Russian parts of the USSR such as the Ukraine; religious believers, particularly Baptists and sectarians who have actively stood up for their faith or opposed state interference with it. It is difficult to tell what the proportion of common criminals to political prisoners is, but it seems certain that, just as in Stalin's time, conditions are much harsher for the 'politicals', though they are no longer confined together with criminals and terrorised by them.

The great reduction in numbers of prisoners means, of course, that they no longer play a key part in the Soviet economy. In Stalin's day there were huge areas (such as North Kazakhstan, equal in size to France), where the factories, mines, and even the farms were run largely by forced labour. This no longer appears to be true, though there are rumoured to be 'death camps' in one or two very remote areas (uranium mines near Norilsk, and rocket installations in the Arctic) to which it is not easy to attract 'free' labour by the lure of high wages. Marchenko's book confirms the impression that most important political prisoners are now sent to the cluster of camps in the neighbourhood of Potma, about 500 kilometres east of Moscow. It is by no means the only camp for political prisoners (the names and location of about ninety others distributed all over Soviet territory are known and Marchenko refers to the continued existence of camps in the traditional areas of Vorkuta and Kazakhstan), but it would seem that major political offenders, including foreigners such as Gary Powers and Gerald Brooke, are sent to Potma. Foreigners are, however, treated somewhat differently – on the whole better – than Soviet citizens. Here most of them are employed in making furniture, cabinets for television sets and – as in Brooke's case – chessmen. They work a forty-eight hour week and are expected to fulfil the usual high 'production norms'. This is not easy on a full stomach – and impossible on a semi-starvation diet, with its lack of fat and vitamins. In this respect the camps are as bad as, if not worse than, they were under Stalin.

It is also clear from Marchenko's account (as from others that have filtered out in recent years) that this inadequate diet is now used as a deliberate means of pressure on political prisoners. Those who are 'uncooperative', e.g. refuse to act as informers, are not allowed to receive parcels from their relatives and have no hope of a remission of their sentences. This is probably the main respect in which the camps are now worse than they were under Stalin. In many other ways they are much the same: the physical lay-out, the guards and punishment cells are all more or less as described in Solzhenitsyn's *One Day in the Life of Ivan Denisovich*. Even the name of the Potma camp area, Dubrovlag, is a sinister relic from Stalin's day: in 1947, Stalin personally ordered the setting-up of special camps with bucolic-sounding code names – Ozerlag ('lake camp'), Rechlag ('river camp'), Dubrovlag ('oak forest camp') in which he wished to concentrate all political prisoners to facilitate their speedy liquidation in case of a new war.

Not much is known about Marchenko except what he states about himself in his book. He was born in the small western Siberian town of Barabinsk, where both his parents were railway workers. He left school after eight classes, that is, two years short of a full secondary education, and went to work on the Novosibirsk hydro-electric station, and then on similar projects all over Siberia and Kazakhstan. His troubles began in 1958, when he was twenty years old, as the result of a fight in a workers' hostel. In typical fashion the police indiscriminately arrested the innocent and the guilty, and Marchenko was sent with all the others involved to a camp near Karaganda (also a relic of Stalin's time – it is the camp described from his own experiences by Solzhenitsyn in *One Day in the Life of Ivan Denisovich*). After escaping from this camp, Marchenko made his way down to Ashkhabad on the Iranian frontier, where he was arrested while trying to leave the country. He was charged with 'treason' and sentenced in 1961 to a further six years imprisonment.

After his release in 1966 he was subjected to all the usual restrictions applied to former political prisoners, that is, he was not allowed to take up residence in the capital or in any other major city. There were also the usual difficulties about getting work (and since 'there is no unemployment in the Soviet Union', there are also no unemployment benefits). After nearly a year, however, he was at last permitted to live in the small town of Alexandrov, not far from Moscow. From May 1968 he began work in Moscow as a loader, though he was still forced by the regulations to live outside the city limits in Alexandrov. It was here, during 1967, that he wrote this book. After writing the book, which he could not hope to get published in the Soviet Union, he wrote a number of open letters, addressed to the President of the Soviet branch of the Red Cross, and to several Soviet writers.* In one of them he said:

The present day Soviet camps for political prisoners are just as terrible as under Stalin. In some things they are better, but in others they are worse. It is essential that everybody should know about this – both those who want to know the truth . . . and those who do not wish to know it, [preferring] to close their eyes and ears so that one day they will again be able to absolve themselves ('O God, we didn't know'). I would like this testimony of mine about Soviet camps and prisons for political prisoners to become known to the humanitarians and progressive people of other countries, to those

* See Appendix, p. 411.

who speak up in defence of political prisoners in Greece, Portugal, South Africa and Spain . . .'

These activities of Marchenko were, needless to say, highly 'inconvenient' to the Soviet authorities, and they soon found a pretext to silence him. On 22 July 1968, Marchenko wrote another open letter, this time addressed to the people of Czechoslovakia. In it he welcomed the signs of restoration of freedom and democracy for the Czechs and Slovaks, protested against the systematic misrepresentation of events in Czechoslovakia in the Soviet press and said that any attempt to interfere would be nothing less than criminal. Seven days after sending this letter, on 29 July, Marchenko was arrested.

Larisa Daniel described the circumstances of his arrest in her open letter of 1 August 1968:

Why should the authorities set the machine of arbitrary power in motion against him? It's easy to guess the answer when you have read the appeal of Anatoly Marchenko's friends.

His book, in which he tells the truth about the camps for political prisoners, aroused such hatred for him in the KGB that they began to bait him like a hare. KGB agents followed on his heels for months on end – I've spotted them so often that I know many of them by sight. And not only in Moscow, where he works, and in Alexandrov, where he lives: he went to visit relations in Ryazan but wasn't allowed to leave the train and had to return to Moscow. He was seized on the street almost as soon as he had been discharged from hospital; his face was smashed up as he was being pushed into a car when he came to Moscow for a literary evening. Marchenko's open letter to *Rude Pravo* and other papers evidently infuriated the KGB to such an extent that they couldn't wait any longer to put this Marchenko behind bars by any means and on any pretext. On the morning of 29 July he was picked up in the street on his way to work and now he's in prison again. *

* For full text see Appendix, p. 426.

With characteristic disingenuousness the authorities charged him not on political grounds, but for the technical offence of allegedly having infringed the regulations on residence permits which debarred him from living in Moscow. Since he had in fact established residence outside the city limits, this charge too was trumped up. For his 'offence' he has been sentenced by a Moscow court to a year's imprisonment in a 'strict regime' camp, this time in the region of Perm. He is known to have been sent there in December 1968 to begin serving his sentence.

According to some reports in the Western press (see *The Observer*, 6 July 1969) he has since been retried once more, presumably on account of his book having been published abroad in Russian, and sentenced to a further three years.*

The arrest of Marchenko caused great indignation in Moscow intellectual circles. An open letter in his defence was signed by Larisa Daniel (whose husband Marchenko had met in Potma), Pavel Litvinov, General Grigorenko, and others. They pointed out that his arrest was a breach of Soviet law – it had taken place on the day of his arrival in Moscow from Alexandrov, though as a non-resident he would have been entitled under the regulations to spend three days in the city. †

Larisa Daniel and Pavel Litvinov were themselves arrested in August for organising a demonstration on Red Square against the invasion of Czechoslovakia, and have been deported to remote places in Siberia after a closed trial. General Grigorenko was arrested in Tashkent at the beginning of May 1969. Also arrested in August 1968, for having in her possession copies of the petition on behalf of Marchenko, was a young woman engineer, Irina Belogorodskaya, who is reported to be the daughter of a retired colonel of the KGB. In February 1969 she was sentenced to one year in a labour camp for 'slander'. ‡

Finally, a word about Marchenko as a writer. What immediately strikes one is the soberness of his account, and the care

---

* It has become known since this introduction was written for the first edition (1969) that Marchenko's latest term is in fact two years. See Appendix, p. 453.

† See Appendix, p. 432.

‡ See Appendix, p. 436, for an account of this trial.

with which he distinguishes between what he has witnessed himself and hearsay evidence. He does not harangue or preach, but just tries to tell us in a straightforward way the things that we want to know. He also succeeds, incidentally – though this was not his conscious intention – in giving very revealing glimpses of Soviet life in general. Not only is there a wealth of information about social habits (including sexual *mores*), but the reader is given the 'feel' of real life at the humbler levels of existence in the Soviet Union. Marchenko introduces us to the vast submerged reality which few foreigners or even educated Russians ever see.

Despite his relative lack of formal education, he writes in good literate Russian, yet avoids the temptation to treat his material in an obviously 'literary' way. He is clearly a person of great natural gifts, integrity and will-power. Despite all the odds he has made his voice heard. It is heartening that there are still such people in Russia.

Max Hayward

Surely we will be joined by all free minds and all passionate hearts?

Let them join together, let them write and speak out!

Let them try together with us to enlighten public opinion and all those poor and humble people who are now being lashed into a frenzy by poisonous propaganda! The soul of our fatherland, its energy and its greatness, can be expressed only in its justice and magnanimity.

I am concerned with one thing only, and that is that the light of truth should be spread as far and as quickly as possible. A trial behind closed doors after a secret investigation will prove nothing. The real trial will only begin then, for one must speak out, since silence would mean complicity.

What madness to think you can stop history being written! No, it will be written, and then no one, however small his responsibility, will escape retribution.

Emile Zola: *Letter to France*
(Pamphlet, Fasquelle, 1898)

AUTHOR'S PREFACE

When I was locked up in Vladimir Prison I was often seized by despair. Hunger, illness, and above all helplessness, the sheer impossibility of struggling against evil, provoked me to the point where I was ready to hurl myself upon my jailers with the sole aim of being killed. Or to put an end to myself in some other way. Or to maim myself as I had seen others do.

One thing alone prevented me, one thing alone gave me the strength to live through that nightmare: the hope that I would eventually come out and tell the whole world what I had seen and experienced. I promised myself that for the sake of this aim I would suffer and endure everything. And I gave my word on this to my comrades who were doomed to spend many more years behind bars and barbed wire.

I wondered how to carry out this task. It seemed to me that in our country, with its conditions of cruel censorship and KGB* control over every word uttered, such a thing would be impossible. And also pointless: our people are so oppressed by fear and enslaved by the harsh conditions of life that nobody even wants to know the truth. Therefore, I thought, I will have to flee abroad in order to leave my evidence at least as a document, as a small contribution to history.

A year ago my imprisonment ended. I emerged into freedom. And I realised that I had been mistaken, that my testimony is needed by my countrymen. The people want to know the truth.

The main aim of these notes is to tell the truth about today's

* Soviet secret police. The initials stand for Commissariat for State Security.

camps and prisons for political prisoners – to those who wish to hear it. I am convinced that publicity is the sole effective means of combating the evil and lawlessness that is rampant in my country today.

In recent years a number of fictional and documentary works have appeared in print on the subject of the camps. In many other works, furthermore, this subject is mentioned either in passing or by implication. Lastly it has been very fully and powerfully covered in a number of productions disseminated by *Samizdat* – typed and duplicated manuscripts circulated illegally. Thus Stalin's camps have been exposed; and even though the exposures have still not reached all readers, they will, of course, in time. All this is good. But it is also bad – and dangerous. For the impression involuntarily arises that all these descriptions refer only to the past, that such things do not and cannot exist nowadays. Once they are even written about in our press, then everything is sure to have changed already, everything is in order again, and all the perpetrators of these terrible crimes have been punished and all the victims rewarded.

It's a lie! How many victims have been 'rewarded' post-humously, how many of them even now languish forgotten in our camps, how many new ones continue to join them. And how many of those who condemned, who interrogated and tortured them, are still occupying their posts or living peacefully on their well-earned pensions, bearing not one iota of moral responsibility for their acts! Whenever I ride in a Moscow suburban train the coaches are filled with benevolent, peaceable old pensioners. Some of them are reading newspapers, others are taking a basket of strawberries somewhere, while still others are keeping an eye on grandson . . . Maybe these are doctors, workers, engineers now on a pension after long years of strenuous work; maybe that old man over there with the steel teeth lost his others from the 'application of physical methods' or in the mines of Kolyma. But in each such peaceful old pensioner I see rather the interrogator himself, who was himself responsible for knocking out people's teeth.

Because I myself have seen plenty of them – *just the same* – in our present camps. Because today's Soviet camps for political prisoners are just as horrific as in Stalin's time. A few things are better, a few things worse. But everybody must know about it.

Everybody must know, including those who would like to know the truth and instead are given lying, optimistic newspaper articles, designed to lull the public conscience; and also including those who don't wish to know, who close their eyes and stuff up their ears in order to be able at some future date to justify themselves and to emerge from the dirt with their noses clean: 'Good heavens, and we never knew . . .' If they have a single particle of civic conscience or genuine love for their country they will stand up in its defence, just as the true sons of Russia have always done.

I would like my testimony on Soviet camps and prisons for political prisoners to come to the attention of humanists and progressive people in other countries – those who stick up for political prisoners in Greece and Portugal and in Spain and South Africa. Let them ask their Soviet colleagues in the struggle against inhumanity: 'And what have you done in your own country to stop political prisoners from being "re-educated" by starvation?'

I don't consider myself a writer, these notes are not a work of art. For six whole years I tried only to see and to memorise. In these notes of mine there is not a single invented personage nor a single invented incident. Wherever there is a danger of harming others I have omitted names or remained silent about certain episodes and circumstances. But I am prepared to answer for the truth of every detail recounted here. Each incident, each fact can be confirmed by dozens and sometimes by hundreds or even thousands of witnesses and their comrades in the camps. They could also of course, cite horrific facts that I have not included.

It seems a likely supposition that the authorities will try to be revenged on me and to escape the truth that I have told in these pages by an unprovable accusation of 'slander'. Let me declare, therefore, that I am prepared to answer for it at a public trial, provided that the necessary witnesses are invited and that interested representatives of public opinion and the press are allowed to be present. And if instead we are given yet another masquerade known as a 'public trial', where representatives of the KGB stand at the entrance in order to repel ordinary citizens and secret policemen dressed up in civvies are used as the 'public', and where the correspondents of all foreign newspapers (including communist ones) are forced to hang around outside, unable to get any information – as happened at the trials of the writers Sinyavsky and Daniel, Khaustov and Bukovsky and the others – then that will merely confirm the justice of what I have written.

One day our company officer, Captain Usov, said to me:

'You, Marchenko, are always dissatisfied, nothing suits you. But what have you ever done to make things better? All you wanted to do was run away and nothing more!'

If, after writing these notes, I come under Captain Usov again, I shall be able to say:

'I have done everything that was in my power. And here I am – back where I started.'

PART ONE

. . . Guards and sentries check their watches,
The tail of the column winds through the gates,
Ten o'clock sharp in the camp – lights out
Is tolled over the palisades.

Rail thumps hard against rail – lights out!
The con hurries back to his hut – lights out!
Icy railings of tempered steel
Lull Kolymá with their Angelus peal.

It's your turn now, Igarka and Taishet!
Wrap up warm in your jackets, Karaganda!
The chiming rails of the rusty timepiece
Toll out the weeks and the years.

The shadow is half way over now,
The shadow's crept over the Urals . . .
Dubrovlag in its turn comes in
To swell the bedtime chorus.

Songs that didn't get born – lights out!
Stars that have slipped out of sight – lights out!
I cannot sleep in the Moscow calm:
Reveille's in an hour at Kolymá.

Song of the Time Zones, 1967

(Kolyma, Igarka, Taishet, Karaganda and Dubrovlag are prison camps spread over the Soviet Union. The prisoners' day is punctuated by the clanging of a rail on a rail which calls him to work and sends him to bed.)

THE BEGINNING

My name is Marchenko, Anatoly, and I was born in the small Siberian town of Barabinsk. My father, Tikhon Akimovich Marchenko, worked his whole life as a fireman on the railway. My mother was a station cleaner. Both of them were totally illiterate and my mother's letters always had to be written by somebody else.

After eight years of schooling I quit school and went as a Komsomol volunteer to Novosibirsk to work on the hydro-electric power station there. This was the beginning of my independence. I was made a shift foreman with the drilling gang, travelled around to all the new power station sites in Siberia and worked in mines and on geological surveys. My last job was on the Karaganda power station.

It was there that I first fell foul of the law. We young workers lived in a hostel and went dancing at the club. In the same settlement lived some Chechens who had been exiled from the Caucasus. They were terribly embittered: after all, they'd been transported from their homes to this strange Siberia, among a strange and alien people. Between their young people and us constant brawls and punch-ups kept breaking out and sometimes there was a knife fight as well. One day there was a huge brawl in our hostel. When it had all died away of its own accord the police arrived, picked up everyone left in the hostel – the majority of those involved had already run away or gone into hiding – arrested them and put them on trial. I was one of the ones arrested, and they took us away from the settlement, where everyone knew what had happened. They sentenced us all in a single day, with no attempt at finding out who was guilty and who innocent. Thus it was that I found my way to the terrible camps of Karaganda.

After that the circumstances of my life turned out in such a way that I decided to escape abroad. I simply could see no other way out for me. I made my run together with a young fellow called Anatoly Budrovsky. We tried to cross the border into Iran, but were discovered and captured about fifty yards from the border.

That was on 29 October 1960. For five months I was kept under investigation at the special investigation prison of the Ashkhabad KGB. All that time I was kept in solitary confinement, with no parcels or packages and without a singe line from my family. Every day I was interrogated by KGB investigator Sarafyan (and later Shchukin): why did I want to run away? The KGB had entered a charge of treason against me and therefore the investigator was not very pleased with my answers. What he was after was to get the necessary evidence from me, wearing me down by interrogations, threatening that the investigation would go on until I had told them what was required of me, promising me that in return for 'worthwhile' evidence and an admission of guilt, I would have my twice daily prison rations supplemented. Although he didn't get what he was after and got no material whatsoever to support the charges, either from me or from any of the forty witnesses, nevertheless I was tried for treason.

On 2–3 March 1961, our case came before the Supreme Court of the Soviet Socialist Republic of Turkmenia. It was a closed court: not a single person was present in that huge chamber, except for the court officials, two guards armed with tommy guns at our backs and the guard commander at the main entrance. For two days they asked me the same questions as they had been putting during the investigation and I gave them the same answers, rejecting the charge. My fellow escapee, Anatoly Budrovsky, had evidently not been able to stand up to the interrogations and solitary confinement and had yielded under pressure from the investigator. He gave evidence against me, thus shielding and saving himself. The evidence of forty other people was in my favour. I asked why the court paid no attention to this and was told: 'The court itself decides what evidence to believe.'

Although I refused any defence, my lawyer attended the court and pleaded my case. He said that the court had no grounds for convicting me of treason: no trust could be placed in the evidence of Budrovsky in that he was an interested party and was being tried in the same case. The court ought to take account of the evidence of the other witnesses. Marchenko could be convicted for illegally attempting to cross the border, but not for treason.

I refused to take up my right of having the last word: I did not consider myself guilty of treason and had nothing to add to my evidence.

On 3 March the court pronounced its sentence: Budrovsky got two years in the camps (this was even less than the maximum in such cases, which was three years) for illegally attempting to cross the border, while I was given six for treason – this too being considerably less than the permitted maximum penalty – the firing squad.

I was then twenty-three.

Once more I was taken back to prison, to my cell. To tell the truth, the length of my sentence made no impression on me. It was only later that each year of imprisonment stretched out into days and hours and it seemed that six years would never come to an end. Much later I also found out that the label of 'traitor to the Homeland' had crippled me not for six years but for life. At the time, however, I had only one sensation, and that was that an injustice had been committed, a legalised illegality, and that I was powerless; all I could do was to gather and store my outrage and despair inside me, storing it up until it exploded like an overheated boiler.

I recalled the empty rows of seats in the chamber, the indifferent voices of the judge and prosecutor, the court secretary chewing on a roll the whole time, the silent statues of the guards. Why hadn't they let anyone into the court, not even my mother? Why had no witnesses been called? Why wasn't I given a copy of the sentence? What did they mean: 'You can't have a copy of the sentence, it's secret'? A few minutes later a blue paper was pushed through the little trapdoor for food: 'Sign this to say that you've been informed of your sentence.' I signed it and that was that. The sentence was final, with no right of appeal.

I went on hunger strike. I wrote a statement protesting against the trial and sentence, pushed it through the food trap and refused to accept any food. For several days I took nothing into my mouth but cold water. Nobody paid any attention. The warders, after listening to my refusal, would calmly remove my portion of food and soup bowl and bring them back again in the evening. Again I would refuse. Three days later the warders entered my cell with a doctor and commenced the operation known as 'forced artificial feeding'. My hands were twisted behind my back and handcuffed, then they stuffed a spreader into my mouth, stuck a hose down my gullet and began pouring the feeding mixture – something greasy and sweet – in through a funnel at the top. The warders said: 'Call off your hunger strike. You won't gain anything by it and in any case we won't let you lose weight.' The same procedure was repeated on the following day.

I called off my hunger strike. And I never did get a reply to my protest.

Several days later a warder came to fetch me. He led me via a staircase and various corridors to the first floor and directed me through a door lined with black oilcloth. A little nameplate said: 'Prison Governor'. In the office inside sat the prison governor at his desk, beneath a large portrait of Dzerzhinsky;* on the couch were two men familiar to me from the investigation of my case, the Legal Inspector of Prisons and the head of the Investigation Department. The fourth man was a stranger. One glance at him and I shuddered, so unnatural and repulsive was his appearance: a tiny little egg-shaped body, minuscule legs that barely reached to the floor and the thinnest scraggy little neck crowned by an enormous flattened globe – his head. The slits of his eyes, the barely discernible little nose and the thin smiling mouth were sunk in a sea of taut, yellow, gleaming dough. How could that neck hold such a load?

They told me that this was the Deputy Public Prosecutor

---

* A former chief of the Soviet secret police, called the GPU in his time.

of the Turkmen Republic, and invited me to sit down. The conversation was conducted in an informal and familiar tone. They asked me how I felt and whether I had ended my hunger strike. Thanking them for their touching delicacy and interest, I informed them that it was ended and asked in turn: 'Can you tell me, please, when and where will I be sent?'

'You are going to a Komsomol* site. You'll be a Komsomol worker,' answered the monster, absolutely wreathed in smiles as he enjoyed his little joke.

I felt unbearably revolted. On me, who had been sentenced by them for treason to my country, it somehow grated to hear them utter these words here, in this office, and to see their cynical sneers. They all knew perfectly well what it meant. And I knew too.

Back in my cell I thought of the various sites I had worked on. Outside every one there had been a camp, barbed wire, control towers, guards and 'Komsomol workers in reefer-jackets'.† I recalled how as a nineteen-year-old youth I had been sent on a two-month assignment to Bukhtarma power station. The quarters where we free workers lived were at Serebryanka, some way away from the site, and the camp was there too. Both we and the camp convicts were taken to each shift and back again by train. The 'free' train consisted of five or six ancient four-wheeled wagons. It used to stop about fifty yards from the guardhouse and then we would show our passes to the soldier on guard duty and walk through the entrance passage. After this they would open up the gates and the endless train with the cons‡ on board would roll straight inside the site perimeter. This one was not like ours with its hopeless little four-wheelers, but consisted of big, strong, eight-wheeled cars into which the cons were packed like sardines. On every brake platform sat a pair of tommy gunners and the rear of the train was brought up

---

* The Komsomol is the Soviet youth organisation. Many members used to volunteer to go and work on difficult sites just as Marchenko himself had done on leaving school (see p. 29).

† Reefer-jacket is the ironic term used for the quilted-cotton short overcoats issued to prisoners.

‡ i.e. convicts or prisoners.

by an open platform full of soldiers. The soldiers would open the doors, drive out the cons, herd them away from the cars and line them up five deep. Then began the count by fives: the first five, the second, the third, the fifteenth, the fifty-second, the hundred and fifth . . . counting and recounting. Suddenly there would be a mistake and they'd start counting all over again. Shouts, curses and yet another recount. After a thorough check the cons would go to their work places. Then, when the shift was over, the same thing would take place in reverse order. I had worked side by side with them, these 'Komsomol workers in reefer-jackets'. I used to get my pay, go to dances on my days off and never think a thing of it. Only one incident had embedded itself in my memory.

One day at the beginning of August one of the watch towers had suddenly started firing in the direction of the river Irtysh. Everybody downed tools and ran to the river bank, crowding up against the fence, with the free workers and cons all mixed up together. They tried to drive us away, of course, but we stayed put and gaped. A swimmer was already more than halfway across the river, closer to the opposite bank. We could see clearly that he was having difficulty in swimming and that he was trying to go as fast as possible. It was a con. It seemed he had bided his time till the dredger stopped working and then had crawled through the pipe and plunged into the Irtysh some way out from the shore. They hadn't noticed him at first and by the time they opened fire, he was already a long way off. The guard launch had already set off in pursuit and now was about to catch up with the fugitive; it was only about a dozen Yards behind, but the officer with the pistol in his hand was for some reason holding his fire. 'Well, if he shoots and kills him and the con goes to the bottom, how's he going to prove afterwards that he hasn't escaped?' explained the cons in the crowd. 'He's got to have either a living man or a body to show them.'

Meanwhile the fugitive reached the far shore, stood up and staggered a few steps. But the launch's bow had already struck the stones and the officer leapt out and found himself within two paces of the con. I saw him raise his pistol and shoot him in the legs. The con collapsed. Some tommy gunners ran up and as they stood there and in full view of the crowd on the opposite bank, the officer fired several times into the prostrate prisoner. The crowd gasped and somebody swore obscenely.

The body was dragged over the stones like a sack and tossed into the launch. The launch set off downriver in the direction of the camp.

Now I couldn't help but think of Bukhtarma and this incident, and also other sites. No matter where they sent me now I would always be a 'Komsomol worker', I would be soaked and frozen during the checks, I would live behind barbed wire, I would be guarded by armed guards with sheepdogs; and if I couldn't bear it and tried to escape, I would be shot down just like that fellow in the Irtysh.

CONVOYS

The following day I was sent away. They gave me back my clothes, which had been taken away when I was arrested, with the sole exception of my boots – these had been cut up into little pieces in their search for the 'plan of a Soviet factory'. I was ordered to get dressed and was then led out of the prison. A black maria stood right up against the door. I was thrust into a 'box' in the back and locked in. The van moved off. My cage had no windows, so that I couldn't see out but could only feel the van's motion. Suddenly the van slowed, turned and began to back up. So I was being transferred to a train. Then hurry, hurry again out of the van, between two solid ranks of soldiers and straight into the train. The prison coaches (they are still called 'Stolypins'*) are the same as normal passenger coaches: a narrow corridor runs the full length of one side, with the separate cabins or compartments on the other side. The connecting doors, though, are not solid but barred. There are no windows whatever. One side of the coach is completely blank, while the windows facing the corridor are filled with bars. None of this can be seen from outside however – they are covered with blinds – so that to look at it's a coach just like any other coach, and no one would guess that it's carrying convicts. It's true, of course, that all the windows are blocked up and shuttered, nobody looks out and waves to friends on the platform. It's as though all the gloomy and unsociable passengers have gathered together into this one coach.

Each compartment has three shelves on either side, one

* Named after P. A. Stolypin (1863–1911), Tsarist minister of the interior who was assassinated by a revolutionary.

above the other. Between the middle ones a board can be fixed to form a single solid bunk. This means that generally there is sleeping room for seven – eight if you crowd up tight – but usually they cram twelve to fifteen people into each compartment or cage, and sometimes even more. And their luggage as well. And everything is stoppered up tight, so that there is no chance of any fresh air getting in, except perhaps during a halt, when they open the door to take somebody out or shove an extra one in.

The corridor is patrolled by soldiers armed with pistols. If a soldier happens to be a decent sort he will open one of the corridor windows in passing and for a short while a draught of fresh air will blow through the bars of the door. But some of the escorts won't give you any air no matter how much you beg them. And then the cons choke in their cages like fish thrown up on the beach.

From Ashkhabad to Tashkent I travelled like a prince, with a whole cage to myself! The other cages were packed tight. When I asked my neighbours through the wall how many they were, they replied 'seventeen'. It turned out that the explanation of the comfort offered to me was not any special regard for politicals, but a fear of bringing them into contact with ordinary criminals – in case they corrupted them during the journey. As a result, I did not suffer from overcrowding like the others. In every other respect, however, my ride was just as unpleasant as everybody else's.

In Ashkhabad prison I was supplied with victuals for my next journey: a loaf of black bread, one and a half ounces of sugar and a salted herring. No matter how far it is to the next transit point, that is all you get; they don't feed you in the prison coaches. But worse than hunger is the thirst that tortures prisoners on the move. Morning and evening they give you each a mug of hot water and as for cold water, it depends on what soldier you get. If he's a good one he'll bring you two or three kettles, but if he can't be bothered to fetch and carry for you, then you can sit there till you die of thirst.

Towards evening I decided to have some supper. I unwrapped my Ashkhabad ration, tore off half the herring with my fingers and ate it with some bread. Then I asked the soldier for some water, but he refused. 'You can wait till the rest get it.' I waited. About twenty minutes later they started giving out the hot water. A soldier with a kettle walked down the corridor, pouring hot water into the mugs held out through the bars. He came to my cage.

'Where's your mug?'

As it happened, I had no mug, I had lost it during my investigation. So I asked:

'Maybe you could lend me yours . . .'

'What bloody next! Give him my mug! Maybe you'd like my prick as well?'

And he went further on. I started to dip my bread in the sugar and eat it dry. Yet I had a terrible thirst. I hadn't drunk anything for ages, my mouth was all dried up, and on top of it all I had just eaten salted herring. For some reason they always give prisoners salted herrings when they travel – on purpose probably. And later, no matter where or when I travelled, I was always given salted herring. Old cons also told me that they always got salted herrings and nothing to drink.

My neighbours in the next cage, hearing that I had nothing to drink and nothing to drink from, started asking the soldier to pass me one of their mugs of hot water. He swore black and blue, but nevertheless passed it to me. I drank the water down, together with my sugar.

'Keep the mug yourself,' they shouted, 'it will come in handy!' And so it did. It stayed with me wherever I went for the next six years – to Mordovia, to Vladimir prison and back to Mordovia again.

Then came fresh torments. I asked the soldier to let me go to the toilet. He replied:

'You'll have to wait.'

Well, of course I would have to wait, what else could I do?

There is one toilet in each prison coach: one seat and one wash basin. They take you there one by one. First they unlock the barred door of your cage, stand you in the corridor opposite the door with your face to the wall and your hands behind your back, then they lock the door behind you and lead you at the

double down the corridor. While you do your business the door
of the toilet is left wide open and the soldier stands and watches
you. All the time he hurries you up: get a move on, get a move
on! When you've finished you don't even get time to do your
trousers up, but, still at the double and with your hands behind
your back, are rushed back to your cage again. The coach is
packed full, so that by the time you take everyone that way it's
time to start again. But the soldiers are too tired, they don't
want to: why should they have to chase up and down the corridor all day with these damned layabouts? And so they shout:
'You have to wait!' and don't take you, no matter how you
plead with them, even if you were to break into tears. You
have to wait until everyone is taken, and then until it's your
turn.

It's the worst kind of torture you can imagine, both with the
drinking and the toilet. And a very old invention, so they say.
And it's still practised and will probably go on being practised so
long as convicts are transported around Russia.

All the way to Tashkent I slept like a log, was tortured by
thirst and was also hungry. But I really enjoyed hearing the
voices behind the wall: all day long it was one continual sound
of cursing and blinding, either at the soldiers, or else at each
other or more distant neighbours in the other cages. The stream
of obscenities was music to my ears – for five months I hadn't
heard a human voice, except for the KGB investigators and the
people in court.

The following day the train arrived in Tashkent. One by one
we were taken out of the train, driven through a narrow corridor
formed by two ranks of soldiers and crammed into a series of
vans.

As I went up the steps the cons inside were already yelling
that there was no more room. But the escort roared obscenely
at them, grabbed hold of me and shoved me in, right on top of
the others. After me, several more were crammed in in the
same way. The 'black maria', consisting of a closed van, was
divided inside by a barred grille with a gate. On one side of the
grille were us cons, on the other – two escorts. On the escorts'
side there were also two or three 'boxes' – iron lockers for

single prisoners; you had to tie yourself up in a knot in order to get into them at all. But it was even worse in the communal section. Low benches ran right round the walls, with a space in the middle. There was room for about ten men (both sitting and standing), but no more. Into this space about thirty of us had been crammed. The first ones sat down on the benches, tight up against one another. The next ones sat on their knees. And the rest had to stand. This in itself would have been all right, but think what standing meant! The roof was so low that you could only stand by stooping, with your head and shoulders pressed up against the iron top. And there were so many men crammed in that you literally couldn't budge, let alone change position. In you went, and whatever position you ended up in you had to keep till you arrived. Your back, shoulders and neck turned numb and your whole body started to ache from the unnatural position. But even if you were to lift your feet off the floor, you wouldn't fall, you would still be propped up by the bodies around you.

The last one couldn't get in at all, and then the two soldiers put their hands against him, leaned their full weight behind the load and squeezed him into the mass of bodies, afterwards forcing the gate slowly shut. Somehow they got it closed and then locked it. Our van was ready. But the others still had to be crammed full, and so we were forced to wait. The soldiers closed the outer door, sat down and lit cigarettes. Now there was absolutely nothing outside to tell you what sort of van this was or what was going on inside. A closed body with no windows, except for one tiny window over the rear door, where the escorts sat, and even this had a small green curtain drawn over it.

The men began to gasp for air. Somebody started cursing:

'When the fucking hell do we get started?'

'When you've done your time you can ride about in a limousine,' came the sarcastic reply of one of the soldiers, 'but this is a black maria, not a limousine.'

The con couldn't even talk properly, but only croaked:

'What's a fucking fancy boy like you doing worrying about limousines? You've never even been near an ordinary car. Been fucking starving all your life, and now when they put a gun in your hands you take the piss out of us.'

'Go on, go on! We'll see at the end how talkative you are in handcuffs.'

Then some others joined in:

'That's the only way you can do anything, with handcuffs!'

'Fucking fascists! Sticking us in their "gas vans"*!'

'It's the tommy guns that give the orders! Take those away and they'd be kissing our pricks – that's what they're used to!'

We heard an officer come up to the van. The cons fell silent, trying to listen to what he said. Our two soldiers called him 'lieutenant', but we couldn't hear anything that was said, except 'let them wait'. Then the cons started yelling again:

'Boss! Let's go!'

'Making fools of us!'

'Fascists with red notebooks!'

The men here had nothing to lose, they had been driven to despair by all these torments, and so they shouted the first thing that came into their heads. A criminal con, incidentally, can get himself charged on a political count, tried again and given an additional sentence of up to seven years for anti-Soviet agitation. But in these conditions nobody thought of anything like that or looked ahead in any way. Who had thought them up, these 'gas vans' (black marias), the salted herrings and all the rest? Just give him to us, that clever inventor!

The van trembled as the engine started. We set off. We were shaken and thrown about by the journey, but there was no room to fall down. Not even a dead man would have fallen there, but would have remained standing upright, supported on all sides. How long it took I don't remember. All ideas of time got jumbled in those conditions and a minute seemed an age.

When the van slowed and made several turns, we realised we were nearly there. Hurry up! Oh to get out of there, straighten up and take a deep breath. But then when the van

* A reference to the mobile gas extermination trucks used by the Nazis for mass executions.

halted, nobody even bothered to let us out. We no longer had the strength either to beg or swear. At last one of the soldiers started to open up. First he let the separate prisoners out of the boxes, and they were so doubled up when they emerged that they couldn't stand upright at first. Then he opened the door of our grille:

'Get out!'

This turned out to be not so simple. The men had got so compressed and entangled on the way that no one was able to disentangle himself or extricate himself from the general mass. By the time the first had managed to extricate himself he was forced literally to undress, leaving his padded jacket behind in the back of the van. And when almost everybody had left the van, someone brought his jacket out and gave it to him.

Having got out at last I, like the rest of them, was unable to straighten up, nor to walk a step. My whole body was a mass of aches and pains.

We had arrived at the Tashkent transit prison. Over the entrance was a huge slogan printed in white on red calico: 'Under the conditions of Socialism every man who leaves the path of labour is able to return to useful activity.' To begin with we were stuck in a quarantine cell – a gloomy, cavernous chamber with a double tier of bunks round the walls and a tiny barred window. Then they fed us the usual prison supper and took us to the bath house.

Attached to the bath house was a barber's shop. It came as a great surprise to realise that somewhere on earth there existed such clean rooms with white curtains at the windows. And convict barbers in white coats. And mirrors on the wall. What miracle was this? It turned out that this barber's shop served the entire prison administration, from the warders right up to the top brass. And here I too was cropped.

In general, all prisoners are cropped as soon as they are arrested, but this rule doesn't apply in KGB prisons. There they leave your hair on. But this lasts only as far as the first transit point. To the envy of my cell mates, I was still equipped with my usual hairstyle. They were amazed and I explained it to them:

'You and I have different sponsors – yours is the MVD (Ministry of the Interior), while mine is the KGB (Commissariat for State Security).'

Noticing my hair in the bath house, one of the warders grabbed me by the sleeve and led me to the barber's shop. In a trice I was shorn, and now I looked exactly like all the other cons.

The bath house in the Tashkent transit prison was hell upon earth, especially after the neat and clean barber's shop with its mirrors. In the changing room there were two benches – and they herded a hundred of us in there. Underfoot squelched a messy porridge of crumbling, disintegrating plaster, mud from the street and water. When you had undressed, you handed in your underwear to be fumigated and then had to stand there stark naked and wait until everybody else was ready. But some had no room, some took their time, and some had to be taken for haircuts. Meanwhile it was freezing cold in the changing room and the skins of those of us who were naked turned blue and were covered in goose pimples. Everyone was yelling and cursing, not only the warders but also those who were holding up the rest. Only when everyone was ready did a warder unlock the door of the washroom. Everyone was issued a microscopic piece of soap; but a fat chance there was of soaping yourself! Not everyone had had time even to get some water, when: 'All out! Don't make a meal of it, you're not home now!' Somehow or other we rinsed ourselves and went out. When we were out, of course, our underwear still hadn't come back from the fumigator, so once again we had to wait there naked and wet in the freezing cold.

Finally they brought back the enormous hoops on which each of us had hung his underwear before the bath. It was supposed to have been baked so as to destroy the fleas, but it hadn't even had time to get heated up and was only warm. Just so long as the formalities were observed and could be ticked off: the prisoners have been washed and their clothes processed. But then, how could they possibly manage to do everything properly when so many people were herded through day after day?

I got back my underwear and started to dress. And though I can say, I think, that I'm not the sensitive type, still it turned me over to think of pulling my trousers over feet that had been standing in that filth. If I wiped them with my towel, what would I have to wipe my face with the following day? I fished my only vest out of my things, wiped my feet with it, then spread it out on the floor and stood on it. Somehow I managed to dress. Around me, pushing and shoving and bumping into one another, the rest of the cons also got dressed, each one shifting for himself as best he could. And curses, obscenities, the warders shouting: 'Hurry, hurry!'

We were taken back to the same cell as before. We sorted ourselves out somehow or other, but nobody settled for long – soon we would be split up for the next stage of our journeys. In the meantime we amused ourselves as best we could. A game of cards started in the lower bunks, while on the top tier a number of masters of the trade worked at making a new pack. Someone had already been beaten up. Some people had found neighbours or countrymen and were deep in conversation.

After a couple of hours the duty officer came in with a pair of warders, called out twenty-five people on his list and led them away. Later a second party was led away. Then a third. I turned out to be in the fourth.

We were taken to a detention cell, which was exactly like the quarantine cell we had just left. The same grime and suffocating closeness, hardly any light from a tiny window and a light bulb burning around the clock. The bunks had initials cut into them. On the walls there were various inscriptions, most of them bawdy, but there were also messages and information: 'Ivan and Musa of Bokhara have gone to number 114. Greetings to all Bokharans!'

There were about eighty of us in the cell altogether. Some would be there only a day or two, others would have to wait up to a month for their convoy to leave. And all this time on bare planks, without bedding; all this time without exercise – instead of exercise you had half an hour's toilet break twice a day. In one corner of the cell was an enormous, rusty slop-tank, just one for all eighty of us, and the whole cell reeked of its stench.

Supper was brought. They handed out badly-washed, sticky spoons that stuck to our hands, and started to pour out the skilly. A line was formed at the food trap by those still waiting to be served, swearing among themselves and blindly cursing the cookhands. Then, when they got theirs and were carrying their bowls back from the trap, they cursed the skilly as well: 'Gnat's piss, dish water.' There wasn't enough for all of us (including me); somebody had made a mix-up with the lists, and about forty minutes passed before they sorted it out. What we got then was some sort of slop water that had gone completely cold already. There was nowhere to sit for meals. Some settled down on their bunks, others drank their skilly standing up, over the side or 'over the gunwhales', as we used to say. Then somebody would bump into somebody else – which was easy enough to do in such a crush – the skilly was spilled (they would never give you any more in such cases) and there'd be uproar and a fight. Another man might climb up to one of the top bunks to have his supper and spill some; the broth would splash through the cracks between the boards on to those below, and again there'd be an uproar and fighting. And so on every day.

I spent about twelve days in this cell. I got to know it well and found myself a comfortable spot on the upper tier. I got to know one or two people. The occupants were always changing, since some were always being taken away on convoys and new ones came to fill their places. The arrival of new men in the cell was always an event – there weren't any other events in any case. Everybody would stop whatever he was doing to examine the newcomers and call out to old friends. And although I had no expectation of meeting any friends here, nevertheless I too, like all the rest, used to hang down from my bunk to stare at them.

And then one day, when a new bunch was brought in, who should I see but Budrovsky – Anatoly Budrovsky, my co-defendant, who had ditched me in order to save his own skin! Having seen him, I leaned back in my bunk and watched from the safety of darkness, so that he wouldn't see me. As he entered the cell, Budrovsky swept a quick glance over the bunks and cons all around and walked past me. The door was then closed behind the newcomers and locked. At that point I climbed down and sat on one of the lower bunks, gazing straight at Budrovsky. His kisser was plump and well-fed. At last he caught sight of me and his expression changed in an instant. He huddled at the far end of the cell and watched me closely, without approaching. He was afraid, of course, that I would tell the others about him double-crossing me, for then they would beat him up to within an inch of his life, or maybe even kill him. The cell was full of criminal cons and their rule was simple: once you sell a comrade down the river you pay for it!

The time came for our toilet break. Budrovsky stayed where he was and refused to go. I reassured him:

'Come on, don't be scared. I won't tell anyone, and besides I want to talk to you.'

We went out together. And at this point my co-defendant burst into tears:

'Tolik, forgive me. I couldn't help it, I was scared. The investigator told me you had given the necessary testimony and that if I didn't confirm it, that meant I was worse than you. Then, come what may, it would have meant death for both of us . . .'

'And did they show you "my" testimony?'

'No, Tolik, but it made no difference, I couldn't help it. The investigator insisted and threatened to have me shot – you know, for treason.'

'What did they want you to do?'

'To say that you had hostile intentions, that you intended to hand over . . .'

'You damned fool, what could I possibly hand over! And so you thought you'd save yourself and leave me to face the firing squad?'

'No Tolik, not the death sentence, but only six years. It would have been all the same to you if it had been more, you're older than I am, and we agreed that you'd take most of the blame on yourself. Tolik, forgive me!'

'What's the point of talking to you!'

We returned to the cell. When the hot water was brought I took out my provisions – the remains of my day's ration, a pinch of sugar. Budrovsky came up to me with his. He undid a parcel and I gasped: inside were sweets and cakes!

'Where did you get them from?'

'Ashkhabad, the prison.'

'Yes, but how come? Whose money?'

'The investigator had some transferred to me. He said they had a special fund for people under investigation and twice a month had about seven to eight roubles transferred to me at the prison shop. And the cigarettes were free. I didn't realise it at first and used to use the money to buy them with.'

'I don't seem to have had a single copeck transferred to me.'

'No, Tolik, he said it was for people who behaved themselves.'

'Oh, I see, it was for the cigarettes and the seven roubles at the shop!'

'Tolik, forgive me! Here, take some!'

It made me sick to look at him and his yellow, well-fed, tear-stained face.

A few days later Budrovsky was sent with a convoy to Vakhi, to work on some power station. And I remained behind.

One cell-mate of mine, a man who knew the ropes, Volodya, explained to me that I was being held here wrongly, that since I was a political I couldn't be kept in the same cell as criminals. Evidently they had got mixed up in all the confusion and had failed to make the distinction. But I kept quiet about it – I was afraid of ending up alone again. After five months of solitary I was enjoying being here with other men. Then, when I had had enough of this filthy, gloomy cell, I asked the duty officer during inspection one day how much longer they were going to keep me hanging around in there.

'Just as long as we have to, so you just wait.'

'But I'm not supposed to be in here.'

'What do you mean? What are you in for? What was the charge?'

'You just look up my case and you'll find out.'

The officer shot out of the cell and a few minutes later came back with another one.

'Marchenko, pick up your things, quick. How did you get into this cell?'

'Well, I certainly didn't pick it.'

I was transferred to an empty cell and two days later sent on by convoy to Alma-Ata.

Now my life of luxury came to an end, I no longer had a cage to myself. From Tashkent they had so many prisoners and exiles to send that there was no question of obeying rules. All the cages of the prison coaches were packed as tight as they would go. Eight men sat below, four on the middle tier and two lay up on the top. Up there it was hellishly hot and stuffy and they were soaked, with the sweat absolutely pouring off them. However, everybody down below was soaked as well. And they had been known to pack even more in sometimes, regardless of the torture it caused.

From Tashkent they were sending into exile the 'parasites'.

One of the cages had women in it – they had a fraction more room than we did, they were only thirteen (instead of fourteen). But one of them had a baby that was still breast feeding. Throughout the whole coach we could hear the baby crying, the woman asking the soldier for something and the soldier roughly refusing. The woman began to weep and her neighbours to shout and swear at the soldier. At that moment the officer in charge of the coach came into the corridor, a captain:

'Stop this caterwauling! Do you want handcuffs on?'

Sobbing, the woman explained what was the matter. The baby had messed itself and she only had one nappy for it – could she go to the toilet to wash it out?

'Nothing will happen to it, you can wait!'

'But I've got nothing to change the baby into, what shall I do?'

'You should have asked me that before you had it,' replied the captain and walked away.

When the women started to be let out for their toilet break, the child's mother was the first to go. Somehow she managed to wash the baby's things out in the wash basin and leave them there. The next woman rinsed them as much as she had time for and again left them there. And the next and the next. By the time all the women had been led out, the things were well washed and the last one brought them back with her. Then they dried them inside the cage.

It is fortunate that people remained human, even behind bars.

The whole way there were endless checks and inspections. Before you go into the prison coach you are searched – they even poke and prod at the piece of bread you've just been issued with in prison. Then a complete check: surname, name, patronymic, date of birth, charge, sentence, completion date . . . Finally they check you against your photograph. 'Okay, you can go. Next . . .' When you leave the coach again, another check. At the transit prison another search, another check, more questions about your case: surname, name, patronymic, date of birth, charge, sentence . . . When you're called out for the next stage of the journey – yet another search, another check, questions about your case, and so on every day and several times a day.

How far would I have to go? And where? At least as far as Novosibirsk via Alma-Ata and Semipalatinsk. But then where – to the Urals? The far north? Siberia? There are 'Komsomol' sites everywhere . . .

In Alma-Ata, after we had been let out of the 'gas vans', we were lined up in fives according to the regulations and counted and checked by name before being taken to the prison block. At the tail end of the column were the women who had been in our coach. Before they had even had time to recover from the ride the criminal cons started to chat them up. The warders and officers yelled at the cons and drove them away from the women with threats: it was forbidden even to talk at all, let alone with women. 'Get lost, officer, and your cooler with you,' one of the cons would say. 'Let me at least look at a dame and then you can stick me inside. I haven't seen a dame for five years, except for postcards of those fucking Komsomol girls of yours.'

While we were being led through the yard to the prison block, one of the cons started to filter back towards the rear of the column, to where the women were. A warder noticed this, halted the column, pulled the offender out and dragged him up to the front again.

'You fancy boy, you queer!' screeched the con. 'I hope a prick grows out of your forehead!'

The warder began to stutter something about having to

protect the women from types like him. Then the women started:

'Look who's sticking up for us!'

'A rope's too good for you people!'

The commotion brought some other warders running. The resisting con had his arms twisted behind his back and was handcuffed. At the same time he yelled:

'If you feel sorry for these dames, then bring me your own! Or turn round and let me get at that fat arse you've put on with all that free grub!'

They began beating up the troublemaker and the column buzzed with indignant cries. Then they pulled one more out of the column at random, put handcuffs on him too and started to hack him in the legs with their boots. The pair of them were then dragged off and the column continued to the prison block.

The transit prison in Alma-Ata differed from Tashkent only in the abundance of its bugs. There were so many of them that the cell walls were completely red. It was the same in Semipalatinsk, although here they had iron double cots instead of bunks with wooden boards. In no transit prison do they give you any mattresses or pillows, you have to flop there from arrival to departure just on the bare boards or metal mesh. And the trains have bare boards too, on top of which there's no room to stand or lie down, not to speak of the salted herring, nothing to drink and the refusal to let you go to the toilet.

Novosibirsk transit prison was full of rats. They were running about the floor underfoot, running between the men sleeping there and even crawling over them. It was there that I met a group of prisoners in the corridor who didn't stand like the rest of us, but were slumped against the wall. There were about eight of them and they had horribly gaunt faces. We were in the same cell together. I found out that these were religious believers. They had refused to participate in the elections and so had been arrested, tried in closed court and sentenced to exile as 'parasites'. From the very day of their arrest the whole lot had proclaimed a hunger strike and kept it up throughout the investigation and trial. They had been fed artificially, just as I had been at Ashkhabad. After the trial, they still didn't end their hunger strike and so were despatched, half-starving, to Siberia. At every transit prison they had the feeding mixture forcibly poured down their throats before being posted further. 'We are suffering for our faith,' they said.

From Novosibirsk I was sent to Taishet, where there used to be enormous camps for politicals. But when I arrived, there turned out to be not a single one left. Three days earlier the last special convoy had left for Mordovia. Nature abhors a vacuum, however, and the Taishet camps immediately began to fill with criminal cons. They were brought here from all over the Union – the land had to be cleared and the bottom prepared for the future reservoir of the Bratsk Power Station. Who else would come here to 'labour with Komsomol enthusiasm', if not the cons?

In the transit prison at Taishet I found myself for the first time in a cell with other politicals – a few men had somehow got left behind, for various reasons there hadn't been time to despatch them with all the rest. Up till now I had kept wondering to myself what sort of men they would be, what they were in for, how they behaved and what they thought about.

There weren't many of us in the cell. Two older men, both with twenty-five-year terms, one a Volga German – an old man with a bushy grey beard whose name I don't remember – and the other erect and jaunty, with an obviously military bearing. He had indeed been a soldier, first as a captain in the Red Army and then as a commander in General Vlasov's army.* His name was Ivanov. Ivanov was a year older than the German and invariably addressed him as 'young fellow'. There was also one other with twenty-five years, Ivan Tretyakov, a very nice fellow. In addition there was also Sasha, a vociferous character who had been a front-line officer in the Soviet army throughout the war and had been many times wounded. And of us younger men there were three: myself, a student from Leningrad and a young fellow who was cracked. We got along well in the cell, without

---

* General Vlasov was a Soviet officer, captured by the Germans at the beginning of the war, who organised a Russian army to fight on the German side.

quarrelling, and the old men watched over us, teaching us the ropes about how to make the best of camp life – they themselves were old hands at the game, for each of them had ten to fifteen years behind him of the most terrible camps in existence.

At the end of April some fellow from Afghanistan was tossed into our cell. He hardly spoke a word of Russian and we had difficulty in finding out what had happened to him. It turned out that several years ago he had walked across the frontier into the Soviet Union. Life was hard back home in Afghanistan, working as a shepherd for some rich landowner. He was at once clapped into jail, of course, but after a time they satisfied themselves that he was neither a spy nor a saboteur and allowed him to live in the Soviet Union, which was precisely what he wanted. He was sent to a *kolkhoz* (collective farm) to work as a shepherd again. But the Afghan didn't care for the *kolkhoz* and started asking to go back home, but here came the crunch – they wouldn't let him. Well, he didn't stop long to think about it and set off to return by the way he had come. He was caught, tried and sentenced to three years for attempting to cross the border illegally. His three years were now up and he was due in a few days to be released. The Afghan used to walk up and down the cell striking himself on the head and saying: 'Fool, what a fool!'

'Where will you go now? Back to the *kolkhoz*?'

'No, no!' the Afghan shook his head furiously. He didn't want the *kolkhoz* any more. 'Go Afghanistan.'

'But they won't let you go! And if they catch you you'll get ten years – this time for treason.'

'Go Afghanistan,' insisted the Afghan. '*Kolkhoz* no.' Just before his release they gave him a new quilted coat and a pair of black, camp trousers. He was so infuriated that he pushed both the trousers and coat into the sloptank and left in the rags and tatters he was standing up in. What happened after that I don't know. 'I've never met him since in any of the prisons I've known', as they sing in the song.

On 4 May we were all put back on the train and sent away. More convoys. Back to Novosibirsk once more and then westwards: Sverdlovsk, Kazan, Ruzayevka.

En route our ranks were added to by new companions and at one transit prison we picked up a number of Ukrainian 'nationalists'. They were also in for twenty-five years. One of them I remember particularly well, Mikhail Soroka, an extremely calm, goodhearted and strongminded man. Then there was a fellow from Poland. His father had been one of the Polish officers shot in Katyn Forest.* His mother had been arrested and also perished. He himself had been placed in an orphanage, where he stayed till he was sixteen, and when he got his own passport he was entered as a Russian. He kept insisting that he be allowed to go to Poland, but they said he was 'Russian' and wouldn't let him go. He also wrote to the Ministry of Foreign Affairs and the Polish embassy – and ended up in the camps.

In Kazan our 'grandfather', Ivanov, was summoned to the orderly room. He had just completed fifteen years and they informed him that upon arrival at the other end he would have to go to court again. The point was that the twenty-five-year sentence was being done away with and men who had earlier been given the full term were now having their sentences reduced to the new maximum of fifteen.

I was overjoyed for Ivanov and for others serving twenty-five-year terms:

'Now you've got hardly any time to go. By the time we arrive you'll be able to walk straight out! And I'll be there to see you out of the camp too,' I added to the old Volga German.

'No, Tolya, I shan't see freedom again,' he replied. 'I shall be behind barbed wire till I die.'

* In spring 1940, 15,000 Polish officers and men from Soviet POW camps were shot by the Soviet secret police. See *Death in the Forest* by J. K. Zawodny, University of Notre Dame Press, 1962.

MORDOVIA

At the end of May we arrived in Potma. After five months in the remand prison, after the so-called trial, after the convoys and transit prisons, I had made my way at last to the celebrated camps of Mordovia.

The whole south-west corner of Mordovia is criss-crossed with barbed wire and fences of a special kind of construction, strewn with watch towers and lit up at night by the bright beams of coupled searchlights. Here the whole place is littered with signs saying 'Halt! Forbidden Zone' in Russian and Mordovian.

Here you will come across more military escorts and armed guards than Mordovians – and a superabundance of officers. Here there are more dogs per head of population than there are dogs per head of sheep in the Caucasus. Here statistics in general have been turned on their head, including the proportion of men to women and the national composition of the adult population. Russians, Ukrainians, Latvians, Estonians and 'individual representatives' of other nationalities have been living behind barbed wire here for so many years that they've exceeded all requirements for a certificate of permanent settlement. The fathers and elder brothers of today's prisoners have sunk for ever into the soil of Mordovia, either as skeletons or as a miscellaneous scattering of bones mixed up with sand. The children of today's prisoners come 'for an outing' from every corner of this colossal, multinational land of ours. And now I too had arrived here, after all my preliminary ordeals, to give yet one more tiny tilt to the crazy statistics of Mordovia.

From the Potma transit prison I was directed to camp number

ten. Like any novice I took a long, cautious look at my new
companions and surroundings and simultaneously lost no time
in getting myself settled in. You might well ask what sort of
settling in is required of a con, what sort of belongings, chattels
and furniture does he think he has? However, a novice in camp
is up to his ears in jobs. First he has to find himself a place in a
hut and get himself a cot, straw mattress, pillow, blanket and
bedding and regulation overalls for work, and meanwhile sign
for everything and get it back to his place. They pointed out to
me our company 'steward' (also a convict). He took me off to
look for a cot, questioning me on the way about this and that –
where did I come from, what was I in for, what sentence had I
got. When I told him six years he grinned ironically: 'Child's
play!' Many others would also grin later when they heard that I
had only five years and a bit to go.

Behind one corner of the hut, where the steward had led me,
a number of rusty iron cot frames were lying about on the
ground. We picked out one of the better ones and I dragged it
back to the hut. Inside, the whole hut was crammed full with
'sleeping places': the cots stood one on top of the other in two
tiers and pushed tight together in fours. A place was found for
me in the upper tier. I fixed my frame to the lower bunk and
the two of us went off to search for a wooden panel (four narrow
boards nailed together and placed in the frame of the bunk
instead of a wire mesh). After scouring the entire compound we
at last found a suitable one.

The lockers in the hut were allocated on a basis of one to four
people. The steward showed me my half shelf, but I hadn't
anything to put on it yet – not even my own spoon.

By the time I had finished these preparations it was time for
dinner. The cons were already making their way over to the big
canteen hut and I followed them. The inside of the canteen hut
was crowded with long tables consisting of rough boards with
red paint slapped over them, and were flanked by benches of a
similar nature. The canteen was packed solid. Some of the men,
having found themselves a place, were eating their skilly at the
tables. Others ate standing up, wherever they could find a place.
Long queues stretched away from the serving hatches. I stood

at the back of the queue for the first hatch. But how was I going to eat without a spoon? Having noticed my indecision, one of the lads from our company came over and handed me his spoon – he had already finished. The line advanced quickly. I hadn't had time to blink before the server plucked a bent aluminium bowl from the high pile in front of him, splashed a ladle-full of cabbage soup into it and thrust it into my hand. I moved away and looked around me – all the places were taken, there was nowhere to 'settle'. Then I saw a con standing by the window and just finishing up, he was licking his spoon already. I managed to arrive there just as he finished and stepped back, and quickly slipped into his place: standing my bowl on the window-sill, I started to drink the slopwater that somebody had dignified as cabbage soup. Then, leaving my cap and spoon on the sill, I went to stand in the queue for dessert just as nimbly as the first, the server at the second hatch whisked the bowl from my hand, banged a ladle into it and shot it back on to the tin-plated sill of the hatch. On my way back to my place I glanced into it: a watery wheat gruel was spread over the bottom – about three spoonfuls. It didn't take me long to deal with that. I licked my spoon thoroughly all over – 'polished' it, as the cons used to say – and left the canteen.

I was in luck. The stores turned out to be unexpectedly open outside of official hours and I was able to get my camp equipment immediately after dinner. They issued me with a mattress, blanket, pillow – all so ancient that they looked as if they must have been around in my grandfather's time – grey, washed out, unbleached calico sheets, a pillow case, two gingham towels, and an aluminium mug and spoon. I could also have got my overalls at the same time, but for these I was in no hurry – I would have five and some odd years in which to get sick and tired of them.

For today my equipment and arrangements were complete and I could afford to look around. But it turned out that I had an important appointment awaiting me that day: the steward came and said that the company officer had ordered me to see him.

After knocking on a door with 'Company Officer' written up

on a plaque, I went inside. It was a small office, extremely clean
and tidy. The company officer was sitting behind a desk and
rummaging in one of the drawers. On one wall hung a portrait
of Lenin, with a tear-off calendar just below it and a duty roster
for the internal order section. On the opposite wall, exactly
opposite Lenin's picture and eye to eye with it, was a portrait
of Khrushchev, together with a large map of the Soviet Union.
A large cupboard and rows of chairs along the walls completed
the furnishings. Hearing me enter, the officer closed the drawer,
locked it and raised his head:

'Take off your headgear! While talking to representatives of
the camp administration a prisoner is obliged to remove his
headgear – got it?'

I took off my cap.

'A newcomer, eh? Arrived today. Sit down.'

I sat down and the company officer started to leaf through my
file and ask me questions: surname, name, patronymic, charge,
sentence – the usual formal information about a prisoner. Finishing this, he tilted his chair back and rapped out curtly:

'All right, tell me all about it.'

I was astonished – what was I supposed to tell him? Then the
officer explained that he wanted me to tell him about my crime.
I refused:

'I'm not under investigation and I'm not on trial. This is my
jail and I don't want to discuss such things with my jailers.'

The company officer wasn't very pleased with my statement,
he frowned but kept quiet. Then, curtly and coldly, he read out
to me the duties of a prisoner and the rules of internal discipline:
'The prisoner is obliged . . . obliged . . . obliged . . . To appear
for work in the official prison clothing . . . To go to political
training sessions . . .'

I asked him who conducted the political training sessions. It
turned out that he himself did, once a week on Tuesdays. Then
he explained the punishments that awaited me if I failed to turn
up at these sessions, and also for other infringements of the
rules. I could be deprived – at his discretion and command – of
visits from relatives, shop privileges, gift parcels, letters – in
short any or all of the few privileges to which I had a right in

the camp. Besides this, I could also be sent to the punishment block . . . And so on – a list of punishments that was even longer than my duties. Everything was taken into account, every single movement regulated.

'Go to the stores and get your regulation clothing,' concluded the company officer. 'Tomorrow you'll start work. You've been put into the farm gang. You may go now.'

I went out. Back in the hut I was surrounded by the other cons in our company.

'Well, how was it? Did you make the acquaintance of Captain Vasyayev? How did you like him? And he you? Alas, alas, you're soon to be parted – he gets his pension soon . . .'

Someone said irritably:

'They're tough bastards. Look how many of 'em hang on with pensions – public money for nothing. And all earned by breaking our backs, instead of doing any work themselves.'

They asked me what gang I was in and said the farm gang worked outside the compound and went under armed escort.

'And don't try wearing your own clothes to work. They'll have you straight out of the guardhouse and into the cooler for a fortnight!'

Then they asked me about my trial: had it been open or closed? Had I been allowed to see my sentence? And after every answer, heads nodded understandingly. Well, of course, almost everybody here had been sentenced in closed court; and the majority, just like me, hadn't been shown a copy of the sentence, but had signed to say it had been read to them, as if they were all illiterate. There were, it is true, a few dozen men in the camp who had been sentenced in open courts – these were policemen, wartime collaborators, war criminals, men with bloody crimes on their record, crimes against humanity. These they tried openly and they described the trials over the radio in clubs and parks and wrote about them in the newspapers. 'And the charges against them are the same as against you and me, so the people think that all the people in the camps are the same sort of traitors and renegades . . .'

They started asking me about life outside: what was it like now, how did people live, were things getting better – you couldn't tell from the newspapers – was there sugar and butter in the shops?

Then somebody took pity on me:

'Let the lad go, he's late for the stores and tomorrow he has to start work.'

The cons reluctantly dispersed and I went to the stores to get my clothing: cotton trousers and tunic, forage cap, quilted coat, two sets of underwear, foot rags and felt boots. How long would I have to work to pay all this off! By the time I'd settled these debts my ankle boots would be worn out . . .

For supper they gave us some sort of watery soup and a tiny piece of boiled cod. The soup was so thin that there was no point in using a spoon on it, and following the example of the other cons I drank it straight from the bowl. After supper, more hungry than satisfied, I went for a stroll round the camp before lights out. There would be plenty of time to get to know the other people later, when I had had time to size them up.

It was a warm evening in spring. the grass looked green. Dusk was creeping up slowly. The cons wandered about here and there. On one bench beside a table they were playing dominoes, while elsewhere a game of chess was in progress. Many cons had settled down in the open air with a book or magazine. Animated conversation and arguments could be heard here and there. As I walked I passed other strollers going in the opposite direction in ones and twos. The majority were young or middle-aged, but I also noticed that there were a number of old men here, some of them completely senile. Then I was passed by a young fellow of about twenty-five to twenty-eight, who was tapping the ground with a stick, poking it out in front of him and moving it from side to side. As he drew level with me I saw that in place of eyes he had two little blue scars, from which tears were oozing in a constant trickle.

'Where are you off to, Sanya?' somebody called to him.

'I'm going to the medical post, my stomach's giving me pains,' replied the blind man. For a long time I stood watching him go and then I headed in the same direction. The medical post hut was quite close to the guardhouse. I walked all around it. In one wing lived the invalid prisoners and on a bench in front of the hut I saw a whole assembly of cripples: blind men, legless men, armless men, paralytics. I hastened to move away.

'Hey there, countryman! You're fresh here aren't you, just in from outside?' It was a passing con who spoke, short, about forty to look at and going noticeably bald.

I replied: 'Still wet behind the ears – six months remand in solitary.'

We introduced ourselves and later became quite close friends. It turned out that he really was a countryman of mine and what's more my namesake: his name was Anatoly Pavlovich Burov.

Later that evening, but before it was yet dark, lights suddenly flared up all round the camp – these were the lamps and searchlights stationed round the perimeter. I went back to my hut in order to make my bed before lights out, after that it would be impossible to see. When I had finished I went out again, I didn't feel like sitting still.

I had walked as far as a red brick building when I was overtaken by the signal for lights out. Ten o'clock. Ten ringing blows on a rail resounded across the camp. When the last stroke had died away I clearly heard the same signal being repeated in the distance. And then still further strokes, barely audible. And I imagined these chimes continuing right round the country, from camp to camp, and the blows on the rails being answered by the clock chimes on Spassky Tower in the Kremlin . . .

However, it is forbidden to wander about the compound after lights out. It was time to go 'home'. The corridor of our hut was still crowded with cons. Wearing just their underwear, they were having one last smoke before bed or continuing arguments that had been started during the day. Four cons were hurrying to finish letters. Suddenly someone shouted from the doorway: 'Guards!' and everyone rushed for their beds, tossing their home-made fags away as they went. The letter writers jumped up from the table, grabbed their paper and pens and scuttled to their places. And I too hurried to my cot. I undressed by the light of the blue lamp over the door and then turned several circles with my togs in my hand, wondering where to put them. Then I suddenly guessed, thrust them under the foot of my mattress and climbed into my top bunk. The other cons were still conversing in low voices, but gradually the noise was dying down. My neighbour, an old man of sixty or seventy, asked in a whisper:

'Well, my lad, how do you like your new home?'

'Not bad . . . It's paradise after those prison trains and transit prisons.'

I didn't exactly hear, but rather felt the old man laughing: my cot, which was hard up against his, began to tremble. After a moment he explained:

'Man's worse than a hog. Wear him out with a few transit prisons first, then stick him into a camp and he's even grateful. He knows where he is. Well, you'll see what sort of a paradise it is. Time to sleep now, good night to you.'

The old man turned away from me and fell silent. But I didn't feel like sleeping and for a long time I didn't go to sleep, I was thinking. No, I wasn't going back over the camp, my new acquaintances, the conversation with the company officer. At last I was in a camp – and it was time to think of escaping. I had long since decided that I wasn't going to squat behind barbed wire, no matter how much of a bed of roses it might turn out to be. I simply couldn't reconcile myself to the idea of imprisonment. I would run away, even at the risk of my life. It didn't occur to me to pretend that it was worse here than I had expected, or that it wasn't too bad, that I could manage. I would run away. All I had to do was think carefully about how to do it. And who with. Surely I could find a pal? At that point I began to recall all the people I had happened to meet that day. I didn't know a thing about any of them. But maybe one of them was even then thinking the same as I was . . .

I fell asleep towards morning. I was woken again by a swaying motion, my cot was bucking and shaking like a boat – the old man next to me was climbing down from his cot, and our neighbours below had already made their beds. All four cots – two above and two below – were fast secured by ropes to aid stability, and it only needed one of us four to stir for all the rest to be set trembling and swaying. Seeing that I was awake the old man said:

'Well, my lad, what did you see in your dreams in your new home?'

'The public prosecutor, of course, or maybe the judge,' answered my neighbour below. 'Well, am I right?'

'No, you're wrong. I'm not looking at any dreams in my new home, so as not to worry afterwards whether the omens are good or bad.'

'What do you mean? How do you manage not to look if you're dreaming?'

'Well, as soon as a dream starts to show itself I screw my eyes up nice and tight. Try it yourself and you'll see.'

The young man protested:

'I don't agree, I like dreams. They're interesting; and besides I keep dreaming about life outside. At least in dreams there's a chance to live.'

'Ah, just you stay in as long as we have, my lad, and you'll forget even how to dream about it. All you'll see will be those same old warders' gobs,' remarked an elderly Ukrainian with a bushy moustache. 'Not that I wish you a stretch like mine, of course. It was just a manner of speaking.'

The old men all agreed that none of them thought about the world outside any more, not even in their dreams.

Together with the rest I washed myself, swiftly gulped the morning 'soup' and returned to the hut to wait for roll call. My neighbours sat down to drink tea. They call it 'tea', but in fact it's hot water slightly tinted with ersatz coffee. It is 'brewed' in huge cauldrons sufficient for the whole camp and the duty orderlies carry it round the huts in barrels. I had nothing to eat with the tea except my bread ration. My neighbours invited me to join them and treated me to sugar and margarine. In those days, in 1961, food parcels were still allowed in the camps and you could buy food in the camp shop up to ten roubles' worth per month, and not only with the money you earned, for you could also be sent it by your family. All these blessings, it is true, could be banned for the slightest trifle, but nevertheless, in those days many men had their own food.

While we were sipping our tea the time for roll call came around – half past seven. Cons started to gather slowly in front of the guardhouse. Then the work supervisor came out with one of the warders. The supervisor would call out a gang and the cons in that gang would leave the crowd and move closer to the gate. The warder then took a sheaf of cards out of a box – there was a separate compartment in the box for each gang – and began to call out the names. There was a card filled out for each individual (this was only for roll calls; in the orderly room there was a whole file for each man) bearing his name, charge, sentence and photograph. When your name was called out you had to walk over to the gate, past the warder (who would look you up and down from top to toe to see if it was you, whether you were properly dressed and had your hair properly cut) and into the boundary zone, which was separated from the living zone by a barbed wire fence. While the names were being called out the latecomers would come running up, still chewing a last mouthful or buttoning their uniform tunics. They could be punished for arriving late. And the cards of those who didn't answer to their names at all and didn't go out to work were put back in the box by the warder. After the roll call they would receive separate attention, and not from the warder this time but from the company officers.

In the boundary zone we would be searched, after which the gate was opened and the whole gang would go outside the zone. On the side where we were there was yet another boundary zone, where we went through another inspection and roll call and where we were placed under the supervision of armed escorts with dogs (the warders are not allowed to have weapons inside the compound – a precaution that is taken in case the cons should disarm them and take the weapons over for themselves). We were ordered to form a column of fives, counted five at a time, warned that in cases of disobedience the soldiers had orders to shoot and then: 'Quick march!'

Our gang was working in the fields. They led us to our place of work and posted little red flags to mark the forbidden limit; beyond this the guards would shoot without warning, for that already constituted an attempt to escape. The patch where we were was as flat as a pancake and there were seven guards to watch your every step – no, you couldn't escape from there, it was hopeless!

We were planting out young cabbage and tomato plants and sowing potatoes and carrots: ordinary peasant tasks, but enforced with a big stick. The peasant works with one eye on the harvest, but we were purposely not sent to gather them in, except perhaps to dig spuds – you can't eat spuds raw.

And the norm was such that you worked all day bent double and still could only just manage to fulfil it. And those who didn't and worked poorly had their parcels docked, were stopped from going to the camp shops and put on starvation rations as a punishment – these were all measures of a rehabilitatory nature, designed to instil love of labour into the cons.

I worked extremely hard – after all deductions from my monthly earnings I had exactly 48 copecks left in my personal account. Not even enough for the shop! And from the second month I had nothing left at all.

I wouldn't have given a tinker's cuss for this drudgery, whether it meant the cooler, a special regime camp or God knows what. But I had resolved, come what may, to escape, and for that I had to look around and get to know the other cons a bit better. Maybe, somewhere among them, I would find some helpers.

BUROV

One of the men working in my gang was Anatoly Burov, the same one who had called out 'countryman' to me on my first day. In spite of his appearance, he turned out to be not forty but barely gone thirty.

He had still been quite small, about two or three years old, when his family were proclaimed 'kulaks'* and dispossessed. All he remembered was how he and the other children, together with his mother and father and blind grandmother, had been driven out into the winter snow in what they stood up in. Somehow they got by till spring, in somebody or other's cowshed, and then in spring all the dispossessed families were rounded up, loaded on to a steamer and transported down the river Ob. They were put ashore on the deserted bank, hundreds of miles from the nearest habitation, and left to fend for themselves as best they could. And the steamer sailed away again.

At first they dug pits for themselves, then they began to fell trees, build homes and clear the land of undergrowth. With tremendous difficulty they adapted themselves to this new spot and got some sort of small farms going. Sometimes about five or six of the men would get together and go off secretly 'to the mainland', take jobs to earn extra money and bring back cattle, tools and utensils. About three to four years later the steamer returned with officials on board. There was no landing stage at the village, so they rowed over by boat, walked from house to house and inspected the farms and ploughed fields. They were

* Kulak ('fist') was the term used by the Soviet authorities during the collectivisation of agriculture in the thirties for peasants who were better off and employed hired labour. The policy of 'liquidating the kulaks as a class' resulted in the disappearance of five million peasant households.

amazed! There were supposed to be only graves. Just look at these damned kulaks! Exploiters, and even here they manage to survive! The powers that be boarded their boat again, rowed off, the steamer left and in two months returned together with another and larger one. A multitude of armed soldiers disembarked and proceeded once more to dispossess the kulaks: everyone was thrown out of his home, being allowed to take not even a pot or a pan along with him, herded on to the steamer and transported further. What could happen to them – even in a swamp they wouldn't peg out; and if they did, serve them right, and the mosquitoes could eat the corpses. Kulaks and all their breed – they didn't deserve any pity!

It was harder to adapt to this new place, they lived at starvation level. A few of them quietly made their way to 'the mainland'. Burov's father died and the family started to go to pieces. Just then the war broke out and things became very bad. At the end of the war it was time for Anatoly to go and he was called to the army. He was about to be sent to the front, but before arriving he was redirected to Omsk for tank training. Burov, however, didn't want to serve either at the rear or at the front and he ran away from the tank training school. He was caught, charged with desertion and sentenced to five years. Then he found out that he was being sent to Norilsk to do forced labour – from there no one returns. And once you were there escaping was out of the question, like trying to get off the moon. So Burov came to an agreement with three other cons – they resolved to escape from jail while there was still time, before they were sent away. Better to perish here from a bullet than to die a lingering death in Norilsk.

One evening when they were being taken to the toilet, they attacked their warders. They had reckoned on being able to tie them up, gag them and get away – the four of them would easily manage two warders. But at the very last moment, one of the four got cold feet, and three were not enough to deal with the other two properly, especially without making a noise. While two of the cons tied up their warder, the third grappled with the other warder singlehanded. The latter struggled free and made a run for it. The whole plan was collapsing. The con picked up the heavy lid of the sloptank and let the warder have it on the back of the head. And killed him! Well, it was all up now. They rang for the sentry, killed him too, took his pistol and managed to get out of the jail. They went into hiding and then made their way to Mongolia, travelling at night and sleeping during the day. But when they reached Mongolia and entered a Mongolian village, they were arrested and of course handed over to the Soviet authorities. Their sentence they knew in advance: for killing a warder and a sentry all three were condemned to death.

For seven months Burov and the other two languished in the condemned cell, expecting every day to be taken out and shot. After seven months the first one was called out. With his things. That meant to be shot. Later they led the second one away as well. Burov waited alone for several days. At last his turn also came. He was led down a corridor and at the far end of the corridor was ordered to halt and face the wall. He waited for the end to come. He was so unnerved that it didn't even occur to him that they would hardly shoot him, right there in the corridor. They ordered him to turn and face the warders and he saw an officer in front of him holding some sort of document. Burov was sure that they were going to read the sentence to him again before proceeding to carry it out. The meaning of the words did not get through to him. They repeated them once more: '. . . the death penalty to be commuted to twenty years' hard labour.' But only when they led him to the bath house did he believe it – condemned men are not given a bath first.

Soon Burov was sent away to the river Amur, to the camps outside Komsomolsk. There he met prisoners who had been inside since the thirties, who had built this town and now were building roads and factories around it. The town was named Komsomolsk in honour of the Komsomol volunteers, but there had never been any to speak of. It had been built by cons, and all around it were camps, camps, camps . . .

Burov ran away from the camp. This time he lasted three days outside. He was picked up in town by the police. Another trial, another term to be added to his twenty years' hard labour. And this time it was Norilsk. By 1961 he already had sixteen years of camps and prisons under his belt. From Norilsk he was

transferred to some camp in Siberia, then to another and a third.
When he had been in Tobolsk prison in 1959, some warders had
beaten him and three other cons unconscious. In doing so they
had broken Burov's arm. Then, to get rid of him, they packed
him off to Mordovia.

I liked Burov – he was a dare-devil. We became good friends
and began to plan our escape.

RICHARDAS'S STORY

Burov and I started sizing up the people around us. Who would join us in our bid to escape? First we would cautiously sound them out in conversation, get to know them better, and only then would we ask straight out: 'Will you risk escaping with us?' In this way we got quite a group together: Anatoly Ozerov, Anatoly Burov, myself and several others whose names I don't wish to give. We decided to dig a tunnel – no other way out of a camp exists. We decided that we three Anatolys would undertake a reconnaissance to find out where it was best to dig and then we would tell the others.

We all knew perfectly well what risks we were taking. We knew that if political prisoners are caught trying to escape only a miracle can ensure their survival. The usual procedure is first to beat them up, maim them and set the dogs on them, and only then to have them shot.

One of the prisoners here in camp number ten was a Lithuanian, Richardas K. He had once taken part in an escape bid and he told me how they had been caught. Three of them, all Lithuanians, had somehow managed to elude their escorts while at work in the fields and had only been noticed when near a wood. They came under fire, but it was already too late. Then the tommy gunners were called up from division headquarters; they put a cordon round the wood and soldiers with dogs began to hunt the fugitives. It was not long before the dogs found the scent and soon Richardas and his comrades heard the chase almost at their heels. They realised that come what may they could not avoid it, but still they tried to hide in the hope that the guards with the dogs would plunge straight past them. The other two shinned up an oak tree and hid in the foliage, while

Richardas buried himself in fallen leaves (the time was autumn) beneath a bush. The scene that followed happened literally before his very eyes.

He had not even had time to camouflage himself properly with the leaves when two soldiers appeared with dogs. The dogs circled the oak trees and clawed at the bark with their front paws. A further six tommy gunners ran up together with an officer holding a pistol. The young men in the tree were discovered at once. The officer shouted: 'So you wanted freedom, you mother-fuckers? Come on, get down!'

The lowest branch was about six feet off the ground. Richardas saw one of his companions put his feet on the branch, then crouch down and ease his stomach on to the branch, so that he was hanging across it, with his hands on the branch and his legs in the air, ready to jump down. At that moment he heard the sound of several bursts from a tommy gun and the young man fell to the ground like a sack. But he was still alive, he writhed and squirmed with pain. The officer fired another shot into him and ordered the dogs to be unleashed. The man on the ground, meanwhile, was unable even to defend himself. When the dogs had been dragged off, he remained lying motionless on the ground. The officer ordered him to be picked up and carried away. They dug the toes of their boots into him, but he did not rise. Then the officer said: 'Why spoil your boots on him? What do you think your weapons are for?' The soldiers started stabbing the wounded man with their bayonets and jeering: 'Come on, come on, stand up, don't try to pretend!' The wounded man laboured to get to his feet. His bullet-riddled arms flapped like empty sleeves. His tattered clothes had slipped off down to his waist. He was completely smothered in blood. Prodding him along with their bayonets, they led him to the next tree. The officer called out: 'Guard halt!' The fugitive collapsed at the foot of the tree. Two soldiers and a dog remained to keep watch on him while the rest turned their attention to the second youth. He too was ordered to climb down from the tree. Having decided, evidently, to be more clever, he did not go as far as the lower branches, but plummetted on to the ground at the very feet of the soldiers. No one had time to fire. As he lay there on the ground the officer bounded over to him and fired several shots into his legs. Then he received the same treatment as the first: he was kicked unconscious, savaged by the dogs and stabbed by bayonets. Finally the officer ordered the beating to stop, went over to the youth and said: 'All right, free and independent Lithuania, tell me, where's the third?' The youth was silent. The officer swung his boot into him and repeated the question. Richardas heard his comrade croak: 'I'd call you a fascist, but you're worse than that.' The officer was outraged: 'I fought against the fascists myself! In the front line. And with fascists like you as well. How many of us did you shoot back home in Lithuania?'

Again they threw themselves on the wounded youth and started to beat him. Then the officer ordered him to crawl on his hands and knees to the tree where the first man lay: 'If you don't want to walk you can crawl!'

And the wounded youth, with his legs broken, started to crawl, egged on by bayonets like the first. The officer walked along beside him and jeered: 'Free Lithuania! Go on, crawl, you'll get your independence!' Richardas told me that this youth was a student from Vilnius and had got seven years for distributing pamphlets.

When the two fugitives were together they were beaten and bayonetted again, this time to death. Finally there were no more groans or cries. The officer assured himself that they were dead and sent to the settlement for a cart. He evidently counted on dealing with the third one by the time the cart arrived. Richardas, however, took quite some time to find. Whether it was the dogs who were tired, or perhaps the smell of decomposing leaves that threw them off the scent, they were quite unable to find him. Soldiers ran about the wood, almost stepping on him and the officer stood no more than two yards away from his bush. Richardas said that on several occasions he was ready to leap up and run for it. And it was only when Richardas could already hear the sound of cart wheels grinding along the road that the officer came up to the pile of leaves, prodded them with his toe and instantly yelled; 'Here he is, the bastard! Get up!' At that moment the cart came along. 'Where are the escaped prisoners, comrade major?' Richardas stood up. The major was aiming his pistol straight at him. Instinctively Richardas jerked round at the very instant the shot rang out, then felt a searing pain in his chest and shoulder and fell to the ground. He did not lose consciousness, but lay there motionless, trying not to stir or groan. Other men gathered around and somebody asked 'Maybe he's still alive, comrade major?' And the major replied: 'Alive my foot! I shot him point blank in the chest.' He could not have noticed how Richardas had turned away.

Richardas was thrown into the bottom of the cart – even then he managed not to groan – and the two corpses were piled on top of him. The cart moved off towards the camp. Richardas heard someone approach the cart and heard the major say: 'Killed while trying to escape.' It was obvious from the tone of voice that both the questioner and the major were fully aware of what that meant. Then the cart came to a halt – they must have reached the guardhouse. Somebody ordered the corpses to be unloaded and left there but when they laid hold of Richardas he groaned. 'Look, he's still alive,' they said. He opened his eyes. It was still light, not even the lamps on the fence had been lit. That same major detached himself from a group of officers and came towards him, dragging his pistol out as he advanced. Richardas thought: 'Now I've had it.' But the chief officer followed him and grasped his arm: 'It's too late, stop! Everyone's looking.' It was true. Lots of people had crowded round the guardhouse, both soldiers and civilians; they had all come running to see the fugitives brought in.

Richardas was tipped out of the cart. Someone in the administration gave instructions to the soldiers. They came up to him and asked if he could walk on his own. He said he could. They led him to the guardhouse and once inside the warders immediately ushered him into the cells.

There he was left alone for the first few days. Nobody came to see him, although he had asked to be bandaged. Only on the fourth or fifth day had a con orderly come and bandaged his wound. And the following day a woman doctor came and examined him and said he should be taken to hospital. He had a fever and his arm was in great pain. In the hospital they cut off his arm at the shoulder – it was too late to heal it. Then he was tried, his sentence was extended and he was sent to Vladimir prison. That was three years before I got there and many still remembered this incident.

But a trial's only a trial and escaping prisoners are intentionally killed while being caught so as to put off the rest from trying. And the injured and beaten are purposely not healed. Seeing someone like Richardas without an arm, many men think twice about whether it's worth the risk. But a trial, a prison sentence – that would stop nobody under the conditions that exist in our prison camps.

But even without Richardas's story I well remembered the incident at the Bukhtarma power station. There the officer had fired practically point blank at an unarmed fugitive. I had seen that myself. And I and all the others knew that if we were caught the odds were against us remaining alive. But nonetheless we decided to take the risk.

EXCAVATIONS

The first thing the three of us did was to investigate the ground. In our camp they had dug trenches under the huts, and these trenches always had water in them. Perhaps, though, it wasn't the same all over the camp? We got hold of a strip of iron (there were no shovels inside the compound, nor any other sort of tool) and one night after lights out, round about eleven o'clock, slipped out of the hut one by one as if going to the toilet. Then we crawled under the front steps and found ourselves beneath the hut. All the huts in the camp were raised on high foundations and every week the warders checked with hooks and pointed metal rods to see if there were any tunnels. Burov and I crawled farther back and started digging, while Ozerov kept watch. We removed the top layer of stones and chips and then came to sand, which was easy to dig. But two feet down we came to water. It was useless to go any further. We filled in the hole and sprinkled rubbish over the top again so that the warders wouldn't notice anything when they checked, and crawled back to Ozerov. We showed him by signs that nothing had come of it – water! Now we had to hurry back to our places. At two o'clock they made an inspection of all the huts, the warders would come in, switch on the light and check the number of sleepers. If somebody was missing from his bunk at that time, it aroused suspicion that a con was preparing to escape. For this you got strictly punished – a spell in the cooler or perhaps even prison. But we were in time. Everything had passed off successfully.

The following night we investigated the remaining huts, even the ones that were a long way from the perimeter. Everywhere it was the same: water. Not a single place for a tunnel could we find in the living zone. Then we decided to try the work zone as well.

The work zone in camp ten was small, consisting of a bakery, a garage for three vehicles, a sawing shed, a small machine shop and a shed where rabbits were reared. And there, next to the rabbit shed, a new machine shop was being built. The work area was right next to our living zone and was separated from it only by two strands of barbed wire, moreover this fence had no lighting of its own. Only the sentries in the watchtowers would aim their searchlights at it from time to time. So it was possible to get in there all right. But when? The second shift used to work there until one a.m., and at two a.m. the huts were inspected. There was nothing for it, we would have to work between two o'clock and dawn, although it was very dangerous. And what if somebody in our hut was not sleeping? What would he think if he saw one of the cons dressing and leaving the hut fully dressed and staying away not for ten minutes but for several hours? Every hut had its grasses. Go outside at night and there were warders and watchmen prowling round, trusties with special armbands from the internal order section. And then there were three of us, not just one, although it was sufficient for only one to be noticed.

In spite of all these dangers we were somehow lucky, they didn't catch us once. We had decided in advance where we were going to dig. The bakery was out of the question, it was working all round the clock. The garage workshop had a concrete floor. We settled on the machine shop – it was closer to the perimeter fence, so that if the ground turned out to be dry we wouldn't have far to dig.

We made an arrangement to meet by the rabbit hut after the night inspection was over. We managed to make our way safely into the work zone, avoiding the night watchman, and creep up to the machine shop. The door was padlocked, but we easily opened it with a nail. Ozerov again stayed on guard while Burov and I went into the workshop. The lights were switched off but it was easy to see: the perimeter lights shone in through the window. The workshop itself was no good, it had a raised wooden floor. We went round the various storerooms and found one that seemed suitable: the floor consisted of bricks laid straight on top of sand, with no cement. Just take the bricks out anywhere and dig. What's more the storeroom was littered with wooden blocks, so that after digging we had only to strew them about again and nothing would be noticed. If only the ground was dry, what a marvellous place it would be! Only four to five yards from the inner fence, then twenty-two yards between the two fences that flanked the main palisade, then a few yards more from the far fence to freedom – thirty to thirty-five yards would do it. That was nothing, that could easily be dug. And the hole in the storeroom could be covered with a wooden platform – there was enough material lying around – sand could be sprinkled on top, the bricks laid back in place, camouflaged, and left till the next night's work.

Burov and I let our dreams have their head. But now it was time to leave, soon it would be getting light. We agreed to start digging the next time. We chose a suitable night, crept into the workshop, then into the store-room, and started to dig. Another failure! Just as in the living zone, water came into the hole at a depth of two feet. This one too had to be filled in and stamped down and the place of our reconnaissance camouflaged with bricks and components.

All we had had till now was one failure after another, with the one possible exception that at least we hadn't been caught. Obviously we had to think up another plan. Maybe we would have to give up the idea of a tunnel altogether, although not all the places had been checked yet. Until we could think of something better, however, we would have to go on looking for a place without water. We couldn't possibly give up the whole idea of escaping and we still couldn't believe that the whole camp was standing on water.

Meanwhile our strength was giving out. It was no joke going without sleep so many nights and spending them digging, and then going out to work again during the day. On camp rations at that. And Burov an invalid with his broken arm. Then I was transferred to the construction gang, which was even tougher than working in the fields. And in June I fell ill.

THE COOLER

I had caught a chill in the Karaganda camps already and had received no treatment. Since then I had suffered from a chronic inflammation of both ears, which from time to time would become acute. This time also it was my ears that caused the trouble. My head was splitting in two, I had shooting pains in my ears, it was difficult to fall asleep at night and painful to open my mouth at meals. On top of that I had fits of nausea and dizziness.

I went to the camp medical post, although the old hands warned me that it was useless, that the ear specialist came once a year and summoned everyone who had complained of ear trouble during the past year to come to him at the same time. There were quite a few. 'What's wrong?' 'My ears.' Without further ado the specialist would note it down in his notebook and write out a prescription for hydrogen peroxide. No further inquiries and no proper examination, and there was no chance of being excused from work – it was out of the question. Only if you turned out to have a high temperature would they consider excusing you from work for a few days.

I appealed to the doctor several times and each time heard only insulting assertions that since I didn't have a temperature I must be well and therefore was simply trying to dodge work. And at the end of June, for failing to fulfil my norm, I was given seven days in the PB or punishment block, in other words the cooler. I found nothing surprising in this: given that I was failing to fulfil my daily norm, the cooler was inevitable. At first they call you up in front of your company officer to listen to a sermon about every con having to redeem his sin in the eyes of the people by honest labour.

'Why didn't you fulfil your norm?' asks the officer when his

homily is finished. This when he can see that the man in front
of him can barely stand up. 'Sick? How can you be when you've
got no temperature! It's very bad to pretend, to dissimulate, to
try and dodge your work.' And just to make the point clear he
gives you several days in the cooler.

Now what did the punishment block look like in 1961? First
there was an ordinary camp barrack block, divided into cells.
The cells were various: some were for solitary, others for two
people, five or even twenty, and if necessary they would pack
up to thirty or even forty in them. It was situated in a special
regime camp about a quarter of a mile from camp ten. A tiny
exercise yard had been specially fenced off; it was pitted and
trampled hard and in it, even in summer, there was not a single
blade of grass – the least shoot of green would be swallowed at
once by the starving cons in the cooler.

The cells themselves were equipped with bare bunks consisting of thick planks – no mattresses or bedding were allowed.
The bunks were short, you had to sleep bent double; when
I tried to straighten out, my legs hung over the end. In the
centre of the bunk, running crosswise and holding the planks together, was a thick iron bar. Now what if this bar had been
placed beneath the planks? Or set in a groove, if it had to
be on top, so that it didn't stick out? But no, this iron bar, two
inches wide and almost an inch thick, was left sticking up in the
very middle of the bunk, so that no matter how you lay it
was bound to cut into your body, which had no protection from
it.

The window was covered with stout iron bars and the door
had a peephole. In one corner stood the prisoner's inseparable
companion, the sloptank – a rusty vessel holding about twelve
gallons, with a lid linked to it by a stout chain. Attached to one
side of the tank was a long iron rod threaded at the other end.
This was passed through a special aperture in the wall and on
the other side, in the corridor, the warder would screw a big
nut on to it. In this way the sloptank was fixed immovably to
the wall. During toilet break the nut would be unscrewed so
that the cons could carry the tank out and empty it. This
procedure took place daily in the morning. The rest of the time

the sloptank stood in its appointed place, filling the cell with an unspeakable stench . . .

At six a.m. came a knocking at all doors: 'Wake up! Wake up for toilet break!' They started taking us to get washed. At last it was our cell's turn. However, it was washing only in name. You had hardly had time to wet your hands when you were already being prodded from behind: 'Hurry, hurry, you can get all the washing you want after you've been released!' Less than a minute is the regulation time for a con to wash in, and whoever fails to get washed has to rinse his face over the sloptank in the cell.

And so, back in our cell once more, we waited for breakfast – alas nothing but a name: a mug of hot water and a ration of bread – fourteen ounces for the whole day. For dinner they gave us a bowl of thin cabbage soup consisting of almost pure water, in which some leaves of stinking pickled cabbage had been boiled – though little enough even of that found its way into the bowl. I don't think even cattle would have touched this soup of ours, but in the cooler the con not only drinks it straight from the side of the bowl, but even wipes the bowl with his bread and eagerly looks forward to supper. For supper we got a morsel of boiled cod the size of a matchbox, stale and slimy. Not a grain of sugar or fat is allowed to prisoners in the cooler.

I hate to think what we prisoners were driven to by starvation in the cooler. Return to the compound was awaited with even greater eagerness than the end of your sentence. Even the normal camp hunger rations seemed an unimaginable feast in the cooler. I hate to think how I starved in there. And it is even more horrible to realise that now, even as I write this, my comrades are still being starved in punishment cells . . .

The time drags agonisingly between breakfast and dinner and between dinner and supper. No books, no newspapers, no letters, no chess. Inspection twice a day and after dinner a half-hour walk in the bare exercise yard behind barbed wire – that's the extent of your entertainment. During inspections the warders take their time: the prisoners in each cell are counted and recounted and then checked with the number on the board. Then a meticulous examination of the cell is carried out. With big wooden mallets the warders sound out the walls, bunks, floor and window bars to see whether any tunnels are being dug or any bars have been sawn through and whether the prisoners are planning to escape. They also check for any inscriptions on the walls. During the whole of this time the prisoners all have to stand with their caps off (I will explain later why this is done).

During the thirty-minute exercise period you can also go to the latrines. If there are twenty of you in a cell, however, it is difficult to manage in time. There are two latrines, a line forms and again you are chivvied: 'Hurry, hurry, our time's nearly up, what are you sitting around for!' If you don't manage it, there's always the sloptank back in the cell, and they never let you out to go to the latrines again, not even if you're an old man or ill. Inside, during the day, the cell is stifling and stinks to high heaven. At night, even in summer, it is cold – the cell block is built of stone and the floor is cement: they are specially built that way so as to be as cold and damp as possible. There is no bedding and nothing to cover yourself with, except for your reefer jacket. This, like all your other warm clothes, is taken away when you are searched before being stuck in the cooler, but they give it back to you at night.

There is not the slightest chance of taking a morsel of food with you to the cooler, or even half a puff's worth of cigarette butt or paper or the lead of a pencil – everything is taken away when you are searched. You yourself and the underwear, trousers and jacket that you are forced to take off are all poked and prodded through and through.

From ten o'clock at night till six in the morning you lie huddled on your bare boards, with the iron bar digging into your side and a cold damp draught from the floor blowing through the cracks between them. And you long to fall asleep, so that sleeping, at least, you can forget the day's torments and the fact that tomorrow will be just the same. But no, it won't work. And you can't get up and run about the cell, the warder will see you through the peephole. So you languish there, tossing and turning from side to side until it is almost light again; and no sooner do you doze off than: 'Get up! Get up! Toilet break!'

Incarceration in the punishment block is supposed to be limited to not more than fifteen days, but the officers can easily get round this rule. They let you out to go back to camp one evening and the next morning condemn you to another fifteen days. What for? A reason can always be found. You stood in your cell so as to block the peephole; picked up a cigarette butt during your exercise period (that one of your camp friends had tossed over the fence to you); answered a warder rudely . . . Yes, you can get a further fifteen days for absolutely nothing at all. Because if you really rebel and allow yourself to be provoked into making a protest, you get not simply fifteen days in the cooler but a new trial by decree.

In Karaganda I was once kept in the cooler for forty-eight days, being let out each time only so that a new directive could be read to me ordering my 'confinement to a punishment cell'. The writer, Yuli Daniel, was once given two successive spells in the cooler at Dubrovlag camp eleven for 'swearing at a sentry' – this happened quite recently, in 1966.

Some men can't bear the inhuman conditions and the hunger and end up by mutilating themselves: they hope they will be taken to hospital and will escape, if only for a week, the bare boards and stinking cell, and will be given more human nourishment. While I was in the cooler, two of the cons acted as follows: they broke the handles off their spoons and swallowed them; then, after stamping on the bowls of the spoons to flatten them, they swallowed these too. But even this wasn't enough – they broke the pane of glass in the window and by the time the warders had managed to unlock the door each had succeeded in swallowing several pieces of glass. They were taken away and I never saw them again; I merely heard that they were operated on in the hospital at camp number three.

When a con slits his veins or swallows barbed wire, or sprinkles ground glass in his eyes, his cell-mates don't usually intervene. Every man is free to dispose of himself and his life as best he can and in whatever way he wishes, every man has the right to put an end to his sufferings if he is unable to bear them any longer.

There is also usually one cell in the punishment block that is filled with people on hunger strike. One day, as a mark of protest, a con decides to go on hunger strike, so he writes out an official complaint (to the camp governor, the Central Committee, Khrushchev – it is all the same who to, it has absolutely no significance; it's simply that a hunger strike 'doesn't count' without an official complaint, even if you starve to death anyway) and refuses to take any more food. For the first few days no one takes a blind bit of notice. Then, after several days – sometimes as many as ten or twelve – they transfer you to a special cell set aside for such people, and start to feed you artificially, through a pipe. It is useless to resist, for whatever you do they twist your arms behind your back and handcuff you. This procedure is carried out in the camps even more brutally than in the remand prison – by the time you've been 'force-fed' once or twice you are often minus your teeth. And what you are given is not the feeding mixture that I got at Ashkhabad, but the same old camp skilly, only even thinner, so that the pipe doesn't get clogged. Furthermore the skilly you get in the cells is lukewarm, but in artificial feeding they try to make it as hot as possible, for they know that this is a sure way of ruining your stomach.

Very few men are able to sustain a hunger strike for long and get their own way, although I have heard of cases where prisoners kept it up for two to three months. The main thing is though, that it's completely useless. In every instance the answer to the protest is exactly the same as to all other complaints, the only difference being that the governor himself comes to see the hunger striker, in so far as the enfeebled con is unable to walk:

'Your protest is unjustified, call off your hunger strike. Whatever you do, we won't let you die. Death would save you from your punishment and your term isn't up yet. When you go free from here you are welcome to die. You have made a complaint, you are complaining about us to the higher authorities. Well, you can write away – it's your right. But all the same it is we who will be examining your complaint . . .'

And this was the sanatorium I had been sent to on account of my illness. I served my seven days and came out, as they say, holding on to the walls – they had worn me to a shadow. Nevertheless, despite my weakness, I still had to go out to work the next day in order not to earn myself another spell in the cooler.

THE LAST ATTEMPT

While I was doing my seven days, Burov and Ozerov fell into despair and lost all hope of digging a tunnel. It wasn't that I was the leading light in the affair, but simply that two people tend to lose hope quicker than three. One of them, say, suddenly begins to doubt that there is anywhere at all to dig when there is water everywhere, and then the other involuntarily falls in with him. And there is no third to say: 'So what, brothers, we can't wait around with our arms folded, let's find another way to escape while we're all still alive . . .'

In short, after I was let out of the cooler and had had time to get my strength back a bit, we again started to make plans for our escape. We decided to have one more go at digging in the work zone – this time in the half-built workshop hut. Our decision was reinforced this time by the special advantages of this new place for a tunnel: the walls, already up to roof height, would screen us from the sentries and security guards, the piles of fresh earth around the hut would help us in disguising the traces of our tunnel, and finally, we could easily get in through the window opening, so that there would be no messing around with locks . . . I find it hard to decide now, but I have a feeling that if we had been forced to think up a new plan, and then another and another, we would always have found advantages in every new variant, so intolerable was the thought of having to stay there much longer.

We agreed among ourselves to make our way the following night to the uncompleted hut to see how far down the water was there. A film show had been announced for the night in question. In summer, films were shown in the open air in front of the canteen. They began after supper, when it was already getting dark, and went on late till well after the usual time for lights out. So that twice a month in summer the cons were able to wander round the place till late at night breathing in the fresh night air, for hardly anybody watched the films; bit by bit, after the newsreel, they would slip away in ones and twos, trying, of course, not to get noticed by the warders. And it was for just such an ideal evening that we made our plan: we would go to the film show, sitting in different places, and then after the newsreel skedaddle to the work zone. We also talked, of course, about the kind of risks threatening us in this new spot. It was near one of the watch towers – we would have to be very careful making our way there and to work without making a sound. We decided that Burov would act as look-out for the night watchmen, while Ozerov and I would do the digging. Burov, who had been working during the day in the rabbit shed next to 'our' hut, explained that the construction gang always left their hand-barrows overnight – which was excellent, they would come in handy – but that their tools, as usual, were always taken back and handed in. Still, there was all sorts of lumber lying about, we would do our best to dig with sticks and pieces of wood.

On the agreed evening I was strolling about the living zone, waiting for the show to begin, when suddenly I heard the voice of our company commander, Captain Vasyayev – or rather not his voice but his yell:

'I see you're asking for more PB, parasite!' he was roaring at some unfortunate, who, like myself, had only just come out of the cooler. 'You're falling short of the norm again! Do you think the state's going to feed you for nothing? We've got too many of you damned skivers here!'

'I didn't ask to come here and get my grub free,' replied the con. 'I used to work in a factory – the pay was rotten but still I used to keep myself and my family, so how does that make me a parasite?'

A knot of cons had gathered round to listen to this argument, obviously sympathising with their comrade, and at this the captain lost his temper even more.

'I don't know what you earned there, but here you get your

rations for nothing,' he went on, continuing his task of education.

The con also lost his temper and couldn't keep quiet, although he knew what he would get for it:

'It's not for the likes of you to count what I earned, captain. I was paid for my *work* at least, but why should somebody like you get paid twice as much as a worker? For standing over us workers with a stick?'

'I'm serving my country!'

'Serving your country? Proud of it, are you? That's in here, but I bet when you go on holiday you don't tell the others where you serve? You're too damned ashamed to come out in the open and admit to people what you get your fat salary for!'

While this was going on the captain caught sight of a couple of warders at the back of the crowd of cons.

'Get him!' he pointed to his opponent, 'And take him to the guardroom!' And he went off to write the order for another fifteen days.

This time the argument had ended relatively luckily for the con: more often than not such lippy prisoners are sent for trial again on a charge of 'anti-Soviet propaganda' and the whole affair ends with another sentence added on, or else 'special regime' or prison.

'He would have to go and get into a row with him!' said the cons quietly as they dispersed. 'Found a right one to try and teach lessons to. You can't make no impression on 'em!'

'So it's better to keep quiet, is it? Keep quiet, no matter what they say or what they do to you,' exploded somebody, probably one of the younger ones – fortunately it was too dark now to see who it was. Captain Vasyayev had already gone away, but even among us cons there could easily be informers: they'd only have to grass and then this young fellow would get exactly the same treatment as the man in the quarrel.

Escape, come what may, no matter what the risk, only escape. We're not humans in this place, we can't even defend ourselves from insults . . .

It was dark. Going over to the canteen, where the screen was already in place, I peered into the crowd. Burov and Ozerov were both there. They also exchanged glances with me and each other and then the three of us immediately looked away again. Even a silent exchange of glances could seem suspicious to one or other of the grasses, all of whom couldn't wait to curry favour with the bosses.

After the newsreels, just as we had reckoned, we were able to melt away unnoticed. Three rows of barbed wire and the low little fence separating the living and work zones – all were negotiated successfully: it was dark here, the searchlights were trained only on the outer fence. By the rabbit shed we had to move about in absolute silence: the night watchmen were very much on the alert to guard the rabbits against hungry prisoners.

At last we were in our half-built hut and could breathe more easily, for the walls blocked us from view. We looked around. Here was the wall that was nearest the main fence, this was where we would dig. If only the ground would turn out to be suitable, with no water! Then we would disguise the hole with boards – there were plenty about – sprinkle-earth over the top and continue the trench on later nights. Silently, without even whispering to one another, we took up our places: Burov crawled out of the hut to keep an eye on the watchmen, while Ozerov and I started digging. Ozerov turned out to have a strip of iron, the same piece he had had when we crawled under our own hut: he had managed to keep it hidden till now. The work got under way. As we were digging a beam of bright light would slide over the hut from time to time – the sentry in the watch tower was shining his searchlight back and forth over the work zone – and inside the hut it would turn as light as day. Down we would crouch on the ground. The beam slid over us and past, and then we would dig again, trying not to bang or clink anything. When we had dug down to a depth of about twenty inches the sand grew damp; another foot and the bottom of the hole filled with water. Failure again! We had still not realised that our whole plan had folded when Burov came crawling back into the hut:

'A watchman just walked past the window here.'

Had he heard us digging? He could even have seen us if he had looked through the window.

'Which way did he go?'

'Over there,' Burov pointed in the opposite direction to the guardhouse.

If he had heard anything and wanted to tell the guards, he would have to pass us again on his way to the guardhouse. We decided to start filling in the hole as quickly as possible until the watchman passed us on his way to the guardhouse, and only then to run for it. For if they discovered traces of our work, they would turn the whole zone upside down and search for those who were planning to escape. And even if they didn't catch up with us, nevertheless the sentries would be on their guard and would start keeping a close watch on every single con – where he went, what he had in his hand, who he exchanged whispers with . . . We would have to give up our escape plans indefinitely, perhaps even forever. No, that was something we had to avoid at all costs. If a tunnel was out of the question, then we would put our minds to it and think up some other means of escape.

Hurry, hurry, fill up the hole! Burov crawled outside again to keep an eye on the watchman: as soon as he headed for the guardhouse we would abandon our work and make a dash for the fence. Maybe in the living zone we would be able to lose ourselves among the rest of the cons. If they caught us they wouldn't exactly kill us – the warders weren't allowed weapons inside the perimeter – but we'd be beaten half to death and maybe even crippled for life.

Ozerov and I started hurling soil into the hole without even bothering to keep quiet. Several minutes later Burov appeared again: 'The warders are coming!' Then we realised that the watchman who had heard us, instead of going to the guardhouse had gone to the other watchmen and they had informed the guard.

We sprang out of the hut. All around was bathed in bright light: the sentry was training his searchlight directly on the hut and us. Blinded by the brilliant light, we made a dash in the direction of the living zone. I hardly remember how I came to be in the rabbit shed, I jumped on to the low fence by the barbed wire fence and saw a line of warders already stationed along its entire length. I jumped down again, back into the rabbit shed, and crawled under the hutches. Somewhere nearby were my companions: I had seen Burov at my side several seconds ago.

Warders ran into the shed, each one armed with a lantern and a sharpened thick stick.

'Surround them and make sure no one gets away!' I heard the voice of Major Ageyev who was directing the hunt.

The warders started poking under the hutches with their sharp sticks. The first to be found was Ozerov.

'Come out!' they ordered.

But when he attempted to crawl out they prodded him so cruelly with the sticks that he retreated even farther under the hutches. Nevertheless they succeeded in driving him out and I saw and heard several warders start pounding him with their boots and jabbing him with their sticks. Meanwhile the others went on with the search. Burov and I were discovered practically simultaneously, we were under neighbouring hutches. And we received the same treatment as Ozerov. I don't know how long the beating went on for. Probably not long, for no bones were broken.

The noise and the shouts brought other prisoners running and they crowded up to the barbed wire fence on the living zone side. Some other warders attempted to disperse them, but they resisted, and from the crowd came shouts of 'Murderers!' and 'Butchers!' Then the sentries in the watch towers fired several bursts from their tommy guns over the cons' heads, but that didn't help either. Major Ageyev ran up to the wire:

'Aren't your sentences long enough? We'll soon see to that! There's plenty of room in prison still – and in the special camps. Get back!'

But the crowd didn't get back. The three of us were picked up and prodded away from the fence in the direction of the guardhouse in the work zone. As they drove us along they continued to beat us. From behind we were jabbed continually with the sharp sticks. Now and again one of the warders would take a run at us and hack us in the legs with his steel-shod boots. Or the boots would be aimed higher – a running jump would land them on our ribs or somewhere else in that region – it didn't matter where, so long as it hurt as much as possible. I bent my head low as I walked and hunched myself up as best I could, with my hands clasped over the back of my head: these were to protect my head from blows, while my elbows covered my ribs. My arms were numb and indeed my whole body had long since ceased to feel any pain from the blows.

In the guardhouse the beating continued. Then Major Ageyev conducted a brief interrogation.

'Who else wanted to escape with you?'

Each of us replied that there was nobody apart from the three of us. After the interrogation we were due to be taken from the guardhouse to the cooler, and the cooler, as I have already mentioned, was in another compound. And so the three of us had only one thought in our heads: would they handcuff us or not? If they didn't, it meant they had decided to shoot us *en route*. They would shoot us in the back and then report us as 'killed while trying to escape from their guards on their way to the punishment block'. How many times had it happened before.

We automatically answered Ageyev's questions and waited to see what would happen – handcuffs or an immediate command to leave.

At last some more warders came in – carrying handcuffs. We exchanged glances and I was aware that Burov and Ozerov were thinking the same as me.

One pair of handcuffs fastened me to Burov on one side and another to Ozerov on the other. The major himself secured me and Burov, while the sergeant major put on the other pair. The major was out to do his best and hammered the handcuffs tight with the butt of his pistol. My wrist was twisted so tightly that I almost whimpered. Burov's face was distorted with pain.

'Tighter, tighter, make 'em remember it for the rest of their lives,' the major commanded the sergeant and Ozerov grimaced and groaned.

We were pushed through several narrow doors and led across the railway track to the next compound. I was still afraid they'd shoot us on the way for here, outside the compounds, our escorts were armed with tommy guns and Major Ageyev had his pistol in his hand. But no, even this reign of lawlessness evidently had its own laws: a con in handcuffs may not be shot. All the major did was hammer us under the ribs with his pistol butt.

Leaving their weapons at the guardhouse entrance the major and our escorts took us to the guardroom. Here they stood us up against the wall and started to beat us again. We for our part, imprisoned in the handcuffs, couldn't even cover our faces to ward off the blows. Then they threw us on to the floor and started kicking and trampling on us.

'That'll teach the fucking bastards,' chanted Ageyev. 'Make sure they remember and tell the others what it means to escape.'

Finally they removed the handcuffs, dragged us down a corridor and threw us into a cell.

For three or four days we lay there without getting up. The door would open and the cookhand would call us to come and get our rations or dinner, and we were unable to stand. Then the cookhand would call a warder who, merely glancing at us from the doorway, without stepping inside, would order the cell to be locked again. Only after about three days did we begin to get up for dinner and our bread ration. One morning they read out a decree awarding us each fifteen days in the cooler. That was from the administration. Then we would be put on trial and would be sentenced to two or three years in prison according to the legal code. Thus, when our fifteen days in the cooler were over, we would stay in that same cell waiting for trial, only now under normal conditions: camp meals, bedding on the bunks, books, exercise once a day and permission to smoke. That's why unsuccessful fugitives were given a fortnight in the cooler to start off with – it was the tradition already – so that they didn't get too much enjoyment out of all that luxury.

Our cell was a small one, for three people, but on the other hand it was in a busy spot. Situated at one corner of the hut, it had a barred window overlooking two exercise yards and facing the latrines, and you could see the guardhouse from it. So that during the last few days of cooler, when we had recovered enough to walk about our cell, all we did was crowd to the window all day, gaping at the cons exercising (and they at us) and at the new arrivals being led from the guardhouse to the huts. Sometimes we also managed to get a few words in unnoticed with the cons in the exercise yard.

These cons were on special regime. The camp too was called a 'special'. 'Done special' the cons used to say.

SPECIAL REGIME

During my first spell in the cooler I hadn't really got to know either the camp or the men in it, except for my cell-mates. But now, during my second stay in the cooler and subsequently on remand, awaiting trial, I and my companions not only got a closer look at the special regime but also got to know a few of the cons doing special. In some of the camps I stayed in later, and also at the prisoners' hospital, I met many cons who had at some time done special, so that I know very well what it amounts to.

The living zone of a special regime camp is equipped with cell blocks about eighty yards long and twenty-five to thirty yards wide. A long corridor runs down the middle of the block from end to end, while a transverse corridor bisects it in half. Both corridors terminate at each end in doors that are equipped with a variety of locks and bolts. The long corridor has rows of doors on either side that lead into the cells, these being the same as you find in the punishment block: plank bunks, bars on the windows, a sloptank in one corner and doors equipped with shuttered peepholes (the shutters are on the outside, of course, so that only the warders can move them – otherwise the cons might look out into the corridor). The cells are divided from the corridor by double doors: on the corridor side there is a massive iron-lined door double-locked with a conventional lock and a padlock; the door on the inside, which is also kept permanently locked, consists of a grille formed by heavy iron bars set into a heavy frame, as in a cage for wild beasts. Set into the barred door is a food trap, which is also kept locked and is opened only when food is being served. The barred door is opened only to let cons in and out, for they are driven out to work, in the words of Captain Vasyayev, so as to pay for the bread they eat.

The appearance of the living zone in a special regime camp is completely different from that of an ordinary or strict regime camp: the zone is completely deserted. After work everyone is kept under lock and key until morning, until the parade for work again. The whole of your free time is spent in the cells, with the warders padding noiselessly up and down the corridors in their felt knee-boots, eavesdropping and peering through the peep-holes . . . But who are the people held on special regime, behind thick bars and behind locked and bolted doors, behind rows and rows of barbed wire and behind a high wall? What fearsome, bestial bandits are these?

Officially, special regime, like prison, is reserved for particularly dangerous and hardened offenders, and also for cons who have committed an offence in camp. That is the rule for ordinary, everyday criminals: first normal regime, then intensified, then strict regime and finally special regime or prison. Politicals begin their camp career at once on strict regime – we are all 'particularly dangerous' from the very beginning, so that for us the path to special regime or prison is significantly shorter.

You can also get special regime as part of your court sentence – for a second political offence. The most common course, however, is for cons to come here from strict regime camps – either for escaping (if, of course, they're not shot on being caught), or attempting an escape, or else for refusing to work, failing to fulfil the norm, 'resisting a guard or a warder' . . . To become a bandit or a vicious hooligan in camp is easier than falling off a chair: all you have to do is preserve an elementary sense of your own dignity and one way or another you are certain to end up as 'a vicious wrecker of discipline', while developments after that depend entirely on the whim of admin – will they limit themselves to administrative measures of correction or have you tried in court again?

Here is an example. I have already pointed out that in the cooler they don't give you a chance to have a decent wash; and there isn't the remotest chance of being allowed to clean your teeth – do it back in the cell, if you please, over that stinking sloptank. The very desire of a con even to do such a thing provokes righteous indignation and anger on the part of the warder: what, a common criminal, and he's talking of cleaning his teeth! But they don't even let you have an ordinary wash. No sooner have you wet your hands in the basin than: 'Enough! Back to your cell!' And if you don't step back on the instant, they grab hold of you and pull you away. At this point, God forbid that you should resist even instinctively or ward off the hand that is dragging you away from the basin. The warders will then drag you into the guardroom and start insulting you, mocking you, prodding you. They only want one thing – that the con should bear all this in silence, submit, so that it is clear for all to see: the con knows his place. And if you dare to answer an insult or a blow – there's your 'vicious hooliganism' for you, 'resistance to the representatives of law and order', followed by a report to the prison authorities, a new trial and sentence by decree, which can be anything up to and including the death penalty. At the very least your term will be extended and you'll be put on special regime.

Somewhat later, in the Potma transit prison, I met several cons from camp ten who had been sent to special regime camps or to prison for 'organising a political party' in the camp. Chinghiz Dzhafarov said something, an informer grassed to the fuzz (a KGB detective in this case): and they started to round people up – not only those who took part in the conversation, but also anybody who happened to be around and might have heard it.

In practice any con that the authorities take a dislike to is liable to end up on special regime or in prison – if he's too difficult, say, or independently minded, or popular with the other cons. Everybody has more than enough of such crimes in his book as failure to fulfil the norm or breaking the camp rules. And sometimes it's simply a matter of chance, the result of sheer bad luck. After I had been taken out of camp ten, for instance, it was decided for various internal reasons to transform it from a political into an ordinary criminal camp. But what to do with the political prisoners? Some of them were distributed to other political camps, but the majority were sent to a special regime camp – it was the closest to hand. And on my way back to the camps in 1963, as I passed through the familiar territory, I saw that several new cell blocks with barred windows had been added to the special regime camp. Inside were my comrades from camp ten.

Iron bars, bolts, extra guards, confinement to cells outside of working hours – all this, of course, is only part of the corrective measures applied to these particularly dangerous offenders. Here the work is also heavier than in the other camps.

First you build a brick factory, for instance, and then you have to work in it. A brick factory, even in normal conditions, is no bed of roses, and in the camps it is even worse. The main machine is the celebrated OSO – two handles and a wheel – plus handbarrows, and that's the extent of the mechanisation. Working in the damp and the cold, the cons get soaked and freezing; then comes the long, long roll-call. One cell at a time they are taken from the work zone to the living zone. Before passing through they are thoroughly searched, one by one, while the rest are forced to wait all this time in the rain, the snow or the frost, stamping their feet to keep warm. Finally they are back in their cells with not the slightest chance to warm themselves or change their boots or clothing: all they have is what they stand up in, both for work and for indoors in the cell after work – filthy, damp and sweaty. Somehow or other the con tries to dry out his clothes overnight with the warmth of his own body; before he's finished, however, it is already morning, time to get up, parade for work, and again it's hurry-hurry, don't stand around, if you don't fulfil your norm you go on punishment rations. And the norms are such, of course, that it is impossible to fulfil them, so that any con can at any time be punished for falling short of them.

The main punishment and the strongest corrective measure in the camps, easy to carry out and well tried in practice, is starvation. On special regime this measure is particularly sensitive: parcels and packages are in general forbidden. All you can get from the camp shop is toothpaste, toothbrushes and soap; in order to buy tobacco you have to write a special application to admin and then it's up to them to decide. No food from outside is ever allowed in, all you get is rations. And everyone knows what camp rations are like: you won't quite kick the bucket, but you won't be in a hurry to shit either – you've got nothing to shit. And even then, if you don't fulfil your norm, admin can put you on punishment rations – the same as in the cooler.

And so men sentenced to special regime camps live for years in these terrible, inhuman, indescribable conditions. It isn't too difficult, it seems, to reduce a man to the condition of a beast, to force him to forget his own human dignity, to forget honour and morality. On top of this the cells are apportioned in such a way that there are never less than two grasses to each cell – to report on their comrades and each other. But what can a grass gain on special regime? First, he doesn't get put on punishment rations; secondly, he may not have his visits cut out. Here a con is permitted one visit a year lasting up to three hours – this is usually reduced to half an hour, and more often than not is not allowed at all. The main thing, though, is that admin can make representations to the judiciary for a prisoner to be transferred from special regime back to strict regime before his time is up, for 'responding to corrective training'. Not before half his term is served, true, but still it's a hope! Somehow to break out of this hell six months or a year ahead of schedule, this is the lure that leads men to become informers and provocateurs and to sell their comrades.

I have already mentioned self-mutilation in the cooler and such cases are even more frequent on special regime. Men gouge their eyes out, throw ground glass in them, or hang themselves. At night, sometimes, they slit their veins under the blankets; and if their neighbour doesn't wake up soaked in blood, yet one more martyr is freed of his burden.

One day three cons agreed to put an end to themselves in the usual way, that is with the help of the sentries. At about three in the afternoon they took three planks from the brick factory and placed them against the palisade. The sentry in the watch tower shouted:

'Stand back or I'll fire!'

'By all means, and deliver us from this happy life,' replied one of the cons and started climbing. Having reached the top, he got entangled in the barbed wire there. At this moment there was a burst of tommy gun fire from the tower and he slumped across the wire and hung there. Then the second man climbed up and calmly awaited his turn. A short burst of fire and he fell to the ground at the foot of the fence. The third man followed and he too fell beside the first.

I was told later that one of them had remained alive, he had been seen in the hospital at camp three. So at least he had escaped from special regime for a time. The other two, of course, had escaped for ever, shot dead on the spot. In general this suicide was just like many others, differing only in that it was a group affair. Individual instances are common, and not only in special regime camps.

A sentry who picks off such an 'escaper' in this way gets rewarded with extra leave to show admin's gratitude. But the attitude of the other soldiers to the marksman doesn't always coincide with admin's. Once, in camp seven in the autumn of 1963, a sentry shot a routine suicide case, a fellow who was ill, when he was on the palisade. He got his leave all right, but he was black and blue when he set off for home: that night the other soldiers had organised a little farewell party for him, though under a different pretext, of course.

On the whole, many soldiers are ashamed of this type of service and don't even tell their families that they are guarding prisoners. Sometimes it happens that when you get talking to one, and he's sure you won't give him away, he'll say quite openly what he thinks of the camps and his duties:

'In a year I'll be free again and this fucking military service can go to hell.'

The way he talks it is clear that his three years are as much a prison sentence to him as the con's years inside. So you say to him:

'But if they order you, you'll shoot me too, and if you're up in the watch tower you'll fire on a con just the same, even when you know he's not escaping but simply doing it in desperation . . .'

'Of course,' he agrees. 'If they order me I'll fire and I'll shoot to kill. What else can I do when it's an order?'

'Yes, what can we do?' says another.

'I don't like the idea of being put inside myself,' replies a third.

Many soldiers perform their duties out of fear, and not because they're conscientious. And when Burov, Ozerov and I were beaten up, the soldiers did it more for show than in earnest. The warders, though, are a different kettle of fish. It's true they're not conscientious and work only for the money, but they try to suck up to admin, try to last out till they're pensioned off and try not to get thrown out beforehand; then they also like to be praised and they hope, perhaps, for promotion to senior warder. Moreover their absolute power over the cons corrupts them (and the higher administration too for that matter).

Nonetheless in a large camp, where there are very many cons, the warders sometimes try to ingratiate themselves with the prisoners. Now and again they will turn a blind eye to the fact that you have brought away a packet of cigarettes from a meeting with relatives, or for a bribe will pass you a pick-me-up (a bit of extra food). Some of them speculate in tea and vodka, especially in the criminal camps. They exploit the cons and their families and at the same time want to be popular and pass for decent fellows among the cons. After all they have to stay in the camps for days at a time, and you never know what to expect from men who have been bitterly antagonised and driven to despair.

The authorities justifiably place no trust either in the soldiers who serve as guards or in the warders. Both groups are infiltrated with informers. Strict watch is kept to see that the soldiers don't talk to the cons, especially political cons. As guards for the Mordovian camps they try to bring in soldiers from the national minorities or from distant republics (though never from the Baltic republics!), in other words those who don't know much Russian.

Here, in the special regime camp, I also saw something I had only heard about before, but hadn't been able to confirm: inscriptions tattooed not only on men's arms and bodies, but also on the face – on the cheeks and forehead. Usually they are criminal cons, of whom there are quite a few nowadays in the political camps.

Criminal cons often, so to speak, 'volunteer' to be transferred to political camps. There is a persistent legend going around the criminal camps that conditions for politicals are not too bad, that they are fed better, the work is easier, they are treated more humanely, the guards don't beat you up and so on. At the root of this legend lies the rumour of an actually existing Mordovian camp for foreigners who have been sentenced for espionage: conditions there are indeed almost like a holiday camp – unlimited parcels, as much food as you can eat, no work norms demanded: if you feel like it – work; if not, you can play volleyball in the compound. Returning home after his time is up the foreigner can find nothing bad to say about our camps and prisons. And among our own people, of course, the newspapers create an impression that every one of our political prisoners is bound to be a spy and a foreign intelligence agent, and so the rumour goes about the camps that politicals live in a kind of paradise. In actual fact conditions in the political camps are far worse than in the criminal ones. But there is also a grain of truth in the legend. Politicals are no longer sent to do logging and lumbering, they are guarded more carefully now, for logging means working almost without guards, and then it also means having axes and saws. Furthermore politicals have different attitudes among themselves: they don't kill one another or slit one another's throats, and in general they respect their comrades and do their best to help them out in time of trouble. And this means that the guards in such camps hesitate to beat the prisoners up in public.

And so a criminal resolves to commit a state crime in order to get into a political camp, even if it means getting an extra sentence. He writes a denunciation of Khrushchev or the party – usually half the words are obscenities. Or else he puts some rags together to make an 'American flag', drawing as many stars on it as he can manage (he hasn't a clue how many there are, all he knows is that it's a lot). Then he has to get caught. He hands out copies of his denunciation to the other cons, somebody is bound to inform admin. Or else he sticks it on a wall in the work zone for everybody to see. The flag is hung up in a prominent position or perhaps he parades with it at roll call. Thus a new state criminal is prepared.

In the political camp he starves even worse than in the criminal one. On one occasion or another he gets a spell in the cooler and on the way there gets beaten up in the guardroom by the warders. He starts to write official complaints, but is soon convinced that this is useless. Meanwhile, he has a long term ahead of him; and he has brought his own forms of protest with him from the underworld, together with its customs and point of view. And this is where the tattoos come in.

Once I saw two former criminal cons, then politicals, who were nicknamed Mussa and Mazai. On their foreheads and cheeks they had tattoos: 'Communists = butchers' and 'Communists drink the blood of the people'. Later I met many more cons with such sayings tattooed on their faces. The most common of all, tattooed in big letters across the forehead, was: 'Khrushchev's slave' or 'Slave of the CPSU' (Communist Party of the Soviet Union).

Here in the special regime camp, in our hut, there was a fellow called Nikolai Shcherbakov. When I caught sight of him in the exercise yard through the window I almost collapsed; there wasn't a single clear spot on his whole face. On one cheek he had 'Lenin was a butcher' and on the other it continued: 'Millions are suffering because of him'. Under his eyes was: 'Khrushchev, Brezhnev, Voroshilov are butchers'. On his pale, skinny neck a hand had been tattooed in black ink. It was gripping his throat and on the back of the hand were the letters CPSU, while the middle finger, ending on his adam's apple, was labelled KGB.

Shcherbakov was in another corner cell similar to ours, only at the other end of the hut. At first I only saw him through the window when their cell was taken out for exercise. Later, though, we three were transferred to another cell and we often exercised simultaneously in adjoining yards. In secret conversation, unnoticed by the warders, we got to know one another. I became convinced that he was normal and not cracked, as I had thought at first. He was far from stupid, he used to read quite a lot and he knew all the news in the newspapers. Together with him in one cell were Mazai and the homosexual, Misha, both with tattooed faces!

In late September 1961, when our cell was taken out for exercise, Nikolai asked us in sign language whether anyone had a razor blade. In such cases it is not done to ask what for – if somebody asks, it means they need it, and if you've got one you hand it over, with no questions asked. I had three blades at that time which I still had from camp ten, before landing in the cooler, and I had hidden them in the peak of my cap as a necessary precaution; in spite of all the searches they had never been found. I went into the latrines, ripped open the seam under the peak with my teeth and took out one blade. Back in the yard, when the warder's attention was distracted, I stuck it into a crack on one of the wooden fence posts to which the barbed wire was secured. Nikolai watched me from his window. The blade stayed there in the crack all day long. Many other cons saw it – the boys used to scour every corner of the exercise yard while outside, every pebble, every crack, in the hope of finding something useful. But once a blade has been placed somewhere, that means it already has an owner waiting to pick it up; in such a case nobody will touch it. Furthermore Nikolai spent the whole day at the window, keeping watch on the blade just in case. While exercising the following day he picked out the blade and took it back to his cell.

Later that evening a rumour passed from cell to cell: 'Shcherbakov has cut off his ear'. And later we learned the details. He had already tattooed the ear: 'A gift to the 22nd Congress of the CPSU'. Evidently he had done it beforehand, otherwise all the blood would have run out while it was being tattooed. Then, having amputated it, he started knocking on the door and when the warder had unlocked the outer door, Shcherbakov threw his ear through the bars to him and said: 'Here's a present for the 22nd Congress.'

This incident is well known to all cons in Mordovia.

The next day we saw Shcherbakov at the window of his cell. His head was bandaged and in the place where his right ear should have been the bandage was soaked with blood, and blood was on his face, neck and hands. A couple of days later he was taken off to hospital, but what happened to him after that I do not know.

And that is the reason why cons always have to be without their caps during inspection and to uncover their foreheads, so that they can be checked for tattoos. Men with tattoos are first sent to the cooler and then put in separate cells, so as not to corrupt the others. Wherever they go after that they are always accompanied by a special section in their files, listing the location and texts of their tattoos; and during inspections the tattoos are checked against these lists to see whether any new ones have been added.

Shcherbakov's cell-mates, by the way, were all hauled in for helping him – for taking part in anti-Soviet propaganda.

But how do cons in the cooler and in prison contrive to tattoo themselves? How do they get the needles and ink? I have often seen it done, both in special regime camps, in transit camps and in Vladimir prison. They take a nail out of their boots or pick up a scrap of wire in the exercise yard, sharpen it on a stone – and there's your needle. Then, to make the ink, they set fire to a piece of black rubber sole from their boots and mix the ash with urine.

But it wasn't the technique so much as the very idea of such activity that astonished me. What did these unfortunates want? Why and to what end did they deform themselves for life? For to do that meant to brand yourself forever, to brand your whole life, it meant you felt yourself to be, in the words of the song, 'an eternal convict', if you disfigured your face in such a way. Or, say, cut off an ear. Why? But sometimes, in moments of helpless despair, I too caught myself thinking: my God, if only I could do something – hurl a piece of my body into the faces of my torturers! Why? At such moments the question doesn't arise.

In time I grew used to those faces and bodies smothered with decorations and inscriptions, and was able to laugh at the newcomers when they almost collapsed at the sight of them, just as I had done on arrival: 'Just you wait awhile and you'll see worse than that!'

We stayed in the special regime cell for three months. First we spent a fortnight in the cooler. Then, in accordance with the regulations, the pre-trial investigation began. On the sixteenth day we began to be called out one by one for interrogation in the governor's office. The three interrogators were an officer from admin, Major Danilchenko and the governor of camp ten. Ozerov was the first to be called. Major Danilchenko asked him:

'Who else wanted to escape with you?'

Ozerov, just as Burov and I did later, replied that there was no one else, only the three of us. That was all, and then they started to lecture him. Ozerov said that we had been beaten up both inside the compound, and in the guardhouse, and on the way to the cooler, while we were handcuffed, and then again in the second guardroom:

'Major Ageyev was present during the beating. He himself battered us with a thick stick and beat us with his revolver.'

'That's a slander!' shouted the officer. 'Who will believe you? You don't show any traces of beating!'

'It was sixteen days ago. We demanded a doctor at the time, but nobody came to see us, not even the warders.'

After Ozerov they summoned Burov and the same sort of conversation took place. Only when they informed Burov that the bit about being beaten up was a slander, he replied:

'Well, all right, I shall probably never get out of here and will die as a con. But those two are both young still, they'll sit out their six to eight years inside and then go free. You might at least preserve appearances, because when they get out they might tell someone what Soviet prison camps are really like.'

'If they do they'll only find themselves back in here again, do you think they don't realise that? Thousands of others go free all the time, without those two, and they keep their mouths shut. And anybody they do talk to makes a note of it and tries not to come here himself.'

When I was called I didn't bother to ruin my nerves with senseless conversations. The interrogation came to a swift conclusion.

'Yes, we were beaten up, me, Ozerov and Burov.'

'Why did you keep quiet about it? Your fellow conspirators made official protests.'

'You would also call my protest a slander, although you know just as well as we do that it's the truth. You, for instance,' I turned to Danilchenko, 'were just the same as Ageyev before you became a governor, and you used to do the same things . . .'

'Take him away!' broke in Danilchenko.

The warder standing behind me pushed his fist into my side and led me back to the cell.

There were no more interrogations and we 'rested' in our cell for about three months, until the trial. This was indeed a break: we weren't driven out to work, they gave us normal camp rations and books, we were allowed to smoke and our exercise period was extended to one hour a day. At first we were held in that same corner cell for three, but shortly before the trial began we were transferred to a larger cell with about twenty men in it. The rest of our cell-mates were also waiting to go on trial, some for refusing to work, some for consistently failing to fulfil their norms, and others for their religious beliefs. In the neighbouring cell there were another twenty men awaiting trial.

At the end of September (a few days after the Shcherbakov affair) the court arrived at our camp, consisting of a judge, a procurator and two people's assessors. The court was held in the office where we had been questioned. One after another the cons were led away, first from the adjoining cell and then from ours. Returning literally after only a few minutes, each one announced: two or three years of prison, at Vladimir. The time came for Burov to be led away and brought back again: two years in Vladimir. I was next. The warder ushered me into the office and remained standing behind me. Apart from the members of the court the office also had its own 'public' – a crowd of officers and staff from the camp administration. The judge, a substantial man wearing a well cut suit, was sitting at a table covered with some red material, with the two people's assessors sitting on either side of him. I wasn't thinking either of the trial or my fate (it was a foregone conclusion), but watched the two assessors.

They looked completely alien and lost in this office among the men in military uniform and the impeccably turned-out judge. One of them was an elderly man wearing a threadbare cotton jacket and a dark-grey shirt that showed signs of repeated washing. He didn't know what to do with his calloused, almost completely black hands, poor fellow, sometimes placing them on the table in front of him and then shyly removing them to his knees. The second assessor was a woman with a wrinkled face, a scarf tied in a knot beneath her chin and work-worn hands. She had an even more pitiful, downtrodden and hunted look about her than her partner. I felt extremely sorry for them, they were looking about them so apprehensively, and then they didn't understand their role in the court and their subordinate positions. Nobody paid the least attention to them for the duration of the trial, as though they were voiceless puppets; nobody asked if they had any questions and the decisions were reached without any reference to them.

When the judge started to ask me the usual procedural questions, I at once announced that I refused to take part in this farce or to play the game called 'people's court'. This announcement caused no surprise at all. My company officer, Captain Vasyayev, read out my character assessment: Marchenko is a vicious parasite, a vicious malingerer and a vicious disrupter of camp regulations; he has not responded to corrective training, he has absented himself from political instruction sessions, he has refused to take part . . . failed to repent . . . been a bad influence . . . After that came a brief but pointed speech by the procurator; without going into detail, he said:

'Three years in jail is what I think.'

Not bothering, even for the sake of appearance, to whisper to his assessors, the judge at once informed me that three years of my camp term would be substituted by a prison sentence.

I was led away and the next one called. Back in the cell they asked:

'How many, two or three?'

All three of us – Burov, Ozerov and I – got the same treatment, so that 'none of us would be offended' as our cell-mates put it.

In the days remaining before our dispatch the more experienced of our companions, who had already been inside Vladimir or had heard about it, told us what awaited us. It added up to little that was good of course. Everyone agreed that prison was even worse than doing special – and special was what we saw all around us. And we felt even worse when we remembered the convoys, prison coaches and transit jails that lay ahead of us.

Soon after the trial they brought our things from camp ten and five days afterwards the first party was dispatched. We three landed up in the second party, which left the special regime camp for Potma at the beginning of October. Then came two days in Potma transit jail, prison coach, two days in Ruzayevka transit jail, prison coach, transit jail in Gorky. And the same transit jails and prison coaches as everywhere else.

In Ruzayevka one prisoner in our party fell ill and was unable to get up at inspection time. The duty officer and warders started to heap obscene curses on his head and forced him to stand. The men in the cell began to mutter, and demanded that this mockery be ended and a doctor called. The result was the usual one: they grabbed hold of a number of men at random, dragged them outside and proceeded to beat them up.

From the Ruzayevka transit jail we were taken to the station during the day. The black marias stopped on the far side of the railway tracks, opposite the station, for the jail was out of town. We were taken out of the vans, lined up in fives and herded across the tracks – beneath a footbridge – to the station. On all sides the column was surrounded by armed guards and dogs and the guards kept yelling at us: 'Stop talking! March, march, quickly, stop dragging your feet!' A large number of people had gathered on the footbridge and their numbers were constantly being added to. They called down to us:

'Hey, lads, where have you come from? Where are you going?'

Packets of cigarettes and money wrapped in paper rained down on the column from the bridge. And at this point some character in civvies appeared from somewhere, asked for the officer in charge of the convoy and at once started to bawl him out:

'What the hell's all this in aid of? You've been told before not to parade prisoners in front of the whole town!'

The officer tried to excuse himself:

'Well, they won't give us any night trains, we've asked and asked for them. We ourselves don't like it either. Just listen to what they're saying about us on the bridge.'

'I should think so! You've got enough audience here to fill a theatre. And then the police have to disperse them, I suppose!'

I remembered how often I had read that always in Russia, throughout her history, the common folk had taken pity on convicts, had given them bread and in the villages brought them milk to drink. Dostoyevsky writes that on holidays their jail used to be snowed under with all sorts of holiday fare: fancy bread, cakes, meat.

Nowadays they just herd you from place to place and people aren't even allowed to look.

PART TWO

I'll tell such truth about you
That lies will be eclipsed . . .

Griboyedov,
(*Woe From Wit,* 1824)

VLADIMIR

The passenger train to which our prison coach had been coupled arrived in Vladimir at three in the morning. The black marias had already been backed up to the platform and we were crammed into them like sprats in a barrel; then we were rushed through the deserted nocturnal streets of this ancient Russian city.

I remembered reading how Herzen,* before his departure abroad, used to stand on the balcony of his house here in Vladimir and watch the convicts, all in chains, being driven along the famous 'Vladimir road' – 'from Russia to the wastes of Siberia'. I remembered Levitan's† 'Vladimir Road' – I had once seen a postcard with a reproduction of it. Probably that well-beaten road, trodden down by the feet of convicts, no longer existed. Nor did the chains. Nobody would see us and no one remember us, except for our jailers. And there was no contemporary Levitan or Herzen to tell the world about our prison convoys in the year 1961.

While I was thinking this the van came to a halt. We had arrived. 'Get out!' The door opened and I stepped straight out of the van and into the door of a building to which we had been backed up. I was led down some corridors and into a large hall which was already full of prisoners who had arrived in the night – some of whom I knew and most I didn't. There were also criminal cons there – all the way from Gorky to Vladimir we had kept stopping to pick them up. We were kept apart, though,

* Alexander Herzen (1812–70), writer, philosopher and publicist, lived in exile (chiefly London) from 1847.
† I. I. Levitan (1860–1900), Russian landscape painter.

and here too we were split up into different cells; I saw them only while in the hall, and then not for long before they were taken away.

We were thrust into 'boxes' – tiny chambers set into the stone wall, one man to each. From there we were summoned one at a time, together with our things. There were the usual questions: surname, name, patronymic, charge, sentence . . . Then a meticulous search. They made us take off all our clothes, inspected us carefully from head to feet, even separated our toes to look between them, pinched the soles of our feet and peered into our back passages. Every single thread of our personal belongings was squeezed and poked and then they took away everything but what we stood up in. We were allowed to take with us two pairs of cotton socks, two handkerchiefs, a tooth brush and tooth powder. And that was all. Not even a change of underpants, not even woollen socks, nothing. All the things taken away from us were listed on receipt forms and in place of the con's pitifully meagre possessions – which were nonetheless extremely dear to him (the handkerchiefs may have been keepsakes, a present from his wife or mother; warm socks were needed for the winter ahead, they would come in just right for the cold floors of those stone cells) – in exchange for the things taken away each man received a piece of paper. The only food we were able to take was our convoy rations – twenty-five ounces of bread (black only) and one salted herring. Thus whoever had managed to save something or other from the camp – ten days' worth of uneaten sugar, say, the remains of some food parcel or something bought at the camp shop – was forced to part with it here.

After being questioned and searched we were taken into the prison yard. Separate from all the other blocks, behind the hospital block and barricaded off from the rest of the prison by a high wall, was the special block for political prisoners. Not even the prison warders were allowed in there without special permission. We were being led past the hospital block when suddenly we heard a cry: 'Help, the Communists are taking it out on me!' – evidently they had mental patients here too. The warders at once started to chivvy us: 'Hurry, hurry, there's no need to gawp all over the place.'

We were halted by the last door in the block. The warder unlocked the door, let us in and then locked the door behind us again. From the vestibule in which we found ourselves a staircase led to the upper storeys, at the top of which was another locked door. The warder unlocked it and let us into the corridor on the first floor. The door behind us was again at once locked and bolted and we were put into the various cells. The cells were empty and we were being put into them temporarily until we had been given baths and assigned to permanent cells. And it was here we experienced our first prison reveille. A very loud bell was sounded, or rather it wasn't a bell but some booming mechanical hooter, and at once the corridors filled with warders banging their keys on the doors and shouting: 'Get up! Get up!' And to dawdlers: 'Is it the cooler you want?' Five minutes later keys rattled in the lock of our door and we were taken out for the toilet break. Then we got breakfast: eighteen ounces of black bread for the whole day, about seven or eight rusty sprats all runny like melting jelly, and a bowl of soup without a single trace of fat or meal in it or a morsel of cabbage or potato, but consisting of lukewarm cloudy wash that we drank straight over the sides. After such a soup the bowls didn't even need cleaning.

At about nine o'clock we were taken for a bath. The main point of this exercise was not to get washed but to have our heads cropped. Stark naked and covered in goose pimples (although it was called a bath house it was pretty cold inside), we submitted one by one to the tender mercies of the barber (one of the criminal cons). They shave not only your head but also all beards and moustaches – such embellishments are not permitted in jail. Seeing this, one old Ukrainian with luxuriant moustaches almost burst into tears: 'I'm sixty-five years old and I've worn a moustache since I was a youngster.'

He refused point-blank to submit. Immediately a number of warders seized him by the arms and legs and dragged him away. (I met him a year later in that same prison – moustacheless, of course. He told me that they had dragged him into some dark sort of cage, then manacled him and given him a thorough beating before taking him back in handcuffs to have his moustache shaved off. He got ten days in the cooler for 'rebellion'.)

I also had a moustache, while many of the religious prisoners had both beards and moustaches. We all faced the same fate as the elderly Ukrainian. My turn came after his. I sat down on the bench and the barber set about my head. After running his clippers over it several times he made a move towards my moustache. I said I didn't want it cut off; even in my file all the photographs showed me with a moustache. The barber went over to one of the warders: 'Here's another one that refuses.' Two warders (Vanya and Sanya) grabbed hold of me, twisted my arms behind my back and threw me on the ground, then the two of them held me down while a third twisted my head back by the ears and the barber in a jiffy relieved me of my moustache. The same thing happened to two of the religious believers while the rest no longer objected. We weren't sent to the cooler; the first had been sent as a warning to the rest of us and that satisfied them for the present, or perhaps there was no more room.

After the barber we were all let into the washroom: several benches, a couple of dozen basins and one hot and one cold tap. Lines formed immediately in front of the taps. Hardly had the last ones had time to get any water when the warders set about pushing us out again: 'Enough, that's good enough!' And to underline their point they turned off the hot water. Willy-nilly we were forced to return to the changing room, where we dried ourselves on some sort of grey rags of towels that had been issued to us. We were not allowed to dress, however. Everything that we had been wearing before had to be handed in to the store and in exchange we were issued with prison clothing. I can't possibly convey how sick I felt putting on that regulation underwear for the first time – God knows how many prisoners had been in it before me. Long underpants, a shirt, regulation cotton trousers and tunic, canvas boots with minuscule tattered foot-rags, a regulation convict's cap, a padded or 'reefer' jacket, everything worn and worn again, everything patched and patched again. The underwear was so threadbare that you were almost frightened to put it on – before you knew where you

were it might crumble to bits in your fingers. Our own things
had to be tied up in bundles and whoever had bags or suitcases
put the things inside, then a tag with your name on was hung
on each bundle and in exchange you received yet another receipt.

After our bath we were locked up in our original cells on the
first floor and then called out one by one. At last it was my turn.
A warder took me down to some sort of store-room. There I
was ordered to strip to the buff once more. While one of the
warders examined my gear – the outfit I had just that minute
received in that same jail – several of the others searched me as
I stood there stark naked. I was ordered to stretch my arms
out in front of me and perform a series of knee-bends, while
they felt me all over in each different position. Then I was
allowed to get dressed and sign out some bedding: a mattress
that was so hard and heavy it seemed to be filled with bricks; a
grey mattress cover that did duty as a sheet; a lumpy pillow on
the same lines as the mattress; a flannel blanket that barely held
together. Also they gave me an aluminium bowl, mug and spoon.
Then I was taken with all my belongings along the prison corridor
to cell No. 54, where we halted. The warder unlocked the door
and I found myself inside, in the cell in which I might be spending
the next three years of my life.

PRISON CELL, PRISON REGIME

It was a cell for five. When I was let in there were already three men inside, all newcomers from the same convoy as myself. Hardly had I time to look round when the keys rattled in the lock again, the door opened and into the cell, weighed down with a mattress and all the rest, walked Ozerov. That meant we were now complete. We began to examine our surroundings. The cell was cramped, about five yards long by three yards wide, in other words about fifteen square yards or three square yards apiece. Directly opposite the door, high up in the wall, was a tiny window filled with cloudy, opaque glass reinforced with wire mesh (unbreakable). Nothing could be seen through such glass, of course, and so little light got through even in the daytime that an electric light bulb was kept on in the cell right round the clock. The window, of course, was barred, and in addition was protected outside by a shield or 'muzzle' (not all the prison windows have muzzles, only cells for prisoners on strict regime; there is also normal regime and these cells have no muzzles over the window). In the older blocks dating from before the revolution the windows had been four times as big – they had been bricked up later, for the new masonry still showed clearly in the old walls.

A pair of iron cots stood against each of the blank walls and a fifth stood under the window. The cots consisted of an iron lattice and were attached to the wall in such a way that they could be lifted and hung on the wall with their legs folded flat. Against the right-hand wall, by the window, was an iron box bound in iron and fixed immovably to the wall – the 'sideboard'; it was divided inside into several compartments in which we kept our soup bowls, spoons, mugs and bread. Attached to the floor in the middle of the cell was a small table with iron legs, with a pair of small benches flanking it, also with iron legs and also attached to the floor. One other item of the furnishing remains to be mentioned – the inevitable sloptank by the door: without this object prison wouldn't be prison. Oh, and then there was the door, of course, an ordinary prison door with a peephole and a food trap, iron-bound and always locked from outside. The peephole was made of glass with a shutter on the corridor side; and the food trap was also kept locked and bolted. The entire furnishings of the cell – tables, benches, 'sideboard', door – were painted dark red.

Cells for prisoners on normal regime are also equipped with a radio – usually an ancient speaker hanging over the door. It is on from six in the morning until ten o'clock at night, being switched most of the time to the internal prison station. This offers the cons information on infringements of the rules – committed, of course, by 'individual' prisoners and quite untypical – and then they read out various orders and decrees on how the culprits are to be punished. Quite often the prison doctors give lectures on 'How to Avoid Tuberculosis', 'How to Prevent Stomach and Bowel Diseases', 'On the Dangers of Alcoholism', or 'How to Guard Against Venereal Diseases'. The advice is well-known: observe personal hygiene, eat clean food, avoid chance relationships, don't mix too closely with invalids, and so on. Both the healthy and those with TB sit and listen to these broadcasts with great amusement: how do you divide up a sloptank between cons, how do you get to breathe air that isn't infected with dampness? The other advice (wash vegetables in running water, chew your food thoroughly, observe a proper diet) might even come in handy in later life, say in five, ten, fifteen years time . . . Cons on strict regime, however, are deprived even of this entertainment.

These were the sort of cells that stretched down both sides of the corridors, though there were also cells for three – 'triple-headers'. One side of the cell block faced inwards, towards the exercise yards and the other blocks. On the other it faced the cemetery (which was also divided from us, like the rest of the outside world, by a stone wall, a ploughed strip and barbed wire). It's true you still couldn't see anything out of the prison windows but occasionally, on the cemetery side, you caught the sounds of a funeral march being played – the sole living evidence that beyond the prison walls life was still following its normal course: aha, somebody's number was up. Our cell was on the cemetery side. The cell block was pierced on the inner or courtyard side by three entrances, one in the middle and one at each end. We were always led in through one of the end doors; inside there was a landing on each floor and a locked door leading to the corridor. A staircase also led from the middle entrance to the upper storeys. Here the stair landings divided the long corridors exactly into half: a barred gate, locked on the landing side, led into each half of the corridor. Inside each half-corridor and locked in, as in a cage, were warders who padded up and down in soft, felt knee-boots and spent their time peering through the peepholes, one after another. According to regulations the warders upstairs were not supposed to have keys to the barred gates – during working hours they too were locked in – but at Vladimir, as everywhere else, this regulation was disobeyed. All keys to all the floors were kept by the chief duty warder, who sat downstairs in the guardroom (and there was also a duty officer in charge of the whole block).

I have already mentioned that our block was divided from the others by a high wall. On one side of the wall was a series of tiny exercise yards for political prisoners; on the other were blocks for civil prisoners, criminals, the hospital and the bath-house. A part of the buildings had been constructed before the revolution. When we were taken to the bath we tried to make out the date – it was something like 1903 or 1905.

One difference between the pre-revolutionary buildings and the Soviet ones, as I have said before, was in the size of the windows. Another was something you couldn't see: it was much colder in the newer blocks. The cells were damp and made you shiver even in summer, while in winter, even wearing a reefer jacket, it was impossible to get warm. Thrusting their hands into their jacket sleeves and with the collars well turned up, the cons would stamp about the cell and bang their feet together, while those who didn't have room to walk about would sit hunched up on the benches with their knees thrust up to their stomachs and their noses tucked into their jackets. Everybody's prison cap, meanwhile, would be pulled right down to the eyebrows: if you leant your head to the right you could warm your right ear, but the left would almost drop off. In the old, pre-revolutionary blocks, although they were also built of stone, it was much warmer and drier.

The politicals' block, alas, was a new one.

The entire prison was enclosed by a ten-foot high stone wall, on both sides of which, as in the camps, were barbed wire fences consisting of several strands; between them was a ploughed and raked strip of land designed to show footprints. The watch towers were manned by sentries with tommy guns and at night the whole barrier was illuminated by powerful searchlights. It says in books that in former times men simply used to escape from prison. Now there are no prison escapes, particularly from political prisons. The cell is locked, the corridor is locked, then comes the inner fence, the ploughed strip and the wall. And even if you stumbled across a sympathetic warder, he still couldn't help you. The security and supervision system is so worked out that the warders control each other – one has the keys to the cell, the other the keys to the floor. And you won't get away with sawing through the bars and hanging a rope-ladder out of the window either: every day there's an inspection, everything is minutely examined, pinched, tapped. In short there's no getting away from it, they make a first-class job of jail.

The daily schedule of prisoners in jail is the same as on special regime in the camps, the only difference being that you aren't sent out to work. At six a.m. it's reveille, followed by toilet break, inspection, breakfast, dinner (with exercise either before or after dinner), supper, inspection, lights out at ten o'clock. From reveille to lights out it is forbidden to lie on your bunk: if you do you earn yourself one to two weeks in the cooler. Sit, walk, stand, doze off standing up or sitting down, but don't on any account lie down. It is also forbidden to go near the window. That is to say, you can go up to it to open the ventilation flap or close it, but if they notice you craning up to it and attempting even with half an eye to look out at the free world outside, the cooler's a dead cert. Singing, talking loudly or making any sort of noise in the cell is also forbidden and for violations the whole cell is punished.

So what is there to do during those sixteen hours out of the twenty-four? Just read or write. You can buy exercise books in the prison shop; you are allowed two school-type books, twelve pages in each, per month. What you write is checked by the warders – if anything looks suspicious the notebook is taken away. They also let you have chess and dominoes. Books and newspapers can be had from the prison library, two books per person every ten days. After a certain time, however, with sixteen hours a day available, even reading loses its charm for the man with a permanently empty stomach. What's more, if a warder sees the prisoners reading in the cell he switches off the light. He has a right to, of course. After all, it's broad daylight outside and the fact that it's dark in the cell is of no concern.

One prisoner in each cell has to be on duty – the duty goes by turns. It is his responsibility to sweep and scrub the cell, to carry out and wash the sloptank during the toilet break, report to the prison officers during inspection or non-regulation visits on how many prisoners there are in the cell and whether there have been any incidents or not. And woe betide the prisoner who makes a bad job of his duties!

I have already said that there are two regimes for prisoners in jail: normal and strict. When I came to Vladimir the system was as follows. Prisoners coming to jail for the first time were held on strict regime for the first two months; those who had been in jail before got six months (thus Burov, for example, faced six months of strict regime, while Ozerov and I were due for two). Prisoners were then put on normal regime and strict regime was reserved for punishment. Since 1964 these obligatory two or six months have been abolished and now the matter is entirely at the discretion of the prison administration. Normally all prisoners are now kept permanently on strict regime, being transferred to normal regime only for periods of six to eight weeks at a time and even then only after a special prison commission (with the invariable assistance of a doctor) has decided that retention on strict regime will endanger a prisoner's life. So they keep a man on normal regime for a while and when he perks up again they send him back to strict.

And so it goes on for years and years – there are men in Vladimir prison with sentences of ten, fifteen, twenty-five years. The difference between these regimes might seem infinitesimal to someone who hasn't experienced them on his own back, but for a prisoner it is enormous. On normal regime there's a radio, on strict regime not; on normal regime you get an hour's exercise a day, on strict regime half an hour, with nothing at all on Sundays; on normal regime you're allowed one visit a year lasting thirty minutes . . .

HUNGER

The most basic difference of all, however, is in the food you get. Here is what a prisoner on normal prison regime receives: eighteen ounces of black bread per day; half an ounce of sugar – he usually gets five days' worth at a go: two and a half ounces. For breakfast he gets seven or eight stale sprats, a bowl of 'soup' (twelve and a half oz.) such as we had the first day after our arrival and a mug of hot water – this you can drink as 'tea' with sugar. Dinner consists of two courses, the first being twelve and a half ounces of cabbage soup (water with leaves of rotten cabbage in it, sometimes you get a tiny fragment of potato), the second three and a half to five ounces of watery gruel, usually made with wheat but very occasionally with oats. For supper you get three and a half to five ounces of mashed potato – so watery and so little that when you peer into the bowl you see the tiny blob of your supper spread out like a minuscule pancake, with the aluminium bottom showing through. On very rare occasions, instead of mashed potato you get a so-called 'vinaigrette' for supper: the same old rotten pickled cabbage with the occasional piece of rotten pickled tomato. But even this pig swill was considered a delicacy by the prisoners. They say that on normal regime it is stipulated that a few grains of fat should be included in the food. Maybe it's true, but I must say that I was never able to notice it in any of the soup or gruel that came to me.

On strict regime the rations are even more meagre: no sugar and no fat is permitted, not even a single grain. You get fourteen ounces of black bread, only sprats and hot water for breakfast, just cabbage soup for dinner (no second course) and the same supper as on normal regime.

Also included in the rations is a packet of cheap tobacco (one and threequarter ounces) every six days. What's more the prisoner on normal regime can also take advantage of the prison shop – until 15 November 1961, he was allowed to spend up to three roubles a month, but since that time the allowance has been reduced to two roubles and fifty copecks. And once a year he is allowed to receive one parcel weighing not more than ten pounds – ten pounds of food!

The prison 'shop', however, deserves a word of explanation. It refers to a process that takes place once a fortnight. Several days beforehand the prisoners start trying to guess which particular day it will be. One day at dinner time the warder puts a list of products available through the food trap, together with blank forms for each prisoner. After dinner he collects the completed forms, showing who wants to buy what, and then he brings the things either the same evening or else on the following morning. Everyone looks forward to this moment. Or rather almost everyone: one man, perhaps, has been deprived of shop privileges, another has no money because he's got no one to send him any. A friend might ask his family to send something to a comrade – two and a half roubles a month wouldn't break anybody – but the trouble is that all letters are censored and that's the sort of request they won't let through. And so some are impatient while others await with sadness the day when orders may be made.

The question is: what to buy and how to dispose of this princely sum of one rouble and twenty-five copecks? I have the right to buy up to four pounds of bread (only black since 1961), up to seven ounces of margarine, up to seven ounces of sausages, up to seven ounces of cheese (you are not allowed to buy butter and sugar). But the permitted sum is not enough to buy what I have a right to, the more so since they only have the more expensive sorts of sausage and cheese – at one and a half to one and three-quarter roubles a pound. And besides, I need soap, tooth powder, socks, envelopes, so that I shall have to take even less margarine, sausage and cheese than I am allowed (nobody refuses the bread; it's cheap and you can fill yourself up with it at least once in a fortnight). For those who smoke, though, it's far worse, since practically all your money goes on smokes. In prison they smoke a lot, a packet of shag lasts for barely two days; but from the shop you can't buy tobacco – only cigarettes: 'Byelomor' at twenty-two copecks a packet, or 'Sever' at fourteen copecks. A packet a day is only just enough, which means that on top of the shag you'd need another twenty packets a month. Two and a half roubles don't go very far . . .

At last they bring the things you've ordered. Men who have been starved for two weeks hurl themselves upon them and eat the lot within the first two or three hours: four pounds of bread with margarine, sausage and cheese – everything they've bought. Far from everyone has the strength of mind to stretch the pleasure out over two or three days. And then back to starvation rations again for another two weeks, at the end of which you again stuff your stomach with four pounds of bread at a single go. (I also decided to stuff myself full one day. I ate my loaf of bread straight off and then at once felt extremely unwell, I got heartburn and almost threw up, but I still had no sense of being full and my eyes were still greedy for more.)

Prisoners in jail soon begin to fall prey to stomach disorders – catarrh, colitis, ulcers. The sedentary life gives rise to haemorrhoids and heart disease. And all this together leads to nervous complaints. In prison you won't find a single healthy man, except perhaps for newcomers – and they don't last long. At any rate those with whom fate and prison authorities threw me together between 1961 and 1963 included not one healthy man.

No, it is impossible to convey the essence of it, this torture by starvation. He who has never experienced it will find it difficult to comprehend.

. . . It is almost morning. Long before reveille not one of the five of us is sleeping. We are all waiting for reveille and then – bread. The moment the hooter sounds we are up. The more impatient among us start to pace about the cell: two steps forward and two steps back. Not everyone can walk about, there's not enough room, therefore the rest are sitting. Sitting and waiting. Toilet break is over. The food trap is open and the server peeps in – he is checking the numbers against his list. The entire cell is already lined up at the food trap: hurry, hurry!

One prisoner takes his ration quickly and moves away, another lingers by the food trap as long as possible, trying to size up the rations and choose the biggest bit and jealously comparing his own piece with that of his companions – as if that fraction of an ounce could save him from hunger! The next one carries his bread off to the 'sideboard' and puts it into his compartment. Another carefully and neatly breaks his bread into three – for breakfast, dinner and supper. At the same time he meticulously gathers all the crumbs and puts them into his mouth. Yet another can't resist and swallows the whole of his ration on the spot, right beside the food trap, before breakfast. And how he watches for the rest of that day as his more patient comrades eat their breakfast, dinner and supper with their bread!

But then how does it feel to be tortured by hunger all day, knowing that in your compartment lies the bread you have saved for dinner and supper! You think about that bread all day and night up to supper time, so long as there's a morsel left. What a magnet it is! How you long to take it out and eat it! Sometimes you can't endure it, you go over to the box, break off a tiny fragment of the crust and place it on your tongue or in the back of your cheek, where you start to suck on it, trying to stretch it out as long as possible, and you suck on it like a child with a sweet, only this morsel of bread is far, far tastier. But then the crust comes to an end, and how you long to go back to that bread again!

So it goes, day after day. You go to bed and you think: let the night go quickly so we can have some more bread again. You get up, wait for your bread and skilly, and before you've finished drinking it you are already thinking: let it be dinner time. Then you hurry the evening along: let it be supper time. Wiping a crust (if you've got one left) over the last traces of the mashed potato in the bottom of your bowl you are already dreaming: let it be lights out, morning, ration time . . . The con's chronometer and the con's diary in prison is simple: bread – breakfast – dinner – supper, and again bread – breakfast – dinner – supper, day after day, month after month, year after year.

Prisoners in a cell need great discipline and great moral strength in order to preserve themselves in such inhuman conditions, in order to preserve their human dignity and human relations with one another. After you've sat in the same cell for several months, everything about the next man begins to irritate you: how he stands, how he sits, how he walks, how he eats, how he sleeps. And you in turn are irritating him. Even with outwardly peaceable relations, everybody's nerves are stretched to the limit and you hold on only because you can't allow yourself to go to pieces and pour out your spite on the others. But think of the situation in cells with civil and criminal prisoners, which are full of men unused to controlling themselves! Scandals, hysterics, fights – and it always ends up, of course, with the cooler for the lot of them, both the innocent and the guilty. But you get scandals and fights in politicals' cells too: it takes all sorts (and there are plenty who become 'politicals' by accident), everyone's nerves are shot to pieces, and the circumstances are such as to drive even the calmest and most stable of men to extremes. There is no way of getting away from them, except perhaps in the cooler.

In winter the most frequent cause of quarrels is the ventilation flap. The point is that one is permitted to open the ventilator at any time (between six in the morning and ten at night) in order to air the cell, but at the same time there is no chance to clear the stench of the sloptank and of all those stale, badly washed human bodies and the tobacco smoke – you can cut the smell with a knife. And so one of the five cell-mates prefers to freeze so long as he can breathe fresh air. The others, though, are not in a condition to stand the cold – they are emaciated, even without the vent open their teeth are chattering. There are old men among them, and sick men in a cold sweat from their illnesses. And here you have grounds for a quarrel, a rumpus – and the pros and cons of the argument are bound to be settled by the cooler.

Even more common are quarrels over food. Just think of it, one part of the prisoners in a cell are on normal regime, while the rest will be on 'strict quota of nourishment'. This is another form of punishment – normal living conditions combined with reduced rations. Then one man will have shop privileges, another will be without; one is allowed food parcels, the other isn't. It makes things difficult for both of them. How can those who are allowed no parcels or shop privileges prevent themselves from staring hungrily at their comrade with a parcel? Or the man with a loaf of bread just bought from the camp shop? Or even the man with a five-day sugar ration – two and a half ounces? And what about the man who has a bit more than the others – what is he to do? Should the hungry man share with the one who's still hungrier? Ignore him and eat his own food, knowing all the while that it gives his comrade hunger spasms just to look at him?

Not every prisoner has the strength to share his parcel or his shop food with his cell-mates. But in my opinion, to eat and look upon those starving, pain-filled eyes is even harder and more intolerable. That's why some prisoners, when they do get a parcel, eat the food on the sly, so the others won't see them – at night, say, under the blanket. Everyone who is free, of course, will condemn such a man – how can you refuse to share with a comrade? But I'm not so sure that he who condemns that prisoner, after going through six months of strict regime, wouldn't hoard his sugar under the pillow and fish out one lump at a time in the night – secretly, so that the others wouldn't hear and be jealous. And how many men who not only have never taken anything from their neighbour but have never even coveted anything of his, now become thieves and steal their neighbour's food from the 'sideboard'? Hunger proves an insuperable ordeal. When he reaches this ultimate degree of degradation a man is prepared for anything. Admin usually knows who these scum are and use them for their own ends – if only to introduce discord into a 'quiet' cell. It is enough to bring in just one of these and then it begins: one man notices some bread missing, another misses some of his sugar – who has taken it? They all start to look at one another with suspicion – and that is exactly what admin wants. Now they have a pretext for handing out punishments right and left, and in any case men lose their self-control and become easy bait, if necessary, for calling out for 'mischief' or a 'violation'.

IVAN MORDVIN

Our cell No. 54 was a peaceful one, we tried not to make life any more miserable for one another than it already was. By December 1961 there were only four of us left (the fifth had been transferred elsewhere): Tolya Ozerov, Nikolai Korolev – the 'terrorist', Nikolai Shorokhov – I think he'd got himself reclassified as a 'political' after being in a criminal camp, and me. One day in the middle of December they moved a fifth man into our cell: Ivan Mordvin. I don't remember either his surname or what he was in for, everybody called him simply Ivan Mordvin – Ivan the Mordovian.

No sooner had he arrived than he started to tell us, keeping nothing back, why and how he had been transferred to our cell. It turned out that beforehand he had been next door. One of his cell-mates was Oleg Danilkin, a 'religious believer' (I later shared a cell with him myself for several months), and one day Oleg received a parcel from his sister in Moscow. Inside were the regulation ten pounds of food. He treated all his cell-mates, including Ivan Mordvin, to the contents, but put aside one eighteen-ounce packet of sugar for later: some sort of religious holiday was approaching and he wanted to save the sugar until then, when he intended to celebrate the holiday by treating the whole cell to tea with sugar. The sugar was left not in his compartment but on top of the iron box. Ivan could not control himself – there was the sugar in front of him, all he had to do was stretch out his hand. In the daytime, of course, in full view of everybody, there was no chance of taking it. But at night you could get up to relieve yourself at the sloptank and there was the sugar right next to you. Ivan couldn't resist the temptation: he took it once, then again, and after that it entered his system.

Night after night he would get up as if to relieve himself, listen – and if all was quiet and everyone sleeping, would slip over to the packet and take some; then, after waiting a while to be sure, he would get up and take some more. The fact that the sugar was disappearing was unknown to the others; there lay the packet and it stayed there, and its owner didn't bother to check the contents – why torture himself for nothing?

And so Ivan Mordvin went on stealing the sugar until someone caught him right by the 'sideboard'. Ivan bellowed loud enough for the whole block to hear, as though his throat were being cut – he explained to us that he did this on purpose so that the warders could come as quickly as possible, before they beat him up. The warders did in fact get there before a fight broke out and after establishing what the matter was, took him out together with his things (i.e. for good) and put him for the time being in one of the 'triple-headers', which was empty at this time. Afterwards he was taken to see the officer in charge of the block. Ivan made a clean breast of everything, telling him all about the stealing and why he had kicked up such a rumpus. In return he was given no punishment and was transferred into our cell.

Ivan told us all this without the least trace of shame and even as though proud of himself, as if to say: look how clever I am, look how crafty I am – I managed to steal the stuff and I got away scot free.

I don't know whether he really didn't realise the vileness of his behaviour and expected us to applaud him, or whether he hoped to win our trust by the frankness of his confession. In the event, of course, he won neither trust nor applause. We all despised him equally and avoided talking to him. But soon our cell too was subjected to a similar incident.

At that particular time we had all just completed two months on strict regime and had just reverted to normal regime. The muzzle had been removed from the window and our exercise period lengthened again. Now we were waiting for our permitted parcels. The first to receive one, from his mother, was Nikolai Korolev: five pounds of sugar – in five packets – plus some food and a home-made cake: his mother had baked it herself. Nikolai shared his parcel with everyone – each of us got one packet of sugar. And he also shared the cake round, leaving a slightly bigger bit for himself. After all, it didn't represent only food to him but also his mother's care – Nikolai deeply loved his mother and was doing time because of her. We all realised this perfectly well. Ivan Mordvin ate his share up at once, including the whole pound of sugar. The rest of us, without discussing the matter, all decided to stretch our food for as long as possible. I, for instance, decided to take four lumps of sugar a day and no more – two in the morning and two in the evening – so as to drink not just hot water but sweet tea (in general I've got a sweet tooth and two lumps per mug is too little for me; here I had to economise, however, and not indulge myself).

The following evening, just before lights out, Nikolai collected all the food left from his parcel, put it into his pillowcase and stowed it under his head for the night. We all exchanged glances in silence. Both I and the others, I think, felt awkward and somehow ashamed, as if each of us suspected the others of some sort of underhand conduct. I couldn't go to sleep all night or obtain any peace of mind. After all, nobody had forced Nikolai to share out his parcel, so why should he have to hide his precious things away from us now, as if he feared for them and didn't trust us? Only in the small hours did I grow exhausted and doze off. But I hadn't had time to fall asleep properly before reveille sounded and I had to get up again in order to steer clear of the cooler and avoid being put back on special regime. We all got up, tidied our cots and settled down to wait for toilet break and breakfast. Ivan was pacing up and down the cell impatiently, Ozerov and Shorokhov sat on their made-up bunks with their arms clasped round their knees and reefer jackets over their heads – this was the best way to snatch forty winks, keeping yourself warm and dozing until the warder shouted at you. Evidently they had also spent a bad night. Korolev was reading some book or other with large print. I also picked up a book and looked at it, but it was impossible to read, so uncomfortable was the atmosphere in the cell. Nor could I look at anyone – it would be too shaming and painful.

The warders were running along the corridor, rattling their

keys and looking into the peepholes: 'No more sleep, no more sleep, is it the cooler you want?' This was addressed to Ozerov and Shorokhov, but more for form's sake than anything else; they were dozing sitting up and not lying down. At last there came a bang on the door: 'Toilet break!' We stood up and took off our padded reefer jackets – no matter how cold it was it was forbidden to wear your outer clothing for toilet break. Today Shorokhov was on duty and it was his job to carry out the sloptank. But the sloptank was heavy and after two months of starvation on strict regime he didn't have the strength any more. Usually two men carry the sloptank, one always helps the man on duty. This time we two carried it out. Shorokhov and I. While we were doing our stuff they came banging on the door, as usual, and the warders shouted: Come on, come on, don't hang around, you're not the only ones here, have you forgotten where you are?' – and more in the same vein.

By the time we were making our way along the corridor the servers were already bustling about at the far end of it and the old man who heated the water (a prisoner) was distributing his hot water. No sooner had the door been locked behind us than the food trap was opened: 'Give us your kettle for the hot water!' We handed out the empty kettle and received it back full again together with our rations. Hot water is awaited in winter with even greater impatience than the skilly: it's hot and at least warms you for half an hour, while the skilly's the same water, only luke-warm. We started to drink our tea – with sugar, for everyone now (except Ivan Mordvin) had a pound of sugar from Korolev's parcel. I took two lumps from my packet and sat warming myself with my tea. At the same time I didn't look up at a soul, I still couldn't recover my composure after yesterday's events.

I didn't see how Shorokhov went to get his sugar and how he arrived at Ivan's side. I woke up only when Shorokhov let Ivan have it full in the face. Ivan leapt up and they started to grapple. Shorokhov turned out to be the stronger (although he looked punier than Ivan), or perhaps the madder: he split Ivan's lips, knocked out some of his teeth and bloodied his whole face. The rest of us, having jumped up from our places, stood around in silence while the fight took its course, without interfering. We still couldn't make out who was attacking whom or for what. And one shouldn't imagine this scene as being like some ordinary street brawl. Prisoners who have done a good stretch in prison, and on strict regime what's more, haven't the strength to punch an opponent properly, nor to stay on their feet after a gentle push. They fasten their fingers on to each other's faces and are afraid even to break away – in case they fall down. And so they just stand there, swaying from weakness, and endeavour with their fingers to tear at each other's faces . . . It is a pitiful, degrading picture!

We came to our senses only when the door opened and the warders came bursting into the cell. The fight was immediately stopped. When the warders left again they said that both Shorokhov and Ivan would be punished.

Later, after the skilly, Shorokhov explained to us what had happened. It turned out that when he went to get his sugar, more than half of the packet had disappeared since the day before. He had immediately thought of Ivan – he couldn't possibly have suspected one of us – and Ivan didn't deny it, but merely sat there silently on his cot. After that Korolev said that on the first night after his parcel arrived he had lost half the food and half the sugar out of it – that was why on the second night he had decided to hide everything under his pillow, so as not to lose the rest. Ozerov said that he too had found several lumps of sugar missing.

I also wanted to have a look at my packet, but I put it off till the evening – for some reason I felt too embarrassed to check it right away. In the evening, when I took out some lumps for tea, I secretly counted the top layer – seven lumps were missing. (This was extremely easy to do: a con keeps track of every single lump of sugar, he remembers how many he ate yesterday, the day before and even a week ago, and also how many layers there are in a packet, how many rows in a layer, how many lumps in a row – all this is carefully calculated in advance and just as carefully apportioned.) And so I was short of seven lumps. I thought back once more to how many lumps I had taken the day before yesterday, how many yesterday and how many today – still there were seven short. That was too many for me to have made a mistake – two, say, or three, that was possible, but not seven. But then how come I hadn't noticed it before? Of course, I used to get my sugar without taking the whole packet out and it had never occurred to me to count. Nevertheless I told no one that I too was short – perhaps I was too embarrassed. But I was mortally offended. Why, that meant practically two whole days' worth of sugar . . .

That same day the block officer called out both Shorokhov and Ivan Mordvin. Ivan got off with a reprimand, while Shorokhov was put on strict regime rations but left in the cell with us.

HUNGER STRIKE

Several days after these events Ozerov was removed from our cell, for no particular reason, and replaced by a young fellow from next door, Andrei Novozhitsky. Andrei was in for treason. He had been serving in a tank unit in East Germany, had crossed over to West Germany and after about a year there, feeling homesick for his native land, had decided to go back. They didn't dissuade him in the West but warned him that once back in Russia he would be sent to a camp. He didn't believe them, putting it down to bourgeois propaganda. So he came back and was sent straight to a camp (he had been sentenced *in absentia* to ten years). It was an ordinary story. I met many men in the camps who had returned from abroad, and not only soldiers either. As for Vladimir prison, Novozhitsky had landed up there for failing to fulfil his norm in the camp.

Not long after being transferred to our cell Andrei decided to go on hunger strike – evidently he had been planning this move for some time. He wrote a statement into which he crammed a whole pile of reasons impelling him to go on hunger strike. He protested against his trial behind closed doors, against the fact that he hadn't been given a copy of his sentence, against being sent to prison for failing to fulfil his norm – he was too ill, he said, to fulfil it, and against the inhuman conditions under which political prisoners were being held in Vladimir jail. A few days afterwards Shorokhov also went on hunger strike. In his statement, addressed to the Central Committee of the CPSU and the Presidium of the Supreme Soviet of the USSR, he also protested against his closed trial, unjust and unfair sentence (whose text, like almost everyone else, he had never seen) and the starvation conditions in the jail.

Now we had two people in our cell on hunger strike. They were left where they were, in the same cell as us, although this was against the regulations: hunger strikers are supposed to be isolated. The prison authorities always break this rule – go hungry in the communal cell, watch your companions getting their skilly and munching their bread! Some men can't hold out – it's a real ordeal after all! – and give up their strike after three or four days. I too have endured that ordeal and will write about my hunger strike in the Karaganda camps.

Hunger strikers have one 'advantage': they can lie whole days in their cot without getting up. Now, during the morning inspection, the duty prisoner, in addition to his normal report: 'Cell No. 54, five prisoners, sir!' had to add: 'Two on hunger strike.' For the first five or six days after their statements nobody pays any attention to them. On the fourth or fifth day the officer says: 'Hunger strike? Well, and to the devil with you!' Or something juicier and more colourful. Then a warder glances through the peephole, sees two cons lying in their cots and bangs his keys on the door: 'Get up! Is it the cooler you want, you fucking bastards?' But seeing that they don't get up but just lie there without stirring, he remembers that they are hunger strikers and walks away from the door, cursing. Another, though, doesn't immediately realise what's going on (how can he remember them all when almost every cell has one or two of them?), opens the door and goes up to the cots. Only at this point does he catch on; and then someone in the cell says sarcastically: 'Get him up, get him up, off to the cooler with him, who does he think he is, lolling about like a lord?' The warder moves away again, cussing blue murder, and threatens the wag with the cooler (for 'arguing with a warder') – it's been done before, if the warder's mad enough. On the fifth or sixth day one of the warders will go up to the bed of a hunger striker and throw the blanket back from his face to check if he's still alive; and at the same time to see if he's tattooed his forehead.

The other men in the cell with hunger strikers get edgy and wound up to an unbearable degree. The indifference and even gloating of the prison officers drives you to distraction. Nobody cares two hoots about the prison regulations, and if you protest nobody bats an eyelid. It's absolute murder eating your rations in front of comrades who are on hunger strike. I myself always felt somehow guilty for not being able to help them and we always tried to swallow our food as quickly and inconspicuously as possible.

Novozhitsky and Shorokhov always turned their faces to the wall during breakfast, dinner and supper. All these days they took not a single crumb into their mouths. Sometimes they would ask for a drink – when you raised the mug of water to their lips they would take a few swallows and then turn to face the wall again. Another time one of the rest of us would be unable to endure it any longer and would try to persuade Andrei or Nikolai: take some of my ration, go on, you can eat it secretly; it's all the bloody same – you know they won't take you out until ten days are up; come on now, just a crust, the warders will never know. Novozhitsky usually refused politely, while Shorokhov would swear blue murder at you for your pains. And why not? Why interfere when things are tough enough as they are?

Every day they would bring bread and skilly to the cell for all five of us. The duty prisoner was obliged to ask a hunger striker whether he wanted his food that day. On getting a refusal he was supposed to return it to the warder. Thus the man on hunger strike was obliged to refuse his food three times a day; and the man on duty was also sickened at having to take part in this recurring torture. Novozhitsky and Shorokhov had both come to an agreement with us beforehand that each of us, when on duty, would hand back their bread and soup without asking them. We agreed, of course – this was the only service we were able to do for them. And that is what usually happens, even among the criminal cons, although the duty prisoner risks punishment if he's found out.

Andrei and Nikolai got terribly chilled, even though they lay on their cots fully dressed with their blankets pulled over their heads. But then even we who were getting our minuscule portions of food and were able to walk about the cell in our padded jackets – even we managed to get warm for a moment only twice a day, i.e. morning and evening when they brought the hot water. It was so cold in the cell that if you put the kettle of hot water on the floor it would go cold in quarter of an hour. Yet these men were completely without food – or even hot water, for they refused to drink anything hot. Furthermore both of them, after several years of short rations in the camps, had just undergone a period of genuine starvation on strict regime in prison. Their bodies retained not a single drop of the reserves that a man has in normal conditions. And from the very first day of a hunger strike such a wasted organism begins to feed off itself.

Andrei no longer got up from his cot after the third day and after the ninth day no longer spoke. Nikolai was able to get to his feet up to the eighth day after his hunger strike began; and he went on talking, although with difficulty, until the very end, when they took him away from us. Not once, during the time they stayed in our cell, did the doctor look in to see them. The nurse, as usual, used to come to the food trap every day (except Sundays) and ask her usual questions: 'Is anyone ill in here?' – and then, without so much as a glance at the hunger strikers, would continue to the next cell.

The three of us who were left wrote protests practically every day, complaining that the hunger strikers hadn't been transferred to a special cell but were being kept in with us. And whenever one of the officers came in to see us we protested again. But the answer was always the same: 'Admin knows best where to keep them. We're still in charge here, not you.'

On the eleventh day after Novozhitsky had begun his strike, towards evening, a group of warders came into the cell. The duty prisoner made the necessary report. The warders went up to Novozhitsky and lifted the blanket. He lay there quite still in his bed, wearing his jacket, trousers and boots, and his face was like that of a corpse. The warders examined him to make sure he was still alive. Then the senior warder ordered one of us to collect up his belongings, and carry them out of the cell. I picked up Andrei's mug, bowl and spoon and together with Korolev went over to Andrei to help him out. He himself was unable to stand, we lifted him and assisted him into the corridor. He was so light that not even we, who were so exhausted and weakened that the two of us were hardly able to carry the sloptank, felt his weight at all. He was a living skeleton dressed up in the regulation clothing of a prisoner. A warder walked ahead of us down the corridor and let us into an empty cell. He ordered us to sit Andrei on the bare cot and Andrei slumped further and further to one side until his shoulder rested against the wall. I lingered there beside him, it was terrible to have to leave him there, half-dead, in an empty cell. But the warder drove me away:

'Scram, scram! There's nothing the matter with him. Nobody forced him to go on hunger strike, it was his own decision not to eat anything.'

I couldn't stop myself and growled back:

'And we, of course, eat like princes, I suppose!'

'Oh, I see your ration's got too big for you,' he replied, 'maybe we ought to clip a few ounces off.'

I got the message and kept quiet. The warder locked Andrei in and led us back to our cell. In there, meanwhile, the other warders had completed their search of Andrei's belongings and were conducting an ideological discussion with Shorokhov: why bother, they said, this hunger strike won't get you anywhere, give it up, you're only signing your own death warrant . . .

They ordered us to carry Andrei's things to his new cell. Korolev and I took the bedding, and truly the mattress was several times heavier than he himself had been. We found Andrei slumped in exactly the same position we had left him in: he was half lying with his face up against the wall. The warder ordered Korolev to lay the bedding out on an empty cot. And me he commanded to lift Andrei and support him under the armpits so that he did not fall. Then, on this body hanging from my arms, he carried out a search.

Afterwards we placed Andrei on the bed, covered him with a blanket and his reefer jacket on top of that, and went out. The warder locked the cell.

Although we had already heard from other prisoners that hunger strikers were kept in their normal cells for up to ten or eleven days, we still hadn't been able to believe that such a mockery was usual or the norm (nowadays it is only seven or eight days). Now, however, we were to learn the truth of this for ourselves. And Shorokhov too, who was on his seventh or eighth day, now knew what an ordeal awaited him during the next four to five days. Nevertheless he still didn't call his strike off and on the twelfth day they took him away. Korolev and Ivan Mordvin were the two who took him. Nikolai looked a bit perkier than Andrei had done, in spite of the fact that he had gone a day longer and what's more had been on strict regime just before his strike because of his fight with Ivan.

I never saw Shorokhov again, nor heard what became of him. Novozhitsky, however, was brought back to our cell about a week later. To describe what he looked like is impossible. He had called off his hunger strike: you can starve and starve, but you can never persuade anyone in authority even to listen to your complaint, let alone to go into it for you . . . Nor do they let you die. The very day that Andrei was taken away from us they began to feed him artificially. Another thing: both we and the two hunger strikers, Shorokhov and Novozhitsky, had demanded that they be removed from our communal cell, as is laid down in the regulations, because we all thought that this would save the hunger strikers from unnecessary torture. But it turned out that getting a separate cell was only a prelude to further cruel indignities. The artificial feeding itself was turned into a daily torture. What's more, I know from my own experience that the feeling of hunger doesn't disappear, nor even lessen: all you get is a sensation of heaviness in the stomach, as though some sort of alien object has been placed inside you. And then they had invented a supplementary form of torment – Andrei Novozhitsky told us about it.

Every morning the warders bring into the cell a ration of bread and a bowl of skilly and place them on a stool beside the head of the bed. Then they go out and leave the breakfast there half a day under the nose of the man on hunger strike. At dinner time they change the skilly and leave it there till the evening. The next morning they change the bread and say 'Are you going to eat your bread today?' 'Are you going to eat your breakfast today?' 'Are you going to eat your supper?' And so on three times a day. We at least were able to shield our friends from this ritual.

One day the block officer went in to see Novozhitsky:

'Hunger strike? A waste of time, you can easily write complaints without going on hunger strike. Go on, complain, write, we won't deprive you of this right . . .'

'But how and who can I complain to about you wild beasts in here?'

'We're not wild beasts, we act strictly according to the regulations. If you think we're breaking the regulations, go on and complain, it's your right . . .'

Novozhitsky, of course, received the standard answers to his protests, despite the fact that his protests were reinforced with a hunger strike: 'Correctly sentenced. Regarding the conditions of his internment in jail, this complaint has been passed back for local consideration.' Truly it makes you wonder whether a hunger strike is worth such answers.

Nevertheless, the fact that they have even been given some sort of answer fills some inexperienced protesters with hope. They call off their hunger strike and wait for the local authorities to 'do justice' to their complaint. So much the greater is their despair, therefore, when one of the prison officers informs them that what they consider to be 'inhuman cruelty' is really 'in conformity with the regulations' – and this is usually communicated to them with a maximum of cynical sarcasm and sneering commentaries. Very often, after this sort of final reply, the prisoner who has not yet recovered from his first hunger strike immediately starts a second, or else does something to himself that is conditioned solely by his despair.

SELF-MUTILATION

Here is one out of a number of similar stories, from which it differs only in its originality. It took place before my very own eyes in the spring of 1963. One of my cell-mates, Sergei K., who had been reduced to utter despair by the hopelessness of various protests and hunger strikes and by the sheer tyranny and injustice of it all, resolved, come what may, to maim himself. Somewhere or other he got hold of a piece of wire, fashioned a hook out of it and tied it to some home-made twine (to make which he had unravelled his socks and plaited the threads). Earlier still he had obtained two nails and hidden them in his pocket during the searches. Now he took one of the nails, the smaller of the two, and with his soup bowl started to hammer it into the food flap – very, very gently, trying not to clink and let the warders hear – after which he tied the twine with the hook to the nail. We, the rest of the cons in the cell, watched him in silence. I don't know who was feeling what while this was going on, but to interfere, as I have already pointed out, is out of the question: every man has the right to dispose of himself and his life in any way he thinks fit.

Sergei went to the table in the middle of the room, undressed stark naked, sat down on one of the benches at the table and swallowed his hook. Now, if the warders started to open the door or the food flap, they would drag Sergei like a pike out of a pond. But this still wasn't enough for him: if they pulled he would willy-nilly be dragged towards the door and it would be possible to cut the twine through the aperture for the food flap. To be absolutely sure, therefore, Sergei took the second nail and began to nail his scrotum to the bench on which he was sitting. Now he hammered the nail loudly, making no attempt to keep quiet. It was clear that he had thought out the whole plan in advance and calculated and reckoned that he would have time to drive in this nail before the warder arrived. And he actually did succeed in driving it right in to the very head. At the sound of the hammering and banging the warder came, slid the shutter aside from the peephole and peered into the cell. All he realised at first, probably, was that one of the prisoners had a nail, one of the prisoners was hammering a nail! And his first impulse, evidently, was to take it away. He began to open the cell door; and then Sergei explained the situation to him. The warder was nonplussed.

Soon a whole group of warders had gathered in the corridor by our door. They took turns at peering through the peephole and shouting at Sergei to snap the twine. Then, realising that he had no intention of doing so, the warders demanded that one of us break the twine. We remained sitting on our bunks without moving; somebody only poured out a stream of curses from time to time in answer to their threats and demands. But now it came up to dinner time, we could hear the servers bustling up and down the corridor, from neighbouring cells came the sound of food flaps opening and the clink of food bowls. One fellow in the cell could endure it no longer – before you knew it we'd be going without our dinner – he snapped the cord by the food flap. The warders burst into the cell. They clustered around Sergei, but there was nothing they could do: the nail was driven deep into the bench and Sergei just went on sitting there in his birthday suit, nailed down by the balls. One of the warders ran to admin to find out what they should do with him. When he came back he ordered us all to gather up our things and move to another cell.

I don't know what happened to Sergei after that. Probably he went to the prison hospital – there were plenty of mutilated prisoners there: some with ripped open stomachs, some who had sprinkled powdered glass in their eyes and some who had swallowed assorted objects – spoons, toothbrushes, wire. Some people used to grind sugar down to dust and inhale it – until they got an abscess of the lung . . . Wounds sewn up with thread, two lines of buttons stitched to the bare skin, these were such trifles that hardly anybody ever paid attention to them.

The surgeon in the prison hospital was a man of rich experience. His most frequent job was opening up stomachs, and if there had been a museum of objects taken out of stomachs, it would surely have been the most astonishing collection in the world.

Operations for removing tattoos were also very common. I don't know how it is now, but from 1963 to 1965 these operations were fairly primitive: all they did was cut out the offending patch of skin, then draw the edges together and stitch them up. I remember one con who had been operated on three times in that way. The first time they had cut out a strip of skin from his forehead with the usual sort of inscription in such cases: 'Khrushchev's Slave'. The skin was then cobbled together with rough stitches. He was released and again tattooed his forehead: 'Slave of the USSR.' Again he was taken to hospital and operated on. And again, for a third time, he covered his whole forehead with 'Slave of the CPSU'. This tattoo was also cut out at the hospital and now, after three operations, the skin was so tightly stretched across his forehead that he could no longer close his eyes. We called him 'The Stare'.

In the same place, in Vladimir, I once happened to spend several days in a cell with Subbotin. This was a fellow the same age as myself and a homosexual. There were few homosexuals in Vladimir and everyone knew who they were. There was nothing they could earn there. He had been classed as a 'political' after being in an ordinary criminal camp and making an official complaint – thus 'letting the tone down'. One day, after having sent about forty or fifty complaints to Brezhnev and the Presidium of the Supreme Council and to Khrushchev and the Central Committee of the Communist Party of the Soviet Union, he swallowed a whole set of dominoes – twenty-eight pieces. When the whole of our cell was being led down the corridor to the exercise yard – he had swallowed the dominoes just before our exercise period – he clapped himself on the stomach and said to one con from prison service who was coming the other way: 'Listen, Valery!' I don't know whether Valery really heard the sound of dominoes knocking together in Subbotin's stomach, but he asked him: 'What have you got there?' and Subbotin drawled 'Dominoes'.

The doctors wouldn't operate on Subbotin. They simply ordered him to count the pieces during defecation, saying that they would have to come out on their own. Subbotin conscientiously counted them each time and on his return to the cell ticked off in pencil on a special chart the number that had come out. No matter how diligently he counted, however, four pieces still remained unaccounted for. After several days of agonising suspense he washed his hands of them: if they stayed in his stomach it was all right as long as they didn't interfere, and if they were out already, then to the devil with them.

THE 'TERRORIST'

Nikolai Korolev was somewhat over thirty and was now serving his fifteenth year of imprisonment. Before his crime he had been living with his mother in a village near Tver. Both of them worked in the local *kolkhoz** and they worked hard there, from dawn to dusk. It was 1947. At that time there were practically no men in the villages, all the work was shouldered by women and by adolescents like Nikolai. Meanwhile the few men that remained in the village occupied all the important posts – chairmen, foremen, stock takers. Usually they drank like fish and lorded it over the *kolkhoz* workers however they liked.

Nikolai noticed that his mother's eyes were tear-stained when she returned from work and at nights she would weep at home. He asked her what the matter was, but she only replied: 'Don't worry, Kolya, it's nothing. It's a dog's life, that's all . . .' But a friend told him that the foreman had got his knife into his mother and used to swear at her obscenely and humiliate her in front of the others.

One day Nikolai had been riding the oxen past the seed store. From inside came the sound of the foreman's voice – he was shouting, pouring out a stream of filthy language. Nikolai halted the oxen and went into the yard. Inside he saw his mother standing there, weeping, distressed and in fear, with her arms lowered, while the foreman sat on horseback in front of her, holding a switch and bellowing at her for all he was worth. Nikolai stepped forward:

'Leave her alone, you drunken pig!'

The foreman answered:

* Collective farm.

'Mummy's boy, what do you think you can do!' and poured out a stream of filth on him too. Then he leaned down from his horse and grabbed the peak of Nikolai's cap, intending, evidently, to pull it down over his eyes. Nikolai ducked, the foreman crowded him with his horse, and then, shifting his switch from one hand to the other, slashed Nikolai with it. The mother rushed to shield her son, put her arms round him and cried:

'Monster, monster! Crowing over us women's not enough for you, now you have to start on the children!'

Nikolai tore himself away from his mother and ran home, beside himself with rage, with his mother's cry still ringing in his ears. Back in the house he seized his father's shotgun from the wall, loaded it and ran out into the street. The foreman was riding towards him, evidently on his way back from the stores. Nikolai raised the gun. He was hardly able to aim it for the mist covering his eyes. All he could see was the horse's muzzle, which seemed to be right in front of him, and so he aimed higher at some point above it. Having fired the shot he lowered the gun and went home without a single backward glance. Only when his mother ran up saying: 'Kolya, Kolya, what have you done?' did he understand that he had killed the foreman.

He sat at home and waited for them to take him. They came, took him out, put him in a van and took him first to the district headquarters and then to Tver, to prison. He was tried behind closed doors; not a soul was in court and no witnesses were called. Killing a *kolkhoz* foreman was interpreted as an act of terrorism. And since terrorism was a political crime, he was sentenced to twenty-five years. Nikolai at that time was just eighteen.

Later he was sent to Vladimir, like me, for attempting to escape. While doing special in camp ten he had got friendly with a 'secessionist Ukrainian', Vasily Pugach, and the two of them had participated in a group dig in the work zone. I knew Vasily. He had been about twenty-five then, with a twenty-five-year sentence round his neck, and his mother was also behind barbed wire somewhere in Mordovia. He and I had been in the same convoy to Vladimir and had both been forcibly cropped – Pugach had also been deprived of his luxuriant Ukrainian moustache. I had been very fond of Vasily Pugach and therefore was well disposed to his comrade and friend from the very beginning. And indeed, Nikolai turned out to be an extremely nice fellow, calm and collected, and that was of great value in a prison cell, where everyone tends to be so nervous and on edge. He used to get letters and parcels from his mother and I have already told how he shared out the parcel, which not everyone was capable of doing.

Nikolai asked me to write an official petition for him – he hadn't really mastered reading and writing. I of course knew that it was useless, but how do you tell that to a man who has already spent fifteen years inside and has another ten left to do? By that time the criminal cons with twenty-five-year sentences had had them commuted to fifteen: that was the maximum sentence under the new criminal code. But the changes in prison sentences didn't affect politicals and to this day they are serving out their twenty to twenty-five years.

I wrote a petition as best I could: that Nikolai had committed murder in a state of extreme disturbance, that this murder could not be construed as an act of terrorism, because Nikolai had had no political ends in view; that he had been illegally tried behind closed doors and that a copy of his sentence was being illegally withheld from him. It ended with a request that his sentence be reconsidered and that his crime be requalified as murder and not terrorism.

I read the petition aloud. Nikolai listened to it together with the rest of the members of the cell. We decided to address it to the Presidium of the Supreme Soviet, to Brezhnev, I think it was. Then Nikolai put his signature on the bottom and the following morning handed it to the warder through the food trap. About three days afterwards they brought him a printed form informing him that his petition had been forwarded to Moscow. He signed this also and settled down to wait.

All the time he was in our cell he waited and then, when he was transferred elsewhere, wrote again and again. He sent off dozens of petitions asking for his case to be reconsidered. The answer was always the same: 'Correctly sentenced, no grounds for the case to be reconsidered.'

In 1963 I heard he was in a special regime camp, coming up to his nineteenth year of imprisonment.

HARD TO STAY HUMAN

Soon they started to break up our cell for some reason. The first to go was Novozhitsky. He was so weak he was unable to carry his own things. We helped him gather them up, carried his gear out into the corridor and said farewell. (We met again only in 1966, in camp eleven in Mordovia.) After that they removed Korolev.

For two days there were only two of us in the cell, Ivan Mordvin and myself. I found this very unpleasant, I couldn't forget the stolen sugar. And now on top of it all Ivan took it into his head to try and excuse himself. I listened in silence and then cut him short fairly sharply. He stopped after that, but not for long. The next morning he started a different tune – how he was due to receive a parcel. I can see him now: tall and skinny as a rake, in prison rig, with his hands in his pockets, pacing about the cell – three steps forward, three steps back – and talking without a break. Any day now he'd be getting a parcel with honey and butter and sugar. And he'd give me some of it too. And how he'd eat then . . . I realised it was the hunger in him talking, but still I couldn't overcome my irritation: for God's sake, we were fed on the same skilly, weren't we, but I controlled myself, while he simply didn't give a damn for other people's feelings!

Luckily some new prisoners were brought in. First an old man, a religious believer, about 65 to 70 years old. He was called Pavel Ivanovich, but I've forgotten his surname. Then they brought an Azerbaijanian, Ilal-ogly, a taciturn fellow of about 35 – short, dark, black-haired, and skinny like the rest of us. I don't know what he was in for, his Russian wasn't up to much. Three days or so later they brought Boris Vlasov – I particularly remember his arrival. The keys clattered in the locks, the door opened and a fellow on crutches came into the cell, accompanied by several warders. He went over to his cot, spread out his bedding and lay down, after which the warders immediately picked the crutches up and took them away with them.

It turned out that Boris Vlasov had been brought to us straight from the hospital. He had been in prison for ages now, and unable to stand the torture any longer had one day upped and swallowed two spoons, his own and another man's. That wasn't enough, however. He also swallowed, piece by piece, a complete set of dominoes. First they dragged him off for an X-ray and then to the operating table. They slit open his stomach, extracted all the official property and stitched him up again. Then, still in hospital, Vlasov went on hunger strike. After fasting for a month he broke down. He called off the hunger strike and immediately slit the veins on his leg. They had noticed in time, bandaged him up and had now brought him straight to our cell. He still couldn't walk and for the first few days the nurse used to change his bandages right there in the cell. A week later, however, he was able to hobble about on his own and began going to the medical post to get them changed – luckily it was on our floor and he had no stairs to climb.

Vlasov became friends with Ivan Mordvin. Both of them had fifteen-year terms, both were old hands, and for days on end they would natter on about the camps and prison: they had already forgotten about life outside and didn't even dream about it any more.

As time went on Ivan told Boris about this and about that and one day came to the incident that had occurred in our cell. And then what did I hear but Ivan (and they weren't speaking in whispers but aloud, with no sense of embarrassment) starting to heap all sorts of abuse on Ozerov, Korolev and Shorokhov. No doubt if I hadn't been there he would have said the same sort of things about me. Not knowing our former cell-mates the others listened to Ivan and drank it all in, looking at me from time to time to see what I would say. At this point all the indignation that I had been feeling against Ivan, that had been accumulating since the very day of his arrival and that I had succeeded in suppressing till now, suddenly boiled up inside me. I cut him off sharply: he shouldn't lie about men behind their backs, he'd be too scared if they were there. Ivan had already lost his temper and called me some sort of dirty name in reply. I was even half pleased by this, I took a swing and let him have it full in the face – now I'd found an outlet for my rage. I was so incensed that I was ready to tear him to pieces. Ivan grabbed hold of the kettle with the cooled remains of our hot water in it and swung it at me. I knocked it out of his hand and it clattered on the cement floor and rolled over, spilling water over the whole cell. Ivan and I grappled. I had managed to punch him several times in the face already and it was covered in blood: blood was running from his nose and oozing from his teeth and split lips. I don't know what I looked like, I was so enraged that I didn't feel any pain. I punched him again, and he fell on to my cot. I turned and walked away, still quivering with rage, and sat down on Pavel Ivanovich's cot in order to get a grip on myself. But just then Ivan jumped up and made a rush at me. I pushed him away, got him down on the table and pressed him flat, though I don't remember how. His foot came into my hand. I grabbed hold of it and gave it a sharp twist. Ivan moaned. I twisted still harder. Then suddenly I heard a crack. In a flash I cooled down, my rage and fury might never have been, I felt unbearably ashamed and sorry for Ivan. I let him go and moved back from the table. Had I really just broken a man's bone, feeling how my heart had stopped and my throat was constricted with rage? I was ashamed to look at Ivan and the other cons.

At that moment the door opened and the warders came running in. There was nobody to drag apart by now so they stopped and examined the cell and all of us. The duty wardress, a spiteful little old woman, pointed at me and Ivan and began to explain:

'I was looking through the peephole.' (She was such a dwarf, in fact, that she couldn't reach the peepholes and always carried a little stool with her; she used to go from cell to cell, place her stool in position and climb up to have a look. And she was dangerous. You only had to feel a bit off colour or sleepy and lie down for a second and if she was on duty she'd be sure to spot you and report you, and then you'd be for the cooler.) 'I was looking through the peephole and this one hit that one with the kettle . . .' For some reason it came out according to her that I had been the one with the kettle. Still, who cared, it wouldn't make the slightest bit of difference.

A couple of hours later we were both taken to see the officer in charge of the block. 'How shall we take you in – together or one at a time?' asked the warder maliciously. The point was that when an officer is handing out punishments for a fight – suspending shop privileges, putting you on strict regime rations or strict regime in full – the accused often start to beg forgiveness or cry, each blaming the other and trying to shield himself. Scenes like these give enormous pleasure to the warders and our escort, evidently, was anticipating a similar sort of spectacle, if only we asked to go in separately.

'It's all the same to me, I don't care if I don't go in at all,' I replied. 'They could just as well tell me in the cell what I'm going to get for it, that would be the best of all.'

'I don't care either,' said Ivan after a moment's hesitation.

The officer in charge of the block, Major Tsuplyak, was talking to the warders in his office when we arrived. As we were led in he broke off his conversation and looked in our direction, looking longer at Ivan. Evidently he remembered him.

'Number 54? A pretty sight you've made of yourselves. Stealing food again. A month on reduced rations for the two of them! Take them away, bring in the ones from 78 . . .'

Ivan stammered:

'Excuse me, sir . . .'

But they pushed the two of us out and led us down the corridor and back to our cell.

The following morning we received only fourteen ounces of bread in our ration and only a single sprat for breakfast, without soup. The thing that bothered me most was that Ivan had been put on short rations because of me. What's more he found it harder than most to endure hunger. It seemed to him that he would never last out a month on strict regime food. He decided to put an end to himself. Two days after our fight he got hold of a razor blade from somewhere and slit both his wrists. This happened just after the bread had been distributed. Ivan had received his reduced bread ration and swallowed it down so as not to waste it (what if he were to die or get carted off to hospital with the bread still uneaten?) before slashing the blade across his veins. It was the time when breakfast was being served and so longer than usual went by without the warders looking through the peep-hole. Our cell got breakfast too. Ivan, who had fountains of blood spurting from both wrists by now, asked us not to touch his sprat. He threw up the bread he had just finished eating and the vomit mixed with the blood all over the floor. The rest of us, however, ate our breakfast as usual, feeling nothing except our hunger. Pavel Ivanovich, after wiping his bowl round with a crust of bread, placed the remainder of his bread ration in the box and began to pray. And that day perhaps he prayed a bit longer than usual.

At last a warder looked through the peephole and discovered what had happened. He summoned the nurse. She put tourniquets on both Ivan's arms and started to bandage him up, talking away as she worked:

'Now what do you mean by going and cutting yourself like that? Who's going to say a good word for you when you're dead? These, I suppose,' she nodded in our direction, 'yes, if you're a good man . . .'

The warders stood around Ivan, smoking and talking among themselves. The senior warder threatened to give the whole cell a going over if Ivan didn't say what he had cut himself with. Then Ivan himself handed the razor blade over, so that we weren't all searched because of him.

The bandaging was finished, the nurse and the warders went away. Somehow or other we cleaned up the cell and scrubbed the blood and vomit off the floor. Ivan lay on his bunk, long, skinny and even whiter than usual, and covered in blood. His shirt sleeves were rolled up right to the shoulders and his arms swathed in bandages. Time for dinner came and they brought our skilly, with reduced portions for Ivan and me. Ivan was unable to stand and we handed him his bowl on the cot. He took it in his bandaged and bloody hands, drank it over the side, licked it clean and asked for his sprat from breakfast. Then he gulped it down greedily on its own – he had eaten his bread, every last crumb, in the morning.

Looking at Ivan I thought to myself: there lies a man who because of you went hungrier than usual; and because of you he wanted to die. What if he did exasperate you with his greediness and his constant talk about eating, what if he did stoop to petty thieving – is he really to blame for it? And are you any better, do you think? Hurling yourself on someone who was just as defenceless and unfortunate as yourself! And anyway, if you're really so weak that you can't control yourself and your nerves, why don't you punch the face of one of those warders who insult you every day? Because for hitting a luckless con you face only reduced rations, or at the most the cooler, while for hitting a warder you can be shot by decree. That means you've been poisoned by fear and fear dictates your actions.

Then I thought about myself. What had I been reduced to by a few months in prison! When I first arrived in a cell I had thought I wouldn't be able to last a day in it. I even found it hard to bring myself to use the slop tank. I went cold at the very thought of having to eat and sleep there, and of other cons eating and sleeping and evacuating themselves there . . . But now I could greedily swallow my sprat in the midst of blood and vomit and it seemed to me that there was nothing in the world tastier than that sprat of mine. A man pours out his blood before my very eyes and I lick my soup bowl clean and think only about how long it is till the next meal. Did anything human remain in me, or in any of us, in that prison?

Ivan lay there for two or three days without rising. Then he began to get up and after several days they insisted on driving him out for exercise periods and forbade him to lie down during the day, threatening him with the cooler. They read him a decree depriving him of parcels for four months for self-mutilation and introducing a razor blade into the cell. It was painful to look at Ivan – he had been so looking forward to that parcel! And on top of that, reduced rations! Every day at dishing-out time Ivan Mordvin would stand at the food trap and wheedle: 'Go on, just one little crumb more! Just half a spoon more!' Not once did they add even a fraction of an ounce, but nevertheless he would stand there three times a day and whine and weep at the food trap. At first every one of us, and I especially, felt sorry for him. But afterwards we all began to get irritated and annoyed. But no matter how we swore at him, Ivan continued to beg for more every day. He no longer had any shame, he could feel nothing but hunger, hunger, hunger.

OUR NEIGHBOUR POWERS

One day they announced over the prison radio that the American flyer, Gary Powers, was to be pardoned. Taking into account his frank and sincere admission of guilt, as they put it, and his good conduct, and also in response to the numerous requests of his family, a pardon had been granted to him.

This at once become the subject of discussions, arguments and quarrels in our cell. Powers had served not even a quarter of his term and here they were pardoning him; we, though, had to sit there from bell to bell, which meant that, according to them, Kolya Korolev, the 'terrorist', Pavel Ivanovich – in for his religion – or Andrei Novozhitsky, an unsuccessful fugitive – in short, any one of us was considered more of a threat and a danger than a capitalist spy . . . However, some people also came to more realistic conclusions: one of our spies, they said, must have been caught in America and now the governments had agreed to make an exchange (subsequently I learnt that this was indeed the case: Powers was exchanged for Abel).

Powers's pardon aroused particular interest among us at Vladimir, because everyone knew that he was there in the same prison. A prison is always chock full of gossip and stories: they get passed on by look-outs – cons who work for the prison service – and are told around whenever the cells are shuffled. We knew that Powers occupied a cell for two on the second floor of the hospital block. Some had even managed to catch a glimpse of him and his cell-mate strolling in the exercise yard. Risking the cooler in the process, they had hauled themselves up to the ventilation shaft in order to take a look at this exotic bird. They said that Powers and his companion wore all their own clothes instead of prison rig, that they were clean shaven – not like us, gone over once every ten days with an electric razor – and that their heads, on the contrary, were not close shaven but were covered in hair. Powers's companion was said to be either an Estonian or a Latvian, in any case from one of the Baltic states, and an educated man who spoke excellent English. This Estonian had been prepared as Powers's partner even before the trial was over. His sentence was twenty-five years and they had promised him that if he fulfilled the necessary conditions he would be pardoned and freed immediately after Powers. As for Powers, they said, it was obvious he wouldn't be in for long. And then, of course, they tempted him with special privileges. On the other hand, if he broke the conditions he would spend the rest of his life in Vladimir prison and even die there. (Incidentally, such life imprisonment is not unknown in Vladimir: one forester had been there for twenty years already after he had accidentally witnessed the slaughter of the Polish officers in the Katyn Forest.)

But what sort of conditions were they? First, the Estonian was not to tell Powers about the real situation of the prisoners in Soviet prisons, but on the contrary should do everything he could to strengthen the conviction that all political prisoners were kept in the same conditions as he himself. There were plenty of accidents that could happen: an emaciated figure in prison dress might somehow pop up while they were exercising, somebody in the hospital might suddenly shriek out (like the time we had heard it) – in such cases the Estonian was to think up plausible and convincing explanations for his American companion. Secondly the Estonian was told to say as little as possible about the ordinary way of life in the Soviet Union: let him keep Powers busy with conversation about the cinema, literature, sport . . .

Powers had even been taken to Vladimir differently from us – no black marias or special prisoners' coaches for him, he had never even seen such things. Oh no, his arrival in Vladimir had been by limousine direct from Moscow.

So that it was in vain, of course, that some of our prisoners hoped that when he was back home, the American flyer would be able to tell them there about our particular circle of hell. Powers was not allowed even a sniff of our real prison life.

Not everybody, though, would believe that Powers was being held under special conditions. I knew of one such 'disbeliever' whose name was Gennady. Gennady used to work himself up into a frenzy arguing with his cell-mates that this could not be, that once the prison rules existed they were bound to be the same for everybody. Naturally they made fun of him; and it was then that he swore that he would see Powers for himself and prove the truth of his words. So it came about that a few days later a comrade informed the warders that Gennady had swallowed two spoons, his own and his comrade's. It was nothing unusual. They made a search of the cell and needless to say found that two spoons were missing. Gennady was dragged off to the hospital block for an X-ray – via that very corridor where Powers's cell was situated. On his way past, Gennady suddenly dashed to the door of the cell (he had found out the number beforehand), pushed the flap to one side and glued his eye to the peephole. And by the time the startled warder had recovered and dragged him away he had managed to see what he wanted.

Well, Gennady's fate after that followed its normal course: he was taken back to his cell and then locked up in the cooler for ten days – both for looking through the peephole and for organising that trip to the hospital (the X-ray, of course, revealed nothing). But while he was back in his cell waiting for marching orders for the cooler he told his companions what he had seen in Powers's cell. Everything was the way the others had said it was: the hair, the civilian clothes, and an appearance that showed that there was clearly no shortage of food.

Of the cons in our cell only Boris Vlasov had seen Powers – also out walking in the exercise yard – and he confirmed that both Powers and the Estonian were held in special conditions.

Many men envied the Estonian his special conditions and the fact that he was now going to be released: if it had not been for Powers he would have had to sit there from bell to bell like the rest of us. But even more of the cons condemned him: sitting there alone with that American, how could he fail to tell him about the tortures being inflicted on all the other prisoners there?

In any case they envied him for nothing. We heard afterwards that the authorities refused to let the Estonian go, that they cheated him, and that after Powers's release, they moved him back to an ordinary cell under ordinary conditions, and that the next day he committed suicide. There was also another story that he really had been released. And another that he was moved to a different prison. I don't know which one was true. Only one thing is sure: the Estonian disappeared and nobody ever saw him again.

BERIA'S MEN

At one time a cell of former Beria* men used to exercise in the next yard to ours. The old fence that divided the yards was full of cracks and so we had a good view of them. They too were held under special conditions, not at all as we were. While exercising, for instance, they always walked about in their expensive overcoats and I never once saw them in prison uniform. I remember one of them. Short and stocky, he used to stride about the yard importantly in a warm overcoat and black Caucasian fur hat. There was another who also wore a Caucasian fur hat and a grey overcoat that somehow looked like a greatcoat on him. They used to say that the latter was not a Beria man but a general whose name, I think, was Schrönberg.

The Beria men's cell was next to ours and on our way to or from exercise we were able to see into it (while the members of a cell are exercising the doors are left wide open to air the cell, and we were always led out either a fraction before or after the Beria men). We could hardly believe our eyes. All the cells in Vladimir jail were so alike that if you blindfolded a con, led him into the wrong cell and uncovered his eyes, he would automatically go to his usual place without even noticing where he was. But the Beria men's cell looked like a luxurious apartment to us. Their beds were covered with warm domestic blankets and a fetching tablecloth covered the table. They were allowed to lie down for as long as they liked during the day and they were allowed an unlimited number of parcels from their families. What sort of rations they got I don't know, or whether

* Lavrenty Beria was Stalin's secret police chief. He was executed by Stalin's successors shortly after Stalin's death in 1953.

they were given the normal skilly, but in any case they had so many parcels that they could live on normal, everyday food.

How they were hated, those five co-prisoners of ours. 'Those bastards, queers and bloodsuckers used to live off our blood when they were free and even here inside they're not doing badly for themselves,' said the cons. There was even gossip that they had done a deal with the government, with obligations on both sides: the Beria men would keep quiet about certain other important violations of 'socialist legality', in return for which they got special privileges in jail. They also said that the Beria men had been heard to say, either among themselves or to someone doing orderly duty: 'Well, what about Lavrenty Beria? Do you think he was the only one and that those men up there now had nothing to do with it? All decisions were taken unanimously. He's just the one they used as a whipping boy!'

Similar stories and conversations in prison (and outside too for that matter) were reinforced by the fact that all the Beria men, and Beria himself, had been tried behind closed doors. Clean and honest actions are not done in the dark. If they had been tried publicly it might not have been necessary later to fill even a single cell in Vladimir with genuine state criminals . . .

Nevertheless, not long afterwards, in 1963, an enigmatic change occurred in the treatment of Beria's men. Their blankets were taken away, the cloth disappeared from the table and their cell became more like all the rest. Parcels for them were also limited to the usual norm: two a year of no more than ten pounds apiece. Instantly a change took place in the men themselves and in the relations between them. The calm, friendly atmosphere disappeared in a trice. The Beria men's cell became one of the most disorderly in the whole block. Hardly had these recent heroes finished the food from their last parcel than they fell upon one another over a stinking prison sprat. The sprats were usually given to a whole cell in a single bowl. The cons would each take one in a special order, so that everyone had a fair chance. But the Beria men could never agree on who was to go first and so they always went out of turn and quarrelled.

In our cell at that time there was a fellow called Volodya. The moment he heard the servers giving out the sprats to the Beria

men next door he used to jeer loudly about the friendship and
solidarity shown by these prize sons of the people. Once or
twice he got the cooler for it, but still he could never resist it.
Not even wolves, he said, would attack one another, yet these
savaged each other over a rotten sprat. They were worse than
wolves.

EXERCISE

Prisoners are let out for exercise once a day – for an hour on normal regime and half an hour on strict. You would think they would be in a tearing hurry to burst out of their stinking cells into the open air, and that it would be far more fun to move about an exercise yard than to take it in turns pacing a narrow cell. Nevertheless in winter the warders have to drive the cons out for exercise, nobody wants to go, although in the end they are forced to, for it's in the regulations. Exercise in winter is just one more form of punishment and torture, particularly for the old and the sick (the doctors excuse you from it only when you're on your last legs).

Twenty to thirty degrees of frost. All we have to wear over our cotton prison rig are our reefer jackets or quilted coats, and these are all tattered and torn, patched and patched again, washed and washed again. 'Older than Soviet power', as the cons say, or: 'Seven quarters have been buried in this jacket already' (a 'quarter' is a con with a twenty-five-year sentence). The remaining padding has gone into lumps and the wind blows straight through you. On your head you have an equally ancient padded cap with ear flaps. You have nothing to wrap round your neck – whoever had a scarf or a sweater, or warm underwear or warm socks, had it all taken away on the very first day. On your feet you have ankle boots over the thinnest and scantiest of already transparent foot-rags. Gloves are forbidden. We are all haggard and emaciated and haven't a trace of body heat, we have been too frozen in our cells. We stamp about the tiny yard, with our hands in our sleeves and our heads lowered, trying with our shoulders, if nothing else, to protect our noses from the frost and the wind. Some of the men, those who have no strength left at all, slump down in the corner by the fence and just sit there huddled up for a whole hour, slowly freezing.

Returning to the cell after an exercise period it is impossible to get warm for the rest of the day. And how can you? Hot water comes twice a day, morning and evening. It is so cold in the cell that when the kettle is brought you have to cover it with somebody's jacket and a blanket to stop it going cold in the twenty minutes before breakfast is brought. At night, in order not to freeze completely to death, you pile on top of you all the rags you can find. Nobody ever uses the mattress covers, which are supposed to take the place of sheets, the way they are intended. Instead of covering the mattress with it you put it on top, pile on your blanket, reefer jacket, cotton jacket and trousers and then crawl inside. But for me even that wasn't enough, I used to get right underneath. After all, it meant two layers instead of one and the mattress prevented draughts from underneath. And even then I froze, and I was only twenty-four to twenty-five years old. What must it have been like for the old men?

In my early days at Vladimir the exercise periods were nonetheless jollier than they became later. We used to be let out into the old exercise yards, which were fairly big – for three to four cells at a time. And only a ramshackle wooden fence separated us from the adjoining yard with another fifteen to twenty cons in it. At that time I got to know lots of cons from the other cells. You could even push a note to a friend through one of the cracks in the fence, though of course you had to make sure you weren't seen by the warder. The warder during this time used to walk up and down a raised board-walk overlooking the yard, while others would keep watch on us through the peephole. Still, they couldn't keep their eye on us all when there were so many of us.

But then one day they built new exercise yards in Vladimir prison. Each one the size of a cell for five, each one equipped with a door with a peephole, and with a concrete floor and concrete walls (those were plastered with roughcast so that nothing could be scratched on them). In other words, another cell only with the roof off. And they started taking us out one cell at a time. In winter it was intolerably cold in that concrete box. But in summer, although it was dreary and not a leaf or a blade of grass was to be seen, still the sun shone overhead and not even the warder on his board-walk could cut off its rays or keep out the fresh, free smells.

On the other hand you lost your exercise period for the slightest infringement in summer. But in winter they never deprived you of it!

TKACH

I don't remember which cell this happened in: like all the other cons I was frequently transferred from cell to cell. As usual there were five of us: Richardas Kekshtas, Pyotr Glynya, Kostya Pintya from Moldavia, old man Tkach and myself. Tkach was a Ukrainian and had been inside, so he said, for seventeen years already – for belonging to a national liberation movement. Like the rest of us he started off in Mordovia and had then been transferred to the prison at Vladimir for failing to fulfil his norm, for his religious beliefs and one or two other crimes of a similar sort. The old man was a bit peculiar and no longer quite normal, or 'gone' as the cons used to say, putting a finger to their temple and eloquently twisting it round. Quite small, with a large bald patch on his head, a long emaciated face and incredibly huge ears, he used to sit on his bunk and spend all his time gazing tensely and fearfully at his cell-mates. He feared everyone and everything. Whenever one of us joked that Tkach's ears weren't his own and must have been stolen, the old man didn't fully understand the joke and would smile at us timidly and ingratiatingly.

One day he secretly asked Kekshtas what sort of a man I was and why I was always silent – it was true that I hardly ever talked. Kekshtas knew me very well, we had been inside together over a year by now, migrating from cell to cell, and he also knew my ingrown character and that my reluctance to talk was partly explained by my constantly increasing deafness. To Tkach, though, he said:

'Don't you know he's a cannibal? He's in for eating one old fellow just like yourself. There was one con sleeping here in this bunk of ours and he chewed off both his heels.'

The old man didn't want to believe him at first.

'You just watch out and see the way he looks at your ears', said Kekshtas, 'you'd better take care of them, otherwise he might eat them'.

Tkach was alarmed. I had only to sit down on the bench beside him and he would jump up and move to somewhere else. He even started to eat his meals in his bunk instead of coming to the table. At night he continued to go to bed with his hat on just as he had done before, because of the cold, but now he also started to wrap up his ears. Kekshtas had told me about his joke during one of the exercise periods and I played up to it. As soon as I caught Tkach's fearful glance upon me I would begin to stare at one or the other of his ears; and once, when he was sitting on the bench, I came up behind him and tweaked his ear. The poor fellow glanced round, caught sight of me and turned to stone. He clapped his hands over his ears, ran to his bunk and for a long time remained sitting there, unable to bring himself to lower his hands from his head. The whole cell rocked with laughter. Kekshtas, after he had recovered from his merriment, asked me:

'Well, tell us then, Anatoly, which are tastier – Tkach's ears or Volodya's heels?'

And I replied seriously:

'Tkach's ears, I should think: I'm sure if they were grilled they'd be as crunchy as a piglet's.'

Tkach looked at me in horror, he was thoroughly convinced now that he was facing a cannibal.

I should point out that Tkach believed in Kekshtas's story not only because he was cracked; everyone who had done time in Vladimir knew of cases even more horrifying than cannibalism. In one cell, for instance, the cons had done as follows: they had got hold of a razor blade somewhere and for several days collected up paper. When everything was ready they each cut a piece of flesh from their bodies – some from the stomach, others from the leg. Everybody's blood was collected into one bowl, the flesh was thrown in, a small fire was made from the paper and some books and then they started to half-fry, half-stew their feast. When the warders noticed that something was wrong and burst into the cell the stew was still not cooked and the cons, falling over themselves and burning their fingers, grabbed the pieces from the bowl and stuffed them into their mouths. Even the warders said afterwards that it was a horrible sight.

I can well imagine that this story is hard to believe! But later I personally met some of the participants in that terrible feast and talked with them. The most remarkable thing of all was that they were fully normal people. I am not Tkach and this is no cock-and-bull story. I myself saw Yuri Panov from that cell – there wasn't a clear place on his whole body. Apart from this instance when Panov and the others decided to feast on their own flesh, he was known more than once to have cut off pieces of his body and thrown them out to the warders through the food flap. Several times he slit his stomach open so that his innards came flopping out; he also slit his veins, went on prolonged hunger strikes and swallowed all sorts of odds and ends, so that they used to have to cut open his stomach and belly in hospital . . . Nevertheless he emerged alive from Vladimir and went on to camp seven and later eleven. We used to talk about him to Yuli Daniel when he turned up in camp eleven and became friendly with our group. Yuli didn't want to believe it at first and then started to ask us to introduce him to Panov. But it turned out that he and Panov met each other not through us but through admin: Yuli landed up in the cooler and Panov was there too, and then they were all taken to the bath house . . . Yuli told us afterwards that he almost fainted when he saw Panov naked.

And yet Yuri Panov was completely normal, not at all cracked, though it was true he was no political, although he was in on a political charge.

In our group in camp eleven we often discussed the problem of how to explain to people outside about all these incidents, which were difficult even to believe. Well, all right, suppose that all these people were abnormal. Why, then, should they be held in prison or in a work camp? Even according to the law they should have been transferred to a psychiatric sanatorium or handed over to their relatives for safe keeping. And if nevertheless they are kept in prison and if all the doctors and commissions consider them normal, then what sort of conditions must they be that drive them to such savage acts? Outside prison that same Panov wouldn't have dreamed of cutting off and frying his own flesh – unless he had truly gone mad. These are the sort of things that our society should ponder, except that of course nobody knows a thing about it . . .

But let me continue with Tkach's story. For a certain time he believed I was a cannibal and carefully guarded his ears. Then one day we got food from the shop. All of us were allowed provisions to the value of one rouble twenty-five copecks – all, that is, except Tkach. He had nobody left at all who could send him money for the shop: some of his family had been driven out or shot by the Germans, others had been exiled to Siberia and had disappeared from view. We subsequently attempted to write to our own families to send money to Tkach, but all our requests were struck out by the censorship. And so we were obliged to share with the luckless old man. Pintya, Kekshtas and I had each bought two loaves of bread, a little margarine and some cheese or sausage. Each of us gave half a loaf to Tkach so that all three had one and a half loaves each. The same took place with the margarine and all the rest. After he had drunk a bit and started on the bread and margarine, Tkach said:

'No, Tolik's no cannibal.'

Kekshtas endeavoured to keep the joke going:

'Do you mean to say that because he shares with you he's not a cannibal? He's cunning. I know him of old. He's just fattening you up. You don't think he'd feed you his bread for nothing!'

Tkach was on the point of believing him and looked fearfully in my direction, but I couldn't keep a straight face any longer and burst out laughing. Then Tkach laughed too and after him everyone else joined in. After that, although he still kept his cap on in bed, he didn't wrap his ears up any more.

This old man of ours was not only cracked but also very weak physically. He was always complaining about pains in his head, pains in his spine, pains in his heart. One day the two of us applied to see the doctor. During her rounds the nurse always asks through the food trap: 'Is anybody sick?' Almost all the cons complain about some ailment or other, especially in winter, and then the nurse, not bothering to examine the patient, gives him some sort of powder. But if the complaint exceeds her competence she registers the con for a visit to the block doctor. The list is usually massive: practically everyone is sick. Then the nurse takes it upon herself, at her own discretion, to cross off the 'unnecessary' ones. The session with the doctor takes place in the presence of a warder and all the patients from one cell are taken together. Thus Tkach and I were taken by a warder to see the doctor. Unfortunately I don't remember her surname, but her first name was Galina. She started off by asking the old man her usual question:

'What's wrong with you?'

'Oh, doctor, I've got pains everywhere, help me.'

'You can't have them everywhere.'

'I've got pains all over, my dear . . .'

'Venereal pains as well?' asked Galina sarcastically, exchanging glances with the warder.

'What's that?'

'I mean have you got pains in your trousers?'

'Oh, yes, yes, in my trousers too.'

'Shame on you, old man, getting mixed up with pederasts at your time of life.'

Only then did Tkach realise what the young woman meant. He told her that on prison rations not even young men could feel desire for a pederast, nor for a woman either. What he meant was that he was passing blood and suffered from sharp pains (in our cell only Pintya was without haemorrhoids, and then, probably, only because he was a 'new boy' – just in from outside). Galina told Tkach to drop his trousers, turn round and bend over.

'Yes, you've got haemorrhoids. How many times a day do you evacuate?'

'Once every two days, or sometimes three.'

'Well, what do you expect then? You should evacuate at least twice a day.'

'Evacuate what, my dear? The skilly? There's nothing in it but water.'

'I can't help you there, the food isn't my department. All I'm telling you is: with haemorrhoids you should evacuate twice a day. And also bathe the place with warm water . . .'

Tkach complained about the pains in his head and spine. They measured his blood pressure – it was high.

'It's all right, everyone has high blood pressure at your age, and they also get pains in the spine.'

'Doctor, at least give me permission to lie down during the day.'

Galina wouldn't hear of it. If she let people like Tkach lie down she'd have to put the whole block on hospital regime.

Then I went through exactly the same procedure: 'Turn round . . . haemorrhoids . . . you should evacuate more often . . . bathe in warm water.' My ears were extremely painful, but Galina refused to look at them: 'I'm not a specialist, we don't have an ear specialist in the jail, you have to wait until they get one from town.'

In the two years I was there the ear specialist visited Vladimir jail just once. I managed to see him and he prescribed me hydrogen peroxide for two weeks. The drops didn't help me, of course, but there was no one to check up on this, and who knew when the ear specialist would be invited back to the prison? Anyway, not only Galina but I myself even could have prescribed hydrogen peroxide – you don't need to be a specialist for that. Galina, however, wouldn't do it. She was there not so much to treat the sick as to see that the formalities were carried out. I don't know whether today there are any doctors in the camps and jails who try to alleviate the sufferings of people who are in any case so unfortunate to begin with. There were once, but in the years from 1961 to 1966 I didn't meet any.

And so Tkach and I returned to our cell equipped with the valuable advice to evacuate more often and bathe ourselves with warm water. But how? Hot water was brought to the cell just before breakfast and supper, and it cooled in fifteen to twenty minutes. This meant that we would have to bathe our backsides just as our cell-mates were sitting down to their grub – and under their very noses. Such curative treatment had to be renounced.

Tkach grew worse and worse, he groaned with pain, froze and was unable to warm himself. If only they would let the man lie down, if only they would excuse him the exercise periods – it was the middle of winter! But no. We, his cell-mates, appealed to the prison authorities; and we complained to the warders and the officers that the old man was weakening and that they might at least let him lie down for a while during the day. They told us that the doctor knew best who was fit and who sick. Tkach got so chilled that he couldn't bend his fingers any more and was unable to roll himself any cigarettes. Kekshtas used to make him enough in the mornings to last the whole day. I also tried rolling him some, but it didn't work, I had never smoked in my life. On the other hand I gave the old man all my tobacco, so that at least he had enough smokes. He grew very attached to us and was always afraid that they might take him out of our cell.

One evening they brought us our supper – the usual, watery mashed potato. As always we dealt with it in thirty seconds, licked out our bowls and were already starting to rinse them when we noticed that Tkach was still fiddling with his.

'Hello, grandad,' said Pintya, 'I see you've got a piece of meat in your bowl by mistake. And seeing that you're toothless, you can give it to me if you like.'

Everyone laughed. Tkach finished his mashed potato, poured some water into his bowl from the kettle, rinsed it sitting down and then went to the sloptank to empty it. Beside the sloptank the bowl fell from his fingers and rolled over the concrete floor, while he himself started to grope and feel for the wall – and then collapsed on the ground. We rushed over to him, lifted him and placed him on his cot. He seemed still alive. We started banging on the door and calling the warder. We heard his voice from the far end of the corridor:

'What's all that banging for? Is it the cooler you want?'

He came along and looked through the peephole. Learning what the matter was, he went to call the senior warder. About fifteen minutes went by, nobody came and we started to bang on the door again. The duty warder bellowed:

'Stop that noise! The senior warder will be here as soon as he's free – you're not important!'

After another ten minutes or so the senior warder came, unlocked the door and entered the cell.

'Well, what's going on in here?'

Once more we explained what had happened. He took Tkach's wrist and felt for the pulse. The old man was lying there without moving or breathing. But the senior warder was in no hurry to call the nurse or the doctor, he started to question us instead: how did it happen, who was doing what at the time, who had seen what. Then he left with a promise to call the nurse. Another ten minutes passed and the nurse arrived, accompanied, as always, by a retinue of warders. She too felt for the pulse – there wasn't any. Then she soaked a piece of cotton wool in sal-ammoniac and held it under the old man's nose. It was no use. Tkach didn't move. She left the cotton wool on his upper lip and gave him some sort of injection. Tkach didn't come round. Then the nurse asked the senior warder to fetch the duty doctor from the hospital block. The doctor came, looked at Tkach, felt his pulse and quietly laid the limp arm across his breast. Then, after questioning us as to what had happened, she called the senior warder outside. She never appeared again, but the senior warder came back and ordered Kekshtas and me to carry the old man out. I took him under the arms, Kekshtas took the legs, and we dragged the body into an empty cell that was indicated to us. There the warder ordered us to lay the dead man on a bare cot and then hurried us out again. The cell was locked. I said to the warder:

'I suppose Tkach can lie on his cot till lights out now, can he?'

'Do you want to go in the cooler?' roared the warder as usual.

Tkach was dead. He had been completely alone, nobody had ever helped him and he never ever received any letters from anyone. But maybe he has relatives somewhere who lost touch with him and don't know what became of him. And so: old man Tkach starved for many years, suffered, fell ill, froze and died in Vladimir Prison in the winter of 1962.

PYOTR GLYNYA

Glynya had also been in a long time and always in prison – he had never been in a camp. His very first sentence, therefore, must have been direct to prison. But nobody knew what he had been sentenced for and it was absolutely impossible to understand him.

Glynya was formally insane and totally cracked. He was always muttering to himself and occasionally he would come out with a phrase like: 'I'm a Soviet agent!' He used to tell us quite seriously that Stalin himself had called him into his office and held a secret conversation with him, at which only Beria had been present. What the conversation was about, Glynya never said: evidently he didn't want to broadcast this important secret. He had been given some sort of task by Stalin and Beria and that was all.

Occasionally he talked as though he had a wife and daughter in Paris and would start to tell us all about France and Germany. None of us had ever been there so we couldn't check on how much of it was true or not. Anyway, you can't make much sense of the ravings of a lunatic. Nevertheless he really did know German and apparently knew it well.

One day Glynya asked me to write him a petition to the Director of Military Prosecutions. My cell-mates also persuaded me: 'Go on, Tolik, write it!' I realised that what they all wanted to find out was what this fellow was in for. I was also curious and so I agreed: 'Go on then, tell me all about it.'

At this, Glynya started babbling such utter nonsense that there was no question of being able to make sense of it: some swamp where he had collected duck eggs and chased snakes, tasks given him by Stalin and Beria, Soviet agent, France, Germany, and again the swamp with the duck eggs.

And so we never did discover what it was that Glynya had been given twenty-five years for.

VITYA KEDROV

At one time I shared a cell with a former criminal con named Vitya Kedrov. Now he was in on a political charge – 'anti-Soviet agitation', I think – which he had acquired in a criminal camp. He had been imprisoned many times before and had been in those terrifying camps about which stories and anecdotes are gradually beginning to appear. Thus there's no point, I think, in me retelling the recollections of Vitya and those other cons who had done time in the logging camps, the pits and the mines, in Kolyma, Norilsk, Vorkuta, Taishet, Magadan, Djezkazgan . . . Vitya had lost the fingers of one hand – he had caught them in a circular saw. There was nothing new in this incident either.

Vitya tortured us in the way Ivan Mordvin had done in my other cell: for hours he used to stand at the food trap begging for something to eat. 'Keep me here as long as you like,' he used to whine, 'but don't kill me with hunger!' Naturally they never once gave him anything, but every day he would insist: 'Keep me here as long as you like, but don't kill me with hunger!'

We tried to shame him out of it – what did he think he was doing! He told me that in other cells they had even beaten him up because of it; and in our cell too it almost came to a fight. Nevertheless he just had to keep clinging to that food trap: 'Go on, give me something. Keep me here as long as you like, but don't kill me with hunger!'

THE BATH HOUSE

We were taken to the bath house at Vladimir once every ten days. There you got a change of underwear, a fresh so-called towel (which was just as much of a rag as the one you handed in), and on every other visit – that is, once every twenty days – a change of 'bed linen', i.e. mattress cover and pillow case. There they also cropped us – head and face at the same time, it was all the same to them. Over ten days, of course, we used to acquire quite a growth, so that we were afraid to look at one another. And we all looked so wild that anyone seeing us would be bound to think: 'Real desperadoes, wild beasts.'

In the summer we awaited our bath with impatience and counted the days, we couldn't wait to splash about in that water! And to have an extra walk in the sunshine, in the fresh air. They used to take us through the prison yard, with not a tree or a bush in sight, only the grey walls of the blocks with their barred windows and the bare asphalt underfoot. And nevertheless, sometimes you would catch sight of a pitiful blade of grass forcing its way upwards. But you couldn't go up to it, much less bend down: 'Not one step out of line. Keep your hands behind your back. No talking and no smoking.' That's what we were warned every time they took us to the bath house.

But although every step and every action in prison is anticipated and laid down, point by point, paragraph by paragraph, unforeseen incidents do sometimes occur. One day we were on our way to the bath house. We were passing the hospital block when we ran into the hospital director, a woman. Evidently she was on her way to work (it was about nine o'clock in the morning). Suddenly we heard a yell from the top storey of the hospital block and something fell right at her feet. The woman bent over, looked at it, and spat. Just then we arrived opposite her and saw, lying on the asphalt, a bloody, amputated penis. Apparently some poor creature in the hospital had resolved to mutilate himself in that way and then, peeping out of the window, had tossed this 'present' to her through the ventilation flap. What, I wonder, had she done to him to provoke him to such a terrible revenge.

The bath house had two sorts of facilities for washing – one a room with benches and basins, the others with showers in individual cubicles. We were sent in two cells at a time, one into the washroom, the other to the showers. To get a shower was tremendous luck and sheer bliss: you were able to wash properly, instead of standing in line for basins and then for water. You were able to stand there and spend the whole time scrubbing yourself, with the water pouring over you ceaselessly (although even then they used to push two or three into a cubicle meant for one). The only trouble was that this bliss always ended too quickly – you never had time to soap yourself a second time before the warders turned the water off and herded you outside again. That's why everyone tried to give himself at least one thorough soaping and to fill his dipper with a second lot of clean water, so as to rinse himself off at the end. If you managed it you were lucky, but sometimes you wouldn't even have time to get the soap off, and then you simply had to rub it off with your towel. In between baths the whole cell would be guessing: will it be the showers next time, or the washroom?

In winter, on the other hand, the bath house is just another form of torture. The newcomer, who still doesn't know about it, looks forward to having a thorough wash and warming himself up with hot water – after all, it's a bath, isn't it? If only it were like that! In winter it's so cold in the changing room that steam comes out of your mouth and the walls are sometimes covered with white frost. You undress and stand there naked and blue, your skin covered in goose pimples. Then you wait there, in a filthy temper, for them to let you into the washroom, and you can feel the cold piercing you to the very kidneys. Afterwards you dress in that same icy cold and shuffle back through the frost to your block . . . Old men were particularly afraid of the baths in winter and Tkach, for example, had to be driven there by force, just as he had for exercise.

Washing of any kind in prison in winter is real torture. Even washing during the toilet break. The water comes out of the tap so cold that even I, a Siberian and a young man, used to feel my hands go numb and lose all sensation. Possibly, of course, this wasn't because of the iciness of the water but because of our permanent state of general exhaustion.

We were usually taken to the bath house by two warders, Vanya and Sanya. Vanya was short, dark and bad-tempered. His nickname was 'Gipsy'. At the slightest excuse he started bellowing, cursing, threatening and pummelling you. Sanya, his bosom pal, was the complete opposite: tall, pale, leisurely and calm. He was calm when he stuck you in the cooler and calm when beating up a prisoner in the company of other warders. Sanya's nickname was 'The Beak' (he had a really enormous nose). And so it was usually Vanya the Gipsy and Sanya the Beak who took us to the bath house – if they weren't both together then invariably one or the other went along. Their greatest pleasure was to turn the water off in such a way that some of us were still covered in soap. It was they, too, who forcibly cropped the newcomers – that Ukrainian with the moustache I mentioned was one of their victims and the two of them had also manhandled me and held me down for the barber.

EQUALITY OF THE SEXES

There was an official linen store in the bath house and in charge of it at that time was a woman of about thirty-five: she was a 'free' worker from outside and her name was Shura. Sanya the Beak was courting her. Courting her, did I say? Well, in his own way, of course – mauling her and pinching her. As far as we cons were concerned, who were forced willy-nilly to be present during their games, neither of them paid the slightest bit of attention. And anyway 'present' wasn't really the word! Naked as the day we were born, we had to wait there in the corridor to be shorn before going on to get washed. Shura never once missed this performance and used to sit there in front of us, messing around with Sanya. I think that having us naked men there looking at them even gave a special piquancy to their slapping and tickling. Or maybe they just didn't notice us – cons weren't really people, were they?

Apart from men warders we also had some women warders in our block. And they too used to watch us through the peephole and could come into the cell at any time. You could be standing at the sloptank to relieve yourself and it was quite possible that at that moment you were being watched by a wardress. And because of this, even though we were used to it, we constantly felt even more humiliated and embittered.

One day the following incident occurred in the cell I was in. One of the prisoners, called Yuri, went to the sloptank to relieve himself; and the sloptank stood right in front of the peephole. A wardress peered in and saw a con standing in front of her blocking the whole cell (usually, if somebody in the cell was working at a tattoo or at something else forbidden by the regulations, one of the others would stand 'on guard', blocking the peephole. By the time the warder had had a slanging match with him and then opened the cell, the 'working' cons would have had time to clear everything away, hide it and adopt completely innocent expressions.) The wardress, therefore, started to shout at Yuri to move away from the door. Her shouts brought the senior warder running and they opened the door, came in and suspiciously inspected us and the whole cell. The wardress pointed to Yuri: 'He's the one who was blocking the peephole.'

The senior warder threatened him with the cooler for breaking regulations. Then Yuri proposed that they either move the sloptank away from the door, or else put a peephole down lower:

'This way she couldn't see what I had in my hand and now I'll never be forgiven for it . . .'

As usual the warders swore at us, threatened us with the cooler and went out. We had got off lightly – Yuri could easily have got the cooler for his impudence.

When the wardresses were on duty they also used to take us out for the toilet break. And they would watch through the latrine peephole to make sure that we broke no regulations. And male warders used to look after women prisoners. And they too used to take them out for toilet break and peer through the peepholes into their cells at any time of the day or night.

At first the women politicals were kept on the second floor of our block. Among them were dozens from the Ukraine and the Baltic states – in for 'nationalism'; and there were also religious believers. Some of them had been in Vladimir jail for ten to fifteen years or more. One day we were coming back from our bath and the women were returning from exercise, when we saw them at a distance. We also saw some old women being helped along by their younger companions. The women, just like us, had had all their warm clothes taken away and were also being driven out to exercise in winter in flimsy jackets and cold boots and also made to take cold baths and were also worn down with hunger. Prison regime was exactly the same for everyone, for both men and women alike. In this respect there was complete equality of the sexes.

PRISON SERVICE

In prison there are all sorts of unskilled jobs that have to be done outside the cells: cleaning, serving the food, stoking the boilers, and so on. Prisoners are appointed to do this work from within the block, so that the cleaners, servers and 'boilermen' were cons just like the rest of us. In the store-room the assistant to the storekeeper, Shura, was an Estonian prisoner called Jan – he it was who did all the work for her, carrying bales about, changing our underwear and handing out the bed linen. Only when somebody received something that was in absolute tatters and impossible to put on, and then kicked up a fuss about it to Jan, did Shura herself intervene.

The cons on prison service lived in two separate cells, but also under lock and key the whole time, just like the rest of us. They were taken out only for the duration of their duties. They also got the same rations as the rest of us, except that they had an extra four ounces of bread – twenty-two ounces instead of eighteen. Thus life for them was marginally better, they were four ounces fuller – and freer to about the same degree.

Nevertheless working in prison service was not easy, especially for the food servers. They, after all, spent their whole time trying to feed starving men – and with what? The kitchen would send along huge insulated urns full of skilly, but when the servers started to ladle it into the bowls it turned out to be all water. Yet in every cell the cons would be crowding up to the food trap and begging for some of the thicker stuff, and then would listen to hear what sort of skilly was being poured into the bowls at the next cell. Each prisoner thought that the next man was getting a better portion. If somebody got a potato in his bowl two days running they immediately suspected the server of favouring 'one of his own'. And it went without saying, of course, that the server always had thick stuff out of the bottom and lived only for his belly. What this thick stuff was thought to be, god only knows, when the whole urn had nothing but water in it, without a solid grain to be found.

Some of the cons on prison service were widely respected, you could see that they were honest and fair to the highest degree. Others were regarded with suspicion and distrust, and some even with hatred. Threats were made: 'Just you wait till we're in the same camp together and then I'll get even with you.' I remember a certain server called Roman who came from Vladimir to camp seven. On his very first day in the canteen, Kolya Grigoryev – also an old Vladimir hand – poured a bowl of hot soup over his head; and later that same Roman was secretly beaten up – he must have given good cause to be hated.

RELIGIOUS PRISONERS

This is the term to describe prisoners who have been jailed for believing in God. They aren't the only people who believe in God, there are other cons who believe as well. But religious prisoners are the ones who have been arrested and tried precisely because of their religion. And what variety there is! Moslems from the Caucasus and Central Asia, Orthodox Christians, Baptists, Jehovah's Witnesses, Evangelists, Sabbatarians and many others.

Our newspapers sometimes carry stories about the crimes of various fanatical sects and about ritual murders, the torturing of children and so on. I find them difficult to believe. How many people did I see at Vladimir or in the camps who belonged to these various sects and not one of them had committed a murder. They were all dead set against killing and the use of force. And of the religious prisoners in the political camps not one had ever been convicted of murder. Those accused of murder are usually tried for 'anti-Soviet propaganda' – if, for example, they say that all political power, including Soviet power, comes not from God but the devil, or from possessing and distributing anti-Soviet literature. Like the rest of us they are tried in secret, and only the ones tried for murder are brought before an open court. Then they say of all religious believers and members of sects: 'Look what they're like – fanatics!'

The fanaticism of religious prisoners finds expression only in their insistence on retaining their own religious beliefs and customs. They are extremely quiet and humble people, old men for the most part of about sixty or over, although there are young ones among them as well. Their attitude to imprisonment is somewhat different from that of the other cons: they take consolation from the fact that they are suffering for their God and their faith, and they are patient in bearing their sufferings and pain. Once I heard some of them sing the following song:

> . . . *The Saviour bore His cross with nought but prayer,*
> *He did not complain to the Father about His foes,*
> *His was a marvellous example of suffering*
> *For the flame that burned inside Him was holy love.*

And nevertheless these men, who were humble and obedient in everything not touching upon their faith, were dispatched to Vladimir – for failing to fulfil the norm, for refusing to work on religious holidays. Here, in the cells, I was thrown together with large numbers of them. Almost every cell had its Evangelist, Sabbatarian, or Jehovah's Witness, and in some cells there were several together. The prison authorities humiliated them in every possible way. I had seen that on my very first day. Many believers had a rule that they must wear beards, yet they were all forcibly shaven while wearing handcuffs.

And what about fasting? You might well wonder how fasting could possibly come into it when in general there was nothing to eat, when day in and day out consisted of nothing but one long fast lasting for years on end and when men were half dead with exhaustion! But most believers wanted to observe the rules of fasting even here, when the right time came around, even though they were in prison where you eat what you're given! 'Even with a microscope you won't find any fat in prison skilly', we argued with them, 'every day's the same!' 'Ah, but you never know,' they replied. 'A little bit of fat is supposed to be included according to regulations and maybe they put it in.'

The warders knew this. And so on fast days they would serve the skilly first to those cells with believers in them. In a full urn, perhaps, there would be one little blob of fat floating on top – so why not make sure that it went into the bowl of someone who observed the fasts? That way he wouldn't eat it and nobody else would get a chance. Generally speaking the religious believers, knowing they would be served from the top of a full urn, were afraid to eat for fear of committing a sin. And when they had tumbled to this trick of the warders they started refusing any hot food at all on fast days and abided by bread and water.

In the starvation conditions prevailing at Vladimir not everyone had the strength to keep up the fasts and refuse food. Then the warders and officers would start to jeer at them: 'You're talking a load of old rubbish when you say you believe, what sort of God is that, it's all put on!' And whenever a religious prisoner went to the doctor in prison they would say: 'Don't come to see me, sign up for an examination with that God of yours and let him make you better.'

THE MENTALLY SICK

I often heard various cons say that if you thought seriously about it, there wasn't one normal man amongst us. In such inhuman conditions and seeing the sort of things that we were forced to see, it was impossible to preserve a sound mind. Especially at Vladimir.

But apart from this universal deviation from the norm, there was hardly a cell in Vladimir Prison that was without at least one con who was well and truly 'cracked'. Some used to gabble nonsense, while others made up all sorts of untrue stories about themselves. And there were also violent ones. I don't know whether they first cracked up as a result of long years of imprisonment or whether that's how they were when they were jailed, but sharing a cell with them was sheer torture. And the authorities purposely didn't segregate them. On the contrary: if there were two lunatics in one cell, they would be split up and put in separate ones so as to poison the existence of two cells instead of one. And it was useless to complain.

In one cell there was a con called Screwy Sanya. By day he was quiet and meek, sitting on his bunk without talking to anyone and plunged in thought the whole time. When lights out was called, Sanya would lie down and wait till all the others were sleeping. Then he would get up, go over to somebody's cot and urinate all over his sleeping cell-mate. What's more he tried, if possible, to make sure it went in his face, and this every night. They tried keeping watch over him and took it in turns not to sleep. But the whole thing was impossible: all cons had to be in bed after lights out, it was forbidden either to stand, to sit or to read lying down. Just try not to sleep, especially when you can't catch up during the day. And so it came about that the 'watchman', more often than not, awoke soaking wet. They also tried beating Sanya, although they realised he was a sick man. But if the warders found out about it, they would whisk the culprit away to the cooler while Sanya, as before, continued to do his business every night.

In another cell there was a completely quiet lunatic who never touched anyone. He even bore himself with a special kind of dignity and looked down on the others. His peculiarity, however, was that he insisted on mixing all his food with the contents of the sloptank. Whenever dinner or supper was brought, each man would take his bowl and sit somewhere to eat. He, though would go over to the sloptank, lift the lid, scoop some of the contents into his bowl and begin diligently to stir it. But that wasn't all. He would then walk round to everyone in the cell and press them to have some: 'Try it. My mummy used to make my porridge that way when I was small, it's very tasty!' Then he would stick it under their noses while they were trying to eat. Afterwards he would sit at the communal table and eat it, forgetting his dignity now and champing away, smacking his lips and covering himself all over in 'mummy's porridge'. After dinner he would pour water into his bowl, rinse it round and then drink it.

There were also the sort of lunatics who used to tear all their clothing off and walk about the cell naked. Whatever clothes they were given they would rip to shreds and stuff into the sloptank. At least they weren't sent out to exercise. But they never lasted long. They caught pneumonia and died.

THE MAN WHO HANGED HIMSELF

At one time I shared a cell with a fellow called Sergei and he told me the following story concerning himself.

Once he had spent fifteen days in the cooler and he came out half dead, 'holding on to the wall'. He thought and he thought: how could he improve his conditions a bit, if only a fraction, if only for a short time? The best would be to go to hospital, but how? He made up his mind to 'hang himself' – not completely, not so as to die, but enough to be taken to hospital.

At that particular moment he was alone in the cell. He tore his mattress cover into strips, plaited them into rope, made a loop and prepared to hang himself. There was a lamp over the door of the cell, set back in a niche with a grille over the front. Sergei calculated the time when the warder would be walking away from his cell, climbed up on to the sloptank, tied the rope to the grille, put the noose around his neck and waited. And everything happened just the way he had calculated.

The warder came back to the peephole, looked inside and saw a con's stomach directly in front of him. He guessed at once: 'The con has hanged himself!' As he began rattling his keys and unlocking the door, Sergei slowly slid off the sloptank. The rope went taut and he hung there, but he still hadn't lost consciousness because the noose hadn't tightened. Sergei knew in advance that he wouldn't have time to be strangled: the warder was already opening the door and entering, and soon would be taking him down. He was already choking as he felt the warder take him by the wrist, feel for his pulse and realise that he was still alive. But then, instead of taking him down, the warder began to pull on Sergei's legs in order to draw the noose tighter. And Sergei lost consciousness.

He came to his senses in the block's medical post. When he was fully conscious again he questioned the nurse on how he had come to be there. The nurse knew nothing of the fact that Sergei had only half hanged himself or that the warder had tried to finish him off. And it came out that only an accident had saved him from death. Just at the time when the warder was in his cell, another warder had come into the corridor from the stairs. He had come on business. The man in the cell had then let go of Sergei and called to the other to come and help him get the hanged man down. With the two of them there, one of whom would be a witness, he no longer dared to go ahead with the murder. They were all afraid of one another and always informed on each other.

Sergei pointed out 'his' warder to me. It was our senior warder, nicknamed 'Ginger' – a real angel without wings. Courteous and good mannered, he never shouted or swore, but spoke with a voice of sweetest balsam.

Now I understood why Sergei twitched all over whenever Ginger came into our cell.

CELL NO. 79

I was kept for a time in cell no. 92 and opposite ours was cell no 79. We usually exercised together, all ten of us, and got to know one another fairly well. I particularly liked one of their prisoners whose name was Stepan. He had been a geography teacher at home in the Ukraine and had already done thirteen to fourteen years in jail when I met him, out of a total sentence of twenty-five. He was such a calm and restrained fellow that I envied him.

One day the Legal Inspector of Prisons came into our cell and asked his usual question: 'Any complaints, any questions?' And registering our silence left immediately. He used to make a visit to all the cells. In the early days a few of the cons had gone to him with complaints and protests, but the response was exactly the same as to letters to the Central Committee, to the Public Prosecutor of the USSR and the Presidium of the Supreme Soviet. And so the cons stopped.

Out at exercise the following day we asked the cons from cell 79 whether the Legal Inspector had been to see them.

'Yes, I'll say he has. He and Stepan are old pals.'

Evidently the Inspector had entered cell 79, caught sight of Stepan and looked startled. Then he spoke familiarly to him and asked:

'Are you still here then?'

'As you see!'

The inspector wriggled and squirmed, said good-bye and went out.

Stepan then told them that they had once shared a cell together for two years, in this same jail. In 1956 the other man had been rehabilitated. And now they had met once more in a prison cell, though no longer as two cons but as con and authority. But what could Stepan say to him, this Legal Inspector, what could he complain about? The Inspector knew it all already and had seen for himself, for he wasn't blind.

In the same cell with Stepan were two former criminal cons, Sergei Oransky and Nikolai Kovalyov, nicknamed Vorkuta. They were 'former' criminals only in a legal sense, for they had merely been re-tried on political grounds and had their sentences lengthened, as was usually the case. In everything else they were dyed-in-the-wool criminals, corrupt, disorderly and completely crazy.

Both of them, as was customary, were tattooed. Sergei Oransky had on his forehead in tiny, almost imperceptible lettering: 'Slave of the CPSU', while Vorkuta was absolutely smothered in tattoos, with not a clear place to be seen either on his face or body. Later he was put into our cell for a while and I saw how he removed one of the tattoos from his forehead. This is how he did it.

First he took a razor blade and slashed the place all over. Then he began to knead the slits apart with his fingers rubbing away for ages, all smothered in blood, until what covered his forehead was not so much skin as some sort of bloody shreds. Then he sprinkled his forehead liberally with permanganate of potash – it was issued specially for this purpose at the medical post. The permanganate of potash ate into the wounds and Vorkuta writhed and howled with pain. The following day his forehead was swollen, black, seared by the permanganate of potash and beginning to go septic. But a short time afterwards the skin began to peel off and new skin formed over the wound. The tattoo was gone and in its place remained a huge, ugly scar.

Nevertheless many men with tattoos preferred to get rid of their 'anti-Soviet slogans' in this way, rather than be operated on in the hospital. There they simply cut the skin out without giving any form of anaesthetic, so as to persuade cons not to repeat the process. Sergei Oransky also got rid of his tattoo himself.

After his 'operation' Vorkuta said that the scar would stay big only for a while and afterwards, in the camp, would be tanned by the sun and wind and become almost unnoticeable. We laughed: 'You would need to be born all over again for your tattoos to be unnoticeable.' Nevertheless he also removed the other tattoos from his face. The scars so disfigured him that he was horrible to look at. Neither time nor sun helped: even after three years you could hardly call his face human.

Both Vorkuta and Sergei used to slash their wrists, while Sergei used to slit open his stomach and let his guts fall out, and also swallow all sorts of rubbish. One day the following incident occurred in their cell. One of the inmates was a Hungarian called Anton. I don't remember his surname, but everyone called him The Magyar. The Magyar asked Vorkuta if, the next time he slit his veins open, he could collect the blood in a bowl instead of letting it run to waste on the floor. Vorkuta was taken aback at first and then agreed: 'Why not, why shouldn't I? It will be wasted anyway.'

And so the time came for Vorkuta to slash himself again, for the usual sort of reason, and The Magyar held up his bowl to catch the blood. The other cons in the cell didn't see this. As soon as they learned that Vorkuta was going to slash himself, they turned their backs and stuck their noses into books. They couldn't help but notice that somebody was moving about behind them, but interfering in such cases was out of the question. Nobody knew of The Magyar's deal with Vorkuta and nobody guessed that he was an interested party.

The Magyar collected half a bowlful of blood, crumbled his bread into it and then started to drink this potage. Turning round at the click of the spoon, Stepan and another Ukrainian called Mikhail saw the following little scene: there sat The Magyar on his cot with the bowl on his knees, scooping up the bloody soup with his spoon and greedily gulping it down. His lips and chin were drenched in blood, blood dripped from his spoon and he kept raising and turning the spoon over in order to lick it clean with his tongue. Realising what was afoot, Mikhail didn't even make it to the sloptank, but threw up on the spot.

They told us about this incident and said The Magyar had explained to them, without a trace of embarrassment: 'Well, the blood was going to be shed anyway, why let it go to waste?'

Later, that same Magyar resolved to go on a secret hunger strike. A secret hunger strike is far more terrible than the usual open one. It usually means that a con has come to the absolute end of his tether and really intends to die. He didn't make any announcements, didn't refuse his food and always accepted his bread, skilly and dinner. But none of it went into his stomach, he secretly handed it round to his cellmates. So it went on for over a week. And all this time, just like the rest of us, he was obliged to go out for toilet breaks and exercise periods and was forbidden to lie down during the day. I used to see him every day in the exercise yard while this was going on and I saw him literally turn into a shadow. How he managed to get up the stairs I will never know! The rest of us had to hang on to the wall as it was.

On one of these days we were being taken out for our exercise period in the normal way. The Magyar was walking behind me. Suddenly I felt a shove in the back – and he slumped down on to the concrete steps, turned a somersault and rolled down the stairs to the vestibule, where he remained lying. The warders chivvied us and prodded us past him. He lay there like a corpse, with wide-open, glassy eyes.

The next day we learned from cell 79 that The Magyar was alive. Then he was dumped back in his cell and continued his hunger strike, which was official now and not secret.

RETURN JOURNEY

Unexpectedly for me I was sent back to the camps a year before my prison term was due to end. At that time, at the beginning of the summer of 1963, they started sending quite a lot of cons away from Vladimir – those who only had a short prison term still to do. Who knows, perhaps they needed the space for new arrivals?

In the transit cell I met up with Anatoly Ozerov again, he was also being sent back to Mordovia. During his spell in prison he had gone almost completely blind and it was painful to think how he would now have to grope his way about the camp with a stick, like Blind Sanya. But then I too had gone almost completely deaf and Ozerov was probably regarding me with the same sort of pained sympathy as I him. 'Yes, Tolik, we're not the men we were when we came,' he said.

Burov wasn't there. Could they be making him do the full term?

Black marias, identical prison coaches, the same old transit prisons, only this time in reverse order: Gorky, Ruzayevka, Potma.

At the Gorky transit prison we were taken for a bath. Inside the bath house, in the changing room, sat a duty officer who examined us before we entered the wash room: had anyone tattooed himself on the train? Those with tattoos on their bodies had them copied down – the officer made a list of what and where things were written. Then came the turn of Vorkuta (he too was going back to the camp). Naturally he provided the officer with enough work for an hour! Vorkuta stood in front of him in his dark blue briefs and slowly turned round and round. When the list was finished, the officer said: 'That's the lot, I take it. We haven't left anything out, have we?'

'Yes, we've left out Khrushchev,' replied Vorkuta.

'Khrushchev, where?'

'Khrushchev on my prick.'

'What did you say? Do you want a spell in the cooler?'

'You asked me where Khrushchev was tattooed and I merely told you the truth: on my prick.'

'Show me!'

To the roar of laughter from the other cons, Vorkuta lowered his drawers and showed him: tattooed in large letters along the full length of his penis was: 'Khrushchev'.

'Handsome, isn't it?' said Vorkuta innocently, stroking his Khrushchev tenderly. 'But he's lonely on his own, poor fellow. What he needs is Furtseva* for a bit of collective leadership.'

Lowering his head the officer completed the list.

The bath house at Gorky transit prison is excellent, the best I have ever seen. All the cons praise it and the fame of the Gorky bath house has travelled to all our prison camps.

As usual we travelled the whole way behind tightly closed curtains. They hung between the glass and the bars. From outside you would never have guessed that those ordinary curtains concealed stout iron bars, and that behind the bars were pale faces all covered in coarse stubble. And we, for our part, couldn't see outside.

In Saransk a soldier in the corridor threw back the curtain immediately opposite our barred door. We all rushed to look out. On the platform stood an old woman with a sack, pitifully dressed and wearing bark sandals – a countrywoman of the astronaut Nikolayev.

---

* Mrs Furtseva is Soviet minister for cultural affairs.

PART THREE

Dubrovlag

The trial is long since over, the documents prepared.
So Dubrovlag's the place where our life is to be shared,
Where we'll waken at reveille and sit waiting for lights out . . .
Counting the days of capture, counting the days of capture is to
    be our fate.

Day and night our heads will ache, swarming with thoughts till
    they burst,
So grit your teeth and keep silent to stop it from getting worse,
And don't torment your conscience with regrets that are in vain
For this is strict regime, this is strict regime for dangerous
    men.

Here hours will seem to linger like weeks as they slowly pass,
Wild dogs are at the ready, machine guns manned by armed
    guards,
And it is not at all an accident that barbed wire encircles the
    zones –
These are special camps, these are special camps for political
    cons.

Do not grudge us, oh Russia, our bowls of convict's skilly!
That band of Decembrists[1] too, became convicts willy nilly.
Chernyshevsky[2] was here, and the People's Will[3] also came,
And now it's our turn, and now it's our turn, to be the same.

Song, 1966

1. An aristocratic revolutionary group that vainly attempted to overthrow
Tsar Nicholas 1 in 1825. Many of the leaders were exiled to Siberia.
2. A well-known radical critic and publicist of the mid-19th century who was
imprisoned in 1862, and subsequently exiled to Siberia, for publishing revolutionary pamphlets.
3. A revolutionary party of the 19th century that advocated violence and
organised the assassination of Alexander II (1881).

BACK IN CAMP

We arrived in Potma at the beginning of summer and spent several days in the transit jail there. We had to go before a medical commission to be classified for the kind of work we could do. Everybody except Stepan was classified A1, while Stepan, with one leg cut off above the knee, was put in the second or possibly even third category. Our other ailments – haemorrhoids, ruptures and so on – didn't weigh in the balance.

Already here, in the Potma transit prison, I was struck by certain changes and innovations. One block was crammed full with prisoners on special regime and they were all wearing a striped uniform. This uniform is still in use and the cons wearing it are called 'stripeys' or 'tigers'. At Potma at that time they were mainly religious prisoners – for some reason they were now being segregated from the rest and all going on special regime.

After about three or four days we were loaded into 'Stolypins' and distributed around the camps. I landed up in camp seven, together with Ozerov. The station was Sosnovka, not far from Potma.

We were marched from the station under armed guard – tommy gunners with dogs walked ahead, behind and to either side of us. But the road gave me such pleasure that I even forgot about the guards. How fine it was to walk down that simple, trodden road and through a hamlet with a wood standing just behind it! Grass grew on both sides of the road – I hadn't seen any for two years. And now some little wooden houses came into sight and although I knew that guards and warders lived inside them, still the very sight of those peaceful cottages with their two or three windows brought a feeling of joy and relief. As we walked along we filled our lungs with the fresh, tree-scented air and we knew that tomorrow and the next day we would be breathing that same air all the time, and no longer the stifling air of the cells and the exhalations of the slop-tank.

And here was the camp, exactly the same as all the other camps: watch towers, barbed wire, perimeter fence, search-lights . . . Ah, what the hell! At least it wasn't prison with its grey walls and muzzled windows! We waited about forty minutes at the guardhouse. Roll-call, counting, recounting; then we were called out in groups, searched – and let into the camp.

A crowd of cons was waiting inside the guardhouse – those who worked the afternoon and night shifts had come to meet the regular convoy. No sooner had I stepped down from the porch than I was ringed with prisoners and peppered with questions: who was I, what was I in for, how long? But the first question was: 'From Vladimir, eh? You can see that! You'd go to the grave looking better.'

The very first thing they did was take us to the canteen, continuing to question us on the way: do you happen to know so-and-so? Or so-and-so? Do they still stop you from lying down during the day? Did you see Powers? Who's the governor now – Grishin or Tsuplyak? The canteen at camp seven was the same as everywhere else: bare, painted tables, long benches, serving hatches at one end and a stage at the other, with a dais and a large white cloth for a cinema screen. Above and behind the stage and all around the canteen walls hung slogans, placards and photo-montages. But the surroundings were of little interest to me now.

I was made to sit at a table where several cons from our convoy were already hard at work with their spoons. We new-comers were surrounded by a crowd of local veterans, cook-house hands and cooks in their grey and white overalls. At once a bowl of noodle soup was pushed in front of me and a whole pile of cut bread was placed at my elbow, then they thrust a spoon into my hand and said: 'Eat, dig in.' I stirred the soup with my spoon. It was thin and fatless, even though the cooks had served us with the thick stuff from the bottom. But it seemed to me on that occasion that not even at home had I eaten better noodle soup.

'Well now, brother, is it the same as at Vladimir?'

I replied that you'd get five Vladimir helpings out of a bowl like that.

I wasn't aware of how I had emptied the bowl in a flash. At once they took it away and brought it back again brim full: 'Eat up, eat up!' I realised that if I finished this they would bring me yet another. I felt embarrassed at eating so greedily and decided to recoup on the bread. The slices of bread had been cut the full width of the loaf; one slice took me four bites to get through; I was trying to stuff a whole mouthful of bread in at one go with each spoonful of soup; and therefore I had to keep stretching out my hand for fresh slices. But this too began to make me feel ashamed. I managed to slow down and not take the bread so often, and when they offered me a third bowl of soup I refused, saying I was already full. In truth I felt that although I had stuffed my belly full, I could have gone on eating and eating.

As we stood up to leave the canteen the local cons suggested we take some bread with us. Supper was at five, but at four they served hot water and that way we would have something to eat with it. We almost wept with gratitude.

Such generosity with the bread continued at number seven for about another month or two, you could eat as much as you wanted. But after that, they too started rationing it. But in the camp it didn't matter so much, as I will explain later.

After dinner I went for a walk round the compound. After feeding me they left me alone to look around. The first thing I noticed was the abundance of greenery: there were lots of trees and shrubs, and flower beds had been laid out round the huts, though the flowers hadn't come out yet. There were just as many slogans and placards, but I ignored them and didn't look at them, admiring instead the trees and the grass. There were lots and lots of cons about the compound, in fact there were over three and a half thousand men in the camp, and therefore there were plenty of people about, even during the day when the first shift was at work.

I also noticed that the cons were all dressed identically now, in black cotton tunics, similar trousers, and with black uniform caps on their shaven heads. Two years ago it had been different, then you had been able to wear your own clothes in the living zone. On that hot day, it is true, many had bare heads and wore their tunics flapping open, while a few, stripped to the waist, were even tanning themselves in the sun. (Later, during my last year in camp, we were thoroughly persecuted if we took such liberties and were forced to keep our tunics on no matter how hot it was: 'You're not on holiday now!')

I strolled about in the hope of meeting old acquaintances, but none turned up. A few I recognised by their faces, remembering that I had seen them, I thought, at camp ten, but I couldn't really say I knew them. After all, I had only been there a few months before landing up in jail. And nobody recognised me. Many looked round, it is true, and asked: 'Just out of Vladimir?' And when this was confirmed, remarked: 'I could see you were.'

I went to the barber's. Here there were five con barbers, hard at work and long lines of people waiting in front of each one. Once again, though, I experienced an extraordinarily friendly and solicitous attitude towards me on the part of others: guessing that I had just come from prison, they immediately let me go first, without waiting. I sat in the chair of a lame Lithuanian barber and while he shaved me questions rained down on me from all sides. They came from both barbers and customers and the Lithuanian repeated everything into my ear to make sure I understood. How pleasant it was to sit with a clean towel around my neck and to feel for the first time in two years the touch of a shaving brush and soap. Overcome with pleasure, I closed my eyes and tried to let my mind go blank.

After my shave I walked out of the barber's shop, running my hand over my freshly shaved chin and not finding the usual stubble! And just then I caught sight of a familiar face. Tapping his way past the barber's shop with a stick came Blind Sanya, that same Sanya I had met on my first day in camp ten, just over two years ago. My exalted mood vanished in a trice. What was I feeling so pleased about, idiot? I was still in Mordovia, wasn't I, the camp was just as much a prison, only with the walls pushed back a bit and the sky visible overhead.

By four o'clock I also had time to glance into the library. It was full of people and there was nowhere to sit, so I merely walked up and down. As in the canteen and outside there were placards everywhere, together with newspaper and magazine cuttings, quotes from the classics and slogans, slogans, slogans: 'He who doesn't work shan't eat'; 'Today's generation of Soviet citizens will one day live under Communism'; 'Communism is the bright future of all mankind'; 'Lenin is always with us'. The largest number of sayings and quotations came from the speeches and reports of Khrushchev; wherever you looked you saw 'N. S. Khrushchev' looking back at you, together with his face on various photographs and cuttings.

But it was time to go to headquarters for my first interview. A group of new arrivals was already waiting outside HQ and was constantly being joined by more people coming up. We discussed the work that lay ahead of us and who was likely to get what. We had no choice in the matter: we would have to go where we were told. They called us in one by one and each con as he emerged again would say: 'Eighth company', 'twenty-seventh', 'foundry'. At last my turn came.

A spacious office contained what seemed the whole of admin: the Camp Commander himself – Lieutenant-Colonel Kolo- mytsev, his various aides and deputies, majors, captains, lieuten- ants, young and old. I was spoken to by some major with tattoos on his hands and with a scar across the whole of his cheek and upper lip. (The cons told me later that this was the Deputy Camp Commander, Major Ageyev, nicknamed The Lip, a terribly foulmouthed officer and a great troublemaker. They said he was the brother of that other Ageyev who had beaten us in camp ten, that he had been disfigured by some criminal con in revenge and that he himself was a former criminal con. I don't know how much truth there was in all this but he certainly used to behave like a thug, foully cursing everyone to beat the band and bellow- ing from one end of the camp to the other; on the other hand he never took umbrage and never punished cons if they gave as good as they got – it seemed that he even liked it.) Anyway it was this same Ageyev who asked me all the standard questions, inquired whether I was intending to escape again (naturally I said no, I would sit out my term) and informed me that I would work in the stand-by gang as a loader.

'What sort of gang is that? And what work is it?'

A young lieutenant explained to me that this gang unloaded coal, logs and timber from railway wagons and loaded them again with finished products. I said:

'But I'm deaf, how can I work on loading and unloading? I won't hear the commands, I'll be crushed to death.'

'Never mind, you'll hear if you try hard enough,' replied the lieutenant, 'we've got worse than you working at it.'

This was my company officer, Lieutenant Alyoshin. That evening I had an interview with him above in his own office. Again I heard the same old sickening questions that I had to answer every day: name, charge, sentence. And then a new question:

'Do you repent, are you sorry for what you did?'

'All I need to be sorry for in here is not that I tried to escape, but that I failed.'

Alyoshin was silent in response to this and then briefly outlined my duties and the camp rules and regulations. Soon I was to get to know them in practice.

Meanwhile I set off for my hut and my section in order to get myself organised. It turned out that our section was the best in the entire camp: the cots stood not in a double circle, as in all the other sections, but in one. I was shown where to put my cot (it was a lucky place, they said: a twenty-five-year-termer had slept in this spot and only yesterday had been freed after doing twenty-one years), where to get a sack for my mattress and where to get all the rest of a con's camp equipment and clothing, including a cap like the ones I had noticed earlier. This black cotton cap was somewhat reminiscent of a fore-and-aft cap with a peak and was called a 'Cuban' in the camps, while in camp ten we had still worn forage caps à la Stalin. The cons used to joke that in this too Khrushchev was eradicating the cult of Stalin and currying favour with Fidel. Tomorrow I would have to put on this black prisoner's uniform and keep it on for the next three years.

Later our orderly, Andrei Trofrimchuk (also a twenty-five-year prisoner, a Ukrainian from Kiev, he had already done sixteen to seventeen years; in general there were lots of cons with twenty-five years in number seven at that time) took me into the work zone to stuff my mattress. At first they didn't want to let me through the guardhouse in the clothes I was wearing, but then Andrei persuaded the warder and we passed through. Just as we had entered the work zone a flood of women came walking the other way – they were free workers in good clean clothes. The working day had just finished in the office and the other institutions where they worked, and almost all the office workers were the wives or daughters of officers and warders. The women passed Andrei without so much as noticing him, looking straight through him as if he were made of glass. With me, on the other hand, many of them exchanged greetings. I was astonished and Andrei explained laughingly that they must certainly have taken me for one of 'theirs', a free worker, because I wasn't dressed like a con, and the fact that I was on my last legs wasn't noticeable at a distance.

We came to a shed where some cons were using a planing machine to turn miscellaneous planks and blocks into shavings – these were 'feathers' for the camp mattresses and pillows. We picked out one of the drier bales of shavings, filled the mattress cover and pillow case and set off back for the living zone (at the guardhouse they searched us, of course, and the sacks of shavings – everything was back to normal).

The whole of our gang was already back in the hut. The men had returned from work, eaten their supper, received their food from the shop and were now drinking tea. The ganger, Anton Gaida, came over to me and told me to take the paper packets that were on the table. It turned out that every con in the gang had put aside from the food he had bought a spoonful of margarine and a handful of toffees, so that now I had my own food and just as much as the rest of them. Everybody persuaded me to take it without being shy, for they all knew what Vladimir jail was like and some of them had been there themselves. As for the shop, I'd have to wait a good month and a half till I could use it, till I had earned five roubles from my work. But there was no hope of lasting out on nothing but camp rations, it was only at the beginning that it seemed you could eat your fill in the canteen; once you got on a bit and had to work, you soon found out that without food of your own, without the shop, you would snuff it in no time.

Thus they persuaded me to take the food, explaining at the same time what sort of life lay ahead of me. Deeply touched by their thoughtfulness and sympathy, I took the packets and carried them off to my locker.

As I began to get a closer look at my gang-mates I suddenly saw a familiar face and managed to remember who it was. He was a con called Ivan Tretyakov, who had travelled with me from Taishet via all those transit jails to Mordovia. At the end of it, though, I had been sent to number ten, while he had come straight here to seven. He was pleased to see me too, and also that we would be working in the same gang. Examining me closely, he said that I was unrecognisable, that he himself would never have known me – I had changed enormously since 1961, I was so far gone I was terrifying to look at. And moustachless too, what had I done with it, eaten it in desperation? We gossiped away and exchanged information about our former travelling companions. Then Ivan suddenly stopped short, excused himself and dragged me over to the corner, to his cot, to drink tea. Again I felt ashamed of my starved appearance. I had already eaten plenty that day, but my eyes still looked insatiably hungry and probably it showed quite plainly.

Ivan fetched two mugs of hot water, took some bread, margarine and toffees out of his locker and offered them to me. We sat on his cot drinking our hot water and talking, recalling all our convoy ordeals. Ivan showed me some photos of his family – his wife and two daughters. They lived in Balkhash and the elder daughter was already married.

I remembered Ivan's past. He and his family had originally lived in Western Byelorussia and when the Germans came Ivan had joined the police under the occupation. There was a man from the same village in camp seven and he later told me that when Ivan was a policeman he had never run wild or oppressed people in any way, but had simply done his duty. Ivan himself now deeply regretted it, but never sought to excuse himself, merely explaining his error by the fact that he had to find a way of feeding his wife and children.

Well, I don't really know what happened in those times during the war and I can't pretend to judge, but I do know that both in the convoy and here in camp, Ivan behaved like a decent fellow and a good comrade. Everybody thought the same of him in our gang and because of this they immediately treated me not only with sympathy but also with trust: Tretyakov would never be friends with a grass. And you had to be careful, because often the authorities would transfer their grasses from camp to camp and pretend that they were simply newcomers.

Anyway, after the Germans, Ivan went into the Soviet Army and fought with them to the very last day – after which they sentenced him to twenty-five years inside. For a while he was transferred to a free colony at Balkhash and was joined there by his family, which remained there still. But he himself, like the majority of the settlers, was locked up in a camp again and then sent to Taishet. It was there that the two of us met.

Ivan suddenly remembered something and said:

'By the way, Tolik, you were a bad prophet.'

'What do you mean?'

'Do you remember the two old men who travelled with us from Taishet – Ivanov and another one with grey hair and a big beard, a Volga German? You prophesied that they would soon go free and that you would see them off when they left. Do you remember? Well, you can go and say hello to Ivanov tomorrow, he's here.'

'And the German?'

'Yes, the German left,' replied Ivan, 'feet first. He told you, didn't he: "I shall be here for the rest of my life, Tolik. I shan't be released, I shall die behind barbed wire." Well, he died in here.'

Ivan and I talked right up until lights out. He advised me to join his team unloading coal and timber. The work in the other team was slightly easier – loading finished products, unloading barrels, spare parts, cases of paper, but on the other hand you couldn't earn much for the shop in that team, while in the 'big' team you at least got credited with an extra twenty roubles a month, and sometimes even more. What's more, you weren't got up so often at night – it was rarely more than once. I agreed and it was a simple matter to arrange it with the ganger.

For my first three days the ganger didn't call me out to work, he let me rest and get my strength back. The whole gang had agreed in asking him to do this. It was done, of course, without the knowledge of admin. I was marked down on the chart as working, otherwise I would have ended up in the cooler as an absentee. Only in the stand-by gang were such tricks possible. There were sixteen men in the big team, of whom twelve were needed for unloading. Thus four always remained behind. At the next call twelve cons would have to go again – the four who had rested plus eight from the first twelve, and so on, by turns, with four cons always left behind in the living zone. And so I was left behind for three whole days, but I had to steer clear of the company officer, of course. And then by the fourth day I had been carried long enough on the backs of others and it was time to bend my own.

My first time out was in the early evening – we were called out to unload a wagon of timber. The logs were loaded in a double stack, end to end, with a 'cap' of logs over the joins to stop them shifting, and all the work was done by hand. At first it went easily: we set up our 'roller' (a simple log with a hook on the end to hook on the side of the wagon), several men climbed up on top and started shoving the 'cap' off, while the rest used crooks to roll the logs away from the wagon. You just had to shove and away they rolled. The hard part began, however, when we got half way down the stack inside. All of us had to take hold of the log together and at the command: 'one, two, three!' had to raise it aloft and throw it over the side of the box-shaped wagon. As for the bottom logs, there was no hope of throwing them out and they had to be dragged and pushed out at the back.

By the time I had helped unload this one wagon I thought I

would never get back to the hut. The work itself was killing, and on top of that I was completely out of condition after two years in Vladimir jail. I could hardly walk. But the boys cheered me up: it was nothing to worry about, I would soon get used to it. Back in the hut I collapsed on to my cot and went straight to sleep, without even eating. I awoke what seemed like a minute later. When I had gone to bed the others were taking off their clothes after work. Now, when I opened my eyes again, they were still undressing, noisily discussing the job, the timber and the 'rub-down' at the guardhouse. My body ached all over, as though I hadn't slept at all, yet it turned out that the night was already over and the gang had just returned from its third call – twice more during the night they had been out unloading wagons. On me, however, they had taken pity, not wanting to wake me.

With difficulty I got out of bed and was hardly able to straighten up, I had pains in my waist, arms, legs, neck. I went out to get washed and I couldn't even walk straight – my legs wouldn't bend and the whole of me was swaying. And I waddled like a duck as I went. I was kidded for ages afterwards about that duck's waddle of mine.

When I came to the washroom I was told that a con had just hanged himself in one of the section washrooms, he was cold when they cut him down that morning. He was a Latvian or Lithuanian with a twenty-five-year term. He had already done sixteen when he was re-tried for a possible reduction to the new regulation fifteen. But the court refused, leaving him nine more years to do. So he hanged himself.

NEW DESIGNS

The new year comes and with it new designs
The camp is ringed with a barbed wire barricade
Stern eyes keep watch, regard us from all sides
And hungry death is everywhere on guard

> (Sung to the tune of a favourite old tango
> from the twenties and thirties)

Gradually I really did get used to the work and I settled down in camp seven. And I learned of changes other than the obvious ones I had been so quick to notice before. Since the autumn of 1961 the situation in the camps had taken a big turn for the worse and it still continues to get worse with every succeeding year. So what was the regime for political prisoners between the years 1963–65? And since it has remained the same, what is it like now in 1967?*

First, the prisoners have their heads shaved and are not allowed to wear their own clothing or footwear. The con is forced to spend his whole time in the black cotton camp uniform, with heavy ankle or knee boots on his feet (women too) and in winter a padded coat or jacket (reefer jacket) on top of his cotton tunic. If a warder catches sight of a con in a civilian shirt or a cap, he will chase him all over the compound until he catches him and takes it away, after which the con is dispatched to the cooler. The same thing happens if they find any civvies on your cot during a search. The huts are searched frequently and usually when the cons are away at work. Those waiting for the second shift are usually chased out during this time. Everything is

---

* Considerable documentary evidence shows it to be the same in 1969.

turned upside down, they rummage through your bedding and your lockers and read through all your newspapers and letters and anything you might have written. What they want, they take.

The writing of letters is limited to two a month. And the fact that you can receive as many as you like, and from whomever you like, is just one more proof of what it is the authorities are afraid of. All the means at their disposal are used to limit information about the camps, so that the public knows as little as possible about what goes on there. Furthermore the prisoners are warned that it is forbidden to write about the camp organisation and the rules to relatives. All letters are examined by the censor. You have to hand each letter over in an open envelope. If he doesn't approve of something in it, he sends it back to you. And letters from outside are opened before arrival. Sometimes one or two sentences are blacked out. Some letters disappear completely: the censor confiscates them and adds them to the prisoner's file, or else simply refuses to hand them over. Who can you ask about them? The minister of communications?

You may also receive printed matter: books, magazines, newspapers, Soviet only. Not even Polish and Czech are allowed. Not even humorous ones. Many of our cons knew or had studied foreign languages. In the camps you can find an expert in almost any language you care to name, from English down to some remote Indian or African dialect. Some of them know half a dozen languages, so that there are plenty of teachers available. But the only books and newspapers you can get in these languages are ones published in the Soviet Union. And the same goes for text books.

It is also possible to have soap, toothpaste and notebooks sent in printed packets. And handkerchiefs. All printed packets are prodded and felt, closely examined and minutely studied before being passed on.

In the big camp, of course, it happens that a con gets away with wearing a sweater under his uniform tunic and puts on a normal cap or beret instead of that sickening 'Cuban'. Sometimes a pair of socks get through in a printed packet, or a warm scarf. But this is the result of an oversight on the part of the censor or warders – it's not so easy to keep an eye on everything and everybody when you've got three thousand-odd different men milling around under your eyes. And a con who commits a 'violation' in this way takes good care not to be seen and gives all officers the widest possible berth.

Receiving food or even smokes from outside when you're on strict regime is completely forbidden. No parcels, no packages. The con has no right to them. The camp administration has the right to permit parcels as a form of reward for exemplary conduct, to show that a con 'is responding to corrective training'. But even then only to prisoners who have completed half their term. That means you serve at least half your time without parcels and after that you may or may not be allowed a 'concession' – one ten-pound parcel once a quarter, forty pounds of food a year, or just over three pounds a month! And after this you have to work till you drop, bashing out your norm, and not once break a single one of the camp regulations. And needless to say, that's not all. A prisoner, for instance, gets fed up with admin and says:

'I've served half my time, I always do the norm and I haven't broken the rules – why can't I have a parcel?'

And the company officer clarifies the matter.

'Well, well! So you haven't broken any rules! But we *punish* for breaking the rules and concessions have to be worked for, concessions have to be deserved.'

It is well known what 'deserved' means: suck up to the powers that be at all times and in all places, beginning with the warders; cooperate with admin, be an 'activist', prey on your comrades, become a grass. And in general it means that you're thrown on the mercy of the camp authorities. For a food parcel means a lot in camp. Even those pitiful three pounds a month. And each time, every three months, you have to ask for your 'reward': you go to the company officer, make your application, get in return a sermon and – nine times out of ten – refusal.

Applications since 1965 have grown very rare. Now you have to appear before a commission consisting of your company officer, the camp commander, representatives of the KGB and PEU (Political Education Unit) and the KGB Security Officer for the camp. This lofty body sits in judgement on whether a con shall be allowed his ten pounds of food, or whether he has failed to deserve such magnanimity.

The majority of prisoners serve their whole term without receiving a single parcel. In all my six years inside I received only one package from my mother – ten pounds of food – and that was when I was lying in the camp hospital. One girl I knew sent some apples. They were a birthday present. I only learned about it a month afterwards, from one of her letters. I wrote back telling her she was naive to think that a prisoner in Mordovia was allowed to eat apples. Maybe she had been reading about prison parcels in the newspaper, in an article about some 'difficult pages'.* My letter was confiscated and added to my file and I was called in by the KGB and warned that for writing like that I wasn't far from having my sentence extended. I expect the apples went rotten on their way back to my friend.

If a parcel should weigh a couple of ounces over ten pounds together with its wrappings it is sent straight back again. If a parcel comes from a friend and you happen not to recognise the sender's address on the box, it is sent straight back again.

Well, and what about a prisoner's rights? There is his right to correspond (with limitations and censorship). His right to have visits from relatives – I will write about these a bit later. His right to buy up to five roubles' worth of food in the camp shop, though only with money earned inside the camp. If he has nothing left after deductions have been made – too bad, he can make do without, even if his relatives are prepared to send money. Not on sale in the camp shop and forbidden because of the regime regulations are: sugar, butter, tinned meat and fish, bread. All you can buy is tinned vegetables or fruit (hardly anybody buys these because they are too dear, they take your whole five roubles), cheap sweets and margarine. There is also soap, cigarettes, cheap tobacco, toothbrushes, envelopes, notebooks, and you can buy camp clothing if you like – not that anybody does on five roubles a month.

---

* This is the euphemism used in the Soviet press to refer to the existence of labour camps.

But all these rights are no better than a dream, a mirage. Admin has the right to deprive a prisoner of all of them. This is done for violations, and who can say that he commits no violations – if admin wants to find some? And so they take away your rights – to the shop, for instance, for a month, two months, three. And then you have to get by on 'basic' – on camp rations that have been worked out on scientific principles to be just enough to keep you from dying off.

The daily norm is 2,400 calories: twenty-five ounces of bread, three ounces of cod, two ounces of meat (the sheepdog guarding the cons gets one pound), one pound of vegetables – potatoes and cabbage, about one ounce of meal or noodles, three-quarters of an ounce of fat and half an ounce of sugar. And that's all. It adds up to one and a half times less than a normal man needs on light work. You will say: what about the shop? But then they deprive you of the shop! Keeping strictly to all the rules and regulations they condemn you to an empty belly!

But anyway, not even all of this finds its way into the prisoner's bowl. A cart, for instance, comes into the compound carrying meat for the whole camp, 300 pounds for three thousand men. You look at this meat and you hardly know what to think: is it carrion or something still worse? All blue, it seems to consist entirely of bone and gristle. Then it goes to be stewed and you're lucky if half an ounce finds its way into your mouth. You're eating cabbage and you can't make out to begin with what it is: some sort of black, slimy, stinking globes. How much out of the established quota gets thrown on the rubbish heap? And in spring and summer the cookhouse hands can't even bring themselves to throw out the bad potatoes any more, otherwise there would be nothing to put in the soup. And so they throw in the black and rotten ones. If you go near the cookhouse in summer the stench turns you over. Stinking cod, rotten cabbage. The bread is like we had in the war. In number seven we had a bakery in which we baked two kinds of bread, black for the camp, white for outside. Sugar, though, you would think was fool-proof. It won't rot, you don't have to measure it. But then they give it to you damp so that it weighs more. And they give you ten days' ration at a time – five ounces – because if they gave you your half ounce daily, it wouldn't so much be a question of having nothing to eat as of nothing to see.

During six years in camp and jail I had bread with butter twice – when I received visits. I also ate two cucumbers – one in 1964 and another in 1966. Not once did I eat a tomato or an apple. All this was forbidden.

Every month you have thirteen to fourteen roubles of your wages deducted for food. Outside now as a free man I go to a cafe where dinners are cheap. Cabbage soup costs me twenty-three copecks, a main dish twenty-five to twenty-seven copecks without meat, a dish of stewed fruit seven copecks, and then I have four to five copecks' worth of bread. That means sixty copecks a day on dinner alone, or eighteen roubles a month. And breakfast and supper costs about the same. Thus I alone spend about fifty roubles a month on food, almost the whole of my salary, and you wouldn't say I was eating well. But a con spends thirteen roubles!* Even if he ate only canteen soup once a day and his twenty-five ounces of bread, that would take almost the whole sum, and he'd have three roubles a month to pay for all the rest. No subsidies are allowed for prisoners, they have to pay for all their food out of their own paltry wages. Everybody can figure that out and see what sort of grub that must mean. And then basic's nothing in comparison with the cooler and a reduced quota of food. Reduced – that means 1,300 calories, one third of what a man needs: fourteen to eighteen ounces of bread, skilly that's all water and cod once a day – the usual three ounces or perhaps less. And not a grain of sugar, not a shred of meat, not a granule of fat. At the same time you still have to go out to work, and if you're unable to and refuse, you'll be tried and stuck in jail.

It happens that starving cons who have longed for years for a touch of green or a fresh vegetable sometimes get hold of some seeds and sow them in the compound, say carrots or onions in some distant corner. Sooner or later, however, the

---

* At the official rate, there are 1.11 roubles to the dollar and 2.16 roubles to the pound sterling, but a more realistic rate would be three times as many roubles in each case. There are 100 copecks in a rouble.

warders always see them and kick them out. It's not allowed! Caucasians have more success with their edible sweet grass. It grows to the cons' advantage: the warders can't recognise it or distinguish it from other grasses.

And that is what strict regime looks like today. Strict regime, for the most part, is for political prisoners, because among criminals only the persistent offenders get put on strict regime, or those who commit a crime or a violation already in the camps, and even then not for their whole term – they do a stint on strict regime and then go back to normal regime again. For criminals and civil prisoners strict regime is the harshest form of punishment. But for us politicals it is the mildest, our imprisonment begins with this, because it is the minimum awarded by the courts. From strict regime political prisoners can go only on to special regime or to jail. And that is even worse.

WORK

While I was at camp seven I tried almost all the different sorts of work there were. We had a big output of furniture – out of three and a half thousand cons practically all, with the exception of some of the invalids, worked in the factory. We had a sawmill, a cutting out shop, a machine shop, assembly shops, a finishing shop, our own foundry, a blacksmith's shop, our own timber yard and our own builders. Only the skilled craftsmen and supervisors came from outside. All the workers were prisoners.

For a month or two I worked in the finishing shop. It was full of unhealthy fumes, the stink of varnish and acetone, and the workers used to suffer from dizziness and vomiting. True, the finishers used to get a supplementary ration consisting of fourteen ounces of milk a day, and the foundry workers too. But as often as not the milk didn't come every day. And then many cons tried to share with their friends, who otherwise after five or ten years without it would forget even the taste of milk. So how could you possibly drink it all on your own?

The foundry, at the time when I worked in it, was absolute hell. It was used for smelting and casting spare parts out of an alloy consisting of zinc, aluminium and copper. The furnace was an old one with a poor ventilation system, so that your lungs would be filled with zinc fumes, gases and smoke and you would run out with the sweat pouring off you to take a few gulps of fresh air.

The law decreeing a shorter working day for unhealthy types of work doesn't extend to prisoners – you still have to do a full eight hours. When you come off the shift you are trembling from head to foot, as in a fever, and then you have to wait outside the guardhouse for an hour for roll-call. After I left they built a new foundry, so I don't know what it's like now. But our norms were impossible to fulfil. And all the time they were being raised, while our rates were steadily lowered. Some cons, in order to earn more, used to pitch in in pairs and then book it down to only one of them. Thus one would be credited with 150 per cent, while the other would get only 20–30 per cent, which was okay, just so long as you weren't put on reduced rations. Then the first one would share his bonus with the second. Or maybe he would leave it in his own name and accumulate money for the shop. After a few months, half a year or a year of such work, one man at least would have something to take out with him when he was released, enough to see him through for a while. And then, once outside, he would try to help his friend still in the camp. But this was a dangerous game: the authorities might take their cue from such a 'star' and raise the quotas for everyone else.

Some would have to go without their dinner and work two shifts in succession. They would still only be booked for a single shift, but a working day of fourteen to sixteen hours would enable them to turn out up to 150–170 per cent of the norm. Thus they killed two birds with one stone: their pay was higher and they earned the approval of admin. For generally speaking admin knew of these various tricks. And with regard to overtime they sometimes had a direct agreement with some of 'their own' cons: these would then be listed as the star workers and on the basis of their performance the norms would be raised for everybody else. 'If he can do it, then you have to as well!'

It is generally thought, I suppose, that production goes up at the expense of mechanisation, but in fact any increase is at the expense of the con's sweat and blood. In the finishing shop the norm was originally to polish six 'Yugdon' radiogram cabinets, but while I was there this was pushed up to thirteen. In 1964 the norm for 'Radius-V' television cabinets was four, and in 1965 six. But the work stayed exactly the same: a wad of cotton wool soaked in acetone with which you polished the cabinet by hand until you had brought it to a high sheen.

Basically, however, I worked as a loader in the stand-by gang. I have already described the first job of unloading I did and that is how it continued day after day, with five to seven wagons to unload every twenty-four hours. In the autumn and winter our clothes would never have time to dry out in the drying room before the next call came and we would have to pull them on, still wet, and go out. The work was so heavy because there were only sixteen loaders for the whole factory.

Even worse than timber was the coal. It used to come in a steady stream, great mountains of coal would be piled on both sides of the track and there would be nowhere to put the latest consignment. Two or three wagonloads would arrive and they would be practically invisible behind the heaps. That meant it was impossible to open the hatches: there was nowhere to shovel the coal and it would all slide under the wagon. Like the timber, therefore, it had to be thrown over the sides, only much farther away, of course. And in winter it would be frozen solid, we would have to break it up with crowbars before unloading it. Even before that, though, we would have to roll the wagons into position ourselves ready for unloading, because the track was poor and they wouldn't let the locomotives on to it. So we'd have to heave and push a wagon of sixty-two tons 200 yards up the slope, and at least an hour would go on that. But neither the time nor the work involved in this was taken into consideration or paid for, because it was held that our gang was working 'with the assistance of light machinery', and the fact that we, a gang powered by fourteen to sixteen cons, had been harnessed to a wagon in place of a locomotive wasn't entered in the records at all. And the whole of our 'light machinery' in unloading consisted of crowbars, crooks, staves and a roller.

In the spring of 1965 they equipped our timber yard with a crane for unloading timber. And at once a part of the loaders was transferred to the factory, for fear that we might have a bit less work to do. The remainder now had to go on call every time and couldn't take turns any more. And the work was just as hard as before: we still had to shovel the coal and every now and then the crane had a breakdown. And you couldn't put the crane on special regime as a shirker.

In general, though, a prisoner's work differs little in essence from work outside. I'm a free man now and since April 1967 I

have been working as a loader – we do the same uncredited
overtime and we also push wagons about from store to store,
and our earnings are about the same: seventy to seventy-five
roubles (if you don't do extra work). The only difference is that
you get a bit more to eat and the deductions from your wage
packet are bigger, especially for childlessness. In the camp, too,
you pay the same taxes (and they also make deductions from
cons for childlessness!) and then 50 per cent of the remainder
is assigned for maintenance of the camp and its staff – from
warders to the administration and doctors; and it also goes on
hut maintenance and supporting the sick and invalids. Out of the
remaining 50 per cent they take thirteen roubles for food and
you have to pay out several roubles a month for that wretched
camp uniform that is issued on deferred payment. And out of
what's left five roubles goes on the shop (if you're allowed) . . .
So that you won't get rich as they imply in the advertisements:
'Save up and buy a motor car!' God grant that in the course of
your term you can save enough for a suit and a pair of boots.

It's no different outside, however.

There was a time in the camps when, just as elsewhere, we
had a wave of 'work on a social basis'. The company officer
would call in a number of activists among the cons and prompt
them to some valuable new initiative. In our library we had a
librarian and in return for his work he received, although it was
tiny, something that could nevertheless be called a salary. Under
pressure from admin the prisoners organised themselves in
shifts to look after the library voluntarily, in their free time. The
librarian was dismissed ('You can hang around hungry if you like,
you don't have to work, you're an invalid. Otherwise go and get
stuck in at the factory.') But that was only a library! Later we
were forced, 'on a social basis', to renovate our own hut. And
why not? After all, ordinary workers go and build houses for
nothing in their free time. But then if workers go to work on
such social projects (and who knows whether they go voluntarily?) they stand a chance of getting a flat in that building, while
in our case it turns out that we're forced, 'on a social basis', to
repair our own jail! And we repaired it: if you refused you got
no parcels and a black mark on your record.

Our cons also built a new Visitors' Hostel for free in their spare time. Some of them even volunteered for this project, because the old hostel really was very bad and small. A mother or wife would arrive and would have to wait around for two weeks or more. And some of them had a long way to come, so that their holiday wasn't long enough and they had to ask for unpaid leave from work, and then they would spend the whole of their holiday time in Mordovia, standing around outside the guardhouse. Because of this a large number of wives couldn't come at all. But now admin had suddenly turned generous: here's the material, build it yourselves.

The cons built a new hostel with twenty rooms in it and were overjoyed: now my wife can come too! Even though they were working for the camp, still it was somehow for themselves as well.

But when it was finished admin took twelve of the twenty rooms for its staff. Here they set out their desks and hung up their curtains. So the cons, 'on a social basis', had been putting up offices for their jailers! Still, they did at least leave eight rooms for family visits and at least the waiting got shorter: now it was eight to ten days instead of the former two weeks.

Admin and HQ got a double advantage from this unpaid work: first they would be praised for their success in 'educating' the prisoners; but second and more important – they made considerable savings. For no matter what happened 50 per cent of the cons' wages would be deducted to pay for all the repairs and building work in the camp. And in this way they both deducted the money and got their building work free. Admin, moreover, used to be liberally rewarded for any savings they made, while the cons, of course, got sweet Fanny Adams.

But the biggest evil of camp work is not that it is cruelly heavy, nor that you work for virtually nothing, for a morsel of bread, or for even less. The main reason why you hate this work is because it's slavery, arbitrarily enforced and humiliating, and all the time you have those parasitical warders standing over you, grudging you the crust of bread that you've earned with your own sweat.

When I was released and came to Moscow, I would always

stop by the windows of shops selling furniture and radio and television sets. There inside would be a polished table, a handsome, shining wardrobe and familiar cabinets: 'Radius-V', 'Yugdon', 'Melodia'.

So you buy yourself a new wardrobe and you sit there in the evening in your cosy room, in front of the television set. You've paid 360 whole roubles for that TV of yours and now you are going to enjoy your right to a bit of comfort and relaxation. That television set has cost me and my friends our sweat, our health, roasting in the cooler and long hours during roll-call in the rain and snow. Look closely at that polished surface: can you not see reflected in it the close-shaven head, the yellow, emaciated face, and the black cotton tunic of a convict? Maybe a former friend of yours?

THE CONS' ECONOMY – DOUBLE-ENTRY BOOK-KEEPING

'Yes, but wait a minute,' some of my readers will say, 'if those were the conditions you lived under in Dubrovlag, how is it the whole lot of you didn't just bite the dust? We know that there used to be really terrible camps: Kolyma, Vorkuta, Taishet. There they used to die like flies from exhaustion, "goners" would literally tremble in the wind, dysentery and scurvy were practically universal. But at least you haven't got that any more and I don't understand, there's something wrong somewhere.'

Old Kolyma and Vorkuta hands who have remained prisoners to this day explain it as follows: the grub is the same or even worse, there are no parcels, and the shop privileges are limited and often withheld altogether; in the logging camps, the pits and the mines no con would have lasted even a season under present conditions, he'd go under. At least the work is human now. That's one thing. And the other is that there were millions stuck in the camps in those days, there was hardly anyone outside to help, and in any case how could they in those hungry days of the war and postwar period?

And there is a third reason which I will now explain.

If men aren't dying of starvation in the camps of Mordovia, this is because there exist all sorts of illegal, forbidden ways of getting hold of food. For the con here isn't shut up inside four walls like he is at Vladimir. Work truly saves the compound from hunger. And the reason is that all sorts of free workers also work at the factory, such as supervisors and foremen, and the lorries that bring loads into the compound are driven by drivers from outside. All these people also find it hard to make ends meet on the wages they get. Of course they are warned against us in various ways. We are said to be cut-throats and desperate criminals. But this sort of propaganda has little effect. When they mix with the cons the free workers soon see that the cons are just the same as they are, and that in general they think the same . . . Every one of them realises that if he were to speak his mind out loud he would be inside too, a con like all the rest.

Free workers value the opportunity to work in the compound because of the bonus they get on top of their wages. They get 15–20 per cent added on 'for danger' – a danger that is less than outside, where the workers can easily get blind drunk and end up by crippling or killing their foreman. So the bonus is prized. But even then the wages aren't high enough. And it is here that the possibility of trading with the prisoners arises, or speculating on the side, which is more profitable in camp than anywhere else you care to name. True, there's a danger of being not only fired but also arrested and charged. But on the other hand, how difficult it is to resist temptation!

The most profitable trade of all is in tea. It's easy to smuggle in – easier than butter or sugar – and the rake-off is big. For a packet of tea costing thirty-eight to forty copecks in the shop a con will pay a free worker from one and a half to two roubles. Ten packets means fifteen to twenty roubles of clear profit – as much as a foreman gets for five days' work in the factory. Once the tea is inside the compound it passes through several more hands, bringing a profit to each new trader.

A camp trader, say, buys some tea in bulk from one of the free workers and then splits it up and sells it to his friends in two and a half to three rouble packets. After that it becomes currency. One con has done a deal with a warder and when his wife comes she brings him thirty-odd pounds of foodstuffs (out of which the warder, of course, gets a bribe). Not only does he not starve himself. but he starts to barter his vegetables for tea, and the tea he sells to a 'dealer'. Another is himself a 'dealer' and sells his shop food for tea. And so on and so forth.

If the officers find out that some of the cons have tea, they will turn the whole zone upside down. And if they find any they put the owner in the cooler. But that, of course, doesn't stop anyone.

In our gang we had a prisoner called Konchakovsky. The whole camp knew that he traded in tea. He had an agreement with one of the drivers and the latter used to bring him about fifty packets at a time. Konchakovsky used to hide the tea in the work zone. He didn't sell it himself, though, but did it through an intermediary, Sanya the Beak (the exact double of the warder at Vladimir jail), who was also in our gang. Sanya would find a buyer among the cons and sell him a couple of packets, usually still in the work zone. That way there was no risk of being picked up during the search at roll-call and no loss through having the tea confiscated. And it was up to the buyer to smuggle it through without being caught. The most common method was to hide it in your boot, spread out over the whole sole. After all, they could hardly make everyone take his boots off at roll-call, otherwise they would need the whole day to search everyone, and when would the cons get their work done? And anyway the warders used to get bored and they too used to hustle while on duty. Sanya the Beak also used to take tea through to the living zone on occasion. The price was two to three roubles a packet (this depended on demand, but was never less than two roubles), while Konchakovsky paid the driver one and a half roubles a packet.

This group went on speculating over a period of several years, but still came to grief in the end. This happened in about 1963–4. Probably they were given away by some warder or officer whom they failed to bribe properly. Certainly such a major enterprise can't get by without bribes: the driver, for instance, bribes the warder at the gate and treats him to vodka or gives him presents.

As for the warders, it is difficult for them to resist. Sometimes they even complain to the prisoners themselves that although the work's not dirty and you're not likely to rupture yourself with it, still you have to eat and drink and feed the kids and the pay's not much. And even the officers, although they've got more to fear, are unable at times to resist temptation. Thus gradually a whole lot of people get to know about this commercial enterprise but keep quiet about it in return for a kick-back. If a lone prisoner with tea gets caught it's the cooler, but big speculators are left alone. And so it goes for as long as everyone is paid or until the participants fall out. Then somebody squeals, there's a search and the culprits are caught redhanded. Then comes the trial and a sentence for speculation. That, evidently, is how Konchakovsky's group came to grief.

Four of them were tried in court: Konchakovsky, Sanya the Beak, the driver and the shop assistant who had sold the tea to the driver and shared the rake-off with him (within the whole territory of Dubrovlag, shop assistants in the settlements were forbidden to sell more than one or two packets to one person at a time). All of them got three to five years of camp. Sanya and Konchakovsky, moreover, being sent to do theirs in a special regime camp. Konchakovsky came off worst of all: he had already done fourteen years out of a twenty-five-year sentence and had hoped to be released in a year owing to the reduction in the maximum. But now there could be no question of that: to his remaining eleven years they added a further four, bringing it up to a full fifteen. Thus having done fourteen and with fifteen still to go, he would have a total term of twenty-nine years! And now special regime too! Some price he paid for his tea and the benefits it brought with it – money, butter, sugar, vodka and the shortlived indulgence of the authorities.

In 1965 the warder Vasya Vasek came to grief by trading in tea. He was a really savage animal, he used to go to extremes during the searches, yet was himself a speculator. Probably his savagery was his undoing and one of the cons betrayed him for it. The only thing that happened to Vasek, however, was that he was dismissed from his job. Generally speaking, if one or other of the warders gets caught, they try not to bring charges in order to avoid publicity.

Vodka is also a profitable commodity – you make about five roubles clear profit on a pint. But it's harder to smuggle, of course, like tinned food. But nevertheless both manage to find their way into the compound by way of the free workers.

The camp bakeries and shops are also a great help. Wherever there's a bakery you can have enough bread – provided the money is there. The bakers (who are cons) always 'arrange' to have left-overs and these they sell. At camp seven, five two-pound loaves of black bread used to cost a rouble, or you could have three loaves of white bread (baked for outside) for the same. The cons would either settle up with the bakers when they bought it or else pay a sum in advance. I used to pay ten roubles in cash in advance and then take the bread when I needed it until I had used up my credit. The bakers used to share their profits with their civilian supervisor from outside.

The shop, too, always had a brisk trade going. The civilian who ran it always used to bring in more food than was necessary for the camp. He did it supposedly secretly. A share used to go to the quartermaster who let him bring his stuff into the zone, and then he also used to bribe the officers, who pretended they didn't know about it. And after that, of course, it was simple. At camp seven we had two selling points, the so-called shop and the buffet. Basically they were both the same and in both places the cons paid not cash but with vouchers (not in any circumstances is the con allowed to have money in his hands). The man selling the stuff was a civilian from outside, but the buffet keeper was a con and it was through him that trade was conducted – not in vouchers but in cash. All the food was three times as dear, of course, but what can the con do? He will pay five times the price if there's something going.

Where do prisoners get their money from? From outside, of course. You bring it back from a meeting with one of your family or in some other way. A whole host of stratagems have been thought up for doing this, but I won't describe them – let the cons go on using them for a bit. One thing only can be said: the screws knew how to look and we knew how to hide. Furthermore we have a fundamental interest in the matter, for us it's a question of life and death, whereas for them, when all's said and done, it's only a matter of duty.

In any case admin isn't really interested in cutting off all the streams of food and money into the compound from outside. A hungry con, a 'goner', is a poor worker, and who's going to keep the factory going then? If the plan's fulfilled the whole of admin is rewarded and that's not something you want to lose. Certainly not. That's why, in general, they hunt lazily, mainly to keep the con on tenterhooks and also to exhibit the necessary degree of diligence to their superiors. There are, of course, people who enjoy their work – these try their very best and work hard.

On the whole these camp fiddles keep everybody going. It

saves the cons from starving to death, helps hard-working civilians to feed their families and assures the bosses of a suitable standard of living.

And even the worst-off cons, those who receive nothing from outside and never take part in these trading deals, even they gain from them. For instance, there's no point in a man like Konchakovsky drinking his skilly every day and he's certainly not going to make a rush for a smelly sprat; sometimes he doesn't even finish his bread. And there are plenty like that in the camps. Maybe they aren't so rich as Konchakovsky, but they're still more or less comfortable, with a thing or two tucked away in their lockers. And so the penniless con gets hold of a spare helping of skilly, or sometimes even a spare bit of bread. One man I knew used to say: 'Yes, that way it's possible to live.'

But without these backdoor supplies strict regime would be just the same as Vladimir Prison or special regime.

One day, I remember, we had 'vinaigrette' for supper. Nobody ever refused this, not even a camp millionaire: it might be rotten underneath, but it had vegetables in it! We came back tired from unloading something, soaking wet, hungry as wolves, and at once rushed to the canteen. But the cooks always dish out vinaigrette strictly according to ration, because absolutely everybody eats it and there is never anything left. Two spoonfuls is the ration, no more. Kolya Yusupov looked into his bowl and went off the deep end: 'You work like an elephant and they feed you like a rabbit!' What use to him, this six-foot giant of a loader, were these two spoonfuls of silage and this blob of revolting sprat? It was as the cooks used to say: 'Be grateful that it's not like this every day. If everybody came to the canteen every day you wouldn't last longer than a couple of months before kicking the bucket.'

And that is the whole secret of the prisoner's existence today.

EVERYTHING HERE IS JUST LIKE OUTSIDE

The hut is chock-full of people, they've rounded up as many as can be found. Behind a table sits the presidium, the chairman is conducting a general meeting of the company. The presidium is made up of prisoners – beside them sit the company officers. Democracy! On the agenda are elections to the Council of the Collective. Does anyone have any proposals?

Some con or other gets to his feet and reads out a list, the assembled prisoners take yet one more yoke on their necks, for the benefit of admin, and go back to their work. But at least it's quick.

Another time there's a new craze: the men are proposed and elected one by one, with a 'discussion' of the candidates. The same tame prisoner gets up:

'I propose Ivanov. We all know him as an exemplary production worker of exemplary conduct. He takes an active part in the life of the collective (not camp! Such words are never uttered at meetings – we're nothing but a friendly collective, and that's all!) and he participates in amateur art activities.'

Literally the same thing, word for word, is said about Sidorov and Petrov, except that perhaps the wall newspaper takes the place of amateur art, or the IOS – Internal Order Section, or something else of that sort. And although 'we all know' that he was a *polizei** sentenced for bloody crimes, we all vote 'for' in order to get away as quickly as possible.

Why do we do it? The answer is simple. For in fact the candidates are proposed not by prisoners but by admin through its previously prepared stooges. Whether you want it or not,

---

* A collaborator who worked as a policeman under the German occupation.

the bosses will insist on getting their own way and only those
that admin wants will end up in the Council. On several occasions
it has happened that the voting machine 'seizes up' – the cons
refuse to vote for some complete rat. Then the company officer
stands up:

'You there, why are you refusing to vote for our activist?' he
will say to one of the uncooperative' cons.

'Because he's a grass, a rat and as slippery as an eel.'

'It doesn't matter, it's not going to be the way you want it
but the way I want it,' replies the candid officer. And he drags
the meeting out *ad infinitum* until they elect the ones he has
chosen.

Anyway, what difference does it make who you elect to the
Council? It is never allowed to act of its own volition, to go
against the decision of admin, to refuse to carry out its demands:
it acts under admin's control and admin always has the right to
dissolve a Council it disapproves of or to expel any con from its
membership. Thus this organisation hasn't even a semblance of
self-government, nor indeed a semblance of anything. Everyone
knows that the Council of a company or camp collective is
nothing but a willing instrument, a bludgeon in the hands of the
authorities, and with the aid of this bludgeon the authorities can
terrorise any prisoner they want – and make it look as though
it's by the will of the other prisoners. It may be that this
produces an impression outside the camp that, say, the prisoners
themselves have insisted on their comrade being punished.
Inside the camp, however, everybody knows exactly what this
means.

There are also idealists among us who say: 'Look at us. We
chose these scum ourselves and then complain. We need to
have decent men in the Council' – and they volunteer to join.
Sometimes admin doesn't object: come what may the Council
will do what it's told to do, while on the other hand the cons
can't keep needling them with: 'You've only got *polizeis* and
creeps on the Council.' How does it all end? With the rout of
the idealists, as usual: either they themselves seize on the first
pretext to leave the Council or else they are simply expelled.

The function of this organ is an extremely unsavoury one.

Every single decision it takes is a blow against the prisoners, either all together or some of them individually. One day it's a decision to repair and redecorate the huts in the cons' spare time – so when you've finished your eight hours of compulsory slavery you can use your free time to build a prison for yourself and others. Another day they discuss and condemn somebody's behaviour and force another man to work beyond his strength, knowing that he is sick and not in a condition to maintain his norm. And how does such a discussion end? 'We beg the administration to deprive such and such a prisoner of shop privileges and parcels, to place him on a reduced quota of nourishment and to confine him to a punishment cell.' When jailers do this sort of thing it is at least understandable, but who among the prisoners will consent to condemn his comrade to starvation? Only swine of the lowest possible kind!

And so you get a situation that is the only one acceptable to the authorities and yet for all that very ugly: the Council of the collective is actually made up almost exclusively of former *polizeis*. Earlier they collaborated with the fascists and now with the administration of our camps for political prisoners – after all, it's all the same to them, as long as they can have a quiet life and get out as soon as possible. Even outside they manage to get on better than the rest: they are released with excellent character references, all the official organisations help them, they take a careful look round, adapt themselves – and prosper. They might even make the grade as minor bosses somewhere.

When you say to a company officer: 'Just look at who's working with you!' he starts to squirm like an eel in a frying pan. And truly it's embarrassing. We don't, of course, know about all the members of the Council or what they were sentenced for (and we wouldn't be interested in the first place if they were to behave themselves decently). But then one day the court comes to re-examine their sentences, if they've 'earned' it. These sessions are open. And at this point it emerges that one 'activist' collaborated with the Nazis, another worked on a special punishment squad, and a third was in the same business.

Thus I learned accidentally at camp ten that the chairman of the Council of our company collective had also been an 'activist' in a Nazi death camp. During the trial he broke down and wept. 'I didn't do anything wrong, I only opened and closed the crematorium doors.' God knows, maybe he really wasn't a traitor there, but merely served so as not to go to the gas chamber himself . . .

What goes for the Council of the collective is equally true of the IOS – it has the same reputation, the same composition and the same aims: to assist admin terrorise their fellow prisoners. And the reward for this is the same: parcels, a good reference – 'responding favourably to corrective training'. The IOS is the Internal Order Section, the camp militia. The same as the 'Kapos', the prisoners chosen to police the others, in the Nazi concentration camps.

Perhaps someone who doesn't know may be wondering what is wrong with the prisoners maintaining order among themselves, after all you get upsets and fights in camp, and brawls and drunkenness – and there are criminals there too. But the chief function of the IOS is not to maintain order, but to keep watch over and spy on the prisoners and to inform the authorities on who says what and who has forbidden contacts with outside. And again to deprive the con of his shop, parcels and visits, or rather, to 'beg the administration to deprive . . .'

The members of IOS wear a red armband on duty with the three letters printed on it, and not long ago a new rule was introduced: now they must constantly wear a red diamond on their tunic or reefer jacket, because the armband is only for when they are on duty – and when a warder in the zone has to identify his faithful aides in a hurry it is usually too late – after all, they serve out of fear, not conviction.

All the bosses, especially higher up, are very proud of themselves: everything here in camp is just like outside – self-government, the prisoners are being reformed, they keep order themselves, how's that for putting faith in the prisoners? Maybe they've forgotten about the 'Kapos'. Maybe they don't know how prisoners are recruited for the Council and the IOS? Maybe they don't know, higher up, who it is that enters these camp organisations? The camp administration knows perfectly well – these are the same 'Kapos' and *polizeis*, and the percentage of 'reformed prisoners' depends directly on the number of skunks in the zone.

The prisoners loathe them. Seeing the red diamond with the letters IOS on it they say: 'Ah, the skunk has come out for a stroll!' (and on top of that you get a badge – you put it on, sell yourself, everybody turns away from you and there's no way back). But resisting a con with an armband is punishable in just the same way as resisting a warder – you end up in court. Just like outside.

A MORDOVIAN IDYLL

In the autumn they started driving us out under a double armed escort to pick potatoes. We went willingly – who knows, maybe we would get to eat a baked potato if the guards turned out to be human and didn't stamp out the fire. Only cons nearing the end of their sentences were allowed to go, that way there was less danger of escapes. One day I went along too.

Leaving the compound for the first time in two years I looked at the free life outside as at a totally different and forgotten world: houses along the streets, free people, free horses, non-working dogs (excluding the ones guarding our column, of course), chickens scratching in the dust. There was a sign outside a club: 'Dancing'. Good God, do you mean to say that here, no more than a hundred yards from our huts, people are dancing, listening to music, making love?

We passed some schoolboys carrying satchels. They skipped past our column without even looking at us, coolly made their way past men who were being guarded by tommy gunners and dogs. It was clear that the local people had long been used to such a spectacle . . .

There was the club itself, a squat, ramshackle structure on a crumbling foundation. And next to it the camp commander's mansion, looking particularly sumptuous in comparison with the miserable cottages surrounding it. All around it ran a high fence and there was a gate with a sign on it: 'Beware of the dog'.

'What's he got the sign for?' quipped one of the cons, 'All he needs to put is the master's name – that in itself would keep everyone away.'

PEU – SINGING, DANCING AND SPORT

From time immemorial, from the days of Stalin's camps, there have been 'spontaneous activities' in camp. Who knows, perhaps they really were spontaneous once upon a time, men gathered together and sang and read poetry. They say they even used to act in little plays, put on shows and perform operettas. They say the theatre in Vorkuta even came into being as a result of this kind of spontaneous activities. It existed first of all independently and then under the patronage and supervision of the CEU – the Cultural Education Unit, whose organisers placed more faith in the cons than in themselves where questions of art were concerned.

Now it is no longer the CEU but the PEU – Political Education Unit – and it doesn't so much patronize the arts as control them and run them. And in general it's no longer a spontaneous activity but a form of forced labour – another one to add to the extra work you have to do.

And why is this? Not one concert programme can get by without the help of the PEU. 'Help', did I say? The PEU runs the damn thing from start to finish! And you're lucky if, between the anthems and the marches, you can squeeze in a lyrical song or two, a romance, or a poem by Pushkin, Blok, or Esenin. In the first place a concert is supposed to 'educate' its listeners; in the second it is supposed to offer evidence that the participants have been fully 'reformed'; and in the third it has to please the commission and help our camp 'outspit' its neighbours in the competition (and how do you do that? – 'The golden grove was ablaze'* is problematical, you don't know whether it's good or

* A poem by Esenin.

bad, it depends on your taste, but 'Lines on my Soviet passport'*
is absolutely bound to please everybody without question);
fourthly, the concert itself just might as well not take place, to
hell with it, but you need a tick in the right place on the report.
This it is that determines everything: the programme, the people
who take part and the attitude of the cons to 'spontaneous
activities'.

And so the company officer starts recruiting people for the
choir or the poetry-reading circle. Some he approaches himself,
others are called into his office. One is promised a parcel,
another a good character reference (when I say 'promised a
parcel' I don't mean that he gets some sort of extra parcel – no,
I mean his lawful, regular one, which he still has to 'earn'). The
poetry lover answers: 'To whom would it occur to sing on an
empty stomach?' And the master of diction replies: 'Get fucked
with your amateur activities before dinner.' There are some,
though, who agree. A few for the parcel, but this makes an
unreliable group, and too slippery: a man turns up to all the
rehearsals, gets his parcel – and you can't get him on the stage
whatever you do. The basic membership of the choir and similar
groups is made up of cons with twenty-five-year terms – they
hope to get known, earn themselves good character references
before they go to court, and then maybe their sentences will be
cut.

And so a concert is announced. The next job for the warders
and educationalists is to round up an audience. And here they
really get on their high horses when the necessity arises. Why
aren't you going to the concert? Sick? Have you got a doctor's
certificate? Oh, so you don't want to go? Why not? You don't
like it? What don't you like? You won't answer? But the con is
bound to answer for he is obliged to be polite to all representatives of admin and the camp security services. Violation! One,
two, three such violations and your shop privileges are stopped
– not for not attending the concert, oh no, that's a voluntary
matter, but for 'disrespect to . . .'

Newcomers go to the concerts – out of curiosity. I too went

* A poem by Mayakovsky.

along several times to get an eyeful. What a joke! If the PEU chief, Major Sveshnikov, had specifically wanted to demoralise the cons with negative propaganda, he couldn't possibly have bettered this. On the stage a choir of policemen sings 'The Party is our Helmsman' and 'Lenin is always with You'. From the auditorium come loud guffaws and whistling. The warders bellow: 'You'll get the cooler for interrupting the programme!' The choir, even though it's full of old men, sings loudly to drown the racket in the audience. And pretty much in tune – they are mostly Ukrainians and Ukrainians know how to sing. What do they sing? Once they gave a rendering of 'Buchenwald Alarm', but for some reason admin didn't like this very much.

It's the same story with sporting arrangements. Force is applied (moral, of course – the same parcels and references) to get the cons to join the sports sections, where they are obliged to participate in athletics tournaments. When you see these sporting competitions you don't know whether to laugh or cry.

Old men, all but legless already, run up and down or leap about the 'stadium' (no more and no less – under the sensitive leadership of Camp Commander Pivkin the parade ground was turned into a stadium; camp eleven has its 'Pivkins' too), their skinny, crooked legs with knotted veins clothed in baggy shorts and their mouths gasping for air. Having run the required distance, they are checked off by the company officer and hurry off to their bunks to lie down and rest a bit.

On the other hand, what singers and guitarists there really are in the camps! Sometimes we'd get together in the evenings after work, in some corner of the compound, and what songs we'd strike up – underground songs and old ballads, all accompanied by the guitar. Once the Estonians organised a concert of their folk music. And we had literary evenings – in honour of Shevchenko or Herzen. Somebody would talk about the writer and others would read Shevchenko's poetry in Ukrainian. Yet others would read their own poetry or translations into Russian. But all this, of course, went on not only separately from the PEU but in secret from admin – at such evenings, after all, each man said what he thought and read what he wanted.

There were even more amateur sportsmen who were genuine

and admin usually left them alone and didn't persecute them. I myself went in for soccer and there were also lovers of table tennis and skating. The basketball always used to attract large numbers of spectators; there were high class teams of Lithuanians, Latvians and Estonians, lads who were the pick of the camp, young, tall and agile. The only thing was that they all had shaven heads . . .

PIS – POLITICAL INSTRUCTION SESSIONS

At seven o'clock in the evening the canteen closes and the cons working on the first shift wander out all over the compound. The time from now until lights out is our own. Some go to the library, some to the volleyball court, some sit in the hut and write letters home, domino fans settle down around some table or other, friends gather to talk or argue, and some simply walk up and down inside the fence on their own – a hundred yards in one direction and then about turn and back again – eyes down and thinking about something.

But today is Thursday, the day of our political instruction session. At seven on the dot every single man has to be back in his hut: attendance at the political instruction sessions is one of the con's most important duties. Nevertheless, everybody does what he can to slip out of this duty. What's the good of it, what's the use of it? Just sit there like an idiot and listen to your company officer, stammering and stumbling over every other word, as he reads you a regulation 'lecture' from previously prepared notes in an exercise book. The majority of the company officers are completely uneducated, particularly the older ones, and are not able to prepare even this sort of talk on their own – and anyway they wouldn't be trusted to: who knows what they mightn't blurt out in their ignorance? Each talk is prepared by Sveshnikov himself. Before each session he dictates it to the company officers, who painstakingly copy it down in their exercise books (I can just imagine how many grammatical mistakes there are in those notes!) and then interpret it to us.

What do we get from such a talk? We are all quite capable of reading and understanding the newspapers ourselves, the clichés and slogans there have long since tired and sickened us,

dating from when we were still free. The majority of the prisoners have completed high school, many of them also had a
higher education and have doctoral dissertations to their name,
men who have learned to think independently, who have made
special studies of philosophy and the works of Marx, Lenin,
Hegel, Kant and contemporary philosophers and sociologists:
willy-nilly, 'politicians'.

It's sheer farce when the company officer, repeating somebody else's words parrot-fashion and unable to make head or
tail of his own notes, conducts a political discussion with them
on the level of class four in school. And in our camp, which was
a political camp, even the criminal cons knew and understood
more than the company officers, for they would listen to the
conversations of the other prisoners and join in their arguments.
I myself entered the camps completely ignorant. I had had only
eight years of schooling and the most I could say was that I tried
to think for myself, without prompting. But once I decided to
sort out what was what, why should I want to listen to the
company officer's burblings? I had read the whole of Lenin,
volume by volume, and was now starting on Plekhanov.

Having been along a few times out of curiosity, I didn't go to
political instruction sessions any more and for this I was constantly having my shop privileges taken away. During the whole
of my time inside I was only allowed a single parcel.

I remember my first chat with the company officer on this
theme. Alyoshin called me into his office:

'Sit down. Marchenko, you've only just come back to the
camp from prison and you're already breaking the camp rules.
Why? You were transferred from prison before your term was
up, weren't you? Are you in a hurry to go back there and get a
sniff of the sloptank?'

I replied that I saw nothing in these talks that was interesting
or useful to me. Then, seeing that I couldn't be swayed by
threats, he attempted another tack:

'The others go! Do you consider that you're cleverer than the
others? That you know everything already?'

'No, I don't think at all that I know everything already. On
the contrary, I know too little, and that's why I value my time.

I have never considered myself cleverer than the others. But I'm certainly no more stupid than the people who run the sessions. The fact that others go is their own affair. I decide for myself and I'll carry on deciding.'

Alyoshin started telling me that attendance at political instruction sessions was obligatory. I could go and not listen if I liked, so long as I came and sat for the regulation two hours. But like it or not, I would be forced to give in: 'If you don't give in I'll punish you.'

'Of course I don't mind going to the sessions now and again just to see this comedy for myself, but – compulsorily every week? Under duress? I didn't ask to come to this camp of yours and I don't want you to "educate" me. What's more I'm a political prisoner, maybe I have my own opinions, my own point of view on facts and events, maybe I'm an idealist, a religious man. After all, it's not a discussion you're inviting me to. If I begin to say what I think at your talks you always answer me with threats of force – the cooler, a new trial, prison!'

In short, prisoners are driven to the political instruction sessions by threats of punishment. If you don't go – no shop, no parcel, visits are cut short, you get a bad character reference: '. . . persists in his errors, isn't responding to corrective training . . .' So that only those who value their parcels or references go 'voluntarily'. But the majority of prisoners in the camp have nothing to lose: they've already been deprived of the shop for something else; their next visit's not due for a long time – next year; they've still a long way to go until their term is half over, so there's no hope of having any parcels; they're in admin's bad books anyway, so the character reference has gone to the devil; and they've just got to sweat it out from bell to bell, because only the cons with twenty-five years can hope to get their sentences cut. Cons such as these don't go. But it is essential for everyone to go, the company officers are required to ensure a hundred per cent participation in political education. And you can't blow up the figures in your report – Sveshnikov himself might come round at any moment, or another officer squeal on you. And so you have to tie yourself up in knots all the time.

. . . Ten to seven. They close the library at this time on

Thursdays and drive everyone out of the reading room. But on the volleyball court the ball is still flying from end to end, the dominoes are still clicking on the domino table and cons are strolling about here and there. The door of the staff offices opens and a crowd of about thirty company officers comes spilling out into the compound. They are on their way to 'catch' their cons. Warders are running about the compound winkling cons out of various secluded corners. Several officers approach the volleyball court:

'Stop the game, it's time for political instruction!'

Nobody answers and the game continues. The cons appear to be deaf. Then one of the officers or warders runs up to the player with the ball.

'Give it to me!'

The con silently tosses the ball to another con. The officer goes across to him but the ball is already being held by a third. And so it goes on until it reaches the most timid con. He himself won't take the ball over to the officer, but now they have taken it away so what is to be done? The warders lose no time in dragging the culprits off to the cooler – not for refusing to attend the political instruction session but quite legally for insubordination to an officer.

The same thing happens with the domino players. 'Stop the game! Give me the dominoes!' And it ends the same way: the officer scoops up the dominoes from the table and several men are dispatched to the cooler.

At last they've rounded up everyone they can find; and some have come themselves. The session begins. The officer mumbles into his beard, following his notes, while the cons occupy themselves in various ways – finishing off letters or reading books. The officer tries not to notice this. Only if they read or write openly in the front row does he suggest to them that they move farther back, so that Sveshnikov doesn't see them should he happen to come in. Sometimes this responsible job – reading out the notes or a newspaper article, or an article from the magazine 'Kommunist' – is entrusted to one of the 'activist' cons so as to give the appearance of prisoner participation in the political instruction sessions. These activists usually turn out to be semi-illiterate old men who can barely read, so that corrective work is hardly possible. And on extremely rare occasions the company officer steels himself to ask someone a question on the subject of the previous week's session. But whom? That one over there is no good, he's illiterate and can't string two words together; and that one's even worse – he's too literate.

On the other hand the cons themselves, having been forcibly driven to the session, often pepper their instructor with questions of their own, mainly about material matters. 'You say that we have to live honestly without deceiving the state, but how can a family get by on fifty to seventy roubles a month? What salary do you get? You just mentioned the increasing prosperity of the workers – how do you relate the concept of "increasing prosperity" to the rise in food prices and the raising of the norms in industry?'

This last question was asked by Kolya Yusupov one day when I was there. Our company officer was lost for words and then said: 'You, Yusupov, misunderstand our political situation. You purposely draw attention to individual shortcomings which are only temporary.' All the cons laughed and I asked:

'How long does your "temporary" last and on what time scale is it to be calculated? We know, for instance, that the decree on censorship was accepted as a "temporary" measure and even for a "short time" only. That was approximately fifty years ago and the censorship is still with us . . .'

'Your sentence was too short, Marchenko, it ought to be extended. And there are one or two more here, I see, who would like a spell in the cooler!'

'We're convinced, we're convinced!' roared the cons boisterously.

The session ended and the cons dispersed, cursing all 'instructors' and 'propagandists' to kingdom come. Everybody laughs at them, even the grasses.

BIG BOSSES AND LITTLE BOSSES

> Power comes from the people . . .
> But on what does it feed?
> Where does it lead?
> What does it breed?
>   Bertolt Brecht – *Songs*

As soon as word goes round that Gromov is on his way to the camp there's a terrible hustle and bustle. It's no joke – Gromov in person! The camp commandant runs in circles and hustles the company officers, these hustle the warders and the lot of them together, of course, hustle the cons. There is a general clean-up, an exhaustive search of the huts and you start to overfulfil all norms. Are you sneaking off work? The cooler! Are you improperly dressed, has your hair grown a couple of centimetres? Haircut! No shop privileges!

Gromov is feared like the plague – and by everyone: free workers, officers, even the camp commander; and also the local inhabitants. In all the settlements from Potma to Barashevo, in all the camps – male and female, criminal and political, special regime, normal regime, strict regime – everyone trembles at the mere mention of Gromov's name. He can do anything, he is a feudal prince in these parts. Colonel Gromov is Commander-in-Chief of the whole of Dubrovlag. And the main thing is that you never know what he is going to praise you for and what will cause him to blow up. It can happen that what inspires his gratitude the first time will bring a tongue-lashing the next.

Here he comes now, leaving the staff offices at camp seven for the compound. He is accompanied by a deferential retinue consisting of aides from HQ and the camp bosses. The officers divide their time between casting apprehensively obsequious glances in Gromov's direction and glaring at us cons – there mustn't be any violations or disturbances. Nevertheless they aren't watchful enough. Right outside the offices an old man, leaning on a stick, comes up to Gromov and starts telling him something. Whether he is complaining or perhaps asking for something I can't hear. All I can hear is Gromov snapping at the camp commander: 'This won't do!', before moving on impassively.

Confusion overtakes the retinue. One of the company officers goes up to the old man and scolds him in a loud voice:

'Why didn't you say so earlier? Come to my office tomorrow and we'll sort it out for you.'

The old man, thanking the officer profusely, hobbles away in the direction of his hut. At that moment Gromov turns and roars:

'Where? I said to the cooler with him, the cooler! This won't do! You've let your prisoners get out of hand, they won't even let me pass! Why didn't you make it clear that he should register to see me when I'm receiving prisoners and should come at the proper time?'

While he thus dresses our camp bosses down, two warders run up to the old man, snatch his stick from his hand, throw it away and drag the poor fellow straight off to the cooler – and he has just been overjoyed to think that Gromov had interceded for him.

Gromov came to us another time because our plan was on the rocks. He must have really blown up the staff inside, because when Ageyev scrambled out into the zone behind Gromov he was as red as a beet. He had been ordered to send all the invalids to the factory, that is those cons who were unfit for work but somehow managed to do little jobs around the living zone, acting as orderlies, keeping the compound clean and so on. For a beginning there was to be a general muster of invalids, they were to be rounded up into a single hut for a meeting to be held. Gromov was giving instructions as he walked and Ageyev, absolutely quaking with fear, was running alongside and asking:

'Comrade Colonel, what shall we do with the bed-ridden? Carry them to the meeting or leave them?'

'Carry out your orders, major!'

And so it was everywhere, no matter where he appeared. The officers would scurry about with their eyes bulging out of their sockets, petrified with fear, and punishments would rain down on us poor cons from right and left. When Gromov used to come to us (much later) in the hospital at camp eight, Major Petrushevsky himself, the Chief of the Dubrovlag Medical Department, who used to pack medical orderlies off to the cooler in droves – the windows were all dusty, there were cobwebs in the corners and coal was falling out of the stove – Petrushevsky himself used to trot at Gromov's heels and then look sideways into his eyes to see whether he was angry or satisfied. And it goes without saying that a day or two before Gromov's arrival we orderlies were transferred from our blocks back to the communal huts – God forbid that he should ever discover that the con orderlies were living two and three to a room: what luxury, maybe they'd like to have separate flats or their wives sent out to them?

One day Gromov came to the hospital with a commission from Moscow – representing the Ministry of the Interior. The commission proceeded through the wards, the doctors answered questions, the director of the hospital, as usual in Gromov's presence, smiled ingratiatingly, nodded her head and hastened to agree with everything he said. Nobody, of course, even looked at the cons – patients and orderlies – or asked them any questions. But in one ward the patients spoke up for themselves, complaining that it was cold. Gromov didn't deign to answer them. But a visiting colonel, taking a look at the thermometer on the wall (it was fifteen degrees in the ward), went over to one of the bunks: 'Who are you, where from, what's your name, what were you sentenced for?'

The patient replied. He had an ulcer and had only just been brought in from the camp in a very serious condition. His name was Sikk, he was from one of the Baltic states and he was in for 'nationalism'. After hearing all this the Moscow colonel shouted so that the whole block could hear:

'And you have the nerve to complain that you're cold! People like you should be kept out in the snow, and not in hospital! The whole lot of you Baltic people are enemies and gangsters! You fought against us with weapons in your hands and now you're asking us to coddle you!'

He went on bellowing like that for ages. Gromov stood there the whole time completely calmly, without interfering, and in no way hurrying to support his superior. On the whole he always behaved independently and didn't suck up to anyone.

On the other hand he found an excuse on this occasion to pick on another prisoner, a doctor's assistant named Ryskov. Ryskov was not a bad fellow, a Moscow journalist and poet, though physically not very strong. For that reason some of his friends among the cons had helped him to get light work in the hospital, as a doctor's assistant (he had had some medical training). It seemed to Gromov that Ryskov held himself with a dignity not prescribed for a con – and he answered questions without a hint of servility. He called Ryskov into the office and questioned him as to who and what he was and why he was here in the hospital. Ryskov replied that he worked there.

'Why do you talk so provocatively to your superiors?'

'I don't talk provocatively, but simply the way I do to everyone else.'

There was nothing to pick on and nothing to justify the cooler. Nevertheless, Ryskov was sent back to camp with the next convoy, to do general work. In such cases there's no point in asking why. Admin knows best, admin makes its own arrangements.

Gromov has been serving in labour camps for a very long time, ever since the time of Stalin. In those days he was commander of a camp that was building an oil refinery at Omsk. In Mordovia you can still meet cons who used to work in that camp. I shared a cell with one who had been foreman there. Listening to his stories used to make your blood run cold. Anyway, it's well known what camps were like in Stalin's time, in the fifties! And now Gromov was in command not just of one camp, but of the directorate of a whole network, with dozens of camps under his control. The methods had changed a bit, but he himself was still the same and just the same despot that he had always been. All that had changed was that he had gone up in rank and was now a colonel. Doubtless he would be a general by the time he retired.

On the whole a great many camp personnel had toppled from their posts since Beria was shot in 1953. The lower ranks had been simply dismissed or demoted. To the bigger (and older) fish it was suggested that they accept an early retirement and these retreated with their fat pensions for a well-earned rest in the Crimea, cultivating vineyards confiscated from the Crimean Tartars. But even those dismissed or demoted former MVD* men managed to set themselves up in comfortable little jobs, with good rates of pay, in or around the remaining camps. They became production managers, supply managers, warders and even just foremen – anything to get back into a camp where you were paid not for the work you did but for squeezing cons to the very last drop. They settled in there and bided their time. They were confident that their experience would be needed again, that they would be recalled. And they were right.

They themselves will admit that they received in some cases advice, in others instructions, from 'above' to send in official complaints and petitions asking to be restored to their posts and for their good name to be rehabilitated. Naturally each of them wrote that he had served faithfully and honourably, that he had been slandered and treated unjustly, that he had never exceeded his powers but had acted only on orders from above, and that he promised to do the same in the future. Slowly and on the sly they began to be restored to their posts and to return to their favourite form of work. They took out their uniforms – which hadn't yet had time to fade – and again appeared in the roles of camp commanders, company officers and aides at Dubrovlag HQ.

Former members of Stalin's cadres at camp seven included the Commander, Kolomitsev, and his deputy, Ageyev. One of

---

* Ministry of Internal Affairs. Beria used it to consolidate his position after Stalin's death by fusing it with the Ministry of State Security, but the security service was separated from the MVD after Beria's downfall.

our company officers for a time, after Alyoshin and Lubayev, was a former lieutenant-colonel who had been reduced to the ranks and subsequently rehabilitated. A con who had been imprisoned in Mordovia since 1949 told me about the Chief Officer's deputy at camp seven, Shved: that Shved had taken an active part in the mass shootings of cons while they were on parade. At that time they used to lead all captured Ukrainian 'secessionists' into the forest, ostensibly to gather firewood, and then gun the whole column down under the pretext of an 'organised mass escape'. Thus the cons knew that if they were taken out to gather firewood there would be no return. And the cons on parade started refusing to go into the forest. Shved, who was then a major, used to go up to the prisoners who refused and shoot them point blank with his revolver – the con who told me this had seen it with his own eyes. Shved was later dismissed and reduced to the ranks, but afterwards returned to work in the camps, although without his former rank.

In my time he was merely a senior sergeant, although already pushing fifty. He was an extremely brawny Ukrainian, calm and leisurely in his movements, with a singsong Ukrainian accent (about which we always teased our Ukrainians: look, we said, you're always complaining about 'big brother' Russians taking it out on you here in Mordovia, but what about this beloved countryman of yours? He makes mincemeat of both you and us, without distinction). Shved was short, stocky, round-faced and bullnecked and both his face and his neck were always red – the cons said it was from the amount of our blood he had drunk, like a bedbug. In so far as he was deputy to the Chief Officer he wielded great power. And he used to do everything he could to make life unpleasant for us.

We in the stand-by gang used to have to go to the work zone three or four times every day, and sometimes even more. As soon as the wagons were brought up for loading or unloading we would have to go out – day-time, night-time, at any time of the day or night and in all weathers. And so Shved thought himself up a little amusement: long before the wagons were ready, Shved would call us out to the guardhouse. When we arrived there would be no warder – he had gone off to the work zone to hunt for 'malingerers' who might be sleeping in odd corners during working hours. We would hang around, growing steadily more irritable, and a whole hour or more would go by before we could get to work. Having done our stint and unloaded the wagons, we would set off 'home' again – and again the same thing would happen, we would have to wait for more than an hour, come rain, come snow, standing by the guardhouse gate. All this when we might easily be called out again in another three to four hours! Shved would come out of the guardhouse to gloat. And when we complained would reply:

'What can Shved do? I can't tear the warder in two so that one half goes looking for shirkers and the other half stays in the guardhouse. We're short of warders, you're costing the state too much already.'

One evening I was called to the guardroom to see Shved: during one of the searches a civilian cap had been found under my pillow. That meant I faced an explanation and most likely punishment.

After knocking on the door, I entered the office. Shved was sitting there playing draughts with a warder. Two more warders were just sitting around. They glanced at me and went on playing. I just stood there. After about three minutes had passed, Shved tore himself away from the board: 'Company?' I replied. There was silence again and then, after another move: 'Gang?' Again a pause, a move and then the question: 'Surname?' I answered the questions and stood there waiting.

At last the game finished. Shved had won and beamed with gratification. He carefully packed the pieces into their box and then, before turning his attention to me, spoke to the warder: 'Slip down to the visitors' hostel and put an end to that visit there, he's had long enough. And tell Tarasova she's not to let any food through, not even an ounce. Then bring the prisoner here – I'll search him.' (Shved usually searched the cons himself after visits – either he didn't trust the warders or else he just loved the work.) Then he turned to me:

'Do you know what you've been brought here for? Do you want to guess?'

'Why should I guess? You'll tell me yourself.'

'What are you doing with a cap of a civilian model? What have you thought up to answer?'

I hadn't time to reply before the other con was brought in from his visit – an old man of about sixty. Shved stood up, went over to him and said banteringly:

'Well, grandad, did you hold the old woman's tits for a bit?'

The old man was lost for words for a moment, but then nevertheless responded:

'That's all over for me, I'm too old.'

'You should have called me if you couldn't manage it yourself. I would have come down and done her a favour.'

'Yes, but she's an old woman too . . .'

'It doesn't matter if she's old. I wouldn't have turned my nose up at her. What's your score?'

'Eleven years to go.'

Shved burst out laughing.

'You mean you hope to live another eleven years? I'm not talking about your sentence, blockhead – how old are you, I said. Never mind, let me search you.'

Shved removed the 'Cuban' from the old man's head, felt it all over, seam by seam, and then laid it to one side. Meanwhile the old man had already taken off his tunic. Feeling it carefully, Shved asked in friendly fashion:

'Tell me right away, grandad, how much money have you got on you?'

'What money? I haven't got even a rouble. Once a year the old lady's allowed to come and she can't even give me a lump of sugar.'

Shved replied just as good-humouredly: 'It's nothing to do with me. The law's the law. If the law says a prisoner's not allowed to have sugar, lard and other kinds of food then that's the way it has to be. The law has to be obeyed. If Shved's told tomorrow that parcels are allowed, Shved will let a whole wagon-load in.'

My skin used to crawl at the tone of his voice and those abominable jokes. 'The law's the law . . . If Shved's told not to send the cons out to work, Shved won't send them . . .' I could see him so vividly intoning these sayings of his, pacing up and down with his revolver on parade, that my fists clenched involuntarily.

Shved had already felt his grey undershirt all over and ordered the old man to take off his boots. Grunting and groaning, the old man removed his felt knee-boots and gave one to the sergeant. The latter groped around inside the boot, found nothing there, took out the inner sole, examined it and pinched the leg of the boot – there was nothing. Just as calmly he examined the second boot and when he fished out the inner sole his face lit up with a happy smile: a ten-rouble note had been glued to the under-side. Shved started to shame the old man:

'And you said you had no money on you! An old man, a Christian too, no doubt – aren't you ashamed of telling lies?'

The old man was silent, he had been caught red-handed, there was nothing he could say. Shved meticulously peeled the note from the inner sole, smoothed it out, laid it on the table and went on with his search. He felt the trousers that the old man had just taken off, ordered him to drop his underpants, turn round, turn back again and squat on his haunches (in doing which the old man almost toppled over) and then examined the underpants. There was nothing else hidden anywhere. But Shved was pleased: he knew that no con would come away from a visit empty-handed – they were all the same, all swindlers and liars!

With relish he wrote out a report, signed it, gave it to the warders to sign and then ordered one of them to give the ten roubles back to the old woman and get her to sign for them. The old man, meanwhile, was already getting dressed and mumbling something about being allowed to have no food and no money, not even if you were dying of starvation.

But Shved had already lost all interest in the old man and after rapping back at him as he walked away: 'I'll deal with you later' turned his attention to me. Evidently he was now 'tired' of working, for he told me curtly that he would write out a report on me and hand it to the Chief Officer, let him deal with it and punish me himself.

'You can go.'

The old man and I left the guardroom together. When we had

gone some way from the guardhouse I took the old man to task: how was it he hadn't found a better place in which to hide his ten roubles? The old man grinned cunningly:

'It wasn't me who was diddled, it was Shved.'

And he explained to me where the trick lay. His visit had been from his wife and son-in-law, and his son-in-law had already knocked around a bit – including ten years spent in the camps at Kolyma. His wife, too, had left the camps only five years beforehand and they were both well used to such visits. While still at home the son-in-law had concealed twenty-five roubles in the heel of one of his boots and here had exchanged boots with the old man.

'These are my son-in-law's boots. We knew Shved was bound to suspect I had money hidden somewhere, so we put the tenner in the sole on purpose. He's pleased as punch with himself and I've got something to add to my regular fiver.'

After so many years, how could he fail to learn how to pull a fast one on the screws?

The marketing director of the furniture factory at camp seven was Chekunov. They said that earlier he had worked for the MVD but was later demoted. We, however, only knew of him from work, for it was with him that we in the standby gang had to deal: he was in charge of the loading and authorised our worksheets. He and the chief of the timber yard (for unloading) constituted our immediate bosses at the factory and on them depended our work and our pay.

This Chekunov not only never let the least bit of extra pay through on to the worksheets, but would even refuse to pay us for work done. For instance we used to push both full and empty wagons from place to place by hand – it was heavy work, but we never got a penny for it. Not only that but Chekunov even used to sermonize: 'What, do you expect to get money from the state for nothing? To squander the people's wealth, plunder the state? I as a Communist am guarding the people's property!'

And suddenly there came a rumour: Chekunov's been caught for misappropriation, Chekunov's going to be tried. It turned out that he had been writing off good furniture as defective; after first setting himself up, he had supplied all the officers of

Dubrovlag with furniture on the cheap and all the representatives of local government absolutely free. And in general he had been up to various machinations with defective goods: whenever furniture came back after being damaged in transit, he would write it off as defective, then get the cons to repair it and send it out again as new. I think that's how it was, or maybe he found some other way of lining his pockets, but in any case he was a natural swindler. Somewhere or other along the line, though, he failed to share with the Party boss, the latter then informed on him and thus our Chekunov was awaiting his trial.

We celebrated too soon, however. It didn't come to a trial initially; all he got was a strict reprimand from the Party. And the Party chief was thanked for his vigilance. Once again Chekunov returned to the ranks of the bosses, once again we had to listen to his ranting: 'Sitting on your arses at the people's expense?' And a little later the Party Chief was removed and transferred elsewhere.

But evidently he wouldn't rest and wrote a letter to Moscow – not only about Chekunov this time but also about his cronies, who were covering up for him. Willy-nilly the local authorities had to take the matter up properly. Chekunov was their man through and through, but it was better not to tangle with Moscow. He was relieved of his post and charged. But they didn't stick him in jail before the trial, like the rest of us, but left him at liberty while the case was being investigated. He covered his tracks, did deals with the witnesses, shot his furniture off to various friends. And he also came to the camp, to the work zone, to talk to us in the stand-by gang – but of course in quite a different tone from before, politely and even kindly, insisting on the conversation himself, so that it was clear he was afraid of something.

Later the trial was held. All the free workers from the factory and the offices went to hear it, even abandoning their work in order to do so. They told us afterwards what had happened. Chekunov got three years on modified regime and was to serve this term here in Mordovia. That meant he would come under some officer whom he himself had supplied with free furniture, would be free to go about without armed guards and would get parcels every month. Living off the fat of the land! Life in camp for Chekunov wouldn't be just easy, but seventh heaven.

More often than not, however, it never gets as far as a trial, they try to hush everything up, not to wash their dirty linen in public. One of our camp bosses, for instance, built himself a great big house on the side – using government materials and free labour: cons. He set himself up with furniture from the factory and lived like a lord. But it still wasn't enough, his greed was too much for him and he came to grief over some further manipulations. They didn't put him on trial but suggested he should apply for his pension. He sold his home, loaded all his belongings into packing cases and departed for some place in the south, where he settled down to live out his days in peace.

Everybody knew he was a swindler. We cons learned about it from the free workers, and anyway it was all the warders could talk about: just look at that skunk – feathered his own nest very nicely with not so honest labour and wouldn't even give us firewood from the factory.

The cons needled the officers for ages afterwards about it: what's this about teaching us to live by honest labour while your own boss is a thief – and what's more wriggled out of everything without being punished? At first they tried to persuade us that it wasn't true, but then gave up – how could you hide it anyway? – and merely got out of it by saying that 'every family has its black sheep'.

Not one of the camp officers or employees can resist fiddling something or other. Taking stuff out of the compound, for instance – that doesn't rank as pilfering. How can it? It's nothing, it's government stuff, and the government won't go broke (at this point they somehow manage to forget their political instruction sessions and little talks; those are just the necessary words, the correct things to say, and anyway they're one thing, but here we're talking about trifles, small stuff, some three cubic yards of firewood, and that's a different matter entirely). Even less would it occur to any of them to 'ask' a con to work for them, whether in or out of working hours – it is crystal clear that the con is dying to do favours for his bosses.

Our company officer, Lieutenant Alyoshin, 'asked' his cons to load him up a lorryful of firewood. It's true that this meant not only loading it up, but sawing and chopping it first. But who would refuse? For on that same Alyoshin depended such questions as whether you were to have shop privileges or not, or parcels, or visits – in short the whole of your camp existence. So we sawed and chopped it and loaded it under the watchful gaze of a warder (he had to watch the lorry being loaded in case somebody was hidden underneath – at the guardhouse too they would thoroughly prod the whole load with a pointed iron rod and examine it from all sides). The truck rolled up to the guardhouse. And who should turn up at this moment but the commandant of the compound.

'Where'd you get that wood? Who's it for? Where's your receipt?'

The warder sitting on top of the wood handed him the receipt to show that the wood was paid for. The commandant looked from the paper to the truck and back again:

'Christ, the fucking bastard, he's signed for one yard and loaded up four! Turn your lorry round and start unloading! Unless Alyoshin pays up at the cashier's.'

Alyoshin came up and a first-class row broke out. There was a parade just at that moment, a crowd of cons were standing by the guardhouse and they rocked with laughter as they listened to the exchange. The conversation went like this:

'You've got a fucking brass neck, you great prick! Signed for a yard and taking out four.'

'Well, it's all the fucking same to you, isn't it? Is it yours or something?'

'I don't give a fuck, turn the fucking truck round, or else pay for the rest!'

'Wait a minute, what the fucking hell are you shouting about?'

'Fuck off with your "wait a minute!" Turn it round!'

And so on for about fifteen minutes to the general merriment of the cons. I don't know how long it would have continued, but at that point the Camp Commander came over to the guardhouse (Kolomitsev had already retired by that time and been replaced by Dvoretskov). Both of them dashed to meet him, the commandant with a complaint and Alyoshin with a request to be allowed to take the wood out. The Camp Commander was at a loss. He didn't really want to offend Alyoshin, but it was awkward to give him permission in front of the cons. He neither agreed nor disagreed, but excused himself by saying he was busy, that they would have to sort it out themselves, and walked away. Alyoshin spat, gave a wave of his hand and ordered us to unload the three extra yards. He would make up for it later, there was no point in paying out money unnecessarily.

That same firewood later caused me to have a personal skirmish with another company officer. The incident occurred in the autumn of 1965, not long before my departure for hospital in camp three. I was working on night shift in the foundry at the time. I came back one morning from work, drank my skilly and lay down to sleep. I was absolutely dog tired from work, my ears were hurting, my head aching, and I couldn't even fall asleep for the pain. Then, when I had just dozed off, I was woken by the orderly:

'Go to the company officer, he wants to see you.'

How reluctant I was and how hard it was to get up! While I got dressed I kept wondering to myself what it was all about, why was I being called? I couldn't think of anything I had done to give cause for going to the cooler. I thought and thought and decided that an answer must have come to one of my complaints about my illness.

Knocking on the door, I entered the office and the company officer said something that I couldn't hear properly – I had a steady roaring in my ears. The orderly bent down and whispered to the officer to speak louder. The latter repeated loudly:

'Go to the factory with the orderly. You must go now.'

Half asleep, I was able to make very little of it and I stumbled to the guardhouse. Several cons from our gang were already waiting there, they were also from the night shift. Well, they led us, as usual, through the gate and only in the work zone did I suddenly come to my senses and ask:

'Hey, where are they taking us? And what for?'

'What for, what for? To load wood for the company officer, of course.'

God, what a fool, stumbling off like a donkey to break my

back for an officer! I was so infuriated, both with myself, the orderly and the officer – and with the whole world – that I turned round and walked back. But it wasn't so easy! Who was going to let me out of the work zone all on my own? I would have to wait at the factory until they finished with the wood. So on top of everything else I was going to have to go without my dinner: I was in the work zone now and my dinner would be in the living zone. There was nothing to be done. I found a secluded corner and flopped down to have a sleep – I was damned if I was going to slave for my jailer.

I dozed off – and again was woken up. A warder was digging me roughly in the ribs:

'Aha, skiving off, eh? Let's go to the cooler!'

I tried to explain to him that I wasn't on duty, that I had done my stint and was resting, but he wouldn't listen to me and dragged me off to the guardhouse. It was useless to resist. All right, I thought, it will all be cleared up at the guardhouse. But just for the purpose, the warder who had searched us and taken us into the work zone wasn't there. I tried again to explain that I'd only just come off work and would have to go back that night – what a hope! He took me straight through the guardhouse and into the cooler. To kick up a fuss, insist, call for the company officer – all this was to invite a certain ten to fifteen days in the cooler for disorderly conduct and resisting a warder. I gave up in disgust and lay on the bare boards. For dinner I had the cooler skilly, with no bread. Then round about four o'clock, I was let out: they had checked with the records office and assured themselves that I was working on the night shift. All they said when they let me out was: 'Why the bloody hell did you have to sleep in the work zone?'

After supper I was again called in to see the company officer.

'Why did you leave the others and refuse to work?'

After everything that had happened I was fighting mad and in no mood to restrain myself. I said that although I was a con, not a man, nevertheless I neither desired nor intended to wait upon my jailers. And there was nothing said in my sentence about acting as labourer to company officers.

'But nobody forced you to go, you were only asked to help.

If you didn't want to, you shouldn't have gone. And the others didn't refuse, they volunteered to go.'

'Yes, of course they volunteered – otherwise you'd find an excuse to stop them getting any more parcels. A prisoner's got to earn his parcels – and that means sawing your firewood, doesn't it?'

The officer said he had no time to argue with me now but would deal with me later. I could go and get ready for work. I left convinced that I would get no shop privileges that month. And so it was.

KHRUSHCHEV GETS THE BOOT

In the autumn of 1964 we were on our way to dinner from work when we saw the following little scene: three warders dragging a con off to the cooler while he struggled and yelled so that the whole camp could hear. Many people in the zone knew this prisoner, he was a former criminal con, a rowdy and even violent fellow. As he was being dragged through the whole camp, the cons who passed him asked:

'What for?'

'For Khrushchev, you cunts, for Khrushchev!'

Soon afterwards we learned what the matter was. Now the story is well known to all the cons in Mordovia, just like the story of Kolya Shcherbakov's ear.

It turned out that Khrushchev had been ousted and we in the camp still didn't know about it. The camp administration, however, had hastened to put an end to the cult of Khrushchev. Early one morning, long before reveille, they had roused the camp artist – a con – from his bunk and brought him to the staff offices. The top brass was already there, and not just the camp KGB but their superiors. The artist was ordered to erase the name of Khrushchev from all the placards as swiftly as possible, while all the cons were still in their huts. There was far too much work for only one man, however, for the whole camp was plastered with placards and slogans and on all of them was written: N. S. Khrushchev. Therefore they summoned several 'activists' as well – grasses, members of the Internal Order Section and Council of the collective. And this special task force set to work.

It was clear that they still wouldn't finish before reveille, so they hurried to expel the former head of the government from at least all the more prominent places: inside the staff offices, on the outside walls of the offices and in the area immediately surrounding the offices. Over the cinema screen on the open-air stage hung a lengthy red banner: 'Under Socialist conditions every man who leaves the path of labour is able to return to useful activity.' And in even bigger letters the signature: 'N. S. Khrushchev.' This banner was very high up and couldn't be reached without a ladder – which was the last thing you could expect to find in a prison camp! While they were getting a ladder and moving it into place, reveille was sounded and the stage was surrounded by gaping prisoners. And when the artist started to scrape off the name of Khrushchev, everybody at once guessed what was up. And what a scene there was! Whistles, hoots, curses – many were inside because of Khrushchev, including almost all the criminals. Nobody from admin dared show themselves to the prisoners that morning, but just sat tight in their offices.

But now the time came to open the library and they suddenly remembered that all the walls inside were plastered with newspaper and magazine cuttings and photographs and placards. Something had to be done quickly. And then they called in a number of out and out scum – well known to admin – of whom it was known that even if they couldn't be forced they could always be bought.

One of them was invited into the office of Sveshnikov, head of the Political Education Unit (he himself talked about this afterwards in great detail). Sveshnikov took several packets of Indian tea from his desk and spread them out for the con to see:

'Go to the reading room, destroy all the photographs of Khrushchev in any way you like – and this tea is yours.'

Before the criminal con lay the tea. This in camp terms was a whole fortune – you could buy quite a few people with tea.* Sveshnikov and the other officers present from the KGB all knew this and were thoroughly confident of success. They looked at the con and he looked at the tea. Of course he was calculating in his mind how much tea there was – in a minute

* This is a reference to 'tea addicts'. A very powerful stimulant can be brewed from tea.

he'd agree. Or else he'd bargain in the hope of adding to it. The con transferred his gaze from the tea to the officer and then back to the tea again. At last he said in a businesslike tone:

'Tea makes everything possible. But . . . you know, officer' – this to Sveshnikov – 'you've got such a lovely arse as to make any woman jealous. You've fattened it at our expense. Let me just shag you once and in return I'll bring you twice as much tea and every single photo in the camp of your faithful Leninist.'

Naturally they dragged him straight off to the cooler. And as he went he bellowed to the whole camp and everyone he met on the way:

'Look at these cunts! Not so long ago they were kissing Khrushchev's cock and arse themselves and now they want us to take his mug off the walls! I got seven years added on for Khrushchev, you nancy boys, they made me a political because of him! You should be letting me go now! But no, because of him you're dumping me in the cooler again!'

We in the stand-by gang had been working since before dawn and not having been in the living zone that morning still knew nothing. Thus we heard the news about Khrushchev's downfall, interspersed with obscenities, from the mouth of that unfortunate criminal. He continued to yell the same in the cooler and could be heard all over the camp.

But of course they found people ready to sell themselves for tea – 'tea makes everything possible'. They appeared in the reading-room and set about tearing down the placards and cuttings in front of everybody, to the accompaniment of general laughter. This important operation soon became a game. A con would go up to a photograph, wet his index finger with spit, give a push and a twist and there would be Khrushchev headless on the photograph, while his head stayed on the cons' index finger. Then the con would creep up on one of his friends, strike suddenly with his finger, and the friend's forehead would be decorated with that all-too-familiar physiognomy. In the noise and confusion they started to tear down the pictures of other members of the Central Committee and government too: Brezhnev's body suddenly acquired Khrushchev's face, and vice-versa. And they managed to destroy practically all the photographs of Podgorny, explaining afterwards with an innocent expression on their faces: 'Sorry, I got mixed up, they all look the same to me.'

A day or two later they started to 'reshape' the reading room The disturbances died down of their own accord. But then new ones took their place: cons who had been sentenced because of Khrushchev started demanding to be set free. They said that in camp eleven they even packed their bags and moved on the guardhouse: 'We were imprisoned for criticising Khrushchev and now we've been proved right. Let us go!' Instead they were dispersed, of course.

In order to calm the prisoners down a bit they started calling in everybody who was in for Khrushchev, one by one, to talk to the KGB. There they were advised to write to the Praesidium of the Supreme Soviet petitioning for pardons; the latter, so the argument went, would be bound to respond to such petitions, now it was merely a question of letting them know of your existence. The calculation was a simple one: by the time the cons had written their petitions and sent them off, and then waited for some kind of reply, two or three months or even half a year might go by. In the meantime the agitation would die down; and in any case the answers would come in bit by bit – while some were reacting indignantly to the refusals, others would still be waiting and hoping.

Many prisoners to whom it was suggested they write refused: 'What pardon? We were proved right, we ought to be rehabilitated.' But the majority nonetheless begged for pardons – anything to be released, who cared how it was done? And who would want to spend any more time than was necessary in camp?

Perhaps a few of them really were rehabilitated – I don't know of any such cases and never heard of any. Even pardons, at camp seven at least, were granted to only a handful out of hundreds, and only to those who had not more than a year left to serve and had good references from admin.

One of the men to be pardoned a few months before the end of his term was Sanya Klimov, my neighbour at the time of my meeting with my mother. After that meeting I got to know him better and learned that he had been charged under Article 70 'for criticising Khrushchev'.

Klimov had been a building worker formerly. One day he and his friends had picked up a couple of bottles on pay day and gone into a restaurant. This was just at the time when the price of butter and meat had gone up, so the dinners must have gone up too. They behaved rowdily and loudly criticised Khrushchev: first it was the damned vodka going up, now it's butter and meat. By the time we overtake America the bread will be dearer too. In other words it was the normal sort of workman's conversation. Sanya, most probably, talked louder and more sharply than the others – and he was just unlucky. Some KGB man must have been in the vicinity, or a Party worker. Sanya was picked up within minutes, there in the restaurant, and his friends whisked off as witnesses.

Now he wrote a petition for pardon and at least got out before the end of his term. But a fellow from our stand-by gang, Potapov, another Sanya, is inside even to this day, although he too was in for Khrushchev.

Sanya Potapov had been an active Komsomol worker and a convinced Leninist. He served in the navy and was Komsomol Organiser of his unit. After demobilisation he became secretary of the Komsomol town committee in Lipetsk. He married an equally convinced and enthusiastic Komsomol worker who was also a Komsomol secretary. An exemplary family came into being, a genuine Komsomol cell – two secretaries. And a child was born – also a future Komsomol member.

But the trouble was that young Potapov was an honest and thinking sort of fellow. To begin with, mixing with the young workers, he saw that they weren't burning with enthusiasm at all, that many of them were dissatisfied with their life and their pay and used to make fun of Khrushchev almost openly. He started to meditate on the situation in the country, on the role of politics in economic life, and came to the conclusion that the current policy was wrong and the methods of management no good (after 1964 they came to be characterised as 'voluntarist').

Sanya tried to talk about these things in the town committee where he was secretary, but he was called to order, as they say, and put in his place. But he was no longer able or willing to suppress his views and so he embarked on underground activity in the spirit of the best models to be found in our own literature: he started to write leaflets and distribute them round the town. By day he would work in the local party headquarters, delivering lectures and reports to the youth of the town, and everything in them was 'proper' and 'acceptable'. But coming home in the evenings he would sit at his desk, take paper and pen and write out one of his leaflets: that Khrushchev and his Central Committee were following an anti-people's policy that threatened the country with economic collapse; that an adventurist foreign policy was bringing us to the verge of catastrophe; that the raising of food prices and the raising of work norms were cutting the workers' wages back at both ends. These handwritten leaflets he would stick up in prominent places during the night or put into people's letter boxes.

One day one of the members of the town Party committee caught Sanya just as he was dropping a leaflet into his box. He knew Sanya very well and now he knew who had been supplying him with the regular leaflets. But he didn't run straight off to tell the KGB. Instead he tried to persuade Sanva that this form of activity was useless. It would make no difference, he said, for our people were incapable of acting decisively and incapable of standing up for themselves. 'You will just become a useless victim,' he said to Sanya. And then he warned Sanya that if he continued to put leaflets in his letter box he would go to the KGB. He himself understood the situation even better than Sanya, there was no need to convince him, but he had no intention of going to prison for nothing: 'My life and my freedom are too dear to me.'

After this Sanya continued to write and distribute his leaflets, but missed out the home of his friend. And so it went on for about two years. All this time the KGB was searching for an 'anti-Khrushchev organisation' and couldn't find one – they couldn't even imagine that all this was being done by one man. In 1963 the military commission started calling in everyone in Lipetsk liable for military service and proposing to them that they either write their curriculum vitae or fill in a questionnaire. Sanya realised that they were collecting samples of handwriting and attempted to change his own as best he could. Whether this didn't help or whether he was betrayed isn't clear, but soon afterwards he was arrested. He was tried, like most of the rest of us, in secret session, and condemned, under Article 70, to four years in camp. Then he was brought to Mordovia.

Sanya suffered a great deal on account of his family. By 1963 a second child had been born. After his arrest his wife, of course, was kicked out of her job in the Party committee and found work as a typist. But how could a typist feed two little children on her salary alone? What's more she was often ill and had to spend long periods in hospital, for she had a weak heart. And if it hadn't been for his and her parents, goodness knows how they would have got by.

Knowing of his difficult family situation the camp KGB, even before Khrushchev was toppled, had called Potapov in several times and suggested that he write a statement admitting that he had wrongly interpreted the policy of Khrushchev, that he had slandered him and now repented. Then they would see about getting him pardoned. But Sanya always refused. Then, when Khrushchev was removed, they called him in again together with the rest to petition for a pardon. Sanya said:

'How can that be? Some months ago you suggested to me to write that I had been wrong and was repenting. Now it turns out that I was right, that I was correct in criticising Khrushchev, yet I still have to beg for pardon. What do you want me to write in my petition?'

Their reply was: 'Isn't it all the same to you, just so long as you go free?'

He refused to write and is still doing time in camp eleven. But even of those who did petition, far from all of them were released. Particularly the ones whose cases were similar to Potapov: they were refused on the grounds that 'agitating against Khrushchev they were also agitating against the Central Committee' or on the grounds of the 'special gravity of the crime that was committed'.

A VISIT

'Marchenko, your mother's here,' said a fellow from a gang that worked outside the camp. Returning from work they had seen an elderly woman standing by the guardhouse and eagerly staring at the passing cons. As usual they asked her who she had come to see. She said Anatoly Marchenko, her son, and also managed to add that she had been waiting for three days already to see my company officer and get him to sign a permit for a visit.

I hadn't seen my mother for many years. I had gone away to work on construction sites, then I went to the camps, escaped, was caught again, sent to Vladimir prison . . . Six or seven years had gone by. I had left home an eighteen-year-old youth, strong and fit, and now I was already a con with a sizeable stretch behind me, deaf and sick. And what had happened to my mother during these years? She had written me letters, or rather not written them herself but dictated them to the girl next door, for she herself couldn't write. There was little I could learn from them about her or father. I knew only that father still worked on the railway, that my kid brother had grown up and was due to go into the army. I knew, or felt, that my mother loved and felt sorry for me, that she grieved. And now my legs even wobbled when I realised that I was about to see her again.

It is difficult to convey what a con feels, knowing that his mother is nearby, and that he can't see her or help her. Why, she had travelled thousands of miles to get here from Siberia; she had had to make preparations, endure three to four days of hard travelling, and now she had spent three days knocking on doors, walking around the camp, hoping against hope to see me or at least find out something about me. I was overwhelmed with rage, it rose in a ball in my throat. I tried to suppress it, to keep it inside, to remain at least outwardly calm, for if I allowed myself the luxury of addressing various cutting remarks to admin, both I and my mother could say good-bye to any visit.

I went to the deputy camp commander, Major Ageyev: for the first time in all my stay there I decided to ask admin for something. And although I made a great effort to keep calm, I didn't make a very good job of it. As a result of my agitation, my suppressed fury and the necessity of having to ask for something, I was incapable for several minutes of uttering a single word (I in any case tend to stutter, and when I'm worked up the words just refuse to come). At last I mastered myself. I asked that my mother either be given permission to make a visit or else be given a refusal, so that at least she wouldn't have to worry, to linger on in uncertainty and to wait in vain.

As it happened, I was lucky: my company officer, Lubayev, was away, he was off for two days at the end of his spell of duty. There was somebody to put the blame on, and besides, the officers always had their own little scores to settle. Lubayev wouldn't have given me a three-day visit for anything in the world and he would have forced my mother to wait in the queue for fifteen days (the queues for visits were enormous at that time, some people had to wait for two weeks and more and it even happened that they went away empty-handed – not everyone, after all, has the time to wait so long, or can pay for a room and afford the expense of food for a fortnight). Ageyev evidently knew that I was on bad terms with Lubayev and allowed the visit just to spite him. More than that, he allowed my mother and me to bypass the queues and meet in the cookhouse – if the adjutant would give his permission. I rushed to see the adjutant. He at first refused:

'If I allow this you'll complain afterwards that the visit took place on improperly equipped premises.'

I started to beg him and promised him that I wouldn't complain, having requested it myself. And in truth, I wasn't being visited by a wife – I was going to be with my mother in a room without bars; and if there was only one bed in it then I'd return to my hut every night. After I had written out an application in which

I requested to be assigned a visit in the cookhouse and declared that I would make no complaints on the subject, the adjutant gave his permission. I went back to Ageyev again – his signature was the decisive one. He took my application:

'How many days shall I sign this for? Lubayev knows you better than I do, but that great cunt has fucked off somewhere, and I don't know a monkey's tit. Okay, fuck off with you, here!' And he handed me the signed application. It was for three days! Tremendous luck!

Several hours later I was summoned to the guardhouse, searched more carefully than ever before (I was about to mix with someone from Outside) and taken to the end of the corridor. The corridor was barred by a door with a peephole in it and the lock was on the guardhouse side. On the other side was the room for visits and adjoining it the cookhouse. They let me through this door and locked it behind me. I took one step along the corridor towards the cookhouse and stopped dead – I couldn't walk. I felt as if I would never ever be able to move from the spot. At last I forced myself to go up to the door and knock. I would never in any case have heard the answer from the other side; I waited for several seconds, then opened the door and went in.

Mother was standing at a table piled high with food of all kinds; she had evidently been waiting for me for some time already and was aimlessly fiddling with the things and moving them around. I stopped in the doorway, she too was incapable of moving towards me. I don't remember how we came to be close to one another, how we embraced. Mother stroked me and kept saying over and over again:

'It's all right, son, it's all right, keep calm, son, keep calm.' Probably she wasn't so much calming me as attempting to calm herself, so as not to burst into tears on the spot, before my very eyes.

Then there came a knock at the door – not the one that led into the corridor but the one that linked the cookhouse with the visiting room. An extremely plump woman came through the door, still young, about thirty to thirty-three. She greeted me and said to my mother:

'There, you see, now you've met your son, and you were so worried the whole time.'

She was followed into the cookhouse by her husband. We were acquainted already and knew one another by sight, although, as so often happens in the camps, we knew no first names or surnames. Here I learned that his name was Alexander Klimov. Later, after the visits, we got to know one another better and I learned his story. At the time, though, we merely exchanged a few words, and the conversation with Klimov helped mother and me to compose ourselves. When they had gone back into their room we already found it easier to talk. Mother started to tell me all the news from home – about my father, my brother Boris, the neighbours; who had left Barabinsk, who had got married, who had had children. While she talked she kept trying to thrust into my mouth some of the food she had brought. But I could get nothing down, I was too agitated by our meeting. Mother talked very loudly to make sure I could hear, but not once did she inquire how bad my deafness was; obviously she wanted to avoid upsetting me with too many questions. I reassured her that I was feeling well, that I was fit and that everything was all right. It was only after several hours that I made out that she had aged considerably and looked exhausted; at fifty she looked like a real old woman already. That was because of me, grief had aged her prematurely. And then life in general had never been a bed of roses for her: hard work, three of us children (one brother had died while still small, Boris and I had remained), constant need, shortages . . .

That night I went back to the zone to sleep. And at six the next morning I was back again. In the stand-by gang we worked not on shifts but on call, and for those three days the ganger didn't call me and gave me the chance to spend the time with my mother. Klimov, however, was made to go to work every day and came to his wife only in the evening and then spent the night with her. One day he tried to take a piece of lard back with him from the meeting, hiding it under his belt. Sometimes it can be done. But he was unlucky: they searched him diligently, found the lard and threatened to stop his visit.

We and the Klimovs cooked our food jointly and ate breakfast, dinner and supper together. Klimov's wife told us about herself and her baby and what it was like living in Saratov. Mother talked about life in Barabinsk. It turned out that everywhere was much the same: people were barely able to make ends meet, hanging on from payday to payday. My folks had it a bit easier, it seemed, because they had their own vegetable patch and a cow. Alexander's wife, however, had a really tight time of it, what with the poor pay she got in the kindergarten and having to earn for herself and the child.

On the last day of the visit the door opened and in came Lubayev without knocking. It was obvious he was in a filthy temper: he had failed to screw up my visit from my mother, the permit had been signed in his absence. When he came in I was sitting at the table, eating jam straight out of the pot with a spoon – mother knew what a sweet tooth I had and had brought loads of sweet things with her. I didn't dream of standing up when Lubayev came in – what a nerve, he keeps my mother kicking her heels for three days and then walks in on us uninvited. He gave me a sidelong look and greeted my mother. She invited him to sit down. The company officer started complaining about me: I was rude and insolent and behaved myself badly, and I obviously didn't want any remission so as to get out early. When my mother heard this, her eyes opened wide with amazement: what, did I really not want to leave the camp?

'No, he doesn't,' said Lubayev. 'And it all depends on him, on the way he behaves.'

'Why, what's he doing,' said my mother anxiously, 'refusing to work?'

'Oh, he does his work all right,' began Lubayev, and then went on to explain how bad I was and how they were forced willy-nilly to punish me, to deprive me of shopping privileges and stick me in the cooler on starvation rations. At this I could stand it no longer, I didn't want my mother to get all worried and start weeping over my hunger and difficulties, I hadn't complained to her at all. I cut in on Lubayev and said, turning to my mother:

'And you ask the company officer what one has to do in order to be in his good books. He will tell you that you have to suck up to your superiors, spy on your comrades and inform on your fellow prisoners.'

'Oh my, there's never been any of that sort of thing in our family!' exclaimed my mother. Then I turned to Lubayev:

'You came here to this meeting even though you weren't invited, you came to distress an old woman with your tales. We've only got three days to meet in and we've got plenty to talk about without you coming in here. And it's not as if you're going to lengthen our visits afterwards by the time that you're wasting. If you have to, call me out of the zone any time you like and talk away. But leave my mother alone.'

Lubayev left the room without a word, which was all I wanted – so long as he didn't have time to tell mother just how bad it was here. Mother looked at me in horror for talking to a boss that way. Throughout her whole life she had got used to the idea that bosses were to be feared, that it was better not to tangle with them, for you could only do yourself more harm. I felt very very sorry for her.

The visit came to an end and we parted. I was gladdened by our meeting and simply happy, I seemed to melt during those three days after all the years of loneliness. But I didn't want mother to come to see me again. I had three years to run to the end of my sentence, it was better somehow to be patient during this time, rather than for her to have to torture herself with travelling, to beg, to humble herself and to sit for three days behind bars – it was better not to see each other at all for three years than for her to see her son in those surroundings.

I was also glad again later that mother listened to my advice, and that she didn't come to see me in prison at Vladimir. Meeting there was even more painful. Once upon a time, about ten years ago, they used to have personal visits too, but what visits! In a cell-like room with bars on the windows and a peephole in the door. The light in the room used to burn all night and the wardress would patrol the corridor and keep peering through the keyhole, especially, of course, if it was a man and wife inside. Now even that doesn't exist any more, Vladimir has no personal visits. Sometimes they give you one or perhaps two visits a year – up to half an hour each; but even these can be taken away for the slightest excuse, or even without an excuse.

One day one of my cell-mates, Alexei Ivanov, had a visit from his mother – this happened quite recently, in the spring of 1963. She lives in Vladimir province and since she didn't have far to go she decided to take her little granddaughter along, Alexei's sister's child, who was five years old. Later he told us what had happened. A wardress sat in the room the whole time, listening and watching to make sure there were no 'infringements'. It is forbidden not only to embrace your family but even to approach them: you have to talk across a table. Alexei's mother had to wait a long time outside the prison, the little girl got tired and started playing up, so grandma bought her an ice cream. And so they went into the room still carrying the ice cream. The little girl held it out across the table for her uncle to have a lick. The wardress swooped on her, ripped the ice cream out of her hand as though it were an atom bomb and at once put an end to the visit.

This story of Alexei's came back to me quite recently when I was listening to extracts from Svetlana Alliluyeva Stalin's memoirs over the radio. In one particular episode* she talked about meeting her brother in Vladimir prison. Why, those were the very years when we were there and not one of us had an inkling as to whom we had the honour of sharing the prison with! Powers we knew about, and 'Beria's generals', but not a whisper reached us about the 'heir apparent', Vasily Stalin.

I've no idea what conditions he was held in, or what soup they gave him in place of skilly; but how different was his meeting with his wife and sister from Alexei's meeting with his mother and niece. It's clear that not all citizens in our country are subject to the same laws and the same regulations.

---

* See letter 19 in *Twenty Letters to a Friend*, Hutchinson (London); Harper & Row (NY).

THE SUICIDE

. . . What if I go up the wire, okay?
Or onto the strip? If I wish
you to go, get lost, disappear –
will this favour make us quits?

Go on then, fire! You're also sick and tired
of Mordovia, godforsaken hole!
They'll give you leave for it, off you go
to your mother and sister waiting at home . . .
. . . And you won't remember how I hung on the wire,
a semi-quaver on an empty stave.

Yuli Daniel: 'The Sentry' (1966)

This incident occurred on Sunday 4 October 1964. We came
back from loading and unloading at five in the morning and went
straight to bed. Round about eight o'clock I got up feeling
extremely hungry. I was about to wake Valery, but he was
sleeping so sweetly that I took pity on him: it was better to go
short of food than short of sleep. I took my spoon, cut a piece
of bread from my ration and went over to the canteen.

It was a clear, sunny morning and everyone was pleased that
it would be warm by dinner time. Warm weather for the con is
a gift of providence. I was also in a good mood as I walked to
the canteen. On Sunday mornings the canteen stays open until
nine, but almost everyone had had breakfast a great deal earlier
and there was no more queue, merely a few dozen cons sitting
around on the benches and waiting for breakfast to end – perhaps

the cook would have a few bowls of skilly left over and would give them second helpings.

I have a feeling that the breakfast on the menu that morning was called noodle soup – and a few luckless noodles were indeed floating inside the bowl. A spoon was superfluous here, so I stuck it in my pocket and emptied the bowl over the side – a few swallows were enough. All that remained to be done was to inspect the sides for any stray noodles that might be stuck there.

Suddenly a lone shot rang out. Everyone raised his head and kept perfectly still. Nobody dared clink a bowl. After about a minute, somebody said quietly: 'From the corner tower, by the bakery.' We listened and waited. There ought to be two more shots. A long minute passed and no shots were fired. What could it mean?

The shot had been fired by a tommy gunner in one of the watch towers, so a con must have climbed onto the palisade in order to put an end to himself. In such cases the sentry is supposed to fire two warning shots and aim only the third at the 'escaper'. But usually it is done in reverse order: the first shot is fired at the living target and then two shots into the air. Well, what difference does it damn well make – the con's bound to die so what's the use of fooling around? You let fly into the air and maybe he even changes his mind about it, and then good-bye gratitude, good-bye extra leave and a nice trip home. In short, none of us knew of a case where a sentry had fired according to the regulations – the main thing was to spend three cartridges.

One way or another there should have been three shots and we only heard one. What could it mean? We left the canteen to find out, but just as we emerged on the front porch a series of further shots rang out. The firing came from the same direction, near the bakery, but the sound was different from the first.

Cons from all over the camp were converging on the bakery. I was overtaken by a group of cons that included my old acquaintance from Vladimir prison, Sergei Oransky. As he walked past he called out: 'Somebody's been shot again!'

Oh, those 'agains'! How many 'escapes' had there been during my time alone at camp seven? The last time had been several months earlier, in June or July. Then, hearing the regulation three shots, we had rushed to the perimeter. The tommy gunner had shot the fugitive at the foot of the wooden palisade and he lay there with his nose digging into the warm earth of the softly raked strip. Evidently he was still alive: he was scrabbling at the soil with his hands and trying to raise himself on one leg. Some cons ran to the medical post and fetched the medical orderly. But what could they do? The wounded man lay on the raked strip, behind two rows of barbed wire, and the sentry wouldn't let them go anywhere near the wire: cons were forbidden to go on the strip and anyway the dead or the wounded con first had to be photographed on the spot, then a report had to be drawn up in the presence of several officers, and only afterwards could the body be moved and medical aid given.

The injured man lay there, jerking convulsively from time to time. The prisoners were noisy and shouting, paying no attention to the bellows of the warders and the bursts of tommy gun fire over their heads. So it went on for ages, at least an hour and a half. At last the officers appeared on the other side of the wire: Lieutenant-Colonel Kolomitsev ordered the palisade to be broken – it was forbidden to carry an injured or dead con through the camp. They made a hole in the palisade and two warders, taking hold of the man by his legs, dragged the body outside the compound. His head bounced up and down as it was pulled over the ground, leaving a bloody trail behind it. The cons roared and howled. Then Ageyev's face appeared in the gap in the palisade and yelled:

'Well, what the fucking hell makes you go on the strip in the first place?'

Later, our medical orderly was called to the guardhouse 'to administer first-aid', and later a nurse and a doctor came. The orderly said that he was still alive and was dispatched alive to the hospital in camp three. But he didn't arrive there in time and died on the way.

I thought of this incident – and others like it – as I made my way with the others to the bakery. What had happened this time? Who was the luckless con?

At the bakery a huge crowd had gathered, almost the entire

camp. I found some of my gang-mates there. Kolya Yusupov pointed out the place on the palisade to me – there on the 'peak',* his clothing caught in the barbed wire, hung one of the cons. Only his legs could be seen from the side where we were, the rest of him hung outside – in freedom.

Kolya and I climbed to the roof of a low building nearby – the former parcel-sorting office. From there we had an excellent view of the raked strip, the palisade and 'freedom' beyond. A crowd had gathered on the far side as well: officers, tommy gunners and free workers. Beside us on the roof sat a con who had seen the whole thing from the beginning. He was terribly agitated and shaken. And he told us how it had happened.

'I was sitting with Kiryukha in the stokehole,' he said, 'where I'd gone for a natter and some bread. All of a sudden we heard this sentry yelling from his watch tower: "Get back, I'll fire! Get back you fucking idiot, I'll kill you! Where the fuck d'you think you're going in broad daylight?"

'Kiryukha and I ran out of the stokehole and saw this con. He'd already cleared one of the barbed wire fences and was tangled up in the other. And he was carrying a plank with him. I recognised him – we had been in the cooler together. He was sick, couldn't fulfil his norm and then stopped away from work: Kolomitsev himself had given him fifteen days. I called out to him:

'"Romashev, have you gone crazy, come back, they'll kill you."

'"I couldn't give a fuck if they do, it's all the bloody same to me. It'll be a quick release."

'He was in bad health all the time and the doctors wouldn't give him a certificate. Not only that but they insisted on driving him out to work and squeezing the norm out of him. I ran along the barbed wire fence, trying to persuade him to come back, but he waved me away, scrambled over the second fence and made for the palisade. He was almost directly under the watch tower by now. But the sentry, evidently, was a decent sort – the first one I've ever seen. He was swearing blue murder at

---

* Inclined rows of barbed wire along the top of the palisade.

Romashev, but he didn't fire. Then I heard him ringing the guardhouse: '"There's a con here on the strip, tell the warders to come and get him."

'I couldn't hear what they said from the guardhouse end, but then I heard him yelling into the receiver:

'"He can be shot quick enough, but you can come and get him, he's still tangled up in the second fence."

'Then he added really harshly and angrily:

'"What the bloody hell are you sitting on your arses for? It's my job to keep a look-out and warn you and yours to pick 'em up, so pick the bastard up, you mother-fuckers! I'm warning you, I shan't fire."

'And he didn't fire until Romashev was on the palisade. Then the sentry fired once into the air and went on bellowing to the con to get down and scarper back to the compound. But it was as though Romashev couldn't hear. He was crouched on all fours on top of the palisade, with his feet on the "peak" and his hands resting on the points of the boards. And it looked as though he had no intention of coming down.

'Then the sound of a motorbike engine came from the far side of the palisade and it could be heard approaching Romashev and stopping just opposite him. Somebody shouted at the sentry:

'"What the hell are you staring at? You've got a con on the palisade!"

'We didn't hear the sentry's reply because the shout was immediately followed by several pistol shots in succession. Romashev took his hands off the palisade, stood up to his full height and slowly tumbled backwards and outwards, towards the farther side. Then his trousers caught on the wire and he hung there, and was hanging there still . . .'

Kolya asked the eye witness who had fired the pistol. The latter replied: 'I can't say for sure. I climbed up here as soon as possible to have a look, but the motorbike was already on its way back. Judging by the voice and red kisser it was Shved.'

While we were listening to this story a group of officers appeared on the far side of the palisade, including Ageyev and Shved. They walked up and down, looked, asked the sentry something, and then Ageyev entered the compound while Shved remained outside. Soon Ageyev reappeared on our side of the palisade and walked through the crowd of cons accompanied by officers and warders. He walked unhurriedly, paying no attention to the indignant cries of the cons: 'Murderers!' 'Cannibals!' 'Go on, take him down, maybe he's still alive!' The officers went right up to the barbed wire and Ageyev shouted to someone on the other side of the palisade: 'All right, get cracking!' The photographer focused his camera and took several pictures from various positions. A few moments later the face of Shved appeared over the top of the palisade. He looked down at the cons and smiled. The cons went wild. From the crowd came shouts of 'Blood-sucker!' 'That's who the grave's waiting for!' and 'One day you'll burst with all the blood you've drunk!'

A warder then appeared beside Shved and without paying the slightest attention to the shouts, the two of them set about their work. First they disentangled Romashev from the wire, tearing his pants, it seems, in the process. The crowd fell silent and there was such a hush that I even thought I heard the sound of material ripping. When nothing more held the body, Shved and the warder held the body still for a moment, head down, and then let it drop, and we heard Romashev hit the ground with a sickening thud. A low hiss, half sigh and half exclamation travelled through the compound. And then at once a dreadful din broke out – shouts, protests, hysterics almost. I myself saw several cons – old Kolyma and Vorkuta hands – break down in tears. Torture and starvation had never managed to squeeze tears out of men like this, but now they wept with mortification and impotent rage.

Meanwhile Shved stood on his ladder, looked over the palisade at us and smiled.

Later the nurse told us that Romashev had been dead when they took him down. Evidently he had been shot point-blank.

FRIENDS AND COMRADES

During the years I spent in Vladimir jail and in camps I got to know large numbers of prisoners and with some of them I became close friends. How many different stories did I hear! And I can't write about all of them. I will try, however, to describe just a few.

First, though, let me repeat what I have already pointed out before: people here vary, just as they do everywhere. You have marvellous people and you have rotten ones, you have brave men and cowards, you have honest men with principles and you have unprincipled swine who are prepared for any kind of betrayal. Here there are men who have been imprisoned for their beliefs, and there are more than a few who have come here by accident. Some stay faithful to themselves, serving out their entire sentence from bell to bell. Others disavow everything, and even publicly – themselves, their views and their friends. I can say absolutely categorically – and many will confirm this: the majority of the 'disavowers' (if not all) do it in order to ease their life in the camps and perhaps later outside.

Imprisoned in the political camps of Mordovia are writers, scientists, students, workers and semi-illiterate peasants. And also genuine 'politicians' with their own systematised views and criminal cons who have been transformed into 'politicians'.

I would like to talk about some of my friends and acquaintances without making any distinction among them, just as it was in real life.

One of my companions in the stand-by gang in camp seven was Iosip Klimkovich, a fine, simple fellow. Later we were in camp three together, in hospital, and got to know each other even better. He told me what he was in for, why he had been sentenced to twenty-five years.

At the end of the 1940s Iosip had still been a young boy and lived in Stanislav *oblast* with his mother and sister. At that time armed partisan warfare was in progress over the whole of the Western Ukraine and many Ukrainian peasants had taken to the woods. Among them – with the partisans – was Iosip's uncle, or so they said at least. One day, when Iosip was sitting at a friend's hut, some canvas-covered trucks entered the village and disgorged a number of soldiers with tommy guns, who then proceeded to surround certain of the huts. Through the window they could see how a truck stopped at the Klimkoviches' hut and the soldiers surrounded it too. Iosip dashed to the door: his sick mother lay at home. But his friend's grandfather seized hold of the boy and prevented him from going out. And as he held him he said:

'What are you, weak in the head or something? Can't you see – they're sending them to Siberia. If you go out now they'll take you away too.'

He frogmarched Iosip from the door to the window: 'Take a good look, my lad, and take note.'

Iosip pressed up against the glass. He saw the soldiers running about his yard, looking behind the firewood and into the barn – probably for him. Then he saw them drive his sister out of the hut and tie her hands behind her back before throwing her into the back of the truck. His sick mother was unable to walk – she was dragged along by the arms and also tossed into the truck. Outside several other huts the same story was repeated. The scene was fixed in Iosip's memory for ever, but most clearly engraved of all was the face of the officer in command of the operation.

Afterwards Iosip learned that everyone taken away had been driven to the main town in the district and herded into a single barn. Iosip found the barn and prowled around in the vicinity, but couldn't bring himself to approach it: it was being guarded by soldiers. They said that the people inside were given nothing to eat or drink. Several days later Iosip learned that his mother had died and his sister, with the rest, had been transported to

Siberia. Then he left his home, but not to go to the woods to
join the partisans – he went to the town. He got himself a pistol
(it wasn't difficult at that time) and started to hunt for that
officer. For several days he drew a blank. People said that the
officer was away at other villages doing similar work. But at last
Iosip caught up with him when he was leaving the local military
HQ in the company of a tommy gunner. Iosip followed them,
made sure it was the same officer that had taken his mother and
sister away, went right up behind him and shot him point-blank.
The officer fell without even a cry. The soldier turned and jerked
up his tommy gun, but had no time to fire – Iosip shot him
too.

Iosip Klimkovich was subsequently sentenced as a Ukrainian
nationalist and bandit and given twenty-five years. The trial was
a closed one. That was in the late forties and Iosip is still doing
time.

A similar story to this belonged to the man in the next cot to
me at camp seven, Vladas Mataitis. He was a Lithuanian and
also a peasant. He and his father and brother were with the
partisans in the forest, while the third brother was a student in
town. One day the student came home and the old man and his
two other sons came out to meet him. Just then there was a
raid, all three of them were seized, taken outside the village and
shot. Vladas managed to escape. Later he learned that the three
dead ones had been loaded on to a cart and brought back to
the village. When Vladas's mother saw the three corpses all
at once – her husband and two sons – she went mad. In
this state, together with her daughter, she was transported
to Siberia. He, meanwhile, was captured heavily wounded
and sentenced (also behind closed doors) to twenty-five
years.

He was still in Mordovia when his mother and sister were
permitted to return to Lithuania.

Mataitis twice went before the courts to have his sentence
reduced to fifteen years, but both times was refused because
the camp authorities wouldn't give him a good character reference: he didn't want to become an 'activist' (serve in the IOS)!
But he didn't want to stay inside either, so Vladas signed up in

the camp sanitary section. That's what many people did to get a good reference for the courts: the older ones went into the camp sanitary section, while the younger and fitter ones went into the sports section. Although you were cooperating with admin, at least it wasn't at the expense of your fellow prisoners – all you had to do was observe the formalities and those alone, if the worst came to the worst, would be enough to satisfy the authorities.

Vladas went before the court yet a third time and at last got his sentence reduced. He was released. But he still wasn't allowed to go back to Lithuania.

In that same camp seven, in the finished goods warehouse, there was an old man who was also from the Baltic. I don't remember either his surname or his real first name – we called him Fedya, just as we used the Russian name Volodya for Mataitis and Kolya for Yusupov. Fedya was also in for twenty-five years, just like all the so-called 'nationalists' from the Baltic states and the Ukraine who had been convicted in the forties.

Fedya spent all his free time writing petitions. This is a common disease in the camps – people write and write day after day: to the Central Committee, to the Presidium of the Supreme Soviet, to Khrushchev, to Brezhnev, to the Public Prosecutor's office; and Fedya wrote too.

He hadn't been sentenced alone – somewhere in Mordovia were his wife and son. I don't know what exactly he wrote in his petitions, but they all came down to the same thing: he had never been a partisan and a nationalist, he and his family had been wrongly convicted, by mistake. The cons used to laugh at him: 'Aren't you fed up with writing after eighteen years?' The company officer would hand Fedya the routine 'Application Refused' and start cussing him:

'All you do is write, write, write! Writers, the lot of you! Nobody's guilty, it's all been a mistake! Once you've been sentenced, sit it out and don't be in such a hurry. As if it's not obvious the kind of tree you were picked from!'

And all the answers came back the same: 'Correctly sentenced, there are no grounds for re-examining the case.'

And then one day the cons came running: 'Fedya, go to the guardhouse, they've come for you!' And in the guardhouse he found his wife and son – they had been released first and had come to find him, while he still knew nothing. It turned out that all three had been rehabilitated. After eighteen years justice had triumphed at last!

We had another similar 'writer', a country fellow known to the whole camp, whose name was Pyotr Ilyich Izotov. Both cons and officers called him simply 'Ilyich'. This Ilyich used to write several letters and petitions a day and used to receive at least two replies daily in return. He had organised a whole office for himself: copies of all his petitions were stored in a special suitcase, later the answers were affixed to them, and he kept a special exercise book in which he noted down when he had sent out each petition and when he received the answers. The answers that he got were identical to Fedya's and the cons used to pull his leg in just the same way. But now, whenever the company officer started his 'Write, write, write, what's the use, none of you are guilty, but all this scribbling won't do you a scrap of good, better join the IOS instead' – the cons would stick up for Ilyich:

'You used to tell Fedya it was a waste of time and he got rehabilitated.'

Although Ilyich used to make a point of sending several petitions every day, he evidently had little faith in them himself. True he didn't join the IOS, but he joined the school instead, in class four, hoping no doubt that they would give him a good reference for his pardon.

In the autumn of 1963 a new man was put into our gang – Najmuddin Mahometovich Yusupov. I became very good friends with him and we were together right up until my release. We worked together, lived in the same section, slept next to one another, kept our bread in the same locker and shared all the victuals and money we had with the rest of our group: whoever managed to get anything shared it around. He was an extremely kind and loyal friend, ready to help anyone. Our gang rechristened him Kolya – we couldn't get our tongues round his other name at all. Kolya was young and a fine figure of a man, well over six feet tall; he was built like a giant, strong and handsome, with large regular features and thick brows over big, deepset brown eyes. He arrived in the camp beardless but once inside decided to grow one – there were lots of men with beards in the camp. But some get permission and some don't. Several times Kolya was forced to shave: for a beard they take away your parcel or shop privileges. And then sometimes they don't even do that, but the shop simply refuses to give you any food: you're clean shaven on this identity card, they say, and then you come to us with a beard. How do we know it's you? It was a very handsome beard, coppery chestnut and framed his face in such a way as to give it great expressiveness.

Kolya is now 37 or 38. He is an Avar, his old folk live in the mountains of Daghestan, where he too grew up. Having completed at the teacher training college in town, he went back to his village as a teacher for a while and then into the army. He was in the paratroops, stayed on after his conscription time was up and did eight years altogether. During this time he saw the world a bit, tasted city life, and when he was demobilised was reluctant to return to his remote village. He decided to go for the big money and return to his family with full pockets, not as he was on demobilisation.

The biggest wages are earned by miners, so Kolya decided to go down the mines. He worked away there like nobody's business. He liked work and knew how to go about it: all of us in the gang had seen him doing the work of three. But somehow or other he never managed to accumulate anything, he was always spending just as much as he earned, except, perhaps, for a trifle here and there. And no matter how hard he tried, he could never knock out more than 150–200 roubles a month. If he worked any harder the rates went down and the norms went up. Leaving the mine wasn't any better – not even one person could live on a teacher's salary. And all the time food prices were rising. All the other miners were also discontented and used to mutter and grumble and curse, but always among themselves, in their own circles. And Kolya was just like the rest.

One Sunday he had been out drinking with his friends and was on his way back to the workers' hostel. He wasn't exactly drunk, but, as they say, one over the eight. He walked through the market and at every corner of the market place there were loudspeakers bawling out: 'Khrushchev, Khrushchev – a faithful follower of Lenin! The people's welfare, the growth of prosperity!'

Kolya got his dander up. He climbed on to some barrels and started spouting himself:

'People! Listen, they're babbling on the radio about us living better and richer every day. Have you noticed that you're living better? Nikita says that in Stalin's day things were bad. But in Stalin's day norms were lower and pay rates higher. In Stalin's day a miner used to get seven to eight thousand, and now under Nikita I can hardly scrape up 150–200. And what's it worth anyway? In Stalin's day butter was 2.70 a kilo, and now it's 3.60. Meat is dearer – who wants this sort of life? In the old days in the Caucasus, so the old men say, they used to eat mutton and there were mountains of mutton bones outside each village. But now we hardly know what mutton tastes like. And instead of mutton bones we've got Khrushchev's maize.'

Kolya talked for a long time, stamping his foot so hard that he even broke the barrel. The barrel's owner came dashing over with fists ready to let fly, but when he heard him abusing Khrushchev and praising Stalin he stepped back again: 'All right, talk away, my lad.' (Many Caucasians idolise Stalin even to this day.) They let Kolya finish what he was saying and then several of the lads led him away. For a week nobody touched him, but then they caught up with him after all, jailed him and tried him for anti-Soviet propaganda and for slandering the Soviet system and state. The court, as usual, was closed, and they gave him four years. When Khrushchev fell, Kolya, together with the others, was called in and asked if he would like to apply for a pardon. He refused, served his full term and was released some time after me, on 28 May 1967.

Gennady Krivtsov was one who had had an extremely turbulent and adventurous life. He was a countryman of mine, by the way, being also from Novosibirsk *oblast*. He had completed at the Artillery College in Odessa at the end of the war and became

an officer just in time to take part in it. But when his unit was
passing through Czechoslovakia he deserted: he had fallen in
love with a Czech girl. Then he married her and stayed there.
To avoid being hauled before a tribunal he later fled to Austria;
and on returning to collect his wife he was arrested. Next,
inevitably, came the tribunal, sentence, camps, exile. Fleeing
from exile he was caught, tried again and sentenced to a new
term. In one of the camps Gennady wrote an article for the
camp newspaper and it was printed. Shortly afterwards they
decided it was anti-Soviet and added another term to his previous
one.

In general Genka Krivtsov was the sort of man who figures
in the prison song: '. . . Forever to you tied, my youth and
talent have died within your walls.' And he really did seem to
be in 'forever'. His whole life had consisted of camps and exile
and escapes and new terms. I can't even remember all the
camps he had been in, how many times he had escaped or all
the things he got 'supplements' for. And still he could never
manage to subdue himself, could never manage to come to terms
with his fate. Or didn't want to.

He was short and weedy and painfully skinny – even in
Vladimir jail I had seen few so far gone. But as belligerent as
they come. Already in the old camps he had been nicknamed
'Trotsky's Son' – for his flashing tongue. The company officers
were simply scared to cross swords with him: you could never
under any circumstances out-argue Krivtsov, only make a fool
of yourself. People like him were to be avoided like the plague
so far as they were concerned. But of course they wouldn't kick
him out to freedom, only into the cooler or jail. I got to know
him in jail and then we were together in camp seven.

In jail he had started writing a long story whose title I can
remember – 'In the Devil's Claws'. It was about life in the camps
and prison. He had already written several chapters when it was
taken away and he was thrown into the prison cooler for a start,
with the warning: 'Krivtsov, you'll soon be earning yourself
another term!' When his spell in the cooler was over the educational measures were then continued. Genka was taken to an
office where he talked with a poet from Vladimir named Nikitin.

Nikitin tried to persuade Genka to repent and write on other subjects. He, Krivtsov, had an undoubted gift, he said, and if only he would change the tendency of his writings so that they could be published, he would probably be pardoned and could then stay on in Vladimir as a normal citizen and would be accepted into the Writer's Union . . . These shining prospects failed to attract Genka. He remained 'forever tied' to the prison.

Krivtsov also had a married sister living in Novosibirsk. Both she and her husband were Party members – he was Party Organiser at his factory in the ideological department of the town committee. The prison authorities found out about this and suggested to Genka that he enter into an open discussion with his sister, that is that he write to her as often as he liked and whatever he liked, expressing all his views. They promised him that there would be no comeback, that the censor would let his letters through. And so a polemic sprang up between brother and sister. Genka was a believer, she an atheist, and it was on this topic that their first exchange of views took place. It turned out that the convinced atheist was none too steady in her convictions, or at least not able to defend her views. So the authorities soon put an end to the dispute and brought Genka's correspondence back within the established limits.

Whenever a lecturer came from outside to give us a lecture in camp seven, Krivtsov, Rodygin, Nikols and others of that ilk were always locked up in the cooler for a day or two before his arrival. Thus we always knew: if Krivtsov and Rodygin were dragged off to the cooler, there'd be a lecture on the following day.

Valery and I were introduced to Rodygin by Krivtsov. Or rather, we had noticed him even earlier. We were walking past the staff offices one day when we saw the chief of the Dubrovlag KGB standing there, Major Postnikov, and some cons arguing with him and trying to persuade him of something. We passed them several times and later Valery told me what they had been talking about. It seems the con had said to Postnikov: 'You say that Soviet power derives from the people, that in this lies its strength and its might. But if you, the representatives of that power, were truly convinced of your strength, you wouldn't

imprison us. How many people are you holding in camps and
jails? A simple peasant gets ten years from you for the merest
word, that means you fear that peasant and are not at all sure
of the people's support . . .' What Postnikov answered to this
Valery didn't hear. Later we asked Genka if he knew this fellow
and Genka introduced us.

Tolik Rodygin was from Leningrad and was still very young
– he was born in 1936. He had also been an officer, but whereas
Krivtsov was in the artillery, Rodygin was in the navy. Krivtsov
wrote prose and Rodygin wrote verse. In Leningrad he had
published a volume of poetry and had become a member of the
Writer's Union. When he first came to camp seven he found a
copy of his book in the camp library and removed it, refusing to
show it to anyone; they were bad poems, he said, and made
him feel ashamed.

Somehow or other he left the navy and went to the Far East
to catch fish as captain of a trawler. He was imprisoned in 1962
for the same thing as me – attempting to go abroad: he had tried
to get away by swimming the Black Sea, either to Turkey or to
some foreign ship. He was picked up and got eight years in
Mordovia.

He and Krivtsov were good friends. When they got started
on an argument, half the camp would come running, it wasn't
like our 'political talks' or lectures. Rodygin was an atheist,
Krivtsov, as I have said already, was a believer, and so they
would have a debate. It was usually held in our section – the
stand-by gang's. Sometimes it went to the extent that the
listeners would even miss their suppers. They didn't debate
only religion, of course, but also politics, literature, art, the role
of contemporary science, ethics, where do moral values come
from, and then religion again. For the officers these debates
were a thorn in the flesh: they were too frightened to join in
because Krivtsov and Rodygin would pin them down in a flash
from opposite sides, and so they would be furious. A company
officer would come running into the section and say: 'What's this
meeting about? There's nothing here worth listening to! Break
it up! Obey your officers!' This last argument was usually
conclusive.

In the autumn of 1965 Rodygin, Krivtsov, Mart Niklus and other dyed-in-the-wool 'politicians' were clapped in the punishment block for six months. Valery and I saw them only rarely, when the punishment block was taken out for exercise. Soon afterwards I was sent to the hospital in camp three and while I was there camp seven was dispersed to other camps. Rodygin and Krivtsov went to camp eleven, but only stayed there for two weeks or so before being tried again and sentenced to three years in prison. So that when I came back from number three I no longer found my friends in the camp. But I remember one of the last conversations between Rodygin, Krivtsov and an officer shortly before they went to the punishment block.

Somebody came to give us a lecture – a Mordovian writer (for some reason they had failed to stick Rodygin and Krivtsov in the cooler beforehand and they were present too). The writer talked about some writers' congress he had attended or some conferences or something – who had made the speeches and who had said what. Sometimes after lectures they allowed questions to be asked by the audience or proposed that anyone wanting to ask something should go up on the stage to 'chat among themselves', depending upon the subject of the lecture. This time those who wished to ask questions were invited to go over to the staff building. But Krivtsov, Rodygin and several others stopped the lecturer on the front steps of the staff building, so that nonetheless the conversation took place before a large number of people.

The lecturer was being 'assisted' by Major Postnikov, our top KGB officer. Krivtsov asked why at the writers' congress or conference no opportunity to speak was given to any of the more progressive writers, such as Nekrasov* or Solzhenitsyn.† The lecturer replied that it was impossible for everyone to

---

* Viktor Nekrasov (b. 1915), author of *In the Trenches of Stalingrad, Kira Gheorgievna* and controversial travel sketches on the USA and Italy (trans. as *Both Sides of the Ocean*).

† Alexander Solzhenitsyn (b. 1919) a former camp inmate and the Soviet Union's most famous and controversial living writer. Author of *One Day in the Life of Ivan Denisovich, Cancer Ward, The First Circle* and a number of short stories and plays.

speak. But at this point Postnikov intervened (with him, as with all the officers, warders and KGB men in the camp, to pronounce the very name of Solzhenitsyn was like waving a red flag in front of a bull – they literally foamed at the mouth):

'Get lost with your Solzhenitsyn! What makes you think he's a writer? He's nothing but a disgrace to the profession of writer!'

'Why don't you like what he writes?' asked Genka sardonically.

'Who the hell does like it? It's an insult to the Russian language! What about all this 'mucking wick' or 'muck all '* on every other page?'

At that moment some con asked the duty warder to let him through into the work zone to visit the dentist. He showed the warder his certificate, but the latter brushed him aside and yelled:

'Fuck off with your bloody certificate! Wait till the shift goes through, until then you can go and get fucking well stuffed!'

'And what words,' asked Rodygin, 'would you recommend to describe that little scene?'

'There's no need to describe it at all. It's pointless and even harmful to draw attention to the dark side of life, to petty details and individual shortcomings,' replied Postnikov didactically.

'If Shchedrin† hadn't written about life's "petty details" and Ostrovsky‡ hadn't denounced the kingdom of darkness no one would remember them now; and it's impossible to fight against shortcomings, whether petty or major, when you sweep them under the carpet, keep quiet about them and draw some cheaply painted veil over them to hide them,' said Krivtsov, speaking not so much to Postnikov as for the benefit of the cons crowding

---

* A reference to euphemisms (for obscenities) used by Solzhenitsyn in his novel of camp life, *One Day in the Life of Ivan Denisovich*. These words are never printed in the Soviet Union and appear only rarely, as in Marchenko's book, represented by the first letter followed by dots.

† Saltykov-Shchedrin, M. Y. (1826–1889). Political and social satirist who exposed conditions of his time in his novels and stories. He was in government service, was banished, and retired as vice-governor of a province in order to write.

‡ Ostrovsky, A. K. (1823–1886). Playwright whose works are concerned with the evils of Russia in his time.

round him. But Postnikov wasn't worried about Shchedrin and Ostrovsky, he still hadn't finished with Solzhenitsyn.

'Your Solzhenitsyn distorts life! My two daughters – at school both of them – went and read *Ivan Denisovich* and then imagined that they could start criticising their father. Questions, reproaches, tears almost every evening! In the beginning I explained it all to them nicely, but later I had to throw the magazine* on the fire and that was the end of it.'

'Well,' said Rodygin, 'and did that convince your daughters? You always have one infallible argument: put the magazine in the fire and us in the cooler.'

---

* *One Day in the Life of Ivan Denisovich* was first published in the monthly literary magazine, *Novy Mir*.

YOUTH

The cons serving nowadays in the Internal Order Sections, prisoners' councils and other prisoners' organisations are for the most part old men. But even these old men finish their terms sooner or later and the camps are filling up with youth – students, workers, young writers, scientists. The camps are 'growing younger'.

But with youth the administration is having much more trouble in finding a common language, as the authorities like to put it. If they squeeze the young people harder, they only get angrier. They don't bend before the authorities and won't keep quiet – there's a continuous stream of protests in various spheres.

They tried replacing the stick with the carrot: youth gangs were formed, and huts only for youth. They hoped it would be easier to control them in this way. But the opposite happened. Finding themselves together, the young Ukrainians and Lithuanians, Estonians and Russians, workers and students, soon found that 'common language'.

And the warders complain: 'You should see the con nowadays! Say a word and you get two back again. You cuss him blind and he outcusses you. And he's not afraid of the cooler!'

THE BOUQUET

Political prisoners are brought to Mordovia from all corners of the Soviet Union and from all republics. There are particularly many Ukrainians and people from the Baltic republics – Lithuania, Latvia and Estonia. And it's not enough to bring them to a camp in Russia – they are even forced to speak Russian during visits from their relatives, so that the warder can understand. Between themselves, however, these prisoners speak in their own language, sing their own songs and organise secret celebrations in honour of their poets and writers.

Apart from this the camps are sometimes visited by representatives of the public of the various republics. These 'representatives' don't look to see what conditions their countrymen are being held in, they don't ask them how they are getting on and they even go out of their way to avoid any direct contact with the cons, fearing that they will be accused of interference in the affairs of the camp. All the conversations they have are conducted exclusively in the presence of members of admin or the KGB (sometimes the representative himself is a KGB man, and even in uniform). On the whole they don't want to know or hear anything at all about the camp, they would prefer to keep their eyes tightly closed and their ears tightly stuffed. They talk, on the other hand, about life in their republics, and this the cons don't want to hear: how can you believe a man when you can see his knees knocking in the presence of the KGB? And on top of all this he says how nicely everybody lives and how free they all are!

At first very few people went to these 'meetings with representatives', the cons had to be forced to go, just as to the political talks. Then the public representatives began to be accompanied by amateur artists. Now you could hardly get into the canteen at all for these occasions, not only Latvians or Lithuanians went, but all the other cons as well. Everyone liked to listen to the songs and poetry and look at the dancing. On the stage there would be people in national costume, not cons in their camp rags. They were given a very friendly reception (not like the speakers) and offered flowers and heartfelt thanks.

In the summer of 1965 we had an official visit at camp seven from representatives of one of the Baltic republics: after the speeches a concert was promised. The canteen was full to overflowing. At first, as usual, we had to listen to the 'representative'! When he had finished, the audience peppered him with questions – that was also quite usual. The speaker couldn't answer them, he was pinned to the wall – cons have no embarrassment and aren't afraid to ask questions that don't get asked outside. The discussions are usually ended by the officers: 'Comrades, pay no attention to provocative questions, we have plenty of provocateurs in here.'

And to the cons: 'Some of you are fed up with strict regime, it seems. Don't forget that special's just around the corner!'

Suddenly a young con made his way up on to the stage, a former law student from one of the Baltic republics. In his hand he held a bouquet tightly wrapped in paper. Evidently he wanted to present the bouquet to his countryman. And this was unprecedented: flowers were presented to the artists, but never to speakers.

There was a hush in the audience. The young man turned to the speaker: 'Permit me, in the name of all my countrymen, to present to our Homeland these flowers, which grow here so far away from her.'

He spoke with an accent, but in Russian, so that all could understand him. And while he was uttering this short speech, the audience began to show its consternation. From all sides came shouts of:

'Scum!'

'Arselicker!'

'Grass!'

I was boiling with indignation: to think that Krivtsov and Rodygin had been friends with this fellow! But the con had finished speaking now and was offering his bouquet to the speaker. The latter grasped it in his hand and at that moment the youth tore the paper off: it was a bouquet of barbed wire!

For the first moment everyone on the stage and in the audience just sat there rigid with mouths gaping, not knowing what to think. The speaker, holding on to his bouquet, shifted from foot to foot beside the table. A minute later the audience exploded. Never in my life, either before or after, have I heard such applause as I heard then. Literally every man jack of them was clapping, including well-known grasses and members of the IOS wearing armbands.

The KGB man on the stage regained his presence of mind. He ran over to the speaker and snatched the bouquet from his hand. But he himself had no idea what to do with it – he could hardly run through the audience in order to take it outside. He sat down in his seat again and laid the 'flowers' on the table in front of him. Then he snatched them off again and thrust them under his chair. The hubbub in the audience continued.

The young fellow who had presented the bouquet left the stage and made his way through the crowd. The warders made a dash towards him, but the cons fell to yelling and howling. The chief of political instruction gave orders to an officer and he dashed after the warders and told them something, after which they left the young fellow alone. We all understood that this would be only a short respite, while the visitors were here.

Somehow the audience calmed down. Another of the guests took the rostrum and started to say that this was merely a provocation 'as the comrade captain has just pointed out'. And he added: 'But we know that the majority of those present have correctly understood this incident and will condemn their comrade.'

Somebody shouted back in reply: 'You saw and heard the attitude of the majority. Don't pretend!'

The speaker fell silent. And then at once they hastened to begin the concert.

After the concert the performers were presented with flowers

– genuine ones. And when the bouquets were handed over the cons and performers exchanged glances and smiled.

That evening the young fellow was thrown in the cooler and fifteen days later transferred to a restricted form of special regime.

Several days after the incident we read in the Dubrovlag newspaper, 'For Outstanding Labour, that . . . in unit seven a meeting with national representatives was held in a warm, friendly atmosphere . . .'

FLOWERS IN THE COMPOUND

The thing that most amazes the visiting stranger from outside in the camps is that the compound is full of flowers and greenery. 'The territory of the unit is overflowing with flowers', as the camp newspaper puts it. And it is true.

The people who spend most time on the flowers are the old men and invalids, especially the ones who aren't driven out to work. There aren't many, but it is enough for the gardening. They are absolutely useless for work any longer, but they can't be let out till their time is up. Flower seeds are sent in by relatives – this is allowed. And many of the younger men help too. Everybody likes flowers.

The authorities don't order the flowers to be grown, but they don't forbid them either, and they don't trample on them like they do on carrots or onions. Let the visitors see them and say how well our prisoners live!

Quite often the officers and warders take flowers home with them to give to their wives. And on 31 August, before the start of the school year, all free workers leave the compound carrying flowers: the following day their kids will be giving them to their teachers.

One day a speaker came to visit us and the cons got into an argument with him about conditions in the camps.

'Well, what are you complaining about?' asked the speaker in surprise. 'You've got a sports ground, a volleyball court, a library, and a camp full of flowers!'

'Don't you know,' replied Rodygin, 'that flowers also grow on graves.'

HOSPITAL (CAMP DIVISION 3)

And those whom the torturer cripples
they patch up and darn and mend
and back for more torture send.

B. Brecht – 'Song'
(*The Fears and Miseries of the Third Reich*)

At about eight o'clock on the morning of 17 September 1965, all of us who were going to hospital had to gather at the guardhouse with our things. Already the day before we had filled in our release forms showing that we had handed in all our camp equipment – mattress, pillow, etc., and had had our work payments settled. And now about twenty of us had gathered there: those who were able came on foot, the more serious cases were brought on stretchers. Then the stretchers were placed straight on the ground.

We were waiting to be searched. The warders began to call us one by one into the guardhouse (those on the stretchers were carried into the guardhouse). Every single one of us, without exception, had to strip stark naked and then they examined and pinched us all over, pinched and felt every seam of our gear and took away everything that was forbidden to a con to possess: money, sharp or pointed objects, tea. Everything, in short, was as usual.

The main thing they were looking for was notes or letters: maybe a con would try to use the opportunity for dropping a few lines to a friend elsewhere, another con, and correspondence between prisoners was strictly forbidden. When they finished with one they would take him into the outer boundary zone, which was fenced off both from the inner boundary zone and the compound proper, and call the next.

By the time they had searched us, lined us up in fives, checked our personal belongings against the documents and counted us again, two hours or so went by. Finally we set off: those who could walk went in formation, escorted by armed guards, while those who couldn't were transported in carts – also accompanied, of course, by armed guards.

We arrived at the station and waited for the train. It was the same small train that did the usual run from Potma to Barachevo – just a few coaches with a prison coach usually at the back, so that you couldn't enter it from the platform but had to do it straight from the ground. For us who could walk it didn't matter, but with the stretchers it was a hell of a job: the coach was terribly high off the ground, the doors were narrow and you couldn't turn in the corridor. The stretchers had to be turned from side to side and almost stood on end to get them in.

Luckily the stretcher-bearers had the knack of it through doing the job so often. Every Tuesday and Friday there was a convoy to camp three the whole length of the railway line, from every camp in the group; the other two days were reserved for civil prisoners. Here it is necessary to point out that although there are trains to the hospital every week, the number of the sick in the camp never decreases: almost half the inmates of every camp suffer from ulcers or stomach complaints alone, and there simply isn't room for them all in number three. In any case they don't cure patients in camp three, they merely examine them, get them back on their feet somehow or other and send them back to work in the camps again. Their places are then taken by new arrivals, and so it goes on in perpetual rotation.

In the prison coach it makes not the slightest difference that sick men are being transported, the crush is as bad as ever and there is nowhere to sit down. No sooner have the stretchers been put inside than the others have to crowd in as best they can. Never mind, you'll get there somehow, it's only a couple of hours till we arrive. And they don't give you any sort of toilet break either because again, as they say, its only a couple of hours, you can wait. In actual fact we were chased out early that morning, so that it's not at all a case of waiting two hours but from eight o'clock in the morning. And sick men at that. But you can cry as much as you like, you still have to wait.

At every station they put more sick men on board and then lock everything up again.

At last we arrived. Here it was – number three – the hospital camp. And a camp like all the rest: palisade, barbed wire, watch towers, and a number of huts inside.

The distance from the station to the guardhouse was very small, about a hundred yards. But rules were still rules: the officer in command of the prison coach handed us over to the officer in command of the armed escort, just as he had received us, counting us and our files. The armed escort, having led us these hundred yards, handed us over yet again to the warder in the guardhouse, counting and checking each con against his photograph in the file. Then we had to go through another search. We were all gathered together into one big cell in the guardhouse and driven one at a time down a narrow corridor into another. In the corridor sat several warders; they ordered us to strip naked and pinched and felt every thread of our clothes and every hidden place on our bodies. However, they still didn't return our things to us but handed them all in to the stores. Then we were dispatched to different blocks – some to the surgical block, some to the psychiatric and some to the therapeutic – and once there we were issued with a towel, long underpants, an undershirt, and slippers for our bare feet. Now you were a patient and nothing else was prescribed, though you could also take with you a toothbrush, toothpaste, soap, a book or two and whatever food you happened to have. On the whole it was like when I went to hospital at home, the only difference being that I got no pyjamas and that the first 'examination' was carried out not by a doctor but by warders.

I was sent to block seven – the therapeutic block. A long hut with a corridor running its full length, on either side of the corridor small wards containing from twelve to twenty cots, then the doctor's office, a treatment room, and a pantry (all the people who work in the block live here too – orderlies, food servers, and so on). The ward was clean, the cots, although close together, weren't arranged in a double tier. White bed linen. Dressing gowns hung on one wall – about five or six per ward: whoever needed to go into the corridor took one down and put it on, though people also used to walk about in their underwear. It was all very similar, I must say, to an ordinary hospital. The difference was that whereas in an ordinary hospital the patients are always in a hurry to get out and go back home again, here it was the opposite: stay in as long as you can, for the way out of here lay not homewards but back to the camp, to those same officers, re-educators and warders, back to parades, searches, and that hated forced labour . . .

Then again, in a normal hospital you look forward to visiting hours, when your family will come to see you and bring you some delicacies to eat. Here in the camp hospital nobody comes to see you, your friends perhaps merely send you greetings via one of the regular convoys. And there are no parcels, no 'pick-me-ups', unless you happen to be due for a parcel in the ordinary way (and so long as you haven't been deprived of the right to receive one). Healthy or sick, a con's a con and should expect no extra privileges – God grant only that his lawful ones aren't taken away.

On the other hand the food in hospital is better than in the camps. Patients with ulcer or kidney trouble, post-operational patients and patients suffering from undernourishment – each gets a suitable diet. For one man the food is strained, another gets a saltless diet. Even the general diet in number three is better than in the ordinary camps. In the first place, you really do get everything that is prescribed in the daily rations: if, say, it is two ounces of meat a day, you don't get a sniff of it in a normal camp, whereas in number three, even if you don't get the whole two ounces you get one and a half in the form of rissoles or meat balls. The skilly for breakfast and dinner is the same, the gruel is the same and you get the same amount but on the other hand you also get a dish of stewed fruit in the mornings, and half an ounce of butter. And every sick person gets a glass of milk a day. The bread ration is smaller: eighteen ounces, but then seven ounces is white bread.

It may be that the calorie count of the camp hospital rations is no higher than a con's normal camp ration, but the quality of the calories is undoubtedly higher. Needless to say, such hospital delicacies as eggs, curd cakes, apples, are beyond the con's wildest dreams, he'll die before he sees any . . . But then there's the milk, the stewed fruit . . .

For so long as you're in a serious condition or very weak, the hospital rations are fully satisfactory and sometimes there's even a bit left over, but once you start to get better the situation's grim, you feel hungrier than in camp. For in the camp, as I have said before, nobody lives on 'basic', everybody contrives some way out of it: one man buys bread with money smuggled to him from home, another speculates, and even the man with nothing gets a part of somebody else's rations – the leftovers of some more resourceful con. Here in number three, though, you eat meatballs and drink milk, but you can't for the life of you get beyond the authorised norm, nor is there anywhere where you can get more than the prescribed eighteen ounces of bread. There is a shop in the camp, it's true, but everything is done to prevent the con from using it. You're transferred to hospital, for instance, and you've no idea when the money from your personal account will arrive, and then, while you're waiting, you're discharged again and when you get back to your camp your money is still travelling about somewhere, so that there too you have to go without the shop . . .

Free people can hardly comprehend all these problems and what seem at first to be the petty practical complications that fill a con's life. Take, for example, the question of whether to apply to go to hospital or not. On the one hand you feel like death warmed up, treatment is absolutely essential, you haven't the strength to work: on the other hand you will lose your shop privileges, perhaps for two or three months, so that if you go you'll have to live on an empty stomach for a month or two . . .

I felt that I was turning into an invalid, that I simply wasn't strong enough to stay in the gang. Day and night we would be ordered out – unload, push the wagon up, shovel coal, shovel grit, haul logs. The work was enough to break even a healthy man's back. And on top of this, autumn was setting in, to be followed by winter – rain, cold winds, frost. You'd get soaking wet at work, the autumn wind would blow right through you while you waited at the guardhouse – and by the spring you'd be either dead or a permanent invalid. So the lads advised me nonetheless to apply for hospital and to try and hang on there for as long as possible.

And so I had come to camp three. The ear specialist, with scarcely a glance at my ears, prescribed me some drops. The treatment was timed to last five days. That meant that in a week when convoy time came around, I would be on my way back to camp, to my dearly beloved stand-by gang.

Fortunately I met up with an acquaintance of mine in the surgical block – Nikolai Senik, a senior orderly working for the camp service. And there was a doctor's assistant too, also a con, who knew me slightly. They advised me to apply for work as an orderly: it was close to the doctors, just in case, and they would treat me a bit on the side. And the work too, although not easy, was at least indoors, out of the weather.

On the whole cons are unwilling to take work as orderlies and do so only in cases of extreme necessity or in order to get a good character reference. The point is that a hospital camp has no income, it is pure expense as far as the authorities are concerned, and so they do all they can to reduce this expense as far as possible. A whole block will have only two or three orderlies. And the work includes lighting stoves, washing and cleaning, laundering the doctors' white coats, serving out food, washing dishes and attending to the bed-ridden. What's more they ask far more of a camp orderly than one in a normal hospital: there, if you wear the orderly out with too many demands, she will simply ask for her cards and go elsewhere; and just you try and find another to take her place on the miserable pay she gets. That's why I have never seen a free hospital as clean as our camp hospital. Our doctor on his rounds used to take a piece of white cotton wool and rub it over the walls and window panes and even over the leaves of the flowers – and God forbid that he should find any dust! Thus the orderly has to dash about all day long. What's more, fifty per cent of his pay, just as elsewhere, is deducted for his keep, so that after deductions for food and clothing there is nothing left – not even enough to go to the shop. And so only cons like me used to volunteer for work as orderlies – in the hope of getting some treatment.

Here too, of course, the authorities tried to operate with administrative measures: once you were appointed an orderly, willy-nilly you had to work and knuckle under. If you refused – off to the cooler. But here in the hospital these measures didn't help. One con would be stuck in the cooler, another let out, again they would refuse and again go back to the cooler; but somebody had to do the work anyway. And so the authorities were forced to adopt an uncharacteristically liberal approach: the nurses or doctors would themselves pick suitable cons for particular kinds of work, or else interested cons would come to an agreement with them independently. Then, even though you were working unpaid in point of fact, at least it was voluntary.

I decided to apply for work as an orderly in the surgical block: here there were tiny rooms for two for members of the hospital service; and it was an enormous blessing, after living in communal huts, to have almost a separate room to yourself (actually we lived there 'illegally'; all members of the hospital service had a separate hut to themselves and whenever a commission came we were hurriedly evacuated there from our cubby-holes in the block).

Senik recommended me to the matron. She talked to the head doctor, the head doctor pleaded my case with the Chief Officer – and I became an orderly. My friends' advice turned out to be correct: I continued to receive treatment and was even given some sort of injections. The work too, although there was plenty of it, didn't bother me: my mother had been a cleaner and as a boy I had been used to helping her. The only difficult bit was lighting the stoves. The firewood they brought us was in such big pieces that it wouldn't go into the stove – and a chopper, of course, was not allowed into camp! Use your teeth, seemed to be the motto. As always, of course, I found a way out: I got myself a chopper. But I still couldn't chop anything outside, where it could be seen – I had the chopper, but had to pretend that I hadn't. And so I was forced to crawl under the front porch and there, bent double and practically on my knees, hack away at the billets in secret – as though I was gaining something for myself instead of providing fuel for the hospital.

Our complement for the surgical block was supposed to be two orderlies. I was taken on in excess of the complement and later they had to take two more: one assisted Senik in his duties and the other assisted me. We were registered officially as patients, so that no pay at all was credited to us and we worked solely in exchange for treatment. We were also fed as patients. The patients in our block also worked a bit: some volunteered to help with the washing up or to do some cleaning. As soon as their condition permitted they would ask for some little job or other. Not, of course, for lack of anything to do, but for an extra bowl of skilly or some bread: the orderly would go to the cookhouse and wheedle for some and then give it to whoever had helped him.

In our block we also had criminal prisoners and cons from special regime camps, and for a while they even brought women to us from the women's compound for operations, because their operating theatre was being renovated.

Patients from special regime camps were held in separate hospital cells, which were equipped with barred windows and sloptanks and always kept locked. After an operation, a 'stripey' (cons doing special have to wear striped uniform) was put into the general post-operative ward where he lay until he began to come round a bit from his operation, say for two to three days. Then, the moment he began to stir, it was off to the cell with him and under lock and key. These hospital cells were triple-headers, the keys to them were supposed to be held by the duty warder in the guardhouse. We tried to badger the duty warder as much as possible: at one moment we would be running to him to open up the cell for cleaning, the next it would be for treatment – injections had to be given or an enema administered; then the doctor's assistant had to check a patient's condition; then it was time to let the patients out for exercise (in hospital they were authorised to have half-an-hour's exercise in the corridor per day, but the time was determined by the assistant doctor). The upshot of all this was that the duty warder used to get fed up with this running back and forth and would give the keys into the safe keeping of the assistant doctor. The assistant doctor, of course, had no intention of holding convalescent patients under lock and key and allowed them to wander up and down the corridor – 'they've just been getting their injections' or 'the orderlies are washing the floor' – there was no shortage of excuses.

Senik tried to feed these patients up as much as he could; and in any case we all knew what it was like on special regime and had seen what pathetic 'goners' used to come from there.

We used to scrounge left-over bits of black bread from the bread-cutting room and dry them out for the cons doing special, so that when they went back to camp they could at least take these 'rusks' with them for themselves and their cell-mates. Whatever else they took back with them would be confiscated during the search, but rusks made of black bread were allowed. As for the other cons from strict regime camps, they could always shift for themselves in the matter of food, but on special regime, just as in prison, there is no way at all.

Surgical patients from among the criminal prisoners also had separate wards (therapeutic patients had a separate compound altogether), but they were not kept locked in and used to troop down the corridor all together. On the whole the authorities try to separate the criminal prisoners from political prisoners not because the latter have to be protected against bandits, but on the contrary – they are afraid in case the 'politicals' with their views and conversation might somehow corrupt these honest and respectable swindlers and hoodlums.

The women's hospital compound was just behind that of the criminal prisoners. That winter the women were operated on in our theatre. Senik and I were usually sent to bring the patients who couldn't stand, and it was we who usually took them back again. On operation days we would be summoned to the guardhouse of the women's compound, where we would go under armed escort, put the patient, who had already been prepared by the women orderlies, on to our stretcher and carry her straight to our block. There we would place the stretcher in a narrow passageway in front of the operating theatre, undress the patient to her undershirt and then carry her in on our arms and place her on the operating table. Meanwhile the convalescent men would crowd at the door to the passageway just for a chance to set eyes on a woman, especially one that was almost completely undressed. It didn't matter that she was sick and wasn't even able to walk, but had to be brought in on a stretcher.

After the operation, while the patient was still under the influence of the anaesthetic, we would remove her from the table, place her on a stretcher, wrap her up as warmly as we could (it was wintertime, frosty) and carry her to our guard-house. Here we would have to lower the stretcher and begin to beg the duty warder to get us an escort quickly – he always insisted on taking his time. Officers and doctors would walk past the stretcher as it rested directly on the ground and not one of them gave a damn for us and our patient – every free worker here had long since got used to the idea that cons weren't human beings. Then we would begin to lose our tempers and rush from one to the other: 'We've got a patient here fresh from the operating table, the anaesthetic will wear off in a minute and when she starts to move about she'll uncover herself and catch cold! Hurry up with the escort!'

The officers replied: 'We're not doctors, our job is to guard you. Anaesthetics and patients are none of our business.'

Just then an elderly, dignified lady in a light-brown overcoat with a fur collar would pass by. This was the hospital director, Shimkanis, a major in the medical corps. Without even a glance at the stretcher, she would reply: 'We're doctors, our job is to heal and perform operations. Escorts are nothing to do with us. What do you want me to do?'

We tried complaining about such inhuman methods. The Chief Officer replied by putting us in our place:

'It's none of your business! You've brought the stretcher to the guardhouse, now wait! People can only complain for themselves, not for others. Have you forgotten that?'

And the same reply was given to us by Major Petrushevsky, chief of the Sanitation Department of the Dubrovlag directorate: 'Why can't you mind your own business! The authorities will answer for everything!'

Yes, and they do! A healthy man is sent to the camp and he

comes out an invalid – will Major Petrushevsky or Major Shimkanis have to answer for that one day? And to whom? . . .

And so we stand and stand, wait and wait. At last the armed guards crawl out and lead us to the guardhouse of the women's compound. We walk slowly, fearing to fall: it is slippery, our boots skid on the frozen snow – and we are carrying a patient in a serious condition. Before we get there we stop several times to take a breather, obliged each time to lower the stretcher directly on to the snow. At the guardhouse we are received by two wardresses – coarse, fat women wearing greatcoats with striped epaulettes – who take us to the block. Here we are obliged to wait in the corridor while the women orderlies remove the patient and free our stretcher. That's another joke: we are one administration, in essence a single hospital compound, although divided up into a women's, political and criminal prisoners' compound – yet each division has its own equipment, its own stretchers; and for the sake of these and in order that we should remain responsible for them, they allow us to remain for a while among the women prisoners. Although any contact between men and women is forbidden and harshly punished, nevertheless when it comes to even such a trivial piece of equipment as a stretcher, the rules can all go to hell!

While we are waiting for the stretcher we are surrounded in the corridor by women prisoners, both patients and orderlies. They are delighted just to see or talk to a man who is not a guard and not a warder. The majority of them are criminal prisoners – and the things you get to hear while you're waiting! Some of them have friends in the men's camps and these ask to see us to pass on greetings or notes to them – after all, patients come to us from every corner of Dubrovlag. And we also look around us as though in a different world. We don't notice either the skinniness or the pitiful clothing of the women surrounding us. Or rather, we notice it, we pity them for it, but in spite of their unfortunate appearance they seem terribly attractive to us. One door off the corridor opens into a small ward from where we can hear the sound of a sort of high pitched squeaking, like the miaowing of cats. We look in. Round the walls runs a double line of cots, just like the ones we have in the men's compound, and across the cots, several to each, lie little squeaking bundles: new-born babes.

'Whose are these?' we ask.

'Gulag's* children,' answers a cheerful young woman con.

There are quite a few women among the patients who have had children born to them in the camp. 'My Valery's two already!' 'My Nina's going on five!' Where there are no families outside to take the children, they grow up inside the camp and are brought up in the camp nurseries and orphanages. The mother stays in the compound behind barbed wire, while the child stays with her for a time and then goes into a special orphanage – but still not a free one. And so they grow up . . .

Sometimes women used to come on their own for operations – under armed escort, of course, but not on stretchers. They usually didn't feel too bad and were awaiting some simple sort of operation. They would bring half a dozen to the block all at once and take them to the treatment room, where they would undress (also to their undershirts) and wait to be called for their operation. In the corridor would be a crowd of convalescent men. The politicals tended to be more reticent, but the criminal prisoners simply went wild over the women; and then the women were of different types too. One of the cons would start to beg Nikolai Senik:

'Listen, you bring her to the toilets and I'll already be there. Go on, just for ten minutes, eh?'

After the operations, of course, some have to be carried back on a stretcher, others shuffle back on their own. But they're not up to anything by that time, least of all men . . .

Our surgical block was also good in that our doctors were young, they hadn't yet been worn down by the system, hadn't become accustomed to it and hadn't adapted themselves to it. Having finished their studies they had been drafted here, and they were only waiting for the day when they could get back 'to freedom' again. From every one of them I heard the same:

'All I want to do is get these three years over with and then

* Gulag is an acronym for Main Administration of Camps.

get away from here to wherever I can, even to the devil himself if necessary!'

On the other hand, the work in camp three was beyond even the wildest dreams of a beginning doctor: operations of all degrees of complexity, traumas, even bullet-wounds.

One day they brought us a young fellow from one of the criminal camps – his chest had been shot away by a tommy gun. It had happened like this: a group of cons had been standing on a porch in the compound and having a slanging match with the sentry in the watch tower. The latter lost his temper and trained his tommy gun on them. The rest of the cons ran into the hut, but this one stayed behind – it wasn't conceivable for a sentry to fire into the compound. Well, the sentry did let off a burst. I don't know whether he was punished or not, but the con came to us in the surgical block.

So here was the chance to get experience and independent work and reasonable conditions (although, of course, it was a pretty poor hole to be stuck in) – and yet the young doctors were anxious to get away from this work to 'wherever they could'. One of the main reasons was that they were unable to help their patients properly – and all around them they could see injustices and hunger. Here they were undergoing a training in heartlessness and indifference: do what directly concerns you and don't interfere with anything. For a doctor, of course, it is difficult to reconcile this principle with the principles of his profession. But some accustomed themselves to it, remained there forever and themselves became like admin and the officers – like Shimkanis for example. But then there were lots more like her, especially in the camps themselves.

Our surgeons, however, were quite different, including both the chief surgeon, Zaborovsky, and the two other doctors, Kabirov and Sokolova. They used to talk to the patients and would turn a blind eye to us orderlies meeting late at night in the treatment room. How many times did our doctors go to the hospital director to ask for more firewood for our block! Sokolova was the sort of woman who would order me not to light her stove during the frosty weather and would sit in her office in her fur coat – so that there would be more firewood for the wards and because it was better for the patients to be warm. In actual fact, this was about all the doctors could do for us, apart from giving treatment. Another characteristic feature was that they lacked the arrogance with which most free workers regarded prisoners. Our assistant doctor, Nikolai, had a twenty-five-year term to serve, he had long experience, and our young doctors always sought his advice: his diagnoses were considered the best of all.

Here I again came into close contact with various 'self-mutilation' cases, tattooed cons and failed suicides. Almost every operation day included some sort of stomach operation, when they cut out whatever it was the con had swallowed. I won't talk about them all in detail, since this would only be a repetition of what I saw and described in Vladimir jail: barbed wire hooks, pieces of glass, bent kettle spouts . . .

A young fellow from the Baltic coast was brought in one day from the psychiatric block. I had got to know him earlier when in hospital for the first time. Then he had just cut off one ear. They healed the wound and put him in the psychiatric block. And now, when he had only a few months to go till his release, he had cut off his second ear and swallowed a spoon and some pieces of barbed wire. He was operated on by Sokolova, but two months later came back again: this time he had swallowed a whole set of chessmen, both the black and white pieces, with the exception of two knights. Only about forty days remained till his release. I don't know whether he was really crazy. I had often talked to him and he gave me the impression of being fully normal – far more normal, at any rate, than many cons in the camps who passed for normal. He was the son of a priest, a literate, well-read fellow. And he read a lot in hospital too. The second operation was also done by Sokolova: Senik asked her afterwards if he could have the chessmen from the stomach. He and I preserved this museum exhibit – we couldn't play with it, two of the knights were missing.

I also met another old acquaintance of mine here – Boris Vlasov, the one who had come into our cell at Vladimir on crutches. Soon after that, Boris had been taken out of prison and put on special regime, and all this time he had been doing special. He was brought in wearing a striped uniform and put in a cell with the other 'stripeys'. While in the special regime camp he had tattooed himself all over, including on the face and chest, and had all the usual slogans: 'Slave of the CPSU' and so on. In our block they cut out his tattoos and he didn't stay with us long. As soon as his wounds began to heal he was transferred to the therapeutic block, which he didn't like for one minute! Only in our block did the 'stripeys' live relatively freely, stroll up and down the corridor and talk to the other cons. In the other blocks they kept strictly to instructions: in the cell they stayed, under lock and key.

One day they brought a young fellow in from one of the camps. While doing special he had swallowed several rusty nails, two spoons and some pieces of barbed wire. He knew that as soon as he recovered from his operation he would be taken away again and put back on special regime. And so, immediately after his operation, before he had hardly come round, he tore off his bandages and split open the seam on his stomach. They were forced to sew him up again. And he lay there, tied down in his cot, until the scar healed. Naturally he was put back on special regime. There he got hold of a razor blade, ripped open his stomach again and again got sent to us; and again we were forced to tie him down in his cot . . .

These are just ordinary, everyday stories of camp life to which cons, doctors and admin have grown fully accustomed. But one day one of our nurses (they were all free workers from outside) went on holiday to some nurses' holiday home. Once there she avoided telling her companions that she worked in a camp, no, she was just a nurse in a hospital. But, as happens on holiday, she got to telling them about the kind of things that happened at work: they took a spoon out of one patient's stomach, another one had nails inside him, or chessmen, or glass . . . And lo and behold, after she had told these stories, her companions at the holiday home decided that she was abnormal, that she was psychologically unbalanced, and they even began to be afraid of her. After her holiday she told us this on one of the evenings when we gathered in the treatment room. And all of a sudden we seemed to see properly for the first time everything that surrounded us, the whole savagery and fantastic incredibility of the situation we were in, of these ordinary stories of ours, and of this hospital behind barbed wire under the armed guard of tommy gunners in watch towers.

LOVE

Earlier the men's and women's hospital compounds had been next door to one another, separated only by a wooden fence, some strands of barbed wire and a ploughed and raked strip. We were able not only to see the women but even to talk to them secretly and throw notes over. And even later, when the women's hospital camp was moved farther away, our orderlies and patients managed to keep contact with them, and this is how it was done. Sometimes we stretcher bearers would have to take the women to and from operations, while the nurses used to take our linen and steriliser over to the women's camp, at which times a note could be passed over. Admin persecuted prisoners remorselessly for any relations with women and if a note was ever discovered and they succeeded in tracking down its author and the addressee, the cooler was a cert for all three of them, that is for both 'partners in the relationship' and the person who passed on the note. And if a nurse was to blame, she was dismissed immediately.

It is not quite clear to me why these platonic affairs should so arouse admin's ire and indignation. Was it that they imagined more in them than there really was? Sheer malice (not even the slightest pleasure can be permitted)? Or simply because the regulations were being broken? But no prohibitions or persecutions in the world could stop men and women who for years had been deprived of any natural relations with one another. And so these forbidden camp affairs would break out, a paper love that might last a week, but sometimes went on for years. They began always with introductions ('my name is so-and-so' – 'and my name is so-and-so'; often the first note was sent completely at random). Well, and then – declarations of love,

dreams of a meeting, and sometimes even a photo got passed.
And so a con dreamed no longer of kissing a woman in the
abstract but thought of his Nadia or his Lucy, and she would tell
him that she loved him and write tender words, and he would
wait for the next note and undergo agonies of uncertainty – did
she still love him, had she found another? . . . Gone is the camp,
the barbed wire, the loneliness; all that seems real is the
separation from your loved one . . . Sometimes, though very
rarely of course, this camp love survives even release.

Nikolai Senik once had his own 'sweetheart' – her name was
Lyuba and she was an assistant doctor in the women's hospital.
Both Lyuba and Nikolai had been working in their respective
hospitals for ages, for five years already. They had got to know
one another when the women's camp was still next to ours and
used to send each other notes and look at one another from a
distance. Nikolai knew that Lyuba had a husband outside, some
of the boys had even seen him when he came to visit her and
said he was a nice sort of fellow. Nikolai himself was alone: his
wife had left him and married somebody else. The fact that
Lyuba was married didn't stop them loving one another. Anyway,
they were two different lives: the outside world, a husband,
visits once a year; and against this the camp, love notes and
dreams of a meeting. I don't know which of these two lives was
the reality and which of them existed only in the imagination.

When the women's camp was moved away, Nikolai and Lyuba
continued to correspond through the nurses. Now they even
managed to see one another from time to time, for our orderlies
used to take the women to be operated on. For the first time
they were able to see one another close up, for the first time
they were able to talk. Nikolai always tried to go himself with
the stretchers to the women's camp in order to have an extra
chance of swapping a few words with Lyuba. And we used to
help him as best we could. We could either take over his duty
in the operating theatre or try to fiddle about with the stretchers
in the women's camp as long as possible, so as to distract the
wardresses. Sometimes Nikolai and Lyuba even managed to be
alone for a few minutes.

Not long before Lyuba's release she was operated on for

varicose veins. She came over herself for the operation. The women orderlies had picked out the best smock they could find for her, with no holes and more or less the right size. And Nikolai himself had prepared in advance the most becoming dressing gown and the best slippers. He had also washed and ironed it himself. But he didn't go to the operation, in order not to embarrass Lyuba, and asked me to go on duty instead. The doctors knew of their love and Kabirov, who was doing the operation, permitted Lyuba to keep her panties on on the operating table – usually the patients remained naked under their smocks.

When the operation was over, Nikolai helped me to carry Lyuba back to the women's hospital. They continued to write letters to each other as before, but it didn't last much longer. Lyuba was soon released. Nikolai and I wrote a last letter to her together – of farewell . . .

I also had offers to introduce me to one of the women prisoners – to 'get married', as they say – but I didn't want to. I knew that I wouldn't be here much longer and that soon I would have to return to my camp.

Paper love gets carried on not only in hospital but in any camp, particularly if there are men's and women's camps in the same settlement. In camp eleven a number of friendships were struck up when our construction gang was working in the women's camp. Knowing that their affairs would have to be broken up as soon as the construction gang finished its work, the women and the cons made plans in advance about how to keep in touch – through relatives and through the hospital. And what quarrels, scandals and even fights took place over love! Suddenly somebody would find out that one woman was writing to two or three at the same time, or on the contrary, a con would be writing to one and her friend would then start writing to him and 'steal' him – tears, despair, jealousy . . .

There were also cases, of course, of more 'material' love, for there were women working in the camps as medical staff or teachers in the school. Many prisoners used to go to school only to look at the women teachers. But this in any event wasn't love – it was a case of many looking at one, and in a certain sense she belonged to them all. Well, and then there were instances of a con getting together with one of the unskilled women working inside the camp. I've no idea, I'm sure, of where and how they managed it. Sometimes an affair was the result of mutual attraction, and sometimes because of some sort of present. One of our cons had an affair with a free worker after giving her a watch. And that's all there was to it. The most intriguing thing about this whole business was that most of the free women in the camps were the daughters and wives of the officers and warders.

But the majority of prisoners live all these years and the whole of their sentences – five, ten, fifteen, twenty-five years – without any kind of love whatsoever, either paper or genuine. This is why in the ordinary camps, among the criminal prisoners, homosexuality is rampant. Practically one hundred per cent of them indulge in it, despite the fact that homosexuality is punishable by law. If they catch you out you can get a new stretch for it – but then they can't catch everybody. I remember when I was at Karaganda, in Stepnoy Camp, all the homosexuals there – the ones that were known, that is, and caught in the act – were herded into a single hut with 180 men in it, in an attempt to segregate them from the rest. 180 men – these were only the ones that got caught and the ones who played the woman in the couples. Those who played the men were not considered as homosexuals. The former were universally despised, while the latter went about like heroes, boasting of their masculine strength and their 'conquests' not only to each other but even to the guards. One day I heard Vorkuta, a famous pederast known to the whole camp, stand next to a company commander and say to him about another commander (who was just walking past): I wouldn't mind getting hold of him and doing this, that and the other to him: and the two of them lingered lovingly over all the details. That was not in a criminal camp, but a political one.

In general homosexuality is also spreading to the political camps, together with the criminals who find their way there. But the position of homosexuals there is far different from in the ordinary camps. They are despised by the whole camp, but on the other hand are beloved of admin. If anyone is ever caught at the game, they don't send him for trial but merely threaten him with a trial and publicity. That way they blackmail them and enlist a whole army of grasses and provocateurs. It's true, though, that admin don't get much use out of them: there are few homosexuals in the political camps, you can practically count them on the fingers of one hand, and the prisoners know who they are even better than admin and do their best not to mix with them.

I used to know several homosexuals: in Vladimir and later in Mordovia there was a certain Subbotin (the one who swallowed the dominoes), also Yuri Karmanov – nicknamed Lyubka – a homosexual since the time of the Byelomor Canal, and then the celebrated Vorkuta. They were all scum, the lowest of the low, cynical and foul-mouthed. As far as obscenities went, however, the officers and guards and all the members of admin could compete with them any time, and I don't know who would have won. Once Vorkuta got into such a competition with our censor. He was lining up for printed packets when, all of a sudden, he let loose a terrific hail of curses. The censor evidently decided to show that he wasn't born yesterday either and also knew a thing or two – and sent back an even bluer reply. Vorkuta then started fucking everything up hill and down dale – his God, his soul, his mother, and the censor likewise. I was also in the same line and to stand by and listen to it was both comic and disturbing.

The married cons, of course, were a different matter entirely, they didn't need any paper love. They lived on memories of their families, letters, and their wives were allowed a visit once a year. But the KGB and admin tried to use the con's right to one visit per annum as one more means of exerting pressure, a means of enslaving the prisoner. At first, while a case is still under investigation and immediately after it's over, they endeavour to persuade the wife to disown her criminal husband. And a few wives disown them of their own accord: all the unpleasantness, the troubles, the journeying, bringing up the children on your own, and on top of that to wait for ten or fifteen years. The wife of one of my camp friends demanded not only a divorce from her husband but also that he give up all rights of paternity.

The law went out of its way to satisfy such demands, even when a normal divorce in our country was complicated by all sorts of formalities – they just went ahead and divorced and took away paternity rights with no red tape whatsoever, and without saying a word to the convicted husband. My friend asked: how was it, then, that they had divorced him from his wife and taken away his children without any consent from him (in those days you still needed the consent of both parties for a divorce)? They replied that he had betrayed his country – that was the article he was convicted under – and by virtue of that very fact had obviously betrayed his wife as well, and that was why she was disowning him.

And if a wife doesn't disown her husband and travels to visit him, they call her in for a talk before the visit in the hope that she will influence her husband and persuade him to give up his beliefs and his friends in the camp and cooperate with the administration. In return they promise that he can have a visit lasting three whole days and have parcels, and that his lot will be improved. On the other hand 'obstinate' prisoners, who stubbornly maintain their convictions, have their visit shortened to two days, one day, or one working day (in other words sixteen hours); and they dream up all sorts of excuses in order to deprive him of his personal (with no warders present) visit – his one and only visit a year.

The unmarried cons – and there are quite a few of them now in the political camps, more and more young people have been coming in in recent years – suffer badly from the lack of women. You get the following sort of thing. While outside, a young fellow lived with a girl as man and wife, only the marriage was never registered. And then suddenly he's put away and she can't come on a visit, not even a communal one, because the camp administration recognises only legal marriages, confirmed by the register office's rubber stamp. True, they might permit a visit if the unofficial wife gets a certificate from the district or village council testifying that she had in fact been cohabiting with so-and-so. And although it was humiliating for a woman to have to ask for such a certificate, still a great number used to accept the humiliation in order to be able to meet their beloved. And it even used to happen that unknown girls, after becoming friends through correspondence, would come armed with such certificates to see their pen pals – if they were lucky enough to get one from the village council (and what could the council do, how the devil could they know who was living with whom?).

They say that not so long ago, about two years before I came to Mordovia, the village council's confirmation or certificate of marriage was insufficient. Then, so the boys told me, a woman also had to have a certificate from the VD clinic that she wasn't suffering from any venereal disease. So a husband would end up writing to his wife: 'Darling, I'm allowed a visit. Please come, but don't forget to pick up a certificate from the doctor saying that you haven't got syphilis or gonorrhea . . .' The wife, of course, would be in tears: 'We've got children, I'm waiting for you – and you don't trust me.' 'I trust you, my dear, it's my commandant who's so suspicious.'

Particularly amusing was the fact that if the wife was a Party member, she didn't need such evidence – instead of a doctor's certificate she could show her membership card. This gave rise to a multitude of questions: did an applicant for Party membership need a certificate? Did you have to have a certificate from the clinic before being accepted into the Party? If not, then had it been established by science that entry into the Party would cleanse and cure you of syphilis caught earlier? . . . In brief, there was no shortage of jokes on this theme.

I was too late to see this rule in operation. In my time it was sufficient to have evidence of marriage or a certificate from the village council. I wrote about this to a girl-friend of mine and in 1964, having obtained the necessary certificate in her village, she came to pay me a visit. At that time I had no black marks to my name and they gave me three days; and the ganger didn't call me to work on those days. I was lucky: in six years of imprisonment I managed to spend three days with a woman.

After that I didn't ask her again. What was the point of her tying her life to a con, what fun was it for her to travel once a year just to spend three days with me? After all, she wasn't my wife.

THE LOONY BIN

Apart from the therapeutic and surgical blocks in camp three we also had a psychiatric block – everybody called it the 'loony bin' (from 'lunatic asylum', I suppose; there are other words for it too). What horror stories you hear outside about madmen and about mental hospitals! I was overwhelmed with curiosity: although it was frightening, I was irresistibly drawn to have a look at the madmen close up. And the more so since everybody feels flattered by such a confrontation: looking at lunatics you rise in your own estimation – they are lunatics, but I'm clever. I had heard, of course, that sometimes perfectly healthy people were incarcerated in lunatic asylums if they had displeased the authorities in some way. But still, a loony bin was a loony bin . . .

I went on a visit to the orderlies in the psychiatric block. The block was divided off from the others by a high fence. I rang at the gate and it was opened for me. Cautiously I entered the yard. All over the yard there were cons walking up and down – patients who were quietly talking to one another. Maybe these were the mild cases, only slightly cracked? I walked through the whole block and visited every one of the cells – everywhere it was the same picture. Reading, playing chess, quietly talking together. The orderlies made fun of me for trying to find the lunatics: 'Are you cracked yourself, or something? Don't you know where the madmen are? Didn't you see them in the camps?'

I recollected that in the camps and in jail – in the communal cells – I really had met cons who were genuinely mentally sick and in some cases even violent. Many of them absolutely poison the lives – which God knows are miserable enough already – of their fellow cons: they make a racket at night, shout things out, howl, steal food, create uproar, start fights; there are even those who defecate on the floor and then eat their own faeces. How often did we complain to the authorities and beg for them to be taken away and isolated from the healthy cons, but the answer was always the same: 'It's none of your business, you're not in charge here!' And at the best we might hear: 'What do you want us to do with them? We can't take them home with us!'

'Do you mean to say that everyone here is normal, that there are no genuine madmen here at all?' I asked an orderly one day. He explained to me that indeed there were a few genuine ones, but these were kept there for a short time only and then sent back to the camps. Sometimes they would be sent to the Serbsky Institute in Leningrad for expert diagnosis. There, more often than not, they would be pronounced normal and admin would be given an authorisation to treat them as normal. People under investigation for a crime are a different matter, of course: the Serbsky Institute can proclaim as mad almost anyone with even the slightest abnormalities in his psychology, or even completely normal people – if that is what the KGB wants.

Afterwards I often used to go to the loony bin, and in any case our 'lunatics', secretly from the administration, used to wander all over the camp, even though it was strictly forbidden. The orderlies weren't in the least afraid of letting them out: they knew that they need fear no unpleasantness from their patients.

Among the 'lunatics' I met several people I knew. On my very first visit there I was astonished to recognise one of the patients as a con I had known in camp ten – he was that same man who had tangled with Captain Vasyayev on the memorable evening of our failure to dig a tunnel. I was told by other cons that he used to enter into discussion not only with the officers who were our 'teachers', but also with visiting lecturers – and always floored them with his questions and arguments. The prisoners used to listen to these discussions with enormous interest, but admin used to get furious. How many times did they stick him in the cooler, but he still wouldn't let up. He and I talked together, recalled that evening and acquaintances we had in common, including Burov, whom he had known very well. I

cautiously asked him how he had come to land up among the
'lunatics'. He laughed at my embarrassment and said that there
were lots here like himself: admin felt much happier with them
in the loony bin than in camp.

Kolya Shcherbakov was also there, minus both ears and blue
all over from the slogans and sayings that were tattooed on his
face and body. I also met a genuine madman, Nurmsaar, from
the Baltic coast. I had known him earlier at camp seven, we had
lived in the same section. He was more or less quiet in his
behaviour and caused more trouble to himself than others. Every
now and then he would refuse to go to work; when the time
came to go on parade, he would walk off in the other direction.
We used to stop him: 'Nurmsaar, where are you going? It's time
to go to work!' But he seemed not to hear and would look straight
through us. Several times our company officer, Alyoshin, gave
him two weeks in the cooler for failure to go to work. And now
he had been brought to the loony bin – correctly in this case,
you could hardly drive him out to work and demand a norm from
him as if he were normal. I went over to him in order to ask
about my friends in number seven, but it seemed he didn't
understand me, and maybe he didn't even recognise me either.
Thus, having got nothing out of him, I went away. Later, after
my release, I learned that Nurmsaar was back in camp again and
had also been stuck back in the cooler.

It was another meeting, however, that produced the biggest
impression on me. I went, as was customary, to meet one of
the regular convoys, to pick up patients and bring them back to
the surgical block. And who should I see among the new arrivals
but a close acquaintance of mine, Mart Niklus. He had been a
friend of my own friends, Genka Krivtsov and Tolik Rodygin.
All three of them had been put into an intensified regime block
(IRB)* ostensibly for failing to fulfil their norms, but the whole
camp knew that they had been put in the block for their 'obstinacy' – in other words because they stood up for their beliefs.
I knew that their term on intensified regime wasn't up yet, so I
was all the more pleased to see Niklus – both because he himself

* A kind of 'special regime' administered to a small number of prisoners
within a 'strict regime' camp.

had managed to get out of the IRB (this happens very rarely, usually they say: 'Finish your punishment first, then you can go for treatment') and for the sake of news of my friends. Mart passed on greetings to me from Genka and Tolik and I told him a bit about life in number three – so as to help him orientate himself as quickly as possible. Then I asked him what had happened and how he had managed to get himself out of the IRB and into hospital. And although by this time I was used to just about everything, nevertheless I was stunned by his reply: 'Well, don't you see – I'm mad now, that's why they've brought me to the loony bin!' Somehow I just couldn't fit this news into my head. Mart explained that he had gone on hunger strike as a mark of protest against the starvation rations. They threatened that if he didn't call off his strike they would lock him up in the lunatic asylum – and here he was: 'Now,' said Niklus, 'I can live among the same sort of lunatics as myself.'

Sometimes Niklus would come secretly to join us in our block. Four of us – he and I and two of our orderlies, countrymen of his, named Karl and Jan – used to spend our evenings in conversation. He stayed for about a month and then was sent back to the IRB – to finish out his term. When that was over, he and Krivtsov and Rodygin were 'tried' and sentenced to three years in Vladimir jail. Niklus was soon let out again, but Genka and Tolik are in jail even now.

What an interesting situation: the same man turns out to be normal at one moment and abnormal the next, and then normal again – all according to the whim of the authorities. Niklus, for instance, was considered normal – he was obliged to keep up with his work and observe all the conditions of the regime; he went on hunger strike, became 'insane' and landed up in the loony bin; then he went back to the IRB and was tried by a camp court as though fully normal (and on the same charge that had cost him six months in the IRB already – perhaps if he went on hunger strike at Vladimir he would be pronounced a lunatic again).

And here is another case: one day in camp three a warder detained a patient from the psychiatric ward outside the library

– the patient was not supposed to go beyond the fence. This patient had been pronounced abnormal by the Serbsky Institute and I think he really was cracked. Nevertheless the warder started dragging him off to the cooler for breaking regulations. The patient broke away and made a run for it, the warder caught up with him and grabbed him, then the patient started to fight him off and in the ensuing struggle tore off one of the warder's shoulder-straps. The patient was put on a charge. But so long as a man's a lunatic, he cannot be tried. And so a few days later the madman was pronounced normal, tried for resisting a member of the security services, for causing him bodily harm and for tearing off one of his shoulder-straps. So they tried a sick man solely to frighten off the others, so that others wouldn't be tempted. His sentence was extended to fifteen years; and still he was lucky that he wasn't shot!

A SKIRMISH WITH AUTHORITY

On a normal convoy day at the end of February, Karl and I set off for the reception centre to meet the surgical patients. We travelled light: wearing just our backless slippers, capless, without our oversleeves and not even wearing our padded jackets.

With our hands in our pockets and the stretcher tucked under our arms, we set off at a run. Although there was more than thirty degrees of frost, we weren't afraid of getting cold: the reception centre was about one minute's walk from our block.

When we got there we found two patients unable to walk – that meant we needed another stretcher. I dashed out on to the porch and hesitated: where was the best place to go? Our block had only one stretcher. As I looked around I saw some officer standing by the guardhouse and beckoning me with his hand. Just my luck, I thought, for him to want to see me in this frost. But I ran anyway, there was no question of not obeying. I kept my hands in my pockets, my bare feet flip-flopped in the slippers and I could feel the frost already nipping at my toes. I arrived. The officer was wearing a warm great-coat with the epaulettes of a full lieutenant, the ear flaps of his cap hung down but weren't fastened, he had felt knee-boots, fur gloves and evidently was also wearing something warm under his greatcoat. His face was unfamiliar to me. Still, we knew very few of the officers and guards at number three, they rarely bothered us and we thanked God for it.

The officer moved his lips – he was saying something to me, but not very loudly. I said:

'Speak louder, please, I'm hard of hearing.'

He really bellowed then:

'Ah, so all at once you're hard of hearing! What's your name?'

'Marchenko.'

'What block are you from?'

'Number one, surgical.'

While this exchange was taking place I got thoroughly frozen: all I had on was a cotton tunic over a cotton undershirt – and I was practically barefoot. I was in a filthy temper. Couldn't he see that I was completely undressed? What was he keeping me out in this frost for? And he was shouting:

'Why have you got your hands in your pockets? Have you forgotten how to speak to your officers? That rule goes for the deaf as well!'

I was so taken aback that I couldn't even think of anything to say. And he went on shouting, without a pause: 'What are you bobbing up and down and jerking about for? Can't you stand still when you're being spoken to by a representative of the camp administration?'

I was silent. Then he started again: 'Why don't you say something? You are obliged to reply when asked a question by a representative of the camp administration! Take your hands out of your pockets, stand up straight as you're supposed to! Why won't you obey your superior? Why don't you answer any questions?'

'Because your questions are idiotic!' I replied bitterly, with my teeth already chattering from the cold.

His eyes popped. But at this point, remembering himself, he shouted to two warders in the guardhouse to come and cart me off to the cooler. 'I shall sort you out a little later, we will finish this talk elsewhere,' he snapped threateningly. I was at least glad to be able to move at last and go indoors, even if only to the cooler – it was better than standing out in the frost.

While I stood with the warder by the gate in the fence surrounding the cooler, waiting for it to be opened, I thought I would freeze solid. We went inside. The usual procedure followed – I was stripped to the skin, searched, ordered to dress and thrust into a cell. It was a small cell for two, about a good pace wide and eight feet long. From wall to wall and not very high off the floor stretched a row of continuous boards; there was a tiny window and in one corner a sloptank. Over the door a hole in the wall held an electric light bulb.

It was so bitterly cold in the cell that you didn't dare sit or lie down – you'd freeze to death. The glass in the window hadn't been puttied and a draught was blowing through the cracks. I started to stamp about in the small space left free at one end of the boards: one step from the door to the boards, one step along the boards from wall to wall and then round again in the same little circle. Soon I noticed that the draught got stronger from time to time, just like that, and an icy wind would chill me to the marrow. This would happen when a door was opened in the corridor – the wind came through all the cracks in the window and the hole for the bulb went right through from cell to corridor. Because of my deafness I couldn't hear the door being slammed, but I could see the glass shuddering in the window frame.

For dinner they gave me a bowl of luke-warm skilly and about two hours later a warder came to take me to the chief officer's office. Behind the desk sat that same lieutenant. His cap and gloves lay on the desk. He invited me to sit down and invited the warder to leave the room.

'Why are you behaving in this way?' was his first question.

'What way?'

'You behave like a scoundrel.'

'And you behave like a fascist!'

The officer leapt from his chair: 'I am a Soviet officer! How dare you call me a fascist! Do you know what can happen to you for that?'

I said that only fascists would make a point of freezing people to death. He himself (and I pointed to his cap, gloves, boots and greatcoat) had been warmly dressed, while I, with almost no clothes on, with no cap or jacket and only slippers on my feet, had been made to stand there and be questioned in the frost, what's more he had forced me to take my hands out of my pockets and stand to attention without moving. After all, it was only because of the frost that I had been shifting from foot to foot.

The officer calmed down a bit after this, and even seemed to excuse himself.

'You should have done as you were told and taken your hands out of your pockets. Now you've got three days in the cooler. And you can thank your lucky stars you're in a hospital – in a normal camp you'd have got ten to fourteen days!'

After that he began to ask what I was in for, how long my sentence was and where I had been tried.

'Probably a student, eh?' And without waiting for an answer he went on didactically:

'You young people, why do you always have to get mixed up in politics? You don't understand a thing about it, yet you insist on going ahead. You should get on with your studies, but no, you have to poke your nose into everything! . . .'

I didn't bother to enter into discussion with him on this point, but merely asked:

'Why did you call me over to see you in the frost? Specially to find fault with something and put me in the cooler?'

'There you are again, behaving provocatively,' said the officer sadly. 'I called you over because prisoners are not authorised to come near the guardhouse when a convoy arrives.'

'But I'm an orderly, I was near the guardhouse on business, it's my duty to receive patients.'

'Well, why didn't you tell me that?'

'But you never asked.'

'Oh well, it's too late to sort it out now. While you're doing your three days in the cooler you can think things over a bit. Maybe you'll pipe down a bit next time, and won't be so impertinent to a representative of the camp administration.'

I was led back to my cell and immediately set to work. Pouring the rest of the water from my soup bowl into the sloptank, so that just a tiny drop was left on the bottom, I picked some plaster off the wall, crumpled it up in the water and mixed a thick paste. Then I stuck this home-made putty over all the cracks in the window frame and round all the edges of the glass. It was a good job the cell window was small! By evening the work was finished. Now there was no draught from the window, not even when the corridor door was opened. And later it became completely cosy: a con came and lit the stove in the cooler. I was warm, there was no draught and I could sleep right through until the next morning, until the stove went cold again. Even on the bare boards I didn't freeze. It got colder towards morning, however, and I froze all day until the following evening: then they lit the stove again.

There was no getting away from it, the hospital cooler was far better than any of the coolers in the camps!

BACK TO THE COMPOUND

While I was in camp three they transferred the politicals from camp seven, where I had come from, to camp eleven. And they filled up camp seven with criminal prisoners.

Soon we began to hear reports about various scandalous incidents in number seven. The criminal cons raped several of the women working there, including a cashier and the daughter of one of the company officers who had a job in the camp. Two cons also came to number three from camp seven – they had drunk huge quantities of acetone. Three other cons had had their stomachs pumped out in time, while these two were dispatched unconscious to the hospital. They didn't get there, however, but died on the way, so that two corpses arrived. Now the officers began to moan: how nice it had been, and how quiet, to work with fifty-eighters (we politicals are still usually referred to as being under the old article 58, although a new criminal code has been in force since 1961).

I was no longer a patients' orderly, having been transferred to work for headquarters. But I had a foreboding that this wouldn't last for very long, and so it turned out. Soon after my skirmish with Chief Officer Ketsai I got another three days in the cooler, and when I came out, Nikolai informed me that I was being sacked and would be sent away with the next convoy. I finally left camp three at the very end of February 1966. Still, I had been able to take it easy throughout the whole autumn and winter and maybe this is what saved me.

On the day of my departure I went to the guardhouse with my gear. The other prisoners in the convoy were already being searched. On my way through the reception room I passed some new arrivals – a group of prisoners still on their feet and two on stretchers. One of them was covered by a sheet of canvas up to his chin, with a reefer jacket on top. And both the jacket and his face were smothered in blood. He must have been vomiting blood – probably had an ulcer or had swallowed something. The other one on the stretcher I immediately recognised, although he looked terrible. His face was covered in whiskers, his cheeks were sunken and his cheekbones stuck out under the skin – they said he had been on hunger strike in one of the camps for twenty days and now they were transferring him to hospital. I had known him at Vladimir. He was a sturdy chap then, his name was Volodya, but his surname escapes me now. His eyes were open and I greeted him, but he did not answer, he must have been pretty far gone.

I passed on through the reception room and entered the cell where the discharged prisoners were waiting. Here there was also a group still on its feet and three men on stretchers: a completely paralysed old man, a younger man, also paralysed, and a third whose illness I don't remember. It was only a short while since they had been brought to the hospital camp, about two or three weeks ago, and now they were already on their way back again – still on stretchers, just as they had arrived.

Everything followed its usual course: a painstaking search, the walk to the station under armed guard, the loading up – with the same antics with the stretchers – the airlessness and stench of the prison coach, groans, somebody vomiting, halts at every camp station and then finally Yavas.

I had arrived at camp eleven.

When I returned to the camp from the hospital compound I didn't go to number seven, but to camp eleven. There were lots and lots of cons there from camp seven and I was delighted to meet some of my friends again. How lucky to be with Valery, Kolya Yusupov, Burov and other old acquaintances of mine! Another awful thing about the camps is that close ties of friendship are always being broken. Once admin learns of any friendship between prisoners, it hastens to split them up into different compounds. And then you can't even exchange letters, for correspondence between prisoners is forbidden. But this time we had been lucky: we were together again.

Camp eleven was crammed to overflowing, there were even cons living in the attics for a while, for there was no more room in the huts. But my friends helped me to find a place – and in any case I was no novice in camp. I was assigned once again to the stand-by gang. I didn't even try to explain to them that with my health and hearing it was impossible for me to work at unloading – you could explain until you were blue in the face, it still wouldn't do any good. Admin knows best. On the following day, 28 February 1966, I was supposed to start working already.

Meanwhile Valery, Kolya and I got together to exchange our news. What were their families writing, how were things outside? In eight months' time my term was due to end and from my first day in camp eleven we started discussing my release and what I would do outside. It was no easy problem: where would I be allowed to live, what work could I get? Because of my deafness I would never again be able to work at my trade as a drilling foreman. And in the camp there was no hope of getting a different profession. Evidently I would have to sign up as a loader outside as well, there was no other course open to me. But what about my health? Valery insisted that I should first concentrate on getting cured. Well, never mind, I still had eight months to go – plenty of time in which to think things over. And who knew what else might turn up in the meantime?

YULI DANIEL

We talked about one event that interested all of us politicals at that time – the trial of the two writers, Sinyavsky and Daniel. The first news of them had reached me at camp three already, but now that the trial was over they would soon be coming to Mordovia. One of them was bound to join us in camp eleven: they always separate co-defendants, stick them in different camps and employ different tactics in working on them. For the time being we knew neither of them.

The cons in the camp quarrelled a lot about this trial and also about the two writers themselves. In the beginning, after the first newspaper stories had appeared and before the trial began, everyone agreed unanimously that they were either scum, or cowards, or maybe provocateurs. After all, it was absolutely unprecedented – an open political trial, an open hearing of a case brought under Article 70. We still didn't know that the whole world was talking of their arrest and that this was the only reason the case could not be hushed up. Anyway, these two were bound to weep and recant, to confess that they had taken their orders from abroad, that they had sold themselves for dollars. How many more of their like were already in the camps, and not one of them had been tried in open court. That meant we were in line for the standard sort of show trial where the accused would play their parts without a murmur.

But then we began to read the first accounts of the trial itself. The accused were not admitting their guilt! No admissions of guilt, no pleas for forgiveness – they were even arguing with the court, standing up for their right to freedom of speech. This was clear even from the accounts in our own press, just as it was equally obvious that our newspapers were distorting the heart of the matter and the course of the trial. This last detail, however, did not bother us: soon we would be hearing it all from the writers themselves. Bravo, Sinyavsky and Daniel! For the first time the KGB was openly trying someone other than scum – and how they were catching it! But what was at the bottom of it? Why an open trial, why were the newspapers writing about it? Some prisoners guessed that the West must have somehow got to hear of it. Oh well, we would soon know.

As for the sentences, we fixed those at once, on the very first day: Sinyavsky would get seven years and Daniel five. Say what you like, but we were men of experience. A few predicted prison at Vladimir, but the majority were confident they would come to us. Everybody, though, agreed unanimously on one thing: whatever the sentence might be, this time the KGB had suffered a crushing defeat. And it wasn't just because the accused had behaved honourably. The main thing was that now the whole world would know that the Soviet Union had political prisoners. Khrushchev had bayed to the whole world that there were no political prisoners in the Soviet Union, that people were not imprisoned for their beliefs. What would he do now with these two? Build a special camp for them?

Valery, Kolya and I discussed the trial. What did they think in camp eleven? And what about number three? We decided that to begin with we would help whichever of the two came to us; and if we couldn't then others would, somebody would always be found. The young people in particular were the first to show admiration for the two writers.

On my very first day back in camp eleven I had a meeting with our section boss, Captain Usov: 'Well, Marchenko, I hope you've had a change of heart and are starting to mend your ways. Why don't you join the IOS, help the administration, and we'll see to it that you get packages and can see your family.' I replied that I had almost finished my sentence and that I could easily manage the remaining eight months without any packages. Then, when free again, I would still be able to look my fellow prisoners in the eye if we met outside.

'Marchenko, you have a false conception of honour and conscience. How will you be able to live outside with the views that
you hold?'

'Oh, I'll manage somehow.'

The following day the captain summoned me again to read me
a homily about attending political indoctrination sessions. At the
end he said:

'You young people are all the same, always dissatisfied with
everything, nothing ever suits you. You should get down to
some hard work here, but no, you wanted to run abroad instead.'

'All right, so I did. But even if people ask you openly you
won't let them go.'

'I should think not!'

'Well then, why did the Soviet Union sign the Declaration of
Human Rights? It says there that every man has the right to
live where he wants and to choose the country that he prefers.
They signed it all right, but they haven't the least intention of
carrying it out.'

'How do you come to know what's written in the Declaration,
Marchenko? Where did you read it? Who gave it to you? Who
told you what's in it?'

'It's been published in the UNESCO *Courier*. And although
not many people in our country get a chance to look at that
journal, you, sir, can get hold of a copy if you wish to. Incidentally, perhaps you can explain to me why the contents of this
Declaration are never mentioned in our press?'

'I don't know. I work for the Ministry of the Interior, not
External Affairs' – the abbreviation he used (MVD) was the old
Stalinist one, not the new name; even the younger officials still
use the old name. 'But you are wrong to think that the workers
in America live better than ours. Why do they go on strike if
they're living so well?'

'Do you mean to say that the reason ours don't go on strike
is because they live so well?'

'Of course. It's beyond dispute.'

At this point I made a comparison between the wages of
our workers and those in America. He knew how much our
construction workers earned because he himself signed the

wage sheets: if there was no faking it came to seventy roubles a month. But in America it was 500 dollars!

'How do you know that, Marchenko? Who told you? I've never read it anywhere.'

'I have, though. And you can too if you like, in *An International Comparison of World Economics*.'

'But dollars are worth less than roubles!'

'According to the official exchange rate they are. But in real value? On a wage of 500 dollars an American worker can buy a television set like our "Radius B" for ninety-nine dollars. Five television sets out of a single month's wage! And how many television sets at 360 roubles a time can you buy out of one month's wages here?'

'Marchenko, you've been reading too much bourgeois propaganda and now you've been led astray!'

'And where could I get it! I don't know about bourgeois propaganda, but your camp censors stop even letters from my own mother.'

'Don't you lecture me, Marchenko. I'm here to teach you, not you me.'

'All right, then, teacher (here Usov grimaced), convince me that I'm going astray. Go on. Convince me that our workers live better than the Americans and that that's why they don't go on strike – that's where you began, I believe.'

'According to you our workers don't earn very much and live poorly. Okay. But what about those two,' he pointed to an old newspaper with an article about Sinyavsky and Daniel in it, 'what was the matter with them? They also didn't earn very much, I suppose? They both had cars, you bet, just like ministers! But still that wasn't enough, so they sold themselves for dollars and francs, working for the CIA. Men of conviction! We know their sort!'

'Are you sure about their connection with the CIA, sir? There's been nothing in the newspapers about it.'

'Not yet, but there will be! There's bound to be.'

'Well, we'll see. And we'll get to know them ourselves. They're coming here, aren't they?'

'Knowing them's got nothing to do with it. I'm telling you

straight, they sold themselves. And you, Marchenko, had better think about your own position a bit. Come to your senses. We can't let you out, you know, with your ideas about life in the Soviet Union.'

On this note the conversation ended. Usov had similar talks with Valery and Kolya and with many other cons.

A couple of days after these pep-talks I came back from working in the zone and looked for Valery in our block. He wasn't there. I went to the changing room to change. Just then Izotov poked his head round the door and seeing me yelled:

'He's here! He's here!'

'Who?'

'The writer.'

'What? Well, where is he?'

'He's been put in our gang and he'll be living in your block. Valery's taken him over to the canteen.'

I didn't ask which of them it was. So long as Valery was with him it was all right – he would show him and tell him everything.

Valery came back while I was still changing. With him was a fellow of about thirty-five to forty. The new man was wearing his own clothes still, but had clearly made preparations for camp life: a quilted jacket with buttons, knee-boots and a ginger fur cap with ear flaps. The jacket was unbuttoned and beneath it could be seen a heavy sweater. His general appearance struck me as funny: the collarless jacket somehow didn't fit with the expensive cap, he was bandy-legged when he walked, like a bear, his back had a pronounced hunch to it and his whole bearing was somewhat embarrassed and uncertain. We introduced ourselves. It was Yuli Daniel. When we talked he turned his right ear to me and asked me to speak louder. And since his own voice was low I turned around so that my right ear was towards him and cupped it in my palm. So we were two of a pair – he was just as deaf as I was. And both of us found it very funny.

Others of our gang mates came up, surrounded the new man and began to ask him what was going on outside. Every now and then people would come running into the hut from other huts to stare at Daniel – he was a celebrity! Questions were showered upon him from all sides. We learned that the trial had been open in name only, and that only people with special passes had been allowed inside. Of his friends and family in the court he had seen only his wife and the wife of Sinyavsky. He was sure his friends would have come, he said, but they weren't allowed in. The majority of the people in the courtroom were typical KGB stooges, but there were also some writers there, some of whom Yuli had recognised from their well-known pictures and others whom he knew personally. Some of them had lowered their eyes and turned away; two or three had nodded to him in sympathy.

'Yes, but why do you think there was so much publicity?'

It turned out that Yuli thought the same as some of us: they must have kicked up a big fuss in the West. Sitting under arrest in the investigation prison he could know nothing, of course. But he had deduced a thing or two from what the judge said and the answers of the witnesses under cross-examination.

'Were you wearing your own or did they put you into prison clothes while you were under arrest?'

'My own, of course. Both during the investigation and during the trial.'

'And alone in a cell?'

'Only for the first few days. The rest of the time there were two of us. A good companion he was too, we played a hundred games of chess together . . .'

'Good God, another Powers. We were all stuck into prison clothes from the day of our arrest. I was kept in solitary for the whole five months, and the others were too. Whereas these two – oh well, they were being kept ready for their "open trial".'

'What did you and Sinyavsky write?'

'What sort of car have you got? One of ours or a foreign model?'

'The same as yours.'

Captain Usov passed through the room where we were talking. As he went by he said:

'A new man? Hand your cap and sweater in to the quartermaster's today – they're not allowed.'

Yuli started to ask us about the work. We did our best to reassure him, the way we did all newcomers:

'It's hard work, but don't be scared, you soon get used to it. You're not the only one, we've got plenty of others who've never held anything heavier than a fountain pen before and now they're experts with a spade. Cheer up. You'll come through!'

Yuli talked more about Andrei Sinyavsky than about himself:

'Now there's a man for you! And as a writer there can't be more than maybe one or two to equal him in the whole of Russia today.' He was extremely worried about his friend, how he had settled down in camp, what sort of work he would be put on and whether it would be too hard for him or not. And this, of course, pleased us all very much.

Although Daniel was supposed to go to work the next day, our gang decided not to take him on assignments for the first three days, just as they had done with me when I came back from Vladimir prison. Let him look around the compound first. Furthermore we knew that he had a broken right arm that hadn't knit together properly – a legacy from the war. So it must have been on purpose that they put him on the heaviest kind of hard labour in the camps. How, with his crippled arm, would he be able to lift logs and shift coal? The bosses knew what they were about: smother him in this hell until he could bear it no longer and begged for some sort of lighter work. Then they would have him right where they wanted. First let him write to the camp newspaper and go on the radio, in return they'd make him a librarian and the doctors would certify him for third category work only. If not in a week then in a month – it was all the same, this intellectual was sure to cave in. No submission in court – all right, let him submit here. He'd soon learn what trouble was.

We advised Yuli to hold out, no matter how hard it would be for him, and not to ask the bosses for anything. But he wasn't thinking of it anyway, he was prepared for hardship.

Far from all the cons reacted to Daniel favourably. Some of them waited suspiciously to see how he behaved in camp. And some gloated openly: 'Let him knuckle under with the rest of us! We know these writers, they're all corrupt, they live off the fat of the land themselves and then write about our heavenly conditions. These two have been caught, so now let 'em redeem their real sins.'

Cons usually detest all writers. How many times have they read in books or newspapers about 'reforming criminals with honest labour', or the stern but just reforming governor. But where does anyone ever write about our starvation, about the brutal tyranny that drives so many cons to suicide? Only Solzhenitsyn has dared to write the truth, and then not all of it. All the rest are scum, and because of those bastards they stiffened the regime in '61. Made a pretty picture of the camps they did – thanks very much. 'Send them to us in the stand-by gang, governor,' yelled our criminal cons, Footman and Vorkuta, before Yuli arrived, 'and we'll find the biggest coal shovels we can for them!' While others said: 'And what makes you think Daniel's going to stand at a machine or handle a shovel? He'll find himself a cosy little nook here too, the Jews always get away with it everywhere.' We already knew from the newspapers that Daniel was a Jew. In the camps, just as outside, there is no lack of anti-semites, even though here too some of the Jewish cons pitched in on the same terms as the rest of us, while others looked for a cushy number – in this too differing in no way from the cons of other nationalities.

The administration played on these feelings in their little 'chats', fully aware that the majority of the cons were well disposed toward Sinyavsky and Daniel for their honest behaviour at the trial. And they also stuck Yuli into the stand-by gang so as to compromise him in the eyes of the hard workers, so that his authority would be undermined by his physical weakness.

'Hold on, Yuli, hold on for all you're worth,' said Valery to him, 'show them all that they haven't succeeded in breaking you.'

Footman's and even Vorkuta's attitude to Daniel changed after the first few days. It might have been that the admiration of the others rubbed off on them, but more likely he won them over himself. For he was a simple and straightforward fellow, fame and celebrity had not turned his head in the least. His own view was that he had become famous by accident, that he had simply had the luck denied to others just like himself. And it also meant a great deal that he deeply sympathised with the others around him and didn't remain indifferent to their troubles. Soon everyone was sure that Yuli was not looking for an easier life than the rest of us. When unloading he would pitch in as best he could, but of course he did less than the others: what chance did he have of keeping up with people like Kolya Yusupov? Yet at the end of it all he was more tired and worn out than anyone. He also suffered from being unused to physical labour – he had not had to do any physical work since being wounded in the war – and from his arm. Very soon he began to get pains in his shoulder, in the spot where the bone had been shattered. But even then Yuli didn't ask any favours of the administration, and we in our gang decided to pick out for him the sort of work he could manage. We had such jobs, for instance, as cleaning up the timber sheds. After the timber had been unloaded there was always lots of litter left behind – boards of various kinds, sticks, small logs and the straps that held the timber tight in the wagons. There was enough work for the whole shift, but it didn't require much strength. The hardest part was rolling the logs away with crowbars, but then they were never very big. And at night-time they are just left there: once you've done your shift it's straight off to bed. Anyway we insisted that the ganger put Yuli onto this work, but it only lasted a few days. Admin found out about it and the camp KGB immediately insisted that he be transferred back to unloading again, although nothing came of their plans even then. Daniel absolutely refused to ask for any concessions, and all the cons helped him as best they could. Kolya Yusupov asked the ganger to let him take Yuli's turn but the ganger was afraid of admin and refused. When coal was unloaded, however, Footman, Yusupov and Valery used to finish their own hatches and then go over and help Yuli.

Our gang started to be called in by the KGB.

'Who's helping Daniel with his work?'

'All of us.'

'Why? Can't he do it himself? He's shirking! Maybe you'd like to serve his sentence for him as well?'

One talkative fellow had the presence of mind to answer back: 'And what does it say in your moral code? That mutual help should be the rule among comrades, that man should be a friend, comrade and brother to his fellows.'

There was nothing the KGB could do with this sort of thing. Then they took Daniel away from our gang and transferred him to the machine shop, making out that they were doing him a favour on account of his crippled arm. The point was, though, that he hadn't just crippled his arm yesterday; they had known about it from the very beginning and still they had assigned him to the stand-by gang and forced him to work at unloading. We all got the point: it wasn't a question of any sudden generosity on admin's part, but simply that they didn't like the other cons helping him out. And in any case, where was the generosity? In the machine shop the racket of the lathes would set even a sound head ringing and Daniel suffered with his ears, a fact that was just as well known to admin as the business with his arm. What's more, lathe work also puts quite a strain on the arm, though not as much, of course, as shovelling coal. Still, nobody could help here, because each man had his norm to fulfil.

Yuli continued to stay friends with us. Although we lived in separate barracks now, we kept up our old ties and whatever one of us got was divided among all. Footman too became one of us now. He grew fonder than anyone of Yuli, protected him in various ways and was even jealous of the other cons. How many times did the following little scene take place? Yuli would be lying on his upper bunk, reading or writing a letter or perhaps writing poetry. Someone who was not in our circle would come in and ask: 'Where's Daniel?' Every now and then somebody would come along to ask him something or tell him about their troubles, or else just to chew the fat. They didn't even give him time to rest in the early days. Footman would be there every time: 'Whoever disturbs Daniel is going to have to deal with me.' Needless to say, there were no takers.

The one thing Footman didn't like was to hear references to one of his first conversations with Yuli. The whole group of us had been standing in the corridor one day, by a window, and every now and then first one con and then another would come by and stare into our hut. They just wanted to see and get to know him, and kept coming along. So Footman said:

'Hey, look at those whores of Jewboys come running and hanging around.'

'Don't forget that I'm a Jew too.'

'Ha, I couldn't give a shit who you are.'

After this conversation, however, Footman never again spoke disrespectfully of the Jews in Yuli's presence.

Footman in general, after making friends with Daniel, underwent a significant change. Beforehand he had been the criminal to end all criminals, a permanent con, as they say. He had fallen foul of politics in the same way as other criminals. He didn't give a damn about anything or anyone – he cursed the lot of them, admin and cons alike, he was scared of nothing. In some situations he wouldn't have hesitated, in my opinion, to use a knife as well. And he didn't expect ever to live outside. Now, however, Footman grew much quieter, started to read a lot and to think seriously about his future. Perhaps for the first time in his life he was experiencing a human relationship with someone. Admin didn't like this at all. They called in first Yuli and then Footman and attempted to set them against one another, telling each of them disgusting stories about the other. And when they failed to smash the friendship, they transferred Daniel to another camp. That was after I had already been released and I heard about it outside.

Of course, it wasn't only Daniel's friendship with us and Footman that annoyed admin. Daniel was liked, I should think, by everyone in the camp. He involuntarily became the centre that united diverse groups and nationalities. One day it would be the Lithuanians inviting him into their circle to listen to their songs, another it was some young people from Leningrad inviting him for coffee, or else the Ukrainians would read their poetry to him. One day one of the groups offered him some 'Mordovian special', in other words the varnish that cons drink in place of vodka. Valery advised him against it. 'Earlier,' he said, 'you could have drunk yourself silly on it, but now you don't have the right. What's more, there's no point in giving admin an excuse to get at you.' Yuli had great respect for Valery and always listened to his advice.

A certain amount of time passed and everyone got used to Daniel, he became just another con among cons, like the rest of us. He told us how it had been on his way to the camp: 'Where were they taking me, I wondered. Just like in the song: *Oh, where, oh where am I going? Who will I be meeting there?* All the political prisoners had been released ten years ago. True I had heard of some Kiev Jew being sent down for having a connection with Israel, was it, or something of that sort. He and I and Sinyavsky made three. Well, and maybe there were a couple of dozen more of the same kind as this Jew. Probably they would stick us in with the criminals. I had already worked out how I could get on with them. I remembered the war – there were some convicts in our unit. Then in Ruzayevka I was told about the thousands of politicals. There's no doubt about it, they certainly know how to pull the wool over our eyes.'

And there were also lots of laughs when we heard what he had taken with him.

'My wife,' he said, 'brought along enough things to clothe an army just before I was due to leave. Warm stuff it was – evidently all my friends had collected it up, each one giving me what he had. There were my father-in-law's fur mittens – from his own days in the camp; the quilted jacket, I remember, had been tried on for size by one of her friends; and there was warm underwear – which I had never had in my life before. Well, and then there were a few things of mine: a sweater, a cap, my one and only suit and a white shirt. And she also gave me some new felt boots and leather knee-boots – what was I to do with it all? I picked out some of the warm stuff and also took my suit, best shoes and a shirt. During their time in the camps the old cons still used to wear their own clothes. These best clothes, I thought, might come in handy for group activities, reading poetry at a camp show. And what do I find? Warders on stage warbling "The Party is at the helm". And every damn one of us in prison togs . . .'

We all burst out laughing, and Yuli too. Now he sports a camp beaver to cover his shaven head. Once he tried to compensate for the lack of hair on his head by growing a moustache, but it came out a sort of splotchy ginger colour. He didn't like it and shaved it off again.

Occasionally it still happened that some unknown con would pester Daniel about having his own car. But we all knew now how writers like Sinyavsky and Daniel lived. Sometimes on nothing more than bread. And Sinyavsky, according to Daniel, wrote all his articles and stories in a basement because there was nowhere else for him to work. Perhaps it was this that helped Yuli to endure the deprivations in camp; his life had never been a bed of roses.

Unable to bully Daniel one way, admin decided to try another tack. In June 1966 they gave him fifteen days solitary for 'malingering and failing to fill his quota'. Both the cons and admin knew that his old wound had turned septic and that a splinter of bone lay at the root of the sepsis. But the doctors wouldn't let him off work and then Yuli refused to go out, so he landed up in the cooler and spent fifteen days inside. Coming out the last evening he was sent straight back in again the next morning for another ten days, and again everyone knew it was for nothing, they simply wanted to give the poor fellow a roasting. Some of the cons made an official protest about it. I know, for instance, that a prisoner named Belov sent protests to the Central Committee and to the Praesidium of the Supreme Court, demanding that an end be put to the victimisation of political prisoner Daniel and that he be granted medical aid. These protests brought no results, of course, they never did in such cases. They continued to bully Daniel right up to the time I was released; never once did they let him have a full meeting with his wife and he was not even allowed to take any cigarettes back with him after a meeting. But then it was all done on instructions, so that there was no point even in protesting.

We were all pleased to see that Yuli was made of too stern a stuff to be easily broken. Never for any reason did he complain, nor ask for anything for himself, though he was always ready to stick up for someone else.

EARS

In camp eleven, as in all the other big compounds, we had our own medical post: a doctor's office, dispensary and laboratory. If you fell ill you could go to the doctor. In the beginning there were up to four thousand of us cons in the camp and the office was manned by one woman doctor. If she were to fall ill or for some other reason was unable to come to work, patients were received by the husband of the medical post's director – a surgeon from the local civilian hospital nearby. Attached to the medical post was a small infirmary with twenty-five beds in it. Eight to ten of them were more or less permanently occupied by motionless paralytics (nowadays they are not 'signed out' any more, so they stay cons until they die). The remaining beds are usually empty. To get into the infirmary you have to be carried in practically unconscious on a stretcher. That's the way I got there too.

On 17 March they brought up three wagons of sawn-off birch trunks for us to unload – the wagons were full of huge blocks about five feet in diameter. We had to unload them by hand – the crane, as usual, was out of action – the blocks were wet and we worked in the rain and the snow. And when we had finished the work we stood about for another hour or so in the wind outside the guardhouse, waiting for them to provide us with an escort. I got so chilled that even in my cot under the blanket I was unable to get warm and I shivered the whole night long. During the night they also brought up two wagons of coal and a further three wagons of birch logs. The ganger started to rouse me, but I was unable to get up. Valery said: 'Leave him alone, he's ill, can't you see?' And the ganger left me in peace. In the morning, though, I'd have to have a meeting with the company officer and it was quite possible that I had already earned myself a spell in the cooler.

I could hardly wait for the morning in order to go to the medical post. My head was splitting apart. I attempted to rise from my cot, but my head spun and I felt horribly sick. I lay down again: doubtless it would pass and I would be able to go. But it got worse and worse with every moment. I could no longer even move my head. The slightest motion brought on giddiness and vomiting. Footman ran to the medical post and fetched the doctor. She examined me and ordered Footman and Valery to carry me to the infirmary. The lads placed me on top of a padded coat and carried me away.

On the first day no one came to examine me. On the second the rounds were being done by the surgeon from the local hospital. 'Where does it hurt?' I even had difficulty in speaking. The con who worked as medical technician in the infirmary explained that I had been brought in with giddiness and vomiting and when the surgeon had gone he told me that they were calling in the ear specialist from camp three because the surgeon could do nothing, it wasn't his speciality. Two days later on his rounds the surgeon repeated that I needed an ear specialist and that the specialist had promised to come as soon as he had some free time. 'And what if the specialist doesn't have any free time?' cracked the con in the next bed to me sarcastically. For five days I had been lying there, and there was no thought even of giving me some treatment.

In the meantime I was getting worse, I could no longer move my eyes from one object to another. So long as I kept looking at a single point it was all right, but the moment I moved my eyes – more giddiness and vomiting. There was a basin by my bed all the time – I was vomiting very, very frequently. Every time he came round the surgeon would say: 'There's nothing I can do, I'm not a specialist, wait for the ear specialist.'

At last, on the sixth or seventh day, the ear specialist came, it was the same one who had examined me at camp three. He behaved in a friendly fashion to me, questioned me and prescribed some injections. I asked him:

'Doctor, what is this I've got?'

'It's nothing serious. Just take it easy for a while and it will pass.'

In the evening the technician came to give me an injection. It turned out that the ear specialist had prescribed penicillin. At camp three, however, I remember him telling me that penicillin had no effect on me.

For three days I had injections and my condition still didn't get any better. All this time I was unable to eat, the very sight of food would turn my stomach. In a whole day I would get down a few swallows of hospital stewed fruit, and that was all. The rest of my rations I gave to the con lying next to me.

On the fourth day after the ear specialist's visit my temperature rose still higher – 103.6. The technician told this to the surgeon on his next walk round and the latter suspended the injections, since they didn't seem to be helping. I asked them to call in the ear specialist again, but he never came and after a while they told me that he never would come either. He had gone away for four months on some course or other.

And so I threshed around in my hospital bed for about three weeks or so, and in all this time the only one to help me was the con in the next bed – he gave me water to drink and changed the cold compresses on my head. I felt so ill that I was sure I was going to snuff it. Then everything would be all right – the con had died in hospital and not out working, what could we possibly do? Medicine is not yet infallible. And the fact that I had received no treatment, that the ear specialist had examined me only once, that for nine days they had been unable to get the results of my blood analysis – who cared about that? In any case nobody would ever find out about it!

After about twenty days or so my condition began to ease and I gradually started to come round: at first I was able to turn in my bed without giddiness or vomiting, then I began to get up and even to walk about a little, holding on to the wall. Only the sight of food continued to disgust me. At last I managed to crawl outside. It was already the middle of April, sunny and warm. Valery dragged some doctor along to see me, a prisoner. Outside he had been a doctor, here he was a construction worker. He questioned me closely and was amazed: 'Well, well, well, now you'll live to be a hundred since you haven't died already. You had meningitis!'

My temperature fell and, although unsteady, I was able to stay on my feet. Now the surgeon on his rounds used to look at me with suspicion and would say:

'Marchenko, you've got no temperature. It's time to send you back to the compound.'

'But doctor, I can hardly walk, how can I possibly do any work? And my ears are still painful just the same.'

'I know nothing about ears, there's nobody here to treat your ears and I can't keep you in hospital any longer. For two more days, okay, you can skive around a bit, but that's all. In two more days you go back to the compound.'

I looked at his tattooed arms (the same old thing, I had seen it a hundred times already: 'life is full of sorrow') and I thought: 'It is you who's skiving, you skunk, you bastard! Call yourself a doctor! You know what condition I'm in and you're sending me back to shovel coal. You're no better than the officers!' I was afraid that after a few days of unloading I would be carried back in again on a padded jacket, and I didn't want to die, especially when I had only six months to go until my release.

That same day I wrote a long petition to the Central Committee. I complained that I was ill and that I was receiving no treatment even though I had twice been held for a while in the hospital in camp three and once in the camp infirmary in camp eleven. I wrote that although a sick man and deaf, I was constantly being obliged to work in the stand-by gang, doing the heaviest camp work there was. Also that the camp doctors always gave the same recommendation: 'Prisoner Marchenko has no need of medical treatment and is fit for all kinds of work' – and that as a result of this I had narrowly avoided a trip to the next world. And if they continued to refuse me medical aid here I would be obliged to turn for assistance to the International Red Cross.

I knew in advance that this petition would do me no good and might even do me harm. I knew that I would never be allowed to turn to the Red Cross even if I were free, let alone as a

prisoner in camp. But let them at least have it as a document –
I was keeping a copy for myself anyway.

Two days later I was discharged and sent back to the compound – and straight out to work again. It was a good job I had
friends. Valery and Tolya Footman now helped me the way they
helped Yuli Daniel. I went out on calls day and night, but they
wouldn't let me do a stroke of work. The only thing was that it
worried Yuli and me to be an extra burden to the others – it
was hard enough for them without us on top. Better to spend
the rest of our days in the cooler! But the lads talked us round
and reassured us: our turn would come to help the others one
day.

Two weeks afterwards we received a visit from a Medical
Board commission – it had come to interview the cons and
re-define work categories. Two strange men in civilian clothes,
three women and our surgeon with his arms tattooed like a
jailbird: all of them clean, well dressed and well fed. Doctors!
When they asked me I told them about my condition.

'Where do you work?'

'In the stand-by gang.'

'What sort of work do you have to do?'

I explained.

'When the ear specialist comes he will examine you. Now you
may go. Category A1.'

I went out of the room gritting my teeth with rage.

After about another two months I was summoned to the
infirmary: 'You wrote a complaint? An answer has come. Sign
here to say it's been read to you.' (They never give you a copy
to keep. All you can do is write down the number and the date).
I read: 'Your complaint has been received and forwarded to the
Medical Board of Dubrovlag for consideration.' Well, of course!
It's them I'm complaining about, so let them decide. That's
the answer they give everyone. I read further: 'It has been
established by the medical unit of camp division eleven that
Prisoner Marchenko, A.T., is in no need of treatment. Signed:
Chief of the Medical Board of Dubrovlag, Major Petrushevsky
(Medical Corps).'

Four months after this reply, after I had been released, I

went to a doctor. Doctor G. B. Skurkevich, MD, examined me and gave the following verdict: 'The left ear must be operated on immediately, after that the right ear will also need operating on'. He himself did the operation and afterwards he told me that he had rarely seen a patient in such a neglected and dangerous condition. Dr Skurkevich did everything he could to return my hearing to me, but with no success, it was too late. On the other hand he did clean out all the pus that had accumulated in my suppurating ears: he said that when he cut open the vestibule the pus came squirting out, as though under high pressure.

It was lucky I was released in time, otherwise I would almost certainly have kicked the bucket in the camp from suppurant meningitis – still, of course, 'in no need of medical treatment'.

MISHKA KONUKHOV

In the spring of 1966 a new man came to camp eleven and was assigned to us in the stand-by gang. This was Mishka Konukhov, a stevedore from the port of Arkhangelsk.

Mishka was a young man of about twenty-five. His childhood had been difficult, he grew up without parents. He became a stevedore and worked at unloading foreign ships; and although the pay was better than if he had worked on our ships, say, or, in some railway warehouse, nevertheless he could only just manage to get by. For he was all on his own, with no one to help him: usually, if there are young people in the family, the parents provide board and lodging and your pay goes on getting some gear together and amusements. Mishka, moreover, had married early so that he also had a family to support. True, his wife also worked – in a laundry – but on her miserable pay (fifty roubles a month) she barely had enough to buy food for herself. Well it's clear, in other words, what sort of life they led: you worked in order to eat and ate in order to work.

But in the port and on the ships he worked on Mishka used to see the foreign sailors – they were well dressed, and although they spoke no Russian, it was clear they hadn't much to complain about and were in no hurry to dash over to our side, to live in the homeland of the world proletariat. Not even the Negroes. Of course all this was bourgeois propaganda, but Mishka didn't understand. He merely became terribly enraged – and, evidently remembering something from his orphan childhood, found the sole form of protest open to him: across his chest he tattooed the words: 'Victim of communism.' And then stevedore Mishka Konukhov became the focus of political passions.

Someone among the foreigners photographed him stripped to

the waist and this photograph appeared in the newspapers over there. Then the KGB started to pull Mishka in: let him make a statement, they said, pointing out that he was a victim of the underworld, that he had let himself be tattooed because of his youth and foolishness, and that now the gutter press was exploiting this without his knowledge. Mishka refused. Then all sorts of strange incidents started happening to him: one day some characters he didn't know would tag on to him in the street and start calling him names and insulting him; another day a brawl would suddenly break out right beside him and the participants would try to involve him in the mêlée; or else some 'hooligans' would fall upon him all of a sudden and beat him up in some dark alley. Mishka didn't respond to these provocations and kept out of brawls and didn't drink in company, and after every incident he went to the police station, made a statement and signed a charge. But the police somehow had no success at all in finding the culprits and in the meantime he continued to be called in by the KGB, who warned him on several occasions that anything might happen to him, that our patriotic-spirited youth was up in arms over his conduct and might easily take the law in to their own hands and make short work of him, and the police, of course, would be powerless to protect him against the wrath of the crowd.

Konukhov finally got tired of this comedy and took a train to Moscow. He wandered round the streets looking for the British embassy. He had already worked out how to get in. He knew that if he hesitated he would be stopped by our policemen on guard outside the embassy. Therefore he walked swiftly past the front of the embassy, as though hurrying somewhere on business, then directly opposite the door, took a sharp ninety-degree turn and ran into the vestibule. The policemen didn't realise at first what was happening and they were well behind him when he heard them shout: 'Where are you going young man? Halt!' But he was already inside.

In the vestibule he was detained by some employee or other – the doorman or a guard. Mishka explained that he absolutely had to see the English ambassador. 'The ambassador is engaged at the moment, but you may speak to one of the embassy secretaries; perhaps your business can be settled without the aid of the ambassador.' He was ushered into an office and invited to sit down.

An interpreter remained present during Mishka Konukhov's chat with the English embassy secretary, but he was being paid, it seemed, for nothing – the secretary himself spoke perfectly good Russian. To begin with he offered Mishka some dinner. Mishka politely declined: he had just had a meal in a cafeteria, he was full. Then the secretary ordered coffee for the two of them – chatting over coffee was somehow easier. Well, coffee was all right, Mishka wouldn't say no to a coffee. He explained the nature of his request: he was asking them to assist him in going to England, he no longer wanted to live in the USSR. They asked him who he was, where he worked and why he wanted to leave the country. And the secretary listened very carefully to all his explanations. Then he began to speak himself. He said that in order to leave the country, Mister Konukhov would first have to renounce his Soviet citizenship. Then he would be able to take any nationality he liked, including British, and the embassy would assist him in this. But the secretary advised him to think his decision over once again. 'It happens quite often', said the secretary, that a Soviet tourist or member of a delegation remains in England, asks for political asylum, and then realises that he finds it hard to live away from his homeland, his family and his friends. For a very long time after that, for dozens of years, your government doesn't allow such people to return and visit them. Some emigrants decide sooner or later to return to their homeland. We understand their feelings and our government places no obstacles in their way. However it happens quite often that upon their return to the USSR these people explain their decision not by homesickness and a desire to see their country and family, but by the bad living conditions in our country. What is more, they make it sound as though they were obliged to remain in England almost by force or by trickery, and as though they were not allowed to go home. Statements such as these, quite naturally, are extremely distasteful to us, they impugn our honour and cause diplomatic friction. Therefore we are obliged to be extremely cautious in approaching requests such as yours. And in general, Mister Konukhov, perhaps you don't know our country and are idealising it? We have our problems and our difficulties, you know, and when you run up against them you may, perhaps, regret your hasty decision.'

In short the Englishman was politely dissuading Mishka from fleeing to England, rather than luring and decoying him, and Mishka was taken aback. In conclusion the secretary explained to Mishka that if, on mature consideration, he did not wish to change his mind, he should go to the Ministry of Foreign Affairs and renounce his Soviet citizenship. Thus, although the embassy did not refuse to accept him as an English citizen, the business would obviously take some time.

Mishka resolved to carry it through. But when he left the embassy he noticed three unknown men following closely at his heels and beside him, in the street, a slowly moving car. Mishka tried to merge with the crowd, but he knew it was useless, that he wouldn't be able to get away. At one of the crossroads the three men came right up to him, laughing and joking, embraced him tightly, like an old friend, and bundled him into the car. It all took place in a moment and probably not one of the crowd on the pavement either saw or understood what had happened.

They drove him – it goes without saying – to the KGB. There they threw him into a cell and began to question him. Why had he gone to the embassy? With whom had he talked? What about? Had he not left something there? Mishka told them everything as it had happened – he had nothing to hide. While he was there he also wrote an application to the Ministry of Foreign Affairs informing them that he wished to renounce his citizenship and requesting permission to go to England. Both the KGB officials and representatives of the Ministry of Foreign Affairs came to talk to him, persuading him to withdraw his application and write that he had changed his mind. Well, what sort of 'persuasion' did they use? 'Anyway we'll never let you leave, do you understand?' Mishka insisted on having his own way. Three days later they let him go, ordered him to return to Arkhangelsk and made him sign that he wouldn't leave without permission.

In Arkhangelsk, of course, he was no longer permitted to

work on foreign ships and was transferred to a different sector. Here his pay was lower too. They continued hauling him in to the KGB and trying to provoke him into 'hooliganism' on the street. But Mishka didn't fall for the provocation and he didn't give up either. Several times he wrote to the Foreign Ministry and in the end received a questionnaire. In answer to the question: 'Why do you want to leave the USSR?' he wrote: 'Because I don't like its political system and ideology.'

And why should he lie – say that he wanted to visit a second cousin or something? They still wouldn't let him go.

And so they kept pulling him in to the KGB, to the party committee, working him over at meetings – all the stevedores had long known that Mishka was trying to go to England and wasn't being allowed. The time came round for his annual holiday and although he couldn't go anywhere because of the undertaking he had signed, Mishka handed in an application:. 'I wish to be granted a month's holiday.' A month, and the regulation holiday was twelve days! Konukhov was interviewed on this subject by the first secretary of the regional party himself, and Mishka again dug his heels in and insisted on having his own way. 'The workers in Sweden, by striking, have long since obtained a month's paid holiday during a year, and I demand the same.' To the astonishment of all the other stevedores he got his month's holiday and even got the same for his wife. What the devil next and what if they upped and sent him to England – what would he be telling them about life over here!

Shortly after this a letter came from the Foreign Ministry: Konuhkov was required to pay a duty of ninety roubles for the drawing up of his renunciation of citizenship. Mishka sent off the money. Three days later they came for him at home in a car, took him away by force and drove him somewhere. He ended up in some camp or other, in the camp hospital, with a ward to himself. The surgeon came and said: 'Konukhov, do you agree to an operation to remove this embellishment from your chest?'

'And what happens if I refuse?'

The surgeon laughed:

'Sooner or later you'll agree, it's better not to drag it out.'

And Mishka agreed.

After the operation, however, he was sent not to Arkhangelsk, but to solitary confinement in a KGB investigation prison: 'You see, Konukhov, we warned you we would put you inside, that we would find a way if you didn't pack it in. Now you have only yourself to blame.'

He was tried for possessing foreign currency and some sort of printed matter – God knows if he really did have a few dollars or whether it was all trumped up from beginning to end. The court, as usual, was closed and Mishka was not given a copy of the sentence.

And so our gang acquired a practically fully-qualified Englishman. He looked around him with the same lively curiosity as he would have done had he landed up in England. He was particularly interested in cons who had come back from abroad: what was life really like there, why had they come back, how had they landed in Mordovia? He remembered his conversation with the secretary in the English embassy and was checking on both him and himself.

We had plenty of such cons in the camp and there were several in our gang alone: Volodya Pronin had come back from West Germany; Anton Nakashidze, a dancer in the Georgian State Song and Dance Ensemble, had stayed on in England and then returned; Pyotr Varenkov, Budyonny, Bessonov and the Ossetian, Pyotr Tibilov, had all come back from abroad. All these 'returnees' said that the material standard of living in the West was far better than in our country and everywhere, of course, there was freedom: nobody forces you to do anything. 'Then what the bloody hell brought you back if life was so good over there?' They replied that they felt homesick for their country and their families – one would have a mother here, another a father, a third a wife (the biologist Golub, for instance, about whom so much was written in the newspapers at one time, returned because his wife implored him; when he was jailed she renounced him). They came back free men as far as the frontier and from the frontier on – under armed guard to prison and then to camp for a term of ten to twelve years. Golub, it is true, and other such 'celebrities' are not jailed right away, but six to twelve months afterwards when their stories are forgotten. 'Well, now you should be pleased,' say the cons to those who have come back, 'here's your homeland and this is your family – Mordovia and the fraternal collective of the camps!'

Maybe if these people would agree to appear in public and announce how badly they had lived in the West, how they had been recruited as spies or something of that sort – maybe a few of them wouldn't have been jailed or would have been pardoned and released. But even then not all of them: it is easy enough to get into a camp, but few manage to get out again before their term is up, even at the price of a public recantation.

Mishka Konukhov no longer dreams of going to England and they haven't even returned his ninety roubles to him, although the official application was never drawn up. Now he dreams of something else: how to train to be a medical technician, at least he would have cleaner work. And greater respect.

In the summer of 1966 a routine 'accident' occurred – our hut was burnt down. They tried Yurka Karmanov for it, an old friend of mine from Vladimir and camp seven. There were different accounts of how it happened. Some people thought it was a routine provocation on the part of admin in order to have an excuse for tightening up the regime still further. They alleged that the sentry in the watch tower had stated during his evidence: 'I was instructed to sound the alarm as soon as I saw the fire.' I don't know. I think that Yurka Karmanov was indeed capable of setting fire to it out of despair and helplessness. Just as Romashev and many others deliberately put themselves in the tommy gunners' sights; as Sherstyanoy in camp seven set fire to the machine shop; as men slash, hang, poison and tattoo themselves. Whoever hasn't been in a camp can never understand the actions and behaviour of a con.

RELEASE

Two or three months before I was due to be released I was called into the KGB office for a chat. There were three people there: our KGB officer, the chief of the Political Education Unit and company officer Usov. I remember that conversation well: it was their last attempt to convert me, to re-educate me 'by peaceful means'.

'Marchenko, you're due to be released soon. Do you realise that, once back outside, you will have to behave and think like everyone else? It's not like in camp, where everybody has his own opinion.'

'Citizen officer, even outside I doubt if everybody's thinking alike. Times have changed. Even the communists have fallen out among themselves.'

'Don't speak such slander, Marchenko! Communists form a united front.'

'What about the Chinese? And the Albanians? And the splits in all sorts of communist parties?'

'What about the Chinese! There's a black sheep in every family.'

'Citizen officers, you are all communists, aren't you? But what sort of communists are you – straightforward or parallel?'

They looked at me hard, as much as to say – are you cracked or something? Usov said: 'I've heard all sorts of rubbish from prisoners in my time, but this is the first time I've heard that one. What are you babbling about?'

'In yesterday's newspaper I read that the government of India had released thirty communists from jail – members of the parallel CP of India. So I'm asking you what sort you are: parallel, perpendicular or oblique?'

The KGB officer took a file down from the wall and began to leaf through it. From where I was sitting I showed him the place where it was written. After that they changed the subject, going back to the beginning again: 'Take thought, Marchenko! With your beliefs you'll be coming back here again.'

'You can say that again, I know that already. The moment someone disagrees with you – to the camps with him. Tomorrow you'll be singing a different tune and again you'll all be unanimous about it. In six years, thank God, I've had time to see plenty of traitors like myself – your camps are full of them. But what I don't understand is how can you communists put me in jail for my beliefs? In other countries whole opposition parties exist quite legally, including communist parties dedicated to changing the system. These communists, when they go back home from a routine conference in Moscow, aren't then tried for betraying their country. But me, a worker who belongs to no party whatsoever, you have been holding behind barbed wire for six whole years and now you're threatening me with more.'

'What's the point of telling us about other countries! They have their own laws and we have ours. You people are always throwing America in our faces – a fine country you've picked to show us freedom! If they had freedom there, why would all the Negroes be rebelling? And the workers striking?'

'Lenin said that strikes and the Negroes' struggle in the USA were themselves indications of freedom and democracy.'

When I said this my educators literally leapt up from their seats and all three of them pounced on me together:

'How dare you slander Lenin!'

'Where did you hear such a lie?'

'Repeat what you've just said!'

I remembered this passage word for word and repeated it, even naming the number of the volume it was in. The PEU chief went to the door: 'What volume did you say? Just a moment, I'll be right back.' He returned from his office carrying the book in its dark-blue binding – the latest edition, I had seen the whole set in his bookcase, pressed tightly together, cover to cover, behind the glass doors. He handed it to me:

'Go on, show us where it contains what you've just said.'

While I was leafing through the tightly pressed pages the three of them waited like hounds on the leash: now they would catch their game, now they would catch me out. They were convinced that Lenin never said any such thing, that he couldn't have said such a thing. An important consideration here was that their minds couldn't contain the idea of an uneducated fellow like me actually reading Lenin – or anything else for that matter. They themselves had read only 'from here to here'. They tried not to argue with a con who was a historian. But when somebody like me referred to an article in a magazine or a document, in short any printed source, they were convinced he was repeating it from hearsay, that one of the cons in the camp was spreading hostile propaganda, and that's why they always pounced: where did you hear that? Who told you that? And now it would turn out that I was talking through my hat and these questions would rain down on me.

I handed them the open book. The political education chief read out the lines I had indicated. Usov gazed at him in perplexity. The KGB officer went over to him:

'Here, give it to me.'

Together they turned the pages over, hoping, no doubt, to find some appropriate explanation or refutation of the passage they had just read. But nothing was to be found there and the KGB captain said to me, not in the least put out:

'Marchenko, you must have misinterpreted Lenin. With your views you interpret him in your own special way, and that's bad. You won't last very long outside.'

'But how else can these words be interpreted? After all, it's really true that strikes and mass disorders occur only in democratic countries, whereas totalitarian regimes repress the people with terror. Under Hitler, for instance, there were never any strikes in Germany.'

Then it began again: 'How dare you! You ought to be stood up against a wall for saying that!' Then, cooling off a little, they again set about 'educating' me: 'The peoples of the whole world are moving towards communism, every day it is winning more and more followers . . .'

'If these followers knew that they were leading their peoples towards prisons and camps they might, perhaps, think again. But you usually don't mention these things aloud, except when you start scrapping. One day almost every newspaper was full of: "China on the path to communism!" or "The successes of socialist construction in China!" And what is it now? "A hundred million Chinese in concentration camps" – what do you think, that they imprisoned them all in a single day?'

'Did you read that in Lenin as well – a hundred million? Where on earth do you get this rubbish from, Marchenko? A hundred million – why, that's one seventh of the entire population! These are the ravings of a madman!'

'Then it's not me who's mad but that lecturer who came to camp seven last summer. But why ravings? Didn't we have tens of millions in camps ourselves? If it were me alone, perhaps, I wouldn't believe it, I'd think I misheard about China. But I'm not the only one: all the cons heard it and laughed to think that the pupils had outstripped their masters.'

'A hundred million – that's slander! Here, take a pencil and paper and write that there are a hundred million prisoners in China. You know what will happen to you if it's untrue, don't you?'

I took a piece of paper and wrote: 'I, Prisoner Marchenko, A.T., heard during a lecture on such and such a day and at such and such a place that there are now a hundred million prisoners in China. During a talk with representatives of the KGB and PEU I mentioned this fact and referred to the lecturer, but was told that it was untrue. I would like the truth or falsity of this statement to be investigated and to be informed of the answer.' I wrote the date and signed it. Then I asked:

'When will I know the answer?'

'We'll check everything and when the time comes we'll call you in. You may go.'

I know that when people outside read of this conversation they will say to themselves: 'What the devil, there's more freedom in the camps than out here! Even at home I'd think twice before saying what Marchenko gabbed to his

officers! And all they say afterwards is "you may go" –
why, here I'd be clapped in a cell immediately if I talked like
that!'

Of course, if I'd taken it into my head to talk like that
to strangers in the compound, the grasses would have squealed
on me and I'd have had my sentence extended for 'agitation
among the prisoners', but an officer in his room is bound to
convince me with his arguments, and if the opposite occurs,
what's it to do with me? He can hardly nail me for agitating among
himself!

Nevertheless they might still have drummed up a charge and
slung me into Vladimir jail – but only if it had been just me,
whereas it was everyone, the entire youth. So that it couldn't
really go beyond the cooler and the cooler in camp is in any case
inevitable.

I landed up in the cooler almost on the very eve of my release,
on 30 September. The day before we had worked through the
entire day, from eight till five, then during the night we had heen
called out to unload cement and the following morning were
pushed out for a third time. But I was suffering from chills and
giddiness again. I didn't go, I refused. Anton Nakashidze (the
one from the Georgian Ensemble) also remained behind, he was
too exhausted to get up.

In the morning I dragged myself over to the medical
post, registered and settled down to wait my turn. The doctor
handed me a thermometer. I thrust it under my arm and
sat there thinking: 'I probably don't have a temperature,
it was a week before it went up last time. But they won't
put me in the infirmary anyway: I came myself, on my own
two feet. So what is to be done?' The doctor took the thermometer:

'Almost normal. What's the matter with you?'

'It's still the same as before – giddiness, headaches.'

'Well, why have you come here to me, Marchenko? You know
very well that it's the ear specialist you need! Take some pills
for your headache, that's all I can do for you.'

I got some pills at the hatch and went back to the hut. Our
gang had already returned from work and were sleeping, except

for Anton. The company officer had already given him fifteen days in the cooler. Soon afterwards our orderly, Davlianidze, came in: 'Marchenko, the company officer wants to see you!' Well, I'd better go.

'Why did you refuse to work last night?'

I explained why and it seemed to me that Usov believed me.

'All right, you can go.'

Back in the hut Anton asked me:

'How many? Ten or fifteen?'

'Well, nothing it seems.'

Anton couldn't believe me:

'Get away with you! I wouldn't have expected it.'

I climbed into my cot and endeavoured to go to sleep. But I had only just dozed off when somebody dug me in the ribs and started pulling on my leg. I opened my eyes and saw a warder.

'Come on, get ready!'

'What for?'

'Don't you know where shirkers go?'

Oh well, to hell with it, if it was the cooler, so be it. I still didn't know which was worse – the cooler or unloading timber. Anton and I started to get ready, putting on as many warm things as possible, but the warder warned us: 'You're wasting your time dressing up, we shall take it off you just the same.' Of course they would. It was so long since I had been in the cooler that I had forgotten. We picked up our padded jackets, our toothbrushes, some soap and a towel – and we were ready. I didn't even ask how long I had got. When we arrived they told me it was fifteen days.

Anton and I were separated and put into different cells. Mine turned out to be tiny, six feet by nine, but I was the only one in it. This is what they always try to do: either you're alone or they cram about twenty people into one small cell. I was pleased to think that at least I could sleep peacefully, but I was in too much of a hurry. Instead of cots the cell had two wooden shelves, as in a railway compartment, and both of them were folded flat against the wall and padlocked. You were able to lie down only between lights out and reveille. Still, it was a good thing I was alone, for at least I could sit down. But when there are two of you, one sits on the small block of wood that is fixed to the floor and the other has to stand: there is seating only for one. Unless you sit on the sloptank.

At night they brought the padded jacket that had earlier been confiscated and unlocked one of the shelves. I lay down. At first I had the jacket underneath me. But soon I was frozen stiff. It was bitterly cold, October was only one day away and the stoves weren't lit until the eighteenth. I dragged my jacket out from underneath me, huddled myself up and tucked it in around me. Now the cold began to come from underneath: the shelf was made of boards with cracks several inches wide between them, and the floor was the same. In short, I was unable to sleep for the cold and spent the whole night tramping about the cell in an attempt to get warm. Yuli had been lucky, it was summer when he was in here – in June!

In the morning my couch was locked up, the padded jacket was removed until the following night, and I myself was led to a small yard to work. It was old woman's work – the whole of the intensified regime block and the cooler was put on knotting shopping-nets. The norm was seven or eight nets a day. Nobody, of course, ever got anywhere near the norm, or even half the norm. Once we tried an experiment: we worked one whole day without a breather. And nevertheless, even the hardest workers got stuck on the third net. When I first went in they didn't insist on us fulfilling the norm: so long as we didn't refuse to work we at least got our basic. But after a week they announced that anyone who finished less than three nets would be put on a reduced food intake. Nobody could manage this target and we were all put on 1,300 calories a day. For us in the cooler it wasn't too bad – a week or two of starvation was nothing; but what about the men in the IRB? They had up to six months to do – and all that time on starvation rations! No parcels, no shop, not even allowed to buy smokes: you had to make a special application to the camp commandant. Then some would get permission, others not. In the cooler, of course, smoking was completely forbidden, tobacco was confiscated if they found any on you.

As in all prisons, the toilet break here was misery. There was no time even to wash, let alone clean your teeth. And there was one latrine for the whole jail, with only two holes. Two cells would be led out at a time, consisting of twelve to fifteen men, and there was no chance of them all having time. When they put you in the cooler they search you down to the last stitch of clothing and any paper is taken away; and they don't give you any paper when you go for your toilet break:

'Think you're an intellectual, eh? Well, you can wipe your arse with your fingers, it won't hurt you.'

It's a wonder no one's thought of keeping the sloptank locked and bolted.

In these conditions deceiving admin is a matter of life and death for the con. 'They know how to search and we know how to hide' is what they say in the camps. The compound even manages to get help to the IRB and the cooler. Friends who are 'free' – the compound, of course, is free compared to the cooler – manage to get smokes over to them, a bit of bread, sugar and margarine. And to do this the cons have invented the 'pony'.

What is a pony? The lads in the compound wrap some tobacco, bread or something else of that sort in a bit of rag, roll it into a tight little bundle and then wind a slender thread round it in which they make dozens of little loops. Then, at a convenient moment, they lob it over the fence so that it lands under the cooler windows. Meanwhile the cons inside are already prepared. They bend a piece of wire to make a hook, get hold of some thread – one usually sacrifices a sock – and they throw this line out so that the hook lands on the far side of the packet. Now they have to pull it slowly towards them. As it slides over the packet the hook is bound to catch in one of the loops.

If the bundle with the pick-me-up inside is too big and won't go through the bars on the window, they unwrap it right there on the far side of the bars, separate it with their hands and pull it into the cell bit by bit. So long as somebody manages to haul the pony in, and once the pick-me-up is inside the prison walls, it is bound to go to whoever it is intended for; the cons pass it

over either during the toilet break, or else at work or somewhere. Passing things from the compound to the cooler or from
cell to cell is severely punished, but nobody takes any notice of
that. If you were to fear punishment and obey all the regulations,
you wouldn't last a year in there. And we all had terms of five,
ten, fifteen years.

The pony was used right up until the summer of 1965. They
had become so clever at it that the whole operation took no
more than a minute: in a single moment the pony would be
lobbed over and already inside the cell. But word got round to
admin. The chief officer took steps to intensify vigilance and to
put an end to this lawlessness. And so they welded extra steel
bars on to the windows. Now the openings were three times as
narrow and the bars formed not so much a grill as a net. Not
only could you not get a hand through any more, but you could
barely get two fingers in the hole.

When I was in the cooler that autumn the pony was already
a thing of the past, it had served its turn. And the cons still
hadn't found a new trick to replace it. But they are bound to think
of something soon, I'm sure of it. For how could it possibly be
otherwise?

On 15 October I left the cooler to go back to the compound; I
was staggering like a drunkard after those scientifically calculated
1,300 calories. Till the end of my term, till the time of my
release, I had precisely seventeen days to go.

Just as before I went out to unload, lifted tree trunks, shovelled coal and cement. I got up at night when called, went with
the others to the guardhouse, waited for the armed escort.
Just as before I still suffered from giddiness, but I no longer
refused to go to work: I didn't want to spend my last few
days shut up in the cooler, I wanted to spend them with my
friends.

We were together for every free moment we had. The subject
of conversation was always the same: where would I go, where
and how would I get myself a job outside? The head of the
records office had already warned me that 'on account of the
passport regulations' I was forbidden to live in the districts of
Moscow or Leningrad, in ports or in frontier regions. Besides

these there were restricted-access towns where I also wouldn't be allowed to register.

'What does that mean, restricted-access towns, which ones?'

'If you're not allowed to register there, that means it's a restricted-access town.'

'Okay, where can I live then?'

'You'll find out when you're released. Just tell me for the time being where you want your ticket and certificate made out for.'

'Well, what about Kalinin?'

The major grinned:

'You can't register in Kalinin.'

'Make it Kursk then.'

'I can give you a certificate with Kursk on it. But let me tell you straight, Marchenko: it would be better for you to go to the far north or Siberia through a special recruitment office, so as not to waste your time chasing about.'

'Go from one camp to another just like this one, only without the barbed wire? No thanks. Anyway, they wouldn't take me in a special recruitment office with this health of mine.'

'Do as you like, but if you insist on having your own way you'll end up by coming back here again and we'll register you for another five to seven years in Mordovia without the least trouble at all.'

The thing that concerned my friends most was whether I would manage to get myself treated by a decent ear specialist. They also made more distant plans for my future. Valery insisted that I should definitely go to school: 'Finish night school and you'll be able to go to a research institute. It's not too late.'

'Valery, what kind of a pupil do you think I'd make? I'm as dumb as an ox at mathematics.'

Valery began to demonstrate that nobody is incapable of learning, except for congenital idiots. It was just that maths was always taught badly. 'You can learn if you want to.'

'But I'm deaf, I won't even hear the lessons.'

Yuli said that in Moscow you could buy a hearing aid. They cost a pretty penny. But on the other hand the girls would never notice you were deaf. All you had to do was let your hair grow long – to hide the loop that went over your ear.

We discussed everything down to the smallest detail: how I would dress outside, where to buy what so that it was both cheap and practical. I would have to travel in my camp reefer jacket, since it turned out that all that was left of my clothes was an old skiing suit and a pair of boots. What a hurry I was in to strip off that reefer jacket, how sick and tired of it I was by now!

The lads started bringing me clippings from various magazines: fashionable men's wear, what tie to wear with which suit. One might have thought that I was going to have at least three of these suits, that I would be spending my time rushing from concert hall to diplomatic reception.

My last days in the camp were particularly painful: they dragged on and on until it seemed they would never come to an end and I could hardly believe that the day of my release would really come, and I didn't know what to expect afterwards.

Already on the day before my release I had handed in my regulation equipment and overalls and early on the morning of 2 November my friends and acquaintances on the first shift came in to say goodbye: they were going off now and we wouldn't be seeing one another again. Among them were Burov, the two Valerys from Leningrad – Ronkin and Smolkin, Vadim, and also a number of others that I knew. They all hoped I would settle down all right outside, gave me their families' addresses and asked me to call in if it was on my way. They asked me not to forget them – those who were sitting in Vladimir prison as well as those remaining in Mordovia. When they left for their shift only my closest friends stayed behind – Valery, Yuli, Kolya, Tolik, Footman, Anton. Yuli presented me with Lebedev's book on Chaadayev – he knew that I was very fond of it. And on the fly-leaf he had written:

> Not bad on the whole
> Your fate is amusing:
> Your ears here were closed,

Your eyes here were opened.
Be proud of your uncommon feat –
Not everyone seeing sees.

To Tolya Marchenko with respect and
affectionate best wishes, Yuli Daniel.

Footman and Valery presented me with Prévost's 'Manon Lescaut', probably as a hint. At ten o'clock the whole group of them accompanied me to the guardhouse. Here we again embraced and said our farewells. It is impossible to convey my feelings. All my joy evaporated, a lump rose in my throat and I was afraid of bursting into tears. I deeply regretted parting from my friends, leaving those who had become so dear to me behind barbed wire. For a moment I wanted to return.

'Go on, Tolya, you'll miss the train!' they said, hurrying and encouraging me at the same time.

I walked through the outer zone – a barbed wire fence already divided us. Waving my hand to them one last time, I entered the guardhouse and the door banged shut behind me. Now I faced quite a different sort of leave-taking.

I was taken into an office.

'Strip! Stand over here! Knees bend and hold out your arms! Go into the corner!'

After this they began to feel and examine my clothing. Every seam of my shirt, then my underpants, then all the rest. One warder examined the shirt before passing it to another; he then felt it and passed it on to an officer, who passed it to a second who passed it to a third who passed it to a fourth and then on to me. I then put it on. Present at the search were: the Chief Officer, the chief of camp security and the chief of the camp KGB.

Next came the turn of my suitcase. There was practically nothing in it: towel, soap, toothbrush, a few handkerchiefs, some exercise books with my study notes and some books. Everything was inspected just as painstakingly as my clothes, every object was poked and felt by five or six pairs of hands. The exercise books and books were checked with particular care and leafed through page by page. What were they looking for? The warder opened Chaadayev and saw Yuli's inscription. He immediately showed it to the KGB man who took it and left the office with it. They also kept taking my exercise books out into the corridor, showing them to someone and getting advice. Returning with my copy of Chaadayev, the KGB man put it to one side.

As I watched them rummaging through my things I suddenly remembered something. Not long before me a Muscovite called Rybkin had been released. As soon as he came to the guardhouse they had pounced:

'Come on, give us Daniel's poems! We know all about it!'

Rybkin was astonished, he had never exchanged a single word with Daniel, he didn't even know him. They set about searching him and when they reached his papers one of the warders dragged out a notebook with some verses: 'Here they are, we were right!' Their triumph was shortlived however. These verses were not by Daniel but by Ryskov (a former medical orderly in camp three). One of the grasses had seen Ryskov giving them to Rybkin and had squealed. Therefore they knew in the guardhouse that Rybkin was trying to take some verses out of the camp, a whole notebook-full. But whose verses? No one was in any doubt – they must be Daniel's! And it turned out they weren't Daniel's at all, but a collection of love lyrics! What a disappointment! And now they must be looking for Yuli's poems on me. Let them look! They had already found his inscription in the book.

Meanwhile they had already finished turning my gear upside down and the chief officer was examining, poking, tapping and thrusting a steel spike clean through my suitcase, which had in any case already been examined by the others. Then he set about a toy I had been given – a plastic fisherman with a fishing rod. The fisherman was completely soft and all but transparent. Only the head was hard, having been stuffed with something. The chief officer squeezed it and squeezed it, pinched it and pinched it, but was evidently unable to make up his mind and took the fisherman out into the corridor. A little while later he returned and tossed the fisherman back into my case – failed again!

Into the office came Major Postnikov himself, head of the KGB for all the camps in Mordovia. They showed him Chaadayev. Postnikov turned the book round in his hands, read the inscription and commanded:

'Cut it out and make a record of it.'

I asked him to explain what was wrong with the inscription and why they were confiscating it.

'You see, Marchenko, in my opinion Daniel was expressing his views in that verse.'

'Well, of course he was, you wouldn't expect him to express someone else's. But what's subversive about them?'

Postnikov didn't reply. He started to look through my exercise books.

'I see, Marchenko, that you've been reading the whole of Lenin. On the whole that's a good thing, of course, but . . . I fear that with your views we shall be seeing you back again.'

With this farewell ringing in my ears and having received back my case, my mutilated Chaadayev, my internal passport and my certificate of release. I walked to the exit, accompanied by the major in charge of the records office. We passed through several doors. At each one the major handed some documents through a tiny window, after which the door would open and then close after us again. At last the last door opened and banged shut behind me and I walked out into the street.

Past the guardhouse and down the road between the living and work zones, past the festive posters and slogans, came a column of women prisoners. I could hear the rough shouts of the armed guards with their tommy guns: 'Stop talking! What did I tell you!' The women were walking slowly, dragging their feet in their clumsy felt boots. Dark grey padded jackets, padded trousers, greyish-yellow faces. I gazed at them – that one, perhaps, I had carried in for an operation; perhaps that one over there had said: 'My Valery's a year old already!' No, I didn't recognise any of them. They were all exactly alike in this column – cons.

The column passed. I filled my lungs with fresh air – although Mordovian it was unguarded and free – and walked away from the guardhouse. It was snowing. Big snow-flakes settled and immediately melted on my still warm clothing, which had not had time to cool. It was the latter half of the day of 2 November 1966, five days to go to the forty-ninth anniversary of Soviet power.

APPENDIX

1. Open letter by Marchenko to Alexander Chakovsky,
Editor of the Literary Gazette

Citizen Chakovsky,

I have read your article, 'Answer to a Reader', in No. 13 of the *Literary Gazette*. Among other things it contains the following: '. . . instead of feeding such persons at the nation's expense in prisons and corrective labour colonies . . .'.

You adopt the stance in your article of a man with a civic conscience, as if you were sincerely concerned about the fate and prestige of our country. A man who takes such a stand on civic grounds cannot possibly justify himself with a plea of ignorance or shortage of information. If you really didn't know beforehand, nevertheless you *could* have known and therefore *should* have known just how prisoners in corrective labour colonies are fed, and at whose expense. It appears, however, that you are not making any effort to find out, that the problem does not interest you and that the lines quoted above were written merely for effect so as to make a great play of exposing 'criminals'. Let me, therefore, not so much for your sake as for that of your readers, introduce a slight amendment to your remarks.

A prisoner in a strict regime corrective labour camp (all political prisoners are in this category) receives 2,400 calories a day – sufficient for a seven- to eleven-year-old child. This means a helping (about two cupfuls) of watery, fatless skilly in the morning; the same amount of rotted cabbage soup at lunchtime with two spoonfuls of thin gruel; and two spoonfuls of the same gruel in the evening together with a morsel of boiled cod about the size of a matchbox. All these soups and gruels taken together are supposed to contain not more than five-sevenths of an ounce of fat (not butter, of course), and one is also allowed twenty-eight and a half-ounces of black bread and half an ounce of sugar a day. And that is all.

These are the normal rations. For 'obstinate' prisoners there is the so-called 'strict' food quota – punishment rations. These consist of a mug of hot water for breakfast, fourteen and a quarter ounces of cabbage soup and two spoonfuls of watery gruel for lunch, and the same little piece of boiled cod, but without gruel, for supper. Moreover this 'punishment soup' is prepared separately – it contains no fat at all. And sugar is also forbidden. The sixteen ounces of black bread you get on this regime is the equivalent of 1,300 calories (sufficient for an infant of one to three years).

That is how 'such persons' are fed today. As for at whose expense – that is another question.

Prisoners in corrective labour camps work eight hours a day, forty-eight hours a week. It was in the corrective labour camp of Dubrovlag that prisoners made that television set that you and your family so love to watch, and that radiogram on which – by accident, of course – you heard the Voice of America, and that soft couch of yours and that desk. But don't imagine that those who make your furniture and are fed 'at the nation's expense' have an easy time of it. In those 'easy' furniture factories, prisoners who work as loaders (including former artists, writers, scientists, Party and Komsomol workers) overstrain themselves unloading heavy timber and stone by hand. In unhealthy workshops former colleagues of yours, polishing *your* table perhaps, are ruining their health for life. And in return they get – gruel, black bread, empty stomachs day after day for years on end.

Is this what you had in mind when you wrote that 'such persons are fed by the nation'? What lofty humanism, writer Chakovsky! Is this how the nation – including the prisoners of Dubrovlag, Vorkuta, Siberia and Kazakhstan – feeds you and the other writers, the 'nation's conscience'? Perhaps the lofty civic passion of your article is explained precisely by the fact that you receive somewhat more for it than a bowl of skilly and a hunk of black bread?

If you are told to answer this letter, you will no doubt cite examples of the conditions of prisoners in the USA or China. You might even go beyond these two examples to Greece or Southern Rhodesia. Or why not bring in Hitler's concentration camps? You will probably keep quiet about Stalin's camps, however, even though you exhort the public to 'cast their eyes back to the comparatively recent past'. But what about the situation in our country today? This is what citizens with such a lofty awareness as yourself should first and foremost be directing their civic passion towards.

Finally, I would like this open letter to you to reach my fellow citizens not via the Voice of America or the BBC, but through publication in your newspaper. Only then will we be able to talk of 'perfecting socialism', and our ideological enemies abroad won't be able to use the shameful facts given here for their own ends.

27 March, 1968

A. Marchenko (Loader and former political prisoner),
Noviskaya ulitsa 27,
Alexandrov (Vladimir Oblast).

2. Open letter by Marchenko to the Chairman of the Soviet Red Cross and others

To:
The Chairman of the Red Cross Society of the USSR,
G. A. Mitiryov;
Minister of Health of the USSR, B. V. Petrovsky;
Director of the Food Institute at the Academy of Medical Sciences,
A. A. Pokrovsky:
Patriarch of All Russia, Alexy;
President of the Academy of Sciences of the USSR, M. V. Keldysh;
President of the Academy of Medical Sciences of the USSR, V. D. Timakov;
Director of the Institute of State and Law, Chikvadze;
Rector of Moscow State University, I. G. Petrovsky;
Chairman of the Board of the Journalists' Union of the USSR, Zimyanin;
First Secretary of the Board of the Writers' Union of the USSR,
K. Fedin;
K. Simonov, R. Gamzatov, R. Rozhdestvensky, E. Evtushenko, writers.

(Copies to the UN Human Rights Commission and the International Human Rights Conference of UNO)

Five months ago I completed a book, *My Testimony*, on the six years (1960–66) that I spent in Vladimir Prison and in camps for political prisoners. In the introduction I wrote:

'Today's Soviet camps for political prisoners are just as horrific as in Stalin's time. A few things are better, a few things worse. But everybody must know about it.

'Everybody must know, including those who would like to know the truth and are given lying, optimistic newspaper articles instead, designed to lull the public conscience; and also including those who don't wish to know, who close their eyes and stop up their ears in order to be able at some future date to justify themselves and to emerge from the dirt with their noses clean: "Good heavens, and we never knew . . ." If they possess a single particle of civic conscience or genuine love for their country, they will stand up in its defence, just as the true sons of Russia have always done.

'I would like my testimony on Soviet camps and prisons for political prisoners to come to the attention of humanists and progressive people in other countries – those who stick up for political prisoners in Greece and Portugal and in Spain and South Africa. Let them ask their Soviet colleagues in the struggle against inhumanity: "And what have you done in your country to prevent political prisoners from being 're-educated' by starvation?"'

I have done my best to make my book known to the public. However, there has been no official reaction at all so far (except for a chat with a KGB officer about my 'anti-social' activities). Conditions in the camps remain the same. Thus I am forced to turn to certain personalities who, by virtue of their social position, are among the people most responsible for the state of our society and its level of humanity and legality.

You should know the following. Our country's camps and prisons contain thousands of political prisoners. Most of them have been sentenced in closed courts, there have been virtually no really open trials (with the exception of trials of war criminals) and in all cases a fundamental principle of legal procedure has been violated – publicity. Thus society has not paid attention, and still does not pay any, either to the observance of legality or to the extent of political repression.

The situation of our political prisoners is generally the same as that of criminal convicts and in some respects is considerably worse: the best that political prisoners can hope for is 'strict' regime conditions, whereas for the criminals there is both a 'normal' regime and an even lighter one. Criminals may be released after serving two-thirds or a half of their sentence, while political prisoners have to serve every single day, 'from bell to bell'. Thus political prisoners are in all respects put on a par with the most dangerous criminals and recidivists. No juridical or legal distinction is made between them.

Political prisoners, as a rule, are people who, before their arrest, were engaged in socially useful work: engineers, workers, writers, artists, scientists. In the camps, by way of 're-educational measures', they are obliged to do forced labour. Furthermore, work is used by the camp administration as a means of punishment: sickly persons are forced to perform heavy physical labour, intellectuals are compelled to do unskilled physical work. Failure to fulfil the norm is regarded as a violation of the regulations and serves as a pretext for various administrative punishments, ranging from a ban on visitors to the punishment cell or solitary confinement.

The most powerful measure for manipulating the prisoners, however, is starvation. The normal rations are such as to make a man feel perpetual hunger and perpetual malnutrition. The daily camp ration contains 2,400 calories (sufficient for a seven- to eleven-year old child) and has to suffice for an adult doing physical work day after day for many years – sometimes as many as fifteen or twenty-five! Those calories are supplied mainly by black bread (twenty-eight and a half ounces a day). The cons never even set eyes on fresh vegetables, butter, or many other indispensable foods and these are prohibited from sale at the camp shop (as also is sugar).

Let me say at once that camp food as well as camp clothing is paid for by the prisoners themselves out of the earnings accredited to them. (Fifty per cent is in any case deducted at source for the upkeep of the camp: barrack huts, equipment, fences, watch towers, etc). Only five roubles a month, out of the money that remains after all deductions, can be spent on products (including tobacco) at the camp shop. But you can be deprived of even this right to spend seventeen copecks a day for 'violating the regulations'. For example, the historian Rendel, who got ten years for participating in an illegal Marxist circle, was banned from the shop for two months for bringing supper to his sick comrades in their hut. So was the imprisoned writer, Sinyavsky, for exchanging a few words with his friend, Daniel, when the latter was in the camp jail.

To punish a prisoner for 'violating camp regulations', e.g. for failure to fulfil his work norm, they may put him on a 'strict' food quota – 1,300 calories (sufficient for an infant of one to three years). This is what they did, for example, with the writer, Daniel, and the engineer, Ronkin (seven years for illegal Marxist activity) at the end of summer 1967.

Food parcels from relatives are 'not authorised' for prisoners sentenced to strict regime. Only occasionally, as encouragement for good behaviour (i.e. recantation, informing on others, collaborating with the camp administration) do the camp authorities allow a prisoner to receive a food parcel, but even then not before he has served half his sentence, not more than four times a year and not more than ten pounds at a time.

Thus the camp administration wields a powerful weapon for exerting physical pressure on political prisoners – a whole system of escalating hunger and starvation. The application of this system results in emaciation and vitamin deficiency.

Some prisoners are driven by permanent malnutrition to kill and eat crows and, if they are lucky, dogs. In the autumn of 1967, one prisoner at Dubrovlag camp two found a way of getting potatoes while he was in the hospital zone. He overate them and died (the potatoes were raw). And starvation rules even more harshly in Vladimir Prison and in the special regime camps, where political prisoners are also numerous.

In comparison with this permanent malnutrition, the other 'administrative measures' appear relatively harmless. It is perhaps worth mentioning a few, such as banning meetings with relatives, shaving the head, prohibiting the wearing of your own garments (including warm underwear in winter), obstructing creative work and the observance of religious rites.

Prisoners' official complaints and petitions addressed to the Procuracy, the Prasidium of the Supreme Soviet of the USSR or the Central Committee of the Communist Party are unfailingly returned to the camp administration. The top bodies send them to the Ministry for the Preservation of Public Order or to the Main Administration of Places of Confinement, and from there they go on a multi-stage journey round the departments and end up, one way or another, in the hands of the very people complained about – 'for checking'. All these complaints naturally end in the same way, with the camp administration replying that 'the statements cannot be confirmed' or that 'the punishment was correctly administered', and the petitioner's position becomes intolerable. Sometimes he is even transferred to the camp cells or to solitary confinement for this latest 'violation of the regulations'. And then the 'educator-officers' enjoy taunting dissatisfied prisoners: 'Go on, lodge a complaint against us, go on, write a letter, it's your right.' Others, more simple-minded, offer warnings: 'Why protest? You know the administration can always get its own back on any of the prisoners. You're only making things worse for yourself, better put up with it.'

And indeed, the 'Regulations for Camps and Prisons' passed by the Supreme Soviet in 1961 give camp administrations almost unlimited scope to apply physical and moral pressure. The prohibition of food parcels, the banning of purchases from the camp shop, starvation rations, the curtailment of visits, the punishment cell, handcuffs, solitary confinement – all these are legalized by the Regulations and applied regularly to political prisoners. For the camp administrations find these measures much to their taste, all the more so in that the 'educators' include not a few officials from Stalin's concentration camps, men who are accustomed to arbitrary power (which, incidentally, was quite in line with their instructions at that time).

Since the prisoners lack all rights, they are driven to dreadful and disastrous forms of protest: hunger strikes, self-mutilation, suicide. In broad daylight, for instance, a prisoner will walk over to the perimeter fence and climb the wire, and there the guard shoots him down for 'attempted escape'.

I don't know of a single country in the whole world, except ours, where, in the 1960s, political prisoners have such a status – legalized deprivation of rights plus legalized starvation plus legalized forced labour. I am convinced of one thing: these conditions are possible in our country only because no one knows of their existence, except the people responsible for organising and enforcing them. For if the public knew of them, how could they possibly protest against the conditions of political prisoners in other countries? At the moment, however, it is only the political prisoners themselves, when they read of these protests in the newspapers, who are able to appreciate the monstrous hypocrisy of our situation and the extreme contradiction between our propaganda 'for export' and our actual practice here at home.

Some among you bear direct responsibility for the present situation; the responsibility of others is determined by their public position. But I am appealing to you as fellow citizens: we are all equally responsible to our motherland, to the young generation, to the country's future. Let it suffice that the generation of the thirties and forties put up with crimes committed 'in the name of the people'. It is impossible and impermissible to display once more the criminal indifference that turned a whole nation into accomplices in bloody crimes.

I appeal to you.

Demand a public investigation into the situation of political prisoners.

Demand wide dissemination of the 'Regulations for Camps and Prisons' and try to get special rules drawn up for the confinement of political prisoners.

Demand publication of the food rations for prisoners. Demand the immediate dismissal from 'educational' work of former staff from Stalin's concentration camps and of camp officials who have more recently displayed cruelty and inhumanity towards prisoners. Demand a public trial for them.

It is our civic duty, the duty of our human conscience, to put a stop to crimes against humanity. For these crimes begin not with smoking chimneys and crematoria, nor with steamers packed with prisoners bound for Magadan – they begin with public indifference.

2 April 1968

A. Marchenko,
Novinskaya ulitsa 27,
Alexandrov (Vladimir Oblast).

3. Reply by the Soviet Red Cross Society to the letter from Marchenko

USSR. Order of Lenin Executive Committee of the
Union of Red Cross and Red Crescent Societies,
First Cheremushkinsky Proyezd 5,
Moscow, V–36.
   No. 182/125 yur. 29 April 1968

To:
Citizen A. Marchenko,
Novinskaya ulitsa 27,
Alexandrov (Vladimir Oblast).

The letter sent in your name to the Executive Committee of the USSR URC and RCS has not, unfortunately, been signed by anyone,* which makes it impossible and unnecessary to give detailed consideration to its contents.

   Nevertheless the Executive Committee considers it necessary to point out briefly that our legislation and the Soviet concept of law regard people who have attacked the achievements of the October Revolution as having committed a most serious offence against the nation and as deserving of severe punishment, rather than any kind of indulgence or leniency.

   In the light of the foregoing, the entirely groundless nature of your other assertions becomes apparent.

F. Zakharov (Deputy Chairman of
the Executive Committee of the
URC and RCS of the USSR).

---

* Marchenko probably confined himself to a typewritten signature and forgot to affix a handwritten one.

4. Open letter by Marchenko to the International Committee of the Red Cross

To:

Mr S. Gonard,
President,
International Committee of the Red Cross.

I am sending you a copy of the letter I sent in April 1968 to the addresses indicated.* The only reply I received was from the Executive Committee of the USSR Red Cross and Red Crescent Societies, of which I am also sending you a copy. I received, in addition, a reply from the writer, K. Simonov, but that was a personal letter to myself.

The reply of the USSR Red Cross does not, in my opinion, conform to the humanitarian aims of this organisation. Therefore, Mr President, I would like to make the following request: 'Please send to the USSR a representative mission of the International Committee of the Red Cross to study the position of Soviet political prisoners in the camps of Mordovia (Mordovskaya ASSR *stantsia* Potma, Dubrovlag, camp nos. 11, 17, 10 and 3 – the hospital zone. Also Vladimir Prison at Vladimir) and give them all necessary help.' (This request of mine is almost identical in its wording with the appeal from the Executive Committee of the Soviet Red Cross and the Communist Party of the Soviet Union concerning the position of political prisoners in Indonesia. I enclose a copy of that appeal as published in *Izvestia* on 22 June 1968.)

I also request the International Committee of the Red Cross to join with me in making the demands set out in my letter.

4 July 1968

A. Marchenko.

5. Letter from the Rev Sergei Zheludkov concerning Marchenko's book, My Testimony

To:
Professor Josef Hromadka, President of the Christian Peace Conference, Prague, Czechoslovakia.
His Holiness the Ecumenical Patriarch Athenogoras, Istanbul, Turkey.
Dr Eugene C. Blake, Secretary-General of the World Council of Churches, Geneva, Switzerland.

* See document No. 2 above.

His Eminence Cardinal Bea, Rome, Italy.

His Eminence Cardinal Stefan Wyszinski, Warsaw, Poland.

His Grace the Archbishop of Canterbury, Michael Ramsey, London, England.

Archpriest Father Vladimir Rodzianko, BBC, London, England.

His Reverence the Bishop of Woolwich, John Robinson, London, England.

Archpriest Father Shmeman, Professor of Columbia University and of the Orthodox Academy of St Vladimir, New York, USA.

CHRIST IS RISEN

Dear Professor,

I am appealing to you and also, in similar letters, to a number of other eminent representatives of world Christendom known to me. I make this appeal not as the representative of any corporate body, but entirely on my own personal responsibility. I have regarded it as my personal duty as a Christian and a priest to convey to you my impressions of the evidence presented in the manuscript *My Testimony* (written in Alexandrov in 1967) by Anatoly Tikhonovich Marchenko, who recently returned from a concentration camp at Potma in the Mordovian ASSR. He writes not about the accursed past, but about things that are happening at the present time.

1. Political detainees held in our prisons and camps today are being subjected to inhuman treatment. The conditions under which they are transported from place to place are nightmarish. Thereafter, throughout the whole term of their sentences, they suffer from hunger, chronic malnutrition and at times outright torture by starvation: 2,400 calories each per day, with only 1,300 calories for those who have committed an offence. They are also subject to forced labour, which is intolerably severe when combined with such inadequate food, to living conditions that constitute a danger to health, and to a completely unsatisfactory medical service. The writer of the book emerged from the camps a disabled man – he had become deaf owing to lack of treatment for septic meningitis. He testifies, and is prepared to corroborate it in open court, to prisoners being unmercifully beaten, to captured escapees being killed, and to all manner of persecution that reduces men to madness, self-mutilation and suicide.

The camp administration is totally arbitrary and it is useless to protest. The tradition of Stalin's camps still prevails and is fully operative today: suppression of the prisoners' human dignity and severe punishment for anyone who resists; deprivation of visits, parcels and books; the 'cooler' or camp jail on punishment rations. All this taken together is termed 'strict regime' – in actual fact it amounts to a system of accelerated death.

2. Besides political prisoners this system is now applied to so-called 'religious prisoners' as well. As the author testifies: 'This is the term used to describe prisoners who have been jailed for believing in God. They aren't the only people who believe in God, there are other cons who believe as well. But religious prisoners are the ones who have been arrested and tried precisely because of their religion. And what variety there is! Moslems from the Caucasus and Central Asia, Orthodox Christians, Baptists, Jehovah's Witnesses, Evangelists, Sabbatarians and many others . . . The fanaticism of religious prisoners finds expression only in their insistence on retaining their own religious beliefs and customs. They are extremely peaceful and humble people, old men for the most part of about sixty or over, although there are young ones among them as well. Their attitude to imprisonment is somewhat different from that of the other cons: they take consolation from the fact that they are suffering for their God and their faith and they are patient in bearing their suffering and pain.'

3. The author became closely acquainted in the prison camp with the writer, Yuli Daniel, who, together with Andrei Sinyavsky, was sentenced in 1966; they were given five and seven years respectively of 'strict regime' for literary works that adopted a critical attitude towards present-day realities. It is common knowledge that Alexander Ginzburg was subsequently sentenced to five years of strict regime for compiling a collection of documents about the trial of these two writers. At the same time the chronically ill Yuri Galanskov was sentenced to seven years of the same murderous strict regime for compiling the handwritten literary review, *Phoenix*. Unfortunately it is impossible from Marchenko's testimony to determine the approximate number of other persons suffering under this kind of treatment. Formally they are regarded as criminal offenders, but they have not committed or conspired to commit any offence. They have merely sought to give effect to some of the human rights proclaimed as long ago as 1948 by the United Nations. And these are human rights that, at the same time, constitute a man's religious duty. A Christian is bound before God to be a whole man, a free man: free to think, not to be untruthful or to act deceitfully either towards himself or towards others. To persecute a person for exercising this freedom of peaceful, personal beliefs, this freedom to express the truth, is Caesar attempting to take something that belongs to God. It is essentially a crime

against humanity, against that free and sacred humanity bestowed on us by God in Christ, Our Lord. The above-mentioned representatives of the Russian intelligentsia, together with others unknown, are today suffering in strict regime conditions on behalf of that Christian principle.

Such, briefly stated, is the testimony, whose truth, if so desired, can be easily verified. I offer it for the consideration of your Christian consciences. I believe that the practical attitude we assume towards these facts today will be the real test of the sincerity and spiritual strength of our Christianity.

Yours sincerely,

St Nicholas' and Victory Day,
9 May 1968

Sergei Zheludkov (Priest).
Pskovskaya ulitsa 6,
Pskov 14.

6. Open letter by Marchenko to Czechoslovak Newspapers

To: *Rude Pravo, Literarni Listi, Prace.*
Copies to: *L'Humanité, L'Unità, Morning Star*, BBC.

At the recently concluded session of the Supreme Soviet of the RSFSR, all the deputies dwelt upon one question: the events in Czechoslovakia. The deputies unanimously supported the CPSU Central Committee plenum on this question and also unanimously approved the Warsaw Letter of the five Communist parties to the Central Committee of the Communist Party of Czechoslovakia. They approved and supported the entire policy of the Party and government on this question.

If Communists endorse this policy as a model of proper Marxist-Leninist policy in relations between fraternal parties, that is their business and a matter for their party conscience. But here at this session, this policy was unanimously endorsed by the deputies to the RSFSR Supreme Soviet, who express the opinion of the voters, i.e. the people, the overwhelming majority of whom, including myself, are not Communists.

Even before *Izvestia* had had time to reach the entire population with its reports on the work done by this session of the Supreme Soviet, the newspaper suddenly launched a campaign in its succeeding issues in support of the decisions adopted by the session on behalf of 'all' the people and 'all the workers'. I have my own opinion in this regard and would like to avail myself of the right, guaranteed me by the constitution, to express my opinion and my stand on this question.

I have been closely following (as far as this is possible in our country) the events in Czechoslovakia and I cannot remain calm and indifferent in the face of the reaction that these events are provoking in our press. For half a year our newspapers have been trying to misinform public opinion in our country, and at the same time to misinform world public opinion on our people's attitude towards these events. The newspapers represent the position of the Party leadership as being the position – even the unanimous position – of all the people. All Brezhnev had to do was to pin the labels of 'imperialist intrigue', 'menace to socialism', 'offensive by anti-socialist elements', etc. on current developments in Czechoslovakia and in a trice the entire press and numerous public resolutions took up the same refrain, even though today, just as half a year ago, our people essentially do not know the real state of affairs in Czechoslovakia. Workers' letters to the newspapers and the resolutions of mass meetings are nothing but repetitions of prepared formulae handed down from 'above' and have nothing to do with expressions of independent opinion based on a knowledge of concrete facts. Obedient voices repeat after the Party leadership: 'The waging of a resolute battle to preserve the socialist order in Czechoslovakia is not only the task of the Czechoslovak Communists, but also our common task as well'. Or 'I support the plenum's conclusions on the necessity of waging the struggle for the cause of socialism in Czechoslovakia', and so on (*Izvestia*, no. 168).

The authors of these letters and declarations probably did not even ask themselves why decisions concerning the struggle for socialism in *Czechoslovakia* are being made by a Central Committee plenum of the Communist Party of the *Soviet Union*. It probably did not occur to them that our appeal to 'healthy forces' in Czechoslovakia might possibly be an appeal to anti-government elements and an incitement to armed attack on their own legal government. They probably did not realise that the words 'this is our task' could mean, at the very least, political pressure on a sovereign nation and, at worst, possible intervention by our troops in the Czechoslovak Socialist Republic. It is probable, too, that the authors of these letters, in endorsing the policy of the Central Committee, did not realise that this policy is strikingly reminiscent, for example, of US policy in the Dominican Republic, which was denounced a hundred times in our press.

On the basis of articles in the Czechoslovak press, of western radio reports, and the few facts that have been reported in our own press,

I believe that the Czechoslovak Socialist Republic has been making genuine progress towards the development of a healthy society. There is a struggle of ideas and opinions, freedom to criticise, an attempt to implement in practice the declared ideals of socialism that up to now have existed everywhere only in the form of slogans or promises for the distant future. This is why the Warsaw Letter of the five Communist parties and the decisions of the Central Committee plenum of the Communist Party of the Soviet Union, unanimously supported by our press, have evoked in me feelings of shame and outrage.

In view of all the words we have uttered about the need for a people to decide its own fate, just why is the fate of the Czechs and Slovaks being decided not in Prague, but rather in Warsaw and Moscow? What leads Brezhnev and Ulbricht to believe that they can make a better assessment of the situation in Czechoslovakia than Dubček and the Czechs and Slovaks themselves?

I do not believe in either the mythical imperialist plots against Czechoslovakia, or the 'offensive of internal forces of reaction'. I do not think that even the authors of these myths believe them. These accusatory formulae have been thought up as a pretext and with the aim of befogging the brains of our fellow citizens.

Are our leaders really disturbed by what is happening in Czechoslovakia? In my opinion they are not merely disturbed, they are scared stiff – not because what is happening there poses a threat to socialist development or to the security of the Warsaw Pact nations, but because the events in Czechoslovakia could undermine the authority of the leaders of these nations and discredit the very principles and governing methods that presently prevail in the socialist camp.

One might well ask: what could be more horrible and scandalous than Chinese Communism? Every day our newspapers expose the bloody Chinese terror, the collapse of their economy, the theoretical errors of the Chinese Communist Party, etc. The Chinese leaders reply in kind. There is no longer any question of friendly cooperation between such recent brothers and great peoples. Yet no meeting or plenum of the Central Committee has adopted a resolution on the need to defend the cause of socialism in China, nor has there been any discussion of the responsibility of the fraternal parties towards their own peoples or towards the people of China, who have been drowning in blood for many years now. To be sure, the Communist Party of China has not relinquished the reins of government. But what of it? Are the results of its rule any better than the prospects offered by free, democratic development in Czechoslovakia? Is the open hostility of the Chinese Communist Party towards our nation better than friendly relations with the present Czechoslovak government?

Yet our leaders do not remind the Chinese leadership that we liberated China from Japanese militarism and do not lay claim, on that basis, to the role of defender of the Chinese people against internal reaction. We do not appeal to 'healthy forces' and 'true Communists' in China and promise that 'Communists and all Soviet people, in fulfilment of their international duty, will lend those forces all possible aid and support!' (speech by N. V. Podgorny at the third session of the Supreme Soviet of the RSFSR on 19 July 1968, reported in *Izvestia*, no. 168). However, our Chinese brothers, who are being physically destroyed, probably need this aid far more than the 'true Communists' in Czechoslovakia, who are not only free and secure, but also enjoy the same freedom of speech as all other citizens. With respect to China our leaders assume the position of detached observers and there has been no joint initiative such as that by Party Committee Secretary V. Prokopenko, Brigade Leader Akhmatseyev and Candidate of Sciences Antosenkov (*Izvestia*, no. 168). to offer 'all-out aid' to the Chinese people. Can it really be that our sense of collective responsibility is less aroused by the bloody terror which the Central Committee of the Chinese Communist Party has unleashed against its own people, than by the basically peaceful development of democracy in Czechoslovakia? How can one explain such a contradictory reaction?

In my opinion, the first explanation is that we dare not talk to China from a position of strength, whereas from force of habit we permit ourselves to speak to Czechoslovakia in bullying tones. No less important is the fact that, despite Chinese hostility towards the Soviet Communist Party, China's internal policy strengthens rather than undermines the position of the Communist Party in our country. 'In China there are public executions, in our country there are none!' our press rejoices (see Chakovsky's 'Answer to a Reader' in the *Literary Gazette*). Compared with the regime in China, our present regime is one not of terror but merely of suppression – almost liberal, in fact, almost like in the nineteenth century. But if Czechoslovakia should really succeed in organising democratic socialism, then there would be no justification for the absence of democratic freedoms in our own country, and then, who knows, our workers, peasants and intelligentsia might start demanding freedom of speech in fact and not merely on paper.

And that is the real meaning of the Warsaw Letter: 'we cannot allow'. And it has nothing whatever to do with a mythical threat to socialism in Czechoslovakia.

Our leaders have voiced concern about 'true Communists' supposedly being slandered and subjected to 'moral terror' by Czechoslovak anti-socialists who have seized the means of propaganda (one would think there had been an armed seizure of the postal, telegraph and radio services in Prague). But somehow they omit to mention that these Communists themselves have the opportunity to refute these slanders publicly. True, the justifications uttered by the Former Chairman of the Supreme Court of the Czechoslovak Socialist Republic, Dr Urvalek, for example, sound unconvincing, but what does this have to do with anti-socialists? He has said all that he wanted to say and all that he could say. But it is understandable why our leaders hasten to intercede for the likes of Urvalek and Novotny: the precedent of making party and government leaders personally responsible to the people is a dangerous and contagious one. What if our own leaders should suddenly be called to account for the deeds that have timidly been called 'errors' and 'excesses', or, even more mildly and obscurely, 'difficulties experienced in the heroic past' (this when it was a matter of millions of people unjustly condemned and murdered, of torture in KGB dungeons, of entire peoples being declared enemies, of the collapse of the nation's agriculture and similar trivia)? Today the Czechs and Slovaks are asking questions of Urvalek and Novotny, but tomorrow – who knows? – our own multi-national people might put similar questions to Brezhnev: 'And what were *you* doing up until . . . 1953?' And until the matter has been cleared up they might well remove him temporarily from office . . .

In their Warsaw Letter to the Communist Party of Czechoslovakia, the five parties propose the use of all available means in the arsenal of the socialist nations to combat 'anti-socialist' forces. It is too bad that the fraternal parties do not specify what exactly these means would be. Kolyma? Norilsk? Khunviiny? 'Open' trials? Political concentration camps and prisons? Or merely conventional censorship and extrajudicial reprisals, such as dismissing people from their jobs?

And in the light of the situation that has developed, we are still offended that Czechoslovakia should demand the withdrawal of Soviet troops from its territory! In fact, after our pronouncements and resolutions and with our military units present on Czechoslovak soil, these are no longer the troops of an ally, they are a threat to a nation's sovereignty.

In this letter I should also like to express my own position on these events, a position that differs from the 'unanimous' support of the decisions of our Central Committee plenum. The newspaper campaign of recent weeks has aroused in me the apprehension that it may be paving the way for intervention under any pretext that might arise or be artificially created.

I should like to remind the authors of these letters and the participants in the meetings and gatherings being held in support of the policy of the Central Committee that all the so-called 'errors' and 'excesses' in our nation's history took place to the accompaniment of stormy, sustained applause swelling into a crescendo of ovations, and amid shouts of approval from our highly conscious citizenry. But it turned out that obedience is not the highest of civic virtues.

I should also like to recall more remote historical events – how the valorous Russian army, having liberated the peoples of Europe from Napoleon, just as valorously drowned the Polish uprising in blood. Davydov, the Russian hero of the War of 1812, was prouder of his feats during the reprisals against the Polish patriots than of his feats during the Great Fatherland War.

I am ashamed for my country, which is once more assuming the disgraceful role of gendarme of Europe.

I would also be ashamed of my countrymen if I thought that they were truly unanimous in supporting the policy of the Central Committee and the government in respect of Czechoslovakia. I am confident, however, that this is not the case and that my letter is not the only one – but such letters are not published in our country. Here too, the unanimity of our citizens is a fiction, created artificially by violating that same freedom of speech that is being upheld in Czechoslovakia. But even if I were the only one of this opinion, I still would not renounce it, for it is the voice of my conscience. In my estimation, conscience is a more reliable guide than the constantly changing line of the Central Committee and the resolutions passed by various assemblies in step with the fluctuations of that line.

Permit me to tender my admiration and sympathy for the process of democratisation in your country.

22 July 1968

A. T. Marchenko,
Novinskaya ulitsa 27,
Alexandrov (Vladimir Oblast),
USSR

[On 29 July 1968, Marchenko was arrested for 'violating the passport regulations'.]

7. Open letter by Larisa Bogoraz [Daniel] on the arrest of Marchenko

Anatoly Marchenko has been arrested and is in Butyrka Prison. A case of infringement of the passport regulations is being fabricated against him, which claims that he was living in Moscow without being registered.

This is not the time to talk about article 198 of the RSFSR Criminal Code (deprivation of liberty for an infringement of the passport regulations) as a hangover from eighteenth century serfdom or Stalin's enslavement of the Population. This is not the time to demonstrate that it is in complete contradiction to the Declaration of Human Rights, or to discuss the hypocrisy of a government that, for propaganda reasons, demands of the whole world such a minimum freedom for man as the freedom to choose his place of residence, while at home arranging criminal proceedings for those who claim the same. It is too late now to analyse the legal ambiguity of the wording of this article,* which is such that, in practice, every single citizen might find himself guilty of infringing it – and without ever being aware of it, for the article refers to 'special rules' which are not only unknown to the general public, but are actually secret. All one need note is that article 198, by virtue of its utter ambivalence and ambiguity, allows the authorities the utmost freedom of arbitrary repression, and this can now be brought to bear against Anatoly Marchenko.

Now it is his fate that is at stake and it is essential, leaving aside general legal, social and even moral questions, to protect this man from arbitrary repression.

With regard to the law on registration (article 198 of the Criminal Code), Marchenko acted exactly like other citizens and they are not at this moment under arrest and investigation. Like all of us,

---

* RSFSR Criminal Code, Article 198: Infringement of Passport Regulations. 'Malicious infringement of the passport regulations in localities where special rules for residence and registration have been introduced, if such infringement takes the form of residence without a passport or without registration and if the person concerned has already been subject to administrative penalties for this, shall be punished by deprivation of liberty for a term not exceeding one year, or by corrective labour for the same term, or by a fine not exceeding 50 roubles.'

Marchenko had a passport that was duly registered at his place of residence. He worked as a loader at a factory and lived off his earnings. He had friends in Moscow, visited them and sometimes stayed the night. Not once did he disturb public order or cause anyone the slightest material damage. So why should the authorities set the machinery of repression in motion precisely against him? It is easy to guess the answer when you have read the appeal by Marchenko's friends.

His book, in which he tells the truth about the camps for political prisoners, aroused such hatred for him in the KGB that they began to bait him like a hare. KGB agents followed on his heels for months on end – I have spotted them so often that I know many of them by sight. And not only in Moscow, where he works, or Alexandrov, where he lives. He went to visit relatives in Ryazan one day, but wasn't allowed to leave the train and had to return to Moscow. He was also seized on the street almost the moment he had been discharged from hospital; and his face was smashed in as he was being pushed into a car when he came to Moscow for a literary evening.

Marchenko's open letter to *Rude Pravo* and other newspapers evidently infuriated the KGB so much that they couldn't wait any longer to put Marchenko behind bars at all costs and under any pretext. On the morning of 29 July he was picked up in the street on his way to work and now he's in prison again. And his second book remains unfinished.

The last time he was arrested, they wanted to make Marchenko into a political criminal – and they succeeded, although he hadn't been one. This time political revenge comes in the guise of a criminal case. The fact that there are political motives behind it and that the KGB is involved is borne out by the following circumstances. In connection with a mere infringement of the passport regulations, a search was made and Marchenko's papers, manuscripts and notes were confiscated. And on suspicion of this trivial offence they applied the severest possible means of restraint, namely arrest. Yet there are plenty of available measures of interim restraint, such as a signed undertaking not to leave one's domicile, personal surety, bail and the surety of social organisations. Arrests are made only in exceptional cases.

Marchenko's whole personal history, right up to the day of his arrest, convinces me that he is in serious danger. If he is condemned to a year in the camps, he may never emerge alive. How much can be done to a man in camp conditions in the space of a year, especially if there is a special reason for wanting to settle accounts with him!

I am sure that no decent person will remain indifferent to Marchenko's fate. If you haven't read it yet, read his book, *My Testimony*, and read his open letters – you can get them all in manuscript versions. Read them and you will see for yourself that Marchenko is not some plausible rogue or adventurer, but a talented, original writer and publicist and an uncompromising and courageous man. And his courage is on behalf of the rest of us, each one of us.

Marchenko did not count on anyone to intercede for him. He realised that they might decide to settle scores with him at any moment. But do we have the right to permit this? I have had occasion to hear many arguments, even from decent people, to the effect that, in view of the overall situation – the threat to Czechoslovakia and so on – it is too much to trouble society with the fate of one individual. And in any case, we are used to far greater tragedies than this. But in my opinion it is impossible to get accustomed to such things. And as for the fate of one individual, remember how all the foremost men of France came forward to defend Dreyfus and how all the best people of Russia found a way to defend Beylis,* and that was also in a pretty serious overall situation, namely on the eve of a world war. Furthermore, there is a direct connection between the course of historical events and such an incidental detail as the price of an individual human life.

1 August 1968

Larisa Bogoraz [Daniel]
Moscow.
Tel. 134–68–98

8. *Open letter of the Eight in defence of Marchenko*

On 29 July 1968, Anatoly Marchenko was arrested in Moscow. We, the prisoner's friends, feel it our duty to relate what led up to this arrest. Everyone must know what has happened to Marchenko.

Anatoly Marchenko was born in 1938 in a working-class family in Barabinsk. After leaving school he worked as a foreman driller on Komsomol construction sites in Siberia and Kazakhstan. On one of these sites a fight broke out between non-local workers and the local ones, or rather deportees, who had broken into their hostel. Anatoly, who all his life had felt it was monstrous to strike a man, could not stand idly by. He had not instigated the fight, he hadn't injured

* A Jew who was tried in Kiev in 1911–13 on charges of ritual murder.

anyone, but he was one of the people detained in custody and he was subsequently convicted and sent to a camp. At the time he was still under twenty years old. The sequel was escape from the camp, re-arrest and a further term of imprisonment on an unsubstantiated political charge.

From 1960 to 1966 Marchenko was a political prisoner in the camps of Mordovia, in Vladimir Prison and again in Mordovia. After surviving miraculously, without treatment, an attack of meningitis, he emerged disabled at the age of twenty-eight suffering from deafness, migraine and intestinal haemorrhages. After his imprisonment he was twice on the verge of death. He had two serious operations and six blood transfusions. Then came five months in hospital and five gruelling months of wandering in search of work – Kursk, Kaluga, Maloyaroslavets, Vladimir, Kalinin – but nowhere would they register him for residence. Finally he was given permission to live in Barabinsk and then in Alexandrov in Vladimir *Oblast*. From May 1968, while continuing to reside in Alexandrov, he worked as a loader in Moscow. Though forbidden by the doctor to do heavy physical work, there was no other alternative.

Even so, this was not Marchenko's principal work. In 1967 he wrote *My Testimony*, a book that is at the same time an epoch-making document. People know of Stalin's torture chambers and concentration camps and the endless bloodletting of those years. And most of them regard these things as a nightmare of the past. But it is our duty to know that today, at this very moment, thousands of political prisoners are languishing in our prisons and camps; and it is also our duty to know the situation of these prisoners. We refer here not to war criminals, but to people sentenced for their beliefs, for having dared in some way or other to express their disagreement with the existing order of things in our country. It is true there are not millions of them, as in Stalin's day, but thousands, and that is the difference. But we are acquainted with history: today thousands, tomorrow millions if this inhuman machine isn't stopped.

Yet the machine has not stopped: trials that are to all intents and purposes closed, political prisoners deprived of all rights, human dignity trampled underfoot, 're-education' by starvation, and for those who refuse to submit to arbitrary repression there are special forms of coercion – deprivation of shop privileges, a ban on visits and parcels from relatives, punishment rations, the cooler, handcuffs. Then comes despair and disastrous forms of protest: hunger strikes, self-mutilation, suicide, open attempts to climb the perimeter fence and the barbed wire, so that the sentry can shoot them down 'while attempting to escape'. Such is the lot of political prisoners in the post-Stalin era, for whom 'strict regime' camps constitute the minimum degree of severity. But there are also 'special regime' camps, where the convicts wear striped uniforms and where the cells are locked. And then there is also the deadly Vladimir Prison.

Marchenko's is the first book ever to write about all this. Everything described in it was seen and experienced by the author himself, which explains why the book is so strikingly authentic and its exposures so compelling. The bosses of these strict and special regime camps, those masters of the prisoners' fates, are unmasked and given a name. They include quite a number of professional torturers trained in the Stalin school. But the camp experience of these veterans is fully equalled by that of some of the prisoners too, victims of Stalin's terror who have been passed over by all the amnesties and rehabilitations. Their sufferings have lasted over decades, they have been buried alive. Marchenko's voice is the voice of all these silent sufferers behind barbed wire and in our country at large, so the scale of his testimony is nationwide and historic, the scale of all mankind.

Marchenko did not succeed in publishing his book for fully comprehensible reasons. But he could not abandon his comrades, just as his grandfather, a peasant shot by Kolchak, could not give up his land. His book was followed by open letters and a letter on the situation of political prisoners addressed to a number of responsible people, including the Chairman of the Soviet Red Cross and several writers. Here is an extract from that letter.

'Today's Soviet camps for political prisoners are just as horrific as in Stalin's time. A few things are better, a few things worse. But everybody must know about it.

'Everybody must know, including those who would like to know the truth and are given lying, optimistic newspaper articles instead, designed to lull the public conscience; and also including those who don't wish to know, who close their eyes and stop up their ears in order to be able at some future date to justify themselves and to emerge from the dirt with their noses clean: "Good heavens, and we never knew . . ." If they possess a single particle of civic conscience or genuine love for their country, they will stand up in its defence, just as the true sons of Russia have always done.

'I would like my testimony on Soviet camps and prisons for political prisoners to come to the attention of humanists and progressive people in other countries – those who stick up for political prisoners in Greece and Portugal and in Spain and South Africa. Let them ask their Soviet colleagues in the struggle against inhumanity: "And what have you done in your country to prevent political prisoners from being 're-educated' by starvation?"'

The Executive Committee of the Red Cross and Red Crescent Societies replied in a manner that could hardly have been outdone by the KGB: political prisoners are 'deserving of severe punishment, rather than any kind of indulgence or leniency'.

Another open letter was sent to the editor of the *Literary Gazette*, Chakovsky, who in an article had complained bitterly that political prisoners 'are fed at the nation's expense in prisons and corrective labour colonies', and this when a political prisoner on 'hard labour' gets a daily ration of 2,400 calories (the norm for a child of seven to eleven years old), while punishment rations amount to 1,300 calories – sufficient for a one-year-old infant. Incidentally, Marchenko also wrote the following to Chakovsky: 'Is this how the nation – including the prisoners of Dubrovlag, Vorkuta, Siberia and Kazakhstan – feeds *you* and the other writers, the "nation's conscience"? Perhaps the lofty civic passion of your article is explained precisely by the fact that you receive somewhat more for it than a bowl of skilly and a hunk of black bread?'

Marchenko's actions are totally devoid of pretentiousness, affectation or a desire to show off. He cannot behave differently. Gorky once compared Yesenin to an organ emitting poetry. Similarly, Marchenko can be compared to an organ emitting the truth, an organ of the naked conscience. In order to fight for truth, however, one needs scientific knowledge, as well as an instinct for justice and knowledge of life. And in their time the camp authorities were dismayed to find this lad, with only eight years of regular schooling, studying socio-political works and poring, volume by volume, over the complete works of Lenin.

Marchenko's last open letter was addressed to the people of Czechoslovakia. He welcomed that country's civic renaissance, its re-establishment of freedom and democracy. He protested against the systematic misinformation of the Soviet public regarding events in Czechoslovakia and asserted that armed intervention, should it ever take place, would be totally unacceptable. The letter was sent on 26 July, and on 30 July* Marchenko was arrested.

* This appears to be an oversight. The date is named as 29 July in all other sources.

It must now be clear to any honest thinking man that the time has come when everyone must be responsible for everything, and not just Marchenko and people like him for everybody else. The compact of fear and servility must be replaced by a compact of humanity and civic courage. Raise your voices in defence of Anatoly Marchenko.

2–6 August 1968

Ludmila Alexeyeva, tel. 258–70–34
Larisa Bogoraz, tel. 134–68–98
Yuri Gerchuk, tel. 141–57–45
Natalya Gorbanevskaya, tel. 257–77–08
Pyotr Grigorenko, tel. 246–27–37
Victor Krasin, 2nd Novogireyevsky prospekt.
Pavel Litvinov, tel. 299–38–05
Anatoly Yakobson, 17 Perekopskaya ulitsa, Block 5, flat 66.

9. Petition of the Five to the Procurator of the Timiriazevsky District, Moscow

We have learned that on the morning of 29 July our friend, Anatoly Tikhonovich Marchenko, was detained by the police on a suspected passport violation (Article 192/1 of the RSFSR Criminal Code) and is being held in a pre-trial detention cell at station no. 64. We consider this detention illegal for the following reasons:

1. There was no passport violation in this case because Anatoly Marchenko departed from Alexandrov, where he lives, on the evening of 27 July (this can be confirmed by his landlady in Alexandrov) and did not spend even the three days in Moscow that are allowed under the law.

2. Although, formally, this is Marchenko's third detention, the first two warnings were, in fact, also illegal. In the first instance, Marchenko had undergone one and a half months of hospital treatment and was suffering from the after-effects of an operation. In the second, he was detained the very day he came to Moscow after having been invited to attend a literary evening at the Central House of Writers.

3. Even if he really had violated the passport regulations, this would be no reason to hold him in a pre-trial detention cell, since such a violation is not in itself a dangerous crime. It endangers no one, and there is no reason to believe that Marchenko would have sought to evade investigation. He is in regular employment and has a fixed place of residence.

In addition to the foregoing, we would also like to point out that a search was made of L. Bogoraz's flat, where Marchenko was staying in Moscow and where he also kept his personal papers. In the course of the search, not only Marchenko's legal papers and medical documents were confiscated, but also his private files: personal letters, letters concerning the situation in the camps for political prisoners, replies to these letters from official sources, rough drafts, synopses of the works of Marx, Engels, Plekhanov and Lenin, articles from political and economic journals and articles on literary criticism. Such confiscation of documents can have no connection whatsoever with a violation of the passport regulations.

In addition to this, some papers and a book belonging to L. Bogoraz personally were also confiscated. These were in her briefcase.

All these things go to show that the charge of a passport violation lodged against Anatoly Marchenko is nothing but a pretext for political reprisals against a man who is known to society as the author of a documentary book about political camps and the author of a number of protests against the treatment of political prisoners in our country.

We demand the immediate release of Anatoly Marchenko and an investigation into the circumstances of his detention.

Leninsky Prospekt 85, Flat 3,
Moscow V–261.

P. Litvinov,
P. Grigorenko,
I. Rudakov,
I. Belogorodskaya,
L. Bogoraz.

[On 7 August 1968, one of the signatories of the above letter, Irina Belogorodskaya, was arrested for being in possession of copies of the Open Letter by Larisa Bogoraz (document no. 7) and the Open Letter of the Eight (document no. 8). On 21 August 1968, Marchenko was sentenced to one year in a corrective labour camp for violating the passport regulations.]

10. *Extracts from an open letter to the Procurator of the RSFSR*

It has come to our attention that during the latter part of December, 1968, the Leningrad City Court examined in open session the case of

Yu. L. Gendler, L. V. Kvachevsky and A. M. Studenkov, when they were charged under article 70 of the Criminal Code of the RSFSR. All three were found guilty of the charge and sentenced to various terms of imprisonment. According to the verdict, the accused were found guilty of keeping at home and reading various materials that can be divided provisionally into two groups. The first group comprises the works of foreign authors published abroad and found in the possession of the accused. The second includes typewritten copies of several letters of appeal by Soviet citizens to public opinion, to state and party organisations and to private individuals, . . . and a typewritten copy of A. Marchenko's book, *My Testimony*.

All these documents carry their proper signatures. The authors have signed not only their first and second names, but also their addresses. The documents themselves quote not only facts, but also the places where things are said to have occurred and the names of offenders. Neither the court nor the investigator were in possession of evidence to throw even the slightest suspicion on the genuineness of the facts or the authenticity of any of the signatures. But in order to throw the fantasies of the investigatory and judicial organs into the sharpest possible relief, let us just examine in greater detail but one of the documents adjudged by the court to be anti-Soviet. Let us, for this purpose, take Anatoly Marchenko's book, *My Testimony*.

In it the author takes upon himself full responsibility for relating the facts about the astonishing tyranny that reigns in places of detention for people convicted of state crimes. This document was sent to the Praesidium of the Supreme Soviet of the USSR, to the Council of Ministers of the USSR, to the General Procuracy of the USSR and of the KGB, attached to the Council of Ministers, to several organs of the Soviet press, to leaders of the Soviet Red Cross and to a number of representatives of Soviet public opinion. The author regarded the facts of this tyranny as being so scandalous that he lost no time in giving them wide publicity and employed all the means at his disposal to obtain an inquiry into the situation of political prisoners in our camps and prisons. In letters he asserted that although, in his book, he had quoted only facts that were known to him personally or in whose authenticity he had not the slightest doubt, in reality the situation might well be even worse. In spite of this, no one bothered to inquire into the facts cited by Marchenko. At least, nothing on this subject was communicated to the author of *My Testimony*. We have it on reliable grounds that neither the investigators nor the court were in possession of documents refuting the facts set out in the book under scrutiny. Consequently, the court had every reason to regard everything in it, from beginning to end, as the plain truth.

We think there is no need to demonstrate that these prosecutions also amount to a blatant violation of Soviet law. And the author of *My Testimony* has also been prosecuted. But they did not take the risk of telling him that it was unethical to write the truth about the camps. Instead they trumped up a 'crime' that had nothing to do with his book, so that they have now succeeded in trying the book without its author and the author without his book. While three people were languishing in prison in Leningrad for disseminating this 'anti-Soviet work' by Marchenko, the latter was standing trial in Moscow for 'violating the passport regulations'.

Leaving aside for the time being the fact that to be prosecuted for going to work where work is available and where it is convenient to do so contradicts both international declarations on human rights and all the dictates of human reason and conscience, may we point out that Marchenko violated neither the letter nor the spirit of even these rules. In spite of this, the court inflicted on him the severest possible punishment laid down for such 'crimes'. His judges took not the slightest account of the fact that he is a gravely sick man and that imprisonment under such cruel conditions might well cost him his life.

A comparison of the trial of Marchenko with the investigation into the case of the Leningrad 'anti-Soviet agitators' convincingly demonstrates that this was a well organised and centrally directed *provocation*. Its aim was to conceal the truth about today's camps for political prisoners, to place a ban on the book and settle accounts with the book's author without an inquiry into it or any public discussion of its contents. This is the true explanation of the fact that the investigatory organs in Leningrad were 'proving' the book's 'anti-Soviet character', while its author, who was uniquely qualified to throw the most light on it and best equipped and qualified to defend its contents, was being quietly shipped as far as possible from Leningrad – to a strict regime camp in the northern Urals in conditions of the greatest danger to the life of this courageous but gravely sick man.

P. Grigorenko, Komsomolsky prospekt 14/1, Flat 96, Moscow G–21.
I. Gabai, Novolesnaya ulitsa, Block 2, Flat 83, Moscow A–55.
Yu. Kim, Ryazansky prospekt 73, Flat 90, Moscow Zh–456.
P. Yakir, Avtozavodskaya ulitsa, Flat 75, Moscow Zh–280.

V. Krasin, Shkolnaya ulitsa 44, Petrovo polye, Moscow.

Z. Asanova, Bekobad, Uzbek SSR

A. Kaplan, Leninsky prospekt 976, Block 101, Flat 66, Moscow.

V. Kozharinov, V. Pervomaiskaya ulitsa, 45, Block 3, Flat 28, Moscow.

A. Krasnov-Levitin, Tretya Novokuznetskaya ulitsa, Moscow IS–377.

Yu. Telesin, Malaya Bronnaya ulitsa 20, Flat 6, Moscow K–104.

11. Extracts from 'Brief transcript of the trial of Engineer Irina Belogorodskaya, with a commentary by Pyotr Grigorenko '

The trial took place in the Baumansky District Court in Moscow, 19 February 1969.

Judge: Monakhov
Procurator: Mme Biryukova
Defence advocate: Romm

1. CHARGE

'A lady's handbag was handed to the KGB by taxi garage no. 7. It was found to contain a passport, a pass and reader's ticket for the Lenin Library in the name of Irina Mikhailovna Belogorodskaya, eight blank envelopes and six with addresses on them (to the writers Volodin, Granin, Gorbovsky, Aitmatov, Suleiman, etc.) and eighty-eight type-written copies (on 211 sheets of paper) of two documents. One of these documents was signed Bogoraz-Bruchman* and the other bore eight signatures at the bottom.† Both documents contained slanderous allegations about Soviet reality.

'Belogorodskaya is acquainted with all the authors of this second document and is a cousin of Bogoraz-Bruchman, whom she frequently visits. On 6 August she was there until late in the evening. She left in the company of three men. All four of them took a taxi on Leninsky prospekt and drove to Kazan Station. *En route*, Belogorodskaya and one of the men left the taxi at the main post office. The others continued to Kazan Station. After they too had alighted from the taxi, the driver, Kudryavtsev, found a lady's handbag between the front two seats. Unable to find the departed passengers, he handed the bag

---

* See document no. 7, p. 426. Larisa Bogoraz has never used the double surname quoted in court.

† See document no. 8, p. 428.

in to the duty clerk, Anna Surina, when he returned to the garage at the end of his shift.

'The letters found in the taxi distort the facts of Marchenko's life, representing him as an innocent victim when in fact he has two convictions to his name, the first for hooliganism and the second for attempted treason. At the moment he is serving a term in a strict regime camp for "violating the passport regulations". The letters also contain slanders against existing criminal legislation and Soviet judicial procedure, as well as giving slanderous statements about illegal repressions of political prisoners and their situation, alleging that they are detained under inhuman conditions and that criminal charges are fabricated against them. They also heap baseless praise on Marchenko, who emerges from their description as almost an ideal personality.'

Two quotations from Larisa Bogoraz's letter were submitted in support of these wholly unfounded accusations: 1. 'This is not the time to talk of article 198 of the RSFSR Criminal Code (deprivation of liberty for an infringement of the passport regulations) as a hangover from eighteenth century serfdom or Stalin's enslavement of the populations'; and 2. 'It is too late now to analyse the legal ambiguity of the wording of this article, which is such that, in practice, every single citizen might find himself guilty of infringing it – and without ever being aware of it, for the article refers to "special rules" which are not only unknown to the general public, but are actually secret.'*

Belogorodskaya had good references from her place of work. She pleaded not guilty, although she admitted that she was preparing to distribute the letters in question.

2. QUESTIONING OF THE ACCUSED

In describing the circumstances of the case and replying to questions from the procurator and the judge, Belogorodskaya spoke as follows:

---

* These two quotations are separated in the original by the following sentence: 'This is not the time to demonstrate that it is in complete contradiction to the Declaration of Human Rights, nor to discuss the hypocrisy of a government that, for propaganda reasons, demands of the whole world such a minimum freedom for man as the freedom to choose his place of residence, while at home arranging criminal proceedings for those who claim the same.' It is clear why this sentence was omitted from the charge, since its authors were aware that not only was it not slanderous, but rather exposed the slander embodied in the charges against the authors of the letter and against Marchenko. – Note by Grigorenko.

'After learning of the contents of Larisa Bogoraz's letter and the appeal of the Eight, I wished to help this man who was in trouble. I addressed the letters to people whose sense of justice, sympathy and humanity I could rely on and whose position in society was such that the authorities would have to reckon with their views. I collected the letters from Larisa myself. I put them in my handbag and left Larisa's flat together with three other persons. With one of them, Ivan Rudakov,* I alighted at the main post office. I missed the handbag as soon as I had left the taxi. We immediately went in search of another taxi and rushed to the station. Unable to find the first car, we returned home, rang the taxi garage and the lost-property bureau, but failed to locate the bag. The following day I reported the loss of my bag and my documents.

'No one gave me the letters in defence of Marchenko. I read them myself at Larisa's flat and the contents so moved me that I decided to take them and distribute them, in order to help a good man in trouble. I have been acquainted with Marchenko since 1967 and know him very well. I know the kind of crimes he has been accused of in the past from his own account of them and I am sure that he spoke truthfully. The article under which he was convicted the first time was concerned with hooliganism, but, knowing Marchenko as I do, I am convinced that he is incapable either of insulting anyone or of doing them a wanton injury. In the case for the prosecution at his trial, a copy of which I was shown during the investigation of my own case, it is written that he was not the instigator of the brawl, nor did he injure anyone. This is sufficient reason for maintaining that at his first trial he was unjustly convicted.

'He was tried a second time for attempted treason. The entire case for the prosecution rested on the evidence of Burovsky,† who was being tried on the same charge as Marchenko. Therefore his testimony does not inspire confidence. Marchenko hardly knew this singular witness. He had met him shortly before attempting to cross the border. Burovsky testified that Marchenko had said he wanted to cross the border in order to work against the Soviet Union for money. Marchenko denied this both during his interrogation and at the trial. I am inclined to believe Marchenko in preference to this witness, since Marchenko is known to me as a man incapable of lies, whereas Burovsky might have been giving false evidence in order to lighten his own sentence.'

Mme. Biryukova, the procurator, attempted to shake the confidence of the accused in Marchenko's innocence by reading an extract from

* Belogorodskaya's husband.
† Portrayed under the name of Budrovsky in Marchenko's book.

his case to the effect that he had been arrested, simultaneously with Burovsky, 400 yards from the Iranian border. The accused replied that she had never denied that Marchenko attempted to cross the border. She was merely disagreeing with the statement that he had wanted to betray his country, i.e. she was convinced he had never done what he was convicted of.

Later the procurator moved on to the question of Marchenko's third arrest. She asked:

'Do you know what he was arrested for, or do you consider that the case was fabricated against him and that the court sentenced him unjustly?'

The accused replied that when she began her preparations for distributing the letters, Marchenko had not yet been sentenced, but she was well aware that he had not broken the passport regulations, since he had never spent more than one night at a time in Moscow.

Procurator: 'But he had had two warnings already!'

The accused repeated that he had never spent more than one night at a time in Moscow. Then the judge intervened and remarked:

'He was registered in Alexandrov and had no right to be in Moscow at all.'*

This disconcerted the accused and she said distractedly:

'Well, I don't know.'

Procurator, swiftly: 'So he really did infringe the passport regulations?'

The accused, still disconcerted, shrugged her shoulders and said uncertainly:

'Well, . . . maybe.'

The procurator, obviously well pleased with this answer, went on to ask further questions. The accused said in reply that she considered the letters in defence of Marchenko to be truthful, since, knowing the writers and knowing Marchenko, she could not conceive of them lying in any respect. She did not think of Marchenko as an ideal man, but she had a high opinion of him. The blank envelopes found in her possession had been intended for sending letters in defence of Marchenko. She had counted on sending them to about 40 people. She was not acquainted with the persons she intended sending them to, but had judged them on the basis of their writings and concluded that they could not be worse than their works. Therefore she had counted on their sympathy and humanity.

---

* Not even these inhuman regulations are as savage as that. The judge, to put it mildly, was uttering a deliberate untruth. – Note by Grigorenko.

In an effort to discredit the accused's evidence and disturb the tone she had adopted, the procurator then produced an obviously irrelevant question:

'What have you read by Suleiman?'

Evidently the procurator was unacquainted with this author and counted on the accused not knowing him either, but the latter replied calmly:

'I have read a collection of his verse and I liked it very much. I did not think that these people would bring pressure to bear on the judiciary, but I hoped that their intervention would help to ensure that justice was observed. I hoped that they would appeal to the institutions responsible for Marchenko's fate, to the procuracy, and thus help to rescue this man – who has endured so many hardships already – from harsh new ordeals.'

At this point the procurator again asked a question with a hidden trap:

'But why did *you* have to take up his defence? Isn't he capable of appealing to the procuracy himself?'

'Yes, of course he is,' she replied, 'but that doesn't prevent others from interceding on his behalf. I wanted to bring the question of Marchenko's defence to the attention of a wider public. I counted on the people I sent letters to taking an interest in this matter, reading his book and open letters and experiencing sympathy and fellow-feeling for him. It doesn't have to be only the relatives of a man under arrest who take up his case. Neither I nor the authors of the letters wanted to thrust our opinions down other people's throats. We thought that those who read the letters would draw their own conclusions.'

After this the procurator returned to the contents of the letters, seeking to put her questions in such a way that the accused, if only by implication, would discredit the arguments in the letters.

Procurator: 'Bogoraz writes in her letter that the case against Marchenko was fabricated. What do you think?'

The accused replied that she had complete faith in the authors.

In an attempt to get the accused to admit that the letters contained slanderous allegations about the situation of political prisoners in the camps, the procurator imperceptibly switched from the strict regime camps in which political prisoners are actually held to corrective labour colonies of a general nature. She said:

'The letters assert that prisoners are subjected to arbitrary tyranny. But are you aware that while undergoing his first punishment, Marchenko was given official encouragement?'

The accused replied: 'During the preliminary investigation of my own case, I was shown extracts from a case dating from ten years ago. They included evidence from a warder to the effect that, while undergoing his punishment, Marchenko received official encouragement and rewards. But I have no idea what this has to do with my case.'

Procurator: 'It is to show that the statements made in your letters are untrue. At the beginning, when Marchenko behaved badly, he was put in the punishment cell. But when he began to behave properly, he was rewarded and given encouragement. This, as you see, was justice, and not arbitrary tyranny. He was even pardoned and released before the end of his sentence. Your letters make out that Marchenko attempted to flee abroad because of the hopelessness of his position, whereas he did it after the order had been signed for his pardon and release.'

The procurator supported her statement by showing the accused a certificate, from which it was clear that the date of the signature on the release order preceded the date of Marchenko's arrest while attempting to cross the border.

'Therefore,' went on the procurator, 'it was not because of the hopelessness of his position that he attempted to cross the border, but because he intended to betray his country.'*

---

* This part of the procurator's speech was so formulated that a person in the body of the court, if he did not know the truth, would get the impression that Marchenko had been shown clemency, having been released and pardoned, and that, after his release, he attempted to go beyond the bounds of the Soviet Union. In actual fact the matter stands as follows. No clemency was shown to Marchenko. He was supposed to be released almost at the very end of his term of imprisonment because the article under which he was convicted had just been rescinded. He was to be released simultaneously with all the other prisoners convicted under that article. He was supposed to be, but he wasn't, and the procurator did her level best to hush this fact up. Marchenko was not released because he had escaped from the camp before the order for his release had come through. And he tried crossing the border because he feared the consequences of his escape, not knowing that, back in the camp, they had 'released him from serving the remainder of his sentence'. Furthermore, the procurator distorted the substance of the question by playing on the subtleties of the Russian language. She alleged that the accused and the authors of the letters she wanted to distribute had stated that Marchenko's position was 'hopeless' (Russian – *bezvykhodnoye*, literally 'exitless' – Translator's note), whereas the authors, and Marchenko himself in his book, *My Testimony*, had referred to him attempting to escape 'because he could see no way out of his position' (*ne naidya* vykhoda *iz polozheniye*). Note by Grigorenko.

3. QUESTIONING OF WITNESSES

The driver of the taxi was Kudryavtsev, thirty-five years old. In his evidence he confirmed the information given in the charge concerning the journey made by Belogorodskaya and her companions from the Leninsky prospekt to Kazan Station and the fact that he had found the forgotten handbag only after his passengers had gone. He had tried to find them again, but without success. Therefore he had kept the handbag in his vehicle and taken it to the garage at the end of his shift (about 1 a.m.). There he found some comrades waiting for him 'who were interested in the handbag' (i.e. agents of the KGB). 'They asked the number of my taxi and inquired after the whereabouts of the handbag. Learning that I had it, they told me to hand it in in the regulation manner. I handed the bag to the duty clerk, Surina, and together we compiled a list of the contents.'

He then named the same number of things as mentioned in the charge and confirmed the accuracy of a list that was handed to him. In answer to a question from the judge, he said that the usual procedure in such cases, when something was left behind in a taxi, was for the lost article to remain with the duty clerk for a few days and then, if not claimed by the owner, to be handed to the lost-property bureau.

Surina, the duty clerk, confirmed Kudryavtsev's account in her evidence.

Ivan Rudakov (the defendant's husband) related how, during their ride in the taxi, he had placed the bag between the two front seats. On getting out at the post office he completely forgot about it and by the time he missed it the taxi had already disappeared. He went on to relate how they had endeavoured to recover the bag, first by going to the Kazan Station and then in a series of telephone calls. He was unaware, right up till the time of his wife's arrest, that there were any criminal documents in the bag. Nor did he know the contents of these documents. He found out only after he himself had begun to distribute them. This statement clearly astounded both the judge and the procurator. There followed an awkward pause, which the judge interrupted with a question:

'Where do you work?'

'I haven't worked since the 25 September 1968, because I can't find a job.'

'Why were you dismissed?'

'They called it "at my own request".'

The judge decided not to risk going into this question in further detail.

4. PROCURATOR'S SPEECH

'In the period when Communism is being constructed on a large scale it is of prime importance to develop the activity of individual citizens and social organisations and encourage their participation in social and state activities. But this should not be confused with attempts by individual citizens to exploit democracy for the purpose of making slanderous allegations defamatory of the Soviet social and state system. Slander, at the present time, is the favourite device of bourgeois propaganda. Article 125 of the Constitution of the USSR* grants broad democratic rights to Soviet citizens, but we cannot countenance the employment of these rights to the detriment of Communist construction. The present case is a typical instance of an attempt to use the rights granted by the constitution in that way.'

The procurator went on at interminable length to enumerate all the details of the evidence already given in the course of the trial – how they had taken a taxi, how they had forgotten the handbag, how they had looked for it and what was found in the bag when it was opened by the duty clerk, Surina. Only one highly curious detail was 'forgotten' by the procurator – how the taxi driver was already awaited at the garage by those 'who were interested in Belogorodskaya's handbag'.

Then the procurator proceeded to an analysis of the documents. They were said to contain, on the basis of nothing but her own unsupported assertions, slanders against the existing legal and judicial system of the state, against existing criminal legislation and against the situation of political prisoners.

'They contain,' said the procurator, 'slanderous allegations about the fabrication of criminal charges against dissenters, about them being sentenced on trumped-up charges for their beliefs, and also baseless eulogies of Marchenko, who is pictured in them as being an almost ideal man. One of the letters says, for instance, that after school,

* 'In conformity with the interests of the working people and in order to strengthen the socialist system, the citizens of the USSR are guaranteed by law:
  (a) freedom of speech;
  (b) freedom of the press;
  (c) freedom of assembly, including the holding of mass meetings;
  (d) freedom of street processions and demonstrations.
These civil rights are ensured by placing at the disposal of the working people and their organisations printing presses, stocks of paper, public buildings, the streets, communications facilities and other material requisites for the exercise of these rights.'

Marchenko worked as a foreman driller at Komsomol sites in Siberia and Kazakhstan. But what sort of a worker was he? His work record before the attempt to escape abroad covers no more than four years' work, of which one year and nine months were spent in a camp.* The letter also says that Marchenko escaped from the camp and because of this decided to flee abroad, yet in actual fact the order for his release pre-dates the attempted crossing of the border, therefore there can be no doubt that he made this attempt not in order to see what life was like abroad, as he himself maintains, but with the aim of working against the Soviet Union for financial gain, as Burovsky testified. Furthermore, Marchenko's guilt has been confirmed by no less authoritative an organ than the Supreme Court of the Turkmenian Soviet Socialist Republic. This court's sentence now has the force of law, which means that to oppose it is to slander Soviet judicial procedure. He was convicted for treason, which means that to allege that he was convicted on unsubstantiated political grounds is to slander our existing legal system.

'These people are endeavouring to parade Marchenko as the victim of judicial repression, whereas in fact he was treated with leniency, indulgence and magnanimity. In sentencing him the court drew attention to the fact that he was still young (just over 20 years old), had left his parents at an early age to live away from them and was deprived of parental care and support. Taking all this into consideration, the court prescribed a sentence that was less than the minimum for this gravest of all state crimes.'†

When she had finished this paean of praise to Soviet justice, the procurator returned once more to the theme of the camps: 'When

---

* This is an obvious fraud. The procurator was well aware that Marchenko's first sentence had been so unjust that not only was it rescinded, but his time in the camp was included in his work record. This is not normally done either with those who serve out their sentences, or with those who are pardoned and released. – Note by Grigorenko.

† It is true that Marchenko got less than the minimum – 6 years – whereas the normal minimum for treason is 10 years. But the procurator omitted to mention that the charge of treason was not proven, and it was precisely this circumstance that evoked the 'magnanimity' of the court. It saw that Marchenko could be convicted only for attempting an illegal crossing of the border, but, not wishing to spoil its relations with the KGB, showed 'magnanimity' by sentencing him to 6 years in strict regime camps, although the maximum sentence for crossing the border illegally is 3 years in a corrective labour colony of a general type. Such was the 'magnanimity' of the court that the procurator praises. – Note by Grigorenko.

Marchenko behaved himself,' she enthused, 'he was encouraged and even released ahead of time.'*

After this she turned to the question of his behaviour after his second release from camp. He had been registered in Alexandrov, but systematically travelled into Moscow.† He had been warned twice, but still came into Moscow again on 29 July.‡

'Belogorodskaya,' went on the procurator, 'has a good reference from her place of work. But she could not fail to be aware of the slanderous nature of these documents and yet she wished to distribute them. She failed to do so only as a result of circumstances that were beyond her control. During the preliminary investigation of her case she steadfastly maintained the truthfulness of the two slanderous documents found in her possession. And in court, although she admits that she cannot substantiate all the statements made in the letters,

* Another sleight of hand. The procurator returned yet again to Marchenko's first illegal detention and spoke as though the rescindment of the sentences of all who had been convicted under the now rescinded article was the equivalent of a premature release of Marchenko alone, although it was precisely Marchenko who was unable to take advantage of his release because he had 'prematurely', i.e. before the court order had been received at the camp, made good his escape. Such was the price of objectivity, magnanimity, etc., in the eyes of this procurator. – Note by Grigorenko.

† The procurator omitted to mention that Marchenko was unable to travel to Moscow other than systematically, since Moscow is where his work was. – Note by Grigorenko.

‡ The procurator again omitted to mention that the passport regulations do not make it a crime to travel to Moscow. It is a crime to spend more than three consecutive nights in Moscow. She did not say, could not say, had no wish to say – and moreover strove with all her might to conceal the fact – that his arrival in Moscow was preceded by an event that made his arrest absolutely certain. One week beforehand, Marchenko had written an open letter addressed to numerous newspapers, including several Czechoslovak newspapers, in which he warned that an invasion of Czechoslovakia was being prepared, and denounced the injustice of such an invasion. The 'vigilant' Soviet post office did not, of course, permit these letters to go abroad, but the men who already knew at that time that there was going to be an invasion understood that the man who wrote *My Testimony* was not the sort to remain silent. So he had to be got back into prison. And a pretext was found. Every day thousands and thousands of workers who live, like Marchenko, outside of Moscow, travel in and out to work. And not one of them is called to criminal account for this. And cannot be, even under our passport regulations that are so redolent of the age of serfdom. Only for Marchenko did it all end so tragically. Only for him were special laws required. – Note by Grigorenko.

she has affirmed her unlimited faith in the authors and therefore her belief in their writings. It follows from this that she has not admitted her guilt and does not repent of her crime. She will not even admit the injustice and slanderous nature of the charge made in L. Bogoraz's letter that, during his last trial, an attempt was made to turn Marchenko into a political criminal when he was no such thing, whereas now he is being tried on a criminal charge for what were essentially political activities. This is a lie, since he has been tried in fact for "violating the passport regulations". Since she will not admit any of this, Belogorodskaya is a socially dangerous element and her punishment must be such as to ensure that she is isolated from society. Her actions are fully covered by articles 190(9) and 15 of the Criminal Code of the RSFSR. I ask the court to sentence her to one year's detention in a corrective labour colony of a general type.'

COMMENTARY

The essence of what took place at this trial, even in my brief transcript of it, is so crystal clear that any commentary, as they say, would be superfluous. If, in spite of this, I nevertheless undertake to provide one, it is not in the least for the purpose of discussing the trial itself. No, what I would like to clarify are some important attendant circumstances.

1. It has long been known that political trials in our country are held not for the purpose of *trying* people, but for *condemning* them. Nevertheless, in former times some attempt was made to provide at least a semblance of evidence, material proof, testimony by witnesses and logical deductions about the guilt of the accused . . . In Belogorodskaya's trial, however, there was not the faintest whiff of any of this. It is impossible, for instance, to regard six addressed envelopes as material proof of preparations to commit a 'crime'. But the court solemnly examined not only the addressed envelopes, but also the blank ones (eight of them). And examined them in such a way as to create the impression that if these blank envelopes had not been inside the handbag, it would have been impossible to send the letters.

The witnesses' testimony was no better, for the taxi driver and duty clerk can hardly be regarded as valid witnesses in this affair. All they could confirm was the already obvious fact that the handbag contained eighty-eight letters and some blank and addressed envelopes. Nevertheless, the driver, Kudryavtsev, did offer one interesting little piece of evidence. Those who 'were interested in the handbag' evidently knew already the number of the vehicle in which the defendant and her companions had been travelling (she herself did not remember it), which shows that the taxi was under observation and was being followed by a KGB squad car. Secondly it shows that Belogorodskaya's phone was being tapped. Otherwise there was no possible way of knowing that the bag had been lost in the first place. On the basis of these two facts alone a thinking man might easily deduce what serious and useful work was occupying Moscow's organs of state security that evening . . .

The third witness, Ivan Rudakov, also let slip some interesting information, though there again not from a realm of particular interest to the court. He informed them first that for his marriage to the defendant he had paid with his job, and second that the letters were being distributed even without Belogorodskaya's help.

Oh, what a weird and wonderful trial! In the dock sits a young woman accused of *preparing to distribute* certain documents, while the man who *actually distributed* them stands in the witness box giving evidence. Furthermore, those who wrote the documents and are prepared to accept full responsibility not only for their contents, but also for their distribution, are left hanging around outside the door to the court, unable to gain admittance, even though they have spent six whole months stubbornly demonstrating to the procuracy Belogorodskaya's innocence and their right to defend their own writings.

Belogorodskaya's innocence is so obvious and irrefutable that the prosecution did not even attempt to prove otherwise. Guilt, in this case, was totally unprovable. There is no article in the Criminal Code with reference to which, even casuistically, it could be argued that a desire to help a man in trouble constitutes a crime. That is why the prosecution resorted to an absolutely incredible stunt. Throughout the trial it attempted to prove not Belogorodskaya's guilt, but the criminal nature of Marchenko's personality and the criminal character of documents that Belogorodskaya had never written. Marchenko, in view of his physical absence, was naturally unable to defend himself. The documents in themselves were also, as it were, defenceless, and their authors, as has already been pointed out, were prevented from defending their own productions. Not one of the participants in the trial stuck up for Marchenko or the documents. Belogorodskaya, evidently, was unable to withstand the casuistical devices of the procurator, while her defence advocate, taking his own view of his defendant's interests, presumably thought his own position strong enough anyway, without shouldering extra burdens, which would have meant dispersing his energy and taking risks.

Whether this is a correct reading of the case or not, the fact remains that no one pulled the procurator up short when she twisted the facts or substituted one question for another, so that an onlooker, sitting in court and uninitiated into the truth of the matter by objective evidence, would have formed the impression that Marchenko is a criminal type. And from this it is but a short distance to the conclusion that whoever defends a criminal is himself guilty of a crime. This was the aim of the tactics employed by the procurator. And she achieved it. Therefore, in order to expose the blatant unscrupulousness of the prosecution, it will be necessary to subject the whole 'Marchenko case' to a more detailed and objective investigation, taking into account all the attendant circumstances of his life from the moment when he started out as an independent worker.

2. After finishing eight classes of middle school, this patriotically inspired youth received a Komsomol warrant and set off full of enthusiasm to work on 'the great construction projects of Communism'. The procurator maintained that he was a bad worker. She based her argument on the fact that in the course of his short working life, which included one year and nine months in the camp, he left his job four times voluntarily and twice for 'violations of labour discipline'. I have no way of checking whether there is any trickery here or not. But I cannot help asking myself: how did the procurator define Marchenko's departure from work at the time of his first sentence to a camp, and also his subsequent departure when he attempted to cross the border? As 'voluntary' departures, or as dismissals for 'violations of labour discipline'? But even if everything really had been the way the procurator said it was, would this really characterise Marchenko's attitude to work? Is this not to a large extent a result of the conditions in which enthusiastic youths, little more than children and totally unprepared for life, find themselves? If she had taken a little more thought the procurator would have realised that it was not at all in her interests to raise this particular matter. For Marchenko, despite the harsh physical and living conditions, didn't abandon everything and run home to his parents, as tens of thousands of other enthusiastic youths have done upon encountering the realistic prose of life on these construction sites. Marchenko stayed on the job and earned his own independent way. By today he might well have become a universally respected and highly qualified construction worker, or perhaps even an engineer, a senior administrator or a party functionary. Might have! Had it not been for the intervention of . . . Soviet justice!

The procurator maintained that Marchenko was first brought to court for hooliganism. But this assertion openly contradicts even the official documents. Marchenko was convicted under an article of the Criminal Code whose inhuman character was so blatant that the Supreme Soviet of Turkmenia was obliged not only to repeal it, but also to release all who had been imprisoned under it and grant them free pardons. If she were to observe both the letter and the spirit of the law, the procurator could rightfully have referred to Marchenko's first conviction as nothing but a judicial mistake, or, at the very most, should have omitted to mention it at all. Even without the documents, however, no one acquainted with Marchenko could possibly believe the charge of hooliganism. He is an extremely sensitive and impressionable man, with a profound natural intelligence and an easily injured temperament. He is incapable of offending his fellow man without cause, not to speak of doing him physical violence. The question might also arise – could he not have been guilty of hooliganism while under the influence of alcohol? But the whole point is that Marchenko doesn't and never did drink.

In brief, at the time of his first trial, Marchenko had committed no crime at all and was perfectly aware of it. The unjustified conviction dealt a heavy blow to his sensitive spirit. After this came the camp with its unnatural conditions, where this single resentment was gradually transformed into a stubborn desire to abandon the country that had treated him so heartlessly. Not knowing that the order for his release had already been signed, he escaped from the camp, worked for a while not far from the border and decided to attempt a crossing. He was arrested and found himself once again at the mercy of Soviet justice.

It is well known that criminal prosecution for an illegal attempt to cross the border is in glaring contradiction with the generally accepted spirit of the Universal Declaration on Human Rights and other international legal agreements signed by our country. But Marchenko did not know this at the time. And if he had been convicted for illegally crossing the border, he would most certainly have acknowledged his guilt and accepted any sentence as just. He would have emerged from the camp a second time with his wings clipped, a man with no more illusions, and would have raised a family and settled down with his everyday cares like millions of other middle-class self-centred citizens. But he was charged with high treason instead, in other words with a crime he did not commit.

The reason why Marchenko's co-defendant, Burovsky, gave false evidence is absolutely clear. In his book, *My Testimony*, the author describes his meeting with Burovsky in a transit prison. The latter fell on his knees before Marchenko, wept and begged forgiveness, and also begged him not to tell the other 'cons' about his false testimony. He knew what to expect if his vile behaviour were discovered. Explaining his reason for giving the false evidence, he swore the investigator had threatened that, if he failed to give the necessary evidence against Marchenko, the latter would be invited to do the same against him, and Marchenko was hardly likely to turn out to be such a fool as Burovsky. In other words, the investigator had more or less said: 'One of you has to be convicted of treason. And one of you will be! So take your choice while you've got a chance.' Meanwhile Marchenko told no one about it. He marked Burovsky down as 'scum' and advised him to make himself scarce.

And so Burovsky is clear. But what it was that prompted the investigator to slap a false charge of treason on a twenty-year-old youth is more difficult to make out. It is quite possible, of course, that he had fallen short of his norm for uncovering crimes of treason. Or perhaps personal antipathy played a part in it. All this is obscure for the time being. But it is absolutely obvious what motivated the court to pass a clearly unjust sentence. It simply had no wish to 'wash dirty linen in public', realising that this would provoke the resentment of such a powerful organ as the KGB. But still the youth was innocent and the court was perfectly aware of it. And being aware of it, hit upon a 'judgement of Solomon': it covered the crime of the security organ by passing an unjust sentence. Then, taking into account the 'mitigating circumstances', it sentenced Marchenko to 'less than the minimum term'. But Marchenko failed to grasp the court's 'magnanimity'. He failed to grasp it not only because this 'magnanimous' sentence was twice the maximum laid down for 'illegally crossing the border' – for you have to know Marchenko. His sensitive nature was also stunned not by the length of the sentence, but by the blatant *injustice* of it. And he then faced the question: *why?*

He began to seek an answer. He sought it in the classics of Marxism-Leninism, in literature, in his relations with other people, in the world of the political camps of Mordovia in which he now found himself. He mastered Marxism-Leninism in the most primitive possible way – he simply took the complete works of Lenin and worked his way through the lot of them, tome by tome. Let anyone reading this just imagine what a truly sisyphean task that was! This man, who was politically almost illiterate, was forced to excavate those 55 fat tomes, in which the real Lenin had been safely interred. But he mastered his legacy. And not only his. He used the same method to work through the complete works of Marx and Engels.

When I met Marchenko in 1967 he was already profoundly erudite in the field of Marxism-Leninism. I hadn't met a man of such erudition since the 'oppositionists of all hues '* had been liquidated. He was also a highly cultivated, thoughtful, conscious, determined and courageous political fighter. The book that he wrote and offered for our opinion shattered us not only by its truthfulness and documentary realism, but also by its literary qualities. It revealed a genuine major artist.

I will not conceal that some of us, who subsequently became his close friends, hesitated to distribute his book, warning him that it threatened to bring disaster down on his head. But he was adamant: 'My friends are still there, every day they are under the threat of death. How can I stay silent! Come what may, I refuse to stay silent. It is scandalous that people have remained silent about it for so long!'

25 February 1969

P. Grigorenko,
Komsomolsky prospekt 14/1, Flat 96,
Moscow G–21.
Tel. 246–27–37.

12. Extract from the Chronicle of Current Events No. 8,†
30 June 1969

The fate of Anatoly Marchenko, author of the book *My Testimony*, is well known to readers of the *Chronicle*. On 21 August 1968, he was sentenced to one year in a strict regime camp for 'a violation of the passport regulations'. The statement issued by Marchenko's friends saying that the charge against him was trumped up was borne out at every stage of the legal proceedings. As additional proof of this, mention may be made of how the two People's Assessors were 'instructed'. They were told that they were dealing with a criminal so cunning and insidious that he had not even broken the law, and that this article of the Criminal Code was the only means of getting him into jail.

Anatoly Marchenko is a very sick man. In the camps of Mordovia he contracted meningitis and became deaf. After he emerged he

* A reference to a particular phase of Stalin's purges in the thirties.
† An unofficial typewritten journal that appears in the Soviet Union every two months.

underwent a trepanning operation on the skull. He also suffered from heavy internal bleeding in the stomach and a dangerously high loss of haemoglobin, and was saved only by a series of blood transfusions. The court had access to Marchenko's medical reports, but despite this he was sent to a camp in the extreme north of Perm Province, with a very severe climate. He was put to work in a construction gang in the camp. In April 1969 he was incarcerated in the punishment cell for fifteen days for refusing to work in a basement without the requisite protective clothing authorised for that particular job.

Marchenko's term of imprisonment ends on 29 July, but in May the Perm Province Procuracy instituted new proceedings against him under article 190(1) of the Russian Criminal Code. Marchenko was transferred to Solikamsk Prison. His book, in which he told the truth about life in the prisons and camps for political prisoners, aroused a personal hatred for himself in the KGB and Ministry of the Interior and it cannot be excluded that those who ordered these new proceedings are intent on physically destroying Marchenko. Three years in a strict regime camp for a man in Marchenko's condition would be sufficient to kill him.

13. Extract from a letter to the Human Rights Commission of the UN

As a supplement to our letter to you sent last May, we would like to inform you of new and particularly bitter instances of the violation of human rights in our country.

1. Soon there is to be a new trial of Anatoly Marchenko, author of the book, *My Testimony*, which has been circulating in typewritten copies. It is well known that Anatoly Marchenko, although his health and hearing had already been destroyed during the years he spent in political camps and in Vladimir Prison, was sent into the sub-Arctic region of north Perm Province. It is possible that those responsible for this decision were motivated by the hope that Marchenko wouldn't survive the hard, months-long journey there and a cruel winter in the camp. But Marchenko remained alive. The date of his release is drawing near (29 July). But now, all of a sudden, the Perm Province Procuracy has instituted a new investigation of Anatoly Marchenko. This time he is being charged under the notorious article 190(1) of the Criminal Code of the RSFSR, which is applied exclusively in cases of persecution of individuals for their beliefs or for communicating information that is forcibly concealed by official propaganda. It was precisely the truthful information about camps and prisons for political

prisoners contained in Marchenko's book that aroused the hostility of the punitive organs and was the real reason for his arrest and conviction.

This man, who is unbroken in spirit but at the same time dangerously ill in body, is now threatened with three more years' detention in a camp. It is no longer a question of a man's fate, but of his life. Now he is to be tried – far from his friends, far from the public eye and beyond the reach of publicity, so that it will be all the easier for them to go ahead with this trial with its exposures highly disagreeable to the KGB and the Ministry of the Interior.

30 June 1969
Initiative Group for the Defence of Human Rights*

*14. Extract from the Chronicle of Current Events No. 9
31 August 1969*

On 26 August Anatoly Marchenko was sentenced under article 190(1) of the Criminal Code of the RSFSR to a new term of imprisonment – two years. The trial took place at the settlement of Nyrob in Perm Province, within the labour camp zone. The witnesses consisted of prisoners convicted of serious crimes as habitual criminals, and of camp administration workers. They alleged that Marchenko had uttered slanderous statements about Soviet policy towards Czechoslovakia, about the Sino-Soviet conflict and about the position of writers in the Soviet Union. Apart from these verbal utterances, no other accusations were made against Marchenko. Marchenko pleaded not guilty and denied ever having made these statements. At the moment Marchenko is in the transit prison of Solikamsk. Another exhausting journey is in store for him – to an unknown destination.

*15. Extract from the Chronicle of Current Events No. 10,
31 September 1969*

The *Chronicle* has already reported that Anatoly Marchenko has been sentenced once more – this time to two years' imprisonment in a strict regime camp under article 190(1) of the Russian Criminal Code. Marchenko's trial was held on 22 August 1969, in the reading-room of the labour camp at Nyrob, a settlement in Perm Province. The

* This letter bore 46 signatures altogether, including those of A. Yesenin-Volpin, N. Gorbanevskaya, V. Krasin, P. Grigorenko, P. Yakir and A. Yakobson.

trial was formally considered open, although, of course, no one but prisoners and camp staff is ever allowed into a camp.

Anatoly Marchenko was charged with uttering the following statements: 'the Soviet Union is violating the sovereignty of other nations and Soviet troops were sent into Czechoslovakia to suppress freedom with tanks'; 'there is no democracy in the USSR, freedom of expression of the press and of creative writing does not exist'; 'the Soviet Union is to blame' for events on the Sino-Soviet border. Apart from making these statements, Marchenko was also charged with refusing to report for work and with declaring, while in the punishment cell: 'the Communists have drunk all my blood'. This last charge was based on the testimony of two punishment-cell warders, Lepanitsyn and Sobinin. Since they contradicted one another in their evidence concerning the date on which Marchenko was supposed to have uttered this statement, the text of the charge, and later of the sentence, stated that he had uttered it twice – on 14 and 15 May. After the warders had reported it to the KGB security officer in the camp, Antonov, to whom the warders are subordinate in their work, he began to collect further evidence against Marchenko and on 31 May instituted criminal proceedings.

The charge was confirmed during the preliminary investigation by the warders Sedov and Dmitrienko, and also by other warders. Sedov was not summoned to appear at the trial, but his testimony, in violation of the law, was read out and duly incorporated in the verdict. Dmitrienko declared at the trial that he had not known Marchenko before but had 'decided' that the statement attributed to him in the charge must have been uttered by him. Now, however, having seen Marchenko in court and heard his voice, he was firmly convinced that Marchenko hadn't spoken these words. Furthermore, Dmitrienko knew who *had* spoken them and could name him and have him summoned to the court. The court failed to react to this statement and ignored Dmitrienko's evidence in its verdict, although a court is obliged by law to explain why it has rejected any testimony that is in conflict with its conclusions. Marchenko's fellow-prisoners in the punishment cell, who had been summoned to the court at his request, stated that they had not heard him utter the statement mentioned in the charge.

On the subject of the other statements he was charged with uttering, Marchenko said that he had indeed held conversations with other prisoners on the subjects mentioned, but that his statements had been distorted out of all recognition in the witnesses' testimony. Marchenko said he had been offended by the statement of witness Burtsev to the effect that 'Czechoslovakia ought to be crushed once and for all', since he thought the idea of crushing an individual, a nation or a people to reveal hatred of mankind. In the course of conversations about freedom of expression, press and creative writing, Marchenko had in fact replied to prisoners that no ideal freedom of expression, press and creative writing existed anywhere, nor did pure democracy, and that included the Soviet Union. Every country had its limitations.

The witnesses for the prosecution had related Marchenko's views in a primitive and arbitrary form. Not one witness had reproduced them accurately and there were contradictions in their testimony. According to Marchenko, the case against him had been fabricated, by Antonov, the camp KGB security officer, who had put pressure on the witnesses – who depended on him – to make them give suitable testimony.

The court declared that 'there was no reason not to believe the witnesses questioned at the trial, since many of them had given explanations even before proceedings had been opened – some in their own handwriting – which confirmed the facts brought to light in court and had led to criminal proceedings being instituted in the first place.' These 'explanations', of course, on the basis of which proceedings had been instituted, had been provided by KGB officer Antonov in the course of his investigations. The court's second argument for proving the reliability of the witnesses was that the investigation had been headed by the Deputy Procurator of Perm Province, 'the court having no reason to doubt his objectivity'.

The composition of the court was as follows. Chairman: Khrenovsky; People's Assessors: Rzhevin and Biryukova; Procurator: Baiborodina. Marchenko conducted his own defence.

On 30 September the Supreme Court of the RSFSR heard Marchenko's appeal and an additional appeal by the advocate, Monakhov, who spoke at the hearing. The composition of the court was as follows. Chairman: Ostroukhova; Members of the court: Lukanov and Timofeyev; Procurator: Sorokina. The verdict of the Perm Province court was upheld.

16. Extract from the Chronicle of Current Events No. 11,
31 December 1969

For reasons unknown, Anatoly Marchenko, who was convicted under article 190(1) by a camp trial on 22 August 1969, is still in Solikamsk Prison. His address is: Permskaya Oblast, Solikamsk P.O. Box 1Z 57/2.

Readers will recall that Marchenko is the author of the world-famous book about camps for political prisoners in the post-Stalin period, *My Testimony*.

17. Extract from the Chronicle of Current Events No. 12, 28 February 1970

Anatoly Tikhonovich Marchenko has been sent to a camp. His present address is: Permskaya Oblast, Solikamsky rayon, P.O. Krasny Bereg, Box AM 244/7–8.

GALINA VISHNEVSKAYA

GALINA

Once, Galina Vishnevskaya was the Soviet Union's most celebrated diva. Born into bitter poverty in Stalinist Russia she rose to fame through the purges, the famine, the Nazi blockade, to become an intimate in the circles of Russia's most famous men – Khrushchev, Rostropovich, Brezhnev, Yevtushenko and Solzhenitsyn. Then, in 1978, Galina defected from her homeland. Her autobiography stands as a moving testament to the singer they could never silence.

'A devastating and compulsively readable autobiography'
Standard

'This book is epic in its scale . . . Imperative reading for anyone interested in the lives of Russian artists'
The Literary Review

'Vishnevskaya's life story proves just as absorbing as her artistic achievements'
Daily Telegraph

sceptre

GEOFFREY MOORHOUSE

AGAINST ALL REASON

AGAINST ALL REASON is a unique and illuminating account of the monastic life, which met with critical acclaim when first published in 1969. Today, more than fifteen years later, it is as perceptive and relevant as ever.

'Mr Moorhouse combines radical criticism with much inner understanding . . . an enquiry which might have been superficial and rather sensational is neither'
Michael Ramsey, then Archbishop of Canterbury,
in the Spectator

'I have learned more from this outsider than from a dozen books by professionals within'
Martin Jarrett-Kerr CR in the Guardian

'I think it is a noble achievement . . . a splendid book'
Paul Jennings in The Times

'I must say at once that I find this an appalling book, but that is partly because it is so good. If Mr Moorhouse were sentimental, or had less sympathy and were less thorough, if his judgement was not so obviously balanced, the picture of conventional life he brings before us would have less force and therefore less power to disturb'
Stevie Smith in the New Statesman

sceptre

BERNARD LEVIN

HANNIBAL'S FOOTSTEPS

In the winter of 218 BC, Hannibal marched to war across the Alps with 60,000 infantry, 9,000 cavalry and 37 elephants. His journey 'captured the imagination of the world'.

2,000 years later, Bernard Levin retraces his hero's steps. With great reluctance he abandoned the idea of taking elephants. The story of his travels is a marvellous blend of history, travel, anecdote and personal philosophy.

'The benign, inquiring spirit of ENTHUSIASMS is still present in HANNIBAL'S FOOTSTEPS, still enjoying and seeking something "beyond the next mountain"'
Bel Mooney in the Listener

'Who could be a more amusing or provocative cicerone on a journey from the Rhône across the Alps towards Turin, following Hannibal's legendary elephantine dash of 218 BC into Italy?'
Peter Jones in The Times

WINSTON S. CHURCHILL

THE RIVER WAR

In 1881 the Mahdi's rebellion plunged the Sudan into bloodshed and confusion. Egyptian armies sent to recover the territory were routed and destroyed. All outside control and administration had been wiped out. Mr Gladstone's Government decided that British interests in the area were to be withdrawn. General Gordon was sent to Khartoum to bring out the surviving officials, soldiers and Egyptian subjects. But, as the Mahdi's forces surrounded Khartoum, Gordon was trapped and doomed.

THE RIVER WAR tells of the expedition of reconquest that, under General Kitchener, fought its way up the Nile. The young Winston Churchill was there. This is his classic account of the expedition and the final Battle of Omdurman.

Current and forthcoming titles from Sceptre

GALINA VISHNEVSKAYA

GALINA

BERNARD LEVIN

HANNIBAL'S FOOTSTEPS

GEOFFREY MOORHOUSE

AGAINST ALL REASON

WINSTON S. CHURCHILL

THE RIVER WAR

JULIAN FANE

MORNING

BOOKS OF DISTINCTION